ERICA JAMES
The Romantic Comedies

Erica James

Three Great Novels: The Romantic Comedies

A Sense of Belonging

Act of Faith

The Holiday

ORION

A *Sense of Belonging* Copyright © 1998 Erica James
Act of Faith Copyright © 1999 Erica James
The Holiday Copyright © 2000 Erica James

This omnibus edition first published in Great Britain in 2003
by Orion, an imprint of the Orion Publishing Group Ltd.

The moral right of Erica James to be identified as the
author of this work has been asserted in accordance
with the Copyright, Designs and Patents Act of 1988.

A CIP catalogue record for this book
is available from the British Library.

ISBN 0 75285 658 8

Typeset by Deltatype Ltd, Birkenhead, Merseyside

Set in Minion

Printed in Great Britain by Clays Ltd, St Ives plc

The Orion Publishing Group Ltd
Orion House
5 Upper Saint Martin's Lane
London, WC2H 9EA

Contents

A Sense of
Belonging

To Edward and Samuel

Acknowledgements

This book couldn't have been written without the help and support of so many people and whether they want the credit (or the blame) or not, they're going to get it.

Life-saving thanks must go to Big G for those quiet, calming moments.

Glass-raising thanks to Helena who listened to numerous silly ideas being tossed around her kitchen while I poured the wine and she cooked the lunch.

Side-splitting thanks to Maureen for saying, 'Come on, that's just not on!' As ever she made me laugh at just the right time.

Courteous thanks to Morris Phillips for allowing me to pry into his business.

And the same to Susan Howard of Avocado Cards in Huddersfield.

Respectful thanks to Jane Wood at Orion, along with Selina Walker and Sarah Yorke.

Appreciative thanks to Helen Spencer for the over-the-phone consultations.

Humble thanks to all those people who shared their personal experiences of MS with me, especially Sue Argent who never minded me ringing her with yet another query. Her outlook on life, together with her extraordinary strength of character, is a truly inspiring example to us all. Thank you, Sue.

Devoted and adoring thanks to the two back-room boys, Edward and Samuel, who know exactly when to run for cover when things are going badly, and whose survival skills are improving with each book I write.

And, finally, forelock-tugging thanks to Jonathan Lloyd at Curtis Brown for being nothing like Piers Lambert!

A novel is a mirror which passes over a highway. Sometimes it reflects to your eye the blue of the skies, at others the churned-up mud of the road.

Henri Beyle (called Stendhal) 1783–1842

The Beginning

1

THE END

Jessica Lloyd looked at what she'd just typed, considered it for a few seconds, then allowed herself a small wry smile.

This wasn't because she had at last finished her latest novel, or indeed that these two perfectly innocuous words would irritate the hell out of her exacting agent – 'I know when it ends, Jessica, there's no need to tell me, I'm not a fool' – but because, and heaven forbid that anyone would accuse her of spouting high-sounding humbug, she happened to believe that there was no such thing as an ending. In her experience life was all about beginnings.

And today of all days she had to believe that this was true.

She switched off the laptop, stood up, stretched her arms over her head and went and leant against the white-painted wall that separated her small terrace from the rocky drop below. She rested her elbows on the sun-warmed stone and gazed out at the sweep of bay with its crystal-clear water that was holiday-brochure blue. It was a breathlessly hot June morning and the sea was calm and tranquil, benign even, but Jessica knew well enough that by early afternoon there would be a strong wind blowing in across the water, bringing with it the kind of crashing waves that wind-surfers delighted in and for which this part of Corfu was renowned.

But for now, all was still.

She went back to the shade of her vine-covered pergola, to the wooden table she had been working at, and gathered up her things and took them inside. She plugged the laptop into the printer, which squatted incongruously next to the bread bin on top of the fridge in the tiny kitchen, and set it to print her final chapter of *A Carefree Life*. While she waited for the machine to do its work she poured herself a glass of ice-cold mineral water and gulped it down. It was eleven o'clock and she had been working on the terrace since a little after seven, having got up early to finish her novel. And now that it was done she could use the rest of the day to say her goodbyes.

She had lived on Corfu for six years and for the most part she had cherished every magical timeless day that had drifted by. She had come to the island not long after her thirtieth birthday and had fallen for the charming, carefree way of life the Corfiotes so enjoyed. It had suited her own temperament perfectly.

She had also fallen in love, or what she had thought was love at the time. Now she wasn't so sure.

First there had been Christos who, if nothing else, had tried to teach her to cook, or rather his mother had. But when it finally dawned on Christos that she had absolutely no interest in cooking, and that if he wanted anything worthwhile to eat he either had to do it himself or go home to his mother, he went in search of a nice local girl who would know exactly how to produce his favourite meal of arni brizoles. There had been no bitter recriminations between them when they'd parted, just a shared sense of better luck next time.

Luck had given her Gavin.

Gavin, so sure, so confident and so amusing. He was the original free spirit, as he'd never stopped letting her know.

He had come to the island some two years before, to work as a sailing instructor, and when they'd met, like Christos, he had set about teaching her what was important to him. In his case it was sailing. She hated sailing almost as much as cooking, but had been so captivated by Gavin that she hadn't let on and had tried her best to listen to his enthusiastic instructions. She'd then tried even harder to carry them out. But it had been hopeless. Tacking into the wind was a concept she never mastered. Each lesson she would capsize the small boat at least half a dozen times – it didn't help that Gavin would shout from the shore that a child of ten could sail the wretched thing. 'Then let it!' she shouted back at him one day, abandoning the boat and swimming away from it in a monumental sulk.

If the sailing was a nightmare, the sex was a dream.

And always afterwards, whether they were lying on her bed in the moonlight or in the sun on her secluded terrace, he would sing to her or tell her jokes.

But the sex, the singing and the jokes – and thank goodness, the sailing – were all about to become things of the past.

She hadn't told Gavin what she was doing because she knew what his reaction would be if she did try and explain to him why she was leaving. There would be that little-boy-lost look, accompanied by the words, 'But you can't really mean it' – in Gavin's world, nobody ever meant what they said. He would then open a bottle of wine and insist they discuss it on the terrace beneath the stars and moon, where he knew she'd be unable to stay angry with him for more than two minutes. And because of his arrogance he would assume she was going because of him and he'd say, 'But it's just the way I am, it doesn't mean anything' and lead her to the bedroom. Then, once they'd made love, he would whisper in her ear, 'Stay, Jessica, don't go.'

And she'd give in. Just like that.

She sighed. It wasn't good to think about Gavin too much. Not at this stage. Not when she knew how weak he could make her feel. His greatest skill, she had long since decided, was that he knew exactly how to keep her dangling. She was ashamed to admit it, but basically it was all down to sex. And it wasn't even that Gavin understood her body and knew all the right things to do with it that made him so appealing, it was more a case of the sheer force of his energy in bed that had her gasping for more. Without a doubt, if sex were ever made an Olympic sport, Gavin would be the Mark Spitz of the event.

She smiled to herself and imagined Gavin putting his latest round of infidelity down to essential training.

She poured another glass of water, quickly drank it, then decided to have a swim before taking her motor boat into Kassiopi. She went in search of her swimming costume. Just as she had changed, the phone rang.

It was her mother.

Instantly Jessica was filled with alarm. Her mother rarely called. It was always Jessica who did the phoning. The last time Anna had phoned was six months ago and it was to announce that she was being admitted into hospital for a heart bypass operation. Very calmly she had said, 'Don't go doing anything silly, Jessica, like rushing over, but I'm going into hospital for a few days. There seems to be a problem with my heart. A lot of fuss over nothing, very probably.' Within hours of the call Jessica was sitting on a plane bound for Manchester, panic-stricken that she might never see her mother again. It was a thought that had stayed with her throughout the flight and had reduced her to a tearful, sniffling wreck, much to the consternation of the man in the seat next to her.

They had never been overtly close, not like other mothers and daughters Jessica knew, who needed constantly to be together, but their love for one another was just as strong. Unfortunately, so was the need for both of them to live independently of each other.

'What is it?' Jessica asked. 'What's happened?'

'Don't fuss. I'm fine. I just wanted to see if it wasn't too late to make you change your mind.'

'No chance,' Jessica said with a light laugh. 'Everything's arranged this end and you know jolly well that I've exchanged contracts on Cholmford Hall Mews, so you can expect me as I'd originally said.'

'Remind me.'

Jessica tutted. 'Does that mean you've lost the letter I sent you?'

'I might have.'

'Honestly, Mum, you're hopeless.'

'I'm nothing of the sort. After years of having a head for paperwork I've given it up. Now get on and tell me what time you'll be arriving tonight, this call's costing me a fortune.'

'With a bit of luck I'll see you some time after eleven.'

'As early as that?'

'You really know how to make a daughter feel loved.'

'I'm working on it, Jessica, but it's not easy.'

A few moments later, when Jessica put down the phone, she found herself almost wishing the hours away until her flight. She wanted to go home. Which was strange because England hadn't been home for years.

She picked up a large towel from the back of a chair and made her way down the steep hillside path at the end of her sun terrace. At a sharp turn she paused and stood still in the fierce heat, and gazed across the expanse of sparkling water. In the distance was the Albanian coastline, its mountainous bumps blurred and hazy in the baking sunshine. All around her was the sweet smell of cypress trees and the ever present noise of cicadas hidden in the olive trees. Surely she should feel something, she thought, as she stood taking in the view and the moment. Shouldn't there be at least some feeling of regret at leaving all this, this island that had once been such a blissful paradise?

But that was the point, she supposed. It no longer was a blissful paradise.

She carried on down the path, taking care where she placed her feet on the stones that in places were loose and wobbly.

When she reached the tiny sheltered area of pebble beach that she called her own, where she kept her small boat tied to an overhanging branch of a eucalyptus tree, she placed her towel on a rock and slipped into the clear turquoise water. It was wonderfully cool and refreshing, and leaning her slim brown body forward she began swimming away from the shore, moving her arms and legs slowly and rhythmically.

Perhaps this might be something she would miss when she returned to England.

But even the thought of a chilly chlorine dip at the local swimming baths back in Cheshire could not persuade her that what she was doing was wrong.

It was in January, when her mother had gone into hospital, that Jessica had begun to feel uneasy. It was the first time that she wondered whether she hadn't been a little selfish all her adult life.

The trouble was she had been brought up by a strong, clear-minded and very independent woman, and raised with the expectation that she would be the same. Which had meant that at the earliest opportunity she had been encouraged to fly the nest and spread her wings. At no stage had she thought about marriage or ever having children, the two things just didn't come into her thinking. As a child there had been no bedtime stories of young girls being rescued by handsome princes on the look-out for a compliant, pretty wife, instead there had been tales of heroic women battling against the odds; of Joan of Arc, Amy Johnson, Florence Nightingale and even Ginger Rogers who, according to her mother, did everything Fred Astaire did but backwards and in high heels. 'Whatever you want to do,' her mother would say when kissing her good-night, 'believe you can do it and you will. And more important than anything else, make sure you enjoy what you do.'

Which might well have provoked some children into becoming high-flying achievers, but not Jessica. What it did was convince her from an early age that whatever she did it would be because she wanted to do it. She grew to be extremely single-minded and able to turn her hand to anything she chose. Her scholastic education came to an end at the age of eighteen and because she already had a passion for skiing, but couldn't afford to fund it, she decided to work as a chalet maid in a ski resort in the French Alps, where she spent what little free time she had on the slopes perfecting her technique. She'd then gone to live in Colorado, where she worked as a skiing instructor. From there she'd returned to Europe and while island hopping round Greece, with only a bulging backpack to her name, had chanced upon a holiday company desperate for an extra rep to help them out for a couple of weeks on Corfu. By the time the job came to an end Jessica knew that she had chanced upon a place that she had no desire to leave. She began working in a taverna, which was where she had met Christos, and when she wasn't serving plates of moussaka and feta salad to the tourists, along with retsina and ouzo, she was to be found on the beach with a notebook and pen. Quite unexpectedly she had discovered she had a new craving and was instantly keen to satisfy it. She had started writing a novel. It took her a year and when it was finished she posted the set of notebooks to her mother to read. Unbeknown to Jessica, Anna had then secretly typed it out and sent it off to an agent in London. Several months later, not long after Christos had given up on Jessica, she had received a letter from her mother with the news that a publisher was interested in her book. 'They're offering real money,' she wrote, 'not buttons, but hard cash. You'd better come over right away and see what you think.'

And she had. First she had met the agent to whom her mother had sent the manuscript, then the publisher. A contract was signed and when she flew back to Corfu a week later the first thing she did was to give up working at the taverna and buy herself a new set of notebooks and pens, and start writing another novel.

Now, as she climbed up the steep path to her small whitewashed house that nestled comfortably into the unspoilt hillside, she thought of the third book she had completed today, which she would take with her to England that evening on the plane, along with just a few carefully selected possessions that would remind her of Corfu. The house was rented, as was the furniture, and much as she'd come to love her locally carved olive-wood knick-knacks and brightly coloured rugs and wall hangings, it was only right that they should stay behind. They would look out of place in her new house; it would be like taking holiday souvenirs home and finding they looked silly away from their own environment, just as cheap holiday wine was best enjoyed *in situ*.

She threw her wet towel over the clothes line tied between two olive trees and experienced the uneasy feeling that her decision to leave Gavin and her idyllic life-style and return home to England was all about her finally growing up.

No more could she justify her carefree life. No more could she ignore what she felt she owed her mother. And whether her mother was prepared to admit it or not, Anna needed her daughter's help.

Just occasionally, though, Jessica had the strange and dangerous feeling that perhaps this wasn't so, that in actual fact, by some quirk of human nature, it was she who wanted her mother to need her.

Either way, it didn't matter. The truth was, at the age of thirty-six she had discovered that Corfu could not offer her what she now found she wanted more than anything else.

She went inside the house to shower and get ready to go out, more convinced than ever that what she had suspected for some time was true – she had outstayed her welcome on this lovely Ionian island. It was definitely time to move on, to go back to England where she had a new home waiting for her, not with her mother – that would be a disaster for them both – but somewhere close by, where she hoped to be able to keep a surreptitious eye on Anna.

And maybe she might even find what it was she was looking for, that setting up home at Cholmford Hall Mews would satisfy the very real sense of belonging that she was now seeking.

2

Kate Morris stared with pleasure through the large arched window in the sun-filled sitting-room of 5 Cholmford Hall Mews and experienced the sensation of having died and gone to heaven. She wondered how she would ever get anything done in the house with this beautiful view of rolling fields and woodland to gaze at all day.

Well, one thing was for sure, today was not the day to stand and dream. There was such a lot to do and she wanted most of it done before Alec came home from work that evening. She wished to surprise him, wanted very much to make their new home together perfect.

They had only moved in yesterday, so she knew that it was just possible that she was setting her sights too high, but she badly desired everything to be right.

She moved away from the window and turned her attention to one of the large packing cases in the middle of the room. She opened it, took off the protective layers of scrunched-up paper and pulled out a parcel to unwrap. It was a framed photograph of Alec and his family – the McLaren clan as she called them – taken last Christmas. There was Alec's daughter Ruth, who wasn't much younger than Kate, and her husband Adam, and their son, little Oscar, four years old and utterly adorable; dark-eyed and winsome, and Kate's favourite member of the McLaren family, other than the man she loved. And looking very much the patriarchal figure, Alec was in the middle of the picture, his tall frame dominating the photograph as he stood proudly, surrounded by his family. She ran her finger over his face, taking in the flecks of grey at his temples, the smile that had put her so thoroughly at ease when they'd first met and the new pair of gold-rimmed glasses she had helped him choose the week before Christmas. She was in the picture too. She gazed critically at herself and saw a tall girl in her late twenties looking more like a gawky schoolgirl with shoulders slightly stooped as though this would make her less visible and less out of place among a family in which she felt she didn't belong. It was a sad truth, but it was exactly how she'd always looked in her own family photographs. The final figure in the group portrait was perhaps the most important member of the family . . . in terms of Kate's future happiness, she suspected. It was Melissa McLaren.

Melissa and Alec had been divorced now for over two years, but Kate was astute enough to know that a formal piece of paper could never fully untie the bond that existed between a couple who had not only been married for as long as Alec and Melissa had, but who also still saw one another on a daily basis running their jointly owned company together. Kate recognised all too well that some women in her position would be unhappy with the situation in which her partner still had so much contact with his ex, but Kate was determined never to let something as petty as jealousy ruin what she and Alec had between them. Though they had only known one another for less than a year their love was as precious to Kate as anything she'd ever known.

She placed the photograph on the mantelpiece, along with some other ornaments she'd already unwrapped after seeing Alec off to work earlier that morning. It was a shame he'd needed to go in to the office today of all days, it would have been lovely to have had him here with her setting up home together.

They had met last autumn through, of all things, a dating agency – a fact that nobody in the McLaren clan was ever to know about. 'I couldn't bear for Melissa to know I'd resorted to meeting somebody this way,' Alec had told Kate. It wasn't perhaps the most flattering thing for him to say to her, but she knew and understood what he meant, and had respected his need to protect his pride. Hadn't she felt exactly the same herself?

In theory they should never have met, because of their age difference, but that particular week the computer at the agency had had a glitch and had sent out hundreds of profiles to mismatched prospective partners and, with curiosity on both their parts to blame, she and Alec had arranged to meet for a drink in a wine bar in Knutsford.

'Excuse my lack of originality,' he'd said on the phone, 'but how will I recognise you? I've never done this kind of thing before.'

'I'm tall for my age,' she'd joked, 'and I have rather a lot of hair.'

She had liked the look of him from the very first second she'd seen him enter the wine bar, without even knowing that he was her date. He'd been dressed in a loose-fitting raincoat over a linen suit and pale-green shirt that later in the evening she had realised had reflected the colour of his eyes. She had liked him even more when he'd approached her without hesitating and said, 'You have to be Kate Morris, I love your hair, it makes you look like an ethereal Burne-Jones beauty.'

According to the advice offered by the dating agency, when two people meet for the first time they should plan to spend a maximum of thirty minutes in each other's company. She and Alec had spent all evening together. They'd had a couple of drinks in the wine bar and moved on to a nearby restaurant. She had found his manner easy and comfortable. He was softly spoken, with just the merest hint of a Scottish accent, and appeared confident and perfectly composed, even though he admitted to her the following day that he had been terrified that she would think him old and boring. But there was nothing old and boring about Alec, he was spontaneous and fun, and she had fallen in love with him by the time they'd finished their meal. Later, when he had walked her to her car and had said how much he'd enjoyed the evening, he'd added, 'I don't suppose there's any hope of you humouring a middle-aged man and having dinner with me next week, is there?'

'No,' she'd answered, 'no, I don't think so.'

He'd lowered his eyes, disappointed – ever since that moment she'd never seen him look so downcast. 'I just thought it was worth asking,' he'd mumbled awkwardly, staring into the shop window behind him, 'but I quite understand, I suppose that's how this dating thing works.'

She'd reached out and rested her hand on his coat sleeve. 'You don't understand at all,' she'd said, 'I said no because I can't wait until next week. How about tomorrow evening?'

His handsome face had instantly broken into a delighted smile. 'You mean it?'

'Yes.' She'd smiled back at him. 'Why wouldn't I?'

He'd thrown his arms in the air. 'A million and one reasons why not. Like I'm twenty years older than you.'

'Actually you're twenty-one years older.'

He groaned. 'That bad, eh?'

'Old enough to be my father.'

'Doesn't it bother you?'

'So where shall we eat?'

'Here? Wherever. Wherever you want. Oh Kate, give me something that belongs to you so that I don't wake up in the morning and find you were nothing but a dream.'

Kate smiled and hoped she would never forget the memory of their first meeting. She carried on with the unpacking. When she'd cleared another two boxes she was interrupted by the sound of the doorbell. She clambered over the chaos of yet more unopened boxes in the hall and opened the front door. She was met by the sight of a woman holding a large bouquet of flowers.

'Kate Morris?'

'Yes, that's me.'

'For you.'

Kate took the flowers and watched the woman turn her florist's van round in the gravelled courtyard in front of all the mews houses and drive out through the central archway. She closed the door and walked through to the kitchen. She laid the flowers on the table and read the small accompanying card. *To my darling Kate, sorry I can't be with you on this special day. Please don't work too hard. All my love, Alec.*

Kate swallowed back tears of happiness. Nobody had ever treated her so lovingly.

3

From the kitchen window of 2 Cholmford Hall Mews Amanda Fergusson watched the florist's van drive away and felt a stab of jealousy at the sight of such a beautiful bouquet of flowers. Tony wasn't a flower person, chocolates yes, occasionally, but rarely flowers. But then that was all right, because she wasn't a sentimental person either.

She closed the dishwasher and moved on to tidying up the breakfast bar. But her thoughts were still with the pretty young girl over in number five, who she decided was probably sickeningly sentimental and was on the receiving end of similarly romantic gestures all the time from her ... Amanda hesitated. Her what, precisely?

Husband?

No. The man who had stood on the doorstep that morning kissing her goodbye as though he couldn't bear to be parted from her was no husband. Amanda had one of those and she knew the difference: in broad daylight husbands pecked, while lovers embraced.

On the other hand, they might be newly-weds. That was it, probably. Recently married and still going through the honeymoon period. It would soon be over, just as it was with her and Tony. It hadn't slipped her notice either that there was a considerable age gap between the happy couple.

She carried on with the clearing up. In the adjoining family room she could hear the sound of Tony's six-year-old daughter Hattie, singing along to a programme on Children's BBC. Amanda listened to the little girl. She sounded relaxed and cheerful. Which wasn't always the case.

When Amanda had met Tony eighteen months before, he was still trying to get over the loss of his wife, who had died in a car accident the previous year. He was also finding it difficult to cope with the demands of his job and his young daughter. A succession of unreliable nannies hadn't helped either and had served only to disrupt Hattie's life further.

But now, at least, thanks to her, both Tony and Hattie seemed to be on a more even keel, even if at times Amanda felt she was out of her depth. Marriage to Tony wasn't all that she'd imagined it would be, but she was working on it. Tony, however, wasn't her real problem, that was Hattie. She wished at times that Tony would trust her more with his daughter. He was too prone to step in and undermine her when she was trying her best to discipline the girl.

They had argued again last night. Hattie had been in and out of bed, one minute claiming she was thirsty, the next that she was too hot. 'I can't sleep,' she'd said. Tony had immediately suggested that Hattie come downstairs and sit with them for a while, but she had known the answer was to be firm and make Hattie realise that grown-ups needed their time together. Tony had had his way, and Hattie had sat between them on the sofa and had consequently refused to go back upstairs. Eventually she had fallen asleep, lying across Tony's chest, and he had carried her up to her room. By which time it was nearly midnight and they too had gone to bed, exhausted and bad-tempered.

'May I have a drink?'

Amanda turned round to see Hattie standing in the doorway. 'Please,' she said. '*Please* may I have a drink?'

'Please,' repeated Hattie in a bored tone.

Amanda poured out a plastic cup of apple juice. She placed it on the breakfast bar. 'Climb up on to your stool, then.'

'I want it in there,' Hattie said, pointing towards the family room and the television.

'In here or not at all. What's it to be?'

Hattie stared back at her.

Amanda sensed a battle of wills looming. 'You know the rules,' she said, 'where there are carpets, new carpets at that, you're not allowed to eat or drink.'

'Daddy lets –'

'Then Daddy's wrong.'

Hattie's eyes opened wide.

Amanda was cross with herself. Once again, not only had she cast herself as the wicked stepmother, but she had broken the cardinal rule: Daddy was never wrong. And the only way out of the problem now was either to give in – which she wouldn't – or provide a distraction. 'Why don't we go out,' she said. 'Let's go and meet the nice new lady who moved in yesterday.'

Kate had almost cleared the sitting-room of packing cases and was just considering a well-earned coffee break when she heard the doorbell for a second time that day and went to answer it.

It was the little girl she noticed first. She decided that she was a couple of years older than Oscar.

'We thought we'd come and introduce ourselves,' said the woman behind the small fair-haired child, 'we live in number two over in the corner. I'm Amanda and this is Hattie.' Hattie immediately tried to hide herself behind Amanda.

'Come on now, don't be shy,' Amanda said, giving her a little shove. 'I'm afraid she can be very silly at times.'

Kate bent down and smiled at Hattie. 'Hello,' she said, 'I'm Kate. Would you like to come in and help me unpack a few boxes? I've got so much to do, it would be lovely to have another pair of hands.'

Hattie considered Kate for a moment, then pushed past Amanda and followed her inside the house.

'I was just going to make myself a cup of coffee, would you like one?'

'Please,' Amanda answered, 'but only if we're not keeping you. I can see you've still got a lot to do.'

Kate led the way through to the kitchen and swept her long hair up from her face. She held it in that position for a few seconds and looked back at the mess in the hall, which she had yet to make an impression on. 'You're so right.' She sighed, letting go of her hair and sending it cascading down her back. 'But not to worry, I'm sure I'll get it all done by this evening, especially now that I've got Hattie to help me.' She smiled down at the little girl who was busy staring at her.

'You've got lovely hair,' Hattie said unexpectedly.

'Thank you and so have you.'

'No I haven't, mine's horrible. I'd like it long like yours, but Amanda says it's easier to keep it short like this.'

'And Amanda is quite right,' Kate said diplomatically, wondering what Amanda's relationship was to this sweet girl – aunt, stepmother or child-minder? Surely not her mother. 'But maybe when you're a big girl and can look after your own hair you'll be able to have it just as you want.'

'I will,' Hattie said flatly. She gave Amanda a sideways glance.

'Now what would you like to drink?' Kate asked, aware that the rapport between her two visitors was not all that it could be.

'May I have some apple juice, please?'

'What beautiful manners you have, but I'm afraid I've only got orange juice or grape juice. Or how about some milk?'

'Milk please.'

Amanda watched the scene between her new neighbour and Hattie. If she had been jealous at the sight of the flowers arriving in the courtyard earlier this morning, she now felt an even greater sense of envy witnessing the ease with which this willowy beauty could strike up such a friendly alliance with her stepdaughter. It had taken Amanda the best part of six months to get Hattie so much as to smile at her.

'There now,' Kate said, picking up the tray of drinks, 'I think that's everything we shall need. Oh, Hattie, could you carry that tin of biscuits for me? Yes, that's the one, the large red tin. Can you manage it? Splendid.'

'Where are we going to have our drinks?' asked Hattie.

'In the sitting-room, it's the only tidy room in the house.'

'Is there a carpet in there?'

'Yes,' Kate said, puzzled. 'Why?'

Hattie didn't answer but she threw another look at her stepmother.

Amanda followed behind, feeling cross and slightly left out. 'What lovely flowers,' she said, when they went into the sitting-room and she saw the enormous arrangement on a highly polished corner table. 'I saw them arrive earlier, lucky you.' She went over to take a closer look and to read the card propped up in front of the vase. When she looked back at Kate she was surprised to see that she was blushing.

'Alec is very romantic, he does things like that.'

'Is Alec your husband?' asked Hattie, taking off her shoes and making herself at home in a large comfortable wing-back armchair.

'Sort of,' Kate said, handing Amanda her cup of coffee. 'Milk?'

Amanda shook her head, hoping that Hattie would ask what 'sort of' meant.

'Sugar?'

'No, thank you.' She waited for Hattie to oblige, but the silly girl was too busy smiling at Kate, who was now passing her a glass of milk. She almost wished that Hattie would misbehave and spill the drink all over the expensive-looking fabric of the chair in which she was sitting, as she did at home sometimes, then they'd see how this beautiful serene creature would handle things.

'So when did you move in?' Kate asked, as she settled herself on a low footstool beside Hattie's chair and offered her a biscuit.

'Last week. We were the first. It's been strange being here all on our own. It's very quiet. I'm just so glad I've got a car or I'd feel completely isolated.'

Kate stared out through the large arched window that took up nearly the entire width of the far end of the room. 'But it's wonderful, isn't it? The countryside is so pretty. I don't think I shall ever want to leave. There's such a good feeling about the place. Do you feel it too?'

'Ah . . . yes,' lied Amanda. All she had felt since they'd moved in was a colossal sense of exhaustion. Running herself ragged over unpacking, then gathering swatches of fabrics and wallpaper samples was not her idea of fun, especially as she was now looking after Hattie full time because they'd taken her out of school before the end of term so that they could move house and area. For the first time since her marriage to Tony, when she'd given up her job in the building society in order to be a stay-at-home mum for Hattie, she longed for her old way of life – chasing unpaid mortgage payments was a doddle in comparison.

'Is there anybody else living here, or are we the only ones to have moved in?' Kate asked, offering Amanda a biscuit.

Amanda had a pretty good idea what was going on with the development as she'd made it her business to befriend Sue, the sales negotiator who worked in the show house three days a week. Though even Sue hadn't been entirely sure what the set-up between Kate and Alec was. 'Contracts have been exchanged on number one and completion has already taken place on number four,' she said.

'Any idea what the other people are like?'

'Apparently your immediate neighbour is a well-known author, a romantic novelist, but I've never heard of her, not that I read that kind of book. I prefer something with a bit more substance when I do have the time to read.'

'How interesting. Do you know her name?'

'Jessica . . . Jessica Somebody or other. I can't remember her surname, which just goes to show she can't be that well-known.'

'Her name's Jessica Lloyd,' Hattie said, her mouth full of biscuit crumbs.

'Hattie,' reprimanded Amanda, 'don't speak with your mouth full.' She then turned to Kate. 'I think Hattie might be right though.'

'I know I'm right,' Hattie continued, 'because when the lady in the show house said her name yesterday I thought of Vanessa Lloyd at my old school. Is she famous?'

Kate smiled. 'I don't know about that, but I used to work in a library and Jessica Lloyd's books were never on the shelves, they were always out on loan. She's very good.'

'Oh, well then,' Amanda laughed, 'we shall have to watch ourselves and be on our guard, or we'll all end up in her next novel.'

'And what about number one, do you know who's moving in there?'

'According to Sue in the show house, he's a lonesome bachelor. She thinks he's the sort to keep himself very much to himself.'

4

'You're out of your mind!'

Josh ignored his brother and continued to drive along the narrow lane with its high hedges that in places were brushing both sides of his Shogun. He hoped they wouldn't meet an oncoming car, because if his memory served him correctly there wasn't another space to pull in for at least a quarter of a mile.

'I mean it,' Charlie persisted. 'You must be mad thinking of living out here, there'll be no night-life other than owls tu-whit, tu-whooing all hours and driving you round the bend. What's got into you?'

Still Josh didn't say anything. He had anticipated this reaction from Charlie, which was why he had deliberately only brought his brother to see the house when he'd exchanged contracts and had set a date for the removal men to move his stuff out of his flat in Bowdon. And he knew very well that his brother wasn't at all concerned about the lack of available social life that there would be out here in the country. The real line of Charlie's argument was yet to come. He didn't want to hear it, but he knew there could be no avoidance. It was inevitable. Just as so many other things in his life were inevitable.

'Is there any chance of you answering me?'

'And is there any chance of you keeping an open mind?' Josh said evenly, slowing the Shogun to negotiate a small bridge that crossed the canal. He stopped the car to admire the view, hoping it might impress his brother – that it might disarm Charlie of some of his resounding disapproval. To the right of the bridge and moored further along the tow-path was a brightly painted barge and on the bow of the boat was a Jack Russell terrier with a red spotted scarf tied round its neck; it was barking frantically at a swan passing serenely by. On the other side of the bridge and to the left was an attractive white-painted cottage with a garden that was in full flower, which led down to the tow-path where willow trees dipped their elegant branches into the water.

'Well?' said Josh.

'Okay,' Charlie muttered crossly, 'an open mind it is.'

Josh drove on. The narrow lane began to open out and the hedges shrank sufficiently to reveal fields of ripening corn swaying gently in the rippling breeze. They came to a turning to the right, which took them through an avenue of chestnut trees so large and majestic that the branches reached out across the road and formed a long leafy tunnel.

Charlie continued to sit in the front passenger seat unmoved by all the picture-postcard settings they were driving through. For the life of him he couldn't work out what Josh had been up to. Why in heaven's name had he done this crazy thing? And in secret. What had possessed him to buy a house out here in the middle of nowhere? 'Is that it?' he asked, seeing a large building ahead of them.

'Yes,' said Josh. He slowed the car and drove through the archway of Cholmford Hall Mews. He parked outside number one, which was the end property on the left-hand side of the horseshoe-shaped barn conversion. 'I'll get the keys,' he said.

He walked slowly and stiffly across the courtyard to the show house where he found the sales negotiator in the kitchen. She was perched on a bar stool reading a magazine. She closed it and slipped it under a property brochure as soon as she saw him.

'Okay if I have the key?' he asked. 'I want to show somebody round.'

'Of course, Mr Crawford. No problem.' She went to a filing cabinet tucked into a corner of the kitchen and pulled out an envelope of labelled keys. She handed him his set. 'You're moving in next week, aren't you?' she said, hoping to engage him in conversation. He really was quite good-looking, in that smooth, clean-cut kind of way you usually only saw on the telly. He had a neat dress sense too, but then she'd always liked a man in black. A shame she could never get him to talk, though. He was always polite, but not what she'd call forthcoming. He thanked her for the keys and left.

There was no sign of Charlie when Josh went back across the courtyard, but the small gate to the garden of number one was open. He found his brother standing in the middle of the recently turfed lawn. This garden mirrored exactly number five's and they were the largest plots on the development, both extending to almost half an acre, and the views across to Bosley Cloud and the Peak District were stunning.

'Admiring the view?' asked Josh.

'Not particularly, I'm getting agoraphobia. Give me the suburbs any day.'

'Philistine. Come and see inside the house.'

As they moved from one empty, echoing room to another Josh waited for his brother finally to get to the point. Charlie was rarely quiet and the uncomfortable silence growing between them was getting on his nerves. It had been the same at work recently. Without a word, Charlie was syphoning off jobs that would normally come Josh's way. Even when they had been planning their last trip to Hong Kong, Charlie had assumed that Josh would stay behind. He'd tried to make out that Josh was needed in Manchester to make sure everything was in order for their next trade fair.

'Okay,' Charlie said at last, when they'd done the full tour and were back in the sitting-room where they'd started. They stood in front of a large arched window and stared out at the garden and hills beyond. 'I'll concede that it's a great house. I'll even go so far as to say I like where it is. It has a certain countrified-meets-chic charm to it, though I couldn't see myself here, not ever. I'd feel too cut off.'

'But?'

A couple of moments passed before Charlie spoke. 'Oh, come off it, Josh, you know perfectly well what the "but" is.'

Josh shook his head. 'Please. Explain it to me.'

Charlie kept his eyes on the patchwork of uneven turf outside. He couldn't bring himself to say the words. How could he? How could he tell his brother – his best mate – that the odds were against him, that one morning in the not too distant future he could wake up unable to manage the stairs in his own home, never mind push a bloody great mower round that huge garden out there.

'You're not saying anything, Charlie. Don't tell me you're struggling to find the right words.'

Charlie turned away from the window. He faced his brother. 'Don't taunt me, it's not fair.'

Josh's face hardened. 'You're right,' he said, 'you're absolutely right. It isn't fair. It's not fair that I've got multiple sclerosis and that I should want to live in this house. I should behave myself and conform, and become the disabled person you want me to be. I should throw in the towel and move into a crappy, depressing little bungalow and have the whole place kitted out with ramps and God knows what else.'

'I didn't say that.'

'No. You didn't need to. It's been written all over your face ever since last night when I told you about this place.'

Charlie ran his hand through his hair. It was nine months now since Josh had been diagnosed as having MS and he knew he should be getting used to these sudden outbursts of anger from his younger brother, but he wasn't. If anything he was finding it more and more difficult to come up with the right response. If he were honest, he found his brother's anger frightening because he knew that it betrayed Josh's fear of his illness.

'Who said anything about a bungalow?' he said, trying to make light of Josh's accusation. 'And anyway, what was so wrong with your flat? Why the sudden need to up sticks and be so far away from everyone you know?'

Josh moved slowly across the room and went and leaned against the carved oak mantelpiece. He could feel the underside of his left foot beginning to tingle, which he knew in a matter of hours would turn into full-blown pins and needles and would spread up his leg, leaving him with barely any feeling in that part of his body. If he was lucky it would be gone by the morning. If not, it could last for days, maybe even weeks. 'If you must know, I'm tired of you all staring at me,' he said, 'you, Mum and Dad, and everyone at work, you're all giving me those same pitying looks. Poor Josh, you're thinking, only thirty-seven and destined soon to be little more than a vegetable in a wheelchair.'

Charlie flinched at his brother's words, but he couldn't stop his concern now turning to anger. He stuffed his fists into his trouser pockets. 'It's because we care about you, you ungrateful bastard!'

'And I'm sick of it,' Josh shouted back at him. 'If I haven't got much worthwhile life left then I'm bloody well going to enjoy what I have got, which means living out here in the country and being allowed to be *me*, and not some stereotyped image of a crippo that you've got in mind.'

'But it's so isolated here,' Charlie tried to reason.

But Josh was past reason. 'Good,' he shouted, 'because then you won't hear me screaming when I've had enough and done myself in!'

5

Before heading for Kassiopi, Jessica steered her boat towards a secluded bay that contained nothing but a couple of extravagantly large holiday villas surrounded by bushes of purple-flowering oleander and soaring cypress trees. Both villas had direct access on to the small sandy beach where Jessica could see and smell a lunch-time barbecue in progress. Exuberant English voices drifted across the water as children chased and splashed each other in the rock pools and parents, stretched out on sun-loungers, instinctively called out to them to be careful.

Jessica smiled at the children as they waved at her and carefully manoeuvred the boat alongside the rickety wooden jetty that had been built to serve the two holiday properties, as well as her friends' more modest house higher up the hillside. She switched off the engine, hopped out and tied the boat to the post Helen and Jack used. She then began the climb up the steep wooded slope to where they lived.

She was hot and short of breath by the time she reached their little house with its buttermilk walls partially draped in bougainvillaea and topped with a delicate coral-coloured roof. She found them both lying languidly in deck-chairs in the shade of the terrace that Jack had spent the winter months constructing. For once, Jack was wearing shorts, but as usual, apart from a sun visor, Helen didn't have a stitch on.

'Hi there,' Helen said when she saw Jessica. 'You look like you could do with something to drink.'

Jessica flopped on to a nearby chair and fanned herself with her hand. 'Please,' she said, lifting off her sun-glasses and wiping the sweat from her face, 'a keg of water should just about do it, along with the same quantity of ice that sank the *Titanic*.'

Helen laughed, which had the effect of making her large tanned breasts wobble. Jessica had always been fascinated by Helen's body: splendidly Rubensesque and the colour of terracotta, its voluptuous form compared with her own, which was a rather straight-up-and-down affair with just a hint of a bump here and there, had made her feel slightly less of a woman than her friend. Before Helen and Jack had made their home here on the island Helen had dressed in what she herself described as mumsy chain-store separates. Looking at her now, it was difficult to imagine that such a sensual, generous body could ever be restrained by anything so criminally dull. Helen's body was made for being on show and these days she chose to do exactly that, and proudly. She'd told Jessica how when she and Jack had arrived and they'd first stripped off their inhibited Englishness, Jack had been in a permanent state of arousal, which Helen had further boasted had done wonders for their sex life, which she said had begun to run out of steam back in Huddersfield.

'You just never learn, do you?' Helen said. 'How many years have you lived here and you still go rushing about in the heat of the day when any sensible-minded person does little more than open a bottle of wine.'

'Not sure we've got any icebergs lurking in the freezer, Jessica,' Jack said, getting to his feet, 'but I'll see what I can rustle up for you.'

Jessica watched Jack go inside and not for the first time wondered what his ex-work colleagues from the bank in Huddersfield would make of his current life-style.

Forty-eight-year-old finance managers didn't normally go in for such bohemian mores, but when Jack and Helen had come to Corfu on holiday three years ago they had returned home to Huddersfield after two weeks of bliss and decided that their lives were no longer suited to the confines of a nine-to-five existence on a smart housing estate on the edge of town. Jack had told Jessica how one morning, with his resignation neatly typed up, he had gone in to work ready to end twenty years of company loyalty and to discuss the effect this decision would have on his pension. What he hadn't been prepared for was a generous redundancy package being solicitously offered across his boss's desk. He immediately feigned disappointment and desk-thumping outrage at such treatment, then rushed to the staff toilets to dispose of his resignation.

They quickly sold their executive five-bedroomed house and moved to Corfu, and with Jack's redundancy money they bought a couple of tiny villas; one to live in and the other to rent out to tourists. And to go the whole hog, Helen rekindled an old hobby from her pre-teaching days and started painting. She now sold tasteful water-colours of the surrounding area to the very same kind of holiday-maker she had once been. Jessica affectionately called them the Tom and Barbara Good of Corfu.

'Do you think you'll ever leave here?' Jessica suddenly asked Helen.

Helen looked at her. 'What an absurd question. Are you feeling okay?'

Jack joined them on the terrace, carrying a tray of drinks. He handed Jessica a large beer mug of water with several cubes of ice, as well as another glass which contained white wine. He passed a glass of wine to his wife, who said, 'Jessica's just asked me the strangest of questions. Go on, Jessica, ask Jack and see what kind of response you get from him.'

'Fire away,' Jack said, settling himself in his deck-chair.

Jessica smiled. 'I only asked if you could ever see yourselves leaving the island.'

'It's a possibility, but only to go somewhere equally perfect.' Jack stared at Jessica. 'So what's the deal? Why the question?'

Jessica drained her beer mug of water and let a few ice cubes slip into her mouth. She crunched on them noisily.

'Well,' Helen said, 'like Jack says, what's the deal?'

'Not much, it's just that I've come to say goodbye.'

'Goodbye?' Helen and Jack looked at each other, horrified. 'What do you mean?' they said together.

'I'm going back to England.'

Helen sat up aghast. She leant forwards, her legs akimbo, completely oblivious to her nakedness.

'A-hem,' Jack said, raising his eyebrows, 'you're showing your sexy bits, Helen.'

Jessica smiled, amused that Jack hadn't lost all of his nine-to-five conventions.

Helen tutted and to please Jack slapped her legs together. 'Why, Jessica?' she asked. 'I don't understand it. It's paradise here.'

'I know,' Jessica said, 'but I think that's part of the problem. It's all too easy living as we do. It's as if we're all caught up in this wonderful balloon of a life that encapsulates the very best of everything we could ever want and ... and I've got the feeling my own particular balloon of perfection has burst.'

Helen looked confused. 'I'm not sure I understand. What's wrong with enjoying ourselves?'

'Nothing ... so long as it feels right.'

'And it doesn't feel right for you any more?'

Jessica turned to Jack and shook her head. 'Not any more, no. It's not enough.'

'How much paradise do you want, for heaven's sake?' cried Helen.

'I don't think it's paradise I'm searching for. Perhaps it's the opposite. I feel like I haven't earned myself a proper slot in life yet.'

'Oh, my fathers, you're not on some kind of guilt trip, are you? Don't tell me you're about to embark on some personal crusade of masochistic pleasure. You've had it too good and now it's time for a bit of punishment, is that what you're after? A hair shirt and a steady job?'

'Helen,' warned Jack, 'stop trivialising what Jessica's got to say.'

'I'm not,' she said crossly.

Jessica suddenly laughed. 'Stop it, you two. And Helen, for goodness sake stop looking so thoroughly indignant, it doesn't suit that wonderful body of yours.'

'So come on, Jessica,' Jack said, 'why the Shirley Valentine in reverse? What's brought it on?'

'I'm not sure I can explain it to you. All I know is that I no longer feel a part of life here. I don't feel I belong.'

'What does Gavin have to say?' Helen asked.

'Er ... he doesn't know I'm going.'

'What?'

'When are you leaving?' asked Jack.

'Tonight.'

'*What!*'

'Helen, will you stop saying *what* all the time.'

'Listen, Jack, I'll say what as many times as it takes to talk some sense into this girl. She can't go, she simply can't.'

*

Jessica said goodbye and left her friends to carry on their bickering. She took the steep path down to the beach, untied her boat, started up the engine and headed towards Kassiopi where she hoped her next round of farewells wouldn't be quite so interrogative.

When she reached the busy harbour with its myriad fishing boats jostling for position with the many caiques waiting to take tourists for a trip along the coast she made her way to Costas's restaurant and decided that, to be on the safe side, she would simply tell him and his family that she was returning to England to look after her mother. A Greek man like Costas would understand all about family duty and responsibility.

Costas hugged her warmly when he saw her. He kissed her many times over and slipped his arms around her waist. He took her to the back of the restaurant away from all his customers. He kissed her again and asked her in one breath how she was, how her writing was going and when was she going to get around to casting him as her next romantic hero? His English was perfect, if slightly Americanised, having been learnt while working in Chicago in a restaurant owned by one of his many cousins. He called through to the kitchen at the back of the restaurant. Instantly his mother appeared through the beaded curtain and shuffling behind her came an even older woman, Costas's grandmother. The two women beamed at Jessica. They were very fond of her, especially as she had immortalised them both in the opening chapter of her first novel which had been set in Corfu. They spoke hardly any English and even though Jessica could speak passable Greek, Costas always insisted that she spoke in English so that he could practise his interpreting skills. Jessica suspected it was because he liked to show off in front of his womenfolk.

'I can't stay long,' she said, refusing his offer of a drink and a plate or two of mezéthes, 'I've just come to say goodbye.'

'Goodbye?' he repeated, 'why?'

'I'm going back to England.'

Costas forgot all about translating for his mother and grandmother. They waited patiently for him to speak to them. But he didn't. 'For good?' was all he said to Jessica.

She nodded. 'I think so.'

He smiled.

'You don't seem surprised.'

'I'm not. I've seen it many times before. For visitors to the island its magic only lasts for so long.'

Jessica kissed him.

'What's that for?' he asked.

'For being the first to understand. Thank you.'

After leaving Costas and his family Jessica walked along the crowded harbour and crossed the square to Dimitrios, the owner of her house who, with his wife Anastasia, ran a noisy bar that unashamedly pandered to the needs of a particular type of English tourist. They served up steak and kidney pudding with mushy peas, even in August when the heat could be in the high nineties, and in the evenings they didn't bother playing bouzouki music, but showed videos of *Fawlty Towers* and *Men Behaving Badly* to amuse their customers over their beers.

Jessica chatted for a while with Dimitrios – unfortunately Anastasia was out visiting her mother – then handed him her spare set of keys to her house. She signed the necessary forms and returned to her boat.

When she finally reached Coyevinas she found Gavin waiting for her on the sun terrace.

Having said goodbye to her closest friends and dealt with the formalities of relinquishing her home, Jessica was already mentally flying back to England, ready to start her future.

But here was Gavin. Here was the present.

And just one look at him was enough to make her undo all her well-made plans.

He was leaning lazily against the wall, looking down at her as she approached the last few steps. His shoulder-length, sun-bleached hair was blowing in the afternoon sea breeze that had just started to pick up and his white T-shirt was rippling across his chest. She couldn't make out the expression on his face because he was wearing his favourite Ray-Bans, but she had the feeling that he had been waiting for her for some time and that he must have seen her little boat appear round the rocky promontory from Kassiopi and that he must also have watched her climb the steep hill path. She wondered what had brought him here at this time of day when normally he would be out teaching tourists to sail before the sea became too rough.

'Why aren't you working?' she asked, going straight inside the house.

'Pete's covering for me,' he said, following behind her and pushing his glasses up over his head.

'Why?' She frowned. *Why* was a word she'd heard too often today.

'Helen phoned me.'

'Oh.'

'What were you going to do, Jessica, write me a letter?'

She thought of the envelope in her bag. 'I'm sorry,' she said guiltily.

'No you're not.' His face took on an expression of bewilderment and reduced him to the hurt boy she had predicted.

'And are *you*?' she asked. 'Are you sorry I'm going, or are you just put out, a little inconvenienced perhaps?'

He didn't answer her. 'Helen didn't seem very clear about your reasons for leaving.'

Jessica smiled. 'She wouldn't be, she's too busy being punch drunk on Ionian nectar.'

Her metaphor was lost on him. He frowned and came towards her. 'Are you okay?'

'I think so,' she said, suddenly aware of the warmth of his body next to hers. She held her breath, knowing that if she breathed in the smell of him she would be caught in his spell and be reminded of all the pleasures soon to be denied her.

'Is it me? Is that why you're going?'

His arrogance gave her the strength she needed. How typical that he should think the world revolved around him. She took a step back from him and went outside to the terrace. He followed her and to the sound of the cicadas chirruping noisily in the nearby olive trees they both stood gazing at the sea and the shimmering outline of Albania where so much needless fighting had recently taken place.

'Your sleeping with other women did hurt me at first,' she said, determined to be honest with Gavin, but equally so that her last memory of him wouldn't be an acrimonious one. 'But then I began to realise that it wasn't our relationship that was bothering me. It was something much more significant. I woke up to the fact that there's nothing here for me any more.'

'Not even me?'

Still that arrogance! 'No, Gavin, not even you. Besides, there are plenty of other women for you, you don't need me. And I'm afraid that's something I want, I want somebody to need me.'

'Like your mother?'

She smiled. 'How perceptive of you ... and how very out of character.'

He shrugged. 'All things to all men, that's me.'

'Don't you mean all things to all women?'

He had the grace to turn away.

'By the way,' she said, sensing that their conversation was coming to an end, 'I know you don't approve of boats with engines, but you can have mine anyway. Do with it what you want.'

'Thanks.' He placed his hands on her shoulders and kissed her. 'Good luck, Jessica, I hope you find what you're looking for. Do you want a lift to the airport?'

6

Alec thought of ringing Kate to let her know that he was on his way, but he was in such a hurry to see her he didn't want to do anything that might slow him down, so he locked up the office, threw his briefcase into the rear of his Saab 900, pushed back the soft top and headed for home along the A34 going south.

It was strange not to be driving in a northerly direction on this familiar stretch of road – through Alderley Edge, then on to Wilmslow – as he'd done for as long as he could remember, but he guessed that his new route home would soon become second nature to him. He passed Capesthorne Hall on his right with its extraordinary turreted façade and toyed with the idea of getting tickets for him and Kate for the open-air summer concert that would be held there next month. Thinking of Kate again made him want to get home even faster and he pressed down on the accelerator.

He wondered if he'd ever lose this feeling of euphoria every time he thought of her. He still couldn't believe his good fortune, that a girl like Kate would even be interested in him, let alone love him.

But then so much had happened to him that he was convinced that no matter how predictable one thought one's life was, it was anything but. He for one had never imagined he would end up running such a successful greetings card company.

Neither had he ever considered ending up a divorcé.

While he would admit that his marriage with Melissa had never been perfect, he had thought that there had been enough common ground between them – namely their daughter and the jointly owned business – to keep them together no matter what. There had been the usual conflicts that life bestowed so generously on any married couple, especially a couple who lived and worked together, but he had accepted the arguments and irritations as all part and parcel of marriage. Looking back on it, perhaps he had been too passive, too inclined to remember his vows of *for better or for worse* and had simply gone along with things. But in the end Melissa had not. Melissa had seen fit to give up on what she referred to as a bad job. She had likened their marriage to a rather tedious book that one is told to read because it's a classic and never mind the boring bits, one must stick with it and see it through. Rather graphically, she'd told him that she had grown tired of wading through the same book, she wanted something new to read. 'There isn't anybody else,' she'd told him, as if this would make him feel better, 'I just don't want to be married to you any more.' Her pragmatic approach, he realised later, had at least made them both behave in a civilised manner throughout the divorce.

Initially, though, shock had rendered him unable to comprehend a life without Melissa when, one wet, miserable November evening she had moved out of their house in Wilmslow. 'I shan't be one of those grasping women,' she'd told him in the office the following morning. 'I shall just expect what is currently mine: half of the house, half of the savings and half of the business. Here's the name of my solicitor.'

That was the thing about Melissa, she was very businesslike, very organised and very together. Nothing fazed her.

No. That wasn't quite true. He had seen Melissa floored once, completely so. It was last Christmas when she'd first set eyes on Kate.

He'd heard the intake of breath, as well as the comment that followed. 'Pretty enough wrapping,' she'd whispered to their daughter Ruth, 'but is there anything worthwhile beneath those liquid eyes and the bewitching smile?'

He smiled, turned off the main road and drove through the avenue of chestnut trees towards Cholmford Hall Mews. 'Oh yes, Melissa,' he said out loud, a triumphant note to his voice, 'there's something more worthwhile than you'll ever know.'

He parked the car in front of the house and through the kitchen window that faced the courtyard he caught sight of Kate. She must have just taken a shower for he could see that she was wearing her white towelling bathrobe and had a towel wrapped around her head.

He let himself in and placing his briefcase at the foot of the stairs in the hall he called out jokingly in true Hollywood style, 'Hi, honey, I'm home.'

She came and wrapped her arms around him. 'So you are.'

He held her tightly, pressed her slight body against his own and kissed her slender neck. He breathed in the perfume of her fragrant skin. 'You smell wonderful.'

'So does supper, I hope. It's nearly ready.'

He kissed her and began loosening her bathrobe. 'Can it wait?'

'Can you?'

He pulled the towel away from her head and let her wet hair fall to her waist. 'No,' he said and took her upstairs.

Later, when they sat down to eat, Alec poured out some wine and handed Kate a glass. 'A toast,' he said, 'to our first proper meal in our very own home.'

They chinked their glasses and smiled happily at each other in the candle-light.

'You don't mind eating in the kitchen, do you?' Kate asked. She had hoped to have had the dining-room sorted out in time, but in the end she had been too exhausted to start unpacking all of Alec's cut glass and china. Even so, she had gone to great lengths to make everything just right for them in the kitchen, setting the table perfectly for a romantic supper; napkins, scented candles, even a few flowers taken from Alec's bouquet.

'Of course I don't mind.' He laughed. 'This is wonderful. I don't know how you managed to get so much done today and cook a meal. The house looks fantastic. You're a marvel, you are, really.' He leant over and kissed her.

'So what was your day like?' she asked, basking in his praise.

'Busy. We've got trouble in the warehouse down in Oxford. I shall probably have to go and take a look some time in the next few weeks.'

'Can't Melissa go?' Kate knew it was silly, but she didn't want Alec going down to Oxford, not if it meant he might spend the night away from her.

'She could, but I'd rather do it myself. Why don't you come with me?'

'Are you sure?'

'Of course I am. We could stop the night in a nice hotel. It would give you a break from all the hard work you're putting in here.'

'I wouldn't be in the way?'

'Not at all. I'd much prefer it if you came. And besides, expensive hotel rooms have an aphrodisiac charm all of their own.'

She smiled. 'My own charm wearing thin already?'

He covered her hand with his. 'Not in a million years.'

Amanda tipped the remains of Tony's uneaten supper into the bin. Another disastrous evening was behind them. If only Tony didn't always give in to Hattie. Surely he could see that the child had him tightly wrapped around her little finger? How many bedtime stories did it take, for heaven's sake?

She went back into the sitting-room, switched on the television and began sorting out the swatches of fabric and wallpaper samples that she had collected over the past week. She really had to decide what colour scheme to have in the sitting-room. She was fed up with not having any curtains.

Upstairs in Hattie's bedroom Tony was sitting on the floor alongside his daughter. They were leaning against her bed looking at a book all about dolphins, which they'd bought on their holiday in America last year when they'd visited Sea World in Orlando.

'Do you remember when we were all splashed by that huge whale?' Hattie asked her father.

He smiled, remembering the holiday with fondness, not because it was supposed to have been his honeymoon with Amanda, but because it had brought his daughter such pleasure. 'Yes, we were drenched good and proper, weren't we?' He drew her closer to him.

'And then the whale came round the pool a second time and splashed us some more. Can we go again?'

Tony closed the book and placed it on Hattie's bedside table next to a framed photograph of her mother. 'Come on,' he said, 'time your pretty little head was on the pillow.'

Hattie reluctantly climbed into bed. Tony covered her with the white frilled duvet.

'So can we go again?' Hattie asked, looking up at him, her arms outstretched, waiting for a final hug.

'We'll have to see,' he said. He leant down and kissed her soft cheek. She quickly reached out to him and held on to his neck and pulled him down so that he ended up lying beside her.

'We went to see the new lady who moved in yesterday,' she said, hoping to keep her father's attention for a little longer.

'And is she nice?' he asked.

'Very nice. She's got lovely hair. It goes all the way down her back.'

'I'll look out for her. Now you really should go to sleep.' He kissed her again and made his escape.

He turned out the light and went downstairs, his head aching with tiredness. He was exhausted. He'd been up since five that morning and on the road by half past in order to see a customer in Reading for nine o'clock. The meeting had gone on until two, then he'd driven to Birmingham for another appointment. He'd finally reached home just after eight, only to find Amanda cross and out of sorts because Hattie had played her up over tea.

'Fancy a drink?' he said, when he found Amanda in the sitting-room watching the television.

'I'll make us some coffee, shall I?' she said, rising from the sofa.

He shook his head. 'I need something stronger.'

'There's some wine in the fridge. I'll get that.'

He collapsed on to the sofa, pushed aside the mess on the coffee table in front of him and put his feet up. He closed his eyes to some poor devil of a politician having his bones picked clean by a predatory Jeremy Paxman and tried hard not to think of what lay ahead after the weekend when he had an all-day meeting with one of the company bigwigs who was flying over from the States to determine the effectiveness of their UK office. 'Nothing to worry about, Tony,' Bradley Hurst had said on the phone yesterday morning, 'I want you to know that Arc is deeply invested in the UK. All I want to do is simply have ourselves a head-to-head to clarify our position.' The last time their position had been clarified by Bradley-Dewhurst-the-Butcher's-Boy, as all the sales guys in the office referred to the recently appointed vice-president of Arc Computers, their numbers had been dramatically reduced. As director of sales in the UK, Tony was only too aware that no matter how well the figures looked they would always be vulnerable to another attack from Bradley Hurst. The man was ruthless and probably went to bed at night chanting his own personal mantra – one employee less equals a dollar saved; two employees less equals two dollars saved; three employees less . . . It was a short-sighted way to run a company and long term it couldn't work.

When Amanda came back into the room with a bottle of wine and two glasses she found her carefully ordered wallpaper and fabric samples scattered all over the floor and Tony fast asleep. 'Happy bloody families,' she muttered to herself.

The flight had been delayed by nearly an hour and Jessica hoped her mother wouldn't be worrying. She had tried ringing from the airport at Corfu to warn her that she'd be late, but she hadn't been able to raise an answer. She had tried again when she'd landed at Manchester, but still there was no reply from Willow Cottage. She had fought against the rapidly forming image in her mind of her mother lying prostrate on the floor, her hand inches away from the phone. Instead, she had forced herself to picture her mother doing some late-night weeding in her immaculate garden, happily ignorant of the time or of the ringing telephone inside the house.

Now, as she sat in the back of a taxi driving at a snail's pace through the dark Cheshire countryside and with only a few minutes to go before her journey would be completed, Jessica chided herself for her stupidity. Her mother had managed just fine all these years without having anyone fretting over her, especially the kind of fretting that was turning her daughter into a neurotic idiot.

Idiot had been the word that Helen had used so vociferously at the airport when she and Jack had seen her off. Gavin had offered to come as well when she'd told him that Jack was driving her to the airport, but she had said she'd rather he didn't. 'Tears and sentiment would do me no good at this stage,' she'd told him.

There had been no danger of tears or sentiment with Helen, though. She was still cross with Jessica for leaving. 'You're an idiot, Jessica. A complete idiot. But mark my words, when you've been back in England for a few months you'll wonder what you've done.'

'You're probably right,' Jessica had said, 'but I'm going anyway.'

'And another thing,' Helen had gone on, 'why didn't you tell us what you were up to?'

'Because you would have tried to stop me.'

And that was the truth. She knew she'd hurt Helen and Jack with her secrecy, but she couldn't have taken the risk of letting them know what was in her mind. If she'd told them that on her last visit to England, when her mother had gone into hospital, she'd seen a house that she was considering buying they would have gone out of their way to dissuade her.

'Been on holiday, then?' the taxi driver asked, opening his mouth to speak for the first time.

'Yes,' she said, not wanting to explain yet again why she was returning to England. The pair of chatty young lads sitting next to her on the plane, with their scalped heads, noserings and sunburnt faces and bulging carrier bags of duty free, had been at a loss to understand why she didn't want to live in Corfu for the rest of her life. 'Give me a life of sun, sex and ouzo any day,' one of them had said.

'Somewhere hot and nice?' the driver asked her.

'Very hot and very nice,' she said truthfully.

'Ah well, it'll be back to normal and the real world now, won't it? That's the thing about holidays, there's nothing lasting about them, just a few out-of-focus photographs.'

Too tired to add anything of any worth to the conversation, Jessica let the man ramble on with his personal philosophy and anxiously watched the road. Now that the driver had opened up the floodgates of dialogue he seemed to have lost interest in keeping his eyes on the dark, narrow lanes and kept turning round to emphasise a point to her.

'You'll have to slow down here,' she said, suddenly leaning forward in her seat, 'there's a small bridge and almost immediately there'll be a turning to the left. That's it.'

In the clear moonlit sky Willow Cottage looked enchanting with its white rendered walls almost hidden beneath a swathe of sweet-smelling blooms from several ancient climbing roses, as well as a clematis that had competed for space over the porch. It was exactly how Jessica always pictured the house in which she'd grown up. Her own life might have taken a few twists and turns, but Willow Cottage had not.

The taxi driver was impressed. 'If I lived here I wouldn't need to go on holiday.'

Jessica waited impatiently for the man to amble his way round to the boot for her things. Come on, come on, she muttered to herself. 'How much do I owe you?' she asked, when finally a collection of overstuffed holdalls was gathered around her feet.

'Call it twenty-four.'

I'd sooner call it highway robbery, Jessica thought as she watched the red tail-lights of the car disappear. She looked up at the house and wondered why her mother hadn't already come to the door.

No! she told herself. Keep that writer's brain firmly under control, your mother is not lying dead on the Axminster!

She tried the doorbell, but got no response. In the end she let herself in with the key that was kept hidden beneath a large stone that Anna had brought back with her in her hand luggage after one of her stays in Corfu.

She found her mother upstairs in the spare room; it was stripped of all its furniture and old flannelette sheets covered the floor. Anna was standing on the top rung of a pair of step-ladders, a paintbrush in one hand and a pot of undercoat in the other; beneath her, a ghetto blaster was blaring out *The Three Tenors* and Pavarotti was 'Nessun dorma'-ing.

Jessica went over to Pavarotti and turned him down. Her mother suddenly caught sight of her and visibly jumped out of her skin. She gave a loud scream. 'What are you trying to do, Jessica, creeping up on me like that? You frightened me to death.'

'I'm sorry,' Jessica said, immediately horrified at what she'd done – *good grief, she could have killed her mother with shock!* 'I should have thought. I'm sorry. Are you okay? Do you need to sit down?'

'I'm fine,' Anna said irritably. She came down the step-ladder and put the pot of paint on a piece of newspaper. She then looked up at her daughter and, seeing the distress in her face, thought, poor Jessica, how fragile she thinks I've become. 'It'll take more than a little bit of shock to finish me off,' she said more good-humouredly. 'Now let me put this brush in a jar of white spirit, then I'll make us a drink. How was your flight? Oh, and by the way, welcome home.'

7

It was a difficult weekend for both Jessica and Anna. Jessica spent most of it hovering anxiously over her mother, watching her every move. In turn, Anna took every possible opportunity of trying to escape her daughter's infernal gaze.

'Should you be doing that?' was Jessica's automatic response to almost anything Anna did. She said it when she found her in the spare room finishing off the undercoating to the picture rail that she had started while waiting for Jessica to arrive the night before. She said it again when she found her mother standing on a chair in the downstairs loo, changing a light bulb.

'Look, Jessica,' Anna said, 'this can't go on.'

'You're right. It can't. Now get down from that chair and let me do that.'

By Sunday afternoon the strain was really telling. Jessica found Anna struggling with a heavily loaded wheelbarrow in the garden. 'What on earth do you think you're doing?' she cried out, running across the lawn to her mother. 'You have Dermot twice a week to help you in the garden. Leave him to do the heavy work.'

'This is not heavy work. Now kindly leave me alone,' Anna said, gripping the handles of the wheelbarrow through her tattered gardening gloves and doing her best not to lose her temper. 'Go and do something useful. Go for a walk. Go and look at your new house. Anything. So long as you leave me to dig in this manure in peace.' She then pointedly turned up the volume on the Walkman that she had strapped around her waist and staggered further down the garden listening to a piece of Chopin, which Jessica could hear tinkling through the headphones.

Jessica stood and watched her mother angrily tossing fork-loads of manure on to the rose beds and, realising that her own anger needed to be assuaged, decided to go for a walk. She stamped off across the lawn towards the front of the house and to the willow trees either side of the brick steps that led down to the canal.

At first she marched furiously along the tow-path, snatching out at long blades of grass and swishing them against the undergrowth of dock leaves and buttercups, at the same time mentally shouting at her mother for her stubbornness and her stupidity, but gradually the calming effect of the canal worked its magic on her and she felt herself beginning to think more rationally.

It had been the same when she'd been a teenager. The canal had been the perfect place of refuge after she'd argued with Anna over something as trivial as the colour of her hair or the skimpiness of her clothes. They'd shout at one another, each convinced the other was wrong, then she'd race out of the house in a fit of adolescent angst and make for the tow-path. But always by the time she'd even reached the first sweeping curve in the waterway and her favourite tree, her temper would have fizzled out and she would lean against the sycamore and wonder what all the fuss had been about.

She reached the sycamore tree now and as she leant against its huge trunk, a pretty red-and-green-painted narrow boat came into view. Its occupants smiled and nodded at her. She smiled back and watched them slowly chug on with their journey.

Her anger and frustration now gone, she admitted to herself that it was obvious she would have to move into Cholmford Hall Mews sooner than she had originally planned. The idea had been for her to stay for over a week at Willow Cottage, then move into her new home, but even a weekend was turning out to be too nerve-racking an ordeal for them. She suspected that her mother was trying to prove a point with all her displays of independence and that it was merely a device for marking out the territory that belonged to Anna, which she clearly wished to retain.

With this in mind, the first thing Jessica did the next day, Monday morning, was to phone the sales negotiator in the show house at Cholmford Hall Mews. 'I know I said it would be the following week I'd move in and we'd agreed that you needed the show house for as long as possible, but is there any chance I could arrive sooner?'

'You're in luck. We've finished work on number three and we're going to use that as an impromptu show house. It's not a patch on this one, but at least it'll be somewhere for me to sit. I'm actually in the process of moving my stuff across at the moment. I should be finished by this afternoon. I don't see why you couldn't move in tomorrow if you can get your solicitor to arrange for completion to take place by then. Everything's ready for you, the carpets were cleaned on Saturday and the furniture not included in the sale has been shifted across to number three. Do you want to come and check anything?'

Jessica's first reaction was to say no, but then, thinking that it would do her and her mother good to have a break from each other, she said, 'Yes, I'll come down later, about two.'

She phoned her solicitor who said he'd arrange everything in time and after lunch she set off for Cholmford Hall Mews, which was little more than a mile away from Willow Cottage.

The day was warm and sunny, and as Jessica strolled along the lane and entered the cool tunnel of chestnut trees she found herself remembering all the times she'd played here as a child. With her mother's help she had even learnt to ride a bike properly on this flat stretch of road. Anna had never tired of telling the story of the day when Jessica had demanded that the stabilisers be removed from her bicycle. This act of 'big girlness' had meant that her poor mother had had to spend hours running alongside her, one hand on the saddle, the other nudging the handlebars whenever Jessica starting going too fast and out of control.

'Let go, let go,' she had screamed at Anna. 'I can do it, take your hand away.' And of course, the first time Anna had let go, Jessica had tumbled straight off the little bike and had ended up in a heap, with two grazed knees and a blow to her pride.

Jessica smiled to herself, thinking that her mother would probably view her as no better now than that skinny, demanding, four-and-a-half-year-old.

When she'd been that horrible child, Cholmford Hall Mews had been nothing but a sad, derelict stable block – the only surviving bricks and mortar from Cholmford Hall, which according to the local history books had originally been a grand shooting lodge. Just after the First World War the Hall was completely burnt down to its eighteenth-century foundations and for years after nobody saw fit to rebuild the house – the Cholmford family had long since run out of money. In the fifties the land was finally sold to a neighbouring farmer, who immediately cleared away the great pile of rubble and used the land for grazing. The stable block was then relegated to housing tractors and other assorted agricultural equipment and it wasn't until last year when a local building firm, on the look-out for a suitable conversion project, discovered the now thoroughly dilapidated barn and made an offer on it.

When Anna had first told Jessica about the development that was being built she had felt pangs of sorrow that her childhood haunt was to be spoiled and turned into a hideous eyesore. But then, when a few months later her mother had had her heart operation, Jessica had quickly made the decision to go and take a look at the building work. Far from spoiling the barn and the surrounding area, the builder had gone out of his way to create five good-sized homes of considerable quality that blended in perfectly with the incomparable setting. Jessica had come away impressed and within days had made up her mind to buy one of the houses. She didn't tell Anna straight away what she was doing – she needed the shock of her own actions to settle down before she could start explaining herself to her mother.

When Anna had been admitted to hospital, all Jessica had been able to think about was how much she loved her and what a happy childhood she had given her. Even her father's death when she was six years old had done nothing to dent the rosy picture she had of her formative years. She supposed it was because Anna had more than made up for the potential deficit in that area.

And now it was down to Jessica to make sure that her mother's love and kindness were returned.

Jessica moved in to Cholmford Hall Mews on Tuesday afternoon. Anna helped her. They were both the happier for it, knowing that the sooner Jessica was installed in her own home, away from Willow Cottage, the sooner they would start adapting to having each other around.

In terms of moving in there wasn't much to do. The only things that needed unpacking were the holdalls Jessica had arrived with from Corfu, along with several carrier bags of supermarket provisions and a bag of basic crockery borrowed from her mother for Jessica's empty kitchen. Between them they carried everything into the house from the boot of Anna's Fiesta parked outside in the gravelled courtyard.

'It's quite lavish, isn't it?' Anna remarked when everything was in and they'd closed the front door and she looked about the place.

'You said that the first time you saw it.'

'I know. I suppose I was hoping it might have calmed down a bit since then. It's all a bit chichi, don't you think?'

Jessica laughed. She knew exactly what her mother was getting at. The show-house-style furnishings and décor were not at all to her liking, but at the time she'd made her offer on the house it had made sense to Jessica to have everything all done – it was a bit like moving house the *Blue Peter* way; *and here's one I made earlier.*

'And those sofas will be a nightmare to keep clean,' Anna said, going over to inspect the two enormous cream sofas that were placed either side of the fireplace with a distressed-oak table between them. 'It's straight out of *Homes and Garden*. I'm not sure it's really you, Jessica.'

'What, you think I'd be better suited to something a bit more down-market? Some sawdust on the floor and a couple of barrels to sit on?'

'Don't be clever. I only meant it's hardly what you've been used to.'

'That's true enough. Come on, let's go upstairs, the bathrooms are quite something. You'll be green with envy.'

'Why do you need two bathrooms?' Anna said when she followed her daughter up the stairs.

'I don't,' Jessica said, opening a door at the top of the landing. 'It's what builders think people want nowadays. Now what do you think of that, it's the last word in des. res. luxury, isn't it?'

'Goodness, what a lot of edges and corners,' Anna said, peering in at the Wedgwood-blue bathroom with its white tiles and dado border decorated with Grecian urns. Opposite the bath and built around a low-level toilet and a pair of basins was a bank of cupboards and drawers. She went over and opened them all, one by one. 'What on earth will you keep in all these?' she asked.

'I've no idea. Old manuscripts, perhaps. Come and see my bathroom, it's even grander than this one. It looks over towards Mow Cop and the builders have set the cast-iron bath on a raised platform, so I'll be able to enjoy the view while having a soak.'

When they had finished inspecting the bathrooms and Anna had marvelled at the jacuzzi facility to Jessica's bath they went back downstairs. 'How about a cup of tea?' she suggested.

'Good idea, I'll put the kettle on. Oh, but I can't. I don't have one.'

'Oh, well, we'll go shopping later,' Anna said, forever practical, 'meanwhile I'll fill the teapot with water and boil it in the microwave.'

'What microwave?' Jessica asked, looking about the streamlined kitchen and seeing only a row of light-oak cupboards and a runway of spotless work surface.

Anna went over to the built-in cooker unit. 'This one,' she said. She pressed a button and a small door sprang open revealing the spotless interior of a microwave. 'You'll have to get yourself better acquainted with modern-day kitchen equipment, Jessica. I never did like that kitchen of yours in Corfu, it was so basic. The ancient Greeks were such a go-ahead lot, but I'm afraid their descendants are way behind in the white goods department these days. Ooh look, you're not the only one moving in today.'

They stood at the window and stared at a removal van as it rumbled its way into the courtyard and came to a stop outside number one. A few seconds later it was joined by a dark-blue Shogun. Anna and Jessica watched the driver get out. He was quite tall, with a slim build, and was dressed entirely in black – black T-shirt tucked into black jeans, a black denim jacket slung over his shoulder and black shoes with thick chunky soles. He started walking across the courtyard, his progress slightly hampered by a limp to his left leg.

'I do believe he's coming here,' Anna said as the figure in black drew nearer.

'I think you're right,' Jessica concurred, slipping out of view from the window. 'I wonder what he wants.'

They waited for him to ring the doorbell. But he didn't. To their amazement they heard him turn the door handle and suddenly he appeared in the kitchen.

'Keys,' was all he said. But then he looked about him and when he'd taken in the sight of Jessica's few possessions already making themselves at home on the breakfast bar his face coloured. 'Ah,' he said uncomfortably.

Jessica was a nanosecond ahead of him. 'This isn't the show house any more,' she said helpfully, 'it's number three you want.'

He looked at her as though he were going to speak and certainly Jessica could have sworn she saw his mouth open, but something must have made him change his mind, for he quickly turned and left.

'What a rude man,' Jessica said as they took up a discreet position in front of the kitchen window once more and watched him make his way over to the new show house. 'He didn't even have the manners to apologise for barging his way in here.'

'I thought he was rather dishy,' Anna said, 'in an awkward, boyish kind of way. He reminds me of that chap from *The X-Files*, you know, the one with the lovely skin and the silly surname.'

'Oh, stop being so modern, Mum. Now come and show me how this blasted microwave works.'

Josh collected his keys from the woman in the show house, thankful that she'd been on the phone and had been unable to try and engage him in conversation. It was the last thing he needed right now. He hadn't been able to believe it when he'd woken this morning and found that today of all days, when he needed all his faculties to cope with the move, the power of speech was to be denied him. It was like that some mornings. He never knew what he would wake up to. Sometimes it was his hands that refused to work properly. Other days it could be his legs and this morning it had been his speech. He could form a sentence perfectly in his head, but when he actually said the words they came out all joined together like a string of sausages. It was so frustrating.

And so bloody demeaning.

He dreaded to think what those two women must have thought of him. Bad enough that he had barged his way into their house as he had, but even worse that he couldn't apologise for what he'd done.

He joined the removal men who were now all out of the van and were having a quick smoke before unloading his things. He let himself into the house. From his jacket pocket he pulled out a pen and a pad of yellow Post-its and on each page began writing: sitting-room, dining-room, study, kitchen and so on, until he had identified each room. He then went round the house sticking the appropriate piece of paper on each door. That way he hoped the men wouldn't have to keep asking him where everything had to go as each packing box had been appropriately labelled. He'd spent most of the day trying to keep himself to himself so as not to invite conversation, but there had been times when they'd been packing up at the flat when it had been impossible not to answer their questions. He'd tried his best to give them clear instructions, but he knew that they either had him down as a drunk, because his speech was so slurred, or worse, had concluded that he was a half-wit.

It was nearly seven o'clock when the removal men left Josh alone. He found the emergency box of supplies that he had packed himself – coffee, milk, tea-bags, biscuits, Mars bars, pain-killers and some Southern Comfort. He pulled out the bottle and without bothering to look for a glass he slowly climbed the stairs, taking each step with infinite care, steadying himself with his free hand against the white-painted banister. When he reached his bedroom he had to fight his way through the packing boxes to where his bed had been placed. It was exactly where he didn't want it. But no matter. He sat on the edge of it and took several large gulps of Southern Comfort. It burnt his throat and left a warm glow of apparent strength there. He knew he shouldn't drink, that the alcohol would make his co-ordination even worse, as well as slur his speech more than it already was, but he didn't care. He was exhausted and had no intention of talking to another soul that day. He planned to sleep for at least the next twelve hours. He drank some more, then tried screwing the lid on the bottle, but this simple task took all his concentration and when he'd managed it he dropped the bottle on the floor and collapsed back on to the bed.

He was asleep within seconds.

The phone rang an hour later. It wasn't easy to find as somebody – one of the removal men – had placed it under the bed. He eventually located it and fumbled with the receiver.

'Josh, it's Charlie. How's it going?'

'Iwasleep.'

'What? You're not very clear. Do you need a hand? I could come over if you want.'

'Sodoff!'

Josh banged the receiver down and lay on the bed. He tried to go back to sleep, but in spite of his exhaustion he knew he wouldn't be able to. He knew also that Charlie would ring again.

He was right. The phone rang almost at once.

'Sawry,' he managed to say.

'It's okay,' Charlie said, 'don't worry, is it a bad speech day?'

'Yess.'

'Do you need any help?'

Josh could hear that Charlie was suddenly emphasising his own clear diction, as if this would in some way help Josh's words come out right. He knew that Charlie couldn't help it, it was a knee-jerk reaction, like clearing your throat for somebody else. The last time they'd been in this situation Josh had felt angry and humiliated by Charlie talking to him as though he were a simpleton, but tonight he was too tired to feel anything.

'Josh, are you still there?'

'Yesss,' he said wearily.

'Are you very knackered?'

'Yesss.'

'Would you like some company?'

'No.'

8

Amanda wondered what on earth she was going to do.

Her mother was supposed to be baby-sitting for Hattie that evening and she had just rung to say that she couldn't make it. Tony would go mad. The relationship between the pair of them was bad enough without Rita further worsening the situation – one that had developed from the day she had taken Tony to meet her parents for the first time: the dreaded Sunday-lunch scenario – roast boyfriend and apple pie. Her mother didn't have a very high opinion of men and was never slow in publicly declaring them a species incapable of making a commitment. 'Commitment my foot,' she would often say, 'men don't know the meaning of the word. A piece of soggy loo roll has more staying power than a man.'

When she had uttered these familiar words in front of Tony he had laughed politely and asked where that left Amanda's father. 'You've been married for over thirty years, Amanda tells me, that's quite a commitment, wouldn't you say?' Since then Rita had viewed Tony with suspicion. She didn't like to be questioned.

Even on their wedding day, Rita had approached Amanda while she was slipping into her dress and suggested that it wasn't too late to change her mind.

'But I don't want to change my mind,' she had told her mother.

'Then maybe you should consider it. I'm not entirely sure you've thought this through. Is he really the right man for you? It's all been so quick.'

'A two-year engagement would be too quick for you, Mother. Now help me with my zip. And please don't worry, I know exactly what I'm doing.' Which was true, she was not the sort of woman to leave things to chance. Her mother might not realise it, but Tony was perfect for her.

She had thought that moving to Cholmford, where they would be only a few miles away from Rita, would perhaps ease the situation between the three of them. She had had visions of Rita becoming more involved with her and Tony, and especially with Hattie. She had seen her mother in the role of doting grandmother wanting to spend time with her newly acquired granddaughter. 'That's all right, Amanda,' she had imagined her mother saying, 'I'll take charge while you and Tony have some time to yourselves. A long weekend alone is just what you both need.'

She must have been crazy thinking that life could be that simple.

And what was she going to do about tonight? In an hour's time she was supposed to be having dinner with Tony and Bradley Hurst and his wife. It wasn't often that Tony discussed his work with her, but she knew that his all-day meeting with Hurst was an important one. She was aware, also, of the importance of tonight's little get-together and the part that she was expected to play. Which, if she was honest, she enjoyed. The role of corporate wife appealed to her. If she herself couldn't work, then making a career on the back of her husband's was quite possibly the next best thing. And it was another reason why she didn't want to lose this evening's opportunity of presenting herself and Tony as the perfect couple to Bradley Hurst. She quite fancied the trappings that came with Arc Computers, more important, she had her eye on the perks that came further up the organisation. Currently Tony was the UK sales director for Arc and while he seemed happy with his lot, she had other ideas. Who knows, if only Tony could show a bit more ambition, one day they might end up in America where the standard of living was so incredible.

But all this was pie in the sky. So much for being the force behind the successful husband, she couldn't even organise a baby-sitter for that evening. There just wasn't anybody to whom she could turn. Having moved here to the back of beyond where they didn't know a living soul, apart from Rita, there wasn't anyone to whom she could shout for help. Everyone they knew lived at least twenty-five miles away. It was hopeless. Well, there was nothing else for it but to ring Tony and explain. She would have to lie through her teeth and make out that her mother was, at the very least, at death's door. Which would probably bring a smile to Tony's face.

'When will Grandma Rita be here?' asked Hattie, coming into the bedroom where Amanda was staring out of the window. Hattie was all ready for bed, dressed in her Beauty and the Beast nightie and chewing on her toothbrush.

'She's not,' Amanda said flatly. 'She can't make it.'

Hattie sucked on her toothbrush. 'Does that mean you can't go out?'

Amanda moved away from the window. She went and sat in front of the dressing-table mirror and began taking out the heated rollers from her hair. 'Got it in one.'

Hattie came and stood next to her. 'Are you disappointed?'

Amanda stared back at Hattie in the mirror. 'Yes,' she said truthfully, 'yes I am, and I think your father's going to be more disappointed. In fact, I'd better ring him now while he's still at the office, before he leaves for the restaurant.'

'Isn't there anybody else who could baby-sit?' Hattie didn't like the idea of her father being upset.

Amanda took the last of the rollers out and shook her hair. She started brushing it. 'We don't know anybody else here, that's the problem.'

'We know Kate.'

Amanda stopped what she was doing. She thought of last Friday when the sickeningly *lovely* Kate had had Hattie eating out of her hand. She had certainly shown that she had a knack for dealing with small children, which was more than Amanda had, and she had come away after their visit consumed with jealousy that anyone could be that good with her stepdaughter. When they'd finished their cups of coffee Kate had let Hattie plunder several packing cases of books out in the hall and had even allowed her to play with her jewellery box – little more than a cheap trinket box as far as Amanda could see – which she had brought down from her bedroom. 'I'd be so grateful if you sort it out for me,' she'd said to a smiling Hattie, 'the move has made it all topsy-turvy. Do you think you could manage that?'

Amanda turned and faced Hattie. 'You're right,' she said, a glimmer of hope twinkling in the far distance, 'we do know Kate, but do you think she'd do it?'

'She might, she was very nice to me.'

The words 'to me' were not lost on Amanda. 'She's probably got plans for tonight already,' she said, brushing her hair once more. 'And anyway, what would your father say about somebody he doesn't know looking after you?'

Hattie kept quiet and carried on chewing her toothbrush.

Stupid question, thought Amanda, if there was one person who could convince Tony a bad idea was a good one it was Hattie. 'Okay,' she said, getting up from the padded stool and stepping into her black patent shoes. 'I'll go across and see Kate. It's worth a try.'

The taxi dropped Amanda off just outside the restaurant. She couldn't believe her luck that Kate had agreed only too readily to help out.

'Alec won't be home till late, so I'd be happy to look after Hattie,' she'd said. 'Let me write a note for him and I'll be over.'

Not being a child person herself, Amanda couldn't understand anyone being so keen to spend an evening cooped up with somebody else's offspring. But she was more than glad that there were people like Kate who were fool enough to do so.

She saw Tony attracting her attention from the far side of the busy restaurant and she weaved her way through the maze of tables to reach him. He kissed her cheek and introduced her to the Hursts. She had never met Bradley Hurst before and she was taken completely unawares by the sight of him. He was one of the best-looking men she had ever had the good fortune to meet. He was tall, very tall, with piercing, icy blue eyes behind a pair of rimless glasses and he had a head of thick blond hair that made him more Robert Redford – in his younger days – than the man himself; he also looked and smelt the very epitome of power and success. His wife complemented him exactly – she could have been straight out of *Murder One*; a smart-arse lawyer type, all suit, lipstick and shiny hair. They made a glamorous couple and in comparison Amanda felt like little wifey who'd forgotten to take off her pinny and slippers.

'So great to meet you,' Bradley said, up on his feet and clasping her hand in his, 'Tony's told us all about you. We even know your shoe size.' He laughed warmly and Amanda didn't doubt his words for a minute. She knew how Arc operated from the way Tony had to spend hours genning up on the people who worked for the company.

'Hi, I'm Errol,' the suit and lipstick said, now taking her turn to shake hands.

As in Flynn? Amanda wanted to ask, but she knew better than to question an American about his or her name.

They sat down and Amanda waited to see which way the conversation would go, now that she had arrived. Would there be the routine polite questions about her busy day as a stay-at-home mother? She hoped not. It was too tedious for words.

'Tony's been telling us about the new home you've just moved into,' Bradley opened up with. 'Sounds kinda interesting. A converted barn. Errol and I would just love something like that, out in New England perhaps. Connecticut would be great. Ever been to New England, Amanda?'

'No.'

'Sure thing? Tony, you'll have to fix that. Amanda would love New England, I just know it. It's the neatest place for a vacation.'

Tony made the appropriate response and retreated behind the head-nodding diplomacy he'd employed for most of that day. He'd like to fix Bradley-Dewhurst-the-Butcher's-Boy good and proper. How dare the man sit here in this bloody expensive restaurant telling him to take his wife on a lavish holiday to the States when he'd just informed him today that three of his best men would have to go. 'We're reshaping things as we head towards the millennium, Tony,' he'd started with first thing that morning, before Tony had even removed his jacket and sat down at his desk. 'We need to create a new vision, a new direction. It's all about concentrating the focus. You should see what we're doing back home, it's an exciting time for Arc. Tough, but exciting.'

Exciting for whom? Tony wanted to know. For the fortunate few who still had a job? And how the hell was he going to keep up morale in the office with everyone terrified about what would happen next? He'd be treated as a leper. He would become the enemy. Nobody would want to speak to him for fear that raising a head above the parapet would be reason enough to have it blown off.

Tony drove home listening to Amanda talking about how much she'd enjoyed the evening. 'You never told me what an interesting man that Bradley is.'

'I never told you that because he isn't.'

Amanda laughed. 'Nonsense.'

'I'm serious. The man's ruthless.'

'That's his business persona. If you're running a company like Arc you've got to be tough and stand up to people.' Secretly Amanda wished that Tony would show a bit more backbone. He'd been a right wet rag round the table during the meal, hardly opening his mouth, and when he did speak it was to come up with something as tactless as questioning Bradley's views on the state of the world's economy. Of course Bradley knew what he was talking about. As vice-president of Arc he was certainly better placed to understand these things than Tony.

'Now tell me about this woman who's looking after Hattie,' Tony said, breaking into her thoughts. 'You did leave a phone number with her, didn't you, just in case –'

'Don't worry. Of course I did. And believe me, there wouldn't have been a problem. I've never seen Hattie behave so well as she does with Kate. We should thank our lucky stars that we've got her living so close, she'll prove to be an absolute godsend, especially as your daughter seems to have fallen for her in such a big way.'

There were no lights on in the house upstairs when they reached home and when they let themselves in, all was quiet. Either Hattie was fast asleep or ... or there was something wrong. Tony hurried through to the sitting-room, which was lit by a single lamp. When he saw Kate rise from the floor where she'd been sitting cross-legged reading a book in the soft light cast from the lamp behind her he could understand perfectly why Hattie had fallen for her. She was beautiful. Stunning.

And though the situation was completely different, he was reminded of the very first moment when he had met Hattie's mother Eve.

It had been love at first sight.

9

About an hour after leaving Tony and Amanda, Kate got into bed. She snuggled up close to Alec and laid her head in the crook of his arm. 'You didn't mind me not being here when you got home, did you?'

'Of course not,' he answered. 'What a silly question to ask.'

But Alec had minded, more than he cared to admit. He knew it was irrational, but when he'd let himself into the house and called out Kate's name and there'd been no response – only the message propped up by the microwave where his supper was waiting for him – he'd felt deflated and let down. Ever since their relationship had begun, and more particularly since Kate's job as a librarian had come to an end, he'd become used to her always being there for him when he came home from work.

Within weeks of meeting one another he had asked Kate to move in with him, to the cheerless house that he'd been renting after he and Melissa had sold what their solicitors had coldly referred to as *the matrimonial home* – he could have bought out Melissa's share in the property and stayed where he was, but he hadn't seen any point in remaining in the large family house, not when every room, every square inch of it, would remind him of the past. In what seemed no time at all after Kate had moved in with him the small, ugly house had undergone a magical transformation, it was suddenly alive and felt like a home; a proper home that was comfortable and inviting. It was as if Kate had bottled her unique, understated charm and liberally sprayed it around all the rooms. He realised very soon that the house had responded to Kate in exactly the same way that he had when she had saved him from a life that was leaden and interminably dull.

And it was that old life that he had been reminded of this evening when he had waited for Kate to come home. The empty house had dredged up memories of his being on his own after Melissa had left him. He had hated the long solitary evenings when all he'd had for company was the television and a meal for one on his lap. He had been wretched and depressed. Inevitably, it hadn't taken him long to slip into the bad habit of staying late at work, then going home for a liquid supper followed by an early night.

Melissa had been only too quick to point out that he was letting himself go. 'You're a mess, Alec,' she said one morning at work, when he'd turned up late and heavy-headed. 'And your clothes stink of whisky. Go home and change, and take a good look at yourself.'

Melissa had never believed in pulling her punches. But she had been right, as she so often was, and with more strength than he'd known he possessed he'd hauled himself out of the trough of despair and begun to think about his future. And while clearing up several months' worth of self-pitying squalor from around the house, including a bin liner of old newspapers, his eye had fallen upon the 'Encounters' page of the *Sunday Times*. Was this the answer? he'd asked himself as he'd run his finger over the numerous dating agency advertisements. In a moment of decisiveness he'd picked up the phone and rung one of the numbers. Afterwards he'd regretted what he'd done and had needed a large whisky to calm himself down. His sense of shame and embarrassment was enormous, that he, Alec McLaren, had sunk to such a pathetic point that he was prepared to meet a total stranger in the belief that somehow his life would be miraculously improved by such a meeting.

But it had been. And how!

Kate was his life. He never wanted to be apart from her, which was why he had been so miserable all on his own that evening.

Of course, he could have simply strolled across the courtyard and joined Kate at number two, but in a way he had wanted to test himself. Just how dependent on her was he?

'So tell me about your day,' Kate said, slipping over on to her side and looking into his face.

He kissed her forehead and held her close. 'Nothing special,' he said, 'though I managed to convince our friends at W. H. Smith to give us more shelf space later in the year. You wouldn't believe how tight the whole thing's becoming. Oh, and by the way, Ruth phoned.'

'What did she want?' – other than more money, Kate wanted to add, but she had promised herself that she would never criticise Alec's family, no matter how tempted she was. In her opinion, Alec's daughter was a spoilt brat; a spoilt ungrateful brat at that, who shamelessly used her father whenever she needed to.

A few months before, Ruth had told Alec that Adam's one-man-band architectural firm was going through a lean time. 'People are so miserly these days,' she had moaned to Alec over Sunday lunch, 'they just don't seem to understand that to invest in one of Adam's exclusive designs is the best investment they could ever make.'

Alec had dutifully helped out in the only way Ruth understood and had parted with a large amount of cash. 'It's only money,' he'd told Kate, when a few weeks later Ruth announced that she and Adam were leaving little Oscar in the care of a child-minder and taking a holiday in St Lucia for a couple of weeks.

'She's after a favour,' Alec said, shifting his hand from Kate's neck and following the contour of her shoulder and then planting soft kisses on her throat.

'What kind of favour?' Kate asked nervously, raising Alec's head to her own. What on earth could Ruth want from *her*?

'I'll tell you in the morning.' He smiled and went back to kissing her.

When Tony awoke the next morning he found that Amanda's side of the bed was empty. He turned over and looked at the alarm clock. It was half past six. He closed his eyes, wishing the clock were wrong. Then he wondered where Amanda was. She was never up before him. 'You'll find I'm not a morning person,' she had told him the first night they'd slept together.

It was just one of the many little incompatibilities between them.

He pulled the duvet up over his head and wondered at the mess he had made of his life. He should never have married Amanda. Anyone could see they were wrong for each other. But then, how many other men in his position wouldn't have done the same?

Nothing could have prepared him for coping with the shock of Eve's death. One moment she had been on the telephone saying that she was just on her way to pick up Hattie from nursery and the next she was dead.

A freak accident.

A lorry with a man asleep at the wheel. It could have been anyone crushed to death on that wet, windy afternoon.

But it hadn't been anyone. It had been *his* wife. *His* Eve.

For months afterwards he'd gone around as if he too were dead. Nothing had made any sense any more. Even little Hattie had meant nothing but another problem for him to cope with. His work colleagues had helped as best they could by covering for him and continually making allowances. Friends, too, had played their part, but even the closest of them had gradually tired of the same sad story being replayed over and over.

In the end, and quite understandably, he had been left to stand on his own feet. Then he'd met Amanda at a party that his friends had insisted he went to. 'You've got to get out, Tony,' they'd repeatedly told him.

He'd given in, on the basis that after an hour he could leave if he wanted, and five minutes before his allotted time was up Amanda had walked into the kitchen where he'd been occupying himself arranging the magnetic letters on his hostess's fridge to form the words *I've had enough.*

'Enough of what?' she had asked.

If he'd been drunk he would have told her the truth, that he'd had enough of life, but because he was stone-cold sober, he'd said, 'Enough to eat.'

'Me too,' she'd said. 'Does Julie always force-feed her guests this way?'

'I wouldn't know. I've never been here before.'

'We've a lot in common then, me neither.'

Tony pushed back the duvet and thought that Amanda couldn't have been more wrong. They had nothing in common. He could see that so clearly now. He had married her because he had been a fool, a calculating fool to boot. He had seen her as a mother for Hattie, someone to organise his private life while he kept his professional one intact.

Poor Hattie, he thought as he got out of bed and went through to the bathroom for a shower. Poor, poor Hattie. He had thought he was doing the right thing in providing her with a mother, but the truth was he'd made things worse. He knew Hattie would never view Amanda as a proper mother and in a way he felt sorry for Amanda too. She was no Mary Poppins, but then neither was she Cruella De Vil. She was just Amanda, a woman who had made the mistake of getting herself involved with a man who still hadn't got over the death of his wife.

His first wife, he corrected himself. For better or for worse, Amanda was his wife now.

Downstairs in the kitchen Amanda was busy making breakfast. For a non-morning person she was feeling surprisingly cheerful. Her good mood was directly attributable to the previous evening. Late last night in bed, while Tony was asleep, she had made a few resolutions. From now on things were going to be different.

She had known all along that Tony had married her because he thought she would make his life easier. She had never deluded herself over the role she had been expected to play in his life and, more to the point, the role expected of her in Hattie's life. And that was fine, she liked nothing better than to know where she stood. But Tony had to be prepared to accept that as much as he was using her, she would use him. It was a fair bargain, in her opinion. If it was her job to take Hattie off Tony's hands, then in return it was only reasonable that his was to provide her with the life-style she wanted.

But after last night she had come to the conclusion that to get the best out of Tony – and ultimately the life-style she craved – she was going to have to work at their marriage a little harder than she'd originally imagined. She would have to appear to be giving him her unfailing support in everything that mattered to him – his daughter and his career.

It was listening to Bradley and Errol describing their 'honey pie' marriage that had made her reconsider her own. The gist of what they were saying was that if she were to shoulder the greater part of Tony's life, the more there would be for them to gain as a couple. 'I always treat Bradley's job as much mine as his,' Errol had said.

Amanda's initial response to such a comment was to scoff – only an American could have such a crass and idealistic view – but then she'd begun to wonder at what they were saying.

'Success is down to sharing the commitment of a career,' Bradley had said, 'I rely on Errol one hundred per cent. She's at home so that I can function at my best and be the success I am. Old-fashioned values keep it together, am I right, hon?'

'Absolutely,' Errol had said, 'I've had to make a few sacrifices here and there, but the rewards have certainly made up for anything I thought I'd lost.'

'And she's not just talking about the rewards of a perfectly cooked muffin.' Bradley had laughed.

Looking at the woman across the table in her smart-arsy suit, Amanda had found the image of Errol at home with a tray of blueberry muffins at the ready rather an unlikely picture.

'Brad's right,' Errol had said, 'I used to work as an attorney, but we soon found that we were pulling against each other and we just weren't getting anywhere. I suppose you could say we're centred on Brad now, we've invested my skills into his.'

'But hey, hon, you're talking to the converted. That's exactly what Tony and Amanda have done. Am I right, Amanda?'

The notion of centring herself on Tony had never before entered Amanda's head – what woman in the nineties *would ever* think of doing that?

In bed, she had asked herself the same question over and over – was it really possible that by turning herself into an Errol she could make Tony a power-hungry executive like Bradley? In the end she had decided that it was worth a try . . . even if she did only pretend to be doing all that centring rubbish.

She scooped out Tony's egg from the pan of boiling water and took it to the table where she carefully placed it in the china egg-cup. Hearing footsteps on the stairs, she hurriedly poured out a cup of freshly made coffee.

Tony stood in the doorway amazed.

'Good-morning,' she said brightly, 'did you sleep well?'

He came over and continued to look amazed. He had never known Amanda to be up this early and he had certainly never heard her talk to him as though she were an air stewardess. 'It's not some kind of anniversary, is it?' he asked warily, looking at the table where he saw mats, napkins, glasses of orange juice, a pot of proper coffee and even a boiled egg. What was she up to?

She laughed and guided him to his chair. 'It's a celebration of sorts,' she said, 'it's the start of me getting my act together. Now tell me what you'd like for supper tonight.'

Supper! Good grief, it was as much as he could do to contemplate the egg in front of him. He knew he was being ungrateful, but more than anything he wished that Amanda were upstairs in bed as she usually was at this time of day, leaving him in peace with his normal hurried bowl of cereal while hovering over the sink looking out at the surrounding countryside with nothing but his own troubled thoughts for company.

Sinking into his chair and taking a fortifying sip of his coffee, he let his thoughts turn to last night. To that incredible moment when he'd first set eyes on Kate. She looked absolutely nothing like his first wife, but his whole body had responded in the same way as when he'd met Eve. His heart had jolted and his pulse had quickened, and as he'd crossed the room and held out his hand to her he had felt as though they'd met already. 'This was so good of you. I hope Hattie wasn't any trouble,' he'd said, holding on to her hand and not showing any sign of letting go of it.

'Not at all,' she'd answered, 'we chatted and then I read to her.'

'Let me guess. *The Secret Garden?*'

Kate had laughed. 'Yes, a few chapters, then we had *The Tale of Mrs Tiggy-Winkle.*'

Tony had been shocked. Not since Eve's death had Hattie let anyone read that book to her. She had loved the way her mother had read the story. Amanda had once tried it and Hattie had snatched the book out of her hands.

'We ought to thank Kate properly for last night,' he heard Amanda say.

He snapped out of his reverie. 'Yes,' he said, 'yes, you're right. How about some flowers?'

'Flowers,' Amanda repeated, her hand poised over the cafetiere to top up his coffee – flowers for a complete stranger, but rarely for her, she thought. 'We could do that, but I'm not sure it's the right thing to do,' she said slowly, thinking that Errol's marital professionalism would never allow her to stoop to anything as base or unworthy as jealousy. 'I know for a fact that her partner Alec has just bought her some.'

'Oh,' Tony said flatly. Partner. Alec. *Her partner.* He didn't want to hear words like that.

'I've got a much better idea,' Amanda carried on. 'Why don't we invite them for supper one evening, that way we can start being more neighbourly. Living out here and being so isolated it makes sense to build up a rapport with people whom we might need to rely on occasionally. What do you think?'

'Fine,' he said, pushing away his half-eaten egg. 'See what you can fix up. I'd better get going. Bradley wanted to see me in the office early this morning before he heads off to the airport.'

'Oh, well, give him my best and tell him to stay longer next time so that we can see more of him and his lovely wife.'

Tony grimaced. The less he saw of Bradley-Dewhurst-the-Butcher's-Boy the better.

10

When Alec had left for work and Kate had finished the toast and marmalade that he had kindly brought upstairs on a tray for her, she thought about what they had discussed while Alec was getting dressed.

'You don't have to do it, if you don't want to,' he had said, 'you mustn't feel duty bound to accept because it's Ruth who's asked you.'

But Kate had known that she would accept Ruth's proposal. That it was irresistible. Looking after Oscar would be a delight. In fact, it was just what she needed until she had decided what she was going to do about getting another job.

She got dressed and went downstairs, and found that the postman had been. A scattering of assorted-sized envelopes lay on the carpet in the hall. She picked them up and carried the pile through to the kitchen where she switched on the radio and was met with a snappy John Humphrys berating some poor soul for being incompetent. She turned the dial until she found Terry Wogan being accused of the same crime by one of his loyal listeners and to the sound of the Irishman's mock outrage she began opening the mail. The envelopes were all addressed to *Mr Alec McLaren and Miss Kate Morris* and were cards wishing them well in their new home, except for one which was addressed to her only. It was from Caroline with whom she had shared a tiny terraced cottage in Knutsford before she'd moved in with Alec, and with whom she'd also worked for two years at the library.

'I've lost your new phone number, so have resorted to this – let's get together for an evening out.' Caroline had used a green felt-tip pen to scrawl her message on the inside page of the card and her writing was large and loopy – not unlike Caroline, Kate thought with a smile. The card itself was also typical Caroline and the picture showed an oil-smeared, bronzed, muscly man in the skimpiest of leopardskin swimming trunks and to one side of his bottom her friend had written, 'Now he's what I call a man!'

To say that Caroline was interested in men was a huge understatement. She was pretty much obsessed with the male species. 'I'm always hungry for a good man,' she would joke, 'the only trouble is most of them are like a Big Mac, you have one and then a few hours later you're ready for another.'

No man ever stayed long in Caroline's life.

'I don't know what's wrong with men these days,' she would complain after the door of her love life had been slammed in her face yet again.

'You frighten them to death, that's what's wrong with them,' Kate had told her. 'Try not to be so pushy. Let them come up for air occasionally.'

'I'm only being me,' she would retort, 'I'll be damned if I'm going to pretend to be something I'm not.'

And if there was one quality about Caroline that Kate was in awe of it was her friend's incredible self-confidence and her implicit assumption that she was right and others were wrong. Whereas Kate had grown up believing it was she who was usually to blame for anything that went wrong and that it was her place to yield to those around her in order to make a situation work, Caroline was convinced of the opposite. The word sorry never appeared in her vocabulary, nor did the concept of being helpful, biddable or compliant ever occur to her, as her behaviour at the library showed only too plainly.

Caroline hated *the public.* She saw them as an unpleasant nuisance that got in the way of her carrying out her job as she roared about the shelves with a sense of urgency that frightened some of the more timid browsers who liked to while away their time quietly flicking through the papers and magazines. They certainly weren't up to being physically moved on when Caroline felt the need to tidy up the tables of paper-strewn reading matter. She didn't care that some of the braver users of the library called her the Gestapo behind her back.

Untidy customers Caroline could just about tolerate, but people who interrupted her and expected an answer to a daft question were the kind she had no time for. One afternoon an elderly pensioner had taken his life into his hands and had approached the desk where Caroline was hiding behind the computer reading the latest Penny Vincenzi and had asked, 'I wonder, have you got that book, you know the one all about life in a Cheshire village during the war?'

'How the hell should I know,' Caroline had snapped back. And seeing the poor man almost reduced to tears Kate had stepped in and taken him reassuringly by the arm to the selection of local history books.

Another time Caroline had caught a woman furtively eating a prawn and mayonnaise sandwich while reading a book in what she had thought was a quiet corner in among Travel and Careers. Unfortunately she had chosen a book that had made her laugh out loud and Caroline had pounced on her, not just for disturbing fellow library users, but for defacing council property by smearing page fifty-eight of *Caught in the Act* with a blob of mayonnaise.

Kate was just recalling the look of shock and bewilderment on the face of the woman when she remembered that *Caught in the Act* was one of Jessica Lloyd's novels.

Kate had noticed signs of their new neighbour moving in yesterday and she had badly wanted to pluck up the courage to go and knock on the door and introduce herself. Perhaps today she might.

But first she had to ring Ruth. She looked up at the clock – her Ikea station clock that her colleagues at the library had given her on her last day – and saw that it was nearly a quarter to nine. She went through to Alec's study and flipped through the address book to find Ruth's number. She pressed the buttons on the phone and prepared herself for a conversation with Ruth by taking several deep breaths. When the phone was picked up at the other end she was greeted with an explosion of noise. It sounded like an angry scene from a soap opera on the television, but Kate quickly realised that it was Ruth and Adam arguing. So who had answered the telephone?

'Hello,' she said cautiously.

'Hello,' said a small voice.

'Oscar, is that you?'

'Yes.'

'It's Kate.'

'Hello, I've just had my breakfast. I had a big bowl of Honey Pops.'

'Mm ... delicious, do you think I could speak to Mummy?'

'She hasn't had her breakfast and she's very cross with Daddy. He used all the milk.'

'I'm sorry to hear that, but can you tell her I'm on the phone?'

Kate listened to Oscar banging down the receiver on something hard, then strained her ear to catch him interrupting the shouting match that was still in full flow. She couldn't hear his gentle voice, but she caught Ruth's loud and clear.

'Who's on the phone? Well, why didn't you tell me, Oscar? Really, you can be so naughty at times. Kate, is that you?'

'Hello Ruth, I hope I haven't called at an awkward time.'

'It's always an awkward time in this house,' Ruth said bad-temperedly, 'it's called being married to a fool. Now has Dad put my proposal to you? He did explain that I want this done on a proper footing? I'll be paying you.'

'Yes, Alec did mention that.'

'And?'

'I'd love to help out.'

'But?'

'There is no but,' Kate said. Poor Ruth, she was so cynical and unhelpful herself she couldn't imagine anybody wanting to help her.

'You mean you'll do it?'

'Of course I will.' And feeling in control with a member of Alec's family for the first time, Kate added, 'Why don't you and Oscar come over for lunch today and we can sort out the details?'

They agreed a time and said goodbye, and after Kate had tidied up the kitchen and found that she was still feeling flushed with success at having managed a conversation without Ruth making her feel slightly less worthy than a toe-nail clipping, she decided to introduce herself to Jessica Lloyd.

Jessica took one look at the stunning girl in front of her and wanted to reach for her notebook and pen. As classic images of romantic heroines went, this one was the princess of them all. Peas under the mattress, mirrors on the wall, mislaid glass slippers, she could show them a thing or two!

'I'm Kate and ... and I don't want you to think I'm an interfering neighbour,' she said hesitantly, 'but I live next door and thought I'd just pop round to say hello. If you're busy I could come back another time.'

'I'm not busy at all. Come on in. I'm Jessica, by the way.' *Yes, come on in and let me get a better look at you!*

Jessica took Kate through to the sitting-room. 'Now before you say anything about the furniture and décor,' she laughed, 'I didn't choose any of it, so in no way does it reflect my character.'

Kate laughed too. 'It must be strange knowing that so many people have walked through your home just for the Sunday afternoon experience of poking about in a show house.'

Jessica pulled a face. 'Do you know, I hadn't thought of it quite like that. But you're right. What a horrid thought. Would you like a drink?'

'Tea would be lovely, but only if you're sure I'm not stopping you from doing anything.'

'You're not interrupting, honestly.'

Out in the kitchen Jessica filled the kettle – newly bought yesterday afternoon with her mother – plugged it in and reached for the nearest piece of paper to hand, which turned out to be an envelope from British Gas. She wrote quickly and spontaneously on the back of the envelope, trying her best to capture the stunning girl in the sitting-room. *Hair to die for*, she scribbled, *masses of copper waves right down to her waist – colour of a good sweet sherry. Tall and very slim – does she eat? Long, long legs hidden beneath faded jeans. Looks about twenty-one and makes me feel about a hundred and twenty-one! Pale complexion, probably never had a spot in her life! Greeny eyes, sort of misty in a sad kind of way. Irish background? Reminds me of those girls from* Riverdance. *Dread to think what Gavin's reaction to her would be!*

She crossed out this last comment and wrote, *Gavin Who?*

When she was satisfied with the thumbnail sketch, she made a pot of tea, grabbed a couple of her mother's cast-off mugs and slopped some milk into a cracked jug, also from Willow Cottage. Sooner, rather than later, she simply had to do some serious crockery shopping.

'Sorry I was so long,' she said when she joined Kate in the sitting-room. 'And I apologise for the state of this china. It's all borrowed from my mother until I get myself sorted. These poor old mugs look dreadful in here among all this chic furniture, rather out of place. A bit eccentric even. One could almost feel sorry for them.'

Kate wanted to say that everything looked fine and that anyway writers were allowed to be as eccentric as they wanted, that it was expected of them, but instead she said, 'Where have you moved from?'

'Corfu.'

Kate's eyes widened. 'Corfu? How wonderful. This is going to feel very different then, isn't it?' She suddenly lowered her gaze, conscious that Jessica was staring at her.

'I'm sorry,' Jessica said, realising that she'd been caught out. She quickly turned her attention to pouring the tea. 'I have a terrible habit of staring at people. An occupational hazard you could call it. I watch people all the time. They fascinate me.' She passed Kate her mug of tea.

'Thank you. Perhaps that's what makes you such a good writer.'

Disarming as well, thought Jessica. 'I don't know,' she said, 'am I?'

'A lot of people seem to think so, including me.'

Jessica looked awkwardly at her mother's chipped teapot. She found praise difficult to handle. Probably because she never trusted it. 'So how did you know I was a writer?' she asked.

'The woman over in number two told me ... and the sales negotiator told her. But I'd already heard of you. I'm a librarian, or rather I used to be.'

'Used to be?'

'I was made redundant. I was the last to be taken on and so naturally when all the cutbacks came into force a few months ago I was first to be asked to leave.'

'Any idea what you'll do next?'

Kate shrugged. 'I don't hold out much hope of getting another librarian job locally, but for the time being and perhaps until I really know what I want to do next I'm going to be looking after my partner's grandson.'

'Ah,' said Jessica – and thereby hangs a tale I'd like to know more about, she thought. But instead of immediately pursuing that particular line of conversation, she decided to keep it for when she and Kate knew one another a little better. She tucked her legs up underneath her on the sofa, reached for her mug of tea and settled herself in for a good gossiping session about her new bedfellows. 'When did you actually move in?' she began.

'On Thursday last week.'

'And were you the first?'

'No. There's a family over in number two –'

'With the woman who'd spoken to the sales negotiator, who'd told her all about me?'

Kate smiled. 'Yes, they were first to move in.'

'So what are they like?'

'They've a little girl called Hattie. She's really sweet.'

'And the parents, are they as sweet?'

Kate wasn't a gossiper by nature and she was reluctant to pass on what Hattie had told her last night while she had been looking after her, but having recently spent so much time alone she now found it almost impossible not to chat away with her new neighbour. And it wouldn't be gossip, really, would it, because Amanda had told her herself on Friday last week that she was Hattie's stepmother? It wasn't as if it were a secret. If it were, Amanda wouldn't have told her. 'They're very nice,' she said, 'she's his second wife ... the first was killed in a car crash. From the little I've seen of her I think Amanda finds the role of stepmother difficult. It can't be easy if you don't have a natural rapport with children.'

'And she doesn't?'

Kate shook her head, then regretted it. 'That was probably very unkind of me.'

'No worries,' Jessica said, 'I shall strike it from the record.' She was amused at Kate's discretion. Beauty as well as a conscience. A beguiling combination.

They fell silent for a moment or two, until Kate said, 'We could lend you some china and anything else you're short of, if you like. Alec and I have got plenty of stuff we probably won't ever use.'

Jessica was touched. And intrigued. She wanted to know more about this Alec. She knew she was being unashamedly nosy, but meeting somebody for the first time often gave her an insatiable appetite for a dose of interrogation, especially when she was on the verge of writing a new novel and therefore on the look-out for a likely source of inspiration. 'That's really kind of you,' she said, 'but tell you what, would you like to come shopping with me this week and help me choose some things?'

Ruth finally arrived for lunch with Kate. She was over an hour late, uptight and overdressed in a Jackie Onassis-style cream suit with matching handbag, high heels and sun-glasses. She was cross, having just wasted an entire morning on an unsuccessful shopping trip to buy herself a suitable wardrobe for her new career, and while she took out her temper on her father's new home, tutting at the unimaginative design – Adam could have made so much better a job of it – Kate took Oscar outside to set the wooden table for lunch in the garden. Normally she would have had everything all neatly arranged, but she knew how Oscar liked to help her.

'Shall I put this knife here?' he asked.

'Yes please,' Kate said, 'and can you put the napkin next to it?'

They worked happily together until Ruth, tired of tutting inside alone, came out to the garden and tutted some more, saying that it was foolish to consider having lunch outside. 'The wasps will be swarming round as soon as we sit down.'

Kate held her ground and, as it turned out, the only person the wasps annoyed was Ruth. A pair hovered menacingly around her, dive-bombing her glass of orange juice or threatening an assault on her salad with its honey-and-mustard dressing. In the end they grew bored of the sport and flew away.

Kate ventured to enquire about the arrangements for Oscar. 'How many days a week will it be for?' she asked, watching Oscar who had finished his lunch and was now exploring the large empty garden.

'To begin with just two, that's until things pick up. But eventually I see myself working more or less full time. Adam needs somebody to get to grips with the administrative side of the business. The woman he's got now is hopeless. I know she's got problems at home, but these days one has to rise above that kind of thing and be the complete professional, otherwise there's simply no point.'

After hearing the sparring professionalism of Ruth and Adam arguing that morning, Kate couldn't help but wonder what the effect of their relationship might have on the business. It appalled her enough imagining the effect it must already be having on their son.

'So what time will you be wanting to drop Oscar off in the mornings?'

'Quite early, so you'll have to get your skates on. There'll be no more being spoilt by Dad bringing you breakfast in bed.'

Kate coloured and wished the wasps would come back. How did Ruth know these things? Surely Alec didn't tell her?

'Then in September, when he starts school, you'll have to take him. He's to be there at nine and he'll finish at three thirty. When you've collected him he'll need his tea. And by the way, I don't want him eating any old rubbish when he's here with you. He's to have fresh vegetables and fruit, plenty of fibre. I've got a list in my bag of meals he's to have. He's not to have any red meat, or fish fingers, or orange squash, fresh juice only. And definitely no sweets or biscuits.'

Poor Oscar, thought Kate. 'What time will you be picking him up?' She was wondering how much love she could cram into the precious hours Oscar would be with her.

'Heaven knows, to begin with. We'll both need to be flexible if this is to work.'

'Just a rough idea?' Kate persisted.

'Now don't try and pin me down, Kate. It's all very well you having worked in a cushy library where the hours are set, but outside the world of subsidy, in the real world, people have to graft all hours to get things done. I'm sure we'll soon slip into a pattern.'

'I'm sure we will,' Kate said, glancing over to Oscar who was fully absorbed in gathering buttercups and daisies by reaching one of his tiny hands through the picket fence to the weed-infested area of the neighbouring field.

'Oscar! Stop that at once,' called out Ruth, 'you'll get horrid stains all over your new Osh Kosh trousers. Now come back here where I can keep an eye on you.'

Oscar slowly withdrew his hand and wandered over to where they were sitting. He smiled up at Kate and handed her his bunch of squashed flowers.

'Thank you,' she said and gave his sun-warmed cheek a kiss. She was looking forward to having Oscar all to herself. It would be like having a child of her own.

11

More than a week after he'd moved house Josh drove through the central archway of Cholmford Hall Mews and set off to work.

It wasn't yet eight o'clock, but already the day was warm. He activated the sun roof and as it slid back he switched off the radio. He wanted to enjoy his drive in to work that morning and had no desire for his good mood to be jeopardised by the tedium of listening to bad news. He didn't want to hear another word from some unknown MEP whinging on about why Britain should or should not touch a single currency. Neither was he interested in the latest round of Northern Ireland peace talks breaking down again.

On the other hand, nor did he want any good news to eclipse his own.

It was nothing short of a miracle that he was feeling better than he had for days. This morning he'd woken up with nothing more annoying than a stiff leg to bother him. Now that was what he called bloody fantastic news! Sod the government's latest unemployment figures – the lowest on record for years – and to hell with the pre-summer bonanza of high street spending, he, Joshua Crawford, was up and running!

Okay then. He wasn't exactly running, but he was up and ready to get back to work.

He drove through the suffused green light of the avenue of chestnut trees and thought how it was that in such a relatively short space of time his expectations had been so dramatically reduced. It wasn't that long ago that if he'd have woken up with a stiff leg he would have been filled with fear, panic and anger.

When he reached the small bridge that spanned the canal he slowed the car and looked over to the pretty white cottage that he admired whenever he was passing. He envied whoever lived there. It was an idyllic spot. But then for that matter so was Cholmford Hall Mews. He drove on.

He would never admit it to his brother, or his parents, but the effort of setting up a new home on his own had been more debilitating than he'd expected. They'd all offered to help him, but he'd turned them down, wanting to prove to himself that he could manage. For the first few days after moving in he'd cursed his weakened body constantly, then he'd cursed himself for having collected so much junk. He made several trips to the council tip and jettisoned piles of stuff that should have been thrown away before the move, if not years before that. He also paid a visit to the nearest charity shop and donated countless bags of clothes that no longer fitted him because of the weight he'd lost in the past months. As well as this he handed over a bag of unused Christmas presents, including a Whistling Key Finder; some Resonating Energy Chimes, designed to relax and uplift; a Mini Carpet Bowls set and a rubber-sealed radio designed to be listened to while in the shower. They were absurd gifts and were all from his father, who took a perverse pleasure in browsing through the hundreds of mail-order catalogues that came his way. His taste for the impractical meant that for some time now both Josh and Charlie, as well as their mother, had ended up with a series of ludicrous presents.

It was while he was at the charity shop that his ego had taken an unexpected battering. He'd asked an elderly white-haired assistant whether the things in his car would be of any use. 'Always glad to have whatever's going,' she'd said and had promptly raced outside to his Shogun parked on the double-yellow lines, eager to help him unload the bags of clothes. It was a while before she realised that he wasn't able to keep pace and that he was still inside the shop, limping his way through the racks of second-hand goods. 'You should have said something, you poor old duck,' she'd said, looking pointedly at his legs, 'we'd have arranged to collect this lot from you, it would have saved you all the bother.'

His sense of frustration was enormous as he was then forced to watch a woman, who had to be at least thirty years older than him, manhandling the heavy bags from the back of his car. He'd hated himself and his situation.

Worse was to come later in the day when he started unpacking yet more boxes and came across his squash and tennis rackets, along with his skis and boots. The objects lay on the floor in the hall, reminding him, just in case he'd forgotten, that they would be of no use to him now. He banished them to the garage where they could no longer sneer at him. He hid the offending items behind an old blanket. He'd then spent the rest of the day struggling to put together a simple rack of shelves, but with each turn of the screwdriver his hands and wrists had burned until, two hours later, when all sense of feeling had gone from them he'd finally put in the last screw.

Triumphant, but knackered, he'd slept on the sofa that night, too exhausted to contemplate the stairs.

'Multiple sclerosis,' he'd been told last year by the neurologist, who had confirmed the illness to Josh, 'will take over your life and destroy it if you let it. There are certain things that you are going to have to face up to, like the chaos it will bring. Each day will be different. There's not a lot you can do to stop the unpredictable nature of MS, so the best advice I can give you is to take each day as it comes.'

The doctor had gone on to explain how the central nervous system worked and how his own was unable to send out and receive messages, which was why his body didn't work as it should. And as Josh had listened to what he was being told a feeling of relief had swept over him – he wasn't going mad after all. He hadn't imagined the weakness in his arms and legs; the occasional loss of balance and co-ordination; the heavy tiredness that without warning would suddenly come over him just as if he'd been drugged; the pins and needles; the numbness. For nearly two years he had experienced all these problems off and on, but because they came and went so quickly, as if by the flick of a switch, he had kept them to himself, but had always wondered after each occurrence whether he wasn't turning into some kind of hypochondriac. He had tried all this time to ignore what was going on, but when one morning he'd woken up and found that he couldn't see properly – everything through his right eye was blurred – he'd been terrified that he was going blind. He rushed to the nearby busy health practice, where he was quickly referred to an eye specialist, who in turn sent Josh to a neurologist. A whole series of tests followed. By this stage he had convinced himself that he was dying.

'You'll be with us for a few years yet,' the neurologist had said, when Josh had voiced his fears after he'd been given the diagnosis. 'But first things first. We need to set you up on a course of steroids to sort out the inflammation of your optic nerve.'

'Is that what's causing the blurred vision?'

'Yes. It's quite common in MS. Often it's the first conclusive evidence we have as to what we're dealing with.'

'And will it go back to normal? Will I be able to see?'

'Yes, the eye will be fine. Don't worry.'

But that was exactly what Josh started to do. Once the initial feeling of relief, that he now knew what was wrong with him, had gone, he realised that though the neurologist had given him varying degrees of help and advice, he had omitted to explain to him that there was no cure for what he had. When pressed, he admitted that there wasn't even a drug he could take to stop the illness from getting any worse.

Worry kicked in.

And anger.

How could this have happened to him? He'd always been so fit. He'd rarely been ill, not with anything significant. So why should he have multiple sclerosis? And what was there to come? He began to read up on the illness, and what he discovered only fuelled his anger and his ever-growing terror of what lay ahead.

But now, as he drove into the centre of Manchester and headed towards Deansgate, he was determined not to think about the future. It was too depressing. He joined the slow-moving queue of cars at the traffic lights and suddenly wished he weren't there, that he were back in Cholmford, in his new home.

Charlie might have joked that the place gave him agoraphobia, but Josh knew that he'd done the right thing in buying the house. He loved it already. He loved being in the sitting-room overlooking the fields of corn, bright and golden, and sharply contrasted against the adjoining fields of lush green grass, edged now and then with rows of hawthorns, oaks and beech trees, and all set against a magnificent backdrop of soft-focus hills.

What had appealed to Josh, when he'd first driven out to Cholmford after reading about the barn conversion in *Cheshire Life*, was the sense of freedom the house offered. Its isolation had immediately struck a chord with him. He had a desire to be alone, or at least to *feel* alone – given his circumstances, the coward in him reasoned that having a few people living close by wouldn't be a bad idea.

For some time he had been wanting to move as far away from Manchester as he sensibly could – the daily drive in to work had to be a realistic journey – and not just because he wanted a bit of space around him. He needed to distance himself from those closest to him.

Since his illness had been diagnosed he had felt confined – trapped even. He knew that Charlie meant well, his parents too, but their constantly looking out for him was beginning to have a suffocating effect. Trying to accommodate their response to his MS, as well as his own, was too much for him; it was like having to cope with yet another symptom of the illness. He believed, and hoped, that by moving away from their good intentions he would be able to sort himself out. God knows, he needed to.

All this he could see so clearly on a day like this when his body didn't feel as heavy as lead. When he felt comparatively well and normal it was easy to think logically and marshal his thoughts and fears. But it wasn't always so. He knew that. Too often he was irrational and as moody as hell.

He parked his car alongside his brother's TVR in the car-park behind their offices. Crawford and Sons was situated on the second floor of what had once been a Victorian warehouse, but had been converted into office space in the seventies. The first floor was occupied by a firm of solicitors and the top by a company of financial advisers. Josh had always joked that he and his brother were the only honest souls among a den of thieves.

Josh and Charlie had never considered working in anything other than the garment industry and when, thirteen years ago, their father had decided he wanted to retire early, he'd handed the business over to them. 'It's yours now,' he'd said, 'and I promise I shan't poke my nose in, it's up to you how you run it.' He'd been true to his word. Not once had he interfered with any decision they'd made.

They had worked for their father since leaving college and before that, spending all their vacations learning their craft from him, as well as developing a crucial sixth sense for a potential quickest selling line – an asset which had proved invaluable during the heady days of the Thatcherite era when there were fast bucks to be made in the garment trade and even faster bucks to be lost.

Crawford's had gone from strength to strength during the eighties and at one stage they'd had as many as forty employees. But that was then. Now things were different. With margins as tight as they were, the traditional layer of middle management had been removed from the company and they had pared themselves right down to the bone, numbering just fourteen employees to date. It was at least satisfying to know that, given the medicine they'd forced down their throats, they were still turning over the same profits as they had in the years of plenty, whereas many of their competitors who had resisted any honing down of their businesses had gone under.

Josh was convinced that their current success was due as much to their father as it was to the way in which he and Charlie had guided Crawford's through the recession and had then had the courage gradually to broaden the base of high street stores whom they supplied. The reputation and longevity of the company were just as important. Crawford's was well-known in Hong Kong where the bulk of what they sold in the UK was produced and as a consequence of their good name they were seen as a low risk. Maybe they were even liked. A few of their suppliers, the older ones in particular, still asked after their father. One always asked the same question: 'How's William?' he'd say, 'still pruning his roses?' He thought that was what all Englishmen did when they retired.

The other contributing factor to their survival was that Josh and Charlie knew their strengths. They were not innovators in the world of fashion, but followers. It was a clear distinction and so long as they remembered it Josh was sure they would continue to be a success.

He took the lift up to the second floor. When Mo, their receptionist, saw him she quickly stuffed a book under her desk. Josh was amused. For ages he and Charlie had known that Mo did most of her night-school homework during office hours, but so long as she kept doing her job as well as she did, neither of them had any complaints. He could also see that she must have raided the rail of finished samples in his office while he'd been away, for he recognised at once that she was wearing a knitted top that was part of next spring's line, as well as a pair of black PVC trousers – currently their fastest selling item. She grinned at him. 'Couldn't keep away, eh?'

'Got it in one.' He tried to sound as upbeat as he could, then attempted to stride past Mo, but the stiffness in his leg wouldn't let him. 'Charlie in his office?' he asked.

'Yes, but I've just put a call through. Shall I get you some coffee?'

'Thanks, that would be great.'

Charlie was still on the phone when Josh pushed against his door. When Charlie realised he was there he hurriedly brought his conversation to an end.

'Josh, what are you doing here? I thought you were off for another week?'

'I was getting bored,' he lied. He hadn't been bored at all. What had made him come in to work was something quite different. It was fear. He was frightened that if he stayed away too long there might not be a proper job for him to come back to. He wasn't worried that his brother would take advantage of his illness and try and squeeze him out of the business – Charlie would never do that – it was more that he was concerned that people would get used to him not being there. He was conscious, too, that for the past few months his brother had been working ridiculously long hours in order to cover for him. It couldn't go on.

He sat in the chair opposite Charlie and Mo brought in their coffee. She placed the mugs on the desk between them, which was almost buried beneath a tidal wave of faxes, contracts and specifications.

'So, how about you bring me up to date?' Josh said when Mo had left them. 'What's happened over that faulty batch of black jeans? Have they managed to get the dye fixed?'

Charlie leant back in his chair. 'Yes, after much verbal abuse they agreed there was a problem. I gave them an ultimatum by the way; one more cock-up like that and we ditch them. Is that okay with you?'

'Sure it is.' Josh felt the net of good intentions creeping over him. A year ago and Charlie wouldn't have put that question. 'And how about the problem at the warehouse?'

'I'm still dealing with that one.'

'Well, seeing as I'm back, let me sort it out.'

'Actually,' Charlie said slowly, 'I thought I'd go up there later today.'

'Meaning what?'

Charlie began sliding bits of paper across his desk. He didn't look up. 'Meaning exactly that. I'll go there later.'

Josh felt his body go taut with angry frustration. He got to his feet, placed both hands on the desk and leant forward. 'Meaning poor old Josh isn't up to it, I suppose. For pity's sake, Charlie, I'm quite capable of driving to Failsworth.' Then, summoning every ounce of energy, he marched out, slamming the door behind him. He ignored the stares of curiosity from everyone in the design area as his footsteps banged out angrily on the wooden floor. When he reached the safety of his own office he sank into his chair, sick with bitter exhaustion. He clasped his head in his hands.

A few moments later he looked up to see Charlie standing in the doorway. He came in. 'I'm sorry,' he said.

'Yeah, so am I.'

They fell silent. Then Josh spoke. 'Listen, Charlie, we need to talk. We can't go on like this . . . apart from anything else I don't have the energy. And what strength I do have I don't want to waste proving to you that I'm still capable of pulling my weight around here.'

Charlie nodded. 'Point made. Do you want to go out for lunch later and put me straight?'

'No, I've a better idea. Come back to my place tonight for supper. Meanwhile, I'll drive up to Failsworth and sort out the warehouse. Okay?'

Charlie nodded. 'Okay.'

12

Jessica had a surprise call from her agent.

It was a surprise for two reasons: one, it was so early in the morning – early enough for Jessica to be dozing in bed still – and two, to her knowledge Piers rarely called anyone until late in the afternoon – not because he was still dozing in bed, but because he'd always given her the impression that he was far too busy a man to pick up the phone before lunch-time.

He was a curious agent, with none of the smooth-tongued charm Jessica had come across in her limited dealings with the world of publishing, and his opening gambit to their conversation now was a typical example of his complete disregard for the social conventions usually employed in such circumstances.

'Jessica, is that you?' he demanded – he never announced himself; if Piers was benevolent enough to ring somebody they were supposed to have sufficient wits about them to know who he was. At the other end of the line she could make out a strange vibrating noise. Then she recognised what it was. It was Piers shaving. The cheek of the man! He was too stingy to give her his undivided attention. He was probably sitting at his desk, his phone on monitor, one of his hands guiding a Braun multi-shaver across his coal-face craggy chin and the other scrolling through an author's royalty statement on his computer screen.

'Hello, Piers, how are you?' she said defiantly. She might be in bed and still not fully *compos mentis*, but she was prepared to give the social conventions an airing, even if he wasn't.

'Flat out and with no time for small talk. I finished *A Carefree Life*.'

'And?'

'Not bad.'

Praise indeed, thought Jessica. For Piers to offer up such a charitable comment was quite something. 'Thank you,' she said.

'Much better than the previous one you churned out,' he said, the sound of the Braun still whirring away in the background.

'Kind of you to say.' *It had only reached the bestseller lists!* Why the hell did she stay with him? There were plenty of other literary agents in London she could switch to. Why did she put up with him?

Easy. She put up with him because he was dead straight with her. There was never any beating about the bush. No fawning. No bullshit. No literary snobbery. No ego massaging. And if there had ever been the merest hint of any skin-crawling sycophancy she would have dropped Piers like the proverbial hot brick. Or was it a hot potato? Well, whatever. Something mighty hot.

There was also the small matter of his undeniable talent for negotiating a cracking good contract. The advances Jessica had received since writing her first novel had been more than enough to satisfy her modest needs and had enabled her to buy her house in Cholmford Hall Mews. She had no delusions that Piers was partly responsible for her good fortune. It was just a shame he couldn't employ a touch more sweetness in his manner. A few words of encouragement wouldn't go amiss.

'I want you to come down and see me,' he said.

She sat bolt upright, terrifyingly *compos mentis* now. A summons? What had she done wrong? Did he no longer want to act for her, was that it? Or worse, had her publishers decided not to offer her another contract? Had they found themselves a new Jessica Lloyd? After all, no writer was indispensable.

'When were you thinking?' she said calmly, already worrying about her next mortgage payment.

'Day after tomorrow.'

'Day after tomorrow?' repeated Jessica, more convinced than ever that the summons was in order to impart bad news. 'But I've just moved house,' she said, grasping at any excuse to put Piers off, 'I've got so much to do. I need to –'

'I know all that, Jessica.' His tone of voice implied, don't bother me with domestic details, I'm a busy man. 'But this is important.'

'Okay, what time?'

'Be here for twelve thirty. I'll book us a table for lunch.'

She heard him switch off the razor, which was all the goodbye she received.

She went downstairs and made herself a cup of coffee, and determined not to fret over her conversation with Piers she took a kitchen chair and went outside to sit on the unimaginative rectangle of patio. She stared at her empty plot of garden and tried to visualise how it would look by the time her mother had taken it by the scruff of the neck. Anna was full of enthusiasm for creating all manner of curvy-shaped beds and filling them with seedlings and cuttings from Willow Cottage. 'I'll plant some rudbeckia against the fence for you,' she'd said only the other day, 'and then I'll throw in some campanula and verbascum. Maybe some columbine as well, though not too much, it can be very short-lived. And a hibiscus would love the sunny aspect as well as the rich soil.' Jessica was no gardener and she was more than happy to let her mother's green fingers take charge, just so long as she didn't overdo things.

She yawned and stretched out her legs in the warm early-morning sun. She glanced down at the T-shirt she was wearing and the words written across her chest – *Wind Surfers Do It Wet And Standing Up.* It was Gavin's and had been part of a small selection of his clothes that he had kept at her house. It was months since he had worn it, yet Jessica could smell him in every fibre. She had intended to leave it behind in Corfu, but at the last minute, and in a moment of weakness and indulgence, she had relented and tucked it into one of the bags. Then last night, while lying in bed unable to sleep, she had pathetically sought it out. Slipping the garment over her head, the soft, well-worn fabric had felt familiar and comfortable against her skin, and had brought back happy memories of Gavin. Within seconds she had fallen asleep.

But this morning – and before Piers's phone call – she had woken up to the smell of Gavin and had longed for him, every bit of her missing him. Well, perhaps only the physical bits – she didn't miss the mental pain he'd inflicted on her by refusing to commit himself to their relationship. But really the missing and longing had started ages ago when she had become conscious of the loss of what had attracted her to him in the beginning. When they'd first met, Gavin's sense of fun and happy-go-lucky nature had matched her own carefree persona. They had been in perfect accord with the shared view that life was best enjoyed with no more thought given for tomorrow than for yesterday.

But then things had changed.

She had started wanting to plan her tomorrows.

And it had proved fatal.

She drank the rest of her coffee, then ran a lingering hand over the front of Gavin's T-shirt. She hadn't expected to feel his absence so keenly. She had imagined that she would simply start a new way of life and that it would be without Gavin. After all, she had done it before. Each time she had moved about the world she had managed quite easily to piece together a new existence on her own. But she suspected that this time it was going to be a little more difficult because the memory of Gavin was going to be more persistent than she had anticipated.

She had thought that she would miss Corfu itself, but strangely she didn't. Every now and then she would think fondly of the quiet bay that had been home for so long and of the friends she had made. Sometimes she would recall Helen and Jack and imagine them on their terrace happily bickering like a couple of noisy cicadas. But for how long would they remain so happy? was the question that came into her mind. Might even their contentment turn on them one day and poison their bickering into something altogether more damaging? She hoped not. She wanted them to be happy.

She wanted Gavin to be happy, too.

She smiled. Who was she kidding? Gavin would always be happy. He was too straightforward to be anything else. Nothing ever troubled him because he was incapable of taking anything seriously. That was why he was able to be unfaithful and not wonder at his actions. If it didn't matter to him, then why would it matter to anybody else? was his unspoken philosophy.

She hadn't thought of it before, but Gavin and Piers were quite similar. In many ways they couldn't be more different, but in other ways they were worryingly alike. It probably never crossed Piers's mind that a chance remark on his part – *Much better than the previous one you churned out –* would be deeply hurtful.

She thought now of her impending day to be spent in London and the thought appalled her. It would be stinking hot and horrendously crowded, full of worn-out tourists pointing at screwed-up maps and asking her for directions. Which would be futile because she knew London about as well as they did. On any previous trips to see Piers, or her editor, she had afterwards flown back to Corfu desperate for her little house and the peaceful tranquillity it gave her. She wasn't a city person and a day in London was just about as much as she could take.

She began to worry again what it was that Piers had to tell her. What was so important that he couldn't discuss it on the phone? Was it something to do with her recently delivered manuscript? She wondered about ringing her editor, but remembered that Cara would still be away on holiday and that *A Carefree Life* would be lying unread on her desk, awaiting her return.

Well, whatever it was that Piers had to tell her would have to wait until Friday, today she was going shopping with Kate. It was a funny thing, but the more times she saw Kate, the older and more worldly she felt. In the past all her friends had been older than her and she had been happy to play her part accordingly. But Kate was almost ten years her junior and being in her company forced Jessica to behave quite differently. So what did that say about her? The trick cyclists might mutter something about her suffering from that well-known Peter Pan syndrome and that Corfu had been her Never-Never Land. Well, the trick cyclists could say all they wanted. They could pedal themselves up their inner tubes for all she cared. She wasn't afraid of adulthood. Wasn't that the very reason she had left Corfu? Responsibility for her mother had fairly smacked her in the face and made her see where her duty lay.

And on that grown-up thought she went indoors to get dressed.

Kate was just turning the key in the lock before going to call on Jessica when she heard footsteps coming across the courtyard. It was Amanda.

'I'm so pleased to have caught you,' Amanda said, hurrying the last few paces. 'I've been meaning to have a word with you for days. Tony and I wanted to thank you for helping us out the other night and we wondered whether you and Alec would come for dinner on Saturday.'

'There's no need to go to all that trouble,' Kate said, 'it was a pleasure looking after Hattie.'

'Well, come for dinner anyway. We'd love to see you both. About eight o'clock?'

'Thank you,' Kate said. She hoped that her voice conveyed at least a hint of sincerity. 'Would you like me to bring anything?'

Amanda laughed. 'Yes, some of your magic to work on Hattie, at least then we'll get an evening without her bothering us. She can be such a nuisance at bedtime.'

'I'll see what I can do,' Kate said stiffly. She suddenly decided that what she'd suspected from her first meeting with Amanda was true. She didn't like her one little bit. She started to move away from her front door.

'Off out, then?'

The enquiry was perfectly reasonable, but Kate was reluctant to satisfy Amanda's curiosity. Just because they were neighbours it didn't mean that they had to know one another's business. And besides, she didn't want Amanda suggesting that she come along for the ride as well. She had been looking forward to her day out with Jessica and had no desire for Amanda to spoil it.

'I'm just going shopping,' she said, in an effort to be economical with the truth.

'Anywhere nice?' asked Amanda.

Before Kate could reply Jessica's front door opened and she appeared on the step. Now we're for it, thought Kate.

Amanda looked over to Jessica and gave her a little wave. She hadn't yet had an opportunity to introduce herself to this supposedly well-known author – of whose supposed fame she was yet to be convinced – and she immediately seized her chance. She moved towards Jessica. 'Hello,' she said, 'I'm Amanda and I live in number two, over in the corner.'

'Hi, Kate tells me you were first to move in. How are you getting on?'

'Slowly getting things straight, you know how it is.'

Looking at Amanda in her commodore outfit – navy blazer and perfectly pressed knee-length white shorts with creases standing to attention and two-tone blue-and-white shoes – Jessica had a sneaky feeling that Amanda's idea of getting things straight would be entirely different from her own.

'I just came over to invite Kate and Alec for dinner on Saturday,' Amanda went on, 'I don't suppose you'd like to join us, would you?'

Kate hoped that Jessica would say yes. She didn't relish an evening of Alec talking to Tony and her being stuck with Amanda. Her wish was granted. 'Thank you,' she heard Jessica say, 'I'd love to come. What time?'

'Eight-ish and don't feel you have to dress up, it's casual.'

'One man's casual is another man's Sunday best,' Jessica said with a light laugh.

Amanda stared blankly at her, then returned her attention to Kate, 'I hope you enjoy your shopping.'

As they drove through the archway in Kate's little Mini, she said, 'Thank you for saying yes to Amanda's invitation. I'm not sure I could have coped with a whole evening of her without some kind of moral support.'

'Well, don't you dare back out at the last minute and leave me on my own. But tell me, and bearing in mind that I've known Amanda for all of two minutes, does she have the same effect on you? Does she make you want to say or do something outrageously rude, just to see how she would react?'

Kate smiled. 'Not exactly. To be honest she makes me feel awkward and nervous. But then lots of people make me feel like that.'

'What an extraordinary thing to say.'

'But it's true.'

'I hope I don't make you feel awkward.'

When Kate didn't reply Jessica said, 'Shall I take your silence as confirmation that I thoroughly put the wind up you?'

'No. No, I was quiet because I was just thinking that you don't make me feel nervous and I was trying to work out why.' She slowed down to negotiate the bridge over the canal and noticed that Jessica was craning her neck to look at the cottage on the right. She remembered then that Jessica had told her that this was where her mother lived. 'It's a beautiful house,' she said as they drove on.

Jessica wrenched her gaze away from Willow Cottage. She knew perfectly well that Anna wasn't at home, that she was staying with friends for a few days, but she couldn't rid herself of the need to be continually checking on her mother. It was quite alarming that in such a short space of time she had become a fanatic worrier about her mother's well-being. She realised now, with a sense of very real shame, that previously she had worried less over Anna because it had been a clear case of out of sight, out of mind.

'And did you grow up there?' asked Kate.

'Born and raised, as the expression goes.'

'It's lovely,' said Kate, 'I wish I'd grown up somewhere like this.'

Jessica caught the wistfulness in Kate's words. 'Don't be fooled by a few pretty roses round the door,' she said lightly. 'Now come on, tell me where we're going.'

'I thought perhaps we could go to Macclesfield. It's fairly easy to park there and I'm sure you'll be able to get most of what you want.'

'Brilliant, the sooner I get this over and done with the better. And thanks, by the way, for driving. Mum was all set to lend me her car, but then she was invited to spend a few days with friends over in Abersoch. And that's another thing I've got to arrange.'

'What's that?'

'A car. I'll go mad if I don't get one organised soon.'

'Did you have one in Corfu?'

'No. I either walked or used my boat.'

'It sounds very romantic. Don't you miss it all? This must seem quite ordinary in comparison.'

'It's all relative. Even shopping by boat becomes ordinary in the end.'

'I suppose so.' After a while Kate added, 'I hope that's not true of love.'

'That's quite a leap of thought,' Jessica said, intrigued and hoping for some further comment.

But Kate didn't say anything else. She kept her eyes on the road and her thoughts to herself. There were times when if she thought about how much she loved Alec she became convinced that something so precious could never last. She wasn't a pessimistic person by nature, but it was as if she were waiting for their relationship to go wrong.

13

Kate and Jessica finally returned home just after six o'clock. Kate's tiny car was brimming over with carrier bags, and boxes of china and glassware and bed linen, and the larger items that they hadn't been able to squeeze into the Mini were being delivered a few days later.

Kate helped Jessica carry everything inside and after she'd said goodbye she went next door to find a message on the answerphone from Ruth telling her – not asking her – to call back immediately.

Kate took the unprecedented step of ignoring a member of Alec's family and started preparing supper. She crushed a clove of garlic, put it into a frying pan along with a large spoonful of olive oil, then chopped up an onion and while that was softening in the hot oil with the garlic she peeled and chopped some tomatoes and added them to the pan. She was just reaching for the pot of fresh basil on the window-sill when the phone rang. She had forgotten to turn off the answerphone and Ruth's voice bellowed at her from the hall.

'You can't surely *still* be out,' Ruth said bad-temperedly.

Kate was tempted to ignore Ruth again, but remembering that, to all intents and purposes, she was now an employee of Alec's daughter she decided she'd better answer the phone. She took the frying pan off the hob and went and put Ruth out of her misery.

'Sorry about that, I've just got in,' she said, stretching the truth by about twenty minutes. 'If it's Alec you want to speak to I'm afraid he's not back yet.'

'No, it's not Dad I want, it's you. I need you to look after Oscar tomorrow. I'll drop him off at about half past eight.'

'But I thought you didn't want me to have him until the week after next.'

'I know that's what we agreed, but something's come up.'

Yes, thought Kate, lunch with a friend probably. 'I'm sorry, Ruth,' she said, 'but I can't help you, not tomorrow.'

'What? What do you mean you can't do it?'

'Alec's got to go down to Oxford to the warehouse tomorrow and I'm going with him.'

'Well, surely you can go another time; Dad's always going down there.'

Kate gripped the receiver. She really mustn't let Ruth push her around in this way. 'Alec was quite keen for me to go. We were going to stop the night in a hotel and then come back the following day.'

A loud snort from the other end of the line told Kate exactly what Ruth thought about her father spending a night in a hotel with a woman twenty-one years his junior.

'Well, all I'll say on the matter is that poor Oscar is going to be devastated,' Ruth went on. 'I promised him he'd be spending the day with you and now he'll probably cry himself to sleep with disappointment. If there's one thing children need, Kate, it's stability and consistency. I didn't think I'd have to remind *you* of that.'

Kate flinched. She'd known that she would regret ever letting Ruth wheedle out of her the details of her unhappy childhood. It had been a chance remark on Boxing Day when she had met Alec's family for the first time that had led to the mortifying disclosure. She had spent all morning in the kitchen preparing lunch and trying to take her mind off the impending show-down, and while she had been willing the day not to happen Alec had been insistent that all would be well. His calmness had surprised her. She hadn't expected him to be as nervous as she was, but his jovial manner – to the point of seemingly enjoying the prospect of his ex-wife meeting her – had only added to her own anxiety. The words *trophy girlfriend* had entered her head as he'd helped her choose what to wear. By the time they arrived she was rigid with fear and she let Alec greet his family while she hid in the kitchen and listened to him taking coats and offering drinks.

'They'll love you,' he whispered into her ear when inevitably he came to find her, 'who could fail to?'

'Melissa for one,' she whispered back.

He kissed her and took her by the hand to the sitting-room.

'This is Kate,' Alec announced, his arm around her shoulder. Predictably all eyes – especially Melissa's – were on her and, wishing herself anywhere but in that room, she made a few polite noises and sought refuge in Alec's grandson Oscar, who was sitting on the floor looking at a book.

'Hello,' she said, going over to the little boy and slipping down to the floor beside him. 'Is that a Christmas present?'

He raised his head warily, stared at her with his large, thoughtful brown eyes, then said, 'Yes. Will you read it to me?'

She didn't need asking twice and leaving Alec to entertain the rest of his family she took the book from Oscar and began reading aloud to him, but in a lowered voice so as not to draw attention to herself. After a few minutes, Ruth came over and joined them. She sat in the wing-back chair in front of Kate and Oscar, and with a glass of wine in her hand she watched the pair of them closely. She also listened. Kate struggled to keep her nerves at bay and continued reading as best she could. When the story was over Oscar, who was now sitting on her lap, turned the pages back to the beginning and said, 'Read it again, *please.*' She smiled and gave him a hug, glad that she had at least made one friend in Alec's family.

'Do all children lap you up in this way?' Ruth asked.

'I . . . don't know,' she answered.

'I've always thought that it's the childlike who relate best to children. Wouldn't you agree?'

The insult was glaringly obvious and Kate said the first thing that came into her head. It proved to be entirely the wrong thing to say. 'I just like children to be happy. I know what it's like to be unhappy.'

The expression on Ruth's face changed. She snapped forward in her chair and began the process of interrogation that she must have been dying to do ever since she had learnt of her father's scandalously young girlfriend. Kate tried hard to parry the questions that were being fired at her, but her nervousness and natural distaste for deception rendered her incapable of defending herself against such a determined inquisitor. By the time Ruth had finished with her, the full details had been drawn out of her and an unspoken conclusion reached – not only had Kate's unstable upbringing set her on a course of seeking out a lover to make up for the father she had never known, but her love of children was to compensate for the love she'd never received from her own mother, who had flitted from one disastrous relationship to another. But what was wrong if that was the case? Did it really matter? Wasn't it true that everybody's actions were attributable in one way or another to their upbringing? But any amount of self-justification wouldn't quell the tide of unhappiness Ruth's questioning was causing her.

Several times during Ruth's cross-examination Kate had looked across the room for help, to where Alec was talking to Melissa, but he had been unaware of her distress.

In the end it was Oscar who came to her rescue. 'I'm hungry,' he announced. 'What's for lunch?'

'I'd better go and see,' she said, quickly lifting him off her lap and getting to her feet. He had followed her out to the kitchen and they had remained the best of friends ever since.

But now as Kate thought of her little friend her heart ached at the distress she would cause him if she didn't do what his mother wanted. She couldn't bear the thought of him crying himself to sleep that night. She tried to think of a way round the problem; a solution that would suit them all. She didn't want to let Alec down, but neither did she want to hurt Oscar. An idea came into her head. She wasn't sure how Alec would take it, but Oscar was his grandson after all, so he couldn't object too much, could he?

But Alec did object.

'What?' he demanded, later that evening when Kate told him what she had agreed with Ruth.

'Ruth wanted me to look after Oscar and I said if it was all right with her he could come with us to Oxford . . . I thought he'd enjoy it,' she faltered. 'I thought you would, too.'

'You mean, you thought *you'd* enjoy it.'

Kate was dumbfounded. She had never heard Alec's voice so cold, or so sharp. 'I . . . I don't understand, you know I enjoy having Oscar around, I love him dearly.'

Alec turned on his heel and marched out of the kitchen. He went upstairs to the bedroom, yanked off his tie and threw it on the bed, followed by his jacket. He went and stood in front of the window and gazed out at the distant hills. After a few minutes, when his anger had subsided, a far worse emotion took hold of him. Shame. He was shattered at his sudden outburst of anger.

He didn't need to try and reason out his actions. It was all about his own insecurity. He was so terrified that he would lose Kate he was becoming irrationally possessive. He couldn't handle her wanting to spend time with anyone but himself.

Hell! He was even jealous of her spending time with Oscar.

He'd heard people talk about the demon of jealousy and what a powerful destructive force it could be, but he'd had no idea until now just how destructive.

All he wanted was to have Kate entirely to himself while they were in Oxford. He'd planned to get his visit at the warehouse over and done with as quickly as possible, then spend the rest of the time with Kate. He'd even ordered champagne to be waiting for them when they arrived at the hotel. He'd had in mind a night of seduction.

Not a night of baby-sitting!

He banged his fist down on the window-sill and Kate's small china trinket box close to his hand rattled its lid.

From downstairs he heard the sound of a door shutting and as he continued to stare out of the window he caught sight of Kate walking away from the house. He knew he ought to rush out to her, but he stayed where he was. Motionless. Bewildered. He had never known such pain. He watched her cross the courtyard and walk past the block of garages. Then she began to run, her beautiful hair fanning out behind her as she ran across the field where the nearby farmer sometimes grazed his sheep. She went into the darkness of the small copse and vanished out of sight.

'What are you staring at?'

Charlie turned away from the window and faced his brother who had just come into the room.

'You never told me you had such terrific-looking neighbours.'

'I didn't know I had.'

'Well this one was a beauty and she was running into the sunset like a frightened gazelle.'

Josh thought of the only female neighbour he'd met at Cholmford Hall Mews, bearing in mind that he'd felt like death when he'd encountered her. All he could recall of the woman from number four was that she was slim, with a terrific tan. He had the feeling, though, that she wasn't what his brother would describe as a beauty. He knew Charlie's taste in women and they were usually of the very tall, curvy variety. And as far as he knew there wasn't anybody of that description on his doorstep. But then he hadn't exactly gone out of his way to meet his neighbours, having kept himself to himself since moving in.

'So what did she look like?' he asked, going over to the leather sofa and settling himself down, glad to take the strain off his left leg, which had been hanging off him like a dead weight for most of the day. He picked up his can of beer from the glass-topped table in front of him.

Charlie came and joined him. 'I think I've just fallen in love with an angel straight from heaven.'

Josh nearly choked on his beer. 'You what?'

Charlie smiled. 'Okay then. Maybe not. But she was all willowy and gorgeous, like something out of a picture, you know, one of those Pre-Raphaelite paintings.'

'What, the ones where the women look like they've got disjointed necks?'

'Yeah, those are the ones.'

'So let me get this right. There's a woman out there in the fields with a broken neck and you fancy her?'

Charlie sighed. 'You put it so well.'

Josh got to his feet. 'I think you need another beer.'

Charlie followed him out to the kitchen and while Josh opened the fridge he lifted the lid on the pan of curry gently simmering on the hob. 'When's supper ready? I'm starving.'

Josh tossed him a can of beer. 'When we've had our conversation.' He went and sat on a stool at the island unit in the middle of the kitchen.

'Oh, it's the serious stuff now, is it?'

'Got it in one.'

Charlie sat opposite his brother. 'Look,' he said, 'I'm sorry about this morning.'

'Yeah, and so am I, I over-reacted. But if we're going to avoid any repeat performances of that little fiasco we've got to come to some kind of understanding. My body might be doing its best to convince me – and everybody else – that I'm about as useful as a chocolate teapot, but there's nothing wrong with my brain. Okay?'

Charlie nodded. 'I know that, Josh. It's just that –'

'I know what the just is, it's you thinking that you've got to cover for me. But how long do you think you can keep that up? You're shattered with all the extra work you're taking on and I don't know whether you've looked in the mirror recently, but your looks are definitely going.'

'Cheeky sod!'

'Yeah, well, do something about it. Stop treating me like a charity case and let me do my job as best I can, and get yourself home and in bed at a more realistic time each night. Otherwise we'll end up with no company to run because we'll both have blown it.'

Charlie took a long swig of beer. He looked thoughtfully at his brother. 'I hear what you're saying and in principle I agree. But . . .' he raised his hand as Josh opened his mouth to speak, 'don't leap down my throat, but how long do you think *you* can keep this up?'

'Honest answer?'

'Yes.'

'I don't know. Some days I feel fine, as if I could plod on for ever. Other days, I feel like death. But you know that already.'

'You don't think, then, that by easing off work you might . . . you know, you might prolong . . .' But he couldn't finish the question.

Josh did it for him. 'You mean, if I give up work and take it easy will I live to be sixty instead of perhaps snuffing it when I'm in my forties?'

Charlie swallowed. 'I wish you weren't so bloody blunt.'

'But that's the gist of your question, isn't it? Well?' Josh prompted when Charlie didn't answer him.

'Yes,' Charlie muttered morosely. He kept his gaze firmly on the can in his hands. He couldn't begin to imagine life without Josh. It was inconceivable. They weren't like other brothers. There was an extraordinary affinity between them that had enabled the pair of them never to tire of one another's company. They had grown up together; played together; studied together; worked together and even holidayed together. Some might say it was an unnatural relationship, that siblings could never be that close without there being something strange or sinister going on. But the truth was quite straightforward, he loved his brother and would do anything to protect him. He looked up, suddenly realising that Josh was answering his question.

'I have no idea if by taking it easy now my life will be extended, but I can only do what feels right. And what's important to me at the moment is to be able to carry on as though this whole nightmare had never started.'

'So how can I best help?'

'By supporting me, I guess.'

'That's what I've been doing.'

Josh shook his head. 'No. You've been feeling sorry for me. Pity's the last thing I need.'

Charlie crushed the empty beer can in his hand. 'Okay then. I'll try my best.' And wanting to lighten the mood – there was only so much of this he could handle – he said, 'But in return you've got to introduce me to your neighbours. I want to meet that fantastic girl who's just taken flight across the fields.'

Josh stared at the crushed can in front of him and felt a bit demolished himself. 'She's probably not real,' he said, slowly getting to his feet. 'It's just some mythical vision your body has created to taunt you with.'

It was almost dark when Alec heard footsteps on the stairs. Soft, wary footsteps.

He hadn't moved since Kate had fled. He was still standing in the bedroom, his head slumped against the cool glass of the window. He turned and faced her when she came in. She stared at him, the hurt on her face only too visible. She looked pale and fragile, her eyes wide with the pain he'd inflicted on her. He could see that she had been crying and his heart twisted with shame and guilt.

'I'm sorry,' she murmured. 'I should have asked you first about Oscar. I should have thought.'

That she could think herself in the wrong appalled Alec and in an instant he was across the room with his arms around her. He held her so tightly he heard her gasp.

'It's me who should be sorry,' he whispered, burrowing his face into her lovely hair and keeping it there. He couldn't look at her expression. Not because he couldn't risk seeing the anguish he had caused, but because he didn't want her to see the tears in his own eyes.

14

Thanks be to Richard Branson, thought Jessica as her train pulled into Euston Station precisely on time; the journey from hell was over.

The fat man in the seat directly opposite her – the cause of two hours and fifteen minutes of purgatory – closed his laptop and began tidying away his portable office, which, as the train had hurtled its way through the sun-dried countryside of Middle England, had steadily encroached further and further towards the small space that Jessica had tried in vain to claim as her own.

As far as Jessica was concerned journeys had a peculiar tendency to bring out the territorial, if not the killer instinct in the most passive of people. Motorways were bad enough with every driver seeing himself as king of the road, but there was nothing like a train journey really to threaten somebody's personal space. Especially if the very latest in high-tech weaponry was being employed – the mobile phone.

And the fat man opposite her must have been a top gun in the use of his.

Of course, she should have known better than to occupy a seat in the same compartment as Porky, never mind sit barely three feet away, but it had been a choice between him or a screaming baby further down the train.

Once she'd made up her mind where to sit she had offered up a smile in the hope of at least setting off on the right foot. But he had ignored her. Fine by me, she had thought, settling herself into her seat and sorting out where to put her large leather bag, which was loaded up with reading matter for the journey.

But it was clear from the word go that nobody but Porky was going to get a moment's peace all the way to London. If he wasn't shuffling through sheaves of paper or rattling the keys on his laptop, he was on the phone. And there was nothing discreet about Porky's manner of conducting business.

'Yah!' he would holler into the small phone pressed into the pudgy flesh of his face, 'Yah. Yah. Yah. Yah, just do it. Yah, thanks. Let me know how you get on. Speak to you soon.'

By the time the train reached Watford Gap, Jessica and her fellow passengers had had enough. But nobody, it seemed, was brave enough to do anything. One or two people shook their newspapers, hoping that this might be enough to shame Porky into quietening down. Someone even tutted. But it was Jessica who decided it was time for action when the horrible man heaved himself out of his seat and headed towards the buffet car. When he was completely out of sight, she leaned forward, reached for one of his yellow Post-its and wrote in large letters – *One more noise from you, Porkster, and you're DEAD!* She stuck it on the screen of his laptop. Her immediate neighbours read what she'd written and smiled their thanks and support.

'Couldn't have put it better myself,' said a tiny grey-haired lady who had been sucking Polo mints all the way from Stoke.

Porky returned with several paper carrier bags of food and drink. He squeezed his bulky frame back into his seat. But just as he'd levelled off he saw the note. He snatched it off the laptop and held it up. 'Who's responsible for this?' he demanded, glaring round at the compartment like a teacher with a class of fifth-form pranksters.

Nobody spoke. Nobody even looked at him. It was as if he didn't exist. The remaining half-hour of the journey was wonderfully quiet.

As soon as she could, Jessica squeezed past Porky and bolted off the train. She made her way along the busy platform towards the escalator for the underground. She was in luck, a train had just pulled in and she found herself a space jammed up against a George Michael look-alike, extraordinary whiskers and all. He smelt delicious and was rather good-looking, but then after two joyful hours of Porky, Robin Cook would have scored a ten-out-of-ten rating on the hunkometer.

She got out at Charing Cross and began the short walk to Piers's office, which was situated just off Haymarket. It was now, as she made her way through the tourists sunning themselves on the steps of the National Gallery, that she began to worry – at least the awful train journey had kept her mind off her impending doom.

Jessica was convinced that her writing career was over. Last night in bed, she had tossed and turned – even Gavin's T-shirt had been of no use – as her mind had worked through the same scenario again and again: her publishers were no longer interested in her and Piers was unable to find anybody else to take her on, which was probably why he had been so uncharacteristically generous about *A Carefree Life*. Though convinced that this was the case, there was the small voice of reason suggesting that if so, Piers would be the last person to have any qualms about breaking the news to her over the phone. If an author was past her sell-by date Piers would have no problem in sending her packing. 'Jessica,' he would say, 'it's time to clear your desk. Pick up your P45 on your way out.'

By the time she reached the glass-fronted building where Piers hung out on the second floor she was sweating and her stomach was somersaulting a treat. She could barely breathe and there was a dull ache clawing at the back of her head. Nervous tension was a real killer!

She pressed the button and when the doors opened she stepped into the mirror-lined lift and hunted through her bag for a strip of pain-killers. But all she found were a couple of loose Paracetamols, chipped and coated in fluff. She gave them a rub and put them in her mouth and swallowed. One went down, but the other stuck to her tongue and at the foul taste her face twisted into the kind of distorted shape a champion gurner would have been proud of. The lift came to a sudden halt, the doors opened and in front of her stood an immaculately dressed Piers – pin-stripe trousers, light-blue shirt and Old School-style tie. Through her discomfort she was conscious that he blended in nicely with the navy-blue carpet at his feet.

'Les Dawson, I presume,' he said, when he saw her grimacing face.

It was the nearest she'd ever heard Piers get to making a joke. 'I need a glass of water,' she croaked. The tablet was firmly lodged at the back of her throat now and her taste-buds were sending out emergency distress signals. Mayday! Mayday! Poison alert! Prepare to abandon ship. Which was a smart way for her body to say that if something wasn't done soon, Piers would have a revolting mess on his office carpet.

Stella, Piers's assistant, was sent for and was given the task of sorting Jessica out, and when she finally emerged from the toilet she composed herself and allowed Stella to escort her to Piers's office. He was waiting for her.

'Sorry about that,' she said, 'it must be the air down here in London, it doesn't agree with me.'

He gave her a look as if to say, are you quite finished? Then lifted his jacket from the back of his chair and pulled it on. 'Let's go and eat.'

Jessica had rather hoped that Piers would put her out of her misery before they went to the restaurant. Perhaps he was such a sadist that he was enjoying the moment of keeping her in an agony of suspense. Oh well, if that was the case, she'd have the most expensive meal the restaurant had to offer. That would serve him right.

He took her to the Caprice.

'I was here with Nick Hornby last week,' he told her as they perused their menus.

'Who?' Jessica asked, knowing full well whom Piers meant; she'd read *Fever Pitch* as soon as the book had made it to the shelves in Kassiopi. It was the first time she'd known Piers even hint at trying to impress her. What was going on? A joke earlier and now a blatant case of social climbing. He'd be telling her next that he was a drinking chum of A. A. Gill. She shuddered at the thought.

He lowered his menu and contemplated her. 'You're going to have to get your act together, Jessica,' he said sternly. 'Now that you're back in England you'll have no excuse for being out of touch.'

Her act of out-of-touchness was her deliberate way of showing up other people's hoity-toity pretentiousness. And anyway she had never been out of touch with England. The *Sunday Times* had always been available to her in Corfu and her mother had regularly sent her videos of all the best in TV drama, though she had begun to question Anna's taste when tapes of *Star Trek: The Next Generation* had arrived in the post. 'Why should I have to get my act together?' she asked Piers. She was being bold now. Well, why not? If she was being given the old heave-ho, she might just as well go out fighting to the last.

He didn't answer her. Instead he caught the eye of a passing waitress and began ordering his lunch. When he'd finished he looked pointedly at Jessica. So did the waitress.

'I'll have the duck whatsit on a bed of asparagus, followed by the pan-fried chicken liver with rosti, and I want the liver cooked. I don't want to cut into it and find lumps of strawberry jelly.' She slapped the menu down on the table and leant back in her chair. She was really getting into the part now: recalcitrant and thoroughly obnoxious.

'In that case we'll have a bottle of red wine,' Piers said, ignoring her performance and making her feel like a naughty child. 'I think the 1994 St Chinian will be suitable.'

When they were alone he said, 'How's the new house?'

Now this was going too far. Piers making small talk. No, really. This had to stop. 'Piers,' she said, 'would you please get to the point?'

'The point?'

'Yes. Just why on earth have you dragged me all the way down here?'

He smiled. Well, it was almost a smile; a slight lifting of the corners of his mouth. For a split second he looked almost handsome. Jessica had never before considered Piers as a good-looking man, but she decided that if he could only get the hang of this smiling thing he would stand a chance of being half decent; marriage material even. To her knowledge – Stella being her main source of information – Piers had never been married and at the age of forty-seven he gave the impression of having no desire to do so. Jessica would put money on him not being gay, though why she felt so strongly on this score she had no idea. Perhaps it was his brusqueness that precluded this possibility. Not that all gay men had to go around gushing like Julian Clary.

Their wine arrived and Piers instructed the waitress to leave them to it. He poured out a large glass for Jessica and one for himself.

'I think this is what the clever-arsed folk would call a champagne moment,' he said, raising his glass, 'but you know me well enough to know that I'm not a champagne person, or clever-arsed for that matter, so this will do well enough instead. Come on, raise your glass.'

Jessica did as she was told, but viewed Piers suspiciously. He was up to something. A spot of softening up before delivering the blow perhaps?

'To your next contract,' he said. 'Congratulations.'

'My what?'

'You heard. Go on, drink up.'

She took a sip, then a gulp. Followed by an even larger mouthful. 'So why didn't you tell me this on the phone?'

He leant back in his chair. 'I wanted to tell you in person. I think the occasion merits such treatment. Nothing's definite and it's all down to you to make the final decision, but how do you feel about switching horses?'

'I think you'd better explain.'

Their first course arrived and while they flapped napkins open, sprinkled salt and pepper and poured out more wine, Piers explained. 'As you know, now that you've delivered *A Carefree Life* you've fulfilled your contract which means –'

'Which means I'm now out of contract.'

'Precisely. And I think you've outgrown where you are.'

'How do you work that out?'

'I've had an offer from another publisher who's prepared to pay a substantial amount of money for you.'

Jessica reached for her wineglass. 'How much? And which publisher?'

'One question at a time.'

She gulped her wine and tried to stop her knees from shaking under the table. It was all turning out so differently from how she'd imagined, and the combination of shock and relief was transforming her into a jittery mess. She planted both feet firmly on the ground in the hope it would keep her legs from moving. But it didn't work. They carried on banging away like pistons.

'You're being offered a two-book contract,' she heard Piers say. But suddenly he stopped and stared at her. 'Jessica,' he said, 'are you playing footsie with me?'

'Certainly not!' she squeaked. And with enormous will-power she forced her legs to be still.

He carried on, but with a curious expression on his face. 'As I was saying, it's a two-book contract and three times what you're currently being paid.'

Jessica drained her glass and goggled. The cutlery on the table began to rattle as her legs started up again.

Piers refilled her glass and said, 'Got anything to say?'

'Um . . . supposing I don't like my new editor?'

Piers rolled his eyes. 'For this kind of money, Jessica, I'd make an effort to get on with Genghis Khan.'

'But I like where I am.'

'In that case you'll have to accept their lower offer.'

'Which is?'

'A two-book contract and only twice what you're currently getting.'

Jessica considered what Piers had just told her. It was difficult to take it in. One minute she was worrying about her mortgage and the next she was feeling like Barbara Taylor Bradford. 'Even if I take the lower offer, it's still a lot of money, isn't it? I mean, it's oodles more than I ever thought I'd get paid. Squillions more in fact.'

'Such a precise command of the English language you have when it comes to money, Jessica. But it's only what an author of mine deserves. How's your duck by the way?'

They left the restaurant a little after three and took a cab back to the office. Jessica had been too shocked and excited to eat a thing and had drunk far more than was good for her. She tried to sit upright in the back of the cab, but somehow she kept slipping to one side. At one point she ended up with her head on Piers's shoulder. In a more sober state she would sooner have put it inside a tandoori oven.

They sat in his office and Stella was instructed to bring them coffee. And lots of it.

'I'm not drunk,' she told Piers as she sank into a chair.

'And I'm the Archbishop of Canterbury,' he said drily.

She giggled and found she couldn't stop. She laughed and laughed until tears were rolling down her cheeks. He came over and passed her his handkerchief.

'Thank you,' she said, pressing the hanky to her face. The square of crisp linen smelt of aftershave. *Piers wore aftershave?* Why hadn't she noticed that before? She tried to picture him at home in his bachelor bathroom splashing about with bottles of Givenchy or Chanel for Men. But it was no good. All she could imagine was Piers shaving in his office, too busy to bother with anything as trivial as men's toiletries.

She looked up at him as he stood leaning against his desk, his hands placed either side of him. She suspected that he was having a crack at smiling again, that mouth of his was definitely slightly more curved than it had been a few moments ago. She suddenly wondered what he was like in bed. Underneath that stern façade was there a passionate man who was dynamite between the sheets? Never mind the bedroom, how about the office, spread-eagled across the desk? The thought that she would like to find out had the effect of instantly sobering her up. *Arrgh! She'd actually just considered the possibility of having sex with Piers!*

She reached for the cup of coffee Stella had brought in some time ago and quickly drank it, even though it was nearly cold.

'Fully recovered now?' Piers asked, regrouping to the other side of his desk.

'Er . . . yes, thank you,' she said. She tried to make her voice sound sure and businesslike, and made an even bigger effort to sit up straight. 'Sorry about that, it's the shock. You know, the excitement of it all.'

He stared at her, his head slightly tilted to one side.

He knows, she thought. He knows what I was just thinking. She squirmed in her seat.

'So,' he said slowly, 'what's your decision?'

She cleared her throat. 'Um . . . I don't know.'

He tutted. Sentiment, his expression said. Nothing but woolly-minded sentiment. 'I'm sure I don't need to remind you that you have to think of your long-term future.'

'I know all that, but it's not just the money,' she said lamely, 'it's the personal side of the working relationship that counts as well. Cara and I get on. I might not like my new editor.'

'I thought we'd already covered that.'

She frowned.

He held up his hands. 'Okay. If you don't want to make the move that's fine by me. It's entirely your decision.'

Jessica needed some time on her own to work things out. So she went to the toilet to make up her mind. It was a ridiculous thing to do, but after ten minutes of deliberation she decided that if the loo flushed perfectly first go she would stay where she was. If it took two yanks of the handle, as it normally did whenever she used a strange toilet, then she would take the money and run. She held her breath and gave the loo handle an almighty shove – Frank Bruno couldn't have put more into it.

She went back to Piers. 'I'm staying with Cara and the team,' she said firmly, but not looking him in the eye – her decision to accept a lower offer meant that Piers had just lost out financially as well.

He made no comment, but offered her another cup of coffee and insisted on personally taking her back to Euston for her train.

'It's to be the red-carpet treatment from now on, is it?' she said, as they walked along the station platform, 'now that I'm one of your big earners.'

'I've always treated you well, Jessica.'

She came to a stop. 'Piers, you've never once walked me to my train and as far as I'm concerned you've treated me abominably ever since I've known you. You take a tenth of anything I earn and make me feel like shit.'

He raised an eyebrow. 'Good to know that I'm so good at my job. And if you really want to know why I'm escorting you to your train it's because in your current state of mind I wouldn't trust you to find the end of your nose.'

15

Jessica found herself a seat in a relatively uncrowded compartment. She hoped that there wasn't a clone of Porky lurking somewhere in the carriage.

As the train pulled out of the station she closed her eyes. Her head was beginning to ache again. What was needed was a quick forty winks.

But a nap didn't work and by the time they reached Rugby she knew she was in for a migraine. The dull ache had spread to the right side of her head and was throbbing with all the intensity of a pneumatic drill. She kept her eyes shut to stop the pain caused by the blinding overhead light and when the train stopped at Crewe she went and stood in the corridor by an open window, hoping that the cool evening air would help.

But it didn't and twenty minutes later, when the train finally pulled into Cholmford Station, Jessica walked like a zombie along the deserted platform. The station was unmanned and there was no sign of a phone. She was completely alone. She cursed herself for not having arranged for a taxi to pick her up. There was nothing else for it but to walk.

She staggered along the empty lanes for almost a mile, her head feeling as though it were going to explode. She felt so desperately ill that she was tempted to lie down in the road and wait for a passing car to run her over and put her out of her misery – if only there were any cars about. She had reached the stage now where the migraine was making her feel sick and light-headed. She reckoned that her mother's house was only a mile away so she struggled on. But it was no good. She couldn't go another step. There was a gap in the hedgerow and seeing that there was a small stump of a tree hidden in the long grass of the verge, she sat down and tried to breathe slowly and deeply. All around her it was very quiet. It wasn't yet dark, but the light was fading fast. She had never felt so isolated. A perfect night for a murder, she thought. No one to hear her screams. No one to appear on the *Six O'Clock News* as a key witness. She was just cursing her mother for living in the most remote spot in the whole of Cheshire when she heard the sound of a car coming along the lane.

'Oh please, God,' she said, seeing the headlights and getting to her feet, 'let it be someone prepared to help a damsel in distress.' She stood in the middle of the road determined that the driver would have no choice but to stop for her. She didn't give a thought to her safety – the person behind the wheel could be the mad axeman of Cholmford on the look-out for his latest victim for all she cared. He could chop her up into convenient bite-sized pieces and it would be fine by her – she'd even hold herself steady so that he could get make a better job of it – because at least then her head would stop hurting. Perhaps she could insist that he start by chopping her head off first.

Josh slowed down. He switched off Michael Nyman's *The Draughtsman's Contract* and as he approached the strange figure in the road he recognised who it was. It was his neighbour from number four. He got out of the Shogun and went to her. She didn't look at all well. She was very pale and her eyes were unfocused. She was shivering, too.

'Please,' she said, 'whoever you are, can you give me a lift to Cholmford Hall Mews? And if you are a mad axeman, do you think you could treat yourself to a night off?'

He smiled. 'Okay, but just this once.' He helped her into the car.

She didn't speak for the next hundred yards, then suddenly she blurted out, 'Stop!'

He slammed on the brakes and before he could get out of the car to offer his assistance she was on the roadside bent over a clump of stinging nettles.

After a few moments she got back into the car. He handed her the box of tissues he kept in the glove compartment. 'I'm not drunk,' she murmured, 'if that's what you're thinking. I've got a migraine, it always gets me like this. I'm sorry.'

'Let me know if you need to stop again,' he said.

'Don't worry, I will.' She put her head back against the head-rest and closed her eyes. She looked really ill now. He wondered if she had recognised who he was yet.

In all, they stopped three times. When they finally reached Cholmford Hall Mews, Josh parked as close to number four as he could. He went round to her side of the car and opened the door. 'Okay?' he said. 'You're home. Have you got your keys?'

She stepped down, took a couple of paces and lurched forward, almost knocking Josh clean off his feet as she fainted against him.

Regaining his balance, he decided the best thing he could do was to push her back into the car and take her over to his place. It didn't seem fair to leave her all alone.

She came to just as he started up the engine. 'I thought I'd already got out of the car,' she said drowsily.

'You did, but you also fainted.' He drove across the courtyard.

'Oh dear, I'm making a nuisance of myself, aren't I?' she said in a small voice. 'Where are we going?'

He pulled on the handbrake. 'My house. I don't think you should be on your own. And don't worry, I promise you, hand on heart, I've taken the evening off from axe murdering.'

She looked at him for the first time. 'I've just realised who you are. You're my rude neighbour, aren't you?'

Josh frowned at this description of himself.

'Right,' he said, when they were inside the house. 'What do you normally do when you have a bad migraine like this?'

She leant back against the wall, light-headed and dizzy. 'Bed, hot-water bottle and complete darkness.'

'Okay, can you manage the stairs?' It was strange asking somebody else this question. Usually it was asked of him. They made slow progress and Josh was glad that his neighbour was unable to go any faster, at least it meant he could keep up with her.

At the top of the stairs he led her to the spare room. The bed wasn't made up, but he opened a cupboard and pulled out a duvet. He threw it on the bed, followed by a couple of pillows. He also found a hot-water bottle. 'I'll be back in a minute with this,' he said.

Downstairs in the kitchen he boiled a kettle, found a bucket – just in case – from under the sink in the utility room, filled the hot-water bottle and grabbing a box of tissues from the window-sill he slowly made his way back up the stairs. He tapped lightly on the door and went in. She was already in bed, fully dressed, judging by the lone pair of shoes on the floor. She was very nearly asleep. He handed her the hot-water bottle and put the other things on the floor beside her.

'I'll leave you to it,' he whispered, 'just give me a shout if you need anything.'

She nodded and he crept quietly away.

Jessica opened her eyes, but then immediately closed them. She didn't want to wake up. She wanted to stay where she was in Gavin's arms. They had been making love on the hot sand beneath a cloudless sky – it had been like *From Here to Eternity*, but in colour and without the messy crashing waves. But try as she might to recapture the dream, she couldn't, it was gone.

And so was her migraine.

She opened her eyes again and remembered where she was – her neighbour's spare room. She peeped under the duvet. She was fully dressed. Well, that was okay then. She looked at her watch and saw that she'd been asleep for just over an hour. She sat up slowly. Very slowly. If she moved too quickly at this stage the blinding pain would come back. She shifted the pillows behind her shoulders and looked about her, taking in the room in the semi-darkness. For a man who had just moved house there was very little sign of him having done so. All was neat and tidy. Apart from there not being any curtains up at the window.

She could make out the sound of music coming from downstairs. It was a familiar opera, but one she couldn't remember the name of. It irritated her that she couldn't recall its title. Puccini, she decided. It was definitely Puccini. But which opera?

After ten minutes of sitting quietly she ventured out of bed. She stood up and found that the dizziness had gone, as had the nausea. She felt a bit embarrassed going downstairs. It wasn't every day that she ended up sleeping in the house of a man whom she barely knew and who had taken on more than his fair share of neighbourly kindness.

She found him in the sitting-room, bent over a mound of paperwork. From an impressive-looking hi-fi system in the corner of the room Puccini was still doing his stuff.

'Hi,' he said, when he saw that she was there. He put down his work, took off his glasses and got to his feet. 'How are you feeling?'

'Like I've been beaten over the head with a frying pan,' she said, squinting against the light.

'Is it too much for you? I'll turn it off if you like and just leave a lamp on.'

She nodded her thanks and watched him move across the room. He seemed to be limping much more than she remembered when she'd first seen him.

He caught her looking at his leg. 'It's an old skiing injury,' he said hurriedly, 'it comes and goes. Please, sit down.'

She hesitated. 'I really ought to go. You've done so much to help me, the least I can do is leave you in peace.'

'Nonsense. I'll make you a drink. What would you like?'

'Tea would be great.' She was glad that he wasn't making her feel that she should be off straight away and while he was out of the room she settled herself in a chair as far away from the lamp as possible.

Whoever her neighbour was he had good taste. The room, though sparsely furnished, was comfortable and homely. The chair she was sitting in matched the leather sofa, which was black and well worn and had a couple of terracotta-coloured cushions placed at each end. In front of it was a glass-topped coffee table that her neighbour had been working at, and on the floor was a large rectangular black-and-red rug that had Rothko stamped all over it. The other pieces of furniture were all modern in design and appeared to be made of beechwood; they contrasted stylishly with the wrought-iron lamps. There were several Italianate architectural prints in gilt frames covering the walls and either side of the fireplace were hundreds of books crammed into the built-in shelves that went right up to the ceiling. Jessica was pleased to conclude that her Good Samaritan was a man who liked to read.

Unlike Gavin.

She was sure that the last book Gavin had read was *Noddy Gets Into Trouble.*

It was a shame that she was still feeling so groggy as she would have loved to have prowled round the room and explored her neighbour's belongings.

'Have you managed to take any pain-killers, yet?' he asked, coming back with two large mugs and a packet of something under his arm.

'No,' she said, 'and that was the problem. I didn't have any with me.'

He put the mugs on the glass-topped table and handed her the packet he'd been carrying. 'Try those,' he said, sitting down on the sofa, 'they usually do the trick for me.'

'You get migraines as well?'

'Not so much these days.' Which was true. He might have a lot else going wrong with him, but hey, the migraines had eased up. Fair exchange was no robbery, as they say.

Jessica read the back of the packet, popped two tablets out of the foil packaging and swallowed them down with a gulp of tea. 'This is really kind of you,' she said. 'I don't know what I would have done if you hadn't come along.'

'It's no problem.' He smiled.

And what a smile, thought Jessica. Here's a man who could teach Piers a thing or two.

'My name's Josh, by the way,' he said, leaning back into the soft leather of the sofa and straightening his long legs, 'Josh Crawford.'

'And I'm Jessica Lloyd and I can assure you I don't normally go around throwing up in the bushes for an evening's entertainment.'

He smiled again.

Wow! When the sex appeal was being handed out this guy must have been first in the queue.

'You know, I've always meant to apologise to you,' he said.

'What on earth for?'

'For that day when I barged my way into your house for my keys. I had no idea the show house had changed.'

'Oh that. Forget it. And if it makes you feel any better my mother thought you were rather dishy. That's her phraseology, not mine.'

'And what did you think?'

'I thought you were exceptionally rude.'

He lowered his gaze, surprised at her candour. 'Then I have to hope that my rescue of you tonight has in some way made up for my appalling behaviour that day.'

Jessica smiled. 'Put like that, I have no choice but to agree fully with my mother's description of you.'

He looked up and saw from her face that she was gently making fun of him. 'Good,' he said, entering into the spirit of the conversation. 'So this mother of yours, who has such impeccable taste in men, does she live nearby?'

Jessica laughed. 'Yes, very close by. We passed her house on the way here. I would have pointed it out to you, only I was otherwise engaged. It's the one just by the canal bridge.'

He raised an eyebrow. 'There? It's a lovely house. Great situation as well.'

'Everyone says that.'

'And is that where you grew up?'

Jessica nodded and as she finished her tea the music on the hi-fi came to an end. It seemed the right time to leave. 'I really should go now,' she said, stretching forward to put her empty mug on the table.

'Must you?' he asked. It had been a while since Josh had enjoyed the company of a woman in this way and he was reluctant for the evening to come to an end.

'It's quite late,' she said, 'I'd hate to outstay my welcome.' Much as she thought she ought to be making a move, Jessica was more than happy to stay and chat. Having decided that her rude neighbour wasn't at all the uncouth monster she'd thought he was, she was keen to find out a little more about him.

'You're more than welcome to stay,' he said. 'In fact, I'd rather you did, it would stop me from working.'

Jessica glanced at the open files at the far end of the table. 'Okay,' she said, 'it's a deal.'

'Good. Would you like something to eat?'

'No thanks, but another cup of tea would be good.'

She watched him limp out of the room, then she too got up. She went over to the CD player and inspected the two tall beechwood columns of CDs. There was practically every taste in music accounted for: Northern Soul, Choral, Reggae, Frank Sinatra – *Frank Sinatra?* – Rock, Classical and Blues. She then checked the CD that they'd been listening to and found that she had been wrong. It hadn't been Puccini at all. It had been Verdi's *La Traviata*.

When Josh came back into the room, she said, 'Can we have this on again, please?'

'Sure.' He put their mugs on the table and came over and pressed the start button. They were standing very close, so close that even in the half-light Jessica could see the intense dark hue to his brown eyes as he looked at her. She could also see how dilated his pupils were. *Talk about the stuff of romantic fiction!* She cleared her throat – unnecessarily – and moved away, back to the chair in which she'd been sitting.

'So where have you been today?' he asked, also resuming his earlier position. 'You look too smartly dressed to have been out rambling.'

She cast her eyes over her sleep-crumpled suit – her one and only suit. 'I'd been down to London,' she said.

'For pleasure or for business?'

'Could London ever be for pleasure?'

'Depends on your viewpoint.'

'Well this was definitely for business and I'm afraid to say I behaved very badly at one point.'

'Oh?'

'I was given some fantastically brilliant news, having expected the reverse, and the shock of it made me drink too much over lunch, which I couldn't eat, and I very nearly made a pass at my agent, so that tells you how bad I was.' She groaned and hung her head, recalling her behaviour in the taxi and in Piers's office.

He laughed. 'There's a lot of information packed into that one sentence. Any hope of you disentangling it for me?'

She looked up and smiled. 'It'll have to be another time. I'm too tired now.'

'Well, when you've drunk your tea I'll be the perfect gentleman and see you safely across the courtyard.'

'I wouldn't want to put you to all that bother, not with your dodgy leg.' As soon as her words were out, Jessica knew she'd said the wrong thing. It was as if a cloud as black as the shirt he was wearing passed over Josh's face. 'You'll have to go easy on the skiing in future,' she said, trying to make light of the situation. 'Bones, ligaments, muscles, they're all tricky blighters, they take for ever to mend.'

'Yes,' he said flatly. 'I guess you're right.'

When Jessica had gone, Josh turned up the volume on the CD player and the final act of *La Traviata* filled the sitting-room. He threw himself on to the sofa.

He was angry.

Not with Jessica – she couldn't have had any idea that what she'd said would have meant anything to him. No, he was furious with himself. Why did he let these things get to him? Why couldn't he just brush it off? It was a chance remark. Nothing more. They were getting on fine until he'd acted like an idiot.

And there was another thing. Why had he lied? *Skiing injury! It comes and goes!* Too bloody right it does. Just what the hell had he thought he was doing?

Apart from wanting to make a good impression on Jessica.

Apart from wanting her to view him as a whole man.

Apart from convincing her that he wasn't some weak, uninspiring invalid.

Oh, to hell with it! What was the point anyway?

In spite of his anger he couldn't help but smile at the memory of the pair of them over by the hi-fi. There'd been a split second when he had thought of kissing Jessica. In the old days he wouldn't have hesitated. He would have swooped in on her and steered her towards the sofa.

He got up and went in search of something to drink. He found some Scotch in the dining-room, poured himself a large glassful and took it back to the sitting-room.

Like in the old days, he repeated to himself. The good old days before . . . before everything had started going wrong. Before he'd started having trouble with his balance. Before his legs had begun to feel like lead. And before that humiliating night in Hong Kong when he'd fallen down a short flight of stairs and everyone had thought he was drunk.

He took another swig of Scotch.

His last girlfriend had run a mile when she'd found out that she was dating a guy who was likely to end up in a wheelchair.

Well, lucky old her that she could run a bloody mile. Good bloody riddance!

16

It was Saturday afternoon. The sun was high and very hot, and as it shone through the window it beckoned Tony to leave the confines of his study, where he was checking through that month's sales figures, and go outside.

It was a tempting thought and one he was inclined to take up as it would give him a welcome break from Amanda endlessly rushing about the house getting it ready for that evening's dinner party. She had dusted, cleaned and polished from the minute she had got out of bed and, for no good reason that he could understand, she seemed intent on ruthlessly cleansing the entire house from top to bottom. She was now vacuuming the hall and as she approached the study he experienced the sensation of his breath being sucked out of his body.

A walk with Hattie was definitely what he needed. He switched off his computer, stood up and turned to confront the turbo-powered monster making its way into his study.

'Why don't you take Hattie for a walk?' Amanda shouted above the din. She seemed to Tony in that moment just as much a turbo-powered monster as the machine she was wielding. 'I'm sure she'd like that.'

'Good idea,' he said, thoroughly irritated that Amanda had suggested what was already in his mind.

Hattie ran on ahead, while he strolled behind at a more leisurely pace. They took the path leading away from the development and began walking through the long grass, and as the distance between them and the house grew he thought how strange it was to be on his own with Hattie with Amanda's blessing. It was an unusual occurrence. Invariably Amanda wanted him to spend more time with her.

He knew that she had found it hard adjusting to her role as stepmother, but there had been times in the past few months – though not this week – when he had found himself impossibly torn between his wife and his daughter. Maybe it was to be expected. Perhaps a second wife had more to be insecure about than a first. With an unknown act to follow, and if the relationship was to work, it was more than likely that the new partner needed, *and deserved*, a much greater depth of love and reassurance than the previous wife. If this was true, and Tony suspected it was, then he knew with certainty that he was unable to offer Amanda what she needed most from him.

When they reached the cool shade of the copse of trees Hattie said, 'Shall we climb a tree?'

They found a suitable candidate: a small oak with a branch that was just low enough for Tony to hoist Hattie up on to it. She began moving along the thick branch to a hollow spot nearer the trunk of the tree and waited for him to join her. He jumped, caught hold of the bough and hauled himself up.

'It's great, isn't it?' Hattie said, squeezing herself close to him. 'We can see for miles. Look, there's our house, right over there.'

He stared to where she was pointing and dangled his legs beneath him. It was years since he'd climbed anything other than the corporate ladder and being here with Hattie brought back happy carefree memories from his own childhood. Days when the biggest dilemma he had had to face was whether there was time to play another game of tag in the street with his friends before his mother would call him in for tea. Now he was head to head with perhaps the biggest dilemma of his life – how to carry on with his marriage.

He had reached this depressing conclusion while driving home from work last night. He had had a lousy day, having delivered the news to three of his most experienced salesmen that they were no longer required by Arc. Throughout each session he had cursed Bradley Hurst for his short-sightedness. Letting go of good men like Dave, Alan and Richard didn't make sense. Not when they would eventually end up working for their main rivals, taking with them years of accrued knowledge and invaluable experience.

Dave had been gracious enough to say, 'No personal ill feelings, Tony. I know it's not your fault. It's the way things are done.'

But both Alan and Richard had been furious, particularly Alan, and with good reason, as his wife was expecting their third child any day. 'You're nothing but a yes man, Tony,' he'd snarled across the desk. 'And don't think we don't know how chummy you are with that bastard Hurst. Each time he comes over and gives you the latest edict you're practically kissing his arse to keep in with him.'

The insults had escalated until Tony had insisted that Alan get out of his office, which he did, leaving Tony in no doubt that Alan held him directly responsible for the loss of his job. And when driving home late last night, having the roads practically to himself, Tony had been filled with the desire to jack it all in. He'd had enough of being in a no-win situation at work. He hadn't slogged his guts out ever since leaving school to be on the receiving end of such dog's abuse.

At the entrance to the avenue of chestnut trees he had stopped his Porsche and wondered what the hell he was doing at Arc Computers. Was this really the life he had imagined for himself? And as he'd sat in the car in the gathering dark, he couldn't figure out which depressed him more, his job or his loveless marriage.

'Daddy?'

He turned and faced Hattie. He could see from her expression in the dappled sunlight that she must have been trying to attract his attention for some time.

'I'm sorry. What did you say?'

'Why do you look so sad, Daddy? Is it Mummy, do you still miss her?'

His heart twisted. 'Yes,' he said honestly. And he truly did. Every time he looked at his daughter's face he was reminded of Eve.

'Are you missing her now?'

'A little,' he confessed. The truth was that a part of him – that bit he kept from the rest of the world, including Hattie – missed Eve every day. It now occurred to him that since her death his life had lacked direction. With Eve, he had seemed set on a particular course – a shared course – and one that he'd been keen to follow. But now none of those life goals seemed important. Everything seemed shallow and trivial and uninteresting. Work. Marriage. Even the new house that he and Amanda had been so keen to buy. Though if he was honest it had been Amanda who had settled on Cholmford Hall Mews. She had hated moving into the house that he and Hattie lived in and had started going round the various estate agents in the area picking up details on all manner of properties. But then at least she'd been straight with him and said how she felt about sharing the home that he and Eve had created. Not that he would have been so insensitive as to have expected Amanda to slip neatly into Eve's shoes.

He wondered now about Amanda's sudden change of heart. Or whatever it was that had happened to her these past few days. Ever since that night out with the Hursts she had been acting differently. It was as if she had turned over a new leaf and was going out of her way to please him. It was callous of him, but he couldn't help likening her to a Stepford Wife. He'd noticed too that she was trying harder to get along with Hattie and of that he realised he should be glad. But deep down he knew that whatever Amanda was doing, without a monumental change of heart within himself it was pointless.

'It's like we've run away, isn't it?' Hattie said, looking up into his face. 'Nobody knows we're here. We could just stay here in this tree for ever and ever.'

And ever – he echoed in his head. He smiled and gave her a hug, and pulled out a packet of Opal Fruits from his back pocket. 'I sneaked them from the tin in the cupboard in the kitchen,' he confessed. He offered her the first one.

She chewed noisily on the strawberry-flavoured sweet, making great sucking noises. When she'd finished she said, 'When Kate came to baby-sit she told me that there was a pond here somewhere. Shall we see if we can find it? Maybe we could go for a paddle.'

'If you like.'

They climbed down from the tree, Tony first and then Hattie. She slipped with a light thud into his waiting arms. As they walked further into the copse, Tony had to acknowledge that his daughter's mention of Kate was stirring up yet more disquieting thoughts in him – innermost thoughts that so far he'd been unable to formulate or, more truthfully, hadn't had the courage to express with any clarity for fear of what he might discover about himself. Was it possible that whatever it was he felt for Kate was because his life was in such a mess? Were chaos and turmoil making him behave irrationally? Was his troubled mind causing him to imagine himself in love with a woman whom he didn't know? And if all this was true, what was to become of him? Was he one step away from the funny farm?

'Yucky!' said Hattie, pulling a face when they came to the edge of a large pool of murky green water, 'I don't want to paddle in that. What shall we do now?'

'How about a game of hide and seek?'

'Good idea. I'll hide first.'

'All right,' agreed Tony, 'but only on condition that you don't go anywhere near the water. Got that?'

She nodded and scampered away. 'Close your eyes and count down from fifty,' she shouted over her shoulder.

Tony did as she said and as he called out the numbers he had the sinking feeling that he was performing a countdown on his life.

When at last they had exhausted all possible hiding places Tony swung Hattie up on to his shoulders and slowly they made their way home in the hot afternoon sunshine. He was in no hurry to get back – he had no desire to be caught up in Amanda's determined attempts to impress their new neighbours – and if it weren't so hot and Hattie weren't desperate for a drink he'd have willingly stayed out longer. He had enjoyed his afternoon with Hattie and, giving her tired little legs a squeeze as they dangled over his shoulders, he made up his mind that whatever madness he was on the brink of he would spend more time with her.

As they drew level with the front door of number one he caught sight of their immediate neighbour just getting into his Shogun. He hadn't yet had the opportunity to introduce himself and seizing the moment, Tony went over to say hello.

17

At long, long last Oscar had fallen asleep.

Alec switched off the cassette player and brought a much needed end to his ordeal. Since leaving Oxford it seemed as if he'd heard the same banal song over and over – if he was forced to hear one more squeaked 'eh-oh' from the Teletubbies he'd throw the wretched tape out of the car window. He glanced sideways at Kate and saw that she was looking at him.

'Has it been very awful for you?' she asked.

'Yes,' he said, but then he smiled and reached out for her hand and squeezed it. 'Only joking. It's hard work, though, isn't it, keeping him entertained the whole time?'

Kate didn't agree, but she wasn't going to risk upsetting Alec by saying so. Their trip down to Oxford had been fun and had helped to heal the damage caused by their argument of Thursday night, but even so, Kate was anxious not to rock the boat and say the wrong thing to Alec.

He couldn't have apologised more for what he'd said to her, but she still felt the sting of his words – You thought *you'd* enjoy it. Never before had she heard Alec's usually soft voice weighted with such coldness and never would she have imagined him capable of wanting to hurt her. But he hadn't meant to hurt her, he'd told her that repeatedly in bed after she'd come back from sitting outside in the dark.

'I don't know what came over me,' he'd said, cradling her in his arms. 'I'm sorry, truly I am.' He had fallen asleep almost immediately, but she had lain awake, for the first time unsure about her future with Alec.

Only a few days ago she had thought she had discovered perfect peace at last, that the sense of belonging she had craved all her life was to be found through Alec. But lying there in the dark emptiness of the night she had begun to worry that this was not the case.

She had slipped out of bed and crept quietly downstairs and while making herself a drink she had wondered if out of need for that most basic of human requirements – to love and to be loved – she had been too hasty and unrealistic in her expectations of Alec. In her ready acceptance of a man she thought could offer her all the love and reassurance she had ever wanted, had she deliberately overlooked the one vital question she should have asked herself before she'd got so inextricably involved with him: had her upbringing led her into a situation that was doomed to fail?

But who was to say what was and what wasn't an acceptable basis for a loving relationship? What did it matter that she loved a man who was old enough to be her father? Surely all that mattered was that she loved him.

And she did love Alec.

So much so, that for him she was willing to sacrifice her desire to have children.

She had always wanted to have a child of her own, but Alec had made it very clear, right from the start of their relationship, that he didn't want any more. 'I'm too old to go through all that again,' he'd told her, 'much too old. I want to be able to enjoy myself with you, not be up in the night chasing bottles and nappies.'

And because she had felt so wonderfully secure, wrapped in his love and affection, she had been confident that she could come to terms with this ultimate sacrifice. But the longing for a child was never far away and Oscar's ever-increasing presence in her life was a poignant reminder of what she was to miss out on.

But perhaps this too was another example of her subconscious searching to resolve her own childhood.

'Penny for them?' Alec suddenly said.

'I was thinking about supper over at number two tonight,' she said. It was her first lie to Alec. Was this the start, then? Was this when they began to cover up their true feelings for fear of hurting or upsetting each other?

'Are we in for a deadly dull evening, do you think?' he asked, interrupting her thoughts once more.

She smiled, determined to put her anxiety aside. 'It would be worse if Jessica weren't going.'

'You seem to have made a good friend there; I'm glad about that.'

'Are you?' Immediately she regretted the words.

Alec took his eyes off the motorway and looked at her. 'What a strange question,' he said. 'Why wouldn't I be pleased?'

She didn't say anything, but Alec knew why she had asked it. And it served him right for playing the part of possessive lover the other night. His behaviour had told her in no uncertain terms that he wanted her all to himself, that he couldn't bear to share her with anyone. He badly wished that Thursday could be erased from their memories, but he knew it couldn't. His complete sense of unworthiness compelled him to go on seeking confirmation from Kate that he hadn't hurt her as much as he knew he had. More than anything he needed to believe that she had forgiven him. 'Are you still upset about the other night?' he asked gently.

But before Kate had a chance to reply a sleepy voice from the back of the car said, 'I need a wee.'

At four o'clock they pulled up outside Ruth and Adam's beautifully proportioned Georgian cottage. It constantly amused Kate that Adam chose to live in such an exquisite home himself, but designed for others some of the oddest houses she'd ever seen.

The sight of a bright-red MR2 on the driveway didn't amuse her, though. It was Melissa's car. And while Alec switched off the engine and unbuckled his seat-belt, she fought back the urge to brush her hair and check her face in the mirror.

Oscar ran on ahead and banged on the front door, while Kate and Alec followed behind, carrying between them an assortment of his luggage, along with his car seat. Ruth opened the door.

'I've been to Oxford,' Oscar announced excitedly. 'Kate took me on a big bus that didn't have a roof and we saw lots of –'

But Ruth wasn't listening. 'There you are at last,' she said, directing her words at Kate. 'Why didn't you phone to say you were going to be so late?'

'I didn't think we were late,' Kate answered.

'Come on, Ruth,' Alec said, oblivious to his daughter's rudeness, 'out of the way so we can off-load this little lot.'

She let them pass. 'No, not there, Dad,' she said, 'you're cluttering up the hall. Take it through to the playroom.'

Kate followed behind Alec, their footsteps echoing on the polished wooden floor. They deposited Oscar's car seat beside a row of boxes containing tidied-away building bricks and puzzles and farm animals. Kate had never seen the room littered with toys and she had the awful feeling that Oscar was rarely allowed to spoil the neatly arranged boxes.

'I don't suppose there's a drink on offer, is there?' Alec prompted.

If there was, Kate didn't want it. She wanted to be off. She didn't feel up to an encounter with Melissa. But Alec was hell-bent on a drink.

'After what I've put up with since yesterday, at the very least I deserve a triple whisky.'

Ruth took them out to the garden. It was beautifully kept, and so it should be, thought Kate, who knew that Ruth had a gardener in twice a week to see to the lawns and borders. She watched Oscar go up to his father and heard him tell him about his trip round Oxford on an open-topped bus, but like Ruth, Adam wasn't paying his son any attention, he was deep in conversation with a smartly dressed man about the same age as Alec. Kate didn't recognise the man and wondered who he was.

Disappointed, Oscar left his father's side and came back to Kate. He tucked his hand inside hers. 'They're not listening to me,' he said, his words reflecting the sadness in his face.

'Not to worry,' she whispered, 'they're just busy at the moment. Who's that man talking to your father?'

'Don't know.' Oscar shrugged miserably. 'I'm going in for a drink.'

For a few minutes Kate found herself standing alone. With a large tumbler of whisky in his hand, Alec had now joined Adam and was being introduced to the stranger.

'Hello Kate,' came a silky voice from behind her. It was Melissa. 'How was Oxford? I thought you were very brave taking Oscar away with you. I bet Alec hated every minute of it. But good for you for trying to turn him into a more participating grandparent. Though to be honest, I think you're wasting your time.'

'Alec thoroughly enjoyed himself,' lied Kate.

'I doubt that very much,' Melissa said with a laugh. 'He couldn't bear Ruth when she was that age, so there's no reason to suppose that Oscar will stand any higher in his estimation. Now if you'll excuse me I must go and have a word with Alec. Poor devil, he looks quite worn-out.'

Kate watched Melissa move away, the heels of her shoes sinking slightly into the soft lawn. Much as she didn't like Alec's ex-wife, Kate had to admit that Melissa was still a very attractive woman. She dressed in what Kate called expensive grown-up clothes and gave off an air of relaxed confidence, which in turn had the effect of making Kate feel plain and gawky, and about fifteen years old. There was an aura of poise and sophistication to Melissa which Kate knew she would never possess and she often wondered what it was that Alec saw in a girl like her, when for so long he had been married to such a beautiful woman.

As Kate watched Melissa move in on Alec, who was now on his own with Adam, she experienced the familiar wave of jealousy whenever she saw them together.

'Hello there.'

She turned to her right and realised that the unknown man, who earlier had been talking to Adam and Alec, was now at her side. At such close range, she decided that he wasn't particularly good-looking – his eyes were too pale and his jaw too square – and that he was one of those slightly overweight middle-aged men who looked as good as he did because of the expensive clothes he wore.

He held out his hand. 'Tim Wilson,' he said.

She shook hands with him. 'And I'm Kate.'

'I know,' he said. 'In fact I know lots about you.'

'You do?'

'You're Alec's girlfriend, aren't you?'

She nodded. 'So who are you?'

'I suppose you'd call me Melissa's boyfriend.'

The surprise on Kate's face must have shown.

'She's not mentioned me before, then?'

Kate shook her head.

He seemed disappointed. 'Well, it's a recent thing.'

Kate was curious and wondered why Melissa hadn't shown off the fact that she had a boyfriend. 'How did you meet?' she asked.

'Oh, the usual; dinner party, eyes across the table. How about you and Alec?'

'Much the same,' she lied.

'And how do you get on with this business of them still seeing one another every day?'

Kate followed his gaze across the garden to where Alec and Melissa were chatting.

'It doesn't bother me at all,' Kate lied again. How many lies was that today? she thought wretchedly.

He eyed her closely. 'It bothers me,' he said flatly, 'it bothers the hell out of me.'

'But Tony,' cried Amanda, 'how could you do this to me? Now the whole meal will be a disaster!'

'Nonsense, just don't give everyone such big helpings.'

Amanda tried desperately hard to keep her anger in check. But it wasn't easy. Not when she had put so much effort into that evening's meal and it had all been ruined by Tony waltzing in with Hattie after their walk saying he'd invited their other neighbour for dinner. She wasn't given to acts of the miraculous involving loaves and fishes, so just what exactly did Tony think she was going to do?

'I'm sorry,' he said, 'I should have thought. What can I do to help?'

At the sound of Tony's words she suddenly thought of her role model. Now what would Errol Hurst do if she were presented with the same situation? How would she react if Bradley were to turn up from work with an unexpected car-load of Japanese clients for supper? Calmly and proficiently capable, that was how Errol would be. There'd be no domestic histrionics. No apportionment of blame. Just a professional willingness to provide her husband with that all-important back-up so necessary in order for him to get on. Errol would be so resourceful she'd probably raid next door's fish tank just so that she could serve a meal of sushi if she thought it would help Bradley's career. Well, anything Errol could do, she could do better.

'Do you want me to go over and explain to him that we haven't got enough food?' Tony suggested. 'I'm sure he'd understand, he seemed a nice enough bloke.'

Amanda stared at Tony and slowly forced a smile to her lips. 'Oh, don't be silly. Of course I can rustle up something. Just leave it to me. And at least now the numbers around the table will be equal.' She turned away from Tony, amazed at how sincere she'd sounded. It almost made her want to laugh.

Tony was amazed too. How could Amanda be so angry one minute and apparently so understanding the next? It was bizarre. Was this a hormonal thing, he wondered, or just a case of schizophrenia?

18

At a minute past eight Jessica peeped out of her kitchen window to see if there was any sign of Kate and Alec heading for number two. But there was no sign of anybody and determined that she wasn't going to be the first to arrive she decided to ring her mother for a chat – anything to forestall the inevitable.

She had almost finished dialling the number when she remembered that Anna was still away. Damn, now what? She couldn't just sit here twiddling her thumbs. She caught sight of last Sunday's partially unread copy of the *Sunday Times*. She began idly flicking through it, until she came to the book section. She looked to see who had said what and about whom and, only too thankful that she hadn't written any of the novels that had been given the sniffy literati treatment, turned to the television guide to see what she would be missing that evening.

Mm ... *Prime Suspect* was on at nine o'clock. Aha! The ideal delaying tactic, right in her lap, setting the new video would take for ever. She'd be drawing her pension before she made it to Amanda's dinner-table. 'Oh, sorry I'm late,' she'd be able to say, 'but videos, aren't they just the worst?' Playing the helpless bimbo would appeal to Amanda's superior air, she suspected.

At seven minutes past eight Josh looked at his watch. He then glanced out of his kitchen window, checking for some sign of movement from across the courtyard. In particular from number four.

When Tony had introduced himself that afternoon and had invited Josh for dinner, he had very nearly refused, but when Tony had said who else would be there he had instantly changed his mind. He'd enjoyed Jessica's company last night and saw no reason to be antisocial and miss out on an opportunity of seeing her again.

At ten minutes past eight Kate slipped out of Alec's arms and said, 'Come on, we'd better get a move on, we're already late.'

He pulled her back down on to the bed and kissed her. 'I wish we didn't have to go.'

'So do I, but I promised Jessica I wouldn't back out at the last minute. So hurry up and get dressed.'

He smiled. 'One more kiss and I'll think about it.'

*

At twenty-one minutes past eight, and much to Jessica's amazement, she found that she had managed to set the video recorder and with nothing else for it she picked up the box of chocolates for Amanda and made a move.

At twenty-two minutes past eight Josh pulled out a bottle of red wine from the wine rack in the kitchen and decided he might just as well be the first to arrive.

At twenty-three minutes past eight three front doors opened simultaneously and four dinner guests faced each other across the courtyard. Josh waited for the others to join him on his side of the development.

After the necessary introductions had been made, Jessica said to Josh, 'I didn't know you'd been invited.'

'I think I was an afterthought.'

'That makes two of us.'

They fell in step behind Kate and Alec as they led the way. Josh could quite see why his brother had been struck by the sight of Kate, she was stunning, but personally he was more taken with Jessica. She looked so much better than she had last night. Gone were the pale face and the dark-rimmed eyes, and in their place was a very attractive woman. She looked great in a tight-fitting lycra top – Crawford's had sold thousands like it last year, as they had the long wrap-around skirt that she was wearing. He noted how it fell open with each step she took and he wondered how such a fantastic pair of legs had slipped his attention last night.

They were greeted by Amanda who, after being handed an assortment of flowers, bottles and chocolates, took them through to the sitting-room. Sparkling white wine with cassis was offered and as the drink was already poured out and waiting for them on a tray Josh took his fluted glass politely, wishing, though, that he'd been given the choice of a beer. He caught Jessica pulling a face at the sight of her drink and they exchanged a small knowing smile.

'Tony will be down in a minute,' Amanda said, handing Alec and Kate their glasses, 'he's just putting Hattie to bed. Why don't you all sit down?'

Jessica waited to see where Amanda would sit, then chose the sofa which was as far away as she could get from their hostess.

Josh came and joined her. 'How are you feeling?' he asked in a low voice.

'Much better, thanks. You were great last night, by the way, a true hero.'

He smiled. 'Glad to be of service.'

'What's all this, then?' asked Amanda, rudely interrupting Alec, who in answer to her question had just been explaining what business he was in. 'Who's been a hero?'

Jessica considered inventing an outrageous story about herself and Josh, but as she couldn't be sure of her audience, or that Josh would be willing to play along with her, she decided to keep the fiction to a minimum. 'Let's just say that despite the unusual circumstances we found ourselves in last night,' she said, unable to resist leading Amanda on, 'this fine young man behaved as a perfect gentleman.'

She needn't have doubted Josh.

'And it would be far from correct of me to elaborate on what Jessica has told you all,' he said, 'my lips are sealed, a gentleman never betrays a lady.'

Alec and Kate laughed, but Amanda, who was waiting for a full explanation of what was being implied, was distracted by a movement in the doorway. Jessica followed her gaze and saw a small, pretty girl dressed ready for bed. Holding her hand was a good-looking fair-haired man. Tony and Hattie, she assumed.

'Now Hattie, what did I tell you?' Amanda said. Though her words revealed little more than a hint of mild irritation, there was nothing mild about the expression on her face. Jessica could see that she was clearly cross and she remembered what Kate had said about Amanda not being ideal stepmother material.

'Hattie just wanted to come down and meet everybody,' Tony said affably. He brought his daughter further into the room.

'Well, a few seconds won't do any harm, I suppose,' conceded Amanda, 'but then it's straight to bed, young lady,' she added, 'and no nonsense. This is grown-up time.'

'Oh dear.' Jessica laughed. 'On that basis I'd better join Hattie.' The expression on Amanda's face gave Jessica every reason to suspect that she had just made herself public enemy number one.

Not long after Hattie was dispatched to bed the rest of them were ordered into the dining-room. They were told where to sit and what they were eating.

'It's a Gary Rhodes recipe,' Amanda told them in a loud voice, interrupting Tony, who was talking to Kate and Alec at his end of the table. 'I know he's a bit showy and that there's a lot of window dressing to him, but his recipes do actually work. What do you think, Kate?'

Oh Lord, thought Jessica, recognising that Amanda was going to insist that everybody participated in her dinner party, whether they wanted to or not. There would be no skulking behind napkins for any of them.

Kate took a few moments to finish what was in her mouth and politely agreed with Amanda. 'Though I quite like the Two Fat Ladies,' she added.

'Really?' asked Amanda. 'You do surprise me.'

'It's their originality that –'

'Original, I agree, but so unhygienic,' Amanda said dismissively. She then turned from Kate and fixed her attention on Josh. 'And Josh, how about you? Do you like to cook? Or are you one of those terrible *Men Behaving Badly* types in the kitchen?'

Jessica couldn't believe the crassness of the woman. Somebody shove a bread roll into that great big mouth! she wanted to shout across the table. But she was pleased to see that if Josh was at all put out by Amanda's assumption that because he was a single man he was therefore a complete dick-head when it came to feeding himself, he didn't show it.

'I manage pretty well,' he answered smoothly. 'I particularly enjoy Thai cooking.'

Jessica silently applauded Josh for his subtle slap in the chops of their hostess.

But after a long silent pause, the weight of which could have equalled any number of lead balloons, Jessica scooped up the last of her salmon mousse and thought, well, this *is* going splendidly. What fun we're all having. She wondered how Helen Mirren was getting along.

'So tell us about your writing, Jessica,' Amanda said, moving her attention around the table. 'It's not every day we have an author in our midst. I thought of writing a book once.'

Oh, here we go, thought Jessica. If she had a pound for every person who had ever said that to her she'd be up there with Jeffrey Archer.

'But I've never had the time,' Amanda went on. 'I've always been too busy.'

Yeah, yeah, yeah. She'd heard it all before.

'It must be wonderful to be able to earn a living from something as easy as writing.'

Jessica was nearly out of her seat and reaching for a gob-stopping bread roll. *Easy! She'd give her bloody easy!*

'I don't think it's quite as simple as that,' Kate said diplomatically. 'If it were, too busy or not, we'd all be doing it, wouldn't we?'

Jessica gave Kate a grateful look.

'Well, I wouldn't know about that,' Amanda carried on. 'Do you sell many books, Jessica? I saw one in the supermarket yesterday.'

'I get by,' replied Jessica. Tight bitch, she thought, noting that Amanda had said 'saw' and not 'bought'.

'I didn't know you were a writer,' Josh said, seizing a few seconds of conversational lull while Amanda chewed on a piece of cucumber.

'It's not something I go out of my way to advertise,' Jessica said – *was it any wonder when there were people like Amanda in the world?*

'Jessica's an excellent writer,' Kate said generously. 'I've read both her books.'

'So what kind of novels do you write?' Josh asked.

'Romantic comedies,' Jessica replied. 'Probably not your cup of tea; not enough explosions or car chases.'

Alec laughed. 'From what Kate tells me, your sex scenes are pretty explosive.'

'But all done in the best possible taste,' Jessica joked.

'I suppose you must have to do an inordinate amount of research,' Josh said with a playful smile.

'Oh, an inordinate amount of research,' Jessica said, matching his expression.

Josh slowly leant back in his chair. 'You must let me know if there's anything I could help you with in the future,' he said, his eyes still fixed on her.

Jessica's own gaze held firm. She took a long, deliberate sip of her wine. 'And who knows,' she said, 'I might just do that.'

Aghast at the way in which Jessica and Josh were carrying on, Amanda began gathering up the plates and cutlery. She gave Tony a get-up-and-do-something look and he immediately got to his feet and went round the table refilling glasses. He was secretly envious of the way in which Jessica and Josh were flirting with each other. It reminded him of himself and Eve. They had met on a management training course and he had been determined from the moment he'd set eyes on her to get her into bed before the end of the three-day course. By the close of day one, when they'd spent five hours solving what the tutor had called 'Mind Opening Puzzles' they had built up a flirtatious rapport. By day two they were found kissing in the hotel lift and on the final day, when they should have been attending an afternoon talk on 'There's More than One Way to Look at a Problem' they were in his hotel room making love. The memory of such a happy time in his life made him risk a glance in Kate's direction. How he longed for the evening to be over. Sitting in the same room as Kate without being able to talk to her, in the way he wanted, was unbearable.

Even more unbearable was Alec's presence.

What made it so bad was that Tony found himself liking the man. It was beyond him that he could chat so effortlessly to Alec when all the time he was imagining what it would be like to hold Kate in his arms.

'No more wine for me, thanks.'

Tony looked down to see Josh's hand covering his wineglass.

'Sorry,' he said distractedly. 'What can I get you instead?'

'Water would be fine, thanks.'

Josh watched Tony fill his water glass, then he raised his eyes to look at Jessica. She was turned slightly to her left, talking to Alec, but he had the feeling she knew full well that he was staring at her.

Last night when he'd gone to bed and thought about his evening with Jessica, he'd known that he was attracted to her and now, as he viewed her across the table, he realised that for the first time in a long while he was experiencing the urge of wanting a woman. The impulse was so strong that it was outweighing the fear and loss of confidence that had crept over him since his illness had been diagnosed. One of the aspects of MS that appalled him most was the threat of impotence. What if he couldn't perform? What if his useless body let him down? One of the specialists he'd seen at the hospital a few months ago had waved the subject aside when Josh had put it to him. 'You don't need to concern yourself about that now,' the man had said – a man who in Josh's opinion looked like he'd lost interest in sex years ago – 'worry about that when it happens,' the doctor had added. Easy for you to say, Josh had thought angrily.

And since his last girlfriend had done a runner, the subject of sex had become nothing more than a hypothetical conundrum anyway.

But now ... well now, it was very much on Josh's mind. He had the feeling that it was on Jessica's too. Or was that just wishful thinking?

Jessica was the first to say that she was tired and that she ought to be getting off home. 'It's been a wonderful evening,' she said, faking a yawn. She wasn't lying completely. Excluding Amanda, she'd enjoyed everybody's company once they'd all relaxed. She pushed her empty coffee cup away from her and stood up.

'I hadn't realised it was so late,' Josh said in turn, also getting to his feet. He didn't want Jessica rushing off without him.

Which caused Alec to say that he and Kate had had a long day and that they had better be going as well.

Thanks were made, goodbyes said, and finally the four dinner guests departed. It was past midnight and the dark sky above the courtyard was pricked with bright, twinkling stars. It was very quiet. And very still.

'Well, good-night then,' Alec said to Jessica and Josh, 'it was good to meet you both. If there's anything in the neighbourly department you need, don't hesitate to knock on our door.'

'The same goes for my door,' Jessica said, 'knock any time you need to. See you for coffee during the week, Kate.'

Kate and Alec walked away, arm in arm, their feet crunching noisily on the gravel.

'Well,' said Josh, turning to face Jessica.

'Well indeed,' she repeated.

'I don't suppose you'd fancy a nightcap, would you?'

'I thought you'd never ask.'

19

When Jessica awoke the following morning it was very late. It was getting on for lunch-time.

In Corfu she had never slept in. Early morning, before anyone else was about, had been her favourite part of the day. It was so quiet sometimes that she could hear the distant sound of goat bells high up in the hills behind her house. On days like that it was as if she had the island to herself. It was when she worked at her best. She would make a pot of coffee and a plate of toast dripping with butter – not for her the local breakfast of yoghurt and honey and the occasional fig that Helen and Jack relished – and go and sit outside on the terrace. She had never tired of the view and each morning she had lost herself in admiring the tranquil setting. She had often wished that instead of being a novelist she had Helen's skill as an artist. She would have loved to have been able to paint the myriad shades of blue, green and white that for her epitomised where she lived – sand as silvery as the moon; beaches whitened by sun-bleached pebbles; water the colour of pure turquoise; and cypress trees, lush and green, their verdant tips spearing a cloudless sky of china-blue.

Then, once she had had her fix of admiring the view, she would get down to work. The hours would slip by effortlessly as she lost herself in her latest cast of characters who were facing all manner of dramas as a result of her vivid imagination.

Thinking of work reminded Jessica that it was high time she got stuck into her next novel. When she'd had lunch with Piers on Friday he had asked her only once what she had in mind to write next – he'd probably decided not to push her, thinking that it would be unlikely that he'd get any sense out of somebody who was making such a fool of herself.

And he would have been right. He would have got more reason out of the salt and pepper pots on the table than her.

It wasn't often that she let the side down so appallingly, but on that occasion she'd certainly gone all the way. She cringed at the memory and buried her head deep into the pillow. Gavin would have loved seeing her behave so badly and wouldn't have thought twice about using it against her if she'd ever dared to show so much as the merest hint of disapproval over one of his frequent drunken binges.

She turned on to her back and stared up at the hideous lace canopy above the bed and thought of Gavin.

She wondered what he'd be doing right now. Probably he was down on the beach at Avlaki: Ray-Bans on, hair catching the breeze and no doubt putting his breath-taking charm to good use on some keen-to-please female tourist whom he'd met the previous night in a bar in Kassiopi. 'I've never tried sailing before,' the silly girl would have simpered, which was all the opening Gavin would need. 'Then I'll teach you' – his stock reply to anybody stupid enough to give him the opportunity to show off how good he was in and on the water – 'be on the beach for ten-thirty tomorrow,' he'd add, 'and I'll take you through the theory, then we'll get down to the exciting stuff. I guarantee you'll be sailing single-handedly by late afternoon and to celebrate your success we'll have a drink afterwards at the nearby taverna.' His technique was persuasive and irresistible.

She ought to know, she'd fallen for it herself.

Since leaving Corfu, Jessica hadn't once deluded herself that Gavin would be pining for her. But she did wonder whether he missed her. Just a little.

She supposed not.

If he had, he might have been in touch with her. But there had been nothing. Not one phone call. Not even a letter.

But then, what could she expect? It had been she who had chosen to end things between them.

It was a strange phenomenon, though, that one could be so involved, so wrapped up in another person, then be so entirely separate.

Mind you, with Gavin it had been a basic physical wrapped-upness rather than any meeting of minds. Jack had often asked her what she saw in Gavin and Helen had laughed at him.

'You imbecile, Jack, the man's an Adonis, what do you think she sees in him?'

Helen had been quite right. The physical attraction between them had been like a white-knuckle ride; no matter how often they made love the thrill was as great as the time before.

But gradually it had dawned on Jessica that a physical thrill was only as good as the moment it took to fulfil itself. She had then begun to want more. And poor Gavin didn't have more to offer. It had been a sad realisation, that. It had also made her feel old. Expectations in one's youth are delightfully low and straightforward, you put up with anything. But age brings with it higher and more complicated expectations from a partner, such as consideration, respect, faithfulness, understanding and, worse still, something as horrifying as a planned future.

Gavin's idea of a planned future was choosing what he was going to eat for lunch.

She sighed and got out of bed. She pushed back the curtains and leant her elbows on the window-sill. It was a glorious morning and beyond her garden, a sun-filled landscape of fields and clumps of trees presented itself to her. It was beautiful. Very different from what she had been used to for the past few years, but just as captivating. She opened the window and leant out over the white-painted sill.

She thought of Josh. He, too, was different from anybody she'd previously known.

It would have been the easiest thing in the world to have carried on their flirting to its natural conclusion last night, but when, after a couple of drinks, things had started hotting up on the sofa she had thought, Whoa! I've been here before and I'm not sure I'm in the market for a casual affair.

She had, of course, only herself to blame. She really shouldn't have encouraged him.

Mutterings of 'I'm sorry, I'm not sure I can do this' had seemed slightly ridiculous when he'd tried to kiss her – and just for the record his technique had been faultless: a subtle inching along the sofa so that their legs were almost touching, a beautifully timed silence, a lowering of his eyes to her lips, a lifting of his hand to her shoulder and then the final tilt of his head – always a heart melter that one – as he moved in for the big finish.

Except she had gone and spoilt things for him.

'My mistake,' he'd said, when he'd felt her resistance. He'd backed away from her as though she had a gun pointed at his head.

They'd then metaphorically dusted themselves down and catching sight of the awkwardness on one another's faces they had suddenly burst out laughing.

'Sorry about that,' he'd said with a grin that had enough sex appeal in it to cause her very nearly to say, oh what the heck, let's go for it, anyway!

'I'm sorry too,' she'd said, 'I've behaved outrageously all evening. It's either the fault of that awful woman Amanda, or . . .'

'Or?'

'Or it's your fault.'

He laughed. 'Fancy another drink?'

They finished a bottle of Southern Comfort and moved on to coffee, and all the time they talked. He told her about the company he and his brother ran – he had talked a lot about Charlie – and about all the travelling the pair of them had done, but he wasn't one of those men who only spoke about himself. He prompted her to speak about her own life, about growing up in Cholmford and what had led her to live such a nomadic life, and what had brought her back home. She told him about her mother and her heart condition. She even told him about Gavin. Then there was her writing. He wanted to know all about that, unlike Gavin who had never been interested in what she did, having dismissed her books as the kind of commercial nonsense anyone could do if they put their mind to it – he and Amanda would get on like a house on fire.

She had felt extremely comfortable in Josh's company, so much so that the time had flown by, and before they knew it it was nearly four in the morning. She had tiptoed her way across the gravel and let herself in, just as the first signs of dawn had begun to filter through the bruised night sky.

'Dirty stop-out,' she said with a smile, now turning away from the bedroom window and going into the bathroom, 'what *will* the neighbours think?'

In the make-do show house of plot number three Sue Fletcher, the negotiator, was tidying up her things. Her work at Cholmford Hall Mews was over. Tomorrow she would start work at a new site. She was going to miss Cholmford, it had been one of her more enjoyable assignments. It was a shame, though, that she hadn't managed to sell the last remaining plot, but she'd had a feeling all along that number three was going to stick. Everybody she had shown round the house had had the same criticisms of it – they didn't like the property being divided by the archway; they didn't like the garden; but mostly they didn't like the price. So now it would be down to an estate agent to do his best, but Sue knew as well as the next person that without a substantial drop in the asking price it would be an uphill struggle to find a buyer.

Still, it wasn't her problem. Her next challenge was an exclusive block of apartments in Altrincham.

Happy that everything was in order, she locked the door behind her for the final time and as she turned round she saw the man from number one driving out through the archway. She returned his smile and wished that all the clients she dealt with were as easy on the eye.

Josh drove like the wind to his parents' house in Prestbury. He parked his car alongside Charlie's and because it was such a hot day he walked slowly round to the back of the house, assuming that everybody would be sitting in the garden.

He was right. His brother, dressed in shorts and a T-shirt, was lolling in a hammock slung between two apple trees and his father was coughing and spluttering over the barbecue, where the coals were sending up great lung-threatening clouds of smoke.

His mother was sitting in her usual sun-lounger and was doing the usual crossword. She looked up when she realised he was there. 'Hello, Joshua,' she said, putting her newspaper down. 'We'd nearly given up on you. I was about to send Charles in to give you a call. We were getting worried.'

He went and kissed her. 'A late night,' he said by way of explanation for turning up unprecedentedly late for their monthly family get-together. He'd also woken up unprecedentedly late. Normally an early riser, he had surfaced just after twelve o'clock and it wasn't until he was munching on a bowl of muesli in the kitchen and thinking about Jessica that he'd caught sight of the calendar hanging beside the telephone on the wall. With a thud of realisation he'd remembered that he was supposed to be washed, dressed, shaved and in Prestbury within the hour. Dumping the half-eaten cereal in the sink, he had gone back upstairs to do something about his appearance. Glad that his body was at least continuing to keep up with him, as he'd stood in the shower, and conscious that he was feeling okay for yet another day, he dared to hope that his MS was entering a period of remission; that the symptoms of his illness were lessening. It had happened before. So why not again?

'Shall I get you a beer?' his father offered.

'That's all right, Dad. I'll go and help myself.'

When he went into the kitchen and pulled open the fridge door he heard footsteps following in behind him. It was Charlie. 'You want one as well?' he asked.

'Please.'

Josh handed him a can. 'I met your wondrous creature last night,' he said.

'And?'

Josh smiled. 'She's really not your type.'

'Hey, I'll be the judge of that.'

'And she's also fairly well partnered up.'

'Shit!'

'Language, Charles.'

'Sorry, Mum,' Charlie said, turning to see their mother coming into the kitchen.

'So how are things?' she asked Josh as she went over to a chopping board beside the sink and picked up a plate of vegetable kebabs.

Josh tried not to over-react. He knew his mother had to ask and that she did her best to put it in such a way as to imply that a general enquiry was being made of him, but in reality the question was much more specific. It was stupid of him, but he'd much prefer his mother to come straight out with, 'So which bit of you isn't working properly today?'

'I'm fine,' he said and, going for a deflection he added, 'and the house is pretty well organised now. You and Dad will have to come over.'

'We'd like that,' she said. 'Now go back into the garden and get some sun on you. You look far too pale and all that black doesn't help. Don't you have any clothes in any other colour these days?'

'She's right,' Charlie said as they went outside and found themselves a couple of chairs away from the smoke, 'you do look pale.'

'If you'd drunk as much as I did last night you'd be pale.'

Charlie raised an eyebrow. 'Tell me all.'

Josh told him about being invited to dinner with his new neighbours.

'So that's how you got to meet my scampering angel,' Charlie interrupted. 'What's the husband like?'

'I never said she was married. She lives with somebody, a guy called Alec.'

Charlie leant forward in his chair. 'Not actually married, eh? So all is not lost. What's he like? A right Smart Alec? Or is he some kind of brainless gladiatorial hunk who's charmed her with his pecs?'

Josh laughed. 'She's a whole lot smarter than that.'

'So come on then, what am I up against?'

'You're not going to believe it. He's got to be about fifty, grey-haired and –'

'You're winding me up!'

'Nope.'

'You mean that fantastic creature has thrown herself at a man nearly twice her age. Why?'

Josh shrugged. 'He's a nice bloke, maybe she just goes for the father-figure type. It takes all sorts.'

'Who likes the father-figure type?' asked their father, coming over and seizing the opportunity of his wife's absence from the garden to stand easy from his barbecue duties for a couple of seconds.

'A neighbour of mine whom Charlie has decided he's fallen in love with.'

Their father laughed. 'Missed the boat again, Charles, have you?'

'I wouldn't say that exactly. I reckon I'm a worthy match for a grey-haired has-been any day.'

'Nothing wrong with grey hair,' William Crawford said, running his hand through his own. 'And may I remind you that you're not short of a few threads of silver yourself.'

'Thanks, Dad.'

'William,' called a voice from inside the house, 'those chops, they're burning!'

He hurried back to his sentry post.

'So what are your other neighbours like?' Charlie asked.

'A couple with a young daughter and . . .' he hesitated.

'And?'

'And a writer.'

'Really. What's he like?'

'*She.*'

'Oh. Any good?'

'Not sure about her writing skills, but she's . . .' Josh's voice faltered. How exactly should he describe Jessica? The usual adjectives of striking and attractive somehow didn't seem appropriate. She was more than that. But what? Interesting? Was that how he would describe her? Or how about sententious? She was certainly to the point. She was also extremely funny. But these were hardly the normal descriptions a man would use of a woman whom he had every intention of getting into bed.

'She's what?' prompted Charlie.

Josh smiled. 'Never you mind.'

'Oh, like that, is it?'

'I should be so lucky.' Josh told his brother about Jessica's migraine and his rescue of her. He also told him about last night.

Charlie laughed. 'Well, one thing's for sure, I'll have to take back all I said about no night-life being on offer out there in the sticks. Perhaps your paleness has nothing to do with an over-indulgence of alcohol but an excess of carnal pleasure.'

'I wish.'

'You mean, she was there all that time with you last night and you didn't manage –'

'I was taking the subtle approach.'

'Get away. She didn't fancy you, did she?'

'Course she did.'

'But not enough, evidently.'

They both laughed and drank their beers. Josh listened to his parents battling it out round the hot coals – the chops were done, but the kebabs were not – and felt unaccountably relaxed. Talking to Charlie in this light-hearted way reminded him how it always used to be when they'd teased one another about their sexual prowess. It was one of the things he'd noticed when his illness had been diagnosed; overnight Charlie stopped treating him as the brother he'd always been and had started talking to him like some ancient maiden aunt. The teasing abruptly stopped. So did the mateyness. It was as if it was in bad taste to rib somebody who wasn't a hundred per cent – mocking the afflicted just wasn't on.

'What's her name?' asked Charlie, breaking into Josh's thoughts.

'Who?'

'Don't give me any of that. The woman who turned you down.'

'I told you, she didn't turn me down.'

'If you say so.'

'Her name's Jessica, Jessica Lloyd.'

'Mm . . . nice name. So what kind of writer is she?'

'She writes romantic comedies and according to your darling Kate she writes brilliant sex scenes.'

Charlie held up his hands as though giving thanks to the Lord. 'My darling Kate. How sweet the name doth sound.'

'Put a sock in it, will you? And take my advice. She won't give you a second look. She and Alec are very much a couple.'

Charlie pulled a face. 'Just because you were shunned last night, don't go sour-graping all over me.'

'I didn't say I was shunned.'

'Well what were you then?'

'I was . . . if you must know I was spoken to like I was a normal human being.'

Charlie looked at him closely. 'Meaning what?'

'I mean she didn't talk to me in that does-he-take-sugar-with-it? way so many other people do.'

'Are you getting at me?'

Josh shook his head. 'All I'm saying is that Jessica treated me like a normal bloke because she doesn't know anything to the contrary.'

'She doesn't know about your MS?'

'That's right.'

'But what if –'

'There are no what ifs. I have no intention of telling her about my illness, because at least then I won't have to put up with any crap from her.' His face broke into an expression of intense seriousness. 'She'll treat me as a man, not an invalid. And who knows, I might even get lucky.'

Charlie turned away and looked down the length of the garden, to the old rope swing hanging from the silver birch where he and Josh had played as boys – their mother joked that she still kept the rope swing as a hint that one day she hoped to have grandchildren playing on it.

He thought about what his brother had just said. He had the feeling that Josh liked this Jessica, that he viewed her as being more than just a potential one-night stand. If that was the case, and if Josh really thought there was any chance of a relationship with her, then surely it had to be founded on honesty. Not on deception.

He'd be a fool to think otherwise.

20

It was Monday lunch-time and at first glance the car-park of the Vicarage looked as if it were full. But driving round to the back of the pub, Kate spied a small space that had been ignored by everybody else and with breath-holding care she squeezed her Mini between an ugly people carrier on her left and a white-painted wooden barrel on her right, which was stocked with a large flowering hydrangea and an abundance of yellow and purple pansies that clashed horribly with the blue of the hydrangea.

She found Caroline perched on a bar stool, pretending to be reading the lunch-time menu on the blackboard to the right of her. In reality, Kate knew better. Caroline was eyeing up a group of noisy businessmen at the far end of the bar. Nothing changes, she thought. 'Hi, Caroline,' she said, tapping her friend on the shoulder.

Caroline whipped round. 'And about time, too. I've been sitting here on my own for ages. It gives a girl a bad name.'

'Sorry, the traffic was terrible, but I'm sure you've been able to amuse yourself in my absence.'

'Definitely not my type,' Caroline said, catching Kate's eyes straying over to the far end of the bar. 'They've done nothing but discuss company cars and Manchester United. What are you drinking?'

'I'll get them,' Kate said, reaching into her bag. 'What would you like?'

'Dry white wine, please.'

Kate attracted the attention of the woman behind the bar and when they'd got their drinks and ordered two prawn salads they went outside to the garden. They chose a table which had an umbrella above it. Kate sat in the shade and Caroline positioned her chair to catch the sun, and pulling off a loose-fitting silk shirt she revealed a skimpy strapless top and a pair of deeply tanned shoulders.

'It must be hell being you,' said Caroline smugly. 'You can keep your dazzling head of red hair and perfect pale skin, I'd sooner be a boring brunette any day and soak up the rays.'

'Well, at least I shan't look like a prune when I'm fifty.'

'Don't give it another thought. I shall have had the very latest in drastic surgery by then. I'll have my face stretched right round to the back of my head. I'll look sensational.'

'You'll look like Bette Davis.'

Caroline laughed. 'My word, but you're frisky today. Now tell me what you've been up to. I want to know everything. How's the big relationship going and is the sex still as good and have you found yourself another job yet?'

There was never any chicanery to Caroline's conversation. 'If I were a stronger person I'd tell you to mind your own business,' Kate said.

Caroline smiled. 'Yeah, but I know that deep down you're just dying to tell me what a wonderful time you're having so that you can rub in what a dreary depressing life I lead. Hey, do you mind moving slightly to the right? There's a drop-dead gorgeous guy sitting over there and he can't see what he's missing out on with you in the way.'

Kate obliged and finding that the sun was now in her eyes she put on her sun-glasses.

'Do you have to do that?' Caroline asked, 'those shades make you look even more glamorous; you look like Julia Roberts. Take them off at once.'

'No,' Kate said firmly, 'now stop treating me like one of the poor pensioners in the library you bully so sadistically and tell me what *you*'ve been up to.'

Caroline raised an eyebrow. 'My, my, Kate, who's been teaching you how to be so assertive?'

'It's you! You've taught me everything I know.'

'So that's it, I'm to be hoist by my own petard, am I?'

Their lunch arrived and when they were left alone again Caroline said, 'You're looking particularly well. Dare I ask, is that what the love of a good man does for you?'

Kate smiled and reached for her knife and fork. 'You should try it some time.'

'Ouchy-ouch! You're turning into a nasty piece of work, Kate Morris.'

'So there's still no decent man in your life, then?'

Caroline sighed. 'Chance would be a fine thing. Do you know, I'm so desperate I've thought about joining one of those dreadful introduction agencies, you know, the ones you see advertised in the paper all the time.'

Kate held her tongue. She had never confided in Caroline about how she had met Alec and she certainly wasn't about to start now – Caroline was the last person on earth that she'd trust with such a delicate and private piece of information. It still amazed her that she'd had the courage to join the agency in the first place and had done so in secret. She had thought about it for months before finally taking the plunge. It wasn't so much that there had been a lack of boyfriends in her life, it was just that they were all the wrong kind. They were either too serious or not serious enough; too quiet or too noisy; too nervous or over-confident. Having your personality traits matched to those of a like-minded man seemed a good way to cut through all the toe-curling embarrassment of a first date that was obviously going nowhere. But it hadn't been anywhere near as simple as that – there was only so much a computer could come up with – and there followed several disastrous evenings before she'd struck gold with Alec. 'So why don't you join an agency?' she asked Caroline innocently.

'But it's so desperate. I mean, the whole set-up must attract all the wrong kind of men, the flaky ones whose trousers are too short, and who wear grey slip-on shoes and want to unburden themselves on some equally sad woman.'

How tempting it was to prove Caroline wrong. 'But how do you know it would be like that?'

'Believe me, Kate. I just know.'

'Well, perhaps you should give it a try. You never know, you might meet somebody really special. I'm sure it would be worth a go. What have you got to lose?'

Caroline chewed thoughtfully on a prawn. 'Do you really think so?'

I know so, Kate wanted to say, but instead she nodded her head and sipped her fizzy water.

'Anyway, enough about my non-existent love life, tell me about yours. Any sign of the clanging of wedding bells yet?'

'Alec and I are happy enough without getting married.'

Caroline contemplated her friend. 'If you don't mind me saying, that sounded just an itsy-bitsy bit too pat; it also had the distinctive ring of an untruth behind it.'

Kate blushed.

'Doesn't he want to get married?'

'It's not something we talk about.'

Caroline scoffed. 'He's taking you for a ride, girl.'

'He's not,' Kate said indignantly, quick to leap to Alec's defence. 'And why should we change things when we're both happy with what we've got? Everything's perfect between us.'

'Mm . . .' said Caroline. She sounded far from convinced. 'Okay then,' she said, 'you give me no alternative but to test your idea of perfection. Suppose I were to put the question of, let's say, how could you possibly improve on your relationship? And don't give me any bullshit about your lives resembling a day in the life of Adam and Eve before the wily snake made his appearance.'

'That's a silly question.'

'So what if it is, give me an answer.'

Kate didn't want to. She knew what her answer was and she was frightened that hearing herself actually say the words out loud might court disaster for her relationship with Alec.

'Come on,' pressed Caroline. 'It doesn't have to be something monumental. It could be something as simple as changing the colour of his socks. Or guiding him through the tricky transition from Y-fronts to boxers.'

Kate relaxed and smiled.

'Or, of course,' Caroline went on, 'it could be something more earthshattering like you . . . like you wanting to have a baby and him not being interested because he's done that scene already.'

Don't react, Kate told herself. She's only fishing. She has no way of knowing.

'Well?'

There was no avoiding the question. She would have to come up with something credible in order to make Caroline drop the subject. 'I'd like to be rid of Alec's ex-wife,' she said with a sudden flash of inspiration. It was even true.

'Why?' latched on Caroline, 'is she a problem? He doesn't still have a thing for her, does he?'

'Heavens no!'

'How can you be so sure?'

'Really, Caroline, are you so jealous of me that you want to unravel my relationship with Alec completely?'

Caroline had the grace to look shamefaced. 'Spoil-sport,' she said. 'Come on, eat up and I'll go and fetch us another round of drinks. Same again?'

'Please.'

When Caroline returned she said, 'So if you're going to be boring and not tell me anything about you and Alec, tell me how you're managing financially and what you're doing about getting another job.'

This was much safer ground and Kate pushed her finished plate to one side and said, 'I had a bit saved for a rainy day, so I'm okay for a while, but ... but I think I'm going for a career move.'

'Oh, sounds interesting. What are you thinking of doing? With your new-found assertiveness you'd make an ideal doctor's receptionist.'

Kate smiled, but thought about what her friend had said. Had she changed? Was she really standing up for herself more these days? 'With all the cutbacks going on I really don't hold out much hope of getting another librarian's job in the immediate area, so the obvious answer is to retrain.'

'Go on.'

'What do you think about teaching?'

Caroline groaned. 'The only kind of teaching I'd consider would be in an all-boys' school with an excessive amount of sixth-form testosterone to drool over. So what age do you see yourself with?'

'Infants.'

Caroline groaned again. 'Well, you always were the only one at the library who could control the little horrors. You should have seen the state Maggie got into on Saturday when we had the first of the summer holiday story-time sessions. I thought she was going to hit this one boy who kept interrupting her. "Please Miss, please Miss," he kept whining. It was only after Maggie had finished the story and all the children stood up that she realised why the pest had been wittering on at her. He'd wanted the loo and had used the carpet in the end. Oh happy days.'

'The poor boy.'

'Poor Maggie, you mean. You know how obsessive she is about hygiene. She's becoming even more of a basket case these days. She's started wearing gloves, saying that the average library book contains more germs than a public lavatory. She reckons the books taken out by men are the worst. She's probably right.'

Kate laughed.

'So what does Alec think about you becoming a schoolmarm?'

'I haven't talked to him about it yet.'

'Why not?'

'Because I only started thinking about it over the weekend.' It was while she had been waiting for Alec to finish talking with Melissa on Saturday afternoon that the idea had begun to take root. Melissa's boyfriend, Tim, had asked her what she did for a living. When she had explained, he'd said, 'I don't recall librarians being as attractive as you.' She had felt the colour rising in her cheeks and had hoped that Melissa hadn't overheard what he'd said.

'So why aren't you still stamping books and telling people to ssh?' he'd asked.

'I was made redundant.'

'I'm sorry. Any idea what you'll do next?'

'I'm not sure, to be honest. Which I know sounds pathetically feeble.'

'Not at all, but what would you most like to do if you had the pick of any job?'

She had thought about this for a few seconds, then, seeing Oscar coming towards her, she had found her answer. 'I like children, so maybe I could do something in that line.'

'Teaching perhaps?'

'Yes,' she'd said, and responding to Oscar's hand searching for hers she'd added, 'I think I'd like that a lot.'

'Hello. Anybody at home?'

'Sorry, Caroline,' Kate said. 'I was miles away then.'

'I could tell. So what are you going to do about this career change? If you act fast now you might be able to join a teacher training course starting this autumn. Why don't you come over to the library and go through all the further education information?'

Kate drove home full of optimism, which made her realise that she must have been feeling the opposite before she'd arrived for lunch.

Since losing her job and moving in with Alec she had perhaps been too quick to put her life on hold. Being content to drift along was all very well, but it couldn't go on that way. She would spend the rest of the summer taking care of Oscar, as she'd promised Ruth, but come the autumn there would be her own life to see to.

It had been good to see Caroline again. One of her friend's greatest strengths was bullying people into sorting out their lives.

She decided to stop off at the supermarket on the way home and buy something special for supper that evening. She felt the need to celebrate the fact that a twinkling of an idea had been turned into a fully fledged decision.

She saw it as an important decision; one that she was convinced was going to make everything right again between her and Alec.

Having a new career to work for would stop her wanting something she couldn't have.

21

Jessica was fooling herself that she was working. Or rather, she was trying to fool herself that she was working.

Sitting with her head bent over a pad of foolscap and sucking pensively on the end of a pencil, she was giving an impressive performance of a writer. Only trouble was, the paper was blank and the pencil, completely unused, was as sharp as a pin.

Her attempt at putting a story-line together was not going well.

In fact, it was going depressingly badly. Not a word had been written since eight o'clock that morning. It was now ten thirty and the great Muse of romantic fiction had yet to get out of bed, apply her make-up, don her heels and make an appearance in Jessica's study.

The worry was, perhaps she never would.

Maybe the goddess who had worked so well for Jessica in the past had deserted her and had stayed behind in Corfu. 'Forget it,' the mythical Greek goddess had said to her many sisters when she'd learnt of Jessica's plans to leave the island, 'I ain't working my butt off in some freezing outpost called England!'

Jessica flung down her pencil. It bounced off the desk, hit the corner of the printer and broke its sharp point clean off.

'Serves you right,' Jessica said with childish satisfaction.

Starting a new novel in the past had never been a problem for Jessica. In fact, she had invariably enjoyed the anticipatory element of staring at a blank piece of paper and waiting for ideas to start to flow. It was at this stage, before she had progressed to working on her laptop, that she had the most fun. So long as she didn't have a single word written she could kid herself that her next novel would be her crowning glory; her *magnum opus*. It would win universal critical acclaim, the like of which had never been heard before – even Germaine Greer and A. S. Byatt would find it amusing, in a deceptively meaningful and thought-provoking way. It would race straight to the No. 1 slot of the *Sunday Times* bestseller list and it would stay there longer than Helen Fielding's *Bridget Jones's Diary*. Not only that, it would have every known television and film producer champing at the bit to serialise or Merchant Ivory it.

But that was the stuff of dreams. It was not to be taken seriously.

She stood up. It was time for another cup of coffee. Her sixth of the day so far.

Not that she was counting.

Not that she was becoming paranoid.

While she waited in the kitchen for the kettle to boil she thought of her phone call with her editor yesterday afternoon – another timely reminder that she should be getting on with the next novel. Fresh from her holiday, Cara had read *A Carefree Life* over the weekend and had phoned to say how much she'd enjoyed it. 'It's great, Jessica, definitely your best.'

'Thank you, Piers thought so, too.'

'In that case we must be sitting on the book of the decade!'

They'd both laughed, then Cara had congratulated Jessica on her new two-book contract. 'We're all thrilled here that you're staying with us.'

'You know how it is,' she had joked, 'better the devil you know.'

'We're planning a massive promotional campaign for *A Carefree Life*,' Cara had gone on to explain, 'and just as soon as the art department have done their stuff I'll let you have a copy of the jacket. Any ideas for the next book?'

'Um . . . I'd rather not say just yet.'

'That's fine, don't worry, Jessica. We can always trust you to come up with something good.'

Thinking of Cara's praise now, as Jessica dunked a digestive biscuit into her coffee while staring out of the kitchen window, she felt riddled with worry – *we can always trust you to come up with something good.* Well, supposing she couldn't do it this time? Supposing she'd only ever had the three books in her and that anything she wrote now would be contrived, samey and destined for the cut-price four-books-for-a-pound stores to be found in every high street?

And there was so much money involved.

It was a frightening thought to be trusted with such an incredible weight of responsibility. This, of course, was one of the reasons why she'd turned down the more lucrative offer Piers had negotiated – the more the advance, the greater the responsibility.

What a wimp she was!

And what a dreadful and unnerving revelation it was to know that deep down she was as scared as Gavin to take on the mantle of responsibility.

She dunked another digestive into her cup and seeing it disintegrate into her coffee, she decided she needed shaking up.

The best person to do that was her mother. They'd spoken on the phone late last night, not long after Anna had arrived home from her jaunt to North Wales, and Jessica had said that she would see her some time today. Now was as good a time as any.

As she walked along the lane to her mother's cottage Jessica tried not to think about the fruitless morning spent in her study. Think of anything, she told herself, anything so long as it has nothing to do with writing.

So she forced herself to count how many flowers in the hedgerow she recognised. She got the easy ones, the daisies and buttercups and dandelions, and even identified the patches of tufted vetch with its pretty pale-lilac flowers and the covering of groundsel greedily spreading itself along the roadside. But it was no good. No amount of nature-trailing was going to stop her worrying. Just what was she going to write about in her next novel? An idiot's guide to Cheshire's least-trodden pathways?

This whole business of not being able to write was getting her down. It was a new phenomenon to her. She had never experienced the dreaded writer's block before. But now she had. And in spades.

The inspiration for her previous books had come mostly from some of her own experiences – her first novel had featured a young backpacker; her second, *Caught in the Act*, not surprisingly had starred Gavin; and *A Carefree Life* had more than a passing similarity to her own life. Oh, but heaven help her if she was relying on her new situation to throw a shaft of illuminating light on a potential story-line, because so far, Cholmford seemed to be doing its best to keep her permanently in the dark.

Since she'd been living back in Cholmford, she had tried several times to get started, but on each occasion she had failed. And miserably. It was as if she were clean out of ideas. She had blamed it on her new surroundings to begin with, convincing herself, after each failed attempt, that the next day she would crack it. It wasn't even as though she was having trouble in getting chapter one off the ground, it was worse. Much worse. She had no characters. She had no setting. She had no story-line. In short she had a resounding zippo. No wonder she'd nearly throttled Amanda on Saturday night – *It must be wonderful to be able to earn a living from something as easy as writing*. Hah! The horrible woman should try it some time. She should try rolling up her sleeves for a day of creative black-out.

The strange thing was she could say with great authority – enormous authority in fact – what she wasn't going to write next. That was easy. She didn't want to write some thinly disguised copy of a classic. The bookshelves were full of contemporary reworkings of *Jane Eyre*, *Pride and Prejudice*, *Emma*, and more recently *Rebecca* had been given the same treatment. She was sick of bright young things always getting their man.

The other kind of novel she didn't want to write was the one about the bored, frumpy housewife, who manages overnight to shed three stone and with little more than a wave of a new mascara wand makes the sexy love interest fall at her feet.

If she was sick of bright young things getting their man, she was equally sick of middle-aged women making good.

Where was the reality?

Where was the nitty-gritty, hard-up-against-the-wall portrayal that all men were bastards and weren't worth the effort?

So, having condemned most of the popular romantic fiction currently on offer, what exactly did that leave her to get her teeth into?

A good juicy murder story?

It would be her own if Piers got wind of the mess she was in.

Oh Lord, what on earth had happened to her? Why was she so thoroughly cynical about love and romance all of a sudden?

She came to an abrupt stop in the road.

Gavin!

That was what was wrong with her. It was all his fault that she couldn't write. He had knocked the stuff of love right out of her and now she couldn't write about it.

'Damn you, Gavin!' she said out loud. A startled sparrow flew out of the undergrowth and disappeared into the safety of a hawthorn tree.

And what's more, she thought as she stomped her way along the road, having stolen her creative Muse, Gavin was very probably having his nautical way with her.

By the time she reached Willow Cottage Jessica's fury was just waiting to unleash itself.

She found her mother heaving a large rock out of the back of her Fiesta.

'Oh hell,' muttered Anna, when she saw the look of fuming anger on her daughter's face. 'I'd hoped to hide this before you arrived.'

'I bet you did!' stormed Jessica, going over to the car and pushing her mother's hands away from the enormous filched lump of North Wales coastline. 'Just what do you think you're doing?'

'I would have thought that was quite obvious.'

Jessica struggled with the rock, then pitched it into the wheelbarrow which her mother had positioned against the car. The barrow shuddered and nearly toppled under the weight of its cargo.

'In heaven's name, couldn't you have found something smaller?'

Anna smiled. 'The others are.'

'Others!' cried Jessica, now following after her mother, who was staggering behind the barrow and pushing it round to the back of the house.

'I'm building a rockery,' Anna said over her shoulder.

'I don't believe this,' Jessica said when they stood looking at a pile of stones. 'You've got enough here to rival Stonehenge.'

'Oh, don't exaggerate.'

'Well if you're not worried about your own suspension, what about the car's? You must have been dragging the boot on the ground the whole way home from George and Emily's.'

'It's my body, my car, I'll do as I please.'

Jessica frowned. Why couldn't her mother behave as she was supposed to? Why couldn't she be happy with a little light weeding and the odd coffee morning to keep her out of mischief? Why this bloody need to kill herself! 'And what was George thinking, letting you do this? I thought I could trust him.'

'Look, Jessica, I know you mean well, but do you think you could ease up a bit? And for your information, George wasn't around when Emily and I loaded the car. So don't go blaming him. Here, just help me tip the barrow to get this rock out.'

Jessica did as her mother asked. 'I'm sorry,' she said, when the stone rolled away from them and joined its compatriots, 'it's just that I can't help but worry about you.' She knew that she'd just taken out her anger and frustration on Anna.

'I know, dear. But honestly, I'm fine. Which is more than I can say for you. Now why don't you sit down for a few moments and tell me what you've been up to while I was away. Oh, and before I forget, George and

Emily send their best wishes and they both loved your last book. They want to know when the next one comes out. I said you'd write and tell them yourself.'

Jessica rolled her eyes. 'Letters will be all I'll be good for at the rate I'm going.'

Anna could see that her daughter was unusually upset. 'Come on,' she said, 'sit on the swing and tell me all about it while I prune the roses.' Without waiting for a response from Jessica, she led the way.

The swing had been one of Anna's proudest achievements in the garden. It had been a present for Jessica on her tenth birthday. It was built out of a sturdy combination of wooden sleepers and metal girders, and Anna had trained clusters of baby pink roses to grow over it. Now, after all these years it resembled the prettiest of rose arbours.

Jessica sat on the wooden seat and breathed in the sweet smell of roses; the perfume was as fragrant as she remembered from her childhood. She suddenly felt sad. The time would come when one day, these beautiful roses would be nothing but a memory.

'So what's the problem?' Anna asked, pulling out a pair of secateurs from her skirt pocket and snipping away at the deadheads; she dropped them tidily into a trug on the ground.

Jessica picked up her feet and gently began swinging to and fro, setting off a steady rhythmic creaking. 'I can't write,' she said simply.

Anna carried on with what she was doing. 'You mean you've got writer's block?'

'Something like that.'

'So what are you going to do about it?'

'I wish I knew.'

'Remind me to fetch some oil out here, that swing sounds as fed up as you. Any idea what's caused this block?'

'Promise you won't tut or scoff?'

'Have I ever?'

'Frequently. Especially over Gavin. When you met him for the first time you did nothing but tut and scoff.'

Anna turned and faced her daughter. What Jessica had just said was true. She had never really taken to Gavin. 'Are you saying he's the reason for your writer's block?'

Jessica nodded.

'Dear me,' was all Anna said. She went back to her roses.

'He's made me so cynical about love and romance that I don't think I can write about it as I used to.'

Anna tutted.

'You promised!'

'No I didn't. And the answer is simple. Find somebody new to love. Have a bit of a fling to restore your faith in all things romantic.'

'I can't possibly do that!'

'Whyever not? There's nothing like a casual affair to put the spring back in your step. Now tell me how your house is coming along.'

Jessica was amazed at her mother's extraordinary suggestion. Mothers weren't supposed to go around saying things like that! Little did Anna know that Jessica had already had the offer of something to put the spring back in her step, but had turned it down. She wondered, now, why she'd done that. Why had she backed off from Josh Crawford in the way she had? Was it simply that it was too soon after Gavin? Well, chances were she was going to find out. Last night, Josh had called over to invite her to dinner this evening.

'Jessica,' Anna said with a frown, 'I'm getting more attention from that creaking swing than from you. I asked you how your house was.'

'Sorry,' Jessica said, dragging her attention back to her mother. 'It's fine, though I'm not sure how much longer I can put up with some of the décor.'

'Then do something about it.'

'I will.' Jessica smiled. How clearly her mother saw things. If there was something wrong, then Anna's immediate response was to put it right – have a fling, redecorate, whatever. She never wasted any energy complaining about a thing.

'Which room bothers you the most?' Anna asked.

'Um . . . the kitchen probably, it's too slick, too much like an operating theatre.'

'Then let me decorate it for you.'

'What about Stonehenge?'

'I am capable of doing more than two things at once you know.'

'All right,' said Jessica. 'You're on.' At least if her mother was helping her it meant she could keep an eye on what she was getting up to. 'Do you think you could help me with something else?'

'Depends what it is. It's nothing to do with Gavin, is it?'

'No it isn't,' Jessica said crossly. 'I need to buy a car, and I wondered if you'd like to chauffeur me round a few garages and help me choose one?'

'When?'

'This afternoon?'

Anna looked disappointed. 'I wanted to make a start on the rockery.'

'Please.'

'Oh, all right. And don't think for one moment that by putting me off today I shall lose interest and not get around to doing it.'

'Hadn't crossed my mind.'

'Liar.'

Jessica stayed for lunch with Anna and told her about her new publishing contract.

'Does this mean you're going to be fabulously wealthy?'

'Don't be daft. It means there's a lot of hard work ahead of me . . . if only I could get started.'

After lunch they went in search of a car.

'What are you thinking of buying?' Anna asked Jessica as they drove away from Cholmford. 'Something with a decent engine I hope. Will your ill-gotten gains run to something brand new and swanky? I quite fancy being driven around in style. How about a little sports car? We'd look good in that.'

'I was thinking more along the lines of a second-hand runabout.' Even though Jessica knew she was about to start earning what in anyone's book was a decent amount of money, the years of living with little more than a backpack stuffed full of frugal uncertainty had made her unable to splash out too lavishly.

'You're surely not telling me you want a boring old Metro that's been driven by a dull old dear who's never pushed it beyond third gear?'

'It'd be better than your Fiesta that's been used as a skip. Honestly, Mum, the state of this car's disgusting. When was the last time you cleared it out?' She held up a pork pie wrapper that had been stuffed into the space where cassettes were supposed to be stored.

'You're turning into a right old whinge. Where, oh where, did I go wrong with you?'

'You didn't. I'm the voice of reason.'

Anna groaned. 'Now that you've come home, I'm not going to see too much of you, am I?'

'Thanks, Mum. Love you too.'

'One can have too much of a good thing, you know.'

'I'm beginning to see that.'

'Good. Just so long as we know where we stand. Now tell me about your neighbours, what are they like? And more to the point, what's the story behind the good-looking man we saw the day you moved in? Single, married, divorced or gay?'

Jessica laughed. 'I've a good mind not to tell you.'

'You could always walk to the garage.'

'Okay, I give in.' Jessica began by telling her mother about Tony and Amanda, then moved on to Kate and Alec next door. 'I like them, they're nice. They're not married but they're very much in *lurve*. She's a lot younger than him and a real stunner, but one of those who doesn't realise it.'

'You mean, she's stupid?'

'No. There's a naïvety about her that's really quite refreshing. I'd love to use her as a character in a book one day.'

'And what about him? Is he a middle-aged lech?'

'Not at all. He's the kind of man I'd have liked as a father.' She immediately wished she hadn't said that.

'I'm sorry not to have obliged you, Jessica.'

'I didn't mean it like that.'

Anna smiled kindly at her daughter. Years ago, Jessica had always been on at her to find a husband. But what with bringing up a child on her own and running a busy employment agency, the opportunity had never shown itself. Perhaps if it had, Jessica wouldn't now be so overly attentive.

'So,' she said, 'we've covered Mrs Social-Climber and her cute husband, and Mr and Mrs Lovey-Dovey next door, how about our good-looking young man? What have you got to tell me about him? I see that you've kept him till last. Would he be any good at helping you over your writer's block?'

'Honestly, Mum, why don't you just come right out and ask if I fancy sleeping with him?'

'I thought I just had.'

Jessica feigned a look of shock and told Anna all about being rescued after her trip down to London. She went on to give an edited version of the nightcap session following Tony and Amanda's dinner party.

'And?' Anna said when she'd finished.

'And, there isn't anything else to tell.'

'You sure?'

'Kindly remember there are certain things a daughter can't share with her mother.'

'It must have slipped my memory. Didn't I ever tell you that you were adopted?'

Jessica laughed. 'Forget it. I'm not telling you any more about him. So keep your nose out of my private life and your eyes on the road, I'd forgotten what an appalling driver you are.'

She had decided not to tell her mother that she was having dinner with Josh that evening and would keep it that way until she had made up her mind where she stood with him. It was all very well her mother suggesting that she have a fling with one of her neighbours, but how would it be when it was over and she and Josh had to face each other across the courtyard?

And surely Anna was wrong? Rushing headlong into the arms of somebody, for whatever reason, so soon after Gavin didn't seem like the most sensible of ideas.

It sounded like a perfect recipe for disaster.

22

Josh read through the recipe for Thai salmon parcels one more time and got down to work.

He grated the small stump of fresh ginger, crushed the clove of garlic, squeezed the juice out of two limes, chopped up a spring onion together with some coriander, then put it all in a pyrex bowl. Next he melted a chunk of butter in the microwave, then laid out the first of the sheets of filo pastry. As he began brushing the melted butter over the thin layer of pastry he had to concentrate hard on keeping his right hand moving.

It's fine, he told himself, determined to ignore the pins and needles and stiffness that were building up in his fingers. There's nothing to worry about. It'll pass.

But the cruel voice of Past Experience said otherwise. *If you're struggling to hold a pastry brush now*, it sneered at him, *how do you think you're going to relieve Jessica of her clothing later on tonight? Just think of all those buttons and fastenings to get through.*

He told Past Experience to bugger off and carried on with what he was doing, but the brush slipped out of his hand, rolled off the edge of the island unit and landed on the floor. He picked it up and threw it into the sink, then hunted through the drawer for another. When he found one, he laid a second sheet of filo pastry on top of the first and smeared it with the melted butter.

I'll be fine, he told himself. It's only the one hand that's playing up and anyway, I could always claim I'd hurt it during the day.

How? the gloating voice sneered at him again, *a squash injury perhaps?*

He blotted out what he didn't want to face, just as he had his brother's expression on Sunday afternoon when he'd told him about Jessica. He could tell what Charlie was thinking, but he didn't care.

'I'm not looking for a big relationship that's heavy on commitment,' he'd said to Charlie, when they'd eaten lunch and were tidying the kitchen, while outside in the garden their parents dozed in the sun. 'There's no point anyway. I just want a bit of fun ... while I still can.'

'But wouldn't you rather have something that's more meaningful?'

'Like I say, there's no point. What can I offer anyone?'

Josh knew that he was being selfish, that what he had in mind that evening was all about himself. Jessica might not have wanted to go to bed with him the other night, but he had every intention of making things turn out differently tonight. And to hell with the consequences.

He finished making the salmon parcels and went through to the dining-room to check there was nothing he'd forgotten. Everything looked in order. He'd set the table earlier when he'd got back from seeing a customer in Stoke and all that remained to be done was to light the candles when Jessica arrived.

In the sitting-room he went over to the flowers he had bought on the way home. They were large creamy white lilies and had been the most impressive-looking flowers in the shop. 'They'll last for days,' the florist had said, 'and the scent's terrific.' Now he wondered if they were a bit too much; the room seemed to be filled with their rich, powerful fragrance. He carefully picked up the vase and carried it away from the mantelpiece and positioned it on a small table beneath the open window where a cool breeze gently blew in. He stood back and stared at the lilies. He didn't know why, but they didn't look right. There was nowhere else to put them so he returned the vase to the mantelpiece. He then fiddled about with the cushions on the sofa and chairs, and straightened the magazines on the coffee table.

Bloody hell, he thought, what was he doing, turning into some neurotic housewife plumping up the cushions?

All the same, he couldn't resist going upstairs and checking the bedroom. He smoothed out the duvet which he had changed earlier, kicked his work shoes under the bed and pulled open his bedside drawer. A new packet of condoms winked back at him and before the malevolent voice that had taunted him in the kitchen had a chance to say anything, he shut the drawer and went and inspected the bathroom. All was clean and tidy. No hairs in the bath plughole and not a sign of any shavings in the basin. Even the towels were hanging straight.

He went back downstairs to the kitchen, where the tantalising smell of garlic and lime was making itself at home. He poured out a glass of wine from the bottle already uncorked in the fridge and congratulated himself. The stage was perfectly set for an evening of seduction. All that was needed was for Jessica to make her appearance.

Jessica was totally unaware of the time.

After an exhausting but successful afternoon spent car hunting with her mother, she had come home and run herself a bath. While lying back in the hot scented water and thinking about the evening ahead, the miraculous had happened – inspiration for her next novel had leapt out at her. What's more, the title had even presented itself.

And amazingly it was all down to her mother. Though heaven forbid that Anna should ever know that the credit was hers!

Not wanting to lose a single precious idea, Jessica had made a fast exit from the bathroom and with only a towel tied around her she had hurried down to the study where, on a creative high, she began throwing together a cast of characters along with a rough outline for a story.

Only when her neck and shoulders started to ache from being hunched over her desk for so long did she wonder what time it was and, remembering that she was supposed to have been getting ready to go out, she went through to the kitchen. The digital clock on the oven unit told her it was twenty to nine. She gasped in horror. She was nearly half an hour late for Josh.

She flew upstairs and threw on the first things to hand – the long wraparound skirt she had worn the other night for supper at Tony and Amanda's and a loose-fitting sleeveless top the colour of ivory, which made her look browner than ever. She slipped a pair of gold hooped ear-rings through her ears, brushed her hair and was downstairs in a matter of seconds, ready to open the front door. It was then that she realised she'd forgotten to put on any knickers. Back up the stairs, she yanked open a drawer and found that she was down to her last pair – they were years old and had seen rather more action than was decent. She wriggled into the worn-out pinky-grey cotton-and-lycra mixture and dashed downstairs again, remembering on her way out of the house to grab the bottle she'd bought for Josh.

When she knocked on his door she was flushed and out of breath.

In contrast, Josh looked like he deserved better than her cobbled-together appearance and antique knickers.

He stood there smiling at her, every inch of him heart-stoppingly, stomach-lurchingly gorgeous. And she was so busy taking him in – every little bit of his clean-cut splendid self, dressed in black jeans and crisp white T-shirt – that she almost missed the kiss being planted on her cheek. She reacted just in time and caught the benefit of his lips brushing against her skin.

'Here, this is for you,' she said. She handed him the bottle of Southern Comfort. 'Seeing as I helped you polish off the last one.'

'Thanks, we'll have a go with this later, perhaps. Come on through to the kitchen, I'm just in the middle of something.'

She followed behind him. Mm . . . nice bum, she found herself thinking. She even thought his limp was attractive and decided that it gave him an interesting air of vulnerability. As they passed what she took to be the downstairs loo, she was aware of a heady nose-clearing cocktail of Pine-O-Fresh toilet cleaner and some kind of air freshener. Bless him. The bachelor boy had been busy.

In the kitchen, she watched him open the oven door and take out a tray of croûtons. Her taste-buds responded to the delicious smell of garlic and olive oil. 'Sorry I'm so late, by the way,' she said.

'I was beginning to wonder whether I was going to be stood up,' he said, closing the oven door with his foot and tipping the perfectly cooked croûtons into a yellow-and-blue pottery bowl. 'I would have been very disappointed.'

'Oh, I wouldn't have done that,' she said, 'standing people up isn't my style.' She had the feeling that they were flirting with one another again.

'Good, I'm glad to hear it. So what's your excuse for being late? And I shall expect something highly imaginative and original from you, no ordinary explanation will do, not from a writer.'

She laughed. 'Well, Crawford – you don't mind if I call you that, do you?'

'If it amuses you, go ahead. Though I'd like to know why.'

'How very tedious of you. But let's just say that a little formality never does any harm. It's a useful device for putting people at their ease.'

He moved across the kitchen and slid the baking tray into the sink. 'An interesting concept, with more than a hint of Oscar Wilde to it.'

'You're not accusing me of plagiarism, are you?'

He turned round and laughed. 'Oh I wouldn't dare. Now, about your excuse for being late.'

'Heavens, you're like a dog with a bone. Would you believe me if I said that burglars broke into my house in the middle of the night and stole all my clocks, thereby leaving me unable to keep track of the time?'

'No. Try again.'

'Localised earthquake?'

'Hopeless.'

'I overslept?'

He shook his head.

'Okay, I admit it, I was with another man having great but meaningless sex.'

He smiled. 'The truth at last. Glass of wine?'

'Thanks.'

He poured out a glass and handed it to her.

'Actually, I'm late because I've at last started work on my next novel.' She told him how depressed she'd been that morning. 'You can't imagine what a relief it is for me to get going again. There were a few nasty moments today when I thought I'd lost it.'

'I'm delighted to hear that you haven't. Am I allowed to know the title?'

She hesitated. Normally she didn't share too much of a new novel with anyone, not until it was firmly in her mind – a new book was like a tiny flickering candle flame, blow too hard on it and it would be completely snuffed out. But she decided to tell him. He would probably think it funny. Well, he would if he knew what her mother had suggested today. 'It's going to be called *A Casual Affair*,' she said, 'what do you think?'

It was his turn to hesitate.

'Don't you like it?' she asked, concerned.

'No. I mean, yes. Yes I do, it's great.' He lowered his gaze and busied his hands with adding the croûtons to the bowl of salad. *A Casual Affair*, he repeated to himself. Well, considering what he had in mind it was perfect.

When they sat down to eat Jessica was impressed. 'You've gone to a lot of trouble, Crawford,' she said mockingly, watching him light the candles on the table. 'Or is this the way you always eat?'

He smiled. 'Only when I want to impress somebody special.'

'Oh,' she said in a coy girlie voice, 'does that make me special?'

He passed her a dish of Jersey Royals that were coated in butter as well as a sprinkling of chopped chives. 'What do you think?'

'I think that you've a manner smooth enough to charm the devil and that I should be very wary of you. And,' she continued, helping herself to a couple of potatoes and adding them to her plate of salmon, 'a man who can cook as well as this is clearly to be viewed with the utmost suspicion. The bottom line, Crawford my boy, is that you're too good to be true. There has to be another side to you that you're keeping under wraps.'

He shook his head. 'See, there's the thing, I'm told that all the time.'

'I can well believe it. Take it from me, this new man stuff of being a whizz in the kitchen will do you no good at all. It only serves to undermine the majority of women and frighten the pants off them.'

He grinned. 'Sounds like justification enough to me. *Bon appetit!*'

The salmon was perfect, as was everything about the meal, and when they'd finished eating Josh told Jessica to go and relax in the sitting-room while he made some coffee.

Alone in the kitchen, he punched a fist in the air. *Yesss!*

Everything was going exactly to plan. They were getting along just fine. All he had to do was get some coffee down Jessica, followed by a couple of glasses of Southern Comfort, then it would be up those stairs. Yes, yes, *yesss!*

The fact that he had hardly any feeling in his right hand did nothing to dampen his confidence and he congratulated himself on his performance over dinner – he'd managed to eat with the fork in his right hand, which didn't need too much manipulative skill, and had used his left for the trickier business of cutting up his food.

And if his luck continued to hold out he was certain he was going to get away with the rest of the evening.

He filled the cafetiere with Sainsbury's Colombian coffee, placed it on the tray with the cups and saucers, along with a box of mint chocolates, and took it through to the sitting-room, where he found Jessica standing in front of the bookcase. She turned to look at him when she heard him come into the room.

'What's the interest in multiple sclerosis?' she asked. She showed him the book in her hands, *Multiple Sclerosis – And How to Get the Better of It.*

He gripped the edges of the tray and carefully moved across the room; all his euphoria instantly gone. He lowered the tray on to the glass-topped table, sank into the sofa and swallowed back his shock. He racked his brain for something convincing to say.

She came over and joined him, the book still in her hands. 'It's an illness I know nothing about,' she said.

'The majority of people don't need to know anything about it,' he said flatly.

'I suppose not. But do you know somebody with MS, then? Is that why you've got this?'

He swallowed and hoped that Charlie would forgive him. 'Yes,' he said, 'my brother Charlie.'

She put down the book on the table. 'Oh, I'm sorry.'

Aware that he could still save the situation, he poured out the coffee with his good hand and began the not so subtle web of lies that he hoped would satisfy Jessica and get him off the hook. 'Charlie's not got it too badly,' he said, trying to sound casual, 'it's just every now and again that he gets caught out, he gets tired easily. But most of the time you'd never know there was anything wrong.'

'When did it start?'

'A few years back. It was quite out of the blue.' He paused, then said, 'Do you think we could drop the subject of my brother?'

'Of course,' she said, 'I'm sorry, I was being nosy.' Jessica had already concluded that Josh and his brother were close, but going by the tone of Josh's voice, it was clear that he was also extremely concerned about Charlie. She felt annoyed with herself for her insensitivity.

'How about some music?' Josh asked, already on his feet and going over to the CD player. 'What do you fancy?'

She was tipsy enough to say 'You,' but sober enough to refrain. 'You choose,' she said.

He put on *The Best of Chris Rea* and 'The Road to Hell' started up. The irony was not lost on him. He went back to the sofa and poured out two glasses of Southern Comfort.

They sat in silence for a while listening to the music and, conscious that they were only a few inches apart, Josh decided it was now or never. It was time to make a move on Jessica. He turned and faced her, and found that she was staring at him. He reached out to her hand on her lap, but was cheated of the touch of her; his fingers were completely numb. He raised his good hand to stroke her face and when she made no attempt to push him away, he kissed her, slowly and lingeringly, and for the first time that night he felt his entire body relax. It was wonderful. He hadn't realised just how uptight he'd been. He gently pushed her along the length of the sofa and began parting the front of her skirt. It was going to be easier than he'd thought.

Dead easy.

He was home and dry.

She was as keen as he was.

But from nowhere he experienced a bolt of self-revulsion; it caught him like a punch in the stomach. He saw what he was doing for what it really was – he was using Jessica as a means to boost his self-esteem. By bedding her, he hoped to chalk up a point of victory over his illness.

And with this clarity of thought came a wave of nausea. He wanted to put it down to the overpowering smell coming from the lilies on the mantelpiece, but he knew deep down that it was something more. He felt cheap and shabby, and knew he couldn't go through the motions of seducing Jessica in the contrived manner he had planned so exactly. It was all wrong. With a shock he realised that instead of the desire for a mindless easy lay upstairs on the clean sheets, he was overcome with the need for something more.

But what?

Charlie's words came into his head – *Wouldn't you rather have something more meaningful?*

No! he wanted to shout.

No. No. *No!* I'm not capable of anything more. What the hell can I offer anyone in a long-term relationship?

23

It was the first wet day in over three weeks and as Alec drove past Capesthorne Hall the rain came down even harder. He switched the windscreen wipers on to full and dropped his speed as he joined the queue of cars which stretched back almost two hundred yards from the traffic lights at the junction ahead. It was always busy at this time in the morning and every day as he waited in this same stream of traffic he promised himself to leave the house earlier in order to avoid the rush.

He thought the same now.

But as the wipers tump-tumped across the windscreen he suddenly thought, why? Why should he?

Why should he deprive himself of a few precious minutes at home with Kate just so that he could reach the office at eight thirty instead of eight forty? What possible difference would it make?

None.

None whatsoever. He would still get exactly the same amount of work done. So why bother?

Because the old Alec McLaren had spent a lifetime on the treadmill convinced that the only way to be was to adhere to the puritanical work ethic that his father had drilled into him – a busy mind is a pure mind.

He smiled and not for the first time wondered what his poor father would have made of his relationship with Kate. The old man's verdict would probably have been that Alec hadn't kept himself busy enough. 'Your mind has wandered,' he'd have said, 'and wandered badly into the mire of evil.'

Alec had been terrified of his father as a child and had never attached himself to any of the religious views he propounded, finding the commitment to such an apparently cold and unforgiving deity too austere a concept to consider as having any value or relevance.

He preferred his mother's God. While his father had frightened him with his tales of hell and purgatory, his mother had told him reassuring stories of a merciful God who was more interested in seeing a smile on Alec's face, rather than a grim expression of servitude.

His mother had been a quiet, affectionate woman whom Alec had adored. Being her only child she had spoilt him as much as she dared and, without ever defying her husband or the strict code of conduct by which he expected them all to live, she had managed to ensure that Alec's childhood was a happy one.

He wasn't quite sure that it was something he should admit, or ever explore in any depth, but there were definitely times when Kate reminded him of his mother. Physically the two women were quite different – his mother had been a tiny dark-haired woman – but they both had the same ability to give him a sense of true well-being. Often when he left work and drove home to Kate he experienced the same degree of comfort and anchorage as when he'd been a ten-year-old boy arriving home from school on a cold, wintry afternoon to find his mother pulling a tray of freshly baked oatcakes out of the oven.

If he wanted to offer up a superficial analysis of any of this, he supposed it was possible that he loved Kate as much as he did because, like his mother who had eased the severity of his father's treatment of him, Kate had wiped away the shock and pain of what Melissa had done.

In the end, time had helped him to resolve the difficult relationship with his father. As an adult, Alec had grown to understand, and on occasion almost respect, the strong will and reserved manner that had kept them apart. To this day, though, it saddened Alec that they hadn't been closer. When his father was dying and he and his mother had spent so many hours by his hospital bedside there had still been that impenetrable barrier of stiff formality between them. What would have seemed the most natural thing in the world to have done was to have hugged his father and said that he loved him. But it hadn't happened. Even at so poignant a moment to have shown the slightest flicker of emotion in front of this formidable man was unthinkable. And perhaps that's the way it should have been. It was probably what his father would have wanted. No emotion. Just a quiet acceptance that his life was over.

Except it wasn't.

No life was ever over. It could never be that clear-cut. There was always a legacy that kept the deceased well and truly alive. And in his father's case he had bequeathed Alec a confusion of conflicting attitudes that was hard to shake off. It was frightening just how good a job his father had done, because sure enough, the work-till-you-drop ethic was clearly ingrained in Alec, which was why from time to time he had to force himself to stand firm and veto this edict from the grave.

So, no, he now said as the lights changed to green and he turned left on to the Chelford Road. No, he would not leave the house any earlier to avoid the traffic just so that he could gain an extra ten minutes at his desk.

He reached the office at the same time as Melissa and parked alongside her MR2. She let them into the redbrick building that had once been the local village school. With its distinctive Victorian arched windows, it still looked exactly like a school from the outside, but inside it was completely different, with many of the walls knocked down to open up what had originally been small cramped classrooms into large areas of creative working space. The windows were perfect for letting in plenty of natural light so that the three artists they currently employed could work at their best. Where the light wasn't quite so good, Melissa and Alec had their offices, along with other members of the team who carried out the administrative side of the business.

Many of the people whom they employed had been with them since Thistle Cards had moved to these premises back in 1981. Before those days the business had been little more than a dream, consisting of him and Melissa putting in a full day's work for a small advertising agency where they were both employed as designers, then taking it in turns to look after Ruth or spend an evening inhaling the fumes of turpentine-based ink in a rented basement room beneath Squeaky Clean, a dog parlour that was a local harbouring ground for fleas, ticks and any other ghastly canine parasite you'd care to think of. Alec didn't know which was worse, the stink of the turpentine in that tiny dank room as they worked until gone midnight producing a limited range of cards, or the permanent smell of wet dog seeping through the rotten floorboards above their heads.

'What are you smiling about?' Melissa said, catching the expression on his face as she looked up from sorting through the mail in her hands.

'Sorry,' he said, 'I didn't realise I was. I was just reminiscing.'

She followed him through to his office. 'Reminiscing about anything in particular?'

'I was thinking about Squeaky Clean.'

Melissa shuddered. 'I gave up thinking about those awful days a long time ago. I much prefer to think of the present.'

He sat in his swivel chair and considered what she'd just said. 'In all ways?' he asked.

The question hung in the air while Melissa returned his gaze. She thought about answering it, but decided not to – cheap shots at an ex-husband were two a penny. Instead she said, 'I want to check a few things with you about Birmingham.'

At this time of the year the Birmingham trade fair was their biggest concern. There was a colossal amount of work involved in order to be ready for the September event. But despite the organisational headache both he and Melissa thrived on it. They always had. It was where the bulk of their business was done and where most importantly they found their entrée into the export markets; a third of their money was made in the USA, Japan, Australia and more recently Iceland had been added to their order books. The trade fairs were a fundamental part of the greetings card industry, without them they might just as well pack up and go home.

'What is it?' he asked. 'A problem?'

She sat in the chair opposite him. 'Of course not, stop thinking the worst.'

He was reminded of Kate on Monday evening when he'd got back from work and found her eager to share some news with him. 'Sit down,' she'd said, 'I've got something to tell you, and don't go jumping to conclusions and thinking the worst.'

'What is it?' he'd asked warily. The awful thought had gone through his mind that Kate was about to tell him that she was pregnant. He'd sat awkwardly in the armchair petrified that his expression would betray him. He knew that Kate would love to have a baby and knew too how she would want him to react to such a piece of news. But when she'd told him that she'd decided that she wanted to retrain and become a teacher he had pulled her on to his lap and hugged her.

'That's a brilliant idea,' he'd said, kissing her. 'That's fantastic.'

Thinking now about his relief that Kate wasn't pregnant it struck him how utterly selfish he was. It wasn't a pleasant realisation. In fact, it was a rather unpalatable conclusion that spoke volumes about their relationship. Without doubt he loved Kate more than he'd loved anyone, but it was all too clear that he didn't love her sufficiently to give her complete happiness. Whereas Kate loved him selflessly. Because of her love for him she was prepared to deny herself something she desperately wanted – a family of her own.

What was he prepared to sacrifice for Kate? Good God, he hadn't even had the decency to marry her.

When he and Melissa had finished discussing the Birmingham trade fair Alec phoned Kate. He suddenly wanted to hear her gentle, loving voice. He needed confirmation that he wasn't a complete heel.

Kate put down the phone and went back to pouring out a small mug of Ribena for Oscar.

'Was that Gramps?' he asked from the table where he was busy painting.

'Yes,' she said, handing him his drink.

He put down his paintbrush, taking care to keep it on the newspaper that Kate had partially covered the table with.

'Would you like a rice cake?'

He shook his head.

'A biscuit?'

His face lit up. 'Yes please.'

Kate fetched the biscuit tin from the cupboard and came back and sat next to him. She prised the lid off and offered him the tin. He took a custard cream and began nibbling on one of its corners. He stared at her thoughtfully. 'If you were married to Gramps, would that make you my grandma?'

Kate smiled. 'I don't think so,' she said, amused at the notion of being a grandmother.

'Good,' he said. 'I don't want you to be like Grandma Melissa.'

Much as a good bitching session about Melissa would intrigue her, Kate knew better than to draw Oscar on the subject. 'Grandma Melissa and I are very different,' she said tactfully.

'I don't like her,' he confessed, his eyes lowered. 'She tells me off.'

'Well,' Kate said slowly, 'if you've been naughty then she has every right to tell you off.'

He raised his eyes and looked indignant. 'But I wasn't naughty. I only said that I liked you better than her.'

'Oh, Oscar,' Kate said, 'you mustn't say things like that.'

'Why not?'

'Because ... because you must have hurt Grandma Melissa by saying what you did and that's something you mustn't do, you mustn't go around hurting people. It's not nice.'

'I didn't mean to hurt her,' he said, his face full of concern. 'Mummy says I mustn't tell lies . . . I was telling the truth. I only told Grandma Melissa that I liked you better than anyone else. What was wrong with that?'

Nothing, thought Kate, if you were a four-and-a-half-year-old boy. 'Come on,' she said by way of distraction, 'how's this picture coming along?'

Oscar drained his mug of Ribena, set it down next to the jam jar of greeny-grey water and picked up his paintbrush. 'I'm going to do the sky next. Will you help me?'

'If you want. But you go first and I'll do a tiny bit at the end.'

Kate watched Oscar dip his brush into the jar of water and select his colour from the plastic tray of paints. He covered the stumpy bristles in blue and started stroking the brush across the top two inches of his picture. He worked carefully and slowly, and Kate watched his face closely. It was rigid with concentration, his tongue poking out of the corner of his mouth, his smudgy little eyebrows furrowed lest he make a mistake.

This was Oscar's first day with Kate – and Ruth's first day working alongside Adam. She had arrived late, having told Kate on the phone last night to expect her at eight o'clock. She'd eventually turned up at a quarter to nine. 'The roads are a nightmare,' she'd said to Kate, bundling Oscar out of the car as the rain had lashed down on them, 'I can't believe how selfish people are all travelling in separate cars. Haven't they heard of public transport, or car pools for that matter?'

Kate would have liked to suggest that maybe Ruth ought to travel to work with Adam and save yet another car from adding to the congestion, but she hadn't; instead she had taken Oscar's hand and led him through to the kitchen.

'I've brought his jacket and boots so that you can take him for a walk,' Ruth had added, throwing the things down on the floor in the hall, 'he must have at least half an hour of fresh air.' She made him sound like a dog. 'And here are some rice cakes for him to eat instead of biscuits. I don't want you filling him up with rubbish. I'll see you at about six.'

She'd flown out of the house without so much as a kiss for Oscar and together he and Kate had waved goodbye from the doorstep.

'There,' Oscar said, turning to face Kate and handing her the paintbrush. 'I've left you the bit in the corner.'

'Thank you. But tell you what, why don't we put a bright jolly sun in that space? What do you think?'

He turned away and looked out of the kitchen window to the scene of the courtyard that he'd been painting. 'But there isn't a sun today, it's still raining,' he said.

She smiled. 'But we're using our imaginations to do this, aren't we? Let's paint a sun in, then maybe if we're really lucky it might make the rain go away and we could go for a walk.'

'I'll need some clean water.'

She got up and took the jam jar over to the sink. She refilled it and cleaned the brush under the tap. When she went back to Oscar the phone rang.

It was Caroline. 'Hi,' she said, 'have you got a minute?'

'Of course, but not too many, I've got Oscar here with me.'

'Oscar? Who's he? Some gorgeous hunk?'

'Gorgeous, but not a hunk. He's Alec's grandson.'

'Oh, yes, I remember you saying something about a child. But never mind all that. You're not going to believe this, but I've taken your advice.'

'You're right, I don't believe you. You never listen to anything I say, never mind act on it.'

'Well, this time I have. I've joined an introductions agency.' These last two words were whispered into the phone. 'And if you breathe a word about this to anyone I'll kill you. Got that?'

Kate smiled. 'Don't worry, I shan't say a word to anyone. So tell me all about it.'

'I won't bore you with all the details now, but hopefully by this time next week I shall be fixed up with my first date. I just hope it isn't somebody I know. Can you imagine the shame?'

'Well, don't forget, it will be the same for him. He'll be just as embarrassed.'

'That would be impossible.'

'But it's true. The men are bound to feel as awkward as you.' She recalled Alec telling her how anxious he'd been about meeting her. 'I very nearly bottled out,' he'd admitted. 'I parked the car and as I walked to the wine bar I thought I was going to be sick with nerves.'

'So how come you're suddenly such an expert on the matter?' Caroline demanded.

'I'm not,' Kate said quickly, 'I'm just imagining how it must be, that's all.'

'Look, I'm going to have to go now, the place is swarming with creepy old men in macs with nothing better to do than make a nuisance of themselves in the library. First drop of rain in weeks and they bloody well come in here dripping wet umbrellas on the carpet. By the way, when will you be in for that teacher training info?'

'How about first thing next week?'

'Come in on Tuesday morning and we can have lunch afterwards.'

'I might have Oscar with me.'

'He can come so long as you put a muzzle on him. Bye.'

Kate put down the phone and when she looked up she saw two figures hurrying across the courtyard in the rain. Amanda and Hattie.

Oh, heavens, what did Amanda want now?

24

Amanda removed the heated rollers from her hair and carefully began brushing it. She framed her face with her full bob of hair in the way that she normally wore it. Then she looked critically at herself in the mirror and changed her mind. She decided to go for a completely different look and, sweeping back her hair, she tucked it behind her ears, and before it had a chance to flop forward she quickly fixed it into place with some maximum-hold hair spray. When she'd finished she stared at her reflection and smiled at herself. Not bad, she thought. Not bad at all.

But then, at that precise moment she was feeling particularly pleased with herself anyway.

Not only had she finally decided on the fabric and wallpaper for the sitting-room – and found a decorator who wasn't fully booked up until Christmas – but she had managed to off-load Hattie on to Cholmford's very own equivalent to Maria von Trapp for that evening, leaving her and Tony free to take her mother out to dinner. And if all went well tonight, and there was no reason to suspect that it wouldn't, the outcome would be that her mother would baby-sit Hattie next month, enabling her and Tony to go away for an all-expenses-paid weekend that Arc was putting on.

'It's nothing special,' Tony had said at breakfast that morning, 'it's just the usual Arc "do" to encourage the team.'

Tony might not think that a long weekend spent at Gleneagles was special, but she had other ideas. Compared with what she was used to, three days of pampering would be bliss and she had every intention of indulging herself to the full. The first thing she planned to do, once Tony and his boring colleagues had gone off to the golf course, or whatever it was they were expected to do, was to hit the hotel fitness centre, followed by the beauty salon where she would gratify herself for as long as she wanted. And after three days of being steamed, covered in seaweed, plucked, waxed, massaged and manicured she would emerge a new woman. It would be fantastic. She couldn't wait.

The only thing that could conceivably get in the way of this wonderful weekend was Rita refusing to do her bit.

Downstairs she heard the sound of the doorbell. Good. That meant the ever reliable, ever sweet Kate had arrived.

Tony let Kate in. He took her through to the kitchen where he was in the middle of tidying up Hattie's tea things. 'This is very good of you,' he said, 'I hope you don't think we're taking advantage.'

She smiled and shook her head. 'Of course I don't.'

He tried not to stare at her, but he couldn't help himself and as he watched her push her wonderful hair away from her face he experienced a wave of something he hadn't felt in a long time.

It was a wave of desire.

And not some piddly ebb and flow of desire.

This was a roller.

A breaker.

A torrent.

A ruddy great tidal wave.

To hell with that, it was the Niagara Falls of desire.

He cleared his throat and went back to scraping the remains of Hattie's tea into the bin. Watch it, Tony, he said to himself as he dolloped tomato ketchup on to a half-eaten apple, you're imagining things. Nobody could have that effect on anyone.

Wrong!

Eve had. Eve had bowled him over the second they'd met.

He swallowed. Why was it that every time he was in Kate's company he was reminded of Eve? Was it because she had the same effect on him?

'Hello Kate.' It was Hattie. She was not long out of the bath and as she came into the kitchen Tony could smell the sweetness of her; a combination of bubble bath and talc. He watched her approach Kate and envied the warm hug she received. 'Will you read to me like you did last time?' she asked Kate.

'I should think so,' Kate answered. 'Why don't you go upstairs and choose which books you'd like.'

Hattie smiled. 'I've done that already.'

Tony laughed, went over to Hattie and lifted her up into his arms. 'What a terrible little opportunist you are,' he said, holding her aloft. He kissed her cheek and she kissed him back, smack on the lips, her hands clasped tightly around his neck.

'Will you come up and say good-night to me before you go out?' she asked him, her eyes wide and appealing.

'Try and stop me.' He gently lowered her to the floor. 'Go on, off you go, I'll be up in a minute.' He watched her leave the kitchen, then turned to Kate. 'Would you like a drink?' he asked.

'No thank you,' she said.

'Sure?'

'Yes.'

'How about something to eat?'

She smiled. 'I had a sandwich earlier.'

'Is that all?'

'I'm fine, really.'

'So there's nothing I can offer you?' Bloody hell! What did he sound like? – *So there's nothing I can offer you?* Why didn't he have done with it and start wearing a chunky gold bracelet and a fake tan, and take a crash course in *doubles entendres* for the intellectually challenged?

'*Kate,*' came a voice from the landing, 'are you coming up now?'

But before Kate could answer, Amanda made her appearance in the kitchen, her high heels clickety-clicking across the tiled floor. 'You really mustn't let Hattie boss you about, Kate,' she said, opening her small leather purse and slipping a tissue inside, then snapping it shut.

Hattie isn't bossing Kate about, Tony wanted to snipe back at Amanda, and without meaning to he ran a critical eye over what his wife was wearing.

She was smartly dressed in a pair of oatmeal-coloured linen trousers with a navy blazer and she had on just the right amount of gold jewellery – she'd got the balance exactly right, any more and she would have looked ostentatious. Her make-up had been carefully applied and enhanced her high cheek-bones, as well as smoothing away the fine lines round her eyes. He sensed that there was something different about her hair, but he couldn't put his finger on what exactly. He also sensed that anyone meeting Amanda for the first time, dressed as she was, would say that she was a most poised and elegant woman, that she was the epitome of a woman in her mid-thirties who knew what she was about – a no-nonsense woman who was completely in control of her life. Which was what had attracted him to her in the first place. He had recognised in her an ability to take charge of his disorganised life. He had seen in her someone to resolve all his problems.

But she hadn't, he now realised, she had only added to them.

He risked a sideways glance at Kate. The contrast between the two women couldn't have been greater. Kate was dressed in faded blue jeans with a tiny sort of misshapen cotton cardigan that was not only low-necked but also so short it didn't quite meet the top of her jeans and revealed about an inch of tantalising waistline. She wore no jewellery and as far as Tony could see, no make-up either. She was delightfully natural and fresh-faced, and standing beside Amanda she made her look overdressed and starchy.

'I'll just go and say good-night to Hattie,' he said, hastily retreating from the kitchen before the expression on his face gave him away. He wasn't imagining it, he told himself as he climbed the stairs. What he felt for Kate was no trick of the mind. His feelings for her were as real as those he'd felt for Eve. So why the bloody hell had fate done this to him? Why had it let him marry the wrong woman, then taunted him with exactly the kind of woman whom he could have loved and been happy with?

Back in the kitchen, Amanda was saying, 'Now you know where everything is. Just help yourself to teas and coffees and anything else you might need. We shan't be that late, about eleven-thirty I should think.'

'That's fine,' said Kate, 'please don't worry about the time.'

'I hope Alec doesn't mind you doing this for us.'

'He doesn't mind at all. He's working late tonight anyway, but he might join me when he gets back. Is that okay?'

'Of course.'

Uncomfortable in Amanda's presence and anxious not to prolong their conversation, Kate said, 'I think I'll go up and start reading to Hattie. Have a good evening.'

When she reached Hattie's bedroom door she paused, suddenly unsure whether to go in or not. She felt as if she might be barging in on Hattie and her father. She could hear them talking, their voices low and confiding. She thought about going back downstairs, but as she turned to go the floor betrayed her presence and gave off a loud creak.

'Is that you, Kate?' asked Hattie.

She pushed open the door and went in. Tony was sitting on the bed beside Hattie. He had one of his arms around her shoulders and from nowhere Kate was reminded of what she'd missed out on as a child. She couldn't ever recall being tucked into bed when she'd been little. Her mother had always been too busy arranging her own life to be bothered with sitting on the edge of a bed to kiss her good-night. Even now her mother was too busy to bother about Kate. The only contact between them was a Christmas card enclosing a cheque each year and the occasional birthday card sent from her latest home, which she shared with her third husband in Sydney, Australia. It had been like that for years. Kate didn't hold it against her mother, there was no point, some people just weren't designed to be parents.

Kate looked at Tony and realised that he was openly staring at her in a way that made her feel unaccountably confused.

The meal was dreadful and the company diabolical.

Bloody Rita was the last person on earth with whom Tony wanted to spend an evening. And as he picked out the artificially red cherries from the enormous slice of black forest gateau in front of him he found himself wishing that Amanda's father was there with them instead of taking the minutes at the AGM of his local history group – Roy might be one of the most boring men on the planet, in fact he could bore for the entire universe on the subject of ancient burial sites in the area, but his company would at least have had a sedative effect.

Tony forced himself to listen with half an ear to what his wife and mother-in-law were rattling on about. But he had no interest in their conversation – what did he care that some neighbour of Bloody Rita's was applying for planning permission to extend his house? With a more than willing mind he turned his thoughts to Kate.

He was trying to work out how he was ever going to see her alone. He knew he was playing with fire, but he couldn't help himself. He wanted to be with her. He wanted, just once, to be able to touch her, maybe even kiss her. Because perhaps then the spell she had cast on him would be lifted. He was trying to convince himself that what he felt for her had to be little more than infatuation and that no harm would come to either of them if he could just touch her and make the fantasy disappear.

'Isn't that right, Tony?'

'Sorry,' he said, suddenly alert to having been caught out not listening to the conversation.

Amanda frowned at him. 'I was just telling Mum about the important weekend away that Arc have asked us to host.'

It was his turn to frown. It was news to him that they were supposed to be hosting the event. But a kick under the table told him that Amanda was deliberately exaggerating the importance of the weekend in order to enlist her mother's help.

'Yes,' he lied, 'it should be quite an interesting weekend.' Hell's teeth, it would be the usual boring routine of trying to rally the troops – such as they were – to keep them working themselves into the ground in order to please Arc. He couldn't imagine anything worse.

No. That wasn't true. A weekend with Bloody Rita would win hands down.

He didn't know what it was about the woman, but she had an uncanny knack for metaphorically disembowelling him each time they met. He prided himself on getting on with most people, but here was somebody he'd failed to impress. She made it very clear to him that he didn't match her expectations for her only daughter. If he'd been a doctor or a barrister, or even an accountant, he might have given her something to be pleased about, but in her opinion being a sales director was nothing short of making a living out of knocking on doors with a suitcase of polishing cloths to peddle.

It was a class thing, of course. In her eyes he was nothing but a cloth-capped lad in clogs from Rochdale. 'Rochdale?' she'd said in a disappointed tone of voice, at their first meeting when she'd asked 'And from where do you hail?' – *from where do you hail?* – did any normal human being talk like that these days? He had no obvious accent to speak of, but her cross-examination of his upbringing had made him want to return to his roots and stretch out his vowels.

Rita's dislike of him was set in stone from that day on.

Even on the phone she couldn't bring herself to communicate with him more than was necessary. 'Is my daughter there?' would be her opening gambit if he ever picked up the phone when she called – she made no pretence at small talk.

Her generosity was as abundant as her conversation. Her Christmas present to them last year had been a pair of salt and pepper pots. Except they weren't a pair. They didn't match.

A bit like him and Amanda really.

Maybe Bloody Rita had known this right from the outset and had been trying to tell him something.

He tuned in again to what Amanda was saying. It sounded as if she was getting to the crucial bit.

'So we thought that perhaps you might like to help us out.'

'How exactly?' said Bloody Rita, her eyes narrowing, her lips tightening to a point.

How do you think, you stupid woman! Tony wanted to yell across the table.

'With Hattie,' Amanda carried on bravely, 'we wondered whether you could come and look after her for us. There's nobody else we can ask.'

The eyes had almost disappeared, as had the lips, which had been sucked in, in an expression of wary mistrust. 'For how long?' she asked, when a few seconds had passed.

'It'll only be a couple of days.'

Rita stared at her daughter. 'Be more specific, please.'

'From Friday morning through till Sunday evening,' interceded Tony, who could be as specific as the next person when he chose.

'I don't know,' Rita said, without even bothering to look at Tony, 'I haven't brought my diary with me. I'm away on a bowling trip during August.'

'Yes I know,' said Amanda, 'you're going the first weekend, our weekend is the second.'

Tony had to admire Amanda's persistence, but he didn't hold out much hope of Bloody Rita being persuaded into any kind of agreement. He understood her well enough to know that they were a long way from clinching the deal. But to be honest he didn't care. He wasn't fussed about a ra-ra weekend of team bonding, not when he was so disillusioned with the whole show. It had been different last year; company morale had been good and he'd gone to great lengths to organise a nanny to take care of Hattie so that he could join in with the fun, but what would be the point this time? With Bradley Hurst's blood-stained butcher's knife hanging over everybody, what fun would there be for any of them?

On top of all that, he wasn't keen on the idea of Hattie being looked after by Bloody Rita. In fact, the more he thought about it, the less he liked the prospect of his daughter having to put up with this witch of a woman.

'Perhaps we've been too presumptuous,' he heard himself say, 'we shouldn't have put you on the spot like this, Rita. Forget we ever mentioned it.'

He got a sharp kick from Amanda and a look that would have withered the strongest of men. He also received a sceptical lifting of an over-plucked eyebrow from his mother-in-law.

The atmosphere in the car after they'd dropped Rita off at home was deadly. Tony had no intention of speaking. He knew Amanda was cross with him, so it was just a matter of waiting until she'd calmed down enough to spit out the words in the right order.

Inevitably she did. 'What the hell did you think you were doing back there?' she hissed. 'After all the softening up I'd done you just waded in and blew it all away.'

He decided to be honest, which was a dangerous thing to do, but he was past caring. 'I don't want your mother looking after Hattie. If you really want to know, I don't ever want her to take care of my daughter.'

'What!'

'You heard.'

'I don't believe I'm hearing this.'

'You did ask. And you'd better believe it.'

They drove on in silence for a further mile and as they approached the small bridge over the canal Amanda found her voice once more. 'Are you serious, or are you just annoyed with her? I know the pair of you don't exactly get on.'

What an understatement! 'I'm serious. I want Hattie to be with someone who is genuinely fond of her. Your mother clearly isn't. She would only be doing it out of a sense of duty, which is never the right motivation to do anything.' He of all people knew how true that was.

Amanda was stunned. 'Well, that's that then. We shan't be able to go. Unless . . .'

'Unless what?'

'Unless Maria von Trapp would do it.'

'Who?'

'Kate, of course, who else.'

'No,' he said firmly. 'Absolutely not. We've imposed on her enough. You're not to ask her, it wouldn't be fair.'

They remained silent for the remainder of the journey.

Amanda stared out into the blackened fields. She was furious with Tony, but was determined not to be cheated out of her weekend of indulgence; she knew very well that she *would* ask Kate. Probably tomorrow. She would buy some flowers and pop over as she had this morning.

When they reached home they found Kate in the sitting-room reading. She was alone.

'Alec didn't show, then?' Tony said, his spirits lifted by the sight of Kate.

She stood up. 'No, he had some work he wanted to do on the computer at home.'

Amanda flopped into a chair. 'These shoes are killing me,' she said bad-temperedly. She kicked them off and rubbed her aching feet.

'Everything all right with Hattie?' Tony asked.

'No problem. She was fine.'

'Good. That's great. I'll see you out.'

He led her to the hall and as she reached to open the door he did exactly what he'd planned to do while sitting in the restaurant – he placed his hand over hers. 'Here, let me get that for you, it can be awkward at times.'

For a fraction of a second their hands were together and knowing that he had no more than a moment to ensure the final part of his plan was carried out he opened the door, said good-night and quickly kissed her cheek.

– A kiss that was as innocent as a neighbourly debt of gratitude.

– A kiss that was as guilty as a lover's act of adultery.

He watched her cross the courtyard in the darkness and as she let herself into number five she turned and glanced back at him.

He gave her a little wave and knew that he had to touch her again. Once wasn't enough.

But then he'd known it wouldn't be. He'd merely been fooling himself that the fantasy could be disarmed so easily.

25

Dear Cara,

Synopsis of A Casual Affair

The story so far!

Our heroine, Clare (aged twenty-eight and as feisty as a Tabasco sandwich) is bored with her going-nowhere job with a large insurance company and on the point of handing in her notice when her boss obligingly drops down dead. A replacement is quickly found who turns out to be Miles – thirty-something, attractive-ish but shy, unmarried and, according to the office gossip on the third floor from where he's been plucked, sexually inexperienced, with a preference for putting all his energy into his work rather than chasing women. Clare immediately sees the potential her new boss can offer her and, into scheming overdrive and with designs not just on promotion but on Miles, she decides that a casual affair with him would be as good a way as any to relieve her current boredom and further her career. But attracting Miles's attention proves to be more difficult than she imagined.

Hope this meets with your approval, Cara.

Best wishes,

Copy to Piers Lambert.

Jessica printed three copies of the letter – one for Cara, one for Piers and one for her file – and when she'd signed them and addressed the envelopes she looked out of her study window, over to Josh's house and wondered if she was using the wrong deodorant.

It was now a week since Tuesday night and she had the sneaky feeling that, like Clare's new boss in *A Casual Affair*, Crawford – the slimy toe-rag – was ignoring her; there hadn't been so much as a call or a visit from him.

Well, let him ignore her.

What did she care if he had decided that she was the last person on earth with whom he wanted to spend any time?

Unfortunately – and this was the annoying part – she did care. Oh boy, she cared. Josh Crawford, she had come to the conclusion, with his sexy smile and neat bum, had seemed an ideal antidote to the malaise that Gavin had left her with.

Put like that, it did seem a bit calculating to have viewed Josh in such a way, so perhaps it served her right that things had turned out the way they had. But what the heck, it was all hypothetical now anyway. Clearly Josh wasn't the slightest bit interested in her.

She lowered her gaze from his house and let it rest on the card on her window-sill. It was a familiar picturesque view of the harbour at Kassiopi: fishing boats and pleasure craft were neatly lined up around the small quay, and in the background shops and tavernas with stripy awnings were bustling with sun-tanned tourists, and above the jumble of pastel-painted buildings the sky was an unbelievable shade of blue.

But then the card itself was pretty unbelievable.

It was from Gavin. And all that was written overleaf, apart from her address, were the words – *Wish you were here, missing you something rotten. Come back!*

Yeah right! And just who did he think he was kidding? had been her initial response to this unexpected communication.

Did he really think that a few scribbled words would have her leaping on the next available flight to Corfu?

Did he truly imagine her sitting in England, sad and lonely, strumming her fingers to the beat of her aching heart?

She looked down and caught sight of her fingers playing over the desk. She snatched up her hand and frowned.

She was not sad.

She was not lonely.

And she certainly wasn't longing for Gavin – any more than he was longing for her.

Not in her wildest dreams did she think it remotely possible that if she were to go back to Corfu she would find a heart-broken Gavin wasting away, yearning for her.

Fat chance of that! More likely she'd find him busy rubbing sun-tan oil all over the sleek, man-made body of Silicone Sal. And if not her, then some other beach babe.

But deep down, somewhere deep in the dark, romantically candle-lit recesses of her childlike gullibility, where she still wanted to believe in fairies and Father Christmas, she also wanted to believe in Gavin. She wanted him to be missing her, for him to have come crashing to his senses and realise what he'd lost.

At the sound of a car she glanced out of the window and saw Josh's midnight-blue Shogun sweep into the courtyard, followed by a flashy open-top sports car, the engine of which gave off an impressive and satisfying throaty roar as it came to a stop. Very nice, thought Jessica. She watched Josh get out of his car, then the other driver as he emerged from his. He held a briefcase in one hand and a small brown paper carrier bag in the other – which, with its tell-tale splodges of grease, made it look suspiciously like a take-away. Whoever it was who was dining at 1 Cholmford Hall Mews that night, he was slightly shorter than Josh, but equally good-looking and as well-dressed, but in marked contrast to Josh's usual black attire he was wearing a vivid orange-and-green check shirt with a light-coloured suede jacket hanging off one of his shoulders.

The thought of the tasty meal that Josh and his friend were about to tuck into made Jessica leave her study and go in search of something to eat for herself.

She suddenly realised that she was famished and as she began rooting through the near empty fridge for some kind of culinary inspiration – she really must get into the habit of shopping more regularly – she thought of the supper Josh had cooked for her.

He really had gone to a lot of trouble that evening – and not just in the kitchen. In her experience single men rarely reached for the Pine-O-Fresh without there being an ulterior motive behind such an out-of-character activity, namely that of luring a woman upstairs and into their beds.

So why the sudden red light that night?

One minute they had been on the verge of a repeat performance of their *après* Tony and Amanda dinner-party session – except this time she had planned on being a willing participant – and the next Josh had been up on his feet saying it was late and that he had an early start the next day.

It didn't make sense.

Unless it had all been a deliberate ploy to get his own back on her for having messed him around previously. Had he played dirty to prove a point with her? No girl teases Josh Crawford and gets away with it. Had that been his game?

Could he really be that proud and petty?

Charlie was worried about Josh. Which was why when they had finished work he had suggested that they pick up a take-away and spend the evening together.

Not since Josh's illness had been diagnosed had Charlie seen his brother so low and despondent. There was an awful emptiness to him that concerned Charlie. The past few days had been particularly bad, with Josh seemingly distancing himself from those around him. He had become morose and deeply withdrawn, punctuating his moody silences with a level of cynicism that was cruel and barbed, and aimed at anyone who got in his way.

Yesterday at work, Charlie had found Mo in a full-blown tearful strop. 'I only asked him if he was okay when I took him in a cup of coffee,' she'd told Charlie, 'and he bit my head off. He can make his own coffee in future.'

Charlie knew that not only did Mo have a soft spot for Josh, but that under normal circumstances she wouldn't have thought twice about blasting off at him for treating her in such a way, but since his illness had become general knowledge at work she, like everybody else, had tended to shy away from speaking her mind. 'What's got into him?' she'd asked Charlie, when Josh had gone to Failsworth to check on a lost delivery and had given everybody the chance to come out from hiding for a couple of hours.

'I wish I knew,' he'd said in answer to Mo's question.

More than anything, Charlie wished he knew exactly what was going on inside his brother's head. Which was why he was here now. He had no intention of leaving until he'd got to the bottom of what was making Josh so unbearable at work.

'Another beer?'

Charlie looked up from his lamb korma. 'I'll get them,' he said.

He was almost on his feet when Josh said, 'Sit down. This is my sodding house and if I'm offering you a drink I'll bloody well get it myself. Okay?'

Charlie watched Josh limp across the kitchen and open the fridge. When he came back to the island unit he handed him a can of Budweiser. Charlie took it and experienced the urge to smash the can into his brother's face. Appalled at the level of anger he felt for Josh, he wondered if their lives would ever be the way they used to be. But then they couldn't be, could they? Josh could never be the man he had been. It was unfair and selfish to expect that of him. Charlie wasn't proud of himself for thinking it, but he didn't know how much longer he could put up with his brother's mood-swings.

They continued their meal without speaking, each forking up his food and washing it down with the occasional mouthful of beer. Charlie couldn't bear it and in the end he pushed his unfinished plate away. 'I've had enough of this,' he said.

Josh raised his eyes. 'I hope you're referring to your meal because if you're about to start on one of your bloody lectures you might just as well leave now. I'm not in the mood.'

'That's just the point. What kind of mood are you in? You seem to be going out of your way to upset everyone.'

Josh gave an indifferent shrug of his shoulders. 'Can't say I'd noticed.'

Charlie silently counted to five before saying in as calm a voice as he could, 'What the hell's got into you, Josh? Why are you acting like this?'

Josh stood up and went over to the window, which looked out over the courtyard. He saw Jessica moving about in her kitchen. He turned away. 'You just don't get it, do you?'

'All I can see is you intent on punishing everyone else for your MS and if you want my honest opinion on that, I think it sucks.'

'Maybe you're right,' Josh said flatly, 'but you should try having all your dreams taken away from you. Imagine . . . imagine wanting something and knowing you couldn't have it . . . that all that was on offer to you was something so second-rate it wasn't worth having.'

Charlie didn't know what to say. Who was he to make a comment on what Josh had just said? He hadn't had his dreams taken away. He didn't know what it felt like. He hoped he never would. 'Are we talking generally or specifically?' he asked.

'What the hell do you think?'

Charlie had no idea. 'Josh, I'm not a mind-reader, so just cut the crap and tell me what's going on.'

Josh came and sat down. He picked up his can of beer and began turning it round in his hands. 'I'm not sure I understand it myself,' he said. He badly wanted to say what he'd been feeling all this week, but each time he tried to put it into words, even to himself, it only served to fuel his anger and bitter frustration. Ever since that evening with Jessica, when the realisation had hit him that he wanted much more from her than he'd bargained for, he'd felt confused, depressed and demoralised. His low sense of self-worth told him that he couldn't expect a woman like Jessica to be the slightest bit interested in him when he had so little to offer. And supposing she did allow herself to become involved with him, when she knew the truth, how long would it last? How long would it be before she decided she wanted to be with a man who wasn't going to become a burden?

He looked up and saw that Charlie was waiting for him to speak. He suddenly felt sorry for him. Poor Charlie, so keen to help and so clearly out of his depth. Not unlike himself really. 'Do you remember at Mum and Dad's the other Sunday,' he said, 'when you asked me if I wouldn't prefer a relationship that was a touch more meaningful than a one-night stand?'

'Yes,' Charlie said cautiously.

'Well, you were right ... and that's the problem.'

'Is this to do with your neighbour Jessica?'

Josh nodded and slipping off the stool, began slowly prowling round the kitchen. When his leg started to ache he stopped in front of the window and stared out across the courtyard. Charlie came and joined him.

'So what's the problem?' he asked. He now had a pretty good idea what was going through Josh's mind, but he wanted his brother to go through the process of actually explaining it to him.

'Like I said to you that day, what's the point in me getting into a serious relationship, or even considering one? What could I offer Jessica?'

'Quite a lot, I should think.'

Josh shook his head. 'Maybe a few good years ... and when my health really starts to deteriorate, what then? I'm hardly the pull of the decade, am I?'

'Isn't that for her to decide?'

'I wouldn't want her pity.'

'Is she the pitying kind?'

Josh considered this. He thought of the way Jessica called him Crawford and accused him of having a manner smooth enough to charm the devil. He also thought of her vibrant face and slightly mocking eyes. There was an energy to her that he found exciting. Each time he had been with her he'd been aware of her vitality and her strength of character. 'No,' he said with a hint of a smile. 'No, she's not the pitying kind.'

'Well then, why not give it a go and see what happens? And if it doesn't work out, I guarantee it's because she catches on to what a pillock you are.'

'You reckon?'

Charlie smiled. 'I reckon. Now, when do I get to meet her?'

It was just gone ten o'clock when Josh watched Charlie's car disappear through the archway and for a few moments he stayed where he was on the doorstep, contemplating his brother's pep talk.

Was Charlie right? Was Jessica worth pursuing?

With an evening's worth of beer inside him he decided that there was no better time to find out. He'd go over now and ask her out to dinner later in the week. What's more, he'd be honest with her and to hell with the consequences. If she didn't like the idea of him being a potential cripple, then tough. Humiliation was something he was going to have to learn to deal with.

He put his front door on the latch and started walking across the courtyard, but with each step he took his confidence began to wane.

He was mad. Mad to think that Jessica would be remotely interested in him. He glanced at his watch. Surely it was too late to call on her? But as he looked up, all set to do a quick turn-about, he saw her gazing at him from her kitchen window. *Hell!* Now what? What excuse could he give for going across to see her?

But there was no time to think of anything, her front door suddenly opened and there she was, staring straight at him. She looked as if she was dressed ready for bed. All she had on was a T-shirt emblazoned with the slogan *Wind Surfers Do It Wet And Standing Up.* It was difficult not to stare at her long legs.

'Hi,' she said, aware of his gaze, 'and what brings you here at this time of night?'

'I . . .' He paused, ran a hand through his hair, shifted a little to the right, then back to the left. 'I was just wondering –'

'You were just passing and wondered if I had any sugar, is that it?'

'Not exactly.'

'Coffee, then?'

He shook his head. Oh shit, why was he so nervous? And where the hell was his alcohol-induced confidence when he needed it?

'Well, Crawford, I know I'm a writer, but I'm running out of lines here; you're going to have to help me out.'

He swallowed. Or rather he would have if his throat hadn't dried up – was it from desire at the sight of Jessica's legs, or just plain nerves? 'I wondered whether you'd like to come for a walk,' he said. *A walk!* He couldn't believe he was hearing himself. Was he completely out of his mind? He'd be suggesting a quick jog around the block next.

She stared at him, then up at the night sky. 'Mm . . .' she said, 'the moon and stars look pretty enough. Why not? Give me a couple of minutes and I'll put something on. Come in while you wait.'

He stood in the hall and listened to Jessica moving about upstairs. He stupidly hoped she wasn't putting on too much. Within minutes she was back with him – the T-shirt had been exchanged for a baggy sweat-shirt and her lovely legs had been covered with a pair of jeans.

'You've put your legs away,' he said, disappointed.

'And you've been ignoring me all this week.' She shut the door behind them and led the way across the courtyard. He struggled to keep up. She turned and faced him. 'Sorry, was I going too fast?'

'Yes,' he admitted, 'and I haven't been ignoring you.'

'So where have you been? I tried several times to thank you for dinner last week, but each time I knocked on your door there was no answer. In the end I shoved a note through your letter-box.'

'I got it, thanks. There was no need, though.'

'Yes there was. You went to a lot of trouble.'

'Not really.'

'Are you going to dispute everything I say?'

He didn't answer and they carried on without speaking. The night was warm and very still, and as they approached the copse, bone-dry twigs crackled noisily beneath their feet and the moon shone down on them, intermittently lighting their way as it filtered its silvery brightness through the leafy branches of the trees. It wasn't long before Josh's leg was giving out on him. He needed to rest and spying a fallen oak, he grabbed Jessica's hand and pulled her towards it.

'So,' she said, sitting beside him on the moss-covered trunk and drawing up a knee to rest her chin on.

'So?'

'So, why are we here, Josh?'

He shrugged. 'I fancied a walk and thought you might like to join me.'

'And is this something you do a lot of, nocturnal wanderings?'

'Not really. I just wanted the opportunity to talk to you.'

'Aha, in that case, I'm all ears.' She lowered her leg and turned to face him, her eyes flashing with that mocking humour he had come to know. 'Fire away.'

He cleared his throat, ready to launch himself into what he had to say. *See, here's the situation: I'm thirty-seven, not unattractive – so I'm told – I'm financially solvent. I have my own home and car, and a more than healthy interest in sex – especially with the right partner. The only downside is that there's a strong possibility that I'll be a dead weight hanging round your neck within a few years. So how about it? How about you and me getting it together?* Oh sod it! He couldn't do it. 'Will you have dinner with me again?'

A slow smile crept over her face. 'Yes. But on one condition.'

'What's that?'

'That you stop messing about and make full use of the romantic opportunity offered here beneath the stars and kiss me. I've waited long enough.'

He laughed out loud, and as his laughter drifted away into the darkness, it was as if all the tension of the past week went with it, as though if he watched closely, he would see the bits of himself he hated and despised being cast into the night sky. If there was one thing he had come to realise in the short time he'd known Jessica it was that when he was with her, she had a fantastic effect on him. Her sense of fun was wonderfully recuperative.

'I'm waiting.'

'Are you coming on to me, Jessica?' he asked with a smile.

'Certainly not. I just want a kiss.'

'And would this be for research purposes?'

'It might be.'

'Well, we'd better get it right, then, hadn't we? What kind of kiss did you have in mind, exactly?'

'Let me see what you've got to offer.'

He gave her a chaste peck on the cheek.

'Sorry, but I don't write that kind of novel. My readers expect a little more from my romantic heroes.'

He moved closer and kissed her lightly on the lips.

'Better, but I was hoping for something a little more melt-in-the-mouth, like the other night.'

'You should have said.' He held her face in his hands and gave her a long, deep kiss. 'Now was that more what you had in mind?'

'I'm not sure,' she said breathlessly. 'Could you run it by me one more time?'

He did, and as their mouths came together, he slipped one of his hands under her sweat-shirt. He felt the tremor in her body as he found her breast and her instant response to his touch exploded within him. With only one thought in his mind, he very gently began pushing her backwards. But he'd forgotten what they were sitting on and the next moment they were lying in a heap on the soft bedding of leaves and ferns the other side of the fallen tree. Their happy laughter filled the dark copse and after they'd disentangled themselves they sat down again.

Jessica rested her head against Josh's shoulder. 'Why did you give me the brush-off at your place last week?' she asked.

He reached out for her hand and wondered what to say. Was this the bit when he told her the truth?

No. No, he couldn't. Not yet. He couldn't face it right now. He didn't want anything to spoil what he was feeling. 'I didn't give you the brush-off,' he lied.

She raised her head and looked at him. Straight at him. 'You did. You couldn't wait to get me out of your house, my feet didn't touch.'

He flinched at the strength of her directness. 'Okay,' he said, 'you're right.' And determined to give at least part of the truth, he tried to explain his actions. 'I wasn't very subtle that night, was I? I'd planned to get you into bed and suddenly I felt ashamed of myself in the way I'd gone about it. It seemed too contrived . . . and I didn't want it to be like that. I'm not sure I really understand it myself, but I suddenly realised that I wanted something more than what I'd intended to make happen . . . and it had to be something that you wanted as well.' He watched her closely while she took in his words. 'I'm sorry,' he added.

She regarded him with a steady gaze. Then she smiled. 'Crawford,' she said, 'you're a man of surprises.'

Aren't I just, he thought. 'Come on,' he said, 'let's go back, it's getting cold.'

When they reached Jessica's house she let them in. 'Would you like a drink?' she asked. 'Wine, coffee, brandy, or . . .' But her voice broke off as Josh, with unexpected force, took her in his arms, pressed her against the wall and kissed her.

'Or tea?' she managed to say when he finally let her come up for air.

'I'm not thirsty,' he whispered.

'Me neither,' she whispered back. 'Josh, why are we whispering?'

He smiled. 'It's supposed to be romantic.'

'I must remember that.'

'Isn't that what romantic heroes get up to? I thought they only spoke in hoarse whispers.'

'Not in my books, they don't.'

'Oh well, never mind . . . Jessica?'

'Yes.'

He looked deep, deep into her eyes and she felt herself go limp with longing. She watched his Adam's apple bob about as he swallowed.

'Do you think there's any chance that –'

'You've stopped whispering,' she interrupted him, 'does that mean the romantic interlude has passed?'

'No, it means we're on to the serious stuff now.'

'Serious stuff?'

'Yes. I'm about to ask if you'd like to go upstairs.'

'To do what?'

'I thought I could slowly undress that beautiful body of yours and make love to you. But only if you wanted me to.'

'I'd need to think about that.'

'Take your time. I'm in no hurry.'

'Would there be much kissing, like just now?'

'Comes as standard.'

'Caresses?'

'Lots.'

'All over?'

'Definitely.'

'Of the light-as-a-butterfly's-wing variety?'

'Lighter.'

'Pounding hearts?'

'Like steam hammers.'

'Gasps of pleasure?'

'Loud enough to wake the neighbours.'

'Bodies as one?'

'A perfect synthesis of intimacy.'

'Soaring high as a bird?'

'Spinning into orbit.'

'The "Hallelujah Chorus"? I would have to insist on that.'

'It's yours, followed by the *1812 Overture*.'

'With cannons?'

'Fireworks as well.'

She smiled. 'You paint a tempting picture.'

'And your answer?'

'Oh, the answer was always going to be yes.'

The Middle

26

Kate stared and stared at the small white stick in her hand. What she had suspected since the August Bank Holiday, just over a week ago, was now confirmed. She was pregnant.

Pregnant!

She hugged the secret to her. She hadn't shared with anyone the thought that she might be pregnant; not Caroline, not Jessica, not even Alec.

Definitely not Alec.

But now she would have to. Tonight, Alec would be arriving back from his week away at the Birmingham trade fair. He had wanted her to go down with him, but knowing that Melissa was going to be there, too, she had cried off – staying in the same hotel as Melissa for a whole week was not something she had any desire to do. Instead, she had stayed at home and mentally ticked off the days on the calendar waiting for the first possible opportunity to use the pregnancy test kit that she had already sneaked into the house.

She continued to gaze at the little white stick and despite the sense of foreboding about breaking the news to Alec, a warm feeling of euphoric happiness crept over her. Her greatest wish had been granted. She wanted to leap in the air, clap her hands, even dance a little jig round the kitchen, and she would have done exactly that if the phone hadn't rung. She skipped across to it and snatched up the receiver. 'Hello,' she said, hoping that it was Alec – while he'd been away he had called her at least twice a day.

But it wasn't, it was Melissa. 'Kate, I haven't got long, it's unbelievably busy here, but over breakfast I spoke to Alec and he suggested I talk to you. Have you got your diary to hand?'

'It's in the study, hang on a minute.' Light-headed with happiness, Kate went through to the study. *I'm going to have a baby*, she chanted delightedly to herself. She found the diary Alec always kept on his desk and picked up the phone extension. *I'm going to have a baby!*

'Melissa, are you there?' *I'm going to have a baby.* How wonderful it would be to let the words trip off her tongue.

'Yes, I'm still here. Now flick through to 22 November. It's a Saturday, are you both free?'

A baby! Her very own baby! 'Yes we are.'

'Good. I'm giving a dinner party for Alec that night, seeing as it's a special year for him.'

Kate froze. 'Special,' she repeated. 'What do you mean?'

'Good Lord, Kate, don't tell me you've forgotten that it's Alec's fiftieth birthday on 15 November. Surely you're doing something for him? I deliberately chose the following weekend because I thought you would be organising some kind of party on the actual day.'

Kate was mortified. Alec's fiftieth! How could she have made such an oversight?

'Clearly you had forgotten. Anyway, I must go, Alec and I are having lunch with some Japanese distributors.'

Kate replaced the receiver and sank into the chair in front of the desk. She was devastated, not because she hadn't given Alec's birthday any thought, but because Melissa had. The ex-wife of the man she loved – *the father of her child* – had shown her up, had pipped her to the post good and proper.

And what was more, she hated the idea of *Alec and I are having lunch.* Breakfast, too.

She should have gone with Alec to the trade fair. He had wanted her to go and she had let him down, preferring instead to stay selfishly at home nursing the possible gestation of her greatest desire.

So now what? What was she to do? Pretend that she'd arranged a party all along? And if so, whom should she invite?

She decided to go next door and see Jessica. She would know what to do.

Throughout the summer, she and Jessica had formed a strong friendship and when her writing wasn't going well they would go for long walks. Some days it was just the two of them, occasionally it would be Oscar. When he was with them they would put a picnic together and Jessica would tell him they were going exploring. She knew the surrounding area well and had taken them on some wonderful walks, but her favourite route was along the banks of the canal. It had become Oscar's favourite place to potter as well, especially if there were any passing boats to watch. Invariably he would be too tired to walk all the way back to the house and they would take it in turns to carry him home.

But it wasn't just during the day that she and Jessica got together. Now and again, they would go out as a foursome; she and Alec, and Jessica and Josh. Only the other week, Alec had commented to Kate that he thought their neighbours made a great couple. Kate thought so too. Jessica's sharp wit, which might have threatened and undermined another man, was always met with an equal measure of mercurial humour from Josh. But there were times when Kate felt there was another side to Josh's character: a more intense facet of his make-up that she suspected was only glimpsed when his guard was down. On one of their recent evenings out together she had noticed that Josh had been unusually quiet and that his normally handsome face had borne an expression of painful weariness. At the time she had put it down to tiredness, knowing that he had just spent a hectic week down in London, but a few days later when they'd all been having a drink at Jessica's she had seen the same exhausted countenance. She wondered if he was working too hard, was maybe under a lot of pressure.

But Josh's problems were not hers to solve. She had enough of her own.

She went back to the kitchen, tidied away the pregnancy test kit and called on Jessica. 'Is it a bad moment?' she asked, when Jessica let her in. She was always wary of disturbing her when she was working.

'Your timing couldn't be better. I'm getting nowhere with chapter eleven so a distraction is perfect. Fancy some fresh air?'

They took the path towards the copse, then set off in a south-easterly direction between recently harvested fields of corn. Though it was September and the midday sun wasn't as high in the cloud-dotted sky as it had been a few weeks ago, it was still warm enough to make Jessica strip off her sweat-shirt and tie it round her waist. 'So what's eating you?' she suddenly asked.

Kate looked up. 'Oh dear, is it that obvious?'

'Sure is. The long face is a dead give-away.'

'I've just let Alec's ex-wife get one over me,' Kate said miserably.

'Go on.'

'And what's worse, it was through my own selfishness. I've been so preoccupied with myself these past weeks I'd forgotten all about Alec's birthday.'

'And Melissa remembered?'

Kate nodded.

'Oh dear, well that certainly sounds like a life-threatening situation. I mean to say, you forgot and she remembered. Wow! Sorry, but I can't see what the fuss is all about. She was married to the man for goodness knows how long, she's going to have the date permanently etched on her brain.'

'It gets worse. It's his fiftieth.'

'So?'

'It's special. Melissa's doing a dinner party for him to mark the occasion.'

'Mark the occasion, my foot! She wants to rub his nose in the fact that he's getting on.'

'He's not getting on,' Kate said defensively.

'Sorry, I could have put that better, but you know what I mean.'

'I think she's done it to make it look as if I don't care about Alec. That I'm not up to the job.'

Jessica could see the distress in Kate's face and knew that it was real enough, but in all honesty she doubted whether there were many women who would go to so much trouble just to undermine their ex-husband's new partner. Over the summer, she had got to know Kate sufficiently to realise that at times she allowed her insecurity to get the better of her. 'Alec knows how you feel about him and that's all that matters,' she said.

'But it's not enough, is it? It's not just a case of pleasing Alec, I've got to prove myself to Melissa.'

'Oh come on, Kate, think about what you've just said; it's ridiculous.'

'No it's not and I have thought about it – there are times when I think of nothing else. Proving ourselves is what all second wives and girlfriends have to do. We're constantly having to compete with the wretched person we've replaced; it's all part of the bloody awful triangle.'

Jessica had never heard Kate swear before. The mild-mannered Kate whom she knew rarely broke into anything more vitriolic than a sneeze.

Clearly something was wrong. 'Ever thought that it might be the other way around?' she suggested.

'You mean Melissa competing with me?' Kate shook her head. 'You've never met her, she's not the type to need to prove herself. She's so confident and together.'

'You sound like you're frightened of her.'

'I'm terrified of her . . . and jealous. I'm convinced that if she ever wanted to make a play for Alec she could do so.'

'And so what if she did? From what I've seen of you and Alec he's potty about you, his eyes barely leave your face and I've noticed how he struggles to keep his hands off you when we've been out together. It's like being with a couple of teenagers.'

Kate blushed. 'But supposing Alec's only infatuated with me, supposing it's not love at all?'

Jessica needed time to think about this. Were Kate and Alec having problems? Was that why Kate was so edgy? And if so, what sort of advice should she be offering?

They had come to the end of the footpath that crossed the open fields and they now had to climb over a stile and join another path, which led down to the canal and would eventually wend its way to Willow Cottage.

'You haven't answered my question,' Kate said, as she stepped over the wooden stile.

'I haven't because I'm trying to work out what's behind this sudden loss of confidence in your relationship. It can't just be that Melissa has decided to treat her ex to a meal; you've told me yourself there are endless family get-togethers, so why is this one any different? You sure there isn't something else that's bothering you?'

Bothering was not the word for it. Kate could hardly believe that only an hour ago she had been thrilled to bits knowing that she was expecting a baby, but then Melissa, straight out of the blue, had phoned and like a bird of prey had swooped down on her and plucked her happiness right out of her hands.

Except she knew in her heart that wasn't really what had happened. Melissa's call had simply tugged on one of the slippery silk ribbons that held her and Alec's relationship together. With startling clarity she now saw that it wasn't, as she'd always thought, Melissa who held the key to her happiness, it was Alec. How would he react when she told him about the baby? If he was only infatuated with her then their relationship was over – he had made it very clear that he wasn't interested in having any more children. Only a man who truly loved her would stick with her in the circumstances.

'I've just found out that I'm pregnant,' she said, 'and I know that Alec is going to hate the idea of being a father again.'

'Ah,' Jessica said, 'well, cheer up, just think, that's one hell of a birthday present Melissa can't give him.'

Kate tried to laugh, but she couldn't. 'I was so happy when I found out, but now I'm frightened how Alec will react when I tell him. He'll be furious. He might even want me to get rid –'

'I doubt that very much,' cut in Jessica. 'Most men hate the idea of babies littering the house, but when confronted with the reality of the fruits of their loins they usually manage to step into the role of proud father without too much persuasion. Mark my words, Alec will be as proud as anything. There's great kudos involved when an older man starts begetting wee ones. There's nothing like an offspring to prove a man's virility.'

Kate looked up hopefully. 'Do you really think so?'

Jessica smiled. 'Not for sure, but it sounds about right, doesn't it?'

They were now walking along the tow-path of the canal. It had rained the day before and the ground, in parts, was damp and slightly soft underfoot. Everything looked lush and green. Tall, upright stems of ragwort leant casually over the bank as if, while nobody was looking, the vibrant yellow flower-heads were trying to catch their reflection in the still water. Red clover speckled the long tufts of grass and the occasional bee staggered from flower to flower with its heavy load of nectar. Seeing a straggly bush of blackberries, Jessica came to a stop and helped herself to a handful of fat juicy berries. 'Mm ... beautiful,' she said, when she'd tasted one. She offered her hand to Kate. 'Eat up, you'll need all the vitamin C you can get from now on.'

'I'm going to need more than vitamin C to get me through the ordeal of telling Alec about the baby,' Kate said despondently. She started to cry. 'Oh dear, you must think me very silly.'

'Nonsense, you're at the mercy of your hormones, you're allowed to cry over the slightest of things, spilt milk even. Dare I ask how it happened? I assume at least one of you was doing something to prevent this happy event ever taking place.'

'I've never liked taking the pill and the idea of a coil makes me cross my legs, so it was down to Alec. I guess something just went wrong.'

'Well, at least he can't accuse you of being deliberately careless, not unless he thinks you're not above sabotage, you know, sticking pins into certain things behind his back.'

Kate wiped her eyes and almost smiled. 'But you do see the problem, don't you? Alec is so against us having a family, he's had one ghastly child and the thought of another like Ruth must terrify him. How do you think Josh would react if you were to tell him you were pregnant?'

Jessica gave a loud snort of laughter. 'Josh and I don't have that kind of relationship.'

Kate frowned. 'You mean you don't ... you don't ...'

'Oh we have sex right enough. No, I just meant that our relationship is very different from what you and Alec have.'

'What do you mean?'

'Good question,' Jessica said thoughtfully. What exactly did she and Josh mean to each other? There was no doubt that they got on well together, more than that, there were times when she felt so close to him it was as if she'd always known him. He was fun to be with and she respected his quick and alert mind. He was urbane and erudite, and had rapidly gained her respect. And since that day in July when they'd gone for a late-night walk in the copse, he had proved to be as good in bed as he was in the kitchen – two qualities, in her opinion, no woman should ever underestimate when choosing a partner. It amused her to think of Josh on that unforgettable night when they'd first made love. He had been so nervous when she'd opened the door to him – she'd seen less nerves in a dentist's waiting-room. His awkwardness had touched her and had made him utterly irresistible, prompting her in the woods to demand a kiss from him. But by the time they'd made it to the bedroom his nervousness had vanished and he'd made love to her with a gentle skill that made Gavin's technique seem more like a Grand Prix driver racing round the track of her body, hell-bent on clocking up as many erogenous zones as possible on his way to the finishing line – which at the time had been breathtakingly exhilarating, but which now appeared to be a little lacking compared with Josh's more loving approach. In short, sex with Gavin had left her wanting more, whereas sex with Josh left her feeling wonderfully content.

And quite apart from any physical compatibility between them, she had come to value Josh's opinion, to such a degree that she had actually allowed him to read a few chapters of *A Casual Affair*, something she had never done in the past with anyone – an unfinished manuscript was such a fragile and vulnerable thing. But Josh had been awarded special status in this respect. The question was, why?

Especially when, just recently, she had begun to feel a little uneasy about their relationship. He rarely invited her over to his house these days, saying that he preferred to come to her, and often he would arrive straight from work and cook them supper while she finished off what she was doing. And whenever they made love – and they did frequently – it was strange, but he never stayed the night.

If she wanted to be objective about his behaviour she would say that Josh was a man who had to compartmentalise his life, as though anything he did with her had to be completely isolated from anything else he chose to do, which probably meant that no matter how close they became, there would always be a part of Josh that would remain shut to her.

But if she wanted to be subjective she would say that Josh was turning out to be just like Gavin – allergic to commitment.

And like Gavin, Josh was showing signs of being unreliable. On several occasions in the past couple of weeks when they had arranged to go out, he had backed out at the last minute. On one particular evening somebody from work, possibly a secretary, had called to say that he was sorry, but he'd been held up in a meeting, which was likely to go on for quite a few hours yet.

It didn't take a fool to wonder if Josh was leading a double life. Heaven forbid, but the situation had the signs of a Gavin and Silicone Sal scenario stamped all over it.

What was it with men? Why did they always have this need to cheat and double-cross?

And why hadn't she kicked Josh into touch yet?

Well, because if she was honest she was intrigued to see how long he thought he could go on fooling her, and so long as she didn't get herself too emotionally involved – whatever that might mean – she was sure that he wouldn't be able to hurt her in the way Gavin had.

And, so much for the lying, cheating wretch in Corfu who was supposedly *missing her something rotten,* she'd not heard another peep out of him since that postcard back in July.

Realising that Kate was still waiting for an answer, she said, 'Josh and I are nothing like you and Alec. Commitment is written all over Alec's face. As the old line goes, Josh and I are just good friends.'

'Do you think it will stay that way?'

Jessica laughed. 'With my track record, yes. I know it's a corny thing to say, but I long for the day when a man will be sufficiently nuts about me to want to spend his every waking moment in my company. The nearest I ever get to being with my ideal man is writing about him. You don't know how lucky you are with Alec.'

But it was the wrong thing to say.

Kate's face crumpled and she started to cry again. 'I know exactly how lucky I am ... that's why I'm convinced that I'm going to lose him.'

27

Josh took off his glasses and flung them down on to the desk. He ran a hand over his face, then rubbed his eyes. He felt dreadful. Like death.

It was only four o'clock and normally he wouldn't dream of leaving work at this time of day, not when he still had so much to get through, but today he would have to – if he left it much later there was a very real danger that he might not be able to drive himself home.

Both his legs felt as though they were on fire; the heat was radiating through his trousers as if he had a fever. It had been going on like this for a few days now, the mornings would start off okay, but by the afternoon the tingling would kick in and the excruciating burning sensation would follow. He'd experienced something similar last year, but nowhere near as bad as this, and certainly not in both legs. Which probably meant his MS was getting a firmer hold on him.

For a short while during the summer he had thought he was on top of the illness. The symptoms had lessened and his energy levels had definitely increased; even his leg had shown signs of loosening up. And certainly his relationship with Jessica had gone a long way to revitalising him, bringing about a resurgence in his confidence as well as a general sense of well-being. For a few wonderful weeks it was as if the clock had been turned back and he was his old self.

But the period of remission – if that was indeed what it was – had been cruelly short-lived. The only warning he got that the holiday was over was a feeling of extreme tiredness creeping over him as he and Charlie had driven back from London after their week at the Earls Court trade show. By the time Charlie had dropped him off at Cholmford his arms and legs had felt heavy and sluggish. He'd gone out that night with Jessica and Kate and Alec, but had been far from good company for them – just trying to join in with the conversation had taken all his concentration. By the time he'd reached the safety of his own house, having fobbed off Jessica with some lame excuse about being tired, he'd crashed out in bed and woken up the following afternoon to find that his co-ordination was all over the place, as was his balance, and when he'd eventually mastered the art of walking upright and without falling over, his feet, which were virtually numb, gave him the sensation that he was walking on thick cotton wool. It had been a grim weekend.

He put his glasses back on and tried to focus his mind on the design specifications for their summer range for the following year. But it was no good. He couldn't concentrate. All he could think of was the agonising pain in his legs and the desire to immerse himself in a bath of icy cold water. He had to get home. He slapped the pile of papers into his briefcase, in the hope of working on them later that night, and got to his feet, then suddenly found himself plunged into darkness.

When he opened his eyes, Charlie was kneeling on the floor beside him. He couldn't see Mo, but he could hear her anxious voice in the background.

'Is he okay? Shall I get a doctor or something?'

He wondered in the confused fog of his mind what a 'something' could possibly be. He tried to sit up, but a hammering immediately set off inside his head. He tentatively touched his left temple where the worst of the hammering seemed to be located and when he looked at his hand it was covered in blood.

'It looks worse than it actually is,' Charlie said at once, handing him his handkerchief. 'Mo, will you go and get the first-aid kit, please?'

When Mo had discreetly shut the door behind her Charlie said, 'What happened?'

'How the hell should I know,' Josh snapped. He pushed Charlie's hands away and got determinedly to his feet. 'One minute I was packing up to go home and the next you're in here acting like Florence frigging Nightingale.'

There was a knock at the door. Mo stepped into the office and handed Charlie the first-aid kit. She tried not to stare at Josh and at the amount of blood trickling down his face. 'I'll put all calls on hold, shall I?' she asked.

'Yes,' said Charlie, 'whoever it is, say we'll get back to them tomorrow.'

When they were alone, Charlie made Josh sit down so that he could assess the damage. 'Like I said, it looks worse than it really is. I don't think you need stitches, but I'm going to put a dressing on it.'

While his brother fussed with antiseptic, squares of lint and plasters, Josh rummaged in the red plastic box for some pain-killers. There was nothing stronger than Paracetamol, so he swallowed four and hoped they might take the edge off not just the pain in his head but the burning sensation in his legs. He tried to reason what could have happened. He must have caught his foot on something and tripped, and head-butted his desk. It was the only logical explanation.

It had to be.

Oh God, please let it be that, he thought desperately. Not black-outs. He couldn't take that. He wouldn't be allowed to drive. It would mean the end of his independence, of everything.

'There,' Charlie said when he'd finished. 'Now what?'

'I want to go home,' Josh said bleakly.

'Okay. I'll drive you.'

Josh felt too awful to argue that he was capable of driving himself. He knew he couldn't, that he was beaten. He even doubted his ability to walk out of his office, never mind make it to the car-park.

They waited until everybody else had gone home, then Charlie helped Josh to the lift and took him down to the ground floor. He went and fetched his car, and brought it round to the front of the building where Josh was waiting for him. They drove out of Manchester, through the rush-hour traffic and down the A34. Neither of them spoke. Josh's head was back against the head-rest, his eyes closed.

When they reached Cholmford Hall Mews, Charlie parked as near to the house as he could. 'Don't try and help me,' Josh said, opening the car door, 'I don't want –'

'Don't be so bloody stupid!'

Too weak to fight back, Josh found himself willingly putting his arm round his brother's neck as he helped him into the house. Just once he looked over his shoulder to see if Jessica had seen him. But there was no sign of her.

Charlie took him through to the sitting-room, where he collapsed, exhausted, on to the sofa. Every bit of him ached, particularly the joints in his legs. The burning sensation had now spread to the rest of his body. He started kicking off his shoes, pulling at his jacket, then the buttons on his shirt.

'What do you need? What can I get you?' Charlie asked, suddenly aware just how ill his brother looked. His face was flushed and tiny beads of sweat were forming on his forehead, his lips were pale and drawn. He looked terrible.

'Run me a bath,' Josh murmured, leaning back on the sofa, his eyes tightly closed, 'a cold one, I'm burning up.'

Charlie went over and touched him. 'Shit!' he said, 'you're right. You sure you haven't got flu?'

'I wish!'

Charlie went upstairs and began running a bath. He stood over it, watching the water gush out from the taps, wishing he could do more for Josh. Perhaps Mo had been right earlier, maybe they should have called a doctor.

When he went back downstairs he found Josh in the kitchen. He was stripped down to his boxer shorts, lying stretched out on the tiled floor, a bag of frozen peas on one knee, a frozen loaf of bread balanced on the other. It was reminiscent of years gone by when at a party they'd both ended up so drunk that they'd crashed out on their friend's kitchen floor, surrounded by a knocked-over vegetable rack. But that had been fun. This was different. This was Josh suffering God knows what.

'It's bliss,' Josh said, when he realised Charlie was there, 'better than sex.'

'You'd better not let Jessica hear you say that.'

'She's a very understanding woman,' Josh said, shifting the bag of peas to his ankle.

'And why, if she's so understanding, haven't you told her about your MS?'

Josh scowled. 'How do you know I haven't?'

'Don't bullshit me! I saw the way you were peering over your shoulder when I helped you into the house. You were terrified she'd see you . . . that she'd see the real you.'

Very slowly, Josh got to his feet. He returned the peas and loaf of bread to the freezer and walked stiffly out of the kitchen, every now and again reaching out to the wall to support himself.

Charlie followed him to the hall and up the stairs. 'Well?' he said, when Josh had immersed himself in the bath. 'Have you told her the truth?'

Josh continued to ignore his brother. He slipped under the cool water. He opened his eyes and through the ripples could make out Charlie's distorted face staring down at him. How easy it would be to finish it all like this one day, he thought. All it would take would be some pills and a bottle of Scotch, and for him to let himself simply sink beneath the surface of what was left of his life.

He closed his eyes and stayed where he was, feeling nothing beyond the stabbing pressure on his lungs. But then he was suddenly being hauled out of the water and Charlie's face, a picture of fury, was glaring at him. 'Don't even think about it, you bastard!' he yelled. 'Just don't even think about it!' There was real anger in his face ... and tears in his eyes.

Bowing his head in shame, Josh coughed and spluttered as his chest heaved at the sudden intake of oxygen. When his breathing had steadied he said, 'I'm sorry. Let's just say it's been a bad week.'

Charlie grabbed a towel and dried his hands and arms, then settled himself on the loo seat. 'With your fondness for irony, I assume that has to be a colossal understatement.'

Josh rested his head back against the bath. 'Look,' he said wearily, 'I've told you before, I don't have any spare energy to try and help you understand what I'm going through. I've barely enough for myself. I'm just trying to learn to cope with this on my own, that's all. I can't keep dumping on you.'

'Well, you just have, big time. How do you think it makes me feel realising you're going through hell knows what and you won't let me help? You can't go on shutting us all out; me, Mum, Dad ... even Jessica for that matter.'

'She doesn't need to know,' Josh said sharply.

'Why? What makes you think you have the right to go round operating on some stupid need-to-know basis?'

'She doesn't need to know because ... because I'm probably going to stop seeing her.'

'What?' Charlie was bewildered. He had yet to meet Jessica, but from what Josh had shared with him he got the impression that she was good for him. Certainly up until the past couple of weeks Josh's mood-swings had levelled out and he'd seemed much better in himself.

'Don't look at me like that,' Josh said, reaching for the plug. He was shivering now and wrapping himself in a large towel he carefully stepped out of the bath, his movements awkward and clumsy. 'Why don't you do something useful like make us some supper? There's a lasagne in the fridge, bung it in the microwave. I'll be down soon.'

On his own, Josh lay on his bed and stared up at the ceiling. His body had miraculously cooled down, but his head still ached. He touched Charlie's dressing. It was sopping wet and fresh blood was beginning to seep out. He breathed in deeply, then exhaled slowly. What was he going to do? And not just about coping with what was happening to him, but with Jessica. Was he really going to stop seeing her?

No, he wasn't. He'd only said that as a knee-jerk reaction to what Charlie was saying.

He had no idea how he'd managed to hide the truth from Jessica for as long as he had. He hated the deception – and himself for what he was doing – and had lost track of the number of lies he'd told her. Not once had she questioned him, not even when he'd let her down. He was ashamed of his selfishness, that by hiding the truth from her he'd tried to ensure their relationship could continue. He covered his face with his hands in an agony of shame, appalled at the depth of his deceit as he recalled the catalogue of lies he'd devised: getting Mo to ring Jessica to say that he was held up in a meeting, when the truth was he'd been having a bad-speech day and had been unable to string more than two words together; backing out of dinner dates at the last minute because some bit of his body had given up on him; and worst of the lot, refusing to spend one single night with her.

That bit of deception seemed particularly hurtful. After making love he would immediately start pulling on his clothes and get ready to leave her. 'Crawford,' she'd said once, 'is my bed not good for anything more than a bonk?' And he had laughed, kissed her good-night and slowly made his way across the courtyard in the dark to the loneliness of his own bed, when all the time he'd wanted to lie next to Jessica and hear the steady rhythm of her breathing and feel the warmth of her arms around him. But he couldn't take the risk of enjoying that particular pleasure because he never knew what he would wake up to. If he had woken beside her and found he was unable to walk properly, or that his speech was slurred, or his hands refused to grip anything, she would have wanted to know what was wrong and the game would have been up.

Not that he saw their relationship as a game, far from it. He was dangerously close to admitting that he cared deeply for Jessica, in a way he'd never experienced before. And to make matters worse, because he'd been so adroit at keeping her at arm's length he had no idea what she really felt for him.

He wished now that he had told her about his MS in the first place. If he'd had the courage at the outset, he wouldn't be in the mess he was in now. But he'd been so terrified of losing her that he'd kept quiet, living each day as it came, hoping that by some miracle there would never be the need to tell her the truth. For he knew that when she did find out the truth it would destroy their relationship. Much as he hated the lies, he had no choice but to carry on with them . . . it was the only way he could be sure of seeing Jessica.

In the kitchen, the microwave hummed its tuneless tune, then pinged intrusively. Charlie finished setting the table for supper and went upstairs to see if Josh was ready. He found him asleep on the bed, still wrapped in the damp towel. Carefully, he manoeuvred it away and covered his brother with the duvet.

Downstairs again, he helped himself to a plate of lasagne. It was only when he'd finished eating that he remembered he was supposed to be somewhere else – having dinner with Rachel. Rachel had joined the firm of solicitors below Crawford's a few weeks ago. She wasn't really his type, but these days it seemed he couldn't be choosy. He reached for his jacket hanging on the back of the chair and pulled out his mobile phone.

Rachel wasn't impressed when he made his apologies and explained that something had come up. He didn't blame her, he wasn't exactly chuffed with the way things had worked out either.

But then, nor was Josh, he suspected.

28

While preparing supper, Kate could hear Alec running the shower upstairs. He was just back from Birmingham. The M6 had been a nightmare and having contended with roadworks and an accident just north of Stafford, he'd finally made it home an hour and a half later than he'd originally told her to expect him. He'd spoken to her several times on his mobile to warn her that he was held up, as well as wanting to pass the time by talking to her.

'What are you doing now?' he'd asked, when he'd called her twenty minutes after their first conversation.

'Talking to you,' she'd said evasively. She couldn't tell him that she was actually standing in front of the hall mirror, sideways on, foolishly checking to see if there was any discernible change in her shape. She had also been trying to work out how best to break the news to Alec.

As she was now.

There were any number of ways of going about it, but she had yet to decide on the right one.

Darling, she could say, *I've got some news.* But that sounded awful, like some trite piece of sit-com dialogue.

Or there was: *Alec, you'll never believe it but I'm –*

That sounded horribly flippant.

Almost as bad as *Guess what, Alec?*

She carried on chopping up pieces of bacon for the carbonara and flung them into the frying pan. She gave them a half-hearted prod with a wooden spatula. Oh, how she sympathised with poor Mary! What must the poor girl have gone through after the Angel Gabriel had paid his little visit and she'd had to wait for Joseph to appear after a hard day's toiling with his chisels – Joseph, trust me, and doubt me not, but behold, I am with child. Joseph, why dost thou look at me with eyes of disbelieving scorn?

She prodded the bacon again and let out a sigh.

'What's that for?'

She spun round at the sound of Alec's voice and forgetting the wooden spatula in her hand, whacked him smack on the chest with it. She reached for the dishcloth but he caught her hand and raised it to his lips.

'I've missed you so much,' he said. He drew her into his arms. 'Promise you'll come with me to the Harrogate fair in February; a week's too long to be without you.'

'I'll do my best,' she said and slipping out of his arms she quickly turned her attention to the pan of spaghetti that was threatening to boil over.

Alec watched Kate moving about the kitchen. Something was wrong. He could see it in her body; the lovely fluidity of her movements was gone. She looked stiff and awkward, like she did whenever Melissa was in the same room as her.

'Did Melissa ring you?' he asked, knowing full well that she had. He helped himself to a handful of grated cheese from the dish next to the cooker, wondering if his ex-wife, with her blunt way of speaking, had upset Kate in some way. He should have phoned Kate himself and not suggested Melissa speak to her.

'Yes, she did,' Kate said, hoping that she could hide behind the conversation she'd had with Melissa until she'd finally summoned up sufficient courage to tell Alec her news.

But as the evening wore on she realised that she was no nearer to making her confession. They ate their meal in the sitting-room with trays on their laps, while watching a Channel Four programme on the changing face of the British work-force. Kate had no interest in it, but Alec was engrossed, occasionally shaking his head and pointing his fork at the television screen in disagreement. 'It's all hyperbole, jingoistic rhetoric of the day. It's common sense that if you pay a man a decent wage he'll do a better job.' He turned to Kate. 'These idiots don't have a clue . . . Kate, are you okay? You haven't eaten a thing.'

She pushed her untouched meal away from her. 'I'm just tired,' she said, 'take no notice.'

Alec put his tray on the floor, reached for the remote control and switched off a fat-cat industrialist expounding on the lack of motivation in your average Brit. 'Kate,' he said gently, 'I know there's something wrong. Is it . . . are you still upset about not doing the teacher training?'

Kate shook her head guiltily. Guiltily because she had lied to Alec. She had been all set to make her formal application to the college when she had begun to suspect that she was pregnant. She had then decided against the course. There seemed no point, not when she would soon have a baby to take care of. She had told Alec that her application had been turned down by the college because she had missed the last date for enrolment.

'You're not upset about Melissa organising that dinner party, are you?' Alec persisted.

She shook her head again, desperately hoping that the right words would magically pop into her head. But they didn't. Instead she blurted out, 'Would you like me to do a party for your birthday? I didn't go ahead and organise anything because I wanted to know what you'd like to do. Not everyone wants a party, do they? And I know that you don't like a lot of fuss. Oh . . . I'm sorry, Alec, but the truth is I forgot all about your birthday. I'm sorry.'

Alec smiled at her kindly, relieved to know at last what had caused Kate to be so unhappy. 'It's okay,' he said, 'I don't particularly want to be reminded of how old I'm going to be.'

'But you're not old,' Kate said vehemently, 'and I love the way you are.'

She suddenly threw her arms around him and hugged him tightly. 'I don't ever want things to change between us.'

'They won't,' he whispered into her ear, 'I won't ever let anything change between us.' Then, pulling back from her, he said, 'And anyway, I've decided what I'm doing for my birthday, I'm taking you away for a romantic weekend. Just the two of us, no family or friends to worry about. Just us.'

Kate buried her face in his neck and clung to him. *Just us.* She couldn't tell him now, not now.

Alec smiled to himself, thinking of his plan to take Kate to Venice, where to mark the occasion of his fiftieth birthday he intended to ask her to marry him, something he should have done months ago. He just hoped she'd say yes.

29

Late that night Tony brought the car to a slow and steady stop. He didn't want to jolt Hattie awake. She was fast asleep in the back and had been so since they'd joined the motorway at Exeter. Amanda was also asleep with her head lolling to one side, but as he opened his door and activated the interior light she stirred. She stretched her legs. 'Good,' she said, 'we're home. At last.'

Her words didn't come anywhere near his own thoughts. He was more than glad to be home. Never before had home been such an attraction. Their last-minute booked holiday – a cottage in Devon – had been nothing short of a lifetime in Purgatory and he'd spent most of the week wishing he were back in Cholmford. The thatched cottage that they had rented had been advertised as being idyllically situated, quaint and cosy. It had been none of these things. It had been cramped, damp and dismal, and had made the tiny terraced house in which he'd grown up seem like a palace in comparison. And with the rain that had poured down almost every day they had been forced either to stay indoors and risk cabin fever, or go out and join the other miserable holiday-makers wandering wretchedly around butterfly farms, cheese-making factories and any other lucrative enterprise that had been set up to entertain bored and depressed tourists too bedraggled to fight back and say to hell with your so-called attractions, I'm off! He suspected that if some local had stuck up a sign outside his garage and declared it to be a Museum of Post-War Horticultural Implements, he and hoards of other suicidally depressed holiday-makers would willingly have got in line to stare at a bench of B & Q garden tools. What was it with people on holiday that made them put up with being taken for such a monumental ride?

He'd expected Amanda to be the first to say she wanted none of it, but some perversity must have taken hold of her because she'd actually admitted to enjoying herself. Extraordinary.

He reached into the back of the car for Hattie. He carried her indoors, up to her bedroom where he carefully removed her sandals and snuggled her into bed. He kissed her forehead. In response she turned on to her side. He kissed her again, unable to resist her warm little cheek.

Downstairs, he found Amanda going through the mail that Kate had thoughtfully placed on the breakfast bar for their return. 'Anything urgent?' he asked, thinking of the present he and Hattie had picked out specially for Kate.

It had been Amanda's suggestion that they go away and also her idea that they ask Kate to keep an eye on things in their absence. 'She won't mind watering a few plants,' Amanda had said. 'After all, what else has she to do all day while Alec's at work?'

In return for Kate watering the patio tubs of geraniums and trailing lobelia, Amanda had suggested that they reward her with a half-pound tin of Devonshire cream toffees. But Tony had had other ideas and had gone shopping with Hattie, and between them they had settled on a hand-painted silk scarf for Kate. They found it in a smart little shop selling quality-produced arts and crafts. He didn't tell Amanda how much he'd paid for the scarf and hoped that Hattie wouldn't attach any significance to his using his Barclaycard rather than cash.

It was picturing the smile on Kate's face when she opened the present that had mainly kept him going during the week. There had been other thoughts that had gone through his head as well during the interminable days of rain and boredom, but he had tried to dismiss them as nothing more than the wild imaginings of a desperate man.

Wild imaginings or not, they had come to him in the long empty nights in that poky cottage where he had no escape from Amanda. Initially he'd tried to resist the powerful images in his head of him and Kate together – whichever way he tried to justify it, lying next to Amanda and wishing that she were Kate was wrong – but in the end, and because it was the only way he could get to sleep, he had given in to the fantasy.

And now he was doing it again, but not in that hole of a bedroom that had mould-spotted wallpaper held up in places with drawing-pins and Sellotape, but lying in their own comfortable bed.

Here it felt even more wrong.

This was their marital bed. This wasn't some anonymous cheap plywood divan and damp mattress that a thousand other unfortunate couples had shared.

Guiltily, he turned his thoughts to something altogether less shameful.

It was Hattie's first day at her new school tomorrow and to surprise her he had specially taken an extra day off work to drive her in himself. He wouldn't hang around, he'd just help her find her new classroom and leave quietly. Once that was done, he planned to take the silk scarf over to Kate, when ... when Alec would be out of the way and Amanda at the supermarket stocking up for the week ahead.

The house was wonderfully quiet and Amanda was revelling in it.

Having taken Hattie to school, Tony was now in the sitting-room reading the newspaper and she was in the kitchen – her lovely, spacious, airy kitchen, at least four times the size of that hateful kitchenette she'd suffered in Devon. She was putting a shopping list together: *Lurpak. Olio Spread. Fromage frais.* But her thoughts soon strayed from Sainsbury's dairy produce to their week in Devon.

It had been an unmitigated disaster. She had never seen Tony so fed-up and she was glad of it. He deserved to be miserable. It served him right for the humiliating weekend he'd put her through last month.

The Arc weekend at Gleneagles – the jolly that she had been so looking forward to – had turned out to be nothing of the kind. There had been none of the manicures and massages that she had imagined, nor any of the elegant dinners enjoying excellent food and interesting company set amid stylish surroundings.

What she'd got instead was a shambles of a doss-house that couldn't provide sufficient hot water for a bath after she'd spent most of each day being drenched and covered in mud – and not the expensive stuff that was so good for the skin.

She shuddered at the memory.

It had been humiliating.

And downright unfair.

Having dumped Hattie on Kate and Alec, much against Tony's wishes but very much in line with Hattie's, they had arrived at the hotel in the depths of the Shropshire countryside, only to find that everyone else had got there at least three hours ahead of them and, judging from their boisterous behaviour, must have settled themselves into the Anne Boleyn bar for most of that time.

The owner of the hotel, not in evidence himself – he was away on holiday in Marbella – was a fan of Henry VIII, and had gone out of his way to share his love of the man with his guests and had named all the rooms accordingly. She and Tony were staying in the Sir Thomas More suite and after they'd unpacked they joined everyone in the bar. Tony introduced her to the other wives, then abandoned her and went and chatted with his colleagues. The women all knew one another and it soon became clear that in the current climate of job insecurity at Arc she was, as Tony's wife, classed as the enemy. One of the wives, a tiny woman with a strong Mancunian accent and the longest nail extensions Amanda had ever seen, asked her which of Agatha Christie's novels she thought most resembled Arc's attitude to its employees. Amanda had said, 'I'm sorry, I've no idea.'

'*Ten Little Niggers*, of course ... *and then there were none.*'

She had laughed politely, but then realised that she was laughing alone. It wasn't a joke.

Embarrassed, she had struggled through the rest of the evening, picking out ominous curly brown hairs from her coq au vin in the Thomas Cranmer dining-room and trying very hard to ingratiate herself with the two men either side of her. She gave up when one of them, no doubt rendered brain-dead from the amount of beer he'd earlier chucked down his throat and which he was now topping up with Piesporter plonk, kept referring to her as Eve.

'Well, Eve,' he said, 'how's that sweet little daughter of yours that Tony's always on about?' He repeated the question a further five times, despite the looks others were throwing him.

She barely slept that night, due to the Thomas More suite being situated directly above the Anne Boleyn bar, the staff of which couldn't have been acquainted with the phrase 'last orders', and in the morning, as they dressed for breakfast, Tony told her what they would be doing that day.

'What?' she'd cried, looking out of the dirty window at the rain beating down on the weed-infested tennis court, making it resemble a large rectangular pond. 'Orienteering? But I haven't brought anything to wear to go tramping through woods.'

'You don't need to worry about that, the hotel specialises in these kinds of activities; they provide boots, waterproofs, everything you could possibly need.'

'The hell they do! I haven't seen anything here that remotely resembles a beauty salon or a personal fitness centre.'

'I did warn you,' he'd said, 'I told you that it wasn't going to be the normal event. In view of the downsizing going on at work, Marty decided that the usual extravagant do at Gleneagles would be inappropriate.'

'And this is appropriate?'

He'd shrugged his shoulders in that pathetic way he did sometimes – you wouldn't catch a man like Bradley Hurst shrugging his shoulders.

'Why didn't you tell me exactly what it was going to be like?'

'I didn't know anything about it. Marty organised the whole thing. It was to be a surprise.'

It was a surprise all right.

She was put into a group with the woman with the nail extensions, whose name was Wendy, along with Marty – the one who had kept calling her Eve the previous evening.

'Right then, Wend and Mand,' Marty said, rubbing his hands together and obviously deciding that in their group he was the only one qualified to take charge. 'This isn't a race exactly, but I want us to get back to base at least twenty minutes ahead of the others. Remember, there are no winners, only losers. Mand, sweetheart, you ever done this kind of thing before? Any good with a compass?'

They'd finished last, which probably was due to the sit-down row she'd had with Marty. Not that he'd seemed to notice. The man had a skin thicker than tarmac and with about as much sensitivity.

'I'm not going any further,' she'd screamed at him, after she'd slipped in the mud for the third time. The rain was pouring off her ill-fitting sou'wester, cascading into her face and streaking what wasn't already streaked of the make-up she'd applied before Tony had broken the news to her. 'I've been out here in this bloody awful rain for over five hours, I'm not taking another step. I've had enough.' And she'd thrown herself down on the muddy ground and added, 'You'll have to carry me back.'

'Hey, Mand, sweetheart,' Marty had said, adopting a let's-be-reasonable tone of voice and squatting down beside her, 'this is the bit where you have to apply your mind. Your body's tired and is attempting a mental coup of your brain, you've gotta step right in there and put a stop to it.'

'Balls!'

Wendy had laughed out loud. 'That's what I like to hear, a bit of plain speaking.'

'And you can shut up as well!'

Wendy ignored her. 'When the going gets tough, it's time for a bevvy.' She leant against a tree, pulled out a hip flask from a pocket and began swigging on it. The forethought of the woman had incensed Amanda even more.

The weekend didn't get any better and by the time they were safely heading for home Amanda had promised herself that, if it was the last thing she would do, it would be to teach Tony a lesson. Of course he'd known what Marty would organise. Wasn't it his job to know what was going on?

So when they'd arrived in Devon last weekend, to find that the cottage they'd booked through the small ads in the *Sunday Times* was little more than a thatched coal shed, she had been delighted. The expression on Tony's face as they'd let themselves in was one to savour.

'It's disgusting,' he'd said, after taking one look at the grimy sofa and coffee-cup-ringed table in the sitting-room that measured less than their *en suite* bathroom. 'We can't stay here. The place stinks.'

'Oh, do you think so?' she'd said, 'I think it's rather quaint.'

As the days slowly went by and the rain came down, she could see that Tony was becoming more and more depressed. Now you know what it feels like, she thought maliciously. This is nothing compared with what you put me through in Shropshire.

Amanda looked down at her shopping list. She hadn't got very far with it.

Which was how she felt about her marriage. Her attempts back in June to try and inject some kind of purpose into her life with Tony had fallen foul of the realisation that Tony was never going to be another Bradley Hurst. He didn't have the killer instinct. All he seemed to care about was Hattie.

Was Hattie happy?

Would Hattie cope with her new school?

Of course she would. That girl, with her uncanny knack for manipulating people, was one of life's great survivors. Just look at the way she could get Kate drooling over her. And as for the way she wound Tony round her little finger, well, that was plain sickening – a day off work just to take her to school! Pathetic. Surely he had more important things to be doing. Bradley Hurst hadn't got to where he was by fussing over a devious child.

She finished her shopping list and as she underlined the last entry, she forced herself to swallow the unpalatable truth that the way things were going between her and Tony, their marriage was heading for a fall. What had seemed at the outset to be a marriage of happy convenience on both sides was now proving to be a battleground of silent dissatisfaction. She had accepted for some time that Hattie resented her, and equally so, she resented Hattie. But now she was beginning to feel the same for Tony.

In fact, she felt little else for him.

Tony thought Amanda would never go off to the supermarket. How long did it take to put a shopping list together, for heaven's sake?

He checked himself one more time in the hall mirror. His hair was newly washed, he was wearing fresh clean clothes – he'd spent ages deciding what to put on – and had poured enough aftershave all over himself to knock 'em dead in John o'Groats.

But was it enough to make an impression on Kate?

Well, it was time to find out.

He locked up the house, straightened his collar, cleared his throat and strode across the courtyard. He knocked lightly – in view of what was on his mind, anything louder would have been a flagrant announcement of his intentions.

He waited for her to come to the door.

And waited.

He knocked again, this time slightly louder.

Still no answer.

He looked over his shoulder at the staring windows behind him. His guilt was so palpable he was convinced that if anyone was watching him they would know exactly what he was up to. He was about to give up and accept that maybe Kate was out when he heard a movement from within.

Very slowly the door opened and Kate appeared. She was crying. More than that, her whole body was shaking as tears streamed down her pale face. Something terrible must have happened.

Overcome with concern at the sight of her distress, Tony stepped over the threshold, took her in his arms and closed the door behind him.

30

Jessica was in her study where she was trying to heighten the tension between Clare and Miles. She'd got to the tricky bit in the middle of her first draft of *A Casual Affair*, the bit where there had to be some kind of romantic action going on between her two main characters, and if Clare didn't get Miles to surrender to her charms in the next few pages then the reader was going to get bored and give up on the book – and on Jessica Lloyd.

Jessica knew as well as the next novelist that a loyal reader is the best friend an author can have and that they should always be treated with respect. As Piers had once said to her, 'To short-change a loyal reader is an act of gross stupidity, Jessica. Take care that you're never foolish enough to make that mistake.' It was as basic as knowing that every story had to have a beginning, a middle and an end.

So come on, she told herself as she stared at the blank screen in front of her, it was time for Clare to get tough with Miles. So far Clare had been pussy-footing about with him – casually dropping hints over the photocopier along the lines of there being more to her than met the eye was never going to crash through Miles's shy reserve. She was going to have to come up with something infinitely more to the point, like . . . like cornering him in his office and grabbing him by his insurance bonds.

Jessica laughed, suddenly recollecting the scene in Piers's office when her vivid imagination had run riot and had wondered what it would be like to have its wicked way with her agent across his desk.

Mm . . . she wondered. What if . . . what if Clare tries that?

And what if Miles responds? Unbridled passion across the spread-sheets would certainly hot up the pace.

She started tapping away at the laptop, the scenario in her mind rapidly taking shape.

'Jessica,' came a voice from somewhere beyond the study.

'Yes,' answered Jessica absent-mindedly. In her ability totally to absorb herself in her writing she had forgotten that Anna was spending the day with her and that she was making a start on redecorating the kitchen.

'Isn't it about time for a coffee break?'

Clare and Miles's big moment was put on hold as Jessica left the study and went and joined her mother in the kitchen. Anna was half-way up a pair of aluminium step-ladders and was stripping wallpaper from around the window that faced the courtyard. Jessica watched her pull at a piece of wallpaper; it came away in one long, satisfying piece. She made some coffee and they sat at the kitchen table. It was covered with colour charts and several back issues of *Ideal Home*, which Anna had brought with her to help Jessica choose a new look for her kitchen. Between them they had decided on 'clotted cream' for the walls and 'summer blue' for the skirting and kitchen cupboards – Anna had assured her that sanding down the expensive units and repainting them would be simplicity itself. 'I've seen them doing it on the television, it looks straightforward enough. We'll change the doorknobs as well while we're about it.' Jessica had had no idea how expert at DIY her mother had become. She watched her now as she picked over the biscuit tin hunting for one of the few remaining chocolate bickies.

She was enjoying having her mother around. Since the rockery argument, when Anna had made her feelings about her independence very clear, she had managed to curb the desire to watch over her too zealously. It wasn't always easy, as Anna at times seemed to have a death-wish. She'd recently taken up going to the local swimming baths first thing in the morning and after she'd been boasting about the number of lengths she could notch up in an hour Jessica occasionally made the effort to join her so that she could keep a surreptitious eye on her and make sure she didn't overdo it, especially as her mother had recently bought a black Speedo costume, an obscene-looking rubber hat and a pair of goggles.

Breaking into her thoughts, Anna said, 'I should have the rest of the wallpaper off by tomorrow, then I can make a start on rubbing down the units.'

'There's no need to rush things.'

'No point in not.'

That was the trouble, thought Jessica. Every minute counted to Anna, not a single second was to be wasted. She doubted whether she would ever view life in the same way. It wasn't that Jessica was idle, well, she didn't think she was, it was more a case of having lived such a happy-go-lucky existence for so many years – Corfiotes were not people to rush things – that she tended to take a more relaxed approach to getting things done. Her mother on the other hand was a human dynamo and didn't know how to slow down.

'So how's the writing going?' Anna asked, digging around in the biscuit tin again.

'Not bad, I was having trouble getting the main character and her love interest together, but just before you called me through I found a way round the problem.'

Anna raised her eyes from the biscuit that she was dunking in her coffee. 'And how's Josh? I've not heard you mention him recently.'

Jessica laughed. 'So subtle, Mother dear. I don't know how you do it.'

'Well? How is he?'

'Good question, I haven't seen him for a few days.'

'How many days?'

'Over a week.'

'Mm . . . that doesn't sound good.'

'Thanks!'

'You must face up to these things, Jessica. If he were seriously interested in you he'd be banging that front door down and pulling you by the hair across to his place and . . . well, I think I can safely leave the rest to you. I wonder if he'd consider a more mature woman?'

'Forget it, there's mature and there's downright gone off.'

But Jessica knew that her mother was right. The way Josh had vanished from her life so suddenly hardly gave a girl cause to hope. And yes, she was well aware that she could quite easily go over and see him herself. Or for that matter, she could phone him. But that wasn't the point. It was *she* who had phoned him last, it was now down to him to make the next move. No way in the world was she going to go crawling to him. Her begging days were over. Fool that she'd been, she'd done enough of that with Gavin.

From his bed, Josh gazed out of the window, across the fields and towards the distant lumpy shapes of the Peak District. It didn't seem that long ago since he and Charlie used to go off to Derbyshire for walking weekends – weekends which usually had a habit of turning into long-distance pub crawls. But wallowing in memories never did him any good.

He pushed back the duvet, slowly slid his legs out of the bed and placed his feet firmly on the floor. So far so good. Then, holding his breath, he stood up. That was good, too. Okay, now it was time to move. Still holding his breath, he took a couple of paces.

Yesss! He was mobile.

When he'd lain on the bed last night, his head aching from where he'd struck it at work, the rest of his body had felt as though it would never move again. It was a huge relief to him now to know that this was not the case.

Spurred on, he shuffled over to the wardrobe and knowing there was no chance of him making it in to work that day, he pulled out a pair of black jeans. He considered a shirt, but thought of the buttons and instantly dismissed the idea – his fingers had all the dexterity of a bunch of bananas. He chose a T-shirt instead. Next it was over to the chest of drawers for some socks and boxer shorts, followed by the staggering journey right across the bedroom to the adjoining bathroom. He was exhausted by the time he reached it and leant against the basin for support. But at least he'd made it. By shit he'd made it!

He didn't bother with shaving, but once he'd washed and dressed he stood at the top of the stairs and geared himself up for what today, for him, was his very own equivalent to the downward climb of the north face of the Eiger.

As he'd suspected, when he finally entered the kitchen Charlie was already there and was making breakfast. He'd known that his brother would stay the night, that he would never have left him alone. He was grateful, touched by Charlie's concern, but too much of him was angry at the circumstances in which he found himself to be able to thank him in the way he ought.

'You look better than you did last night,' was Charlie's only comment when he saw him.

'Thanks. So do you.'

They ate in the kitchen. Josh would have liked to have had breakfast outside on the patio in the warm morning sun, but the thought of traversing the entire length of the hall, sitting-room and the two steps down to reach the garden made him settle for where they were.

'I thought I'd hang around here for the day,' Charlie said, 'if that's okay with you?'

Josh shrugged. 'Sure.'

'I've phoned Mo and explained we won't be in. I thought if you were feeling up to it we could go for a pub lunch later on?'

'And maybe a walk afterwards?' The sarcasm in Josh's voice made Charlie throw down his knife.

'Sod it, Josh! I'm just trying to help, that's all.'

Josh buried his head in his hands. 'I know,' he said, 'I know.' He looked up. 'I can't help myself at times. It's like there's more anger in me than I know what to do with. I'm ... I'm sorry.'

'Will you promise me one thing,' Charlie said, his face suddenly earnest. 'What went through your mind in the bath last night ... you ... you wouldn't ever ...'

'What, top myself?'

Charlie nodded.

'I don't think that's a promise I can make ... or perhaps anyone is capable of making. The dark demons of the mind leap out on you when you're least expecting them, a bit like Jehovah's Witnesses really.'

'That's hardly the reassuring response I need, though.'

'Yeah, well, right now it's the best I can do.'

'But you've got so much going for you.'

'Have I?' Josh's voice was expressionless.

'Yes!' Charlie was defiantly adamant. 'There are so many people who care about you and apart from anything else, how the hell would I run the business on my own?'

'You'd manage.' Again the same flat voice.

'But I don't want to run it alone, I want you there with me, or ... or there'd be no point.'

Josh turned away. He couldn't cope with Charlie's honesty. 'Look, can we drop this?' he muttered. 'It's really not helping either of us.'

'And what about Jessica?' Charlie had the bit between his teeth now.

Josh looked up sharply. 'What about her?'

'Last night you said you weren't going to carry on seeing her. Why? Isn't she someone who'd be worth living for?'

'Don't you think I haven't thought of that!' Josh rounded on him.

'Then stop bloody well pissing about and do something. Go over there and tell her the truth. Give her time to think about it and start treating her with the respect she deserves instead of palming her off with all those lies you've been dishing out. Yes, Mo told me about the phone call you asked her to make. I dread to think what else you've been up to.'

Josh stared angrily at his brother. 'Have you quite finished?'

'No!' Charlie retorted, 'no, I haven't.' But as he tried to think of what else he wanted verbally to throw at his brother, he realised that his fury at Josh's stubbornness had suddenly rendered him impotent. He could think of nothing else to say. Nothing that would be of any help. He stood up. 'This is no good,' he said, 'I can't cope with you when you're like this. I'll be at work if you need me.'

Unable to get to his feet fast enough to go after his brother, Josh listened to the sound of the front door shutting, then the unmistakable rumble of Charlie's TVR starting up.

He slowly lowered his head into his hands, saddened beyond measure that he continually treated Charlie so badly.

31

Acting as a shoulder to cry on wasn't exactly what Tony had had in mind when he'd knocked on Kate's door half an hour ago, but it was all he could do in the circumstances.

She had stopped crying now, but was still sitting hunched on the bottom step of the stairs – she'd been there since she'd let him in. In front of her was a half-empty box of Kleenex, beside it, a pile of soggy screwed-up tissues. His present for her was lying unopened on the hall table next to the phone, which she kept glancing at. She was doing so now. 'When he's calmed down, he'll ring, won't he?' she said, her bloodshot eyes filling with tears once more as she hugged her knees to her.

'Maybe,' Tony said softly beside her. From what Kate had told him it seemed pretty unlikely that Alec would call for a few hours yet. 'He needs time to cool off,' he added. He had to admit, though, that Alec's reaction to Kate telling him that she was pregnant did seem a bit extreme. He remembered how he had felt when Eve had told him she was expecting Hattie. It had come as a complete surprise to them both as they hadn't planned on having children so soon. But his reaction had been one of amazement rather than shock. 'How come?' had been his first astonished words. 'Because you've impregnated my body with your sperm, dummy,' had been Eve's response, followed by a smile that had shown him how pleased she was. They had gone out for a meal to celebrate and later they'd made love. 'It won't harm the baby, will it?' he'd asked afterwards, suddenly concerned. She'd laughed and rolled on top of him. 'Honestly,' she'd said, 'men, they know nothing!'

'It takes time for a man to adjust to the idea of being a father,' he said kindly to Kate. He slipped his hand over hers and squeezed it. 'It took me a while really to get to grips with the idea of Eve being pregnant. I was frightened that a baby might come between us. Men can be very insecure when it comes to sharing the woman they love.'

Kate looked down at Tony's hand holding her own. He had nice hands, she suddenly thought. 'How long did it take for you to come round?'

The truthful answer was less than a few days, but the truth wouldn't help Kate right now. 'A couple of weeks,' he lied. 'It might even have been longer.'

'But Alec might never come round to the idea,' she said, staring into the middle distance. In her mind's eye she could see Alec's face earlier that morning; first the shock in it, then the disappointment and finally the anger.

Over breakfast she had summoned up the courage to tell him about the baby. He had been listening to Sue MacGregor and John Humphrys bringing to the nation's attention that inflation was up – or was it down? – and that as a result home-owners would be worse off, but investors would be happier. And I don't give a damn, she'd thought as she'd got up from the table and switched off the radio and faced Alec. She didn't wrap her announcement in any kind of fancy packaging. She simply stood before him and in a matter-of-fact voice that was vaguely reminiscent of Sue MacGregor reading the news she said, 'Alec, I'm pregnant. I know this isn't what you wanted, but I'm afraid it's definitely something I want.'

His eyes were what she noticed first – they suddenly seemed to grow larger; it was the shock, she supposed. Then it was his hands that caught her attention; they stopped what they were doing and came to rest either side of his plate of half-buttered toast, the palms face down as though feeling for some levitational force that was about to start making the table bounce about.

Very slowly he had begun to move. He stood up. Then he spoke. 'You knew I didn't want this. You knew.' The disappointment in his voice was heart-breaking.

But worse was to come when he walked out of the kitchen. He paused in the doorway, turned back to her and said, 'You've used me. Ruth said you would. She warned me, but I wouldn't listen.'

And that was the anger. Scalding, accusative anger, as though she had planned the whole thing.

Within seconds he was gone, the door closing quietly behind him – Alec wasn't a dramatic man, slamming the door would have been too hackneyed. She watched him get into his car and drive away to work.

To Melissa.

She had started to cry then, tears of sobbing heartache that she had been storing up over the weekend. Or was it longer? Had she always known that it would end like this?

It was while she was trying to pull herself together, at the same time clearing up the breakfast things, that she had heard the sound of knocking. At first she'd ignored it. She didn't want to see anybody. But then she'd wondered if it was Jessica and realising that she was the only other person who knew her predicament and that she might be able to help her, she went to the door. But it had been Tony. The details of what happened next were hazy, but she could remember the sense of relief as he'd held her – she hated crying alone and to be able to cry while somebody held her somehow made the hurt seem slightly more bearable. He'd sat with her on the stairs, handed her tissues and listened while she told him what had happened.

'It's over,' she now whispered. 'I know it is. Alec thinks I've done this deliberately.'

Tony put his arm around her shoulders. How easy it would be to manipulate the situation to his own advantage, he thought, to write off Alec and claim Kate for his own. But he couldn't. Kate's distress touched him too much even to consider what had earlier been in his mind. 'Come on,' he said gently, 'let's get you somewhere more comfortable to sit.'

They went into the sitting-room. Kate curled herself up in one of the armchairs in the bay window. He took the chair opposite. He handed her the present which he'd picked up from the hall table. 'Here,' he said, hoping it would provide a temporary diversion, 'open this, it's a thank-you for looking after the house while we were away.'

She carefully unwrapped the layers of cream tissue paper. 'It's beautiful,' she exclaimed, when she saw what was inside, 'but I don't deserve it, I only watered a few plants.'

'Nonsense, of course you deserve it. Hattie and I chose it together. Are the colours okay? We hoped all those different shades of pale green would suit you.' He was conscious that he was speaking too quickly. He so wanted her to like the present.

She nodded and lovingly stroked the silk scarf. 'It's perfect. Thank you. And will you thank Hattie for me? How is she?'

Brief as the diversion might be, Tony was glad that the scarf had brought about a respite in Kate's unhappiness. 'She's fine. Or rather she was when I left her a few hours ago. It's her first day at her new school. I think I was the more nervous of the two of us when it was time to say goodbye. Do you think you'd be up to a visit later when she comes home? She'd love to see you. Children are wonderful for taking your mind off things.' He saw immediately the pained expression on her face. 'I'm sorry,' he said, 'that was insensitive of me.'

She blinked away the threat of fresh tears. 'I've always wanted children,' she said wistfully. 'I'd love a little Hattie of my own . . . you're very lucky.'

'Yes,' he said softly, 'I know I am.' Then before he could stop himself, he added, 'But it didn't always seem that way, not when . . . not when Eve died.' He clenched his hands in his lap. 'I've never told anyone this before, but . . . but I would have willingly swapped them over.' He leapt to his feet. 'Oh God, what does that make me sound like?' He leant against the window, resting his hands on the sill and, needing time to compose himself, he stared through the glass, concentrating his gaze on the jutting shape of Bosley Cloud in the far-away distance.

After a few seconds he slowly turned round and faced Kate. 'I didn't mean that I wanted Hattie dead, it wasn't like that, I just wanted Eve. I wanted her so desperately . . . I would have done anything to have her alive again.' But as he spoke those last terrible words he felt his composure going again. He had to fight hard to overcome the terrible pain that always threatened to engulf him when he thought of Eve's senseless death. 'I've no idea why I'm telling you all this,' he said, his voice low and shaky, 'but I love Hattie more than I thought possible. Maybe it's guilt. Maybe I'm overcompensating for what I once felt.' He cleared his throat and willed himself to finish what he'd started. 'And as a result I know I've made the biggest mistake of my life. I made the error of thinking that Hattie needed a mother more than . . . more than I needed a woman I could love.'

They stared at one another, the room suddenly still with a taut silence.

'I thought so,' Kate said at last.

He was stunned. He sat down again. 'Is it that obvious?'
She didn't answer his question, but said simply, 'What will you do?'
He shook his head and let out his breath. 'I've no idea.'

32

Alec wasn't interested in what Susan Ashton from the warehouse in Oxford had to say. It didn't bother him that the hand-finishing on one of the Christmas card lines was taking longer than originally estimated; for all he cared Susan could have phoned with the news that the entire factory had burnt down and there were no survivors.

All he could think of was Kate.

Why, oh why had this happened?

They'd been fine as they were. Now everything would be different. All the plans he'd had in mind were ruined. There'd be no more romantic dinners together. And there'd certainly be no chance of any romantic weekends away. In fact, experience told him that there'd be no bloody romance at all.

He could remember all too vividly what it had been like when Ruth was born; the whole house had been given over to her. It was the smell he'd disliked most; whichever way he turned there was the smell of drying nappies, sour milk and sickly talcum powder. There was no escape from it.

He'd become a stranger in his own home, unable to walk into any room for fear of disturbing Ruth who might be sleeping there in her Moses basket – it had always seemed absurd to him that such a tiny being not only possessed its own mini-empire within hours of its birth, but was actually given the power to rule and dominate it.

But the trouble had started way before Ruth's arrival in the world: it had begun when Melissa discovered that she was pregnant. Pregnancy hadn't suited her and from day one it had made her tired and crotchety, and she'd been in bed by eight thirty most nights, with sex clearly no longer a viable proposition. After Ruth was born he'd waited patiently for Melissa to wave the green flag. But there was still no sign of affection between them. By the time Ruth was five months old he was beginning to lose hope of them ever having any kind of sex life again. If he gave so much as a hint that he desired her in bed, Melissa would turn away from him. It was only after she had stopped breast-feeding that things improved. But it was never the same.

It had always been his opinion that it was Ruth's conception that had created the first crack in their marriage.

And exactly the same would happen between him and Kate. A child would come between them. He just knew it.

Kate would, of course, deny that anything would change between them, but he knew better. It was all down to nature. Nature dictated that a woman behaved differently the moment she became pregnant. She didn't realise what was going on herself, but very gradually all her thoughts became wrapped up in that small being that was fast taking her over, allowing no room for anything else in her life, or anyone else for that matter. And when the baby was actually born, nature stepped in to ensure it survived by putting its needs first and foremost in its mother's brain. There was no room for any other thought, all nature allowed the mother to think of was providing nourishment, warmth and a safe environment for her child.

And that was another thing nature did – the child was never *their* child, it was only ever *her* child.

Ruth had never been his. His initial clumsy attempts at bathing or dressing her had been mocked and devalued, and had reduced him to the position of onlooker, where his services were only required in the middle of the night when Melissa was too exhausted to soothe a teething Ruth.

He could imagine Kate saying she would never be like Melissa, that she would never make the same mistakes, but in his heart he suspected that she would be worse – she was so very desperate for a child of her own that she probably wouldn't let him have a single look-in. He would be squeezed out. Surplus to requirements.

It had been just like that when Hattie had stayed with them that weekend last month. Kate had spent nearly all her time entertaining the child. Thinking that he mustn't let his jealousy get the better of him he had left her to it and spent most of Saturday and Sunday at work.

'So what do you want me to do, Alec? Give it one more try?'

Susan's insistent voice at the other end of the line forced Alec back to what she was saying. 'I'm sorry,' he said curtly, 'I've got to go. Speak to Melissa about the problem.'

He replaced the receiver and sank back into his chair. Almost immediately the phone rang again. He snatched it up. 'I'm busy,' he barked at the receptionist who'd put the call through. 'I don't want to be disturbed.'

Was there to be no peace for him?

The answer was obviously no, as at that moment his door opened and in walked the very last person with whom he wanted to speak. Hell, she'd love every minute of this, he thought. He watched Melissa drop a batch of sample cards on his desk and for the first time since Tim had arrived on the scene he experienced a wave of angry jealousy about the relationship she had with him. How simple it must be for the pair of them, he thought enviously, there was no danger of a pregnancy to bugger things up because very conveniently Melissa had had a hysterectomy six years ago. And unable to stomach the idea of her gloating, he stood up quickly and pulled on his jacket. 'Whatever it is, it'll have to wait,' he said. He moved towards the door. 'I'm going for an early lunch.'

Melissa stared after him. Something was wrong. Very wrong. In all the years she had known Alec she had only twice seen such a distraught look on his face – when his mother had died and when she'd told him she wanted a divorce. She had never forgotten that sad, wounded expression. She had hurt him so badly and it had taken all her strength to carry out what she had instigated. He had never known how near she'd come to changing her mind that night.

But it had been the right thing to do. She had never since doubted the decision she'd made. She and Alec got on much better as friends and business partners than they had as husband and wife. She still loved him – she always had – and that was perhaps why she had divorced him; if they'd stayed together they might have ended up hating each other and she'd never have wanted that; it had been a case of being cruel to be kind. It had been difficult at times, though, she'd had to adopt a tough veneer to convince Alec that she no longer cared for him in the way she once had. In the early days after she'd moved out, when he'd taken to drinking the lonely evenings away, she'd had to fight back the urge to comfort him. Instead, she had put on what she called her tough bitch act and bossed him about, ordering him to pull himself together. Little did he know that she had spent many a lonesome night worrying about him.

Still, that was all in the past. She now had Tim and Alec seemed to have found genuine happiness with Kate.

Alec was driving much too fast for his car to cope with the country lanes and after coming within an inch of his life on a tight bend and almost smashing his Saab into the back of a tractor he lowered his speed.

He had been driving recklessly and mindlessly for the past hour, but now as he approached the village of Swettenham he decided he needed a break, as well as something to eat. He headed towards the Swettenham Arms. The car-park was large and not very full, and he easily found himself a space.

Inside the pub he was met by the comforting smell of real ale. He ordered a pint of bitter and a steak and kidney pudding, and took his drink over to the only available table. It was in the window, where not so long ago he and Kate had sat. They had been celebrating some kind of anniversary – five months of knowing one another, or was it six? Whatever it was, happiness and contentment had flowed between them as they'd sat wrapped in each other's love that warm, sunny spring afternoon. There had been a small vase on the wooden table containing a single carnation which he had taken out and tucked into her hair – a silly, sentimental gesture which had made them both laugh, as well as the couple sitting close by.

There was no flower on the table today, just a solitary squashed chip left over from somebody else's lunch.

He drank his beer and when his food arrived he found he wasn't hungry. He managed to force a mouthful of boiled potato down but gave up after a feeling of nausea spread over him.

Eating wasn't going to solve his problem. Nor was drinking. He looked reproachfully at the almost empty glass in his hand. He'd already been down that particular road when Melissa had left him. It hadn't worked then. It wouldn't work now.

So what was the answer?

Go home and talk to Kate?

But what good would that do? Talking would only lead to one of them compromising. And again, what good would that do?

If it was he who compromised there was a danger he would always hold it against Kate, that the slightest disagreement between them would be blown out of proportion because he would feel he'd conceded so much to her already.

And if it was she who compromised – could he really expect her to have an abortion? – then he would never be able to look her in the eye again for fear of seeing the most profound bitter regret in her face. And worse would come – her bitterness would turn to pure hatred for what he'd made her do.

Either way, they couldn't win.

He drained his beer, pushed his uneaten lunch away and made himself accept that because of his selfish love for Kate he had almost certainly lost her. There could be no hope for their relationship now.

Caroline was full of fighting talk. 'The bastard! How dare he say that to you? It's he who's used you.'

'Caroline,' hissed Kate, 'keep your voice down, people are looking.'

'Let them,' Caroline said even louder, staring defiantly round at the faces now glancing their way. 'Let them know what a pig he's been.'

'Caroline, if you don't shut up I'll walk out of here.'

Caroline stared at her friend, mystified. 'Well I must say, you seem to be taking this very calmly. Don't you feel angry at the way he's treating you?'

'I'm too confused and upset to feel angry,' Kate said. 'Now please, can we order what we're going to eat and talk rationally.'

When Tony had left her that morning – having made sure that she was over the worst of the tears – she had phoned Caroline to see if she was free for lunch. She had been in luck: Caroline was enjoying a few days off work. The really good thing about her friendship with Caroline was that she never failed to focus Kate's thoughts and make her feel level-headed, and as she'd driven to the wine bar in Knutsford to meet her she had known that within minutes of listening to her friend's over-the-top reaction to her news she would feel composed and empowered.

A good-looking waiter came and took their order, and when he walked away, after Caroline had tried a bit of small talk with him, she said, 'Now, Kate, he's much more what you should have gone after, not some old duffer who's not prepared to take on his responsibilities.'

Kate frowned. 'Alec is not an old duffer, Caroline, how many times do I have to tell you, he's only forty-nine?'

Caroline snorted. 'Whatever you say. So what are you going to do?'

'I think that depends on what Alec is going to do.'

'Well, as to that, I think you'll find he's had his bit of fun, now he'll be off. Mark my words, he'll have you out of that house before you've had your first antenatal appointment. He'll have some kind of legal document drawn up, stating he knows he's the father and here's the dosh for the next X years, then it'll be a case of it's been nice knowing you, ta ta.'

'He might change his mind,' Kate said, ignoring her friend's damning indictment of Alec, and determined to give him the benefit of the doubt she added, 'Tony says lots of men over-react when they hear they're going to be a father.'

Caroline looked up, interested. 'Who's Tony?'

'He's a neighbour and he . . .'

'And he what?'

'He came over this morning when I was doing my hysterical bit. He was very kind.'

'Was he indeed?' smirked Caroline.

'Don't be ridiculous,' said Kate, but despite herself she couldn't prevent her face from colouring as she thought of Tony. She recalled his hand on hers and the way he'd comforted her. When he'd started talking about his problems she had felt so sorry for him that for a few minutes she had forgotten her own worries and had been concerned only for a man who in the midst of his troubles had shown her such kindness. It was strange that without having acknowledged it to herself she had known all along that Tony wasn't happy with Amanda. Or maybe it wasn't strange; after all, Amanda wasn't a particularly lovable person. There was a coldness to her that was at odds with Tony's naturally warm personality. Perhaps anybody who got to know Tony and Amanda as a couple would quickly realise that he couldn't possibly have married her for love. Equally so, she suspected, they would guess that Amanda's readiness to marry Tony had also had very little to do with love.

'So what's he like?' asked Caroline.

Kate smiled. 'You're impossible, you really are.'

'Answer the question. I want to know what kind of men you're keeping in with. Tell me all.'

'There's nothing to tell.'

'Not much, there isn't. You've gone the colour of my nail varnish.'

Kate gave in. 'He's quite tall.'

'How tall?'

'Five foot ten-ish.'

'Hair?'

'Yes.'

'Don't get clever. What colour?'

'Fair-ish.'

'Eyes?'

'Blue-ish.'

'Age?'

'Mid-thirties-ish.'

'And I suppose if I were to ask what kind of car he drove you'd say it was fast-ish. Are you being deliberately vague?'

Kate smiled. 'He drives a Porsche and it's silvery grey –'

'Don't tell me,' interrupted Caroline, 'it's silvery grey-*ish*.'

They both laughed.

'Well, with or without the babe-catching machine he sounds distinctly eligible. How would he feel about taking on somebody else's child?'

'He's married and has one of his own. So end of story.'

'There's always something to spoil it, isn't there? Oh, good, here's lunch.'

After the waiter had left them alone again, Kate said, 'Caroline, I want to talk seriously with you now.'

'Do you have to? I was just beginning to enjoy myself.'

'I want to ask a favour of you. If Alec . . . if I do have to move out, can I come and stay with you, just until I've got myself sorted?'

Caroline inwardly groaned. The picture of her lovely little house messed up with crate-loads of Pampers and sicked-on Babygros did not appeal, but realising that her attitude was sympathising with the enemy – namely Alec – she said cheerfully, 'Of course you can, so long as we have an understanding; if I'm lucky enough to bring a man back to the house you're to keep out of sight, one look at you and they won't be interested in me. Hey, you're not about to start blubbing, are you?'

Kate swallowed and blinked away the threat of tears. 'I'm just really grateful, that's all. It probably won't come to it. Alec and I will sort everything out, but if I do need a place to go to, it's nice to know there is one.' And, keen to change the subject, she said, 'Tell me how the dating's going.'

Caroline knew that she was one of the least sensitive people around – she knew this because Kate was always quick to tell her that it was the case – but today she could see only too clearly that Kate needed her to distract her and she was more than ready to comply with her friend's wishes. 'You won't believe some of the dorks I've met,' she said. 'It beggars belief that there are so many weirdos out there. There was this one guy who wittered on for hours about his collection of purple ceramic dragons. Well, it would have been for hours if I hadn't pretended to feel violently ill and excused myself. There was one guy who kept going on about all his previous girlfriends. And there was another who was a Buddy Holly freak; he turned up in a fifties suit with those hideous specs and asked if I minded being called Peggy Sue for the evening. I just did a runner, straight out the door, down the high street and to my car. I went home and drooled over my George Clooney scrapbook with a cup of hot chocolate. It's a nightmare, a total nightmare. They sound sane enough on the phone, but believe me they all turn out as dorky as Woody Allen and with twice as many hang-ups.'

'But you must have met at least one decent man,' said Kate.

'If I did, I must have missed him among all the dross.'

They carried on eating for a while, then Kate said in a low voice, 'I've a confession to make.'

'You do fancy that Tony guy? I knew it!'

'I wish I'd never mentioned him now,' Kate said crossly. 'I was going to tell you that it was through an agency that I met Alec.'

Caroline lowered her knife and fork and stared at Kate, then gradually a small, wry smile appeared on her lips. 'Well,' she said, raising her glass of wine, 'I rest my case, m'lud, not a decent man among the lot of them.'

It was late afternoon when Kate drove through the archway of Cholmford Hall Mews. The first thing she saw was Alec's car parked outside the house. She was tempted to reverse straight back out through the arch, but several hours of being in Caroline's company had prepared her for the inevitable confrontation with Alec. 'I will not fall apart,' she told herself firmly as she parked alongside his Saab. 'I am in control of the situation,' she went on, as she locked her car door, 'I will hold my ground.'

She let herself into the house.

He was in the study, bent over his desk, flicking through some letters he must have brought home with him from work. He turned round when she entered the room.

'I think we should get this over with,' she said, her hands gripping her keys behind her back.

'You're right,' he said. He followed her through to the kitchen.

Why was it that so many of life's big decisions were made in the kitchen? Kate wondered as they stood facing each other, the table between them acting like a barrier. So this is it, she thought. This is really it. This is when I make my choice and stand by it. She marvelled at how calm she felt. I've aged about ten years today, she reflected.

All his emotions petrified, Alec stared down at his shoes. He was waiting for Kate to speak. He didn't think he had the courage to go first. But when she didn't say anything he slowly raised his eyes. Not directly at her, but to the window, then to the fridge where Kate had stuck one of Oscar's paintings – it was a picture of him and Kate holding hands, beneath their feet was a thin green strip of grass and above their heads a wobbly stripe of blue sky, and written in pencil in Oscar's four-and-a-half-year-old shaky handwriting were the words, *Grampa Alec and Kate*.

'I'm sorry,' he blurted out, unable to take the silence a moment longer. But still he didn't look at her. He kept his eyes on Oscar's picture – Kate with her impossibly long, matchstick-thin legs and he with a round barrel of a stomach and tiny stumps for legs. 'I'm sorry,' he repeated.

'What are you sorry for, Alec?' she said.

He tore his gaze away from Oscar's artwork and looked at her. The late afternoon sun was pouring in through the window and her hair was glowing a vibrant shade of golden chestnut. It was tied up with a silk scarf he didn't recognise and the colours in the fabric brought out the exquisite shade of green in her eyes – large, sad eyes that were fixed on him. He thought he'd never seen her look more beautiful. And as he thought this, the awful strain and horror of the day suddenly lifted from him and he knew what he had to do.

He went to her, wrapped her in his arms, needing to undo all the harm he'd done – desperate for her forgiveness. 'Oh, Kate,' he whispered, 'I didn't mean what I said this morning. It was the shock. Just give me time to adjust and I promise everything will be all right. I promise.'

33

By Monday evening Josh was feeling a lot better. The burning sensation that had plagued him for most of the previous week had gradually receded over the weekend and other than coping with the usual stiffness in his leg he had felt relatively normal today.

He'd gone in to work for a couple of hours that morning and, after making his peace with Charlie and sorting out a few things that had been left pending since Thursday, he'd come home after lunch with his briefcase stuffed full of faxes to deal with, from their suppliers in Hong Kong. He'd decided – before Charlie had had a chance to suggest it – to take things easy on his first day back.

He'd spent most of the weekend taking it easy. In fact, he'd slept through the best part of it, finding it difficult to stay awake for much of the time. He hated to admit it, but maybe in the future he ought to take more notice of his body. Perhaps if he hadn't struggled on trying to ignore the pain in his legs last week he wouldn't have ended up so exhausted . . . or head-butting his desk. He was now fully convinced that what he'd experienced in his office on Thursday afternoon hadn't been the start of him suffering from black-outs, but had been a one-off case of him collapsing through exhaustion. His body had simply had enough.

The only disturbance to his weekend of recovery was a call on Saturday morning from his mother – he suspected that Charlie had been at work in the background and had prompted her to ring him.

'Everything all right for Sunday lunch next week?' she'd asked. 'You'll be able to make it, won't you?' He had heard the tense wariness in her voice, knowing that she was torn between wanting to rush over and make sure he was all right – but knowing that it would be the last thing he'd want – and pretending that she knew nothing of his latest MS attack.

'Yes, as far as I can tell,' he'd replied, feeling genuinely sorry for her. Ever since he had lost his temper with his mother, the day after he'd been diagnosed as having multiple sclerosis and when he'd felt smothered by everyone's concern, she had been wary of him. She had been so hurt by his lashing out at her that she had never wanted to repeat the episode and had tiptoed round him, scared of saying the wrong thing. He kept meaning to talk to her about it, but somehow the right moment had never presented itself.

Their conversation hadn't lasted long. But using as much tact as she could, she had asked him how he was and in a by-the-way tone of voice had added that Charlie had spoken to her, and in order to circumvent the painful process of her drawing out the grisly details from him he'd said, 'I'm fine, Mum, please don't worry. I'll see you next week. I'll be there as usual.'

As he'd put down the phone he'd made himself promise to find time to speak to his mother, to talk to her properly.

Now as he finished dealing with the last of the faxes that he'd brought home with him he took off his glasses and sat back in his chair. He gazed across the courtyard, through the sash window of his study, and wondered if now was the right time to stop hiding from Jessica and talk to her. He didn't hold out much hope that she'd want to say very much to him, though. It was ages since they'd last spoken – it was when she'd called him and he'd been feeling rotten, and the resulting conversation had been as lively and interesting as a party political broadcast. No wonder she hadn't bothered to ring him again.

He turned away from the window and looked at the bookshelf to the left of his desk. There, in pride of place between a framed photograph of him and Charlie on the slopes at Val d'Isère and another of the pair of them up at Victoria Peak in Hong Kong, were copies of Jessica's books. He'd read them both and much to his surprise – he'd never read a romantic comedy in his life before – had laughed out loud. Her style of writing was incisive, pacey and sardonic – just as she was herself – and he was conscious that given his behaviour towards her of late, she could make short work of him if she so chose. God knows, she was entitled.

He returned his attention to looking out of the window and twirling his glasses round in his hand, and thinking just how much he'd missed Jessica's company he caught sight of her in the room directly opposite. She had just walked into her study.

Without giving himself time to change his mind he leaned forwards, picked up the phone and dialled her number from the piece of paper he had propped against the halogen desk lamp – a piece of paper that had stared reproachfully at him for nearly two weeks now.

He watched her pick up her phone. 'Hi,' he said, 'it's Josh.'

There was a pause, then the sound of her voice. 'Mm . . . now let me see, would that be Josh Reynolds the painter chappie, or that other well-known Josh, the man who led the Israelites to the Promised Land?'

'Neither. It's Josh the pain in the bum who hasn't spoken to you for . . . for quite a while.'

'Oh, that one. Well I have a sketchy picture of him in my mind, but you'll have to help me out, he's little more than a vague memory these days.'

'If you look out of your window you might catch a glimpse of something that could help.'

There was a slight pause. 'Good heavens, there's a mad man out there waving back at me. Fancy that. But hang on, I think you're right, there is something familiar about him. It's beginning to come to me now.'

'How are you, Jessica? I've missed you.'

'Have you?'

'Yes.'

'Really?'

'Really.'

'Like hell you have!'

'But it's true, I have.'

'So why haven't you been in touch?'

'I've been busy.'

'Crawford, save me the bull. Get off the phone and get your butt over here and make your apologies in person.'

'I . . . I can't.'

'Why not?'

'Because . . . because I'm just getting over flu.' Oh hell! He was off again. More lies.

'Why didn't you let me know you'd been ill? I could have come over and made broth, and mopped your brow for you and stood prettily at the end of your bed.'

'Nice idea, but I'm afraid I make a lousy patient.'

'Believe me, most men make lousy patients. So why are you ringing me?'

'I'd like to see you.'

'I'm not sure I want to see you.'

'Jessica, I said I'm sorry. I've been busy, work's been crazy –'

'And don't forget how ill you've been with the flu.'

'Can I see you tomorrow evening?'

'You sure you'll be well enough?'

'I'll make sure I am.'

'Okay. Be here for half past seven. And Crawford –'

'Yes?'

'No excuses this time, okay?'

'As if.'

Josh spent most of Tuesday praying that he'd make it through the day. If something went wrong with him and he didn't get to Jessica's that evening she was never going to believe another word he said.

And as it was the truth he wanted to speak tonight, it was important that nothing prevented him from seeing her.

Speaking to Jessica on the phone yesterday evening, it couldn't have been further from his mind to own up to her about his MS. When she'd suggested he call on her there and then, he'd suddenly lost his nerve and had been terrified that he might get half-way across the courtyard and keel over. So rather than take the risk, he'd backed out and given her some crap about recovering from flu.

How pathetic.

And how cowardly.

It was after he'd put down the phone and he'd made himself some supper that he'd known that he couldn't go on as he was. It was time to come clean with Jessica. He would rather she knew the truth about him than have her condemn him as a complete shyster.

At half past five he gathered up his things and switched off the lights in his office. Out in the reception area Mo was chatting to Charlie. When she saw Josh she handed him a small card. It was an invitation.

'It's my birthday on Friday, I'm having a party, will you come?'

'Of course he will,' Charlie said.

'I'm not sure,' Josh said hesitantly.

'Oh, please,' said Mo. Reluctantly she added, 'You can bring Jessica if you want. Charlie's going to try and persuade Rachel to come.'

'I'll think about it.'

'You're an ungracious bugger,' Charlie said as he and Josh walked to their cars. 'You could have just said yes to Mo.'

'I don't like making promises I might not be able to keep.'

Charlie let it go. He was tired of reasoning with his brother. 'Doing anything tonight?'

'Yes. I'm seeing Jessica. I'm . . . I'm going to tell her.'

Charlie came to a stop. 'About your MS?'

Josh nodded.

Charlie wasn't sure what to say. If he said anything glib like: 'It'll be fine, don't worry,' it would be an insult to Josh's intelligence. And though he himself had urged his brother on many occasions to be honest with Jessica, he didn't for one minute underestimate the risk Josh was taking. His last girl-friend's sudden departure from his life was proof enough that love didn't always conquer all.

'Good luck,' was all he could think to say. 'Give me a ring if . . . well, you know.'

'What, if things don't turn out well?'

However Josh had thought the evening might turn out, he couldn't have predicted the way it did.

He called on Jessica, spot on seven-thirty as she'd instructed, but when she didn't let him into the house as he'd expected, his plan of quietly explaining things to her immediately went on hold.

She led him towards her car and said, 'Get in and don't argue. It's time for you to loosen up. You're going to sit for two whole hours in my company whether you want to or not, and what's more, you're going to do it in the dark and you're going to laugh. I might even let you have some popcorn if you're good.'

The film was billed as a knockabout comedy with Steve Martin playing a love-struck oil tycoon.

'This really isn't my kind of thing,' Josh said petulantly as they took up their seats in the crowded cinema.

'Yeah, I know, this is far too unsophisticated for you, isn't it. But then, that's your trouble, you've let yourself go. You're old before your time and have forgotten how to enjoy yourself. Now, why don't you sit back and let the child within come out to play?'

'I'd rather be an adult at home playing with you.'

'Ssh! The film's about to start. Have some popcorn. And don't look like that, sulking won't get you anywhere with me.'

When the credits began to roll at the end of the film, to the sound of Aretha Franklin singing 'What Now My Love', they joined the stream of people queuing for the exit and left the cinema. It was dark outside and soft rain was beginning to fall.

Jessica unlocked the car and they climbed in. 'Well,' she said, 'it wasn't such a bad film, was it? I distinctly heard you laughing back there.'

'I was laughing to please you,' he conceded.

She threw him a look and for the first time noticed the cut to his temple. 'You've hurt yourself,' she said. 'How did you do that?'

He hesitated. Was this the opening he needed? Was this the perfectly timed moment for him to tell her the truth? That he suffered from MS and it had got the better of him last week at work. 'It's nothing,' he said, turning away from her, 'nothing at all.'

Jessica started up the engine, drove out of the car-park and, as she waited for the traffic lights on the main road to change, she said, 'Josh?'

'Yes?'

'I don't believe you.'

'What don't you believe?'

'That you would want to please me.'

There was an awkward pause between them.

'Well, you're wrong,' Josh said at last. 'Nothing would give me more pleasure than to please you, only –'

'*But* alert! *But* alert!' Jessica said, shifting into first gear and moving off. 'As clear as daylight I sense one looming large on the horizon.'

He frowned and reached out and gently stroked her neck, just in the bit where he knew she liked it. 'The *but* is I don't think I'm up to the task.'

'And if that isn't the sound of a man back-pedalling his way out of a relationship I don't know what is. You'd better take your hand away or we'll smash into the car in front.'

Josh did as she said and decided to wait until they were home before telling her what he had to say. He wanted to be able to see her face when she realised the truth about him, to read her expression. It was crucial.

When they finally drew up alongside her house, Jessica snatched on the handbrake and switched off the engine. Without looking at him and keeping her eyes straight ahead she suddenly said, 'Is there somebody else? Because if there is, do us both a favour and tell me. All I want to know is where I stand. I don't think I'm being unreasonable.'

Oh hell! she thought, I'm sounding like a paranoid middle-aged wife. Any minute and I'll be telling him to consider the children and the effect it will have on them. But much as she disliked the sound of the words coming out of her mouth, she knew that now that she had started, in true *Mastermind* fashion, she was going to bloody well finish and have her say. He was going to get the full force of her anger for the way he'd treated her. In fact, he was probably going to get Gavin's share as well!

'If there is somebody else I think I have the right to be told,' she went on. 'One minute you're there in my life and the next you're not. I'm not a possessive woman, I just don't like being mucked about. I had enough of that with Gavin and I'm not about to start accepting that kind of situation all over again. And of course, if it's the perennial problem of a man being scared of commitment, then –'

'I'm not scared of commitment,' he interrupted her, magically stemming the flow of her anger, 'at least not in the way you mean.' She felt a hand on her shoulder and he slowly turned her round. 'And there's no one else,' he said firmly. 'I'm appalled that you should think there is. Now be quiet long enough for me to kiss you. And when I've done that, can we go inside? There's something I want to discuss with you.'

She swallowed back her relief. *There wasn't anybody else! Oh, thank you, God!*

'So what do you want to talk about? Devolution? Unification? Or global warming?'

Oh, heaven help her, she was rambling again. What was it about him tonight that was making her so nervous?

He shook his head. 'Nothing as trivial as that.'

Another swallow. 'Oh. Something serious then? In that case it must be the escalating cost of the Millennium Dome.'

'More serious than that.'

'Come off it, nothing's more serious than the greatest white elephant this side of Lord Irvine's pad. Not unless you ... but surely you can't mean the Charles and Camilla conundrum. We're not going to discuss that, are we?'

Somebody stop me!

'For pity's sake, Jessica, shut up.' He silenced her with a long kiss. 'Now please, can we go inside before I lose my nerve?'

34

The house was in darkness as Jessica unlocked the front door and let them in.

'*What now my love*,' she sang happily, à la Ms Franklin – there was nothing like a good kiss to calm the nerves. She switched on the hall light. '*Now that you've left me –*'

'Please don't sing that,' Josh said abruptly.

'Why?' She laughed. 'Don't you like my singing?'

He followed her into the half-decorated kitchen and watched her throw her bag and keys on to the table. 'It's not that,' he said.

She came towards him and put her arms around his shoulders. 'What, then?'

'It's the lyrics, they're too sentimental . . . too melancholic.' They were also too close for comfort. Particularly the lines that came next – *How can I live through another day watching my dreams turning into ashes and all of my hopes into bits of clay* – and with what he was about to say to Jessica and her possible reaction, these were sentiments he didn't want to hear.

She smiled. 'There's nothing wrong with a good dose of schmaltzy melancholy, it's good for the heart.'

He didn't return her smile and as he stared down into her eyes Jessica was shocked to realise how changed he was since she'd last seen him. The youthful, handsome face that had come to be so familiar to her was gone and in its place was the expression of a deeply troubled man. He looked pale. His eyes were sad and sombre, and conveyed an impression of intense dread within him, and as her body rested against his she sensed that he was tense and unyielding. 'What did you want to talk to me about?' she asked nervously, suddenly concluding that the change that had come over him had to be connected with what he wanted to discuss with her. Immediately she'd reached this conclusion her mind began stacking up a set of possible explanations for his apprehension – he had lied earlier in the car about not seeing anyone else, or worse . . .

But what could be worse?

What terrible revelation did he have to throw at her that was causing him so much consternation? Come off it, his face didn't so much betray consternation as downright fear.

Oh, my grandfathers, she thought. What was the current nightmare for anyone not in a long-term relationship? What was the spectre at the feast when it came to sex these days?

She slowly released herself from his arms and stepped away from him. No wonder he'd been absent from her life recently. He'd probably been ill ... and not with flu. 'You've got AIDS, haven't you?'

A mixture of horror and incredulous disbelief swept over Josh's face, but before he had a chance to speak the phone rang. It made them both jump.

'I'm letting it ring until you answer me,' Jessica whispered. She was motionless with shock. Rigid with fear. *If he had AIDS then so might she.* Above the insistent shrill of the phone she racked her brain, trying to think if they'd ever had unprotected sex. But they'd always been careful. Even the first time they'd made love, when Josh had been unprepared for the way the night had turned out, she had managed to produce a remnant of her old love life. They had joked about it and pretended to blow the dust away from the small packet. 'Well?' she demanded of him. 'What have you got to say?'

'Please, Jessica, stop being so dramatic and just answer the bloody phone.'

'No! Not until you've told me the truth.'

He shook his head, and went over and picked up the receiver. A few seconds passed before he put it down. 'Jessica,' he said, his face even more anxious than it had been before. 'It's your mother, she's had an accident.'

'Not serious!' Jessica roared at Josh as he sat in the passenger seat of her car once more. 'How the bloody hell do you know it's not serious?'

'Because she said so,' he said calmly. 'She said that she was okay and that you weren't to worry or think the worst.' When he'd answered the phone in Jessica's kitchen, Josh had been surprised to hear a faint voice at the other end of the line saying, 'I've no idea to whom I'm speaking, but don't whatever you do put Jessica on. Just tell her that her mother has had a slight accident and if she'd like to pop over, I'm at home. Be sure to explain that I'm okay and that it's nothing serious.'

He could see now why Jessica's mother had specifically asked not to speak to her daughter. Frantic with worry, Jessica had just rocketed her car through the archway of the development and with her foot jammed down on the accelerator they were speeding along the avenue of chestnut trees.

It was raining harder than when they'd driven back from the cinema and Josh watched her fumble for the switch for the windscreen wipers. 'Some lights might be a good idea,' he suggested.

Jessica flashed him a look of fury. 'Nothing to worry about, my foot,' she muttered while flicking on the headlights. 'Let me tell you, my mother was taken into hospital for what she said was a routine operation and that there was nothing for me to worry about. When I arrived at the hospital I discovered that she was having a triple heart bypass operation. I've since learnt to ignore anything she says.'

'Perhaps you shouldn't. Perhaps it isn't fair to treat her like Cassandra.'

'Like who?'

'Cassandra, the Greek prophetess who was cursed never to be believed.'

'I don't believe I'm hearing this. My mother could well be dying and you're giving me a lecture on Greek mythology? She's my concern, so if I want to worry about her, I bloody well will.'

'Fine, if that's the way you want it.'

'I do. It's exactly how I want it.'

'And by the way, I don't have AIDS, so you needn't worry about that as well. I haven't infected you with anything.'

'Right now I couldn't give a damn whether you have or not,' she fired back. 'All I care about is what in heaven's name my mother's done to herself.' She gripped the steering wheel knowing that she was behaving atrociously, that Josh didn't deserve this, but so long as she was able to take out her anger on somebody it meant that she was just about in control of the situation.

She pulled up in front of Willow Cottage and before Josh had even climbed out of the car was letting herself into the house with the key that she'd insisted Anna give her some weeks ago. She called out to her mother.

'I'm up here,' came a faint reply.

Jessica took the stairs two at a time.

She found Anna on the floor in her bedroom. A pair of step-ladders and the contents of an upturned box of tools lay all around her, as well as the phone from the bedside table.

'I'm sorry, Jessica, but I'm afraid I've broken it.' Her mother nodded towards a decapitated china statue that Jessica had given her when she was a child, the head of which had rolled across the room and now lay with its nose tucked into the carpet pile in front of the dressing-table. 'I caught it with my foot on the window-sill,' Anna added, as though this made everything clear. 'I think I may also have broken my arm,' she said as Jessica crouched beside her, 'and my ribs don't feel so good. Oh, you must be Josh.'

Josh came into the room. 'Hi,' he said with an easy smile and, joining them on the floor, he started to pick up the scattered tools, 'you look like you've been busy.'

'I do my best,' Anna said. She returned his smile and passed him a screwdriver that was clutched in her hand.

'Any chance of making it to the bed?'

'Well you're a fast one, I must say. But I'm not sure Jessica would approve. She looks furious as it is.'

'Of course I'm furious,' exploded Jessica, her anxiety now given rein to turn into full-blown angry relief. 'How many times have I told you to be careful? How could you do this!'

Anna smiled at Josh. 'How long do you give her before she says I told you so?'

'And I'd have every right to say that. This is serious, Mum, you could have killed yourself.'

'What, and missed the opportunity to meet this delightful young man?' Anna said with a wink at Josh. 'No fear.'

Jessica looked even more enraged and opened her mouth to remonstrate further, but Josh intervened. 'Jessica,' he said firmly, 'this isn't helping. Now, Mrs Lloyd, do you think you can manage the stairs? From what I can see of your wrist it most certainly is broken and I think we should drive you straight to a hospital.'

*

Tony was in no mood to speak to Bloody Rita. He didn't make any effort to be polite to her, but handed the phone over to Amanda and went upstairs for a shower. He'd had a tedious day that had got him nowhere. Bradley-Dewhurst-the-Butcher's-Boy had set up a tele-conference late in the afternoon and it had served no purpose other than to delay everybody from getting off home.

On his way to the bathroom he hovered outside Hattie's door. He pushed it open a crack, just to see if she was asleep.

'Is that you, Daddy?'

He smiled and went in. 'Come on, you little pixie, you should have been fast asleep hours ago.'

'I can't get to sleep.'

He smoothed out the rumpled duvet, then sat on the edge of the bed. 'And why's that?' He was instantly worried that maybe her new school was bothering her. He knew that Hattie was by nature a confident child, but it was a dangerous thing to overestimate her ability to accept change. It seemed pretty unlikely, however, that there was anything wrong at school as only yesterday her teacher had told Amanda how well Hattie was fitting in.

'You're not worried about anything, are you?' he asked.

She nodded.

He stroked her hair. 'Is it school?'

She shook her head.

'What, then?'

She pulled him down to her and whispered into his ear, 'It's Grandma Rita.'

'What about Grandma Rita?' he whispered back.

'Amanda says she might be coming to stay with us.'

Tony sat upright. 'That's news to me,' he said.

'Amanda said you wouldn't mind.'

'And when did Amanda discuss this with you?'

'In the car coming home from school. She said it was a surprise, though. It's not a very nice surprise, is it?'

Tony smiled.

'Does she have to come?'

'We'll see. Now off to sleep with you.' He kissed her forehead, then squeezed her hand.

'You won't tell Amanda I said anything, will you? I think she might be cross with me.'

'Of course not. Now go to sleep.'

He was almost out of the room when she sat up and said, 'Daddy, what's a boarding-school?'

He frowned and came back to the bed. 'What do you mean?'

'I heard Amanda talking to Grandma Rita on the phone about something called a boarding-school.'

'Did you indeed?'

'Would I like it?'

He shook his head. 'No,' he said grimly, 'no, you wouldn't. And nor would I.'

'Amanda told Grandma Rita that it would be best for me.'

'Well, she's wrong. Very, very wrong.'

'So what is a boarding-school?'

'It's not something you ever need to think about. Now, it really is time for you to go to sleep. Good-night.' He kissed her again and wondered at the ruthlessness of his wife, that she could plot and scheme about his daughter's future behind his back.

Later, when Tony came out of the shower, he found Amanda in their bedroom sorting through a large plastic laundry basket of ironing. She was a meticulous ironer, everything was steamed and pressed, even his socks. 'How's your mother?' he fished.

'Fine. She sends her love.'

Like hell she does! Bloody Rita would no more send him her love than she would dance naked through the streets of Alderley Edge where she lived. 'That's nice of her,' he said, totally convinced that Hattie must have been right and that Amanda was now switching on to 'softening-up mode' before announcing that Rita was coming to stay. 'We haven't seen her for a while,' he added, 'what's she been up to?' – *something sweet and innocent like evenings out with the Ku-Klux-Klan?*

'Oh, just the usual; bridge and bowling. The bowling club's hoping to go off on tour again.'

'Sounds good.' *Especially if it were a six-month tour of Australia! The further away the better.*

He didn't trust himself to cross-examine Amanda about the boarding-school issue and so got into bed. Well, she could forget that little scheme. He would never allow it to happen.

He closed his eyes and listened to Amanda moving about the room, tidying away clothes into cupboards and drawers. He wondered what Kate was doing. He had no way of knowing what had happened to her since he'd seen her yesterday morning. He didn't know whether she and Alec had resolved things between them, or if Alec was still refusing to accept his child. He hadn't mentioned any of this to Amanda – the thought of her gossiping about Kate was too much for him. He hoped, though, that if Kate needed any help she would feel able to come to him. He'd given her his work number, just in case, and throughout today he had stupidly hoped it was her each time his phone had rung. What kind of help he thought he'd be able to give he wasn't sure. Possibly what he wanted to offer Kate would only complicate matters.

And what exactly was he offering?

He was a married man with a child; the sort of man who would never have imagined himself capable of cheating on his wife. But that was exactly what he'd planned to do, wasn't it? When he'd gone to see Kate yesterday morning he had knocked on her door with the sole expectation of tempting her into an affair with him.

And given half a chance he still would.

He turned on to his side and pulled the duvet up over his head. He wanted the world to disappear.

No, that wasn't true.

He just wanted Amanda and Alec to disappear.

35

A Casual Affair was getting nowhere – Clare and Miles had spent the past week locked in one another's arms and as passionate embraces went, theirs was proving to be the longest in history.

Following Anna's accident on Tuesday night, Jessica had moved into Willow Cottage to look after her mother. She had brought Clare and Miles along with her on her laptop, but much as she cared about their will-they-won't-they relationship, she had found she didn't have a spare minute to devote to them, or if she were honest, the inclination. Her heart just wasn't in it. She was too preoccupied with her mother.

She had thought that Anna's wilfulness would be dramatically reduced by having an arm in a sling, but if anything, the plaster cast was proving a challenge to her obstinate mother – she had even threatened Jessica with it.

'Ask me one more time if I'm comfortable, Jessica, and I shall bring this wretched cast down on your head.'

It wasn't an easy situation, but as Jessica prodded another log into place in the grate with a pair of old brass tongs, she knew that it was down to her to make her mother see sense and keep her from straying from the safe confines of her armchair by the fire.

She put down the tongs and glanced out of the window. The weather, she reflected, was as jittery as she was. Yesterday had been clear and bright, with a warm September sun drying away the early-morning dew and mist, but today a north-easterly wind had chilled the air and there was no sign of the sun as it hid behind the thick banks of grey clouds that threw down the occasional downpour. It was a cold, wet, miserable day. It felt more like winter than autumn and just before lunch Jessica had lit the fire in the sitting-room and insisted Anna sit beside it. But Anna hadn't wanted to and had accused Jessica of treating her like a child. 'That's because you're behaving like one,' Jessica had retorted, 'now please, do as I say.'

Jessica moved away from the fire. She sat in the chair opposite her mother and began pouring out their tea.

It was Friday afternoon and so far they'd been cooped up together at Willow Cottage for three whole days. Jessica didn't know how much longer she could cope. She was exhausted and irritable with worry. The thought that Anna's accident could have ended so differently was never far from her mind. But it hadn't been fatal, she had to keep reminding herself; a broken arm and a cracked rib weren't life-threatening; her mother would be all right. She leant forward and placed a cup of tea on the little table beside her mother's chair.

Anna put down the magazine Jessica had bought for her, which she wasn't really reading, and added it to the pile that had been thoughtfully placed within arm's reach. 'Thank you,' she said, wishing that she actually meant the words. She felt as grateful to Jessica as a blind man would if somebody had helpfully switched on the light for him. She really didn't know how much more of her daughter she could put up with.

What she regretted most about her little mishap – which had happened while she had been trying to fix a window lock in her bedroom – was that it had brought out the worst in both herself and Jessica. In her desire to help, Jessica had turned into a monstrous gaoler and she herself had become a dispirited prisoner with only one aim in her life: to escape.

She raised her cup to her lips, stared across the mahogany table in front of the fire and looked at her daughter's unhappy face. She looked ragged and worn-out. Clearly the situation was doing neither of them any good. They resembled a middle-aged couple who'd been together for a thousand years and now had nothing to say to one another. You saw them all the time, glum-faced people mindlessly stirring cups of over-brewed tea in British Home Stores restaurants all over the country.

Something had to be done.

And soon.

'You know, I'm beginning to feel much better,' Anna said brightly.

The immediate look of scorn on Jessica's face silenced her from trying her luck with suggesting that she could now manage on her own and wasn't it time Jessica went back to her own home?

She stared forlornly out of the window at her deserted garden. How she longed to roll up her sleeves and get her hands dirty. It was most frustrating, especially when there was so much to do. Plums were dropping like manna from heaven from the fruit trees; the stakes and ties for the dahlias needed checking in case the wind got up; the roses were in need of deadheading and it was more than two weeks since she'd last sprayed them for mildew, and goodness only knew what the greenfly were up to while her back was turned. And there were all those dwarf daffodil and tulip bulbs waiting to be planted in the rockery she'd built earlier in the summer. Dermot was all very well, and the lad did his best, but it was her garden and nobody loved it as she did.

If only Jessica were green-fingered, at least then there might have been a chance of her putting something of her over-zealous caring energy into looking after the garden instead of plaguing her.

No, that wasn't fair, she thought, Jessica was only doing what she thought was best.

'Are you sure you shouldn't be working?' Anna tried again – the prisoner had her eye on the imaginary set of keys dangling from her gaoler's belt.

Jessica lowered her cup and looked at her mother. 'You're more important,' she said simply.

The keys were once again moved out of the prisoner's grasp.

'But what about your deadline? You know how much you worry about delivering a manuscript on time.' Desperate now, the prisoner was considering a swift blow to the gaoler's Achilles heel – Jessica's obsession with meeting her publisher's deadline.

'That's not for ages, not until next year, and anyway I can give Piers and Cara a ring, they'll understand.'

Anna frowned, then a tiny idea took hold. An idea that made her realise that she had hit upon a means of tunnelling her way out of her prison cell . . . and all she would need was a sneaky peep at Jessica's address book. But how could she get Jessica out of the way long enough to do that?

Her question was answered sooner than she'd thought possible when the sound of the doorbell broke the dreadful silence that had cloaked the house since her well-meaning daughter had moved in.

Jessica put down her cup and quickly went to answer it. Anna listened to find out who it was – if only it could be a passing member of the SAS expertly trained in dealing with hostage situations. It was a few seconds before she recognised the voice: Josh. A smile spread over her face. Her immediate thought was to leap out of her chair and invite him in, thereby providing a distraction so that she could slip upstairs to Jessica's room and snoop through her things for the precious address book. But she knew it was more than her life was worth even to move from the chair and anyway, if she were painfully honest, the only leaping she was capable of doing was a leap of the imagination.

'If that's Josh, don't keep him on the doorstep, bring him in,' she called out to Jessica. 'It'll be nice to have a visitor' – *yes, it would break the suffocating monotony.*

'Hello, Mrs Lloyd,' Josh said when Jessica brought him into the sitting-room. He held out a pot of white chrysanthemums. 'I saw these on the way home from work and thought you might like them. How are you feeling?'

'Please, you must call me Anna, and I'm feeling much better, thank you.'

Jessica tutted loudly and took the flowers from Josh. She placed them on the oak dresser, alongside the half-eaten box of Thornton's Continental chocolates that Josh had brought earlier in the week. 'She'd be a darn sight better if she kept still for two minutes,' she scolded.

Anna winked at Josh and he smiled back at her.

'Jessica, why don't you make a fresh pot of tea? I'm sure Josh must be thirsty.'

Jessica looked at Josh, her expression clearly indicating that she expected him to refuse any such hospitality.

'That would be great,' he said.

Anna smiled triumphantly and watched her gaoler pick up the tray from the table and retreat from the room. When they were alone she carefully leant forward and whispered to Josh, 'You've got to help me, she's driving me mad.'

'Earl Grey or ordinary?'

Anna jerked her head towards the doorway where Jessica was standing with a grim scowl on her face.

'Ordinary will be fine,' Josh said smoothly. 'What's the problem?' he asked, when he and Anna were sure they were alone.

'She won't leave me be, not even for a few minutes. It's not so much a case of mother's little helper as mother's little tormentor.'

He laughed.

'I'm serious, Josh, she's turned into a monster. I can't do anything without her fussing. She watches me the whole time.'

'So what do you want me to do?'

'I need you to get her out of the house for a few minutes, take her for a walk, anything, so long as it gives me an opportunity to make a call to somebody who'll come to my rescue. Will you do that?'

'I'll try, though I'm not sure it'll work. I'm not exactly her favourite person at the moment.'

'Mm ... I noticed that the other day when you called. What have you done? You've not two-timed her, have you? She's not very keen on men who do that.'

He shook his head. 'No, nothing like that.'

'What, then?'

Josh hesitated. 'I've ... I've hidden something from her, something important which I was about to explain to her on the night of your accident.'

'How intriguing. What is it? Are you really a world-famous drug baron lying low here in Cholmford?'

'Who's a drug baron lying low?' asked Jessica, coming in with a tray and banging it down on the table between Josh and her mother.

'Nobody,' Josh answered, sitting back in his chair. He watched Jessica drop on to the sofa. She looked tired and there was no denying the coldness she was displaying towards him. She had been the same when he'd called on Wednesday on his way home after work. Ostensibly he'd dropped in to see how her mother was, but mainly because he wanted a chance to talk to Jessica. She had made it impossible for him to do so, busying herself in the kitchen with cooking supper for herself and Anna. Even when he'd started to say that he wanted to finish the conversation they'd started on Tuesday night she had pushed past him saying that she didn't have time to listen. She had been close to crying and, sensing that his presence was adding to her distress and the apparent antagonism between them, he had said goodbye and left. He couldn't help feeling confused. It was as if she were blaming him for her mother's accident.

He'd called again today, fool that he was, because he had decided to ask Jessica if she'd go with him to Mo's party that evening. He didn't hold out much hope that she'd say yes, and if the look on her face as she poured out his tea was anything to go by he'd be lucky to escape without having his ears boxed.

'Thank you,' he said when she handed him his cup. 'How's the book going?' He hoped the question would place him on firmer ground than he'd been on previously. He soon found it did no such thing.

'Hah!' she said scornfully, 'as if I've got time for writing.'

He exchanged the briefest of looks with Anna and wondered how he could now suggest that Jessica had time for an evening out. Feet first seemed the only way. He took a fortifying sip of his tea and said, 'I know it's short notice, but I don't suppose you'd like to come to a party with me tonight, would you?'

Anna marvelled at Josh. In the face of her daughter's open hostility towards him the man had real courage. She held her breath and waited for Jessica's reply.

It came in the form of a tut of derision. 'How can you expect me to leave Anna all alone?'

'Oh, what nonsense,' Anna chipped in smartly – *just think of it, a whole evening to herself!* 'I think it's a wonderful idea and just what you need to perk you up.'

'Perk me up?' Jessica said indignantly. 'Who says I need perking up?'

'Not perking up *per se*,' Anna said quickly, 'but it'll give you something to think about other than worrying over me.' *Oh what bliss, to be allowed to settle down to an evening of telly without being interrupted by Jessica continually suggesting that what she really needed was an early night. She'd stretch out on the sofa with a great big martini, at the same time plundering Josh's box of chocolates.* 'I really think you should go,' she added wishfully.

'I'm sure you do,' muttered Jessica, 'so that you can get up to heaven knows what mischief in my absence. I wouldn't put it past you to knock up a quick loft extension while I'm out.'

Anna feigned horror at such an idea. 'Cross my heart and hope to die, I wouldn't get in to any mischief. I've learnt my lesson.'

'And I promise not to keep you out too late, Jessica,' Josh said. He turned to Anna. 'I'll make sure she's back in time to help you into bed.'

'Well, that all seems to be arranged to everybody's satisfaction then,' Anna said happily, secretly hoping that Josh wouldn't stick to his bargain too literally. It was Friday night and there was bound to be a good late-night film on one of the channels.

Jessica stared suspiciously at Anna, then at Josh. 'Yes,' she said slowly, 'it does seem to be arranged to your satisfaction, doesn't it? Anyone would think you'd cooked this up between the pair of you.'

At eight o'clock Josh returned to Willow Cottage. As Jessica climbed into the Shogun he felt the coolness of her manner towards him increase. Once he'd negotiated the narrow bridge over the canal and was driving along the dark lane he said, 'Your mother will be fine, and if there is any problem she's got the number for my mobile.'

'I know that,' Jessica said stiffly.

Without a word Josh suddenly brought the car to a stop. He switched off the engine, turned and faced Jessica. 'Okay,' he said, 'what's this all about? What terrible thing have I done that's caused you to be so cold and rude? You were warmer to me that night when you thought I was the mad axeman of Cholmford.'

Jessica refused to look at him. She didn't say anything either.

'Look, Jessica, a few days ago you were a different woman. Then you were sexy and sarky and made me laugh, now . . . well, now you're moody and miserable; what's got into you?'

'I would have thought it was perfectly obvious. I've got more important things on my mind than providing you with a non-stop twenty-four-hour programme of entertainment. And for your information, unless used with care, alliteration is best avoided.'

He smiled. 'I'll bear that in mind in the future.'

'Good. You do that.'

'Any more advice for me?'

'Yes. You can stop encouraging my mother to flirt with you. She doesn't need a toy boy and I'd hate to read about her in the *Sun*. I can see the headlines now: *Senior Citizen in Sleazy Sex Scandal!*'

'I thought you said alliteration was best avoided.'

She turned and looked at him and he saw that there was a glimmer of a smile on her face, and hoping that maybe he had broken the ice between them he reached out and touched her hands in her lap. 'You love your mother very much, don't you?'

The unexpected frankness of his words cut through Jessica's defences and the pain of the past few days rose up and engulfed her. From nowhere a tiny tear appeared in the corner of her left eye. She lowered her head and bit her lip to stop it from betraying the fact that she was so close to crying. She felt angry with herself. Angry, because crying wasn't something she went in for. It was an emotion she had managed without for as long as she could remember. Crying equalled weakness and she wasn't weak. She was strong, always had been. Just like her mother. It was what had held them together when her father died. 'I need you to be strong,' her mother had said that night after the funeral. It was her only real memory of the day; her mother sitting on the edge of her bed, holding her hand, telling her everything would be all right, they just had to be strong.

She heard Josh unbuckle his seat-belt and when he moved nearer and held her in his arms she knew she couldn't hold back the tears any longer.

'I love her so much,' she sobbed into his shoulder, 'and I'm terrified of losing her. I haven't been a good daughter to her, I've never been there for her.'

He held her tenderly and gently stroked her hair.

'I'm all she's got,' Jessica continued, 'it's down to me to take care of her.'

'But you are.'

She pulled away from him and fumbled for a tissue in her bag. 'No, I'm not,' she said, 'I'm making it worse for her. I'm no good at this saintly caring stuff, I know I'm not.'

'You just need to relax, that's all.'

'But how? I try, but I end up behaving like some ghastly fifties-style matron and bossing Mum about, and biting everyone else's head off . . . you included.'

'Me in particular,' he said.

She smiled. 'I'm sorry. I've been horrible to you, haven't I?'

'Yes,' he agreed.

'I was particularly horrid to you the other night, I'm sorry that I shouted and said all those things. What was it you wanted to talk to me about?'

He ran his hand through her hair and let it linger on the nape of her neck. *Now, tell her now,* he willed himself. *Go on. Just say it. Get it over and done with. Just open your mouth and say, Jessica, I've got MS and I'm sorry that I've lied to you.* 'It'll keep,' he said. He'd tell her tomorrow. Tomorrow, when she wasn't so upset about her mother. He slowly moved away from her, then turned the key in the ignition. 'What you need is a party to cheer you up,' he said.

'Don't you mean to perk me up?'

'That too.'

But once again Josh was to find that the best-laid plans have a habit of going entirely their own way.

36

Back at Willow Cottage, Anna was busy putting her own plan into operation.

Earlier, while Jessica had been in the bathroom getting ready to go out, she had sneaked into her daughter's bedroom and had found what she needed. She was now tapping the number from Jessica's address book into the phone, hardly daring to hope that it would be answered.

It was, almost immediately, which gave her no time to consider what she was going to say.

'Yes,' barked out a cross voice at the other end of the line.

'Good evening, is that Piers Lambert?'

'Of course it is, who else would be answering my private line at this time of night?'

'My word, you're just as Jessica described you.'

'I beg your pardon? Who is this?'

'My name is Anna Lloyd, I'm Jessica's mother.'

'Are you indeed? And what precisely can I do for you?'

Anna told him.

Mo shared a large Victorian house in Rusholme with two female engineering students, a hairdresser – who frequently carried out ground-breaking experiments on Mo's hair, often with hair-raising results – and a night-club bouncer. Josh had been to the house just once before. He'd driven Mo home from work one day when she'd been ill and had come away thinking that its colourful inhabitants made the characters of *This Life* look like wooden extras from *Crossroads*.

There was nowhere to park directly outside Mo's place, but further up the road there was a parking space between an electric-blue VW Beetle and a wreck of a Fiat Panda. Josh squeezed his Shogun into the space and noticed his brother's car across the road where it was parked in front of a house that looked like it had been burnt out; all the windows were boarded up. He wondered if Charlie had persuaded Rachel to come. It probably wasn't Rachel's kind of party. She struck Josh as being more of a canapé-and-spritzer party-goer.

'Am I going to feel very old and out of it here?' Jessica broke into his thoughts. 'You did say Mo was only twenty-five. Won't all her friends be horribly young and trendy?'

Josh smiled. 'Horribly young and trendy.'

Jessica groaned. 'I knew it. It'll be wall-to-wall global hip-hop, oversized jeans with crotches dragging on the floor, drugs in your face and everyone punctuating their sentences with the word shag.'

Josh smiled again and got out of the car. When Jessica joined him on the pavement and he'd activated the alarm, he said, 'You wouldn't be judging others by your own twenty-something behaviour, would you?'

'Certainly not. When I was Mo's age I needed a clear head to chase all those hunks up and down the slopes of Colorado.'

He put his arm around her. 'I'm not sure I like the sound of that.'

She looked up at him with a smile. 'Why's that?'

He returned her gaze. 'Why do you think?'

'I must be particularly dense tonight, I need it spelling out for me.'

'I've always believed that actions speak louder than words.' And manoeuvring her back against the side of the car, Josh pressed his body against hers and kissed her for the longest of moments. 'Now does that give you any kind of a clue?' he asked.

'It was a bit cryptic in places.'

He kissed her again. Longer and deeper. 'We don't have to go to this party,' he said, after they'd been disturbed by an elderly woman passing with her dog, 'we could go back to your place and –'

She laughed. 'Crawford, get your desire in check and lead me on to the party.'

The hum and thud of a thousand decibels spilled out across the untidy front garden as the door was opened to them by a young black man who was wearing a Jimi Hendrix hairdo and a magenta-coloured velvet suit. He ushered them through the house to a large kitchen where a crowd of people were gathered round a selection of bottles that could have stocked a small off-licence.

'Help yourself, man,' Jimi Hendrix said to Josh. He left them to it.

'What do you fancy?' Josh asked Jessica.

'Some kind of white wine would be nice . . . *man.*'

Josh smiled and began opening a new bottle of wine – he'd heard enough morning-after stories from Mo to know that it wouldn't be wise to trust any of the opened bottles. When he'd poured out two plastic cups of plonk, he said, 'Come on, let's go and find the birthday girl.'

They found her outside in the long thin back garden, where some of the trees and bushes had been decorated with fairy lights. There were flaming torches pushed into the ground and candles flickering on all the window-sills of the house. Mo was easy to spot and Josh burst out laughing when he saw her. She was bouncing on a trampoline and showing off a pair of frilly patriotic knickers to a delighted crowd of onlookers. She saw Josh and waved at him mid-bounce. He waved back and caught sight of his brother in the crowd gathered round the trampoline, and surprise, surprise, there didn't seem to be any sign of Rachel. Holding Jessica by the arm, he took her over to meet Charlie.

'At long last we meet,' Charlie said warmly, 'I've heard a lot about you.'

'Not as much as I've heard about you.' Jessica laughed, realising that this was the good-looking man she'd seen with the suspected take-away and the flashy sports car. As brothers went, the resemblance wasn't that strong between them. If she had to guess which was the elder, she'd say it was Charlie. She wondered if he was envious of Josh's youthful looks and the complete absence of grey from his thick dark-brown hair – Charlie's, she noticed, was speckled with grey and was showing signs of receding.

'What's with the trampoline?' asked Josh.

'It's a present from her parents,' Charlie said, 'apparently she always wanted a trampoline as a child, but it's only now that they thought they could trust her with one.'

'How wrong could they be.' Josh smiled.

Jessica turned her attention back to Mo. She'd been joined on the trampoline by a beautiful-looking Asian man, with a long plait of silky black hair swishing behind him like the tail of a frisky pony.

'Who's the guy with her?' asked Jessica.

'That's Sid,' Josh said, 'he's our designer. His parents are from Hong Kong and he's invaluable on any of our buying trips to the Far East.'

'He's also mad about Mo,' Charlie added.

'They look like they'd make a great couple,' Jessica said as she observed the antics going on in front of her.

'And so they would, but unfortunately Mo carries the torch of love for somebody –'

'Give it a rest, Charlie,' Josh interrupted. 'Jessica doesn't want to hear about that.' And draining his plastic cup he said, 'Anyone for another drink?'

'No thanks,' Jessica said – she'd barely touched hers.

'If you're going that way, you can get me something non-alcoholic.' Charlie handed Josh his empty cup.

'So who's Mo carrying a torch for?' Jessica asked Charlie, as soon as Josh was out of earshot.

'Yonder brother, of course.'

Jessica raised an eyebrow. 'And he's never . . . you know . . .'

'Good Lord, no. Mo's been with us since she was seventeen. I guess we both look on her as a kid sister.'

'Which she probably hates.'

'If she does, she's never shown it.'

'But then, as we all know, men are not the most perceptive or sensitive of beings.'

'So how's your mother?'

Jessica laughed out loud. 'Now you're scaring me. In that one simple question you hope to prove that not only do you and Josh communicate with one another, but that you can be sensitive enough to a complete stranger to enquire after a relative's well-being. I like it, the Crawford brothers are the exception to the rule, they have finer feelings just like women.'

'So, how *is* your mother?' Charlie pursued, entertained by Jessica's forthright manner.

Jessica frowned. 'I don't know is the honest answer. She's got a broken arm and a cracked rib, and tries to make out that she's as fit as a fiddle. If she had her way, she'd dispense with her cast and sling, wrap a bit of sticking plaster round her wrist, pull on her gardening gloves and dig up half of Cheshire.'

'Poor you. It's not easy caring for people, is it?'

'You're not kidding,' but then, catching the reflective tone in Charlie's voice and remembering what Josh had told her about his brother, she said, 'I'm sure you'd be easy to look after.'

He gave her a puzzled look. 'Let's hope I'm never in that situation.'

'Ooh, my legs feel all wobbly, like I've been on a boat.' It was Mo and she was breathless and perspiring from all the bouncing. She reached out to Charlie to steady herself.

'Happy birthday,' he said, propping her up and kissing her cheek.

'Where's Josh?'

'Doing what he's best at, fetching drinks. This is Jessica, by the way.'

'Hi,' Jessica said. As Mo turned to face her she was conscious that the young girl was sizing her up. Jessica was surprised how antagonistic she felt towards Mo. When Charlie had said that Mo had a bit of a thing for Josh, her stomach had done silly things like lurch about. It had reminded her of days gone by when she had discovered Gavin had been seeing other women. She glanced around her, suddenly wanting Josh back by her side, where she could see him ... where she could keep an eye on him.

She saw him making his way through the crowd of guests and experienced a wave of relief. No, it wasn't relief, it was something else. But what? She stared at his limping figure as he approached and tried to assimilate what her response to the sight of him really meant. Could the combination of that handsome face and those intense brown eyes really be held responsible for making her feel so extraordinarily weak at the knees? Could that tall slim body truly hold so much attraction for her? Could the thought of those hands that were so gentle and instinctive when they caressed her body actually cause her mouth to go so dry? And while they were on the subject, that mouth of his had a charm all of its own. As kissers went, he was the best. Definitely in a class of his own. When God had been handing out the attributes guaranteed to make a man physically irresistible to a woman, he'd given Josh the top-drawer stuff. There'd been no stinting. Josh, my lad, God would have said when he'd seen what he'd created, with you I am well pleased.

Jessica smiled to herself and suddenly realised that she'd stopped breathing, that her throat was tight with desire. She gulped back her wine, draining the plastic cup in one go. And as she did, she found herself admitting that it wasn't a mere physical desire that she felt for Josh. It was much more. And it scared her.

'Hello, Mo,' he said, when he finally drew level. He handed Charlie his drink, then put his hand in his jacket pocket. He pulled out a small package. 'Happy birthday, it's from Charlie and me.'

Mo's face broke into a smile as her eager fingers slipped off the wrapping paper to reveal a box. She opened it hurriedly and lifted away a layer of cotton wool. 'It's beautiful,' she cried, holding up a silver bangle. 'I love it!

Thank you so much.' She kissed Charlie without thinking, but approached Josh more shyly.

Once again Jessica's stomach gave a sharp involuntary lurch.

At eleven o'clock, when it was too chilly to stay outside in the garden – unless you were prepared to keep warm by flinging yourself about on the trampoline – Jessica and Josh went inside, to a room that on his previous visit Josh was convinced had been the sitting-room. Now it was empty of most of its furniture, the lights had been lowered and people were dancing to boppy music blaring from two enormous loudspeakers.

'We ought to be thinking about going,' Josh said. The last thing he needed was Jessica wanting him to dance with her. He'd been standing for most of the night and his leg was good for nothing now; his knee ached and every now and again a stab of pain seared through him. 'I did promise your mother I wouldn't get you home too late,' he added.

'Oh,' said Jessica, disappointed. 'Couldn't we have one quick boogie?' She'd drunk just enough wine to think that maybe her mother could manage a short while longer without her.

Josh hesitated. 'I ... I'm not very good at dancing.'

Jessica laughed. 'You don't have to be.' And when the record abruptly changed to a slow, smoochy number she said, 'Come on, I actually recognise this, it's Elton John, isn't it?'

'George Michael, you idiot.'

'I knew that.' She took his hands and pulled him towards the other couples.

He held her close as they came together and hoped that she wouldn't notice the lack of movement on his part.

'You feel tense,' she remarked.

'Just tired,' he said and, looking for a way to distract her, he asked, 'Any chance of a kiss?'

'Only the one?'

'Quality, not quantity, that's what I always say.'

'Here goes then.'

And by the time they'd kissed their way through 'You Have Been Loved', Jessica no longer felt scared by her earlier realisation.

After all, what possible harm could she come to by falling in love with Josh Crawford?

While Josh looked for Mo to say goodbye, Jessica went in search of the bathroom. There were numerous bodies to pick her way over as she climbed the stairs and when she reached the landing she found Mo all alone and slumped on the floor. She looked ghastly and was holding a wet flannel to her forehead. 'I don't think Bacardi should be so vigorously shaken,' she moaned.

'Can I get you anything?' Jessica asked, crouching beside her. Suddenly Mo didn't seem like a rival any more. In fact, she seemed more like a poor sick child.

'It was probably the pizza I had afterwards that did it,' Mo whimpered.

'Anchovies don't agree with me. I never learn. The five triple vodkas and Cokes was pushing it a bit, I guess.'

Jessica tried not to laugh. 'Do you think some cold water might be in order?'

Mo groaned. 'Death. That's what I need. Nothing heroic, mind. Just a small affair, me and the grim reaper, face to face. I'd go quietly, I'd be no trouble.'

'And what about the funeral? Any ideas on that?'

'Yes. I want a Princess Di do, lots of flowers and fuss. And I'd like Josh to follow the coffin if that's okay with you.'

'I'm sure he'd oblige.'

Mo lowered the flannel from her face and looked at Jessica. 'You're a lucky bitch. I'd give anything to be in your shoes. You will take care of him, won't you?'

Jessica frowned. 'He doesn't seem to be the sort who needs taking care of.'

Mo tried to smile knowingly, but it came out as a sickly grimace. She returned the wet flannel to her forehead and groaned. 'He pretends he doesn't, but really he does. It's what makes him so bloody moody at times. But then you must have noticed that, one minute he's up and the next he's down.'

Jessica shook her head. 'I'm not sure what you're talking about.'

'It's what MS does to you. And before you jump to the wrong conclusion, I don't love him out of sympathy, I loved him way before his illness was diagnosed. I just hope you're not going to dump him like the last girl-friend did. Oh, bugger, I'm going to be sick again.'

Jessica watched Mo stagger into the bathroom just in time. She slowly went back downstairs and with each body she climbed over she asked herself a question.

Why had he lied?

Why had he wanted to keep it from her?

Was this what he had been trying to talk to her about?

And if it was, why had he turned it into such a big deal?

And what the hell was multiple sclerosis anyway?

She suddenly felt angry, as if Josh had been cheating on her.

When she reached the bottom of the stairs she found him waiting for her by the front door. Charlie was with him.

'We couldn't find Mo,' Josh said, when he saw her, 'somebody said she wasn't feeling well.'

'I've just been talking to her,' Jessica said coolly. 'In fact, we had a surprisingly interesting conversation. Revealing is perhaps the word I'd use. Josh, why did you make me believe that your brother suffered from multiple sclerosis? Why didn't you tell me the truth?'

37

Somebody had turned up the volume of the music and above the sonic-boom effect of Oasis's 'Roll With It' coming at them down the narrow length of the hallway Charlie said, 'I think this is best sorted out between the pair of you.' And without another word, or a backward glance, he opened the front door and shot out into the night.

'Well?' said Jessica, 'I'm waiting for an explanation.'

Josh leant against the wall behind him and lowered his head. 'Not here,' was all he said.

They drove in brooding silence through the streets of Rusholme and only when they joined the A34 did Josh say anything. 'I'll explain it all when we get home.' His face was dark and sombre. He passed her his mobile phone. 'Perhaps you'd better ring your mother and check that she's okay and tell her that you'll be later than you thought.'

When they reached Cholmford Hall Mews, he parked alongside his house and let them in. He went straight to the kitchen where he poured out two large glasses of Southern Comfort. He added some ice and passed one to Jessica. He took her through to the sitting-room. 'Sit down,' he said, gesturing towards the sofa. He didn't join her, but walked stiffly over to a chair and sank gratefully into it, all his energy now gone. He knocked back half his drink in one quick mouthful. 'So what's your first question?' he said, his eyes fixed firmly on the glass in his hand.

Jessica stared thoughtfully across the room at him. 'I'm not sure,' she said. As they'd driven away from the party she'd had all sorts of questions in mind to fire at Josh, but his uncommunicative manner in the car had made it very clear to her that he didn't want to talk to her then and she'd respected his wishes. But now that she was being given the opportunity to speak she found that she couldn't. It was the sight of his obvious discomfort that was unnerving her. He looked so downcast. So defeated. She'd never seen him like this before.

'Don't you want to know why I concealed it from you?' he asked. 'I would have thought you were dying to know that.' There was a hardness to his voice that made his question sound like an accusation. He still didn't look at her.

'Again I'm not sure,' she said. 'I don't understand why you've turned your illness into such a big deal.'

Now he did look up and straight at her. 'Because for me it is a big deal. Don't you know *anything* about MS?'

She shook her head. 'I told you that the night of my migraine attack, don't you remember –?'

'Yes,' he snapped loudly, 'I remember that perfectly well, there's nothing wrong with my memory. I'm not that far gone.' He lowered his eyes and ran a hand through his hair. 'I'm sorry, I didn't mean to . . .' He drained his glass and banged it down on the table in front of him. 'I'm really sorry, Jessica. This is so bloody important to me and I just seem to be making a hash of it.'

She gave him a tiny smile of encouragement. 'Why don't you tell me why you felt the need to hide your illness from me? When we've dealt with that you can explain what MS is. How does that sound?'

He let out his breath, surprised how reasonable she was being. 'How about another drink?'

'Just get on with it,' she said gently.

He ran a hand over his chin. 'Okay, here goes. But first, I want you to know that I did try telling you . . . it was the night your mother had her accident.'

'I guessed that.'

'I'd spent the best part of the day planning what to say.' He paused, then got to his feet. 'It's no good, I definitely need another drink. You sure you won't join me?'

She shook her head. When he came back into the room he sat down again and she watched him nervously turn the glass round in his hands. The room was so quiet she could hear the cubes of ice chinking against the sides of the glass. She wanted to prompt him, but knew she mustn't – whatever it was he had to say, he had to say it in his own time.

At last he spoke. 'The reason I felt so compelled to hide my MS from you,' he said in a low voice, 'is because my last girlfriend beat a hasty retreat the moment I explained it to her and . . . and I thought that so long as you didn't know there was anything wrong with me I could carry on seeing you.'

'And is that what you expect me to do now,' she asked quietly, 'to run off at the double?'

He shrugged. 'Maybe not right away, but in time, yes.'

'Then you have a very poor opinion of people, Josh. What gives you the right to put a ceiling on my feelings for you?'

He looked up. 'But you said yourself that you don't know anything about MS. You don't know the implications.'

'We'll get on to that in a minute. But first I want to know how far your deception went. Did it include avoiding me at times?'

He nodded guiltily. 'More times than I care to think of.'

She smiled, relieved. 'And there was I convinced that you were doing a Gavin on me.'

'Believe me, Jessica, that would have taken more energy than I possess . . . and even if I had the energy I would never do that to you.'

She went to him and knelt on the floor at his feet. She rested her head against his legs.

'Can I ask *you* a question now?' he asked.

'Of course.'

'When you came down the stairs at Mo's and you said that you'd just been talking to her, you seemed angry. Were you?'

She turned and looked at him. 'I was furious, if you must know, I was spitting bricks.'

'Why?'

'The situation reminded me of Gavin. I know it sounds crazy, but from where I was standing I'd suddenly found out something about you and it was like discovering you'd been lying and cheating on me.'

He stroked her hair. 'I'm so very sorry.'

'Don't be.' She lifted his hand from her head and gently squeezed it within her own. 'Now I want you to tell me what's wrong with you. And no glossing over anything. I want the truth. Tell me everything.'

He sighed. 'Where do I start?'

'In true story-telling tradition, try the beginning.'

'Okay. I have what is known as relapsing-remitting multiple sclerosis.' His voice sounded flat and uninteresting, as if he were reading from a script. 'Which means the symptoms I experience come and go as they please. I have no control over them, I'm at the mercy of whatever my body decides to chuck at me.'

'Such as?'

He let go of her hand and stroked her hair again. 'You name it,' he said. 'The most obvious and frequent symptom I have is the lack of mobility in my leg, which seems to be getting steadily worse ... I'm afraid I blatantly lied about that, by the way.'

She smiled cautiously. 'Not a heroic skiing injury then?'

''Fraid not.' He then went on to describe the catalogue of symptoms he'd experienced over the past few years; the slurred speech, the numbness, the tingling, the acute fatigue, the lack of control over his limbs and the most frightening of the lot, the momentary loss of sight in one of his eyes.

When he finished Jessica said, 'But what about a cure?'

He shook his head. 'Nothing. Not even a wonder drug that puts the illness on hold.'

She frowned. 'How bloody unfair! And how bloody awful for you.'

'It isn't always awful,' he said, surprised to hear himself admitting this, 'the symptoms vary in severity, there are some good days.'

'And today?'

He smiled. 'Today's been okay, which was why I plucked up the courage to ask you to come to Mo's party.'

She thought about this. 'Does that mean I've only ever seen you on your good days?'

He nodded. 'Apart from when I moved in and burst in on you and your mother. My speech was all over the place, I could barely get the words out.'

Jessica recalled the day with shame, seeing now his apparently ill-mannered behaviour in a completely different light. 'I'm sorry I thought you'd been rude and even sorrier that I told you so to your face. That was terrible of me.'

'Forget it,' he said lightly. 'You weren't to know. And anyway, that's nothing compared with what I've done to you. I can't begin to think what you must have thought of me each time I deserted you after we'd made love. I hated doing that.'

'I hated it as well. What were you so frightened of?'

'Of the morning ... of you waking to the truth about me and discovering that I wasn't the man you thought I was.'

'And I suppose you didn't really have flu the other week.'

'No. I ... I'd been feeling particularly ill that week and I collapsed at work ... Charlie had to bring me home.'

She looked up at him, full of concern. 'Oh, Josh, I wish you'd told me, I could have helped. I could have been there for you.'

'It's bad enough having to face up to MS oneself without admitting to other people what's going on. Half the time I don't even tell Charlie what's happening, I'm afraid I make his life hell.'

'He strikes me as being able to cope.'

'I'm not sure at times whether he is,' Josh said reflectively, 'he's had to put up with a lot of crap from me. My parents too. Even Mo.'

Jessica smiled. 'Talking of Mo, you do realise that she's completely and utterly in love with you, don't you?'

He didn't answer her. Instead he pulled her on to his lap. 'But more to the point,' he said, 'do you realise that I've gone and let myself fall in love with you?'

'Hang on a moment,' she said with a nervous little laugh, 'it's me who's supposed to write the romantic lines.'

'I'm not kidding, Jessica. God help you, but it's the truth.'

'I'm delighted to hear it, because I reached the same decision about you earlier this evening.'

'You did? My God! When?'

'When I thought that Mo might be a threat, I was so mad with jealousy I could have torn the sweet girl limb from limb.'

He laughed happily and held her close. He couldn't believe the way the evening had turned out. 'I don't suppose there's any chance of you staying the night with me, is there?'

'Mm ... that's a tempting offer, Crawford.' And relaxing into his embrace, she settled herself in for a good long kiss. But suddenly she sat bolt upright. 'I've forgotten all about my mother! What time is it?'

He looked at his watch. 'One o'clock.'

'*What!*' She sprang out of his lap.

'Calm down. If there'd been a problem she would have phoned. Now let me get my keys and I'll drive you back.'

'You sure you're safe to drive,' she asked when they were outside and he was locking his front door. 'You haven't had too much to drink, have you?'

'I'm fine,' he said. He opened her side of the car and just as she was about to climb in he took her in his arms. 'I'm claiming my good-night kiss now,' he said, 'I might not get another chance.'

38

Jessica started buttering a piece of toast for her mother. She spread the low-fat butter substitute evenly, right to the darkened edges of the crusts, then added some of Anna's home-made whisky-spiked marmalade; this too was pressed into place with careful precision, ensuring an equal distribution of finely shredded orange peel. And all the time she was doing this Jessica was thinking of Josh.

Last night he had shared with her two vital pieces of information: first, that he suffered from some illness which he'd gone to great lengths to hide from her, and second ... and second, that he loved her.

He actually loved her.

Amazing!

Getting anybody to fall in love with her in the past had always been such a mighty uphill struggle – in fact, she doubted whether it had ever happened. Certainly Gavin had never loved her.

But Josh did!

And she loved him.

Oh, yes. She loved him right enough. Falling in love with Josh Crawford had been effortless, it had been as easy, as the silly cliché goes, as falling off a log – just like they had that night in the copse.

In a funny way it almost seemed unfair that it had been so easy to fall in love with Josh and he with her, when for more than a year she had tried to make Gavin do the same – or at least care for her exclusively. But it had never happened. It was strange that so much hard work had gone into that particular relationship and it had all gone to waste.

It was very confusing.

As was Josh's illness.

She wasn't quite sure what to make of it. She knew that Josh had found last night an ordeal and that he'd done his best to explain what multiple sclerosis was all about, but when she'd woken up this morning she had realised that not once had he referred to the future.

What was his future?

Would he stay as he was?

Or was he likely to get worse?

And if so, what did that mean precisely?

And could MS be life-threatening?

Oh God! Why didn't she know? Why was she so ignorant?

And another thing. Why hadn't she sensed that there was something wrong with Josh? How blind and insensitive could a person be? For goodness sake, she was a writer, she was supposed to be a keen observer of her fellow human beings.

How damning it was to realise that she had been so shallow. Always, always, her response to Josh had been to consider the effect he had on her. How could she have viewed him in such a two-dimensional manner?

The answer, she suspected, lay in her relationship with Gavin. Determined never to allow another man to hurt her again she had probably been so preoccupied with self-protection that she had become introverted and unaware of those around her, only thinking what the consequences of anything would be to herself.

How selfish she had been.

Which was what she'd felt last night after Josh had dropped her off. When she had found Anna stretched out on the sofa, fast asleep with a throw-over covering her, she had been appalled. The fire had all but gone out and the faintly glowing embers had stared back at her accusingly as though reprimanding her for having neglected her mother that evening. Guilt had overwhelmed her. How could she have left Anna for so long? How could she have abandoned her mother when she needed her most? What kind of daughter was she that could behave so reprehensibly?

She cut the piece of toast diagonally in half and passed it across the table.

'A work of art,' Anna said, having spent the last five minutes watching her daughter closely, 'thank you.'

It was patently clear to Anna that Jessica had something on her mind. But then for that matter so did she.

Although it was only eight-thirty, Anna was willing the phone to ring; it was making her jumpy with nervous expectation. Piers Lambert had said he'd help and ridiculously she was sitting at the breakfast table waiting for him instantly to come to her aid. She had imagined him late last night bursting into action like some mighty Cape Crusader bringing forth with the dawn some way of getting Jessica off her back.

'What do you suggest?' had been his immediate response on the phone, when she'd told him what was going on.

'I don't know, that's why I'm ringing you.'

'You must have had some idea in mind or you wouldn't have called me.'

Jessica had told Anna many times that her agent was direct to the point of rudeness, but she was still taken by surprise at the severity of his manner which, instead of irritating her as she might have expected, did the opposite, it instilled within her a sense of hope – here was somebody who really would get her daughter to step in line and keep her there.

'I want you to crack the whip over Jessica,' Anna had said, 'make her believe that she's got to get on with writing this novel. Can't you make out that the deadline has been brought forward and that she's got to get back to work?'

'That wouldn't be for me to tell Jessica, that would have to come from her publishers. And I'm afraid Jessica's publishers aren't going to start switching round launch dates just to suit you.'

'But surely there must be something you can do.'

'When did she last do any writing?'

'Over a week ago.'

'That's not very long. I think you're exaggerating the case.'

'Look, Mr Lambert, my arm's going to be in plaster for at least another five weeks, maybe longer. Can she afford to take that much time off?'

'Mm ... perhaps you're right. Leave it with me. Good-night.'

Abrupt and to the point Piers Lambert certainly seemed to be, and Anna wished whole-heartedly that his actions would be as forceful and as effective as his behaviour implied.

Tony knew that he was becoming openly hostile towards Bloody Rita – any day now and he'd be lobbing ruddy great grenades at her. He didn't know what it was about her that got his back up most, her haughtiness, or her coldness towards him. He deliberately banged the phone down on the kitchen worktop so as to give his mother-in-law's eardrums a damn good jolt. He called out to Amanda. 'It's your mum,' he yelled at the top of his voice, knowing that such a breach of etiquette would have Bloody Rita blanching into her *Daily Mail* – it could have been worse, he could have referred to her as *mam*.

When Amanda appeared in the kitchen he said, 'I'm off out with Hattie to her ballet lesson, see you about a quarter past eleven.' He was tempted to hang about and eavesdrop on his wife's conversation – he still didn't know what she and her mother were up to – but with Hattie hovering at the front door dressed in her little pink leotard and white tights and her ballet shoes in her hands there was no time for loitering with intent. The thought crossed his mind that it wouldn't be a bad idea to make enquiries into obtaining a few bits and pieces of surveillance equipment, just some useful devices for tapping phones, that kind of thing. He smiled to himself, imagining what might follow if he went down that particular road of madness – he'd end up in a false beard and nose, darting about the streets in a raincoat shadowing Amanda. The idea was so ridiculous it cheered him and patting his daughter's head he said, 'Come on, Hattie, let's hit the road for *Swan Lake*.'

The hall was full of tiny girls, their hair swept back from their gleaming foreheads, their tummies and bottoms sticking out as they held on to the bar in breathless concentration as they bent their knees over their toes. When the music from a bulky ghetto blaster came to a stop, the girls relaxed, curtsied to their teacher and chanted '*Mercy M'dame*', then they stampeded to the back of the hall and their waiting parents, who were on hand with life-saving cartons of juice, bags of crisps and KitKats. Tony gave Hattie a quick kiss and watched her rush away on accentuated tiptoe to join her group – it was her second ever lesson and she was still in the first flourish of enthusiasm for a new-found hobby. He then slipped out of the hall and headed towards the newsagent's in the main street of Holmes Chapel.

The sun was shining and the sky was clear and bright, and it struck Tony as being the most perfect of September mornings. There was that satisfying feeling that the early chill in the air would be long gone by lunch-time and the rest of the day would be warm enough to sit outside with a glass of wine and the newspaper.

Or cut the grass, as Amanda would expect him to do.

He kept meaning to have a word with Josh, who had done the sensible thing and acquired himself a gardener. A gardener was definitely what Tony needed, somebody to take care of the grass and flower beds, leaving him free to plan his future.

In the newsagent's he bought a copy of the *Daily Mail* for Amanda – like mother like daughter – and *The Times* for himself. And while he was there, he couldn't resist scanning the shelves for a magazine aimed at the average man in the street interested in pursuing an innocent hobby of domestic espionage. Surely among the multitudinous and divers selection of magazines on offer there had to be at least one for a dim-witted husband wanting to know what his wife and mother-in-law were up to?

He paid for his papers and went back out on to the street, and weighing up whether he could be bothered to nip into the hardware store for some picture hooks that Amanda had been on at him to get, he suddenly caught sight of a flash of copper hair. It was Kate and she was walking towards the church on the opposite side of the road. Before he could stop himself he was calling out her name. 'Kate!'

She didn't hear him.

He stepped out into the road and immediately leapt back on to the pavement as a car hooted bad-temperedly at him. It was then that she noticed him. He waved over to her and when a flurry of cars had passed, he crossed the road and joined her. 'Hi,' he said. It seemed ages since their last conversation when so much had passed between them.

'Hello,' she said shyly. 'How are you?'

He nodded. 'Okay. How about you?'

'I'm fine.'

'And Alec?'

'Trying to say all the right things.' She lowered her eyes as if regretting what she'd just said.

'He'll come round. It'll be all right in the end.' Tony was surprised how sincere and genuine his voice sounded. Deep down, he didn't want Alec to 'come round'. He wanted him to be a bastard. He wanted Alec to play the Victorian baddie and be booed off the stage, so that he, wonderful, kind, considerate Tony, the young hero, could sweep the badly treated heroine off her feet and give everyone the happy ending they wanted. 'So where are you off to?' he asked, shocked at his shallowness.

She hesitated.

'Sorry, I didn't mean to pry.'

She smiled. 'No. I was just going to sit in St Luke's for a few minutes.'

He looked at the austere sandstone church behind them. He hadn't been inside a church since Eve's funeral, not since that dreadful day when he'd sat in the front pew and silently railed against a supposedly omnipotent and loving God, while all about him people prayed and sang hymns of thanksgiving and everlasting life. For him, though, it had been unthinkable to thank anybody who had seen fit to take away the woman he loved. 'Why?' he asked. 'Why do you want to go in there?'

She looked at him curiously. 'Because it usually makes me feel better.' This was even more unfathomable to Tony. 'Better?' he repeated.

'Yes,' she said simply. 'It's the sense of peace I come away with.'

'Oh.' A sense of peace was the last thing he'd come away with after Eve's funeral service. He didn't know what else to say, so looked along the street at the determined shoppers buzzing in and out of the shops. He was surprised to feel Kate's hand on his arm and even more so to feel her guiding him towards the studded oak door.

He stood in the half-light and swallowed. It wasn't the same church he'd sat in before, but to all intents and purposes it was identical. The pervading smell of age, polish and snuffed-out candles was the same. As was the morgue-like temperature. His body stiffened as feelings of remorse and anger crept over him. Kate began to move away. He quickly followed. He didn't want to be alone. She slipped into a pew and he sat alongside her. He tried to remind himself of the warm sunshine outside, of Hattie happily prancing about in her leotard, anything so long as he didn't have to be reminded of that awful day. He fiddled with the newspapers in his hands, then glanced at Kate, unsure what was expected of him if she was going to apply herself to meaningful contemplation. But instead of finding her deep in prayer he noticed that she was observing him. And closely. 'What is it?' he whispered. 'Why are you staring at me like that?'

'I was looking at the anger in your face,' she said gently.

He turned away. But then found himself face to face with the image of a tortured Christ on the cross in the stained-glass window above the altar. To the right of this was a wooden plaque honouring local men killed in the First World War. Was there no way of getting away from all the senseless suffering in the world?

'I don't think this is a good idea,' he said. 'I ought to be going, Hattie will be waiting for me.' He stumbled out of the pew and hurried towards the escape route. Outside on the pavement he blinked in the bright sunlight and caught his breath. To his horror he realised he was shaking. He breathed out deeply, willing his emotions back into line. But it was no good, it was too reminiscent of the worst day of his life. When the service had finished he'd started shaking and had broken down and wept. He could still remember the reaction from those around him. The older members of the families had frozen in their seats, unprepared and ill-equipped to cope with such a display of loss of control. It had been his closest friends who had comforted him, bundling him out of the church and taking him to the nearest pub for a stiff drink before driving on to the crematorium.

And a stiff drink was what he could do with right now.

The sound of the church door creaking behind him made him turn.

It was Kate. 'Are you okay?' she asked, her face full of anxious concern.

'Sorry about that,' he said, his breathing now back under control. 'You don't fancy a drink, do you?'

'It's a bit early for the pub to be open,' she said, gazing along the street in the direction of the Red Lion, 'you'll probably only get morning coffee served at this time of the day. And didn't you say that Hattie was waiting for you?'

He banged his head with the newspapers in his hands. 'Yeah, of course, stupid me. I'll see you, then.'

'Yes,' she said.

Neither of them made any attempt to move.

'You are okay, aren't you?' she asked again.

'Yes. No. No, I'm not. You have a strange and wonderful effect on me, Kate. You make me remember Eve . . . and you make me want to do crazy things like kiss you.' Which he did, suddenly and intensely. It was the first time since he'd been without Eve that he'd kissed a woman and meant it. His brain told him to stop. It was madness. The consequences could be disastrous. But his heart pounded out a different message.

39

Kate drove home in a state of heart-quickening confusion. She was not in the habit of kissing men so freely. But what made it worse was that deep down she had known Tony was going to do it . . . and that she was going to let him.

Ever since Monday morning she had found it difficult to shake off the effect of not just Tony's kindness towards her, but the desperate sadness of his circumstances, which he had conveyed to her so poignantly during their conversation. When he had spoken of his first wife she had wanted to console him, to show him the compassion he had shown her, but she had been wary of doing so, fearful of the consequences, knowing that in that precise moment they were both dangerously vulnerable; made weak and defenceless by their wretchedness – a heavy heart could be implicitly treacherous.

Later, and over lunch when Caroline had questioned her about Tony, she had refused to allow herself to be drawn into giving anything more than a superficial physical description of him, but inwardly she had been thinking of the soft blue eyes that had been unable to mask his misery; of the hand that had held hers; of the thoughtfully chosen gift; and of the expression on his face that night in Hattie's bedroom when she'd interrupted him chatting with his daughter.

His countenance had puzzled her at the time because she had been unable to define it.

But now she could.

Oh yes, she now knew exactly what it had meant. His actions a few minutes ago had defined it perfectly.

And what of her actions?

How exactly could they be categorised?

And how could she be attracted to Tony when she was carrying Alec's child? It went against everything she'd ever thought herself capable of.

She sped along the road away from Holmes Chapel, as though hoping to distance herself from what had just taken place. It was only a kiss, she told herself. A single kiss, that was all. It was hardly a breach of faith.

Except it was, she knew very well it was.

Afterwards Tony had said, 'I should probably apologise for doing that, but I'm not going to, I meant every second of it. When can I see you?'

Flustered, she had checked the busy street to see if anyone was watching them. But the Saturday-morning shoppers had all seemed safely occupied with their own tasks in hand and with a shake of her head she'd murmured, 'I don't know.' She had then fled to the car-park and had driven away without risking a backward glance.

When can I see you?

The words echoed inside her head as she entered the village of Cholmford. And just as she'd known that Tony would kiss her that morning, she was certain he would do so again and that she would let him ... that she would want him to.

'Did you get the flowers?' Alec asked Kate when she let herself in.

She stared back at him, mystified.

'You know, the flowers for Ruth,' he said.

The flowers! She'd forgotten all about them. They had been one of the reasons for her visit to Holmes Chapel, she was supposed to pick up something nice from the florist to take to Ruth's for lunch that day. 'I um ... I forgot,' she said truthfully.

Alec smiled at her. 'The hormones have started blatting the little grey cells, have they?'

'Something like that,' she said uneasily, wondering if she could ever legitimately lay the responsibility of that morning's breach of faith on her mixed-up hormones.

'Don't look so worried, we'll get something on the way. Did you remember the dry-cleaning?'

'Yes,' she said with relief – thank goodness she had dropped off Alec's suit before she'd decided to cross the road to go into St Luke's.

Since moving to the area she had often visited the small sandstone church, finding herself drawn to the building that quietly dominated the square in the centre of the village. This morning she had felt the pull of its tranquil sanctuary even more keenly and had gone there in search of a few minutes of calm repose. She had wanted to think about Alec and his apparent acceptance of their child.

'Did they say when it would be ready?' he asked.

'Sorry,' she said, 'when will what be ready?'

He smiled indulgently. 'Your memory really is going, isn't it? I was asking about the dry-cleaning.'

'Oh, that. It'll be ready on Tuesday.'

'That's fine. Do you fancy some coffee? I've put the kettle on. It's such a lovely day I thought we could sit on the patio. We won't get many more chances like this. A few more weeks and it'll be autumn for real.'

'I'll have tea, please, I've gone right off coffee.' She left Alec in the kitchen and disappeared out into the garden, where she hoped to pull herself together. The sight and sound of Alec acting as he always did was too much for her. She wanted him to treat her horribly, at least then she could justify what she had done that morning. How could he treat her so courteously when she was considering ... she swallowed hard and tried to force herself to put into words exactly what she was considering.

But she couldn't.

*

Alec drove them to Ruth and Adam's for lunch, stopping on the way at a petrol station to pick up a bunch of rather tired-looking carnations. 'Not as elegantly wrapped as we might have wanted,' he joked when he got back in the car, 'but it'll give Ruth something to be picky about. I swear that girl gets worse. Sometimes I'm ashamed to admit that she's my own.'

Ruth certainly seemed to be on top picky form when she opened the door to them. 'You're early,' she said, clearly annoyed by this lack of thought on their part.

'Hello to you too,' Alec said cheerily, 'have some flowers. And don't worry about us, we won't get in your way, in fact we'll hide in the car if you'd prefer.'

'Dad, you know perfectly well that sarcasm is the lowest form –'

'Of wit,' he finished for her. 'Yes, I know that and don't you just love it? Now point me in the direction of a good bottle of wine and I'll leave you well alone. Hello, Oscar, my fine young man, and how are you?'

Oscar came towards them.

'Shake hands, Oscar,' his mother said.

Oscar extended an awkward hand.

'Other one,' Ruth said sharply.

Kate intervened and stooped down to the little boy. 'I'd rather have a hug.'

Ruth tutted and led the way through to the kitchen. 'Adam!' she called out indiscriminately to some other part of the house, 'Dad and Kate are here, come and entertain them, I've got far too much to do.'

Melissa and Tim arrived late, which caused Ruth further distress. She was so preoccupied with the inconvenience thrust upon her – the pork was overdone and the potatoes were past eating – that she was blind to what was glaringly obvious to the rest of them: Tim and Melissa must have just had an almighty blazing row. Their faces were set like stone, they looked charged and ready to go off at the slightest provocation.

'It's Tim's fault we're so late,' Melissa said as Adam handed her a glass of wine, 'I told him to be ready at twelve, but would he listen?'

'And I told you first thing that I had some important phone calls to make.' Tim's voice was taut with anger, his eyes narrow and threatening.

But by the time they took their seats at the dining-room table the mood had calmed down. Whatever storm had rocked their boat, it seemed to have been lulled. Melissa was now talking about some elderly distant relative in Aberdeen who had recently married his octogenarian neighbour; a woman whom he'd known for the past fifty-five years.

'It was only a small Registry Office do,' Melissa was saying, 'that's why none of us was invited.'

'Can't say that I'd have wanted to go,' Ruth said, pulling a face and passing the first plate of carved meat to her mother. 'Just imagine all those zimmer frames cluttering up the place, to say nothing of the disgusting smell of old age. Oscar, put that book down, it's time to eat.'

'What a kindly view of the elderly you have, Ruth,' Alec said lightheartedly, 'I feel wonderfully reassured by it and can just see you selflessly taking care of me in my dotage. I look forward to that day.'

Ruth passed a plate to Kate. 'Thankfully, I shan't be called upon for that duty; you'll have Kate to swill out your false teeth and change your incontinence pads.'

All trace of the humour that had been on Alec's face was suddenly gone. Kate decided to put Ruth in her place. 'Well,' she said in a clear voice and looking straight at Ruth, 'who knows, Alec might even now end up fathering a child who would *want* to take good care of him if the situation arose.'

Ruth let out a scornful laugh. 'Well, that's the most ridiculous thing I've ever heard. Dad's well past all that, thank God. Oscar, here's your plate.'

His normal composure quickly restored, Alec gave Kate a grateful smile. Earlier in the week he had specifically asked Kate not to tell anyone in his family about the baby. 'I want to be the one who tells them and in my own time,' he'd said to her, but with a certain amount of malicious delight coming to the fore, he concluded that now was as good a time as any to break the news. Indeed, his anger at Ruth's thoughtless words convinced him there could be no better opportunity. 'Actually,' he said, raising his glass of Côte du Rhône and gazing at it intently, then twirling it round in his hand and giving off an air of easy nonchalance, 'you couldn't be more wrong, Ruth. It gives me great pleasure to tell you that Kate and I are expecting our first child.'

The silence was stupendous.

As was the expression on Ruth's face.

It was Tim who was the first to congratulate them. 'Well done, both of you,' he said, then, looking pointedly at Melissa, he added, 'and wouldn't it be a laugh if Melissa and I were to follow suit?' Melissa's eyes glittered back at him. Undaunted, he raised his glass, 'To Alec and Kate's baby, may it be the first of many!'

Half-hearted voices around the table joined in, but Kate sensed that the mood was as congratulatory as a deathbed scene.

'Are you sure?' Ruth said when the initial shock had died away.

Alec laughed. 'Well of course we are. Kate's done one of those tests from the chemist.'

Ruth laughed nastily. 'Those do-it-yourself kits aren't all they're cracked up to be,' she said dismissively, 'they can't be relied upon.'

'I've also been to the doctor,' Kate said with quiet authority as she helped Oscar to some carrots, 'and it's confirmed, it's official.'

'Oh, well, in that case you must be pregnant.'

'You don't sound very pleased, Ruth,' Alec said mischievously, at the same time holding back his surprise that Kate had been to the doctor without telling him, 'don't you like the idea of having a baby brother or sister?' He was enjoying himself now. He knew exactly how his daughter viewed him. Well, this would certainly show her.

'And why would you think that?' Ruth responded directly.

Her tight, scathing voice made Alec hesitate. They were suddenly heading into dangerous territory; sibling rivalry wasn't just for the young, it could kick in at any age. He looked at Melissa, hoping that she might defuse the situation – she'd always been able to calm Ruth in moments of high drama – but all he got from her was an expression that clearly said, 'You've got yourself into this mess, you're on your own.'

'What kind of baby will it be?' asked Oscar, who was chasing a roast potato with his knife and fork – it was so overcooked it was taking all his concentration just to keep it from jumping off the plate.

'A perfect one,' answered Alec, quick as a flash, glad of his grandson's diversion.

Melissa groaned at the other end of the table. 'Not even being a father all over again gives you the right to start talking like that.'

'We'll have to wait and see whether it's a boy or a girl, Oscar,' Kate said. She was trying to work out why she wasn't delighted with Alec for telling his family about the baby, especially as he'd described it as their *first*.

Then it struck her what was wrong. Alec was using her pregnancy as a weapon against his charmless daughter.

Perhaps Melissa as well.

The thought chilled her.

No child of hers was ever going to be used as a weapon. She now wondered if Alec had only accepted the baby because he saw it as a way of scoring points over Ruth and his ex-wife.

40

By early Saturday evening Anna had come to terms with the knowledge that Piers was not going to come to her aid until at least Monday morning, so meanwhile there was nothing for it but to put up with Jessica's infuriating ministrations.

The only phone call they'd received was from Josh. He'd called not long after breakfast and as a consequence Jessica was now thrashing about in the kitchen putting together an unspeakably disgusting supper for the three of them to endure that evening.

When she'd heard her daughter talking to Josh on the phone she'd called out, 'Why don't you invite him for supper tonight?' She liked Josh. The truth was, she was quite taken with him and having his company at Willow Cottage did at least provide her with a welcome break from Jessica's new-found despotic behaviour. It was a shame, though, that her selfishness meant that poor Josh had to stomach one of Jessica's meals.

It was after his phone call that Jessica had explained to her why she had stayed out so late last night. 'I just don't see why he kept it from me,' Jessica had said.

But Anna could quite understand Josh's reasons for keeping quiet. 'The trouble with any serious illness or disability,' she'd told Jessica, 'is that it has a nasty habit of stripping away a person's dignity and that's what that young man is terrified of. He's intelligent and good-looking, and wants to be treated accordingly. He doesn't want shoulder-patting sympathy, no matter how well meant.'

They had then reached for the up-to-date *Family Medical Journal* that Anna had recently purchased from her book club and flicked through it looking for multiple sclerosis.

'*MS is an attack on the central nervous system, i.e. the brain and spinal cord,*' the opening paragraph began. It then went on to talk about something called myelin sheaths being destroyed and exposed nerve fibres preventing impulses from the brain being correctly transmitted. The author of the text wrote in matter-of-fact terms of the twenty per cent of extreme cases of MS sufferers who become so seriously disabled that they end up wheelchair-bound.

When they'd finished reading, Jessica had returned the book to the shelf with a worried expression on her face.

'Best not let on to Josh that we've been researching the subject,' Anna had said. 'And remember,' she'd added firmly, 'he's the same Josh you've come to know these past few months. You haven't treated him as a sick man up to this point, so there's no reason why you should start now.'

'I know that,' Jessica had said.

But Anna wasn't convinced that Jessica did. And hearing the sound of the doorbell and her daughter going to answer it, she sincerely hoped that she would heed her advice.

Josh arrived bearing almost more gifts than he could carry. He came into the sitting-room and Anna tried hard not to notice his limp – previously she'd never given it a second look, but now like a car accident on the motorway it was hard not to take her eyes off the stiffness of his leg and how it affected his gait.

'A fresh supply of chocolates for you,' he said, coming slowly over to where Anna was sitting and offering her a large flat box, 'I thought you might have finished the others by now.'

'Thank you,' she said with a smile, 'how thoughtful and intuitive of you.'

Then he turned to Jessica and handed her a beautifully arranged bouquet of red roses. He kissed her cheek. 'For being so understanding last night,' he whispered into her ear. 'And lastly, but by no means least, something for all of us, a bottle of wine.'

Jessica smiled and took that from him as well. 'Brilliant,' she said, 'it'll go a long way to disguising the awful meal I'm about to make you both eat.'

'Would you like some help?' he asked.

Anna laughed. 'Good idea, Josh. Jessica's told me what an excellent cook you are, why don't you go and see what culinary disaster she's got in store for us? I'm afraid my influence when she was growing up failed to bring out the slightest chance of any cookery expertise in her.'

'I'm sure it won't be that bad,' Josh said, already moving towards the kitchen with Jessica.

'Oh no,' she said to him, 'I'm not having you poking and prying into what I've been slaving over all afternoon and besides, you need to sit down.'

Anna bit her lip. Wrong thing to say, she wanted to shout across the room. She saw it in Josh's face only too plainly. But not in Jessica's. Oh dear, she thought, poor Josh.

When Jessica left the room, Josh came and sat by the fire with Anna. He stared into the burning logs and frowned, his face suddenly pensive, but at the same time painfully vulnerable.

Anna's heart went out to him. She decided to be honest with him. 'Jessica mentioned to me this morning what you told her last night,' she said.

He looked up morosely, his eyes dark and angry. 'What, that I love her, or that I'm a chronic invalid?'

Anna smiled kindly. 'She doesn't see you like that, Josh. Just give her time to understand. And by the way, love wasn't discussed, but I'm delighted that's the way you feel about my daughter. Now why don't you go and join her in the kitchen and help with the supper? At least then I might feel confident that we'll eat something slightly more appetising than wet newspaper.'

That night in bed, Tony lay next to Amanda unable to sleep. Like watching the winning goal in a Cup Final match being replayed over and over in slow motion he was reliving the moment when he'd kissed Kate.

And when *she'd* kissed him.

That it hadn't been a one-sided affair had surprised and delighted him. She hadn't pushed him away as he'd expected. There had been no slap in the face. No enraged 'How dare you!' or 'What the hell do you think you're doing?' None of that, just one long delicious moment of pleasure.

She had willingly kissed him, and kissed him with more passion than he'd dared to hope for. He had no idea when he would get the chance to see her alone again, but somehow he knew he would make it happen.

He got out of bed and went downstairs and looked out of the kitchen window across the moonlit courtyard. Number five was in darkness. Kate and Alec must have gone to bed. He turned away. He didn't want to imagine Kate in bed with Alec, couldn't bear the idea of another man's comforting arms around her.

So this is when the pain starts, he thought miserably.

As though he hadn't suffered enough already.

Kate wasn't lying in bed with Alec's comforting arms around her. She was staring out of the window and looking towards the copse of trees, remembering the evening she had gone there in tears when she and Alec had had their first argument. It seemed that ever since that night things had gone wrong between them.

They had very nearly argued again this afternoon when they'd driven back from Ruth and Adam's. It was only her guilt over Tony that had stopped her from challenging Alec about the way he'd announced to his family that she was pregnant. She recalled Jessica's words when she'd said that sometimes when a man became a father late in life there was an element of kudos to be revelled in. Was that what Alec was doing? Was he now hell-bent on proving his virility to Ruth and Melissa by flaunting his unborn child? She touched her stomach protectively, frightened that Alec might love their baby for all the wrong reasons.

But who was she to say what was the correct way to love a child? No two people experienced love in the same manner and anyway, it was generally agreed that fathers and mothers loved their children quite differently.

She sighed and a small misty patch of condensation appeared on the glass in front of her. She wiped it away with her fingers and wished it would be as simple to wipe away the sense of disappointment that had been steadily growing within her.

She was loved by a wonderful man and was pregnant – not so long ago this would have been all she would have wanted in life. But it was like wishing for a certain Christmas present for months and months, then opening it up on Christmas morning only to discover that it was no longer what you wanted.

So what did she want?

She turned and looked at Alec asleep in bed. He looked so peaceful, so at ease with himself. Tears pricked at her eyes and she swallowed back the painful truth that she no longer wanted Alec.

41

On Monday afternoon, just as the first of Ricki Lake's guests was within a whisker of being confronted with her worst fear in the hope of overcoming it, the phone rang – Anna's worst fear was that her lovely home would never be her own again, that Jessica would sell her house at Cholmford Hall Mews and make herself a permanent fixture at Willow Cottage.

She pointed the remote control at the television and turned down the sound on Ricki's over-excited audience, who were all now screaming and squirming as a large hairy spider was being presented to a visibly sweating, goggle-eyed Kansas mother of six, who in the interest of entertainment was giving a credible performance of a woman going to her death on national television – *you saw it here first, folks!* Out in the hall, Anna could hear Jessica speaking into the phone. From the tone of her voice it didn't sound like Josh. Was it Piers at last? She held her breath and listened in. She also quietly prayed for a small miracle.

'How on earth did you know that I was here, Piers?' Jessica asked.

'It's my job, Jessica, to know where and what you're doing. Haven't I always told you I'm supposed to make your life easier. A shame you couldn't do the same for me. I've been trying your house for days, only to get your maddening squeaky voice telling me you'll get right back to me. And as you haven't had the courtesy to do that, I've been forced into ringing this number which you gave me before you left Corfu.'

'Oh,' said Jessica, taken aback at such a long speech from Piers. Had she given him her mother's number? She couldn't remember ever doing so.

'Oh, indeed,' he said. 'So how's *A Casual Affair?*'

'Um . . .' Piers always made Jessica feel as if she were back at school when he started enquiring about her writing. The second he so much as hinted at wanting a progress report she was back in the classroom, explaining to Mr Hang'em-High-Delaney why she hadn't handed in her history essay on the Battle of Naseby. 'It's on hold for a while,' she said meekly. She took the wise precaution of backing away from the receiver.

'On hold!' roared Piers predictably. 'So that's how it is from now on, is it, Jessica? Suddenly you're earning real money and you're acting like a prima donna. You'll be expecting me to come up there and sort out your shopping next. Or maybe you've ideas of becoming another Barbra Streisand and will be wanting me to put rose petals down the loo for you!'

'I'd rather you cleaned it for me.'

'I bet you would. Now get on and explain what the hell you're playing at.'

'I've got personal problems,' she said – a comment like that to Hang'em-High-Delaney would have had him responding with *You certainly have, it's called scraping yourself off the floor after I've finished with you.* Or, *Miss Lloyd, I have no wish to know about your personal hygiene problems, kindly deal with them and get on with your work.*

'Haven't we all,' said Piers drily.

Which struck Jessica as odd. Piers wasn't the sort to have personal problems, he didn't fit the category at all; to have personal problems one had to have some kind of emotional sensitivity.

'My mother's had an accident,' she said, trying to sound as though she were in the driving seat of the conversation, 'and I'm taking care of her.' Frankly, though, it sounded too much like *Please Sir, the dog chewed up my history book.* 'She's broken her arm and cracked a rib,' she added, just in case Piers needed convincing. *Convincing!* What was she thinking of? What on earth was the matter with her? Why did she let Piers reduce her to this trembling, pathetic state? But it was a familiar question and one that she had never cared to explore too deeply. Delving into her private Pandora's box of lunacy was not a pastime she was keen to pursue. In her opinion it was best simply to nail the lid down on all that jolly psycho-babble and conclude that fathers who died before their daughters had had a chance to become an expensive millstone round their necks, had a lot to answer for.

'I'm sorry to hear about your mother,' Piers said, jolting her out of her thoughts, 'but I'm not sure I see how that prevents you from getting on with *A Casual Affair.*'

Because, you unfeeling soulless man, I can't think straight. Because all my energy's going into worrying about my mother. Surely even a Neanderthal simpleton like you can grasp that small but significant piece of information! And on top of all that I've gone and fallen in love with a man who has some bloody awful incurable disease.

Which was the stark reality of the situation in which she now found herself.

While out food shopping on Saturday afternoon and wondering what on earth she could cook for Josh that evening, she had taken a detour from the supermarket, headed for the nearest bookshop and bought their one and only book on the subject of MS. 'We don't get a lot of call for it,' the woman behind the till had said as she wiped the dust off the small paperback. 'I had an aunt who had MS,' she continued, handing over Jessica's change, 'or maybe it was ME, I get them confused. Anyhow, whatever it was, she died. Her blood got too thick, or was it too thin? She was only young.' Which choice comments had thoroughly depressed Jessica as she'd driven back to Cholmford. It was only late that night after Josh had gone home – having bravely forced down her watery, tasteless shepherd's pie, the lumps in the mashed potato being the only substance to the meal – that she had had an opportunity to open the book. It didn't make for soothing bedtime reading. When she reached the chapter on Sexual Difficulties she had switched off the light. She didn't want to think about that. Sex with Josh was great. Better than great, it was the best she'd ever known. It was chandelier-swingingly fantastic. But would it stay that way?

'Jessica?'

'I'm sorry, Piers, what were you saying?'

'I asked why you weren't getting on with what you're paid to do?'

Jessica muttered something about Anna needing a lot of attention.

'So what am I supposed to tell Cara?'

'Nothing, I'll talk to her.'

'All this is very unprofessional, Jessica, you do realise that, don't you? Especially as I've gone to a lot of trouble to get you a slot on telly, but obviously I can see that it's now out of the question. I'll call the producer back and tell him you're unavailable.'

'Hang on a moment, what slot on telly?'

Having just signed the last two letters that Stella was waiting for, Piers pushed them towards her hovering figure in the doorway of his office and, leaning back in his chair and satisfied that Jessica had taken the bait, he began reeling her in. 'It's not much,' he said airily, 'but it would have coincided nicely with the launch of your next hardback. Cara was delighted when I told her about it this morning.'

'So tell *me* about it.'

'It's one of those new daytime life-style programmes. You know the kind of thing, yesterday's bimbos now all grown up and presenting an hour of uplifting crap. The flavour is feel-good-anything's-possible. The idea was that you would be featured as a young independent woman, attractive and well-travelled, who can rattle off the odd novel while enjoying life to the full. You were supposed to be inspirational.'

Jessica liked the sound of herself. She said modestly, 'I'm not sure about the attractive bit.'

Piers ignored this and reeled her in a few more turns. 'It would be a shame to turn it down, but I can quite see that you wouldn't have the time to fit it in. After all, they'd want to come up and spend an entire day filming with you. It would be very time-consuming.'

'When were they thinking of?'

'They've a busy schedule, Jessica, they said they could only fit you in next week, it's then or never. But don't worry, I'll make the necessary apologetic noises and –'

'It's rather a good opportunity, isn't it? I'd hate to let Cara and the team down.'

Piers had her almost out of the water now; he'd never known an author turn down an opportunity to go on television. 'But like you said, you've got a lot on your plate, they'll understand.'

Jessica was already choosing a new outfit to wear for the programme, something smart, understated, classy, probably black. She'd go to Wilmslow and treat herself. 'No,' she said decisively, 'I've got to be professional about this. Tell them I'll do it.'

Piers snapped forward in his seat, triumphant. 'So long as you're sure,' he said, affecting a casual manner and then going in for the kill. 'Now before I forget, Cara mentioned something about your next book being brought out earlier than originally agreed.'

'How much earlier?'

'May.'

'*What!*'

'You heard, Jessica. Cara said she'll ring you about it. My advice is to crack on.'

He put down the phone, pleased with himself. Jessica had always been one of his most compliant authors. She'd never given him any trouble. Not like some. One author actually expected him to make theatre and restaurant reservations whenever he was up in town. It was the older ones who were the worst; they imagined themselves to be still living in an age when writers were revered as demi-gods. They hadn't sussed that these days nobody gave a monkey's arse for their art-form and that publishers were only interested in profit margins and bestseller lists. Most of the time his job swung between appeasing the appalling egos and vanity of his authors and the ruthless commercialism of their publishers.

And relying on Jessica's vanity had paid off. He had never doubted his ability to get her back to work, but even he hadn't been prepared for the face of good fortune to smile on him so benevolently.

Dinner on Saturday night with an old friend who two years ago had left the murky waters of the publishing industry for the equally shark-infested ones of the BBC had provided him with just the carrot he needed to get Jessica off her backside, or rather on to it and back at her laptop. Max had described the new show he was producing and said they'd been let down by an author and did he have a client – a female client – who had led an ordinary but verging on the interesting life. 'We don't want the bizarre or the surreal. Everybody's sick of publishing success stories achieved on the strength of the writer's dubious background. Ex-prostitutes turned born-again missionaries are out. So are tarnished politicians. We want an ordinary woman to whom the viewer can relate, or even aspire to. Know anyone of that ilk?'

This spectacular piece of good luck was then followed by Cara phoning him first thing that morning to explain that several of their lead titles for next year had been switched about and Jessica's was being brought forward, and did he think it would be a problem for her?

And so what if it was? The amount she was being paid she could bloody well pull her finger out. Not that he'd said as much to Cara. 'I'll put it to Jessica,' he'd told her, 'but you're expecting a lot, that's three months' working time you're cutting from her schedule. She'll expect something in return, like an extra push from the publicity department.'

He clasped his hands behind his head and leant back in his chair. Not a bad day's work all in all. And it would probably please Jessica's mother into the bargain, leaving her to enjoy her broken bones in peace.

But enough of the quiet reflection, there was still work to do. He bent forward in his seat and pulled the telephone towards him. His next task was to deal with a recalcitrant mystery writer suffering from writer's block and a monumental drink problem, who was already two months late for his deadline.

If Anna hadn't had a broken wrist she would have clapped her hands delightedly. Piers had come through for her! She tried hard not to look too pleased and stared solemnly at her daughter. 'So what you're saying is that they're bringing your book out that much earlier, which means you've got to finish it sooner. That's rough on you, isn't it?' She hoped there was enough sympathy in her voice.

'But kind of convenient for you, wouldn't you say?' Jessica said. 'You're thinking, yippee, Jessica won't have time to take care of me now, aren't you?'

'Nonsense, you know how much I've enjoyed having you here – why, it's what's kept me going these long dreary days.'

'Hah! You hate having me around.'

Anna smiled. 'On a permanent basis, yes. A lot of you goes a long way when you're trying to be nice, Jessica; you're a bit like saccharin.'

'Thanks for the recommendation, I'm flattered.'

'In the circumstances, it's the best I can do. When are you leaving?'

Jessica frowned. 'I'm not,' she said stubbornly. 'You need looking after. There are things you can't manage.'

'Such as?'

'A whole load.' Jessica looked helplessly about her. 'For a start, you can't clear out the ashes from the fire and re-lay it, and you certainly can't bring in the logs –'

'Only because you haven't let me. If I take it slowly –'

'No. It's out of the question.' Jessica began pacing the room. 'I can't leave you all alone, I shall have to work from here. I'll set myself up in the dining-room. Just because Cara has changed the goalposts it doesn't mean that I have to leave you.'

Disappointment made Anna want to cry. 'But Jessica, you're driving me mad,' she shouted angrily. 'I want some time on my own, why do you think I never remarried? Why do you think I've always lived in Cholmford where there aren't any neighbours to pester me? Can't you get it into your thick head? *I like being alone.*'

Jessica came to a stop behind the sofa. She rested her hands on the back of it and stared at her mother, amazed at her outburst.

'We've got to reach a compromise,' Anna said more calmly, but wondering whether it was physically possible to throttle her daughter with one hand.

Jessica continued to stare at her mother. Then very slowly she moved across the room and sat in the chair opposite her. 'You're right,' she said. Her voice suddenly sounded dragged down with resignation. 'It's just that I don't know how to compromise where you're concerned; you've done so much for me all my life.'

'I was only doing my job,' Anna said lightly, 'and I'm not sure I've done that much for you.'

'But you have. And now that it's my turn to look after you, you won't let me. You're not being fair.'

Anna smiled. 'When I really need your help I'll let you know. Let's just accept that now isn't that time.'

Jessica frowned, far from convinced that this was the case. She thought of her mother's angry outburst a few moments ago. 'Did you really mean what you just said, about not remarrying because you wanted to be on your own?'

'Absolutely. I've always enjoyed my freedom. Granted it's probably what's made me selfish and difficult to get on with, but it's my life and I'll live it exactly how I want to.'

'So you want me out?'

'Yes, please.'

'But what if something happens?'

'Why don't we do what Josh suggested?'

'What was that?'

'We'll get me a mobile phone and that way, should something go wrong, you know, like I collapse in the bathroom, I'll be able to call you at the flick of a switch.'

'Knowing you, you'll leave the wretched thing somewhere and forget where you've put it.'

'Do you mind! I'm not as daft as all that.'

'Or you'll run the batteries down and for that crucial phone call you won't be able to ring me.'

'Your over-active imagination is running away with you, dear.'

'Don't call me dear, it makes me deeply suspicious. Gavin started calling me *dear* and *darling* before I found out about Silicone Sal. And I don't care what you say, I should sleep here with you every night.'

Anna sighed. 'No,' she said firmly. 'You can pop in for a short while every day, just to make sure I haven't pegged out, but that's as far as it goes. Anyway, wouldn't you rather spend more time with Josh?'

Jessica opened her mouth to refute this, but found she couldn't. The truth was she did want to see more of Josh. Lots more of him. And now that he had nothing to hide from her they could actually spend a whole night together.

Seeing the hesitation in her daughter's face and knowing that the last of her resolve had been weakened, Anna pressed on: 'And as Piers has just told you, you have to concentrate on your writing. He and Cara are relying on you. Now tell me again about the BBC coming to film us.'

'*Us?* It's me, your young, attractive, independent daughter they're interested in,' Jessica said, aware that a feeling very much like relief was creeping over her.

'Really? I didn't know I had one of those. But they'll want to film a snippet or two of where you grew up, won't they?' Anna was thinking about getting the garden into shape ready for the cameras. She and Dermot could sweep up the leaves that were already beginning to fall and they could put them in a neat, tidy pile ready for a bonfire on the day the film crew came; bonfires with a thin trail of smoke hanging in the damp autumn air always looked so atmospheric on the television, she thought. What fun it would be.

42

Mo had spent most of the day in hiding. As soon as she'd caught sight of Josh entering the building earlier that morning she'd made herself scarce by disappearing to the loo. She even conned Sid into taking Josh's coffee to him. Sid knew all about what had happened at the party because after she'd finally made it back downstairs he'd told her what had gone on between Josh and Jessica. 'You're in it deep, Mo,' he'd said, 'about as deep as it gets. The look on the guy's face was awesome. I've never seen anything like it.'

'Oh shit,' she'd cried, realising with horror what she'd done, 'oh shit, oh shit, oh *shit!*'

'Yeah, that's the stuff you're knee-deep in,' Sid had said and, taking her through to the kitchen and pushing everyone out of the way, he'd started making her several gallons of black coffee.

'I don't need that,' she'd wailed hysterically. 'What you've just told me is sobering enough.'

'You're going to drink it,' he'd insisted.

Between forcing down several mugs of Turkish-strength coffee she'd kept saying, 'But I thought she knew. I really thought he must have told her. How was I to know he hadn't?'

'Come on,' Sid had said when she'd refused to drink any more, 'come and dance with me. You need cheering up.'

'No I don't,' she'd said miserably.

'Yes you do and while we dance we can work out what you're going to say to Josh on Monday morning.'

And here they were, half past five on Monday afternoon and still she hadn't plucked up the courage to speak to Josh. Sid had been great to her all day and had taken her out for a sandwich at lunch-time to try and calm her down. She knew that he fancied her and really he was quite cute, with that cool hair of his, and maybe she ought to think about him more seriously . . . now that Josh was probably never going to speak to her again.

She bent down beneath the reception desk and began getting her stuff ready to go home. She slipped a bundle of essay notes into her bag, along with a magazine, both of which she'd been too sick with nerves to so much as glance at during the day. When she stood upright she let out a sudden gasp – Josh was standing straight in front of her.

'Got time for a chat?' he asked.

There was no avoiding him now and with a leaden step she followed him slowly to his office, aware that everybody was staring at them – word had soon gone round that she'd blown her future with Crawford's. She was conscious, too, of the chunky heels of her knee-high PVC boots reverberating loudly on the wooden floor as if beating out a painfully slow death march. It made her remember what she'd said to Jessica about wanting Josh to follow behind her coffin when she was dead. Yes, she thought, he'd follow it all right and then stamp on her grave afterwards. How he must hate her. And with every right. She had committed the one act guaranteed to get up his nose: she had gossiped about his illness behind his back.

As she entered Josh's office she caught sight of Sid giving her an encouraging smile over the top of his computer. Then the door closed ominously behind her.

'How are you feeling?' Josh asked.

She watched him loosen his tie and undo the top button of his Paul Smith shirt; it was one of her favourites and it was attractively crumpled from its day's work. And as he rolled up his sleeves and leant back against his desk she thought, *God, I fancy him.* She then thought, *Jeez, girl, pull yourself together! This is no time for lust. This is the moment you get fired. You're history, kid. You're outta here.* 'I'm fine,' she muttered, suddenly remembering that Josh had asked her a question.

'You sure?'

She gave a little nod and twisted her hands nervously behind her back. Her fingers touched the silver bangle Josh and Charlie had given her. How she wished she could turn the clock back to that lovely precious moment in the garden when she'd opened their present.

He went and sat down and, still regarding her, removed his glasses and added them to a pile of sample T-shirts. 'I haven't been able to thank you for Friday evening,' he said. 'Whenever I went to look for you I couldn't find you.'

She swallowed and wished he'd just get on with it. Why put her through all this agony? Did he want her to suffer? And hadn't she suffered enough all weekend, dreading coming in to work? She moved a little nearer to his desk. It was time to get it over and done with. 'Look,' she said, 'I'm really sorry about the other night. I'd had too much to drink and I was feeling wretched and I shot my big mouth off and I'm really –'

'Yes,' he interrupted, 'Jessica said you weren't well when she spoke to you.'

'I am sorry, honestly.'

He looked at her fondly. 'In a way you did me a favour.'

It was a few seconds before Mo registered that there was a hint of a smile playing at the corners of his tempting mouth. 'A favour?' she repeated.

'Yes, but I don't particularly want to go into that now.' He picked up his glasses and began fiddling with them. The hint of a smile was gone.

'Does that mean you're not going to sack me?'

He frowned. 'Why would I want to do that?'

'Because . . . because of what I told Jessica,' Mo said, wishing he wouldn't frown – didn't he know that it made him even more attractive?

He shook his head tiredly. 'Forget it. At the moment what really concerns me is that you've spent the day hiding from me.'

She lowered her eyes.

'And don't look like that, I'm not a tyrant.'

She didn't know what to say, so she stood staring blankly down at her shiny boots. After a while she said, 'Can I go now? I think I'm going to cry.'

He stood up and went to her.

'It must be the relief,' she sniffed. 'You and Charlie have always been so good to me and then I go and do the worst possible thing to upset you.'

'Come on, Mo,' he said gently, 'I've told you it's all right. It was all my fault anyway, it's me who should be sorry for putting you in such a difficult position.'

She looked up at him. 'Do you really mean that?'

He nodded.

'You're not just saying it to make me feel better?'

'Come on,' he said, 'stop giving yourself such a hard time.'

She managed a small smile.

'Now go home and cheer yourself up on that trampoline of yours. Or better still, make Sid's day and get him to take you out for a drink.'

When he was alone Josh dialled the number for Willow Cottage. He wanted to see if he could make his own day by seeing Jessica that evening.

It was some time before the phone was answered and when it was he was surprised to hear Anna's voice at the other end of the line. 'Hello, Josh,' she said, 'if it's Jessica you want, she's not here, she's gone to one of those late-night-opening stores to buy me a mobile phone, just like you suggested. She's moving back to her own place, isn't that wonderful news?'

'I guess so,' he said, 'you sure you'll be okay?'

'Now don't you start, Josh. I thought if there was one person I could rely on it would be you.'

'Point taken. But ...' He hesitated. Would Anna accept his help? he wondered.

'But what?' she asked.

'I was just thinking if there was ever something you needed and you didn't want Jessica concerned you could always give me a ring, you know that, don't you?'

'That's very kind of you, Josh, and I promise to bear it in mind.'

When he'd finished his call with Anna, Josh caught sight of Mo through his open office door. She had her large Moschino bag slung over her shoulder and was chatting to Sid while he switched off his computer. Josh smiled, hoping that Mo might at last transfer the affection she had for him to poor patient Sid. He put on his glasses and returned his attention to what he'd been dealing with before he'd finally tracked down Mo. But it was no good. He couldn't concentrate. He couldn't shake off the uncomfortable image of himself that Mo had left him with. Did she really think him capable of sacking her, just like that?

First thing that morning when they were going through the post Charlie had said, 'Go easy on Mo, won't you, she looks sick with worry.'

But he'd had no intention of laying into Mo for what she'd done. It was his own fault that it had happened. He should never have played such a potentially dangerous game. It had been unfair of him to expect Mo to be a mind-reader. How was she supposed to know that he hadn't told Jessica the truth?

'How'd it go?'

He looked up to see his brother peering round the door.

'What, when I finally got to speak to Mo?'

Charlie came in. 'Precisely that.'

'She's fine, it's all sorted.'

'Thank heavens.'

'She thought I was going to fire her,' Josh said, a troubled expression on his face.

'So did everybody else.'

'But that's crazy. Why? Why would I do that?'

Charlie shrugged.

'I'm not some wacko jackboot bully.'

But you give a damned good impression of one at times, thought Charlie. 'If you say so,' he said tactfully. 'Any chance of cadging a meal off you tonight?' he added. 'I'm getting bored of solitary take-aways.'

'Sorry, I'm hoping to see Jessica.'

'Oh.'

'How about you and Rachel?'

Charlie shook his head. 'Nothing doing there. Looks like I failed at the first gate . . . unlike you and Jessica.'

Josh leant back in his chair and slowly tapped a pencil on the keyboard by his hand. 'I wouldn't say it's going to be plain sailing from now on,' he said thoughtfully.

'Why do you say that? When I phoned you on Saturday, you said it was all straight between the two of you, that you'd explained everything and she was okay. Sounded to me like she'd taken it pretty well. Better than you could have hoped for in the circumstances.'

'I know. It's just . . .' He let go of the pencil and flicked it across the desk. 'I can't get it out of my head that she's going to over-react.'

'What do you mean?'

He told Charlie about the way Jessica had been driving her mother round the bend with her constant fussing. 'And she started doing it with me on Saturday when I had supper with them. She wouldn't let me help with anything because, to use her words, "*you need to sit down*". She kept watching me, as if she was worried I'd collapse any second.'

'Well maybe *you're* over-reacting,' Charlie said. 'Personally I thought Jessica was great when I met her at Mo's; I just hope you don't go and ruin things by acting like a real lulu. Give her time.'

'Yeah, that's what her mother said.'

Charlie smiled. 'So if nothing else, it sounds like you're well in with the future mother-in-law.'

Tony was doing a Reggie Perrin, he was imagining his mother-in-law as a hippopotamus. It was a pleasing picture and took his mind off Bradley-

Dewhurst-the-Butcher's-Boy who was jawing into the phone about last month's spectacularly good sales figures.

'I just want you to know how much we appreciate what you're doing, Tony. You've really turned things around.'

'There's no reason why this month shouldn't be as good, or the next,' Tony said, wrenching his mind away from Bloody Rita half submerged in a pool of mud. He decided to go on the attack. 'Do we really need to go through with the downsizing we discussed when you were over here?'

'Sure we do, Tony. I know it's tough for those men, but I'm certain I don't have to convince you that these are tough times for us all, we gotta do all we can to concentrate the focus –'

Tony drifted back to the pool of mud. Except now there were two enormous wallowing hippos: Bradley Hurst had joined Bloody Rita.

Later he drove home listening to Dire Straits' *Love Over Gold.* Away from the office he allowed himself the treat of letting his thoughts linger on Kate. There had to be a way of seeing her. But how could he do that when Alec was usually around most evenings? Not to mention the continuous presence of Amanda. Could he suggest that she take up a hobby? Cake icing or something equally fascinating. Anything. Just so long as it got her out of the house one evening a week. But there was still Alec to deal with. Admittedly he was away on business sometimes, but those occasions seemed to be pretty few and far between. He had wanted to ring Kate at home today, but each time he'd got out her number somebody had come into his office. Tomorrow he would definitely do it. He'd get to work early and ring her before anyone else arrived. But not too early, or Alec would still be there.

He wondered if he could prompt Amanda to invite Alec and Kate to dinner.

No!

That was not a good idea.

It would be awful. How did he think he could sit for an entire evening in the same room as Kate without actually touching her?

But a dinner party was exactly what was on Amanda's mind, which was odd because it shouldn't have been, not really.

At nine thirty that morning her mother had arrived on the doorstep and had set the strangest of days in motion. 'There's something you should know,' she'd said, taking off her coat and handing it to Amanda. 'You'd better prepare yourself for a shock. Tony's having an affair.'

But shock is relative and while Amanda wasn't exactly consigning her mother's early-morning revelation to the level of mild irritation caused by a snagged nail, she was not sufficiently shocked to be rendered speechless. She led her mother through to the sitting-room, waited for her to sit down, then said very calmly, 'Are you quite sure?'

'Quite sure. Your father was driving through Holmes Chapel on Saturday morning and he saw Tony kissing her in broad daylight. Bold as you like. The street full of people and the pair of them wrapped in –'

'Yes,' Amanda cut in quickly. 'I think I get the picture.' She was surprised how hurt she felt. Then she realised it wasn't hurt she was experiencing, but anger. She was furious. Tony's betrayal had jeopardised everything. If their marriage could be likened to a business partnership – and it was a fair analogy in her opinion – she had just discovered her co-managing director with his hands in the till, wilfully destroying the company's future. Clamping down on her anger and determining to put it to good use at a later date she said, 'Is Daddy absolutely sure it was Tony?'

'I know he's not the most observant of men, Amanda, but credit him with sufficient sense to recognise his own son-in-law.'

'So why didn't you tell me sooner?'

'Your father didn't want to upset you. He didn't even tell me until late last night. You know what a coward he can be.'

Amanda didn't say anything for a few minutes. Nor did Rita. Amanda went over to the window and looked out to the garden and at the fields beyond. She thought back to Saturday morning. What had they been doing? Or more to the point, what had Tony been doing? Then she remembered – Tony had taken Hattie to her ballet class. It must have been then. While his daughter was tripping the light fantastic he was with somebody. But who?

Unable to take the silence any longer, or restrain herself from blurting out what she'd obviously wanted to say from the moment she'd arrived, Rita said, 'I warned you. I warned you on your wedding day, but would you listen? I told you that you hadn't put enough thought into what you were doing.'

Amanda turned back to her mother. 'This is not the time for a lesson in I-told-you-so. Did Daddy say what the woman looked like?'

'Yes, but I hardly think that's the point right now. We need to discuss what you're going to do. We need to –'

'Please, I want to know.' A sixth sense told Amanda that she knew exactly who Tony had been with.

'Why? Do you think it's somebody you might know? Somebody from the office? Some slip of a secretary who's been making eyes at him?'

Amanda shook her head. 'No. Not somebody from work. Somebody closer to home.' *Very close to home.*

'Your father mentioned something about a lot of red hair.'

Yes! Who else but sweet Kate? That vision of innocent loveliness. Dear, sweet Kate.

Being a practical woman with no time or need for emotional outpourings – what possible use would such a waste of energy be to anyone? – Amanda quickly got rid of her mother, then set her mind to what to do next. She was determined to salvage as much as she could from her marriage and by late afternoon she had worked out a strategy. A whacking great divorce settlement was her objective, but before that she would have some fun . . . and at Tony's expense.

A little dinner party was required.

She would suggest that they invite Alec and Kate to dinner during the week. It would be better, she knew, and much more convenient no doubt for everyone concerned to wait until the weekend, but she really didn't think she could hold out that long – and what the hell did she care for anyone else's convenience anyway? It would be rather amusing to watch the happy lovers passing the salt to one another, maybe even to catch a glimpse of eyes meeting and fingers touching. Perhaps she might drop a few hints, subtle hints, but sharp enough to make them fidget in their seats.

Did she know? they'd ask themselves guiltily.

How did she know?

Oh, yes, she would make them sweat.

She would make them suffer.

Then, when she was sure that she had her own future neatly buttoned up, she would pounce on them.

43

By Friday afternoon Jessica was well into her stride with *A Casual Affair*, another five or six chapters and the first draft would be in the bag.

Since she'd returned to Cholmford Hall Mews – straight after breakfast on Tuesday morning and very much at her mother's insistence – she had set to on her laptop with a vengeance, rattling the keys for hours on end, only pausing for breath to make herself drinks, go to the loo and phone Anna, just as she'd promised she would. But it didn't seem to be improving matters between them.

'You're doing it again, Jessica,' Anna had shouted at her on Wednesday. 'You've phoned me a total of twelve times since you left. Now get on with your work and leave me alone. I'm fine and am doing nothing more energetic than turning the pages of my newspaper.'

'I don't believe you,' Jessica had said, 'you're probably back up that blasted ladder fixing something or other. Prove to me that you're in the sitting-room, put the telly on.'

'I can't do that, because I'm in the bathroom.'

'What are you doing in there?' Jessica had asked suspiciously, 're-tiling?'

'Goodbye, Jessica. Speak to you soon, no doubt.'

Her frustration with her mother was making her vent her feelings on her characters in *A Casual Affair*. Miles was getting it in the neck from Clare, who was wondering if the shy, handsome Miles was worth all the trouble. Jessica knew better than anyone that happy endings were her speciality, but in her current frame of mind she was tempted to split Clare and Miles asunder and be damned. Let Clare be a woman empowered by her own actions. Let her discover that she needed a man as much as she needed . . . as much as she needed a recalcitrant mother.

Damn her mother!

No. She didn't mean that. She loved Anna and wanted desperately to help her. But how to go about it was the thing. How did all these caring and compassionate doctors and nurses get the strength to do what they did? Or maybe they'd never come up against somebody as stubborn as Anna?

She returned her attention to chapter thirty-two and when she was satisfied with its ending she set the printer in motion and looked out of the window. After a short while she saw Josh's Shogun drive into the courtyard.

She smiled. And there was somebody else she loved.

But like the love she felt for her mother, her feelings for Josh were beginning to be made all the more poignant by her anxiety for him. Over the past few days she had noticed a change in him. He was quieter. More tired as well. And, at times, slightly introverted. From what she had come to understand of MS from the book she'd bought, it was possible that these were signs that a relapse was on the cards. But amateur armchair diagnosis was a dangerous occupation and not one that she ought to risk.

It was just gone seven o'clock and the light was already fading outside and with her desk lamp switched on she knew that Josh would be able to see her clearly through her study window. He parked his car and as he locked it he looked over and waved at her. She waved back and he started towards her house.

She watched his progress with concern. Even in the half-light she could see that he was exhausted. His steps were slow and awkward, and greatly exaggerated; his briefcase gave the impression of being much too heavy for him to carry. He looked wrung-out. Her heart ached for him. She went to the door to let him in. 'Good day at the office, darling?' she said mockingly, taking his case from his hand and kissing him. She felt the burnt-out heaviness in his body as he leant against her, but there was nothing burnt-out in the way he kissed her.

'Do we have to go to Tony and Amanda's this evening?' he asked, holding her tight.

'Why, are you too tired?'

He pulled away from her. 'No, I just don't feel like it.'

Conscious that she'd said the wrong thing, she offered him a drink. 'I've just finished work, so your timing is perfect. I'm having a glass of wine, just to put me in the right frame of mind for tonight.'

'I'll have the same,' he said, following her into the kitchen, 'I need something to dull the effect of Amanda. Are you sure we can't lie low and simply not turn up?'

Jessica smiled. 'She'd come and get us; there'd be nowhere for us to hide. And anyway, I promised Kate we'd go. Safety in numbers, etc. The poor girl's terrified of Amanda.'

'Whereas we just loathe the dreadful woman.'

'Something like that.'

Jessica pulled a bottle of wine out of the fridge, but before she had a chance to do anything with it the phone rang. She handed Josh the bottle and said, 'Corkscrew's in the right-hand drawer next to the cooker, glasses are in the dishwasher.'

She took the call in the study and was stunned to hear Helen's voice. 'Helen!' she yelped loudly.

'Is that horror or delight that's making you squeal like a pig?'

'Delight, of course, where are you?'

'Would you believe in Huddersfield?'

'No!'

'Yes. We're over for our usual health and dental checks. Any chance of seeing you?'

'Still not trusting the Corfiotes with your body, then?'

'Oh, I trust the Corfiotes with my body, just not the bones of me. Anyway, when can Jack and I come to see you?'

'How about tomorrow? You could come for lunch and spend the rest of the day here.'

'That'll be fine. I'll hand you over to Jack and you can give him directions.'

After a brief conversation with Jack, Jessica went back into the kitchen, happy at the prospect of seeing her old friends again, but she was met with a crash and the sound of breaking glass.

'Bugger it!' Josh muttered under his breath, then seeing Jessica in the doorway he said, 'It slipped out of my hands.' He stooped down to the floor and started picking up the pieces.

'Not to worry, butter-fingers,' she said brightly. 'Here, let me do that.' She made to push him out of the way.

'Leave it,' he snapped back at her. 'I'm quite capable of clearing it up.'

She looked at him, stung by the fierceness in his voice. 'I know you are, I just ... I just don't want you cutting yourself, that's all.'

He got to his feet. 'Meaning I'm more likely to cut myself than you, is that it?'

'Don't be silly,' she said, forcing a lightness into her words. But his face told her he wasn't taken in and he walked away. She wanted to shout at his retreating figure, to tell him he was being unreasonable. But she didn't trust herself. On top of her mother, Josh acting like a sulky child was the last thing she needed. She cleared up the mess, found another bottle of wine, opened it and when she'd calmed down sufficiently took two glasses through to the sitting-room where she found Josh in the dark staring out into the twilight. She switched on a lamp and cautiously approached him by the window.

He turned round. 'I'm sorry,' he said.

'I'm sorry too.' She passed him his wine. He took it from her awkwardly and catching sight of his hand she suddenly realised why he'd dropped the bottle. His fingers were cruelly distorted and were curled into the palm of his hand.

Shocked, she raised her eyes to his and saw the angry frustration in his face. 'Will we be doing a lot of that?'

'What?' he asked. He knew what Jessica had just been staring at and, uncomfortable with her unspoken concern, switched the glass of wine from his right to his left hand.

'Apologising to one another,' she said.

He shrugged. 'Probably.'

They sat down. 'You need to be more honest with me, Josh,' she said. 'If you had told me that you couldn't open –'

'Believe me,' he cut in, 'it's not as simple as that.'

She put down her glass and took his hand in hers. She stroked it gently. 'What does it feel like right now?' she asked.

He tried to remove his hand from her lap, but she wouldn't let him. 'Tell me,' she said, 'please, I want to know. Does it hurt?'

'A bit.'

'Does this make it worse?'

He shook his head and let out his breath, wanting to be able to admit that what she was doing was good, that it helped. But he couldn't. Instead he said, 'What I hate most is that it makes me so bloody clumsy.'

'And bad-tempered?' she ventured.

'That too.'

She continued stroking the back of his hand, then turned it over and began caressing the palm. Very slowly he flexed and straightened his fingers, and one by one, she stroked those as well, but then like a flower closing at night his hand gradually curled back into the rigid position of before, except now her own hand was held firmly within his.

Kate wished she'd been honest with Amanda earlier in the week. 'No, Amanda,' she should have said, 'Alec and I can't come for dinner on Friday night because your husband is the most physically attractive man I've ever met and I'm worried that if I sit in the same room as him I shall burn up with desire for him.'

Powerful stuff.

Shocking, too.

Was it her hormones again? Or was this what love was really like?

With Alec she had always felt safe. Safe and reassured. Comforted. Protected.

But Tony had a different effect on her. The thought of him made her bold. Tacky though it sounded, he made her want to throw caution to the wind.

And she was certainly doing that!

He had phoned her on Tuesday morning, not long after Ruth had dropped off Oscar, and at the sound of his voice she had experienced a rush of something wonderfully exhilarating flow through her.

'Are you alone?' he'd asked.

'No,' she'd said.

'Is Alec still with you?'

'No. I've got Oscar here with me.'

'Who's Oscar?'

'He's Alec's grandson, I look after him during the week.'

'Does that mean I can't see you for lunch?'

Her heart had pounded. 'No. He goes to nursery school in the afternoons.'

'Tomorrow?'

'I could be free from just after one.'

'Where shall we meet?'

'Somewhere a million miles away from here.'

'It's a bit short notice for lunch on Mars.'

In the end they had decided to meet at John Lewis's in Cheadle. It wasn't a very likely venue for a romantic assignation, but it was at least safe; if they were seen, they could pretend they'd simply bumped into each other while shopping.

'I know you don't approve of what we're doing,' he'd said, as they'd roamed the display shelves of china looking for all the world like a normal married couple, 'and I'm not sure that I do either, all I know is that I have to see you.'

She'd echoed his words, but added what she hoped was a well-grounded warning: 'It'll only last a short while. It's probably a case of caprice. It'll pass and you'll return to Amanda and I'll go back to my life with Alec.'

'I don't believe that for a minute,' he'd said.

In her heart, nor did she.

Nor did she think she had the strength to carry off tonight. Surely the moment she and Tony looked at each other everyone in the room would realise what was going on between them?

She finished dressing and went downstairs to Alec, who had already changed out of his work suit and was wearing a peach-coloured shirt with chinos. He looked younger than his approaching fiftieth birthday.

He looked up from his newspaper when he saw her and gave an appreciative whistle. 'Very nice,' he said, taking in the new dress she'd bought when Tony had left her to go back to his office, 'pregnancy obviously suits you, you look lovely. A regular glowing beauty.'

She turned away guiltily, convinced that it wasn't her pregnancy that was making her glow, but the thought of spending an evening with Tony.

Tony still couldn't believe what was happening. It was like some crazy nightmare from which he couldn't wake himself. There was something horribly different about Amanda. He wished he knew what had got into her. From the minute she'd suggested this dinner party she'd been acting strangely. He'd tried his damnedest to dissuade her from going ahead, but she'd have none of it.

It was on Tuesday evening – the day that he'd seen Kate – that Amanda had announced she was inviting the neighbours to supper again. He'd been horrified and had said the first thing that came into his head, 'I shan't be able to make it, I'm working late that night.'

'But you don't know which night I'm talking about,' she'd said in response, 'and anyway I've checked with your secretary and you're definitely free on Friday evening. I've spoken to everybody else, they're all available. I had a lovely long chat with Alec on the phone, he's such a pleasant man. Did you know that Kate was pregnant? I had no idea. Alec sounded as if he was really looking forward to being a father again.'

'That's not what I'd heard.' Which had been a silly slip on his part, for Amanda had seized on it straight away, probably hoping for some nice juicy gossip to mull over.

'What do you mean?' she'd said.

'Oh nothing, it's just that I'm sure I remember Alec saying that he wasn't keen on having any more children.'

He'd phoned Kate the following morning to see what her reaction was. Half of him wanted her to say that she'd back out at the last minute claiming that she wasn't well, but that was tempting fate and he didn't want her to be ill. The other half of him wanted her to be there, at least that way they would see one another. Her thoughts had been the same as his.

And here they all were. Apart from Alec, who seemed to be as easygoing as ever, the rest of them appeared to be on edge.

Josh and Jessica were certainly quieter than usual, with Josh looking well below par. He'd dropped his fork earlier, as well as knocking over a glass, and he was making slow progress with his meal. He'd also noticed Jessica occasionally casting anxious glances in his direction. Perhaps he was coming down with something.

And, as ever, Kate was looking radiantly beautiful, but again, like Josh and Jessica, she was quiet and only added to the conversation when prompted by Amanda.

As for Amanda, well quite frankly, if he didn't know better he would say that each time she darted out to the kitchen she was having a snort of something. She seemed totally wired and was freaking the hell out of him.

At the other end of the table he suddenly heard her asking Kate when she thought she and Alec would get married. He froze. What would Kate say?

'Because you will, won't you,' Amanda persisted, 'especially now that you're pregnant, such a *sweet* couple as yourselves should do the right thing and tie the knot. I've never seen a couple more in love, isn't that right, Tony?'

'Apart from you and me,' he said silkily.

'Ah, ah, ah.' Amanda's laugh was high-pitched and chilling. 'He's full of talk, just listen to him. But back to you, Kate, you haven't answered my question.'

'I'm . . . I'm not really sure,' Kate said hesitantly.

Alec intervened, aware of Kate's discomfort opposite him. 'Maybe that's for me to decide,' he said jovially.

Jessica laughed. 'Dangerous words, Alec, in this day and age of equality. There's no reason why Kate shouldn't pop the question.'

Amanda turned to Josh. 'And how would you feel, Josh, if Jessica proposed to you, pleased or emasculated?'

Josh swallowed his wine and looked thoughtfully across the table. He contemplated Jessica's face through the flickering candle-light. Her eyes were dark and compelling and so very sure, and she was smiling at him in that challenging way she did. 'I'd be pleased,' he said softly, 'and . . . and I'd say yes.'

The room suddenly went very quiet as Jessica and Josh continued to stare at each other.

Until Amanda, who Tony was convinced had all the sensitivity of a rhinoceros – no, second thoughts, make that a hippopotamus along with her mother and Bradley Hurst – jumped up from the table and said, 'Time for cheese, and why don't we be terribly sophisticated and change seats and swap partners, so to speak.'

Tony stared at her. 'What?' he demanded. He'd have been less surprised if she'd suggested a game of strip poker.

'It's what people do at dinner parties,' she said, 'it makes for better interaction between guests.' She ignored his look of bewilderment and began clearing up the dishes. When she came to Josh's she said, 'You've hardly touched your profiteroles, we can't have you wasting away, you'll have to get Jessica to help feed you in the future and teach you not to be so clumsy.'

Jessica had never wilfully struck another person, not if you discounted the incident at infant school when she hit a girl over the head with her satchel, but she was very tempted to leap up from her chair and smash Josh's bowl into Amanda's face. She'd grind it so hard into that artful countenance that the glaze would come clean off the dish. How dare she speak to Josh in that condescending manner.

But if Josh was riled by what the dinner-party hostess from hell had said he gave no outward sign of it. Jessica was proud of him. As they'd walked across the courtyard earlier that evening he had told her that he didn't want any of their neighbours knowing about his MS. 'Can you imagine what that dreadful woman would say to me?' he'd said, 'she'd probably tell me it's all in my mind and advise me to pull myself together.'

Amanda finished gathering up the dishes, took them through to the kitchen and quietly marvelled at herself. The look on Tony's face when she was asking Kate about getting married, oh, it was priceless. Absolutely priceless.

The shock.

The horror.

The jealousy!

It had all been there in his expression. What a slow-witted fool to have given himself away so easily.

Oh, yes, the evening was definitely a success. And it wasn't over yet. Not by a long way.

She had no idea whether that sharp-tongued Jessica and old limping misery guts knew about Tony and Kate, but she had decided to invite them tonight to find out. She wished she hadn't bothered. Witnessing that excruciating little scene between the pair of them just now had been enough to make her violently sick.

But then, if that didn't make her sick, odds on Kate would. Sitting there like Little Miss Dumb Muffet, convincing everyone that she was the last word in angelic sweetness, was too much. What an act! It would serve the bitch right if she walked straight back into the dining-room and announced that she knew what was going on. 'So Kate,' she could say, 'just who exactly is your baby's father? Alec or Tony? Or maybe you've sampled Josh as well?' That would sure as hell take the smug look off Jessica's face.

It was a tempting thought to stir things up so agreeably, but she wasn't ready yet for such a direct confrontation. She had a much better plan in mind. Since her mother had put her so clearly in the picture she had had plenty of time to consider her options. When her anger had eventually subsided she had wondered – for all of a split second – about doing a Hillary Clinton and turning a blind eye to what Tony was up to; it was one way of ensuring the reins of power stayed firmly within her own grip. But it wasn't in her nature to play the part of forgiving wife and besides, Tony simply wasn't worth it.

What intrigued her most was how she had guessed right away who the 'other woman' was. Funny, that. Without realising it she must have absorbed the connection Tony had made with Kate. And since her subconscious had been forced into a state of acknowledgement she had come face to face with what could only be described as incriminating evidence. Tony's Barclaycard statement, showing the cost of that silk scarf he'd insisted on buying Kate in Devon, was a dead give-away. No wonder he had kicked up such a fuss about a tin of toffees. A bit of overcooked sugar was never going to be good enough to impress a lover. But perhaps the real hard evidence of their affair was the fact that Kate was expecting a baby. Truth would certainly tell on that score.

Hearing a sudden burst of laughter coming from the dining-room, Amanda picked up the plate of cheese that she'd put together earlier along with a basket of oatmeal and Bath Oliver biscuits and went back into the fray for some more fun. 'Well, look at this,' she said, 'you've all moved and yet somehow the shuffling hasn't quite worked. Jessica and Josh are fine, I'll allow that, but Kate, why don't you change places with Alec and sit next to Tony, yes, that's a much better idea. There now, let's see how that improves our intercourse.' She laughed, 'No *double entendre* intended.'

'None taken,' Tony said sharply. Had she been doing a line of Jif out there in the kitchen, or what? And so what if she had? He was past caring. So long as she left him to enjoy the illicit sensation of sitting in such close proximity to Kate, she could do as she pleased. He was now so near her that he hardly dared to move for fear of actually touching her and, the way he was feeling, if he did touch even the tiniest bit of her he was in danger of turning into a freak case of spontaneous combustion.

'Now Jessica,' Amanda said as she passed her the plate of cheese, 'why don't you tell us how your latest book is coming along.'

Jessica helped herself to a piece of Stilton. 'Sorry, Amanda, I'm afraid I can't oblige you. I *never* discuss my work while it's still in progress.'

'How boring. But tell me, do you often write about infidelity?'

'I –'

'Something stuck in your throat, Tony? Kate, you'd better pass Tony that bottle of water, he looks ready to choke to death. Sorry, Jessica, carry on, you were saying…'

'I was just going to say that I covered the subject quite extensively in *Caught in the Act.*'

'Really. You'll have to lend me a copy.'

'And that's something else I never do. You'll have to buy your own, I need the royalties.'

Amanda gave Jessica a hard stare.

In return Jessica yawned and looked pointedly at her watch.

44

When Jessica opened her eyes she felt unaccountably guilty. Then she realised why. She had just been dreaming of Gavin.

She'd been lying in bed with him. Well, more than that, but she didn't want to think about having sex with a man she no longer loved.

She turned over and immediately Gavin was gone and he was replaced with the man she did love.

Josh.

She gazed at his face – a face that at times could be vulnerably sensitive and open, but at other times closed and drawn. She lovingly traced the outline of his jaw with her finger, down his neck, then to his bare chest. She'd never been into hairy men and Josh's sprinkling of fine hair was just perfect. He stirred slightly at her touch, but not enough to wake, and watching him shift position she thought of what he'd said at Tony and Amanda's last night – '*I'd say yes.*'

Would he indeed?

She couldn't have written the scene any better herself. It had been a few seconds of pure magic. The look in his eyes had been so utterly spellbinding that she could have thrown herself down on one knee there and then. But Amanda had put paid to any chance of that.

Honestly, the woman had no soul.

But there again sensitivity was hardly a phenomenon that Amanda was best friends with, it seemed.

Jessica could handle Amanda's snotty comments about her writing – she'd get even one day with her by using her as a character in a future novel – but her manner towards Josh was altogether another matter. The thoughtlessness of the woman had made Jessica want to take her by the throat and shake her till her teeth rattled and her eyes popped out. It was only out of respect for Josh's amazing ability to ignore Amanda that she had restrained herself and kept her anger in check.

When they'd left the scene of what had been the most extraordinary of evenings, Josh had come back with her and they'd gone straight to bed. He was knackered and it was just beginning to dawn on Jessica what life must be like for him. He'd slowly climbed the stairs, collapsed into bed and had fallen asleep almost immediately, leaving her with no opportunity to enquire about tantalising little details such as what he had really meant by '*I'd say yes.*'

But more important, would *she* ever want to pop the question?

Too soon to tell, she told herself. They hadn't known one another long enough.

So how long would it take?

And did his illness have anything to do with her hesitation?

Now look here, what is this? she asked herself defensively, of course Josh's MS had nothing to do with her hesitation. Why, that would make her an *ist* of some kind and she'd never been prejudiced against anything in her life.

No, the truth was they were still in the early stages of their relationship and only time would tell if they had a future together.

Sure, she wrote about people falling madly in love and knowing within a few chapters that they were made for one another, but that was fiction. Real life wasn't like that. Real people took ages dithering about trying to decide whether they would be able to put up with one another for the next five minutes, never mind the next fifty years. And if they weren't doing that they were wondering if it wouldn't be a bad idea to wait and see if somebody better came along.

Well, didn't they?

Wasn't that what Gavin had been doing?

Damn, now she was back to Gavin.

So why exactly had she been dreaming of him?

That was easy – no Freudian worries on that score! – his presence in her subconscious was all down to her seeing Jack and Helen today and their imminent visit had stirred up all sorts of memories.

Thinking about Jack and Helen's impending arrival had her carefully slipping out of bed and tiptoeing downstairs. They would be here in four hours and she really ought to do something about getting the house into some sort of order.

She also needed to think what she could give them to eat.

She opened the fridge for inspiration.

Mm ... not too promising.

The freezer was no greater source of creativity either. Not unless she could get away with serving a deep pan pizza followed by a Magnum – one between them all.

Hell! Now she'd have to go to the supermarket. She groaned. Food shopping and cooking were her two most hated chores in the world. She'd rather spend a fortnight cleaning out an Egyptian public toilet. Okay. Maybe she was exaggerating, make that a week, but who in their right mind enjoyed spending their time browsing along aisle upon aisle searching for yet another way to satiate their stomach? What was happening to them all? Were they turning into a nation of Belly Worshippers? *Oh Great Belly God, unto whom all shopping lists be prepared, receive this miserable sacrifice, a trial special offer of a lime and coriander quorn curry.* There were times when she seriously longed for the simplicity of the small family-run supermarkets in Kassiopi. The less choice, the easier the task. And she was all for an easy life.

She made herself a cup of tea and sat down with a cookery book – her only cookery book and one which Anna had given her years ago. So what was it to be? Could she be crass enough to make moussaka for Jack and

Helen? Or should she be equally silly and cook them roast beef and Yorkshire pudding?

No. Helen was mad enough as it was.

Roast lamb, then. That was easy to do, surely? She could do new potatoes, they wouldn't take too much fiddling about with. But hang on, she was now entering the danger zone of being a hypocrite. It was late September and she was considering new potatoes because the very supermarket she had just condemned for offering too much choice would indeed supply this out-of-season vegetable. Stick to your principles, she told herself. Roast potatoes would have to do instead, a little more work involved, but worth it all the same. And they'd have runner beans and courgettes, they were very much in season.

Her brief shopping list completed, she drank her tea, then poured herself another, as well as one for Josh. She took the mugs upstairs. As she slipped back into bed he awoke.

'Hi,' she said. She bent down to him and kissed the top of his head. 'I've brought you some tea.'

He sat up slowly. 'What time is it?'

'Time I was scurrying around with the Hoover. Jack and Helen will be here at one.'

He glanced at his watch. 'Plenty of time.'

She passed him his mug.

He reached out for it, but then hesitated. She looked at his hand, it was tightly clenched, much worse than last night. 'Still bad?' she asked.

'Yep.' He took the cup with his other hand. 'What time do you want me out of here?'

'Sorry?'

'Well, you won't want me around when your friends are here.'

'Says who?'

'I just assumed.'

'You assumed wrong, Crawford. I'd like you to meet them. I ought to invite Mum for lunch as well, she always got on with Jack and Helen when she used to come and stay.'

'In that case, would you like me to cook for you?'

'Would the Pope like us all to be Catholics?'

He smiled. 'I'll take that as a yes, shall I?'

'A resounding yes.'

'What do you fancy?'

'Apart from you?'

'I think you'll find I won't fit in the oven, Jessica.'

'Spoil-sport. I thought of having a crack at roast lamb, but you're the chef, you decide. Tell me what you want and I'll go shopping for it.'

'That's okay, we'll go together.'

'Wouldn't you rather stay here and . . .?' Her voice trailed away.

'What?' he said, regarding her levelly. 'Rest? Is that what you were going to say?'

'Heavens no. I was going to get you on cleaning duty.'

He let it go. He could see it wasn't easy for Jessica. 'I'd prefer to go shopping,' he said, 'you can be in charge of the cleaning.'

'There,' Jessica said, coming into the kitchen, her hands full of dusters, empty coffee mugs and several weeks' worth of the *Sunday Times* rounded up from all corners of the house, 'I defy anyone to find so much as a speck of dust in this place. Mm . . . that smells good.'

'It's the garlic and rosemary with the lamb,' Josh said, glancing up from the chopping board where he was slowly working his way through a mound of carrots, potatoes, courgettes and baby turnips.

'And what fate awaits them?' she asked, coming over to take a closer look at what he was doing.

'They'll be roasted in olive oil with sprigs of thyme.'

'Delicious. You're a man in a million, Crawford. Anything I can do to help?'

He watched her throw the old newspapers into the bin, store the cleaning things in the cupboard under the sink and wash her hands. He tried hard to overcome his natural desire to struggle on, but though the fingers in his right hand were beginning to straighten he knew they didn't have the strength or the dexterity to enable him to get through the pile of vegetables in front of him. 'You could help with the chopping, if you want.'

Jessica dried her hands and came back to him. She wanted to say, 'Now that wasn't too difficult, was it?' But she didn't dare. She guessed that what had just passed between them was a tiny milestone. Josh had actually swallowed a minuscule piece of his pride. But would it be something he would be prepared to keep on doing?

'Now show me how you want them,' she said, 'big chunks or little chunks?'

'Medium-sized chunks.'

'You would.' She began chopping.

'No, not like that, make the shapes more even or some will be cooked while others will still be raw.'

'Show me then, clever dick.'

He stood behind her and placed his hands over hers. 'Here, this is how you do it.'

His breath tickled her neck and as his warm body pressed against hers she thought of the film *Ghost* and the bit when Demi Moore gets an extra pair of helping hands during her late-night pottery session. She started to giggle.

'What's so funny?' he asked.

'It's you, you're distracting me.'

He nibbled her ear and she laughed some more. 'Stop it,' she said, 'or I'll have one of your fingers off.'

He took the knife from her, put it down and turned her round to face him. She gazed into his eyes and saw that they were dark with desire. It suddenly seemed the perfect time to ask him what he'd meant last night by '*I'd say yes*'.

'Josh,' she said, 'you know at Tony and Amanda's when you –' But she got no further. The sound of a car coming slowly into the courtyard announced the untimely arrival of Jack and Helen.

'I must say you're looking extremely well,' Jack said as he helped himself to another glass of wine from the bottle he and Helen had brought with them.

They were in the kitchen and Jessica was doing her best to finish chopping all the vegetables that Josh had left her in charge of while he went to fetch Anna.

'No guesses for why that's the case,' Helen said with a smile. 'You never mentioned anything in your letters about a new man in your life, not that you've written much to us.' She put on an air of hurt.

Jessica laughed. 'If I spent all my free time writing letters to you I wouldn't have had the opportunity to catch myself such a fine-looking man, now would I?'

'How right you are,' Helen agreed, 'they don't come much finer. So why isn't he already snapped up?'

'Same reason as me I suppose,' Jessica said with a smug smile, 'he's been waiting for that special person.'

Helen stuck her fingers in her mouth. 'Please, somebody pass me the bucket.'

Jack smiled at Jessica. 'She's becoming very cynical in her old age. Ready for some wine yet?'

'Yes,' Jessica said. She flung down the vegetable knife and took the proffered glass. 'Though what Josh wants to do next with this little lot is anybody's guess.'

Helen's eyes opened wide. 'Don't tell me he can cook as well?'

Jessica gave Helen another smug smile. 'He sure can. This is *his* meal.'

Helen gave Jack one of her look-learn-and-take-note looks. Then she said, 'Well, I suppose that really does put the tin lid on Gavin's chances.'

'Helen,' warned Jack in a low voice, 'definitely not the time.'

'What?' asked Jessica, noticing the exchange between her friends.

'Oh, nothing,' said Helen. She reached over to pinch a piece of raw carrot.

'Come on, you're holding back on me. What is it? Jack, you tell me.'

But Jack ignored Jessica. He stared awkwardly at his shoes.

Helen crunched on the carrot. 'Oh, what the hell? It's not much, it's just that we promised Gavin while we were over that we'd try and put a word in for him.'

Jessica gaped. 'What kind of word?'

'Look, Jessica, he's really sorry for what he did.'

'*Hah!*'

'No, let me finish. A more contrite man you could never hope to come across. Silicone Sal is way out of the picture and Gavin . . .'

'And Gavin what?' Jessica prompted her friend.

'And Gavin wanted us to see if there was any chance of a reconciliation.'

'You make it sound as if we were married.'

'Perhaps if you hadn't gone rushing off in such a sulk you might have been.'

'Helen, I don't believe you. He was two-timing me. Probably three-timing if the truth be known. And you know jolly well I didn't leave Corfu because of him.'

'Just as you say, Jessica, but as I said, Gavin's old ways are behind him, he wants to make up with you. He wants to –'

'Well, you can tell him he's too late. Whatever he thinks he's offering, it wouldn't be enough.'

'And what would be enough?'

Jessica picked up the small vegetable knife and drove it through the heart of a piece of potato. 'I want commitment. I want to be really needed. I want to feel that I belong to that person and that he belongs to me . . . that he couldn't live without me.'

Helen banged her empty glass of wine down on the work surface. 'Oh, for heaven's sake, Jessica, that's the stuff of fiction!'

'I don't care. It's what I want. I'm simply not interested in anything less.'

45

Alec had long since gone to work and Kate was alone. She lay on their bed and waited for the feeling of nausea to pass. She closed her eyes and concentrated her mind on what she had resolved to do later that day; what she had concluded at five o'clock that morning as being the only way to resolve matters.

Unable to sleep, she had left Alec slumbering soundly and gone downstairs to the sitting-room where she had sat in one of the armchairs in the bay window and watched the dawn break. Staring out at the dramatically changing sky with its swathes of cobalt-blue darkness giving way to bursts of soft pink light, a diffraction of clarity had suddenly cut through her own confused darkness and with it came the knowledge that today she would bring about an end to the muddle that she had created of her life. It was time to be honest with Alec. She couldn't go on treating him so badly. It wasn't fair. She had to tell him that whatever it was that had brought them together in the first place was not enough to keep them together. She wouldn't tell him about Tony, there was no need for that. Tony wasn't the reason she was leaving him. He had been a symptom of their failing relationship. He was not the cause.

But it wasn't just Alec who had to be told the truth. There was Tony as well.

After that dreadful night last week at Tony and Amanda's, when she came away convinced that Amanda was on to them – all that talk of infidelity and swapping partners had to be for a reason – she had known that what she was doing was wrong. She had gone to bed that night shocked and ashamed. Her duplicity appalled her. All those lies she had told. She hated the woman she had let herself become.

She had no idea how Tony was going to react when she told him she wouldn't be seeing him again, but he had to realise that her leaving Alec didn't mean that she was simply making the way clear to be with him. Tony was a married man. No matter what his feelings were for Kate, or hers for him, he had a wife who could not be ignored.

And like Tony, she too had her own responsibility; that of doing the right thing for the baby she was carrying. She wanted her child's tiny fragile beginnings to be founded on love and honesty. Not on deception. Not on depravity. She didn't want her child to have a mother who could be found culpable for wrecking another person's marriage.

She opened her eyes. The nausea of morning sickness still hadn't passed.

But she couldn't stay lying on the bed all day, she was meeting Tony in less than an hour. She got to her feet, determined to ignore her threatening stomach, and went downstairs. As she glanced at her reflection in the hall mirror she caught sight of her pale, tired face in the glass. Guilt, she told herself. Guilt and shame. It serves you right.

As arranged, Kate met Tony in the car-park of a pub neither of them had been to before – anonymity was, after all, the essence of a perfect assignation.

The first thing Tony said was, 'Are you okay? You look as white as a sheet.'

'I'm fine,' she said, though she knew she wasn't. It's nerves, she told herself. Nerves at what she had to tell Tony.

Though the day was warm, the inside of the pub was dismally cold, so they ordered their drinks and chose a small table in an alcove a few feet away from a gently smouldering log fire where a large, thickset man of indefinable age was jammed into a chair that looked much too small for him. He had tufts of hair sticking out from under a woolly hat and he was nursing a near empty pint glass in a pair of big, strong hands. He nodded at them. 'A fair day, wouldn't you say?'

'Very fair,' Tony responded with a smile.

'Set to continue, I heard this morning on the radio.'

'That's good.'

The man shifted in his seat. 'Well, it's good and it's not good. A splash more rain would do no harm. No harm at all. In fact, we could do a lot worse than have a bloody great lashing.'

Kate inwardly groaned. How could this happen? How could they have ended up, today of all days, with the pub bore chuntering on to them about the weather? She raised her eyes and met Tony's. She could see he was trying not to laugh and her response to his smiling face was to think how much she would miss seeing him. She pushed this dangerous thought aside. She mustn't weaken. Not now.

'Shall I order us something to eat?' he asked.

She shook her head. She felt too sick to eat.

'The ploughman's not up to much,' the pub bore interjected. 'Too much wet green stuff on the plate for my liking. I shouldn't bother with the trout neither. It's never fresh. Nor's the salmon.'

'Kate, are you sure you're all right?'

'Chicken curry's not bad.'

'Kate?'

'Take my word for it, your best bet is the chicken curry.'

Tony's patience was wearing thin. He flashed a look of annoyance at the man in the hope of shutting him up. He turned his attention back to Kate. 'What is it?' he whispered. 'You look dreadful.'

'I'm not sure,' she answered faintly. She rose slowly to her feet. 'I'll be a few minutes.'

He watched her cross the carpeted floor and remembered how Eve had suffered with morning sickness. But even Eve had never looked as ghastly as

Kate did just now. He drank from his glass of mineral water and thought about what he had planned to tell Kate over their lunch.

After Amanda's bizarre behaviour on Friday night he had spent the weekend facing up to the truth that he'd been pushed as far as he was ever going to be pushed. He wanted a divorce. He would be generous to Amanda. More than generous. He would give her everything she wanted. He had the feeling, though, that she wouldn't be slow in defining the parameters of a settlement heavily weighted in her favour, but just so long as she gave him his freedom she could demand as much as she wanted. It would be difficult coping with Hattie on his own again, but he would find a way round the problem. He would have to. Whichever way he looked at it, the situation would be preferable to the madness he'd experienced of late.

And perhaps, just perhaps, his freedom would give him the opportunity to offer Kate something more worthwhile than he was currently able to give her.

'Looks like your lady friend has legged it,' the pub bore said. He gave off a throaty laugh. 'Maybe she got wind of the kitchen and thought better of having lunch here.'

Tony forced a smile to his lips. He glanced down at his watch. He'd been on his own for nearly twenty minutes. He began to worry. He was just wondering what he should do when a woman approached him.

'Are you Tony?' she asked.

'Yes.'

'Your girlfriend told me to tell you that she's waiting for you outside. I think you need to get her to a doctor. She doesn't look at all well.'

Tony raced out of the pub. He found Kate leaning against his car. 'It's the baby,' she whispered, her eyes wide and frightened, 'I think I'm losing it.'

He drove to the nearest hospital. He knew next to nothing about miscarriages, but instinct told him that there would be no chance of saving Kate's child.

While he waited to be told what was happening, he phoned directory enquiries for Alec's work number. When he got through to Thistle Cards he left a message explaining where Kate was. No matter what he felt for Kate, or Alec for that matter, it was only right that Alec should know what was going on; he was the father after all.

A few seconds after Tony had finished his call a nurse came and told him what he'd already suspected. He sat by the side of Kate's bed and held her hand. But she wouldn't speak to him.

'I've left a message for Alec,' he told her, 'I expect he'll be here soon.'

She nodded dumbly.

'Do you want me to stay?'

She shook her head and closed her eyes. Tears trickled down her pale cheeks and splashed on to the crisp white pillowcase. She turned from him and let go of his hand.

He walked quietly away.

He couldn't face going back to the office.

Not yet.

He needed to be on his own, so he drove up the A34 and headed towards the motorway. There was surprisingly little traffic and at the speed he was driving Greater Manchester was soon behind him, while ahead the first sighting of open moorland drew him further on. Seeing the sign for junction 21 he pulled in behind a large haulage wagon. He drove through the familiar roads of Milnrow and when he came to Hollingworth Lake he stopped. Other than a shiny red Nissan Micra, whose elderly occupants were enjoying the view and a flask of something hot, he was alone.

He had often come here as a boy. On a Saturday morning he and his friends would cycle over from Rochdale. It seemed quite a distance now, but in those days he hadn't given the journey a second thought. His mum would put together a parcel of jam sandwiches for him and his mates, and the minute they reached the lake they'd eat the sandwiches while throwing stones into the water. They got told off once by a fierce old lady who came out of her house and accused them of frightening the ducks. They'd called her Old Ma Quackers after that.

How big they thought they were.

And how smart.

They presumed so much.

Little did they know how bloody complicated life could be.

He stared at the rippling surface of the lake and thought of Kate and the loss of her badly wanted child. And because he knew that her loss would be so great to her he was convinced that she was going to shut him out.

If she hadn't already.

He wished now that he'd had the opportunity at the pub to explain to Kate that he was going to ask Amanda for a divorce. If she'd known that she might not have turned away from him in the hospital.

His solitary musings were brought to an abrupt end by the sudden trill of his mobile.

It was Vicki, his secretary. 'Tony, where on earth are you? You're supposed to be in a meeting in ten minutes.'

Damn! He'd forgotten all about that. 'Cancel it,' he said.

'Any reason I can give?'

'No.'

'I've also got a message from your wife,' Vicki went on. 'She says she can't collect Hattie from school today.'

'*What!*'

'I'm sorry, Tony, that's the message.'

'Didn't she give any reason? Any explanation?'

'It seems to be the day for people not wanting to explain things,' she said archly. 'Will you be in later?'

'No. I'll see you tomorrow.'

He looked at his watch. Hattie would be coming out of school in thirty minutes. He phoned home to see what was wrong with Amanda. There was no answer. Next he phoned school and asked them to keep Hattie there until he arrived.

He drove faster than he ought, zigzagging his speeding Porsche through the lanes of traffic and all the time wondering what the hell Amanda was up to.

When he and Hattie finally made it home, the answer was waiting for him.

Amanda had gone.

And so had all their furniture.

'Have we been burgled?' asked Hattie, taking a step closer to her father and reaching for his hand as they stood in the middle of the empty sitting-room. Everything had vanished, the furniture, the hi-fi, the television, the video, the pictures from the walls, the knick-knacks, even the pot plants.

Tony finished reading Amanda's letter, which he had found on the floor of their empty bedroom. He screwed it into a tight hard ball and threw it down at his feet – at least she'd left the carpets!

'No, we haven't been burgled,' he said, suddenly realising that his daughter needed his reassurance. He scooped her up in his arms and smiled. Then he threw back his head and laughed. It echoed horribly in the bare room. Seeing Hattie's uncertain little face, he hugged her tightly and kissed her. 'I'm starving,' he said, 'let's go into town and have ourselves a McDonald's.'

'Really?'

'You bet! You can have whatever you want. Gherkins, fries, the lot.'

'Won't Amanda be cross?'

'Amanda will never *ever* know.'

Tony might have felt that for the first time in months he could breathe properly as he sat in the ultra-clean air-conditioned environment of McDonald's, but he was well aware that there was no getting away from the fact that the swift kick in the groin that Amanda had given him – much as it pleased him in the long term – had precipitated his number-one problem: looking after Hattie.

He stared at his daughter across the small table and for a brief moment she took her lips away from the thick gunky milkshake that she was sucking up with a straw. She didn't seem at all put out by what he had just told her in the car. 'Amanda's decided that she doesn't want to be with us any more,' he had explained, which had been a more elegant way of putting what Amanda had written in her letter.

I've taken only what I think I deserve [the letter had begun]. *You can try and fight me if you want, but really I wouldn't advise it. I'm divorcing you on the grounds of adultery – I know all about you and Kate – and you shan't be hearing from me again, except through my solicitor. I'd just like you to know that marrying you was the biggest mistake I ever made.*

'But why did she take all the furniture?' Hattie had asked, adding quite reasonably, 'It doesn't seem fair.'

'Maybe she liked it a lot,' he'd said. With hindsight, if he'd thought it would have got rid of Amanda sooner he'd have given it to her long ago. He couldn't deny that she had a perfect right to be bitter, she had after all discovered that he was on the verge of having a full-blown affair with Kate – in truth, what had passed between him and Kate could not technically be described as adultery, but nevertheless, the intent was there; if the circumstances had been right he didn't doubt for a single moment that he would have taken Kate to bed. Just thinking about it made him long for her.

He wondered how she was. He hoped that Alec was taking good care of her. He felt no jealousy or animosity towards Alec, only a wish that he would be able to comfort Kate when she needed it most.

'Your chips are getting cold,' Hattie said, pointing at him with one of her own. She tickled the end of his nose with it.

He smiled and resumed eating, marvelling at his daughter. She really didn't have a care in the world.

Just like him as a child when he'd thrown stones into the water at Hollingworth Lake and laughed at Old Ma Quackers behind her back.

By six thirty that evening Kate had swapped one bed for another. She was back at home, with Alec fussing around her, straightening and smoothing the duvet, patting her hands, fiddling with her pillows.

She didn't need to be in bed, but Alec had insisted. 'I'm not listening to you, Kate,' he'd said when he'd brought her home from the hospital and she'd told him she wanted to be in the sitting-room, 'I'm in charge and I want you to go to bed and rest.'

And how did he think she could rest if he was going to spend all his time fussing over her?

She knew what he was doing. He was busying himself so that she couldn't see the relief in his face. But she could hear it in his voice. With each gentle and cajoling word he spoke she could hear how relieved he was that she was no longer pregnant.

'We'll go away,' he was saying, as once again he smoothed and patted the duvet, 'just the two of us, to a nice quiet little hotel, where you can be pampered and thoroughly spoilt.'

Did he have to say *just the two of us*?

'I'll take you to that wonderful hotel in Bath I told you about. We'll go for long country walks and in the evening we'll sit by a log fire and drink champagne. Do you like the sound of that?'

No, she didn't like the sound of it. She had no desire to go anywhere. But she wished Alec would go away, that he would leave her alone.

But still he rambled on about all the wonderful things they would do together.

'We'll have a four-poster bed and a jacuzzi the size of a small swimming pool, you'll love it.'

Was there no way to stop him?

Yes. Yes, there was.

'Alec,' she said finally, staring him straight in the eye, 'I'm very sorry . . . and I wish there were a better way to put this, but I think we both know in our hearts that it's over between us.'

46

Josh recognised Tony's car straight away, as well as Hattie's small figure sitting in the back. Within seconds Tony saw Josh in his rear-view mirror and held up his hand in acknowledgement. They drove the remaining distance to Cholmford Hall Mews in convoy and when Josh had parked in front of his house he went over to Tony to thank him for the other night, not out of any genuine desire to pass on his thanks to Amanda, but out of a sense of solidarity – hell, the man needed some kind of support for putting up with such a weird wife.

'How's it going?' he asked when he drew level with Tony and Hattie.

'Come in and see for yourself.'

Inside, Josh stared round at the empty walls. 'What the –?'

'Amanda's left us,' Hattie said with a big smile on her face. She then went upstairs to her bedroom.

'She's cleared me out,' Tony said, when they were alone. 'Fancy a drink to celebrate?'

Confounded, Josh watched Tony take out a bottle of Scotch from one of the kitchen cupboards. 'She left you that, then?' he said.

'Yes, she left me the cheap and nasty booze and took the decent stuff.' He poured two generous measures into a matching pair of plastic cups that were decorated with Walt Disney characters. 'Sorry about the lack of crystal ware,' he said, passing a cup to Josh, 'but she took that as well, china too, but credit where credit's due, she left all of Hattie's things.'

'I hate to pry, Tony, but did she give a reason why? Did you have any kind of clue that this was on the cards?'

'She found out that I was seeing Kate.'

If Josh had been stunned a few moments ago, he was even more taken aback now. He took a large gulp of Scotch. 'You and Kate,' he said, astonished, 'you mean you were –?'

Tony nodded. 'Though nothing had actually happened between us.' He explained about him and Kate. He then told Josh about Kate losing the baby that afternoon. 'I think she's going to push me away. Guilt will make her want to blame somebody for what happened and I guess I'm the obvious target.'

'It's been quite a day for you,' Josh said, 'I don't know what to say. Were you the father?'

Tony looked shocked. 'No. Absolutely not. I told you, nothing really happened between us.'

'And does Alec know about you and Kate?'

'I don't think so. But then I didn't think Amanda knew. But she obviously did.'

Josh looked round at the empty kitchen. 'Obviously,' he repeated. 'So what happens next?'

Tony drained his cup. '*Next* is my big problem. I'm going to have to organise a child-minder to take care of Hattie after school each day.' He ran his hand through his hair. 'Though at such short notice I don't hold out much hope of getting fixed up this week. I'll just have to take the time off work.'

'Isn't there anyone you can ask for help? Grandparents?'

'All dead.'

'What about the other mothers at Hattie's school?'

'She's only been there a short while. I couldn't tell you who any of her friends are, never mind their mothers' names.'

Josh thought for a moment. 'How about Jessica? You could ask her, just until you've got yourself properly sorted.'

Jessica and Josh gave Tony a wave and drove through the archway.

They'd both just spent the past hour giving Tony a hand. This was after he and Josh had called on Jessica to tell her what had happened and to enlist her services for collecting Hattie from school. 'Do you mind?' Tony had asked. 'I hate to land this on you.'

'It's not a problem,' Jessica had said. 'But what can we do right now for you? If you've not got a stick of furniture you'd better borrow some of mine.'

And though Tony had said he and Hattie would be fine, Jessica had insisted and between the three of them they'd carted Jessica's barely used dining-table and three chairs over to Tony's and from Josh's house they'd put together a basic selection of crockery. When Jessica had pointed out that Tony didn't have a bed to sleep on he'd refused her offer of dragging one of her mattresses across the courtyard and said that he could make do with an old camp-bed he had in the garage.

Which was what they'd just left him searching for. Amanda might have stripped the house from top to bottom, save for Hattie's bedroom, but she'd either forgotten the things in the garage or had felt kind-hearted enough to let Tony keep the lawn-mower, step-ladders and Boy Scout odds and ends of camping gear – somehow Jessica didn't think Amanda would have much use for an old tent and box of billycans; she didn't strike one as being happy-camper material.

'You didn't mind me suggesting to Tony that you might look after Hattie, did you?' Josh asked Jessica as they drove through the avenue of chestnut trees.

'No. Not at all. Why do you ask?'

'You just seemed ... well, a bit quiet at Tony's.'

'I think the word you're searching for is gobsmacked. I still can't believe the Kate and Tony thing. I knew Kate was worried about Alec's reaction to being a father again, but I honestly thought they'd sort that out between them and everything would be sweet. Did you have any idea what was going on?'

'Not a clue. Do you think that's what Friday night was all about?'

'Almost certainly. Amanda must have known what was going on and decided to put Tony and Kate through their paces. All that stuff about *when are you and Alec getting married?* – she mimicked Amanda's voice with unerring accuracy – 'it was just a ploy for twisting the knife in Tony's back and making Kate squirm.'

'But how on earth did Amanda get all the stuff out of the house without any of us seeing?'

'If you think about it that wasn't too tricky. She knew you and Alec would be at work and if you remember back to Friday night she asked both Kate and me what we'd be doing this week. I thought at the time it was odd that she asked specifically about today.'

'You're right, she did rather press the point. Kate said something about seeing a friend for lunch –'

'Who turned out to be Tony.'

'And you said you were going shopping in Wilmslow. I suppose that's what you were up to,' he said with a grin.

She smiled. 'Crawford, you've rumbled me. Guilty as charged. Lock me up and throw away the key.' But suddenly her smile was gone. '*Bloody hell!*'

'What? What is it?'

Jessica slammed on the brakes and brought the car to a shuddering halt just before the brow of the bridge over the canal. 'Look! Just look at that! What the hell does she think she's doing?'

Josh followed Jessica's gaze. In the semi-darkness, sweeping the steps that led from the garden of Willow Cottage down to the tow-path, was Anna. He smiled to himself. Poor woman, she must have thought she was safe from Jessica's ever-watchful eye, having had her daily visit from her daughter a couple of hours ago.

But before Josh could say anything, Jessica was out of the car and running towards the gate of Willow Cottage. She stormed over to her mother and even from where he was Josh could hear her shouting at Anna.

'What do you think you're doing?' she yelled. 'Have you gone completely mad? I thought I'd told you to take it easy.'

Josh opened his door and slowly limped after Jessica. It had been a long day and his leg had given him nothing but trouble for most of it; to-ing and fro-ing to Tony's hadn't helped either. By the time he had managed to drag his worn-out body after Jessica, who was now snatching the broom out of Anna's grasp, he could scarcely feel the ground beneath his left foot. He was ill prepared to put up with one of Jessica's bossy moods. 'Jessica!' he shouted, 'for God's sake, leave your mother alone.' In the dusky lull of early evening his voice bounced off the still water of the canal, ringing out harsh and discordant.

Jessica stared back at him and for a split second he thought she was going to hit him with the broom. To be on the safe side of self-preservation he took it from her and propped it against Anna's wheelbarrow.

'This is none of your business,' she hissed, her eyes wide with astonished anger.

'Oh, stop being such a bloody pain and give your mother some space.' He turned to Anna. 'Shall we go inside for a moment, just the two of us? I said just the two of us, Jessica,' he added firmly, when she started to move with them.

When he and Anna reached the cottage and they stepped into the kitchen his leg finally gave way and he staggered and fell back against the door.

'Josh!' cried Anna, 'are you all right?' She fetched him a chair. 'What can I do?'

'Nothing,' he gasped. He sat down and rubbed at the numb, aching pain in his knee. 'Please ... don't fuss.'

'I wouldn't dream of it, not when we're such good allies.'

He managed a small smile.

'You looked very cross out there with Jessica,' Anna said, as she hovered anxiously round him, 'you won't hold it against her, will you?'

He stared at her. 'What do you mean?'

'I mean, don't judge her too harshly. Her loss of temper is her way of showing how much she cares.'

'I know that,' he said solemnly, 'I just can't bear to see her treating you as though you don't have any say in what you do ... it's too close to home.'

She touched his shoulder and gently squeezed it. 'Don't worry about me, Josh. I can handle Jessica. I'm up to speed with her tantrums.'

'Good. So tell me where your mobile phone is.'

She turned away guiltily.

He sighed. 'Come on, Anna. The deal was Jessica leaves you alone so that you can get up to whatever you want, but you have your mobile permanently with you. Remember, it was my idea for you to have a phone. If something serious ever happened to you and you weren't able to call for help, Jessica would never forgive me. And that's certainly something I can do without.'

'It's over there,' Anna admitted sheepishly. She pointed to the cluttered window-sill. 'I keep forgetting about it. It's not a habit with me yet.'

Josh suddenly tilted his head towards the back door. 'Quick,' he said, 'she's coming, put the damn thing in your sling.'

Anna moved nimbly across the kitchen. She was just in time.

'Well?' said Jessica, coming into the kitchen and casting her eyes first on Josh, then on Anna.

'Well what, dear?' Anna asked innocently.

'I've told you before, don't call me dear or darling, it makes me incredibly suspicious. What have you two been up to in here?'

With the greatest of effort, Josh got stiffly to his feet. 'It's all been taken care of, Jessica,' he said. 'Anna had only been outside for a few minutes and she had her phone with her anyway, so if there had been a problem she would have been fine. Isn't that right, Anna?'

Anna smiled and obligingly pulled out the corroborative evidence from her sling. 'See,' she said.

Jessica scowled. She wasn't convinced that anything was fine. How dare

Josh railroad her in that appalling fashion. Who did he think he was? Taking care of Anna was her responsibility, not his. What right did he think he had to barge his way in like that?

'Off somewhere nice?' Anna asked, keen to change the subject and aware now that Jessica wasn't cross only with her but also with Josh.

'I'm taking Jessica to meet my parents,' he said.

'Oh,' said Anna, 'well, don't let me keep you.' Given her daughter's mood, heaven help Mr and Mrs Crawford, she thought as she waved them off.

Jessica was all set to be furious with Josh after her mother had closed the front door on them, but as soon as she saw how difficult it was for him to walk her anger changed to concern. 'Josh, we shouldn't be going anywhere but home. You said earlier that your leg was a bit stiff and that I ought to drive, but look at you, you can barely walk.'

'Like I really need to be told that, Jessica. Now shut up and give me your arm.'

She helped him to the car. 'Now what?' she asked when she'd settled him in his seat. 'Home?'

'No,' he said, 'to my parents as originally planned. And please don't think you can boss me about as you do your mother.'

Jessica didn't trust herself to retaliate and wanting to make the right impression on Josh's parents, she concentrated on improving her temper. Think of something nice, she told herself as she switched on the engine. She immediately thought of Corfu; of swimming in the crystal-clear water below her little house and of enjoying a perfect sunset while having drinks on the terrace with Helen and Jack. She then recalled Helen and Jack's visit at the weekend. Despite the conversation about Gavin – and not for a single minute did she believe a word of what Helen had said on that particular subject – the day had gone really well. Helen had been on fine form and had started flirting with Josh. To her surprise, and no doubt delight, Josh had flirted back and before he knew where he was Anna had joined in and was declaring him a dirty dog. 'I don't mind sharing you with my daughter,' she'd said, 'but sharing you with a married woman is going too far!' In the end she and Jack had left Josh to defend himself against Anna and Helen, and had disappeared to the kitchen to tidy up.

'My advice is to forget about Gavin,' Jack had said when they were both stacking the dishwasher. 'Josh is by far the better bet.'

'Thanks, Jack,' she'd said, 'I think so too.' She'd given him a big kiss, only to be caught in the act by Helen who had gone straight back into the sitting-room to tell Josh that she was now a free agent and did he fancy a life in the sun with an older woman? He'd told her he'd be five minutes packing his bag, but could Anna join them?

It had been a day of fun and laughter.

Unlike now, thought Jessica miserably. Just what kind of evening lay ahead?

Before setting eyes on Jessica, William and Constance Crawford had long since made up their minds about the woman their younger son was seeing.

They very much liked the sound of her. Charlie was, of course, responsible for influencing his parents in this way, for he had told them in considerable detail what he thought about Josh's latest girlfriend. He was at the house when Josh and Jessica arrived and it was he who greeted them at the door. He saw immediately the state his brother was in and did his best not to react.

'Hi,' he said to Jessica. He kissed her cheek. 'All ready to be put under the spotlight?' he asked with a smile.

He took them through to the sitting-room where William and Constance were standing either side of the fireplace. Constance came forward first. She gave Josh a motherly kiss, chided him lightly for looking tired and offered her hand to Jessica. 'I'm Constance and this is my husband William. Ignore most of what he says, it comes of not knowing the right thing to say.'

Jessica shook hands with Constance and instantly felt at ease. She guessed that Josh's mother was younger than Anna, probably in her early sixties. There was an enviable air of charm and grace about her. She was quite tall and was clearly a woman who knew how to dress. Though Jessica was no expert and didn't know one designer outfit from another, she surmised that the stylish taupe-coloured shift dress Constance was wearing was no knock-down high street bargain. The cream cardigan draped over her shoulders was probably cashmere and the buttons were exquisite mother-of-pearl beauties. Her softly greying hair was elegantly pushed away from her face and seemed to be held in place by nothing more elaborate than sheer will-power. Jessica wondered why she could never get her hair to behave like that.

She then shook hands with William and was immediately aware of the similarity between the two Crawford boys – it was as if their father were the missing link between the pair of them. He was a handsome man and must have been as drop-dead gorgeous as his two sons when he was their age. He insisted that Jessica sit next to him and she didn't refuse.

From across the room, where he was pouring drinks, Charlie winked at her. 'The oldies are having sherry,' he said, 'but what would you like, Jessica?'

'I'll have the same, please.'

He brought the drinks over and handed them round.

Then he turned to Josh, who so far hadn't uttered a word. He was slumped in a chair with his head tilted back. He looked shattered, with deep shadows now showing under his eyes, which were tightly closed. 'Beer, Josh?' asked Charlie.

He opened his eyes and nodded.

'Would you rather sit on the sofa, Joshua?' asked Constance.

He looked at her as if considering her words. 'Why?' was all he said.

Constance turned nervously to her husband, then back to Josh. 'I . . . I just thought that maybe you'd be more comfortable there,' she said in a small voice.

'I'm fine where I am,' he said.

But it was obvious he wasn't and after he'd taken a sip of his beer he put it down and closed his eyes again.

'Well, Jessica, we hear that you're a writer.'

Jessica smiled at William, recognising that with or without Josh's contribution, there was an accepted amount of small talk to get through.

She did her best. So did Charlie. And between them they held the evening together. Every now and then she would look over to Josh and will him to feel better. She also stole a glance or two at the many framed family photographs that adorned the furniture around the large, beautifully decorated room. Constance and William Crawford were rightly proud of their offspring and every stage of their development was there to be seen; from toothless baby grins to formal school portraits to grown men. On a small pedestal table beside Jessica was a lone picture. It was of Josh. She put him at about seventeen or eighteen. He was wearing a baggy sweat-shirt and a pair of John Lennon sunglasses, and looked every inch like a young baby-faced pop star. His hair was much the same as it was now, thick and swept back – and held in place, she now realised, by the same force that Constance applied to hers. He looked just as attractive at that young age as he did now and Jessica knew that if she'd known him then, as a silly, giggling teenager at school, she would have been madly in love with him – his name would have been scribbled all over her books.

As the conversation continued, Jessica could see that both Constance and William were trying hard not to stare at their younger son, though their concern was clearly visible in their anxious faces. And the question that came into her mind was how did they cope with seeing Josh like this? Jessica had no idea what it felt like to be a mother and she could only guess what it was to experience that strong bond of love between parent and child. She didn't doubt for a minute that more than anything Constance was looking at her son, wanting to wrap him in her love and wish away all his pain.

Because as a lover that was certainly what Jessica wanted to do. In the past couple of weeks since she had been allowed to see the real Josh, her love for him had turned fierce and protective, breath-takingly so at times – that monstrous Amanda had been lucky to have survived the other night when she had been so rude to Josh.

Until recently she'd never been aware of what a temper she had, but what with Anna, and now Josh, to worry over, she realised that it was something she was going to have to get the better of.

Josh had been right in the car when he'd warned her not to boss him as she did her mother. It frightened her that he had been so right. But what scared her more was that she had no way of knowing how to stop it. She also knew that if she didn't find a way, and soon, it was probably what was going to come between them.

Alec was determined to convince himself that what Kate had told him a few hours ago was brought on by the shock of her miscarriage.

He was downstairs in his study, the door shut, the lights out, with a near empty bottle of Glenlivet for company. He poured another glass and told himself yet again what he needed to hear. Kate was just upset and confused. Tomorrow she'd wake up and say that she was sorry, that she hadn't meant any of what she'd said. And he would tell her that he understood and that it was behind them.

He drained his glass and pushed it away from him. He could go on telling himself this until he was blue in the face, but deep down he knew what Kate had said was perfectly true.

She had seen right through him. Of course he hadn't really accepted the baby she was carrying as a child he would love and nurture.

Yes, he was relieved that it was over and was that really such a sin? Was it so bad of him to want a partner all to himself?

Damn it! He was going to be fifty in a few weeks' time, what the hell did he want with fatherhood all over again?

He poured himself another drink, swallowed it down in one, lowered his head on to the desk and fell into a heavy drunken sleep.

Kate was awake by five o'clock and by half past six she had packed the bulk of her clothes into two large suitcases. The rest of her things she would have to come back for at a later date.

She sat on the edge of the bed and wondered what to do next. She wanted to go right away, to get this part over with as painlessly as she could, but she didn't want to leave Alec without saying goodbye. To creep away without a final word would be too cruel. She couldn't do that to him; he deserved better.

She crept quietly downstairs, unsure where Alec had slept the night. As she walked past the study she heard a noise. She took her courage in both hands and opened the door. The small room stank of stale alcohol. Alec was on his feet and was opening the sash window above his desk. He turned and stared at her. He looked dreadful: eyes horribly bloodshot, face mottled with a ghastly grey pallor.

'Shall I make us both some coffee?' she asked.

'I'll do it,' he said.

She bit her lip. Even at their parting he was still being the same considerate Alec.

They sat in the kitchen, in their usual seats, directly opposite each other. Kate was reminded of the morning she had told him she was pregnant.

'I don't suppose there's any point in asking you to change your mind, is there?'

'I'm sorry,' she said, 'I really am.'

He nodded. 'So am I.'

'You've always been so wonderful to me, Alec, I'll always –'

'No,' he said, holding up his hand to stop her. 'Please don't, this is bad enough without you telling me something like you love me, but you're not *in* love with me.'

She caught her breath and watched him blink away his tears. He couldn't have put it better. For that was exactly what she felt for him. She wanted to reach across the table and take his hand, but she knew that would only add insult to injury.

'Where will you go?' he asked gruffly.

'To Caroline.'

'Of course.' He looked up at her. 'She never really approved of me, did she?'

'No.' There was no point in lying to him.

They finished their coffee in silence. She made to get up and said, 'I think I'll get going now. I need to call for a taxi.'

He shook his head. 'A last request from a condemned man,' he said.

She frowned. 'You're not a condemned man, Alec.'

'I'll be the judge of that.'

She slipped back into her chair. 'What, then?'

'I don't actually want to see you go, wait until I've gone to work . . . please.'

47

Jessica was not the most organised of people and this morning was proving to be more than usually chaotic. It was the day the BBC were coming to make their film and in an hour's time the luvvies would be arriving, and if she didn't get a move on she would appear on daytime telly with nothing but a towel and a look of panic to cover her modesty.

After an early start she'd washed and dried her hair, and after several attempts at trying to persuade it into something a little more stylish than it was used to she'd given up and let it have its own way. Which meant she looked no different from the way she normally did: a mess!

She now tried to decide what to wear. Spread out on the bed were a variety of clothes, along with more packets of tights than she'd possessed in the whole of her life. On one pillow was a selection of opaque tights, they varied in their opaqueness, ranging from so thick they were bullet proof, down to merely wind resistant. They came in black or barely black; matt or shiny. On the adjacent pillow was a selection of sheer tights in all the different shades of black currently available on the market, as well as barley, beige and natural for that *au naturel* look.

It was a bewildering choice.

If it had been for any other occasion Jessica would simply have bought the first available pair, but because today was important she was doing her best to look the part of a successful novelist – whatever that looked like when it was at home. Prior to her visit to Wilmslow, she'd had the quaint notion that tights were just tights – living in Corfu, she hadn't had much call for them: in summer her legs were always bare and in winter they were covered by jeans. But after yesterday she had come to realise just how wrong she'd been; during her absence from England the buying of the silly things had apparently become an exact science. There were probably obscure universities offering postgraduate courses on the subject.

She hadn't expected to derive any pleasure from her shopping trip, but she had hoped to experience, at the very least, an element of cheap satisfaction. After all, it wasn't everybody who was out that day to spruce themselves up for their fifteen minutes of fame on telly. But as was so often the way with any of her expectations, she was wildly off beam. Cheap satisfaction was not to be had. Only the expensive brand was on offer.

She'd favoured a smart black no-nonsense suit when she'd entered the posh clothes department at Hooper's, but had instantly been pounced upon by an eager assistant who had other ideas and had tried to steer her towards a display of acid-green outfits. After she'd managed to give the girl the slip she made a beeline for the undertaker's rail of funereal black.

The prices were enough to make Jessica drop down dead from shock, but the little voice of temptation inside her head said, *Go on, treat yourself, it is in the line of work, after all.* Trouble came when she couldn't choose between trousers or a skirt. Both fitted her like a dream. Temptation whispered that further television appearances might follow and a second outfit would come in handy. Then it was downstairs to the shoe department. And naturally what went with the trousers didn't go with the skirt. Two pairs of shoes later, with the voice of reason asking her if she was feeling all right and wouldn't she like to sit down, she pressed on to the hosiery department. In the end it was just easiest to take as many pairs as she could carry and choose what to wear at home.

Except it wasn't. She was no nearer deciding what to put on this morning than she'd been yesterday.

She should have asked Josh for his opinion. He had such good taste when it came to clothes, but then he would, wouldn't he, it was his trade. She suspected, though, that in the rag trade or not, he would always have had a knack for making the most of his appearance. It didn't matter what he wore – black jeans and a T-shirt, or one of his trendy suits like the one he'd had on at Mo's party with the little stand-up collar – he always looked as if he'd just been posing for the front cover of *GQ*. She wondered if he was ever disappointed in her abysmal lack of interest in her clothes. If so, he'd never shown it. She looked at the stuff on the bed and wondered whether he'd approve of her choice. It was a shame it was too late to ask him for his advice – she'd heard his Shogun driving out through the courtyard over half an hour ago.

But seeking Josh's guidance on something as trivial as what she should wear seemed in very poor taste after last night. Poor Josh, he must have been in such agony at his parents'.

As the evening had drawn on and she had seen the pain in Josh's face intensify she had twice very nearly suggested that perhaps they should be going, but each time she had opened her mouth to say something she had stopped herself, frightened that her concern to get Josh home would annoy him. She noticed that while she was being careful not to cause Josh any annoyance, so too were his parents. Charlie as well. At no stage in the evening did anybody ask him how he was. Nobody offered to help him as he struggled to his feet when he decided it was time to go. Nobody said anything when he stumbled in the hall. And it wasn't because they didn't care. It was clear that they all cared very deeply about Josh, but they were simply taking their lead from him – if he didn't want to talk about how he felt, then it wasn't their place to refer to it either.

So was that how it was to be?

Was a long-term relationship with Josh going to comprise nervously tiptoeing around him for fear of upsetting him?

And was that really what she wanted? Surely, after being messed about by Gavin, what she needed was an uncomplicated relationship that would allow her to be herself. She thought of Gavin and what Helen had told her.

Could he really have changed? And if he had, why hadn't he let her know this himself?

Wondering if Gavin had changed made her remember the first time she'd caught sight of him. She'd been on the beach with Helen, who for once was quiet, as she concentrated hard on the painting she was working on. Very slowly, a small sailing boat had come into view and as the craft had neared the shore Jessica could make out a head of sun-bleached blond hair and a magnificent bronzed body. Helen had seen him too. 'Jessica,' she'd said, 'you're drooling, put your tongue away.'

They'd watched him jump out of the small boat and pull it up on to the hot white sand. There was nobody else on the beach so it was only to be expected that a conversation would ensue. He came over, pushed his sunglasses up on to his head and took a closer look at what Helen was painting. 'Very nice,' he said. And then as if they'd been expecting him, he settled himself on the sand next to Jessica. 'My name's Gavin, do you fancy a turn around the bay so that we can get better acquainted?'

God, but he'd been sweet. His carefree manner had made it so easy for her to fall for him.

But then everything about Gavin was carefree. Just as her own life had once been. She was shocked to realise that there was a tiny bit of her that was hungry for that way of life again. Since coming back to Cholmford everything she had anything to do with seemed to be so intense – her mother, her writing, and Josh.

Most of all Josh.

There was an intensity to him that Jessica doubted she was capable of handling.

This doubt about Josh had crept over her last night when she had driven them home from Prestbury. He had made it very clear as they approached Cholmford that he wanted to be alone and she had parked outside his house, as close to his front door as was possible, and had helped him inside by offering her arm as support. She had stayed with him for just a few awkward minutes, frightened of doing or saying the wrong thing – having seen his anger once already that evening she had no desire to provoke a repeat performance. She had gone home confused and uncertain as to what she felt for Josh. She had then phoned her mother to check that she was all right.

And to apologise. 'I'm sorry,' she'd said. 'I went at you a bit, didn't I?'

'You most certainly did,' Anna had replied. 'How's Josh and how was your evening?'

'Mixed. I'll tell you about it another time. I'm going to bed now.'

'Yes, you'll want your beauty sleep for the big day tomorrow. You will come and fetch me, won't you? I don't want to miss out on all the fun.'

The sound of the doorbell downstairs jolted Jessica out of her thoughts. She tightened the towel around her and hurried to see who it was, praying like mad that the luvvies hadn't arrived early.

But it wasn't the film crew, it was Kate.

Jessica stared at Kate's pale face and the two suitcases either side of her.

'Oh dear,' she said, weighing up the situation at once. She stood back so that Kate could come in. 'Life has suddenly become very complicated for us all, hasn't it?'

'It's all gone wrong between Alec and me,' Kate said. 'I've left him.'

'I know. Or rather I thought that's what would happen.'

'You did?'

'Josh and I spoke to Tony last night,' Jessica said simply. 'I'm sorry about the baby.'

Kate swallowed nervously. 'You must think I'm terrible,' she said, 'and that I've behaved very badly towards Alec.'

'I don't think anything of the kind,' Jessica said firmly. She could see that Kate was close to tears, that she was wrung out with punishing herself. 'Why don't you come upstairs and talk to me while I get ready for the film crew, they'll be here any minute.'

'Oh dear, I'd forgotten all about that. I'd better let you get on, you don't want me holding you up.'

'Oh no, you don't.' And taking Kate by the arm Jessica led her upstairs. 'I need your help. Someone has to tell me what to wear.'

And while Kate made helpful suggestions, Jessica gently probed about yesterday's events.

'It was all so fast,' Kate said quietly, 'one minute I was pregnant and the next I knew I wasn't. It wasn't particularly painful ... the real pain was knowing that I couldn't do anything to stop it. I felt so helpless.' She reached for a tissue by the side of the bed and wiped her eyes.

Jessica came over and hugged her. 'I've no idea what you've been through, Kate, so I shan't trot out a load of platitudes, but why don't you stay here for the day?'

'Won't I be in the way?'

'Probably. But it'll be a laugh and it will take your mind off things.'

Kate thought about this. She had planned to go to Caroline's and spend the day alone until her friend came home from work. But she suspected that being by herself would only make her more miserable than she already was – solitude would make her think of Alec ... and the baby. She quickly dispelled this last thought from her mind, telling herself that she hadn't been pregnant long enough to warrant such a feeling of loss. But there was no denying what she felt. Physically her body was already recovering from what had happened yesterday – apart from feeling tired and a little weak, it seemed to be getting on with life as if there had never been a tiny baby growing within it – but her emotions were less inclined to carry on as normal and like a tearful child she wanted to shout, *It isn't fair, give me back my baby.*

When she had left the hospital she had been amazed at the ordinariness of the proceedings. The doctor and nurse who had dealt with her had both been kind, but at the same time matter of fact. But then they had to be, she supposed, they must see hundreds of women like her all the time. The doctor had described her miscarriage as being without complication. 'But just to be on the safe side,' she'd added, 'see your GP in a few days' time if you're worried about anything, it's possible that you might need a D & C if the bleeding continues for too long.'

And that was it. It was all over. She was no longer pregnant. It was as if she'd experienced nothing worse than a bad period. She looked up and saw that Jessica was waiting for her to say something. 'Okay,' she said, 'I'll spend the day here, just so long as you're sure I won't be a nuisance.'

'Great.' Jessica smiled. 'Now at least I won't have to worry about making endless cups of coffee for the luvvies; you can do it. Oh, but heavens, listen to me bossing you about. You probably need to spend time with your feet up.'

Kate shook her head. 'I'm okay. In fact I'd rather be busy.'

'Are you sure?'

'Very sure.'

'In that case, I don't suppose you'd do me a real favour and fetch my mother, would you?'

'I'm sorry but I haven't got my car.'

'No problem, you can use mine. Where is yours, by the way?'

'It's still at the pub where Tony and I were having lunch yesterday.'

'Ah,' said Jessica, 'was that where you were when you realised something was wrong?'

Kate nodded and turned, shamefaced, to look out of the window.

'Are you really sure you're doing the right thing in leaving Alec, Kate?'

Kate returned her attention to Jessica. 'I do love Alec, but not in the way . . . not in the way Tony makes me feel about him.'

'Which is?'

Kate lowered her eyes and fiddled with one of Jessica's ear-rings that lay on the bed. 'I'm not sure you'd understand.'

'Try me.'

'I suppose the difference between them is that Alec makes me feel like a young girl, whereas Tony makes me –'

'Feel like a woman?'

Kate coloured. 'Am I that transparent?'

'No.' Jessica smiled. 'I just have above-average intelligence.'

Kate smiled too. Then she said, 'I'm not leaving Alec because of Tony. Or rather, I'm not leaving him *for* Tony.'

'Did you know that Amanda left him yesterday?'

Kate looked startled. 'What?'

Jessica came and joined Kate on the bed. 'The Wicked Witch of the West must have known all about you and Tony, and some time during the day she cleared out the house.'

'I don't believe it.'

'She did. She took the lot, well, everything except Hattie's things and the stuff in the garage.'

'I don't believe it.'

'You're repeating yourself, Kate.'

'But how could she do that? And to Tony of all people.'

'I hate to state the obvious, but I would imagine her motive had something to do with him taking time out of the marriage to see you.'

Kate was horrified. What had she done? By allowing herself to become involved with Tony she had not only wrecked her relationship with Alec, but Tony's marriage. How many more people had she hurt?

As if reading her mind, Jessica said, 'You mustn't take all the blame for what Amanda has done. Tony knew the risk he was taking. I get the feeling he isn't exactly devastated by what's happened.'

Kate thought about this. If Tony's marriage was over, didn't that change things? No, she told herself firmly. She mustn't think of that. She must stop thinking of herself. 'But what about Hattie?' she said, suddenly realising that the little girl had also been affected by her reckless behaviour. 'Who's going to look after her?'

'Tell me about it! I've been roped in to picking her up from school this afternoon, though goodness knows how I'll manage if the filming hasn't finished in time.' Jessica turned her head. 'I can hear a car. It's them and I'm still not ready.' She leapt off the bed and rushed to the window. 'Oh,' she said, relieved, 'it's a taxi. Did you order one?'

'Lord yes! I'd better go down and say I don't need it for now.'

By lunch-time it appeared that the film crew had moved in permanently with Jessica. Bits of her furniture had been shoved aside and replaced with several enormous tripods bearing powerful lights. There seemed to be a ridiculous number of shiny metal cases dotted about the ground floor of the house from which had emerged an even more ridiculous amount of electricity cable and paraphernalia.

The most worrying object for Jessica was what Rodney, the producer of the programme, called a monitor. It was this that he kept his critical eye glued to throughout the proceedings. He was obviously a man who loved his work because he kept wanting to go over the same thing again and again. He was also getting along far too well with Anna for Jessica's liking – the two of them were acting like a regular pair of old buddies.

Kate was busy in the kitchen making drinks and sandwiches for the workers, and Anna and Rodney and his assistant, a young girl called Mel, were crouched over the monitor screen in the study where they and the rest of the film crew were crammed in like sardines. 'Look, Anna,' cried an animated Rodney as he replayed the last bit of the interview they'd just spent two hours filming, 'do you see how Jessica's eyes were darting about when she answered that question? That'll be dreadful on television, she'll look like Marty Feldman. We'll definitely have to redo that bit.'

Mel made a note on her clipboard and Anna said, 'She always does that with her eyes when she's nervous, she did it when she was a little girl whenever I caught her doing something she ought not to have been doing. She does it when she's cross sometimes.'

'Thanks, Mum,' Jessica said, getting up from the chair in which she'd been sitting for the duration of the interview.

The cameraman smiled at her knowingly and the sound man took off his headphones and said, 'Parents, who'd have 'em?'

'Who indeed?'

They ate their lunch in the kitchen while Rodney and Mel discussed the next few scenes they wanted to film. There was a difference of opinion, though. Mel was all in favour of showing an arty-farty Jessica wandering lonely as a cloud through the surrounding woods and fields, but Rodney had been seduced by Anna. 'I think we ought to show the viewer where it all started. Let's have a couple of scenes where Jessica grew up, maybe even have her mother in a shot or two.'

'Oh, do you really think so?' said a delighted Anna.

Jessica rolled her eyes. Then she remembered Marty Feldman.

Rodney was enraptured with Willow Cottage. 'It's perfect,' he crooned, 'just look at the wonderful reflections in the water from those willow trees.' But when he saw the old swing with the last of the summer roses climbing all over it, his artistic cup began to run over in a maelstrom of ecstasy. 'Jessica, Jessica, quick, here, sit on the swing for me.'

'He'll have you looking like something out of a Fragonard painting if you're not careful.' Mel laughed from behind her clipboard. There was more than a hint of cattiness to her voice. She was clearly put out that she hadn't got her way with the woods and fields.

'Something's not right,' Rodney said, disappointed, when Jessica took up her position on the swing.

'The clothes are all wrong,' Mel said smugly.

'Jessica, you look much too severe in that suit, could you be a real sweetheart and go home and change?'

'*Change!*' she squawked. Didn't this man have any idea how much this outfit had cost? And as for severe, well he'd get a dose of that in a minute if he didn't watch his step!

'Yes,' he carried on undaunted, 'slip into something soft and floaty for me, something summery. I know it's autumn, but we'll take a bit of licence with the seasons on this one. Mel, you go with Jessica and help her choose the right look. A long, wafty scarf would be a nice touch.'

Mel drove Jessica the short journey home in the hire car in which the crew had driven up from London. Kate opened the door to them. It was then that Jessica remembered Hattie. 'Hell's bells!' she said, 'what are we going to do? Hattie needs picking up in half an hour and Cecil B. DeMille is nowhere near finished.'

'I could fetch her for you,' Kate said.

'You're a life saver, Kate, truly you are. I'll dedicate the next book to you.'

Suitably attired in a simple cotton top and her longest and most revealing skirt – not her choice, but Mel's – Jessica was driven back to Willow Cottage. She found her mother artfully posing with a rake for the camera, there was even a small bonfire of smoking leaves in the background. Jessica noticed that Anna had removed her sling and was standing so as to disguise the fact that her arm was in a cast.

'Your mother's a natural,' Rodney announced as Jessica stomped her way across the lawn – *whose fifteen minutes of fame was this anyway?*

They filmed the swing scene next. It took nearly forty minutes to get it just the way Rodney had in mind and by the time he was satisfied with what his faithful monitor was showing him Jessica was shivering with cold. Floaty was all very well in the height of summer, but on a sharp autumnal day it was bloody freezing! Piers, she decided, would pay for this.

The filming went on.

And on.

Jessica's childhood was revisited in every shape, form and manner that Rodney could come up with. They filmed her sitting in her old bedroom. They filmed her studying her school reports, which Anna magically unearthed from some overstuffed drawer in the kitchen. She was made to read out her English teacher's comments about her appalling spelling and grammar – 'we want to show the viewer that anyone can be a writer,' Rodney not so tactfully enthused. They filmed her looking at her infant school photograph and had her point out, from the line-up of black and white faces, the smallest and ugliest and skinniest child as herself.

And only when all these avenues of humiliation had been thoroughly explored and Rodney was convinced that Willow Cottage had been fully exploited did he suggest that maybe they could call it a day and head back to London.

There wasn't even a single mention of it being a wrap. It was most disappointing.

After the film crew had packed up and gone, Jessica borrowed an old coat from Anna and walked home. It was nearly half past six when she let herself in. She found Kate in the sitting-room with Hattie; they looked very cosy on the sofa together with Hattie tucked under Kate's arm.

'I'm shattered,' Jessica said, flopping into the nearest chair. 'Remind me never *ever* to be so vain as to want to do anything like this again.'

Kate smiled. 'Cup of tea?'

'Please. That would be lovely. I'll go upstairs and change, I'm nithered to death in these summer rags.'

But she didn't make it as far as the stairs when the doorbell rang. 'Oh, Lord, what now?'

It was Tony. 'Was everything all right with Hattie?' he asked anxiously. 'I'm sorry I couldn't get here sooner. I've been in a meeting all afternoon.'

'Don't worry, she's fine and has been in more than capable hands.'

Hattie came running into the hall. 'Daddy, Daddy, guess who came for me at school.'

He picked her up and swung her round. 'I know who did, it was Jessica and wasn't she kind to do that? We're lucky to have such helpful neighbours.'

'Oh, no, it wasn't Jessica, it was Kate.'

'Kate?' repeated Tony. He turned at the sound of footsteps and as Kate appeared in the doorway he slowly lowered Hattie to the floor. He couldn't think what to say.

But Jessica did. She had written this kind of scene before and knew the score exactly. 'Hattie,' she said, 'why don't you and I go out for some fish and chips for everybody's supper tonight while Kate makes a drink for your father? He looks as though he could do with one.'

48

With Jessica and Hattie's sudden departure, the house fell eerily quiet.

'How are you . . . how are you feeling?' Tony's words were hesitant and barely audible, and magnified the uneasy atmosphere between them.

'I'm fine,' Kate said.

He nodded, then looked down at his shoes. 'That's good. I'm glad. I'm glad you're all right.' He took off his jacket and carefully laid it on the back of a sofa. This was awful. Why couldn't he talk to her? Why was he so terrified? But the answer was simple. One wrong word from him now and he was sure he'd lose Kate for ever.

'How about you?' she asked.

'Me?'

'Yes, you.'

He shrugged. 'I'm okay.' He went over to the patio doors and pretended to look outside into the darkness, but all he could see was his own nervous reflection in the glass staring back at him. He turned away from himself. 'No,' he said abruptly, swinging round to face Kate, 'that's a lie, I'm far from okay.'

She looked concerned. 'Jessica told me about Amanda. I'm sorry, I never meant for anything like this to happen.'

Tony stared at her, then realised the mistake she'd made. 'No,' he said, 'no, you don't understand. Amanda taking things into her own hands is the best thing that could have happened.'

'So why –'

He took a few tentative steps towards her. 'So why am I not okay?'

'Yes.'

A few more steps. 'Yesterday at the hospital I thought you would blame me . . . blame *us*, for what happened . . . that you might not want to see me again.'

She lowered her eyes.

'I'm right, aren't I? That is what you thought.'

'Not entirely,' she said softly.

He was so close now he was almost touching her, could smell her light, fragrant perfume.

'I've left Alec,' she said, suddenly lifting her head and looking at him.

Nothing could have surprised Tony more. He stepped back from her and said the first thing that came into his head: 'Why?'

'Because, without meaning to, I changed. I wasn't right for Alec any more ... and he was no longer right for me.'

He looked away, hardly daring to think of the consequences of what Kate had just told him. Did he have a chance? Was it possible that they could start all over again? And would she want that? Did she think they could be right for one another? An unlikely wave of sympathy for Alec swept over him. What must he be going through? He turned back to Kate and found that she was studying him in the same way she had that day in St Luke's.

'What is it,' he asked uncomfortably, 'why are you looking at me like that?'

'I was wondering if I would ever see you smile again, you look so earnest.'

He shook his head. 'Is it any wonder I feel earnest, Kate?' And with a sudden rush of nervous energy he moved away from her. He began pacing the room. 'Look,' he said, bringing his hands down with a bang on the back of one of Jessica's cream sofas. 'I'm just a simple guy. I'm not clever with words. I can't dress this up. But I'll say it anyway. I need to know where I stand with you. I'm not going to push you into anything and ... and I know you need time to get over Alec, but ... but can I see you from time to time? I'd like to do things properly with you.'

'Properly?'

'Yes. We didn't meet in the right circumstances. I want us to have a fresh start. I want to take you out for dinner and flirt outrageously with you, then drop you off at home and spend the next twenty-four hours ringing you up and agonising over when I'm going to see you again. How does that sound?'

'For a man who can't dress things up it sounds heavenly.'

He came to a standstill and stared at her. 'It does?'

She nodded and went to him. She raised one of her hands and let her fingers drift the length of his jaw, then she kissed him.

'Please don't stop,' he said, when at last he felt her pulling away.

She smiled. 'I'm afraid I need the oxygen,' she said.

He drew her further into his arms. 'By the way, where will home be?'

She lifted her head from his shoulder to answer his question. 'Knutsford. I'm going to stay with a friend until I've got myself sorted. The first thing I need to do is find a job. I don't suppose you'd consider employing me meanwhile, would you?'

'What, at Arc?'

'No, silly. You're going to need somebody to look after Hattie after school, it might just as well be me.'

To her surprise he shook his head. 'No,' he said firmly. 'It's out of the question.'

'But why? It would be perfect.'

'I can't do that. Everyone would say that I was using you.'

'And who's everyone?'

He shook his head again. 'Just people.'

'Well I don't have a problem with it.'

'But I do. I don't want you to be the hired help.'

'Then don't pay me.'

'Now you're being silly.'

She smiled. 'And you're not?'

He let go of her and walked away. He went and sat down. 'I just want it to be right between us, Kate,' he said. 'I did everything wrong with Amanda and I'm not inclined to repeat any past mistakes.'

'Good, so that's settled then. I'll pick Hattie up from school tomorrow.'

'Didn't you hear me?'

'I heard you, Tony. I heard you loud and clear, making life unnecessarily difficult for yourself.' She joined him on the sofa. 'I'm offering to look after Hattie because I'm very fond of her and it just so happens that she's the daughter of the man I'm even more fond of.' She kissed him and as Tony gave himself up to her embrace he realised that there really wasn't any point in disagreeing with Kate. Her mind was obviously made up.

Jessica crawled into bed like a woman suffering from sleep deprivation. She was shattered. Stardom wasn't all it was cracked up to be, especially when it was compounded by a star-struck mother and an evening of running to earth a fish-and-chip shop that was actually open. She and Hattie must have tried nearly half a dozen, only to find they didn't open until eight o'clock, which was no good when they were starving hungry at seven. In the end they'd tracked one down and had then headed for home and found Kate and Tony smiling contentedly like a couple of chipmunks on the sofa.

Love's young dream was written all over their faces and Jessica had felt pleased for them. They'd all sat in the kitchen with their plates of fish and chips, and cracked open a bottle of wine. When they'd finished eating, Tony had driven Kate to her friend's house in Knutsford.

The only downside to the evening for Jessica was that Josh wasn't there to join in. She had tried ringing him several times to see if he wanted to come over, but there was no answer, not even from his mobile. His house, like Alec's, was in darkness and with no sign of his car, she could only assume that he was working late, or was with Charlie.

She lay back on the pillow ready for a good night's sleep – boy, had she earned it. But sleep was to be denied her. The phone rang almost the second she closed her eyes. It was only ten forty-five, but rarely did anyone call her so late. She snatched up the receiver, a vision instantly in her mind of her mother in trouble.

But it wasn't Anna.

'Gavin!' she yelled into the phone, jerking herself into an upright position.

'Yeah, that's the fella. You knew him once. Alas, poor Gavin, I knew him well. And in this case very well.'

'Have you been drinking?'

'Just the merest, teensiest, weensiest bottle or two of Metaxa.'

'What do you want, Gavin?'

'Oh, Jess, don't you know?'

'No, Gavin, I don't.'

'It's you, Jess. I want *you*.'

'You had your chance and you threw it away,' she said nastily.

'But I've changed, Jess.'

'Prove it to me.'

'I've grown a beard.'

'A what?'

'You know, one of those hairy things men wear on their chins.'

'*Yugh!* Why?'

'I thought it would keep the women away.'

'And does it?'

'No.'

'Good-night, Gavin.'

'You're a hard woman, Jessie Lloyd.'

'Thank you. Any other compliments for me?'

'Oh, come on, Jess. I'm trying to tell you that I've changed, that I'm ready to settle down.'

'And I suppose you really expect me to believe that?'

'And why wouldn't you?'

'So let's get this straight. You're telling me you're ready for children and slippers and a Ford Mondeo?'

'Steady on, Jess, I only meant I was ready to settle down for a life of regular sex and a clean pair of trollies every day.'

'*Hah!*'

'Would it help if I sang to you? You used to like me singing to you when we were in bed together.'

'Well, we're not in bed together now, are we?' she snapped back at him.

'Oh, Jess, you've turned into a bitter woman.'

'I'm not bitter!'

'Well that new fella's obviously not treating you right, or you wouldn't be sounding so hard.'

'What do you know about Josh? Oh, don't tell me, Helen told you all about him.'

There was a long pause.

'Well?' demanded Jessica, 'answer me, Gavin.'

'I'm trying to look sheepish down the line, that's why I'm not saying anything.'

Jessica suddenly laughed. 'Gavin, go to bed. If you want to ring me, do so when you're sober.'

'But I'm more romantic when I'm a little the worse for drink, the words come easier.'

'That's a matter for debate.'

'Jess?'

'Yes.'

'I love you, Jess.'

'No you don't, Gavin. Good-night.'

49

'I can't see that you've any choice,' Charlie said bravely.

They were having breakfast and as a consequence of what Charlie had just said a deathly hush had settled on them, but Josh's anger as he continued obstinately to read the front page of the *Financial Times* was as palpable as the strong smell of the coffee Charlie had just made.

It was also as manifestly real as the black cloud of depression that had descended on Josh and it was at times like this that Charlie knew he was way out of his depth. As far as he was concerned, before MS had booted its way into his life Josh had never suffered from depression; the moodiest he'd ever been was when he'd been recovering from a hangover.

But this was different. A glass of Alka-Seltzer was no remedy for what Josh was experiencing. Charlie knew that once the grip of depression was on him there was no instant cure. Sometimes it would only last for a few hours, at others it could be days. He'd read an article once in a magazine about a guy who could never shake off his depression, it was always with him. The poor fellow had likened it to having a parasite in his stomach eating away at the guts of him.

Thank God Josh didn't have it as badly as that.

Charlie poured out the coffee from the cafetière and pushed his brother's mug across the table. He deliberately placed it next to Josh's left hand – he could see that his right was too clenched to get a proper grip on anything.

Still Josh didn't raise his eyes from the newspaper.

'You've got to face up to it, Josh,' Charlie said, determined to pursue the point and to make Josh admit to what was so glaringly obvious. 'You've reached the stage where you need a stick. It would help you.'

But still Josh didn't say anything.

And he didn't need to. Charlie could see well enough what was going through his brother's mind. He knew that this whole MS thing was the most humiliating ordeal for Josh, that it was steadily eroding away his self-esteem, stripping him of his sense of worth. Resorting to a walking stick at his age was bound to be a hell of a blow to his pride. He probably viewed it as giving in to his MS rather than keeping up the fight against it.

But his attitude would have to change. He had no choice.

After work last night when everyone had gone home, Charlie had gone into Josh's office to go over a couple of ideas he'd had on one of their new lines and had found him inching his way round the room for a sample garment hanging on a rail some six yards away from him. Charlie had seen the strain in his face as he completed what to anybody else would have been a few easy steps, but what to Josh at that precise moment was the equivalent of running a half-marathon on one leg.

Much against Josh's wishes, Charlie had insisted he spend the night with him at his house in Hale. As he'd driven them home he had asked Josh when was the last time he'd seen a doctor. But all Josh had said was, 'I know how I feel, I don't need some bloody doctor telling me what I already know.'

And now, as he stared at Josh's sullen face, he decided the silence had gone on for long enough. Josh would have to listen to him. And act on it.

'I just think it would help you,' he said.

Josh lowered his mug of coffee. 'And how the hell would you know?' His words were slow and accusing.

'I'm making an assumption,' Charlie battled on, 'it makes sense, that's all, a stick would give you the support you need. It would stop you from –'

Josh threw down his paper. 'Well, why don't we just get straight to it? Let's not mess about with a stick, let's get me a wheelchair. Would that make you feel better?'

'It's not a question of how it would make *me* feel.'

'Oh, yes it bloody well is! You don't like the sight of me crawling round the office. It embarrasses the hell out of you.'

'That's not true.'

Charlie made a point of staying out of Josh's way that day at work. He knew that if he ventured into his brother's office another argument would ensue. There didn't seem any way of helping him. He appeared determined to ignore what was staring him right in the face. Something, or someone, had to explain to Josh that there were certain things he could do to make his life easier. The thought crossed his mind that perhaps Jessica could help. Could she be the one to get through to Josh?

He didn't have Jessica's phone number so he went in search of Mo. Josh had got her to ring Jessica once and with a bit of luck she might still have a note of the number.

Mo was an obsessive hoarder of bits of paper. Her desk was always a mess, as was the large drawer where she kept everything stashed away. 'I'm pretty sure I've still got it,' she told Charlie as she began taking out her pile of essay notes for that week's homework. At the back of the drawer she found a thick wodge of telephone messages and after sorting through them she finally came up with the one Charlie wanted. 'Why didn't you just ask Josh for it?' she asked.

'Because I'm going behind his back, so not a word, okay?'

'Hey, you're not trying to pinch Jessica, are you? Because if that's your game you can hand that over. I've done enough harm in that department without aiding and abetting you.' She tried to snatch the slip of paper out of his hand.

'Of course I'm not. I just need her help. Now remember, nothing about this to Josh.'

Jessica wasn't in when Charlie phoned her, so he left a message on her answerphone.

*

Jessica was at Willow Cottage. She'd just taken Anna shopping and now they were filling the cupboards and fridge with enough food to ensure that Anna wouldn't go hungry for the next six months. This was partially due to Jessica's desire to appease her conscience over her mother's welfare and also because first thing that morning George and Emily, just back from a holiday touring the west coast of Ireland, had phoned and when they'd heard about Anna's accident had immediately invited themselves to come and stay for a few days.

The arrangement suited Jessica perfectly. At least now there would be somebody keeping a keen eye on Anna. Not Emily, who was as irresponsible as Anna, but George, who was rock solid – forty years as a barrister specialising in Personal Injury had made him reliably cautious. Jessica was more than happy to entrust her mother's well-being to the capable hands of a man who would no more stand for her DIY antics than he would allow her to go bungee jumping.

'Right,' said Jessica. 'That's about everything stored away, do you want me to throw something together for your supper tonight with George and Emily?'

'Heavens no!' cried Anna, 'what have they ever done to you to deserve such a punishment?'

'You're all sweetness, Mum.'

'I know. I do my best. Now off you go and leave me alone. I've got things to do and you've certainly got a book to get on with. Kissy, kissy, bye, bye, and all that.'

Jessica drove home in a despondent mood. She would have liked to have lingered a little longer with her mother. It was silly, but she wanted to talk to her about Gavin's phone call last night. Silly because there really wasn't anything to discuss.

Or was there?

Hadn't she spent most of the night tossing and turning, thinking about Gavin and what he'd said? He'd never before said he loved her. Drunk or sober, the word love had never been a part of his vocabulary. So why, oh why, did he have to go and say it now? Why couldn't he have said it months ago when she wanted him to?

There were two messages waiting for her on the answerphone when she let herself in. She hoped that one of them was from Josh, but she was disappointed. The first was from Charlie asking her to ring him back and the second was . . . was from Gavin.

'I'm not drunk now, Jess, honestly,' he said, sounding hollow and tinny as the machine amplified and distorted his voice. 'And guess what, I meant what I said last night. Not the bit about you being a bitter woman, or being hard, but the other thing. You know, the bit when I said that, well you know, when I said that I –'

But the technology hadn't allowed Gavin time to finish what he was saying and Jessica felt slightly relieved. To have heard Gavin, without the aid of a gallon of Metaxa inside him, saying that he loved her was too much.

She replayed Charlie's message, then phoned him back. She listened to what he had to say. 'I'll try, Charlie,' she said when she'd taken in what he wanted her to do, 'but to be honest I don't think he'll listen to me.'

'But you'll have a go?'

'Of course, but just don't put all your hopes on me. I can't help but think that if you've failed to get through to him there's no chance of me succeeding.'

'It's got to be worth a try, Jessica. But whatever you say to him, don't let on that I put you up to it.'

'Okay.'

'And look, I don't wish to sound alarmist, but I'm convinced he's getting worse. Last night he could barely manage it to the car. If I hadn't been around I don't know how he'd have coped. And another word of warning –'

'Charlie, don't go on, you're making Josh sound like a minefield.'

'That's not a bad way of describing him in his current mood.'

'What do you mean?'

'Put it this way, his mood hasn't improved since the other night at Mum and Dad's.'

'Is he worse?'

'I'd say so.'

'Poor Josh.'

'I've seen it before. It's like he gets caught in a downward spiral and sucked into the darkness. All you can do is go with him and accept that you can't say or do the right thing. You just have to be there for him, a silent support act, you could call it. I only wish I could remember to do it myself. Unfortunately I managed to antagonise him thoroughly this morning.'

'Who's to say I won't?'

'But he feels differently towards you, Jessica. I'm just his boring old brother.'

After they'd finished their conversation Jessica tried to psych herself up for an afternoon of writing, but not surprisingly she found that she couldn't concentrate on *A Casual Affair*. Her thoughts alternated between Gavin, who had been so free and easy with her emotions, and Josh, who even though he was such a troubled person had made her feel like no other man had.

She had only known him for a short while, but within that time he had touched her in an exceptional way. When he wasn't battling with his MS he was all the things Gavin wasn't: gentle and sensitive, thoughtful and astute, and so very loving. She had found him to be the perfect foil to her own personality, which tended to be a little abrasive. She was aware, too, that what she felt for him didn't hinge on what he felt for her. It was almost as if loving him was fulfilment enough. Was this what selfless love meant?

If so, it was the antithesis of what she'd experienced with Gavin. The more she thought she'd loved Gavin, the more she'd wanted him to love her. But he never had.

Until now, apparently.

If he was to be believed.

But she didn't want to think any more about Gavin. He'd taken up far too much of her thoughts today as it was.

She reached for the phone and dialled Josh's mobile, a number which she knew by heart.

He sounded distant when he answered.

'Is it a bad time to talk?' she asked, thinking that maybe he had someone in his office with him.

'I'm a bit busy,' he said.

'Oh.' She wasn't prepared for such a lack of response from him. 'I tried ringing you yesterday evening.'

'I spent the night at Charlie's.'

'Oh.' She cringed. What was happening to her? She was a woman who made her living from words and here she was unable to utter anything more scintillating than *oh*. 'There was a lot of excitement going on last night,' she said, trying to inject some life into their joyless banter. *Why hadn't he asked her about her big day being filmed?*

'Oh?'

Oh great! Now he was at it as well.

She told him about Tony and Kate.

'Good for them,' Josh said uninterestedly.

His lack of enthusiasm annoyed her. He's tired, she told herself when she put down the phone. As Charlie said, this is a definite low period for him.

And just how on earth did Charlie think she was going to be able to broach the subject of Josh seeing a doctor, never mind the other thing she was supposed to bring up casually in conversation that evening – oh, and by the way, Josh, ever thought that a walking stick might come in handy?

So far there had been little conversation passing between them. There hadn't been so much as a kiss or a cuddle.

Nothing.

Zilch.

The atmosphere was distinctly chilly. Any cooler and they'd be chipping the ice off one another.

Jessica had resorted to switching on the television to provide a diversion. But yet another interminable medical drama was not what was required, especially when it was about a small child dying of some muscle-wasting disease. She quickly zapped the telly with the remote control.

Josh turned and gave her an odd look. 'What was wrong with that?' he asked.

Instantly she saw the trap he was setting her. 'Men in masks and gowns give me the willies,' she said. 'Another drink?' Hellfire, he was touchy tonight and obviously just waiting for her to put a foot wrong. Charlie was right. In his current frame of mind Josh really was a minefield.

She fetched the bottle of wine from the kitchen and poured the remains into their glasses. She put the empty bottle under the table and sat down next to Josh. Somehow she had to get him to talk. In the past she'd found it effortless to be light-hearted and flippant with him, but this evening she seemed incapable of the most basic small talk. What had happened to her?

Then she realised what it was. It was her reaction to what Charlie had described as Josh's downward spiral – it was destroying her confidence, making her fearful of him. She had to snap out of it. She might not be able to do anything about Josh's mood, but she had to work on her own.

Tentatively, she touched his hand. 'Josh,' she said, 'talk to me. You've hardly opened your mouth since you got here.'

'What do you want me to say?'

'I . . . I'm not sure.'

'Well, in that case, neither am I.' He removed his hand from hers and reached for his wineglass. He drained it in one go, but when he went to replace it on the table he misjudged the distance and the glass dropped with a soft thud on to the carpet by his feet.

Jessica made no move to pick it up – she'd learnt that much from being with him. Instead, she watched him retrieve the glass and place it with extreme care on the table in front of him.

'See,' he said, 'I managed it all on my own. How about that? Not bad for a disabled person, wouldn't you say?'

Jessica was either going to lose her temper or cry. And deciding that tears were for wimps, she resorted to her old standby. She leapt to her feet. 'Right, that's it!' she shouted at him. 'I've had enough. I've tried to be considerate. I've tried to humour you. I've even tried to do your brother's bidding, but enough is enough. I'm not a patient woman, I've a temper on me like a . . . like a, oh God, I give up, I'm hopeless at similes, but just hear this good and proper, I'm not going to stand here and let you use me like a punchbag. Have you got that?'

He stared at her, his eyes dark and narrowed, his lips drawn in a tight line. 'What do you mean, my brother's bidding?' His voice was frighteningly low.

Jessica's anger was suddenly checked. Damn, she'd given Charlie away.

'Did Charlie put you up to something?'

She swallowed nervously. 'No.'

'Liar.'

She swallowed again, her anger now straining to unleash itself. 'Okay then,' she said, 'you're right. And what of it?'

He continued to stare at her. 'I thought as much,' he said coolly. 'So the pair of you had a little confab behind my back, did you?'

Jessica's anger had fully returned now. And in triple strength. 'God, you're so self-obsessed,' she let rip at him, 'you're so full of self-pity you really can't see what you're doing to those who love you. Your poor parents live in constant fear of saying the wrong thing and as for Charlie, he's so desperate to help he'd chop off one of his own legs if he thought it would be of any use to you. And yes,' she continued, 'Charlie was worried enough to ask if I would talk to you. And what of it? Is that really such a crime? Doesn't it just prove how much he cares about you?'

A cruel smile came over Josh's face. 'Don't tell me, you were supposed to convince me that it was time to put up a neat little sticker in my car window and persuade me to buy the latest in disability accessories? Was that it?'

'If you had a broken leg you'd be more than happy to use a pair of crutches,' she blasted back at him, 'just tell me what the difference is.'

'The difference, Jessica, in case you hadn't cottoned on, is that I've got some fucking disease that is slowly killing me.'

'The only thing that's killing you is your bloody pride, you pig-headed, arrogant bastard!'

His jaw tightened and cold fury sprang into his eyes. 'Well, thanks for informing me of that, Jessica. I'll bear it in mind on the days when I can't put one foot in front of the other. Oh, that's all right, I'll tell myself, Jessica says it's only pride that's preventing me from being able to walk, it's got nothing to do with the gradual breakdown of my central nervous system.'

He began hauling himself to his feet. His movements were heartachingly clumsy. Jessica turned away. She couldn't watch him. It was too painful.

'I think we've said enough,' he said, when he was fully upright. 'In fact, we've probably said all that we ever need to say to one another. Good-night, Jessica. Or perhaps I mean goodbye, but there again that sounds too trite and clichéd even for a romantic novelist.' The bitterness in his voice was total. So was the contempt.

When he'd gone, Jessica threw herself on the sofa and buried her face in the cushion that he'd been leaning against. She could smell his aftershave on the fabric, the redolence of which brought forth the first of the tears; small, pitiful tears that quickly turned into painful sobs of remorse.

How could she have shouted at him like that?

How could she have hurt him when she loved him so much?

And how could she have let him walk away from her?

Why hadn't she tried to stop him? He was so weak, so worn down that she could have stopped him with her little finger.

The answer was ironically clear. The very same thing of which she had accused Josh had stopped her from saying she was sorry. Her pride and anger at the way she felt he had mistreated her, and those closest to him, had killed his love for her.

She had lost him.

Even if he would ever listen to her, which she very much doubted, there was no going back. Those damning words could never be withdrawn.

She stumbled upstairs to bed and cried herself into a restless sleep, tormented by images of Josh reaching out to her and her turning her back on his outstretched hands.

The End

50

While the stolid and reliable George was visiting a branch of his bank in Holmes Chapel and at the same time obtaining his daily fix of *The Times*, Anna and Emily had taken the opportunity to slip in a quick hour's worth of furtive gardening. They were working on the border opposite the back door where they couldn't be seen from the road or the drive, and where Anna had assured Emily that they'd hear George's car in plenty of time so that they could skip back inside the house and pretend they'd been doing nothing more perilous than washing up the lunch things. But their enjoyment of the while-the-cat's-away-the-mice-will-play situation was being marred by Anna's concern for her daughter.

'Do you think Jessica would talk to me?' Emily asked as she pushed the fork into the soft damp earth and waited for Anna to lift out the gladioli corm.

'You could try if you want,' Anna said, taking care not to bruise the corm in her hands as she removed the soil from its surface and cut away all but the last half-inch of its stem with her secateurs, 'but to be honest, I don't think it will work. I've never seen Jessica like this. She's never blocked me out before. We've always been able to talk to one another, but this silence from her is awful.'

Emily looked at her friend's worried face. 'Are you sure you're not over-reacting?'

Anna shook her head. 'I know what you're thinking, that I've got used to having her around and now I can't cope when she's got other things on her mind, apart from me. But it's not like that. Really it isn't. I've always been used to Jessica living away from home and being independent – it was what I wanted for her – and in all that time I've never been really worried about her. I've never needed to. Whenever there was a lack of communication between us I was always confident that she was okay. Don't ask me how I knew, I just did.'

'And you're not confident now?'

'No. It's like she's closed a door on me.' Tears came into Anna's eyes. She wiped them away with the sleeve of her old gardening jacket. 'I never knew that I could miss her so much,' she said quietly, 'or feel so worried for her. Perhaps it's just punishment for the hard time I gave her when she was doing her best to look after me.'

It was nearly a week since Jessica had informed Anna of the argument she'd had with Josh, which had brought about the end of their relationship.

'I don't want to discuss it in any detail,' Jessica had said when she'd come out for a pub lunch with George and Emily last Saturday, 'I'm just telling you what's happened so that you don't go and say something stupid.'

Later that afternoon, when they were alone in the kitchen at Willow Cottage, using all the kid-glove diplomacy she knew Anna had drawn out of her daughter a few more details.

'It strikes me that all you need to do is apologise to one another,' Anna had suggested. She liked Josh and had entertained a very real hope that one day he might become her son-in-law. She felt strangely sad at her own loss.

But in response, Jessica had shaken her head with tears in her eyes. 'I tried ringing him this morning and he refused to speak to me. I tried to apologise, but he was so cold ... so unforgiving. Now please, just don't talk to me about it any more. It's over and I've got work to do. I ought to go. Say goodbye to George and Emily for me.'

And she'd left, just like that, almost running out of the house. Since then, she hadn't phoned. The tables had turned and now it was Anna who was doing all the ringing to check on her daughter. Most of the time Jessica left her answerphone on and on the few occasions when Anna had spoken to her she had claimed she was either too busy to chat, or too tired.

'Shall I call on her when George gets back?' Emily pressed.

But Anna didn't get a chance to reply. 'Quick,' she said, pulling off her gardening gloves and handing her friend the box of lifted gladioli corms, 'it's George. Put those in the shed on the top shelf and I'll go and put my feet up and pretend to be having a snooze.'

'Jess, I can't sleep for thinking of you.'

'Why do you want to sleep? It's only four o'clock in the afternoon.'

'I don't mean now. I'm talking about when I'm in bed at night.'

'Then take something. Treat yourself to some chemically enhanced sleep.'

'So you've turned into a drugs dealer now, have you, Jess?'

'Look, Gavin, please, I'm just not in the mood.'

'I can't remember you ever saying that to me before. If I recall, you were always mad for it.'

'Leave me alone, Gavin.'

'You don't mean that. I know you don't.'

And he was right. These days Gavin was the only person Jessica could talk to without ending the conversation in tears. Over the past week his silly jokes and buffoonery had become a prop to her.

He'd phoned her on Saturday, the day after she'd argued with Josh, and she'd told him what had happened.

'I'm not sure I want to hear you blubbing about some other fella,' he'd said.

'Then don't ring me,' she'd told him through her tears.

'Shall I fly over and beat him up for you; would that make you feel better?'

'No.'

'What would?'

'I don't know.'

He'd phoned every day since.

On Wednesday he'd said, 'I can't hear you snivelling, does that mean you're over the awful fella or back with him?'

On Thursday he'd said, 'Why don't you give yourself a holiday? Dig out your bucket and spade and come and stay with me.'

'Don't be absurd, I've got work to do.'

'Oh, come on, Jess, you can write that penny-dreadful stuff in your sleep.'

On Friday he asked her again to go and stay with him. 'There's hardly any tourists here now, we'd have the place to ourselves. I could take you out in the boat.'

'I hate sailing, you know that.'

'We could have sex if you'd prefer. It could be good for you, you know, in a therapeutic, healing kind of way.'

'Is that your latest chat-up line?'

'Oh no, I've got a much better one than that.'

'Spare me, please.'

And now it was Tuesday and Gavin was complaining to her that he couldn't sleep. She hadn't slept much recently either.

She wondered if Josh was sleeping.

It was exactly eleven days since Josh had finished with her and for most of those days she'd seen him for the briefest of seconds. Every evening while working in her study she would wait for him to come home. Night after night she would watch him across the courtyard as he dragged his tired body from his car to his front door. Not once did he turn and look in her direction. Not once did he even acknowledge that she existed.

But he still existed for her. And each evening the painful sight of him invoked a whole series of responses in her: anger, hurt, regret, but mostly an overwhelming sense of love. Oh yes, she still loved him. She wished that she could tell him that. But he would probably never believe her. His pride and anger would stop him from accepting that she loved him unconditionally; that his MS didn't affect the way she viewed him, that in reality it was just another facet of his personality that had become so precious to her. She wouldn't have cared that their future together would have been full of uncertainty – after all, there wasn't a person alive who could rest secure in the knowledge that his or her own future was clear-cut and perfectly defined.

But there was no point in going over all this. She had to face up to the truth that Josh had no desire to see her, which was why she had taken the step of booking herself on a flight to Corfu. With the first draft of *A Casual Affair* very nearly finished, and with George and Emily staying on for another week at Willow Cottage, she felt able to go away knowing that her mother was in safe hands. Other than Helen and Jack, she had told no one of her plans. But now she told Gavin.

'Great!' he said, 'I'll clean up a bit and change the sheets.'

'No, Gavin, I'm staying with Helen and Jack.'

'You're such a tease, Jess.'

'It's true. Ask them. It's all arranged.'

'All right, then, but let me pick you up at the airport.'

'Okay, that would be nice.'

'Jess?'

'Yes.'

'I'll change the sheets anyway, shall I?'

Anna couldn't believe it.

'What is it?' Emily asked when Anna put down the phone and went and joined her friends in the sitting-room.

'It's Jessica,' she said, 'she's going back to that fool Gavin.'

'What, that chap in Corfu?' asked George, lowering his *Times* crossword and peering at Anna over the top of his glasses.

'The very one.'

'For good?' asked Emily.

'She says she's just going for a few days.'

'Oh, well, I don't suppose too much harm can come of that,' said George, returning his concentration to seven down.

But Anna was far from convinced. 'That place and that man seduced her once before. Why wouldn't the same combination work a second time ... and keep her there for ever?'

'When does she go?'

'Tomorrow.'

Anna had never interfered in her daughter's life before, but she had absolutely no qualms over what she was about to do. It's pay-back time, she told herself as she picked up the phone. All those years when I held my tongue and let her get on with making her own mistakes have to count for something. She dialled the number and waited.

And waited.

Dammit, where was he? Why didn't he answer?

Josh ignored the ringing from his mobile phone. Whoever it was, he didn't want to speak to them. He carried on reading through the latest wad of specifications from Hong Kong.

The ringing eventually stopped. Relieved, Josh took off his glasses and rubbed his eyes. He was unbelievably tired.

Tired of work.

Tired of his failing body.

Tired of trying to banish Jessica from his thoughts.

He was also tired of Charlie.

'For God's sake, ring Jessica and say you're sorry,' Charlie had shouted at him yesterday, 'your life's bad enough without doing this to yourself.'

It was advice he didn't want or need.

Even his parents had phoned him – no guesses who had put them in the picture – 'Are you sure you know what you're doing?' his mother had asked him, 'she seemed such a lovely girl.'

But what none of them could see was that there was no point in any of it.

So much of what Jessica had flung at him he knew to be true. He had hurt his family in the past and without knowing how to stop himself he would probably go on hurting those closest to him.

I'm not going to stand here and let you use me like a punchbag, Jessica had said. It was these very words that had sealed their fate. He could never continue a relationship with Jessica because he would only end up causing her pain and he loved her too much to do that.

His mobile started ringing again. He stared at it, still not wanting to answer it.

'Are you going to let that ring all day?'

It was Charlie. He came into the office and plonked himself in the chair opposite Josh. 'Well?' he said, 'answer it, then.'

'No.'

The ringing stopped and Charlie frowned. 'Who are you afraid of?'

'Nobody,' said Josh sharply.

'Liar.'

Josh leant back in his chair. 'Not another lecture, please.'

The mobile began trilling again. Charlie snatched up the small phone from the desk and answered it. 'No, this isn't Josh, it's his brother, Charlie. Oh, hello, Mrs Lloyd. Yes, we do sound alike, don't we? Hang on and I'll hand you over.'

Josh shook his head. He waved the phone away.

'I'm sorry, Mrs Lloyd, he's rather busy, can I pass on a message or get him to call you back?'

The conversation that followed was brief and to the point, and when Charlie had said goodbye he handed the phone to his brother and said, 'I suggest you speak to Jessica before it's too late.'

'What do you mean?'

'Apparently an old boyfriend is making his presence felt and has persuaded her to go back to Corfu.'

Josh's face dropped. He quickly regained his composure. 'To live there again?' he asked calmly.

But Charlie had seen the expression of alarm in his brother's face. 'I don't know,' he said. 'Her mother just said that Jessica was catching the early-morning flight tomorrow.'

Josh said nothing. He slowly got to his feet and struggled across his office. He came to a stop in front of a large notice-board. He ran his fingers over the samples of stretch denim that were pinned to the green felt. 'So what's any of that got to do with me?' he asked.

'What the hell do you think? Go home and talk to Jessica. Tell her what you feel about her. Be honest for once.'

'It's honesty that's got me where I am.'

'I don't believe that for a single moment.'

'Suit yourself.'

Charlie banged his fist down on the desk. 'It's not a matter of what suits me.'

'Good, so keep out of my life.'

Charlie leapt to his feet. 'I wish I bloody well could! I also wish I could get to the bottom of what's gone wrong between you and Jessica. She's the first woman who's made any real impression on you and you seem absurdly content to let her go. I don't know the full ins and outs of what you and

Jessica argued about, you didn't tell me the whole story, but I bet your bloody pride is involved somewhere.'

Josh turned on him. 'The only reason you're so keen for there to be a neat package of Jessica and Josh is that you hope it'll let you off the hook!'

'*What!*' exploded Charlie.

'That's right. You want me to be conveniently hitched up with Jessica so that you won't have to worry about me any more, you'll have somebody else to do it for you.'

An anger that was raw and violent swept over Charlie. The blood drained from his face. He felt sick with rage. 'Don't ever, ever accuse me again of something as despicable as that.' He spat the words out and turned to walk away, but he changed his mind, and suddenly and without warning he slammed his fist into Josh's face.

Charlie stared in horror at his brother as he lay on the floor. It was a couple of seconds before he took in what he'd done and it took a further split second for him to come to terms with how easy it had been to knock Josh clean off his feet.

Josh's head was spinning. He could taste blood. He gingerly touched his mouth, then looked up to see Charlie offering him his hand.

'I'm not even going to say sorry for doing that,' Charlie said when he was up on his feet, 'you deserved it too much.'

Josh took out a handkerchief from his pocket and pressed it against his lower lip. 'I can't recall you ever hitting me,' he said in a shocked voice. Holding the hanky to his mouth, he went and sat down. 'Do I really get up your nose that much?' he asked.

Charlie pushed his hands into his trouser pockets. 'Yes,' he said simply. 'There've been more times than I'd care to admit when all I've wanted to do is thump the living daylights out of you.'

'So what's stopped you in the past?'

Charlie shrugged. 'Hitting somebody when they're down doesn't seem to be the decent thing to do, I suppose.'

'You mean until now it was pity that was keeping your fists off me.'

Charlie paced the room. 'Why do you have to make pity sound so derogatory? Look it up in the dictionary, it means sadness and compassion felt for another's suffering. I can't help feeling that way about you. You're my brother.'

Josh closed his eyes. His head was still spinning. The shock of Charlie actually hitting him was still with him too. Knowing that he'd pushed his brother to such an extreme appalled him. What had he become? What kind of monster had his illness turned him into? Whoever or whatever he was, he was no longer recognisable to himself.

'There's nothing wrong with people having a genuine concern for you, Josh,' he heard Charlie say. 'It's called love. And it's what Jessica feels for you.'

He flicked his eyes open. 'Yeah well, maybe you're right,' he said matter-of-factly. 'But it's over. We've said our goodbyes. And that's my final word on the subject.'

But Charlie was determined to prove his brother wrong.

*

Jessica's taxi came for her at the unearthly hour of twenty to six in the morning. It was pitch dark when she was driven away from Cholmford Hall Mews, and as the car negotiated the small bridge over the canal and she looked back at Willow Cottage she was reminded of the night she'd returned to England. It seemed an age since then, so much had happened.

But in reality, it wasn't the case.

It was just that what had gone on during the past few months had been so all-consuming. Love was like that, though. Once it got a hold of you it held you in its grip, giving you the impression it would never let you go.

But sometimes it did.

And this was one of those occasions.

At the airport she paid the taxi driver and made her way to the long row of check-in desks in the departure hall. After queuing for a short while she checked in her luggage and went in search of a café where she hoped to force down some breakfast. But the way she was feeling it was unlikely that she would manage it. Her churning stomach was leaving her in no doubt that it wasn't happy at being disturbed so early.

Josh opened his front door. 'What the hell are you doing here?' he asked, bleary-eyed and disorientated – it was six o'clock in the morning and his brother was on his doorstep. *Why?*

Charlie ignored Josh's question. He stepped in and closed the door behind him. 'Get washed, shaved and dressed, you're coming with me.'

Josh opened his mouth to speak, but Charlie raised his hand and pointed a forefinger at him. 'Not a word. Got it?'

Upstairs in Josh's bathroom, Charlie stood over him. 'You've missed a bit,' he said, watching his brother shave, then realising that Josh's hands were shaking and were too stiff to do a proper job he added, 'here, give it to me.'

'I know exactly what you're doing, Charlie,' Josh said above the sound of the razor.

'Good, so let's get on with it.'

'It won't work. I know it won't. It's gone beyond that.'

'Right now, I can't be arsed with your pessimism. Okay, that's the shaving done. Clean your teeth, then splash on something irresistible while I get your clothes. What do you think Jessica would like to see you in?'

'After the way I've treated her a coffin, probably.'

'Would that be teak or mahogany?'

When Charlie parked his car he switched off the engine and reached through to the back seat. He handed Josh a Jiffy bag. 'A present,' he said, 'open it and don't argue.'

'You bastard,' Josh said, when he saw what it was. But instead of there being anger in his face as Charlie had dreaded, there was a look of resigned acceptance as Josh inspected the specially designed fold-away walking stick.

'I got it through one of Dad's catalogues. At least it's black and matches your image.'

'Some bloody image.'

'There's also a slip of paper there for you ... with some addresses you might like to follow up.'

Josh looked inside the Jiffy bag and pulled out the piece of paper. He read what was written on it and, without saying anything, pushed it into his jeans pocket.

They locked the car and slowly made their way to the lift as Josh tried out the new stick. Charlie pressed the button and the doors opened immediately. They stepped inside and as they dropped to the fifth floor Josh alternated between chewing the inside of his mouth and looking at his watch.

'Relax, we'll make it,' Charlie said, 'I checked earlier, the flight won't be called for at least another half-hour.'

'But what if she's gone through passport control already?'

'It never happens that way in all the films,' Charlie said lightly, needing to take the edge off his own apprehension.

The lift stopped, the doors opened and Josh froze. 'I can't go through with this,' he said, suddenly rooted to the spot. 'What if she won't talk to me?'

Charlie took him by the elbow and helped him out. He couldn't answer his brother's question because even he was frightened that Jessica would turn her back on them and simply get on her plane.

They looked everywhere for her, but couldn't find her. They checked out W. H. Smith, searching for her among the shelves of magazines and bestsellers. They moved on to Boots. Then across to the Body Shop. But there was no sign of her anywhere.

Miserable and depressed, Josh was all for giving up, but Charlie wasn't. 'I've got an idea,' he said, 'come on.'

Jessica's stomach was threatening to do its worst. For any normal person there was no decision to be made. It had already been made. The flight was booked. She was at the airport. She was all set for Corfu.

But was she? Was she really?

If she got on that plane there were certain things that would happen as a consequence. She just knew it.

She wiped the sweat from her palms and from her top lip. Lord, she was nervous! She hadn't felt this sick with indecision since that awful day in London with Piers. And as on that surreal day, she was now prepared to let her future be decided by a toilet.

A bloody toilet! I ask you!

To flush or not to flush, that was the question.

This is no time for joking, she told herself severely, just consider the facts, calmly and rationally.

If the toilet flushed first go, she would stay where she was – and that's Cholmford, not Manchester airport, she added for clarification – and she'd talk to Josh. She'd force him to listen to her; he had to realise she was sorry.

And if the toilet didn't flush then she would get on that flight for Corfu.

Well, that seemed clear enough, didn't it?

She reached out to the handle, knowing that she was seconds away from a decision. A crucial one.

Whoa! Just a cotton-picking moment. Was there to be no clarification on the second option? No definition of what Corfu actually stood for? Was the jury to be denied the full facts of the matter? Were the members of the jury not to be told that a few days spent languishing in Corfu licking her wounds was in actual fact an excuse for bailing out at the first sign of difficulty and running straight back into the arms of a previous lover?

She looked round guiltily. So what if it was? What was wrong in doing that? The situation was quite clear. Josh didn't want her. Gavin did.

And besides, a little comforting wouldn't do any harm. Because that's all it would be. She knew how to handle Gavin now. She wouldn't be taken in by those pouty, hurt, little-boy lips whenever he couldn't get his own way with her. Oh, no, those days were gone. She was a much stronger woman than the one who had left Corfu in the summer.

Yes, she thought sarcastically, you're a thoroughly empowered woman, so much so that you're letting a toilet decide your future.

No need to get nasty.

Then get on with it!

She took a deep breath and reached out to the handle.

'Would Miss Jessica Lloyd please go at once to the special assembly area opposite the Lufthansa ticket desk.' The tight nasal voice that came over the PA system threw Jessica into an immediate state of alarm. Something had happened to her mother. She'd had a heart attack and George and Emily were trying to get hold of her. Panic-stricken, she spun round in the small cubicle and head-butted the door.

'Miss Jessica Lloyd to the special assembly area. Thank you.'

'Be quiet you stupid woman!' Jessica muttered under her breath as she fumbled to unlock the door, and with an egg-sized lump already forming on her forehead, she belted out of the Ladies and raced across the arrival hall. Oh God, how could she have thought of leaving her mother? How selfish she'd been.

'Where's the Lufthansa ticket desk?' she shouted at one of the girls on the British Airways check-in desks.

'Straight on and to the right.'

Jessica ran, turned the corner, then stopped dead in her tracks.

She saw Charlie first, then Josh. All at once she realised that her mother was quite safe and that the only heart in trouble was her own. It was pounding so fast it was likely to burst out of her chest.

Charlie smiled at her. He said something to his brother, then walked away.

Josh came slowly towards her. Which was just as well as she was in such a state of shock she didn't think she'd move again – a shock that was compounded by the sight of him having its normal effect on her. Her mouth was instantly chalk dry; she thought he'd never looked more desirable. He was dressed in his usual black jeans and with a baggy V-neck sweater over a white T-shirt he reminded her of the teenage heartbreaker in the photograph at his parents' house.

She then noticed that he was using a stick.

A stick? Had Charlie finally got through to him?

She noticed, too, how terrified he looked.

He was standing in front of her now, so close she could see all the dazzling flecks of colour in his wonderful brown eyes and her stomach twisted itself into the kind of knot she'd learnt as a Girl Guide. *But why was he here? To wave her off? Or . . .*

'You've cut yourself,' she said, lowering her gaze from his eyes to his mouth.

'Charlie hit me.'

'He did what?'

'He said I deserved it.'

'And did you?'

'I think so, yes.'

'That's all right, then. I was brought up to believe that we always get what we deserve.'

'Sound advice. So what have *you* been up to?'

'Me?'

'You've hurt your head.'

She raised her hand and felt the bump on her forehead. 'Nothing gets past you, does it, Crawford?'

'I sincerely hope you're right.'

His voice was suddenly low, which in turn increased the pounding in Jessica's rib-cage. Hardly daring to ask, she said, 'Why are you here, Josh?'

'I would have thought that was obvious.'

She swallowed hard. 'A girl likes to have it properly explained, especially if she's a writer.'

He suddenly smiled. It was the first real smile she'd seen on him for what felt like for ever. Much more of this and she'd be the one needing that stick for support!

'Just my luck that I go and fall in love with a writer,' he said.

Love! He'd mentioned the word love. Was there hope? 'Hey, it could be worse. I could be a civil servant and want it in triplicate.'

He shook his head. 'Believe me, Jessica, nothing could be worse than falling in love with you.'

'I'm not sure how to take that.'

He took a deep breath. 'Look, I'm sorry for the way I've treated you, for all those things I said, please . . . I don't want you to go.'

'Not even for a holiday?'

'No. I hate the thought of you being with that Gavin character. Or any other man for that matter. I love you. And . . . and I need you more than anyone else ever could. Perhaps I . . .' But his voice trailed away and he lowered his gaze.

'Perhaps what?'

'Perhaps I need you too much.'

Hot, stinging tears pricked at her eyes. *He loved her . . . he needed her.* Nobody had ever said that to her before. Nobody. It was all she'd ever wanted to hear. 'You could never want me too much,' she said, and throwing her arms round his neck she kissed him.

When they finally parted he said, 'I'm completely knackered, do you mind if we sit down?'

51

It was a cold, wintry evening in the middle of November and everyone had gathered in Josh's house to enjoy Jessica's fifteen minutes of fame.

Except for Jessica.

She was there with them all, but unlike the others, she held no expectation of deriving a single second of pleasure from watching herself on the television. And determined to put the dreaded moment off for as long as possible she was now opening the first of the bottles of champagne that Josh had specially bought to mark the occasion.

'I think a few toasts are in order,' she announced as she passed the glasses round.

'Oh?' said Anna, 'anything in particular?'

Jessica caught the hopeful glance her mother gave her left hand. 'Yes,' she said, 'for a start I think we should celebrate the removal of your plaster cast this morning and that, despite your worst endeavours, you've been given a clean bill of health.'

'Any chance of having that in writing from you, Jessica, dear?'

'Don't push it, Mum!'

Josh laughed and raised his glass. 'To Anna and her clean bill of health.'

'What's a clean bill of health?' whispered Hattie to her father after she'd taken a gulp from her own tiny glass and had felt the bubbles fizzing up her nose.

'I'll tell you later,' he whispered back. Then putting his arm round Kate, he said, 'I think we should also congratulate Kate on being offered a part-time job where she used to work.'

'That's brilliant news,' said Jessica. 'When did you hear?'

'Yesterday,' Kate answered.

'And after the way they treated you before, you weren't tempted to tell them to shove their job straight up their Dewey System?'

Kate laughed at Jessica. 'No,' she said, 'I'm much too practical for that.'

'You mean you're too nice,' said Jessica.

'Not really. I need the work and besides, for now, the hours are perfect. This way I'll still be able to carry on taking care of Hattie.'

Jessica smiled at Kate, then at Tony and Hattie. 'Well, here's to all three of you and your perfect arrangement.'

They raised their glasses one more time.

'I'm sorry,' Anna suddenly said when the room went quiet, 'but I really can't take the suspense any longer. I'm dying to see a bestselling author's mother on TV. How about it?'

Jessica cringed. 'Do we have to? Can't we have another toast?'

Anna groaned. 'What to this time? The weather?'

Jessica looked thoughtful. 'I know,' she said. 'To the new people moving into number three next week. May they be as –'

'As mad as you,' said Josh. 'At least then there'll be a chance of them fitting in around here.'

Jessica pulled a face at him. 'I was going to say, may they be as sweet-natured as you, lover boy.'

'Please!' cried a thoroughly exasperated Anna, 'before we all die of old age, can we just sit down and watch the video?'

'Okay,' Jessica demurred, 'but only on the condition that I'm in charge of the remote control and I'm allowed to have all the cushions to hide behind.'

'You could always go behind the sofa like you did as a child when you were scared,' Anna said. 'Now come on, I want to see how my garden turned out.'

They settled themselves down: Anna in the armchair nearest the television, Kate and Tony on the floor with Hattie on her father's lap, and Jessica and Josh on the sofa together.

Jessica pointed the remote control at the video, wishing that she hadn't made such a ridiculous pact with her mother and Josh last night – because Josh would be at work when the programme went out, he and Anna had insisted that none of them watched it until they could all be together that evening. 'Now if anybody laughs,' she said, 'I'm warning you, I'll switch it off.'

'Get on with it!'

Amanda was getting ready to go out to a party. As she switched off her hair-drier she could hear her mother arguing with her father downstairs. It was a familiar scene, but one which she had forgotten about until she'd left Tony. Living with her parents for a few months had seemed a good idea, but now it didn't. No wonder her father spent all his time with his head in the past. He had all her sympathy. And just as soon as she'd found herself a job she would be off.

Over the coming weeks she had several interviews arranged, one of which was a follow-up interview, and she was confident that she'd soon be back in full-time employment.

Meanwhile, there was the divorce to organise. Tony had so far acted very decently and had given in to all her requests – no more than he should after everything she'd done for him. Half the house was to be hers, just as soon as it could be sold, as well as a suitable sum of money, part of which was to compensate her for loss of earnings while being stuck at home looking after Hattie. And, of course, she had all that furniture in store just waiting for her to set herself up somewhere new.

When she'd asked her solicitor if it wasn't worth their while pushing for more, the woman's response had been a little disappointing. 'My advice to you, Mrs Fergusson, is to quit while you're ahead,' she'd said.

Well, maybe her solicitor was right. It wouldn't do to be seen as greedy. Not that she thought she was being greedy. In her opinion Tony had been prepared to hand over as much as he had because his conscience had made him do so. He had put no effort into making a go of their marriage and had been only too quick to stray into the arms of another woman. And if it hadn't been for her father catching Tony and Kate red-handed that day in Holmes Chapel, goodness knows how long it would have been before she'd have discovered what he was up to.

She finished applying her make-up and went downstairs. There was no sign of her father, but she found her mother in the sitting-room watching a wildlife programme. Amanda's stomach turned as she caught sight of a panther feasting on a gazelle. She shuddered. Predatory animals, weren't they just the worst?

It was Alec's fiftieth birthday. He wasn't celebrating it in the way he had imagined – in Venice with Kate – but he was enjoying himself. His dinner companion was proving to be good company, but then he wouldn't have expected anything less.

Getting over Kate hadn't been as bad as he'd thought it would be. Initially he had felt sorry for himself and had wanted her back. Unable to stop what he was doing, he had been rather pathetic and pestered poor Jessica and Josh about Kate. They had been very patient with him. And very tactful. When he'd discovered that Kate had been seeing Tony behind his back he had been mortified, distraught with jealousy. But in a way all that deception had helped him to get over her. There was nothing like a little anger to harden one's resolve.

As time wore on, and from the little he could glean from Jessica, his reaction to what had happened between him and Kate changed. It shook him that he actually wished Kate and Tony well. He hoped that one day she would have the children she so badly craved. He was even thankful that it had been Tony who had taken Kate to the hospital that day when she'd lost the baby. He was glad that it hadn't been, as Kate had told him, a stranger who had helped her, but someone who really cared about her.

He saw now that he had fallen for Kate because he'd been unbelievably flattered by her being interested in him. What man wouldn't be? She had stroked and pampered his battered ego – Melissa's departure had left him more devastated than he'd realised at the time – and Kate had made him feel as though he wasn't such a disaster area after all. When it came down to it, it wasn't love that he'd felt for Kate, but gratitude. And feeling grateful to another person leaves you vulnerable – it makes you feel beholden to that person, that you could never be worthy of their love.

He now looked at the person sitting opposite him. Gratitude was something he'd never felt for Melissa – he'd felt a lot of other things for her, but a sense of obligation had never been one of them. Perhaps this was because they'd always viewed one another as equals. Since they'd formed Thistle Cards there had never been a time when they hadn't worked well together – even during their divorce the company had been rock steady under their equal partnership. When it came to business they were of one mind, with an uncanny knack for second-guessing what the other was thinking.

But they weren't conducting business tonight, which meant he had no idea what his ex-wife was thinking. Melissa was one of the most private people he knew and when it came to anything of a personal nature she played things close to the chest. Last week he had spoken to Ruth on the phone and when his daughter had taken a break from complaining about Kate – 'I feel very let down, Dad, decent child-minders are hard to come by' – she had told him that Tim was now history. 'Don't say I said anything,' she went on, 'but Mum sent him packing. She said she couldn't stand him any longer. Something about him having too high an opinion of himself and too low an opinion of others.'

It was certainly news to Alec. Melissa hadn't said a word about any of this at work. But then he wouldn't have expected her to confide in him.

And as they read their menus Alec decided to give Melissa an opportunity to put him in the picture. 'So how's things with you and Tim?' he said as directly as he dared, but at the same time hiding behind his menu.

'Tim who?'

Alec raised his eyes and smiled. 'Like that, is it?'

She didn't return his smile, but kept her gaze on her menu. 'I think I'll have the Dover sole.'

'No starter?'

'No. But you go ahead, I'll pick something from your plate.'

Alec was tempted to say 'like in the old days', but a comment like that deserved to be treated to the derision she would most certainly fling back at him – he and Melissa might spend their days constantly immersed in greetings card sentiment, but there were limits to what either of them would put up with after office hours.

They ordered their food and Alec poured their wine.

'Will you stay in Cholmford?' she asked him.

'I haven't decided yet.' Which was true. At first he'd thought he'd have to move, that he wouldn't be able to cope with seeing Kate's car parked outside Tony's, but when he'd seen the 'for sale' board go up at number two he'd decided to sit tight for a while. There was no point in running away when very soon there wouldn't be anything to run away from. And despite everything that had happened, he liked his house; it was home to him now.

Melissa raised her glass to him. 'Happy fiftieth, by the way,' she said. Then she reached down to her handbag on the floor and pulled out a small parcel for him.

'For me?'

'Who else?'

'You shouldn't have.'

'Save the self-effacing touch and get on and open it.'

He unwrapped the parcel. It was an uninspiring cheaply made notebook, the sort with which the Chinese continually flooded the market. 'Um … thank you,' he said.

She laughed. 'I know exactly what you're thinking, Alec.'

'You do?'

'You're wondering how to thank me for such a cheap and nasty present, aren't you?'

'Of course not.' Then he smiled. 'Okay, then, you're right. Have you bought me an expensive pen to go with it?'

She shook her head. 'That's the present, take it or leave it.'

'Oh, I shall definitely take it,' he said, 'gift horses and all that.'

'It's up to you what you use it for, but it's meant to be symbolic.'

'Of what?'

She reached for her glass of wine. 'Do you remember when I left you, I said I was tired of reading the same book?'

'Yes,' he said, 'I remember very well. I was extremely hurt by what you said.'

'I'm sorry I hurt you, Alec, but I said it because it was true ... at the time.'

Alec had an uncomfortable feeling that he knew what Melissa was going to say next and he wasn't sure what to make of it. 'And now?'

'Well, let's just say that since then, and after what we've been through, both of us must be quite different.'

'You mean improved, like a good wine?'

'Let's not overdo the metaphors.' She smiled. 'What I'm saying is that you're a different book now and one I'd be interested in taking off the shelf. I'm prepared to take the risk ... are you?'

He leant back in his chair and contemplated her. 'I think you've got a bloody nerve, Melissa,' he said slowly.

'But that's what you always liked about me,' she countered. 'You used to say that you admired my strength of character.'

'And what makes you think, after what you did to me, that I'd even consider taking a risk on you again?'

'It was *you* who invited me to dinner tonight.'

'For something called old times' sake.'

'Well, it could be a start.'

'Are you serious, Melissa?'

'We could see if it works.'

Alec shook his head. 'I don't know. We're not the people we used to be, it would be —'

'That's the whole point. It would be different.'

'I still don't know. What about sex?'

'What, right now?'

'*Melissa!*'

She smiled. 'That, too, would be different. I assume you've learnt a new trick or two from Kate. I know I have from Tim. Alec, I don't believe it, you're blushing.'

'Look,' he said, reaching for her hand across the table, 'I'm just an old-fashioned bloke who's beginning to feel his age. I'm not sure I'm up to all this.'

'Nonsense. You'll pick it up as we go along.'

He smiled at her, then laughed. 'You're quite amazing, you know that?'

'It's often been said. And while we're on the subject, you're not so bad yourself. Now, where's my sole? I'm hungry.'

He laughed again. 'There must be some wise-cracking response to that question, but I'm too stunned to come up with anything.'

'Good. Now pour me another glass of wine and let's drink to the future.'

'No, I've a better toast. Here's to better the devil you know.'

'You silly old fool, you.'

'You can come out now,' Josh said as Jessica's face disappeared from the television screen and the presenter of the programme moved on to discuss the relative merits of a home confinement.

Jessica lowered the cushions and emerged. 'I swear that wasn't me,' she said. 'I didn't say half of those things, they've dubbed stuff on afterwards. Nobody could sound that ridiculous.'

'You did say those things,' Anna said. 'I was there; I saw and heard all of it. I was rather good, wasn't I? That bit with the bonfire came across well, I thought.'

'You were both wonderful,' Kate said generously.

'Yes,' agreed Tony, 'quite the double act.'

Jessica groaned. 'My claim to fame, the unfunny half of a double act; the stooge.'

Josh squeezed her hand. 'You were fine, honestly.'

'But what about that bit on the swing?'

He grinned. 'It was the best bit. I'm going to watch it again later.'

She pulled a face. 'For that, you can go and get us all something to eat. And as a real punishment I'll come and help you.'

'Anything I can do?' offered Kate.

'No,' said Jessica, 'I want to bully Josh alone.'

He got to his feet and Jessica slowly followed behind him. When they reached the kitchen they could hear the others replaying the video and laughing out loud.

'Mum was pretty good, wasn't she?' Jessica said as she watched Josh open the oven and pull out a large dish of Cajun-style chicken wings. He placed the hot dish on the hob and gave the pieces of chicken a prod with a sharp knife.

'Perfect,' he said.

'Oh, come on, she wasn't that good.'

'I was talking about the chicken, but you're right, Anna played her part beautifully. So did you.'

'Really? Do you mean that?'

He glanced over at her and frowned. 'I've never seen you in unsure mode before. You okay?'

'Mm . . . I don't know, I think I need a hug.'

He put the chicken back in the oven, took off the oven gloves and held out his arms. She went to him like a small child needing to be comforted. He held her tightly. 'That better?' he asked.

'Nearly.'

He stroked her hair, suddenly worried. With shame he realised that lately life had been so good for him he'd hardly bothered to wonder if the same was true for Jessica. She always appeared so strong, so confident and positive, and had been such a support to him over the weeks that he had come to rely on her vitality to help him through any of his low periods. But had it been too much for her? Was he sapping her of her energy? And was she beginning to regret moving in with him?

A week after he'd stopped her getting on that plane for Corfu he had suggested that they live together and it had been her idea that she move in with him, rather than the other way around. 'Your house is bigger than mine and has the best views,' she'd said in her typically frank manner, 'let's see how it goes, shall we?' He'd thought that the arrangement was working perfectly. Jessica would work in her study in her own house during the day and when she had finished writing, not long after he arrived home, she would come across the courtyard to him. It had seemed an ideal set-up.

But maybe it wasn't. Perhaps she had seen too much of the real him. It was possible that she had found his problems too much to cope with, and he could hardly blame her for that, sometimes they seemed too much for him.

No, that wasn't strictly true these days. Having Jessica in his life and feeling secure in their love for one another had gone a long way to altering his perspective. Though not completely, there were still times when he panicked when he thought of the future, which was reasonable enough – Jessica's love could never be turned into a miracle cure, but it was certainly palliative. She had boosted his self-esteem, which in turn had put him on better terms with his brother and parents, and everyone at work including Mo. They were less cautious of him now. He suspected that this was because they had always taken their cue from him and now that he was more at ease, they were too.

He'd taken his mother out to lunch one day to try and apologise to her, to bridge the gap he had so ruthlessly forced between them. It had been difficult at first to find the right words to express himself because he had become so used to concealing the truth from her. In the end he had resorted to saying that he was sorry and to ask if she would forgive him. 'Nothing to forgive,' she'd said, but the tears in her eyes had told him that this wasn't the case. It also told him just how much he had hurt her.

Undeniably, his mental capacity to cope with his MS was stronger than it had been, which was just as well because it was showing no sign of easing up – but to be positive, it wasn't showing any sign of worsening. The stiffness in his leg was as bad as ever and sometimes it really got to him, but with the help of a physiotherapist whom he'd started seeing recently – and not forgetting the wretched stick Charlie had given him – he was now able to move about more freely. With regard to the wretched stick, his brother hadn't ever said the words 'I told you so', but Josh knew they were there for the prompting, which amused him.

It also amused him when Jessica tried to play the role of Florence Nightingale on speed. He'd found the perfect way to stop her. Instead of over-reacting and blowing up at her, he simply took her in his arms and kissed her till she couldn't breathe. 'A shame I can't do that to her myself,' Anna had said when he'd told her how he had got round Jessica's bossiness.

But it was Jessica's forthright manner that had helped him to take an important step, one that he now saw as being crucial for them both. That day at the airport when Charlie had presented him with the walking stick his brother had also given him the address of the MS Society, as well as the name and phone number of a man who belonged to a self-help group for MS sufferers in the area. His first reaction was that he would have none of it – what would he have in common with a bunch of people who wanted to sit around discussing how ill they were? But he hadn't bargained on Jessica taking things into her own hands. Without him knowing it she phoned the number Charlie had given him and asked the man if he would agree to meet them for a drink.

He came to the house late one evening. His name was Chris Perry and it was only when Jessica had made the necessary introductions that Josh realised what she'd done behind his back. But it was impossible for him to be cross, for two reasons. First, he found he loved Jessica too much to be furious with her and second, the man who had gone to such trouble to meet him was wearing an item of clothing that invariably caused most people to be on their best behaviour, including Josh.

'Sorry, I'm late,' he'd said, settling himself in a chair and taking the glass of wine Jessica was offering him. He knocked back the drink and began removing his dog-collar. 'Do you mind?' he asked, tossing it on the table, 'I hate wearing the damn thing, but I've just been dealing with a woman who thought her house was haunted. She needed the reassurance of a bit of Popery, 'course there wasn't a ghost in sight, just a case of noisy neighbours. Anyway, less of me, more of you, Josh. How's it hanging?'

The Reverend Chris Perry was in his early forties, an Anglican minister, married, with a young son, and before MS – in a relatively mild form – had entered his life, he'd been a compulsive potholer. 'Of course, these days the only hole I get near is the one I've dug myself into from the pulpit,' he told them. 'There's nothing like a controversial vicar to stir up the mob.'

On the face of it he and Chris had nothing in common, but the more the conversation progressed, the more similarities Josh could see between them. Despite the bravado Chris showed, Josh sensed that he was just as concerned for his own future as Josh was. 'I don't mind the possibility of one day being in a wheelchair,' he had said, while driving Josh to meet the rest of the group for the first time two weeks ago, 'it's the crap that goes with it I can't hack. If you can't walk, people assume that you're brain-dead.'

It was a view that was shared by everyone to whom Josh was introduced at the group that evening. If he'd thought the only common thread that would hold these people together would be their depressing list of aches and pains he was proved wrong – it was actually their spirited sense of humour that kept them afloat, offering each other support and understanding. Josh had come away impressed.

And a little humbled. He had a lot to learn.

Which was what Chris said to him in the car on the way home

afterwards. 'It's not just about learning to confront the illness,' he'd said, 'it's learning to laugh at yourself. An illness like MS tends to bring out the worst in us, the challenge is to overcome that and dig out the best in ourselves. No matter how deep you have to go, Josh, just keep on digging.'

On reflection, it was quite a challenge and Josh wasn't entirely sure that he was up for it. But on the other hand, he was aware that in the past few days he'd actually caught himself thinking how happy he was. A milestone in itself.

But suddenly he wasn't so sure.

If Jessica wasn't happy, where did that leave him? Was it possible that she was still hankering for her old way of life in Corfu? Was that where she believed she really belonged? With Gavin . . . a man who didn't have half the problems he had? 'There's nothing wrong, is there?' he finally dared to ask Jessica.

She raised her head from his shoulder. 'No, not really. What made you say that?'

'I was just wondering if you thought that moving in with me wasn't such a good idea.'

'What an extraordinary thing to say. I love being here with you. I wouldn't have it any other way.'

'So why the long face?'

She sighed. 'It's called seeing yourself as others see you. I'm in shock. I looked and sounded dreadful on that programme.'

Relief flooded through him. Nothing had changed between them. Everything was all right. He kissed her. 'Now you know what I have to put up with every morning when I see you lying next to me.'

'You're all charm, now get back to your oven gloves.'

'No,' he said, still holding her in his arms and deciding that now was as good a time as any to let Jessica know what she meant to him, 'there's something I'd like you to ask me.'

'Mm . . .' she said, 'something you want *me* to ask *you*? Sounds a bit tricksy. Any clues?'

He nodded. 'You already know the answer to the question because I gave it to you that awful night at Tony and Amanda's. Do you remember?'

She stared at him, unsure. Then it slowly dawned on her – the flickering candle-light, the way he'd gazed at her and the heart-stopping moment when he'd said *I'd say yes*. She swallowed. 'You mean –?'

'I know I'm not much of a catch, a man who hobbles about with a stick and –'

'Don't go selling yourself short, Crawford,' she said with a smile. 'I know the score.'

He smiled too. 'So, is there any chance that you might ever want to ask me that particular question?'

'Do rabbits like hot-cross buns?'

He raised a puzzled eyebrow. 'Don't you mean carrots?'

'Hey, who's asking the questions? Now tell me, has this got to be a down-on-the-one-knee job?'

He laughed. 'I would think so. Properly or not at all.'

'Like this?'

'Yes, that looks about right.'

'Well, here goes then.' She looked up at him and cleared her throat. 'Joshua, will you –' But she got no further. The phone rang out, loud and shrill.

'I hope that's got nothing to do with fate,' Josh said, disappointed as Jessica got to her feet. 'I'll get it while you serve up the supper for the others,' he added.

He answered the phone, then covered the mouthpiece with his hand. 'It's Piers,' he said, 'do you want to take it in the study while I finish off here?'

Wishing she'd never been so stupid as to give Josh's number to her agent, Jessica picked up the extension in Josh's study. 'Hello, Piers,' she said grumpily, 'this had better be good because your timing is absolutely bloody awful.'

'And good-evening to you, too, Jessica.'

'Don't be sarcastic with me, you've just ruined the greatest moment of my life.'

'Well, if I can tear you away for a little longer, I was ringing to say that you weren't bad on the television this afternoon. Not bad at all. In fact, almost good. A shame you had to go and spoil it by showing your knickers on the swing.'

'How kind of you to share that with me, Piers.' *Argh!* Would he never change? Would he never pay her a clear-cut compliment?

'I'll be in touch.'

'No hurry. Good-night.'

She went back to the kitchen and found everybody helping themselves to something to eat. Another bottle of bubbly had been opened and they all seemed very merry. She wondered if they would miss her and Josh for a while. He came over to her. 'Everything okay?' he asked quietly.

'How's your leg?' she whispered.

'Pardon?'

'Could you manage a short walk?'

'Where to?'

'Just to the woods.'

'Any reason why?'

'I want to get you alone and finish what we started a few minutes ago.'

They sat on what they now referred to as 'their' fallen oak tree. It was a cold and blustery night, and thick black clouds scudded over a full moon; branches swayed, leaves rustled.

'It's like something out of a Hammer House of Horror film, isn't it?' said Jessica with a shiver as she stared up at the restless sky. 'All we need is a howling wolf to complete the scene.'

'And some swirling mist.'

'Vincent Price in a black cloak with blood-red silk lining would be a nice touch.'

'So would Peter Cushing.'

'We shouldn't leave out Christopher Lee.'

'You're right. We'd have to have all three.'

'But what about Boris Karloff?'

'Him, too, if you want.' Josh put his arm around Jessica's shoulder and drew her inside his thick overcoat. He wondered if she was beginning to change her mind. 'You're not getting cold feet, are you?'

She turned her head and smiled up at him. 'You wouldn't be trying to talk me out of proposing to you, would you?'

He suddenly looked serious. 'I wouldn't blame you. We can't pretend my problems won't affect –'

She silenced him by placing a finger on his lips.

'And what about Gavin?' he mumbled against her finger.

She removed her hand. 'I don't believe you. Now you really are getting desperate.'

'He was very upset when you didn't turn up in Corfu. How many times did he ring you?'

'Too many, that's how many. Now please, can we put all the prevaricating aside and get on with what we're here to do? And to put us in the right frame of mind, we'll kick off with a kiss.'

'You sound like you've done this before.'

She laughed and kissed him. And when they stopped, she stared up into his face. 'I'm sorry,' she said in a low voice, 'it's no good, I really can't go through with it. I've changed my mind.'

He looked at her with a horrified gaze. 'But –'

'Don't panic.' She smiled. 'It turns out I'm a traditionalist at heart. In my book the romantic hero has to do the proposing.'

He let out his breath in one long sigh of relief. 'In that case, there's nothing else for it. Miss Jessica Lloyd –'

'*Yes!*'

'I haven't finished. Would you –'

'*Yes!*'

'Do me –'

'*Yes!*'

'The honour –'

'*Yes!*'

'Of marrying me?'

'Yes, yes, yes, yes, yes!'

'Thank goodness for that.'

'Now what do we do?'

'We go home. I'm frozen to death sitting here.'

'You're such a romantic, Crawford.'

'But cute with it, wouldn't you say?'

She helped him to his feet and passed him his stick. 'And as we walk, we'll plan the wedding. St Paul's would be a good choice. We ought to think big.'

'Yes. But if it's booked, we'll make do with Westminster Abbey.'

'And Charlie can be best man.'

'Naturally. And Helen could be your matron of honour.'

'How about Chris to officiate?'

'Good idea. And to hell with convention, Anna can give you away.'

'Brilliant. She'll love doing that.'

'I can hardly wait.'

'Me neither.'

'Jessica?'

'Yes?'

'Where will we live?'

'Your house, of course. Why move again? I've a feeling it's exactly where we both belong.'

THE END

Or to put it another way

THE BEGINNING

Act of Faith

As ever, to Edward and Samuel

Acknowledgements

So many people helped create this book, but to save their blushes (and their reputations) I shan't name them all: they know what part they played and I hope they know how grateful I am.

Thanks must go to everybody at Orion for giving me another year to remember. Jane Wood, Selina Walker and Sarah Yorke need to be singled out for their extraordinary juggling skills and always having time for The Author From Hell. As does Susan Lamb for her patience and determination to get the artwork just right . . . well, almost. Thanks also to everyone at the January sales conference for not eating me alive.

Last, but by no means least, thank you Mr Lloyd at Curtis Brown for the windmill, the go-karting and the freezing North Sea wind in my face. Never again!

The greatest pleasure of life is love,
The greatest treasure, contentment,
The greatest possession health,
The greatest ease is sleep,
The greatest medicine is a true friend.

Sir William Temple

1

Today of all days, Ali Anderson wasn't in the mood for empty-headed foolishness.

'Oh, get a life you silly little man,' she muttered, switching off the car radio and bringing an end to the ramblings of the out-of-his-tree caller from Redditch – a crank who had been advocating a world economy based on a system of homespun bartering. Honestly, was there anything worse than a born-again down-shifter?

She would have liked to vent her feelings further, but the opportunity to do so eluded her as, just in time, she saw the road to Great Budworth. She slowed her speed, made a sharp turn to the right, and took the narrow lane that led to the centre of the small, neat village that, up until a year ago, had been her home. Its picture-book selection of much-photographed quaint houses had long since lost their charm for Ali, and as she passed each familiar pretty cottage, her heartbeat quickened and her throat tightened. She reluctantly thanked Mr Out-Of-His-Tree from Redditch for his momentary distraction and wished for a further miraculous diversion of thought.

But nothing could divert her now. She was on her own, about to come face to face with the tragedy that was made so cruelly poignant at this time of the year. As she switched off the engine, she asked herself the question for which she knew there was no easy reassuring answer: would she ever be able to make this journey without feeling the excruciating pain?

She left her car under the watchful gaze of a well-nourished ginger cat loitering in the post-office window, the panes of which were festively decorated with tinsel and sprayed-on snow, and with her footsteps echoing in the deserted street, she walked, head bowed, into the wind towards the sixteenth-century sandstone church that dominated the top end of the village with its elevated position and massive crenellated tower. It was late afternoon, cold and raw, a wintry day that was cloaked in melancholy. The unforgiving December wind stung her cheeks and snatched at the Cellophane-wrapped roses in her arms. She cradled them protectively against her chest, and breathed in their fragrant scent; a scent that was powerfully redolent of this dreadful place.

There was nobody else in the churchyard. She was glad. It was better to be alone. Last time there had been an elderly man blowing his nose but pretending self-consciously that he wasn't. She followed the path, reading the weathered tombstones that were green with a seasoned patina of lichen as she moved ever nearer to her destination. Scanning the names of Great Budworth's ancient and more recently departed was meant to be a diverting tactic: it was supposed to slow her heart, stop her stomach from coiling itself into a nauseous, tight knot, keep her from reliving the horror of that night two years ago.

But it hadn't worked before and it wasn't working now.

She passed *Robert Ashworth, 1932–1990*, then *Amy Riley, 1929–1992, beloved wife of Joseph Riley*, and knew that there were only three more painful steps to take. She braced herself.

One.

Two.

Three.

And there it was.

Forever precious in our hearts, Isaac Anderson, 1995–1996, dearly loved son of Ali and Elliot Anderson.

She stood perfectly still, staring at the words, afraid to move lest she set off some uncontrollable emotion within her, but wanting more than anything to leave her flowers and run. It was two years to the day since Isaac had died and she hated to remember him this way. This wasn't her son. This wasn't the longed-for baby she had loved from the moment she had held him against her breast in the delivery room. This wasn't the tiny fair-haired Isaac whose smile had melted her heart every morning when she went into his bedroom and picked him out of his cot. This wasn't the little boy who had tottered towards her when she came home from work, and had sat on her lap while she had read him a selection of his favourite stories before they went upstairs to have a bath together, and played at being water buffalo. This wasn't the happy eighteen-month-old boy whom she'd kissed goodbye that fateful morning and had never seen alive again.

An icy gust of wind curled itself round her neck and prompted her to move. She stooped to the small grave, unwrapped the flowers and carefully arranged them. She stuffed the Cellophane into her coat pocket, removed her leather gloves and set about picking at the weeds that were invading the rectangle of space that in theory belonged to Isaac, but in reality belonged to no one. As she worked at the weeds she thought, as she so often did, how the landscape of her life had been changed by her son's death, in particular the disastrous effect it had had on her marriage.

Where there had once been absolute unity between her and Elliot, there was now a terrible division, their lives fragmented into so many badly broken pieces that there was no hope of them being mended. They had become distant and uncommunicative. From loving one another with a passion that had seemed enduring and immutable they had quickly reached a stage where all that connected them was a wall of silent, bitter reproach. It became an insurmountable barrier that neither of them wanted to knock down. They had lived like that for a year, hiding from each other until the inevitable happened and they parted. Divorce had been her suggestion. Elliot had been against taking such a final and drastic step, but she had insisted on going through with it. She had had to. Being with Elliot seemed only to remind her of what she'd lost, and she grew to hate him for it.

Divorce seemed the only way to detach herself from all the pain. But the pain hadn't lessened. Neither had the bitterness between them.

Rigid with cold, her fingers were hurting. She stopped what she was doing and stood up, and with the backs of her hands wiped the tears from her eyes. At the sound of footsteps on the path behind her she whipped round to see who it was.

It was Elliot. He was carrying a bunch of flowers and was on a level with *Robert Ashworth*. Seeing her, he paused, but then continued on and passed *Amy Riley* in one long stride. 'You okay?' was all he said.

She lowered her hands from her face and muttered, 'It's just the wind in my eyes. It's the cold.' As though to prove the point, she pulled on her gloves, hunched her shoulders and stamped her feet on the iron-hard ground.

He glanced up at the dreary leaden sky that was rapidly darkening as the afternoon drew to a cold and bitter dusk. 'It'll probably snow,' he remarked, as though they were merely strangers discussing the weather.

'You could be right,' she responded stiffly, brushing at her eyes again and hating him for being so damnably in control. She was furious that he was here, yet more furious that he had caught her crying and that he was being considerate enough to look away while she composed herself. She didn't want his consideration, not when it reminded her of the past when he'd been so good at it: as a boss; as a lover; as a husband; and as a father. In the beginning it had been one of his attractions, at the end a torment.

She watched him bend down to place his flowers next to hers, glad at least that he was sticking to their agreement – white roses only. 'Never red,' she'd told him when they were preparing for Isaac's funeral. 'Red is too violent, too bloody, too sacrificial.'

'I'll leave you to it,' she said. She turned to go.

He straightened up quickly. 'No.' He placed a hand on her arm. 'Please don't leave because of me. I'll wait in the car while you . . .'

She looked at his hand on her coat sleeve, then at the heavy awkwardness in his face and at the darkness that was eclipsing the natural lightness of his watchful blue eyes. 'While I what?'

'While you do what you need to do.'

She shook her head and withdrew her arm. 'The moment's gone.'

'I'm sorry, I should have timed it better.'

'I shouldn't let it worry you.' She walked away.

He returned his gaze to the flowers he'd just laid on Isaac's grave. Then, as if urged by some hidden voice, he called after her, 'Ali, will you wait for me?'

She stopped moving but she didn't look back at him. 'Why?'

'I'd like to talk to you.'

She began walking again.

'Ali?'

'I'll be in my car.'

2

With Elliot's Jaguar XK8 headlamps following behind her, Ali drove home in the dark wondering what it was he wanted to discuss.

While sitting in her car outside the post office – the ginger cat nowhere to be seen – she had had plenty of time to ponder on Elliot's request to talk to her: twenty minutes in all. When he finally emerged from the churchyard he had asked if she would have a drink with him. Looking at his pale face in the soft light cast from the glowing street-lamp behind him, she had thought that few men had ever looked more in need of a reviving snifter. But glancing at her watch and picturing the pair of them sitting miserable-faced in the empty public bar of the George and Dragon – the scene of many a happy drinking session when it had been their local – she had suggested he came back to her place.

Now she was regretting this rash act of bonhomie and not just because she couldn't recall the state of the bathroom, or the kitchen, or indeed the sitting room – had she cleared away the remains of last night's Chinese takeaway before crashing out on the sofa some time after two and sleeping the sleep of the chronically exhausted? – but because since she and Elliot had separated they had deliberately avoided the come-back-to-my-place scenario.

And with good reason.

Neither of them was equipped to treat one another with anything more cordial than coolness edged with disparagement and crabby fault-finding. It was, she knew, their only way of coping with an impossible situation.

After she had moved out of their home in Great Budworth and had set in motion the wheels of their divorce, they had tried their best to behave in as civil a manner as they could manage. Not easy, given that they were both brimming with unresolved hurt and anger. However, by restricting their infrequent get-togethers to restaurants where it would have been unseemly to hurl abuse – or crockery – they pulled it off. For a more convincing performance, it was better if a third party was involved. Usually this was Elliot's father, Sam, who rarely objected to being caught in the occasional round of crossfire. 'White-flag time,' he would say, when she and Elliot paused for breath before reloading with fresh ammunition. 'Hold your fire.' Only once did they go too far, causing Sam to throw down his napkin and declare that he preferred his drama on the telly and would they kindly stop acting like a couple of spoilt brats. 'Now, behave yourselves, the pair of you, or I shall go home to a nice, quiet, digestibly sound plate of sausage, egg and chips.'

Indicating well in advance of the turning for Little Linton – which could be missed in the blink of an eye, and which concealed itself by merging into the environs of the sprawling neighbouring village of Holmes Chapel – Ali checked her rear-view mirror to make sure that Elliot was still following. He was and, like her, he was now indicating left.

'The boy's no fool,' she said aloud. She smiled, realising that she was relaxing ... was beginning to be herself.

When Isaac had died she had promised herself that she would visit his grave only on the anniversary of his death. She didn't want to turn into one of those people who felt they were keeping a loved one alive by putting in a regular show of graveside attendance. No amount of tombstone weeping was ever going to bring him back, so what was the point? Since the funeral this was the second appearance she had put in at the churchyard, and it had been no easier than the first. It had the effect of turning her into somebody, or something, that wasn't the real her. It brought out the worst in her. It made her angry, self-pitying, bitter, reproachful, but mostly desperate.

Desperate to forget.

Desperate to remember.

Just desperate.

Over breakfast that morning she had considered not visiting Isaac's grave, but how could she not go? What would Elliot and everyone else think of her? That not only in life had she failed her tiny, vulnerable son but in death too?

She indicated again, this time to the right. She checked that Elliot was still on the ball and, slowing, she turned into a narrow gap in the high hedge that lined the road. This was Mill Lane and ahead of her, about a hundred yards or so, was her new home. It was clearly visible in the night sky because it was so cleverly illuminated by a special security lighting system. Windmills weren't common in this part of the country and its seventy-foot-high, brick-built tower made an impressive sight. It no longer had any sails and its tall, looming shape, and white-painted dome-capped top, reminded Ali of a very large pepper-pot. It never failed to amuse her that she was now living in such a curio.

The nasty, unforgiving part of her, that petty bit that held tenaciously on to past grievances and kept her awake at night, hoped that Elliot was impressed. He didn't need to know that this beautifully converted windmill, set in splendid isolation, didn't belong to her, that she had only been renting it for the past month from Owen, one of her expat clients now holed up in some God-awful place on the outskirts of Brussels.

She parked her Saab convertible in front of the small garage and, without waiting for Elliot, hurried to let herself in. If she could just make it up the first flight of stairs before his marathon-running legs sprinted after her, she'd be able to remove, or disguise, the worst of the potential squalor.

But she needn't have worried. As soon as she'd shouldered open the heavy studded door – it could be a devil at times, especially in damp weather – she saw that Lizzie, her priceless treasure inherited from Owen, had paid a call. Relieved, she knew that there wouldn't be so much as an atom of dust in the house, never mind a pair of knickers loitering with intent on the bathroom floor. The evidence that this was the case was on the oak table by the door where Lizzie had left a note. It read:

Out of Hoover bags and Sanilav. Chocolate cake in the tin by the kettle, a minute per slice in the microwave should do it, a pot of whipped cream in the fridge. Love Lizzie. P.S. Have strung up your Christmas cards like Owen used to . . . hope you approve.

'What an improbable place,' said Elliot, appearing in the doorway. 'How long have you lived here?'

'A few weeks,' she said. She slipped off her coat and hung it on the Edwardian coat-rack, which she could only just reach. It had been screwed to the wall by Owen who, like Elliot, was well over six foot. 'And most people wouldn't say improbable, they'd say amazing, interesting, wonderful. Spectacular, even. Close the door, you're letting the heat out.'

Elliot did as she said. He removed his coat and hung it on the hook next to where she'd placed hers. 'What was it used for originally?'

She caught the thin veneer of politeness that only just skimmed his words. 'Corn,' she answered, 'and please don't expect me to explain anything more detailed than that. I wouldn't know a grain bin from a hopper.' She opened a door and took him through to what was the largest room of the mill and where, once in a blue moon, she entertained. But it wasn't a room she cared for. It felt cold and formal. She put this down to the reclaimed slate floor of which Owen was so proud. Lizzie frequently described it as nothing but a bugger to clean.

Ignoring Elliot's look of interest in the thick beams that spanned the low ceiling, she led the way to the next floor via a wooden spiral staircase that creaked noisily. The first floor was Ali's favourite part of the mill and, in her opinion, the best bit of the conversion. It had been designed to provide a comfortable and homely open-plan area for cooking, eating and relaxing, and it was here, when she wasn't at work or in bed, that she spent the majority of her time. The kitchen area had been built by a friend of Owen's who was a joiner and the hand-made pitch pine units and cupboards and ornately carved shelves nestled against the dark-red-painted walls perfectly, so much so that the oddity of the curve was almost lost.

She watched Elliot duck one of the beams as he moved past her to the small-paned window above the sink. She left him to peer out into the darkness and went through to the raised sitting area where she switched on two large table lamps. Soft light bounced off the polished floor and enhanced the rubescent tones in the Oriental rug in front of the fire as well as the Venetian red of the walls. She bent down to the fire, glad once more that Lizzie had chosen today to come in. Four days' worth of accumulated ashes had been cleared away and the grate now contained a fresh supply of logs and kindling, along with a couple of fire-lighters; even the empty log basket had been replenished from the woodpile beside the garage. When she stood up to replace the matches on the mantelpiece she noticed the Christmas cards that stretched from one brass picture light to another. If it weren't for their presence, nobody would have guessed from the look of the room that Christmas was only just round the corner.

'I'll get us a drink,' she said, when Elliot came through from the kitchen. 'Mind that step,' she added. 'It catches everybody. Glenlivet do you?'

He nodded and minded the step.

Chatty so-and-so, she thought, with her back to him as she rummaged in the booze cupboard next to the fridge. Pouring their drinks, she saw the tin by the kettle and remembered Lizzie's note. She prised off the lid and licked her lips. Lunch suddenly seemed an age away. She cut two large slices of chocolate cake, bunged them in the microwave, added a dollop of cream, loaded the plates and glasses on to a tray and took it through to the sitting area, where she found Elliot looking dangerously at home in one of the high-backed armchairs nearest the fire. It was an unnerving scene, too reminiscent of their married days.

Except, she told herself firmly, while lowering the tray on to the table in front of the sofa, if they were still married, he'd have his Gieves & Hawkes suit jacket off, his silk tie slung over the back of the chair and his shoes left just where she'd trip over them.

She pushed a plate towards him, handed him his single malt and wondered whether his silence meant that mentally he was being as rude about her as she was about him. Well, if he was, it was progress of sorts. At least they weren't verbally bashing the living daylights out of each other.

'Cheers,' she said, raising her glass and choosing to sit in the corner of the sofa that was furthest from Elliot. He acknowledged her gesture and took a swallow of his whisky. He seemed quite happy to sit in the formidable silence, but Ali wasn't. 'So what did you want to talk about?' she asked, eager to be rid of him.

He looked uncomfortable, no longer at home, which, Ali noted, had the instant effect of ageing him. But Elliot wasn't old. Far from it. He was only forty-six and could pass for younger with his well-exercised body and light brown hair only faintly shot through with grey. But was that simply because she knew him so well? Wasn't it true that the people one knew best stayed the same age as one viewed oneself? When she looked in the mirror each morning, she didn't see a thirty-eight-year-old woman, she saw a girl of twenty-four. Funny that. Most people when asked how old they felt invariably responded with an age in their mid-twenties.

She watched him take another swallow of his Glenlivet before placing the glass with extreme care on the gold-edged coaster on the table. But still he didn't answer her. He reached for his plate of chocolate cake and began eating it. She knew that these were warning signs that, whatever it was he had to say, he was choosing his words with the utmost caution. It was the way he operated; he never blundered straight in. At work it had always been one of his greatest and most effectively employed weapons. She might not love him any more, but she sure as hell still respected his professional ability and knew as well as anyone who had ever worked with him that nothing clouded his reasoning or his judgement. He had the kind of mind that could play two simultaneous games of chess and win both.

But this wasn't a work situation and she could see that despite his best endeavours to look composed he was edgy. So what was it that he had come here to talk about?

Then it struck her.

He'd met somebody, hadn't he? That's why he was here. Under the guise of wanting to be the one to break the news to her, he was really here to brag that he was getting married again. He probably wanted to rub her face in it. 'See,' he was saying beneath all that outward calm, 'I've moved on. I'm over Isaac. And I'm certainly over you.' The bloody cheek of him, sitting here drinking her expensive whisky and all the time he was trawling his mind to find the right words to boast that he'd been bonking some compliant underling at the office! Bloody, *bloody* cheek of him!

He looked up from his plate and fixed her with his serious blue eyes. 'This is very good. Did you make it yourself?'

'The hell I did. You know perfectly well that baking was never my forte. Now get on and tell me what it is you want to discuss.'

He narrowed his eyes, and she could see that he was figuring out if she'd rumbled him. He looked vaguely perturbed. 'What are you doing for Christmas?' he asked, lowering his gaze and concentrating on scraping up the last of his cake.

'Christmas?' she repeated, wrong-footed.

'Yes, that ritual we go through in the fourth week of December.'

The sarcasm in his voice was in danger of bringing out the crockery-throwing instinct in her. 'Thank you, Elliot, I'm well aware of when Christmas is. Divorce hasn't addled my brain, unlike somebody I could think of.' *Getting married again, hah!*

His gaze was back on her, and it was fierce. 'What's that supposed to mean?'

'Make of it what you will.'

He frowned. 'So *what* are you doing for Christmas?'

'I'm not sure. And I'm not sure that it's any of your business. Now, will you just get to the point and tell me what you wanted to say?'

He looked exasperated. She guessed that they were only seconds away from dispensing with the politeness forced upon them by the circumstances of the day. 'That's what I'm trying to do,' he said. His cool was definitely waning. There was even a hint of clenched teeth. 'Dad and I are going away for Christmas and . . . and, fools that we are, we wondered if you wanted to join us.'

Ali was jaw-droppingly stunned. She corralled what she could of her scattered wits and said, 'An invitation put so elegantly, I hardly know what to say.' It was true. She didn't. Nothing could have taken the wind out of her sails more succinctly. She got to her feet and went and put another log on the fire, playing for time by prodding it into place with a pair of long-handled brass tongs. An invitation to spend Christmas with her ex-husband was the last thing she'd expected to come out of the day.

She was almost touched.

Yet wholly suspicious.

Why had Elliot asked her this when he must have concluded that she would probably repeat last year's Christmas holiday and spend it with her parents down on Hayling Island? He wasn't to know that she had decided not to do that. In fact, the only people who knew that she was planning a home-alone Christmas this year were her parents. Mm . . . she thought, and suspecting that her mother had been at work, she put the tongs down on the hearth and said, 'Have my parents been in touch with you?'

'A brief letter with a Christmas card.'

She tutted. 'And Mum just happened to bring you up to date and mention that I was being a miserable killjoy and staying here on my own, is that it?'

Gone now was his edginess and fully reinstated was his customary detached calm. He crossed one of his long legs over the other. 'Something like that, yes.'

She went back to the sofa. 'And would I be right in thinking that it was Sam's idea for you to invite me to go away with you both?'

He nodded.

'It smacks of charity, Elliot, you realise that, don't you?'

He rolled his eyes heavenwards. 'And you realise that your pig-headedness deserves a damned good smacking.'

'Good, so you'll understand perfectly that it's nothing personal, it's merely my naturally cussed nature forcing me to decline the invitation – as well-meant as Sam intended it to be.'

'So if you won't be spending Christmas with your parents or us, what will you be doing?'

Was she imagining it, or was that the orchestral sound of relief just tuning up behind his words? She could almost feel sorry for him. How shocked he must have been when Sam put that little idea to him. 'I expect I shall eat and drink myself into an exquisite state of catatonic delight,' she answered. 'What will you be doing? A hotel break of candle-lit dinners and log fires interspersed with dancing the conga like last year?'

With what was perilously close to a smile on his face, he said, 'No, I'm weaning Dad off short hotel breaks. I'm taking him to Barbados.'

Ali raised an eyebrow. 'Lucky old Sam.'

'Sure you won't change your mind?'

'You know me better than that, Elliot.'

3

'How'd it go?'

Elliot shut the door behind him and felt that his father had been asking him that same question all his life.

First day at school: How'd it go?

Cross-country race: How'd it go?

Piano exam: How'd it go?

O-levels: How'd it go?

A-levels: How'd it go?

Christ Church College interview: How'd it go?

Job interview: How'd it go?

'Well?' asked Sam.

Elliot hung up his coat in silence. He went into his study and plonked his briefcase on the desk. Sam came and leaned against the doorframe. Always a patient man, he was quite happy to wait for an answer.

Elliot scanned his mail and, without raising his eyes, said, 'Which bit of the day do you want to know about? The bit when I stood by Isaac's grave blaming myself yet again for his death, or the part when I stared across the room at my son's mother and wished I could find a way of undoing all the harm I've done?'

Sam didn't say anything. He kept his gaze firmly on Elliot, regarding him with heartfelt compassion.

Elliot pulled out a Christmas card from one of the envelopes and dropped it unread on to the desk. He looked up at his father and saw the concern in his eyes. He rubbed a hand over his tired face. 'I'm sorry,' he said, 'I shouldn't have said that.'

Sam smiled kindly. 'It's okay. Come and talk to me in the kitchen while I get supper ready. I thought I'd do us one of my famous gut'n'heart-buster specials.'

Elliot followed his father to the kitchen where he could see the beginnings of one of Sam's steak-and-chip dinners taking shape: the potatoes were peeled and chipped, the onion rings were sitting in the frying-pan with half a pack of butter for company, and two enormous steaks the size of a pair of slippers were waiting to be grilled. 'What with this and the chocolate cake at Ali's, you'll be the ruin of me,' he said, forcing a lightness into his voice that he didn't feel. He took hold of one of the chairs at the table, turned it round, and sat on it astride, resting his elbows on the back.

Sam switched on the grill. 'Chocolate cake at Ali's, eh? And she didn't throw it at you?'

'She missed.'

'Now that I don't believe. If Ali meant to hit you, she'd get you all right, moving target or not. You remember that corporate hoopla you arranged a few years back when we all got to have a go on the rifle range? She was a crack shot. Made us both look like rookies.'

Elliot remembered all too well. He recalled also how proud he'd been but, then, he'd always been proud of Ali. She had never been like the other women in the office with whom he worked. And she certainly hadn't been like the rest of the partners' wives. She had been a law unto herself. She'd called a schmuck a schmuck and hadn't given a monkey's for the consequences. Always chronically impatient and restless for a challenge, she had been one of the most sharp-witted people he knew. It had come as no surprise when eventually she had tired of the petty office politics of the big accountancy firm they both worked for and had gone it alone. She had formed her own personal taxation consultancy. It had been exactly the right move for her, though to his regret he had never said so at the time. He'd given her no real support and encouragement. But, then, he'd had none to give. All his emotional energy had been focused on trying to cope with Isaac's death.

'By the way,' he said, getting abruptly to his feet and going over to inspect the wine his father had opened, 'that particular occasion wasn't a *few* years ago, I think you'll find it was more like ten.'

Sam flicked a raw chip at him. 'Don't get smart with me, son.'

They ate their meal in the kitchen, the fittings of which Sam had designed and installed himself. When they'd moved in three months ago, the first thing he'd done was to rip out the previous owners' unworkable layout. Elliot had come home one day after a short trip to the States to find a skip on the drive and the kitchen demolished. 'I'm replacing it with something a touch more user friendly,' Sam had said. And he'd done exactly that. Out with the sterile stainless steel, and in with the natural warmth of maplewood. Out with the breakfast bar with its coiled metal stools, which had had all the comfort of barbed wire and which the previous owners had so generously left them, and in with a large farmhouse table and chairs that Sam had picked up at a local auction and had had stripped and re-waxed.

Tackling his enormous steak, Elliot told his father where Ali was now living.

'A windmill, eh? She's got style, that girl. I didn't know there were any round here. Where did you say it was?'

'Near Holmes Chapel, a tiny village called Little Linton.'

'Never heard of it.'

'Me neither.'

'So what did she say?'

'About the windmill?'

Sam finished chewing what was in his mouth. 'I told you earlier, don't get smart with me. Are we short on wine tonight?'

Elliot refilled their glasses.

'Go on, then, tell me what she said.'

'She said no.'

'You sure?'

'Look, Dad, I know the difference between yes and no.'

Sam gave him a measured stare. 'Oh, aye, I don't doubt it, but how did you phrase the invitation? The way you normally speak to her these days, Charlie Charm? Through clenched teeth?'

Elliot brought the scene to mind. His teeth had been pretty close to clenched, but his hands, for a change, hadn't been balled into tight, angry fists. 'You would have been proud of me, I was the model of diplomacy.'

'Liar! I knew I should have spoken to her. Poor girl, now she really will be all alone for Christmas.'

'Look, I tried. I did. But for all we know she might have something planned that she doesn't want me to know about. Perhaps for once she was acting with a degree of tact and sensitivity.'

'What're you saying?'

Elliot shrugged. 'Surely I don't need to spell it out.'

'Obviously you do. I'm just a working-class bloke after all. Just a thick retired builder from Yorkshire who doesn't—'

Elliot cut in quickly to stem the flow of his father's favourite wind-up. 'I'm not in the mood for the cloth-cap-and-clogs routine,' he snapped. 'What I meant was, maybe Ali's got a new man in her life and is planning on—'

'Oh, I get you. You're saying that, unlike you, she's got more than boring old Rich Tea in the biscuit barrel. That it?'

Elliot rolled his eyes. 'Exactly.'

'So why didn't you ask her if that was the case?'

'*Dad!*'

'It's a reasonable enough question.'

'Not from an ex-husband, it isn't.'

Sam smiled and pushed his finished plate away from him. 'But okay from an ex-father-in-law, I reckon. I'll speak to her tomorrow.' He sat back in his chair and patted his bulging stomach appreciatively. 'Not a bad bit of steak, even if I say so myself.'

Elliot contemplated his father. He wanted to say, 'Leave it, Dad, leave it well alone,' but he knew it would have little effect: Sam always did as he saw fit. It was last night when Sam had cooked up this stupid idea of his. In that morning's post a Christmas card had arrived from Ali's parents. Despite the divorce, Maggie and Lawrence Edwards had remained firmly in touch with him, so the card had been no surprise although its contents were, especially for Sam. 'Maggie says they won't be seeing Ali this year,' he said, as he handed the card to Elliot. 'She says she's staying up here on her own. Why do you suppose she's doing that?'

'How should I know?'

Later that evening, while Elliot was working, Sam had come into his study and said, 'I don't like the thought of Ali being all alone. It's not on. I know what it is to be on your own at this time of the year.'

'But it's hardly any of our business.'

He'd then suggested that Ali could join them in Barbados. 'Well, why not?' he'd said, in response to Elliot's open-mouthed astonishment.

'Because after nine hours of being cooped up together on a plane we'll probably kill one another with our bare hands.'

'There again it might just knock the shit out of you both. Now am I going to ask her, or are you?'

'I will,' he'd said hastily. He knew that if Sam were to invite Ali she would be bound to accept and, coward that he was, he didn't think he could handle that. It was unthinkable that she would turn Sam down. Rarely did anyone refuse him. He was too nice. He was what people used to refer to as the *genuine article*. He was honest, caring and frank: you always knew where you stood with Sam Anderson. He wasn't a big man – he was only five foot five – but he seemed much larger. As Ali once said, 'There's not a lot of your dad, but every inch of him is worth getting to know.' Elliot was well aware that there had always been a special relationship between Ali and his father, and that since the divorce Sam had missed her. But inviting her to spend Christmas with them was going too far, surely?

Looking across the table at his father now, Elliot felt ashamed of himself. He wished he could be more like Sam, put the past behind him and make more of an effort to be nice to Ali. But he couldn't. It hurt too much to see her. On top of all his grief for Isaac, he'd had to cope with her walking away from him when he needed her most. But he could hardly blame her for doing that: because he'd been unable to come to terms with the horrific way in which Isaac had died, he had been of no use to Ali in helping her to deal with her grief; he'd left her to cope on her own. Quite simply she had wanted more from him than he had to give. He had let her down in so many ways and not a day passed when he didn't want to make amends for what had happened. At the time he had done the standard man stuff in the face of a personal tragedy: he'd holed himself up at work and stayed there ridiculously long hours rather than confront the awful emptiness that haunted him at home. To a lesser extent Ali had done the same, and work colleagues had thought it helpful to use their professionalism as a guide to how well they were coping with their child's death. The conclusion was that they were coping extraordinarily well. But they had merely been on the edge of survival, both of them.

Elliot had agreed to their divorce in the belief that by giving in to Ali's request and doing everything she wanted, it would help her, and that maybe they would be able to salvage something worthwhile from their shattered relationship. He had foolishly hoped that, if nothing else, they would be able to be friends. But it hadn't worked. Their separation had added to the friction between them and, like water seeking its level, their confused anger and resentment had dictated their response to each other.

He suspected that, deep within him, there was still a trace of the love he had once felt for Ali, but too many layers of pain and bitterness covered it for it ever to show itself. And all the pain and bitterness inside him made him act as though he couldn't bear the sight of her.

In a way it was true. He found being with Ali almost intolerable. There was so much of Isaac in her face: the same compelling brown eyes; the same fair hair, even the same mouth that, in the days when he saw her smile, was identical to the welcome Isaac would give him when he came home from work and found him in the bath with Ali.

He suddenly blinked hard and cleared his throat of the lump that had formed there. In a determined voice, he said, 'Dad, if you want to speak to Ali, it's up to you, but don't be disappointed if she says no.'

'I know the score, lad, no worries there. So does that mean I have your blessing to talk to her?'

'I've never stopped you from doing that.'

Sam frowned. 'You've not made it easy, though, have you?'

Elliot kept quiet.

'Look, son, I know it's a bugger of a situation, but I still care for her. I need to know that she'll be okay when we're jetting off into the sun. I hate the idea of anyone being on their own for Christmas.'

When Elliot still didn't say anything, Sam got to his feet and said, 'Seeing as I cooked supper, you can clear away. I'm off to read the paper.'

Later that night, long after Sam had gone to bed, Elliot closed his briefcase and switched off the study light. Though it was nearly midnight, he decided to go for a swim.

When he and his father had discovered Timbersbrook House, they had seen at once that it offered them exactly what they both wanted, as well as having the bonus of an indoor swimming-pool. This Elliot now entered by means of a long corridor that led off from the hall in the main part of the house. The previous owners had shown no restraint when it came to creating the opulent and thoroughly showy pool room. They'd gone to town with mosaic tiling, mirrors, pillars, a palm tree – currently decked out by Sam with fairy-lights – and even the thoroughly ostentatious touch of a working fireplace near the shallow end. It was Sam and Elliot's favourite place to read the Sunday papers.

Elliot switched on the wall-lights and stripped off his clothes. He dived into the smooth, glassy surface of the water and swam two lengths before coming up for air. He guessed Sam must have been for a swim earlier that day as the water temperature was a few degrees warmer than last night. He swam, one length after another, slowly, mechanically, each stroke as precise and rhythmic as a metronome; it helped him to think straight, which he needed to do.

It had been a hell of a day. His thoughts had alternated continually between Isaac and Ali. It was difficult sometimes to separate one from the other.

When he'd caught sight of Ali's small, hunched figure bent over Isaac's grave, her face flushed with cold and her eyes wet with tears, he'd wanted so much to comfort her.

And had he?

No.

He'd turned away to give her a few seconds to compose herself and had made some asinine comment about the weather. He had thought he was being considerate, but in all probability she would have interpreted his manner as cool and aloof. For the second time that evening, he wished he could be more like his father. Sam, for all his talk of his working-class background and lack of education, always seemed to do or say the right thing when it came to dealing with anything emotional. Sam would have put his arms around Ali and taken the edge off her pain. He would have held her and let her cry. Unlike Elliot, Sam would have been there for Ali. Just as he'd been there for the pair of them that terrible night at the hospital when Isaac died. Sam had grasped Ali to him while she had screamed and shaken with the shock of what she'd just learned, while he ... while he had stood impotently to one side, already isolating himself from anything that might touch him.

He swam faster, pushing his arms through the water cleanly and noiselessly. He swam on and on, praying that one day there might come a time when he would lose the nightmare memory of that night. That one day the words of the poem Charles Wesley wrote on the death of his own son would cease to impinge on his brain.

> *Dead! Dead! The Child I lov'd so well!*
> *Transported to the world above!*
> *I need no more my heart conceal.*
> *I never dar'd indulge my love;*
> *But may I not indulge my grief,*
> *And seek in tears a sad relief?*
>
> *Mine earthly happiness is fled,*
> *His mother's joy, his father's hope,*
> *(O had I dy'd in Isaac's stead!)*
> *He should have liv'd, my age's prop,*
> *He should have clos'd his father's eyes,*
> *And follow'd me to paradise.*

Buying Timbersbrook House was supposed to have been a start at putting the past behind him. When he had suggested to Sam that they join forces and buy a house together, his father's reaction had taken him by surprise. He had expected hand-throwing-up-in-the-air opposition and indignant declarations of independence, along with the claim that he was only sixty-eight and didn't need anybody cramping his style. But none of this had been said. Sam had agreed readily. 'On one condition,' he'd told Elliot, 'we buy a house that has the potential for me to have my own place within it, and you don't patronise me, I pay my own way. Got that?'

'I make that two conditions,' Elliot had replied.

'Bloody accountants and their obsession with numbers.' Sam had smiled.

Timbersbrook had appealed to them both from the minute they first set eyes on it. Situated a mile from the village of Prestbury, with views across to the Peak District yet within easy driving distance of Manchester where Elliot worked, it was set in an acre and a half of garden with two large outbuildings that had once been stables. One of the outbuildings was the obvious choice to convert into what Sam jokingly referred to as his Lurve

Nest, and the other would suit them perfectly as a workshop, where they would be able to indulge their hobby of restoring left-for-dead classic cars. Within twenty-four hours of viewing the property they had made an offer and subsequently moved in three months ago, with Sam keen to get to work on the Lurve Nest. He prepared plans, checked out materials and local suppliers, then lost interest in the project.

It was ironic. They'd bought the house on the clear understanding that they were both to have their own space, but it soon became evident that they needed the opposite: one another's company.

Elliot hauled himself out of the water. He looked at his watch. He'd been swimming for almost an hour – another hour and he might have got close to working off the excesses of his father's cooking.

He went over to a mirror-fronted cupboard where they kept a supply of towels and old bathrobes. He wrapped himself in a robe, and just as he was about to switch off the lights, a flicker of movement through one of the patio doors caught his attention. He leaned against the glass and cupped his hands around his eyes.

It was snowing, just as he'd predicted.

One of Ali's classic put-down lines came to mind: 'What's it like, Elliot, always being right?'

4

Fifty miles away, in the village of Astley Hope, Sarah Donovan stood at the sitting-room window in Smithy Cottage and listened to her husband coaxing the engine of their tired old car into life. In the still, snow-muffled night, it sounded as glum and ill-disposed as she herself felt. Eventually the engine submitted to Trevor's determined will and the reluctant Ford Sierra disappeared sulkily down the lane, its tyres following in the slushy tracks already made in the snow. Sarah hoped that he would drive carefully, that his current state of near apoplexy wouldn't distract him. She also hoped that he wouldn't embarrass and humiliate Hannah too much when he found her.

She moved away from the window and glanced at her watch. It was twenty-five past twelve. To Trevor's knowledge, Hannah, their eighteen-year-old daughter had never been out this late before on her own. What he didn't realise was that, behind his back, Hannah's social life wasn't the safe, dull routine he imagined it to be. Aided and abetted by Sarah, Hannah had recently, and in secret, started to enjoy a greater degree of freedom than her father would ever allow. As on previous occasions he had thought that Hannah was staying the night with her friend Emily to help each other with their school work. Tonight it was supposed to be a session on Molière's *Le Malade imaginaire.* In reality Hannah and Emily had been in Chester at a nightclub.

Poor Trevor, he just wasn't in tune with the world Hannah lived in. He hadn't realised that he could no longer play the part of omnipotent father to a small hero-worshipping daughter. He had no idea that his role now was to be a middle-aged saddo, who was only to speak when spoken to and was expected to stay in the shadows of his daughter's fast-changing life. He had no comprehension why his authority wasn't respected any more, or why his opinions weren't wanted and the advice he offered went unheeded. It was standard procedure in most households and most fathers went along with it, treating these strange, surly beings as an alien life form temporarily exchanged for their precious little darlings. They knew that they had no choice but to go along with the derision and the tantrums and that, before long, if they played their part accordingly, their loving, sweet-natured daughters would be returned to them.

But Trevor didn't understand any of this and he was fighting Hannah every step of the way towards her becoming a woman. He couldn't see that the struggle was futile – he might just as well have been trying to hold back the tide.

Perhaps if Hannah had been more troublesome when she'd been younger, Trevor might have been prepared for the change in her now, but Hannah had never been a difficult child. Biddable, hard-working and affectionate, she'd adored her father and he'd doted on her. Compared to a lot of girls her age, she had been a late developer, which was probably why they were now experiencing such a radical change in her. Before now she'd never been interested in boys or parties, preferring instead to pursue her musical interests. She'd played the flute since the age of twelve and had recently passed her grade eight exam with distinction. Until the summer she had sung in the school and church choirs. Her teachers had nothing but praise for her. Their only negative comment, which had been made some years ago, was that they thought she ought to make more of an effort to mix with the other girls at school. She wasn't a solitary child, but she took after her mother in that she'd always been happily self-contained and quite content with her own company. But this had changed last year in the lower sixth, when Emily had joined the school. Hannah had been assigned to show the new girl the ropes and, though their characters were very different, they instantly became friends.

The first time Sarah met Emily she had been reminded of her and Ali. They'd been friends since the age of ten, and in the way that Hannah and Emily were chalk and cheese, so were she and Ali. And just as Ali had shown Sarah that another world existed beyond the boundaries of the sheltered one she'd hitherto experienced, Emily had done the same for Hannah.

Which was why, at half past midnight, Trevor was now driving through several inches of snow on a rescue mission to find his daughter.

The plan was always the same, and usually it worked, but this time it hadn't. The arrangement was that whenever Hannah wanted to be out for longer than Trevor would allow she stayed the night with Emily, whose parents had a much more relaxed attitude towards teenage daughters than Trevor, though this was a detail of which he had been kept in ignorance. Sarah had gone to great lengths to ensure that Trevor never met Emily's parents – she knew he would never approve of them: 'Heavens,' she could imagine him saying, 'they don't even go to church!'

Sarah didn't want to lie to Trevor, but if they were to avoid a huge scene every time Hannah wanted to stay out late, which wasn't often, it was the only solution to ensure that Sarah could give her daughter the freedom she felt she deserved. She herself had grown up in a strict, dictatorial, curfew-driven home and had hated it. All the freedom she had ever experienced as a child had been given to her by Ali and her parents. Maggie and Lawrence Edwards had been wonderful to her, including her in their family as if she were one of their own. They still treated her in much the same fashion. Every year they sent her birthday and Christmas gifts, as well as something for Hannah.

It was funny to witness history repeating itself, in that Sarah had had Ali, and Hannah had Emily. Though she sincerely hoped that Hannah's life would turn out differently from hers. She didn't want Hannah to be married to the kind of man from whom she had to hide things. Deceit was no basis for a happy marriage. Too often it had a nasty habit of backfiring, just as it had tonight. Their carefully constructed plan had gone completely wrong. Hannah had telephoned a few moments ago to say that she and Emily were stuck in Chester. Emily was blind drunk and had given away their taxi money to a homeless man whom they'd met outside the nightclub and, to make matters worse, Emily's parents were in London – which Emily had kept quiet about – and they had no way of getting home.

'I'll be there as quickly as I can,' Sarah had told Hannah. 'Don't let Emily out of your sight. And, for goodness sake, don't let her drink any more.'

But the telephone had disturbed Trevor, who had gone to bed for an early night. He had come downstairs bleary-eyed to find her in her coat. 'What's going on?' he'd asked. There was no avoiding the truth now, so she'd told him. He'd flown into an immediate and predictable rage, demanding to know the details.

'Chester! At this time of night! A *nightclub*!'

He'd then insisted on going to Chester himself. 'I'm not having you driving so late and certainly not in this weather.'

She'd pleaded with him that it would be best if she fetched the girls. But he'd refused to listen, dashing upstairs, throwing on the first clothes to hand and rushing out of the house to start the car.

Poor Hannah, thought Sarah. All her recently acquired street cred would be blown away when her father rolled into town in their rusting D-reg Sierra, dressed in what she called his 'Sad Old Man at C & A clothes'.

She bent down to the floor and tidied away the Christmas presents she'd been wrapping before Hannah had phoned. She put the carrier bags in the cupboard under the stairs and wondered what to do next. The bed in the spare room was already made, so at least Emily would have somewhere to sleep, but a couple of hot-water bottles seemed a good idea. She went into the kitchen and filled the kettle, and while she waited for it to boil she decided to ring Ali. As well as wanting to make sure that her friend was all right, she needed to talk to somebody about the impending disaster in the Donovan household.

Ali had been on Sarah's mind for most of that day, and not just because it was the anniversary of Isaac's death: she'd received a card from Maggie and Lawrence that morning. She had wanted to ring Ali earlier, while Trevor was out at a church meeting, but at the last minute the meeting had been cancelled owing to the snow. It was ridiculously late to be ringing anyone, but Sarah knew that Ali hardly ever went to bed before midnight and that in the last two years she'd become even more of a night owl.

The phone was answered almost immediately.

'Ali, it's me, Sarah. You're not in bed, are you?'

'Course not. Hours of fun to get through yet. It's a bit late for you, though, isn't it? What's wrong? A case of insomnia?'

'I'll tell you in a minute. But first, how was your day?'

'It was bloody, bloody, *bloody* awful.'

'I'm sorry.'

'And to make it a hundred times worse, Elliot turned up while I was at Isaac's grave.'

'Oh, Ali, what does that matter?'

'Believe me, it matters.'

'How did he seem?'

'Stiff. Polite. Angry. The usual.'

'A mirror image of yourself, you could say.'

'Look, if I wanted to hear clever-dick comments I'd pay good money to have someone more qualified than you analyse me.'

'More qualified than your oldest friend? You've got to be joking. Did you manage to exchange a few kind words with one another?'

'Put it this way, I was kind enough to invite him back here.'

'Brave as well as kind. And?'

'He'd obviously been instructed by Sam to invite me to spend Christmas with them. Which thoughtful invitation I naturally refused.'

'Naturally.'

'Oh, come on, Sarah. You're not seriously suggesting that I should have considered it?'

'Why not?'

'Because, you fool of a girl, it would be a disaster. Elliot and I can't stand to be near one another, you know that.'

'Maybe you're right. But if I ask you to come and spend Christmas here with us, will you turn me down as well?'

There was a pause.

'Ali?'

'Have you had a Christmas card from my parents?'

'I might have. Why?'

'Because your card probably said the same as Sam and Elliot's. Honestly, how many other people has my mother enlisted in—'

'So why are you planning to spend Christmas alone?' Sarah interrupted. 'Is this just another step down the road of self-inflicted punishment? Because if it is, I think it's high time—'

'Sarah—'

'I haven't finished.'

'Oh, yes, you have. I'll come.'

'I beg your pardon?'

'I said I'd spend Christmas with you. Anything to get you off my case – though God knows how I'll survive Trevor.'

'You'll manage.'

'That remains to be seen. Now tell me what you've been up to.'

Sarah told her about Hannah and Emily and the deception that had been going on behind Trevor's back. 'I can't begin to think how he's going to react when he knows the full story.'

'I can. He'll totally overreact. Just as well I'm coming for Christmas, then. My heathen comments will take the heat off you and poor Hannah. He'll be so busy trying to save my heretical soul from being tossed into the fiery furnace of hell and the Devil's awaiting pleasure that he won't have time to be cross with you.'

'Ali, if there was any such thing as the fiery furnace of hell and the Devil, he'd toss you right back whence you came and we'd have to put up with you for a bit longer.'

'Funny ha-ha.'

'Oh, heavens, Ali, I can hear a car. It's probably Trevor with the girls. Wish me luck.'

'Buckets of it. Give my love to the wayward god-daughter. Tell her I'm proud of her. I'll ring you tomorrow from the office to see how you got on. 'Bye.'

Sarah put down the phone and went out to the hall. She opened the front door and was met by a furious, red-faced Trevor, a tearful Hannah and Emily vomiting copiously into the snow-covered shrubbery.

<h1 style="text-align: center">5</h1>

Not surprisingly, the girls slept late.

Just as predictably, from the moment he was out of bed and dressed, Trevor had been pacing the small kitchen like a caged animal in a zoo, although as Sarah tidied away the remains of their breakfast she wasn't sure that this was quite the right analogy: there was nothing of the majestic lion about Trevor.

Nor the sleek panther.

Nor even a hint of the prowling tiger.

A disoriented gerbil was more the mark.

'But what really disturbs me is that you knew,' he said. Sarah had lost count of how many times he'd thrown this line at her. 'You knew,' he said again, and for added emphasis – just in case she'd missed the point – he slapped his hand down on the worktop and rattled the cutlery in the drawer beneath. 'You knew all along what she was doing. You were even party to the deception.'

She turned on the hot tap and squirted a streak of vivid green washing-up liquid into the sink. Above the rising steam she stared out of the window and took in the serene beauty of the morning. The sky was the clearest of blues with not a cloud to be seen, and the long, thin garden, which had been the recipient of so much of her care and attention in the ten years they had lived at Smithy Cottage, lay hidden beneath a smooth, perfectly formed blanket of snow. A few feet away from the kitchen window, a robin had the wooden bird table to himself and was happily breakfasting on the first-class selection of nuts and seeds on offer. He was a regular visitor to the garden and Sarah called him Gomez. He was such a happy-looking little thing, his only apparent concern being the search for his next meal, which in this neck of the woods wasn't arduous. Sarah envied him the simplicity of his existence.

After she'd settled Hannah and Emily last night, having told Trevor to leave everything to her, she'd put off going to bed for as long as she could. She had hoped that Trevor would go to sleep without her. He hadn't. He'd been waiting for her, sitting bolt upright, his arms folded tightly across his chest, his face grim, his eyes cold and steely. It was the same expression he wore whenever he felt she was challenging him. The last time she'd seen it was in September when, yet again, she had hinted that she would like a job. 'We're fine as we are,' he'd said, his arms slipping into place across his chest in a gesture of first-line defences being erected. 'And anyway,' he'd gone on,

352

'you have a very important job in running the house. It wouldn't be fair to Hannah if you went out to work. She needs you here at home.' Sarah had countered that it wasn't fair to Hannah that she'd had to miss out on the school classics trip to Italy because they couldn't afford it.

For the most part of their marriage they had always been desperate for the money that another income could provide, but Trevor had resolutely denied that this was the case, claiming that they had sufficient to meet their needs. 'Sarah,' he would say, quoting a well-worn line of scripture, '"Life is more than food, and the body more than clothes".' Every time he said this she felt inclined to say, 'I'll remind you of that next time you're hungry or you're hunting for a clean pair of underpants.'

As guilty and disloyal as it sounded, Sarah had to admit that she found Trevor to be that uncomfortable variety of red-hot Christian who gave religion a bad name. He hadn't always been this fervent. When she had first known him as a student teacher, he had been a regular, straightforward churchgoer, but these days he seemed dangerously fired up on an excess of faith. It drove Ali, a passionate, card-carrying atheist, to distraction, especially when he tried to flaunt his spiritual superiority over her. It incensed Sarah too, but in contrast to Ali she kept her thoughts to herself. She didn't think it was right to shake anyone out of their religious beliefs. Not when she had enough doubts and failings of her own. And, besides, there really wasn't any arguing with Trevor: when he had a viewpoint, he stuck limpet-fast to it. As he did whenever the subject of her going out to work raised its head. His old standby of camels, eyes of needles and rich men was usually tossed into the arena of the going-nowhere discussion. His final word was always the same: 'Our Lord's example is very clear on the matter, Sarah. Spiritual wealth is what we seek, not secular riches.'

But Sarah guessed that the real reason behind Trevor not wanting her to work had little to do with scriptural teaching and a lot more to do with his insecurity. As infuriating and absurdly outmoded as it was, he needed her at home so that he could bask in the glory of being the family's sole provider: his position as head of the house had to be maintained. If she were ever to earn more than him, where would that leave him?

But in the end, and employing a huge amount of compromise on her part, she had, at last, got her way. It wasn't a brilliant job, it didn't really pay that well, but it was a job and one that posed no threat to Trevor. For the past six weeks she had been working for an interior-design shop. She'd always been good with her hands and had made all the soft furnishings in Smithy Cottage. Now she was being paid to do the same for other people's homes. She worked upstairs in the spare bedroom and, though the work wasn't stimulating, she enjoyed it. More importantly, it brought in a little more money, which she was putting by for Hannah when she went to university. Trevor had begrudgingly given his approval to what Sarah was doing and had left her to it.

But there had been nothing begrudging or approving about him last night when she had joined him in bed.

'I can't believe that Hannah went to that – that *nightclub*.'

He'd said the word nightclub as though it were foreign to him. Which, of course, it was. To Trevor the word represented another world: a wicked, salacious world frequented only by wicked, salacious people.

The low-life of Chester.

The drug pushers.

The pimps.

The prostitutes.

It wasn't at all the place where a daughter of his should show her face.

Sarah had wanted to say, 'It's probably just the kind of environment in which Christ would have hung out,' but, coward that she was, she hadn't. Instead, she'd said, 'Please, Trevor, it's very late. Can we discuss this in the morning?'

His response had been to look pointedly at the digital alarm clock on his bedside table, his arms still rigidly folded, and say, 'In case you hadn't noticed, Sarah, it's been morning for some hours. You don't seem very shocked by what Hannah's done. You sound almost as if you don't care that she lied to us.'

'That's because I'm not shocked and she hasn't been lying – at least, not as you think she has.'

And out of some kind of defensive anger and wanting to protect Hannah, who had flatly refused to explain anything to her father, she had gone on to tell Trevor the truth. But not the whole truth.

She turned now to where he was breathing like a knight-hungry dragon. 'Why don't you put some of your excess energy into drying the dishes for me? Stomping about the place won't help.'

'I haven't got time,' he snapped, giving his beard a sharp little tug. 'I need to get on.'

'Well, nobody's stopping you.' Really, he was acting in such a ridiculous manner. Anyone would think they were discussing a thirteen-year-old child and not the adult Hannah practically was.

'You know perfectly well I can't, not until we've sorted out this dreadful mess. How can I be creative when things haven't been resolved?'

'There's nothing to resolve.'

He stared at her uncomprehendingly. 'Sarah, you and Hannah both tricked me into believing that she was staying the night with Emily and her parents, where they would be doing nothing more dangerous than their French homework, when all along you knew that they were planning to get themselves dressed like – like a couple of tarts and go into Chester where anything could have happened to them. Did you see how much *makeup* they had on?'

Sarah pulled off her rubber gloves and looked patiently at him. 'Trevor,' she said, with just a trace of firmness, at the same time placing a hand on his arm, 'neither Hannah nor Emily bore any resemblance to women of questionable repute. They were wearing clothes and makeup that make them feel good about themselves, that was all.'

He shrugged away her hand. 'But look at the trouble they got themselves into.'

'That had nothing to do with what they were wearing. Admittedly Emily was silly to have drunk so much, but didn't you ever do that when you were their age?'

He gave what Hannah would call a grade A snort. 'That's an absurd line of argument,' he said. 'You know very well that it's different for boys.'

'Well, it shouldn't be!'

He ignored her heated tone and said. 'None of this excuses you and Hannah for lying to me. Your behaviour is, at best, irresponsible, and at worst—'

'Trevor, please, I did it because it's important that Hannah learns to be more independent. You give her no freedom, none whatsoever. How on earth do you expect her to cope with going away to university next year if she hasn't made any mistakes? She has to make the odd one so that she can learn from it. And, if you want the real truth, she and Emily have done this before. This is the first time the arrangement has gone wrong. You should be proud of her for doing exactly the right thing when she phoned us for help. Far better that than her turning to a stranger for a lift home.'

A stupefied expression covered Trevor's face. He backed away from her. She wouldn't have been at all surprised if he'd held up two crossed fingers to her in a gesture of get-thee-behind-me-Satan. It was a few seconds before he could speak. 'I don't believe I'm hearing this. As Christian parents it's our duty to raise our daughter in a manner pleasing to—'

'Please,' Sarah interrupted, 'don't bring God into this. You do it whenever we have to discuss anything of importance.'

'Sarah,' he said sharply, 'I'm not sure I like your tone of voice. And, what's more, if you'd brought God into your thinking in the first place, none of this would have happened.'

Sarah sighed. All hope of a logical debate was now lost. That was the trouble with Trevor: when he suspected he was losing the fight, he would run home to fetch God to play the part of big, bullying brother. She let his accusation go and reached for a tea towel to dry the breakfast dishes. A few moments later the kitchen door crashed shut and Trevor was gone. She pictured him in his workshop taking out his frustration on an innocent piece of wood, slamming it on to his lathe and attacking it with one of his lethally sharp chisels.

Oh, well, better that than taking it out on me, she thought, glad that he was no longer hovering at her side like an angry bee. And not for the first time she was grateful that, although Trevor worked from home, the nature of his work kept him firmly out of the house.

Nine months ago, Trevor had given up his teaching job to become what he rather grandly referred to as 'a craftsman'. When Sarah had told Ali what he was planning, she had burst out laughing. 'Oh, that's a good one. Trevor the carpenter, just like Christ.'

Sarah had wanted to laugh too, but loyalty wouldn't let her. She'd chided her friend instead: 'Please don't make fun of him, Ali.'

After years of teaching basic woodwork skills to adults with learning difficulties, Trevor was finally doing what he'd always wanted to do and that was to down-shift and work for himself. He'd been a good teacher but never a happy one, and now, in what had once been the village blacksmith's workshop, he was like a dog with two tails. For a long time, he'd been making gifts for friends at church and his skill at woodturning had been much admired. Knocking out candlesticks, little pots with lids, apples, mushrooms, pot-pourri holders and large fruit bowls for church fund-raising events had become a speciality and several people had remarked that he ought to sell his work on a more enterprising scale. But even Trevor had known that giving up a steady teaching job to join the precarious craft-fair circuit was a risk. But the Lord works in mysterious ways, as Trevor would say, and when Sarah's mother had died last June, two years after her father, Sarah had been left enough money to pay off their mortgage. Trevor had announced then that he'd been called by the Holy Spirit to quit the world of teaching.

Business was not what one would call brisk, but it seemed to be picking up, although that was probably due to the season. The proof of Trevor's success would come once they were into the New Year. For now, though, he was busy enough to be happy, supplying a few arty-crafty shops in the area, as well as hawking his wares round the pre-Christmas fairs. His only problem with any of this, and it did cause a genuine moral dilemma for him, was that the fairs sometimes covered an entire weekend, and Sunday, after all, was a day of rest. But, after much prayer, he concluded that he'd been led to do this work so therefore it must be all right.

The kitchen now clean and tidy, and still no sign of the girls, Sarah decided to take Trevor a peace-offering cup of tea. She knew that his anger and silliness stemmed from his love for Hannah and that he would go to any lengths to keep her safe. It was sad, but he would probably prefer her not to blossom into adulthood. He'd been such a good father to her when she was little. He hadn't been, as most other fathers, too busy with his career to participate fully in his child's life. He'd never missed a single concert at which she'd either sung or played in the orchestra, or a performance of a play in which she'd acted, no matter how small the role. Not one parents' evening had gone by without him being there to keep tabs on Hannah's progress.

Yes, he'd been a good father, there was no denying it.

Which was why it was such a shame that he was now spoiling all the good work he'd put into parenthood.

He had to learn to stand back and let her go. He was also going to have to let her make up her own mind about going to church. Hannah had confided in Sarah that she no longer wanted to go to St Cuthbert's, the local church at which she'd been an active member since the age of eight; where she'd played Mary in the Nativity play no fewer than four times; where she'd pretended to be a pumpkin during harvest festival and where more recently she'd helped out with the dwindling Sunday school.

'How can I go, Mum,' she had said, only last week, 'when I don't believe in any of it now? It's real to you and Dad, it makes sense for you. It's not ringing my bell any more. I reckon Buddhism's got more going for it. I think I'll become the first Buddhist in Astley Hope. I'll shave off my hair and go chanting up and down the lanes in an enlightened manner, preaching the four Noble Truths. That should give everyone something to talk about.'

They had laughed together at the idea, even though Sarah was disappointed to hear Hannah talk in such a way. Spiritual faith wasn't to be mocked. It was what underpinned society. It was the fulcrum of one's being. When all else was gone, including hope, it was only faith that shone through the darkness.

And, as Sarah poured Trevor's mug of tea, she hoped that he would understand that Hannah had to discover for herself what did and did not make sense.

6

Sam handed his coat to the waiter and took his seat at the table he'd reserved over the phone that morning. He was early and knowing that punctuality wasn't one of Ali's strong suits, he settled himself in for a minimum wait of ten minutes.

Last night when he had told Elliot that he would speak to Ali, he had known all too well that he was skating on the thinnest of ice, and though he didn't want to do anything to upset his son, he couldn't ignore his feelings for Ali. He missed her keenly: she'd been more to him than just a daughter-in-law. In the days before Isaac's death, and when Elliot had been away on business, as he frequently was, he had often taken Ali out for dinner. Their evenings together were always fun, especially when they were mistaken for a couple, and he and Ali hammed up his supposed role as a sugar daddy. They would howl with laughter after they had left the restaurant and Sam would drive her home high on machismo pride that people thought a short, dumpy old fellow such as he could pull an attractive young woman.

But those evenings no longer existed. Since Isaac had been snatched from them, it seemed that there had been little for any of them to laugh about. Though his own reaction to the death of his young grandson could come nowhere near what Ali and Elliot must have experienced – and still were experiencing – it had had a profound effect on him: the death of a child was never easy to accept. But he'd been through the grieving process before, when Connie, his wife, had died more than twenty years ago, and he knew that although the pain never entirely went away, it did lessen.

He knew also that in some cases grief could separate the bereaved from those closest to them, and that was what had happened to Ali and Elliot. In the immediate aftermath of Isaac's death, he had watched two people who had loved one another with the strongest of passion erect a barrier of bewildered confusion to keep the other out, along with everyone else. Unable to help or stop what they were doing, Sam had seen how difficult it was for them to relate to anything but the pain within themselves and project that hurt on to the other. In the months that followed they turned away from each other and focused what was left of their energy into the routine of work, letting their minds be absorbed by the mechanics of the mundane. Now all that was left between Ali and Elliot was the currency of their disappointment in life itself, which they exercised by attacking the other in the belief that it was the best form of defence.

All Sam could hope for was that this stage in their lives would soon pass, that they would eventually find a way to transcend their grief and anger. His greatest wish was that, at the very least, they could be friends.

Realising that he'd now been waiting for a quarter of an hour, Sam glanced round the smart French restaurant, hoping to catch sight of Ali. He took in a couple of small tables in the arched window that looked out on to the busy street. They were occupied by two pairs of elegantly dressed women who, judging from the carrier bags at their feet, were having a quiet lunch after a hard morning of Christmas shopping. The rest of the diners made up a large, noisy party of exuberant office workers who were presumably enjoying their annual Christmas binge; their faces were rosy-red from the intake of midday booze, their heads decorated with ill-fitting paper hats. Then, out of the corner of his eye, Sam saw the restaurant door open, and a wave of what other men his age and background would have called unmanly sentiment came over him.

The sight of Ali brought home to him just how much he'd missed her all these months and how very fond of her he was. It also reminded him that if anyone were to judge Ali purely on her appearance, they would be in danger of committing the cardinal sin of underestimating her. She was only a fraction over five foot and, with her slight build and delicate features, she looked years younger than thirty-eight. Sam knew that Ali's youthful looks had often been a hindrance to her career and that she hated it when people did not take her seriously and treated her as if she could only be trusted to work the photocopier. Even from this distance across the restaurant, Sam could see the darkness of her eyes – brown eyes that were made to look darker still by the fairness of her skin and her short, slightly wavy blonde hair, which Sam guessed was as genuine as the woman herself. He didn't know anyone else like her. She was sassy, steely and, at times, too full of chutzpah for her own good. He had always known why his son had fallen in love with Ali – hell, he'd have done the same thing if his age hadn't been against him! – and it hadn't been the exterior packing that had attracted Elliot, as delightful as it was. No, it had been deeper than that: Ali had the same tough, incisive mind as Elliot, and he'd respected and admired her for it, seeing her as his soulmate.

When she came over, Sam rose to his feet and they greeted each other with a warm embrace. He let her go and said, 'When was the last time you ate? There's nowt of you. You're much too thin.'

She smiled affectionately at him. 'I'm in training.'

He pulled out a chair for her. 'What the hell for? The one-hundred-metre slipping-between-the-cracks event?'

'Six-pack-Sam, you've lost none of your cheek, have you? Are you going to be as rude as this to me all lunch?'

'Not rude, love, just concerned.' He attracted the attention of a passing waiter and ordered a carafe of Château Maison. 'That okay with you?' he asked, when the waiter had left them.

'It's fine. So what's with all the concern, Sam? Invitations to spend Christmas with you, and now lunch. What's going on?'

He leaned back in his seat; bulls and horns came to mind. 'We've had lunch before, nothing odd in that.'

'But on those occasions I was married to Elliot.'

'Oh, aye, so you were.'

Ali contemplated Sam's round, smiling face. He reminded her of Bob Hoskins with a bit of the dark-eyed Danny DeVito thrown in. Ever since he'd phoned her first thing that morning at work, she'd been speculating as to what he was up to. However, she'd agreed to meet him for lunch, not just to satisfy her curiosity but because she was keen to see him. It was ages since they'd talked on their own and it pained her to think that he had witnessed her and Elliot at their worst, that their divorce and appalling behaviour had put him in an impossible situation, and that he had done his best to make the best of a bad job. She admired him for it. She knew also that there were boundaries that could never be crossed. She could never, for instance, be openly critical of Elliot to Sam. Sam could be as rude as he cared to be about his son, but woe betide anyone else who tried it. As paternal love went, Sam's knew no bounds. In his light-hearted fashion he was fiercely protective of Elliot. Which made the fact that they were having lunch here on their own something of a surprise. Did Elliot know about this? Or had Sam gone behind his back?

She wondered now if Sam's protectiveness went as far as trying to get her and Elliot back together. 'Sam,' she said, fixing him with a penetrating gaze, 'do I have to come right out with it and accuse you of being interfering and devious?'

He laughed heartily. 'If the cap fits, love.'

She laughed too. 'It bloody well fits all right and you know it does.'

'Good, that's settled, then. We've agreed that I'm a sneaky, meddling bugger, so come on, choose your lunch, my stomach's thinking of packing up and going home.'

They ordered their food, and when their wine arrived Sam raised his glass. 'Here's to Christmas and . . .' He hesitated.

'Barbados?' she suggested, with a half-smile.

He lowered his glass. 'A straight answer for a straight question, Ali. Why the hair shirt this year? Why aren't you going down to your parents?'

She shrugged.

He reached for her hand across the table and looked at her with loving eyes. 'I hate the thought of you being on your lonesome for Christmas.'

She squeezed his strong square hand. 'But I shan't be alone,' she said brightly. 'I just had a better invitation than yours, that's all.'

'Better than Barbados?'

'Yep.'

'Oh,' he said. Ali heard the flat tone of disappointment in his voice. 'So Elliot was right,' he added.

'In what way?'

Sam stared at her with a clear, frank gaze. 'The Boy Wonder reckoned that might be the case.'

'Reckoned what might be the case?'

'That you'd gone and got yourself a boyfriend and were—'

'Got myself a boyfriend?' Ali laughed. 'What a joke! And just what the hell would I want with one of those? They're untidy, time-consuming and, like Saturday night curry stains, awkward to shift, and that's just their finer points.'

'There's nothing of the cynic in you, is there?' Sam chuckled. He caught sight of their waiter on the horizon and said, 'Mm ... at last, our food.'

When the plates and side dishes of vegetables had been settled on the table and they were left alone again, Ali said, 'Don't think I'm not grateful for the offer, Sam. I am. But you must have realised that I could never accept it. It would never work. Elliot and I have experienced too much pain at one another's expense to be anything but horribly polite to each other. You must believe me when I say that any kind of reconciliation is out of the question.'

He looked at her, his countenance serious and, with a bolt of what she could only describe as pain, she was reminded of Elliot. Elliot bore practically no resemblance to his father, but there in Sam's face was the same serious expression that had attracted her to Elliot when she'd first met him.

She'd just started as a graduate trainee working for what was then, back in the early eighties, the biggest accountancy firm in Manchester. Eight years her senior, well established in the organisation, and already branded a high flyer – the company's rising star – Elliot hadn't been like the crowd of graduates with whom she was supposed to socialise; thirty of them in total, all of whom still hadn't shaken off their student mores, and without intending to, she had found herself gravitating to his more mature attitude. While her contemporaries were happy to spend their evenings swilling beer before, during and after a vindaloo curry in Rusholme, she was happier to be in Elliot's more thoughtful, sophisticated company. There was an aura of composed calm about him that was enormously appealing. He was a man of few words, claiming that he'd rather speak the right ones than waste his breath on the wrong ones. His taciturn nature made him a good listener and he would fix his candid blue eyes on her and listen intently to whatever she had to say. In the early stages of their relationship, she'd had no way of knowing if he was aware of the devastating effect he had on her, that his subtle but wholly powerful sex appeal was so totally compelling. This was a new phenomenon for Ali. During her time up at Oxford she had been the one firmly in control of her feelings, giving a long line in badly treated boyfriends the runaround. But suddenly she was no longer in control. This man, with his low-key charm and generally acknowledged intellectual brilliance, had taken her heart in one swift movement and was in danger of keeping it.

There was so much in his character that drew her to him, but if she had to name one thing that did it, it was his tendency to look solemn. Even when he was enjoying himself, he rarely smiled. She became fascinated with the man behind the face, and those clear blue eyes, wanting to know what it was that made him tick. The first time he took her back to his house – after several months of discreet dating, neither of them wanting to attract the attention of every busybody at work – she had told him that he was the most understated man she knew. 'You're laconic, droll and about as buttoned-down as a guy could be.' His response had been to kiss her and take her upstairs where he had proved to her for the next two hours that his approach to sex was anything but laconic. Afterwards she'd said, 'Elliot, there's an interesting dichotomy to your character. Beneath that rigidly contained coolness is quite another man.' He'd smiled one of his rare smiles and she'd known from that moment that she loved him.

'I'm really sorry that you feel that way, Ali,' she heard Sam saying. She dispelled the memory of his son lying naked and exhausted beside her, and forced herself to concentrate on what Sam was telling her. 'It would mean a lot to a poor old man to know that you and Elliot could at least be friends.'

She scowled at him. 'Less of the poor-old-man routine, Sam. Any more talk like that and you'll lose all my respect.'

The Elliot-like seriousness was instantly gone and Sam's eyes twinkled with their usual warmth and humour. 'It was worth a try.' He grinned.

'No, it wasn't. It was a cheap shot grounded in sentimentality that wasn't worth an airing. Now, tell me how it's going, you and Elliot living in domestic harmony. I haven't seen you since you cast yourselves as *The Odd Couple.*'

'Not so fast, lass. You're not off the hook yet. You've still not told me how you're spending Christmas.'

'Gracious, everybody's obsessed with my private life.'

'That's because we care about you.'

'Rubbish! You're all a bunch of nosy-parkers. If you must know, I'm going to Sarah's.'

The relief on Sam's face was plainly visible. 'I'm delighted to hear it. How is she?'

'Oh, the usual, a saint for still putting up with Trevor.'

'Didn't he leave his teaching job to try his hand at earning a living from woodturning?'

'Yes, and it makes me mad every time I think of it. When Sarah's mother died and left her that money it should have been used to make their lives financially easier, to give them a few luxuries in life. It should not have been used to give Trevor the excuse to jack in his job. An inheritance, no matter how small, should serve a worthwhile purpose.'

'Just as I've always suspected,' Sam observed. 'We parents are at our most useful and loved when we're six foot under and the will's being read.'

It was Ali's turn to look serious. 'I don't think Elliot, or I, will ever think that of you, Sam.'

He caught the sincerity in her words. He placed his screwed-up napkin beside his finished plate and said, 'Don't go getting sentimental on me, love. Got room for a pud?'

They left the restaurant an hour later. Sam insisted that he walked Ali back to her office. It was a cold, wet, wintry afternoon, and although it was only two-thirty, the light was losing its hold and yesterday's fall of snow, like old news, wasn't worth having around. They made their way slowly through the slush and hordes of Christmas shoppers. The main street was decked out in pseudo-Dickensian style and piped carols tinkled merrily. In the square in front of Marks & Spencer, a small crowd was gathered round a thickly padded Santa. At his side was his pixie helper – a young girl, who in the stiff December wind looked frozen to death in a pair of skimpy, red, fake-fur hot-pants and a pointy hat complete with brass bell; the sleety rain had made her mascara run and she looked thoroughly disenchanted. They were handing out balloons and flyers advertising a new cut-price drugstore that had just opened in town. At the front of the crowd was a small boy in a pushchair, his cold-reddened face a picture of anxious delight as he waited patiently for a balloon. A ghostly shiver went through Ali and, as chilling as an icy hand, it gripped and twisted at her heart. Her whole body froze. Sam put his arm around her shoulder and steered her away. 'Done your shopping, yet?' he asked, by way of distraction.

She shook her head, unable to speak.

'Me neither. Haven't a clue what to buy the Boy Wonder.'

They walked on in silence. 'It's a real bugger, grief, isn't it?' Sam said gruffly, when at last they came to a stop outside the renovated Georgian building where Ali's office was situated on the first floor.

She agreed with a slight tilt of her head, quickly kissed his cheek, wished him a happy Caribbean Christmas and shot inside. She took the stairs two at a time and fled to the toilets where she shut herself inside one of the cubicles. She leaned against the door and sank slowly to the floor. She covered her face with her hands and wept.

7

'I'm fine,' Ali told herself, 'I'm absolutely *fine*.'

She splashed cold water on to her face, looked at her ruined makeup in the mirror above the basin and knew that this was far from the truth. Outwardly the tears had stopped, so had the shaking, but inwardly the choking pain was still there.

She dried her face and hands on a rough paper towel and thought of Sam's words: *It's a real bugger, grief, isn't it?*

Oh, how right he was.

There was nothing so dark, so painful as the agonising torture of bereavement. Losing Isaac had made her realise the extent of love itself, that what she had expressed for her son when he was alive had been only the tip of the iceberg. It was what she felt in her heart, deep below the surface, that caused the pain and tore her apart when she was least expecting it.

There were days when the memory of Isaac was manageable, when she could almost meet her grief head on, confront it, reason with it and accept it. On other days she could work herself into such a state of exhaustion she didn't have a moment to dwell on what had been snatched from her. But then there were the times when, like a stalker hiding in the shadows waiting for its opportunity, the torment of grief would leap out of the darkness and strike her down.

This was what had taken place just now. That little boy in the pushchair with his smiling face had caught her off-guard and razed her defences to the ground.

She closed her eyes and saw Isaac so clearly. He was wrapped from head to toe in his all-in-one quilted suit, his mittens pulled off – she never could get him to keep them on – and his eyes shining with delight. The three of them were Christmas shopping in Manchester. It was a bitterly cold day. The shops were crowded and hectic. They'd just bought Isaac a present – a toy garage complete with cars and trucks – and Elliot was carrying it under his arm while she pushed the buggy through the crowded streets. They were waiting to cross the road to go into Waterstone's when Isaac's eyes rested on two little girls each with a balloon. He was smiling that heart-melting smile of his, the one that was so irresistible. They had tracked down the balloon-seller, who turned out to be a young man with a nose-ring, dressed half-heartedly as Santa – he'd managed a hat and a tuft of cotton wool on his chin, which was in danger of catching light from the cigarette dangling out of his mouth.

The balloon lasted a week, until it wrinkled and shrivelled itself into a flaccid nothingness. She threw it away one evening while Isaac was sleeping.

Two days later, he was dead.

Ali opened her eyes, screwed the paper towel that was still in her hands into a tight, hard ball, then tossed it into the bin. She took a determined breath. She would beat *it*. For Isaac's sake she would not let *it* get the better of her.

Daniel, her business partner, confidant and, after Sarah, her closest friend, was on the phone when she entered the office. He pointed to the pile of messages for her on the corner of his desk where his feet were resting on a file. She picked up the bits of paper and went over to her own. She was glad to discover that one of the messages was from a client cancelling their four-thirty meeting. Good, she now had the rest of the day free to finish the report she'd started that morning.

She heard Daniel trying to wind down his conversation, and from his look of concern as he glanced her way she could see that he knew she'd been crying.

She and Daniel had known one another since their graduate-trainee days, when together they had rented a damp, carpetless flat in Flixton. By day they had worked in the centre of Manchester surrounded by the lavish corporate glamour of the office, and by night they had slummed it like students, surviving on black coffee and takeaway pizzas while getting to grips with the study-load expected of them. Happy days!

When they'd completed their three-year training contracts and qualified they'd looked to the future with enthusiasm. For each of them came a steady, encouraging succession of promotions, but by the time they had reached their early thirties they both realised that, for different reasons, they had reached an immovable glass ceiling. Ali was never going to get the ultimate promotion she desired because she was a woman, and Daniel's future within the organisation was blighted because he was gay. Nothing was ever said, but there had never been a gay senior partner, and the chance of there ever being one was about as probable as hell freezing over. The firm might be riddled with divorce as a result of office affairs, it might be run by lecherous men who couldn't resist sampling younger girls, but perish the thought that a decent, morally minded man who had lived with his partner for more than ten years – longer than a lot of marriages lasted – could manage seven hundred employees without the empire tumbling down because of his sexuality.

Daniel came off the phone and said, 'You okay, Babe?'

She stared at his anxious face and thought how unfair life was for him. There was nothing in his manner or style of dress to hint that Daniel was gay – there was none of the moustachioed, earringed, tight-jeaned extrovert about him. He resembled any straight man she knew who took an above-average interest and pride in his appearance. With his gold-card good looks, and lean, long-limbed frame he made a striking sight in his expensive designer suits, which suggested, rather than flaunted, that he spent a good deal of money on his clothes. Armani and Gucci came as naturally to him as

St Michael underwear did to Ali. He wore his hair short, but not buzz-cut short, and *faux*-tortoiseshell-framed glasses gave his clean-cut features an academic look that was pure Ivy League. His silk ties were never loud and often favoured the sombreness of a man paying his last respects. His voice held no camp timbre and, indeed, for some years now he and his partner, Richard, had sung in their local choral society – they jokingly referred to themselves as the Two Queer Tenors. In Ali's opinion, Daniel couldn't be further from the stereotypical image of a gay man. He once said of himself that he represented what to many was the acceptable face of homosexuality. As cynical as it sounded, it was probably true.

'Babe, you've a face on you like thunder. What's wrong?'

'I'm sorry,' she said. 'I was letting my anger get the better of me. I was thinking of the big bullyboys of corporate accountancy who forced us out of their poxy power games.'

He smiled. 'We weren't forced. And, anyway, they were silly games they played. I much prefer our own.'

She frowned. 'Don't you ever feel bitter?'

He got to his feet and went over to the photocopier. 'No,' he said simply. He set the machine in action, then turned his back on it, leaned with his shoulder against a filing cabinet and said, 'You and I were never cut out for that particular ball-crushing fest. We were, and still are, too independent, too round for the squareness of the peg on offer. Of course, we could have tried our luck at sleeping our respective ways to the top but – I don't know about you – I never fancied any of those overweight, overpaid guys.'

She gave him a wry smile. 'You're forgetting Elliot. He wasn't overweight.'

He lowered his glasses and peered at her over the top. 'I was deliberately forgetting him, Babe. He was always the exception.'

She feigned a look of shock. 'Dan Divine, you're not telling me you fancied him, are you?'

He laughed. 'Too much competition from you, kid. I couldn't get a look in.'

A curious expression worked its way across her face. She sat back in her chair and swivelled in it. 'I've no idea how it happened, but during lunch with Sam I was remembering the first time I ever went to bed with Elliot.'

'And?'

She hesitated.

'Come on, I'm all agog, hanging on your every word.'

She shook her head with finality. 'And nothing.'

Daniel rolled his eyes. 'Well, I clearly recall a young woman returning to the flat experiencing a certain difficulty in walking after she'd spent a weekend with the man in question.'

'I had vertigo.'

'Rubbish! You'd overdosed on Elliot's physical attributes. God knows what kind of state you'd left him in. He was probably a stretcher case.'

She laughed and, as ever, felt enormous gratitude to Daniel for always being able to lift her spirits – a talent that, in recent times, had been frequently put to use. He was one of the most warm-hearted people she knew. He was tolerant too, and although over the years he had been confronted with varying degrees of prejudice in one form or another, he had never allowed it to spoil his easy-going disposition. 'I wish I could be more like you, Daniel,' she said. 'You're one of the nicest people I know. You have such a forgiving nature.'

He gathered his papers from the photocopier and returned to his desk. 'It's a gift,' he said. 'I'll get you one for Christmas. Now, are you going to do any work today, or is it just me running this place?'

It wasn't until Ali was at home that evening, in front of the television and munching the last of Lizzie's chocolate cake, that she remembered she hadn't called Sarah, as she'd promised. Too lazy to move to the kitchen for the phone, she turned the sound down on Kirsty Young – the intelligent face of newsroom drama – and reached for her mobile, which was in her briefcase at the other end of the sofa. She listened to the ringing tone and hoped that Trevor wouldn't answer it.

She was in luck. It was Hannah's voice that greeted her.

'So your father's let you out of the doghouse to answer the phone, has he?'

'He's at a meeting.'

'Which means you and your mother can breathe a sigh or two of relief.'

Hannah laughed. 'Something along those lines. I'll fetch Mum for you. By the way, I'm really glad you're coming for Christmas. It should liven things up no end.'

'Hey, if I'm to be the cabaret turn, I shall expect to be paid. And, I'll warn you now, I don't come cheap.'

'I'll put an extra-specially nice present for you under the tree. One of those tins of gin and tonic do you?'

'Nah, that's a girlie drink. A good single malt's more my style.'

'I prefer vodka and Coke myself. 'Bye.'

While Ali waited for Sarah to come to the phone, she wondered how it was that, in such an impossibly short time, her conversations with Hannah had progressed from vague toddler ramblings to alcohol preferences. Just as well that dear old Trevor wasn't around to hear what had been said: he would have choked on his disapproval and probably accused Ali of leading his daughter astray.

'Hello, Ali.' Sarah sounded breathless, as if she'd been running. 'Sorry to keep you, I was upstairs stripping the spare bed, getting it ready for you.'

'That's what I like to hear. I'm expecting best-quality Egyptian cotton sheets, the covers turned back and a heart-shaped chocolate on the pillow.'

'You can expect all you want, but you'll have to make do with see-through cotton and polyester and a nail-varnish stain on the pillowcase.'

'Sounds just like home. Now, tell me, how did last night pan out? Did Trevor hit the roof and ground you and Hannah for the rest of time?'

'Not exactly.'

'Go on, what did he do?'

There was a pause.

'Sarah?'

'You'll have to talk about something else. He's back, I can hear him putting the key in the lock. Tell me when you're arriving.'

Ali wanted to ignore her friend and demand to be told all the details about what the silly man was up to now, but she knew better. Sarah was ridiculously loyal to Trevor and would never do or say anything to annoy or disparage him. 'Okay, Sarah,' she said, 'I'll go along with you, but I want you to understand that if I get the chance over Christmas to ram home the message to Trevor that I think he's overreacted to this thing with you and Hannah, I will. I'll be there on Monday evening. That okay with you?'

'Christmas Eve, that's great,' Sarah said, in an excessively bright voice. As a cryptic afterthought, she said, 'And there'll certainly be no need for any messages, no need at all. I'd better go now. See you Monday, lots of love.'

Ali switched off her mobile and stared at Kirsty Young, who was still mouthing the news while perched side-saddle fashion on the corner of a desk. She felt angry and wondered, as she so often had over the years, why her friend stayed with Trevor. It never ceased to amaze her that Sarah, an intelligent and attractive woman, could settle for a life that was so appallingly second-rate. Whenever Ali had said as much to her, her friend's reply was invariably the same: 'You're too judgemental, Ali. You refuse to open your eyes to Trevor's good points, you choose only to see his faults, of which you and I both have our own fair share.'

Ali had once admitted to Elliot that she'd never forgiven Sarah for marrying Trevor. 'But, Ali,' he'd said, 'we can't dictate to others how we think they should live their lives. And have you ever considered the possibility that Sarah loves Trevor?'

How anybody could love Trevor was a mystery to Ali. A complete and utter mystery.

8

There was silence. The stony variety that was as portentous as the look on Trevor's face – a face that Ali saw as a cold, unappetising collation of thin, pale lips, beaky nose and beady eyes, which peered at the world through a permanently furrowed brow, an excess of facial fuzz, and seventies-student collar-length hair, which was showing its age by thinning and greying. It was Christmas Eve and Trevor had just raised the inevitable subject of Ali joining the Donovan family at church for the midnight service; he was waiting for her response.

She had only been at Smithy Cottage for two hours but already he was threatening her resolve to be nice to him – made for Sarah's sake. Nothing provoked her more than his supercilious manner; it worked on her with the speed of a class A amphetamine, coursing through her blood and heading straight for her brain where it triggered the desire to shoot down in flames whatever he uttered. When he'd opened the door to her on her arrival, the first thing he'd said was, 'Now, Ali, I know what an independent little soul you are, so what's it to be? Do I help you with your luggage, or do I let you struggle in with it?' She would have preferred a third option, that of her beating him round the head with it. And, not content with patronising her, he went on to lecture and bore her on a subject that was currently close to his heart. 'What I want to know,' he pondered, to nobody in particular as they sat down to eat, 'is why today's clergy are so anti the Devil? There's a modern theory that the Devil doesn't exist, but he most certainly does and the sooner we pin the tail on the donkey and face up to him, the better we'll all be. Why be so wet and talk in terms of shadows and darkness when what we're really dealing with is a very real personification of evil?'

'I couldn't agree more, Trevor,' Ali had said, giving him an ingenuous smile. 'You give me the pin and I'll gladly stick it where it belongs.'

Hannah had sniggered into her glass of orange juice and Sarah had shot them both a behave-yourself-or-I'll-send-you-to-your-room glance across the table. But Trevor, absorbed by the sound of his own voice as he carried on to the next point in his lecture, missed her not so subtle gibe.

And now he was giving her one of his tiresome wheedling looks in the hope of tempting her to go to church. She wasn't the slightest bit tired but she faked an enormous yawn, stretched her arms above her head and said, 'Oh, Trevor, much as I'd enjoy that, I think an early night is all I'm good for.'

He cocked a deprecatory eye in her direction. She smiled back at him and, adopting the I'm-pretending-I-like-and-respect-you-but-really-I-think-you're-a-rattle-head expression she invariably used when dealing with a pernickety tax inspector, she said, 'Yes, a bath followed by an early night is just what I need.' His eye grew chilly. It was very nearly frosty. 'But only if there's enough hot water,' she added sweetly.

'I'll go and check that the immersion heater's on for you,' Hannah said, springing out of the sofa and making for the door.

'There's no need for that, Hannah,' Trevor said lightly. 'I think we'll find that Ali is having another of her little jokes at my expense.'

Perception from old Mutton-chops, thought Ali. Whatever next?

'Your auntie Ali knows full well that our Christmas Eve itinerary wouldn't be complete without going to church.' He laughed one of his mirthless chuckles.

Ali cringed, and not just because she found Trevor such a barrel of unfunny laughs: she hated being called *auntie*. It made her sound wrinkled and dry-boned. Trevor was the only one who insisted on referring to her in this inaccurate way. It was as though he was making her less of the woman she was, that by giving her this title he was taking away her true status. There was something oddly sexless about *auntie*: it had connotations of floral-scented bath cubes, powdery faces and hand-knitted cardies. Elliot had once commented that he suspected Trevor was threatened by her, and not just intellectually. He reckoned that she challenged Trevor sexually and this was his way of making her less of a threat. By turning her into a nice, safe auntie figure, he was protecting himself. Naturally she had scoffed at such a ridiculous far-fetched notion, saying that the only person Trevor was turned on by was Trevor the Almighty.

'I don't think Ali's having a joke,' Hannah said, matter-of-factly. 'I think she's trying very politely to tell you that she doesn't want to go to church tonight.'

Trevor swivelled his beady eyes from Ali to his daughter and gave another of his unamused laughs. 'Nonsense, your auntie Ali is trying one of her intellectual games on me. She loves nothing better than to tease me into a religious debate. We've been doing it for years, haven't we, Ali?' His voice was syrupy with condescension.

'Sure have, Trev.' If he was going to insist on calling her *auntie*, he could have a taste of his own medicine – she knew how he hated his name being abbreviated.

'And she knows perfectly well that we'd like nothing better than for her to accompany us to church.'

'But you're forcing her and it's wrong, Dad.'

Another tight little laugh. 'Goodness, I'd never force anyone to go to church against their will, Hannah. That wasn't how our Lord operated.'

Hannah shrugged. 'Good, so you won't be offended if I don't go tonight.'

Fair play to the girl, thought Ali, with quiet admiration.

Trevor's eyes suddenly fixed on Hannah. Gone was his syrupy tone. Now his voice was sharp and overbearing. 'Now, hold it right there, young lady—'

'No, Dad, I'm not going. And I might just as well tell you what I've wanted to say for some time. I've decided not to go to church any more. I know you won't approve, but that's how I feel.' She opened the door and left the sitting room.

Another silence ensued. It was even stonier than the one before.

Ali wondered whether Trevor would notice her sliding out of her chair and slithering across the threadbare carpet to sound the alarm that would warn Sarah there was trouble at t'mill.

From his chair beside the Christmas tree, Trevor slowly rose to his feet, his lanky, wire-thin body making the room feel claustrophobic. It always surprised Ali that he was so tall: she generally thought of him as being a small, insignificant man. He went and stood with his back to the gas fire and folded his arms across his chest. 'I sense dissension in the troops,' he said, in a low voice.

'I guess you just have to accept that Hannah's old enough to form her own opinions.'

He disregarded her comment with a loud sniff. 'She's at an impressionable age, an age when she could be easily swayed.'

A nice rip-roaring debate on the Church's dubious record of indoctrination was an appealing prospect, but Ali gritted her teeth and resisted the urge to slaughter Trevor with a no-holds-barred row. Thinking that she had probably caused enough trouble for one evening, she slipped out of her chair and went to find Sarah. She was in the kitchen listening to the radio while putting the finishing touches to the Christmas cake. Ali was about to explain what had been going on when Trevor came in and switched off the boy soprano who was giving his all to 'Silent Night' – oh, if only! – and put in his two penn'orth, implying that Ali had been the instigator of Hannah's latest act of insubordination. Ali marvelled at her friend's concentration as she apparently ignored Trevor and, with a steady hand, continued to guide the piping bag across the cake, forming a tracery of green holly leaves. She didn't look up from what she was doing until the last leaf was in place. She wiped her hands on a cloth and said, 'I'm sorry, Trevor, but you can't blame Ali for influencing Hannah. This has been on the cards for some weeks.'

He drew in his breath then exhaled slowly. 'But why is she doing this? We've done everything to ensure that this wouldn't happen.' He sounded genuinely baffled and Ali almost felt sorry for him. It couldn't be easy being a parent when you'd invested so much time and energy into mapping out your child's future and she effectively told you to shove it.

Sarah smiled kindly at him. 'You mustn't blame yourself, Trevor.'

'I wasn't going to,' he said haughtily. 'It's not me who's been encouraging her to throw away all the values we've given her.'

Ali saw Sarah flinch – this was clearly a reference to the nightclub débâcle – and any momentary sympathy she had felt for Trevor was gone. She opened her mouth to stick up for Sarah, but changed her mind when she saw the pleading look on her friend's face. Oh, hell, she thought, and for the sake of damage limitation, she said, 'So, what time's kick-off at St Cuth's? I think I might join you, after all.'

Grateful eyes rested on her, as did a cold, unforgiving pair, the like of which she'd only ever seen in a fish shop.

Ali didn't know how Sarah had persuaded Hannah to don her coat and accompany them in the biting cold for the short walk along the lane to Astley Hope's small sandstone church, but as they leaned into the wind in the amber glow of the street lamps, she was full of admiration for her. But, then, she'd always admired Sarah, right from the beginning of their friendship. They'd met in the playground at junior school when Sarah had come to her rescue. In compensating for her lack of stature, Ali had spent a good deal of her childhood being a real pain in the backside by continually trying to prove herself, especially with her older brother, Alastair. She was always getting herself into scrapes with her peers, boasting that she could outrun, outjump and generally outclass them in anything and everything. On this occasion she had taken on Caroline 'Woof-Woof' Rothwell whose authority was never challenged on account of her being the biggest and most spiteful girl in the school. She was a year older than Ali and that day she hadn't taken kindly to Ali's boasting that she could outrun her and had decided to teach her a lesson. Sarah had come across Ali as Woof-Woof was sitting on top of her forcing her to eat handfuls of grass. Very quietly, Sarah had asked Woof-Woof what she thought she was doing. When she didn't get a reply she had knelt on the ground and stared thoughtfully at the older girl as she continued to stuff grass into Ali's mouth. 'I really don't think you should be doing that,' she'd said. 'She doesn't look as if she's enjoying it.' There had been something so grown-up in the way Sarah had uttered the words that Woof-Woof had stopped and raised her eyes to see who was speaking. It was all the breathing space Ali had needed. Immediately she was on her feet, lip curled, fists raised, her blood well and truly up. But the moment had been defused and Woof-Woof had sauntered away.

For a few seconds Ali had been at a loss as to what to say. It annoyed her that she hadn't been allowed to fight her own battle, she wasn't used to relying on other people for help, and certainly not a girl who was smaller than herself and whom she didn't even know.

'So what's your name?' she asked reluctantly, spitting blades of grass out of her mouth.

'Sarah. What's yours?'

'Alison, but I prefer Ali.'

A few awkward seconds passed. Ali spent the time dusting herself down and running a finger inside her mouth to check for any damage. She hoped that this strange, quiet girl with her enviable head of long dark hair would leave her alone. When she realised that the girl had no intention of moving, she said, 'I didn't need any help just then. I was waiting to catch her off-guard.' Her ungrateful words were met with a smile. A smile that, even at the age of ten, Ali recognised as knowing. It was the way her mother looked at her sometimes. 'How come I haven't seen you here before?' she asked.

'I'm new. This is my first day.'

This piece of information further irritated Ali and, taking in the pristine uniform, she said, 'Do you normally go poking your nose into other people's business on your first day in a new school?'

She shook her head.

Ali frowned. She couldn't make out this girl. She wouldn't make any friends if she carried on being so quiet. She'd probably get picked on. Which meant she would need an eye keeping on her. If Woof-Woof Rothwell decided to come looking for her, she wouldn't stand a chance. 'Tell you what,' she said, 'seeing as you're new, why don't you stick around me, just until you've got the hang of the place?'

Sarah smiled that annoying knowing smile again. 'You mean you could be my guardian angel?'

'Something like that, yes.'

It wasn't until she was a lot older that Ali realised the irony of her friend's words. For ever since that day Sarah had been *her* guardian angel. In her quiet, undemonstrative way she'd always been there for Ali. With her extraordinary gift for defusing moments of cliff-hanging drama – just as she had tonight – she was exactly the friend Ali needed by her side. While she was hot-tempered and impetuous and would incite Armageddon if she thought it would help her cause, Sarah was loving and gentle, patience personified.

It wasn't a big turn-out at St Cuthbert's, and when heads were lowered in prayer, Ali glanced along the Victorian pew towards Trevor. He was the only one in their row who was kneeling, and with his forehead resting on his clasped hands in front of him she was pretty damn sure she was witnessing an excess of reverential zeal. He was red-hot on the liturgy as well and at times raced ahead of the young rector, who seemed to lose the plot every now and then. Poor bloke, thought Ali, as she watched him mumbling his words into his robed chest. He looked washed out with tiredness and was probably sick of the whole concept of Christmas. Trevor, though, was positively getting off on it. Without once referring to his prayer sheet his voice resonated above the mutterings of the rest of the meagre congregation. Now he was declaring himself unfit so much as to gather up the crumbs from under the Lord's table. Hah! What a joke! Trevor Donovan was one of the most swollen-headed people she knew. She didn't know anyone more puffed up with his own self-importance. She felt a nudge in her side. It was Hannah, and she was grinning at her. 'I spy with my little eye,' she whispered, 'something beginning with OG.'

'Obscene Godmother?' Ali whispered back.

'No.'

Ali looked around the church for inspiration, taking in the dried hydrangea flower heads that had been sprayed gold and fixed to the stone pillars; the holly and ivy decorations hanging from the pulpit, and the cobbled-together Nativity scene in the side chapel. Gaining no illumination from her surroundings, she said, 'Obnoxious Gasbags?'

Hannah sniggered and shook her head.

'Opinionated Gibberish?'

'*Ssh!*' It was Trevor, taking a break from bending God's ear and giving Ali the frosty-eye treatment.

'Sorry,' she murmured to Sarah, on her immediate right, when he'd turned away, 'I'll be good from now on. I promise.'

Sarah smiled. 'Don't make promises you can't keep, Ali.'

When they let themselves into Smithy Cottage, Trevor announced that there was something he needed to do in his workshop. 'You won't mind me leaving you girls to have a late-night gossip, will you?'

'Santa's got to see if the elves have finished all the toys, has he?' Ali joked to Sarah and Hannah when they were alone.

Hannah laughed, settled herself on the chair nearest the boiler and warmed her back against it. She drew her long legs to her chest and wrapped her arms around them. 'Seeing as it's Christmas, Mum, any chance of a drink? I could murder a vodka and Coke.'

'And your father would murder you if he found you knocking back that stuff. Don't you think he's had enough shocks for one week?'

'Yes,' joined in Ali. 'Discovering that his precious daughter is hitting the drinks cabinet like Boris Yeltsin would send him completely over the edge. And, apart from anything else, he'd blame me and I'm in enough trouble as it is.'

'In that case I'll go to bed and sulk,' said Hannah good-humouredly. She got to her feet and kissed her mother goodnight.

She was almost out of the kitchen when Ali said, 'Hey, what do you think you're doing scooting off without kissing me?' Hannah came back and hugged her. 'And you'd better put me out of my misery with OG,' Ali added. 'What the hell was it?'

'Old Gits,' said Hannah over her shoulder, as she closed the door.

'She's getting worse,' sighed Sarah. 'Whatever shall I do with her?'

'Absolutely nothing. She's perfect, cast from the same mould as her godmother.'

Sarah raised an eyebrow. 'And would that paragon of modesty like a drink?'

'Mm ... please.'

Sarah opened the fridge and pulled out one of the bottles of Chablis Ali had brought with her. She gave it to Ali to deal with while she arranged two plates of mince pies and put them on the table.

'Home-made?' enquired Ali.

'Of course.'

'Including mincemeat?'

'Naturally.'

Ali bit into the light, buttery pastry and closed her eyes. 'Exquisite,' she said, when she'd finished the first mouthful, and opened her eyes. 'Now I know why I accepted your invitation to spend Christmas with you.'

'Which is as good a cue as any for me to ask you why—'

'No,' interrupted Ali, 'don't spoil it. Like good sex or a good bottle of wine, this pastry should be allowed to have its moment.'

But Sarah wasn't letting her off the hook so easily and, with the quickest of movements, she whipped Ali's plate away from her. 'Now,' she said firmly, 'not another morsel of hedonistic delight until you've explained to me what's going on. I want to know why you were preparing to put yourself through the misery of spending Christmas alone, why, when you're lucky enough to have the best parents in the world, you were choosing not to stay with them. What are you trying to prove to yourself, Ali?'

In the stark brightness from the overhead fluorescent striplight, Sarah's small, pensive face suddenly looked stern. Her perfectly defined eyebrows were slightly knitted and her pursed lips accentuated her elegant cheekbones; dark, determined eyes stared at Ali. 'Well?' she said, pushing back her thick, charcoal-black hair in a graceful flick of her thin wrist.

'I could ask you the same question,' Ali said defensively.

'And what's that supposed to mean?'

Ali looked away.

'Oh, come on, Ali, you can do better than that. It's not in your repertoire to turn down the opportunity to have your say.'

Ali returned her gaze. 'All right, then, I will have my say. I'm talking about Trevor, as well you know. What the hell do you think *you're* trying to prove by staying with him?'

Sarah passed Ali's plate back to her and thought how easy it was for them to slip into the routine of this familiar, but unwelcome, exchange. It was a bit like wearing a mohair sweater: it always irritated in the end. 'I know you've never taken to Trevor, but he is my husband and I'd rather you didn't speak about him in that way.'

Ali dismissed this gentle rebuke with an impatient wave of her hand. 'Oh, please, I've heard it all before. For more than eighteen years I've listened to you trotting out the same loyal line, but tell me this, does he make you happy? Does he make you laugh? Does he make you want to chew great chunks out of the mattress when you have sex? In short, Sarah, does he do it for you?'

Sarah frowned and fiddled with the service sheet that Trevor had left on the table on their return from St Cuthbert's. 'You make marriage sound so one-sided. There's more to it than what's-in-it-for-me?'

'I wasn't implying anything of the kind,' Ali said hotly. 'Marriage should be an equal partnership or it's nothing but a submission of will. No, second thoughts, make that a violation of will. But satisfy my curiosity. What is it you see in him that I don't?'

Sarah ripped the service sheet in half, then in half again and pushed it aside. She reached for her glass of wine and said, 'I don't expect you to understand this, but I've always felt sorry for Trevor. I feel that . . . I just feel that I have to protect him.'

'Protect him? From whom?'

Sarah shook her head sadly. 'From people like you, but mostly from himself.'

9

As usual, Sarah was up first on Christmas Day. She crept quietly downstairs. The house was icy cold and she switched on the boiler, silently cursing the faulty timer. She should have insisted that it was serviced in the autumn as she'd wanted and not listened to Trevor's claims that another year wouldn't do any harm. She filled the kettle, plugged it in, then opened the fridge to tackle the turkey. The sight of the lump of pale, puckered flesh squatting in the old enamel roasting-tin brought to mind the disturbing dream that had nudged her out of her sleep. She'd been dreaming of a much older Trevor: he was in bed with her, naked and fully aroused but his decrepit, loose and ill-fitting body had repelled her.

She knew what had induced the dream: it had been Ali's absurd reference to whether Trevor could make her chew chunks out of the mattress in their more intimate moments.

Trust Ali to be so graphic.

But the truth was they didn't have any intimate moments. There hadn't been any since Trevor had grown worried that Hannah might hear them. She very much doubted if things would change when Hannah left home next year to go off to college. Sarah had long accepted that, first and foremost, Trevor was a father. It was incidental that he was a husband.

She had tried to explain this to Ali last night.

'Feeling sorry for a person and wanting to protect them is no basis for a real marriage,' Ali had argued.

'It's given us a marriage that's lasted eighteen years,' Sarah had countered, 'and has provided a happy and loving environment for Hannah.'

'But at what cost?'

'Ah, well, that's the accountant in you talking.'

'Don't give me any of that, Sarah. You're my closest friend, there's no one I care about more, but ever since you married Trevor I've watched you continually sacrifice and compromise yourself to him. I just want to understand why.'

'Oh, Ali, I wish I had a pound for every one of these conversations we've had.'

'Yes, and I wish I had a pound for every time you've sidestepped the issue. You've always given me the same guff that you were attracted to Trevor because you recognised in him a similar upbringing to your own.'

'I resent the word guff. It's the truth.'

'Okay, so you both had cold, uncaring parents, and I'll go along with the theory that that might be sufficient to spark off a degree of empathy between you, but marriage?'

'There was the small matter of me being pregnant with Hannah, don't forget.'

'But you didn't have to marry him.'

'I wanted her to have stability. And that's what she's had. Trevor's been the best of fathers.'

'And what about the best of husbands?'

'It doesn't always cut both ways. I've been happy with my lot. Have you ever heard me complain?'

'No, but that's because you're a saint. Don't you ever feel the strain of being so damned good?'

Sarah had been on the verge of telling Ali never to call her a saint when the back door had opened and Trevor had joined them in the kitchen, bringing with him a blast of freezing night air. 'Still here, girls?' he'd said. 'There's no stopping you two when you get together, is there?'

Their conversation had ended then, and after they'd locked up, turned out the lights and gone to bed, Sarah had been only too aware that Ali had done her own bit of sidestepping. By attacking Trevor, she had smoothly deflected the question about her wanting to be on her own for Christmas this year.

'Morning, Sarah.' It was Ali. She plodded across the cork-tiled floor in a pair of woolly socks and her thickest winter pyjamas – she knew of old how arctic Smithy Cottage could be. She gave Sarah a hug. 'Happy Christmas. How long have you been toiling away down here?'

'Only a short while.'

'Anything I can help with? Potatoes, sprouts, cranberries, parsnips?'

'Later. For now you can make a pot of tea. The kettle's just boiled.'

While she waited for the tea to brew, Ali went over to the boiler and sat on the chair Hannah had used last night, and as Hannah had, Ali drew her knees up under her chin for extra warmth. She watched Sarah across the cramped kitchen as she chopped a large onion followed by a bunch of fresh sage. There was something intrinsically reassuring and comforting in watching somebody else cook. As a small child she had loved to sit in the big airy kitchen at Sanderling and chat to her grandmother while she worked. Physically her mother's mother had been tiny, but in character she'd been huge: spirited, intrepid, forceful and totally uncompromising. When she was little, Ali had thought there wasn't anything her grandmother couldn't do. 'I want to be like you when I grow up,' she'd told her. 'I want to be able to hold back the waves, just as you can.' It was a family joke that Grandma Hayling, as she was known, was such an indomitable character that she was called upon by the local coastguards to go down to the water's edge and keep the potentially dangerous spring tides at bay. The rest of her family now claimed that Ali's wish had been granted, that she was indeed a carbon copy of her grandmother.

It had been Grandma Hayling who, during the long summer holidays that Ali spent with her, had taught her to swim, to sail, to cook – but, more important than any of this, she had also taught Ali to set her sights on the highest of goals. 'Second best is not an option, Ali,' she had told her. 'Take second best and you'll make do with third, fourth and fifth. Then where will you be? At the bottom of the heap, that's where.' And when Sarah had joined the family trips down to Hayling Island, she also had been taken in hand.

'You look deep in thought,' Sarah said. 'Not regretting coming, are you?'

Ali laughed. 'Not yet.' She uncurled her legs and went and poured their tea. She passed her friend a Forever Friends Christmas mug, a stocking-filler present she'd bought for Sarah more years ago than she cared to recall. 'I was thinking of my grandmother,' she said. 'You were a bit scared of her at first, weren't you?'

'I was terrified of her.'

'But not as terrified as those boys who called round for us late one night. She gave them a right roasting. Do you remember?'

'Not particularly. There were too many of them. They were like driftwood – they came in on the tide each morning.'

'And went out on the evening tide, thank goodness. My ghastly brother was put in charge of keeping an eye on us in the end, wasn't he?'

'I think he rather enjoyed himself, despite having to fend off the rude comments you made in the hope that he would take offence and leave us alone. He was very sweet.'

'Get away. There was nothing sweet about my big bruv. There still isn't.'

'How is he?'

'Still languishing in Singapore, convincing people he's God's gift to the world of finance. If his Christmas card is to be believed, it looks as if he's heading for the altar.'

'After all this time?'

'Exactly.'

'And while we're on the subject of your family, and please don't think you can deflect me as you did last night, would you care to explain why you've ended up here for Christmas?'

Ali resumed her position by the boiler and cradled her hot mug in her hands. She stared into it and said, 'Everyone's made too much of my wanting to be alone. I just felt that it was time I stood on my own two feet. I didn't want people being extra nice to me just because of Isaac and the time of year it was.'

Sarah stopped what she was doing. She lifted her mug, drank from it and peered at Ali over the rim. Very softly she said, 'Why don't you want people to be nice to you?'

Ali shrugged.

'Is it because you feel you don't deserve it?'

'Whoa now, don't start going all deep and meaningful on me.'

Sarah ignored her. 'You wouldn't be the first to feel the need to punish yourself.'

Without looking at Sarah, Ali said, 'I'm not consciously punishing myself.'

'No, you don't need to. Your subconscious is doing far too good a job on its own. But you have to stop it, Ali, and stop it now before it gets out of control. Otherwise we'll be having this same conversation in ten years' time.' She smiled. 'And I really don't think you're cut out for spending too many Christmases with the Donovan household.'

'It'd be all right if it was just you and Hannah,' Ali said grumpily.

Sarah put down her mug and returned her attention to the finely chopped onion that was softening in the frying-pan on the hob. She gave it a stir and added some salt and pepper, followed by the sage. 'I ought to warn you,' she said. 'Trevor will be expecting another full turnout at church this morning.'

'What? But we were there only a few hours ago.'

'It's what we do, Ali. And I think after last night's little confrontation I'd be grateful if you didn't rock the boat too much.'

'But if Hannah doesn't want to go, she shouldn't be pressganged into it.'

'I know that and you know that, but for the sake of a peaceful Christmas, I'd rather we didn't go out of our way to annoy Trevor.'

Ali groaned and thought, It's always about Trevor. Trevor this. Trevor that. Well, Trevor could stick it up his bum.

'Ali?'

'Mm?'

'You will try, won't you?'

'On one condition.'

'It's not another question about my marriage, is it?'

'Nah, I'll just have to put that down as one of life's great mysteries. But while I have you in the hot seat, tell me what got you into all this God stuff. I've never dared to have a heart-to-heart with you about it before in case you roped me in for a quick conversion. Did it all start with you having an Audrey Hepburn crush when you were little and dreaming of being a nun?'

Sarah carefully added a bowl of breadcrumbs to the frying-pan, stirred the mixture a few times, took it off the heat and said, 'Ali, before you completely trivialise everything in my life, consider the words of that famous Quaker, William Penn: "O God, help us not to despise or oppose what we do not understand."'

'Hey, I wasn't trivialising your—'

'Yes, you were.'

'No, honestly, Sarah, it's more a matter of not having the right vocabulary. You know what we atheists are like when you God-squaddie Christians start babbling about Jesus as if he's a best pal! We get all squeamish and hot and bothered and have to resort to the language of profanity.'

Sarah smiled. And then she laughed. 'Ali Anderson, you sit here in my kitchen on Christmas morning with your barefaced creedless cheek imagining you can talk your way out of anything and everything.'

Ali smiled too. 'That's me.'

'And I want it understood that I would never take it upon myself to convert you. Anyone with an ounce of sense would leave that to God.' She returned her attention to the frying-pan and tipped its contents into a shallow Pyrex dish. Ali watched her and thought how strange it was that she had known Sarah since they were ten years old but there was so much about her that she didn't understand. Ali had never been able to get to grips with this God lark of Sarah's. As far as she was aware it had started when they were up at Oxford, and while Ali had frequently wondered what fulfilment her friend was gaining each time she visited the University Church of St Mary the Virgin in the High, she had been careful not to pry too deeply into Sarah's other life for fear of being sucked in.

Or, worse, of losing Sarah.

But she had made it her business to observe Sarah closely, watching for the first sign of a change in her, dreading the appearance of ropy sandals and a beatific expression similar to the one on the gormless face of the first-year linguist in the room next door; a starry-eyed girl who seemed to think that Jesus loved her more if she left off shaving her legs and wore an old greatcoat that stank of wet dogs. But Sarah didn't undergo some dramatic road-to-dementia experience, and whatever heavenly delight it was that she was pursuing, she kept it very private. Just as she still did. Not once had she ever inflicted her views on Ali.

Which could never be said of Trevor.

Put Trevor and religion together and what you ended up with was something similar to herpes – an annoying disorder that would never go away. When Hannah was born and Sarah had said that she wanted Ali to be godmother, Trevor had very nearly suffered a paroxysm of disgust. 'But she's an atheist,' he'd said, staring at Ali as she held the tiny two-week-old Hannah in her arms, and probably thinking that she was already tainting his daughter's pliable soul. 'What kind of spiritual guidance would she ever be able to offer?'

'Well, we'll just have to wait and see,' had been Sarah's rather oblique reply.

Watching Sarah expertly push a large dollop of sausage meat into the turkey's bottom, she said, 'So what is the deal with God, then, Sarah? How did he catch you?'

'That's sounds alarmingly like an agnostic talking, not the atheist I know and love. Are you now saying there is a God?'

'Certainly not. I'm merely trying to understand what it is that makes you believe in something you can't prove.'

'That's the whole point of faith. It's having the courage to trust in the unseen.'

'But isn't that the great universal cop-out?'

Sarah moved over to the sink and washed her hands. 'It might be, but I'm happier with it than without it.'

Trevor ran a tight ship when it came to Christmas. Breakfast was a paltry affair of a bowl of cereal – 'We don't want to eat too much and spoil our lunch, do we, girls?' – and there was to be no frenzied stocking-and-present opening until they were back from church. 'The exchanging of gifts should not be allowed to become the focus of the day,' he intoned, as he frogmarched them down to St Cuthbert's in the raw, blustery wind and rain.

'So why were the three wise men fannying around with those expensive gifts?' Ali shouted above the wind that was slapping her in the face.

He banged a big bony hand down on her shoulder and laughed one of his unfunny laughs. 'God bless you, Ali, I swear you've been put on this earth as a personal challenge for me.'

'Yeah,' she muttered under her breath, as she hurried on ahead to walk with Sarah, 'and I swear that you're the scratchy thorn in my side.'

St Cuthbert's was as exciting as it had been on their last visit, with much talk in the sermon of babies being symbols of hope and new life. Owing to the effectiveness of the sound system there was no avoiding what the rector – who at one stage in the service actually yawned – was saying, and Ali tried in vain not to think of Isaac. Sarah's hand reached out to hers and squeezed it gently. 'Soon be over,' she said. 'Hang on in there.'

Finally the service came to an end, but any hopes Ali had harboured of them making a speedy getaway were dashed by a small segment of the congregation advancing towards Trevor and Sarah to wish them a Happy Christmas.

'AHW,' whispered Hannah in Ali's ear.

'Arse Hole Wankers?' suggested Ali, out of the corner of her mouth.

Hannah laughed loudly. 'Astley Hope's Worthies, but yours is better. Much more accurate. Oh, no, I don't believe it, Dad's inviting them for tea.' She groaned. 'Ali, believe me, this'll be one Christmas you'll never forget.'

Ali suddenly looked grim. 'I've had worse, I assure you.'

Hannah's innocent young face flushed crimson. 'I'm sorry,' she said, 'I was forgetting. I'm really sorry.'

Ali recovered herself and grinned. 'Don't worry. Just help me survive the rest of the day. Do you have a house key?'

'Yes.'

'Well, then, what are we waiting for? Let's leave your mum and dad to socialise and head for home. And, I don't care what your father says, it's time to hit the booze.'

As they walked back to Smithy Cottage, leaning into the squally wind, Ali asked Hannah how the nightclub débâcle had been resolved. 'I haven't had a chance to ask your mother about it, but I guess if it had been truly horrendous she would have told me by now.'

'It sort of just fizzled out,' Hannah said, 'I was expecting Dad to really flip, but he didn't.'

'What, no stern words at all?'

'Oh, there were plenty of those.' She imitated her father's worst pulpit-preaching voice. '"How could you have lied to me? How could you have gone to such a dreadful place? How could you have got dressed up like that?" I think Mum copped more than I did, though. Poor old Mum.'

'Poor old Mum indeed.'

It wasn't long before Trevor and Sarah arrived back and found Ali attending to a green net of Brussels sprouts and Hannah surreptitiously hiding her glass of vodka on the window-sill behind the curtain. The kitchen was comfortably warm and humid with so much cooking going on: the

Christmas pudding was inside a large steamer that was gently bubbling on the hob, and coming from the oven was an appetising smell of roasting turkey. It almost felt like Christmas. So much so that Trevor appeared to lose control of himself. 'I think we might open one or two of the smaller presents,' he announced, rubbing his bony hands together in what he probably thought was an expansive gesture of festive good will to all men, but actually made him look like Uriah Heep. 'We'll save the sharing of the bigger gifts until after the Queen,' he added, just in case there was a danger of anybody getting overexcited.

Ali deliberately ignored his instructions and gave Sarah and Hannah her main presents to them. Hannah loved her black Diesel jacket and immediately tried it on. It fitted perfectly. She checked the label and said, 'Is it the real thing?'

'My life, my life, you think I'd buy you fake schmutter?'

In her delight Hannah did a little pirouette and nearly knocked over the Christmas tree. She came and hugged Ali. 'Thanks,' she said. 'It's great.'

Sarah carefully unwrapped her present and opened her eyes wide when she saw the gold chain Ali had given her. 'It's beautiful,' she said, in a small voice. Ali waited for Sarah to go all boring on her and say that it was much too expensive, that she couldn't possibly accept it, blah, blah, blah. To her relief, Sarah said no such thing. 'Help me put it on,' she said excitedly. 'I'll wear it now.' And as she admired herself in the mirror above the gas fire, Ali handed Trevor his present.

'Oh,' he said, when he saw that she'd bought him Billy Graham's autobiography. 'Thank you, Ali. You've been very thoughtful and most generous.'

Generosity had had nothing to do with it when she'd chosen Trevor's present. She'd been far more devious than that. The idea was that Billy Graham's life story would keep Trevor quiet for most of Christmas.

They sat down to eat at half past one, but though the meal was delicious, it was a sombre affair, a far cry from what Ali was used to. If she were at Sanderling with her parents, things would be very different. For a start, nobody would have been up before nine – having overindulged the night before. Her father would have staggered downstairs first and made tea for everybody. He'd have brought the tray of mugs upstairs and gone knocking on all the bedroom doors telling everyone to rendezvous in five minutes in his and Mum's room for the ceremonial stocking opening. Rubbing the sleep from her eyes, Ali would have crossed the landing and climbed into bed beside her mother, and when Dad had given the word they would have delved into their overstuffed stockings. Even when she was married and she and Elliot had taken Sam to Sanderling for Christmas, this same ritual had continued. Everyone joined in, nobody was excluded. She and her mother would sit in bed spraying themselves with their favourite perfume and munching chocolates, while the men, including Alastair if he was in the country and had honoured them with his presence, would stand around comparing socks and miniatures of malt, the latter invariably being sunk within seconds. 'It's important that we line our stomachs,' they would claim, like the silly boys they were.

It was always Dad's job to take charge in the kitchen at Christmas and every year he threw himself into the task with happy enthusiasm. Breakfast was scrambled eggs on toast with strips of Irish smoked salmon, liberally covered with coarsely ground black pepper, accompanied by a flute of perfectly chilled champagne. A round of present-opening would follow and eventually Dad, armed with a new bottle of eighteen-year-old Glenmorangie – a present from Mum – would retreat to the kitchen where he'd do battle with the beast of a turkey he would have insisted on buying. 'Unless it's big enough to stand up and look me in the eye, it's not worth having,' he'd say each year when he went along to the butcher to place his order. And on Christmas Eve when he came home with the turkey strapped into the passenger seat of his car he would proudly introduce his new friend. 'I met him at the pub,' he'd joke. 'Say hello to Fred, everyone.' By the time they sat down to eat on Christmas Day it would be late afternoon and they'd be so happily pickled that they wouldn't have noticed if Fred had appeared at the head of the table dressed in a jacket and tie with a cigar sticking out of some suitable orifice.

Ali groaned inwardly as she took in the chilly atmosphere of Smithy Cottage – or Coal Scuttle Cottage, as she often referred to it. This was definitely a far cry from what she was used to. In all the years that she had been coming here, she had never once felt comfortable. Come to think of it, she'd never even been warm. She didn't know how Sarah survived it. It was a strange house. From the outside it held great promise: white-painted walls, a slate roof, small-paned windows, a canopy porch and two chimney-pots at each gable end – it had the charming look of a classic hundred-year-old cottage. But inside, and despite Sarah's best efforts, it was charmless and characterless. There were no quaint beams, no funny little nooks and crannies, no original fireplaces, no exposed brickwork and no stripped-pine doors, just a relentless abundance of woodchip and anaglypta and uninspiring square rooms that had had their original features ripped out by the previous owners. Certainly from what she recalled of the family from whom Sarah and Trevor had bought the house, they were not the kind of people to be interested in period restoration. She remembered Sarah bringing her to have a look at the house before Trevor made an offer on it. The garden had been no better, but it was difficult now, after Sarah's green-fingered touch had transformed it, to conceive how it had formerly been a dumping-ground for wooden pallets, discarded furniture and a battered old caravan minus its roof – all of which had appealed to Astley Hope's more discerning rat population. Ali wouldn't have given the owners twopence for it, but Sarah had said, 'Ali, it's cheap, it's all we can afford. We'll do it up, gradually, when we have the money.' All credit to Sarah, she had done her best by trying to brighten the place with superficial touches of paint and cheerful fabrics, but what the house needed was a serious injection of cash to make a real difference.

And money was what they'd never had. Until, that was, Sarah's miserable old parents had popped their clogs. It still rankled with Ali that the money that had been left expressly to Sarah hadn't been used for her benefit. She had tried to advise Sarah on how best to invest or safeguard it, but it had been to no avail. Trevor had seized upon the opportunity it offered him to become a born-again down-shifter, just like that stupid man on the radio last week.

As though picking up on her thoughts, she heard Trevor saying how pleased he was these day to be out of the rat race. Helping himself to a spoonful of cranberry sauce, he said, 'We need more people brave enough to throw away the rule book as I did.' Ali knew well enough that the trick with Trevor was to let him have his say, to let him run down his battery. But the temptation to disagree with him was too great. It was all she could do to stop herself howling with derision, then taking him by the slack of his smug self-importance and booting him up the backside. 'Now, Trevor,' she said, in her silkiest voice, 'just how long do you think it would be before the entire country ground to a shuddering halt if everyone stopped what they were doing? What if every nurse and doctor in Britain decided to wave goodbye to reason and took to growing mung beans?'

'Perhaps if we all took to eating healthier stuff such as beansprouts we wouldn't need conventional doctors and nurses.'

'Hah! That's no argument. No argument at all. That's the trouble with people like you, Trevor. There's no real substance to what you say.'

'Did you know,' said Hannah, skilfully hijacking the conversation, 'that Buddha's disciples, in their search for truth, renounced all worldly goods and begged for their food, and in return people benefited from their wisdom and teaching?'

They all looked at her.

'Just thought you might like to know that,' she said reasonably.

'St Paul and the early Christians did much the same thing,' Sarah said.

'But what I find particularly interesting about Zen Buddhism,' Hannah continued, 'is that it's all about contemplation. Enlightenment comes from disciplined meditation, not from doing good, studying or—'

'You seem very well informed in all this faddish nonsense, Hannah,' Trevor interrupted, with a sharp tone.

'Trevor, please don't insult Hannah's intelligence,' said Sarah. 'Buddhism is not a fad. More turkey, anyone?'

A nice bit of Jack Daniel's-induced nirvana to get through the rest of the day would have suited Ali perfectly. But life just couldn't be that sweet. And at six o'clock that evening, her day got seriously worse.

The AHWs arrived.

Sarah had tried to warn her in advance what to expect. But it was clear within a few minutes of their arrival that she had painted a less than candid picture. They arrived as one, stood on the doorstep and sang the opening verse of 'O Come All Ye Faithful', then proceeded to stand around in the hall chit-chatting while removing their outdoor shoes and exchanging them for slippers, which they'd thoughtfully brought along in carrier bags – though one enterprising man had his stuffed into the pockets of his anorak. They seemed inordinately fond of the cold, draughty hall and in no hurry to leave it, but eventually they trickled through to the sitting room where Ali was introduced. A scary-looking overweight woman in a full flowery skirt with a drawstring waist and frilled hem-line, a large enamelled cross hanging round her neck, sidled up to Ali and, in a waft of Deep Heat fumes, asked her if she was saved.

Ali would have been less shocked if she had asked her if she was into sadomasochism. She stood staring at the woman and frisked her stunned brain for a suitable riposte. 'No, fatso, I ain't,' was not going to cut the mustard of *agape* fellowship that this cranky lot were probably into. But before she had a chance to open her mouth, Sarah tactfully said, 'Ali is partial to playing devil's advocate, Shirley. She hasn't made up her mind yet. How's your back? Any better?'

One look at the salvationist expression on the woman's face and Ali knew that Shirley wasn't interested in her back, not when there was a soul to be saved. Well, she'd have to catch her first, and with a nimble shimmy, she was across the crowded sitting room and by the door offering to put the kettle on. Hannah joined her in the kitchen. 'HB,' she said, as she watched Ali tip spoonfuls of coffee into a long row of mugs.

'Horny Beast?' replied Ali, when she'd finished.

'Nope. Happy Brethren.'

Ali put the lid back on the coffee jar and went to stand by the boiler. 'Are they as cranky as I suspect they are?'

'And some. They're thinking of forming a prayer group with Dad as their leader.'

'What's one of those when it's at home?'

'A gossip and spiritual get-together. We used to have them with our old rector, but since Gordon's been here things haven't worked in quite the same way.'

'Was it Gordon we saw last night and this morning?'

'Yep.'

'He struck me as being dead on his feet.'

'*Aha!* So this is where you're hiding.'

Both Hannah and Ali turned to see Shirley's broad-beamed figure looming in the doorway. To Ali's horror, she came straight towards her, laid a hand on her shoulder and said, 'Ali, I want you to know that I feel called by the Lord to pray for you.'

Ali looked her straight in the eye and said, 'You'll have to excuse me, but I feel called to go to the loo.'

Late that night, when Ali was in bed warming her feet on the hot-water bottle Sarah had just brought in for her, she said, 'Thank you for the quilt you made me. It's beautiful, far more imaginative and creative than the present I gave you.'

Sarah fingered the gold chain around her slender neck. She smiled. 'We each gave the other what we knew they'd appreciate most. I can't remember the last time I received anything so remotely frivolous.'

Ali stared at her friend. 'There's not been a lot of frivolity in your life, has there?'

Sarah frowned. 'There was plenty of that when I was with you at Sanderling. They were happy, carefree days and I treasure the memories.'

'That's a terribly sad thing to say.'

'No, it isn't. Now, come on, I must love you and leave you. Trevor will be wondering where I've got to.'

But as her hand reached for the door handle, Ali said, 'Sarah, those people who came here today, you won't . . . you won't ever become one of them, will you?'

'Not a hope!'

Ali looked relieved. 'You want to watch that Shirley, she's a seriously weird case.'

'Oh, don't let her worry you. She's always going up to people and saying that she's been called to pray for them. It's just something she does.'

'And it doesn't scare the hell out of you?'

'There are worse things in life than that. Now, come on, I want to go to bed. I'm shattered.'

The door closed and Ali lay back against the pillows. She could hear the wind gusting in the trees outside. She could also feel a cold draught whistling through the badly rotting window-frame above the bed. She shivered and tugged at the duvet and the patchwork quilt Sarah had made for her. She thought of the many hours her friend had patiently spent on it and, quite unexpectedly, she began to cry: for the awful life that Sarah led; for not being with her family at Christmas; for Isaac and for the break-up of her marriage. She wondered what Elliot and Sam were doing right now. She had a sudden mental picture of Sam limbo-dancing with some lithe, scantily clad exotic dancer. The thought instantly cheered her. She switched off the bedside lamp and slipped her hand under the duvet feeling for Mr Squeezy, Isaac's teddy: she always slept with him.

10

Elliot closed the door quietly behind him and followed the immaculately swept path down to the palm-fringed beach. Other than a member of the hotel staff raking the sand, it appeared that he had the immediate stretch of coastline to himself. The young black man stopped what he was doing and raised his hand. Elliot returned his greeting and set off. He was aware that he looked downright pretentious as he jogged along the soft golden sand in his running gear and sunglasses, but he didn't give a damn: there were standards to maintain and one of those was that he didn't allow himself to get like the other senior partners at work. Ali used to joke that it was only a matter of time before he became a clone of the men she despised – the fat-faced, chauvinistic lard-lumps, as she had referred to the people he now presided over as partner-in-charge.

He turned up the speed and increased the distance between him and the hotel. It wasn't long before he was beginning to feel the heat from the sun's rays, despite the early hour. He flicked at the sweat working its way into his eyes and pushed himself on. Jogging for him was the same as swimming: it was an act of self-mastery through which he could test his endurance with a ruthless, iron-willed single-mindedness. In other words, he could physically punish himself as no other person could. He occasionally played squash, but after Isaac's death he'd found the pace too sedentary and his opponents had grown thin on the ground, having tired of the silent but ferociously aggressive rallies to which he subjected them. But jogging suited him perfectly. He could run and run, until the blood pounded in his head and he was almost sick he was so breathless.

After thirty minutes he turned round and retraced his steps. When he reached the hotel he saw that, as on previous days, a row of prime waterfront sun-loungers had been claimed with beach towels. According to one of the waiters with whom Sam was now pally, it was always the wives who slipped down in their nightwear first thing in the morning to commandeer the best ones and the umbrellas.

He paused to steady his breathing, sitting on the low wall that separated the beach from the hotel pool area, and stared out to sea. He noticed a woman swimming towards the shore – so he wasn't the only one benefiting from an early start to the day. She emerged from the water, squeezing her long dark hair with each step she took. He watched her bend down to the sand and pick up a multi-coloured sarong, which she tied around her slim waist. She was an attractive woman, nearly as tall as himself with long, straight legs. He decided that she was younger than him, but not as young as Ali. When she drew level, she said, 'Happy Boxing Day. Bit different from home, isn't it?'

He politely returned the greeting and agreed.

'Have you stayed here before?' she asked.

'No.' And, conscious that he sounded curt and unforthcoming, he forced himself to ask how long she'd been at the hotel – judging from her tan, a lot longer than he and Sam had.

'This is our second week,' she said. 'We leave on Saturday. How about you?'

'We arrived on Sunday and leave next Sunday.'

'Too bad you can't stay another week, it's a great place to unwind. You'll have to make the most of it while you can. You're here with your father, aren't you?'

He nodded, not surprised by her question. Sam was one of the most sociable men he knew: in the short space of time that they'd been here, he had established himself on first-name terms with several of the waiters and waitresses, and was hanging out with a number of other guests, including an Irish couple from Dun Laoghaire with whom he'd played cards into the early hours of this morning after the Christmas party had ended. It wasn't beyond the realms of possibility that by now every guest at the hotel knew Sam and Elliot's life history. Not that he was accusing his father of being a gossip. He wasn't. For Sam, striking up conversation with a stranger came as naturally as breathing.

'I'm in the same situation as you,' the woman said. 'I'm here with my mother – maybe we could get them together.' When he didn't say anything, she said, 'I'm going for breakfast now. Perhaps I'll see you around.'

Sam was sitting on the balcony of their ocean-view suite when Elliot let himself in. He was washed, shaved and dressed in a pair of Bermuda shorts with an open-necked shirt. He was reading a Dick Francis novel but hadn't got very far with it – unlike Elliot who was already on his second book.

'Who's the piece with the legs and sarong?' he asked casually, without raising his eyes.

'I've no idea,' Elliot answered, 'but I should watch out, she's got plans to hitch you up with Mother.'

Sam lowered his book. 'What kind of *mother*? The Sophia Loren variety or Vera Duckworth?'

'Not a clue, but I'm sure you'll find out soon enough. I'm going to have a shower.' He stripped off his sweat-stained T-shirt and slung it over his shoulder.

'Yes, please do. I was wondering what the awful pong was. But don't be ages, breakfast beckons.'

'Go on ahead, if you want.'

'You don't mind?'

'Of course not. I shan't be long anyway. Ten minutes at most. Time for you to suss out *Mother*.'

*

In the open-air restaurant, and without Elliot's killjoy, scrutinising eye watching over him, Sam helped himself to four spicy sausages, a few rashers of crispy bacon, a couple of eggs and some fried plantain. He loved these buffet breakfasts: they really set a man up for the day. He knew the Boy Wonder meant well with all his talk of fresh vegetables and white meat, but he'd got this far eating the way he did, and was still as fit as a butcher's dog, so he might as well risk it a bit longer. He poured himself a glass of pineapple juice, exchanged a few good mornings with some of the other guests, then took his plate to their usual table overlooking one of the hotel pools with the twinkling sea beyond. The tape of calypso carols was on again and, to the sound of 'Joy to the World' hammered out on a steel drum, he settled into the comfortably padded wicker chair and made a start on his breakfast. He chewed a mouthful of sausage with relish and took in the view. It was one hell of a spot that Elliot had chosen for them, one hell of a spot. A grand way to spend Christmas, if you wanted to get away from all that tradition and convention. It was certainly a million miles from any Christmas he'd ever known.

He smiled and wondered what dear old Connie would have made of all this. 'Sam,' she would have said, 'pull your stomach in and behave yourself. You're with the smart set now.'

Poor Connie, she'd never felt comfortable with anyone who didn't have the same broad Yorkshire accent as herself.

Other than the Boy Wonder, of course.

Strange, but even from when he was a young lad, his accent had been softer, less noticeable than his mates'. They'd jeered at him for it initially, but after he'd given them a damn good pasting they'd seen the sense in leaving him alone. Connie hadn't approved of the fights Elliot got himself into – which he always won – but Sam had backed his son, saying that sometimes it was the only way.

It was when Elliot was three that they gained an inkling that their only child was loft-extension bright. He was already able to read and soon his head was permanently stuck in any book he could lay his hands on. They had next to no money in those days and couldn't afford to keep him in reading matter, so Connie took him religiously to the library every Saturday morning. By the age of seven he was reading Tolkien and by the time he was nine he'd done with the children's section and was bringing home Charles Dickens. It was one of the women Connie cleaned for who suggested that Elliot should sit the entrance exam for Bradford Grammar. She and Sam had refused to give the suggestion so much as an inch of house room, knowing that they couldn't afford the fees, but when his teachers started making encouraging noises about Elliot being scholarship material, they thought it was worth a try. To this day, Sam could still see Connie's face when she opened that letter from the headmaster to say they were offering Elliot a place. And not just any old place: he'd got a full scholarship. Connie's heart had been near to bursting with pride and she had spent the rest of the day crying. But that night she paced the bedroom floor, wringing her hands, chewing her lip. 'What's up?' he'd said. 'The boy's done it, he's got himself in, just as we hoped he would.'

'Yes, but now he might stop loving us. He might think we're not good enough for him. Oh, Sam, what've we done?'

'There's just no damn pleasing some folk,' he'd said. He'd pulled her into bed and held her tightly, knowing all too well what she'd been agonising over: he'd been doing the same, worrying himself sick for weeks that Elliot would grow away from them, that he'd be educated out of their lives.

But worst fears seldom happen and Elliot didn't change. He remained the same, quiet, introspective and considerate lad he'd always been, gliding effortlessly through the next seven years of school, before going on to Oxford to study economics and surprising no one when he left with a first. Yep, as the football pundits would say, 'The boy done good.'

It was a shame that Connie had never seen the success Elliot had made of himself. Or, for that matter, the success that Sam had made of his own life. He sometimes felt guilty that she had only ever known the tough, lean times. She hadn't lived long enough to see his building business prosper. Even he had been astonished when he retired a few years ago and realised the extent of his ill-gotten gains. Back in the early eighties, and as a sideline to his main business, he'd dabbled in doing up dilapidated terraced houses in Leeds and, instead of selling them on for a quick, easy buck, he'd let them. It proved to be a lucrative venture and one that he enjoyed. He quickly acquired a reputation as a fair-minded landlord who cared about the quality of his properties as much as he cared about the tenants who occupied them. They were mostly young students and found him a refreshing change from the usual cowboy rent collectors. He'd kept on a few houses, just to keep his eye in, but the bulk of his business was now sold and he was reaping the rewards of a lifetime's hard graft. He was determined to bloody well enjoy himself. No point in having a bit of brass and not enjoying it, now, was there?

'How are you this morning, Sam?'

He turned and looked up into the smiling face of Justin, the friendly young waiter who always made sure that this particular table was kept free for Sam and Elliot. 'I'm doing fine, Justin, and yourself?'

'A bit out of it.'

'Late night again at some wild party or other?'

'No, man, it was a family get-together. They're always the worst.'

Sam laughed. 'Depends on the family, Justin, depends on the family.'

'So, what can I get you? Tea or coffee?'

'Tea for me, and if you can throw another bag in the pot, so much the better. I like to see a bit of colour in a brew. Elliot will probably have coffee.'

'He's sleeping in this morning?'

'No, lad. Elliot isn't one for taking it easy.'

Justin looked about himself and said, in his lazy drawl, 'Then what's he doing here, man?'

'Running away,' Sam muttered, under his breath, when Justin had left him. Running away, just as he'd been doing for the past two years.

Elliot appeared a few minutes later. He eyed his father's plate and said, 'Another gut'n'heart-buster?'

'No worries. I'll sweat the calories off later by the pool.'

Elliot tutted. 'I've told you before, Dad, calories need to be burned off.'

'Then I'd best watch myself in this heat or there'll be nowt left of me when we fly home. I ordered you coffee, by the way. Justin only brought it a few seconds ago so it'll still be good and hot.'

'Thanks. I'll go and get something to eat. Can I get you anything? Something with a hint of vitamin C?'

Sam chinked his knife against his untouched glass of pineapple juice. 'This'll do for me, lad.'

When Elliot returned with a large bowl of sliced melon, paw-paw and mango, he said, 'Any sign of *Mother*?'

Sam smiled. 'I'd forgotten all about her.' They both turned their heads and slowly glanced around the restaurant. 'Easy does it,' Sam said, 'I've spotted *Sarong*. To your right, two o'clock by the palm. I can't see if she's sitting with anyone – there's a pillar in the way.'

Elliot followed his father's directions. He raised an eyebrow.

'Does that mean she's in the Sophia Loren category?' asked Sam hopefully. 'Is she hot?'

'How can I best put this, Dad?'

Sam groaned. 'Just my luck. Are we talking Bride of Frankenstein she's had that much surgery, or tight pinky perm and the makings of a moustache?'

'See for yourself, they're coming over.'

11

Ali used to say, 'Never trust a woman with loose skin and gold shoes, especially if she's carrying a matching shoulder-bag. And, whatever you do, approach with extreme care if there's an abundance of red nails and lipstick.'

The swiftest of glances revealed to Elliot that *Mother* had scored a hat-trick and, according to Ali's brief, should be given as wide a berth as possible. But it was her hair that really did it for Elliot: he couldn't take his eyes off its staggeringly rigid auburn form as she and her daughter approached their table.

Both he and Sam rose to their feet. Introductions were made – *Mother* was Pamela and *Sarong* was Rosalind – chairs were pulled out and assertions made that the women had already had their breakfast and were in need of no further sustenance, although another cup of coffee would be nice. Sam immediately assumed the role of genial host, attracted Justin's attention and a fresh pot was fetched.

'Well, isn't this lovely?' said Pamela, curling her long fingernails round her cup and focusing her attention on Sam. 'And what a coincidence you being here with your son and me with my daughter. Have you been to this part of the world before?'

'No, this is my first time and I'm enjoying every minute of it.'

'What about you?' Rosalind asked Elliot.

'Oh, he's been around that one.' Sam laughed. 'You name it, he's been there – Tobago, St Lucia, Antigua. Ask him where he's not been.'

'That's a slight exaggeration,' Elliot murmured, 'but this is my first visit to Barbados.'

'How does it compare with Antigua?' Pamela asked. 'We're toying with the idea of going there next year.'

'Favourably,' was all he said. What else could he say? It was where he and Ali had spent their honeymoon. It had been a fortnight of unimaginable pleasure, when they had experienced nothing but the blissful self-sufficiency of their love. There had been no formal order to their days and nights: the sun and moon had simply dissolved into each other while they ate, swam, slept and made love as the mood took them. Often they would go for a moonlit swim and on one occasion, at two in the morning, they had gone for a long walk along the deserted beach. It had still been warm and the night air thick with the hum of insects and water lapping on the soft white sand. They had taken their clothes off and gone for a swim, and afterwards they'd returned to their hotel room and made love. There had never been any awkwardness between them when it came to sex, and he was a man who enjoyed taking his time over it. Ali had often teased him that he was as meticulous in bed as he was at work. 'You're the most thorough man I know,' she'd said that particular night, as he massaged her neck and shoulders in a way she loved.

'That sounds suspiciously as if you're accusing me of being boring,' he'd replied, turning her on to her back and kissing her warm salty lips. She'd smiled and said, 'No woman who's ever been to bed with you would ever accuse you of being boring. I've told you before, Elliot, you're the sexiest man on the planet ...'

It was inevitable. Sam proposed that they should all meet for lunch. Pamela accepted at once. 'What a lovely idea,' she said, hitching her gold bag on to her padded shoulder. 'Rosalind and I are going into Bridgetown on a little shopping expedition. You're welcome to join us if you wish, though I know how you boys react at the merest mention of the word shopping.'

'I think we'll leave Bridgetown in your capable hands,' Sam said. 'Elliot and I are going to take a dekko at one of the distilleries. If we've time and haven't tasted too much rum we might fit in a drive along the coast.'

She wagged a sharply pointed finger at them. 'Well, you make sure you behave yourselves.'

'Nice woman,' Sam said, when they were alone. 'Daughter's not bad either.'

Elliot eyed him warily and poured another cup of coffee. He saw a slow but predictable smile spread over Sam's face. 'Forget it,' he said. 'I'm not interested.'

'I could help. I could keep Pamela amused leaving you to have the fair Rosalind all to yourself.'

'You'd do that for me?' Elliot responded, in a voice heavy with mock gratitude.

'Come on, son. Didn't you notice the way her eyes were working you over?'

'Frankly, no, I didn't.'

'Then you're more out of touch than I thought you were. Go for it, Elliot. What harm a little holiday romance, eh?'

Elliot drained his coffee-cup and stared at the sea. He squinted against the strong sun and said, 'I told you, I'm not interested.'

Sam frowned. 'Look,' he said, his tone placatory, 'I know that the memory of Ali is powerful and she's one hell of an act to follow, but you have to look to the future. You can't go on living in the past. You've told me many times that there's no hope of you two getting together again, so you've got to start living once more. Self-containment isn't healthy if it goes on too long. Have some fun. Who knows? A bit of a fling might do you the power of good. It might just put the brakes on you running away from yourself.'

*

Elliot was furious. Bad enough that Sam was playing Cupid, but worse that his father should say he was running away from himself.

It was true, of course, and that was the real source of Elliot's anger. Nobody ever enjoyed hearing an unpalatable truth about themselves. And, like the recurrent pain of toothache, Sam's words had continually jibbed at him during the guided tour round the distillery. Not even the heady sweet smell or taste of the island's most famous rum could take the edge off the bitterness of his self-loathing.

He crunched the gears on their hired open-top Mini Moke and slammed his foot to the floor. The diminutive engine whined its disapproval at being treated like a formula-one car, but Elliot didn't care: he kept up the pressure ruthlessly and pushed the car on. Going much too fast, they sped along the narrow lane that cut through the fields of sugar-cane either side of them, the warm tropical wind whipping at their hair and faces as they headed towards Cherry Tree Hill and the east coast of the island. Having climbed higher and higher, they were now bucketing downhill, and as they veered to the left the cane was at its tallest, towering over them and reducing their visibility. Without warning, the road turned sharply to the right, then back to the left. Elliot misjudged it, lost control and, what seemed for ever, they zigzagged perilously across the dusty potholed track. Gripping the wheel with all his strength and praying that no other vehicle would appear, Elliot brought the car under control and they skidded to an abrupt, undignified stop alongside a shallow ditch.

For a few seconds neither man spoke. Sam straightened his Panama and said, 'Well, I certainly hope that's made you feel better.'

Elliot snatched off his sunglasses and raked a shaking hand through his hair. He didn't know what to say. He got out of the car and stalked away. He came to a clearing in the sugar-cane, and from his elevated vantage-point, shielding his eyes from the glare of the midday sun, he looked towards the unspoilt rugged coastline, which in places was treacherous for swimming but in others was perfect for surfing. Knowing the difference was crucial.

As was knowing the right and wrong time to be angry. Now wasn't the right time. He could so very nearly have killed his father. He shuddered at his selfish stupidity. It was reprehensible what he'd done. How many deaths did he need on his conscience? He heard footsteps behind him.

'What maddened you most?' asked Sam, when he joined him and took in the stunning view. 'That I was trying to fix you up with a good-looking woman or that I accused you of running away?'

'Neither,' lied Elliot. 'It was the thought of you and Pamela.' He couldn't bring himself to tell his father that his anger was all to do with his growing conviction that he would never break free of the past. Ali and Isaac weren't just his past, they were his present and his future, and there didn't seem to be a thing he could do to change that.

Sam took off his hat and mopped his forehead with a handkerchief from his shirt pocket. 'Don't you worry about me,' he said. 'I can handle the likes of our Pamela. She's not so bad, I've had worse.'

Slowly Elliot turned his head.

'Don't look so shocked, lad. The celibate life doesn't suit me . . . not like it does you.'

Elliot returned his gaze to the view and pushed his hands into the pockets of his shorts. 'I don't know where you've got this notion from that I enjoy living like a bloody monk.'

'Must be summat to do with the way you refuse to let go of the past and haven't done anything about finding yourself a girl—'

'So a mindless bonk is the answer, is it?' cut in Elliot. 'A quick exchange of bodily fluids and I'll be a new man?'

They fell silent. Until Sam said, 'Don't you miss it . . . you know, the sex?'

Of course I sodding well do, Elliot wanted to shout. After what I had with Ali, don't you think I bloody well miss it? But instead he said, 'Come on, it's hot standing here, we'd better get going.'

They went back to the car, and as Elliot started the engine he thought of their narrow escape from the potential clutches of death. He shook inwardly. Something had to be done. He had to get a grip on himself. He couldn't go on as he was. He said, 'Perhaps you're right, Dad. Maybe it is time for me to take a positive step towards the future.'

'Does that mean a mindless bonk with the fair Rosalind?'

He gave Sam what Ali would have called one of his inscrutable stares.

By the time they arrived back at the hotel, had washed the dusty road off themselves and were being shown to their table by Justin, Elliot had decided that if there was any chance his father was right, there would be no harm in pursuing a transient moment of sexual pleasure if it meant he could be free from the ghosts of the past.

Then, right on cue, he caught sight of Rosalind coming towards them from the other side of the restaurant.

12

A group of local lads were playing a wild and impassioned game of makeshift cricket on the water's edge, and from his seat in the thatched beach bar, Sam watched the spirited goings-on with amusement. He sucked at the straw in his rum punch and waved at the woman who came here every day to set out her stall of locally made knick-knackery. It was the tail end of the afternoon and she was packing her screen-printed T-shirts, leather sandals, bead and shell necklaces and batik sarongs into a couple of tatty cardboard boxes. Next to her was another woman, who spent each day listening to a small radio while braiding tourists' hair. She, too, was packing up to go home.

Sam ordered another drink and continued his wait for Pamela, who had gone to her room to fetch her camera – she and Rosalind were leaving the following morning and it was her last opportunity to photograph a Caribbean sunset. Just as their holiday was coming rapidly to an end, Sam was conscious of his and Elliot's return to a cold, wet England drawing ever nearer. He'd be sorry to go. He'd enjoyed himself immensely and was grateful to Elliot for arranging their trip. He could quite understand why so many guests came back year after year. At breakfast yesterday, he'd been talking to a couple who said they'd got married here five years ago and had returned every year to celebrate their anniversary. There'd been a wedding in the hotel only this morning, a big American do, the full works: the young bride done up like a meringue; the groom as pale and rigid as a corpse in his John Travolta suit, and the bridesmaids bouncing about the place knocking over flower arrangements, while the rest of the guests sweltered in the heat and guzzled champagne. After all the expense, Sam hoped that the marriage would last and, rather tactlessly, had said as much to Elliot. Poor devil. His face had dropped and he'd said, 'Just as well Ali and I insisted on a small cheapskate affair, then.'

'I'm sorry,' Sam had said, 'I didn't mean it that way. It's all the sun and rum punch – my tongue's worked itself loose.'

Thinking of Elliot now, Sam wondered how he was getting on. He and Rosalind had taken out a catamaran and so far had been gone for over three hours. 'Don't they make a nice couple?' Pamela had said archly, as they'd watched them go. 'They seem to have hit it off splendidly.' Though Sam wasn't sure that this was the case, he'd agreed politely.

Since their roadside adventure on Boxing Day, Elliot had done a fair impression of a man enjoying Rosalind's company, but Sam knew his son's heart wasn't in it. It had been difficult for him to encourage Elliot into a holiday fling when he secretly still harboured a hope – forlorn as it was – that his son and Ali could put the past behind them and make a go of things again. But Ali had been so adamant that day over lunch that even he had to admit that there was only one realistic option left on the table and that was for them all to move on.

Including Elliot.

Especially Elliot.

But Sam knew that an 'exchange of bodily fluids' was never going to be a long-term answer to Elliot's problems. At best, a dalliance would take his mind off the past for a few brief moments. And Sam should know: he'd been in a similar situation himself. Most men he knew who had been widowed or divorced had remarried as soon as possible, but after Connie's long-drawn-out battle with breast cancer, which had finally claimed her, nothing could have been further from his mind. For a while the thought of being with another woman had horrified him, but gradually he had come to view things differently, and had found himself seeking out the company of the fairer sex. There was no avoiding it: he was a man who enjoyed the physical aspect of a relationship and saw no reason to go without. But as to marriage, well, he just wasn't interested in that. The way he ran his life suited him perfectly. Admittedly it was haphazard and perhaps a little shallow, but it ticked over pleasantly enough.

But it would never suit a man like Elliot.

Elliot wasn't cut out for such a casual hit-and-miss approach to life. He didn't deal in tombola come-what-may probabilities. He dealt in blue-printed specifics. He'd never had the happy-go-lucky attitude or demeanour that could leave things to chance; his *modus operandi* was to have a goal and work tirelessly towards achieving it.

And he'd done exactly that.

With the foundations set firmly in place, he had ventured into the arena of adulthood with some pretty clear objectives in mind and, to this end, and with meticulous care, he had slowly and steadily built a superstructure of certainty around himself that was meant to be durable and invincible. By carving out the challenging career he wanted, by marrying the woman he desired and by fathering the child he'd hoped for, he must have thought that he had succeeded in masterminding his life down to the very last detail. He had left nothing to chance. All his bases had been covered.

Or so he had thought.

The events of the past two years had proved that even his meticulous approach was fallible. To have lost so much in so short a time was devastating enough, but to blame himself as well was doubly so. It didn't matter how many times Sam told Elliot that it hadn't been his fault, he wouldn't listen. Even the doctors had told him that, given the circumstances, there was nothing anyone could have done. The inquest had spelled out the same message too. But Elliot had refused to believe any of it. He'd also refused to tell anyone in any detail, especially Ali, exactly what had happened that night. 'I'm trying to protect her,' he'd said, when Sam had pressed him on the point, 'I don't want her to remember Isaac that way.

She's never to know.' While Sam had applauded Elliot for wanting to protect his wife, he wasn't so sure that it had been the right thing to do. He had tried on numerous occasions to get Elliot to tell him about those last moments with Isaac, but he wouldn't, and Sam could only wonder at what horrors he was keeping to himself.

'You look like the glummest man in the whole of the Caribbean,' said a chirpy voice. Sam looked up to see Pamela, camera in hand and pointing it in his direction.

'Sorry, love,' he said. 'How's this for you?' He put on his best cheery grin and raised his drink.

'Perfect,' she said. 'That's just how I shall remember you. Now, then, where's that sunset?'

Less than a mile away, Elliot and Rosalind were sitting on a deserted stretch of beach beneath a semi-circle of coconut trees watching the sun slowly sink.

'Thanks for this afternoon,' Rosalind said, breaking the silence that had settled on them for the past few minutes. 'I've really enjoyed myself.'

'Good,' he said, 'so have I.' To a degree it was true. Since their initial meeting he'd found Rosalind's company more agreeable than he'd expected. She was a solicitor from a large practice in Guildford and specialised in family law. 'I doubt I shall ever marry,' she'd told him over dinner last night, when they'd left Sam and Pamela to enjoy the calypso extravaganza at the hotel and had taken a taxi along the coast to St Lawrence Gap. 'I've worked for too long at the sticky end of marriage to be convinced that it could ever be a workable arrangement. I've also had the benefit of experiencing at close quarters my parents' divorce, as well as that of two of my closest friends, and it's not been a pretty sight. Monogamy doesn't stand a chance, these days.' He'd told her about his own divorce, glossing over the details. He hadn't mentioned Isaac. But, then, he rarely did.

He stared at the darkening expanse of sea, and at the sky, which was a luminous mixture of flame-red orange, lilac and inky blue where gossamer strands of cloud had formed. A small sailing-boat was inching its way across the setting sun, which was now within seconds of touching the hard line of the horizon.

'You don't talk much, do you?' he heard Rosalind say.

He caught his breath. It could have been Ali speaking – that day in his office when she'd been assigned to him to work on a big audit. It had been her first day in his department and she'd been standing next to him at his desk going through a client file. She'd paused suddenly in what she was doing and said, 'Are you always this quiet?'

'Yes,' he'd replied, amused at her candour.

She'd smiled and said, 'Good – don't ever change, it suits you.'

He turned and looked at Rosalind, her skin glowing in the reflected luminescent light from the sky. He wanted desperately to dispel the taunting memory of Ali's smiling face so he leaned across and kissed her parted lips. She didn't seem surprised and kissed him back with considerable conviction and urgency. So this is it, he thought, tilting her down on to the soft sand

and pressing his mouth against hers. This is the solution. But almost immediately he realised, with shattering disappointment, that no matter how intensely they kissed he couldn't bring himself to touch her, not as she was touching him. He forced himself to clamp a hand on her thigh and gave it an experimental squeeze. He tried to imagine that it meant something. That any second he'd feel a spark of desire for her – she was, after all, attractive and apparently willing. But as her tongue slid into his mouth he knew he had to stop what they were doing. But how, without offending her? He closed his eyes as if the answer would come to him, and suddenly – suddenly it was Ali in his arms. Instantly he relaxed. Instinctively he moved his hand, gently stroking the warm, smooth skin beneath his fingertips and slowing the pace of their kissing. He was aware of her shifting beneath him and of the change in her breathing. His own breathing had intensified and his body was miraculously alive to the explosion of desire within him. He opened his eyes to stare into Ali's face to tell her how much he loved her, to tell her that—

Horrified, he pulled away.

He didn't know what shocked him more, that his state of mind was unstable enough to have created this situation, or that he still loved Ali. Mortified he sat up and pushed both his hands through his hair.

Beside him, Rosalind righted herself. 'What is it? What's wrong?' Understandably she sounded put out.

Overcome with embarrassment, he mumbled, 'I'm sorry, I – I shouldn't have done that.'

'Oh,' she said flatly. 'Care to talk about it?'

He shook his head.

'Has this happened before, Elliot?' Her voice sounded less cool now.

Again he shook his head.

She touched his arm lightly. 'You wouldn't be the first man to find post-divorce relationships difficult to handle.'

He was about to say, 'And what the hell would you know?' when he remembered what she did for a living: she must have seen plenty of wrecks like him passing through her office.

'Perhaps you need to give yourself more time,' she said.

'Maybe there'll never be enough time,' he said bleakly.

'Do you still love her?'

He swallowed, taken aback by the perceptiveness of her question. 'I didn't think I did, but now ...' His words trailed away.

'But now you're not so sure?'

Afraid to admit, even to himself, what he might feel, he shrugged his shoulders.

'Have you tried talking to her?'

'There'd be no point. She thinks I hate her as much as she hates me.'

'Hate is such an overused word.'

'Substitute it for despise, then. It all comes down to the same thing.'

'Then prove to her she's wrong.'

He almost laughed. 'That would be fatal. Ali doesn't like to be wrong.'

'Nobody does. It's one of the many uncomfortable truths and challenges we sometimes have to face.'

He sighed. 'I feel as if we've both had enough challenges to last us several lifetimes over.'

She squeezed his arm. 'You don't strike me as a man who would give up easily on anything. Didn't you get help when you suspected your marriage was failing?'

He scooped up a handful of sun-warmed sand and let it trickle slowly through his fingers. 'No,' he murmured, 'it was too complicated for that.' It wasn't much of an explanation, but he wasn't prepared to go into any more detail. How could he expect a relative stranger to understand what he and Ali had gone through? That the hell of Isaac's death had thrust them into what he could only describe as a vortex of self-loathing, which they had systematically projected onto each other, and that the presence of a third party prodding their most raw and tender hurts would have served no helpful purpose.

'What are you like on New Year resolutions?'

He turned and looked at her. 'Sorry?'

She smiled. 'The majority of people don't stick to resolutions made in the heat of a booze-filled moment. It's something to do with loss of memory due to a hangover the next morning, which is why I like to make them when I'm stone-cold sober.' She got to her feet. 'Come on, we need some symbolism.'

He followed her to the water's edge and, in the fading light, he watched her bend down to the sand. She picked up a tiny pearly-pink shell. She handed it to him. 'When you're back at home,' she said, 'put this on the shelf in your bathroom. Then, every time you wash or shave, you'll remember the resolution you made on the beach in Barbados with a woman who, if she were given the opportunity again, wouldn't let you get away so easily.'

He raised a questioning eyebrow. 'And the resolution?'

She tutted. 'Don't play silly buggers with me, Elliot. I'm going to leave you to it while I get the boat ready. We ought to be getting back before the light goes completely.'

With all the hesitancy of a small but hopeful child making a wish, Elliot turned his face towards the vastness of the sea, closed his eyes and promised himself that some time in the coming year – he didn't know how or when – he'd try to tell Ali what she still meant to him.

13

It was late March and it was a glorious morning, the air sweet with the scent of a mild spring day. Pale sunlight washed over the rooftops of Astley Hope and cast a tenuous warmth on Sarah's face as she closed the gate of Smithy Cottage behind her. The bitterness of winter had dragged on for too long; it had been unrelentingly cold, wet and windy and it was a heartening thought that they might have seen the back of it. As she set off along the lane, listening to the symphony of birdsong, breathing in the fresh smell of soft damp earth and noticing that the leaf buds in the hawthorn hedge were fatter than when she'd last looked, Sarah was filled with a satisfying sense of well-being. She even slowed her pace to admire the rows of golden yellow daffodils that lined both sides of the road.

Four years ago, the then rector of St Cuthbert's, Christopher Llewellyn, a man of considerable energy, had instigated a campaign called 'Plant a Bulb to Light the World' – an initiative that called upon as many villagers who were physically able to get busy with a trowel. It had taken them three backbreaking weekends to work their way through the village planting hundreds of King Alfred bulbs in the verges and hedgerows, but their efforts had paid off: now, the main road through Astley Hope was not only a focal point of achievement for its inhabitants, giving them roughly four weeks of pleasure each year, but it had also featured several times on the front cover of the Easter issue of *Cheshire Life*.

As claims to fame went, it was all Astley Hope was ever going to be known for: excluding the show of daffodils, it was a remarkably uninspiring place to live. There was no real heart to the village; there was no post office or row of dressed-up little shops; no pub decorated with hanging baskets and ye olde reproduction coach lamps; not even a red-brick Victorian-built infant's school, where the sound of happy laughter could be heard from the playground.

All the village could boast was a selection of houses of varying age and architectural styles ranging from pretty white-painted double-fronted Georgian cottages to 1930s bay-windowed semis and, on the site of what had once been the village dairy, there was a medium-sized housing estate that offered a range of countrified starter homes. That was the extent of Astley Hope, so it was hardly surprising that, in the absence of anywhere better for locals to congregate and gossip, St Cuthbert's, and its shambling wooden-built church hall, was the nerve centre for anything newsworthy going on. As Sarah passed the small church and the path that led to the grey pebble-dashed rectory, which she'd always thought dauntingly austere, she wondered what terrible stories were currently doing the rounds regarding their recently departed rector.

Gordon Watkins, who had been saddled with the predecessor who'd been behind the 'Plant a Bulb' campaign, had not yet made his own mark on St Cuthbert's. Or, more precisely, he hadn't been allowed to. The few changes he had wanted to make since coming to the village back in October – such as overhauling the choir and doing away with all the genuflecting – had been met with a wall of disapproval. It didn't help either that he was such a plain-looking man or that, according to Trevor, he was a little wishy-washy on certain points of scripture. Nostalgic references to the physically robust and spiritually dynamic Christopher Llewellyn had frequently been made within Gordon's hearing. Since Christopher's departure from St Cuthbert's, when he had taken with him his splendidly organised and efficient wife and their two perfectly behaved children, he'd all but been canonised and deified by the heartbroken parishioners he'd left behind. He was a man who had served them well, they maintained, with longing smiles, despite letting them down by moving on to pastures new. Seated staunchly in the right wing fold of the Church of England, where there was little room for doubt or uncertainty, his sermons had had a pulling-no-punches style. Telling it radically how it was in an age of political correctness had surprisingly won him many friends and much support, and if his success was to be measured in bums on pews, he was on his way to being a bishop. But Sarah hadn't always been comfortable with his pulpit dogmatism, and while watching his handsome face playing to the crowd as he delivered his sermons, she had wondered quietly how he would fare if he ever had a crisis of faith.

If Astley Hope had lapped up Christopher Llewellyn and greedily asked for more, they had chewed reluctantly at Gordon Watkins, found him not to their taste and had duly spat him out. They hadn't appreciated his unclear views. Surely homosexuality was wrong? Surely women priests were wrong? And as for purporting to be a fan of that dreadful one-time Bishop of Durham, David Jenkins, well, really! Whereas Christopher had managed to accommodate the various camps within St Cuthbert's, Gordon had not. With his liberal views he had displeased both the fundamentalists as well as the old diehards of traditional Anglicanism.

Before coming to Astley Hope, Gordon's previous church had been in a tough, inner-city parish where he'd presumably tackled more things under heaven and earth than Astley's self-righteous, complacent dwellers could ever dream of. And it was probably this that had been his undoing. The poor man had had a nervous breakdown in the middle of January and, from then on, the rectory had stood empty.

As a consequence tales had been reverberating around the village that he'd been drinking himself into a state of depression.

There was talk of a woman.

There was talk of a man.

There was talk of him losing his faith.

But none of this scaremongering was true. He had simply worn himself out in his last parish. Perhaps the powers that be had thought he could recover his spiritual and physical strength by taking it easy in a cushy, well-behaved parish such as Astley Hope. What a shock he must have had when he'd realised what he was up against. The apathy, the disapproval and criticism that had met him on his arrival must have daily chipped away at his exhausted psyche. Perhaps if he had been married, and had had a wife in whom he could have confided, he might have survived. In the circumstances it was a wonder that he had lasted as long as he had. Would any of them have coped any better in his shoes?

But that was the terrible thing: nobody in the village had been inclined to picture themselves in Gordon's shoes and, though Sarah had thought he looked more and more tired each time she saw him, she was ashamed to admit that she had been too preoccupied with her own life to realise what he was going through.

The sad truth was that each and every one of them had failed him.

Perhaps it was something she should mention at Audrey's coffee morning, which was where she was on her way now. Oh, to be brave enough to say, 'Where were we when our rector was all alone and suffering?' If she had real courage, she'd want to add, 'If Gordon had been the hidden face of Christ, then we all failed to carry out the faith by which we claim to live.'

Yes, that would stir them up.

She mentally rebuked herself. She really shouldn't want to sound such a discordant note. This new prayer group that Trevor had formed in January was, in his words, supposed to be a 'melodic and harmonious blend of spiritual communion and togetherness'. A petulant, dissenting voice was not what was needed.

But it was so difficult to be in full accord with what Trevor believed in: he was so inclined to get overexcited about these things. 'In the absence of a rector, there's the danger that our church could run dry of its vital spiritual water,' he'd said, on the day Gordon had left St Cuthbert's to cope with its period of interregnum, 'so what we need is a hands-on working prayer group.' And after the tiny fledgling group had met in its new official capacity in their sitting room at Smithy Cottage, he'd said, 'It's as if it's meant to be. Who's to say where the Holy Spirit is leading us?'

Who indeed?

And while Trevor had talked enthusiastically about the semantics of timing and the potential power the group could generate in the name of the Lord, a faint warning voice in Sarah's head whispered that Trevor was taking advantage of a situation. She suspected that, while the hierarchy of the Church of England went through the laborious process of finding them a new rector, he would steal his own little bit of limelight while he could. Without a permanent steady hand at the helm of St Cuthbert's, Trevor was employing his own – and he was enjoying every second of it.

Though he had never said as much, Sarah knew that it had always irked Trevor that he hadn't been able to play a key role in the running of the parish. The chosen few on the PCC were a body of men and women whom Trevor described as the Sunday Socialites, who viewed the taking of sacraments as an extension to their golf-club membership and expected to be able to run their village church along similar lines – the more exclusive and élite the better. And while Sarah agreed with Trevor that this was wrong, she couldn't entirely go along with his theory that the PCC actively looked down its collective nose at him because he didn't know a birdie from an eagle. She didn't have the heart to tell him that it was the waving of his hands in church that had blackballed him.

But now, in the absence of a substantial figurehead at St Cuthbert's, Trevor was in his element. Having gathered together a group of misfits from the congregation, he had set himself up as their leader and was maddeningly intent on putting a spiritual spin on the everyday and exerting a worrying amount of fundamentalist muscle-power. Initially Sarah had seen the group as a bit of a hobby for Trevor, something to take his mind off losing his daughter to adulthood, but now she was worried about where it was all going and had shared her concerns with Ali.

'I warned you, girl,' Ali had said last week on the phone, 'I told you at Christmas that Trevor was only one step away from trailing clouds of his own glory. Has he decided on a name for the group, yet? I hope you told him what my suggestion was, the Slipper Gang.'

As appropriate as this name was – as a sign of fellowship respect for their hosts' carpets the members of the group were never without their slippers – Sarah hadn't mentioned it to Trevor. 'He's settled on the Disciples,' Sarah had told Ali.

'How ghastly. And are all disciples equal, with the notable exception of one being more equal than the rest?'

Sarah had now arrived at Woodside House, an unprepossessing thirties semi, the home of Audrey and Maurice Taylor. Audrey greeted Sarah with a plate of shortbread. Sarah's heart sank. She'd clean forgotten that she had offered to bring a cake for Audrey's coffee morning.

'Not to worry,' Audrey said brightly, when Sarah apologised. 'I'm sure I can rustle up something else from my storecupboard.' Sarah didn't doubt it for a minute: Audrey was one of those bracing evangelical types whose talent in the loaves and fishes department was legendary; she would have been able to cater for the Last Supper at a moment's notice. Wartime rationing was held accountable for this singular resourcefulness and she was the only person Sarah knew who still darned socks and stockings, and proudly saved her husband's worn-out Y-fronts to use as dusters.

Audrey led her through to the sitting room, where everyone was already gathered. As the female contingent of the Disciples, the usual faces were there. Squashed on the sofa was Beryl Wade, sporting her Bobby Crush haircut, with Valerie Thompson and Elaine Stewart on either side of her. Sitting in the draught of an open window, with her shoulders hunched, was Brenda Perry, who wouldn't dream of complaining that she was cold although she was shivering in her short-sleeved blouse with its Peter Pan collar. In the most comfortable chair, the furthest from the open window, was Shirley Makepeace, she of the bad back. Propped up with several cushions, she was dressed in bishop's purple – a colour that couldn't have suited her less.

'Sorry I'm late,' Sarah said, despite knowing that she wasn't and that everybody else had arrived early. They paused in their gossip and acknowledged her presence. Audrey pressed a cup of coffee into her hand and she scanned the room for an empty chair. No such luck. Being last to arrive meant she'd landed the piano stool, which was far too high for her short legs and would ensure a gruelling hour of strained calf muscles as her toes skimmed the surface of Audrey's Scotchgarded carpet.

'We were just talking about Anna,' Beryl said loudly, holding her cup out for more coffee from Audrey as she passed – Beryl was one of those infuriating people who specialised in the art of mispronunciation: she continually got Hannah's name wrong and insisted on emphasising certain words in her own annoyingly unique fashion; she drove a red Per-*jo* and she and Martin went away for weekends in their cara-*van*. 'Shirley was saying that we haven't seen her in church for some weeks. Is she busy studying?'

'Very busy,' Sarah said noncommittally.

'One should never be too busy for the Lord,' said Shirley, her countenance po-faced with piety.

But one could go off him, Sarah wanted to say. Wisely she held her tongue: a comment like that would invite Shirley to pray for her. Oh dear, she thought, I'm beginning to sound as cynical as Hannah. Since Christmas, when Hannah had told Trevor she didn't want to go to church any more, the tension between them had increased, as had the rows over free will and the dangers of indoctrination, and as usual Sarah had been the one to mediate and play peacemaker. She had persuaded Hannah that an occasional appearance at St Cuthbert's would go a long way to easing the situation, if not for Trevor's sake, or Hannah's, then for Sarah's. Perhaps it was wrong of her to manipulate her daughter's loyalty in such a crude way, but it was the best she could do in keeping the peace. Unfortunately, though, Hannah still needed to rebel and recently she'd been driving Trevor to distraction by threatening to have her nose pierced. 'And while I'm about it, I might have my belly-button done,' she'd said, revelling in the horror on his face. She was also deliberately shocking him in what she wore, and he would visibly pale when she paraded round the house in what she and Emily called their urban-chic look: a skimpy top that might have fitted her better when she was ten years old, together with a pair of combat trousers that hung off her slim hips and flaunted her enviably flat stomach. He had tried to stop her leaving the house when she was dressed like this, but it had been useless. She had met his disapproving gaze and said, 'If you won't let me go out, I won't revise for my exams, and when I've failed them I'll have to go on the dole, and to make my tedious existence worth living I'll become a heroin addict, and to feed my five-hundred-pound-a-day habit I'll be forced into a life of petty crime and prostitution, and I'll live unhappily ever after in a squat with my drug-crazed pimp. And all because you wouldn't let me go out.' Trevor had never sent Hannah to her bedroom as a punishment, and now, the first time when he wanted to do exactly that, he couldn't for fear of her openly laughing at him. Poor Trevor. He really couldn't cope with the new Hannah.

When her father wasn't around, Hannah dropped her stroppy, belligerent act and behaved quite normally. Sarah had begged her not to treat Trevor so cruelly, but Hannah had said, 'I can't help it, Mum, he makes me do it. He doesn't see that I'm grown-up. He's still treating me as if I was at primary school.'

Sarah had tried reasoning with him, but he wouldn't listen. One day when he'd lost yet another argument with Hannah he'd shouted at Sarah, 'It's all your fault! If you hadn't encouraged her to lie to me, I'd still have some hold over her. You've turned her against her own father.'

Sarah had stared at him, aghast. 'A hold over her?' she'd repeated. 'Is that how you see your relationship with Hannah?'

He'd seen his mistake and tried to bluster his way out of it. 'You know perfectly well I didn't mean it like that. You're – you're twisting my words.'

But that slip of the tongue revealed so much about Trevor. He was trying to control Hannah just as his parents had controlled him. Sarah had never met Trevor's mother and father: they had refused to have anything to do with him after he had told them that he and Sarah were getting married because she was pregnant. As strict old-style Methodists they had been appalled at their son's nefarious behaviour. 'You've let us down,' his father wrote to him. 'You've danced with the Devil. Now you must pay for the consequences.' If Sarah had felt sorry for Trevor before, her heart had ached for him after reading that letter. To be so easily discarded was a terrible thing. She had felt so responsible, but had hoped that, in time, his parents' attitude would mellow. It hadn't. They had stuck rigidly to their resolve and had died ten years ago, never having met their only grandchild. From what Trevor had told her of his upbringing, it had sounded remarkably similar to her own, the only difference being that her parents hadn't been religious. He had been an isolated child with no brothers or sisters, and he had learned from a very young age that if he was to please his parents, by doing exactly what they told him to do, he would go up in their estimation. It was the nearest to love he ever came.

Until he met her.

It was his upbringing of which Sarah continually reminded herself when she found him overbearing and unlovable.

Be patient with him, she would tell herself.

Be understanding.

Try to love him unconditionally.

Be the one to make the difference in his life.

He needs you.

But she was fast tiring of being so patient. She wasn't even sure she could go on understanding Trevor. She'd spent nearly twenty years trying to make the difference and it seemed that, so far, it had got her nowhere. She was growing ever more worried that he would exhaust her supply of patience and that, if pushed, years of tolerance might explode in her and she'd end up doing something she would regret. When her mind had first started wandering down this dangerous avenue just a few days ago, she had recalled the childhood game she and Ali used to play. It had been of Ali's grandmother's invention that the two girls should have an *alter ego*: they were called Sarah the Impudent and Ali the Angel. Ali the Angel was supposed to cool her hot-headedness, and Sarah the Impudent was supposed to develop a sense of daring boldness.

Maybe, Sarah now reflected, it was time to resurrect that second self and see if it would help, if only by amusing her and lightening the effect Trevor had on her. It would be an outlet of sorts through which she might be able to channel the rising bubble of discontent within her.

If all this wasn't enough to worry about, Sarah had become convinced that Trevor was turning to the group for the rewards he felt he wasn't getting at home. Without a doubt the Slipper Gang held his thoughts and opinions in higher regard than either she or Hannah did. In fact, if she hadn't known better, she thought a touch of hero-worship was going on. Women of a particular age invariably had a soft spot for a man with strong, unequivocal views, and Shirley's curly-haired head never tired of bobbing up and down in agreement every time Trevor opened his mouth.

Sarah finished her coffee, looked across Audrey's sitting room, and saw Shirley staring straight at her. She probably had been for some time. Oh, Lord, thought Sarah, with a sinking feeling. She's got that I've-been-called-to-pray-for-you expression on her face. 'Anyone heard how Gordon's getting on?' she asked, knowing that it was a distraction that couldn't fail. But nobody knew anything about Gordon's road to recovery and, with a cold, blatant disrespect for his welfare, they went on to discuss the series of visiting preachers that had graced St Cuthbert's since January. They then lapsed predictably into a period of reminiscence for St Christopher Llewellyn. 'Oh, if only we could be lucky enough to have another Christopher,' Elaine said, with a wistful sigh.

'I disagree,' ventured Sarah, who felt that Elaine's sigh of nostalgia had nothing to do with Christopher's pastoral skills and everything to do with menopausal desire. She also felt that if she didn't defend Gordon she would never forgive herself.

'Oh?' said Valerie, from her end of the crowded sofa. 'What do you mean, Sarah?'

'I think we should have somebody just like Gordon again,' Sarah said. Her words provoked a spontaneous lowering of cups into saucers. 'It would be interesting to see if we all repeated the mistake of showing so little concern.'

In the ensuing silence Shirley, with what Sarah thought was a pointed look in her direction, suggested that they finish the morning with a moment of prayer.

Conversing with one's Maker had always been a personal, solitary matter for Sarah. She wasn't any good at this communal let's-throw-it-to-the-crowd form of worship, but as Shirley began to mutter her way through a shopping list of demands on God's time and attention, Sarah dutifully lowered her head. A lock of her thick hair fell in front of her face and, winding it tightly around her finger, she prayed that she could find the courage to extract herself from any more of these ghastly coffee mornings, wishing with hindsight that she had given them up for Lent along with chocolate. Then, struggling with her Christian conscience, she reminded herself that not only was she meant to like these women she was supposed to love them. They mean well, she told herself. Really they do.

Even Shirley.

She squeezed her eyes shut and did her best to think nice thoughts about everybody, but it didn't work, so she let her mind roam the darkening corridors of her faith and thought how the essence of prayer should be about connecting with a better world ... and a better self. But too often, these days, she found herself on the wrong side of the fence of this better world. It was as if she was there with her face pressed against the chain links waiting for somebody to notice her.

She walked home with a heavy heart, her earlier mood of spring cheerfulness completely gone. Not even the splendour of the 'Plant-a-Bulb-to-Light-the-World' daffodils lifted her weary spirits, and as she neared Smithy Cottage she found herself unwilling to go inside. She decided to pay a call on Astley Hope's newest inhabitant. She had planned several times to visit the lady who, last week, had moved into the tiny bungalow that was the nearest house to theirs, but somehow the time had never been right.

Today it was.

She pushed open the gate and walked up the concrete path, which was cracked in places with shallow-rooted weeds growing in the fissures. The small front garden had recently been tended – the grass had just been mown, judging by the lovely sweet smell, and the flower-beds, though devoid of any colour had been carefully dug over. Sarah could see a long fat worm wriggling about in the rich soil. She reached for the doorbell and hardly had to wait before the glass-paned door was opened. She was expecting an elderly, white-haired woman – a widow, according to the couple who had sold the bungalow to move down to Cornwall – but the sight of a tall man in his late forties, dressed in an O'Neill T-shirt and faded jeans, with dried mud on the knees, made her hesitate. Her expression must have betrayed her confusion for he said, 'You're probably wanting my mother. Hang on a tick and I'll fetch her.'

A few seconds passed, then the woman of Sarah's expectations appeared in the doorway, though she wasn't as elderly as she'd imagined. Sarah explained who she was.

'In that case you must come on in,' said the lady, whose name was Grace – a name that suited her perfectly, Sarah reflected, as she took in the smooth grey hair pushed elegantly back from a face that was only finely lined and brightened by a pair of strong blue eyes, which had not faded with age. 'Callum's just finished doing the garden for me and we were about to have an early lunch. Would you care to join us?'

Sarah hovered awkwardly on the doorstep, held by the clear blue gaze, which was both sure and beguiling. 'I only meant to stop by and say hello. I didn't—'

'It won't be anything fancy, a glass of wine and a bit of bread and cheese, that's all. We thought we'd sit in the conservatory in the sun. It's such a lovely day.'

It sounded heavenly. But still Sarah hesitated.

'Don't overdo it, Mum,' Callum said, from behind his mother. 'Maybe she's got something better to do than have lunch with a couple of strangers.'

'Oh, be quiet, Callum. You'll frighten her away. Please, Sarah, won't you come in? I'd like to get to know the only person in the village who's taken the trouble to call on me.'

Sarah thought of the cold, empty house awaiting her return and of the curtains she was half way through making. She smiled back at the kind, gentle face before her and, feeling irresistibly drawn to her warm-hearted new neighbour, she gladly stepped over the threshold.

14

Sarah was working in the spare bedroom when Hannah arrived home that afternoon from school. It was impossible not to notice the smile on her daughter's face when she came in.

'Good day?' asked Sarah, switching off the sewing-machine and casting aside a swathe of expensive blue and gold Italian brocade.

'Not bad.' Hannah sighed. She went over to the small mirror above the dressing-table where Sarah kept her threads and offcuts. She pushed back her long, dark hair, so obviously inherited from her mother, and studied her face, tilting her head from side to side as if to make a thorough and impartial inspection of herself.

Suppressing the urge to laugh, Sarah said, 'So what's his name?'

Hannah turned and faced her, her cheeks suddenly a charming and delicate shade of pink. 'I don't know what you mean.'

Sarah laughed. 'From what I saw of him I'd say he was quite an attractive proposition.'

'*Mum!* Were you spying on me?'

'Of course I wasn't. I heard voices, glanced out of the window, and saw the pair of you talking at the gate. Who is he?'

Hannah came and sat on the bed. For all her supposed umbrage, Sarah could see that she was itching to talk. She felt glad that her daughter was still prepared to confide in her. 'I met him when I got off the school bus. He was lost and wandering about looking for where his grandmother's just moved to. He was supposed to be meeting his dad there.'

'Is his name Jamie?'

Hannah looked amazed. 'How did you know?'

Sarah smiled. 'Because I'm extraordinarily clever.' She told Hannah where she'd had lunch that day. 'His grandmother and father were very nice. I've offered to make some curtains for Grace. I think we'll being seeing quite a bit of each other.'

Hannah smiled too. 'I'm hoping to see quite a bit of Jamie as well. He's asked me out tonight – he's hoping to borrow his father's car and take me to the Cholmondely Arms. Is that okay?'

Sarah opened her eyes wide. 'You're asking my permission? What's happened to Little-Miss-Bolshy-You're-Doing-My-Head-In?'

'Just trying to keep you sweet.'

'More like you want me to keep your father sweet.'

'You will, though, won't you? I don't want him spoiling this.'

'So what do you want me to tell him?'

Hannah shrugged her shoulders and went back to the mirror to examine her face for spots. 'You could say I'm seeing Emily.'

'I'd sooner tell the truth.'

'But then we'll have the most awful scene. Remember, we're talking about an evening to be spent in the company of a member of the opposite sex. It'll completely freak him out.'

'And, conversely, we'll have the most awful scene if he discovers that we've lied to him again.'

Hannah seemed to consider this. Then, satisfied that no unsightly blemishes were lurking in her perfect complexion, she faced her mother and said, 'You spend your whole life protecting people, Mum. Don't you ever get tired of it?'

Yes, I do, Sarah said to herself, when Hannah had left her alone. I'm extremely tired of it.

After tea, and while Hannah was upstairs washing her hair, Sarah told Trevor that Hannah was getting ready to go out on a date. It was a scene they hadn't previously performed, but definitely one that Sarah felt she was as well rehearsed for as she'd ever be. She'd known that it was only a matter of time before this moment came and, of course, in most households this would have been an issue long since dealt with. But until now Hannah's interest in boys had restricted itself to a crude level of critical analysis; never had she shown an inclination towards singling one out for close-up scrutiny. But now she had. And Sarah couldn't help but admire her choice.

'What kind of a date?' Trevor said sharply, lowering his newspaper a couple of inches.

It was such an absurd question that, from nowhere, Sarah was seized with the mercurial and mischievous nature of her *alter ego* Sarah the Impudent who, with a frantically nodding head and a heated, vociferous voice, was urging her to say, 'Oh, you know, the sort we eat at Christmas, darling. Our daughter's going to ride off into the sunset on the back of a marzipan-stuffed one.' She banished Sarah the Impudent to her bedroom – for some uncanny reason she had not aged a dot from her original creation as a teenager. The ever-restrained Sarah wiped a damp cloth over the kitchen table and said, 'She's having an evening out with a young man she met this afternoon. He's the grandson of the woman I had lunch with.' Sarah the Impudent poked her head round her bedroom door and shouted down the stairs, 'And he probably snogs like a dream!' *Homework, young lady!*

'Precisely what do we know about this *young man*?' Trevor uttered the last two words as if he were dangling them between his thumb and forefinger and keeping them at a healthy arm's distance.

'Hardly anything,' admitted Sarah, 'but if he's anything like his father and grandmother I'd say he'll be both gentlemanly and gracious.'

'What if he's nothing like them? Supposing he's—'

'Then I suggest we cross our fingers and hope for the best.'

He gave her one of his how-can-you-be-so-flippant? stares. 'What time is he coming for Hannah?'

Sarah was suspicious. He was taking it much too calmly. Why wasn't he pacing the floor? Why wasn't he muttering about imminent exams and threatening to shackle Hannah to her desk? 'He's not calling here for Hannah,' she said. 'She's meeting him at Grace's.'

'So much for being a gentleman.' A few seconds passed. Then, after discarding the partially read newspaper, he sat back in his chair and folded his arms across his chest; he resembled a well-behaved schoolboy at the front of the class, smug in the knowledge that he alone had all the right answers. 'In that case, I'll walk down there with her and check him out.'

'Trevor, you can't do that.'

'Sarah, just because you seem to have taken leave of your senses and decided to let Hannah make every mistake possible, don't think for one minute that I'm prepared to do the same.'

Up on the landing, Sarah the Impudent had sneaked out of her bedroom again and was champing at the bit to have her say, but her thunder was stolen by Hannah's appearance in the kitchen. Sarah groaned inwardly when she saw what Hannah had elected to wear for her night out with Jamie. Did skirts really come that small? And wouldn't she freeze to death in that tiny little top? And oh, Lord, look at that those long, long legs. Where had they suddenly come from?

'I'll be off, then,' Hannah said, happily, deliberately ignoring her father's fiercely disapproving stare. She casually threw her black Diesel jacket over her shoulder.

'Not so fast,' said Trevor. He got slowly to his feet and stared at her. 'I suggest you put on the rest of your outfit, which you seem to have forgotten in your hurry, and when you've done that I'll escort you down the road and you can make the necessary introductions.'

Hannah backed away from him. She shoved her fists on to her hips and said, 'No way, Dad. No way. No way.'

'The choice is yours. It's that or nothing.' He sounded horribly distant, not at all the loving father he'd always been.

But Hannah was having none of it. She turned her back on him and headed for the hall. Trevor chased after her. 'You'll do as you're told,' he said, 'or I'll—'

She whirled round on him, her carefully made-up eyes flashing furiously. 'Or you'll what?' she challenged.

Sarah felt scared: scared for Hannah, in case Trevor hit her; scared for Trevor, because if he did raise a hand to his daughter he'd never forgive himself; and scared for herself, because goodness knows what blame would be in store for her.

For that split second while nobody said anything, Hannah opened the front door and slipped outside. Watching her retreating figure, Trevor stood inert and superfluous, as the cold evening air swept into the house like a malevolent spirit.

'You have to let her go,' Sarah said softly, as she closed the door. 'She's an adult now. You have to start treating her as one.'

He turned his head and levelled his bewildered gaze on her. For a moment Sarah thought he was going to admit that she was right. She reached out a gentle, conciliatory hand and rested it on his arm. But his whole body stiffened and he jerked away from her.

'I don't have time for this,' he snapped, 'I need to pray before the group arrives.'

The Slipper Gang was as punctual as ever and arrived together. Sarah didn't know how they did it. Did they ring round and co-ordinate their watches? 'Rendezvous will take place at twenty hundred hours. The time now is nineteen forty-three . . .'

'No, I think you'll find it's nineteen forty-five . . .'

'Sorry but according to my trusty timepiece, which is never wrong, it's exactly nineteen forty-six and thirty seconds.'

'Oh dear, the twenty-four-hour clock always confuses me, what time is it, really?'

Sarah could imagine them twitching for hours over their watches. If there was one aspect of the group that amused her it was its ability to sidetrack itself, which was probably why they were so happy for Trevor to be in charge. They needed somebody to boss them about. 'Leadership is a vital element in evangelism,' Maurice Taylor had said several weeks ago. And there was no doubting Trevor's willingness and commitment to taking command of the 'Lord's soldiers' as he sometimes called them.

As the group filtered through from the hall, outdoor shoes now exchanged for slippers, Sarah glanced at Trevor as he steered them towards their seats. He seemed impatient to get things moving. She wondered how on earth he'd managed to calm himself down after the brief but upsetting altercation with Hannah.

The power of prayer, she told herself wryly.

'Right, then,' he said loudly, when everybody was finally in place but was still intent on wasting vital minutes in chatter. He clapped his hands for good measure.

'Goodness, Trevor,' exclaimed a startled Audrey, 'you quite made me jump.'

Murmurs of agreement were voiced and quickly gave rise to a Mexican-wave of rerouted banter until Trevor held up his hands in a gesture of 'Enough'. 'Five minutes of quiet time,' he announced, 'to get us in the right frame of mind.'

It sounded as if he were putting them under starter's orders. A few seconds of shuffling and clearing of throats followed, then at last eyes were closed and minds supposedly cleared of all unnecessary trivia. Sarah's quiet times usually followed the same unnerving pattern: she'd start off confidently enough, strolling effortlessly through the sunny, buttercupped meadows of her thoughts, but very soon she'd find herself stumbling into the nettles and brambles of her criticism of Trevor and the group. She would spend the rest of the time allocated to meaningful contemplation guiltily dodging God and his thought police.

To help them clear their minds, they were meant to focus on a pertinent image and exclude all other thoughts. Sarah's image, when she bothered to use it, was Holman Hunt's famous painting *The Light of the World*. Its track record was quite good for emptying her head of its hotch-potch of confusion, but this evening, as she tried to focus on its composition, it felt worryingly as if the candle in the lantern Christ carried had been snuffed out. The details of the picture, which were normally so clear and luminous, were now dark and fuzzy. She squeezed her eyes as though to accustom herself to the shadowy darkness of the painting. But the harder she tried to focus on Hunt's figure of Christ, the more it slipped away from her until eventually it was gone.

She flicked open her eyes and checked the room to see if anybody else was having trouble concentrating. On her left Audrey and Maurice were both fully absorbed in whatever it was they had zeroed in on. Maurice's recycled Y-fronts came to Sarah's mind and she quickly moved her gaze to Trevor, who could have been in a coma he was so still and lost in thought. To his left was Martin Wade, whipcord thin and shifting uncomfortably in his seat – he was a rather silly man who believed that anything enjoyable was a sin and of the Devil, which was why he'd opted for the puritanically hard kitchen chair. His wife Beryl was more comfortably positioned, and not just because she professed to have God in her pocket, but because she was on the sofa with Elaine and Tom. And if Sarah was any judge of the angle of that slumped and slightly balding head, Tom was well on his way to dozing nicely. To Tom's left, and seated in a generously cushioned armchair, was Shirley; she was adopting her habitual eyes-closed-palms-up-for-Jesus posture. The recently resurrected Sarah the Impudent whispered in Sarah's ear, 'Hey, wouldn't it be a laugh to drop something cold and slimy into those expectant hands?' *Behave!* And sitting in front of the window were Valerie and her husband Stan. They were wearing a matching pair of whimsical puppy-dog slippers, whose canine heads were bowed, just like their owners', in a perfect composition of his-and-hers unity. And lastly, the newest and youngest – and, in Sarah's opinion, the nicest members of the group – Brenda and Dave Perry with their zip-up Bibles, which were as new and unsullied as their faith. Sarah thought they brought a much-needed breath of fresh air to the proceedings – and more often than not they grasped the wrong end of the stick. Without meaning to, they invariably punctured Trevor's pedantic, inflated views.

Sarah was about to close her eyes and see if *The Light of the World* had resumed normal service, when she noticed Brenda check her watch, then pass a Polo mint to Dave. She smiled to herself, heartened to know that she wasn't the only one struggling to concentrate.

Eventually, Trevor decided that the meter on their quiet time had run into the red, cleared his throat and began to rustle the pages of his notepad. Everyone, except Tom, looked up. Elaine gave her husband a surreptitious nudge in the ribs. 'I'm afraid I'm changing tonight's topic,' said Trevor.

Disappointed, Sarah wondered what he was up to. She'd been looking forward to discussing Gideon, that wonderful Old Testament example of a hero of faith who repeatedly dithered between relying on God's power and his own.

Trevor got to his feet and started handing round pencils and bits of A4 paper. 'We're going to play a little game,' he said. 'I want you to write your name at the top of this paper, then pass it on to your neighbour—'

'Would that be to the right or to the left, Trevor?'

'To the right, Dave.'

'So I give my piece of paper to Brenda?'

'Exactly. Now, as I was saying—'

'And Brenda gives hers to Stan?'

'Yes.'

Brenda giggled. 'It sounds like a game of consequences, doesn't it? Is there a prize?'

Trevor tugged at his beard. 'The prize is enlightenment, Brenda,' he said sternly. 'Right, then, have you all done that? Good. Now, I want you to write underneath that name and, using just the one word, describe that person.' He flashed a look in Dave's direction. 'Is that clear?'

'Clear as daylight, Trevor. You want me to think of a word that best describes Brenda.'

'No! The piece of paper you now have in your hand has Sarah's name on it, doesn't it? It's her you have to describe.'

Dave looked apologetically at Sarah. 'Whoops,' he said. 'I was about to say that you were cuddly. Not that you're not, of course, but that's for Trevor to say, isn't it, not me?'

'Please,' said an exasperated Trevor, 'can we get on? When you've done that, fold the paper so that only the name shows at the top, then pass it on and repeat the exercise until we each end up with our own piece of paper returned to us. And if everybody has done what they should have done,' he flashed another look at the Perry camp, 'we should each have a list of thirteen words that should help us to understand our own personality that little bit better. And I should point out that this only has any merit if we're all honest towards our brothers and sisters in Christ. It also helps not to read what the previous person has written.'

The game got under way.

'Resourceful' wrote Sarah for Audrey. 'Coward,' whispered Sarah the Impudent, '"Show off" is much nearer the mark. That whole Mrs Beeton act is her way of grabbing herself a slice of acclamation pie.'

For Maurice she put down 'Uninhibited'. Glory! She was thinking of those wretched underpants again.

Then it was Trevor's name on her lap. Sarah the Impudent was hurriedly bustled upstairs to her room before she had a chance to open her mouth. *And stay there this time!* Sarah tapped her pencil against her teeth and wondered what to write. She caught Trevor giving her an odd look and was panicked into writing the first risk-free word that came into her head: 'single-minded'. She hoped that hyphenated words were allowed.

So it went on. The only other person she had trouble with was Shirley.

'Misguided.'

'Deluded.'

'Weird.'

They were all possibilities.

'*Crackpot!*' yelled a voice from upstairs.

'Intense' seemed a safer bet.

'There, now,' Trevor said, when they were at last in possession of their original piece of paper. 'Read through the comments and ask for God's guidance if there's anything that particularly challenges you.'

Sarah read through her list starting from the top so that she could work out who had said what about her. Audrey's neat economical handwriting said that she was 'Thoughtful'. Well, that was fair enough. Maurice had put down 'Pensive'. Okay, so there was a theme developing here. She then read what Trevor had written.

But Trevor had cheated and had used three words to describe her: 'Disobedient lost sheep'.

She stared stricken, her mind numb with shock. Then she wanted to laugh out loud, but she knew she mustn't. A horrible realisation dawned: this whole exercise had been nothing but a cowardly and not-so-subtle way of telling her exactly what he thought of her behaviour of late. He must have been notching up all the times she had backed Hannah and not him; now he obviously meant to do something about it.

She folded the piece of paper over and over wondering how many people had seen what he'd written. She looked across the room and caught Shirley and Trevor exchanging a furtive but knowing glance. And knew that he must have confided in her at some time. 'She's going off the altar rails, Shirley,' she imagined him saying. 'Whatever shall I do with her?' 'Pray, Trevor,' she would have advised. 'Get down on your knees and pray.'

And, oh, my God, thought Sarah, that's exactly what the dreadful woman's planning on doing right now. Bad back or not, Shirley was hauling herself out of her armchair and making her way towards Sarah.

15

It was Ali's turn to make the coffee. She took Margaret's Save the Rainforest mug through to the outer office. Margaret enjoyed a reputation for believing that she was the only one who knew what was what, and to a degree it was true. She wasn't only Ali and Daniel's secretary and receptionist, she was also their link to the lurid goings-on in the rest of the building; life would be dull without her. Renting their office space from a trio of whiz-kids, who ran an impressive financial investment outfit and employed a rapidly expanding workforce, had provided Ali and Daniel with continuous soap-opera drama. It was difficult at times to keep abreast of all the dating, hating and slating that went on. But Margaret did her best to keep them informed.

She was on the phone making short work of a delivery company who for the second time in as many weeks had failed to meet its contractual promises. Glad that it wasn't a client on the receiving end of such a vitriolic barrage of abuse, Ali left Margaret's coffee for her and went back to the main office, where she found Daniel with his feet up on his desk studying a set of overhead transparencies – their visual-cum-sexual aids as he referred to them. She gave him his National Trust 'His Lordship' mug.

'What? No biscuits?' he asked.

'Sorry, I ate the last one while I was waiting for the kettle to boil. I didn't want you and Margaret fighting over it.'

'There'd have been no contest. I'd have gladly given it to her. A guy should always know when to do the honourable thing.'

Ali laughed. 'You're nothing but a big girl's blouse.'

'Nonsense. There's something very unseemly about a man and a woman tussling over the last Hob-Nob.'

'Especially when she'd make mincemeat of you.'

'There is that, I'll grant you. Now to business. Our sexual aids are looking a tad jaded. They're losing their integrity. I think we should either tart them up or start again. Any thoughts?'

Ali perched on the corner of his desk and flicked her eyes over the transparencies. 'For now, let's go for the tarting routine.'

At this stage of the year it was their relatively quiet stretch. The tax returns were all done and dusted, and while they were doing some of the straightforward planning work on their clients' files, they took advantage of the lull to promote themselves. They did this by giving a series of presentations, usually to other accountants who felt the need to brush up on expat tax issues. Ali had never intended to specialise in this area, but as a senior manager in Manchester she had been offered the chance to run a new department that was to concentrate entirely on expatriate work. An extra incentive had been thrown in: if she could really make something of the department there was every chance that soon she would join the partnership track. She had leaped at the opportunity, but as the months turned into years and she was no nearer a partnership, she realised that she'd been conned. The incentive had been nothing more than an old trick employed by the senior partners to get the most out of the lower orders, especially women, who were so keen to please and further their careers. By exploiting her ambition and keeping her nose firmly against the grindstone, and claiming at each assessment stage that the time wasn't yet right to promote her, they had got exactly what they wanted from her: an impressively turned-round department that could knock spots off most others and all without any extra effort on their part. She really shouldn't have been so surprised by their deviousness. It was widely known that this was how every male-dominated industry worked. But it still irritated her that she'd been so gullible.

On the other hand, the experience had taught her everything there was to know about expat tax and the law, and it was currently standing her in good stead for their series of forthcoming presentations. This morning they were preparing a talk for the personnel department of a large electronics company which was increasing its number of overseas secondments.

For the next couple of hours she and Daniel worked on rejigging the transparencies with the latest updated information from the Inland Revenue. 'Right, then,' said Daniel, when they were satisfied. 'How about we run through the spiel?'

Ali hated this bit. She wasn't a natural performer in the way Daniel was: she was conscious that whenever she was in front of an audience she sounded stilted and slightly aggressive, and if she allowed her nerves to get the better of her, her voice reached notes a boy treble would have been proud of. Often Daniel would signal to her to slow down and take a deep calming breath under the guise of drinking from the glass of water he made her have beside her notes.

'Do we have to?' she asked, knowing the answer Daniel would give.

He treated her to one of his headmasterly stares over the top of his glasses. 'Babe,' he said, 'you know it makes sense. It's like safe sex. Preparation is all.'

'Well, you go first, then. You need more practice than me.'

'And what colour is the sun in your world?'

'Oh, get on with it, or I'll tell Margaret that it was you who ate the last of the Hob-Nobs.'

'Bitch!'

Daniel gave an effortless performance. He was laid back, he was eloquent, he was to the point, he was funny. He was everything Ali would never be when it came to stand-up delivery.

'Damn you, Dan Divine. Why do you have to be so good?'

'To make you look terrible. Now come on. Up on your feet. Remember, body language is all.'

'I thought you said preparation was all.'

'That too. Now, for heaven's sake, don't stand like that. You resemble a woman who hasn't had a bowel movement for a fortnight. Relax, shoulders back, and give it some of the old Ali sex appeal.'

'Oh, please. Now you're being silly.'

'No, I'm not. Trust me. Sit on the corner of your desk and give me those foxy come-hither eyes.'

'I'd rather eat my own spleen.'

'And if you don't do as I say I'll personally remove it for you. Think sexy, Ali. Be provocative.'

'I can't!' she cried. 'I've forgotten how. I'm all tense.'

He threw his hands in the air. 'Honestly, the things I have to do in the name of work.' Removing his glasses, he crossed the room, grabbed Ali by the shoulders and pushed her down on to the desk. His movements were so quick and deft that she didn't have time to resist. He stared seductively into her eyes, trailed a finger over her lips and said, in his best theatrically camp voice, 'Kiss me, Hardy.'

Her body disintegrated with laughter beneath his and she tried to wriggle away from him. 'No,' he said, pinning her arms either side of her, 'you're not going anywhere until you've snogged me.'

'But you're gay, Daniel!'

He grinned wickedly. 'Then prove to me I'm not.'

As his mouth hovered over hers and their lips made contact, she decided to call his bluff and kissed him long and lingeringly. She expected him to back off, but he didn't and, to her consternation, her heart began to pound faster than it should have. Shocked, she clamped her mouth shut and turned her head. Daniel stared into her eyes and said, in a low voice, 'Darling, I don't know how to break this to you, but it's not working. I'm still gay.'

She laughed and pushed him away. 'God, you're awful – and what's more, I'm going to tell Richard what a terrible little strumpet you are.'

He struck his forehead with his hand. 'Oh, please, anything but that!'

'You're completely mad, Daniel, completely off piste. I don't know why I have anything to do with an old slapper like you.'

'It's because you love me to bits.'

'True.'

'And because I've just successfully managed to relax you.'

'Truer still.'

'Good. So get back to perching on the desk and being provocative.'

She did as he said, struck an over-the-top wanton-woman pose, hitching up her skirt and pouting. 'How am I doing, big boy?'

'Perhaps this isn't the most convenient time to call,' said a voice at the door.

It was Elliot.

Ali sprang off the desk, scattering files, pens, pencils and paperclips. Of all the people to catch her in such a mortifying position it had to be Elliot, didn't it? And just what the hell was he doing here?

After a few polite exchanges, including an explanation for what Ali had been doing – as implausible as it sounded – Daniel made himself scarce under the pretext of needing something from the printer room.

When they were alone, Ali said, 'You're looking well, Elliot.' Even though it was several months since Christmas, she could see that his week in the sun still showed: he looked fit and vaguely bronzed.

'So are you.'

'Well, then,' she said, moving away from him and tidying the mess on her desk, 'we must have nearly exhausted our supply of pleasantries. What can I do for you? Not so short on clients that you've come here to poach some of mine, have you?'

Elliot willed himself not to react to Ali's brusque offhand manner. It's habit, he told himself. Habit that she can't be nice to you. He swallowed hard and threw himself off the cliff edge. 'I wondered whether you'd have lunch with me.'

She stopped what she was doing. 'Lunch?'

'Yes. Lunch.'

'You mean, *lunch*?'

'I mean something to eat in the middle part of the day.'

She narrowed her eyes. 'When were you thinking?'

He looked at his watch. 'How about now?'

They walked the short distance to the restaurant where Ali and Sam had eaten the week before Christmas. Then the weather had been bitingly cold and the sky grey. Today it was clear and blue, and the sun was shining. A few hardy souls were pretending it was warmer than it really was and were wearing T-shirts; one young girl, sitting next to a litter bin in the square and eating from a bag of chips, was bravely displaying a pair of winter white legs.

'I've never been here before,' Elliot said, as he held open the restaurant door for Ali. 'Is the food any good?'

'Of course it is, or why else would I bother with it?'

Her words were as good as a slap in the face and he wondered why he was bothering. But then he heard her say, 'I'm sorry. That was uncalled-for.' It was a minuscule scrap of hope and perhaps all he was entitled to.

Ali watched Elliot hang up their coats on the row of hooks and waited for somebody to come and show them to a table. She was terrifyingly on edge and couldn't believe that she had actually agreed to have lunch with him. She could so easily have said no, she was too busy. Any amount of excuses would have done, but she'd stood there as though she were an idiot, nodding and saying that it would have to be quick.

They were shown to a discreet corner table, and when they were sitting opposite one another, in a familiar awkward silence, Ali felt her nerve going. 'This isn't going to work,' she said. 'Couldn't we just have a drink and leave it at that?'

'Please,' he said, 'for once, let's try and have a normal conversation.'

'But why?'

'Can we order first, then talk?'

'Sure.' Typical Elliot, she thought, further rattled by his calm detachment. How typical of him to be so systematic, so prioritised. She turned her head to her right and scanned the chalkboard menu. She quickly made her choice and switched her thoughts to why he had taken the time and trouble to turn up at her office in the way he had. Why hadn't he phoned? Probably because he knew she would have been better able to fob him off. He would have planned it precisely this way. He'd have wanted to catch her with her guard down, hoping to render her sufficiently witless to be unable to put him off.

But why had he gone to all that effort?

They ordered their meal and when they were alone again Elliot was sensitive to Ali's quick brown eyes darting nervously over him, around him – anywhere, in fact, but actually *on* him. He longed to put her at ease. He made his opening move. 'Ali, I want to apologise.'

With all the hesitancy of a butterfly landing on a flower, her gaze finally came to a quivering rest. She stared at him over the top of her glass of fizzy water. 'Really? What for?' She sounded remote. Hostile.

Good question. Where should he start? There was so much to be sorry for – they'd be here all day if he had to apologise for every wrong thing he'd done. Pinpointing the trivial seemed as good a way as any. 'I'm sorry I didn't make a better job of inviting you to spend Christmas with Dad and me.'

She shrugged. 'Given the circumstances, I thought you did pretty well. How was Barbados? Did Sam enjoy himself?'

There was a glimpse of one of Elliot's rare smiles. But it faded so fast she wondered if she'd imagined it. 'He had a great time. Even fitted in a little romance.'

'Good for him. How about you? Not that it's any of my business.'

'I was my usual boring self, head in a book mostly. How was your Christmas? Dad told me you were going to Sarah's.'

'That's right.' She picked up a roll of bread from the basket in the centre of the table and pulled it apart with her hands. She chewed on a small piece thoughtfully. If she were honest, Christmas at Coal Scuttle Cottage had been unutterably depressing, but loyalty to Sarah would never allow her to admit that.

Their food arrived, and when the waiter left them, Elliot was acutely aware that the conversation had stalled. He seized on a topic that was guaranteed to get Ali talking. 'How did you get on with Trevor when you stayed with them?'

Ali grimaced. 'As badly as ever. The man's become even more of an insufferable fool, if that's possible.'

'And how was Hannah?'

'Growing up fast. She's quite the young lady now. All set for Oxford if her exams go as planned. Brasenose has given her an offer of—' she broke off suddenly and stared blankly at her plate.

'What is it?' he asked. 'Something wrong with your meal?'

She dropped her knife and fork and reached for her napkin. She screwed it into a tight ball. 'It's no good,' she murmured, 'I can't do this. I can't sit here indulging in this mindless small talk.'

'I don't understand.' It was the wrong thing to say.

'You wouldn't,' she said, with scathing bitterness. 'You wouldn't understand how difficult it is for me to be here.'

'You think it's any easier for me?'

She looked up at him, her eyes flashing angrily. Accusingly. 'It was you who wanted this.'

Another slap in the face.

He let out his breath. Would they ever get beyond this? 'Please, Ali, I don't want to fight with you.'

'So what do you want?'

He stared at her reflectively. I want to tell you that . . . that I still love you. I want you to know that I wish we were still married, that I regret all the pain I've caused you. But he didn't say any of this. He couldn't risk that much honesty. It was too soon. There was still too much he didn't understand himself. He said, 'I want us to prove to ourselves, just once, that we can act as normal human beings having a quiet meal together.'

She frowned, unconvinced, but then very slowly, and in a rare act of acquiescence, she picked up her knife and fork.

He sighed inwardly, knowing that he'd come within an inch of being flayed alive by her anger. He'd known from that instant on the beach in Barbados with Rosalind, when he'd been made to confront what he still felt for Ali, that it wasn't going to be easy to talk to her. But this morning while he'd been shaving, and after weeks of ignoring the little pink shell he'd placed on his bathroom shelf, just as Rosalind had suggested, he had decided that today he would do something about his resolution. It had to be a spur-of-the-moment thing, he'd concluded. He would simply appear in Ali's office without warning, offer to take her out for lunch and get her to talk. It would be a start.

What he hadn't bargained on was surprising Ali to the extent that he had: the timing and manner of his appearance had seriously unnerved her, which hadn't been his intention. When he'd climbed the stairs to Ali and Daniel's office there had been no one in the small reception area, so he had decided to announce himself. On the verge of knocking at their door he'd found it slightly ajar and, for a few extraordinary seconds, he'd been treated to the sight of Ali lying temptingly across her desk. He wished now that he had the courage to tell her how fantastically desirable she'd looked.

He risked a glance at her across the table, taking in the softly layered hair, the dark eyes, the small, elegant hands and the close-fitting silvery-grey jacket that matched her short skirt, which just over an hour ago had revealed the full length of her lovely legs. At the memory of her on that desk again, he lowered his gaze lest she could read his thoughts from the expression on his face.

Up until Christmas he'd had no idea how he really felt about Ali. When Isaac had died, he had thought that every other emotion within him had also died. It had been a time of paradox: when he'd most needed the warmth of another human being, he'd made it impossible for anyone to be near him. He had wanted to be isolated. He'd wanted to feel the pain of it. To be comforted was out of the question. He didn't deserve it. And he'd gone to such lengths to punish himself, even denying himself the love of his wife.

It wasn't until he'd been lying on the beach with Rosalind and he had imagined that it was Ali in his arms that he had realised how his feelings towards Ali had changed. Instead of wanting to push away her memory, he wanted to draw it closer to him. More than anything, he wanted her back in his life. That night in the hotel in Barbados, as he'd listened to the water lapping at the sand a few yards from his room, he'd pondered on the irony that the only woman he had ever truly desired was the one who cared least for him . . . and that it was of his own doing. Nobody but he had made Ali hate him. The following day when he'd said goodbye to Rosalind as she was leaving for the airport with her mother, she'd said, 'Don't go back on your resolution, Elliot. If Ali means as much to you as I think she does, be patient with her. But, most of all, be patient with yourself.'

But it hadn't been patience that had made him wait nearly a full three months before getting in touch with Ali: it had been fear. Fear that she'd reject out of hand even the remotest possibility of there ever being some kind of friendship between them.

Determined to banish this fear, he said, 'This hasn't been so bad, has it?' He waited for her reply, searching her face for an honest, unguarded response. But her countenance remained impassive. Her eyes were distant and gave nothing away. She didn't say anything either.

'Do you think you'd risk it again?' he pushed.

'Would there be any point?' Her tone was less acerbic than it had been. Now there was a ring of finality to it.

'There might be.'

'Elliot, I think we can both be satisfied that we've made it through to the end of a meal with a full complement of limbs intact. Sam would be proud of us. But you have to realise that when I'm with you all the pain of Isaac's death comes flooding back . . . and I'm sorry, but it's too much for me to cope with. Can you understand that?'

He nodded sadly. Oh, yes, he could understand that all right. But could she understand that he'd felt exactly the same until now? Now when he looked at her, or thought of her, the worst of the pain of Isaac's death was miraculously kept at bay and, for a few precious seconds, the darkness that he had lived through showed signs of lifting.

16

Ali was a firm believer that, like shoes, houses gave away a lot about their owners and, as she lay back in the enormous, enamel clawfooted bath that took for ever to fill, she thanked Owen for his impeccable taste and for stamping it so effectively on this one particular room. The exquisite décor and characterful fittings spoke volumes of a man who clearly enjoyed dallying over his ablutions, for this was no ordinary bathroom. Owen must have had it tailor-made to suit his own special needs, which presumably extended beyond the perfunctory routine of washing and shaving.

The tiles that covered the sloping walls were predominantly white but were interspersed with a random pattern of blue and white Delft tiles – genuine handmade Delft tiles that Owen himself had chosen when he'd visited the factory on one of his working trips to Holland. Opposite the bath there was a tub-sized marble sink, above which hung a brightly lit gilt-framed mirror with an unruly bunch of chubby cherubs tumbling all over it. Either side of this was a pair of brass sconces, which were wildly and ostentatiously Gothic in their design; the floor was made of polished cherrywood and glowed with the richness of warm honey. At the head-resting end of the bath, within arm's reach, was a low-level built-in cupboard: instead of it being a discreet hidey-hole for the obligatory loo rolls and toilet brush, as one might have expected, it was a drinks cabinet. And when Owen's selection of wines and spirits had been shipped over to Brussels along with the rest of his belongings, Ali had moved in her own supply. She fancied a drink now, and leaning over the rolled edge of the cold enamel, she opened the panelled door of the cupboard and poured herself a large glass of Jack Daniel's. Then she reached for the remote control of the CD player in her adjoining bedroom and activated Bach's *Goldberg Variations*. From the two speakers on the bracketed shelf above the bath, the restrained, smoothly flowing music washed over her. She closed her eyes and began to relax.

It had been quite a day.

She cast her mind back to the morning when Daniel had kissed her.

Or was it she who had kissed him?

Well, whatever. It wasn't that they'd kissed that concerned her, it was her reaction to it. Not since before Isaac's death had she experienced that kind of physical contact and it had awakened in her something she thought she had lost.

Desire.

She knew that she wasn't sexually attracted to Daniel, or he to her. What had taken place was just a silly case of larking around, but there was no getting away from it: the feel of his lips on hers had sparked off arousal in her. She hoped he hadn't realised that and misinterpreted it. It would ruin their relationship if he thought she was lusting after him. But at least she had proved to herself that, if the right man ever came along, she needn't be frightened of not feeling anything for him. This was not something that preyed on her mind, but there had been occasions when she'd doubted she would ever feel for a man as she once had. The combination of bereavement and Elliot's rejection had knocked on the head the very thought of a sex drive. Add to that the fact that she spent the majority of her time on the edge of exhaustion – deliberately so – it was only natural that she didn't squander her energy reserves on anything as superfluous as a sexual encounter.

But now . . . well, now sex might not be such a bad idea, just in the way of recreational therapy, of course.

She took a sip of her drink and sighed. Who was she kidding? Who, this side of full-moon, wolf-howling insanity, would ever want to get entangled with an emotional wreck such as her? No. It would be a whole lot simpler if she could remain uninterested in sex; it would be far easier to be frigidly dispassionate than to try to keep the lid on a revitalised jack-in-a-box libido that would probably spring out at the most inopportune moments.

She smiled at this analogy, set down her glass on the side of the bath and reached for the phone on top of the drinks cabinet. When she had got in from work there had been a message on the answerphone. It had been from Sarah and it had worried her: her friend hadn't sounded at all as she usually did.

It was a while before she heard Sarah's voice at the other end of the line. Her suspicion that something was wrong was confirmed straight away.

'Ali,' said Sarah quietly, 'I need to come and see you.'

'Why? What's wrong?'

'I don't want to talk about it now. Can we meet for lunch?'

'Oh, Sarah, I'd love to, but it's crazy this week at work. Daniel and I are giving—'

'What about Saturday?'

'Yes, that's fine. But what's the urgency?'

'I just need someone to talk to.'

'Has something happened?'

'You could say that.'

Ali had never heard her friend so tense on the phone before. Sarah's voice was always gentle and warm, never terse and tight as it was now. 'Sarah, I know from the sound of you that it must be something serious. Can't you tell me?'

'No. Just let me come and see you.'

'Okay. But why don't you stop over? Let's make a weekend of it. We so rarely get any time to ourselves these days. Leave Hannah in charge of Trevor and stay the night. We'll get a takeaway and have a bottle of—'

'All right, I'll see what Trevor—'

'Never mind what he says, just do it.'

'Ali, please don't tell me what to do. I get enough of that from Trevor. Now, goodnight, I'll see you on Saturday, about three.'

When Sarah had rung off, Ali slipped back into the hot, fragrant water and reached for her drink. She felt curiously hurt by what Sarah had said. *Please don't tell me what to do.* It wasn't so much the words that stung her, it was the way they'd been said. Sarah, so mild-mannered – so reliably mild-mannered – had never spoken so harshly to her. What the hell was going on? Or, more to the point, what the hell had Trevor been up to?

One way or another, the day was getting stranger and stranger.

She still hadn't recovered from the shock of Elliot appearing so unexpectedly in her office. She had wanted to discuss this with Sarah and, while acknowledging how selfish she was being, she felt disappointed that she hadn't been able to offload her thoughts on to her friend.

When she had said goodbye to Elliot, she'd rushed back to the office hoping to catch Daniel before he left for his afternoon appointment with a new client – who was, of all things, a romantic novelist. Trust Daniel to acquire such a kitsch client! But she'd been too late, he'd already gone, and she'd spent the rest of the day trying to rehearse for their series of talks. She hadn't done very well, though: her thoughts had inevitably strayed from the latest changes in taxation law to Elliot. She cringed now as she recalled his face when he had seen her sprawled across her desk. Well, thank God he hadn't arrived any earlier and copped the sight of Daniel on top of her.

She shuddered and groaned out loud. Then the phone rang. It made her jump and she slopped Jack Daniel's down her neck and chest.

'Yes,' she snapped bad-temperedly into the receiver.

'I'm sorry, I must have misdialled.'

'Daniel, is that you?'

'It's me, but is it *you*, Babe?'

'Of course it's me.'

'Then why the harridan act?'

'You made me spill my drink.'

'Does that mean you should be rushing about putting clothes into cold water?'

'There's no need, I'm in the bath. What do you want?'

'All the details about your lunch with Elliot.'

'Oh, that,' she said airily, her tone suggesting that she'd all but forgotten the episode. And just to be deliberately and annoyingly obstructive she asked, 'How did you get on with Jessica Lloyd? Was she a vision in pink with a couple of fluffy pooches under each arm?'

'I shall tell her you said that. She was extremely nice. She reminded me of you, razor sharp and very much to the point.'

'And, like me, did she see right through your fatal charm?'

'Oh, to the bone I should think. She has great taste in men, by the way.'

'I know what a babe magnet you are, Dan Divine, but are you saying she tried to hit on you?'

He laughed. 'I'm saying she's got a class act of a husband. Photographs of him all over her study, including one of him—'

'Yes, all right, all right, I'm getting the message loud and clear that you thought he was a regular sex god. Don't you think of anything else?'

'Ooh-er, touchy, Madam!'

'I'm not being touchy.'

'Yes, you are. You're not cross because I kissed you this morning, are you?'

Ali gulped back the last of her drink. 'Um ... well, seeing as you've brought that up, there is something I wanted to mention in connection with—'

'Aha, you want an appraisal, do you? Well, your technique is perhaps a little rusty – you didn't quite get all the raspberry pips out of my back teeth – but on the whole, and given the dynamics of the situation, it wasn't a bad kiss. Not bad at all.'

'Daniel, you arrogant pig, stop making fun of me.'

'*Moi?*'

'Yes, you. Now, be quiet and let me speak.'

'I ought to warn you, one word of criticism about my technique and I'll never talk to you again.'

'And what a mercy that would be!'

'Are you pre-menstrual?'

'No, I'm not!'

'Then you're probably ovulating. It must be that that's making you overheat.'

'Daniel.'

'Yes?'

'Shut up. Just shut up long enough for me to say that because we kissed ... you know, in the way that we did ... well, it doesn't mean that I fancy you. I wouldn't want you to think that—'

'Ali, please, stop, you're embarrassing me.'

'I'm embarrassing myself.'

'Then quit while you're ahead. I knew precisely what was going through that pretty little head of yours when I had you pinned to the desk.'

'You did?'

'Yeah, you were thinking, Great kisser, shame it's not the right bloke.'

'Mm ... not exactly. But it'll do, you're close enough.'

There was a pause.

'Are you going to tell me about lunch with Elliot now?' asked Daniel. 'Seeing as you've led me all round the houses, down the garden path and on to the motorway of diversion in the hope that I would forget why I'd phoned you.'

Ali gave him the details. 'It was horrible,' she said. 'It was so unreal. He was trying to make me chat as if it was quite normal for us to be having lunch together. He even suggested that we do it again.'

'What did you say?'

'I told him no, that it would be too painful. Oh, Daniel, I don't want all that shallow let's-be-friends stuff, I need to try and get on with my life as if Elliot and Isaac had never been in it.'

'But, Babe, you can't pretend that you weren't married to Elliot, and you certainly can't pretend that you didn't have the most gorgeous son.'

She sighed. 'I know that. It's not that I want to forget Isaac, I don't . . . and I never will. I don't have any choice, he's still a huge part of me. But it is my choice whether I choose to be hurt by seeing Elliot.'

There was another pause.

'Daniel?'

'Ali, I'm going to ask you something so earth-shatteringly obvious you'll probably spill your drink again, so put it down. Why do you think Elliot wanted to see you today? Why do you think he asked if you'd have lunch with him some other time in the future?'

'I don't know. Perhaps he's got nothing better to do. Maybe he's bored and needs a hobby to take his mind off the dull life he leads.'

A long silence ensued.

'Say something, Daniel.'

'I'm waiting for you to say something sensible. Come on, just say the words.'

'What words?'

'Why can't you admit that the man still cares about you? And, if I'm any judge of male lust, I'd say the look on his face when he saw you on the desk with your skirt hitched half way up to your neck was a fair indication that his feelings for you run deep, as they say. But, there again, I'm gay, and what would I know about heterosexual desire?'

'That's not funny, Daniel.'

'It wasn't meant to be.'

'Oh, this is absurd.'

'Is it? Is it really? I'd say you're scared. You're scared that by seeing Elliot again and actually being mutually nice to one another it might remind you of what you once had.'

'And why would I be scared of that?'

'Because then you'd be in danger of having to admit that you were wrong to divorce him.'

17

Invariably there was a disagreement over which music they should listen to while they were in the workshop: this evening Sam had advocated *South Pacific* and Elliot had wanted one of his Leonard Cohen tapes.

Leonard Cohen was a bad sign.

Sam knew that when this particular songster flexed his vocal cords, with his unique ability to make his lyrics sound as if they were being put through the coffee grinder, things were far from good. Which was why he had stuck to his guns and insisted on an hour of inoffensive crowd-pleasing numbers to hum along with. He didn't know what was wrong with Elliot, but he'd been quieter than normal since he got in from work.

While *South Pacific* moved on to 'There is Nothing Like a Dame', Sam lovingly stroked the curvaceous wheel arch of the 1963 Morris Minor four-door saloon that he and Elliot were restoring. They'd bought it as a sad, abandoned heap of rusting metal and had been working on it whenever they could. They'd made templates out of cardboard and tin-plate for some of the repair sections, but for the really tricky structural bits they'd got hold of premanufactured parts. The welding had taken them for ever and had been the worst part, but patience and perseverance had won out. Luckily the engine had been in fine fettle, and with only eighty-five thousand on the clock, Sam reckoned it would be good for at least that again. The next big job they had lined up for Tilly – as they affectionately called the car – was to have her professionally painted. They'd tried doing it themselves: they'd bought a compressor, some primer and five litres of dove-grey paint, but because they'd been stupid enough to spray the car outside, they had ended up with the bodywork covered in hundreds of dead flies. They'd had to strip down their ruined paint job and resign themselves to handing Tilly over to a professional refinisher. That day was fast approaching: only a couple more weeks of work and Sam would arrange to take the car to the Morris Minor specialist in Flint for her final makeover.

When that was done, he and Elliot would have to find another project to work on. Ever since he could remember, the pair of them had messed around with cars. While his peers had been chasing honour and glory on the rugby pitch, Elliot – when he wasn't in his room studying or practising the piano – had been with Sam getting covered in engine oil and grease. By the age of fifteen he had known how to strip down a gearbox and could refit a disc brake calliper without too much trouble. Connie had always been on at him for messing up the Boy Wonder's clothes or, worse, his hands. 'His piano teacher would have a fit if she saw all that oil under his nails,' she'd say in horror, when they came in from the garage so filthy that she made them stand on sheets of newspaper while they washed at the kitchen sink.

Though he didn't hold out much hope of it happening, Sam harboured a very real wish that their next project might be the present he'd planned to give Elliot the Christmas Isaac had died. He'd spent months organising the surprise for his son – getting in touch with the Jaguar Enthusiasts' Club and following leads that took him all over the country until, at last, he had tracked down a viable proposition to restore: a 1964 3.8-litre E-type. The car had been kept in a cowshed for nearly twenty years by the sister of the deceased owner. As it had had nothing done to it in the way of bodged tinkering, it was a real find. More importantly, it was realistically affordable – being a true canny Yorkshireman, Sam wasn't one to be hoodwinked into parting with more money than was necessary. His intention had been that he and Elliot would work on the car and then, ultimately, they would pass it on to Isaac on his eighteenth birthday – Sam had cherished the thought that he would live long enough to see that day. It had never occurred to him that his grandson might not. Not surprisingly, neither of them had had the heart to remove the tarpaulin that, since Isaac's death, had shrouded the car. Looking to the far end of the workshop, where it now rested on bricks, ignored and unwanted, Sam told himself that sooner or later they would have to bite the bullet. If nothing else, they ought to restore it in Isaac's memory.

'Do we have to listen to this drivel?' Elliot asked, from the back of the Morris Minor where he was rubbing down the boot area. Nellie was singing in her determined voice that she was gonna wash that man right out of her hair.

'Hey, bud,' said Sam, affecting the casual air of a US Marine, 'you gotta problem you need to discuss?'

'Not particularly.'

Sam moved round to the rear of Tilly and looked down at Elliot, who was on his knees. 'You sure?' he asked.

A few seconds passed as Elliot apparently applied all his concentration to the area he was working on around the shiny chrome boot hinge. Then, without raising his eyes, he said, 'I had lunch with Ali today.'

So that was it, thought Sam. He switched off the cassette player and, rationing himself to the most restrained response he could manage, said, 'Oh, aye? How was she?'

Elliot got to his feet and wiped his hands on the legs of his overalls. 'She's well and sends her love.'

'That's good. And, um . . . how did all this come about? Did you just happen to run into each other?'

Elliot heard the painfully forced nonchalance in his father's question and decided to be straight with him. 'It was of my doing,' he said. 'I called on her this morning to ask her if she'd have lunch with me.'

Sam couldn't disguise his surprise. Or his delight. Not only had Elliot taken the initiative, but Ali had taken him up on it. 'So has a reciprocal arrangement been made, then? Will there be a return match?'

Elliot knew the conclusion Sam had instantly reached. He didn't want his father to get carried away on a wave of optimism only to have his hopes dashed, so he said, 'It turned out to be a once-only event.' He went over to the workbench and began pulling off his overalls.

'What happened?' Sam's disappointment was as conspicuous as his earlier delight. 'Oh, don't tell me, you blew it. Did you get all defensive and start patronising her? You know how she hates that.'

'I wasn't aware of being defensive or patronising. If you must know, she said it would cause her too much pain to see me again. Are you coming in now? It's getting late.'

Sam sensed that Elliot had made the assumption that he'd just terminated their conversation, but he had other ideas. He wriggled out of his tatty, oil-stained overalls, threw them on the workbench and hurried after his son, who was already switching off the fluorescent strip-lighting. When they were inside the house, washing their hands in the utility room, he said, 'So what brought on this sudden change of heart? What made you want to see Ali?'

Elliot moved away from the sink and picked up a clean towel from the folded pile of washing on top of the tumble-dryer. He looked thoughtfully at the back of his father's head. He knew that, by offering partial truths and explanations, he was being unfair to Sam, and though his natural inclination was not to take the conversation any further, he forced himself to say, 'I'd been thinking about seeing her for some time.'

Sam kept his back to Elliot. He suspected that he'd get more from him by avoiding direct eye-contact. Despite the close relationship they had, he'd never been much good at prising information out of his reserved son. Connie had sometimes managed it. Like that time when Elliot hadn't told them about the school trip to Normandy. 'I didn't fancy going,' he'd said, when they'd found out about it and asked him why he hadn't put his name down for it. In the end Connie had got him to admit that he'd been worried that they couldn't afford for him to go. Sam reached for the nailbrush behind the mixer tap and pretended that his hands needed an in-depth scrubbing session. He said, 'Some time, eh?'

Understanding exactly what his father was doing, and why, Elliot said, 'Dad, if we're going to pursue this conversation, do you think we could do it face to face and over a drink?'

The sitting room was dark, and while Sam switched on lamps and drew the curtains, Elliot poured two glasses of Scotch from the tray of decanters on the table behind the sofa. He handed Sam his crystal tumbler, but instead of sitting in the armchair opposite him, he went and sat at the piano. He lifted the lid of the baby grand and stroked the keys ruefully. He played a languid melancholy scale, then let it grow until his hands were sweeping the full length of the keyboard. He stopped abruptly and listened to the swell of notes echoing in the hush.

He rarely played, these days, and when he did it was for release. In happier times he'd played for Ali: Rachmaninov, Chopin, Haydn, Mozart. One of her favourite pieces had been the *Presto agitato* from Beethoven's *Moonlight Sonata*. 'That namby-pamby *adagio* stuff at the beginning is all very well,' she'd say provocatively, 'but it's so bloody gloomy. Give me the heart-stirring passionate bit any day. It's so sexy.' It was a game of Ali's to make out that she knew next to nothing about classical music, but it was all a front: she loved it when somebody made the fatal error of being musically pretentious. It was a mistake they never repeated. Sometimes when he played she would creep up behind him and join him on the piano stool. She would sit in rapt silence, sometimes with her eyes shut, but more usually they would be open and fixed on his hands. Often her enjoyment of the music would be a prelude to them making love. She would joke afterwards that the combination of watching his hands moving over the keys of the piano and the expression of intense concentration in his face was the fastest and most effective way to arouse her. What his long-suffering piano teacher would have thought of all those lessons serving the rather pleasurable purpose of getting the woman Elliot loved into bed was anybody's guess. Just think how much extra practice he would have put in if he'd been told as a teenager what the rewards might be!

Suddenly he closed the lid of the piano and got to his feet. He crossed the room and joined his father, and took a sip of his Scotch then told him what had led him to see Ali. He even spoke of the humiliating incident on the beach in Barbados with Rosalind. When he'd finished, Sam said, 'So what's to be done? If you still love her, don't diddle about, tell her how you feel.'

Elliot shook his head. 'But how, if she won't see me? She made it very clear that another lunch, or any similar arrangement, isn't going to take place. And don't suggest that I write to her. It wouldn't work – I'd never get the right words down on paper.'

'Do you want me to speak to her?'

'No. Definitely not. Please don't go behind my back either. God knows how, but this is something I have to sort out myself.'

18

Daniel left for the office earlier than usual. He shut the door behind him quietly, envious of Richard who was still lying in bed – he wasn't in court today and was planning to work from home before going to his chambers in Manchester that afternoon. Barristers, thought Daniel, with a smile. Cushy life or what?

It was a beautiful, magical morning: the air was cool and fresh, and from the dew-washed fields that bordered their land came the plaintive bleating of sheep and new-born lambs. Way off in the distance, Daniel could see a scrawny black-legged one gambolling after its mother; it looked so vulnerable and insubstantial he hoped that the current spell of warm spring weather would not revert to a wintry coldness.

But there didn't seem to be any chance of that happening: despite it being so early, the sun was already shining, resembling a highly polished white disc in the clear sky. It was also very low, and after placing his suit jacket and briefcase on the back seat of his Audi A3, Daniel put on his sunglasses – not to pose, as Richard was so quick to imply, but because at this time of year, and at this hour when the sun was hardly above tree level, its blinding brightness could make his cross-country route to work deceptively treacherous.

He switched on the engine and Handel's *Messiah* burst forth, carrying on from where it had left off yesterday evening when he'd driven home after his appointment with Jessica Lloyd. 'For unto us a child is born,' sang the Huddersfield Choral Society, and joining in with more gusto than skill, Daniel turned the car round and set off down the long, sweeping driveway. It had been on a morning such as this five years ago when he and Richard had first clapped eyes on Lane End Farmhouse. And Lane End was exactly what it was. Situated in a dip in the valley between the Cheshire Peak villages of Rainow and Kerridge, and with breathtaking views across to the monument of White Nancy, their nearest neighbours – as the proverbial crow flew – were three-quarters of a mile away.

When he and Richard had decided it was time to buy a place where they could put down roots, they had deliberately only viewed properties that were remote and secluded – they were astute enough to know that not everybody wanted a gay couple living on the other side of the respectable suburban fence. Of course, there would always be those who would say that they had taken the cowardly approach, that they should have moved into a house centre-stage of some backward-thinking homophobic community and flaunted who and what they were. But as far as they were concerned their sexuality was their own business; it wasn't something they needed to prove, share with or justify to anybody else. Neither of them felt inclined to turn their relationship into a crusade for gay rights.

As it turned out, living at Lane End Farmhouse – a modest two-hundred-year-old stone-built gentleman's residence – had given them the best of both worlds: they had all the remoteness and seclusion they desired, including being occasionally cut off by three-foot snowdrifts in winter, but had the benefit of a friendly village a short drive away. It was at the village pub that Richard had made his own inimitable impression on the locals. As a self-confessed news-holic and general-knowledge freak, he was in high demand whenever it was quiz night at the Weary Traveller – his presence usually ensured an easy victory for his team.

As he drove past Adlington Hall and joined the B5358, Daniel turned his thoughts from his hitherto relatively trouble-free life to last night's kamikaze skirmish with Ali. When he'd come off the phone he'd warned Richard that it might be in order to start putting together a guest list for his funeral – just close friends and family, no flowers.

Not surprisingly, Ali had been furious with him for what he'd said. It was just as well domestic hi-tech videophones were still a thing of the future because he really wouldn't have wanted to see the expression on her face when he'd accused her of having made a mistake in divorcing Elliot. He knew that it was either a very brave or very stupid man who told Ali that she was wrong, but the compulsion to do so last night had far outweighed his fear of the consequences. They'd been friends for too long for him to hold back what he truly believed needed saying.

He didn't underestimate what Ali had gone through, and what she was still going through, but seeing her daily as he did, he felt better equipped than anyone else to know that she was no nearer to putting the awful tragedy behind her than she had been this time last year.

He'd actually been with her when it had happened, when she'd received the call from Elliot. They'd been in Frankfurt, on business, visiting a merchant bank in need of specialist expatriate tax advice. There had been no real reason why the pair of them should have been asked to go: as the senior manager of the department and Daniel's immediate boss, Ali was more than able to deal with the matter on her own, but one or two of the partners had said that a man's presence was required – ironically, even a gay man's presence. They had only just arrived at the hotel – their flight had been delayed several hours – and were in the process of reviving themselves from the mini-bar in Ali's room when the phone had rung. He had seen at once the alarm in her face when she'd answered it. She'd been clutching a small bottle of Jack Daniel's and seeing how tightly she was holding it, he'd taken it from her, worried in case she crushed it in her hand. There was no need to ask what was wrong. Her responses to what Elliot was saying were sufficient to let him know that Isaac was seriously ill. 'I'll be on the first plane there is,' she said. 'I'll go straight to the hospital.'

When she came off the phone he called for a taxi for the airport. He went with her and, not wanting her to be alone, tried to insist that he flew back to

Manchester as well, saying that they could cancel the meeting with the bank, that everyone would understand. But she refused to listen. 'No,' she said, 'there's no need. You must stay here. I'll phone you as soon as I know what's going on.'

He'd hugged her taut body, wiped away her frightened tears, and waved her goodbye. He had no idea how she fared during the flight and could only guess at the thoughts that must have gone through her mind. As for him, he'd taken a taxi back to the hotel and willed little Isaac to beat whatever it was that had struck him down so virulently, and so suddenly.

But his efforts had been in vain.

What he and Ali didn't know, was that Isaac was already dead.

Elliot had deliberately lied on the phone to Ali to spare her the ordeal of travelling all that way knowing that her son had just died. He had told her that Isaac was desperately ill and that she had to come back. His motive had been understandable, but Ali never forgave him for that lie. She had never seen it for what it was – a man simply wanting to protect the woman he loved. To this day, Daniel still didn't know what dreadful scene Ali must have walked into when she arrived at the hospital. He couldn't conceive of the courage it must have taken for Elliot to break the news.

And it was courage, admittedly of a much lesser sort, that Daniel was going to need this morning when he confronted Ali. This was why he had left home earlier than usual; he wanted to make sure that he reached the office before she did so that he could greet her with a cup of coffee and a white flag. He'd even raided the cupboard in the kitchen at home and pinched a packet of Richard's favourite almond and chocolate chip cookies as a peace-offering. And though he very much wanted to continue last night's conversation with her when he'd tried to persuade her to consider Elliot in a more favourable light, he knew that it wouldn't help if he did. And, besides, he had a far more pressing objective to fulfil: he had to ensure that she was calm, that she was no longer angry with him. If he failed to do this, then she'd never make it through their presentation this morning. If she was still stoked up with the blind fury he suspected her to be firing on, this morning would be a disaster.

But when Ali breezed into the office at eight thirty-five and dropped her briefcase on the floor by the side of her desk, she appeared to be anything but furious. 'Morning,' she said brightly. Her airy mood made Daniel suspicious and he watched her closely as she removed her suit jacket and slipped it over the back of her chair. He left her to open her mail while he went and made the coffee. When he returned and had cautiously settled her mug on the desk along with a plate of Richard's biscuits, she said, 'Daniel, it's quite all right, I'm not going to bite you.'

Despite her innocent tone, he retreated to the safety of his own desk before saying, 'And why would I think that you would want to bite me?'

She opened another envelope. 'I don't know, you tell me.'

Oh, shit, thought Daniel. This cat-and-mouse routine is much worse than outright anger. A blazing row would be far healthier. He decided to take the light-hearted approach. 'Babe, you're scaring me. I know that somewhere there'll be a sting in the tail. You've not hired a hit-man to take me out, have you?'

'I don't know what you're talking about,' she said uninterestedly, not even bothering to look up from the document in her hand.

Her indifference was too much for Daniel. He threw away his attempt at jocularity and moved on to poker-faced severity. 'Ali,' he said sharply, 'put that down and talk to me.'

She did as he said. 'Well, as you can see, I'm all yours. Now, what is it I'm supposed to be talking to you about?'

He frowned, not sure what he did want her to say. 'I want you to talk about last night,' he said, hoping that if nothing else it would be a good opener.

She turned away. 'There's nothing to discuss.'

'I disagree. We need to clear the air.'

She ignored him and began tearing open another envelope.

Daniel had never seen her act so coolly towards him. 'Look,' he said, realising that it was down to him to make the first move towards apologising, 'I'm sorry for what I said. You probably think I went too far, but I want you to know that I did it for—'

She looked up at him and the directness of her gaze cut him dead. 'You were expressing a point of view, Daniel. A point of view you're perfectly entitled to have.'

'But I never intended to hurt you by giving it—'

'Hurt me?' she interrupted. 'Is that what you think you've done?'

'Well, I can't think why else we'd be having this arctic-temperature conversation if I hadn't upset you.'

She set aside the letter that was in her hand. 'Daniel, let's get this straight once and for all, shall we? You didn't hurt me.'

'I didn't? Are you sure?'

She nodded. 'Very sure.'

'Thank goodness for that.' He relaxed. But he shouldn't have.

'To be fair to you I've put a lot of thought into what you said and I'm going to prove to you that you've got it all wrong.'

He stared at her steadily, sensing that the sting in the tail was looming on the horizon. 'You mean you're going to prove that you're right?'

'Smart boy, Daniel.'

'But what good will that do? I only said what I did to try to make you see things more clearly. It was to help you.'

'And I told you on the phone that I don't need any help. I'm okay. I just wish that everyone else would accept that small but very significant fact. Perhaps we should put out a message on the Internet: "Ali Anderson is fine. Ali Anderson is coping just fine with her grief. It's a slow old process, but she's managing it to the best of her ability." There, how does that sound?'

Daniel thought it sounded a classic case of self-deception. 'So how do you intend to prove me wrong?' he asked.

She gave him a chilling smile. Then, flicking through her Rolodex, she reached for her phone. 'Good morning,' she said, when a few seconds had passed. 'I'd like to speak to Elliot Anderson, please. No, he's not expecting my call, and yes, I know he's busy, he always was. Tell him it's Ali, I'm sure he'll spare me a couple of his valuable minutes.'

Daniel watched in rising horror. What the devil was she doing?

'Elliot, yes, it's me, quite a surprise I know. I just wanted to thank you for lunch yesterday and to say that maybe I was a little hasty in what I said about not wanting to see you again. Are you free for dinner later this week? You are? That's great. How about you come to me and I'll cook. Eight o'clock suit you? Good. I'll see you then.'

She put down the phone and turned to face Daniel. 'There,' she said. 'What do you think of that?'

Daniel got to his feet and went over to her. He leaned forward on to her desk and rested his hands either side of him. He looked her in the eye and said, 'I think the question is more what do *you* think of that?'

She backed away from him, but only an inch or two. She said, 'I'm going to prove to you that I can be pleasant to Elliot without once considering that I was wrong to divorce him. I shall be as nice as pie to him and not regret what I did.'

Daniel stared at Ali in dismay. He didn't want to hear the coldness in her words or see the flinty hardness in her face. He was horrified at what she was doing, but blamed himself. If only he'd kept his great big mouth shut last night. But he'd genuinely thought he was helping her. His intentions had been all for the good. He'd always suspected that Elliot had never really stopped loving Ali, and when yesterday he'd seen the evidence to confirm this in the man's face, he had thought that a nudge or two of common sense might help to set the wheels of a much-needed peace treaty in motion.

But now look at the mess he'd caused. If Ali was cold-heartedly going to use Elliot as a means to prove to the world that she was never wrong, then heaven help the poor guy.

19

Sarah was alone in the kitchen at Smithy Cottage, thinking that she would go quietly mad if she didn't talk to somebody. Trevor had just left to go over to Buxton to collect an order of ebonywood for a set of candlesticks he wanted to make and had left her with the washing-up and specific instructions to open her heart to the Lord. 'Don't tempt me,' she had wanted to say nastily, when he'd driven away in a cloud of burning oil coming from the back of their spluttering Sierra.

Never mind a gentle outpouring of penitent communion with God, what she wanted to do was give Him a piece of her mind. And not the well-behaved bit she normally offered Him. What did He think He was doing by sending Trevor off on this crazy crusade of obsessive evangelism?

The events of Monday night – and subsequent conversations with Trevor – had more than proved to Sarah that spiritual common sense flies out of the window when fanaticism bursts through the door. She was sure that what was happening to the group was a clear case of biblical principles being woefully misapplied, that through blind faith and ignorance they were misusing scripture to suit their own prejudices.

In the past she'd heard terrible cringe-making stories of house churches and breakaway groups getting wildly out of hand; of individuals who started out with an enthusiastic zeal for serving Christ, but who in the end did nothing but serve their own egotistical needs and diminish the God they proclaimed. But could this really be happening to Trevor and the Slipper Gang? Or was she overreacting? Trevor would say that subconsciously she wanted to destroy what they had and she didn't have. And hadn't she said as much to Ali at Christmas when she'd quoted William Penn to her – 'O God, help us not to despise or oppose what we do not understand.'

But this was different.

Surely it was.

It had to be.

When Trevor had played that sly trick on her with that stupid game and had pronounced her a disobedient lost sheep, Shirley had tried to menace her with one of her I've-been-called-to-pray-for-you sessions. Sarah had jumped to her feet and pushed the horrible woman away. She'd tried to make a run for it by saying she'd make the coffee, but Trevor wouldn't let her. He'd stopped her passing him as she'd made for the door and said, in a low voice, 'Perhaps you'd like us to pray for you, Sarah.'

She'd looked at him in astonished disbelief. 'What on earth for?'

He'd lowered his gaze to the Bible on his lap and said, 'Ephesians, chapter five, verse twenty-two.'

She'd wanted to shout, Oh, no, not that old chestnut about wives submitting to their husbands, can't you do better than that? But she'd forced herself to laugh and say lightly, 'I don't think this is the time to air our domestic differences, Trevor. It wouldn't be fair to our friends to bore or embarrass them.'

'As a sister in Christ you could never bore or embarrass us,' Shirley had said, still on her feet and probably hoping to perform a quick laying-on of hands.

'Shirley's right,' Martin Wade intoned. 'Domestic disharmony is one of the Devil's favourite weapons. It should never be allowed too great a foothold.'

'Amen to that,' Stan joined in, crossing his legs and making one of his puppy-dog slippers look as if it were nodding in agreement.

'Have you thought of fasting?'

Sarah turned to Beryl and thought, No, but have you ever considered minding your own business? 'Not ever,' she'd said, with strained dignity. 'I'm not sure that it serves any real kind of purpose . . . other than help one to lose weight.'

Her flippancy had galvanised Trevor and he'd said, in his especially pious voice, 'Sarah, I'm very worried about you. You don't seem to be in step with the rest of us . . . You're not losing your faith, are you?'

An audible hush fell on the room, and while everyone waited for her response she had stood motionless, almost able to believe that it was a bad dream she was experiencing, that she could say whatever she wanted and it wouldn't matter, there would be no comeback. Then, from nowhere, Sarah the Impudent, who until now had been noticeably silent, suddenly came crashing through the door and blurted out, 'My faith is my own affair and it's not up for discussion. But I'll tell you this, the God I pray to isn't the one that you have tucked into your smug-lined pockets.'

Then, horror upon horrors, she'd realised that it hadn't been her *alter ego* speaking it had been *her*. Shocked, she'd fled from the room to the kitchen. A soft pattering of spirit-filled slippered feet had followed her, and the next thing she'd known she was caught in an all-female rugby scrum of evangelical concern. Audrey was praying for her to be renewed, Beryl was calling on her to die to herself and be reborn, and Shirley was asking for the sin that had separated her from God to be removed. And, worst of all, Trevor was hovering by the fridge, tugging at his beard and muttering something about casting out demons.

She hadn't the energy to fight them off.

Even if she'd had the strength she was too scared to do anything about them.

It seemed easier to let them be convinced of their spiritual muscle-power. Let them believe that they had scored a triumphal victory over the dark satanic forces of doubt and evil.

'That better?' enquired Beryl, when at last they let her go.

She nodded and, overcome with the need to be alone, she said, 'I think I'll just go and lie down, I'm feeling a little strange.'

'Aha,' said a smiling Audrey, 'that would be the Holy Spirit working in you.'

'Would you like one of us to come and sit with you?' asked Shirley.

'That's very kind, but no, thank you. I'll be okay on my own.'

She had gone upstairs and stayed there until she'd heard them all leave an hour and a half later.

The next morning Trevor had treated her with a deference she'd never known in him before. He had brought her a cup of tea in bed and insisted that she take it easy. 'You've obviously been under a lot of strain recently,' he said, patting her hand on top of the duvet, 'but you'll be all right from now on. I'm sorry that I had to resort to such drastic measures. But it was worth it, wasn't it? You do feel better, don't you?'

He never actually said the words, but it was terrifyingly clear that he believed she'd been an instrument of the Devil for the past few months. And even clearer was his belief that the power of prayer had chased the Devil away from Smithy Cottage.

She didn't know whether to laugh at him or be angry, so she kept quiet. But when later in the day he had given her a Christian paperback entitled *The Devil and All His Cunning Ways* she'd known for sure that one of them was in dire need of help. That was when she'd left a message on Ali's answerphone.

The washing-up now finished, Sarah wrung out the dishcloth and draped it over the leaking tap that Trevor kept meaning to do something about but never did – he was probably waiting for an angel of the Lord to stop by with a bag of tools and washers. Taking a discarded crust of toast with her, she went outside to the garden where she crumbled it on to the bird table. As soon as she was back inside the kitchen, Gomez appeared. She smiled at the sight of his trim little body and felt marginally better than she had a few minutes ago. She let out a long sigh, realising with sadness how tense and overwrought she was becoming. She really had to find a more effective way of coping with Trevor and the Slipper Gang. Suggesting that they were doing more harm than good would only have them on their knees praying for her confused soul. Going along with them seemed the safest thing to do. At least then she could be the occasional voice of reason. But if she was to do that, she would have to put a gag on Sarah the Impudent. Another outburst such as the one the other night and she'd be done for.

She wondered now about what she had said: 'My faith is my own affair, and it's not up for discussion.'

And what exactly was her faith, these days?

Not so long ago she would have known exactly how to answer that question. But now she wasn't so sure. As with *The Light of the World* painting, which she had tried to focus on on Monday evening, the firm edges of her faith were growing worryingly blurred and fuzzy. Where once it had filled the void in her life, it now added to the vacuous echo of it, resounding like a tolling bell in the growing hollow emptiness.

Another weary sigh.

Oh, where would it all end? And how much more energy was she going to need to keep everything together? Knowing she had no answer to this, she got out the ironing-board and began ironing Hannah's school shirts, grateful at least that her daughter was so preoccupied with her approaching exams that she was blissfully unaware of what had been going on. Her attention had also been conveniently diverted by the appearance of Jamie on the scene.

The inevitable reprimand from Trevor when Hannah had arrived back after her evening with Jamie was met with a casual, 'Sorry, Dad, but you really shouldn't have shouted at me in the way that you did. There was no need, not now that I'm eighteen.' She had sauntered up to her bedroom, leaving Trevor impotent with parental frustration at the foot of the stairs. But perhaps he'd been too exhausted to argue with her. He had, after all, had a busy evening exorcising his wife.

Though it was only two days since she had met Jamie, Hannah was full of him. 'He's really nice,' she'd said yesterday morning, when she came down for breakfast, and while Trevor was still in the shower. 'He lives with his father the other side of Nantwich and he's on a gap year before going to Bristol to read law. He's spending most of the summer travelling round France. God, what I wouldn't do to be able to do that.'

'And how's he funding his little jaunt round France?' Sarah had asked, despising herself for asking the question, but wanting, like all parents, to categorise the poor lad.

'He's spent his year off working for his dad's law firm in Chester. He's just passed his driving test and his father's helping him to buy a car in a few weeks' time.'

'Doesn't sound as if he's short on motivation, does it?' Sarah had said.

Hannah had smiled. 'Believe me, Mum, he's not short on anything.'

'So we'll be seeing more of him, will we?'

'I hope so. He said he'd ring tonight.'

True to his word, Jamie had indeed called last night and they had chatted for nearly half an hour, much to Trevor's concern.

'A boyfriend's out of the question,' he'd said to Sarah in the kitchen, while peering through the crack in the door at Hannah on the phone. 'She's on the brink of her A levels and this is a distraction she can do without.'

Sarah agreed with him: in part, she didn't want anything to get in the way of Hannah fulfilling her potential either, but she also knew that Trevor's condemnation of Jamie was really about him not wanting his hugely important role in his daughter's life being superseded by a mere boy.

The ironing finished, Sarah wondered what to do next. For once she had a free day. Should she open her heart to the Lord, as Trevor had instructed, or should she call on Grace and discuss the bedroom curtains she'd offered to make for her? It would be somebody to talk to; somebody to stop her going quietly mad.

Grace was delighted to see her. 'How extraordinary, I was thinking of calling on you myself,' she said.

'I've brought you this,' Sarah said, as she was shown through to the sitting room, not the conservatory as on Monday. She handed Grace a tin of home-made fruitcake. 'As a thank-you for lunch the other day.'

'How very kind of you. I'll put the kettle on and cut us a couple of slices, shall I? Tea or coffee?'

'Tea, please.'

When Sarah was alone she took the opportunity to survey her surroundings. What struck her first about the room was its immense tidiness. Oh dear, she thought with disappointment, was her new neighbour obsessively house-proud? If so, she'd get a nasty surprise when she visited Smithy Cottage. The contrast between the two houses couldn't have been greater. No matter how hard Sarah tried to keep order it never seemed to work. Between Trevor and Hannah, the house was always a mess, albeit a clean mess. When she took a closer look at Grace's belongings, she realised that it was the lack of them that presented such an orderly effect. There were a couple of framed photographs on the mantelpiece and one or two nice bits of furniture, a dainty satinwood desk, a rosewood pie-crust table and a glass-fronted mahogany bookcase, all of which appeared a bit out of kilter in a modern bungalow with UPVC window-frames and swirly patterned Artexed ceiling. There were no pictures on the walls; nor were there any china bits and bobs of questionable taste. Maybe she hadn't unpacked everything yet.

'There,' said Grace, coming came back into the room and lowering the tray of tea and cake on to the rosewood table. 'Now we're all set for a cosy gossip. Tell me, Sarah, how did Hannah take to Jamie?'

Sarah smiled. 'She liked him a lot.'

'How splendid. I had the distinct feeling when he came here after dropping her off that he'd thoroughly enjoyed himself. There was a smile on his face that hadn't been there before. He's a lucky young man.'

'I don't know about that,' said Sarah.

'Now, then, no false modesty. Jamie brought Hannah in when she called for him and I saw for myself that she's a remarkably pretty girl. I wish I'd had her legs when I was that age.'

Sarah pulled a face. 'I'm afraid her skirt was very short. I hope you weren't shocked.'

Grace laughed. 'I was nothing of the kind. Though I must admit that Callum was rather taken aback. I think it came as a surprise to him that his son could attract such a lovely girl. That's the trouble with being a parent, we so badly underestimate our children.'

'Perhaps that's more true of fathers.'

'Yes,' said Grace thoughtfully. 'You may be right. Generally mothers are more in tune with their children's development, whereas the vast majority of fathers, bless them, come home from work one day and realise that their son or daughter is not only looking them in the eye, but they're on the verge of leaving home. Does Hannah's father fit into that category?'

'In many ways, yes, and he's not doing awfully well at coping with the reality of Hannah not being his little girl any more. He isn't terribly keen on Jamie being around either – her A levels start in May.'

'Jamie mentioned that. He also said that she's hoping to go to Oxford.'

'Yes, that's right,' and, unable to keep the pride out of her voice, Sarah added, 'She's been offered a place at my old college.'

'How wonderful. You must be so proud of her. Does she take after you in all things?'

'Goodness, I hope not,' Sarah said, with a hesitant smile. And as she took the cup of tea Grace had just poured for her she had the feeling that her new neighbour was one of those cleverly intuitive people, whose questions were a lot more probing than they first appeared.

It wasn't until nearly lunch-time that Elliot had a chance to reflect on his telephone conversation with Ali first thing that morning.

As soon as he'd put down the receiver he'd wanted to ring his father and find out what the hell he'd been playing at. He'd expressly told him not to go behind his back – and that was exactly what he must have done, for what else could have made Ali change her mind so suddenly? But there hadn't been a free moment for him to speak to Sam: he'd had to sit through a three-hour meeting with his senior partners, which was only now showing signs of coming to an end.

It was part of Elliot's job to keep everybody in line and, as he stared round the table and observed the egotistical oneupmanship that was rife between his colleagues, he felt that on days like this his position was little more than that of an unpopular teacher trying to control a class of dysfunctional teenagers.

He'd known when he was promoted to partner-in-charge that the decision would not be well received in certain quarters – in particular, by Gervase Merchant-Taylor and Scott Hunt, who had been the two front runners for the job – both considerably older than Elliot, each convinced of their own suitability for the job. Neither had taken kindly to the news from London that Elliot was to run the Manchester office. When the announcement had been made, Elliot had known that London expected him to be the one to defuse the resentment caused by his appointment. It had come at a time when he needed a distraction from the chaos of his personal life, when whipping this lot into shape had seemed a blessing. It had provided him with a much-needed focus, as well as a convenient excuse to work at a blistering pace, thereby minimising the number of hours spent alone dwelling on Isaac.

Mostly, he derived enormous satisfaction from the job and thrived on the challenge of the work, but there were aspects of it that appalled him. The situation of his office didn't help either. Large and ostentatious, situated at the top of the nine-floor building, it rendered him practically inaccessible. But what irritated him more than anything was the skin-crawling sycophancy that went on. He could cope with Gervase and Scott, who disliked each other as much as they disliked him, but what he couldn't tolerate was the constant toadying from the rest of the senior partners who, with the exception of Howard Jenkins, who kept himself to himself, sucked up to him whenever they could. And if that wasn't bad enough, Gervase was constantly pumping him for confidential information about the rest of the partners and what was going on in the firm; he hated the idea that Elliot knew anything before he did. Elliot had quickly learned that he had to make sure he never left any important documents from London lying around in his office. He'd made that mistake once and had caught Gervase snooping through the files on his desk late one evening.

It was a lonely job and made more so by not having a fellow-worker in whom he could put his trust. But he couldn't complain: it was, after all, one of the accepted and inevitable consequences of having achieved so much so young. Being fast-tracked throughout his career from the day he'd started his training contract meant that it had been difficult to form any lasting friendships with his colleagues. He'd always envied Ali that she'd had Daniel's friendship at work; there'd never been any shortage of trust between them. And it was probably this that had been at the root of his proposition to his father that they join forces. Working with embittered rivals and arse-lickers and having no one to talk to at home, was it any wonder that he'd sought out the company of somebody on whom he could rely 100 per cent?

And still the meeting was droning on and on, with Gervase and Scott doing their best to outmanoeuvre each other at every possible turn in the conversation. But at last Elliot had had enough. He mentioned the time pointedly, closed his file, snapped the lid on his fountain-pen and alerted everyone to the fact that he considered their long-winded discussion over. Everyone got up from the table and drifted away to their own offices.

All except Gervase, who seemed to be spending an unnecessary amount of time putting his file in order. 'I wonder if I might have a word,' he said, when they were alone and the door had been shut.

Despite wanting to be rid of everyone so that he could ring his father, Elliot said, 'Sure.' He went and sat behind his desk and regarded the repellent porcine man before him with deep suspicion. 'What is it?' he asked.

'I thought you ought to know that we might have a problem with Scott.'

'Oh?' said Elliot impassively.

Gervase stared back at him with lazy watchfulness. 'It appears that he's keeping more than a weather eye on the job market.' His whole demeanour as he spoke smacked of oily, conspiratorial wanker. 'Just thought you ought to be informed,' he added, 'knowing how difficult it must be for you to keep your ear to the ground stuck up here in your ivory tower, as it were.'

'Thank you, Gervase. I'll bear that in mind. Now, was there anything else?'

A look of annoyance stamped itself across Gervase's fat-jowled face. Obviously this was not the response he had wanted. 'My dear chap,' he drawled, 'you are going to do something about the matter, aren't you? Divided loyalty just isn't on. We can't have it, we really can't.'

Elliot could have struck him to the ground. The man's pompous, monstrously affected pratness had never got up his nose so much as it did now. Every atom of Gervase's refined over-privileged childhood was bringing out the back-street fighter in him. He'd come out on top of enough childhood brawls to know that he could knock the shit out of this posturing prig if he wanted to.

And did he ever want to!

'As I said, Gervase, I'll bear in mind what you've told me. If there really isn't anything else, I have an important phone call to make. Would you excuse me?' He waited for Gervase to get to his feet and cross the office before delivering a well-aimed warning shot across his bows. 'By the way, how's Jim Collins? I believe you had lunch with him last month.'

Gervase's hand fell away from the door handle and his blubbery face reddened all the way to his receding hairline. 'He's very well,' was all he said.

When Elliot was alone he allowed himself a small, wry smile. Jim Collins was his opposite number with a rival firm of accountants in Manchester, and clearly Gervase wasn't privy to the knowledge that they played squash together now and then. Jim had told Elliot over a drink in the bar after their latest game that Gervase had invited him out for lunch, had not so subtly hinted that he might be looking to switch horses – and did Jim know of any likely thoroughbreds in need of a decent jockey?

Gervase might like to labour under the misapprehension that Elliot didn't have his finger on the pulse, but it would take more than a supposed ivory tower to dull his awareness of what was going on around him. Just as he already knew that Scott was looking for another job, he had also heard rumours that Gervase was making himself more unpopular than he already was with some of the women in his department. Elliot was convinced that it was only a matter of time before a formal complaint was made.

He made a note to do something about this, then phoned Sam.

'Hi, it's me,' he said, when his father answered the phone at Timbersbrook; he could hear *The World at One* in the background.

'Hello, son, what can I do for you? Did you forget something?'

'No, nothing like that. But tell me the truth, and no bullshit, did you speak to Ali first thing this morning?'

'No. You made it very clear that I wasn't to do that.'

Elliot heard the indignation in Sam's voice and knew that he was speaking the truth. So, if his father hadn't talked Ali into seeing him again, who, or what, had changed her mind?

20

Ali had regretted her actions from the moment she'd told Daniel on Wednesday morning what she planned to do, and not because she thought there was a grain of truth in what he'd said but because she had, so very plainly, upset him. Though they hadn't actually rowed with an all-out guns-blazing ferocity, there had been a subsequent atmosphere of strained coolness between them, especially in the car when, an hour later, she'd driven them to Macclesfield where they were to give the first of their presentations that week.

How they'd got through it, she didn't know. As the acknowledged ice-breaker of the duo, Daniel had gone first, but she'd been keenly aware that his performance had lacked its usual smooth-paced sparkle; at one point he seemed even to lose the thread of what he was saying. Seeing him unprecedentedly distracted, and knowing that she was the probable cause, she had been unable to concentrate when it came to her turn. Her nerves kicked in and when, half way through her talk, she couldn't work the overhead projector she'd panicked. In her agitation she'd knocked over her glass of water and ruined her notes.

All in all, it had been an unprofessional turn-out on their part. She had hinted as much in the car afterwards when they were on their way back to the office.

'I agree,' he'd said tersely. 'We'd better make sure we do better on Friday when we perform our next freak show.'

'We weren't that bad.'

'Burlesque comes to mind.'

'You don't reckon they'll ask us back for an encore, then?' Her tone had been light, almost throw away, in an attempt to lift his mood. But it hadn't worked.

He turned slowly and gave her a long, hard stare. Glad that she was driving and didn't have to meet his gaze, she focused on the road ahead. After a few minutes he took her by surprise when he said, 'Please don't do it, Ali. Elliot's had enough to cope with without being made to think that there's a chance of being reconciled with you, only then to have his hopes dashed.'

'Oh, don't exaggerate,' she said hotly. 'One dinner does not a reconciliation make. And, anyway, I know for sure that Elliot isn't interested in me in the way you think he is.'

'Oh, and how do you work that out?'

'It's obvious. I'm simply his ticket to easing his conscience. He now feels guilty for the break-up of our marriage and wants to square things so that he can sleep at night. If it'll make you feel better I'll cancel Friday night. I'll ring Elliot and say—'

'Yeah, right, as if this has anything to do with me needing to feel better.'

They'd driven the rest of the journey in silence. It was fortunate that Ali was out of the office meeting several clients the following day, as she had no idea how to handle Daniel in his current frame of mind, or how to deal with what she felt towards him. She felt annoyingly betrayed that he seemed so intent on taking Elliot's side. Why the sympathy for Elliot all of a sudden? *Elliot's had enough to cope with.*

Men!

Straight or gay, they all sided with one another no matter what.

Her anger had stayed with her throughout yesterday as she kept thinking of everything Daniel had accused her of. What he had said, of course, was complete rubbish, a lot of absurd nonsense generated by an over-vivid imagination. It was outrageous that he had suggested that her refusal to see Elliot was because she was scared of feeling anything for him again. And, as she'd told Daniel, she genuinely believed that if Elliot wanted to carry out a post-battle campaign of patch-up-our-differences, it was purely down to his need to use her as a means of softening the sharp edges of his grief. So if anyone was being used it was her.

But it didn't matter how strongly committed to this view she was, it didn't make things right between her and Daniel. She was worried that if their marked difference of opinion was left to its own devices for too long it could force an unbridgeable gap between them. And that was something she wasn't prepared to let happen: Daniel meant the world to her. Which meant she had to do something in the way of climbing down from her precarious position. Sadly, though, she had to admit that self-effacement wasn't something she was terribly well acquainted with.

It was this thought that was with her now on Friday morning as she drove through Stockport's rush-hour traffic to meet up with Daniel at the electronics company where they were giving another presentation. She found him in the prestigious marble-floored, pot-planted foyer, chatting to one of the receptionists. He came over when he saw her.

'Can we have a word before we kick off?' she asked. Apart from desperately wanting to re-establish their friendship, Ali knew that in view of the shambles they'd made of their last presentation they had to regain their happy equilibrium as soon as possible, or they would be in danger of giving a repeat performance of Wednesday's fiasco.

They went and sat on a massive sofa that had a proportionately sized glass and steel table in front of it, the surface of which was covered in an artfully fanned display of that morning's newspapers. Every paper carried the same story that Ali had caught on the news on the car radio, and pictures of a flood-devastated area in Bangladesh stared back at her. Headlines claimed that the floods were the worst in living memory with more than fifteen hundred reported dead and three times that number now homeless, facing poverty and disease. Every paper had its own photograph to portray the disaster but the story behind each grim composition was the same: this was death on a vast, unimaginable scale.

'What is it, Ali?' asked Daniel. 'We don't have much time.'

Suddenly everything Ali had wanted to say wedged itself in her throat in a log-jam of emotionally charged confusion. It had been her determined intention to clear the air with Daniel, but the sight of such mass human suffering so explicitly spread before her stripped her of all her carefully thought-out words and made her realise the shallowness of what she'd really had in mind. In her arrogance she hadn't doubted for a single second her ability to reaffirm what she had already told Daniel and as a consequence extract from *him* the necessary apology to set them on an even keel. So much for a climb-down on her part. This clarity of thought also made her see the truly vindictive nature of her actions towards Elliot when she'd invited him for dinner. Appalled at what she'd done, she continued to sit in mute shame.

'Ali,' Daniel pressed, 'we're supposed to be upstairs in the conference room in five minutes. We ought to go.'

She tore her eyes away from the nearest paper, which showed a distraught young mother crouched in mud, cradling the body of her dead baby. She looks no more than a child herself, Ali reflected, with heartfelt anguish. 'I . . . I just wanted to say that I'm sorry,' she murmured, finding her voice at last. She looked up into Daniel's concerned face. 'I've behaved horribly, haven't I?'

Knowing exactly which photograph would have disturbed Ali most from the selection in front of them, Daniel took one of her hands and held it gently. 'Have you? When was that? I must have missed it.'

'Don't joke with me, Daniel. Not now.'

'I'm sorry. And I'm sorry for some of the things I said to you.'

'Only some?'

'Yes. I'll leave you to figure out which.'

'Well, that won't be too difficult. As soon as we have a spare minute, I'll ring Elliot and cancel tonight. I don't know what could have made me do such a calculating thing. It was very cruel.'

He smiled. 'It was your heavy-handed way of telling me to mind my own business.'

'And to teach you a lesson.'

'That too. And talking of lessons, are you admitting that one of us – a person who is extremely dear to me but who shall remain nameless – was wrong?'

She gave a little nod. 'But I'm only admitting to being wrong in wanting to manipulate Elliot to prove a point. The rest still stands.'

'So why don't you risk dinner with him anyway . . . just for old times' sake?'

She shook her head. 'No, I mustn't. If you're right about Elliot, then it would be unfair to give him the wrong signals.'

'As you wish, Babe. Now, come on, it's show-time. Give me your best Norma Desmond face and let's hit them with one of our Oscar-winning performances.'

*

The day flew by and it wasn't until a quarter to four when they stopped for a short tea-break that Ali found a slot in their busy schedule to excuse herself and ring Elliot's office. When she got through, an overly officious woman told her that Mr Anderson was unavailable.

'But it's extremely important that I speak to him,' Ali said.

'I'm sure it is, but he's not in today.'

'Is he at home?'

'Who is this?'

The question implied that, depending on the answer received, a *pro rata* amount of information would be forthcoming.

Incensed, Ali said, 'Oh, go shove yourself!' cut off her mobile – very probably her nose too – and tossed it into her bag.

'Problem?' asked Daniel, appearing with a cup of tea for her.

'Yes. Elliot isn't in the office today and his dumb secretary was not what we'd call user friendly.'

Daniel deposited the cup of tea on the table that Ali was leaning against, held out a hand and said, 'Give. It's time for our old friend Bob Schlock III to throw his weight around.'

She gave him her mobile and watched him press the redial button. 'Elliot Anderson,' he barked, in a grossly exaggerated American accent which brought a smile to her face. Bob Schlock III was a long-standing device who, every now and again, came in handy when Daniel needed to bypass the occasional annoying obstacle. When he'd been put through to Elliot's unhelpful secretary he slipped even further into character. 'This is Bob Schlock of Texas Incorporates,' he drawled. 'I'm returning Elliot's call. What do you mean, he's not there? Well, where is he? Now you stop right there, little missy, no point in giving me the runaround, I'm not calling for the good of my health, y'know. So just go right ahead and give me a number where I can contact him. No. No message, honey. Now, you be sure to have a nice day.'

Daniel returned Ali's phone to her. 'Nothing to it, honey. You just gotta show them who's boss.'

Ali rolled her eyes affectionately. 'So what's the deal, Schlock III? Where is Elliot?'

'Strategy meeting in London. He's booked on the five-fifteen shuttle out of Heathrow.' He glanced at his watch. 'He's probably already at the airport.'

Ali groaned. 'Now what do I do?'

'Sweetpea, it looks as if you'll just have to don your pinny and entertain him as originally planned.'

'Oh, Daniel, I can't. There has to be a way round it.' She thought for a minute, then said, 'I know, I'll ring Sam and leave a message with him.'

But there was no answer from the phone at Timbersbrook. Not even an irritating message telling her that nobody was there to take her call.

Elliot knew that he was cutting it fine, but he calculated that as long as his flight wasn't delayed, he just had time to make it home for a quick shower and change of clothes before driving to Ali's for eight o'clock. And while he prepared to wait patiently in the executive lounge for the Manchester shuttle to be called, he helped himself to a drink and a copy of the London *Evening Standard.*

Luck was with him and he was shortly stowing his coat and briefcase in the overhead locker, along with the flowers and chocolates he'd bought for Ali, then taking his seat. On average, he made this journey to and from London every other week and was as familiar with the routine as he was with the nature of the head-office meetings he attended on each of his visits – it was the favourite old ploy of attack and defend. The commonly held view in London was that, out of all the regional offices, Manchester was the most efficiently run; it was also known to be the hottest bed of personal ambition. Nothing had ever been said directly, but Elliot was astute enough to know that his promotion had been a carefully orchestrated piece of divide and conquer – London had selected him in the belief that his appointment would clear out some of the dead wood. But twelve months into the job Gervase was still hanging in there, probably hoping that if he made life difficult enough for Elliot he would be the one to clear off. But Elliot was a darned sight more tenacious than that. If there was one single thing he was grateful his father had taught him, it was 'You don't get owt for nowt, son.' It had been a favourite axiom of Sam's and had often been punctuated with further encouraging mantras such as 'Stick with it, lad', 'Make sure you go the distance' and 'Don't let the bastards grind you down.' Sam had never been a pushy parent – he'd never needed to be, not with Elliot being as driven as he was – but he had been a stickler for seeing things through, and Elliot suspected that out of all his father's many qualities this was one of the few he'd inherited. He had often wondered whether he'd been a disappointment to his father when he was growing up. He must have been a boring kid, always reading, always studying, and even when he was at Oxford he hadn't changed. What leisure time he'd allowed himself he'd spent jogging round Christ Church Meadow and along the Cherwell or listening to music in his room, rather than hanging around the college bar seeing how much he could drink before falling down blind drunk. During his second term, one of his tutors had tactfully suggested that he might like to participate in college life a little more enthusiastically. Reluctantly he had made a token gesture to sociability by showing his face in the Junior Common Room once a week and extending his breakfast in hall by five minutes each day. He quickly acquired the sobriquet TSB – That Solitary Bugger – but by the middle of the Trinity term, much to his annoyance and embarrassment, his nearest neighbour's extensive circle of airheaded girlfriends had changed it to QBD: Quiet But Divine. This was after one had missed her footing on the stairs and fallen into his arms as he'd been following her after an hour running in the rain down by the river. Afterwards, when he'd carried her safely to his neighbour, having been taken in by her claim that she'd twisted her ankle, he had heard her giggling through the wall that she'd gladly part with a year's clothing allowance for a night in bed with him. 'Never mind you uncouth, beer-guzzling, rugby louts,' she'd shrieked, at the top of her voice. 'Give me a strong, silent man in a wet T-shirt any day.'

When they landed at Manchester, Elliot made his way through the busy arrivals hall, paid his parking ticket and hurried to the third floor where he'd left his car at half past six that morning. He was home by ten past seven, and after reading Sam's note that he wouldn't be back until late that night, he was in the shower by seven-sixteen. He washed, shaved, cleaned his teeth, dressed and was in the car again by twenty to eight. It was a masterpiece of timing and it was only now as he headed south on the A535 that he allowed himself to think of the evening ahead. So far that day he'd done everything in his power not to imagine what had led Ali to invite him to dinner. He'd convinced himself that, at best, she wanted to apologise for being so curt earlier in the week.

And at worst?

Oh, that was easy.

At worst she wanted to spell out on her own territory, syllable by syllable, exactly why she never wanted to see him again.

'This isn't happening,' Ali muttered to herself, 'it's a bad dream. Any minute now and I'll wake up and find it's morning and I'll be able to ring Elliot to put him off. Or, better still, I'll realise that this whole week has been one long dream sequence.'

She slugged back another mouthful of wine and glanced at the clock again. It was ten minutes to eight. She groaned and wished that she didn't know Elliot as well as she did. It would be futile to hope that he would be late, or that he would fail to show. Elliot was the most punctilious man she knew. He was never late. He'd always managed to make time work in his favour. She didn't know anyone like him. In the days when they used to work together, and there was a big job on that would throw everyone into a maelstrom of frantic activity, he had never once worried about the deadline hanging over them. Instead he had quietly applied himself to the task in hand and had been the epitome of unruffled efficiency. He'd been the same in meetings. No matter the temperature around the table, his body language was always that of inscrutable calm. It was a compelling technique he had cultivated, which had on one occasion, during a lively, heated debate, caught her out. It was in the early days of her training and she had been so mesmerised by the impassive expression on his face that she'd stopped listening to what was being said. When he'd suddenly asked her opinion, Daniel had had to step in and rescue her.

It was not something she had allowed to happen in the workplace again. From then on she had kept her desire for him firmly under control.

But at least that was something she wasn't going to have to concern herself with tonight. There were many things she felt for Elliot now, but desire wasn't one of them. And despite what Daniel thought about Elliot's feelings for her, she was convinced that lust wasn't on his mind either.

When she and Daniel had finally got away from Stockport late that afternoon, they had headed back to the office for a quick catch-up session with Margaret. After they'd gone through their e-mails, returned several clients' calls, were turning out lights and setting the security system, Daniel had said, 'Go easy on Elliot tonight, won't you, Babe? It takes too much energy to keep fighting another person. Give yourselves a break.'

'Hah! Go easy, indeed,' she said, as she brushed egg-yolk on to the puff pastry of the haddock and prawn pie she'd cobbled together when she'd arrived home from work – knowing how particular Elliot was about what he ate, she had decided not to antagonise him by confronting him with a plate of red meat and saturated fats, and had gone for the safe option of fish.

Now, was that going easy enough?

Or would she still be accused of serving him a nice little fricassée of harboured bitterness on a bed of reproachful blame?

She heard the ominous sound of an approaching car, threw back another mouthful of wine and crossed the kitchen to the small window that looked out on to Mill Lane. Sure enough, there in the darkness she could see the headlights of Elliot's distinctive XK8 coming slowly towards the mill. A glance at her watch showed that he was exactly on time.

Damn the man! Would he never surprise her? Would he never defy his own gravitational force of perfection?

She took a deep, steadying breath and braced herself for the evening ahead.

21

Elliot saw at once how uptight Ali was when she opened the door.

'Exactly on time, Elliot,' she said. 'No change there, then.' She banged the door shut with a crash that was so loud and sudden it made him start. 'Sorry about that, don't know my own strength. Overcompensating for the warped wood. No coat? You'll regret that when you go home.'

Seeing the dreadful effect he had on her, Elliot's heart sank with heavy sadness. 'Look,' he wanted to say, 'I know this is difficult, but slow down, relax.' However, a comment such as that would do more harm than good: it would put her on the attack and make her more agitated than she already was.

A friendly kiss on the cheek was plainly out of the question so he handed her the flowers and chocolates. They were received with polite thanks and she led the way up the spiral staircase to the first floor of the mill, to where they'd sat on his only other visit. It looked exactly as before, but minus the cards that had been strung between the brass picture lights. These were switched on, as were two silk-shaded table lamps; soft light reflected off the rich red walls.

'What would you like to drink?' she asked. 'I've made a start on some white wine, but feel free to have what you want.'

'Wine would be nice. Thanks.'

He followed her to the kitchen area and saw that she'd set the table for dinner. He noted that there were no intimate touches of candles and flowers. To the right of the cooker, and waiting to be baked, he saw what he took to be their supper: it had been one of his favourite meals that Ali used to make for them. She handed him his glass of wine and caught him looking at the pie. She opened the oven door and put it inside and said, 'Sorry to be so dull, but my culinary repertoire hasn't had much of an opportunity to move on, since . . .' She trailed off.

He waited awkwardly for her to finish the sentence. When she didn't, he said, 'Since we separated, is that what you were going to say?'

'No,' she said, with an indignant frown. 'I was going to say since work has been so busy and I haven't had time to fiddle around in the kitchen as I used to.'

Rebuffed, he went back to the sitting area and strolled over to a large, old, black-and-white photograph of the mill, taken in the days when it still had its sails. While sipping his wine and apparently studying the picture, he figured out his best chance of changing the course of the evening. As things stood, he'd be shown the door before long. Then, sensing that Ali was standing behind him, he turned and said, 'Any chance of a guided tour?'

She put down her glass. 'If you want, though there's not an awful lot to see.'

Once again Ali took the lead and as they climbed the narrow wooden staircase, she said, 'We'll go right to the top and work our way down.'

A few steps behind her Elliot tried to keep his eyes on something other than Ali's legs and the shortness of her skirt, which barely showed itself beneath the silk blouse she was wearing. She'd flay you alive if she knew what you were thinking, he told himself sharply. 'How many floors are there?' he asked, endeavouring to keep his thoughts on safer lines.

'Five.'

'Any idea how high the mill is?'

'*Exactly* seventy feet,' she said pointedly. They reached the top floor and, slightly out of breath, she stopped and pushed open a stripped-pine door. 'This is supposed to be my study, but I don't use it often. I always seem to end up working on my laptop at the kitchen table.'

Elliot took in the small circular room with its white-painted walls and two tiny windows: it reminded him of a cell. Its diameter was about fourteen feet and its only furniture a desk and chair and two bookcases, which contained several rows of lever-arch files and a selection of standard accounting textbooks. There was a computer, a compact Canon printer, a phone on the desk and nothing else.

They went down to the next floor where there was a bedroom and a small adjoining shower room. The bedroom looked as if it was waiting for a guest: it was meticulously tidy; the double bed was made up with three cushions placed decoratively against the headboard, and on the dressing table beneath one of the three windows was a pastel-coloured tissue box and a cut-glass vase of daffodils.

'Somebody coming to stay?' he asked.

'Yes. Sarah.'

'With or without Trevor?'

'Without. It's going to be a strictly girls-only weekend.'

When they reached the floor below, Ali paused. 'My room,' she said, after a moment's hesitation. She pushed open the door and let him go in first. They stood side by side a few feet away from the corner of the bed. A painful thump of jealousy hit Elliot – had she ever brought a man back here? He willed himself not to picture the scene. But he couldn't stop himself and all too easily he saw her climaxing in the arms of some stranger. He thrust his hands into his trouser pockets, cleared his throat and moved away. 'Cleverly built-in wardrobes,' he said, going over to take a closer look at the workmanship that had ingeniously accommodated the slope and curve of the wall.

'Yes,' she agreed, to his back.

He turned a few degrees to his right and for the first time noticed the bedside table, or rather, he noticed what was on it: a framed photograph of Ali sitting on the beach with their son on her lap. Isaac was wearing the New York Yankees baseball cap that Elliot had bought for him on a recent trip to the States. Much too big for his little head, it had slipped to one side and had given him a cute, jaunty look. With instant recall Elliot could remember the day he had taken the photograph. They'd been down at Hayling, staying with Ali's parents. It had been the most perfect of summer days, hot and sunny with a refreshing breeze blowing in from the sea. They'd spent the afternoon on the beach paddling and building sandcastles and hunting for razor shells. They'd bought ice creams and Isaac had insisted on holding his own, and in the heat of the August sun it had melted and dribbled all over his hands before he'd had a chance to eat any of it. Ali had taken him down to the water's edge to wash him while Elliot had fetched a replacement. The tableau of them all together was so clear and so very real in Elliot's mind that for a split second he was convinced that if he closed his eyes he'd be there on the beach, breathing in the smell of the sea air and hearing the happy sound of Isaac's squealing laughter as the rushing waves whooshed over his tiny feet dragging the grains of sand from under his toes.

He wrenched his eyes from the photograph but then saw something else that brought back another haunting echo of the past. There, almost hidden beneath the duvet, was Mr Squeezy. Without thinking, he went to the bed and picked up the small bear. He held it lovingly in his hands, reacquainting himself with the crooked nose, the long, dangly arms and legs and the soft, well-cuddled body. He swallowed and his jaw tightened as he thought how limp and lifeless the teddy felt . . . limp and lifeless just as Isaac had felt at the end. 'I didn't know you'd kept this,' he murmured, almost inaudibly.

Ali opened her mouth to speak but found that she couldn't. She was completely paralysed with the desperate need to make Elliot put Mr Squeezy back in the bed. She didn't want him touching that small precious bear. It was practically all she had left of Isaac. Irrationally, she knew that she was on the verge of tears and, despising herself for her weakness, she whispered, 'Please, put him down.'

Elliot raised his eyes and saw the agony in Ali's face. Shocked, he immediately did as she said. 'I'm sorry, I didn't mean to—'

She held up a hand to stop him. 'No, don't say anything. Not a word.' Then, turning towards the door, she said stiffly, 'We'd better go downstairs. Supper should be ready by now.'

Ali served the meal while Elliot, at her suggestion, selected a CD. The thought occurred to him as he ran his gaze along the row of CDs that she might be testing him: choose something they both used to be fond of and he'd be accused of cloying sentimentality. His fingers hovered over *Eric Clapton Unplugged*, then flicked away – 'Tears in Heaven' was on that album and he didn't know about Ali but he could never make it through to the end of that song without a colossal amount of desensitising alcohol. He trailed his hand further along the shelf, instinctively bypassing all the classical stuff – Rachmaninov, Brahms, Beethoven and Chopin were dangerously evocative and would dredge up too many poignant, erotic memories. His hand stopped at an album by an artist called Frances Black. He hadn't heard of the singer or the CD. It was called *Talk To Me*. Well, it was appropriate enough. He removed the disc that was already in the hi-fi and looked around for its box. Ali had never been any good at putting things back in their proper place. After extending his search to a wider area, he eventually found it hidden beneath that month's copy of *Taxation*.

'How long does it take for an accountant to put on a CD?' called Ali from the kitchen, where she was refilling their glasses and observing his progress.

'I don't know,' he answered. 'How long *does* it take for an accountant to put on a CD?'

'Apparently twice as long as anybody else.'

He adjusted the volume and, catching the opening lyric of the first track – 'All the lies that you told me, all the tears that I've cried' – hoped he wasn't going to regret his choice. He joined Ali at the table, sat in the chair opposite her and, after he'd complimented her on the meal, to which she made no comment, he asked the question he'd wanted to ask since Wednesday morning when she'd phoned him. 'What made you change your mind about seeing me again?' he said.

Oh, hell, thought Ali. What am I supposed to tell him? That he's only here because I was so mad with Daniel? 'I don't really know,' she lied.

'Oh,' he said flatly. It wasn't a very satisfactory answer. It still left him wondering where he stood with her. Another silence followed and Elliot turned his attention to the CD. The singer had moved on to another track and was now dishing out lyrics with sledgehammer subtlety – 'I wish you would tell me what I'm doing wrong, we could talk it over and try to get along ...' Inwardly recoiling from its hamfisted appropriateness, he put down his knife and fork and reached for his wine, wishing that the singer would get to the end without bludgeoning them any harder with the poignancy of the words. But his hope was in vain. She blundered on, regardless of his discomfort: 'So be my friend or my enemy, be whatever you have to be, but don't, don't be a stranger ...'

Ali was listening to the lyrics too. Puzzled, she couldn't recall buying the album. Nor did she have any recollection of ever hearing it before. But she couldn't deny how apt the words were. She and Elliot had become like strangers to one another. Daniel had told her earlier that day that he thought their divorce had been as senseless a tragedy as Isaac's death. In her heart she knew that he was right. But it didn't help. It didn't change the need she had to keep the distance between her and Elliot. 'But what if there was a way to change some of what's happened?' Daniel had asked. She hadn't answered him because she couldn't bring herself to admit that part of her didn't want her wounds to be healed. Not yet. She wasn't ready. She still needed to kick against the hurt of her grief.

The track came to an end and Ali remembered that Daniel had given her the CD. She recalled what he'd said to her at the time. 'Put it on loud, Babe, and listen to it closely.' She hadn't, of course. But, then, she so rarely did what people told her to do.

Conscious that nobody had spoken for some minutes, Ali looked up from her plate and caught Elliot staring at her. In the lamplight the solemnity of his face was startlingly profound and his eyes, normally so clear and blue, were faded with sadness. Oh, God, she thought, with genuine remorse, he doesn't deserve this. Why had he agreed to come here and put himself through this dreadful misery? Had it been to punish himself? Had she mistaken his motives for using her? Having thought that he wanted to be friends to assuage his guilt, was he in fact here to torture himself by remembering how it had once been? Filled with the need to dispel the mood of gloom that had settled on them, she said, 'How did your day in London go?'

His eyes narrowed fractionally. 'How did you know I was in London?'

She realised her error. If she told him the truth that she'd tried to phone him to cancel this evening, it would lead to him asking why. 'I called your office this afternoon to check that you were still on for dinner,' she lied once more. 'Who's the unhelpful woman you've got masquerading as a secretary, these days?'

He raised an eyebrow. 'Her name's Dawn, and in polite circles she's what one would describe as an acquired taste.'

'And is she your acquired taste?'

'No. I can't stand the woman.'

'Then get rid of her.'

'Other than objecting to her offhand manner, I don't have any real grounds to do so. She's surprisingly good at her job.'

'Historically that's never stopped a partner-in-charge from wielding the great axe of power.'

'True, but misguided as I might be, I pride myself on not being one of those industrial dinosaurs.'

If any other man had said this, Ali would have condemned him for fishing for a compliment, but coming from Elliot she knew better. He'd never been one of those idiots who needed to roll on to his back to have the underbelly of his egotism rubbed. 'So what's this Dawn like? I've money on her being a right old witch.'

He put down his knife and fork and carefully wiped his mouth with his napkin. 'There are some who think she's a vision to behold.'

'Really? With anyone in particular? Or is she not choosy? Perhaps she has a display case of trophy scalps at home?'

'That wouldn't surprise me at all. But for a time it was rumoured that she and Scott had a thing going.'

Ali reached for the bottle of wine. She offered it to Elliot but he shook his head. When she'd refilled her own glass, she said, 'And does this Dawn the Porn have designs on the ultimate prize in the office?'

'Who? Gervase?'

She rolled her eyes. 'I think we can both safely assume that never in a million years would either of us consider Gervase as an ultimate prize. I was referring to the boss. Has she tried to hit on *you*?'

Elliot looked indignant. 'Certainly not.'

Ali smiled to herself. He really doesn't have a clue how attractive he is, she thought, or what an easy target it makes him. 'So how is Gervase?' she asked. 'Still grinding people underfoot if they've dared to get in his way?'

'More or less.'

She groaned. 'The destruction derby of big office politics, nothing else compares with it. How the hell do you stick it, Elliot?'

He shrugged. 'It's just a job.'

'Oh, come off it. Your career means more to you than that.'

He tapped his fingers lightly on the table and almost smiled. 'You're right. Perhaps it's the power struggle I enjoy so much.'

'What? Knowing you've made it and the others haven't?'

'No. It's watching them all fighting with each other and knowing that it's pointless. The real sense of power is accepting that at the end of the day none of it matters.'

'Easy to say when you're sitting comfortably in the coveted office on the ninth floor.'

'Will that be my epitaph? "He made it to the ninth floor".'

'It could be worse. It could be "He only made it to the third floor".'

'Or how about "He cheated and took the lift"?'

'That's not cheating, that's good lateral thinking. Of which I strongly approve.'

'What about you? Do you feel comfortable in your empowered position these days? After all, you're the boss as well.'

'Ah, but a different kind of boss.'

'More human? More caring?'

'Of course, that's real girl power for you.'

'So it all comes down to power, then?'

'I suppose it does when you believe it's something you've been deliberately denied through years of male-dominated prejudice.'

'Does Daniel feel the same way?'

Ali laughed. 'God, no. Not Daniel. He's far too tolerant for his own good.'

Elliot sipped his wine reflectively. After a bit, he said, 'Tolerance is a quality we despise at our peril.'

'Is that what passes through your mind when you're head-to-head with Gervase?'

He leaned back in his chair and stroked the long, slender stem of his glass. 'I'm afraid there's only the one thought that comes into my mind when I'm with that man and that's to knock the hell out of him.'

Ali pretended to be shocked. 'I'm not at all sure that that's the correct way for a partner-in-charge to talk.'

'Then it confirms what Gervase has probably always thought about me.'

'What's that?'

'That I'm the wrong man for the job. My background and credentials are not at all suitable.'

'Aye, lad, as Sam would say. You're a crest short on t' family silver.'

They both laughed.

But then quickly fell silent as they realised what had happened: they'd allowed themselves a brief respite of light-heartedness. They each looked around for a distraction: Ali poked at the few remaining rocket leaves in the salad bowl and Elliot folded his napkin carefully then laid it beside his plate. He wanted to tell Ali how much he was enjoying her company now that she'd relaxed, that chatting with her about the Guano of the Big Practice, as they used to refer to it, seemed the most natural thing in the world to him. He was about to open his mouth to speak when she rose from her chair and began to gather up the dishes. 'I'll get the next course,' she said. 'Why don't you choose another CD?'

Dumping the crockery with a clatter on the draining-board, Ali tried to assimilate the rampant confusion of her thoughts. Only a few hours ago she had been utterly convinced of her distrust for Elliot and his motives for wanting to see her, but now she wasn't so sure. What had passed between them just now was, in essence, little more than an exchange of cordial dinner-party chat, but it made her realise for the first time since they had grown apart what it could be like if the fighting stopped. It tempted her to consider the viability of Daniel's long-held claim that by calling a truce with Elliot, the worst and most debilitating pain of Isaac's death could be disarmed.

Could he be right?

Could it really be that simple?

And was it worth a try?

'Yes,' whispered a faint voice inside her. 'Let it go. Let the past go. Stop fighting him.'

But a more strident, familiar voice asserted itself: 'Why should either of you know peace of mind when you don't deserve it?'

She shook the voices from her head and lifted the cover from the plate of cheese she'd put together earlier in the evening. She placed it on a tray with a basket of wholewheat crackers and took it to the table. Elliot was over by the bookcase behind the sofa inspecting the cover of the CD Daniel had given her, and while he had his back to her, Ali took the opportunity to assess his appearance, which so far that evening she hadn't noticed. He was casually dressed in an open-necked cream shirt, tucked into a pair of sage-green linen trousers with a belt that matched the soft brown leather of his Deck shoes. His hair was shorter than she approved of and made him look a little severe, but for all that, it did nothing to diminish his attractiveness. Then, just as she'd reached this conclusion he turned, saw that she'd been quietly studying him and, very slowly, very hesitantly, he gave her one of his rare smiles.

He could have fired no deadlier a shot. It was as direct and powerful as a cruise missile and caught her thoroughly off-guard.

Holy Moses, she thought, when she'd regained the power of coherent reasoning, where the hell did that come from?

22

It came as no surprise to Ali that her waking thought should be of Elliot. Not that she'd slept much. And when she had it had been fitful and restless.

It was Saturday morning, and instead of being able to enjoy the luxury of a lie-in, her unsettled mind was forcing her to get out of bed. She pushed back the duvet and went downstairs to make a pot of tea. While the kettle boiled, she peered out of the window into the grey half-light of a disappointingly dull and dreary day. The sun was a ghostly orb in the sky and a thin layer of mist covered the surrounding flatness of ploughed fields. In the tall alder trees at the end of the lane she could see the hunched figures of three large crows high up in the tracery of branches that were yet to burst into their spring greenery. There was a sinister and portentous when-shall-we-three-meet-again look about the birds as they surveyed their territory of exposed farmland.

She shivered, left the window and made two rounds of peanut-butter wholemeal toast. She put her breakfast on to a tray, went upstairs and climbed back into bed. She poured herself a large mug of Rose Pouchong and took a bite out of one of the pieces of toast. She chewed thoughtfully, savouring the taste of what had to be at least a hundred calories per square inch.

Now it was time to think about Elliot.

Elliot.

Elliot.

Elliot.

It didn't matter how many times she said his name, it didn't straighten the tangle of knotted thoughts that had kept her awake for most of the night. Impartiality told her that the evening had gone better than she could have hoped for. Apart from that terrible moment here in her bedroom with Mr Squeezy, it really hadn't been too awful. The mood between them might have been wary, but it had certainly been a lot less hostile than on previous meetings.

But there was no denying how relieved she'd felt when Elliot had said that he ought to be going. She had made no attempt to detain him by offering another cup of coffee, but had risen from the sofa and said, 'Give my love to Sam, won't you?'

In return, he'd said, 'And mine to Sarah when you see her tomorrow.'

Neither of them had suggested, 'This was fun, we should do it again,' and it was left that he would call her. There had followed a tricky few seconds downstairs at the front door when they both realised that somehow they had to bring the evening to a close, but on what note?

A formal handshake?

A see-you-around-sometime nod?

Or a cheek-brushing kiss?

She'd stood numb with indecision as the night air had swirled in through the open door and nipped at her ankles like a small snappy dog. But she saw in Elliot's eyes that he had made a decision and with only the merest hint of hesitancy in his movements he reached out a hand, rested it on her arm and bent his head to kiss her. But she'd panicked. Stepping back from him, she'd said, 'Brrr ... it's cold out there. I said you'd regret not bringing a coat.'

She hadn't stayed at the door politely waving him off as he drove away, but had turned the key in the lock, shot the bolt and scuttled back upstairs in a state of red-faced, hackles-up shock.

He'd tried to kiss her!

The bloody cheek of him!

One fish-pie supper and he thought he could make free and bloody easy with her!

The nerve of the man!

These were the thoughts that had passed through her mind as she'd tried in vain to sleep. But now as she finished the last of the toast, she wondered if she hadn't overreacted. The evening may have been a little chilly in places, but there had been one or two tangible flashes of warmth in the conversation, mainly when they'd been discussing work. That had certainly provided them with a conveniently fertile patch of common ground, especially when it came to their mutual dislike of Gervase Merchant-Taylor.

But what about her response when Elliot had given her the benefit of one of his smiles? Was she going to dismiss that as nothing more than a 'flash of warmth'? And wasn't that the real cause of her sleepless night? Hadn't it scared her rigid to know that after everything they'd gone through he could still have the same high-charged effect on her? And that was why she'd panicked when he'd tried to kiss her, wasn't it? She hadn't trusted herself. Go down that road, she'd thought, and goodness knows where she would end up.

She smiled, thinking of Daniel's probable contribution to the conversation if he were here. He'd be smirking and saying, 'Told you so, told you so.'

That afternoon, when what little light there had been during the day had almost faded, Ali banked up the fire with some logs from the wood basket then went over to the window to see if there was any sign of Sarah. It was almost four o'clock; she should have arrived an hour ago.

It wasn't like Sarah to be late and Ali hoped that she hadn't broken down on the way. She knew that Sarah was a slow driver, but even allowing for an extra fifteen minutes on her journey time, she should have been here by now. Ali had already tried ringing Smithy Cottage, but there had been no reply so all she could do was stare into the distance, hoping for a glimpse of her friend's ancient Sierra in the dwindling light. The fields were still shrouded in mist, which Ali had felt, as the day wore on, had seeped its cold, melancholy dampness through the thick walls of the mill and wrapped itself around her.

She'd spent the morning catching up on the tedium of domestic paperwork, a job she hated and which she always put off as long as she could. She'd reluctantly given two hours of her time to sorting through the pile of mail that lived between the fruit bowl and the microwave.

Finally, when she'd finished answering letters, writing cheques for her credit cards and gone through her bank statements, she had decided to go upstairs and see what she could find for Sarah. Sarah rarely spent money on herself, least of all on clothes, but as she and Ali were the same size, Ali had always passed on to her anything she no longer wanted. There was never a feeling of misplaced charity in the gesture and Sarah accepted the clothes in the spirit they were offered. Only once had Ali over-stepped the mark, when she had deliberately bought a MaxMara outfit with Sarah's beautiful dark hair and much darker complexion in mind. She'd given it to her casually and said, 'One of those impulse buys I should never have made. It looks dreadful on me.' But Sarah had seen right through her. 'Ali,' she'd said sternly – well, sternly for Sarah – 'I want your genuine hand-me-downs. Don't ever do this to me again.' She had refused the outfit and forced Ali to take it back to the shop.

It was while she had been sorting through her wardrobe for clothes she could pass off as genuine 'hand-me-downs' that she had come across the shoebox. She should never have opened it, but an urge far stronger than common sense made her carry it to the bed and take off the lid to look at its contents. Carefully wrapped in white tissue paper was one of Isaac's first Babygros, along with a photograph of him wearing it. The picture showed him fast asleep in her arms, his face pale and relaxed, his top lip slightly overlapping the lower one; he was only a week old but unknowingly his tiny being had held the key to what made her complete. She placed the soft fabric comfortingly against her face. She closed her eyes and, just as she knew it would, she let the familiar ache of grief work its way through her body. She stayed like that until tears, unbidden, slowly slid down her cheeks and she dropped to her knees, leaned against the bed and wept loudly and without restraint. And just as freely as her tears flowed, so did the stream of unanswerable questions. Why did Isaac have to die? Why him? Why her child? Why her little boy?

When she was all cried out, she rewrapped the Babygro and photograph and returned the box to the back of the wardrobe. She went into the bathroom and washed her face. She couldn't bring herself to glance in the mirror – she knew that she looked awful and didn't need to have it confirmed. She reached for a freshly laundered hand towel and as she rubbed at her face she breathed in the sweet, fragrant smell of fabric conditioner. Instantly she was reminded of a similar aroma, and of another occasion when she had lost control. It was two months after Isaac's death and she'd been shopping in Sainsbury's. She was pushing the trolley past the shelves of breakfast cereals and as she turned the corner expecting to find household cleaning products she discovered that the supermarket had swapped things about: she was face to face with an aisle of baby products. In previous weeks she'd planned her route to eschew the shelves of nappies and baby foods. But there was no avoiding it that day, and as she forced herself forward the sweet smell of infant hygiene engulfed her – nappies, shampoo, bubble bath, wipes, talc. The sickly smell filled her nostrils, making her feel violently ill. She abandoned the trolley, rushed outside to her car and drove home, unable to stop herself shaking or sobbing. Elliot had been so worried about her he'd called the doctor, who prescribed a cocktail of sleeping pills and tranquillisers. But she had refused to take them and had stuffed the packets unopened into her bedside table.

There was still no sign of Sarah and, moving away from the window, Ali thought of the desolation and bitterness she had felt earlier that afternoon when she'd been crying for Isaac. She had never told anyone this, but it was when she was at her most wretched that she felt closest to Isaac. It was as if she gained a perverse sense of comfort from putting herself through the agony of crying for him. Only when she was in pain could she feel that her love for Isaac was still real, that *he* was still real. Some of her memories of Isaac were already fading – worn out like a treasured photograph with too much handling – and she was worried that if she ever came to terms with his death it would not only be a betrayal of his short life but she would have nothing left of him.

So the pain had to go on. It was her only real source of comfort.

When she arrived and dropped her overnight bag to the floor, Sarah's first words were, 'Please may I have an enormous glass of wine, and after I've gulped it down will you give me another?'

Bemused, Ali opened a bottle of chilled Sauvignon *blanc* and watched, in astonished silence, as her friend plonked herself on the sofa, drained the glass in one go, then held it out for a refill. Ali obliged and when that, too, had disappeared she said, 'And how long do I have to wait before I get an explanation for why my normally sober-as-a-judge friend is suddenly resembling Oliver Reed on an all-out bender?'

'Quite a while,' Sarah replied. 'I want to get drunk. Completely drunk. Then I'll talk. Not before.'

'Has this got something to do with Trevor?'

Sarah said obstinately, 'More wine, please.'

Another glassful disappeared and Ali grew concerned. She moved the bottle away from her friend's field of vision and said, 'Ready to talk yet?'

'No. I want to keep on drinking until everything bad in my life is no longer there.'

'Sarah,' Ali said gently, 'if it were possible to drink one's problems away, don't you think I might have tried it? Now, no more booze until I've had some sense out of you. In fact, I'm going to go and put the kettle on because by the time it's boiled you're going to be feeling the effect of all that wine you've knocked back and in dire need of several mugs of strong black coffee.'

'But I don't want to be sober,' Sarah said, leaping up from the sofa, her cheeks flushed, her voice thick with the onset of tears. 'I've come here to get drunk. Don't you understand? I've come here to be different. I'm tired of being who I am. I don't want to be the Sarah you know, or think you know. I want to be the Sarah I was meant to be.' Her shoulders shook and she sobbed.

Ali went to Sarah and put her arms around her. 'Whatever is it? What's been going on that you've kept from me?'

It was some minutes before Sarah could speak and when she did she realised that Ali had been correct about the effect of all the wine she'd drunk. 'Could I have that coffee now, please?' she said, slightly shamefaced. 'My head feels as if it's floating a couple of inches above my shoulders.'

Ali hurriedly made a large cafetière of coffee, tucked a box of tissues under her arm, went back into the sitting area and joined Sarah on the sofa. 'You were right about this being to do with Trevor,' Sarah said, her composure reinstated once more. 'It is.'

Ali wanted to say, 'Well, of course it is. Who else could push you to this breaking point?' but she wisely held her tongue. This was not the moment for a litany of hatred against the man she held responsible for everything miserable in Sarah's life.

'Trouble is, I'm not sure where or how to begin,' said Sarah, taking a cautious sip of her coffee.

Again Ali wanted to chip in: 'You could go back to when you agreed to marry the stupid man. That's when all your problems started, surely.' But with great restraint she said, 'Why don't you tell me what made you call me on Tuesday evening? You didn't sound at all like you. Had something happened then?'

Without being able to look Ali in the eye Sarah told her what had been going on at Smithy Cottage. She told her of the extent of Trevor's preoccupation with the Slipper Gang and what it was doing to him. Then she told Ali what had gone on at their Tuesday night prayer-group meeting and the pathetic game Trevor had played.

Ali's face blazed with anger. 'Bloody hell!' she thundered. 'This is appalling. The man's stark staring bonkers.'

'It gets worse,' murmured Sarah.

Ali stared at her anxiously. 'He's not hurt you, has he? Because if he's so much as looked at you with intent, I'll—'

Sarah shook her head. 'No. Nothing like that.'

'What, then?'

She told Ali about Jamie.

'Don't tell me, Trevor doesn't approve.'

'That's putting it mildly.'

'But how does that compare with imagining that you're in league with my old mate Beelzebub?'

'This morning he ... he went into Hannah's bedroom and found her diary and—'

'Hold on a moment,' cut in Ali. 'What do you mean by "found"?'

Sarah looked uncomfortable. She put down her mug, took a long lock of her hair and twisted it round her finger.

Ali recognised straight away what she was doing: it was a sign that Sarah was struggling with her conscience. Other people chewed their lip, bit their nails or clasped their hands, but Sarah fiddled with her hair. It amazed Ali that even now, after everything Sarah had just told her, her friend was still torn by loyalty to Trevor.

At last Sarah spoke. 'While Hannah was out in Chester this morning he searched her room until he found where she'd hidden it. Oh, Ali, she'd written about Jamie and what she felt for him. He's her first boyfriend. It was so innocent, so sweet and touching. But Trevor turned it into something sordid and shameful.'

Ali was furious. 'He's got no right to do that,' she roared. 'What kind of father is he?'

'A scared father,' Sarah said quietly.

'You sound almost as if you're defending him.'

'I'm not. It's just that I can understand what drove him to it. He's desperately trying to control something that's no longer within his power. He wants his little girl back. It's as simple as that.'

Ali got up from the sofa to throw another log on the fire. 'Well, he'll lose her for ever if he carries on behaving the way he is. Does Hannah know what he did?'

'Yes. He confronted her with the diary when she came home. I've never seen her so upset or so angry. She burst into tears and screamed and screamed at him. She said some terrible things.'

'There's not a living soul who would criticise her for doing that. You've not left her on her own with him, have you?'

'No. I decided we would all benefit from some time out from one another. I took her to stay with Emily, which was why I was so late coming to you.'

Ali came back to the sofa and sat with her legs tucked underneath her. 'And in what state did you leave Trevor? On his knees praying for both your mortal souls?'

'Not exactly. He was in his workshop taking out his temper on a piece of wood. I've no idea what I'll return to tomorrow.'

'Then don't go back.'

The words hung in the air provocatively.

Sarah raised her eyes to Ali's and knew that she wasn't talking in the short term. 'I have to,' she said softly.

'No, you don't.'

'Ali, I know what you're suggesting, but it's not in me.'

'And it's in you to stay with a man who's unhinged?'

'He's not unhinged,' Sarah said, with a frown. 'I'm sure this is just some kind of mid-life crisis he's going through. He's using the Slipper Gang to replace the relationship Hannah is withdrawing from him. If I can be patient and wait for him to work it out of his system, everything will come right in the end.'

'Oh, Sarah, listen to yourself. You keep on defending him. Why?'

'Because he's my husband.'

'Bugger that for a game of soldiers! No decent husband publicly humiliates his wife and makes out that she's consumed by an evil force that needs exorcising. You have to face up to it. He's hurting and abusing you and will continue to do so for as long as you let him. Just leave him. When Hannah's done her exams come and move in with me. There's plenty of room. We'd have a great time, we'd—'

'Stop it, Ali. Please stop. None of that is possible.'

'Why not?'

'I told you before, he's my husband. I could never leave him.'

'Which means you could never be truly happy. How can you live with that?'

Sarah's face was serious and she gazed across the room at the flickering flames in the fire. 'Because I couldn't live with the knowledge that I'd broken my marriage vows,' she said quietly.

Ali let these words sink in. She had the nasty feeling that Sarah was about to start waving the banner of her religious beliefs as a reason for staying in her incomprehensible marriage. Stalling for time to reassess the situation, she said, 'Sarah, let me ask you a question. Could you ever conceive of living on your own and being happy?'

Sarah returned her gaze to Ali and very slowly a tentative smile appeared on her face, until finally it broke into a radiant expression of happiness. Then she threw back her head and laughed. 'Oh, yes,' she said, her laughter echoing round the room, 'I believe I could be extremely happy without Trevor.'

23

The bright, carefree laughter that had so unexpectedly filled the room came to an abrupt end, and in an altogether more subdued tone, Sarah said, 'You've no idea how good that was, actually to hear myself say what I've thought so many times, but never dared to voice. Are you very shocked?'

Ali *was* shocked. But not for the reason her friend was thinking. She couldn't get over the intense change in Sarah's face as she'd uttered those words: *I believe I could be extremely happy without Trevor.* Not for years had she seen or heard Sarah express herself with such heartfelt joy. Or with such passion.

'Ali?'

Ali kicked herself out of her thoughts. 'Of course I'm not shocked, Sarah, it's more a matter of being stunned that you know how different and infinitely better your life could be, but you're not prepared to do anything about it.'

'It's not as simple as that.'

'It could be.'

Sarah shook her head resolutely. 'No. Divorce is not an option for me.' Then she said, 'I'm sorry that I arrived here in such a hysterical state.'

'Given the circumstances, I'd say you've behaved as you always do, with admirable self-control. If it had been me in your shoes I wouldn't be drinking cups of coffee with a friend, I'd be out there searching for a suitable hiding-place for the recognisable bits of Trevor's dismembered body. Isn't there anything I can say to make you see sense?'

Leaning forward to place her empty mug on the table, Sarah said, 'No, there isn't. I meant it when I said that divorce isn't an option for me.'

Ali drew a knee up to her chest, rested an elbow on it, and gave Sarah one of her no-holds-barred penetrating stares. 'Okay, so give it to me straight. God's lurking at the bottom of all this, isn't he? The God who so graciously dumped Trevor on you expects you to stay with him, no matter what. Even if it makes a mockery of your own existence and robs it of its worth. How am I doing? Am I close?'

'As always, and in your inimitable fashion, you've entirely missed the point,' Sarah said wearily.

'Oh, I know what the point is, all right,' Ali said hotly. 'You expect the wrathful hand of God to strike you down in a fit of retributional malice if you don't do as he commands.'

'Goodness, for an atheist you've got an awful lot to say about something you don't believe exists,' countered Sarah.

'That's because there's so much propaganda put about one can't help but absorb some of it. And while we're on the subject – and I accept full responsibility for the lack of originality to the question, but humour me with a credible answer: if your faith hangs on the belief that God is all-powerful and that nothing's too insignificant or too great for him to handle, why do we spend most of our lives having to cope with so many appalling atrocities? Or is that because we get what we deserve? The punishment fits the crime. You're such a bloody awful sinner God gave you Trevor and, of course, it makes perfect sense that all those poor devils in Bangladesh must have been so inherently bad that they've been given a flood just to make them appreciate the squalor and poverty they already live with. And as for me, well, that's bloody obvious, isn't it? My crimes against humanity were so great I had ... I had—' But her words fell away and, her face suffused with colour, she stared miserably into the middle distance of her anger.

'And you had Isaac taken away from you just to teach you a lesson in humility,' Sarah murmured softly.

'Yeah,' Ali muttered, her eyes dark with bitterness, 'so I did.' She blew her nose, then threw the tissue at the fire but missed. 'I guess in your book that stupid outburst makes me a sodding agnostic, doesn't it?'

Sarah looked at her kindly. 'Chance would be a fine thing. But I have to say, from a theological point of view, you're all over the place with that theory. Isaac didn't die to serve you right, any more than the people of Bangladesh deserved what they're currently experiencing. The question we should ask ourselves is not what sort of God allows thousands of innocent people to die in a disaster, but what kind of person stands by while his neighbour suffers? Our reaction should always be, what can I do to help?'

Ali returned her gaze and said, 'That's what I'm trying to do with you. I want to help you but you won't let me.'

'But, Ali, you are. Right now you're helping me by giving me the opportunity to speak my mind. I'm sure that once I've got everything off my chest and I've calmed down I'll go back home tomorrow and everything will be all right.'

Ali looked at her doubtfully. 'You don't really believe that, do you?'

'I have to believe it.'

'But what if Trevor gets worse? What if he's undergoing some sort of delusory disorder? What if he starts trying to exorcise Hannah?'

'He won't,' Sarah said firmly. 'I'm sure that deep down he thinks she's just going through a typical teenage stage of rebellion.'

'Well, if he thinks that, why can't he adopt the appropriate role of quietly bemused father, instead of going off his head with all this fanatical everything's-of-the-Devil baloney?'

'I don't know the answer to that. I wish I did.'

'And I wish I could understand why you're sacrificing your happiness for the sake of your beliefs. Divorce has been going on in the Church of England long enough for even a saint such as you not to feel guilty about resorting to it.'

Sarah smiled patiently. 'All my adult life I've lived according to my faith –' she raised a hand to stop Ali interrupting – 'and yes, I'm well aware that you'd like to throw in a quick, below-the-belt and-look-where-it's-got-you, but I happen to believe that without it I would have been very much the poorer. I know that when we were at Oxford you suspected that I'd taken up with all that "religious nonsense", as you not so intellectually referred to it, because I was searching for some kind of mental crutch to make—'

'Yes,' Ali was unable to keep quiet any longer, 'you're right, that's exactly what I thought. What's more, I reckon you've hung on to that crutch in the mistaken hope that it would fill the void a loving husband should have filled.'

Sarah opened her eyes wide. 'Ali, I can't believe you just said that! You, the red-hot archetypal independent woman who beats her chest every morning to the chant, "Men, who needs them?"'

'Funny ha-ha. But I notice you've avoided answering my question.'

'I was coming to that before you stepped in so rudely.'

'I'm sorry. Go on.'

'How one views religion, spirituality, faith – call it what you will – is very personal, but for me it doesn't provide one iota of certainty, not even guaranteed peace of mind—'

'So what's the point in it, then?'

Sarah smiled with amused tolerance at yet another interruption. 'It provides the courage to face what we think is beyond us,' she said patiently.

Ali thought about this. 'Are you telling me that it's your faith that's kept you sane throughout your marriage and that it's faith that will keep you there?'

Sarah nodded.

Ali let out her breath. 'Hellfire, that's some act of faith.'

'Marriage is.'

'But . . . but you can still believe in Christ and all his merry apostles and be divorced. Surely the one doesn't preclude the other. Why can't you simply play the Christian trump card of confessing, repenting and moving on? I thought that's what the Resurrection was all about?'

'One has to abide by the basic principles of one's beliefs. I'm afraid I can't subscribe to the view that one can pick and choose from the Bible. If we did that it would fall apart and there'd be nothing left of any value.'

'No leeway, then?'

'No. To disregard a basic tenet of scripture just because it doesn't suit one's current situation is a flagrant breach of faith. If you recall, I did it once before back in Oxford and that's why I'm now married to Trevor.'

'But the bulk of what the Bible says is open to conjecture and how we interpret it. It was written centuries ago and for a very different culture.'

'And to quote something you said to me at Christmas, isn't that the great universal cop-out? Now, if we could drop the subject, I'd love something to eat. I missed lunch and I'm starving.'

They cooked supper together, and while Ali prodded at the lamb chops under the grill, she watched Sarah out of the corner of her eye as she added milk and butter to the potatoes she was mashing. She looked as though she hadn't a care in the world and Ali marvelled at her restored calm. Was it possible that only a few hours ago she had been distraught with frustrated unhappiness?

But wasn't it what they all did? Hadn't she, herself, been on her knees that afternoon consumed by the worst misery? The masks we wear, that's what it was all about. It was always easier to keep the mask in place than let it slip to reveal one's true self. And she should know: she'd been doing it for more than two years now.

'Elliot was here last night,' she said, as casually as she could, deciding that Sarah deserved a break from being under the spotlight. 'He came for dinner, at my invitation.'

'Did he indeed?' said Sarah, joining her at the cooker and putting the saucepan of mashed potatoes on the ring.

'Indeed he did. And afterwards we made love till dawn.'

'Yes, dear, and was that before or after you danced naked around the maypole?'

Ali laughed. 'Why can't I ever make you rise to the bait? If I'd thrown Daniel that line he would have been panting for the sexually explicit details.'

'That's because he's the same as you, incorrigibly nosy.' Without taking her eyes off what she was doing, Sarah went on, 'And did the thought of making love till dawn go through your mind when Elliot was here?'

'Sarah!'

She smiled. 'So it did cross your mind.'

'For no more than a second, I swear.' Ali was part-horrified to hear herself admitting to it but also part-relieved.

Sarah appeared to read her thoughts. 'Come on, Ali,' she said, 'confession is good for the soul. Why don't you tell me what else you thought while he was here? But before that, put me in the picture as to why you invited him for dinner in the first place.'

'I'm afraid you won't approve of my motives.'

'Have I ever approved of any of your motives?'

'But this one was particular unpleasant. Even I'm ashamed of it.'

They served their supper and carried it over to the table. Ali opened another bottle of wine and told Sarah about her week: of Elliot surprising her in the office when she'd been sprawled on her desk showing her all; of him taking her out for lunch; and of Daniel's words of interfering wisdom, which had led her to wanting to prove him wrong.

'And who exactly did you prove wrong in the end?' asked Sarah, when Ali had finished.

'Heaven only knows. Just as I think I've got the answer to all this mess, I realise I haven't. I'm so bloody confused. I thought I had Elliot all neatly buttoned up. I thought I had him sussed. But after last night I'm not so sure. I was dreading him coming here and certainly to begin with my fears were confirmed. We were horribly distant and cold to each other, but then gradually we got talking about work and we seemed to relax. There were moments when it was almost enjoyable.'

'So when did the idea of sex enter your mind?'

'When I was getting the cheese and biscuits. I was sneaking a good long look at him while he had his back to me, then suddenly he turned and ... Oh, God, this is so embarrassing.' She hung her head.

'Go on, what did he say?'

Ali raised her head. 'It wasn't what he said, it was what he did. He flashed me one of his rare-as-gold-dust smiles and I was a goner. *Phwoar* factor big-time.'

'And then?'

Ali grinned. 'Then I ripped off my clothes, threw myself at his feet and said, "It's a wholewheat cracker or me. Make your choice!"'

Sarah didn't return the smile. She sipped her wine and looked serious. 'When you start joking, Ali Anderson, that's when I know I'm getting close. Tell me honestly, how did it make you feel knowing that he could still have that effect on you?'

Ali scowled. 'Confused. Then later, when he tried to kiss me goodnight, I felt cross. Furious.'

'And was that a kiss on the lips or the cheek?'

'It didn't get that far. I ducked out of the way just in time.'

'How fortunate,' Sarah said drily. 'So if he treated you to one of his sexy smiles, which I recall only too well, *and* tried to kiss you, what do you suppose Elliot feels for you, Ali?'

'If you were to ask Daniel, he'd tell you that Elliot—'

'I'm not asking Daniel, I'm asking *you*.'

'Then you're asking the wrong person. I've no idea what Elliot thinks about me.'

'But you're more than capable of making an educated guess.'

Ali reached for the bottle of wine and topped up her glass. 'Are you trying to push me into a corner?'

'Is that how you see it?'

Ali rolled her eyes. 'It's what it bloody well feels like. And if you intend on wheedling away until you get an answer, I'll save you the trouble. Elliot could be doing either of two things. It's possible that he's deliberately trying to punish himself by seeing me, or he could be wanting to use me as a means of assuaging his guilt. Personally, I'd go with the second option.'

Sarah set her glass down on the table and said, 'And that's the last thing you'd want to help him with, isn't it?'

There was a tense pause while Sarah waited for Ali to explode. But she didn't. Neatly changing the subject, she said, 'Oh, I nearly forgot, Elliot sends his love.'

It was tempting to say, 'Give him mine when you see him next,' but Sarah didn't want to antagonise Ali any further. She let her thoughts linger on Elliot and pondered on her own personal loss at not seeing him since the divorce. He was a kind, thoughtful man who had always shown great tact when confronted by Trevor in one of his less than endearing moods. 'Accountants,' Trevor would joke, 'little more than parasites making good on the backs of somebody else's hard graft.' It was quite obvious why Trevor said what he did: it was his way of handling being the odd one out of the foursome. She, Ali and Elliot had all made it to Oxford but Trevor had not: he'd studied at the polytechnic at Headington and had never let anyone forget it. 'Elitist groves of academia are all very well,' he'd pontificate, 'but it's the polytechnics that provide the sound, practical education that industry is after.' The more he went on, the more he made himself the social and academic inferior. It was so embarrassing. Ali would frequently lose her temper with him and tell him not to be such a pig-headed fool, but Elliot would listen patiently then turn the conversation to a subject that showed Trevor in a better light. 'How's Hannah getting on with her music?' he'd ask, and off Trevor would go, happy as Larry to boast of his daughter's skill on the flute. Trevor's pride in Hannah, with his hopes and aspirations for her, was one of those strange but perfectly understandable paradoxes. While he openly disparaged the system that had educated Ali, Elliot and his wife, it was quite within the rules of his prejudice for his daughter to go there. 'Of course, it's different nowadays,' he had said, when Hannah first talked of applying. 'They've had to move with the times and change the whole ethos of what they stand for. It's no longer acceptable to be so elitist.'

It was a not-so-subtle moving of the goalposts but Sarah was more than willing to let him get away with it. Conceding was, after all, something she was good at.

Unlike Ali.

Ali had probably never conceded a point in her life. It was as alien to her nature as it was to forgive and forget. And if only she could do that, thought Sarah with sadness, as she glanced at her friend across the table, she would be so much happier. From what Ali had told her about Elliot, it sounded very much as if he was ready to move on, that he was now wanting to put Isaac's tragic death behind him, and that, for whatever reason, he saw Ali as a crucial part of that process.

As if she'd picked up on the dangerous direction Sarah's thoughts were heading, Ali pushed away her empty plate, rested her elbows on the table and said, 'So let's get back to this divorce thing. I still don't get it. There has to be a way round it.'

She might just as well have rolled up her sleeves, thought Sarah, with a wry smile. Well, two could play at that game. 'Before you subject me to a further onslaught of interrogation,' she said, 'I have a question for you. How much longer do you intend to use Elliot as a focus for your pain and anger?'

24

Ali gave a short contemptuous laugh. 'What is it with everyone?' she asked. 'Suddenly you all fancy yourselves as armchair psychotherapists; first Daniel, now you.'

Undaunted, Sarah said, 'Ten out of ten for a typically defensive response to a question you don't want to answer. Is there any chance of me having some of that wine, or are you going to hog the bottle for the rest of the night?'

Ali pushed it across the table and reflected on why it was that her two closest friends had taken to questioning her. They never had before, so why had they chosen now to start shining the light in her eyes, and giving her the third degree? She decided to be direct. 'Before I submit to your cack-handed grilling technique,' she said, 'am I allowed to ask why the sudden interest in what I do, say or think? What have I done that warrants this special scrutiny?'

Sarah heard the sharpness in Ali's voice. Should she risk all and pursue the conversation in the hope that Ali would finally admit the truth, or should she keep quiet? A true friend would want to help, she told herself. And ignoring Ali's question, she bravely made herself say, 'Knowing you as well as Elliot does, can you imagine the courage it must have taken for him to turn up at your office unexpectedly and ask you out to lunch?'

Ali shrugged indifferently. 'Give him his due, Elliot was never a coward. So where's your point leading?'

'Where it should be leading you.'

'Which is?'

'It strikes me that Elliot is ready to move on. Perhaps he's doing his best to put Isaac's tragic death behind him. I want to know if you're prepared to do the same.'

Ali studied the half-empty glass in her hand. Holding it by the stem, she slowly turned it round and round, the base of the glass scraping on the table. 'Well, bully for him,' she said, without looking up.

'But isn't that what you should be striving for?'

Still fiddling with the glass, Ali didn't say anything.

Sarah knew what Ali was withholding from her and believed that it was the key to unlocking the prison her friend had made for herself. 'Ali,' she said gently, 'look at me and tell me why you don't want to move on?'

Reluctantly Ali raised her eyes. 'Because it would be a betrayal.'

'Of whom?'

'Isaac, of course.'

'So punishing yourself is the way to keep Isaac alive, is that what you're saying?'

'I'm not punishing myself.'

'Oh, but, Ali, you are. And not just you.'

Ali's face darkened. She let go of her glass and shifted uncomfortably in her chair. 'Now you're really scraping the bottom of the trick-cyclist's barrel,' she said airily, letting out her breath as though she was tired of the subject.

Undeceived by Ali's air of dismissive boredom, Sarah took a metaphorical deep breath and pressed on in the unshakeable belief that what she was doing was right. It had to be done. She'd brought Ali this far, she wasn't going to let her slip away. 'I'm talking about your need to punish Elliot,' she said fearlessly. 'By not forgiving him for his rejection of you, you're keeping him in the same hell that you're in. You need his company there because you can't cope with the thought of being all alone in that miserable place. With nobody there to abuse, you'll end up punishing yourself even harder. And, as we all know, nobody punishes us more than ourselves.'

The colour drained slowly from Ali's face. She went very pale. Her hands reached out for her wineglass, then as if thinking better of it she pushed it away. 'I hate it when you get clever,' she said quietly. 'Why couldn't I have chosen a friend who was as dumb as me?'

Sarah smiled at her fondly, relieved that her words hadn't invoked a rage of hot denial. She understood that Ali's flippancy was her way of accepting what she'd just said and lightened the mood by saying, 'You didn't choose me. I chose you. The moment I saw you in the playground with Caroline Rothwell on top of you I thought, Now, there's somebody who goes about everything the wrong way.'

'I haven't changed much, then, have I?' Ali said despondently.

'Strange as it may seem, that's part of your charm. It's why Daniel and I love you as much as we do.'

'Well, I don't feel very charming. I should be more like you, virtuous and perceptively wise.' She smiled awkwardly. 'Do you remember my grandmother making us have an *alter ego*? I was supposed to learn from you how to be more thoughtful and you were supposed to take a leaf out of my book and be more assertive.'

'I think we'd both be the first to admit that we failed that little exercise. But it's funny that you should have mentioned our *alter egos*. After years of not thinking of her, Sarah the Impudent showed up the other day.'

'My God, I'd forgotten we'd given them names. What was mine called?'

'Ali the Angel.'

Ali groaned. 'So it was. Much good she's done me.'

'Perhaps you ought to resurrect her.'

'What, and have her confirm what a terrible person I've become?'

'Don't be too hard on yourself. What you've been through hasn't been easy. Given the extent of your loss, the mistakes you've made are quite understandable.' After a slight pause, she said, 'Why don't you tell me the rest?'

'The rest?'

'Yes. What really drove you to push Elliot away from you?'

Ali frowned with exasperation and chewed her lip. 'But, you know, it wasn't like that. It was *him* who froze me out. He wouldn't let me near him, he—'

Sarah reached across the table and touched Ali's hand lightly. 'In the beginning that's what happened, but what then? Did you talk to him? Did you try to help him, or did you deliberately provoke Elliot by being as cold and unforgiving as you knew how?'

With a sudden, quick-tempered movement, Ali snatched away her hand.

'And isn't it true,' continued Sarah, undeterred, 'that you kept on hurting him until you were convinced that he was in as much pain as you, if not more?'

'That's a terrible thing to say,' hissed Ali, her face blanched with both anger and distress. 'I – I didn't do that. How could you even think that of me?' But her lip trembled and betrayed her. She lowered her head and a painful hush engulfed them. When eventually Ali looked up there were tears in her eyes. 'Oh, Sarah,' she said, all sign of her rancorous denial now gone, 'I didn't mean to do it, I was mad with grief. I couldn't accept that Isaac was dead, it just wasn't possible. And when Elliot turned away from me, I felt – I felt that I had nothing left, that I'd lost everything. I was so angry . . . Then once I'd started hurting him I couldn't stop myself. It was . . . it was like a drug and I kept on going for his jugular until I was sure he hated me. It was the ultimate punishment I could inflict on him – to destroy the love we'd once had. To put him through the hell I was experiencing.'

'Did you never think he was already in hell?'

Ali shuddered. 'I wasn't in any fit state to think logically. All I knew was that if we were both damned, it meant in some crazy way we were connected.'

'Have you ever tried to explain this to Elliot?'

Ali wiped her eyes on the back of her sleeve and sniffed loudly. 'No.'

'Is it time that you did?'

'I don't know. It's probably too late. The harm's done. He'd never understand.'

'I think he does understand, I've a feeling that he's come to terms with a lot more than you give him credit for. The question is, if he's forgiven you, can you do the same for him?'

When Ali didn't respond, Sarah said, 'Forgiving Elliot doesn't necessarily mean that you have to be involved with him again.'

'I'll think about it,' Ali said, getting up from her chair and indicating that she'd had enough of the conversation. 'It's late, we should go to bed now.'

Sarah woke to the sound of tapping on her bedroom door. She muttered a sleepy, 'Yes,' and Ali, still in her pyjamas, came into the room with a large tray. She placed it on top of the duvet and climbed into the double bed beside Sarah.

'It's ten-thirty, time you were stirring,' she said brightly.

'Ten-thirty. You're joking.' Sarah sat up, looked at her watch, and saw that Ali was telling the truth. 'But I never sleep this long,' she said.

Pouring their tea, Ali said, 'That's because the Donovan homestead is the coldest place on earth and if you stay put for too long you'll die of frostbite.'

'It's not that bad. Is it?'

Ali passed her a mug of Rose Pouchong and a plate of toast. 'Bloody freezing with knobs on,' she said.

They ate their breakfast in companionable silence and Sarah thought how glad she was to be here with Ali. Despite the nature of everything they'd discussed since she'd arrived, her usual inner calm seemed to have been fully restored. It was odd that for some weeks now she had begun to doubt her faith, but when yesterday it had come under attack from Ali, she had instinctively leaped to its defence. Which was encouraging. It meant, reassuringly, that it was still intact. After its rough handling of late by Trevor and the Slipper Gang, it was a wonder it hadn't packed its bags and left home in a sulk. She smiled at the thought of this improbable analogy and pictured the sight of Faith pouting and slamming doors and stomping off down the garden path in a state of high dudgeon – *And don't go thinking I'm ever coming back!*

'Something amusing you?' asked Ali.

'A private joke,' Sarah said, 'and one you wouldn't appreciate.'

'It's not Sarah the Impudent showing her face again is it?'

'Not quite.'

'You didn't tell me last night why she suddenly appeared on the scene again.'

'Just a case of needing some inner moral support, I guess.'

'God not enough, then?'

Sarah smiled. 'He was busy watching over you.'

'And having a damn good laugh, no doubt. Did you sleep okay? The bed all right?'

'Fine. How about you?'

'Badly. I kept going over everything we discussed. Or, rather, what you dragged out of me while putting me through open heart surgery without the aid of an anaesthetic.'

'I'm sorry. Am I forgiven?'

'I'll let you know.'

'Well, promise me one thing. Promise you'll talk to Elliot. It would help you both so much in coming to terms with what's happened.'

'Mm . . . Again, I'll let you know. One thing puzzles me, though. Why did you wait until now to push me against the wall and make me admit what I'd been doing?'

'I took a huge gamble last night and simply trusted in my belief that you were willing to listen to me. I wouldn't have dared to try it a year ago. You weren't ready then – you'd probably have ended our friendship.'

Ali thought about this and was forced to agree that Sarah was right. It also made her acknowledge that, without knowing it, she had very slowly been learning to cope with some of her anger at the injustice of losing Isaac. 'I'd like to think that you're wrong about me flying off the handle and ending our friendship, but I'm glad you didn't risk it. Now, enough about my problems, I want to carry on where I left off with you last night.'

Laughing at Ali's ceaseless desire to strip-search her marriage, she said, 'No surprises there, then.'

'And I don't want you slipping in any more of your clever diverting questions. Got that?'

'Standard procedure, Ali. I've learned it all from you.'

'Well, be prepared to be outwitted. First question. When you arrived yesterday afternoon and were hitting the wine like a woman who'd been in the desert for forty days, you said you wanted to be the Sarah you were meant to be. What was that about?'

Sarah proffered her empty mug for some more tea and said, 'I'm afraid I was being a touch melodramatic.'

'That's certainly one way of describing it, but it begs the question why you were being uncharacteristically melodramatic. Especially when I don't think it relates directly to Trevor's bout of madness. I've a strong feeling that whatever drove you to say what you did has less to do with Trevor and more to do with you.'

'You're right. It has. I drove here at screaming pitch realising that I was tired of being Sarah the peacemaker. Just for once I wanted to be Sarah the hellraiser. I wanted a little drama of my own. I've had years and years of being an extra in the drama of other people's lives.'

Ali felt guilty. 'Oh dear,' she said, 'and within no time at all you were back to being Sarah the peacemaker and counselling me on my troubles.'

'But don't you see? That's what I always do. It's of my own doing. I much prefer helping others sort out their troubles than dealing with my own. I'm nothing but a coward.'

'The hell you are! Living with Trevor is a supreme act of bravery.'

'That's not true. I've turned away from Trevor's problems rather than confront them.'

'Such as?'

Sarah hesitated. Her hand rose instinctively to her sleep-tousled hair and pulled at a lock. As ever, the bond of loyalty she felt for Trevor was hard to shrug off. Or was she just plain old-fashioned embarrassed? She took the plunge and said, 'Well, for instance, Trevor and I haven't had sex for nearly ten years.'

Ali goggled. 'Why not?'

'He's not interested. Not since he became worried Hannah might hear us.'

'Does it bother you?'

'It did in the beginning, yes. But not now. I've got used to it not being there. In fact, I'm not sure how I'd react if he suddenly showed a renewed interest.'

Ali knew what her reaction would be: to run in the opposite direction. 'Tricky question on the horizon,' she said, 'and I'm on my guard for any diverting techniques you might have up your sleeve. At Christmas you told me that you've always felt sorry for Trevor. Is that all you feel, or do you love him?'

Sarah dabbed at the toast crumbs on her plate and drew a line through them with her forefinger. She contemplated lying, but in view of the degree of honesty she'd forced out of Ali it didn't seem fair. 'No, I don't love him,' she said, matter-of-factly.

'Have you ever loved him?'

'Sort of, yes.' Again the same reasonable tone.

Ali considered this. 'Okay,' she said, after a bit. 'Let's summarise. You've never truly loved Trevor – not in the heartaching way. You have no real marriage, i.e. there's no nookie on offer. You won't divorce him because of your Christian belief in the sanctity of marriage and, lastly, you know that you could be happier without him. How am I doing? Have I covered everything?'

Sarah frowned. 'It sounds worse when you put it as bluntly as that. There's no mention of the respect I once had for Trevor for being such a good father and for all the—'

'Yes, yes, yes,' Ali cut in impatiently, 'so let's give the man a couple of Brownie points if it makes you feel easier.'

'It's not a matter of awarding—'

Ali held up a hand. 'Sarah, if you're about to embark on some sneaky diverting tactic, stop it now. I've got a seriously important question and I want it answered. According to your absurdly strict and antiquated Christian ethics, is divorce *ever* permissible?'

Sarah sighed. 'Yes,' she said.

'Hallelujah! Finally we're getting somewhere. I knew there'd be some convenient loophole tucked into the depths of all that gobbledegook. So what is it?'

'Adultery.'

Ali stared at Sarah. 'And that makes it permissible in your view? As simple as that?'

'Hypothetically, yes.'

'So if Trevor was to have an affair it would change everything?'

'As I just said, hypothetically, yes.'

Ali threw back her head and laughed. 'So all we need to do is find someone daft enough to go to bed with Trevor and you'd be a free woman?'

Sarah rolled her eyes and tutted at Ali's madness of thought.

'How about that weird Shirley character?' Ali said, when she'd stopped laughing. 'Do you think she's a likely candidate?'

It was Sarah's turn to be amused now. 'About as likely as you!'

Later that day as Ali stood outside the mill in a light drizzle of rain waving Sarah goodbye and wondering what cold misery awaited her at Smithy Cottage, she reflected on what her friend had told her that morning. Adultery, then, so it seemed, was the answer to all Sarah's problems. As easy and as uncomplicated as that. Just one illicit feverish fumble on Trevor's part and it would all be over.

The thought stayed with Ali for the rest of the afternoon, niggling away at her annoyingly as she curled up on the sofa watching television for something to do. Restlessly channel-hopping through a programme selection of golf, football, rugby, a musical adventure and a re-run of *Are You Being Served?*, she kept thinking the craziest of ideas. What if . . . what if *she* slept with Trevor?

No.

No, no, *no*, NO!

It was madness. It was lunacy of the highest order. She loved Sarah to bits, but seducing the ghastly Trevor for the sake of freeing her from her pointless marriage was way beyond even her loyal devotion. Cringing at yet another indelicate reference to Mrs Slocombe's feline companion, she suddenly pictured the scene of a panting, heaving Trevor on top of her. She shuddered with heart-stopping revulsion. *Jeez*, she'd have to be smashed out of her brains on a keg or two of Jack Daniel's to pull off a stunt as selfless as that.

25

It was the end of June, and since the start of Hannah's A-level exams in the middle of May, the weather had been glorious. A baking sun had cruelly taunted Hannah and Emily to abandon their revision and go outside to lie on the parched grass in the seductively hot sunshine. They'd resisted the temptation with admirable determination. And as the temperature had steadily risen, so had the tension inside Smithy Cottage – though in fairness to Hannah, once her exams were under way, there had been only a couple of nail-bitingly fraught days to cope with. This was when she had been utterly convinced that she'd messed up her French literature paper and had taken out her frustration on her father. But now all the hard work was over and Smithy Cottage was a relatively stress-free zone again.

It was also on the verge of becoming a daughter-free zone. As Sarah watched Hannah checking her small black-leather rucksack, which contained her passport and a meagre supply of cash and travellers' cheques, which would hopefully see her through the summer, she tried not to feel too envious. What wouldn't she give to throw a few essentials into a bag and head for six wonderfully carefree weeks in the sun?

For the past fortnight, and since the exams had finished, Hannah had been unable to talk about anything other than her impending holiday. She and Emily were joining Jamie and his friend, Craig, on their trip to France. They were going in Jamie's new car and the plan was to explore Brittany and the Atlantic coast and slowly make their way down to Biarritz, stopping *en route* for a couple of nights with an aunt of Craig's who lived somewhere near La Rochelle. During the last few days a fever pitch of anticipation had been rapidly brewing, with Hannah and Emily constantly making last-minute adjustments to what they would and would not take with them.

Were high-cut shorts in or out?

Did the short silky dress make Hannah's hips look smaller?

Would the bikini or the fluorescent all-in-one make more of Emily's spectacular cleavage?

The backpacks were packed and repacked.

And all the while, Trevor hung about muttering darkly of the potential dangers awaiting Hannah on the other side of the Channel.

'She'll be fine.' Sarah had had to placate him. 'It's not as if she's going to be on her own – there's Emily, Jamie and Craig. She'll be quite safe.'

'Emily's got the sense of a half-wit,' he'd retorted, 'and those boys, well, what do we *really* know about them?'

But Sarah had great faith in Jamie. He was everything she would want in a boyfriend for her daughter. He was polite, caring and mature for his years. As for being a distraction during Hannah's exams, as Trevor had predicted, he'd been the opposite: he'd helped her to revise as well as kick into touch her occasional moments of panic. And much as Trevor had been desperate to consign Jamie to life's overflowing dustbin of no-hopers, Sarah had been delighted when he'd reluctantly admitted that there was little to object to in him – other than that he was not a brother in Christ.

Jamie's friend, Craig, who had been at school with him and was also on a gap year, was 'wacky, but cool', according to Hannah. And this brief description was sufficient to explain his affinity with the dizzy Emily. And no sooner had the perfectly balanced foursome been formed than the suggestion was made that the girls should join Jamie and Craig on their holiday. When Hannah came home one evening and raised the subject, Trevor's response was, 'But what if something went wrong? How would you cope? What would you do? You could be attacked and we wouldn't even know you were in trouble. I really don't think this is a good idea, Hannah.'

'But that could happen to me here, Dad,' Hannah had argued. 'They do have telephones in France, you know.'

Sarah's concern for Hannah's safety was just as great as Trevor's, but she knew there was nothing else for it but to let their daughter go. It was only France, after all. It wasn't as though she wanted to go trekking solo round Bogotá. She's eighteen, she reminded herself, eighteen going on twenty-five. But these reassuring words didn't drive away the worst of Sarah's fears, that Hannah might return home pregnant. In the past, sex was an issue that she and her daughter had discussed quite openly, but that had been in pre-Jamie days. Sarah sensed that Hannah would be a little more guarded on the subject now.

Hannah had now finished checking her bag: a travel packet of tissues had been added, as had a pair of sunglasses, a paperback, some chewing-gum and a stick of strawberry-flavoured lip balm.

'You will be careful, won't you?' Sarah said.

Hannah sat on the bed beside her mother and said, 'Careful to clean my teeth every night or careful with my money?'

'Careful with your body,' Sarah replied.

Hannah gave Sarah one of her grown-up looks that of late had become her stock-in-trade. 'Are you asking me if I intend to have sex with Jamie during this holiday?'

'Something like that, yes.'

Hannah smiled. 'And who's to say we haven't been at it, already?'

'I think I'd know if you had.'

'All parents think that.'

'Am I wrong, then?'

Hannah smiled again. 'Why are we having this conversation, Mum?'

'Because I don't want you coming back from France with any extra luggage. It would spoil your holiday.'

'To say nothing of my future.'

'Exactly.'

'Did I spoil your future, Mum?'

Ouch! thought Sarah. I asked for that.

At an awkwardly precocious age, Hannah had figured out that her arrival in the world had precipitated an early marriage for her parents. 'So I'm a mistake, am I?' she'd said, when she had realised the implications of the date of her birthday coming only a few months after her parents' wedding anniversary. 'Not a mistake,' Sarah had been at pains to point out, 'a surprise, and a lovely one at that.'

Leaving Hannah's question unanswered, Sarah went to the window that overlooked the sun-drenched garden below. The borders were bright with colour: pinks, lavender, nemesia, phlox and petunias held the foreground of the beds, while behind, and standing tall and erect against the rickety old fence that wouldn't see another winter through, were foxgloves, delphiniums and lupins. At the far end of the lawn there were bushes of lavatera, their branches weighed down with soft pink flowers. She had worked hard at creating a loose, natural feel to the garden, just as she'd tried to do in her marriage. With a weary sense of defeat she had to acknowledge that she'd been more successful with one than the other.

Hannah joined her at the window and, from the cluttered sill, picked up one of the many fluffy toys she hadn't yet parted with. 'The question wasn't meant to sound as nasty as it did,' she said, putting an arm around Sarah's shoulders, 'but you must have regretted having to leave Oxford before completing your degree.'

Sarah turned and looked at her – or, rather, looked up at her, for Hannah was a good five inches taller.

'There are always compensations to one's disappointments,' she said.

Hannah hugged her. 'You always say the right thing, Mum. I shall miss that while I'm away.'

'Oh, please, don't start talking like that or you'll have me crying and that would never do.'

Hannah stroked the fluffy toy in her hands, then settled it back amongst its brightly coloured comrades. 'You'll be okay, won't you?'

'In what way?'

'In the coping-with-Dad way.'

'Oh, you know me, I'll manage.'

'I wish you'd tell it to him straight, like I do.'

Sarah smiled, remembering the scene when she and Hannah had returned home after the diary incident. Hannah had certainly given it straight to her father when he'd greeted her with one of his typically graceless apologies. Rather than meet her fiercely defiant gaze he had kept his eyes lowered and practically skewered his bearded chin into the collar of his shirt, giving the impression that he was addressing his creased, old Hush Puppies rather than Hannah. He appeared contrite enough and certainly seemed to be professing that he'd gone too far, blaming his behaviour on an excess of duty to parental care and guidance – but had his performance been sufficiently convincing for Hannah to forgive him? Sarah had waited with bated breath for their daughter's response. It came in the form of a long, bored sigh that contained a pitiful note of contempt. 'Dad,' she said, 'have you looked at me recently?' He raised his head and his puzzled expression indicated that she needed to expand on this question. 'Take a good look,' she continued. 'Do you notice anything different since you last cast your eyes over me? Because, just in case you hadn't realised, I'm now technically a woman. I don't ride about on a tricycle any more, neither do I play with Barbie dolls. So give it up, Dad. Don't keep going with this heavy-father routine.' She'd then gone to her bedroom where she'd taken out her flute and started to play one of her favourite pieces. The clear, silvery, mellifluous sound of Poulenc's flute sonata had drifted down the stairs and had signalled that all was superficially well again. Trevor's relief was so great that he had even enquired after Ali.

'How was she?' he asked, as he watched Sarah getting the tea ready.

'She's fine and sends her best wishes,' she'd lied, then turning to face him she'd said, in a gentle but firm voice, 'Trevor, you must promise never to do anything as potentially harmful as that again to Hannah. You've been very lucky to get off so lightly. A lot of daughters in her place wouldn't have forgiven you.'

Grave-faced, he'd frowned and tugged at his beard. He looked wretched with shame and Sarah's heart went out to him. 'I really don't want to talk about it,' he said, getting up from the table and retreating to the sanctuary of his workshop.

He knows, she thought, that he came within an inch of losing her. She hoped it would be the saving of him.

From that day on, he certainly did his best to treat Hannah with more respect, especially in the weeks before her exams. He even held his tongue when, one evening during supper, after the allegedly botched French literature paper, she attempted to goad him into a discussion on the evils of indoctrination. The scene was uncannily reminiscent of Ali arguing with him, except in this instance, Trevor let his opponent have her inflammatory say then muttered afterwards that he would pray for her.

Now, as Sarah considered her daughter's confident, forthright face before her, she thought, She's right, of course, I should tell it to him straight.

But I probably never will.

'Come on,' she said, glancing over to the bed. 'Is there anything you might have forgotten to pack? No, on second thoughts, forget I said that. I couldn't stand to see you riffle through the contents of that rucksack again.'

Hannah smirked. 'Just wait till I bring it home with six weeks' worth of dirty clothes festering in it.'

Sarah pulled a face. 'I'm counting the days already.'

'But you know I'm worth it, really.'

Sarah smiled indulgently. 'Oh, you're worth it, all right. Every little bit of you. And just for the record, you didn't spoil my future. Far from it, you gave it its focus.'

Hannah hugged her again. 'And for the same record, Jamie and I haven't been to bed with one another.'

When they pulled apart, Sarah said, 'But if or when the time comes, you will be careful, won't you?'

'Hey, wasn't this where we came in?'

'I just need the reassurance.'

'Okay, then, how's this? I've got a handy packet of condoms packed away in my wash-bag . . . just in case.'

Sarah's astonishment was undisguised. 'You have?'

'Wait till you hear how I came by them. It was Ali.'

'*Ali!*'

'Yes, she sent them as a kind of joke present. I wasn't supposed to let on to you, but she said that it was part of her duty as my godmother. She also sent me some money for the holiday, but I wasn't to tell you about that either.'

Sarah rolled her eyes heavenward. 'Well, whatever you do, don't tell your father. He'd kill Ali three times over!'

The thought of what Ali had done stayed with Sarah for the rest of the morning and through till the afternoon when Trevor, poker-faced and brooding, drove them the half-hour journey to Jamie's father's house where everybody was meeting for a farewell drink. She couldn't get over the interfering audacity of Ali's actions and couldn't decide whether she was cross with her or not.

She hadn't seen Ali since that revelatory weekend in March because the past few months had been devoted to Hannah and seeing her through this crucial period. But they had spoken regularly on the phone, usually when Trevor was at a craft fair or visiting one of his specialist wood suppliers. Ali had made her promise that if Trevor started pulling any more pious party tricks on her, she was to call her at once. Mercifully, Trevor seemed happy to believe that he'd hauled his wife back into the fold and, not wanting to disabuse him of this thought, she had played her part. She had gone along with the Slipper Gang who all treated her with sickening solicitude, no doubt worried she might backslide into her old sinful ways. No direct reference had ever been made to that bizarre night when they had prayed for her, but doubtless she was constantly in their self-righteous thoughts. Some evenings when they were together, smugly rejoicing that their names were written in the Lamb's Book of Life, she longed to cause a flutter of God-fearing consternation. But it was too risky and she had no wish to jeopardise the peace that had descended on Smithy Cottage by arousing Trevor's suspicions that she wasn't as committed to the group as he was.

They met twice a week now, having cut themselves off from St Cuthbert's, and held their own service of worship, claiming that it was more meaningful than anything the Church of England had to offer. It was a step Sarah wasn't happy with: she sensed the group was dissociating itself from the real world, that they were beginning to advocate an alternative lifestyle and were putting themselves in a position of authority over others. There was very much an air of complacency to their meetings now, as though the faith anybody else experienced wasn't the real thing.

But more upsetting was that Sarah missed St Cuthbert's. She used to enjoy evensong; it had been a reliable source of solace. Now that was gone and all she had in its place was the inane blathering of the Slipper Gang. They now referred to themselves as a house church and this elevated status was leading them to consider expanding and reaching out to other needy souls. There was much talk of building a community of faith, which amused Sarah as she found it difficult to think of this inept bunch of people building anything more complicated and lasting than a bonfire. But, to be fair to them, the original men of faith in the Bible were always getting it wrong and bickering amongst themselves. Not that there was any bickering going on within the Slipper Gang: rather worryingly, they agreed all too readily with whatever Trevor said. His latest crusade was making them understand how important it was 'not to intellectualise the Lord, but to experience the Lord'. He was very much into 'experience' and was currently immersed in a book on the subject of 'special spiritual gifts'.

The thought of Trevor speaking in tongues was too much for Sarah and she hadn't dared tell Ali about it. She could predict the reaction she'd get: 'I thought he'd been doing that for years.' Signs and Wonders was another of his preoccupations, and just recently he had met a man at one of his craft fairs who had spoken at length to him about something called the Toronto Blessing. He'd told Trevor how the Holy Spirit 'was wonderfully at work in his local church, spiritually slaying great numbers of the congregation'. Sarah had tried not to laugh when Trevor had told her earnestly that this was exactly what the group needed to fire it up. She could think of several members of the Slipper Gang she'd like to see slain, but knew that this wasn't quite what Trevor had in mind.

They arrived at Callum's a few minutes late and added their car to the line of parked vehicles on the driveway. Jamie greeted them at the front door and took them through the elegant Victorian house and out to the impressively well-cared-for garden where his father was pouring drinks for Emily's parents – Craig's parents must have arrived first as they already had near-empty glasses in their hands. Trevor had never met Callum before so that was the first of the introductions to be made, followed by Mr and Mrs Jackson, Craig's parents, whom neither Sarah nor Trevor had met previously. When the handshaking came to an end, Trevor, who had the look of a man still considering a last-ditch attempt to sabotage his daughter's plans, said, 'I caught the forecast at lunch-time. It looks as though the Channel will be a little choppy tonight. Perhaps it wouldn't be a bad idea for them to wait until tomorrow before setting off.'

Callum let out an avuncular laugh. 'A spot of seasickness should set them up nicely,' he said amiably. 'We can't let them have it too easy.'

'Yes,' agreed Emily's father. 'By rights they should be roughing it on public transport, never mind all this luxury of travelling by car. When I was a student I crossed the States in a Greyhound bus. God, it was cramped. Cramped but cheap.'

After numerous ee-by-gum-they-don't-know-they're-born stories had been exchanged, Callum offered Sarah a drink. 'I've got red wine, white wine, beer or soft drinks in the house. Or perhaps you'd like a gin and tonic. What's it to be?'

'White wine would be lovely.'

He took a bottle of Jacob's Creek from a terracotta wine cooler on the wooden table behind him in the shade of a lilac tree, and poured her a large glass. 'By the way,' he said, as he handed it to her, 'Grace is here. She's in the kitchen putting the finishing touches to a surprise she's arranged for the "young people", as she so charmingly refers to them. If you want to go in and see her, feel free.'

'Thanks, I will.' After chatting for a while with Emily's mother, Sarah went in search of Grace. It was hot outside in the south-facing garden, and she was glad of the opportunity to cool off.

They'd seen a lot of each other recently and Sarah viewed Grace as more than just a neighbour: she was now a good friend with whom she had shared a number of confidences.

Mostly about Trevor.

Without letting Sarah know what he was doing, and much to her horror when she did find out, Trevor had called on Grace one afternoon with two objectives in mind: to research the young man who had designs on his daughter, and to learn if their new neighbour had opened her heart to the Lord, or was interested in doing so. Sarah had cringed when Grace told her about his visit.

'I'm so sorry,' she'd said, mortified that she would now be tarred with the same brush of fanaticism.

'No need to be,' Grace had said cheerfully. 'I've seen it all before.'

'You have?'

'Yes, in my last church. There was a man not dissimilar from your Trevor who never went anywhere without his faith on his sleeve. He was very sincere, very hot for Jesus. He had the Bible completely sewn up. There were no grey areas in it for him at all. Sin and retribution were meat and drink to him.'

Up until this point, the subject of religion had never been broached between the two women, and even though it was now out in the open, Sarah was wary of discussing it. But Grace had no problem. 'Trevor was trying to encourage me to come along to your house church,' she said, with a friendly smile. 'Do you think I should give up on St Cuthbert's and join you?'

'No. Definitely not,' Sarah had blurted out, not giving her answer a second thought.

Grace had broadened her smile. 'You don't think it would suit me, then?'

'I wouldn't have thought so.'

'And does it suit you, Sarah?'

That's when the first of the confidences had slipped out. Nothing too personal, nothing too disloyal, just little everyday vexations that occur when you live with a man who is intent on winning souls for Christ.

Compared to the heat outside, the interior of Callum's beautiful house was refreshingly cool, and as she wandered through the polish-fragrant dining room and paused in the hall to admire a pretty Victorian watercolour landscape above a tasteful serpentine-fronted sideboard, she heard the nerve-jarring thump-thump of loud music from above. The light fitting rattled and she wondered how Callum would feel living here all alone when Jamie had left home for college in the autumn. She was already dreading being deprived of Hannah's company permanently and couldn't bring herself to picture the cold emptiness of the days to come.

She found Grace in the Provençal-style kitchen. She was bent over an oval-shaped table, guiding an ancient, discoloured piping bag across the surface of a large square cake on a silver board.

When she realised she wasn't alone she raised her eyes.

'Sarah,' she said, with obvious pleasure in her voice, 'how lovely to see you.' She straightened her back. 'What do you think of my handiwork? Be kind, though, I'm no expert when it comes to icing, and my fingers are too stiff these days anyway.'

Sarah drew near and inspected the cake and its decoration. A cocktail stick had been pushed into the sponge with a French flag glued to it and next to this was a toy car just like Jamie's red Nissan Micra. Written in spidery red icing all the way around the edge were the words '*Bonne Chance*' and '*Bon Voyage*'. 'It's absolutely perfect,' she said.

'Not too childish for the young people?'

'They'll love it.'

'I had wondered about a few of these. What do you think?' She showed Sarah a margarine pot of candles and waited for her verdict.

'No cake's complete without them,' Sarah said with a happy laugh. 'Here, let me help you.'

The cake was a great success, and after the candles had been blown out, Callum decided to embarrass his son by making a speech.

'There's nothing that needs to be said—' he began.

'Then shut up and sit down!' heckled Jamie good-humouredly.

Ignoring him with a grin, Callum carried on, '—other than to say that I wish you all a bloody fantastic time, and don't you dare come back as the same people you went away. I expect horizons to be widened, wills strengthened, perceptions deepened and a bootload of duty-free booze for me!'

An hour later it was time to say goodbye. All the cars on the drive had to be shunted so that Jamie could reverse his out, and after backpacks had been squeezed into position and final instructions issued – Trevor gave Jamie a last-minute test on the Highway Code and reminded him which side of the road to drive on once they reached Cherbourg – they were off. Hands waved out of windows, and the tranquillity of the quiet, respectable road was blasted away by several seconds of ear-splitting noise as Jamie hit the horn, and Craig poked his head out of the sunroof to yell, 'So long, suckers!'

Trevor's face curled itself into a tight knot of disdain, but everybody else laughed. 'Well,' said Callum, when the car had disappeared from sight and Sarah had taken her last look at Hannah for what seemed for ever, 'now we're rid of the rabble, why don't we have another glass of wine?'

There were general murmurs of consent. Sarah had never felt more in need of a drink; she was all set to fall in step with Grace and offer to help her tidy up, when Trevor produced his keys from his trouser pocket and said, 'Thanks, but we really ought to be getting off. Things to do,' and her heart plummeted. She wasn't ready yet to return to an empty Smithy Cottage. She had no inclination to confront what the dismal little house now symbolised without Hannah's presence. And as if sensing her hesitation, and having no truck with it, Trevor started to shake hands with everyone and sealed their departure.

26

A fortnight had passed since Hannah had taken her first real step into the unknown expanse of her future, and Trevor had spent most of it in an agony of anticipatory torment as he hovered conspicuously in the hall each morning waiting for the postman to make his usual seven forty-five delivery.

Today, as Sarah came down the stairs with a small bundle of washing under her arm, she hoped that he would be spared another day of disappointment. 'I think we should take no news as a good sign. It means she's having too good a time to be bothered with letter-writing,' she'd told him yesterday morning when the post had consisted of nothing but a piece of junk mail.

To give Hannah her credit, she had phoned when they'd arrived at Cherbourg, just to let them know that so far all was well: the ferry hadn't sunk; she hadn't been mugged; Craig hadn't got them arrested with his criminal sense of humour and Jamie wasn't driving while under the influence of anything more hallucinatory than a can of Pepsi. Sarah had told her not to worry about ringing again. 'It's much too expensive,' she'd said. 'Just send us a card when you have time.' But Trevor had wanted more and had extracted from Hannah a promise that she would keep them regularly posted as to her exact whereabouts. But his insistence had merely ensured that he was to suffer a daily dose of unease as he waited anxiously for the much-anticipated communication.

Leaving Trevor to stand guard over the letterbox, Sarah went through to the kitchen and pushed the dirty clothes into the washing-machine. She added the powder and turned the dial to the economy half-load sequence. It was extraordinary just how little washing there was without Hannah. She wondered with amusement how she and Emily were surviving on the few clothes they'd taken with them. Or were they already frittering away what little money they had on just-have-to-have skimpy tops to supplement their pared-to-the-bone wardrobes?

The sound of the letterbox scraping open had Sarah silently praying that today might be the day that Trevor was put out of his misery. Just a few scribbled lines on a card would suffice, she added, as a postscript.

Within seconds Trevor was standing in the kitchen, a smile on his face and an airmail letter in his hand. 'At last,' he said, waving it at her, 'she's written, at long last.' He looked as if all his birthdays and Christmas had been rolled into one. Then he sat at the table and picked carefully at the first sealed edge with his thumbnail. Desperate to seize it from him, rip it open and feed off Hannah's writing to satisfy her hunger for some comforting contact with her daughter, Sarah turned away and put the kettle on. She watched Trevor out of the corner of her eye, saw him smooth out the single sheet of paper, handling it as though it were a priceless scroll of papyrus. He started to read.

It didn't take him long.

Annoyingly, though, he went through it one more time. Sarah was itching to know what news it contained. 'Well?' she asked at length. 'How's she getting on?'

'Read it yourself,' he said gloomily. He rose from the table and went over to the bread bin.

Eagerly Sarah scanned her daughter's neat writing, looking for the vital clue that had caused Trevor's mood to change so suddenly.

Dear Mum and Dad,

Guess what, we got bored in Brittany and went to Paris instead. It's the coolest place. We went to Montmartre and Emily nearly got her portrait painted, except it wasn't just her face the piss artist was interested in! We stayed in a campsite just north of Paris and it was the pits. Flies everywhere, especially in the bogs (or crap-holes as Craig calls them) – they stank to hell and back. The site was so rough we had to sleep in the car at night to stop it from being nicked. Emily's father would be proud of us.

Yesterday we went to Chartres. We're now heading for La Rochelle to see Craig's aunt. God, what I wouldn't give for a bath and a decent loo that I can actually park my bum on!

The others all say hi.

Love, Hannah

As Trevor had, Sarah also read the letter twice. She would have done so again had the toaster not decided to play up. While Trevor hoicked charred bread out of the decrepit appliance she threw open the window to get rid of the awful smell. 'It's time we bought a new one,' she remarked. When he didn't respond, she said, 'It's good to know that Hannah's okay and that she's enjoying herself, isn't it?'

He grunted, gave up on the idea of toast, put away his unused plate and helped himself to a bowl of bran flakes.

'What's wrong, Trevor?' she asked. 'She wrote, just as you wanted.'

He raised his eyes from his cereal, which he was eating as he stood with his back to the sink. 'It didn't sound like Hannah,' he said with a sulky frown.

Oh, so that was it, thought Sarah. He'd been expecting a letter from the old Hannah; the little girl who used to go off on Christian-camp holidays, who within a day of being away would dutifully send them a tightly worded I-hope-you-are-well-I-am-having-a-good-time note with a cross at the bottom of the page against a beautifully coloured-in rainbow. The contrast from that to talk of crap-holes and disreputable goings-on in Montmartre couldn't be greater. But surely not even Trevor could have expected a sugar-coated letter from Hannah saying that she was homesick and counting the days until she was back in Astley Hope. She glanced at his furrowed face as he returned his attention to his breakfast. He looked so unhappy. So downcast. Forgetting her own sadness at being parted from her daughter, Sarah considered Trevor's feelings. It was always so easy to disregard anything he said or thought, but couldn't it be the case that he was missing Hannah more than she was? It was generally thought that a child flying the nest affected the mother more than the father. But what if that father had spent the last eighteen years idealising his daughter? What if he had lovingly and selflessly invested every spare minute of his time into her upbringing? Wouldn't that give him just as much right to be lonely and devastated by her leaving as her mother? If not more?

With lightning speed, guilt overtook Sarah's feelings of compassion towards Trevor. While she had been missing Hannah and wallowing in her own trough of self-pity, where had been her support for Trevor? Then a worse thought occurred to her: was it possible that through her thoughtlessness she had driven him to seek understanding from elsewhere? Somebody in the Slipper Gang, perhaps.

But as fast as this thought had presented itself, she dismissed it as erroneous. There was no one to whom Trevor could turn within the group because as their leader he couldn't be seen to be in anything other than full control. That was the trouble with being held aloft as an infallible linchpin: you couldn't have earthly problems. You could wrestle day and night with a thorny spiritual issue – or even have a wife who was in danger of becoming an apostate – but you couldn't have emotional problems because that would mean you weren't in step with the Lord. What kind of example was that for the group? Had St Paul ever admitted to feeling a little wobbly? Had Christ ever said he was having a bad-hair day and that the Sermon on the Mount would have to wait until he'd got his act together? It was hard enough for any man to admit to being unhappy, but for a spiritual guru it was well nigh impossible. Again she glanced at Trevor's miserable face and wondered if he had the same feelings as she had, that having served their purpose with Hannah, their future now comprised nothing but a slow, lonely decline into old age.

Experiencing the familiar need to make everything right for Trevor, Sarah poured him some tea and said brightly, 'What are you doing today? If you're not busy I could put a picnic lunch together and we could go for a walk. Peckforton perhaps. It's such a lovely—'

'I've got too much to do,' he interrupted. 'I've got three craft fairs on the trot and I've my notes to prepare for tonight.'

'Oh,' Sarah said flatly, her compassion for him instantly dispelled. She watched him take his mug of tea with him to his workshop and muttered under her breath, 'Trevor Donovan, you're a difficult man to help.' She didn't even care that it was such an uncharitable thought.

Later that morning, when Sarah had finished the bedroom curtains that she'd been making for Grace and was running the iron over the pretty blue and white fabric, she thought how well the material would look in Ali's bathroom with all those lovely Delft tiles. She had spoken to Ali the day after Hannah had set off for France, to thank her for the extra money she'd given Hannah, as well as refer to the other more dubious gift.

'You're not cross with me, are you?' Ali had asked.

'Now, why would you think that?'

'Oh, my God, you're furious. I can hear it in your voice. You sound as winsome as an avenging Margaret Thatcher.'

'And you sound as guilty as Bill Clinton.'

'My, my, you're sharp this afternoon. Does that mean I'm not your friend any more? Are you going to write me out of your will?'

'I did that years ago.'

'Oh, shucks!'

'So tell me why you did it, Ali.'

'Why I did what?'

'Don't play the innocent with me. Tell me why you gave my daughter a packet of condoms to take on holiday with her.'

'Good heavens, you've got it all wrong. They weren't condoms. They're the latest thing in the world of camping. You use them at night to ward off unwanted insects.'

'*Ali!*'

'Okay, okay. I admit it. I was interfering under the guise of doing my fairy godmother bit. I knew you and Trevor would never be sensible enough to be so practical so I felt I should do it. I didn't want to see history repeating itself.'

'You mean you didn't want to see her ruining her life as I did?'

'Exactly.'

It was absolutely typical of Ali to be so brutally frank. But she'd been right to do what she did, Sarah knew that. Trevor, of course, would never agree with her. He would bang on about the Christian ideal of sex within the bounds of marriage, and that anything less was a sin. How easy it would be for her to throw at him their own flouting of this ideal. But she never would. Not ever.

When she'd finished ironing Grace's curtains she phoned her to see if it was convenient to call round with them.

'Goodness,' Grace said, 'you're a fast worker. I only gave you the fabric the other day.'

'They were very straightforward.'

'For you, maybe. I would have taken for ever fumbling around with my old Singer. Why don't you come now and have an early lunch with me? Or are you too busy to stop that long?'

'No, that's fine. I'll be along just as soon as I've put the washing out and made a sandwich for Trevor. Do you want me to bring anything?'

'Certainly not. I don't approve of people who invite friends for a meal then expect them to supply it.'

When she'd said goodbye, Sarah went out to the garden and pegged the washing on the line. The sun was directly above her head and was hot and bright. Feeling its scorching strength she hoped that Hannah was being careful to use the wickedly expensive high-factor sun cream she'd bought for her. Back inside the house she threw a sandwich together for Trevor, covered it with clingfilm and went to tell him where she was going.

He switched off his lathe, lifted off the white dust mask that covered his mouth and nose and stared at her through his bug-eyed safety goggles. Tapping his chisel on his workbench, he said, 'You're spending a lot of time with that woman, aren't you?'

'*That woman?*' Sarah repeated. 'That doesn't sound very polite. Her name's Grace.'

'Mm ... I'm just not at all sure about her.'

'I'm not with you.' Though, sadly, she was. Trevor didn't approve of Grace, not since he had discovered at Callum's, when they'd been seeing Hannah off, that she was a retired psychotherapist. As Martin Wade of the Slipper Gang would be only too quick to inform anyone stupid enough to listen, psychotherapy was of the Devil, along with yoga, aromatherapy and anything else he felt inclined to condemn.

'People like her have some pretty unorthodox views, in my opinion,' said Trevor, giving the workbench another little tap. 'I'm not at all sure she's our type.'

'What would be our type, Trevor?' she asked innocently.

'You know what I'm getting at, Sarah. She professes to know the Lord, but I'm not sure that she's actually saved.'

Sarah very nearly said, 'Well, in that case I'd have thought it was your Christian duty to get to know her better,' but wisely refrained. A challenge such as that might well stir Trevor to try once more to lure Grace along to the group.

Grace was delighted with the curtains. 'They're beautiful,' she enthused. 'You really are so clever. How much do I owe you?'

'Nothing. They took me next to no time to do.'

'Sarah, I shan't ask you again, how much?'

'I'll let you know later.'

An impasse reached, Grace said, 'Don't think I shall forget to remind you of that. Now, come along, your lunch awaits.' She took Sarah outside to the small garden, which in a strange way reflected the inside of the bungalow. It was very simple, very plain. There was an old, gnarled crabapple tree in the right-hand corner, a perimeter hedge of recently trimmed copper beech, and a tidy square of daisy-spotted lawn. That was all. There were no scent-filled borders, no rockery features, not even a solitary tub of summer bedding plants. Being such a keen gardener herself, it always struck Sarah as odd whenever she looked at Grace's garden that there was so little in it. She'd once asked Grace if she would like some help to brighten it up. Her elderly friend had obviously been amused by her offer. 'Why?' she'd asked. 'Is there something wrong with my garden as it is?'

'No, of course not,' she'd said, instantly worried that Grace would think she'd been poking her nose in where it wasn't wanted. 'I have so much in my garden I wondered if you'd like some cuttings.'

'How very thoughtful. But I'm not a fan of fuss and frills. I prefer everything to be understated. To be seen for what it is.'

And as Sarah took her seat at a small circular table in the dappled shade of the crabapple tree, she could see that Grace had set their lunch in her typically modest, straightforward fashion. This didn't mean she hadn't put any thought into it – Sarah could see that she had – but unlike a lunch table at Audrey's house, which would be decorated to death with silver plate, tiny vases of flowers, fiddly paper doilies, precision-folded napkins and silly little flags to distinguish one plate of food from another, Grace had kept her offering to an unassuming informality. A plain white cloth adorned the garden table and placed on this were two glasses of orange juice, two plates, each containing a slice of quiche, a helping of rice salad and a roll; and in the middle, two glass bowls of mouth-watering strawberries lightly dusted with icing sugar.

'I hope you approve,' Grace said, as she sat opposite Sarah.

'I do. It's much more than I expected. You've gone to such a lot of trouble.'

'Yes, I have, haven't I?'

Sarah caught the mocking tone in Grace's voice and met her eye. 'One of us isn't being sincere,' she said, with a smile.

Reaching for her knife and fork, Grace said, 'Well, eat up, then we'll decide which of us it is. So how are things at Smithy Cottage?'

'Dull is the word I'd use.'

'Oh dear. Missing Hannah?'

'Enormously. I can't begin to think what I shall be like in the autumn when she goes away to college.'

'Then don't think about it. Put it on hold until you have to face it.'

'Isn't that rather silly? I didn't have you down as an ostrich, Grace.'

'Ostrich I'm not. But realist I am. What possible advantage can you gain worrying now about something that won't take place for another four months? And, besides, don't you have enough worries on your mind as it is?'

Sarah stopped eating. 'Is that how you see me? Worried?'

Squinting in the dappled sunlight, Grace fixed her surprisingly strong gaze on Sarah and said, 'Yes. And, more than that, sometimes you give me the impression of being one of the unhappiest people I know.'

'Then I must learn to smile more often in your company,' Sarah said glibly.

'Or be more honest.'

Her glibness evaporated and Sarah was on her guard. 'Why do you say that?'

'Because I suspect it to be the truth.'

Sarah shifted uncomfortably in her seat, remembered that Grace was a qualified psychotherapist and wondered if she was treating her as she would a client. She resumed eating, but for a few minutes avoided looking in Grace's direction, which was no mean feat given that they were sitting so close to each other.

'Have I offended you with my honesty?' Grace asked, after a few minutes had passed. 'Because if so, I'm very sorry.'

Sarah's composure had now fully returned. 'Don't be silly, you haven't offended me in the slightest.'

'But I have unnerved you, haven't I?'

'Only because I'm beginning to think that every conversation I have with you is the equivalent of me lying on your professional couch. Plus the fact that you've just accused me of lying.'

Grace looked serious. 'I was very cross with Callum for telling you and Trevor what my line of work used to be. I knew that it would have this effect on you. If it helps, I really don't go in for analysing friends at the drop of a hat, it's far too exhausting. And as for accusing you of lying, I didn't say that.'

'You implied that I was—'

'No, Sarah, you took my words to mean that. I was suggesting that you're somewhat economical with your feelings and have been so for a long time.'

'If that isn't the sound of me being analysed I don't know what is.'

'I'm merely being honest and objective. If your friend Ali was here in my place, wouldn't she be saying much the same?'

Sarah smiled unexpectedly. 'Outside the work environment, Ali doesn't have an objective bone in her body. She reacts first and thinks later. She's very headstrong, which—'

'Which can preclude a rational conversation on a delicate and personal issue that's worrying you.'

'Exactly. I can never, for instance, discuss Trevor and my marriage with her without her totally overreacting. She always—' Sarah broke off as, too late, she saw how clever Grace had been. 'You did that deliberately, didn't you?' she said crossly. 'You tricked that out of me.'

Again, Grace looked serious. 'Sarah, I'm not some hocus-pocus hypnotherapist sitting here making you do things against your will. We're two friends enjoying lunch together and having what I would hope was a civilised conversation based on my concern for you.'

Sarah felt the severity of Grace's words and apologised immediately. 'I'm sorry. Truly I am. It's just that I've become . . . I've become so very defensive lately.'

'Dare I ask why?'

Sarah leaned back in her chair and considered the question. It required a simple yes or no. The consequences of no would mean that she would go on dodging Grace's well-meant questions. Whereas a yes . . . a yes might help her. Grace's clear, objective thinking might do for her what Ali could never do: she might help her to see her future with Trevor in a more positive light.

She made her decision and, winding her hair round her finger and keeping her eyes on a sparrow hopping through the dusty undergrowth of the copper-beech hedge, she said, 'I've spent the greater part of my life trying to love the unlovable and I don't know if I have the energy to go on doing it.'

If Grace was at all surprised by what Sarah had just told her, she gave no outward sign of being so. 'Trevor?' was all she said.

Sarah slowly turned her gaze back to Grace. 'Trevor,' she confirmed, with a slight nod.

'And you feel you have to go on trying, do you?'

'Oh, yes. I owe it to Trevor and Hannah. And everything I believe in.'

'But not you personally?'

'I don't think I come into it.'

Grace made no immediate response to this comment and they sat in silence, listening to the flutter of a wood-pigeon's wings as it flew overhead and a pair of doves cooing in the sun on the roof of the bungalow. All the antagonism Sarah had felt only moments ago was gone. She let go of her hair and waited patiently for Grace to speak, knowing that, when she did, whatever she said would be worth hearing. She was right.

'Of course,' Grace said slowly, reaching for her orange juice, 'as Christians we're supposed to be following a man whose chief commandment was to love the unlovable . . . even a difficult husband, and there's no denying that there's great virtue in working at a failing relationship. The rewards would be immensely satisfying if one was successful.'

'And if one failed?'

'Ah, well, then I suppose one would have to determine what counts as a failure.'

'I'm sure that deep down Ali thinks that I've been very weak staying with Trevor all these years when I don't love him. In her book that would be a classic example of failing to be true to oneself.'

'Whereas the truth is you've been amazingly strong to stay in a difficult marriage, which makes it a success. Relationships are never easy. My mother used to say that there were more challenges to overcome in a marriage than there ever were in the fiercest of battles. I know you're terrified of me putting on my professional hat, and I assure you I'm talking to you as a friend, but would you mind if I asked you a question?'

'Go on.'

'Just now you said that you thought you didn't come into the matter, as if you're not a part of the equation. Did you really mean that, or did you say those words because you think that's what scripture expects of you? St Paul was a great advocate of self-deprecation, but there's no getting away from it, he had quite an opinion of himself, although that was probably due to his upbringing and culture. Not that I'm suggesting that you have an overinflated opinion of yourself, Sarah, but you're as human as the next person and I would imagine that you harbour the odd hope and expectation for yourself.'

Sarah thought about this. It was hard to admit it, but the truth was she *did* hanker after a better life, and surely that was the root of the problem. Putting others continually before herself was becoming a mighty uphill struggle and she was tired of pushing that cartload of humility before her. She wanted desperately to let go of it. But she couldn't. The consequences were too frightening. 'Yes,' she said, realising that Grace was studying her face and waiting for her answer. 'Yes, I do have hopes for myself. I'm tired of understanding Trevor and constantly making allowances for him. I would love a life of my own.' She decided to tell Grace about her conversation with Ali back in March when she stayed with her at the windmill. 'I said then that I wanted to be the Sarah I was meant to be, not this pretend Sarah I've become.'

'But, Sarah, my dear, there's only one person who's allowed that to happen and that's you.'

'But—'

'One more thought for you to consider while I go inside for our dessertspoons, which I've stupidly left in the kitchen, just how big a sacrifice do you think you have to make?'

27

There was the usual chaos that evening at Smithy Cottage of shoes being exchanged for slippers. There was also the usual exchange of chit-chat – 'Sorry, was that your foot? ... Super weather ... Well into the upper eighties I shouldn't wonder, maybe even the nineties ... It doesn't suit me at all, I can't sleep at night ... Me neither ... No, no, you have that space, my shoes won't fit ... Do you think we'll be in for a hosepipe ban?'

Sarah watched the Slipper Gang in quiet amusement. The scene reminded her of *Dad's Army* and Captain Mainwaring's many frustrated attempts to marshal his platoon into an effective fighting force: the intent was there, but the flesh was weak and much more interested in enjoying a few snippets of gossip rather than jumping smartly into line.

The first to sit down was Shirley, commandeering, as per the norm, the most comfortable armchair over by the window, which tonight was open in the vain hope that a cool breeze might manifest itself from the sultry evening air.

With Trevor still stationed at the door, the rest of them trickled in, and when the last of the group had been rounded up and brought to heel – typically Dave was last, apologising for Brenda's absence – it was eyes down for their quiet time.

Sarah took her seat and closed her eyes gratefully. She gave Holman Hunt's *The Light of the World* a quick going-over, checking that the detailed painting had not been defaced by any new attacks of doubt. She held it firmly in her mind and found that all was well: the seven-sided lantern was glowing softly; the weeds were rampant and untidy; the apples were rolling around on the ground; and best of all, Christ was still there knocking on the door. She then switched her thoughts to that afternoon and her lunch with Grace.

While she had become adept at not answering some of Ali's more probing questions if she so chose, she had discovered that Grace, whose easy manner disguised how intuitive she was, was a far more disarming proposition. A few minutes of the older woman's carefully put questions had soon cut through the layers of self-preservation that Sarah had so skilfully applied to her persona. Grace was quite correct in saying that it was Sarah who was responsible for allowing her marriage to develop as it had. It was true, and she alone was responsible for bringing herself to where she was now. Grace had said, 'And why do you think you've done that?'

'I ... I don't know,' she'd responded.

A kindly smile on Grace's face had told Sarah that she didn't believe her. Very persuasively she had said, 'You're an intelligent woman, Sarah. If you had wanted your husband to treat you better, you would have made it happen. Instead it seems that you have deliberately chosen to let Trevor behave in the manner of a spoilt child. And you've indulged him like a guilty parent, haven't you?'

'I suppose I have.'

'Why?' Again that same quiet, persuasive voice, which was as gentle as the cooing of the doves on the red-tiled roof of the bungalow, but as penetrating as the sun shining its hot rays through the leafy shade of the crabapple tree.

'Because I've always felt so guilty,' Sarah had confessed. She explained about Hannah and their subsequent hurried marriage. 'Trevor's parents never forgave him.'

'Despite him providing them with such a delightful granddaughter?'

'They never saw her. They refused to have anything to do with us. They were very strict traditional Methodists. They didn't drink, they didn't dance and they certainly didn't approve of a child conceived out of wedlock.'

'How sad.'

'And cruel.'

'Yes. It was very cruel of them. And what of your parents? How did they greet their son-in-law?'

'They didn't approve of him. They didn't think he was good enough, and unfairly held him responsible for bringing my education at Oxford to an abrupt end.'

'Do you think Trevor has ever felt guilty about that?'

'I've never looked at it from that angle before.'

'No, I shouldn't think you have. You've been too preoccupied with blaming yourself for cutting Trevor off from his family, haven't you?'

'But that's exactly what I did. If it hadn't been for me—'

'No, Sarah. It wasn't your decision but theirs that removed their son from their blinkered vision. Blaming yourself for somebody else's actions is futile and ultimately harmful. Look where it's got you.'

'Now you're beginning to sound like Ali.'

'I'm sorry. Shall I make us some tea now?'

'Please, won't you let me do it? I feel so lazy sitting here doing nothing.'

'No, you stay where you are, but have a ponder on what I mentioned earlier about the sacrifice you think you have to make – because that's what you're doing by staying with Trevor, isn't it? By lying prostrate across the sacrificial altar of your faith I would imagine you see yourself as a permanent atonement for the past.'

Left alone with this uncomfortably razor-sharp observation, Sarah was seized with the desire to sneak away from Grace's quiet, orderly house and garden and go back to Smithy Cottage where, amongst the clutter and chaos, there would be no danger of anyone seeing through her so clearly.

When Grace returned with a tray of tea-things, she said, 'From the expression on your face I'd say you're cross with me again, aren't you?'

Undeterred by Sarah's hostile silence, she said, 'Good. That means we're getting somewhere. What sort of answer have you prepared for me?'

Sounding distinctly peevish, Sarah said, 'I don't have one.'

Grace smiled. 'You know, Sarah, when our self-interest is at stake, we have the most astonishing ability to convince ourselves that all manner of falsehood is true.'

'Now you're being tiresome and far too esoteric for a sweltering summer's day in the garden.'

'Well, then, let's leave it there, shall we? Have you heard from Hannah? I had a postcard this morning from Jamie. They seem to be having a fabulous time. I'm so envious.'

Without so much as a backward glance at what they'd previously been discussing and at what had threatened Sarah with its unnerving directness, Grace steered the conversation through less rocky water and kept it there until Sarah went home.

'Ahem,' said Trevor's voice from across the room.

Sarah raised her head and saw that everyone was looking at her, including Trevor who must have brought their quiet time to an end a few moments ago. Embarrassed, she tried to appear as though she'd been fully absorbed in contemplative prayer.

Trevor cleared his throat and opened the file on his lap. 'Now I expect you all saw this in your Sunday newspapers at the weekend and will have had the same reaction to it as I did. But for the sake of clarity,' he cast a quick glance towards Dave, 'I thought we'd go through it together, just to be absolutely certain that we know exactly where we stand on the issue, which has repercussions—'

'Um ... sorry, Trevor,' said Dave, 'sorry to interrupt, but we were with Brenda's mother at the weekend. She's having a hip-replacement operation soon. I don't suppose we could pray for her at the end, could we?'

'Of course, Dave, I'll make a note of that,' said Trevor, already scribbling a reminder on his notepad. 'Now, what I wanted to discuss is—'

'Sorry,' Dave interrupted again, 'but what I was trying to say is that Brenda and I didn't see the papers on Sunday, so I don't know what it is that we're all supposed to be reacting to.'

Trevor patiently held up a carefully cut-out half-page from the *Sunday Times*. Just as Dave hadn't seen the papers at the weekend, neither had Sarah: she'd been too busy working in the garden. She glanced at what was in Trevor's hands and took in the headline: 'Bishops Push for Divorcees to be Remarried in Church'. Well, there'd be no prizes for guessing which direction Trevor's comments would be going in.

He began reading aloud from the newspaper cutting: '"Centuries-old doctrine is to be thrown on the scrap heap of outmoded tradition and convention as senior bishops call for change within the Church of England".' He raised his scandalised eyes to them all. 'And there we have it. Once again the Church of England is bowing to secular pressures. By the time the right-on clergy with their woolly-minded views have had their way, there'll be nothing left of what the original Church was founded on.'

'Quite right,' agreed Audrey. 'Remarriage after divorce is adultery in the eyes of the Lord.'

'Absolutely,' nodded Maurice.

'It's the breaking of the seventh commandment, "Thou shall not commit adultery",' Beryl chipped in.

Elaine was flicking through her Bible for a relevant passage, but Shirley was ahead of her. 'Luke states it quite clearly,' she said. 'Chapter sixteen, verse eighteen. "The man who marries a divorced woman commits adultery".'

'Well, I'm glad to see that we're all of one mind on the matter,' said Trevor.

But out of the corner of her eye, and much to her delight, Sarah saw Dave scratching his head. 'Um ... not sure I'm entirely up to speed with you, Trevor.'

'Yes, Dave, what is it that you don't understand?'

'Well, it's Brenda's sister.'

'Yes.'

'She married a divorced man last summer. It was a lovely wedding and his daughter was a bridesmaid, but is that the same as Shirley was just saying?'

'It makes no difference which sex does the divorcing or remarrying,' Trevor said.

But Dave still looked confused. 'So where does that leave Brenda's sister, Susan? If Russell is an adulterer, does that mean that when Susan and Russell first, well, you know, when they first had ... um well, when they—'

'Are you referring to when they first had sexual intercourse, Dave?'

Dave visibly shrank beneath Shirley's forthright question. Even Stan and Valerie's puppy-dog slippers looked embarrassed: their noses were digging into the carpet and their ears had flopped over their eyes. 'Yes,' murmured Dave, and returning his gaze to Trevor, he said, 'So when they had, um ... marital relations, does that mean that they both became adulterers, in that Russell has turned Susan into one?'

Sarah wanted to leap out of her seat and hug Dave. If she didn't know him as well as she did, she'd be tempted to think he was deliberately sending the group up, but as ever his genuine confusion was making a mockery of the Slipper Gang's self-righteous dogmatism. 'Adultery isn't a disease, Dave,' she said, when nobody answered him. 'It's not something you can catch.'

'If I may be so humble as to suggest it, Sarah, that's just where you're wrong,' said Martin, from his God-fearing, bottom-numbing kitchen chair. 'Sin is exactly like a disease. It can spread its micro-organisms without us realising it. We can be jogging along quite happily with not a single thought in our head for the sins of the flesh, then suddenly *wham!* we're up to our armpits in the mire of temptation. Make no mistake, we're in the Devil's laboratory of disease at every minute of the day.'

'Sounds as if we need inoculating,' muttered Sarah, under her breath.

But Trevor heard her and said, 'We have inoculation through God's Word, Sarah.' He gave his Bible an irritating little tap with his index finger.

'So back to Susan and Russell,' persisted Dave. 'Where do you suppose they stand in the eyes of the Lord?'

Sarah waited for somebody to answer Dave's question, but the room had gone unnaturally quiet. Cowards, she thought, as the continued silence and lowered glances condemned the likes of Susan and Russell to whatever hell it was that this crazy lot believed in. 'Dave,' she said, 'if what your sister-in-law and her husband have done is considered a sin, and I'm not convinced it is, then be assured that it's not a greater sin than most of the ones we all commit each and every day of our lives.' She then turned her attention to the rest of the group and said, 'Shall I make the coffee now? Or would you prefer something cold?'

Yes, something as cold as your compassion for your fellow human beings, she thought, when she was out in the kitchen waiting for the kettle to boil and tipping a packet of biscuits on to a plate. Through the open door she could hear Trevor in the sitting room trying to explain to Dave that what she had omitted to say was that Susan and Russell actively needed to seek God's forgiveness. And, though Sarah couldn't see him, she knew that Trevor would be putting on one of his specially earnest and oh-so-humble expressions – the sort that made her want to slap his face. She then heard Dave's concerned voice say, 'But, Trevor, how can they seek forgiveness when they don't even go to church? Or do you suppose it would work if I did it for them on their behalf?'

Oh dear, thought Sarah. How complicated it became when one's beliefs were thrashed to bits like this. Had any of this nonsense been a part of God's original plan? And why is it, she wondered, as she poured boiling water into the mugs of instant coffee, that she believed implacably in the act of redemption for the whole of mankind, but refused point-blank to consider herself worthy of it?

28

That same evening, over in Little Linton, Ali put her key in the lock, hoping to find that the thick-walled windmill was cool inside as it had been since the heatwave began. The temperature wasn't too bad on the ground floor, but after she'd scooped up that morning's mail from the mat and had climbed the stairs to the next level, she was met by a stuffy, airless white heat that took her breath away. She dumped her bag, briefcase and post on the kitchen table then opened the fridge door. She stood in front of it, revelling in the cool blast against her flushed, damp skin and reached inside for a bottle of spring water. She pressed the icy glass to her forehead, rolling it over her face and down her neck. Then she twisted off the metal cap and gulped down the contents.

'You're turning into a slob,' she said, when she'd satisfied her thirst. 'Yeah, and what of it?' she answered herself, wiping her hand across her mouth and returning the bottle to the fridge. Next she kicked off her shoes and peeled away her tights. She stood for a few delicious moments letting her hot, sweaty feet absorb the relative coolness of the wooden floor. Then she crossed the room and unlocked the door to the galleried balcony outside. She attached the wrought-iron handle to the metal hook on the wall and left the door wide open while she went upstairs for a shower.

The drive home from Blackpool, where she'd spent the day with a client, had been the pits. As if it wasn't bad enough that several miles of roadworks had been added to the normal mayhem of the M6, an overheated car engine had brought the scarcely moving traffic to a standstill. The air-conditioning in Ali's Saab had decided not to work and, with the soft top pushed back, she'd been stuck for nearly forty minutes in the vicious heat. She'd had nightmare visions of completing the rest of her journey with her tyres coated in recently laid, melting black tarmac. The thought of a cold shower was all that had kept her sane while she'd tried to ignore the unwelcome, leering glances of truck drivers in their sweaty Bruce Willis vests.

Stripping off her clothes, she stepped under the power-shower. An explosion of freezing cold needles pricked at her skin. Tilting her head, she jet-blasted her face under the force of the water. It was heavenly, wonderfully revitalising.

No two ways about it, it's the little things in life that bring the greatest pleasure, she thought, when an hour later she was sitting on the balcony enjoying the view of cornfields and distant hills to the south that stretched lazily across the heat-hazed horizon like the bumpy back of a sleeping dinosaur. Refreshed and dressed in a pair of old shorts and a Tommy Hilfiger T-shirt, a glass of chilled wine in her hand and a packet of crisps on her lap, she was a new woman.

It was pathetic that such an ordinary moment could be so blissful, but in the barren landscape of her day-to-day existence, it was as good as it got. It made her think of something she'd once read: that if there wasn't any misery in the world, we might be conceited enough to think we were in paradise and would consequently miss out on the best bits. Well, there was no danger of an excess of pleasure diluting what little enjoyment she was currently experiencing.

She popped another crisp into her mouth and savoured it. Mm ... delicious. Was there ever a better combination than good old salt and vinegar for tickling the palate? The only improvement would be if it was a bag of chips on her lap rather than the footballer-endorsed crisps. Chips would be the ultimate perfection. Her mouth watered at the thought, which brought with it the memory of Sarah and her, windblown and bathed in warm sunshine, sharing a portion of fish and chips on the beach at Hayling. And what did they do when they'd finished eating and had licked their fingers clean? What they always did. They'd gone straight to the funfair and ridden the waltzer. How they had kept those chips down she didn't know. If they tried it now they'd be ill within seconds.

Illness wasn't something she associated with her holidays spent with Sarah at Hayling: not once could she remember either of them being sick. It never rained either, or so it seemed. Sun-warmed idyllic days simply drifted from one to the next as the pair roamed the island at will, carefree and happy.

But that was childhood memories for you. Recollections of seaside holidays were the favourite sweets in Nostalgia's tin – the tedium of school and endless hours spent doing homework were the orange cremes that nobody relished.

From this evening on she was supposed to be enjoying a holiday. Officially she was off work, but unofficially she'd slip into the office for the odd day – if she didn't, she'd probably die of boredom. Last week Daniel had got into a regular old strop because she hadn't booked a proper vacation. Ever since he'd returned from a fortnight in a whitewashed villa in Andalucía where he and Richard had done little more than eat, drink and swim in their private pool, he'd been clicking his flamenco fingers at her to organise something for herself.

'Come on, Ali,' he'd said, after he'd told her yet again what a wonderful two weeks he'd had. 'When was the last time you packed a bag and headed out of town?'

Her muttered response of being too busy was rejected out of hand. 'Ali, just get your shit together and book something.'

'It's not as easy as that,' she'd moaned. 'You've got Richard to go away with, but I'd be on my own. I'd be miserable company for myself.'

'Why not try one of those specially arranged activity holidays for singles?'

'What? Abseiling in Aviemore or candlemaking in the Cotswolds? I don't think so, Daniel.'

'Not even bonking in Borneo?'

'Anything as good as that would be booked by now.'

'You don't know that.'

'Yeah, well, I'll tell you what I do know, those activity holidays are for single saddos, and I ain't joining in with them for anybody, not even you.'

'Saddos such as yourself, Babe?'

'Ho bloody ho, you're creasing me up with your humour, these days.'

'And I'm filling up with your self-pity.'

'Then leave me alone.'

She had noticed that for the past few months Daniel had been treating her differently. If she wasn't mistaken, she'd say that he was having a go at bullying her. It had started after that night in March when she'd cooked supper for Elliot. The following Monday, Daniel had come into the office and put her through her paces as to how the evening had gone.

'It was okay,' she'd said noncommittally, switching on her computer and hiding behind it when he'd hit her with the first question.

A lowering of his glasses had told her that he was expecting her to be a touch more revealing.

'All right,' she'd said, 'it was a whisker more than being okay. We didn't accuse, we didn't blame, and we didn't snipe. It was all very dull.'

'Dull?' he'd repeated, unconvinced. 'I doubt that, somehow. The two of you together were never that, not in the good times or the bad times.'

'I meant in the sense of there being no drama to report back to you.'

'Did you feel comfortable with him?'

'If you really want to know, being with Elliot was like wearing an ill-fitting shoe. It pinched now and again.'

He'd smiled at that. 'And when it wasn't pinching how did it feel?'

'Scary.'

'Was that because you realised how it could be between the two of you?'

She had refused to answer him and had made a show of getting on with her work. But Daniel being Daniel had started applying the Chinese water-torture trick of drip-dripping his I-know-better questions and comments to her whenever he could.

Meanwhile, the days and weeks slipped by, and she didn't hear from Elliot. Daniel had suggested she should ring him, but she couldn't bring herself to do it. Elliot had obviously regretted the evening and had thought better of any ideas he might have had for seeing her again.

Sarah had also tried her luck at making Ali ring Elliot. 'After all that open-heart surgery I carried out on you,' she complained, 'and you're not going to do anything about it. I'm disappointed in you. Just see him once more and tell him what you told me. It would help you both so much.'

'I'll think about it,' she'd told Sarah.

But they'd both known that she wouldn't. The impetus to act had been lost.

However, the effect of that conversation she'd had with Sarah, back in March, had not been lost. It was the nearest she'd got to being honest, not just with another person but with herself. It had been the hardest thing for her to do, to admit that she'd deliberately wanted to hurt Elliot. But there was another reason behind her actions; a reason that was so dark and threatening it clouded any thought she had for him. So potentially harmful was it that even now she couldn't own up to it. She wasn't sure that she would ever be able to.

Afraid of the gloomy mood descending upon her, especially in view of the significance of this particular weekend – the day after tomorrow would have been Isaac's fourth birthday – she rose from her chair and went inside to replenish her now empty wineglass. She caught sight of the bundle of mail that she'd put on the table when she'd arrived home. She took it outside, along with her refilled glass, and flicked through it. It was mostly the tedious variety of correspondence that would take up residence beside the fruit bowl, but a flash of blue sky and surf-crested sea hinted at something a lot more interesting. It was a card from Hannah and her writing was microscopic with the amount she had to tell.

Dear Ali, I said I'd write, and so I am. Having a blast of a time. We're now in La Rochelle. We've got our own annexe to stay in – very posh with proper beds and an ace swimming-pool to use. Emily and I are dead brown – don't breathe a word to Dad but we're topless by day and legless by night! Thanks for the money by the way, I've used some of it to buy Mum a present. Love, Hannah

Ali smiled. Good for you, girl. You go for it, kid. Grasp every opportunity of happiness while you can. She took a sip of her wine and stared thoughtfully at the card. She turned it over and looked at the stretch of beach, the impossibly blue sky, the inviting water and the brilliance of the white sand. It made her think of Daniel and his bullying.

Maybe he was right.

Perhaps she shouldn't hang around here being bored out of her skull just for the sake of taking time off work. She put her glass down beside the leg of her chair, went back inside the mill and rooted through her bag for her diary. She studied the entries for the week after next, then reached decisively for her mobile. There was nothing like acting on the spur of the moment. Tapping in her parents' number, she wandered outside again. As she waited for the phone to be answered at Sanderling, she leaned against the wooden rail of the balcony and watched the glowing ball of evening sun slowly sink on the horizon. At last she heard her father's voice. 'Ali,' he said, 'how the devil are you? We were only just talking about you.'

'Kindly, I hope.'

'Of course, what else would I have to say about my best girl?'

'You been at the pop again, Dad?'

'Why? Can you smell the fumes at this distance?'

'Practically keeling over.'

'Cheeky as ever, Ali. But you'll never guess what, Alistair's just phoned to announce that he's officially engaged to Phoebe and is combining a working trip to London with a visit to his lowly parents to show off the bride-to-be.'

'Good God, I don't believe it.'

'Nor can we. We were wondering if we could pull off a right royal family get-together. What do you think? Can I tempt you to come and see us?'

'Don't be so daft, of course I'll be there.'

'That's marvellous. Shall I put the memsahib on so you can finalise the details with her? You know I daren't promote myself to the dizzy heights of social secretary.'

'Hi, Mum,' Ali said, when her mother came on the line. 'How about that, then? The aged bachelor boy has finally gone and done it.'

'I know, your father and I can hardly believe it. After all these years he's succumbed. She must be quite special to have made him change his mind.'

'I'll say. So when are they arriving?'

'Next Saturday, a week tomorrow. You will come, won't you? We'd love to see you.'

'Actually, that's why I rang. I was hoping to cadge a holiday with you. Any chance of there being a bed for a couple of weeks as from Monday?'

'Oh, Ali, that would be lovely. Only trouble is we're away in Dorset for a few days and we leave on Monday morning. But you're more than welcome to make yourself at home while we're not here.'

Ali thought about this. Being at Sanderling on her own would be the same as being here all alone. What would be the point? She'd be just as miserable.

Her mother must have sensed her disappointment. 'Isn't there anyone you could bring with you?'

'What? A nice, handy bit of beefcake to keep me company?'

'Don't be silly, darling, I was thinking of Sarah. Didn't you mention on the phone last week that Hannah was away in France and that Sarah was down in the dumps and missing her? A holiday would cheer her up no end. It would be just like old times for you both.'

'Mum, you're brilliant!'

'Well, if you say so.'

'I'll ring Sarah straight away and see what she thinks. I'll call you in the morning with a yes or a no, shall I?'

'That's fine. But not too early. Your father and I enjoy our lie-ins, these days.'

Sarah answered the phone at Smithy Cottage.

'Hello, Ali,' she said, in a hushed tone that gave a clear indication to Ali that she wasn't alone.

'Is it a bad time to talk?'

'Yes, the group's here.'

'Oh, well, in that case I'll make it short and sweet. How do you feel about coming down to Hayling with me for a holiday? Just the two of us,' she added hastily, keen to ensure that Sarah wouldn't make the mistake of thinking Trevor was invited as well.

'Goodness, I don't know, Ali. When did you have in mind? And for how long?'

'Starting from Monday and for two whole weeks.'

'What?'

'I know it sounds impulsive but it would be fun, wouldn't it? And if you're worried about work, bring your sewing-machine with you. I could even help you.'

'If that's supposed to encourage me, forget it. I'm not having you anywhere near my machine.'

'So what do you say?'

'More to the point, what do I say to Trevor?'

'Tell him the truth, that you're desperately missing Hannah and you need something to take your mind off her. Oh, please say yes. I really want you to come. Mum and Dad will be away for the first week and we'll be able to do exactly as we want.'

'Oh, okay, then. You've twisted my arm.'

'Great! I'll come for you on Monday, about ten. That way we'll miss the early-morning crush on the motorway. Now get back to the Slipper Gang before they wake up and realise that you've gone.'

Ali felt ridiculously happy at the prospect of going away with Sarah and decided to ring Daniel and tell him what she'd done, as well as see if he could cover the extra week she'd decided to take off.

'Nice one, Babe,' he said. 'I knew I'd get through to you in the end. But, hey, this doesn't mean you're dropping out of Richard's barbecue on Sunday, does it?'

'And miss the culinary highlight of the year? I wouldn't dream of it. Though I might be a little late as I'll need to go into the office to sort out a few things.'

'Well, if there's anything you want me to do while you're away, leave a pile of instructions on my desk.'

'Will do. See you Sunday.'

Ali switched off her mobile and leaned back in her chair, pleased with her evening's work.

It was almost dark now, and as she stared into the gathering blackness and listened to the silence all around her, she realised just how quietly inert the evening was. The air was warm and still with hundreds of tiny insects hovering in it as if trapped by the thick humidity of the night. Then, way off in the distance, across the windless fields, she heard barking, but it was a lazy half-hearted bark and probably from a dog that was too hot to make a better job of it.

She found her eyelids drooping and to keep herself awake she began putting together a things-to-do list. First she'd make a start on the packing, then she'd call Lizzie and tell her not to bother coming in for the next fortnight, and when it was late enough she'd ring her parents to confirm the arrangements. Then she'd go shopping for a few essentials – some sun cream and a selection of books to help her while away the long hours she intended to spend on the beach or on a sun-lounger in her parents' garden. Food shopping she'd do when they arrived. Anyway, her mother's freezer was bound to be overflowing with goodies long overdue for consuming: the Bermuda Triangle, her father called it – stuff went in but never came out!

She reached for her glass to drink a toast to herself for having such a good idea and found that a long-legged insect had taken a nose-dive into the remains of her wine. She picked it out and hoped it wasn't an omen of the flies-and-ointment variety. She didn't want anything to spoil the next couple of weeks. For the first time in ages, she had something to look forward to.

It was nearly eleven o'clock when Elliot reached home. The Heathrow--Manchester shuttle had been delayed by nearly two hours and even when they'd been allowed to board the plane, they'd been stuck on the tarmac for a further forty minutes waiting for a slot, without the benefit of air-conditioning. It had been as hot as hell and he'd had the bad luck to be sitting next to a foul-mouthed man who thought he had the right to be as gratuitously unpleasant as he wanted to the young stewardesses.

The house was in darkness when he let himself in. He'd forgotten that Sam was over in Yorkshire with his card-playing cronies. He crossed the hall to his study, put his briefcase by the side of his desk and slipped his suit jacket over the back of his chair, along with his tie. He gave a cursory glance to the post Sam had put there for him and quickly dismissed it as uninteresting. But an envelope at the bottom of the pile stood out from the rest: it was square and very white, with the address written in gold ink, not in a hand he recognised. He slit it open. It was an invitation from Daniel, inviting him to a lunch-time barbecue to celebrate Richard's fortieth birthday. He checked the date and saw that it was for this Sunday.

Now, why had Daniel done that? he wondered, fanning himself with the thick, expensive card. Not since he and Ali had separated, when Daniel had felt that his loyalty lay with Ali, had there been any invitations of this sort.

Puzzled, he left his study and went through to the kitchen where he poured himself a large glass of orange juice from the fridge. He added a couple of ice cubes, swirled it round, then drank it slowly, speculating all the while as to the motive behind Daniel's invitation.

Was it just a harmless gesture of letting bygones be bygones, or was there more to it?

Such as?

Such as Ali putting him up to it because she wanted to see him?

No, he told himself firmly. He was not to let his thoughts go off in that direction. He'd been there earlier in the year and had lived to regret it; he wasn't inclined to make that mistake again.

He decided to go for a swim.

The pool room was airless and stiflingly hot. He switched on the underwater lights, but not the main ones, went over to the three sets of patio doors and slid them open. It was marginally cooler outside and while the temperature inside might not be greatly affected, the strong smell of chlorine would at least be diluted. He flung off his clothes and dived into the cool, refreshing water. It was undoubtedly the best bit of his day. The meeting in London had been a classic example of watch-your-back-and-keep-your-guard-up, and while it was mentally stimulating keeping one step ahead of the game, he also saw it as rather tiresome. For the first time in his career he had wondered if any of it was important to him.

It was a dangerous thought when his work was all he had.

He swam on and blamed the hot weather for making him feel so jaded and cynical. What he needed was a relaxing weekend. He'd do nothing but laze about the house and garden and generally wind down.

But the thought occurred to him that as Sunday would have been Isaac's fourth birthday, it might be better to accept Daniel's invitation and have something to occupy him.

Question was, would Ali be there?

Of course she would.

He hadn't been in touch with her since that night in March when he'd had supper with her. Even now he flinched at the painfully humiliating memory of his attempt to kiss her goodnight and her reaction to it. He hadn't meant it to be anything other than a simple parting act of courtesy, but her response had told him in no uncertain terms that she found him totally repugnant and would no more entertain the idea of physical contact between them than she would with a rattled cobra.

So it would probably be for the best if he phoned Daniel in the morning and politely declined the invitation.

29

It was Sunday, the day of Richard's party, and beneath a swelteringly hot and humid sky, Daniel carried the last of the bowls of salad from the kitchen and added them to the shaded table of food that the caterers from the village had prepared. Running his eye over an adjoining trestle-table laden with drink, and knowing how thirsty everyone would be, he hoped they would have enough. It really was the most incredible weather – nearly as hot as Spain had been. The forecast on the radio that morning had mentioned the possibility of thunderstorms in the north of England; hopefully, though, they would keep until tonight.

A sudden waft of thyme and rosemary met his nostrils and he looked over to the side of the house where the man in charge of the barbecue had just chucked a handful of herbs on to the coals. He helped himself to a glass of sangria and searched the crowd of guests checking for two faces in particular.

There was no sign of either so he widened his search to the garden, then to the shade of the orchard. Again he drew a blank. But his gaze fell on Richard who, like himself and most of the other male guests, was dressed casually in shorts and a polo shirt. His head was turned to one side and Daniel took a moment to admire the cheerfully smiling, dark-eyed countenance that was as familiar to him as his own. Amusing, charming and with a love of witty anecdotal repartee, Richard was lethally intelligent, and Daniel knew that when he was in court he became a dangerous man. He could cut through the most persuasive and carefully constructed cases with a skill envied by anyone who had seen him in action. Right now, though, he looked as benign as the ancient apple tree he was sitting beneath while talking to Julia, a fellow barrister from his chambers who was expecting her second child. Her first, four-year-old Toby, was sitting on what was left of her lap, dipping his fingers into her lemonade then sucking them dry.

A hand tapped his shoulder and Daniel turned round, thinking it might be Ali. It wasn't, it was the barbecue man. 'Everything's about done,' he said. 'Do you want to give folk a shout?' He pulled off his straw boater, which bore a wide ribbon with the words Smoky-Joe's Mobile BBQ printed on it. He mopped his glistening forehead with a paper napkin and stuffed it into the front pocket of his butcher's-style apron.

'That's great,' Daniel said. 'I'll get people moving.' To attract everybody's attention he went over to the house and rang the brass ship's bell beside the door. 'Lunch is served,' he shouted. 'Women and children from steerage class go first, no pushing or shoving.'

'My timing, as ever, is spot on,' came a voice from behind him.

This time it was Ali.

'At last. I'd almost given up on you.' He raised his sunglasses and bent his head to kiss her. Then, tracing a finger over a shoestring strap that was slipping off her bare shoulder, he said, 'Nice dress, Babe. You've buffed yourself up a treat for the occasion.'

'Which is more than I can say for you. That shirt might be Armani's finest, but there's a hole in it, just there.' She pointed to his chest and he lowered his eyes to see. She laughed and flicked him lightly on the nose with the back of her hand. 'Don't mess with me, Dan Divine. Now, where's the birthday boy?'

'Cooling off in the orchard.'

'Sensible man. I'll go and give this to him.'

Daniel eyed with interest the present she was carrying. 'What is it?'

'Never you mind. You see to your other guests and leave me to have a nice, malicious gossip with Richard. And no guesses for who we'll be tearing apart!'

Daniel smiled and watched her make her way through the crush of guests on the terrace, down the three steps that led to the garden and the orchard beyond. He saw Richard get to his feet when he caught sight of her. He hugged her warmly, then pulled up another chair so that she could join him and Julia. Knowing that Ali never gave anyone a gift that she hadn't put a lot of thought into, Daniel was tempted to go over and see what she had brought for Richard.

But this wasn't the only reason he wanted to join them. He was losing his nerve. Sending that invitation to Elliot now seemed the dumbest of ideas and he felt as though he ought to come clean with Ali so that she could prepare herself. On the other hand, it was almost two o'clock and it was just possible Elliot might be a no-show. In which case, if he kept his mouth shut, Ali would be none the wiser.

It was late on Tuesday night when he and Richard were in bed that Daniel had thought of inviting Elliot to the party. 'What do you think?' he'd asked Richard. 'What would they do?'

Glancing up from the brief he was working on, Richard had said, 'Doubtless Elliot would behave impeccably, as he always does, but Ali would probably disembowel you on the spot, toss your tasty little sweetbreads on to the hot coals of the barbecue and then kebab the rest of you.'

'So you reckon I shouldn't do it?'

'I didn't say that.'

'What then?'

'I'm suggesting that you must be prepared for the consequences, should Ali decide that you've been scheming behind her back.'

'But only with her best interests at heart.'

'Naturally. What else could you possibly have in mind?'

'You're beginning to sound as though you're cross-examining me.'

'Just send Elliot the invitation. No real harm can come of it. Ali will always love you, she can't help herself. The worst that could happen is that she'll be cross for a while and then when she's calmed down you'll kiss and make up.'

'And the best that could come of it?'

Returning his attention to the papers on top of the duvet, Richard had said, 'I think we both know the outcome that you're hankering after, don't we? You're a sentimental old fool looking for a happy ending.'

The queue for food was now well established and after Daniel had chatted with some friends from the choral society and made sure that everybody was helping themselves to drinks, he went to check on the tennis court where the older children had congregated. He told them that if they didn't get going all the burgers and sausages would be gone. They threw down their rackets and raced out of the court. Amy, his thirteen-year-old niece, his sister's eldest child, gave him a smile and he flicked at her CK baseball cap as she rushed past. He wondered at their energy in all this sticky heat. I'm getting old, he reflected. And what a depressing thought that was. The noise of an approaching car made him turn and he knew at once who it was. Now, should he go and meet Elliot? Or should he sneak back to the house and hide anything that was long and sharp which Ali could use to disembowel him?

Elliot slowed his speed and parked behind Ali's Saab. He switched off the engine and reached for the bottle of vintage port he had brought for Richard. When he stepped out of the car, he saw Daniel coming towards him.

'Hi,' Daniel said, 'I thought perhaps you weren't going to make it.'

'I wasn't sure that I would,' Elliot said.

And wasn't that the truth? He'd changed his mind about coming so many times since Friday night that in the end, and only an hour ago, he had let the decision rest on the toss of a coin: tails, and he'd stay at home for the afternoon to read the Sunday papers; heads, and he'd put himself through another bit of hell. He inclined his head towards Ali's Saab and said, 'What sort of mood is she in?'

'Relaxed and happy, having a gossip about me with Richard.'

'Does she know I was invited?'

'Er ... no.'

'A surprise, then?'

Daniel nodded guiltily.

'Well, let's hope it's not too horrible for her.'

Passing the long line of cars, they walked up to the house, and when they reached the terrace, Daniel offered Elliot a drink. 'Looks as if we're getting low on sangria,' he said, lifting a large Spanish pottery jug and peering inside it. 'How about some wine?'

'I'd prefer a beer, please.'

'I think I'll join you.' Bending down to one of the cool boxes under the table, Daniel picked out a couple of cans of Budweiser.

'Thanks,' said Elliot, snapping back the ring-pull. 'Cheers.' After they'd both taken a few mouthfuls, and as if it was clearly understood between them exactly why he was here, Elliot said, 'It was good of you to invite me. I appreciate it.'

Daniel responded with a casual shrug, which belied what he really felt. 'It seemed a good idea,' he said, wanting to add, 'at the time.' And doing his utmost not to visualise his entrails being slowly drawn out of him he vowed never, *ever*, to meddle again in Ali's private affairs.

With a hint of a smile, Elliot said, 'Let's hope you still think that later today. Shall we get it over and done with, then?'

Daniel's insides went into liquidised mode. 'Why not?' he muttered, thinking of a million good reasons why not. 'She was in the orchard the last time I saw her. I'll take you.'

They were half way across the lawn when, above the noise of music and party chatter, Elliot heard the unmistakable sound of Ali's laughter. He squinted to find her in the shade of the apple trees. She appeared to be just as Daniel had described, relaxed and happy. She was sitting alone with Richard who was leaning in close, like an attentive lover, and feeding her something from his plate. Her head was tilted back and the pale, slender line of her throat was alluringly exposed. Elliot couldn't remember the last time he'd seen her looking so at ease. Certainly not in his company. His body stiffened as a powerful surge of jealous love for her rose up within him and he knew that he'd made a terrible mistake in coming here. But it was too late to retreat. Richard had caught sight of him and, as they advanced further, Elliot noted the smallest of exchanges pass between him and Daniel.

'How amazingly good it is to see you, Elliot,' said Richard, on his feet now and smiling genially. 'I'm so pleased you accepted my invitation. Daniel, being the ultra-sensitive soul he is, was dead against it, but I insisted. It's my party, I told him, and I'll do as I please. Now, then, you don't have anything to eat. Daniel, why don't you see to that and I'll get Ali another drink? And is that a present I spy in your hands, as the Virgin Queen was heard to remark to Sir Francis Drake on his return to these fair shores of England?'

When they were alone, Elliot motioned towards the wooden chair Richard had vacated. 'May I?'

She nodded and he sat down. She said, 'I know barristers are known for their acting skills, but what, I wonder, am I supposed to make of that little charade?'

The vibrancy of her voice suggested irony rather than displeasure. He ventured a similar tone. 'That Richard was pleased to see me?'

She turned and stared at him suspiciously. 'Possibly. Which was more than Daniel looked. His face wore an expression of abject terror and I swear it had a label attached to it that said, in big black letters, "Shoot me now".'

As usual she was right. Daniel had indeed looked terrified, but not wanting to pursue the hows and whys of this, Elliot opted for the safety of a round or two of small-talk – if there was such a thing with Ali. 'How are you?' he asked, when she'd removed her sceptical gaze from him. 'You look well.'

She leaned back in her seat and adjusted the hem of her dress as well as the strap on her shoulder, which seemed to have a mind of its own. 'Thank you. It's probably the thought of going away on holiday tomorrow.'

'Somewhere nice?'

'Down to Sanderling. Sarah's coming with me.'

'A trip down Memory Lane for you both.'

'Indeed.'

'Sam's away this weekend. He's in Yorkshire with a gang of his poker cronies.'

'Leaving you at liberty to accept lunch-time barbecue invitations.'

'Something like that, yes.'

Their supply of small-talk now used up, Elliot stared straight ahead. His gaze came to rest on a small fair-haired boy in navy blue shorts and a blue and white striped T-shirt. He was sitting at his mother's feet pushing a toy car through the long grass, giving it his entire concentration, *brrming* his lips with noisy enjoyment. His mother, who was about six months pregnant, Elliot guessed, smiled down at him. She then spoke to the man at her side who kissed her while gently passing his hand over their child-to-be in a gesture of protective affection. It was an exquisite cameo of intimacy; a snapshot of a loving family. Elliot tore his eyes away from the scene. 'Look,' he said, his voice thick with emotion, 'if I'm spoiling your afternoon, tell me and I'll leave you alone.'

Ali had been observing the same touching tableau, and it struck at the heart of her: in another life she had been that woman, Elliot had been that man . . . and Isaac had been that son. The poignancy of it made her want the impossible, to turn the clock back, to experience that tender love all over again. The need to feel it once more was so great in her it hurt. But she knew it could never be.

But you could say sorry, she heard Sarah's soft voice whisper in her head.

You could make amends.

Do for Elliot what he can't do for himself.

Forgive him.

Just say the words and you could be nice to one another.

And suddenly Ali knew that the time had come. At last she realised that the pain and bitterness she had lived with for so long had to be eradicated once and for all. She took a deep breath and turned to Elliot. To her surprise, he was on his feet and already moving away from her. Puzzled, she looked at his retreating figure. Then she realised what was wrong. She'd taken too long to answer his question and he'd assumed that her silence meant that she didn't want him near her. Stunned by the discovery that she was now ready to put the past behind her, she watched him march out of the dim light of the orchard and step into the brightness of the garden. She decided to give him time to cool off before going after him.

Elliot had been all for going home, but Daniel had intercepted him with a plate of food and later challenged him to a game of tennis. It had seemed as good a way as any to beat the shit out of himself. He was two sets up and was now serving for the match. Facing into the sun, which was now partially eclipsed by a hazy canopy of thundery clouds, Elliot tossed the ball high into the air. He swung his borrowed racket behind him, then snatched it over his shoulder, throwing all his weight and frustration against it. The ball hurtled over the net and shot past Daniel before he'd even had a chance to prepare for it.

'That's the last time I play tennis with you,' puffed Daniel, when they walked off the court.

'I was on a lucky roll,' Elliot said modestly, wiping the sweat off his face with his hands, then rubbing them on his linen trousers.

'The hell you were. You completely outclassed me.'

They strolled back to the house and helped themselves to two ice-cold beers. 'I don't know about you,' Daniel groaned, 'but I need to sit down. I'm knackered.'

There were no free seats in the orchard so they flopped on to the grass. The small boy Elliot had seen earlier with his parents came and joined them. He had a bowl of raspberries in his hands and set it carefully on his crossed legs as he sat down. 'You look very hot,' he remarked to Daniel.

'That's because I am, Toby. I've just been playing tennis. One of those nice juicy raspberries would make me feel a whole lot better, though.'

The little boy smiled, showing two rows of tiny white teeth, and offered him the bowl. Shyly, and despite there being only a few left, he then passed the dish to Elliot. Touched by the child's generosity, he said, 'No, thanks, it looks as if you're down to your last.'

'Well, we'll soon remedy that,' said Daniel. He rose to his feet and went over to the terrace and the tables of food.

'Is Daniel getting us some more?' asked the little boy.

'I think so.'

He popped the last of the raspberries into his mouth and looked thoughtfully at Elliot. 'Did you know that my mummy's having a baby?'

'I'd guessed that that might be the case.'

'Are you a daddy?'

Elliot said no, and wished that Daniel would hurry back. He didn't want to be alone with this child and his naturally inquisitive chatter. He knew the score only too well. It would be one question after another. Why? Why? Why? That's what children did.

'Don't you like children?'

Oh, here we go. 'I'm very fond of them,' he murmured edgily. He looked across to the terrace for some sign of Daniel. He saw him laughing with a young girl in a baseball cap. Come on, Daniel, he urged silently. A rumble of thunder rolled overhead and he plucked distractedly at the grass between his feet. Without raising his eyes, he wondered how old the boy was. Odds on he was four ... the very age Isaac would have been today. At this thought he felt his throat tighten. He passed a hand over his face and became aware of his heart beginning to thump in his chest. He blinked hard and let out his breath; he was hotter now than when he'd been playing tennis. It's the humidity, he told himself firmly, desperately groping for some reasonable, trivial explanation for what was happening to him. He'd do anything but accept the truth. All he could do was hope that the moment would pass. Then, with relief, he saw Daniel ambling slowly towards them.

The little boy saw him too and when Daniel had lowered himself on to the grass and had stretched out on his side, he said, 'Is your friend like you and Richard? Is that why he doesn't have any children?'

Daniel stared at Toby in amusement. Good God, trust Julia to be so bloody open with her son! But his expression soon changed when he saw Elliot's deathly pale face. Shit, he thought, what the hell's been going on here? He handed Toby the bowl of raspberries that he'd just fetched and said, 'Elliot isn't at all like Richard and me. Now eat up and don't ask any more nosy questions.'

Toby smiled and, leaning into Daniel, he said in a loud whisper, 'Why does he look so cross?'

'He's not cross,' Daniel whispered back.

'Is he sad, then?'

Other than putting a gag on Toby, there seemed no way of stopping the flow of innocent questions, and Daniel looked helplessly at Elliot. Then to his surprise he heard Elliot say, 'I'm not cross, Toby, but you're right about me being sad.'

'Why?'

'Because I had a little boy once. He was quite a bit younger than you and . . . and he died.'

Both Elliot and Daniel expected this to be the conversation stopper it usually was, but all it did was provoke yet another question from Toby. 'Did he die in his sleep? Mummy says that's the best way to die.'

The conversation had now spiralled completely out of his control and, as another rumble of thunder rolled in the distance, a gut-wrenching pain propelled Elliot to his feet. He realised to his horror that his heart was pounding even faster than it had been a few minutes before and that every inch of his body was clammy with sweat. He stumbled away and out of the orchard. He knew with terrible certainty that he was going to be sick. He followed a small path that led down the gentle slope of the valley towards the wood on the edge of Daniel and Richard's land. His head was throbbing and his stomach pitching. He leaned over a crumbling drystone wall and vomited violently.

When at last it came to an end, he slipped his hand into his trouser pocket and pulled out his handkerchief. With shaking hands, he wiped his face and remained where he was, leaning heavily on the wall, his shoulders taut, his chest heaving. But though his eyes were focused on the flock of sheep sheltering in the shade of a tree in the nearby field, his thoughts were with Isaac on the night he died.

There had been nothing peaceful about Isaac's death, nothing of the fairy-tale slipping away to heaven in his sleep that Toby had probably been taught.

The day had started ordinarily enough; there hadn't been a single clue at breakfast that by the end of the day their lives would be so irredeemably smashed apart. The only difference in their routine was that their nanny, who had been with them since Isaac was four months old, had taken a day off and, with Ali flying to Frankfurt that afternoon, Elliot had said that he'd stay at home and take care of Isaac. They'd waved Ali goodbye as she'd left for work and everything had been fine until around five, when Isaac began to look unwell and refused to eat his tea. Thinking that perhaps he was coming down with a cold, Elliot had bathed him and put him to bed. He'd read him a story, kissed him goodnight and gone downstairs to answer the phone. It was Gervase from the office: the wretched man had drivelled on for more than an hour.

When he'd finished on the phone, Elliot had gone back upstairs to check on Isaac. The second he saw him, he knew that something was wrong. His breathing was noisy and painfully laboured; his face pale, his eyes wide and staring. Pulling back the tangle of bedclothes, Elliot touched his flushed skin and realised that his temperature was worryingly high. He unbuttoned his pyjama top and saw that his tiny chest was being sucked in with the struggle to breathe. He knew vaguely about young children suffering from croup, but this seemed far worse than anything he'd read or heard about. He'd gathered Isaac in his arms, rushed him downstairs and outside to the car. He drove as fast as he dared to the nearest hospital, glancing almost every other second in the rear-view mirror, but seeing only what he feared most – that his son was dying.

The noise of twigs crackling underfoot made Elliot spin round. 'What the hell do you want?' he said sharply, when he saw who it was.

Ali hesitated. 'Daniel suggested that I came to look for you,' she said. 'Are you okay?'

He twisted the handkerchief in his hands, screwing it tighter and tighter around his fingers until it hurt. 'No, I'm not okay and I'd rather you left me alone.'

Genuinely alarmed, especially in view of what Daniel had just told her, Ali took a few cautious steps towards him. She leaned against the drystone wall and when she saw what lay the other side of it, she knew that Daniel had been right to make her come and find him. 'Elliot,' she said gently, 'what's wrong?' He turned slowly and she saw an expression of such distilled misery in his face that instinctively she reached out to him and placed a hand on his arm. 'Please, tell me, what is it?'

His jaw tightened. 'Do you really need to ask that?'

'Was it that little boy, Toby?'

He pushed away her hand and squeezed his eyes shut. 'Leave me alone. Just go. You're good at doing that.'

The bitterness in his voice was hard to bear, but she remained where she was. 'Elliot,' she said softly, 'I left you alone once before and it didn't help either of us, did it?'

He opened his eyes and looked at her. 'So what are you saying?'

'I'm saying that we've hidden too much from one another. I think we should put a stop to it. Don't you?'

'What is it that I'm supposed to have hidden from you?'

'Many things. Such as how you feel about me. How you still feel about Isaac. Perhaps even how you feel about what happened that night.'

Her over-simplification of what he was suffering caused something to explode deep inside Elliot. The tortured anguish that had covered his face suddenly turned into an expression of raw anger. 'Okay, then,' he threw nastily at her, 'so you want me to be honest with you, do you? In that case I'll share with you exactly what happened that night. I'll tell you all the grisly details. I'll spare you nothing. You can have the unexpurgated version. Then every day, just as I do, you can live through the hell of it. Is that what you want?'

Ali had never seen or heard Elliot act so savagely and, frightened by the brutality in his voice, she could do nothing but nod in mute agreement.

'Then you're welcome to it.' He moved away from her and as the first soft drops of rain started to fall, he paced the stony path, backwards and forwards, as he pieced together the events of the worst night of his life. He told her how he had driven Isaac to hospital as soon as he'd known something was wrong. 'I don't know who was the more terrified,' he said, 'Isaac because he couldn't breathe or me because I didn't know if I was doing the right thing. We'd only been in the car a few minutes when he literally turned grey. Then he started to drool, and worse – oh, God, much worse – the terrible noise of his tiny lungs struggling for breath began to fade.' He paused, ran a hand through his hair, then rounded on her. He grabbed her shoulders and almost shook her. 'Can you understand what that did to me? Do you have any idea what it feels like having to choose between driving on for help that might be too late anyway, or stopping so that a small, frightened child could at least die in his father's arms?'

Shocked, Ali trembled in his hands. 'What did you do?' Her question was little more than a faint whisper. This wasn't how she'd imagined it. Not at all. She'd needed to believe that there had been no pain for Isaac. That it had been quick – quick, but painless.

The rain was coming down more heavily now, wetting their clothes and faces. Ali's flimsy cotton dress was already drenched and clinging to her. She wasn't cold but she was shivering. Oblivious to the rain, Elliot let go of her and began pacing again. And although the vociferous, accusing fury that had led him to this point had subsided, the desperation was still in his immeasurably wretched face. 'I decided to drive on,' he said, his tone altogether softer. 'All I could think of was getting Isaac to somebody who would know what to do, somebody who would be able to save him. But then he turned blue and when the convulsions started I knew I had to stop. It was awful, his legs and arms were twitching and by the time I got round to the back of the car, he'd lost consciousness . . . He wasn't moving. He was so still. So bloody still and I knew I'd lost him. I tried to resuscitate him. I kept on trying – it seemed like for ever. But it was no good. Nothing I did was of any use. I then – I then—' But his voice cracked with the choking horror of reliving the ordeal. He fixed his gaze on the distant hills and from somewhere, he didn't know where, the strength came to him to carry on. 'I had to drive the rest of the journey to the hospital knowing that our son was dead. I carried him in and he was taken from me. A nurse came and sat with me and when I thought I was calm enough I phoned you.'

He fell silent, closed his eyes and let out his breath in one long sigh. He stood perfectly still, listening to the rain as it pattered all around him, his anger now spent. The worst had passed. Thank God. He was back in control again.

He opened his eyes, turned to look at Ali, but then from nowhere, a sickening wave of agony swept over him as he recalled pressing his lips to Isaac's soft cheek for the last time, his limp body already cool to the touch as he carried him from the car. Unable to stop himself, he started to shake. He covered his face with his hands and wept. He thought that he'd already experienced every conceivable pain there was when he thought of his son, but he hadn't. What he was feeling now, after finally admitting to another person what he'd gone through that night, was the fusion of everything he'd ever suffered.

Then, gradually, he became conscious of Ali moving behind him. He felt her hands on his shoulders. At first he held back from her, rigid and unyielding, but when he realised that she was crying as much as he was, he gave in to her embrace, and in the deluge of rain that had now thoroughly soaked them, they did what they'd never tried to do since losing their son: they cried in one another's arms.

'Oh, Ali,' he sobbed into her neck, 'I swear I did everything I could to save him. It was a nightmare. A total fucking nightmare. It was all so quick and there wasn't anything I could do. You have to believe me.'

30

It was Ali who spoke first. Lifting her head from Elliot's shoulder, she raised her eyes to his ravaged face and said, 'Elliot, we have to talk.'

They took a moment to compose themselves, then followed the path back up to the house, to where all the other guests had now fled for shelter. Without a word to anyone they left the party.

In silent concentration, Elliot drove them to Timbersbrook, the seriousness of his blue eyes and the hard line of his jaw determining that now was not the time to embark on what they had to discuss.

How adept he is at isolating himself, thought Ali, as she sat beside him, sensing that, as physically close as they were, he was far beyond her reach. And wasn't that exactly what he had done since Isaac's death? He'd shut himself off from everyone. Including her. It had been his way of coping with his grief; his naturally quiet, insular disposition had simply brought down the shutters and forced him to retreat into himself. It was obvious now, with the benefit of hindsight, that she should have tried harder to reach him, to infiltrate his defences and knock down that impenetrable shield with which he'd protected himself, but she'd barely had the strength to haul herself through her own misery, never mind sustain Elliott.

If only he had told her what he had really endured that night, how different it all might have been. But her own willingness to accept the original story he'd given – that Isaac's death had been so quick that he'd hardly suffered – was surely partly to blame for that. She had wanted, *needed*, as any mother would, to believe that her son had experienced the minimum of pain. All this time she had believed that Isaac was conscious until Elliot got him to the hospital, that it was only then as he'd arrived that death had taken him. She had believed all too readily Elliot's claim that their child's death had not been precipitated by a gruelling struggle for survival. But now she knew differently. Now she knew that he'd struggled to live, every bit of his small terrified body fighting painfully to the last. To the very last.

She squeezed her eyelids shut as the horror of what Elliot had just revealed to her flashed through her mind. With new and hideously clear understanding, she pictured the chilling scene of Elliot, all alone, trying desperately to revive Isaac and the awful moment when he'd been forced to acknowledge that he'd failed. That there was nothing he could do. How would she have reacted if that had been her? To what depths would she have sunk had she been in his place?

But she had never put herself in Elliot's place. All she had thought about was Isaac. And, selfishly, herself. Her loss.

Not even at the hospital when she had been told what had happened did she pause to think of the ordeal Elliot had just lived through. She had been only half listening to the doctor as he had explained that her son's death was a scenario all medical staff dreaded: there had been so little warning that something was fatally wrong. She had been informed that Isaac had died from a rare case of bacterial croup, epiglottitis, which had resulted in his larynx swelling so much that he couldn't breathe. The doctor had gone on to say, just as he had earlier told Sam and Elliot, that there was nothing Elliot could have done. All that might have saved Isaac was an emergency tracheotomy.

But she had refused to believe the doctor. A child's life could not be snatched away so swiftly. It couldn't end like that. It just couldn't. Somebody had to be accountable.

Cruelly, she had wanted to hold Elliot accountable; he should have got Isaac to hospital in time.

Later, when Sam had driven them home from the hospital, he had insisted on staying the night with them. But no one had slept, and while she had cried alone on the bed upstairs, and Sam had made an endless succession of cups of coffee that nobody drank, Elliot had begun to withdraw into himself. At four in the morning, when it was still dark, she had looked out of the bedroom window and had seen his desolate figure in the shadows at the end of the garden. She had no idea how long he'd been out there, but he must have been frozen for she could see his breath hanging in the wintry air. She knew that he needed her, but her own grief was so great that it overwhelmed anything she felt for him, and with her forehead pressed against the icy pane of glass she had mouthed the words, *You could have saved him ... You could have saved him.*

In one form or another she had been thinking those words ever since.

She had never once verbally blamed Elliot for failing Isaac, but she knew she had done the next best thing: she had punished him relentlessly by making him hate her.

This, then, was the final confession, the truth that not even Sarah had guessed: this was what had really destroyed her marriage. It hadn't just been Elliot's rejection that had fuelled her need to punish him: it had been her terrible, misguided need to make him pay for allowing their son to die. Initially she hadn't been aware of what she was doing, but when she realised the destruction she was causing, she had been beyond caring. It was entirely his fault; he had let their child die.

Consumed now by the heaviest weight of guilt and shame, she wrapped her arms around her wet shoulders and shivered. How could she have behaved so despicably? And towards a man who she now knew had gone through a nightmare far worse than her own. Of course he had done everything he could to save Isaac. Why had she ever thought that he hadn't?

Elliot had loved Isaac with all his heart. He'd never been too busy or too tired to play with his son. Not once had he ever refused to take his share of the disturbed nights when Isaac was teething. He would hold him lovingly in his arms, gently rocking him back to sleep. One night she had heard him talking to Isaac in a low, soothing voice as he'd tried to settle him. He was sharing with Isaac some of the things they would do together when he was old enough. Slipping out of bed, she'd gone and listened at the door.

'I'll take you to Yorkshire,' Elliot was murmuring softly as he rested Isaac, hot and fractious, against his shoulder and stroked the wispy curls of damp, blond hair in the nape of his neck. 'I'll show you where I grew up. We'll take a kite and go up on to the moors. Your grandfather used to do that with me. Perhaps we'll take him with us. Your mother too. And there's something you should know about your mother. I'm sure you've noticed it already, but she's the most beautiful woman in the world. She's also the smartest and you'd do well to watch her. One day you'll realise just how special she is. I'll warn you now, it'll come as a shock. It did to me. Of course, you won't love her as I do, but love her you will, because I promise you, you won't be able to help yourself. And when the time comes for you to fall madly and indescribably in love, I hope that you'll be as lucky as your father and marry the woman who means the world to you. But before all that happens, you've got your parents' love to make do with. And that, I might say, is considerable. There's nothing we wouldn't do for you. We'll always keep you safe. Nothing will ever harm you.'

With tears in her eyes she had wanted to let Elliot know that she was there, that she had heard what he'd said. She had wanted to tell him how touched she was, but knowing that this was the most effusive she'd ever known him, she had crept quietly back to bed and waited for him to join her.

Thinking now of all the love she had so wilfully destroyed, Ali hated herself. She felt physically ill. Worried that she was going to be sick, she opened her eyes and saw that Elliot was watching her. The concern in his face only added to her guilt.

It had stopped raining when Elliot brought the car to a halt and the sun was shining once more. He let them into the house and, without a word, took her through to the sitting room where he poured two enormous glasses of Jack Daniel's. Ali stood awkwardly in the large room watching him. Then, when he passed her drink to her, she caught sight of the group of framed photographs on the baby grand. For something to do, she went over to take a look and was surprised to see an old picture of herself included among the collection. Unnerved, she ran her hand over the lid of the piano and said, 'Do you still play?'

'Hardly ever,' he answered.

'Why's that?'

He took an unsteady gulp of his drink. 'I lost my most appreciative audience.' He didn't wait for her response, but turned on his heel and crossed the room to the French windows. They opened on to the garden, which was flooded with sunlight. He breathed in the freshness of the air, now that the storm had passed.

She came and stood next to him. 'Shall we sit outside?' she asked.

He took her to a wooden bench in a small, shaded area of garden. The ground was flagged with moss-darkened Yorkshire stone and dotted with large pots of hostas and specimen lilies. Everything was washed clean and bright by the downpour of rain and jewel-like droplets of water hung in suspended animation from the drooping leaves and petals. It was very tranquil.

'You should never have kept the truth of that night to yourself,' Ali said, after Elliot had wiped the bench with his handkerchief and they were settled.

'I had to,' he said simply.

'But why?'

'I was trying to protect you ... I didn't want you to have the kind of nightmare memories I have of Isaac.'

'Perhaps if you had told me the truth I wouldn't have added to your pain in the way I did. I might have understood better – been able to help you.'

'It wouldn't have done any good. I wouldn't have let you near me. I hated myself for letting Isaac die.' He lowered his head and stared with unseeing eyes into his glass. 'I still hate myself. For the rest of my life I have to live with the knowledge that if I had realised earlier that Isaac was ill, if I'd shut Gervase up sooner – if I'd got to a hospital quicker—'

She laid a hand on his forearm. 'Elliot, you have to stop thinking those thoughts.'

He raised his head and looked at her. 'I don't think I ever will. Every night when I sleep I'm haunted by his frightened face, I see how betrayed he felt, that his own father was letting him suffer, that I didn't stop it. I hear my voice shouting at him not to die. Again and again I relive that moment when I'm trying to revive him ... Sometimes it works ... but usually he just lies there limp and cold in my arms.' He took a gulp of his drink. 'Sometimes I dream it's you I'm trying to bring back to life.'

Her throat tightened. 'Does it ever work?' she asked.

'No,' he said bleakly. 'I'm always too late ... just as I was with Isaac.'

'Oh, Elliot, why did you never try telling me these things?'

'I'd done too good a job of making you hate me, I guess.'

She frowned. 'No, it's the other way around, I deliberately *made* you hate me.'

'I pushed you away, Ali, because I couldn't stand to have anyone near me, but I never hated you. Please, if nothing else, believe that to be true.'

'Then I got that wrong as well.' She sighed. 'I needed to think you did. It was a crazy way of punishing myself – and you. I wanted to spoil everything we had. By making you feel worse I convinced myself that I was feeling better.'

'Did it work?'

'What do you think?'

'I suppose not.'

She turned to him. 'If I said I was sorry a thousand times would you ever forgive me?'

He stared at her. 'But, Ali, I need *your* forgiveness. If I'd acted sooner Isaac would still be alive, if I'd—'

'No, Elliot, you did all you could. I can accept that, and so must you. You have to stop punishing yourself.'

He didn't say anything but, very gently, he put his arm round her and drew her close until her head was resting on his shoulder. She linked her fingers through his and they sat there silently holding one another, just letting the serenity of the garden wrap itself around them.

'I feel strangely at peace,' Ali said, when at last she moved.

'I know what you mean. I feel it too.'

'If there is such a thing as an afterlife, do you suppose Isaac is looking down on us and saying, "Thank goodness for that."'

'Probably. He was a smart lad.'

'Unlike his parents.'

'Unlike his parents,' agreed Elliot.

They fell silent again. Then Elliot said, 'You might think this inappropriate, but as we ought to get out of these wet clothes anyway, do you fancy a swim?'

She shifted her position and sat up. 'A swim?'

He pulled her to her feet decisively. 'Come on. It'll do us good. It'll help us relax.'

'But I don't have anything to wear,' she protested, when he led her back inside the house and into the pool room.

He pushed open the patio doors. 'I promise I won't look.'

'You mean skinny-dipping?'

He ignored her question and its tone of incredulous propriety. 'Changing rooms are down the other end. I'll get you a robe and a towel.' He opened one of the mirror-fronted cupboards behind him and handed her a bundle of neatly folded white towelling.

When she emerged from the changing room, coyly wrapped in the oversized robe, she saw that Elliot was already in the pool modestly attired in a pair of swimming shorts. True to his word, he didn't look at her until she was fully immersed. It was stupid that she should be embarrassed at the thought of him seeing her naked, but there was something wrong about one's ex-husband viewing the goods that had once been for his eyes only but which were now strictly out of bounds.

Keeping a suitably respectable distance between them, they swam to and fro. Neither spoke. But it wasn't long before she realised that Elliot had been right about feeling better for a swim. She already felt less raw from the painfully honest, vulnerable ordeal they'd just experienced. She hoped he felt better too. Every now and then she looked across the pool to check that he wasn't sneaking the odd glance her way. But as ever, when he wanted it to be, his face was unreadable. She found herself wondering what he was thinking. Were his thoughts running along the same lines as hers? That they had found the key to set themselves free?

What she had said in the garden about being at peace was true. She hadn't ever thought that there would come a time when she would be able to say those words. But it had happened. As if by magic the weight of the past two and a half years had been lifted from her. In real terms nothing had changed – Isaac was still dead and her grief for him was still there – but what had gone was the cruel need to punish herself. By feeling compassionate towards Elliot and knowing, deep in her heart, that she no longer blamed him, she felt almost restored to her former self. Perhaps even a better self.

She was tiring and, knowing that she couldn't keep pace with Elliot's strong arms and shoulders as he cut effortlessly through the water, she watched him swim on ahead of her. He was a difficult man not to admire and she found herself wondering whether there had been any women in his life since their divorce. She suspected the answer had to be yes. She couldn't imagine any woman not falling for his special brand of understated sexual magnetism. It must have been put to excellent use at some stage since their separation. She was smiling at this thought when she noticed that he'd stopped swimming and was waiting for her at the shallow end.

'It's been ages since I've seen you smile like that,' he said. 'What were you thinking?'

'Of you,' she said, as she came to a stop alongside him. 'And don't you dare lower your eyes from my face,' she added, remembering that she didn't have a stitch on, 'not even for a second.'

He was privately amused. 'So what was making you smile?'

'I was wondering whether there'd been many women in your bed since me.'

He raised an eyebrow. 'And do you think you have a right to know?'

'Not really. I gave up that right when I divorced you.'

He sharpened his gaze on her. 'Well, I'll tell you anyway, just to satisfy your curiosity. There hasn't been anyone.'

'Not one?'

He shook his head. 'You seem surprised at my hermetically sealed sex life?'

'Frankly, I'm amazed.' She was also amazed that she felt so irrationally relieved.

'What about you?'

'Hundreds,' she said, with a light-hearted smile.

He frowned. 'What does that mean exactly?'

She laughed and swam away from him. 'It means zippo, lover-boy.'

He went after her and caught her up in one long easy stroke. Matching her pace and swimming barely a few feet away from her, he forgot his earlier promise and allowed his eyes to linger over her sinuous body. In that moment, it seemed to him to be a fluid, shimmering vision of loveliness. Almost at once she saw what he was doing. She ducked and disappeared beneath the water, but not before he'd glimpsed a hint of a smile. He filled his lungs with a gulp of air and dived in after her. Taking her unawares he caught her by the waist and pulled her down to the floor of the pool. He covered her lips with his and gently filled her mouth with air as her surprised resistance gave way and she relaxed into his arms. He kissed her for as long as his breath held out and when eventually they floated to the surface they stared transfixed at each other. It was Ali who made the next move. She pulled him to her and kissed him, urgently and with passion, her body alive to the aching desire she felt for him. Pressing his body against hers and revelling in its familiarity – there wasn't a bit of it she didn't know – she alternated between kissing him and frantically whispering his name, over and over. There seemed no doubt in either of their minds what would happen now. It was more a matter of where. Ali wanted him so badly she would have splashed around in the water and risked drowning. But Elliot had other ideas. He helped her out of the pool, laid her on top of the towels and robes, and just as they always had, they made love with a passion that was tender and uninhibited.

'I was worried that after several years of celibacy I might have lost my touch,' he murmured, when they lay stunned and exhausted, and not a little self-consciously, in one another's arms.

'You have,' she said breathlessly, 'I was faking it.'

He lifted himself up on to one elbow and gazed into her contented face, her features so soft and loving, just as her hands had been a few moments ago. This was the Ali he loved. The Ali who, one minute, could be tough and wildly assertive but who, when they made love, trembled and moaned and became defenceless with desire. It had always knocked him out that he could have such an effect on her.

'Ali—?'

She opened her eyes. 'No,' she whispered, 'don't talk. Not now. Kiss me again and make me believe I'm not dreaming.'

'I can do better than that.' And wrapping themselves in the towelling robes, he took her back inside the house and through to the sitting room.

He sat her on the piano stool next to him and she laughed when she realised what he was doing.

'Well, you know what the outcome will be,' she said warningly.

He flashed her one of his cruise-missile smiles. 'That's exactly what I'm banking on.'

He played from memory and had hardly made it through to the end of the second movement of her favourite Beethoven sonata when she insisted that he take her upstairs. In the falling twilight, and as a warm breeze blew in at the open window, they made love again.

'I believe it,' she said afterwards. 'You've convinced me I'm not dreaming.'

They slept for a short while and when they woke they realised they were hungry. They went downstairs and inspected the fridge. 'How does a plate of cold chicken and a bottle of Chardonnay sound?' asked Elliot.

'Perfect.'

They put a tray together and went back up to his bedroom. He poured their wine and when he handed her a glass, his face grew solemn. 'What should we drink to?'

She knew, though, what he was really asking: was this a one-off or was it the start of a renewal of their relationship? 'I don't know,' she said, in a carefully measured tone. 'What do you think?'

'To the future would seem a safe bet,' he said, equally cautious.

'Do we need to define that?'

His eyes wavered slightly from her face, as though he wasn't sure how best to answer her question. Then setting down their glasses, he kissed her lightly, their lips scarcely touching. He slid a hand inside his shirt that she was wearing and traced the soft, warm curve of her breast. He could feel her heart thumping and pulled away from her so that he could gaze into the dark depths of her eyes. 'Ali, the future without you would be as empty and meaningless as the past two and a half years have been. I need to be with you. I need to have you in my life.'

31

Elliot woke to the brightness of an early-morning sun streaming through his bedroom window. It took him less than a second to recall the events of yesterday and last night, and very carefully, so as not to disturb Ali, he rolled over on to his side and studied her peacefully sleeping face, taking in the smoothness of her cheek and the lovely line of her jaw and chin. His heart swelled with love and more than anything he wanted to linger in bed with her for the rest of that day, but a nine o'clock management meeting put paid to that temptation. He was conscious, as his eyes trailed the length of her body beneath the thin cotton sheet and he listened to the soft rise and fall of her breathing, that he had to treasure this moment in case, when she woke, she regretted what had taken place between them.

There was a very real danger of that, he knew. Through their vulnerability they had sought comfort from each other and maybe now, this morning, when they were feeling less raw and exposed, Ali might view things differently. She might even think that he had exploited her for his own gratification.

But he hadn't. Ali's response in the pool when he had kissed her had been all her own – though he was acutely aware that she had the perfect right to accuse him of classic caveman behaviour, using his strength to overpower her. Certainly there was a strong element of truth in that. In his defence, all he could say was that his desire for her had got the better of his normally restrained nature.

It had been in the way that she had answered him – *It means zippo, lover-boy* – that had made him throw restraint aside and give in to his true feelings. The challenging lightness in her voice had rung out in the echoey pool room with an air of suggestive flirtatiousness, just as it had when they'd first got to know each other. They had been working late one evening, just the two of them, and he had asked if he was keeping her from anything more worthwhile at home – a euphemistic query as to whether there was a boyfriend in tow. Her response had been a slight lifting of an eyebrow and the words, 'Now, what could be more worthwhile than an evening of number-crunching with my immediate boss?'

Other than what was written in her personnel records, all he'd known about Ali Edwards was that she lived with Daniel Delafield who, in those days, before his sexual orientation had become generally known, was attracting above-average interest from most of the women in the office. As a consequence Ali had been a focus of their envy. Unlike most of his colleagues, who were not averse to mixing pleasure with business, Elliot had always believed that it was better not to. He had witnessed all too often the sticky results of the office sexual honey-pot and had wanted none of it. An intensely private man, he had preferred to keep his relationships outside the firm. But despite this self-imposed restriction and Ali's tough reputation – she'd told a partner to bugger off and threatened to knee him in the groin for groping her – Elliot had been drawn to her.

When they'd finished what they were doing, he had plucked up courage to ask if she'd like to go for a drink with him. He had been quite prepared for a thinly disguised, 'Get lost, you're as bad as the rest of them,' but she'd readily agreed and they spent the next two hours in a nearby wine bar. Listening to her barbed but entertaining impressions of some of the senior partners, he had been captivated by her. He'd watched her closely, as if committing to memory the way she ran her hand through her short, wavy hair, the tilt of her head when she laughed and the flashing darkness of her intelligent eyes when she fastened them on his as she asked a question. There was a spirit of assured confidence about her that was immensely appealing, as well as a sparky sense of humour.

It wasn't long into the evening before he found himself wondering what she was like in bed and thinking how very much he'd like to find out. After he had walked her back to her car and was driving out of Manchester, heading for home, he'd known that he would be tireless in his pursuit of her. She was, he decided, the woman he would marry.

He was a steadfastly rational man so it came to him as an eye-opening shock to know that he was capable of such an unreasoned thought. This was not how he ran his life. He never made a judgement based on emotional whim. Clear-headed analytical deduction was what counted.

But red-blooded instinct seemed greater than any cerebral prudence he might have been inclined to exercise, and within a short time he was seeing Ali regularly outside work. The hardest part was keeping the strength of his love and desire for her firmly under control; he was terrified of her feeling trapped so he forced himself not to declare his heart too soon. Exactly a year after that first drink together, he took her on a surprise long weekend to New York and on the eighty-sixth floor of the Empire State Building he had steeled himself to ask her to marry him, having assiduously rehearsed himself throughout the seven-hour flight while she slept.

'I was wondering when you'd get around to proposing,' she'd said, as they stood on the crowded observation deck with Manhattan spread out before them.

'Does that imply you're not opposed to the idea?' he'd asked cautiously.

'You know what you'd be taking on, don't you?' she'd responded, without answering him. 'I'd be hell to live with.'

'It would be a worse hell without you.'

'So I'd be doing you a favour?'

'I'd be for ever in your debt.'

She'd smiled and, with a glint in her eye, had said, 'Did you ever consider the possibility that I might have wanted to propose to you?'

Her question had floored him. 'Er . . . no,' he'd faltered. He should have known that a proposal of marriage to Ali would never have provoked an outright yes or no.

'Did it never cross your mind that there's no one I'd rather spend my life with?' she'd asked. 'Did you never suspect that I think you're the most amazing man I know?'

'More amazing than Daniel?'

She'd laughed. 'Don't push it, Elliot. Daniel's in a class of his own.'

He'd laughed too and taken her in his arms. 'What's your answer?'

But before Ali had opened her mouth to reply, a small elderly American woman with a face as wizened as a Californian raisin had leaned over and said, 'Hey, hon, if she's dumb enough to say no, will you give me a trial run?'

But Ali hadn't said no, and they'd spent the afternoon choosing a ring.

Looking at Ali now, as she lay sleeping beside him, he wondered what she had done with the diamond ring they'd chosen that day. Had she sold it? Or had she thrown it away in a symbolic gesture of casting off a layer of her life of which she wanted no reminders? As for the gold wedding band that they had picked out for him, he had never thought of parting with it and since the divorce it had been stored in the antique wooden chest at the end of his bed where he kept his other bittersweet keepsakes – Isaac's New York Yankees baseball cap and a precious photograph album. Only in moments of real strength was he able to open the chest and look at the photographs of his son, or hold the cap in his hands and allow himself to remember Isaac wearing it. But maybe now it would be different, less painful.

Long into the early hours of the morning, he and Ali had talked about Isaac, as they never had before. They spoke of how much they missed him, what he had meant to them and what he still meant to them. And as intimate as their lovemaking had been, he sensed that in those heartfelt revealing words, as they admitted and shared the pain of losing their son, they had never been closer or more open with each other. Knowing that Ali no longer blamed him for not saving Isaac came as the most profound relief to him. It gave him cause to hope that one day he might fully accept that it wasn't his fault, that Isaac's death had been due to the wrecking ball of fate smashing their world apart rather than his negligence.

Even the memory of his reaction to that small boy at the party yesterday, and the innocent but wholly explosive line of chatter that had brought him to his knees, didn't disturb him as it might otherwise have done. He saw now that without it he would never have been pushed so low as to share with Ali the truth of that night two and a half years ago. Half of him still wished that he had kept her in ignorance of what had really happened to Isaac: he didn't want her menaced by the kind of nightmares he'd experienced all this time.

Glancing at his watch, he saw that it was nearly half past seven. He needed to get a move on. He lowered his head and gently brushed his lips against Ali's. She stirred and slowly opened her eyes.

He held his breath. This, then, was the moment of truth. In the cold light of day, would she regret that she was lying naked in his bed, or would she welcome the unexpected change of direction that their lives had taken?

32

With nearly an hour before Ali was due to arrive, Sarah went out to Trevor in his workshop to tell him that she needed to see Grace. He took off his dust mask and goggles and, above the noisy rumble and whine of the lathe, said, 'But what if Ali comes while you're out?'

'She shouldn't be here until ten but if she's early I'm sure you can talk to her for a short while.'

He looked at her doubtfully. 'You know Ali and I can never find any common ground.'

'That's because neither of you makes the effort.'

Trevor creased his sawdusty brow with a childishly obstinate frown. 'And what's so important that you have to see Grace?'

Without giving an answer she edged away from the workbench. 'I shan't be long. I'll be back before Ali gets here, don't worry.'

Minutes later she was hurrying the short distance to Grace's bungalow in the bright summer sunshine and knocking on her door. Ever since Friday afternoon and their conversation over lunch Sarah had wanted to apologise to Grace. Her churlish manner that day had been very much on her mind over the weekend and she didn't want to go away for the next two weeks leaving Grace thinking she had caused any real offence.

'Goodness, you're out and about early,' said Grace, when she opened the door.

'Is it inconvenient?'

'Of course it isn't. I was on the verge of having a cup of coffee before starting on some jam-making. Would you like to join me?'

'I'd love to,' Sarah said, as she followed Grace through to the kitchen and saw the colander of strawberries waiting on the draining-board to be hulled and washed, 'but I really can't stop.' She explained about the unexpected invitation to go away with Ali.

'What fun. And what good timing.'

Sarah smiled. 'Why is it that when I talk to you I always have the feeling that you're one step ahead of my every move?'

Grace smiled too. 'But I'm right, aren't I? This little holiday with Ali will do you no end of good. How does Trevor feel about being abandoned?'

'Quietly put out, is the best description.'

'Playing the hurt boy?'

'A little.'

'He'll manage well enough. No doubt help will be on hand the minute you've departed.'

Sarah caught the playfulness in Grace's voice. 'Right again. Shirley and Audrey have already offered their services. They'll be falling over themselves in their eagerness to feed him and do his washing. Oh dear, do I sound very heartless?'

'Just shrewdly cynical.'

'I never used to be like this.'

'We're all forced to adapt to the changes around us. And it's not what we used to be that counts, it's where we see ourselves currently that matters.'

'But what if we don't like where we are?'

'Then we must pursue what exactly it is about the present that annoys and irritates us. Identify the root problem and deal with it.'

'And if we can't do that?'

Grace looked at her closely. 'Can't or won't, Sarah?'

Sarah went over to the draining-board and picked up a strawberry. She looked at its perfect ripe form and wondered if, as life itself, its flavour would disappoint. She put it back in the colander and, leaving Grace's question unanswered, said, 'I just wanted to come and apologise for Friday afternoon.'

'Why? What did you do?'

'I got cross with you.'

'I think you were more cross with yourself.'

'Probably, but I'm still sorry for my behaviour.'

'I would imagine that it was little more than a ripple on the surface of what you were really feeling, wasn't it?'

'If you were Ali I'd tell you to shut up.'

Ali knew that she was going to be late, but even so, she still took the time to double-check that she'd locked the door to the windmill – telling Owen that his precious home had been trashed due to her carelessness was something she was keen to avoid. Convinced that all was secure, she heaved her large bag into the boot of the car and set off down the lane. It was only twenty to ten, but already she felt as though she'd put in a full day's work. After Elliot had left her at Timbersbrook House, she'd had to get a taxi to Daniel's to collect her car then tear across half of Cheshire to the mill to change and sort out the last-minute holiday details she was supposed to have done last night.

When she had woken that morning to Elliot's kiss, she had been aroused instantly by the sight and touch of him. Ignoring the bits of her body that ached from their night of mattress antics – and Elliot's half-hearted protestations that they didn't have time – they had made love again. If he had been serious about losing his technique after a prolonged period of celibacy he needn't have worried. If anything, his bedroom skills were even more finely honed. They had showered, eaten a hurried breakfast, and when it was almost time for Elliot to leave for work he had said, 'Ali, we need to discuss what happens next. If there's the slightest chance that you'll go away to Sanderling and regret what we've done, I need to know. I don't think I could cope with the uncertainty.'

She'd kissed him and said, 'Stop worrying, I'm not going to regret it. When I come back we'll decide what we're going to do. But perhaps having a little distance between us at this stage is a good thing. It'll give us time to be absolutely sure what we feel about one another.'

He'd held her tightly against him. 'I've got to go to the States in a fortnight. Can't you shorten your holiday to just the one week?'

'No,' she'd said firmly, then pushed him away and added, 'Now go, or you'll be late and Gervase will score a smug point of office oneupmanship over you.'

'Will you ring me tonight?'

'Yes. I promise. Now *go!*'

She'd watched him drive away reluctantly, sensing that he was terrified that once his back was turned she'd revert to the person she'd been since Isaac's death. If she were honest, a tiny part of her was frightened of that happening too.

But she had to have time away from him to come to terms with the consequences of the past twenty-four hours, as extraordinary as they were, and what Elliot had told her. She doubted whether she would ever justify her son's death and put it down to being part of some greater and higher plan, but she was now able to accept that it was no one's fault he had died.

Least of all Elliot's.

Last night he had spoken at length of the torment of guilt that had plagued him at not being able to save Isaac. He'd also shared with her the pain of looking into her eyes and seeing his culpability reflected back at him.

It was this, more than anything, that she needed to come to terms with: the painful shame of having treated him so unfairly.

She pulled in behind Sarah and Trevor's old Sierra and honked the horn loudly to announce her arrival. Within seconds Sarah was at the front door. 'I was beginning to think I'd dreamed your invitation. What happened? Did you oversleep?'

Much as Ali was bursting to share her incredible news with Sarah, she steeled herself to keep it for later when they were alone and when she could savour the expression on her friend's face. 'Long story,' she said guardedly, 'and one I'll save for the journey. Where's Trevor?'

'In the workshop. I'll give him a shout and let him know you're here.'

While Sarah was fetching him, Ali hurriedly put her friend's luggage into the boot of the car: she was determined to make a speedy getaway.

Trevor greeted Ali patronisingly, with what he thought was humour. 'How's the nefarious world of finance, then, Ali? Still able to sleep at night? Your conscience not keeping you awake?'

Did he have any idea how insulting he was? 'My, what a side-splitter you are this morning, Trevor,' she said with a friendly smile – in her current mood of all's well in the world she was prepared to be magnanimous. 'No worries about my conscience, it's doing just fine. How about yours?'

'Mine?'

'Still shilly-shallying around in your workshop and wasting valuable resources?'

'I don't quite follow you.'

'Wood, Trevor. Rainforests. Scandinavian pineforests. Wildlife threatened in the name of ornamentation.'

He wagged a long, dirty finger at her. 'Now, you know perfectly well that I only use wood that has come from natural waste or from sustainable forests.'

'I think Ali is only teasing you, Trevor,' said Sarah, stepping between them. 'Now, you're sure you'll be okay? I've left plenty of food in the freezer and there's—'

'I'll manage,' he said testily. 'I'm not completely incapable.'

No, thought Ali, just completely incompetent.

At last they were off, and as the distance grew between them and Astley Hope, and the road ahead shimmered in the heat-haze from the hot sun, Sarah was looking forward to the next fourteen days. It was years since she'd had a holiday and she was determined to make the most of this one. Grace had been right when she had said the timing couldn't have been better.

Breaking into her thoughts, Ali said, 'Seeing as this is a bit of a wander down Memory Lane, I thought we could stop off in Oxford for lunch. What do you think?'

'Do we have to?'

'Such keenness, I'm overwhelmed.'

'I'm sorry.'

'You've never been back, have you?'

Sarah shook her head. It was true, she hadn't. Not once. Not even for Hannah's interview last December. Trevor had insisted on accompanying her and she had all too readily stayed at home, maintaining a low profile on the grounds of too many parents spoiling the candidate's broth.

'Is it because you regret not finishing your degree?'

'Hannah asked me that the day she left for France.'

'Well, do you?'

'Of course I do.'

'But you never talk about it.'

'What's to be gained? I can't change anything. I had my opportunity and I threw it away.'

Ali was surprised to hear Sarah speak so vehemently. 'But you could study now, couldn't you?' she said. 'In fact, with Hannah going away in the autumn it's the perfect opportunity. It would give you something to aim for, to focus on.'

'I couldn't afford to study full-time. Anyway, what would be the purpose? It would be a lot of effort just to prove to myself that I could do it.'

'To hell with that! It would improve your job prospects.'

'You don't see me making curtains till the day I drop?'

'If it would make you happy, yes. But I'm convinced that you want more than that.'

'It's funny how we always think we know what's best for another person.'
Ali laughed. 'Mrs Donovan, keep your snidey comments to yourself.'
'And, Mrs Anderson, stop trying to organise me.'

As usual Ali had her way and they stopped for lunch in Oxford. It was now that she planned to tell Sarah about her weekend. They came into the city on the Banbury Road, found a space in Broad Street – despite all expectations to the contrary – and headed in the direction of Turl Street. Cutting through the cool shade of Brasenose Lane, they stepped into Radcliffe Square where the sward of grass and honey-coloured stone buildings were picturesquely bathed in sunlight. A group of noisy foreign summer students were lying stretched out on the parched grass, and a party of Japanese tourists, listening to their fast-talking guide, were gazing intently up at the circular domed building of the Radcliffe Camera.

'It's just the same,' Sarah said, staring round at the scene. 'All these years on and it's just the same.'

'Is that good or bad?'

'I'm not sure.'

Taking her by the arm, Ali led Sarah towards their old college. She was surprised to feel the stiffness in her friend's body as they neared the main gate where an enormous camper van with a German numberplate was parked on the cobbles and an irate college porter was engaged in some pretty unfriendly badinage with the driver.

'Let's go and have lunch first,' Sarah said, holding back as she caught sight of the once familiar porter's lodge and the front quad with its perfectly kept lush green lawn.

'You really have a problem with this, don't you?' Ali said.

She nodded. 'Give me a glass of Dutch courage and I'll be okay.'

Ali looked at her sceptically. 'All right,' she conceded, 'if that's what you want. But we're not eating at Brown's like every other nostalgic idiot who makes the return journey here to relive their youth.'

They found an elegant but unpretentious French restaurant tucked away in a tiny side-street off the High – just the kind of place that as students they would never have been able to afford. They ordered a half-carafe of house red and two plates of melted goat's cheese on a herb salad from a fresh-faced young man in a heavily starched white apron. Only when the food and wine were on the table, accompanied by Annie Lennox doing her rendition of 'A Whiter Shade of Pale', did Ali tell Sarah about her and Elliot.

Sarah listened in silence, amazed and absorbed. She was visibly moved when Ali described Elliot's shock reaction to the small boy at Richard and Daniel's party. And, like Ali, she had to blink away the tears when her friend explained what Elliot had really gone through that night, when, alone and frightened, he had been faced with the certain knowledge that his son was dying and there was nothing he could do. How easily they had all accepted his story that Isaac had barely suffered, that he had slipped painlessly into unconsciousness before dying.

When Ali stopped talking and they had taken a few moments to compose themselves, Sarah said, 'How exactly do you feel about what's happened between you and Elliot?'

Ali looked at her over the top of her wineglass. 'What? No "I told you so"?'

'I'm saving that for later.'

'I don't doubt it. But to answer your question, I feel a whole gamut of emotions: wretched that I abused Elliot in the way that I did, consumed with the most profound relief that we've stopped fighting, and,' she paused to smile, 'bloody exhausted after so much fantastic sex.'

Sarah smiled too. 'Anything else?'

Ali's expression became serious again. 'Yes. I feel extraordinarily at peace.'

'With Isaac?'

Ali nodded. 'Resolving matters with Elliot has somehow taken the edge off all that pain.'

'That's because you weren't only grieving for Isaac. When you lost him, you lost Elliot, your marriage and the future the pair of you had planned for yourselves. It was a quadruple bereavement.'

'It needn't have been,' Ali said despondently. 'If I hadn't been such a bitch—'

'You've been many things, Ali, including pig-headed, stubborn, determined, arrogant, confused, but a bitch isn't one of them.'

'I disagree.'

'That's because you think it's *de rigueur* for you always to have the last word.'

'Nonsense.'

'There you go again.'

'Oh, eat your lunch and be quiet!'

They spent so long over their meal discussing what might or might not lie ahead for Ali and Elliot, that it was a mutually reached decision that they should forgo the delights of doing a *Brasenose Revisited* and carry on with the rest of their journey. 'We'll save it for the return trip if you want,' Sarah said, as they strapped themselves into their seats in the car.

'We'll see,' said Ali, reversing at speed out of the parking space. It was as clear as daylight to Ali that Sarah was enormously relieved not to be retracing their college days with too much exactitude, but it wasn't so clear why this issue had never been raised before. In the intervening years since Sarah had left Oxford, she had hardly ever referred to what she now saw as her lost opportunity. Was it possible that Hannah's hopeful following of her mother's footsteps had triggered this sense of regret in her?

Though it was hardly a new phenomenon when she thought about her friend, Ali felt an acrimonious surge of anger towards Trevor. Why hadn't the stupid idiot taken more care with Sarah all those years ago? If he hadn't got her pregnant, her life would have been infinitely different.

And so much better.

Joining the line of traffic at the lights alongside the Randolph, Ali vowed that at the top of her agenda this holiday was to make Sarah see sense. They would be together for the next fortnight and by the end of those two weeks if Ali hadn't convinced Sarah to take steps towards making a new future for herself then she'd – she'd bloody well sleep with the silly man so that she could give Sarah the necessary conscience-saving grounds for a legitimate divorce in the eyes of her precious God.

Recoiling from the loathsome thought of an all-out adulterous bonking session with Trevor, she turned away from Sarah so that her friend couldn't see her face. She stared at the Martyrs' Memorial on her right, then saw the irony in what she was looking at. Martyrdom and suffering for the cause were hardly her style but . . . but was it possible that just this once she could make an exception? And when you got right down to it, how bad would it really be? All she'd have to do was close her eyes, lie back with gritted teeth and think of England. It would be over and done with in a matter of minutes and it wasn't as though she'd have to repeat it. Suddenly she smiled and shook her head, realising how worryingly close she was to giving the idea serious consideration. I must be out of my mind, she thought. And cocky with it. How could she be so sure it would be that straightforward? Could Trevor really be seduced so easily? She smiled again. Of course he could. For crying out loud, here was a man who hadn't had a sexual encounter in the last decade, he'd be more than up for it. Question was: was she?

As perceptive as ever, Sarah said, 'Something funny, Ali?'

The lights turned to green and Ali slipped into first gear. 'You don't want to know,' she said.

Oh, you *so* don't want to know.

33

Early next morning, and as eager to get started on the day as she had been as a child whenever she was at Sanderling, Ali flung open her bedroom window. She knelt on the cushioned window-seat, rested her elbows on the sill and breathed in the fresh sea air as she looked down on to the large, well-kept garden. It contained so many memories. And they were all good ones. Nothing bad had ever happened here at Sanderling. Or was that merely a childish perception she hadn't yet outgrown?

No. She was convinced it was true. Her grandmother's house, now her parents' home, was a place of true happiness, a haven from all life's travails. Her visits here as an adult – including when she'd brought Isaac – had been just as perfect and idyllic as when she'd been a young girl.

She smiled as she recalled bringing Elliot here for the first time to meet her parents. They'd made a long weekend of it and her mother and father had taken to him straight away, describing him as a step up from the usual wets she dragged behind her.

Without batting an eyelid they had allowed him to sleep with her and in this very room. She looked over her shoulder to the rumpled duvet, remembering how strange it had felt having Elliot in the bed in which she had slept as a child, and which occasionally she had shared with Sarah when there had been more guests at Sanderling than beds. She could also remember how much she had wanted to make love to Elliot that night and how amusingly hesitant he had been, muttering that he didn't want to push it with her parents. 'If you're worried about them hearing the squeaking of old mattress springs,' she'd teased, 'that's easily remedied.' She'd pulled the duvet and pillows on to the floor and proceeded to banish his reluctance.

'Just so long as you don't make your usual noise when the earth moves,' he'd said.

'Can't guarantee that,' she'd answered, with a gasp of pleasure as his lips and hands began working their magic on her.

'Then I'll have to keep you quiet myself.'

And he had. Just at the vital moment, when her body soared heavenward and exploded like a Disneyland firework display, he had covered her mouth with his and kept it there until she relaxed in his arms.

The following morning, when her mother had knocked on the door with a cup of tea, she had found them on the floor and had smiled at her daughter. 'Was there something wrong with the bed?' she had asked ingenuously over breakfast an hour later, with the kind of smile on her face that suggested she knew exactly what had been going on.

'We didn't want to disturb you,' Ali had said, with the kind of smile on *her* face that suggested she was quite prepared to give her mother all the juicy details if provoked. But at her side, deeply engrossed in his boiled egg, Elliot's normally composed face was steadily reddening. The following day he had confessed to Ali that he had expected that to be the last time he ever saw her parents.

'We're a very open family,' she'd told him in the car on the way home, as they headed north.

'So I see.'

For a man as buttoned-down as Elliot, her family's attitude must have come as something of a shock.

Shock was something they'd discussed last night on the phone. It was gone eleven when she called him on her mobile from her bed. He'd just got in from wining and dining a client, and had sounded pleased to hear her voice. She had asked him if, as she was, he was still reeling from the shock of what they'd done.

'Yes,' he'd admitted, 'and it's compounded by not being with you. You haven't changed ... You're not having second thoughts, are you?'

The fear in his voice had touched her and she had been quick to reassure him. 'No,' she said, 'not at all. I told Sarah what happened. You don't mind, do you?'

'Of course not. What did she say?'

'Lots of things. She said that we've experienced a quadruple bereavement: Isaac, losing one another, the loss of our marriage, and the loss of all our dreams.'

'She's right.'

'It's a lot to work through, isn't it?'

'It is.'

She heard him sigh. 'Elliot, are you okay?'

'I miss you,' he said simply.

'I've only been gone a day.'

'In the circumstances that's a day too long.'

She laughed. 'I think it's just as well I'm here and not there with you. My body needs to recover from the onslaught of so much unexpected sex. I must be getting old.'

'I know what you mean. But it was good, wasn't it?'

'Better than good.'

There was a pause.

'Ali?'

'Yes.'

'Ali, I just ... Will you ring me tomorrow night?'

She hesitated. 'Elliot, was that what you really wanted to say?'

Another pause.

'No, but it'll keep.'

'No, that's not fair, you can't do that to me. I'll lie awake all night wondering what it was. Tell me.'

'I – I just wanted to tell you that I love you.'

It was her turn to pause.

'Ali?'

'Say it again – please.'

'I love you.'

'Again.'

'I love – Ali, are you crying?'

'Well, of course I am.'

'I'm sorry. I knew I shouldn't have said anything.'

'Don't be so stupid. It's me. I'd forgotten how wonderful those three words could sound.'

Still sitting in front of the open window and staring into the infinite blue of the sky, Ali drew her knee up under her chin and longed to hear the sound of Elliot's voice. She looked at her watch and thought of ringing him before he set off for the office.

No, she told herself firmly.

If she did that she'd start ringing him up on the hour every hour, and that would never do. A persistent nuisance caller was not what Elliot needed. Tonight would be soon enough. She'd ring him then, just as she'd promised she would.

But there was one phone call she did need to make, and soon. It was to Daniel. He and Richard deserved an explanation for the abrupt manner in which she and Elliot had left their party, and for her leaving her car on their drive overnight. Though presumably the pair of them had not been slow in putting two and two together.

When the taxi had dropped her off at their house yesterday morning both Richard and Daniel had already left for work, but an envelope was tucked under one of the windscreen wipers. The note inside had said, 'Are you still talking to me? If so, fill me in with the details when you've got a moment. Love, Daniel.'

Poor old Daniel, he was probably busting a gut to know what had transpired as a result of his skulduggery. If he hadn't meant so well, and if things hadn't turned out as they had, she might have decided to keep him in the dark for the duration of her holiday. But she loved Daniel too much to torment him so she would ring him later in the day, when he was at the office, and put him out of his misery.

She turned her attention to the garden once more. As the hot weather had been going on so long and there was a hosepipe ban in place, Ali suspected that her mother must have been watering the garden sneakily in the dead of night. The impressive borders that her grandmother had so carefully designed and nurtured were a delight, full of colour, and the lawn was lush and green – there were no dusty dry patches as there were in her garden back in Cheshire. She wouldn't be at all surprised if later that day her mother phoned to give her instructions on the subversive methods Ali would be expected to take on in her parents' absence.

She heard the sound of the letter box being thrust open with what appeared to be above-average paperboy strength, wondered if it was the postman trying to deliver a parcel and went to investigate. Her parents had either forgotten to cancel the papers or had decided to let her and Sarah have the benefit of them. Lying in a heap on the mat was her father's *FT* – the only paper fit for a gentleman, these days, he claimed; the *Daily Mail* for her mother – otherwise known at Sanderling as the *Daily Sniff and Tell* – and a glossy but slightly damaged edition of *Country Life*. Ali carried the bundle through to the kitchen where she was met with the unappetising pong of last night's fish-and-chip supper. She and Sarah had been too lazy to put the plates into the dishwasher and had left them to extend their greasy, vinegary charm to their surroundings. Ali tidied up hastily and closed the dishwasher door on the offending plates and cutlery. She opened a couple of windows and the back door, then filled the kettle. She made herself a pot of tea and, with the papers tucked under her arm, took the tray to the bit of garden that caught the early-morning sun where her parents usually started the day in fine weather. Years ago, and in pre-Alan Titchmarsh and Charlie Dimmock days, before the nation had become obsessed with mirror-backed water features and purple garden fences, Ali's grandmother had had a gazebo built; she'd had it kitted out with comfortably padded seats and a small stow-away table. The cushions had been replaced many times, but it still made the perfect bolthole, especially now that it was covered in a fragrant tumble of honeysuckle.

Ali settled herself in for the next hour or so while she waited for Sarah to surface, poured her tea and set to with the *FT*. She began with a piece about the recently proposed legislation for unapproved share options exercised by non-UK residents, but didn't get beyond the second paragraph before she turned to the *Sniff and Tell*. Though even the shenanigans of some dolly-bird game-show hostess and her aged Viagra-enhanced rock-star boyfriend failed to hold her attention.

Was it any wonder when she had her own shenanigans to dwell on? She lowered the paper and stared up at the house with its pebble-dashed walls, which were almost entirely covered with Virginia creeper.

I love you, Elliot.

She had said it. In response to his declaration on the phone last night she had actually said, '*I love you, Elliot.*'

How was it possible? How was it remotely conceivable that she could have uttered such words?

Because you've always loved him, she imagined Sarah whispering in her ear.

Because you've never stopped loving him, echoed Daniel.

And it was true. That's why the past two and half years had been so awful, so perversely destructive. She had torn herself apart by denying that most essential truth, that she loved Elliot.

She lowered the newspaper to her lap, pushed back her sunglasses and closed her eyes, letting the warmth of the sun wash over her. Then, very slowly, she pictured Elliot that evening at the mill when he had fired that cruise-missile smile at her. She'd known only too well in that moment the effect he could still have on her, and yet she had subsequently talked herself out of it. Which goes to show, she told herself ruefully, that there was no one to touch her when it came to the fatal art of self-delusion.

Just then, a shadow crossed her face and for a wild, fantastical, fleeting second she thought it was Elliot – that he'd put work on hold, had leaped into his car at daybreak and driven all the way down to see her.

But it wasn't Elliot. It was Sarah.

'How long have you been up?' she asked, moving the discarded *FT* and sitting in the seat next to Ali.

'Ages and ages. I've been for an early-morning swim, jogged down to the newsagent's for the papers, and prepared a light brunch.'

'I wish that were true. I'm starving and can't think why.'

'It's the sea air. Don't you remember it does peculiar things to your stomach?'

After a leisurely breakfast in the garden of croissants and locally made blackcurrant jam – all courtesy of Ali's mother's thoughtfulness in stocking up for them – they decided it was time to head for the beach. They didn't have far to go, just a ten-minute walk along the tree-lined road that was home to Sanderling, out into the sunshine, across the main road that joined the east and west of the island, then through the sand dunes and prickly gorse and blackberry bushes that bordered the golf course.

It was all just as Sarah remembered it: the sheltered warmth provided by the dense windbreak of overgrown bushes; the clusters of yellow flowers nestling amongst the purple thistles; the feathery grasses dried by the sun. Even the tyre tracks made by countless bikes on the much-used path looked the same.

Leaving the shelter of the dunes behind them, they came to the open stretch of pebbly beach, already littered with scores of families surrounded by the trappings of a day at the seaside: there were territorial windbreaks pushed into the stones, brightly coloured towels laid out like mosaic tiles, cold boxes, plastic buckets and spades and inflatable beach balls. Down by the shoreline, tiny bare-bottomed toddlers were cautiously dipping their toes into the rushing waves, while older, more adventurous children were splashing about in the deeper water, their shrieks of delight muffled by the breeze that blew in off the sea.

Sarah took in the scene. Apart from the extensive construction of beach defences further along the seashore to keep the threat of erosion to a minimum, there was little evidence of anything different from nearly two decades ago. She felt pleased that the essence of Hayling, like Oxford, had successfully withstood the pressure to change for change's sake.

Last night she had lain awake in bed thinking of how Oxford and its quintessential finery had remained resolutely the same. Conversely, this immutable status quo had reminded her just how much she had conceded to the fickle winds of change.

Getting pregnant had thrown her completely off course; it had meant that overnight she'd had to restructure her life.

Before becoming pregnant she had had a comprehensive plan for her future: she was to graduate from Brasenose with a law degree, follow it up with a stint at law college, then be articled to a provincial firm with a reputation for fair play – the aggressive big-city establishments she would leave to the thrusting types hungry for fame and distinction. She had seen herself working for several years before marrying and having children, then taking some time out while the children were young and, when it seemed right, she would have picked up where she had left off. Her marriage, of course, would have been happy. Her husband would have been loving and supportive, and between them they would have produced two or even three well-behaved, adorable children. They would have been a contented, untroubled, close-knit family. In short she had wanted a duplicate of Ali's family.

Rather naïvely she had hoped that, despite getting the order of events out of sequence – namely the conception of the first, and what proved to be the only, well-behaved, adorable child – the rest of her plan might still follow suit.

The night she had told Trevor she was pregnant was not a night she was ever likely to forget. It had taken her days to summon the courage to put it to him. She knew that he was extremely fond of her and would, as he had told her one evening over a bowl of spaghetti Bolognese in a run-down café on the Iffley Road, do anything for her. 'You know how much I admire and respect you,' he had said. 'There's nothing I wouldn't do for you.' But she couldn't be sure that 'anything' would encompass the commitment of marriage because she was pregnant. Fondness and respect were perfectly valid forms of affection, but were they sufficient to form the basis of a lifelong commitment? Surely it had to be love. But not once had love ever crossed the threshold of their strange, rather lopsided relationship.

At their age, lots of men would have suggested that she abort the child on the grounds that they were too young for the responsibility, that it would ruin everything, that it would hamper them. But Trevor's views were not those of the average twenty-one-year-old, and in the time she had got to know him through the prayer group they both attended, he had voiced his opinions on the murdering of innocent foetuses in the strongest terms. Her fear was that he might suggest the child be given up for adoption. And though it was something she didn't want to consider, she could see how tempting it might be for him: it would conveniently leave them to get on with the rest of their lives with clear consciences.

It was Trevor's conscience and his sense of honour and goodness that she was relying on when he came to her room in college that evening for what he thought would be a cosy couple of hours together. As she waited for him to arrive, she had frantically brushed her teeth several times in the hope of disguising the fact that she'd just knocked back two glasses of vodka from a bottle she had sneaked out of Ali's wardrobe. Ali had been fussing over her appearance in readiness for yet another date with some hapless young man and wouldn't have noticed if there'd been an earthquake, so preoccupied was she with the colour of her eye-shadow.

When Trevor arrived she let him in, made them some coffee, and told him that she was pregnant. The rest she left up to him. His initial reaction had been one of pure astonishment.

'But – but how? I don't understand.'

He was right to wonder how. They had, after all, been to bed together only once.

He started to blame himself. 'This is all my fault,' he said, pacing the small room and running his hand through his collar-length hair, 'I knew it was wrong at the time, but I let my better judgement be ruled by my heart.'

They were strange words coming from a twenty-one-year-old man in the late seventies, but not so strange when one knew his background: he was as he was because through all his formative years he'd been constrained by a strict religious upbringing that would have stunted the most wilful of young men.

Compassion for him made her reach out to him and say, 'It's not your fault, Trevor. You must never say that.'

He looked at her, his eyes glazed with bewilderment. She manoeuvred him into a chair and forced his untouched mug of coffee into his hand. 'I'm not expecting anything from you,' she'd said, a sentence that had taken all her courage to utter. What she really wanted to say was, 'You have to agree to marry me. This baby has to have a father. He or she is entitled to a proper mother and father. This child deserves more than I can give it alone. A loving family is what counts. Right now we might not love each other, but it will come, I know it will.'

He set the mug – still untouched – on the desk beside him and stared out of the window at the view of the front quad where a group of first-year physicists were larking around with a bottle of cheap champagne. He returned his gaze to her. 'Sarah,' he said, 'it strikes me that there's only one option open to us. If you agree, I think we should marry.'

It was not the hearts-and-roses proposal she had dreamed of as a romantically inclined teenager, but it would suffice.

They then discussed what plans they needed to make – Trevor was hoping to take up a teaching post in Sheffield that autumn and he would now have to review the accommodation he had found for himself. When he had finally left her to cycle back to his digs at Headington, she was violently sick.

She wanted to blame it on the stolen vodka, or even late-in-the-day morning sickness, but she knew that the real cause of her nausea was feeling consumed by both relief and regret.

The next morning she told Ali that she and Trevor were to be married in the summer. She would not be returning to college in the Michaelmas term as she would be with Trevor in Sheffield where he was due to start work as a teacher.

She had never before seen Ali lost for words and the sight of her friend's horrified expression appalled her. She had burst into tears.

'But you can't,' Ali said, also now in tears, her arms wrapped around her. 'I won't let you marry him. I won't allow it.'

'But I have to,' she had whispered in shame, 'I'm pregnant.'

Ali had pulled away from her. 'Pregnant?' Her expression of horror now dramatically intensified. 'I don't believe it.'

'Nor did I at first.'

'But, Sarah, this needn't be the disaster you're turning it into.'

'What do you mean?'

'I mean, you don't have to marry Trevor.'

'And how would I manage?'

'I'd help you – so would your parents.'

'You know they wouldn't.'

'Once they'd got over the shock they would. Nobody their age can resist the urge to play grandparent.'

Ali proved to be right, her parents indeed got over their shock – about two years after the wedding took place – and in their undemonstrative way proved more than adequate grandparents to Hannah. Ironically, it seemed they were better suited to this role than the one of parent to Sarah.

But they never took to Trevor. Their disappointment in their daughter's chosen husband was as real as Ali's, and remained so until they died.

After they had risked the cold water for a swim and had sunbathed for a while, they gathered their things together and went in search of something to eat. Beyond the row of brightly painted beach huts was the old kiosk where, as teenagers, they had spent a couple of summers serving beefburgers, hot dogs, questionable meat pies, cans of drink, ice creams and chocolate bars to hungry day-trippers. Ali's grandmother had known the woman who ran it and had inveigled her into taking the girls on while they were staying at Sanderling. The money was good and the perks weren't bad either – they were chatted up by a regular stream of good-looking and not so good-looking boys and, even better, they were allowed to eat the broken ice-lollies that couldn't be sold.

As they approached the kiosk Sarah found that nothing much had changed here either. The pies looked just as questionable and a group of spotty, sunburnt lads were doing a bad job of chatting up the two young girls behind the counter. Sarah smiled at Ali and said, 'Can you believe that used to be us?'

'Away with you! We were much more efficient.'

'Rubbish, you were hopeless with the money, you were always giving out the wrong change.'

'So why do you think I became an accountant?'

They ordered their hot dogs and cans of Fanta and strolled slowly back to the beach.

'You've gone all quiet on me,' Ali said, when they were stretched out on their towels on the pebbles again. 'Are you overdosing on nostalgia?'

'Yes. It's making me feel decidedly old and decrepit.'

'Give over,' laughed Ali, 'there's not a mark on you.'

'We're thirty-eight, Ali, and heading fast for forty.'

'Well, as somebody once said, it ain't over till the fat lady sings. Anyway, what you should be doing instead of dwelling on the past is looking to the future.'

But Sarah knew there wasn't any point in doing that: her future would always be eclipsed by the past.

34

That evening, Ali poured herself a glass of her father's excellent Islay malt and, leaving Sarah in the kitchen working at her sewing-machine, went upstairs for a bath and to ring Elliot. She lay back in the Crabtree and Evelyn scented water and tapped his number into her mobile. While she waited for him to pick up the phone at Timbersbrook, she sipped her drink, savouring its smooth peaty flavour.

'Hang on a minute,' he said, when he realised it was her.

'Is it a bad moment?' she asked, when he spoke again.

'No, I just wanted to close the door.'

'Why? Have you got people there?'

'Only Sam.'

'Aha, so when did the old hustler get back?'

'This morning.'

'And is he richer or poorer?'

'This is my father we're talking about, Ali. Of course he's up on the deal. God knows how many hundreds of pounds he's robbed his friends of.'

Ali laughed. 'Have you told him about us?' She heard him hesitate. 'Elliot?'

'No, I haven't.'

'Why not?'

'I thought it might be tempting fate. Besides, he'd want to know what happens next and I don't have the answer for that.'

'Sarah asked me the same question.'

'What did you tell her?'

'That we need to take things slowly.'

'Not too slowly, I hope.'

'Slow enough to be sure of what it is we both want.'

There was a long pause. Then Elliot said, 'I know exactly what I want, Ali. It's what I've always wanted.'

It was Ali's turn to hesitate and not by choice: her throat was constricted with a mixture of happiness and nervousness. 'Are you saying what I think you're saying?' she asked.

'I'm saying that I want to spend the rest of my life with you.'

Although he had merely voiced what was in her own mind, it still came as a shock to hear him stating the case so boldly. She hadn't imagined either of them taking that step so soon. Not when they had so much to talk through.

When she didn't respond, he said, 'Ali, I'm sorry. I suppose that's going too fast, isn't it? Have I blown it?'

'It could be a terrible risk, Elliot,' she murmured.

'But one worth taking.' His voice was as low as hers.

'You sound so sure,' she said.

'And you sound so unsure.'

'That's because I'm frightened.'

'Of what?'

'Of hurting you again.'

'I'm not prepared to let that happen a second time.'

'You mean you had any control over it the first time?'

'In a way, yes. If I had blamed myself less, hated myself less, I might have worked harder at saving our marriage.'

'Oh, Elliot, it wasn't just you. It was me as well. We both made an appalling mess of it all.'

'In our defence I guess we knew no better.'

'And we do now?'

'Yes, I think we do.'

'I'm still scared, though . . . of myself mostly. I'm not convinced that you, or anyone else for that matter, would ever have much control over my actions, least of all me. You know what Daniel's always said – that I'm a loose cannon on deck.'

'That may well be true, but the issue of control should never be a part of a committed relationship, not one that's based on love.'

She laughed suddenly. 'You know, that's exactly what my parents hoped you'd be able to do. That first weekend I brought you down here, my mother was so impressed with you that she said, "Good choice at last, Ali. He's so much better than the boys you've pushed around to date. This one will actually stand up to you." '

'As fond as I've always been of your mother, she must have been mad to think that I could have any control over you.'

Glad that the tone of their conversation had lightened, Ali went on to tell him how she had been reminiscing about their first night together at Sanderling.

'I remember it well,' he said, 'especially the next morning.'

'Hah! So a boiled egg sticks in your mind more than the brilliant sex we had.'

'Please, don't mention sex. It's not fair when you're so far away and I can't touch you.'

'Did I mention that I'm talking to you while I'm lying in the bath?' she teased.

He groaned. 'I could be there in four hours.'

'I'd be in bed by then.'

'Even better.'

'I'd be asleep.'

'Better still. I'd wake you with a kiss.'

'Is that all?'

'I didn't say where I'd kiss you.'

She laughed again. 'This is turning into one of those sex lines.' Then, in a more subdued voice, 'Elliot, what are you doing at the weekend?'

'I haven't thought that far ahead yet. Why?'

'Why don't you come down here? Mum and Dad will be back by then and, given the circumstances, they'd love to see you again.'

'What shall I tell Sam?'

'The truth.'

'Which is?'

'That you're spending the weekend with your ex-wife with a view to planning a new future together.'

A short while later Elliot put down the phone and shook his head in disbelief. One of the many things about Ali that he'd always loved was her unpredictability. Just as he'd resigned himself to having wrecked everything by revealing his hand too soon and listened with a sinking heart to her less-than-encouraging response, she had floored him.

He got to his feet, left his study and sought out his father. He found him in the kitchen flicking through a magazine on classic cars and singing along to one of his favourite musicals that was being belted out on the CD player next to the wine rack. It was *Mack and Mabel* and the song was 'I Promise You a Happy Ending'.

With a wry smile, Elliot crossed the kitchen and lowered the volume on the hi-fi. 'Dad,' he said, 'I've got something to tell you.'

Sam looked up at him. 'Oh, aye, lad, what's that, then?'

35

Friday was soon upon them and, exerting more energy than they'd used so far during their holiday – the most energetic they'd been in the previous twenty-four hours was to paint their toenails – Ali and Sarah spent the best part of the day tidying the house, making beds and doing the shopping that Ali's mother had asked them to do on the phone last night, as well as going strawberry picking, which had always been a highlight of a summer stay at Sanderling. As children Ali and Sarah had invariably made an afternoon of it: they would cycle up West Lane and spend hours crouched on their hands and knees gathering the sun-ripened fruit and listening to the gossiping women around them who thought the girls were too young to understand what they were talking about. No matter how many baskets they filled, Grandma Hayling would question them on the ones that got away. 'How many did you eat this time?' she'd ask, when they returned with juice-stained hands and sweetly reddened lips.

Now, stretched out on sun-loungers, they were enjoying what the weather forecasters had predicted as the tail end of the hot dry spell. From tomorrow there would be a drop in temperature and a brisk north-westerly wind to spoil everybody's fun.

Ali put down that morning's copy of the *Daily Sniff and Tell* and glanced across at Sarah. She hadn't said a word for the past half-hour and, though her eyes were closed, Ali knew she wasn't asleep because one of her hands was tapping listlessly at the armrest of her wooden chair. If she didn't know better, Sarah, who was inner calm personified, was restless. 'You okay?' Ali asked.

Sarah's fingers came to an abrupt stop. She opened her eyes. 'I'm fine. What made you ask?' Her voice rang with defensiveness.

'You seem on edge.'

After a few moments Sarah said, 'It's called guilt.'

'What on earth have you done to give you an attack of that?'

Sarah leaned forward and swung her legs round so that her bare feet were on the grass between her and Ali. 'It doesn't feel right me being here. I should be at home with Trevor.'

'Aha,' said Ali, 'I was wondering when you'd start beating yourself up. It's a miracle it's taken you this long.'

'That's not kind.'

'No, it isn't. But it's true. Don't spoil it for yourself, Sarah, there's nothing wrong in a wife taking a holiday with a friend. Even the rosiest of marriages can benefit from a bit of time-out space.'

But Sarah looked far from convinced. 'I should never have allowed you to talk me into this,' she muttered.

Ali smiled. 'I don't recall having to twist your arm too far to make you come.'

Sarah frowned and stood up. 'Do you want another drink?'

'No thanks.' Concerned, Ali watched her cross the lawn and go inside the house. She wondered what had provoked Sarah's change of mood. Was she worried that she would be playing gooseberry when Elliot joined them that evening? Or was she uneasy about Alastair and his bride-to-be arriving tomorrow? But that was nonsense! Sarah had no reason to feel like an outsider – she had always fitted in just as if she were a member of the family. Perhaps it wasn't anything as complicated as that. Maybe Sarah *was* feeling guilty about abandoning Trevor for so long. And just as Ali was wishing that Trevor could do the decent thing and drop dead, Sarah reappeared in the garden. 'Ali,' she called, 'your parents have arrived.'

Like most parents, Maggie and Lawrence Edwards were unable to view their offspring as anything but children, Sarah included. Short of patting her head and saying, 'My word, haven't you grown!' they were lavishing upon her every form of parental delight and affection. 'Heavens,' cried Maggie, after she'd hugged her and insisted on an update on life in Astley Hope, especially on Hannah, 'how long is it since you stayed here with us?'

'I know when it was,' said Lawrence, moving his wife aside so that he could have his share of Sarah. 'It was the year you got married.'

'So it was,' Maggie agreed. 'It was Easter.'

'No, it couldn't have been then,' asserted Lawrence, 'it must have been earlier. I remember it snowed. It was February.'

'Goodness,' said Sarah, feeling a little overwhelmed but loving it anyway, 'what an incredible memory you both have.'

'It's their age,' smirked Ali. 'We'll be the same one day. We'll recall everything fifty years back in the tiniest detail but won't be able to remember where we put our slippers and glasses.'

Lawrence laughed, and before Ali had a chance to slip away from him he'd taken her in his arms. 'A little respect,' he said, lifting her a clear twelve inches off the ground, 'that's all I've ever asked of you.'

'Never!' she shouted, as she struggled to get free.

He squeezed harder and tickled her ribs as if she were a small child. 'Can't hear you,' he said. 'I must be going deaf.'

'Well, Sarah,' said Maggie, with a happy smile, 'I think we'll leave them to it, shall we? Let's go inside, I'm gasping for a cup of tea.'

'And that's another sign of old age,' Ali shouted over her father's shoulder as Maggie and Sarah disappeared, 'dodderers spend all their time having nice cups of tea.'

'Whereas you, young lady,' Lawrence said, finally lowering his daughter to the ground, 'have probably been hitting my stash of single malt.'

'Only the cheap stuff.'

'Cheap stuff?' he roared. 'I don't have anything of the kind! For your insubordination you can help me in with the luggage. There's loads of it – you know how fond your mother is of packing for every eventuality.'

By the time Ali had helped her father unload the car and taken the cases upstairs, Sarah and Maggie had put together a tea-tray along with a chocolate cake that Sarah had made especially for the occasion.

'Ali never makes me cakes,' Maggie said, with mock hurt as they sat in the gazebo and she poured their tea.

Ali rolled her eyes and said, 'Oh, here we go, suddenly I'm the daughter from hell.'

'No "suddenly" about it,' said Lawrence, munching his cake appreciatively and fighting off a wasp, 'trouble from the moment you were born.'

'Love you too, Dad.'

He blew her a kiss. 'I'd love you even more if you made delicious cakes like Sarah does.'

Sarah drank her tea quietly and observed the closeness between Ali and her parents, listening wistfully to the warm exchange of affection. It wasn't difficult to see where Ali's sense of humour came from.

The first time Sarah had met her friend's parents was when Ali had taken her home for tea one day after school; the invitation had been made a week after their initial encounter. 'I should warn you that they're completely mad,' Ali had said matter-of-factly, as they waited for her mother to pick them up at the school's main entrance. 'Nutty as two bars of Fruit and Nut. Dad makes the most awful jokes and Mum's silly enough to encourage him.' From this brief description of Mr and Mrs Edwards, Sarah had expected there to be a coolness between her new friend and her parents. According to the girls at school, it was a foregone conclusion that you had to act as if you were superior to your aged and past-it parents. But Sarah quickly realised that Ali's description of her mother and father had been a smokescreen: she clearly adored them as much as they did her, and when she'd used the word 'nutty', she had meant it in the nicest way, because as far as Sarah could see, Ali was as barmy as they were. Mrs Edwards turned out to be exactly the mother Sarah would have chosen, warm-hearted and generous with a subtle skill for putting her at her ease. Ali had never spoken about the kind of house she lived in – unlike so many of the others at their rather pretentious prep school who tried to outdo one another – so Sarah had concluded that, as she herself did, Ali came from a humble background. She couldn't have been more wrong. Ali lived in a vast house that could have consumed Sarah's for breakfast several times over and still had room for a couple of bungalows for elevenses. Sarah had never seen anything so enormous. Or so beautiful. It was light and airy, and full of space. It was the type of house she'd only ever seen on television, or in magazines. The rooms were all large and decorated with pretty patterned wallpaper – she was later to realise that Mrs Edwards was a bit of a chameleon when it came to home décor, and had been going through her Early Laura Ashley Phase before moving on to her Sanderson Days, as Ali described her mother's faddish taste.

Ali's father had come home unexpectedly early that afternoon so they had all eaten together. At first Sarah was a little frightened of him – he seemed so loud and so big, not at all the small, stiff-lipped man her own father was. 'Lawrence, darling, keep your voice down. Can't you see that you're frightening our guest?' Ali's mother had said, when she must have noticed Sarah shrinking away from this larger-than-life man who had burst into the kitchen with all the force of a tornado. 'Don't worry, Sarah,' she had added, 'he's nothing but a six-foot-five giant who wants everybody to play with him.'

Sitting in the prettily decorated kitchen where everything was co-ordinated with red and white polka dots – even the tea-towels matched the curtains and wallpaper – Sarah had tried hard not to appear gauche and unused to such style and lively conversation, which ricocheted around the table at head-spinning speed. But as she'd eaten the lovely meal Ali's mother had served them she had fought back the rising sense of disappointment within her. She had thought that she had made a friend in Ali, but even so young, Sarah knew how the world worked: the differences between them were so great that the first time Ali had tea at her house would be the last. Ali would drop her the minute she realised they came from opposite worlds.

But Ali hadn't dropped her and here they were, almost thirty years on, still the closest of friends. It would have been nice to say that they were older and wiser, but Sarah didn't believe that.

Older, yes, but certainly not wiser.

Between them they had an impressive hoard of academic achievements, but what real good had any of it done them? Had it stopped either of them making some awful mistakes? Had a first-class honours degree taught Ali how to handle bereavement? Had it taught her how to hold her marriage together? And had a failed attempt at getting a degree helped Sarah to be a better wife? Had it helped her come anywhere near accepting the consequences of the selfish, needless risk she'd taken all those years ago?

The answer was a resounding no.

Elliot arrived a little after eight o'clock.

Ali had been watching anxiously from the sitting-room window for his car. When at last she saw the now familiar XK8 sweeping through the brick pillars at the end of the driveway, she jumped off the window-seat and raced out of the room. She would have liked to bundle him into the house unseen, drag him up the stairs and relive a moment of history on her bedroom floor, but her mother appeared in the hall drying her hands on a tea-towel. With her head tilted playfully she said, 'Was that a car I heard?'

'You know perfectly well it was, Mum.'

Lawrence and Sarah joined them in the hall. They were grinning at her.

'You'd better let him in then,' said Lawrence, with a wink.

'I will when you've all backed off. I don't want you scaring him away.'

Nobody moved.

'Oh, I give up! You're hopeless the lot of you.'

She opened the door and went to Elliot. He was reaching for a small bag in his car but let go of it the second he saw her. He took her in his arms and kissed her. It was no brush of lips on cheek, no polite nice-to-see-you kiss.

This was a real passionate show-stopper and, tilting her back against the side of his car, he said, 'Any chance of having my way with you right now?'

She laughed out loud. 'Yes,' she said, 'if you don't mind an audience.'

He straightened up and glanced at the house. Three smiling faces greeted him.

That night in bed, after much concentrated thought, and while applying her special anti-ageing cream to the skin just below her eyes, Maggie asked her husband if he thought there was a chance of Ali and Elliot remarrying.

Lawrence, who had been staring up at the ceiling rose and contemplating much the same line of thought, said, 'If they have any sense they will.'

Maggie turned and looked at him. 'They're like us, aren't they? So right for each another.'

He smiled, took her hand and raised it to his lips. 'You say the mushiest things.'

'But it's true. I just wish we'd tried harder to stop them divorcing in the first place.'

He shook his head firmly. 'Come on, now, there was nothing we could have done. As parents we had no choice but to stand back and let them sort things out.'

'But they've wasted so much precious time.'

'Well, from what we saw of Elliot's arrival this evening, I'm damned sure they'll make up for it one way or another. And before you even suggest it, I don't think they need any help from us in determining the future.'

'You wouldn't be accusing me of interfering, would you?'

He smiled and kissed her. 'Goodnight, Mistress Cupid.'

They switched off their bedside lamps and snuggled comfortably into one another's arms. But Maggie couldn't sleep. She hadn't been able to sleep last night either. She'd been too elated. When Ali had told her on the phone yesterday evening that there would be an extra visitor for the weekend, not in her wildest dreams had she thought it would be Elliot. 'But why didn't you say you were back together again?' she'd demanded, when Ali had explained who the mystery guest would be.

'Because it's all been so sudden, and after everything we've been through I need to be very sure what it is I feel for him.'

'And what do you *think* you feel for him?'

Ali had laughed and said, 'It begins with L and ends with E.'

'Oh, darling, I'm so pleased for you both. Let me tell your father – he'll want to talk to you, don't go away.'

Now, as the moon shone through the gap in the curtains at the open window and streaked across the faded Oriental rug that had belonged to her parents, Maggie smiled to herself as she thought of the happiness in Lawrence's face when she'd told him the news. He'd always been such a big softie when it came to Ali. Many a time in the aftermath of Isaac's death he had wanted to take his daughter in his arms and comfort her. He'd tried it once, on the day of the funeral, but she'd pushed him away tearfully.

'Lawrence?'

'Mm—?'

'I can't sleep.'

'It's easy. Nothing to it. You just close your eyes.'

'Lawrence?'

'Yes.'

'Do you think Sarah's happy?'

He turned over and faced her in the darkness. 'What's brought this on, then?'

'It was seeing Ali so bright and cheerful this evening that made me realise how sad Sarah looks in comparison.'

'I know what you mean. She gives the impression of not being as happy as she could be.'

'I've always thought that.'

'So have I. And, seeing as we're in perfect accord, may I go to sleep now?' He kissed her cheek and resumed his earlier position.

After a couple of minutes Maggie said, 'I wish I could wave a magic wand.'

'Believe me,' Lawrence grunted from the depths of his goosedown pillow, 'so do I. You'd be the first to catch the benefit of it.'

'I'm being serious.'

'So am I.'

'But don't you feel the same? Don't you want to make life better for everybody?'

'I'd settle for making my own better right now.'

'In an ideal world I'd give Sarah the courage to leave that idiot Trevor.'

'In an ideal world I'd never have allowed her to marry him.'

'You've always had a special place in your heart for Sarah, haven't you?'

Lawrence gave up on the idea of sleep and turned on to his back. 'Yes,' he said simply. 'Those parents of hers didn't deserve her. They gave her nothing. No love. No real guidance. And certainly no support.'

'In their defence, they did give her an education they could ill afford.'

'Very big of them, I'm sure. Don't forget she had a sizeable scholarship. They didn't have to dig their cold, unloving hands too deeply into their pockets.'

'I remember when Ali told us about her being pregnant and that she was leaving Oxford to marry Trevor, you were all for driving up there and talking some sense into her. And for taking Trevor by the scruff of his neck.'

He smiled. 'All that stopped me was that I knew it would do no good. In her own quiet way Sarah is, and always has been, as headstrong and tenacious as Ali. How else could she have stuck being married to that drip?'

'Perhaps there's more to him than meets the eye.'

'Oh, yes. Can you name just one finer point you think Trevor might be in possession of?'

'Well, in his own way he's very sincere. Dependable too.'

Lawrence groaned. 'And so very dull.'

Maggie smiled. 'I didn't tell you this, but a few months ago Ali told me that it's all down to Sarah's religious convictions that she stays with him.'

'Well, thank God I'm an atheist, then. Now, are you going to let me go to sleep or shall I go downstairs and make us a drink?'

'I'd rather you made love to me.'

He laughed loudly. 'Good grief, woman, you're as bad as your daughter – sex, sex and more sex.'

'Once would be sufficient.'

'In that case, lie back and prepare yourself to be amazed.'

36

The next morning, when Ali and Elliot finally showed their faces downstairs, long after breakfast had been cleared away, Maggie, with her customary tact and intuition, suggested that they should go for a walk.

'What about the preparations for the return of the ghastly old prodigal?' said Ali.

'All under control,' Lawrence replied from the kitchen sink, where he and Sarah were on new-potato-scrubbing duty. 'We're going out to the fields to kill the fatted calf when we've finished here.'

'Are you sure we can't help? I'd hate to miss out on all the fun.'

Maggie looked up from the onions she was chopping, her eyes brimming with tears. 'Take her away, Elliot,' she sniffed, 'and don't come back until you've exhausted her.'

The weather, as predicted, had indeed taken a turn for the worse. Yesterday's seamless blue sky was now patched with ragged white clouds being hustled by a strong, bullying wind.

They headed towards the beach, cutting through the sand dunes and golf course, then on towards the wooden beach huts before braving the blustery open expanse of the beach. It was high tide and the only people about were a group of hardy windsurfers in wetsuits, preparing to take on the crashing waves, and a lone woman walking a frisky black Labrador. She raised her hand in greeting to Ali and Elliot, and the dog came to inspect their legs, bouncing around them as if expecting them to throw a ball for him. When his owner called him to heel, he bounded away.

'So what's it to be?' asked Ali. 'Which way do you want to walk? To the funfair or the Ferry Boat?'

Elliot pushed his hands into the pockets of his jeans and looked left, then right. 'Mm . . . a ride on the dodgems or a drink. It's a difficult choice. No, second thoughts, it's easy. You were always a devil in a dodgem. We'll go to the pub, at least that way I shan't end the day with my neck in a brace.'

'Chicken!'

Without warning, he snatched her hands and dragged her down to the shoreline. 'What did you call me?'

'Chicken!' She laughed.

He picked her up and held her threateningly near the water. 'I don't suppose you'd care to review your opinion of me, would you?'

'No!' she screamed, clutching his arms. 'You're still a great big chicken!'

He made as if to drop her and, to the amusement of the windsurfers, she screamed again. 'Okay, okay,' she cried, 'I give in. For a mere man you're incredibly smart and very brave.'

He carried her to safety, then when she was back on her feet, he slid his hands around her waist and kissed her.

'Resorting to brute strength is a sure sign of weakness,' she said, with a smile, when he stopped.

'That's an interesting paradox. And one we'll discuss over a drink. Come on.'

They walked hand in hand along the pebbly beach, to the sound of gulls screeching overhead and their shoes crunching noisily on the shelving stones.

'I can't remember when I last felt this happy,' Ali said, then added, 'It takes some getting used to, doesn't it?'

He put his arm around her. 'You're right, it does.'

'I just wish Isaac was here to share it . . . It doesn't feel right to be so happy when he . . .' Her unfinished sentence drifted away on a gust of wind. She came to a standstill and turned to look at the sea, swelling and rolling beneath the grey sky, ominously dark and menacing. She watched a pair of seagulls circle an area of heaving water, their broad, curved wings working against the wind. 'He should be here with us,' she said, in a sad, faraway voice. Then, turning to Elliot, 'If I could just feel him. Just to know, for sure, that there was more to his short life than the eighteen months he was with us. It might make sense to me then.'

A moment passed. 'You never did believe in heaven, did you?' said Elliot.

Surprised at his question, she said, 'Not Trevor's kind of celestial happy-ever-after nonsense.'

'What about Sarah's version?'

'I'm not sure that hers is much different from Trevor's. At the end of the day it all comes down to a lot of allegorical tomfoolery.'

'You don't think religion is a way of making sense of the incomprehensible, of making order of chaos, of making the unattainable—?'

'No. It merely confuses the issue. It conquers and divides.'

'It doesn't strengthen and restore, then?'

She resumed walking. 'It misguides and offers nothing but a bitter drop of false hope.'

He squeezed her shoulder and changed the subject. 'Your parents are looking well.'

'Aren't they just? And all the better for seeing you again.'

'When did you tell them about us?'

'On the phone the night before they came home. I tossed it casually into the conversation, "Oh, by the way, do you mind if we have an extra guest over the weekend?"'

'Were they very surprised?'

'Completely and utterly. Mum was fine to begin with, then she went all gooey and burst into tears and couldn't speak and Dad had to take the helm – except whenever he tried to say anything Mum kept chipping in, wanting to know all the details.'

'I told Sam.'

'And?'

'He wants to know when he can rush out and buy a hat.'

Ali laughed. 'Not just yet, but when the time comes our Sam can have the biggest and most ostentatious hat going – feathers, flowers, veils, the whole shebang. Carmen Miranda or bust.'

Elliot slowed his pace, then stopped. He held Ali firmly in his arms and stared into her face.

'What's wrong?' she asked.

His expression was solemn. 'We are doing the right thing, aren't we, trying again?'

'Cold feet, Elliot?'

He frowned. 'I'm worried that I've rushed you into this.'

'You of all people should know me better than that. Nobody's ever made me do anything against my will.'

'But I need to know that I haven't forced you into something you might later regret.'

'Are you suggesting I don't know my own mind?'

He didn't answer her. Instead his eyes gazed into the depths of hers as if searching for the truth.

'You are, aren't you?' she said.

He stroked her windblown hair out of her face. 'It's just that it's happened so quickly. One minute we can hardly cope with talking to each other and the next we're—'

'—lying exhausted in bed and planning to be together. Bizarre, isn't it?'

'That's one way of describing it.'

'Well, you know what they say, love and hate are two sides of the same coin. We hated one another, now we love each other.'

He flinched. 'I never hated you.'

'And deep down I didn't hate you, but you know what I mean.'

'Supposing the coin flips over again?'

'Then we let it go.'

'As simple as that?'

'Yes.' She stooped to pick up a large flat stone, contemplated it, then threw it into the sea. 'Then we'd just have to resign ourselves to another lifetime of pure hell.'

He, too, chose a stone and skimmed it across the water. 'So we make the most of what we can, when we can. Is that what you're saying?'

'I guess so.'

'It sounds a bit hit-and-miss.'

'Relationships are. Life is. One minute it's there, the next it's not . . . as we both know only too well.'

They stood in silence for a bit. Then Elliot said, 'Ali, what made you abandon the idea of taking things slowly?'

'I suddenly realised there was no point. Playing at courtship after what we've been through seemed the most colossal and futile waste of time.'

'So you're sure, then? You really want us to get back together?'

'Elliot, what is this? Do you need it in writing?'

'You know how thorough I am.'

'Yes,' she smiled, 'and I'm beginning to find it a pain.'

He reached for her hands, drew her near, and lost himself in her soft, dark, loving eyes. 'I'm sorry,' he said. 'Sam told me not to go and ruin things by being too serious.'

'You should listen to Sam more often. Now, come on, let's get going or we'll never get that drink.'

When they reached the Ferry Boat Inn, the clouds had parted sufficiently to let the sun shine through. They paid for their drinks, took them outside and sat on a wooden bench to watch the activity in the harbour. A couple of young, flash types on jet-skis were showing off, sending up plumes of spray in their wake, while a group of shouting men and women over on the concrete ramp were launching a powerful speedboat from the back of a Land Cruiser. Away in the distance was the small ferry that crossed the busy stretch of water between Hayling and Portsmouth – a mode of transport Ali and Sarah had used frequently as teenagers whenever they fancied more action than the island could offer.

'Where shall we live?' asked Elliot, breaking into Ali's thoughts.

She sipped her cider. This was something she had thought of in bed last night while lying next to him and luxuriating in the feel of his body wrapped around her own. Given that she was only renting the windmill from Owen and his secondment to Brussels couldn't go on for ever, the most obvious answer was for her to move in with Elliot. But where would that leave Sam? In fact, wherever they chose to live, where would that leave Sam?

As if reading her mind, Elliot said, 'Dad and I were hoping that you would move in with us at Timbersbrook.'

'But what about—?'

'Sam?'

'Yes. Won't he feel like the proverbial gooseberry?'

'When I bought Timbersbrook the plan was that we would convert one of the outbuildings into a house for him. We were both keen to preserve a degree of privacy between us.'

'So why didn't you?'

'I'm not sure, really. Sam suddenly lost interest in the project.'

'Until now?'

He nodded. 'Yes.'

Ali knew that Elliot's proposition made perfect sense, but she also knew that Sam would do anything for his son when his happiness was at stake. 'I don't know,' she said. 'I'd feel that I'd pushed him out.'

Elliot reached across the table and laid his hand on top of hers. 'He said you'd say that. He also said that you were to talk to him about it so that he could put you right.'

She laughed. 'You mean so that he could sweet-talk me round to his way of thinking.'

'Something like that.' Taking a long swig on his beer, Elliot thought that if anyone could persuade Ali to do something it was Sam. It was, after all, the ideal solution all round.

When Elliot had told his father about him and Ali, Sam had initially, and predictably, made noises about finding himself somewhere else to live, but Elliot had refused to listen to him. 'Timbersbrook won't be the same without you,' he'd said, 'and apart from anything else, it's your home as much as mine.'

What he hadn't said was that there was the future to consider. As improbable as it seemed, given that Sam had the apparent constitution of an ox, there might come a day when he would need a watchful eye kept on him. With everything his father had done for him, this was exactly what Elliot intended on doing.

37

On their return to Sanderling, Ali and Elliot saw an extra car on the driveway.

'Alastair and Phoebe, one supposes,' remarked Ali, as they went round to the back of the house and let themselves in. There was a pile of expensive leather luggage in the hall and voices coming from the sitting room. Maggie and Lawrence must have put Alastair in the picture about Elliot for when they entered the room Ali's brother greeted him as if the past two and a half years had never happened. He then advanced on Ali and, towering over her, gave her a crushing hug. 'And how's my little sis? Still not grown, I see.'

She pushed him away affectionately. 'Get off, you horrid beast, and introduce me to the poor girl who must be crazy to have agreed to marry you. Five minutes with me and I'll soon have her reviewing the situation.'

'Only because she'll worry that there's madness in the family.'

Phoebe was a picture of enviable streamlined looks and youth and was, Ali decided, as near as damn it, probably a whole decade younger than her and Sarah. With the aid of a pair of cripplingly high strappy black sandals she was almost as tall as Alastair, but where he was fair like Ali and their mother, Phoebe was dark and sultry. Her skin had a smooth, Mediterranean quality, and her hair, scraped back from her face and tied into a chic knot at the nape of her neck, gave her an air of refined beauty. She was stunning, and as she stepped forward to be introduced to her sister-in-law-to-be, Ali wondered how on earth her boring old brother had attracted somebody so gorgeous. It must be all his money, she thought, as she shook hands and noted the chunk of dazzling diamond speared by the long, elegant third finger. She was suddenly conscious of her own appearance and wished that her hair wasn't quite so messed up from their walk on the beach. She wished, too, that she wasn't dressed in her seen-better-days T-shirt and battered trainers, or that she didn't reek quite so obviously of the draught cider that she'd spilled down her jeans at the pub. She caught Sarah's eye across the room and when the introductions were over, she joined her friend on the window-seat. 'Quite a babe, isn't she?' she whispered, sure that nobody could hear them as Alastair was now well into his voluble stride, telling Maggie and Lawrence how he and Phoebe had met at a charity ball in Singapore.

'Looks *and* brains,' Sarah whispered back. 'She's an investment banker, like Alastair.'

'Heaven knows how my ugly pain-in-the-butt brother hit the jackpot with her. She's so sophisticated.'

'Come off it, Ali, he's far from ugly. He's really quite handsome.'

'Get away. He's totally gruesome. He's got all the charm of Freddy Krueger.'

Sarah smiled. 'That's because you see him through the eyes of a younger sister.'

'And how do you view him?'

'Slightly more objectively.'

Ali shook her head in disbelief. 'Diplomatic to the end, that's my Sarah.'

Elliot joined them and, in a lowered voice, said, 'All you need are a couple of fans and you'd be dead ringers for those two women from *Dangerous Liaisons*. I can't begin to think what you two are gossiping about.'

Ali moved along the seat and made room for him.

'She is rather lovely, though, isn't she?' Sarah said wistfully.

'Careful how you answer that, Elliot,' warned Ali. 'I can turn very nasty when I'm made to feel jealous. You know how chronically insecure I am.'

Elliot stared across the room to where Phoebe was sitting on the sofa next to Alastair, her long legs elegantly crossed in a pair of tight black leather trousers. She was, as Sarah had just said, a very attractive woman. But for him she was too cool, too poised. There was an unreal quality about her that reminded him of the scores of trophy wives he'd seen at office parties over the years. 'I prefer blondes any day,' he said, taking Ali's hand in his, 'especially the small, ruffled variety.'

'God, but you're smooth,' Ali said, with a happy laugh.

Maggie insisted that everybody dressed for dinner that evening. 'Go on, you two girls,' she said to Ali and Sarah. 'Up those stairs and dollify yourselves.' Ali's protestations that she and Sarah hadn't brought anything remotely glitzy with them were met with a firm, 'We've a lot to celebrate tonight – your brother's engagement and you and Elliot getting back together – so do as you're told and make an effort. I know you probably both pride yourselves in being slimmer than me, but have a rummage through my things and see what you can find.'

Ali took Sarah upstairs to investigate the contents of her mother's fleet of wardrobes, and while Sarah sat on the bed, she threw open the cupboard doors. 'Imelda Marcos or what?' she said, as she stood back and took in the rails of clothes and neatly stored shoeboxes.

'Imelda Marcos, but with a great deal more taste.'

Ali was riffling through the colour-ordered clothes. 'What do you fancy?' she asked. 'Something in emerald or fuchsia, or both?'

'Something a little quieter, please.'

Ali moved along the rails and pulled out a simple shift dress in a warm shade of caramel. It was made of silk and shimmered luxuriously in the light. 'You'd look great in this,' she said.

'Do you think so?' asked Sarah doubtfully, slipping off the bed and taking the dress from Ali. 'It looks terribly expensive.'

Ali tutted. '*Ergo*, unless it costs less than a tenner it won't suit you?'

Sarah ignored her friend's salvo of sarcasm, held the dress against her and went to inspect her reflection in the cheval glass in the bay window. But the sight of Alastair and Phoebe sitting in the gazebo in the garden below deflected her gaze. They were staring up at the house as though Alastair was recounting some part of his childhood that had been spent here. They looked completely at ease with one another. From nowhere Sarah felt a stab of jealousy. All around her people were caught up in the rapture of a happy, loving relationship.

There was Maggie and Lawrence, still as devoted to each other as they'd ever been; there was Ali and Elliot, who had beaten the terrible odds stacked against them and realised that they'd never stopped loving one another; and now there was Alastair, that one time committed bachelor, who had finally found a woman with whom he was prepared to share his life.

And what of her? Oh, dear God, what of her? What real happiness did she have? Or was ever likely to have?

Maggie was delighted with the way the evening was going. Staring round at her family in the flickering candlelight, she felt a rush of matriarchal pride. At the other end of the table, beyond the swathes of damask, cut-glass and best silver, was Lawrence, his face slightly flushed from an excess of good food and wine. He was chatting amiably to Phoebe, who was sitting on his right wearing a glamorous, low-slung number that revealed more than just the string of pearls around her neck.

On Lawrence's left, where he insisted she sat whenever she was at home, was Ali. She was wearing a strapless dress of black velvet which, had she worn it a year ago when she'd been so gaunt and pale, would have looked dreadful on her. Tonight, though, there was nothing wan or haggard about Ali: she was bright-eyed, and glowing with a radiance Maggie hadn't seen in her for a long while. With an elbow on the table she was resting her chin on her hand, leaning in towards Elliot and listening to him intently, watching his face as closely as if she needed to lip-read him. Maggie almost felt sorry for the pair that they had to join in with a family get-together – they'd probably prefer to be alone upstairs.

From the first time she had seen Ali and Elliot together she had known that they were right for each other: there was such an obvious compatibility between them. Before Elliot had made his appearance in her daughter's life, Maggie had been concerned that Ali would make a disastrous match with a man who would be threatened by her forthright, headstrong nature and would either feel compelled to change her or slink off to find a more compliant companion. From the cross-section of young men with whom Ali had dallied, the latter situation had invariably taken place – though frequently it was she who told them to sling their hook. But Elliot had stayed the course. She could remember when, out of the blue, Ali had phoned to say that she'd met somebody 'special' at work. 'He's something else, Mum,' she'd said. 'He never smiles and he hardly speaks, he just stands there and does this amazing thing.'

'And what amazing *thing* would that be?'

'He gives out this spellbinding aura of sexiness. Bucketloads of it. I think I'm in love.'

Their subsequent conversations had run along similar lines and had left Maggie in no doubt that her daughter was indeed in love. She had cherished the fact that she had the sort of relationship with her daughter that enabled them to talk in a way that was usually the reserve of close friends.

And, thinking of close friends, there was Sarah on Elliot's left, talking to Alastair across the table. The silk dress she'd picked out looked particularly well on her and was one Maggie hadn't worn in ages; she wondered whether she dared offer it to Sarah to take home with her. She noticed the pretty gold chain around Sarah's neck and remembered Ali telling her last year that she had bought Sarah a necklace for Christmas but was worried she might refuse it, seeing it as too extravagant. Poor Sarah, thought Maggie, continually having to fend off a best friend's well-meant generosity, not to mention the good intentions of that best friend's family.

She listened to what Sarah and Alastair were discussing and was astonished to hear her son showing an interest in something other than himself – much as she loved him, Maggie had no qualms in admitting that her eldest offspring had a tendency, at times, to behave as an exasperating self-congratulatory big-head. He was asking after Hannah, and Sarah was telling him about her being in France with a group of friends before taking up her place at Oxford.

'Which college has she applied to?'

'Brasenose.'

'Aha. A touch of the old *alma mater*. What do you think her chances are?'

'She needs three straight As.'

'And is that a tall order?'

'Yes and no.'

'You don't sound very sure she'll make it.'

'I don't doubt her academic ability, it's just that one can never be certain how things will turn out.'

Maggie knew that to have been a comment on Sarah's own life. She admired Sarah immensely. So many women in her position would have made a victim of themselves. But not Sarah. Well, she had no need to, did she? In a sense, and not intentionally, the Edwards family had done that for her. When she'd been a child they had taken it upon themselves to improve her lot and had tried to do much the same thing for her as an adult when they'd privately denounced her marriage as little more than a state of prolonged purgatory. Some might say they'd been arrogant to make such a sweeping assumption, but Maggie liked to think it was because they cared for Sarah, as if she were one of their own.

Leaving Sarah and Alastair to their conversation, Maggie turned her attention once more to Phoebe. When Alastair had called to tell them he was engaged, nothing could have surprised Maggie more. She had resigned herself to having a son who lacked the inclination to pursue a meaningful relationship to its logical conclusion. His problem, she suspected, was that he was that infuriatingly restless type of man who couldn't keep still for more than two minutes. It would have to be an exceptional woman to hold his attention long enough to avoid being shown the door. In his late teens, he'd been the same and had annoyed Ali no end: she'd hoped that the presence of a permanent girlfriend would mean he'd spend less time hanging around her and Sarah. On more than one occasion, Ali had been furious when he had overplayed his big-brother role. 'No, you can't come and play tennis with us,' she had shouted at him, when he had tried to follow them on his bike down to the park and the tennis courts. 'We're going to play singles, not triples.' Sarah had been more patient and tolerant, and had suggested he could join them another day. There was no doubt in Maggie's mind that Ali had resented Alastair pitching in on what she clearly saw as her territory, but she had also wondered whether he had been keen on Sarah. Maggie had once hinted as much to Ali, who had fallen about laughing. 'The only person Alastair's keen on is himself,' she'd said. 'That, and getting on, is all that matters to him.' Certainly ever since leaving college 'getting on' had been important to Alastair and had been the focus of all his energy. But looking at the beautiful girl at the far end of the table who was soon to become a member of their family, Maggie could only conclude that her son must have changed – miraculously he had found the time and reason to fall in love. Maybe in the not-too-distant future there was even a chance of him becoming a father. Now that would be a real turn-up for the books.

But it would also be a sad reminder of little Isaac.

How delighted she and Lawrence had been when Elliot had phoned to say that Ali had given birth to a baby boy. 'He's perfect in every way,' Elliot had said ecstatically, 'just as his mother is.' Maggie had never forgotten the rare rush of emotion in his voice as he'd gone on to describe the fairness of their grandson's hair, the smoothness of his skin, the blueness of his eyes and the impossible smallness of his hands and feet. 'His fingers,' he'd burbled on, 'they're so tiny, you wouldn't believe it. So tiny.' It had been particularly touching to hear their laconic son-in-law being so effusive.

How different had been the phone call eighteen months later when he had called to tell them that Isaac was dead. She didn't think she would ever lose the memory of his voice cracking up as he'd tried to break the news. Unable to finish what he was saying, Sam, who was at the hospital with him, had taken over and explained what had happened. She and Lawrence had both wept and lain awake in bed until they could stand it no longer. They had dressed, packed a couple of bags, got into the car and driven up to Cheshire, never once suspecting the extent of the nightmare that lay ahead for Ali and Elliot.

She turned her attention back to them at the dinner table and saw that they were still deeply and exclusively engrossed in one another. It struck her how two people who loved with the intensity that they did could inspire in each other either a blissful happiness, or a crushing sadness.

Oh, let them know only happiness from now on, thought Maggie, as she raised her glass and silently wished her family well.

38

After lunch the following day, Elliot set off for Cheshire.

'I wish you weren't going,' Ali said, when everyone else had wished him a safe journey and discreetly left them alone to say their goodbyes. 'Couldn't you cancel, postpone or delegate whatever it is you have to do?'

He pulled her closer to him. 'If you were in my shoes, would you consider doing any of that with Gervase on the scene?'

'Mm ... maybe not. Will you ring me when you get back?'

'Of course.'

'Give my love to Sam and tell him he's on for a lunch-date when I'm home. Warn him there's a lot we need to discuss.'

'Am I included in this little *tête-à-tête*?'

'No. I want Sam all to myself.'

The traffic was surprisingly light, given that it was a Sunday in the height of summer, and not even the sprawl of cone-lined roadworks on the M6 and endless cavalcades of caravans did much to slow Elliot's progress. He reached Timbersbrook shortly after six o'clock and found a note from his father in the kitchen informing him that he'd gone to the Morris Minor Specialist garage in Flint to fetch Tilly after her paint job and should be home around eight. He poured himself a glass of orange juice, wandered over to the table and looked at the large pieces of paper that Sam must have been studying in his absence: they were the plans he'd drawn up for the Lurve Nest. For some inexplicable reason he hoped that Sam wasn't jumping the gun. Though he had no cause to doubt Ali's love for him, or what he felt for her, there was deep within him an anxiety that something might go wrong between them.

He wanted to put it down to his naturally cautious nature, but he knew that his concern stemmed from that most basic of instincts: fear. He was frightened of being so vulnerable again. Loving Ali as he did put him in a position of excruciating defencelessness.

He had loved Isaac and lost him.

He had loved Ali and truly believed that he had lost her.

The thought of losing her again was too much. What if she had a fatal accident? What if she developed cancer as his mother had when he was at Oxford? How would he cope with watching the vibrant and vital woman he dearly loved slowly die before him? He had held his own son in his arms as he died. Did the same awful fate await him with Ali?

Appalled at the mawkish trajectory of his thoughts, he carefully folded Sam's plans for the future and went through to his study to ring Ali, needing the sound of her voice to dispel the disturbing image of her being taken away from him.

At nine thirty-five the following morning, Elliot was waiting for that week's partners' meeting to get off the ground. Everyone was there around the large oval table in his office – everyone except for Gervase who, annoyingly, was ten minutes late. It was Gervase to whom Elliot needed to speak. The question was, should Elliot talk to him in front of the others, or wait until the meeting was over? A public flogging was an appealing prospect, given the dislike Elliot had of the man, but a private word one-to-one was undoubtedly the more professional approach.

Lying in a file in his desk drawer was a letter of complaint from Paul Davidson, the managing director of Hayes and Clarke, one of their key clients. He had written to Elliot that he was far from happy with the service he had received on an important acquisition project, and that if matters weren't resolved to his satisfaction he would have no choice but to move his firm's business elsewhere.

In Elliot's opinion, to let down a client, especially a well-established, lucrative client, was not only sloppy and unprofessional, it was unforgivable.

And who had been in charge of that particular account?

None other than Gervase Merchant-Taylor.

Elliot was furious that the reputation of the firm had been compromised and he was determined that Gervase would be found accountable and make amends. Right on cue, the door opened and in he strolled. The man's smug face and lack of apology for keeping everybody waiting made Elliot want to confront him on the spot, but he allowed Gervase a few seconds to settle into his chair and arrange his papers. Then, as was Elliot's habit, he opened the file in front of him, removed the lid from his fountain pen and suggested that they get on with the big, crunchy issues of work in progress and the accounts still to be billed – he was conscious that Howard's department had a more than average amount of audit work that had time running up on it and it wasn't unreasonable to expect an explanation, or better still an assurance that matters would improve.

Two hours later and they were done. He rose to his feet and was about to ask Gervase if he'd spare him a moment, when Gervase announced that he and his wife were having an impromptu do at the weekend. 'Nothing special,' he said, in his annoyingly pompous voice, 'but you're all invited. Eight for eight-thirty.' General murmurs of acceptance were made, some marginally more enthusiastic than others.

Poor devils, thought Elliot, moving away from the table and going over to his desk at the far end of the room. None of them had the guts not to be present at one of Gervase's ghastly gin-and-tonic parties for fear of not being there to defend themselves.

'How about you, Elliot?' Gervase said. 'You'll come, won't you? You know what they say, all work and no play makes Elliot Anderson a thoroughly tedious boy.'

In view of their impending conversation, Elliot responded with a noncommittal, 'Thanks, but I'll have to check my diary.' Then he said, 'Have you got a minute? There's something I need to discuss with you.'

'It'll have to be quick and to the point, old chap. I'm expecting—'

'It'll be quick and to the point, I promise you.'

When they were alone, Gervase sat in front of Elliot's desk and said, 'I suppose it's Howard you want to discuss, isn't it? Frankly I'm surprised it's taken this long for the shambles of his department to come to your notice. What do you propose to do about the situation?'

Elliot leaned back in his chair and steepled his fingers together. He considered staying quiet for a bit longer, thereby giving Gervase the opportunity to carry on digging himself a bigger and deeper hole. It would, after all, serve the obnoxious bastard right. But instead he reached for the confidential file in his drawer, opened it, and pushed Paul Davidson's letter across the desk.

'What's this, then?' asked Gervase.

'You tell me,' he remarked casually.

Shrewd enough to be on his guard now, Gervase raised the letter and began reading it. Elliot watched his face closely, noting the change in colour as well as the thought process that was going on behind the piggy eyes that were darting from side to side as they scanned the piece of paper. Elliot's money was on Gervase blustering about some kind of misunderstanding that had occurred and that it was little more than a storm in a tea-cup that Paul Davidson was overreacting to. But when Gervase passed the letter back to him and said, 'I was hoping against all odds that this wouldn't happen,' he was momentarily wrong-footed.

'I think you'd better explain what's been going on,' he said. 'Just what's been the problem?'

Gervase held up his hands in a gesture of resigned weariness. 'Rachel Vincent is the problem. Or, rather, she was.'

Once again Elliot leaned back in his chair and contemplated the man before him, narrowing his eyes imperceptibly. So that was the way he was going to play it – deny all responsibility and shove it on the shoulders of a senior manager who had, much to Elliot's surprise, left the firm unexpectedly a couple of weeks ago. He had viewed Rachel as professional and highly competent. Now Gervase was implying otherwise. 'Rachel always struck me as being one of our most meticulous managers,' Elliot said slowly.

'I thought so too.'

Far from convinced that this was Gervase's true opinion, Elliot said, 'Perhaps you ought to share some of your reservations with me.' He hoped that by giving the man enough rope he would eventually hang himself.

Gervase picked at a minuscule bit of fluff on his pinstripe trouser leg and said, 'Of course, if she were here, she'd deny everything, but the sad truth is she made the classic mistake of not knowing what the left hand was doing from the right. She presented the client with a bill that was well over the agreed fee.'

'If she made such an obvious mistake, why would she deny it?'

'You know how it is with women.'

Instinctively sensing trouble, Elliot said, 'No, Gervase, I don't. How is it with women?'

Gervase laughed one of his infuriating self-important laughs. 'No head for business is the polite way of putting it.'

Elliot thought how Ali would react if she were here. Very probably she would have pushed Gervase's genitals through the shredder by now. 'I'd like to see the billing file,' he said. His words had the satisfying effect of instantly slamming the door on Gervase's pompous men's-locker-room laughter.

'Good Lord, there's no need for that, surely?'

'Sorry?'

'What I mean is, just leave it to me. I'll speak to Paul Davidson and see if we can put matters right by agreeing to write off the excess fee.'

'If anyone is going to speak to Paul it will be me. And until I've seen the billing file I won't do that.' Suddenly he snapped forward in his seat, rested his elbows on his desk, and fixed Gervase with a cold, piercing stare. 'Now, as Rachel was reporting directly to you, I assume you knew exactly what was going on and can tell me the precise figures involved.'

Gervase shifted uncomfortably in his seat. He scratched the back of his neck then fiddled with the knot of his tie. 'I'll get somebody to dig out the file,' he muttered testily.

'Good. I'd like to see it first thing tomorrow morning.'

'Tomorrow morning?'

'Got a problem with that?'

'I'm out for the rest of the day and I've a lot on.'

'So have I. I'm in the States next week and I want this awkward and embarrassing mess cleared up by then.'

When he was alone, Elliot sat back in his chair, considered what Gervase had told him, and knew it to be a monumental work of fiction. The man was lying through his tonsils, never mind his back teeth. He wondered whether he ought to make a pre-emptive strike and go in search of the file himself. He wouldn't put it past Gervase to come back to him and say, in his poncy voice, that it was the strangest thing but he couldn't find the file. Elliot was in no doubt that Gervase had caused the problem and that it was his fault, not Rachel's, that the correct fee hadn't been agreed. Even if Rachel had got it wrong, what Gervase had failed to acknowledge was that as a senior partner the buck stopped with him as regards the actions of one of his managers.

But what rattled Elliot most was that no matter how incompetent the Gervases of this world were, with their moneyed backgrounds and inbred patronising attitudes, they always surfaced from the pit of shit smelling sickly sweet.

Well, not this time. Not if Elliot had anything to do with it. He was determined to expose Gervase for the posturing fraud he was.

To achieve that he needed to do two things: first he had to get his hands on that billing file before anyone else did, and second he had to speak to Rachel Vincent and find out the real reason behind her sudden departure. At no stage had she given him cause to think she wasn't happy in her work.

As far as he was aware, she had had a healthy interest in pursuing what, by all accounts, was a promising career with the firm.

Elliot had a strong suspicion that Gervase had been using his secretary as an extra pair of eyes and ears, so didn't give a moment's thought to enlisting Dawn's help in obtaining Rachel's home address or the information he needed on Hayes and Clarke. He told her he would be unavailable for the next hour and left his office. He took the lift down to the second floor and hoped that he wouldn't bump into Gervase with the same task in mind. He found Rachel's old office, but instead of starting his enquiries there with her replacement, he tapped on the shoulder-high partition next door.

Two graduate trainees looked up at him. They immediately stopped what they were doing and scrambled to their feet as if they were a pair of fifth-formers caught smoking in the loos by the headmaster. This was definitely an aspect of his job that Elliot hated: no matter how hard he'd tried to cast himself as an approachable my-door's-open-any-time-of-the-day boss, his position in the firm made the junior members wary of him. These two girls were no exception. They stared at him nervously, clearly fearing the worst.

He stepped into their small office and, glad that he had the capacity never to forget a name, he said, 'Claire and Louise, could you spare me a few minutes, please?'

With an unconcealed display of edgy distrust, they offered him a seat and the tallest of them, Claire, said, 'Of course, Mr Anderson. There's nothing wrong, is there?'

He refused the chair, preferring to try to put them at ease by leaning against the block of filing cabinets. 'Not at all. I just wondered whether you could help me. Do you know what Rachel's up to now?'

The question took them by surprise. They looked at each other guardedly, then back at him. 'I think she was taking a few weeks' holiday before starting a new job next month,' Louise said.

'Do you know if she was going away on holiday or just staying at home?'

Again the two girls exchanged reticent glances. Neither seemed inclined to answer him. He suddenly realised what was going on. They had him down as another Gervase who wouldn't think twice of using his sex and position to get exactly what he wanted. This, then, was the reality of working in a male-dominated office such as theirs, where an excess of testosterone reigned supreme and where female employees were automatically marginalised and expected to toe the line accordingly. Annoyed and disgusted that he hadn't taken steps sooner to change such a deeply ingrained culture, Elliot decided to be straight with the two young women. 'Look,' he said, 'do you have any idea why Rachel left so unexpectedly? Was she, for instance, recently made to feel unhappy working here?'

From the expression of scorn on both their faces his worst fears were confirmed. He tried an even more direct line and lowered his voice. 'You don't have to go into details if you don't want to, but, please, just tell me, was it, in your view, a case of sexual harassment?'

After the briefest of sideways glances, they both nodded.

Half an hour later, Elliot left the second floor and returned to his office. He now had the file he needed, as well as Rachel Vincent's home phone

number. He locked both vital pieces of information in his desk to deal with
that evening and got on with what he should have been doing instead of
playing amateur detective.

39

When Elliot had told Gervase that he was busy, he had not been exaggerating, and though he had had time at home to go through the Hayes and Clarke billing file – and discover that crucial bits of information were missing – he had not had time to do anything about it. Neither had he been able to make contact with Rachel Vincent: she hadn't responded to any of the messages he'd left on her answerphone, and until he had spoken to her he couldn't make a further move on Gervase. With his trip to the States scheduled for the day after tomorrow, he had no choice but to be patient and hope that the reason Rachel had not contacted him was that she was still away on holiday.

In the meantime he had replaced the billing file and spoken to Paul Davidson to reassure him that the matter was being looked into. He'd also told Gervase that until his return from New York the situation would be on hold. The man's relief had shown itself in the form of a flamboyant wave of a hand. 'I expect we'll just have to treat it as one of those things, old chap,' he'd said airily, 'a damn nuisance, but nothing that can't be smoothed out by exercising a little judicious writing off of the excess fee.'

Elliot would have liked to exercise a little judicious knuckle-flexing into the side of Gervase's arrogant, overfed jaw, but instead, and to lull him into a greater sense of false security, he said, 'Oh, and by the way, I shall be able to make it on Saturday night, after all.'

When he'd told Ali on the phone what he was doing and why, having confided in her his suspicions about Gervase, she had wished him luck. 'I can't think of anything worse,' she'd said, 'than an evening with Gervase and that ghastly wife of his, the Bitch Queen of Prada Accessories.'

'I'm hardly thrilled at the prospect myself.'

She'd laughed. 'A perverse part of me wishes I could be there with you.'

'If you were here, I wouldn't even consider going. I'd have a much better evening planned.'

'Pining for me, are you?'

'What do you think?'

'I think you're running up a terrible phone bill. We've been talking for nearly an hour and mostly about Gervase.'

'I'm sorry, it's just that you and Sam are the only ones I'm prepared to confide in at this stage.'

'Don't worry, it doesn't bother me. But do you really believe Gervase would be dumb enough to think he could get away with it? Most of us girls in the office knew that he and others like him considered us fair game for a bit of slap-and-tickle, though I have to say he never once tried it on with me. This is shaping up into quite a different ball-game, though.'

'Oh, I think he's more than stupid enough. And don't forget, he counted on Rachel being too scared to give her side of the story for fear of jeopardising her career, and so far it's worked beautifully.'

'Well, Elliot, for the sake of the sisterhood, nail the so-and-so!'

Elliot parked his car and, with Ali's words echoing in his ears, approached Gervase's prestigiously large house. It was a centuries-old pile that had been in the Merchant-Taylor family since one of Gervase's ancestors had made an obscene amount of wealth from exploiting men, women and children in his cotton mills. It overlooked the greens and fairways of the nearby golf and country club in one of Cheshire's classiest areas.

He rang the bell and cringed as he heard it clang ostentatiously on the other side of the studded oak door. He planned to stay just long enough to make Gervase think that all was well in the office – an unprepared Gervase was what Elliot wanted when he made his strike.

It was Fiona who answered the door. She was the second Mrs Merchant-Taylor, having replaced the former some seven years previously. Fifteen years Gervase's junior, she had, once upon a time, been little more to him than his secretary – but that was before they embarked on a standard workplace affair. It had been going on in a semi-clandestine manner for several months when one day, Barbara, Gervase's wife, under the influence of whatever alcohol she'd earlier consumed, stormed into the office and dramatically announced to anyone who would listen that she knew exactly what her vile, womanising husband was up to. A messy divorce followed, as did a precipitous marriage between Fiona and Gervase. And according to what Ali had told him from ground-level gossip, Fiona had at once adopted the air of a county-set wife and overnight had become an expensive liability. No longer was she prepared to do anything as menial as sit in an office typing letters or answering the phone. Her new occupation was as a lady who lunched, who filled her days consulting interior designers to be rid of all evidence of her predecessor's taste in her newly acquired home. And when she wasn't agonising over lunch menus or choosing between samples of thirty-pounds-a-roll wallpaper, she was pampering herself at the local country club, tanning on sunbeds and having her gold-digging nails manicured. According to the office gossip, she also spent a staggering amount of money on clothes to ensure that she could play to the hilt the part of glamorous young wife married to older man. Elliot had always thought it a shame that the previous generations of Merchant-Taylors had not taken better care of their wealth; if they had, he would have been spared having to work with a git like Gervase. But gambling debts and reckless investments had ensured that Gervase's generation would be denied the privilege of sitting on their fat backsides living off old money.

'Elliot,' drawled Fiona, as she extended a languid hand that was all varnished nails, emeralds and diamonds, 'Gervase said you'd be coming. We'll all have to be on our best behaviour now, won't we?'

'Not on my account, please.'

She took him through to what she pointedly called the drawing room, and which was high-ceilinged and swagged and draped with the kind of rich, heavy fabric more commonly seen as theatre curtains.

A large number of what Elliot called the Blazer Crowd had already arrived and were standing about in small noisy groups. They were being waited on by a couple of girls in short black skirts, white blouses, thick black tights and huge platform shoes. They looked thoroughly bored as they passed round trays of smoked-salmon canapés, and Elliot hoped they were being well paid to prop up Fiona's status-conscious ego.

Clicking her fingers to attract one of the young girls, Fiona said, 'We had hoped to be outside in the garden, but one can never rely on the weather in England. I've told Gervase that, come the autumn, we shall have to get away for some real sun. I feel so dreadfully pale.'

There wasn't anything Elliot could say in response to this vacuous remark. She was clearly more stupid than he thought.

'What would you like to drink?' she asked, when the summoned waitress was by their side. 'Everyone else is having Pimms or G and T.'

'I'll have orange juice, please.'

'You wouldn't like a splash of something with it? Gin? Vodka?'

'Just ice.'

'How very boring. Hardly worth you coming.'

When the girl returned with his glass of orange, Fiona said, 'Now, then, I've got somebody special for you to meet.'

He nearly choked on his drink. 'Fiona, there's really no need—'

'Nonsense. You'll love her. Look, she's over there, talking to Dawn. Isn't she stunning? It was Gervase's idea. He thought the pair of you would really hit it off. We both think you've been on your own for far too long. It's time to put your silly old divorce behind you and find yourself a new wife.'

Elliot was horrified, and furious, to hear his private life referred to so glibly. He stared across the room and saw the woman to whom Fiona was referring. When she realised he was looking in her direction, she waved coyly at him.

'Her name's Miriam,' Fiona said, 'but everyone calls her Mitzi. Come on, I'll introduce you. I've told her all about you.'

Elliot held his ground, determined not to be ambushed into the arms of a woman who went by the name of a miniature poodle. 'Fiona, you had no right to do this.'

But she threw back her head and laughed. 'You're so set in your ways, Elliot. You really should lighten up.'

He knew that the easiest thing to do was to tell Fiona about him and Ali, but he had no desire to do that: it was absolutely none of her business. Then, to his annoyance, he saw that it was too late to protest further. Mitzi was advancing and he was trapped. As soon as the introductions had been made Fiona made herself scarce, claiming that she had to keep an eye on the hired help. 'You have to watch them the whole time,' she said, with an exaggerated roll of her eyes, 'or they'll knock back all the drink and make off with the silver.'

'Fiona tells me you're divorced,' Mitzi began unimaginatively.

He nodded reluctantly.

'Me too. It was a horrible time, lots of nasty solicitor's letters and no end of rows about money. You wouldn't believe how petty my ex was – we very nearly had a custody battle over Twinkle.'

'Twinkle?'

'My Siamese cat.' Smiling meaningfully at him, she went on, 'But it hasn't put me off men entirely, I'm quite prepared to give marriage a second chance with Mr Right. How about you?'

Elliot inwardly groaned and considered telling her that he was gay. He decided not to and said, in his politest voice, 'I'm sure that's the healthiest and most positive attitude to adopt, but I doubt you'll find him here tonight.' Seeing Howard Jenkins standing on his own, he added, 'Now, if you'll excuse me, there's somebody I need to speak to.'

'Bloody awful party,' Howard said morosely, when Elliot approached. 'I don't know why I bother. Same crowd, same crap being said, and the same traps being set. I watched you being set up with the rent-a-bimbo. A lesser man would have gone for it. But not you, eh, Elliot? Coolest man on the block is what the trainee conscripts say about you, did you know that? Mr Cool. Better than what they probably call me.'

Elliot was surprised to hear Howard speaking so vociferously. He wondered if he'd had too much to drink. 'Everything okay?' he asked.

'Oh, everything's hunky-dory. Hunky-bloody-dory.'

'Annabelle not here with you?'

Howard turned his empty glass around in his hand, then raised his dim watery eyes to Elliot's. 'You might as well know,' he said. 'She's left me – for a man who apparently understands her. God, I thought that was supposed to be our line – "My wife doesn't understand me," and all that rubbish.' He sounded the bitterest of men.

'Howard, I'm sorry. When did this happen?'

He shrugged. 'Been going on for a while. Well, it does, doesn't it? There are always the warning signs, one just chooses not to act on them. But, then, you probably know all about that, don't you?' He frowned. 'Sorry,' he mumbled awkwardly, 'shouldn't have said that. Not my place to pry into why your marriage sank without trace. But do you know what the worst bit is?'

'Go on.'

'It's not seeing the children.' He shook his head and frowned again. 'Sorry, shouldn't have said that either. Keep putting my foot in it, don't I, what with your little Isaac?'

'It's okay, don't worry.'

'I don't know how you coped. Must have been the most bloody awful time for you.'

'It was,' Elliot said simply. 'Is there really no hope of saving your marriage?'

'Don't think I haven't tried – God knows I have – but she's not interested. In a way, I don't blame her. I've not been the best of husbands. I've always put work first, so I guess it serves me right. Now, if you don't mind, I want another drink. An extremely large one. I'm going to get embarrassingly drunk and then vomit messily all over Gervase's expensive carpet. Something I shall enjoy doing. I only hope I can remember it in the morning.'

Elliot watched Howard weave his way through the crowd of guests in search of a waitress. It distressed him to see yet another marriage ruined through work. If it wasn't the stress of the job and the long hours that did it, it was a consequence of the environment: too many middle-aged insecure men with something to prove and usually with the younger women in the office.

But Howard's broken marriage at least explained why he hadn't been running his department with his usual efficiency, and now that he knew what the problem was, Elliot could do something about it. He would ensure that Howard was given the support he needed while he was going through what he knew from his own experience, was a pretty bleak period.

It was odd, but the conversation he'd just had with Howard was the nearest he'd ever got to sharing with a work colleague what he had gone through during the past two and half years. Immediately after Isaac's death he had shunned the merest hint of sympathy from anyone in the office, and very soon he had trained himself to appear – according to accepted male conventions – as though he was fully in control of his grief. No one would have guessed at the extent of his misery. He supposed that this was one of the aspects of his character that had helped perpetuate the office myth that he was Mr Cool. It struck him also that his controlled demeanour worked the other way: nobody here tonight would have the faintest notion that he and Ali were back together and that he was what Sam would call top-dollar happy.

An hour later, when Elliot thought he'd shown his face for long enough, he went in search of Gervase. Unable to find him, he asked Fiona where he was.

'You'll find him in his study,' she said, 'second door on the left. It's the only place I allow him to smoke those disgusting cigars of his.'

Elliot followed her directions and indeed found Gervase.

But he wasn't smoking one of his disgusting cigars.

He was sitting behind his desk, his head tilted back, his eyes closed, his mouth open, with Dawn the Porn astride his lap.

Very quietly, Elliot edged out of the room.

He drove home wondering how much more rope Gervase would need to make a proper job of hanging himself.

40

Their holiday was over and Ali and Sarah were heading north. Although they'd enjoyed themselves immensely at Sanderling, they were both looking forward to getting home – Ali because she would be seeing Elliot that evening, and Sarah because it wouldn't be long before Hannah returned from France.

Sarah had spoken to Trevor on the phone last night and he had said he'd received a postcard from Hannah that morning to say that they were planning to catch a ferry on the 18th of August – two days before the dreaded A-level results would be out.

For most of the fortnight Sarah's conscience had been doing its best to make her feel guilty for leaving Trevor on his own. She had called him frequently but he hadn't once asked how she was or what she and Ali were doing. From their conversations it was evident that he was surviving pretty well without her. Audrey and Shirley were keeping him in wholesome casseroles and iceberg-lettuce salads and, not to be outdone, Elaine had washed and ironed a few shirts. Most of his news revolved around the Slipper Gang. 'Brenda's mother is recovering well from her hip operation,' he told her one evening, 'which comes as no surprise as we've been praying very hard for her.'

His unshakeable belief in the power of prayer had caused Sarah, rather unworthily, to enquire after Shirley's back. 'Is it any better?' she'd asked, knowing perfectly well that it wouldn't be.

'No,' Trevor had answered blithely, 'but then Shirley's come to the conclusion that her sciatic nerve is a special gift from the Lord and that she must use it as a witness to others.'

This last comment had had Sarah quietly sniggering in bed that night as she imagined a bent-double Shirley hobbling through the streets, a placard strapped to her shoulders with the words 'The Lord heals!' As marketing campaigns went, it would not be the most convincing or direct route for establishing God's kingdom here on earth.

She smiled now as she imagined the scene.

'You've been doing a lot of that lately,' Ali remarked, taking her eyes off the motorway for a couple of seconds and flicking her gaze over Sarah.

'A lot of what?'

'Smiling.'

Sarah tutted. 'Oh, why not go straight for the subtext, Ali?'

'Do I need to?'

Ignoring her friend's question, Sarah turned away to look at the stream of traffic they were overtaking. Just as she lived her life, Ali drove at lightning speed in the outside lane and treated anyone who wasn't quick-witted enough to notice her in their rear-view mirror to a battle-cry flash of her headlamps. In contrast, Sarah lived her life meandering along in the inside lane doing her utmost to keep out of harm's way. She knew perfectly well what Ali had been getting at by saying that she had done a lot more smiling of late: it was the effect of Sanderling. As a child she had believed there was something magical in the brickwork of the large, rambling house, which charmed and captivated its many visitors. As an adult she knew better: the magic was all down to its hospitable owners – Ali's grandmother, in those far-off childhood days, and now Maggie and Lawrence. Even the beautiful but cool Phoebe had been warmed by the infectious bonhomie of Maggie and Lawrence and had lost some of her sophisticated aloofness. Alastair had actually got her into a pair of shorts and on a bike and had taken her on a tour of the island, sharing with her his old haunts: the disused railway line, which was now an official leisure trail, the sailing club, and the park with its tennis courts and pitch and putt.

The following day, Alastair and Phoebe had left Sanderling to drive to Bath so that he could meet his future in-laws, and start to plan the wedding. 'It's to be a real old medals-and-swords affair,' Alastair had told them over breakfast on their last morning, 'so, Dad, you'd better start trimming yourself down for that morning suit.'

Lawrence had grinned and said, 'Don't you worry about me. With or without the extra pounds I'll cut a fine old dash in a top hat. Isn't that right, Ali?'

'Only if we can find one big enough, Dad.'

It had been strange seeing Alastair again after all these years. Gone was the thin, gangly, rather intense youth she remembered and in his place was a tall, thickset man with a head of fair hair heavily peppered with grey. His manner was confident and relaxed, and he seemed totally at ease with himself. She wondered if he had found her much changed: she had not gained weight and had only a few strands of grey hair – which she dyed at regular intervals – but to somebody who hadn't laid eyes on her for nearly two decades did she seem an altogether different person? Had the passing of years taken a greater toll on her than she was aware of?

Chiding herself for her vanity – what did it matter what Alastair had thought of her anyway? Compared to the Phoebes of this world she was just a drab little housewife – she said to Ali, 'Thank you for inviting me to come on holiday with you. It's been wonderful.'

'Good. We'll do it again.'

It was a nice idea, but Sarah knew it wouldn't happen. Now that Ali and Elliot were reconciled, there wouldn't be room for an old friend muscling in on their precious leisure time.

'I know what's going through your mind, Sarah Donovan, but I meant what I just said.'

'Ali Anderson, keep your telepathic nose out of my thoughts.'

'I wish I could, but you're so damned easy to read. You might just as well write what you're thinking on your forehead. If I'm offering you a holiday with my parents, that's exactly what I mean, Elliot or no Elliot. Empty gestures are not my forte. Got that?'

'If you say so.'

'And while I'm having my say, what are you going to do about Trevor?' Sarah laughed at the absurdity of the question. 'What do you suggest?'

'Lots of things, all of which you wouldn't approve.'

'Oh, Ali, you just don't give up, do you?'

'I always get my way in the end, you should know that.'

'But not on this occasion.'

Ali heard the firmness in her friend's voice and chose to ignore it. She hadn't forgotten the promise she'd made when they'd been driving out of Oxford two weeks earlier, and was still committed to making Sarah see the sense of planning a new future for herself. Something told her that this might be their last opportunity in a long while to have a real heart-to-heart. 'Sarah,' she said, 'don't be angry with me, but please, just hear me out.'

Sarah took a sideways glance at her but didn't say anything.

Ali plunged in. 'Everything I'm about to say I know will have passed through your head at some stage or other, so don't accuse me of speaking rubbish. When you're with Trevor, you know as well as I do that you're only half alive. His presence literally snuffs you out. Without him I know you could do anything you wanted. So, please, why don't you throw away this partial existence and live? Think how happy you've been these past two weeks. I can't remember the last time I saw you looking so well. Or so relaxed.'

Sarah returned her eyes to the slower moving cars on her left. 'You make it sound as if it's the easiest thing in the world to throw a whole life away then start again from scratch.'

'I'm not saying it would be easy. But it is possible. It really is.'

'What of my commitment to Trevor?'

Ali pursed her lips. 'A commitment that's slowly suffocating you.'

'Don't over-dramatise it, Ali.'

'I don't think I am. And I don't think you were over-dramatising the situation in March when you said you could imagine a better life without Trevor.'

'What we want isn't necessarily what we get ... or what we deserve.'

'No!' shouted Ali, giving the steering-wheel a thump and making Sarah start, especially as they were cruising at a cool ninety-five miles an hour. 'No, no, no! I simply won't allow you to hide behind that worthless disreputable theory. We live in an age when, as women, we don't have to make do with second best. We're entitled to make better and more informed choices these days. It's our right.'

'It's exercising that right that usually leads to there being so much misery in the world.'

Ali's face darkened with exasperation. 'Why do you always have to think of other people? Couldn't you, just for once, put yourself at the top of the list and say to hell with everybody else?'

'Trevor would say that I've done exactly that by coming on holiday with you.'

'Then you should do it more often.'

When Sarah didn't respond, Ali said, 'Nothing to say?'

Suddenly Sarah smiled. 'I was letting you have the last word.'

Ali smiled too. 'You really are the most tiresome friend a girl could have. But I haven't finished with you yet. I'm going to pull off at the next service station for the loos and while we're having a cup of tea you can tell me one more time why you stay with Trevor. As you're talking, try listening to yourself and hear how crazy you sound.'

By the end of their journey, and despite everything Ali had thrown at her, Sarah knew that none of it had changed the resolve she had made during the last few days at Sanderling. Time away from Trevor had given her the space to realise that she had the strength to turn her marriage round. In the days before quick-fix divorces this was exactly what dissatisfied wives had to do. They rolled up their sleeves, straightened the antimacassars and forgave their husbands for their failings and inadequacies.

And, as she'd frequently told Ali, who was she to say that Trevor's failings and inadequacies were any greater than her own?

Revitalised by Maggie and Lawrence's high spirits and affectionate generosity, as well as feeling the benefit of long walks in warm sunshine, she felt better equipped to cope with Trevor than she ever had. There was also the rather amusing idea tucked away at the back of her mind of one day proving Ali wrong. 'There!' Sarah would say. 'We came through the tricky patch and here we are with a happy and enduring marriage. What do you think of that, then?'

They reached Smithy Cottage just as Trevor was locking the front door to go out. He had a large Bible tucked under his arm, and on his face the kind of expression that only a man intent on saving the world would dare to wear.

'Can't stop,' he said, as he hurried to his car. 'Brenda's mother's hip has taken a turn for the worse.'

Off he went without so much as a welcome-home kiss for Sarah or a patronising comment for Ali.

Ali was stunned by his behaviour. But she was more appalled by the look on Sarah's face. She could see in her friend's dejected expression that, in one fell swoop, the happy afterglow of their holiday had been doused.

That's it, thought Ali. That's absolutely it. Nobody hurts my friend and gets away with it.

Trevor bloody Donovan, you insensitive, pig-ignorant fool, you're in for the shock of your life.

41

Ali was met by a loud wolf-whistle from Daniel when she arrived at work the following morning.

'Take a look at you, Babe,' he said, getting up from his desk and coming to greet her. 'I bet you're sun-kissed in places I don't even know exist. You look fabulous.'

Smiling, she put down her briefcase and gave him a hug.

'Mm . . .' he said, breathing in deeply. 'Is that the smell of an old sea-dog, or is it the whiff of a woman in love?'

She laughed, pushed him away, then handed him a package. 'I saw this and immediately thought of you,' she said.

He tore off the paper and held up a china mug that had on it a rear-view shot of a broad-shouldered, tiny-waisted man wearing only a pair of boxer shorts.

'When you pour boiling water into the cup he loses his pants and shows his bum.'

Daniel laughed. 'The cheeky boy. As tacky seaside novelties go, it's perfectly hideous. I love it. And to be sure you weren't conned, I'll make us a drink right now. While the kettle boils you can tell me what it's like to be in touch with your joy button again.'

After spending time away from the office, Ali never found it a problem to get back into the swing of work, but that morning she was unusually distracted and making slow progress on the correspondence Margaret and Daniel had laid on her desk for her return. It wasn't just that Daniel kept bombarding her with questions about her and Elliot, or that she was thinking of Elliot now on his way to New York: she felt as if she was standing on the edge of a precipice.

After she had driven Elliot to the airport at the crack of dawn, she had gone home, sat on the balcony with a cup of tea, listened to the lively chorus of birds, and experienced the remarkable sensation that everything was right with the world.

In particular, her own world. She was filled with a marvellous sense of well-being. It didn't seem possible that the fragments of her life could have been pieced together again, and to such great effect. It had made her think of the occasion at Sanderling when she had accidentally broken one of the Wedgwood vases. Grandma Hayling had carefully picked up the pieces and said, 'Not to worry, a properly mended vase is often stronger than its flawless counterpart.' It was only now that Ali understood what the old lady had meant: her splintered heart had been reassembled and indeed she felt stronger. In fact, she felt invincible, as if there wasn't anything she couldn't do or overcome.

It was then that her thoughts turned to Sarah.

Or, more accurately, to Trevor.

If she had to believe in any kind of mystical mumbo-jumbo she would plump for voodooism. In her current mood, she'd gladly fashion a nice little wax effigy of Trevor and systematically torture him for all the miserable years he'd inflicted on Sarah.

The unthinking brutality of the man when he didn't notice Sarah's hurt yesterday afternoon had incensed Ali to the extent that she'd vowed silently to put an end to the mockery of her friend's marriage.

It wasn't fair that Sarah should have to live that way.

It wasn't right that Sarah believed in a set of unsound rules that precluded her from living the life to which she was entitled.

It was so, *so* wrong that Sarah had shipwrecked herself on the rocks of her faith.

With this in mind, Ali had decided it was time for action. If Sarah's freedom hung on a technicality of faith, as she had admitted to Ali back in March, Ali would provide the means to liberate her. She would lure Trevor into bed with her, then tell Sarah what she'd done.

Except that appearances were going to be highly and convincingly deceptive. If she could pull it off, it would be the illusion of all illusions.

It was while she had been driving into work, chugging slowly behind a heavily laden brewery wagon that she had hit upon the perfect plan: a plan that was so beautifully simple yet such a masterstroke of cunning she didn't know why she hadn't thought of it before. What's more she wouldn't have to endure anything more sexually explicit than the removal of Trevor's clothes. All she had to do was get him so drunk that when he regained consciousness the following morning he'd believe any story she cared to feed him. If he was convinced he'd just experienced a night of passion, then Sarah wouldn't doubt it. And that was the crux of the whole plan. Sarah had to believe that Trevor had done the dirty on her. It didn't matter how or why, just that he had.

It was the sight of all those metal beer barrels on the wagon in front of her that had given her the idea. Initially she had thought that she would have to be the one who got drunk to go through with the plan, but then a thunderbolt of pure logic told her otherwise. If Trevor was out of it, then there would be no need for her to do what, in all honesty, she knew was beyond her. She was no coward but she had her squeamish no-go areas – and sex with a man she so thoroughly despised was at the top of the list.

Even with her track record of impetuous rushing in where angels feared to tread, Ali knew that what she intended to do was daring and shocking. But she so badly wanted Sarah to be happy that she was prepared to be as devious and audacious as it took. She knew, though, with unerring confidence, that once Sarah had recovered from her amazement at what Ali had done for her, she would be relieved and able to look to the future with an enthusiasm she probably hadn't felt in years.

Meanwhile Ali's number-one priority was to do the deed while Elliot was out of the country, which gave her only the next eight days.

It was not long.

It meant that the route to Trevor's supposed seduction was going to have to be simple and direct: it would be via his innate sense of misguided superiority and would appeal to what she'd always called his saviour complex. She would trick him into believing that she was offering herself up for conversion. She could just imagine the evangelical zeal with which he would treat her. He would be so blinded by his own self-importance at saving her and bringing her to Christ – 'Hey, Lord, I've caught you a big one' – that he wouldn't realise what was happening.

It was after lunch that Ali made her opening move. She waited for Daniel to leave the office for a meeting with one of his clients and, having sent Margaret on a spurious errand, she called Smithy Cottage. She was counting on Sarah being out at the shops or catching up on the weeds in the garden, and that Trevor would answer the phone. She was in luck. Hearing Trevor's pompous voice she clamped down her usual reaction of wanting to take him by the throat; instead she asked how he was and then enquired after Brenda's hip.

'It wasn't Brenda's hip, it was her mother's,' he corrected her, 'and she's gone back into hospital.'

'Oh, how awful.'

'Not if it's the best place for her.'

'You're so right, and of course, it could be . . .'

'Could be what?'

Come on! Don't bottle out now! Just start spouting the rubbish he does. 'I was going to say that it could be the will of God.'

Her words must have made him suspect that she was about to make one of her usual off-the-cuff asides, for he said standoffishly, 'I'll tell Sarah you called.'

Quick, you're losing him. Be nice to him. Keep him talking. 'Actually, Trevor, it was you I wanted to talk to.'

'Me?'

Well, who else is there in this conversation, you idiot? 'Yes. Um . . . I don't know how to put this but – and I'd rather you didn't mention this to Sarah – but . . . Well, it's just that in the past few days I've been thinking a lot about some of the conversations we've had over the years.'

'Which conversations would they be, Ali?' His tone was stalagmite hard with suspicion.

She gripped the receiver in her hot, sweating hand, clenched the other on her lap, and curled her toes over till her feet were arching painfully in her shoes. 'It's this whole business of God, Trevor,' she said. 'I've begun to think that there might be something in it, after all.'

There was a pause and then an oleaginous laugh trickled down the line. 'Well, well, well, Ali, I knew it would happen one day. You've finally stopped being cynical long enough to feel the Lord tapping you on the shoulder. Congratulations!'

His unctuous, patronising manner had her wanting to work methodically through the alphabet and hurl every known obscenity at him. Arrogant Arsehole would be first, followed by Banal Bastard. But with strained politeness, and a little stomach-churning meekness and humility thrown in, she said, 'I was wondering, Trevor, and I know that we've not always seen eye to eye, but I was hoping that you might be able to help me make the next step.'

'Ali, the next step is vital and I'd be failing in my duty as a mature, experienced Christian if I didn't offer you the benefit of my relationship with the Lord. Why don't you join us here on Friday when we have our next discipleship meeting?'

'*No!*' she blurted out. 'I mean, that's a nice idea, but I'm not ready yet to join in with a group.'

'I quite understand. Then the ideal solution is for you to come and talk things over one evening with Sarah and me.'

'I'd rather it was just the two of us. Call me a silly, sentimental girl' – *don't you dare!* – 'but I thought I'd surprise Sarah with a *fait accompli*. You know how she's always been so tolerant of my views on religion, well, I feel that I'd like to make amends for some of the things I've said in the past and present myself, with your help, with a clean slate, so to speak.'

'The only person who can clean your slate, Ali, is the Lord, not me.'

Oh, do us both a favour, Trevor, and save the sales pitch for your precious Slipper Gang. 'But you can show me where God puts the Brillo pad and the Mr Muscle, can't you?'

'Indeed I can.'

'So when can you come over to see me?'

'You want me to come to *you*?'

Well, of course I do, you stupid moron. 'Yes, if that's possible.'

'When were you thinking of?'

'This evening?'

'That's a bit short notice, Ali. I have various commitments and you don't exactly live next door.'

'Oh, please.'

A weighty pause followed. 'All right, then.' He capitulated. 'I suppose I'd never forgive myself if I said no and the Devil slipped in and claimed you back.'

The man is completely barking she thought when, minutes later, she put down the phone.

Madness was something Ali accused herself of several times throughout the rest of the day, right up until that evening when she heard a car approaching the mill. It was dusk and she noticed that only one of the Ford Sierra's headlamps was working. She let out a groan of heartfelt torment at the prospect of spending an evening alone with Trevor. Not only was she going to have to survive a one-to-one with him, but she was going to have to be nice and put him at his ease so that he would be relaxed and comfortable with her. She was almost tempted to back out now. But no. She was committed one hundred per cent to saving Sarah from throwing away the rest of her life. Nothing would stop her now.

Not even the thought that had occurred to her in the car on the way home from work; a thought that had made her break into a sweat. What if the unthinkable happened and she had to explain the situation to Elliot?

Her hope – and it was a solid, unequivocal hope – was that Elliot would never find out what she'd done or, more to the point, what it would appear that she had done. It was a dangerous game of double-bluff she was playing but logic dictated that the episode would become a secret that would be safely contained within the consciences of the three parties involved. She couldn't conceive of Trevor wanting his sin of sins to be made general knowledge; he, of all people, would want it kept firmly under wraps. And, of course, Sarah wouldn't breathe a word of it – she would have no cause to anyway.

But if the worst came to the worst and Elliot discovered that she'd apparently gone to bed with Trevor – a lie she would need to keep up for Sarah's sake – she would have to make him see that her actions had been justified. More importantly, she would have to convince him that she hadn't betrayed his love.

When Elliot had arrived at the mill last night and after she'd taken him upstairs to bed, he'd held her in his arms and said that he'd always love her.

'But what if I did something dreadful?' she'd asked guiltily, her face turned away from him as they lay in the dark.

He'd stroked her bare shoulder and said, 'Such as?'

'Oh, I don't know. What if I robbed a bank?'

'I'd still love you.'

'What if I defrauded all my clients of their hard-earned money?'

'I'd still love you.'

'And if I had an affair?'

'Anyone in mind?'

'Um ... how about Trevor?'

He'd raised her face to his, kissed her on the mouth and said, 'I'd know you'd gone clean round the bend and have you certified.'

'But would you still love me?'

'I imagine I would.'

'No matter what?'

'I wouldn't be able to help myself.'

Oh, Elliot, she thought, with a heavy heart, as she heard Trevor hammering on the door downstairs, please don't go back on your word. What I'm about to do has nothing to do with you and me ... You must believe that.

42

Trevor seemed to have brought an extraordinary amount of stuff with him – two Bibles, several A4 notebooks, a bundle of pamphlets and a clutch of biros, one of which he dropped.

'How about a drink?' Ali asked, once she'd shown him up to the sitting room and he'd cast his eyes over his surroundings, commenting on the whimsy of such an unusual home.

'No, thanks, I had a cup of coffee before I came out.'

'I was thinking of something a little stronger, just to kick things off.'

He dismissed this with a further shake of his head, then parked his sawdusty bottom on the sofa and arranged his collection of soul-saving equipment on the low table in front of him. 'I think it would be appropriate if we began with a prayer,' he said, in a distinctly prudish voice, when he'd finished making himself at home.

Putting the fortifying thought of a large whisky on hold and realising that getting Trevor drunk wasn't going to be as easy as she'd thought, Ali moved towards the armchair furthest from him. Then she remembered that she was supposed to be acting the part of repentant simpleton with a bit of fawning coquette thrown in, and sat uneasily on the sofa next to him.

This is by far the scariest moment of my life, she thought, as beside her, and smelling vaguely of wood and linseed oil, Trevor grabbed one of her hands, closed his eyes and began to pray. 'O Father,' he intoned, his voice sepulchral, 'I bring before you Ali, who has for so long hidden her shame in the darkness but whose eyes are now being opened to your shining light. I humbly pray, Lord, that through my guidance she will very soon be kneeling in your awesome grace. Amen.'

There we have it, thought Ali, slipping her hand out of Trevor's hot, damp grasp – *through* **my** *guidance*.

None of this God malarkey had anything to do with serving a higher divine being. It was, as she'd always suspected, nothing but a prop on which Trevor could hang his overstretched ego. How many lost souls did he need to believe he was responsible for saving? And what a monumental kick he must get out of it. No wonder he wasn't interested in having sex with Sarah – he was too busy getting off on the potent combination of self-aggrandisement and narcissistic ambition.

'Now then,' he said, leaning forward and fixing her with what she supposed was an I'm-here-to-help-you stare, 'first things first. We need to discuss eternal life, redemption and the remission of sin. How are you doing on confessing your sins, Ali?'

Hah! Never mind mine, what about yours! 'How do you mean?'

He smiled one of his overly smily smiles that made his eyes disappear into their crinkly crevices, which in turn caused a loose bit of something to come away from his straggly beard. She watched whatever it was drift down on to the rug between his battered Hush Puppies. 'To be saved, Ali,' he said, bringing her attention back to his face, 'you have to open your heart to the Lord. You have to jettison the clutter that you've hoarded and lived your life by and make room for the Holy Spirit to move in and do His work.'

She did her best to appear interested in what he was saying, but her mind was elsewhere – out in the kitchen pouring itself a huge shot of life-saving sanity. 'Um ... this saved business,' she said, 'I'm not sure I really understand it. Perhaps you could explain it to me over a drink?' And before he could say anything to stop her, she leaped up from the sofa and disappeared to the kitchen where she unscrewed the top of the Jack Daniel's bottle and sloshed the dark amber liquid into two large glasses before raising one to her lips and taking a swig. Instantly she felt strengthened by the warm, glowing effect it had on her as it hit the back of her throat. Joining Trevor in the sitting room, she handed him his drink and forced herself to perch girlishly on the arm of the sofa next to him. 'Cheers,' she said.

He looked hard at the cut-glass tumbler, turned it round in his bony hands, and sniffed it. 'I don't normally drink spirits,' he said, 'I'm more of a *vin de* plonk man.' He gave a little chuckle as though he'd just said something terribly amusing. Any other time Ali would have treated him to a look of disdain, but knowing that if she were to get Trevor into a more relaxed state – and therefore oblivious to how much booze he was knocking back – she had to start serenading him with songs of saccharine-sweetness. She mustered an indulgent smile and laughed too. 'You know, you can be very entertaining when you want to be,' she said. 'A *vin de* plonk man, indeed.'

He took a tiny, cautious sip of his drink and, for an unnerving moment, fastened his beady gaze on her. 'I don't think you've always held that opinion of me, have you, Ali?'

It was the most astute comment she'd ever heard him utter, and sliding down on to the sofa she said, in a low, humble, slightly tremulous voice, 'I'm seeing everything and everyone in a different light these days – and I've come to realise I've misjudged you in the past.' *Oh, yuk! Any minute and she'd be giggling and fluttering her eyelashes.*

'That's what happens when you come to know the Lord.'

'I think you must be right, Trevor.'

'I know I am. I know what it is to be blessed by the Spirit.'

'But have you never doubted—?'

He shook his head adamantly and tugged at his beard.

Ali averted her eyes from the shower of dead skin that would surely cascade on to the rug and the polished floor. 'Not even a speck of – I mean an ounce of doubt?' She wondered if he'd notice her running the vacuum over him.

'No. Since the age of sixteen I've always known that I was saved and that God had designated a truly special task for me to perform.'

'Really? And what would that be?' *It wouldn't by any chance have anything to do with annoying the hell out of other people?*

'Like Billy Graham, I've always believed that I was called to bring people to Christ.'

'I thought that it was Christ Himself who knocked on the spiritual door, as it were.'

'Yes, but it's the foot-soldiers here on earth who help that person to open the door.'

'Oh, I get you. So you could say that our lively exchange of banter over the years has been you rattling the doorknob waiting for me to turn it?' *And there was me thinking you were just being a sanctimonious pain in the butt.*

He smiled. 'Exactly. Didn't I tell you last Christmas that I'd always seen you as my greatest challenge? I hoped I'd get you in the end.'

'Gosh, Trevor, you must be so pleased with yourself.'

He misread the sarcasm in her voice, put down his barely touched glass and said, 'Just doing my job. Though I don't mind admitting to you now, Ali, that there was a time, just recently, when I suspected your heart was hardened beyond even my power to bring you to the Lord. But to work! I thought we could go through some of the passages in the New Testament that I think are of paramount importance, cross-referencing them with Old Testament quotes and going over anything you're not sure of. When I've gone, I want you to read through my notes carefully then answer the questions I've prepared for you. I'm going to keep a close eye on you, Ali, and return on Friday evening so that I can check your answers, but more importantly to make sure that our old enemy the Devil hasn't slipped in while my back was turned.'

Holy Moses, homework!

He saw the look on her face. 'Studying scripture is the backbone of our faith, Ali. Without it we're rootless, broken reeds swaying in the breeze, noiseless—'

'Yes, I'm getting the picture.' She was also getting the picture that she wasn't going to get anywhere with Trevor tonight: he was too fired up with the crazy zeal of a man intent on pursuing his own agenda. But Friday night would be different. She was sure of it. Confident, because she'd just come up with Plan B.

The week passed slowly. Each day seemed an eternity. She could hardly sleep and when she did she had nightmares of Trevor's hairy face leering at her in the most unlikely situations: when she was with a client in the office; when she was in the bath; and, scariest and most vivid, when she was lying in bed. The verisimilitude of the dreams had her waking in a hot sweat. Once she had to get out of bed and search the room to convince herself that she really was alone.

He arrived exactly on time and appeared to be revelling in their newly defined roles – he the wise teacher, she the simple child supposedly hanging on his every sagacious word. She noticed after he'd made himself at home on the sofa and set out his books and pens as before that he must have gone to some considerable effort to spruce himself up. The rumpled checked shirt of Monday night had been replaced with a freshly laundered blue and white one, and his dusty, patched old jeans exchanged for a pair of clean brown corduroys. He'd also washed his hair and trimmed his whiskers, and in place of the nose-curling smell of sawdust and linseed oil was a suspiciously strong aroma of eau-de-Cologne. It wasn't at all the sackcloth-and-ashes image she was used to. Well, well, well, she thought, picturing the ascetic Trevor back at Smithy Cottage tarting himself up for his evening with her, 'vanity of vanities; all is vanity'.

'You're looking extremely smart this evening, Trevor,' she said, unable to resist the temptation of seeing how he would respond to her flattery. 'Nice shirt. Suits you.'

Bingo! The hairless bits of his face flushed an incriminating crimson. But then, and with alarm, Ali remembered Elliot's theory that she and Trevor had never got on because subconsciously Trevor was threatened by her strong sexuality. Now – supposing Elliot was right, and let's face it, he usually was – where the hell did that leave her? Playing catch with live dynamite suddenly seemed a safer bet than schmoozing a sexually repressed Trevor.

Shunting this dangerous thought into the sidings of her brain where it could be dealt with at a later stage, she offered him a drink. 'I've got you a nice bottle of red *vin de* plonk. Is that okay?'

'Some red wine would be most agreeable. Thank you.'

She went out to the kitchen, picked up the bottle she'd already opened and poured Trevor a large glass. She then poured herself a tumbler of Jack Daniel's.

'How did you get on with those questions I gave you?' he asked, when she joined him on the sofa and handed him his glass from the tray she'd just settled on the table. 'I kept them as simple and straightforward as I could.'

She feigned a pathetic little shrug of her shoulders, a gesture that she hoped would appeal to his need to feel superior. 'Well, I did my best, Trevor,' she simpered, 'but no doubt you'll be able to put me right with anything I didn't understand.' She passed him the notepad on which she'd written her answers. He read aloud from it. '"Question: After reading Romans 7:15–25 what do you think St Paul was getting at in terms of the law of sin and death?

'"Answer: We want to do good but can't. We know what is right and what is wrong, but can't stop ourselves from doing wrong. Given the choice between right and wrong, we inevitably do what is wrong. We need help. That help comes in the form of Christ."'

Trevor lowered the notepad and stared at Ali. 'That's very good,' he said, 'very spiritually sound. I'm impressed. You were really listening to me the other night.'

'It must be your excellent teaching,' she said, keeping to herself that after he had left her on Monday night she'd logged on to the Internet and got talking to a theology student in a chat room.

'I must say it makes a change to have such a keen student, to have somebody on the same wavelength. Between you and me, one or two members of the Disciples just haven't grasped the hallowed nettle. I spend most of my time covering the same things over and over again.' He sighed. 'I just have to keep reminding myself that we're not all on the same intellectual footing.'

She clicked her tongue in sympathy and topped up his wine. 'That must be very frustrating for you,' she said soothingly.

'It is. And Sarah doesn't help. To be honest, I don't think much of her faith. It's not solid, not at all sound. It's affecting her judgement and the way she treats Hannah.'

Ali stiffened. She wasn't prepared to listen to a single word of criticism against her friend. 'Shall we move on to the second question you set me?' she said.

He smiled approvingly. 'Such eagerness, Ali, it does you credit.'

He checked through the rest of her work, and each time he flicked through his Bible searching for a relevant passage to emphasise his point, Ali surreptitiously refilled his glass. In a state of nervous anxiety, she watched him closely, which he naturally took to be attentiveness.

An interminable hour of Bible-bashing passed but, apart from the odd yawn, Trevor wasn't showing any real sign of succumbing. With a bitter sense of disappointment creeping over her, Ali began to lose confidence in Plan B. But then, suddenly, he swayed to his feet and excused himself to go to the bathroom. She gave him directions and waited anxiously for him to return.

And waited.

After fifteen minutes had passed and there was still no sign of him, she went to investigate. She discovered him lying on the floor, gazing glassy-eyed up at the ceiling. And, Hallelujah, praise the Lord with bells on, he was a multiplicity of sheets to the wind. He looked as happy as a pig in mud. Noticing that he was no longer alone, he grinned inanely at her as she stood over him. 'Ali,' he giggled, 'I can't move.'

She got down to his level and knelt on the floor. This wasn't quite the effect she had been expecting. But it would do. 'Are you okay, Trevor?'

He giggled again, then yawned hugely. 'I'm fine. I've never felt better. I think I'm experiencing something called the Toronto Blessing. I'll explain it to you one day.'

'The Toronto what?'

'It's the work of the Holy Spirit. I'm full of it, Ali, and I'm rejoicing in all its glory. It's what I've been waiting for.'

You're full of something, Trevor, but it ain't holy, that's for sure. 'Do you think you can stand?'

He laughed. 'No, the Lord has put me here on the floor and here I shall stay. Ooh, Ali, when I close my eyes I feel as if I'm flying. Are you sure you can't feel it too?'

'Sorry, but no. You don't think that God might want you nice and comfortable in bed?'

He shook his head from side to side like a small child refusing a dose of nasty medicine, but then very quickly he changed his mind. 'Oh,' he groaned, clutching his forehead, 'I'm feeling a bit dizzy now. Perhaps you're right.'

She hauled him to his feet and, staggering under the weight of him as he leaned against her, she shuffled him through to her bedroom. She pushed him backwards on to the bed and hoped that her punishment for what she'd done, and was going to do, wouldn't be him vomiting all over her duvet.

'Lali,' he said, not noticing that his speech was deteriorating, or that she was slipping off his shoes and tossing them over her shoulder, 'schpeaking as your new-found bluther in Chris', I want to shtell you something. You may blot realise this, but hive always schbeen scared of you. You're sdifferent to other women.'

Too right I am, thought Ali, yanking off his socks and throwing them after his shoes. I'm not one of your sycophantic groupies who's had her brain removed.

'Lali,' he went on, yawning again, 'do you know why you're sdifferent?'

'Surprise me.'

'You've bot galls.'

She laughed out loud.

'Have I schlocked you?'

But before she could answer him, he yawned once more, closed his eyes and fell into the deepest sleep of his life.

Unhindered by his babbling, Ali carried on undressing him. When she finished she went downstairs and phoned Sarah.

'Hello, Ali,' said Sarah. 'I thought perhaps it might be Trevor ringing. He went out several hours ago after acting quite mysteriously. I've no idea where he was going, he—'

'He's here with me,' Ali interrupted.

'With you at the mill?'

'It's a long story but he's stopping the night. He's had some kind of weird experience.'

'Ali, are you winding me up?'

'For once, no, I'm not. Sarah, have you heard of something called the Tornado Blessing?'

'Do you mean the Toronto Blessing?'

'Yes, that's the fella.'

'But what's that got to do with—?'

'It's gripped Trevor by the spirituals and he's crashed out on my bed.'

'Oh, good Lord, Ali, what's he been up to now? Do you want me to come over? I could get a taxi.'

'No. Leave it to me, I'll take good care of him. Come the morning, everything will be all right. Trust me.'

These glibly spoken words stayed with Ali as she climbed the narrow staircase. As she surveyed her bedroom and the comatose, snoring Trevor, the first seeds of doubt began to germinate.

What if her plan went wrong?

43

If there was going to be any credence to the story, Ali knew that when Trevor woke up she had to be by his side in bed. To achieve this, and as appalling as it was to her, she had made herself pass the night balancing on the edge of the mattress as far away from him as she could manage.

But she hadn't slept.

Through the dark, lonely hours as she'd lain awake listening to Trevor while he snorted and muttered, she had watched the luminous hands of the clock on the bedside table move slowly but inexorably towards dawn. It was now a quarter to seven and, through the gap in the curtains that she'd drawn so hastily last night, she could see that it was a bright, sunny day.

It was a brightness that was disquietingly at odds with how she felt.

An apocalyptic, eerie, shadowy darkness covering the land would have been more appropriate. It would match the inauspicious, bleak chill that was clutching at her heart.

She looked again at the clock. Thirteen minutes to seven. Would Trevor never stir? Would he never open his eyes to what she had in store for him?

Unable to lie there a minute longer, she feigned her own awakening: yawning, stretching and gently nudging him with her elbow.

But still he didn't wake.

She pushed her pillow towards him, then decided her only real course of action was a sharp, well-deserved kick.

He responded instantly, snorting himself out of his heavy torpor and turning over. His eyes cracked open and slowly focused on her face, just a few inches away from his. Suddenly, and as dramatically as a rocket being fired, he launched himself into a sitting position. Then, realising that his chest was bare, he looked under the duvet and found that the rest of him was naked too. His mouth dropped open, his eyes popped and he made a grab for the duvet. He pulled it chastely right up to his chin.

His eyes swivelling round the room, he tried to speak, but the only sound that came out was a stammering, 'Wh-wh-what's going on?'

Ali had had all night to consider what her first response would be when Trevor asked this question. 'Hey, big boy, you need me to tell you?' had originally struck her as comically appropriate, but as the clock had softly ticked away the darkness, she had grown subdued. Now she was rendered speechless. All she could do was look abashed and lower her eyes.

It prompted him to peer under the bedclothes again, as if he hoped to find something lurking at the bottom of the bed to allay his fears. He finally returned his horror-stricken face to hers and said, 'What happened, Ali?'

It was time to speak. It was time to lift the curtain on her performance. 'Don't you remember?' she said softly. Demurely. Eyes lowered.

He screwed up his eyes, ran his hands through his hair, then tugged at his beard. In a final gesture of confused frustration he shook his head. From the pained expression on his face, this had clearly been a mistake. 'Ali,' he groaned, 'we didn't, did we? Tell me we didn't.'

Again she lowered her eyes – she felt like one of those classic Hollywood movie actresses who did all their acting with their eyelashes while puffing curls of smoke into the air. 'It was the wine and whisky, Trevor,' she said. 'We both drank too much. I'm not proud of what I've done.' Realising that she was actually speaking the truth, she slipped out of bed and draped her dressing-gown over her shoulders, which were already covered with an old T-shirt that doubled as a nightdress in the winter. 'I don't know how I'm ever going to face Sarah again.' She forced a little wobble to her voice and added, 'She's my best friend and this is how I treat her.' She looked back at Trevor and saw that his face was bone white, his eyes wide and horrified.

'Oh, my God, Ali, you're not trying to tell me that we—' His voice broke off.

She looked straight at him and nodded. 'Yes, Trevor, that's exactly what I am saying.'

His eyes followed her as she went and stood at the end of the bed. 'But we can't have,' he muttered. 'I would have remembered. I would remember something like that.'

'You did knock back a hell of a lot of booze.'

'But, Ali, I don't get drunk. I'm not that sort of a man. In fact, I've never been drunk. Not ever.' His tone had taken on a more pleading and reasoned edge and, frightened that he might piece together the correct sequence of events, Ali knew it was imperative that she kept the upper hand.

'Well, you did last night,' she said waspishly. 'Now, tell me, does your head ache? Do you feel sluggish? Does your mouth feel as if it's been dried out with a blowtorch then scarified with a garden rake? And does everything feel a strange blur?'

'Yes,' he admitted, with a small, pitiful nod.

'Congratulations. You're suffering from your first hangover. And to fill in the blanks for you, I'll tell you what happened. I found you smashed out of your brains on the bathroom floor, wittering on about something called the Toronto Blessing.' She could see that she'd fed him the right line. Recall was slowly dawning on his face.

'I remember being in the sitting room,' he said, in a vague, distant voice, 'and then I went upstairs to the toilet.'

'That's right,' she said, 'and I came to look for you.'

'Why?'

'Because you'd been gone so long.'

'But why? Why was I gone so long?' He sounded like a small child pestering his mother.

'Because you were drunk, Trevor,' she said firmly.

'But I don't remember drinking enough to make me drunk.'

She was losing her patience. It was so bloody typical of the man to lose sight of the big picture and nitpick over the tiniest details. 'I'll show you the empty bottles if you want,' she snapped. Steering him back to the point of it all, she went on, 'When I found you, you were babbling on about feeling so fantastic that you could fly and then you said that I was wonderful and that as my brother in Christ you wanted to make love to me and that it would all be okay because it was what the Holy Spirit wanted. While you lay on the bed you told me how you thought I was different from other women. Afterwards you passed out, which is probably why you don't remember anything.'

He'd been listening open-mouthed to her carefully worded reconstruction of what had happened, no doubt recognising enough bits to make him accept the rest, and now he hung his head.

Overcome with shame, Ali gathered up her clothes – which she'd strewn over the floor for that authentic air of frantic undressing for sex – and left Trevor to his misery.

She couldn't face the thought of breakfast and didn't offer any to Trevor when, at length, he appeared in the kitchen. He was fully dressed now but was as awkward and self-conscious as if he were still naked. Clearing his throat several times, he said, 'Ali, we don't have to tell Sarah, do we? I mean ... we could just ...' but he didn't get any further.

Ali looked straight at him. 'Yes, we do, Trevor,' she said grimly. 'I couldn't ever lie to Sarah.' Hell, she hadn't gone to all this trouble only to have him sweep it under the rug of his conscience. He swallowed nervously and she could see the direction in which his cowardly thoughts were tunnelling: say nothing and nobody gets hurt, especially Trevor. She was incensed by his hypocritical cowardice. 'Surely the Christian response to what we've done is to confess and repent,' she said, hitting him smack on the head of his religious doctrine, while taking pleasure in the knowledge that, when pious push came to sinful shove, Trevor was as committed to his religion as she was.

'But you don't understand the consequences,' he bleated.

Oh, believe me, I do. 'Trevor, if you don't tell her the truth it will haunt you for the rest of your days. Besides, even if you don't feel the need to confess your sins, *I do.*'

This startled him sufficiently to set him pacing the kitchen; the soles of his Hush Puppies filled the silence as they squeaked loudly on the wooden floor. He suddenly turned on her. 'But do you think she would forgive me?'

'Only Sarah knows the answer to that.'

He considered this for a few seconds. 'I suppose it would be her duty, wouldn't it?' he said reflectively. 'As my wife, it would be her Christian duty to forgive me.'

Given what Trevor had done – or what he thought he had done – Ali was outraged that he could talk about Sarah owing him duty. 'Sarah is one of the most forgiving people I know,' she said, 'I'm sure that she'll give you all the redemption you need.' Yeah, and a clean-break divorce.

He nodded decisively. 'You're right,' he said, and as he ran his hand over his beard, Ali was further appalled to see what she could only describe as a tidal wave of relief wash over him. My God, she thought. He really thinks that he can be let off the hook as easily as that. She was about to bring him back down to planet Earth with a crashing bump when he said, 'It's most important that we work this out between the three of us, Ali. The fewer people who know about this, the better. At all costs, I don't want the Disciples to get wind of it. The damage this would do to the group is incalculable. I am their leader, after all.'

Ali was stunned. His marriage was on the line and here he was blatantly more concerned with his standing in the Slipper Gang! Any niggling doubts about her manipulation of him were gone. He deserved everything, and more, that would shortly be coming his way.

They drove the forty-five-minute journey to Astley Hope, Ali following impatiently behind Trevor having insisted that they make a joint confession to Sarah; she wanted to be sure that Trevor owned up exactly to what he thought they'd done.

Driving along the quiet, early-morning sun-filled country lanes, Ali began to think about Sarah and how she would react to the revelation that was about to be sprung on her. Stupefied amazement would come first, perhaps, followed swiftly by understanding and an acknowledgement at what Ali had given her: her freedom. Thank goodness Ali didn't have to worry about Sarah being hurt by Trevor's apparent betrayal, though, of course, Sarah being Sarah she might feel inclined to spare his feelings by playing the aggrieved wife – How could you do this to me? – while secretly relishing the thought of hotfooting it to the nearest solicitor.

On reaching Smithy Cottage, Ali parked her car alongside Trevor's and followed him inside. She had agreed with him that she would stay in the background and let him do most of the talking, but she was determined that if he chose to be selective with his confession, she would jump in smartly and make sure that Sarah was fully aware of the facts – that it wasn't a bit of sofa grappling that he was owning up to but a full-blown case of commandment-breaking adultery.

Sarah greeted them anxiously. She looked first at Ali, then at Trevor's pallid face. 'Are you all right?' she asked him.

He nodded dumbly and went through to the sitting room. Sarah and Ali followed. 'You look as if you could do with a drink,' Sarah said. 'In fact, you both do. What's wrong, Ali?'

Ali saw Trevor's involuntary shudder at the mention of the word 'drink' and said, 'Sarah, I think you'd better sit down. Trevor's got something to tell you.'

Sarah remained where she was but Trevor flopped into the nearest armchair. He rubbed the palms of his hands together then pushed them the length of his corduroy-covered thighs. He let out his breath and, without glancing either at Sarah or Ali, he began his confession. It didn't take long and when he'd finished he raised tormented eyes to Sarah and waited for her to speak.

Ali waited too. The chill that had clutched at her heart earlier that morning returned. This was it, then, she thought, with sickening dread. They were on the brink of a defining moment. From here on, it was all down to Sarah.

Sarah went over to Trevor. She touched his shoulder and, without a trace of bitterness in her voice, said, 'I'd be grateful if you would leave us alone, Trevor. I need to talk to Ali.'

He got clumsily to his feet. 'Are you throwing me out?'

She closed her eyes for a couple of seconds as though overcome with tiredness. 'Just go, Trevor. Come back later. Much later.'

'You will be here when I get back, won't you? You're not leaving me?'

'Trevor, for once in your life will you please just do as I ask?'

He left the room and quietly shut the front door after him. His car wasn't so sensitive to the moment, though, and the engine backfired irreverently as he reversed down the drive and drove off in a cloud of smoke.

Alone now with Sarah, and aware of a terrible silence between them, Ali's heart slipped into another gear and began to beat faster. Always the one with the smartarse response, the one who could outwit any opponent, the one who could sidestep with all the speed and agility of a featherweight boxer, she now felt extraordinarily feeble-minded. It seemed an age before Sarah spoke. When she did, she said, 'Ali, would you care to explain what you've done?'

Ali swallowed nervously. 'I think you know exactly what I've done.'

'But I want you to explain it to me.' Sarah's words resonated in the stillness of the room with chilling restraint.

Ali tried to meet her friend's gaze but found she couldn't. It had all seemed so reasonable in her head when she'd plotted and schemed to rescue Sarah. Even in the car a few moments ago it had seemed perfectly plausible and acceptable, but now . . . but now, hearing the coldness in Sarah's voice, she wasn't so sure. She went over to the open window and stared out at the beautiful garden her friend had brought to life, every inch of it cared for and loved. 'I did it for you,' she said softly.

'At least have the courage to look at me.'

Ali turned.

'Tell me exactly what you did, Ali. Spell it out for me. And, to quote you from only the other day, "Perhaps you'd take the trouble to listen to yourself and hear how crazy you sound."'

'That's not fair.'

'And it's fair what you've done?'

'Yes,' said Ali defiantly, her voice rising. 'Trevor's treated you abominably all your marriage. He worships a God made in his own self-deluded image and has gone around acting like one, keeping you under his thumb like some subjugated acolyte.'

The colour rushed to Sarah's face and her icy calm now gave way to an altogether different emotion: raw anger. 'How dare you accuse Trevor of acting like God,' she threw at Ali, 'when that's exactly what you've done?'

'I have not!'

'Oh, yes, you have. You've played God with my marriage, and that's unforgivable!' To Ali's horror, tears ran down Sarah's flushed cheeks.

'You've no idea what you've done!' she wailed. 'Why, oh, why, did you have to interfere?'

'But I don't understand,' Ali said, genuinely baffled. 'You told me . . . you said that if Trevor had an affair it would leave you free to leave him.'

'But I never said I *would* leave him,' shouted Sarah.

'Why not? Why not leave the stupid man? You don't love him. Or are you going to deny you ever said that?'

'Shut up! Shut up!'

'No, I won't. I've gone to a lot of trouble to provide you with the means to end your marriage with your Christian ethics still intact, so you can bloody well give me a damn good reason why you can't do it.'

'Okay, then.' Sarah rounded on Ali, her eyes flashing white-hot rage, her hands tightly balled at her sides. 'How's this for a reason? It's guilt that's kept me in this marriage and it's guilt that will keep me in it.'

'Guilt? You, the paragon of selfless love and honesty, what the hell have you got to be guilty about?'

Years of self-control, years of suffocating anger and years of bitter disappointment burst the strained banks of Sarah's carefully constructed façade, and in one explosive and irrevocable outpouring the damage was done. 'Trevor isn't Hannah's father,' she bawled, her eyes blazing, her face twisted with anger and fear, 'and I only married him because I was pregnant and desperate. How's that for a paragon of selfless love and honesty?'

44

'Oh, that's complete nonsense,' retaliated Ali, without thinking. 'Of course Trevor's Hannah's father! You told me yourself that—' But her words fell away as, all at once, she felt the full force of Sarah's dark, hollow-eyed expression bearing down on her. Its severity made her gasp. And in that moment the world seemed to rock on its axis. She reached out to the window-sill, needing its support. 'But – but it can't be true,' she stammered. 'You would have told me. You were my best friend. You *are* my best friend. Why didn't you ever tell me?'

Light-headed with shock at what she'd just blurted out, Sarah couldn't speak. She hadn't meant to reveal her shameful secret. She hadn't ever intended another living soul to know the truth. She had kept it to herself these past eighteen years and had sworn to keep it that way for ever.

But now somebody knew.

She felt a faint tremor building in the pit of her stomach and, fearing that she was going to be sick, she breathed deeply and slowly.

'Why didn't you share it with me?' persisted Ali.

Another few breaths and the wave of nausea passed, but in its place came a further and more dangerous surge of fury for what Ali had done. She stared at Ali and said, 'It's always about you, isn't it?' She heard the poisonous hostility in her voice, not recognising it as her own, but then she saw Ali's hurt. With vengeful satisfaction, she knew that she wanted Ali to suffer for her wilful interference. She wanted her to know that her headstrong impetuosity had ruined everything.

Including their friendship.

Oh, yes, that was gone. Destroyed at a single stroke by Ali's arrogant belief that she always knew best.

She crossed the small room purposefully and stood by the open door. 'I want you out of my house,' she said, with ruthless detachment.

Ali remained where she was. 'Look, Sarah—'

'I said, get out of my house. I never want to see you again.'

Close to tears, Ali didn't know what to do. Whatever reaction she had expected from Sarah, it was not the wild, hysterical response of a few minutes ago, nor this cruel, dispassionate dismissal. 'Sarah,' she said, fighting back the lump of fear in her throat, 'please, just talk to me. Let me apologise properly. If I'd known about Trevor not being Hannah's father—'

'Be quiet! I don't want to listen to you. Don't you understand? I don't want anything more to do with you. You've done nothing but try to control me. Poor old Sarah, you've always thought. Well, I'm tired of your pity. And your charity. I don't want it any more.'

'I've never pitied you and I've certainly never tried to control you.'

'Yes, you have. You're always telling me what to do. Well, this time you've gone too far. You've wrecked everything that I've striven to create and preserve.'

'You mean I've forced you to stop flogging the dead horse of a marriage that was unworkable from the start.'

'It was *my* marriage, Ali, and it would have worked just fine if you hadn't been continually poking your nose into it. And while you were plotting to seduce my husband did you never think of what the consequences would be for Hannah?'

Ali swallowed and chewed on her lower lip. The awful truth was, she hadn't. She had thought only of her friend's welfare . . . and the future she thought Sarah secretly craved.

'And what about Elliot in all of this?' Sarah continued. 'What will he make of your betrayal when he hears of it?'

The lump of fear in Ali's throat grew bigger. 'He won't ever know – I shan't tell him.'

Sarah's small, pensive face took on a hardness that Ali would never have imagined possible. 'But I'll tell him,' Sarah said, slowly and menacingly. 'I'll make very sure he knows what a callous bitch you are. Maybe he'll end up hating you as much as I do. Now, please, get out and leave me alone. And don't try contacting me again. Our friendship is over. Do you understand that? I don't want you coming near me ever again. *Not ever!*'

'But, Sarah – please, please don't do this!'

'No, Ali, it's over. This is one act of impetuosity that you're going to regret for the rest of your life.'

As the sound of Ali's car faded into the distance, Sarah's composure went with it. She threw herself on to the sofa and sobbed. She cried so violently that once again she feared she would be sick. With tears blinding her, her breath coming in shallow gasps, she stumbled out of the sitting room and up the stairs, steadying herself with a trembling hand on the rickety banister. She stood over the toilet in the bathroom and retched painfully. Again and again. Finally, when her breathing slowed, she turned on the cold tap and filled the plastic tooth-mug from the shelf above the basin; she managed a few small sips.

She looked at her reflection in the mirror, forcing herself to see beyond the tear-stained miserable mess to the depths of the manipulative woman who had used and abused an innocent man. The irredeemable black despair of her guilt and shame stared back at her. She tore her eyes away and set about tidying herself up. She scrubbed at her face with a steaming flannel, then rubbed a towel roughly over her tingling skin. All the while she cursed herself for her selfishness so many years ago. Rehanging the towel on the rail, she heard knocking. Furious that Ali was refusing to do as she'd asked, she went downstairs and threw open the door.

It was Grace. So profound was her relief that it wasn't Ali, Sarah started to cry again. 'I'm so sorry,' she said through choked sobs as Grace closed the door behind her and took her in her arms, 'I'm so sorry, so very sorry.'

For the next ten minutes Grace didn't say a word. She listened as Sarah told her what Ali had done and her reasons, and how Sarah had told her that she never wanted to see her again – she didn't refer to Trevor not being Hannah's father. When she'd finished, Grace made no comment on the drama that she'd walked into inadvertently, but said, 'Let's get you away from here.' She took the front-door key out of the lock, shut the door behind them and walked Sarah along the lane in the bright sunshine to her own neat little bungalow. 'There, now,' she said, when she had installed Sarah on the sofa and had fetched a bottle of Bristol Cream and two small glasses. 'Slightly early to be hitting the sherry, I agree, but on this occasion quite permissible. Something sweet for the shock.'

'This is very kind of you,' Sarah murmured, her face partially hidden behind a tissue as she took the proffered glass with a shaking hand.

'Yes, it is kind of me, isn't it?'

Hearing the light touch of irony in Grace's words, Sarah looked up at her and saw that Grace was smiling one of her knowing smiles. 'Shall we dispense with the polite comments, Sarah,' she said, 'and get to the nub of things? Or would you rather we ventured further into the field of evasion and discussed the weather?'

'Evasion. Why do you say that?'

'Well, I'd hazard a guess that evasion has been at the heart of all your problems. If it hadn't been there, I suspect your friend Ali wouldn't have needed to go to such mind-blowing lengths to help you. Moreover, her actions wouldn't have had the devastating effect that they've had on you.'

Sarah plucked at another tissue from the box Grace had placed on the rosewood table in front of them. She blew her nose and fought back the instinctive desire to go on hiding the truth. She sipped her sherry and felt its sweet, sticky warmth trickle down to her empty stomach. 'Grace,' she said softly, 'I'm not at all the person you think I am.'

'Ah,' said the older woman, with a slight tilt of her head, 'and who exactly are you, then?'

Sarah sighed. 'A long time ago I did a very wicked thing.'

'And presumably have been paying for it ever since.'

Sarah frowned. 'Please don't patronise me.'

Grace put down her glass and laid a reassuring hand over Sarah's. 'I'm not, truly I'm not. Now, why don't you finally tell someone the truth? The whole truth. It must have been awful for you all these years keeping such a dead weight of a secret to yourself.'

Sarah raised her eyes and stared into Grace's intuitive gaze. She felt the warmth and love of her personality reach out to her. 'You know, don't you?'

Grace nodded. 'Yes, I believe I do.'

'But how?'

'To an objective eye, most children share a fairly balanced proportion of their parents' looks and mannerisms, but Hannah doesn't. There's not a bit of Trevor in her. I can see plenty of you, but nothing of Trevor.'

'But surely that's not enough to make you suspect that he isn't her father?'

'You're right, it isn't. The real clue was that I could find no logical reason, other than a guilty secret or – more accurately – a guilty conscience, that would let such an intelligent woman as you submit your will to Trevor in the way that you do.'

Sarah turned away in shame and instinctively reached for a lock of hair. It was a few minutes before she could speak. 'Oh, Grace, I've used him so badly.'

'Nonsense. You've given him the finest daughter he could have wished for. Some might say that that's better than he deserves.'

'But all the lies—'

Grace dismissed Sarah's unfinished words with a wave of her hand. 'What of Hannah's real father? Was he an older, married man, or a regretted one-night stand you never saw again? Was that why you couldn't turn to him?'

Sarah shook her head sadly. 'No. It wasn't like that. We knew one another and a situation developed – a situation that I should have prevented, but didn't. It was curiosity that made me do it. It was my first time. I was very naïve.'

'And, later, did you tell him you were pregnant?'

'I couldn't. He wasn't around any more. I didn't know what to do. I panicked. I couldn't bear the thought of my child not being part of a happy family. I wanted everything for my baby that my parents hadn't given me – a mother and a father who genuinely loved their child.'

'A perfect replica of Ali's family?'

'Yes. Stupid, wasn't I?'

'Not at all. You were very young. So when did you think of Trevor?'

'Almost straight away. I already knew him from the prayer group we both attended and we'd had meals out together as well as enjoyed a few evenings at the theatre. I knew that he was keen on me and, believe it or not, I was fond of him. He was different in those days, kind and generous, somehow freer. He stood up for what he believed in and I respected him for it. He wasn't like the students I was supposed to be hanging around with, the over-privileged élite who were hell-bent on milking life for all it was worth. Trevor and I had a lot in common, similar backgrounds and similar views. I knew he'd make a good father and that he'd do anything for me, so I . . .'

'So you seduced him?'

A flicker of anguish crossed Sarah's pale face and, wet-eyed, she said, 'Yes, I seduced him. I knew I had to trick him as soon as possible so that he would always believe that he was the father of the child I was already carrying. Call it madness, but I had convinced myself that as long as I stuck to the same story of when I'd conceived, I'd be able to pass off the baby's birth as premature. Very conveniently Hannah's arrival was two weeks later than expected and nobody was any the wiser. Though I did wonder at the time about the midwife. She made some comment about Hannah being a big, bonny baby considering she hadn't gone full-term.' She fell silent, then said, 'Do you want to know how I seduced Trevor?'

Grace sipped her sherry thoughtfully. 'Only if you want to tell me. If it would help.'

Sarah sighed again and, with a resigned shrug of her shoulders, said, 'I've come this far, I might just as well. I invited him to my room in college and, over a bottle of wine, I practically threw myself at him. I knew it was a huge risk. Even then he was a deep-boned fundamentalist and didn't believe in sex outside marriage. The ironic thing was, neither did I. But having done it once, I told myself that one more sin couldn't make my situation any worse. Incredibly, he was a pushover. I hated myself afterwards. I'd compromised not just my own faith but his as well. The next day he came to see me and apologised for what had happened. He blamed himself for his loss of control and promised it would never occur again. Six weeks later, when I was actually twelve weeks gone, I told him I was pregnant and he nobly asked me to marry him. You see now how awful I am?'

'Oh, Sarah, you're not awful – of course you're not. But what is, is that ever since then you've punished yourself so severely. Why could you never allow yourself to be forgiven?'

Sarah pursed her lips until they were almost colourless. 'I never felt I deserved it,' she said, in a tightly controlled voice.

'Yet I'm sure you would have been the first to point somebody else in the direction of their own personal redemption.'

'Oh, yes. I do it all the time. I told Ali to stop punishing herself over Isaac's death, to forgive herself and Elliot. Ironic, isn't it?'

'Not really. Given the amount of agony you've put yourself through, I would imagine there's no better qualified person to dissuade another from taking that particular route to hell. Now that you've had a chance to calm down, how do you really feel about what Ali's done? Do you still feel you hate her?'

'Yes. No. Oh, I don't know what I think. I still can't believe she did it. How could she willingly go to bed with a man she feels nothing for?'

Grace gave her a long, hard stare. 'She could ask the same of you.'

'Oh, that's cruel.'

'I'm sorry. But, from what you've told me, Ali saw it as a means to free you. As misguided as she was, you have to acknowledge that that was quite a sacrifice she made. She clearly has a very strong sense of commitment towards her closest friend.'

'No,' Sarah said angrily. 'It's just another example of her wanting to control me. I didn't need rescuing.'

'So what are you going to do now?'

Sarah let out her breath in a long sigh of despondency. 'I don't know.'

'Do you want to leave Trevor?'

'I can't.'

'Why not?'

'It would destroy him.'

'Staying together might destroy you both.'

'But what Ali did was unforgivable. She tricked him and I can't let him take the blame for that.'

'I hate to point out the obvious, but it seems that Trevor has rather an unfortunate weakness for being tricked by women.'

'That's an exaggeration. Twice is hardly a weakness.'

Grace levelled her gaze on Sarah. 'Still protecting him, Sarah?'

'I don't have any choice. I feel sorry for him. Just as I always have.'

'And now Ali's made you feel even sorrier for him, I suppose?'

'Yes.'

'Which means you'll forgive him and everything will go back to how things were before Ali tried to take charge.'

'I have to hope so.'

'Oh, come on, Sarah, you're deluding yourself. I guarantee that after today nothing is ever going to be the same again. You can't isolate the consequences of what Ali has done. Wasn't it Tennyson who wrote "Our echoes roll from soul to soul"?'

'"And grow for ever and for ever",' Sarah finished for her, in a low whisper, praying desperately that her elderly friend was wrong.

45

Ali had been driving aimlessly for the past half-hour. She didn't know what to do. Or where to go. She didn't want to go home – the thought of being alone terrified her. In her wretchedness the windmill, with its solitary structure and secluded situation, would only emphasise the heart-aching sense of isolation that was consuming her. Even in her confused, desperate state she couldn't fail to realise how ironic it was that she should now be shunning something that, only a short time ago, she had viewed as a symbol of her fierce independence.

I never want to see you again ...

This is one act of impetuosity that you're going to regret for the rest of your life.

I'll make sure he knows what a callous bitch you are ... he'll end up hating you as much as I do.

The bitterness with which Sarah had uttered those dreadful words terrified Ali. What if she had meant what she'd said? What if, when all the furore had fizzled out, Sarah still refused to see her? Ali couldn't imagine life without Sarah. It was inconceivable that they could be separated: they'd been together for ever. She suddenly thought of the Forever Friends Christmas mug she'd given Sarah and burst into tears.

She slowed the car, pulled off the road into a litter-strewn lay-by, slumped over the steering-wheel and howled like a baby.

What had she done?

Why had she been so determined to meddle?

She thumped repeatedly at the wheel then, frightened she might activate the airbag, she stopped. But her frustration was still there, and for the first time in her life she wished that she believed in this God of Sarah's: at least then she'd be able to berate him. 'It's all your bloody fault!' she'd shout at him. 'If it weren't for you, none of this would have happened. Sarah wouldn't have tied herself up in a lot of religious hocus-pocus that's done nothing but made her feel guilty for the last eighteen years. Eighteen bloody years in some misguided act of atonement!'

Having expressed a tiny fragment of her shock and anger, she wiped her eyes and decided what to do next. She drove towards Nantwich, picked up the A534, skirted round Congleton, then joined the A536 for Macclesfield and headed for Daniel.

'Please let him be there,' she murmured over and over to herself as she was bumping along the dusty track towards the farmhouse that looked picture-book perfect in the bright sunshine. The sight of both his and Richard's cars gave her hope that her long drive had not been in vain. Leaving the Saab, she hurried across the terrace and rang the brass ship's bell beside the door.

There was no answer.

She tried again.

Still no answer. A knot of panic gripped her insides. Where, oh, where was Daniel when she needed him? Her lips trembled and the abject misery she had successfully controlled while driving threatened to overwhelm her: it made her want to throw herself at the door until somebody – anybody – came to her rescue.

Suddenly, above her head, a window opened and Daniel stared down at her bleary-eyed, his hair tousled, his chest bare. 'Ali? What on earth are you doing here?'

She gulped back her relief. 'Please, Daniel, I need to talk to you.'

Sitting at the kitchen table with a sedative mug of Earl Grey in her hands and surrounded by the ordinary and commonplace – Richard making toast on the Aga and Daniel ferrying pots of jam, honey and marmalade from the pantry – Ali's composure slowly returned. Everything would be all right, she told herself. Daniel and Richard would know how to help. They'd tell her how to straighten out the mess she'd caused. 'I'm sorry I got you out of bed,' she said.

'That's the third time you've apologised,' Daniel said gently, as he put the last of the breakfast things on the table and slipped into the chair opposite her, 'but I think it's time now to tell us what's wrong. It's not Elliot, is it?'

She willed a stray tear to stay where it was and not breach her defences. 'Elliot's not my immediate problem,' she murmured morosely, 'but he soon will be.'

Richard came over with a rack of toast. 'Would you rather I made myself scarce?' he asked.

Ali was touched by his thoughtfulness. 'It's okay,' she said, 'you can stay, but I don't think you're going to like what you hear.'

Her eyes on the mug of tea in front of her, she told them everything, all the details, and all the reasons why she'd undertaken such a scheme. 'My original plan,' she explained, 'was to get Trevor so inebriated that he'd crash out and come to the following morning with only the sketchiest of memories. But I realised on Monday evening that I couldn't rely on getting him drunk so . . . so I decided when he came to see me for a second time to spike his wine with a couple of tranquillisers and a sleeping pill – stuff I'd been prescribed after Isaac's death but had never used. It worked perfectly. And although I had a few misgivings, I really believed I'd done the right thing by Sarah. Except now I find out that she's stuck fast to Trevor by her guilt. You see, he isn't Hannah's father. She tricked him into marrying her when she discovered she was pregnant. And now she won't speak to me. She says she never wants to see me again – that she hates me for what I've done. Even worse, she says she'll tell Elliot.'

Both men stared at her in deathly silence, their hands poised over their plates of untouched toast, their eyes wide and incredulous. It was Daniel who spoke first. He rose from the table, walked over to the other side of the kitchen, and leaned back against the dishwasher. He ran his hands through his uncombed hair. 'I don't believe I'm hearing this. What in hell were you thinking of, spiking the man's drink with potentially lethal drugs? You could have killed him!'

'I was very careful. I—'

'Oh, good call, Ali. You were careful, were you? *Bullshit!* My God, I've heard of date rape, but this is something else!' He turned from her and stared out through the window. Then he whipped round. 'And what possessed you to think that you had a right to take hold of somebody else's relationship and stamp the viable life out of it? If you could do that to a friend, what the hell would you do to an enemy?'

Ali covered her face. 'I did it with the best of intentions,' she whimpered. 'It was an act of faith in our friendship, it was—'

'An act of faith!' exploded Daniel. 'You have to be joking. It was a malicious act of devious hatred. You've always hated Trevor and you saw this as a way to have Sarah all to yourself and make like a bloody heroic saint into the bargain.'

'That's not true!' cried Ali, springing to her feet and scraping her chair noisily on the tiled floor. 'It wasn't about hating Trevor, it was about loving Sarah and wanting the best for her.'

'Well, no argument there, then. She'll be a darned sight better off without you around.'

Ali glared at him. 'If that's how you feel, then perhaps it would be better if I left. I'm sorry to have disturbed your Saturday morning. Thanks for the tea and sympathy.'

His arms folded across his chest, Daniel stayed where he was. He watched Ali move towards the door, but Richard intervened. He went after Ali, placed both his hands on her shoulders and drew her back into the kitchen. 'Don't go,' he said softly. 'Daniel didn't mean half of what he just said.'

Unconvinced, Ali glanced over to him, but his dark, brooding gaze was fixed on a spot on the floor at his feet. In all the years she had known and loved him, she had never seen such an expression on his face. She realised then what it was. It was disappointment. He was disappointed in her. 'I think Daniel meant exactly what he said,' she murmured sadly, 'and he's probably right.'

'Daniel,' urged Richard, 'Ali needs our help and support, not our animosity.'

Slowly, Daniel raised his eyes from the floor and met Ali's tear-filled gaze. Gradually the darkness cleared from his face, he unfolded his arms and held them out for her. 'I'm sorry, Babe,' he said.

She went to him and held him tightly, desperate for his forgiveness: to be rejected by Daniel was as unthinkable as it was to lose Sarah's friendship. 'I'm sorry too,' she said, 'sorry for what I've done and sorry for letting you down.'

'You haven't let me down.'

She released herself from his arms and looked up into his face. 'I have, I know I have.' She began to cry again, her breath catching in long, choking sobs. 'I've ruined everything. Sarah won't talk to me and God knows what Elliot will do when he finds out. I never intended to hurt so many people. Oh, please help me. Tell me what to do.' Her crying grew louder and she shook violently. Daniel took her in his arms again and held her protectively to his chest.

'Let's get her upstairs to bed,' Richard suggested. 'She needs to rest.'

Between them they helped her into their bed, which was still warm from where they'd been sleeping. She lay in the middle, Richard on one side of her with a box of tissues at the ready and Daniel on the other stroking her cheek and holding her hand.

Shortly afterwards she fell asleep, and when Daniel checked on her five hours later, she opened her eyes and asked him what time it was.

'Half past four, Babe.' He came and lay down with her. 'Feeling any better?'

'I think so.' She sat up and shifted the pillows behind her into a more comfortable position. 'I'm sorry I lost it downstairs.'

He put an arm around her and kissed her forehead. 'Nothing like a bit of drama to nourish the soul.'

Her face broke into a small smile. 'Oh, Daniel, whatever am I going to do?'

'I've no idea, but for now, explain to me one more time what, in the name of all that's wonderful, you thought you were doing.'

'Do I have to?'

'Yes. I want to try and understand what you did.'

As painful as it was, she went through the story again, labouring the point about Sarah's religious convictions. 'She told me she could never leave Trevor because of her beliefs, but that if he was to have an affair it would change everything.'

'So you took her at her word, literally?'

'Yes. I swear I thought she meant it. If I'd doubted her I'd never have dreamed of interfering. I truly believed that my actions would leave her free to be happy and fulfilled. I just wanted her to be happy. Do you understand that?'

'Mm ... I'm getting there. But carry on. Tell me the rest.'

Ali did, and when she'd finished, she said, 'And to make matters a thousand times worse I know I have to tell Elliot.'

Daniel looked at her doubtfully. 'Don't do it, Babe. If you've got any sense you'll leave him well out of this.'

'But I can't. I have to tell him before Sarah does. And I know she'll do it. Oh, Daniel, if you'd seen her face, heard the terrible hardness in her voice. Believe me, she meant every word of what she threatened. Even if she doesn't, Elliot will want to know why the pair of us aren't speaking to one another and the lies will just hang over me. I don't think I could live with the dread of him discovering accidentally that I'd been to bed with Trevor.'

'But, Ali, you didn't go to bed with Trevor. In real terms, you've done absolutely nothing to betray Elliot.'

Ali chewed on her lip. 'But I've got to pretend that I did, for Sarah's sake.'

'Now you're losing me.'

'Look, if I share with Elliot what I really did, he'd make me tell Sarah and Trevor. Elliot is a man of true honour. He's loaded to the gunwales with scruples. He wouldn't let me get away with deceiving them over something as serious as this.'

'Then tell Sarah the truth.'

'If I do that she won't have what she thinks is adultery as a reason to leave Trevor with a free conscience.'

Daniel sighed. 'So, let me get this straight. If you stick with the lie about you and Trevor bonking the night away, you might lose Elliot, and I hate to say it but I think there's a high risk of that happening. But if you tell Elliot what really went on, you get to keep him but have to tell Sarah that Trevor's honour is still intact and she loses her legitimate bid for freedom. How am I doing?'

'On the nail.'

'So, what's the problem? You have to take the second course of action.'

Ali shook her head. 'No, I won't. If I do that Sarah will never leave Trevor and all this would have been for nothing.'

'From what you say it sounds as though she never will. If she's stayed with him this long because of her guilt, she's hardly going to jump ship now.'

'But the point is, she could if I keep quiet. She'd always believe that, at the end of the day, she could take a hike if she really needed to. The get-out clause would still be there for her.'

'If you go for that option, you realise that you're in danger of sacrificing your love for Elliot in favour of your friendship for Sarah?'

She nodded gloomily.

Daniel stared into Ali's miserable face and found himself remembering the radiant smile with which she had greeted him on Monday morning when she'd returned to the office after her holiday. How clearly her happiness had flowed out of her, and equally clear had been the cause of it: her reconciliation with Elliot. And now she was prepared to risk all that for the sake of a friend. He took one of her hands in his and squeezed it between his own. 'Ali, I won't let you do this. After what you and Elliot have been through, I won't let you risk a single moment's happiness with him.'

She slowly withdrew her hand. 'I have to do it, Daniel. I've known Sarah practically all my life and she's always been there for me. I owe her this.'

'And Elliot? What do you owe him?'

'Please,' she whispered, 'don't make it any more difficult for me.'

But Daniel wasn't prepared to be so easily swayed. 'Look,' he said, 'I'll do you a deal. I'll go along with this madness, but only for so long.'

'What kind of a deal?'

'You can tell Elliot all the lies you want in the vain hope that Sarah will kick Trevor into touch, but I'm putting a time limit on your deception with him. If Elliot hasn't forgiven you by the end of next month, you tell him what you really did.'

Ali frowned. 'I don't know, Daniel. That's not long. He'll need time to calm down. He'll need to let—'

'It's that or nothing, Ali. That's the deal. Take it or leave it.'

'If I don't agree?'

'Then I'll speak to him myself.'

She paused. 'Give me until the end of October.'

'Okay,' he said reluctantly, 'but no longer.'

They sat in silence, each with their own thoughts. Then, raising her tearful eyes to his, Ali said, 'So have you forgiven me?'

He smiled. 'Of course I have. I've never been able to stay cross with you for more than two minutes.'

'That's because he worships the ground you walk on, Ali.'

They both turned to see Richard standing in the doorway. He came in with three mugs of tea and a packet of chocolate digestives tucked under his arm.

'How's the patient?' he asked.

'Much better, and I really don't deserve to be spoiled like this.'

'Ulterior motive, my little cuddle-muffin,' laughed Richard, settling himself beside her and offering her a biscuit, 'I'm sweetening you up for a three-in-a-bed romp later tonight.'

Ali laughed, but Daniel rolled his eyes and tutted. 'Barristers,' he said, 'they're full of shite. It comes of spending too much time in a horsehair wig.'

'Language, Danny boy. Now tell me where we're up to, *vis-à-vis* our very own Greek tragedy.'

Recognising that Richard was deliberately lightening the mood for Ali, Daniel filled him in on the details.

When he'd brought him up to date, Ali said, 'Do you think Elliot will forgive me?'

'Well, we have,' Richard said, 'so I don't see why he won't be able to.'

'Yes, but you both know the truth,' said Ali, 'which is—'

'Which is,' cut in Daniel, 'that our reckless Ali didn't actually sleep with the cerebrally challenged Trevor.'

'"Aye, and there's the rub" to quote that greatly troubled prince of Denmark.'

'The rub indeed,' echoed Daniel, reaching out for Ali's hand again. He loved Ali dearly, but he couldn't pretend he wasn't appalled by what she'd done. Or perhaps it was the measure of his love for her that dictated the level of his shock. She'd always been one of the most headstrong, gutsy people he knew, but this was taking daredevil hotheadedness to unimaginably risky heights. This ill-conceived plot of hers was one hell of a quantum leap even for the most foolhardy of desperadoes. 'When's Elliot back from the States?' he asked.

Ali swallowed hard and stared out at the view to which Daniel and Richard woke up each morning. It was lovely, so throat-catchingly beautiful with the sun shining down on the green hills, picking out the ribbons of drystone walls and dots of recently shorn sheep. 'Tomorrow, early lunch-time,' she said, returning her gaze to Daniel. 'I'm meeting him at the airport.'

'Then you'd better stay the night with us,' said Richard, 'and no arguments.'

The following morning Ali said goodbye to Richard and Daniel and drove the half-hour journey to the airport. She would have liked to have their company but she knew that she had to get through the next few hours on her own. She paced the arrivals hall nervously, glancing up at the row of monitors, waiting for one to show that Elliot's plane had landed. So far his flight was twenty minutes late. She wondered whether he would be so jet-lagged that all he'd want to do would be sleep for the rest of the day.

No. That would never happen. She had never seen Elliot suffer from jet-lag. He could get off a twelve-hour flight, go straight into the office, work a high-pressure day, then go home and catch up with the backlog of his correspondence before going to bed at the normal time. It was so typical of him, always able to make time work for him.

It had been the same while he was in New York attending the world-wide partners' conference and meeting several key clients: he had still found space in his busy schedule to call her. Mostly it had been around midday when he phoned – breakfast time for him. He'd said how much he was missing her and that he had been thinking a lot about their future.

What future? she thought now, wretchedly.

An influx of weary-faced travellers pushing trolleys with luggage piled skyscraper high made her study the monitors again. Her stomach churned as she saw that Elliot's plane was on approach. A sudden desire to run seized her. She didn't want to confront Elliot. She didn't want to reveal her shame to him. She wanted only to run away and hide.

She hadn't expected to feel so ashamed – she might as well have had a fully fledged affair with Trevor – but what surprised her most was that she felt sorry for Trevor. Now, that was a blow.

What a hornet's nest she had unwittingly disturbed. Trevor wasn't Hannah's father. Why, oh why hadn't Sarah told her? If only she had shared it with her at Oxford, the last eighteen years might have been so different. And who the hell was the real father? Would Sarah feel compelled to tell Trevor the truth? And what of Hannah? How would she react to being told that Trevor wasn't her biological father?

She looked again at the monitor, and her heart missed a beat. Elliot's plane had landed. He was probably a mere twenty minutes from coming through those doors expecting to see her smiling face.

As self-pitying as it sounded, she doubted that she'd ever smile again after today. On top of losing her dearest friend, Sarah, she was now in danger of losing Elliot.

For the second time.

Oh, if only she could turn back the clock. If only she hadn't been so sure of herself or so confident that she knew how Sarah would react. How arrogant she had been to think that Sarah would accept what she'd done in her customary undemonstrative way, and be gratefully relieved, seeing Ali as her liberator.

But Sarah hadn't acted in her usual way, so she hadn't set in motion the pattern of events Ali had foreseen and relied upon. It was only to be expected that, if she could so wildly miscalculate Sarah's response, she was hoping for too much understanding from Elliot – after all, he would see only that she had slept with another man while his back was turned.

Another posse of travellers came through the automatic doors. Mostly they were casually dressed holidaymakers with expanded waistlines and depleted wallets after enjoying the excesses of a trip to the States. But then, amongst the jostle of brightly coloured shirts, baseball caps, shorts and carrier bags of duty-free purchases, there was Elliot, impeccably dressed in a lightweight pale grey suit, his white shirt open at the neck. Her throat went dry and her stomach lurched as he caught sight of her. She watched him square his shoulders and move impatiently through the crowd of people in his way. When, at last, he was standing next to her, he lowered his suit-carrier and two other bags to the floor, and took her in his arms. He kissed her long and deeply and she responded willingly, thinking, as she gave herself up to the tenderness of his embrace, that this might be the last time he would ever want to kiss her.

'You look tired,' he remarked, when they were driving away from the airport complex.

'I've not been myself these past few days,' she said cryptically. *Oh, and wasn't that the truth!*

'You're okay, though, aren't you?'

She heard the loving concern in his voice and could have wept.

When they reached the windmill and drew up alongside Elliot's car, Ali knew that she could put off her confession no longer. She had to do it now. Each minute that passed was a cruel reminder that she was waiting powerlessly for when Sarah carried out her threat. She, Ali, had to be the one who told Elliot. She owed him that much.

She let them in, and while Elliot was upstairs in the bathroom, she poured them both a drink. When he returned, she suggested he sit down and handed him his glass. 'You're going to need it,' she said flatly. 'There's something I have to tell you.' She saw at once that his senses were keenly on the alert and already piecing together a worst-case scenario.

'It's not Sam, is it?' he asked.

'No, it's not Sam,' she said and, giving him no time to question her further, she blundered on. 'It's me. You won't like what I've got to say and . . . and I've a pretty good idea what the consequences will be.' She sounded so much calmer than she felt.

He sat motionless on the sofa, his watchful gaze following her as she prowled the sitting room and told him what had gone on in his absence. Not once did she look at him – she didn't dare risk seeing the shock in his eyes. Or the anger. Her unworthy tale of guilt and deceit complete, she went and stood outside on the balcony, needing to breathe in the warm afternoon air as though it might purify her. She waited for him to join her and have his say, but then she heard him moving inside. Scared that he might leave with nothing said, she turned to stop him, but then saw that he was coming towards her.

He rested his hands on the balcony rail and leaned against it. 'I don't understand you, Ali.' His voice was scarcely audible. He looked vulnerably tired, his face etched with lines of sadness, his eyes clouded and distant. 'We had it all resolved between us and then you do this. What am I supposed to think? That you could make love to another man and it wouldn't matter? That it wouldn't hurt me?'

'I told you, it meant nothing,' she said lamely. 'It was purely a means to an end.'

He banged his fist down on the rail, sending a shockwave of restrained rage along the wooden bar. His vulnerability was gone and in its place was full-frontal anger. 'And that's supposed to make me feel better? Shit, Ali, I've heard bastards like Gervase come out with comments as low and vile as that and despised them with every ounce of my being.'

'Do you despise me?'

He stared at her, his whole body strained and tense. 'Yes,' he said coldly.

She flinched beneath the candour of his reply. 'But could you forgive me?'

Again he stared at her. Oh, God, she thought, he's trying to make up his mind. She held her breath and waited for his reply.

Finally he spoke. 'No,' he said, with grim resolution. 'No, Ali, I don't think I can find it in my heart to forgive you.'

He turned and went back inside the mill. She went after him. 'But you said the night before you went to New York that you'd always love me. You said that.'

He collected his things together. 'Oh, I'll always love you, Ali. To my cost, I doubt that I'll ever stop loving you.'

'Then why are you leaving?'

'Because I have to. What you did was beneath contempt, and I can't stand to be near you.'

Ali didn't argue with him. There wasn't any point. Everything he'd said was true. She'd lost the will to fight, anyway. The old Ali would have battled on tenaciously to prove that she was right, that the end did indeed justify the means. But this shamed and self-loathing Ali knew she was beaten, that she had made her biggest ever mistake and would pay for it dearly.

She went back outside on to the balcony and waited for Elliot to go. She heard him clatter down the wooden staircase with clumsy urgency, then the sound of the front door shutting behind him. She watched him get into his car and, though he must have known that she was looking down at him, he didn't so much as glance up at her. With more speed than care, he shot off down the lane.

Never had she felt more alone.

Or more unworthy.

She thought of the bargain she had struck with Daniel and suddenly doubted that she was strong enough to stay the course.

Wiping the tears from her cheeks, she closed her eyes and willed both Sarah and Elliot to find a way to forgive her.

46

Sarah was working on some hand-sewing at a trestle table in the shade of her favourite spot in the garden. It was behind the previous owners' ugly old pigeon-loft, which was where she kept her gardening tools and which she had cunningly disguised by trailing honeysuckle over it. After years of selective pruning and encouragement, it was a mass of sweet-scented flowers. In the bright afternoon sunshine it was humming with bumble-bees going about their business. From here she could sit unseen from the house but, more importantly, out of view from Trevor who was in his workshop.

She had stayed with Grace for most of yesterday, leaving her reluctantly in the evening when she knew that avoiding Trevor was no solution to the problem. He was waiting for her when she reached home, his face pinched with fear, his manner edgy and smothering. 'I thought you'd left me,' he said, trying clumsily to embrace her.

'No, Trevor,' she responded, pushing him away, and searching her memory for the last time he'd so much as touched her. 'I haven't left you.'

'Where've you been?'

The question had annoyed her. What did it matter where she'd spent the day? 'I was at Grace's,' she said.

'Why her?' he asked, following her closely as she went into the kitchen.

Again annoyance had flared within her. He'd been to bed with her oldest and dearest friend and he was querying the company *she* kept. 'Grace has become a good friend to me,' she said.

For a man in his current position, his next utterance was outrageous: it was the most blatant piece of blame-shifting she'd ever heard. 'Which is more than we can say of Ali,' he observed, with weighty malevolence.

'What are you trying to tell me, Trevor?'

Shoving his hands into the back pockets of his corduroys, he said, 'I know what I did was wrong, and I have to take my share of the responsibility, but ... but it wasn't just ...' His words petered out.

'Go on,' she said, knowing exactly what he was building up to and despising him for it.

'Ali has to take more responsibility for this than me,' he said, in a voice that suggested he was all but abdicating his own part in the sordid affair. 'It was she who got me drunk.'

Of course, in a sense Sarah knew that he was right. Ali would have planned the whole thing with such consummate skill that Trevor would have been little more than a stooge in the scene she had devised. He wouldn't have stood a chance. She let his comment go and asked him the question she'd been puzzling over since that morning: how had Ali enticed him to the mill? What possible pretext had she come up with?

His manner became more strident and assured. 'She duped me, Sarah. I can see that so clearly now. She phoned on Monday afternoon when you were out and said she wanted my help. I went to see her that evening as well. She told me that she wanted guidance in coming to know the Lord.'

'And you believed her?' she asked, her tone openly ridiculing him.

'Yes,' he'd answered stoically. 'She was very convincing.'

Sarah had wanted to laugh at Ali's brazenness. She'd done a perfect number on Trevor. She had known his weakness and gone for it. No other ruse would have worked so effectively. By appealing to his pick-up-thy-cross-and-follow-me stance she had ensnared him with his own naïve conceit. She could picture the scene, Ali throwing him all the right lines and him thinking of all the heavenly kudos and glory in store for him. Dear God, if this was somebody else's crisis, it would be hilarious.

But it was her crisis and it was far from funny.

As furious as she was with Ali, she was now equally cross with Trevor for having fallen prey to such an obvious ploy. Couldn't he have seen what was coming? He'd told her that Ali must have plied him with drink. Well, fair enough. But did she pinch his nose, hold his mouth open and force in the bottle? Of course not. He had allowed himself to get drunk. He wasn't a child who didn't know the consequences of over-indulging. He was a grown man who knew exactly what he was doing. Perhaps he'd played his part more willingly than he was prepared to admit. How flattered he must have been when Ali turned to him for help – him of all people! And he'd certainly dressed up for the occasion, hadn't he? Clean clothes, trimmed beard, the rarely touched bottle of eau-de-Cologne. Oh, yes, they were all signs that the silly man had gone to Ali's that night like a lamb to the slaughter. What a fool he'd been. What an idiot not even to consider why she would be interested in going to bed with him when she had Elliot. Did he not wonder why she would go for a spin in a Robin Reliant when she had a Ferrari in the garage?

Not that she was defending Ali, but it was scandalous that he should be attempting to heap all the blame on her. He should have been more of a man and seen what she was doing. And if he was so drunk, how on earth had he managed to perform? Or was he going to claim next that Ali had slipped him some Viagra?

Oh, yes, when it really came down to it, she was just as angry with Trevor as she was with Ali. But whereas she had been able to launch a verbal attack on Ali, she couldn't do the same with Trevor. Her own shameless, unprincipled behaviour prevented her from displaying so much as a flicker of what she really felt.

At her suggestion they'd slept in separate bedrooms last night.

'That's quite understandable,' he'd said, in deference to her moving her things into the spare room. 'We each need a period of private cleansing.'

She'd lain awake for hours going over so many of the things she and

Grace had discussed during that exhausting, seemingly endless day. 'Sarah,' Grace had said, 'please listen very carefully to what I'm about to say and don't disregard it out of hand. Not only do I think that you've hidden behind your faith, but I believe very strongly that you've used it as a stick to beat yourself. Would I be right?'

She'd denied it at first, but Grace had said, 'If you hadn't used it as a weapon against yourself, you would have forgiven yourself a long time ago, and who knows what that might have led to? You know, there are too many people in this world who won't allow themselves to be happy or loved, and you're one of them, Sarah. You said earlier that you felt you didn't deserve to be forgiven, which means that you've stuck with Trevor as a penitence for your deception. There was no surer way to punish yourself, was there? Now that really is some stick.'

'You're wrong,' she'd replied, still afraid to admit the truth, even though she knew Grace would see right through her. 'I've stayed with Trevor because he was a good father to Hannah.'

'Yes, I'll grant you that that was always important to you. But what about now? Hannah's an adult, she's flying the nest, she's leaving you both. She doesn't need her mother and father in the same way she used to. How much longer do you think you have to go on paying the price?'

'Beneath all his silliness, Trevor is a good man. He doesn't deserve to have his marriage taken away from him.'

'I applaud your selflessness but wonder where it will take you.'

It was on that thought that she had fallen asleep, and for the first time that day her battered psyche was given a much-needed rest.

Now as she sat in the garden, with a much clearer head, Sarah knew what she had to do. Despite what Grace had said, she owed Trevor so much that she had no choice but to forgive him his part in Ali's madness and carry on as normal. The irony was that the door that Ali had thought she had opened she had actually locked and barred: she had added another ton of guilt to the load Sarah was already carrying.

And what of Trevor's guilt?

Rather cynically she suspected that he wouldn't find too much trouble in coming to terms with it – if he hadn't already by blaming Ali for the whole seedy episode. She imagined that he would have high expectations of their lives returning to normal soon. He might even think their relationship would be strengthened by the crisis.

But one relationship would not have the chance to recover so easily: her friendship with Ali.

When Ali had said, 'I did it for you,' it had seemed to Sarah the most monstrous invasion of her free will. If she wanted to be married to Trevor, it was her choice. What right did Ali think she had to rearrange the furniture of somebody else's marriage?

In her anger, she had accused Ali of pitying her and of wanting to control her, but what she hadn't expressed was the sudden realisation that she was jealous of Ali. She was jealous that she was the kind of person who could do anything she chose. No challenge was too great for her. In their second term at Oxford she had vowed to leave with a First, and she had done exactly that. She'd then gone on to be the career woman Sarah had dreamed of being, and had topped it by marrying a man who was as passionate about her as she was about him.

One only had to scratch the surface of their friendship to realise that, beneath the genuine love she had felt for Ali, she had always been a little envious of her success and happiness. Even when Isaac had died and her marriage had self-combusted, Ali had somehow found the courage and energy to battle on and start up her own business. She was an impressive, enterprising woman, however one viewed her.

When Sarah had first met Ali at school she had seen her as an equal and, in their different and complementing ways, they were a good match, Ali all argumentative debate and Sarah thoughtful and reserved. Although Ali was never bothered by the disparity in their backgrounds, Sarah was constantly aware that there was an element of poor relative about her when she was absorbed into the welcoming bosom of Ali's family. By the time they were at Oxford it bothered her less, but then she had ruined everything by getting pregnant. From then on she had never felt Ali's equal. From her unsatisfactory marriage, Sarah watched Ali go from strength to strength and secretly envied her. And, all the while, Ali told her what a mistake she'd made in marrying Trevor.

As though she needed telling!

Each time Ali made some negative comment Sarah defended Trevor. She had to. She had to convince herself, if not Ali, that she'd done the right thing, that she lived as fulfilling a life as her friend.

So when yesterday Ali had announced that she'd saved Sarah, she was as good as saying that Sarah was a fool and couldn't be trusted to make a right decision for herself. The implication had incensed Sarah, and had led to the appalling outburst in which she'd revealed that Trevor was not Hannah's natural father. She wondered now if she hadn't thrown the confession at Ali to show her that there was more to her than met the eye – 'Hey,' she was subconsciously boasting, 'I'm not the saint you've always made me out to be!'

For more than eighteen years she had kept that secret tucked away deep inside her. In those first few weeks of her pregnancy she had nearly confided in Ali but, knowing that her friend would overreact, she had held her tongue. Then, as the months and years had passed, the secret had been easier to keep. And Trevor was so kind and loving towards Hannah that, to all intents and purposes, he *was* her father.

Sarah put down her sewing and rubbed at her fingers, which were stiff and sore. She leaned back in her chair and saw that her little red-breasted friend Gomez was looking at her from the garden fence. She stared at his cocked head and thought how pleasant it would be to swap lives with him. Dodging predatory cats and surviving the cold months of winter would surely be easier than the chaos she had to cope with.

The sun had moved round now and, feeling the strength of its rays on her neck, she picked up her wide-brimmed straw hat from under her chair and set it on her head. She resumed her sewing, badly wanting to get it finished: Hannah was coming home tomorrow and there was a lot she wanted to get done between now and then. At the top of her list was a talk with Trevor.

She worked for a further hour, and when she'd applied the last of the tassels to the Cluny-style cushion covers she'd been making, she took them inside the house and up to the spare bedroom. She then went to find Trevor, to tell him that, as far as she was concerned, what he and Ali had done was in the past and that it was now a closed book. She was also going to tell him that, for the sake of their marriage, she had decided not to see Ali again.

By getting rid of such a dangerously divisive element, Sarah hoped her marriage would stand a better chance of surviving.

47

It was late October and the weather was damp and cold. Beneath a drab iron-grey sky, the village of Astley Hope looked even drearier than it usually did. A thin, vaporous mist of drizzle hung in the windless air and the trees along the lanes looked black now that they were almost leafless. It was a comfortless, gloomy scene.

Upstairs in the spare bedroom of Smithy Cottage, cold and tired, Sarah was bent over her sewing-machine. She'd been up since six working on this particular pair of curtains – the fabric was a heavy chenille and had been a devil to handle but with a bit of luck she'd be finished by tea-time and could make a start on the next order. She was busier than she'd ever been, but that was of her own choosing: like many other mothers in her situation, she had made the decision, since Hannah had gone away to college, to keep herself fully occupied. The extra money was coming in handy and she was putting regular amounts into a building-society account for Hannah's inevitable rainy days – being a student was costly and Sarah didn't want her daughter to go without.

While Sarah's 'little enterprise', as Trevor referred to it, was flourishing, his was not. He was spending less time in the workshop these days and more hours at the kitchen table applying himself to the Bible. He'd started a home-study course, which took up the majority of his mornings as he laboured over the finer points of the Apocalyptic Age.

Since the summer, life at Smithy Cottage had more or less resumed its normal rhythm, and, as Sarah had predicted, Trevor had turned what might have been a personal humiliation into a blessing. Though what she hadn't bargained on was an all-encompassing attentiveness towards her, which she hadn't encountered from him in years. It reminded her of the brief spell at Oxford when he'd openly held her in such high esteem. But, instead of reassuring her, it stifled her, set her nerves jangling and made her want to withdraw further from him.

In the immediate aftermath of his fall from grace – his own coy euphemism for the act he'd committed – his principal concern had been to keep it from Hannah and the group. He wasn't easy in the knowledge that Sarah had confided in Grace and, despite all her assurances that her elderly friend would never betray a confidence, he saw her as a weak link in the chain of concealment. 'But what if she mentioned it to Callum and he let it slip to Jamie?' he said in bed one night. 'Jamie would be sure to tell Hannah.'

'Grace wouldn't do that.'

'But how can you be so certain?'

'Because I am.'

His desire to screw down the lid on what he'd done was the only tangible sign that the episode held any repercussions for him. Otherwise he acted as if he'd just had the luckiest of escapes. Which he had. How he had squared matters so easily with his own conscience, never mind with God, was a mystery to Sarah, especially when she thought of all the years she had scrubbed at the dirty tidemark of her own guilt. 'Repentance is the watchword,' he'd said to her, when he'd been helping her with the washing-up. In a crazy way, she almost admired him for having faith so strong that he had allowed himself to be forgiven just like that.

On the other hand Grace had said, 'I don't believe a word of it. Classic case of self-deception. He's blamed Ali and washed his hands of the whole affair. When he's least expecting it, the reality will come crashing down on him.'

It seemed a probable and credible interpretation of his behaviour but Sarah was not inclined to suggest it to Trevor and warn him of the potential crisis hanging over him. Not when he was so full of the wonder of the Lord, and how their faith had held them together through the crisis. 'Imagine how Ali must be feeling,' he'd said. 'She has no one to turn to when the chips are down.' His smugness had maddened Sarah.

Though she had stuck fast to her resolution not to see or speak to Ali again, Ali had made one attempt to communicate with her. She had written Sarah a letter. It was short and to the point.

> I'm so very sorry for what I have done. If it makes you feel any better I've lost everything that I held precious. I've lost your friendship – which is bad enough – and I've lost Elliot as well. How careless can a person be?
>
> With all my love, Ali
>
> P.S. I will respect your wishes and steer well clear of you . . . but if you change your mind, you know where I am.
>
> P.P.S Love to Hannah – please don't ever tell her what I did, I couldn't take the shame.

She hadn't shown it to Trevor. She'd known that it had come from Ali's heart and didn't want it tainted by one of his derisive comments. She still had it, hidden in one of the drawers in her workroom where she stored her offcuts. It was also where she kept the gold chain Ali had given her.

Her anger had now subsided sufficiently for Sarah to feel how badly she missed her friend. It made her ineffably sad to know that Ali had lost her second chance of happiness with Elliot. She felt guilty too, convinced that it was as a result of her threat to tell Elliot what Ali had done that had caused their break-up. Again, it was a classic example of Ali's feisty and courageous personality to own up. Anybody else would have kept quiet, but not Ali. Sarah wished now that she had never made such a vindictive threat, especially as, within hours of having made it, she'd calmed down enough to know that she had no intention of carrying it out. But Ali hadn't known that and must have forced herself to tell Elliot before Sarah had a chance to.

There were times in the dead of night, with Trevor asleep at her side, when Sarah longed to ring Ali. But she couldn't bring herself to do it. Seeing Ali again would take them all back to square one and she wasn't prepared to do that. As long as Ali wasn't around to pass judgement on her marriage, it would tick over as well as any other half-hearted union. She had tried to explain this to Grace, but Grace had said, 'It won't work, Sarah. That's as helpful as a surgeon putting a sticking-plaster over a burst appendix.'

Ineffectual or not, it was the decision she had made, and it was the one by which she would stand firm.

The lack of Ali in their lives had come as a relief to Trevor, but not so to Hannah. 'I don't understand,' she'd said a couple of weeks after she'd returned from France with her ears pierced, her hair cut spiky short, and looking vastly more sophisticated than when she'd gone away. She was also revelling in the news that her run of straight As had got her into Oxford. 'If you've had a bust-up with Ali just apologise to one another and it'll be cool again.'

'It's not as simple as that,' Sarah had said, hoping that Hannah would drop the subject. But she hadn't.

'Well, no matter what's gone on between you two,' she asserted, 'she's still my godmother. Are you going to ban me from speaking to her?'

'When did I ever ban you from doing anything?' had been Sarah's reply.

Whether or not Hannah did get in touch with Ali, Sarah never knew, but on the day she and Trevor were due to take Hannah to Oxford for the start of the Michaelmas term, and whether it was a coincidence or not, a good-luck card arrived in the post for Hannah. It was from Ali and contained a cheque. Hannah didn't let on how much it was for, but the smile on her face indicated that it was a hefty and welcome amount.

With Trevor at the wheel of their recently serviced car, the journey to Oxford took them considerably longer than when Ali had driven Sarah there in the summer. It was a trip of mixed emotions. While Sarah was delighted that Hannah's A-level results had secured her place at Brasenose, the sadness of letting her go was too much for her, and at times she'd had to hide her face in her hanky. Worse was to come when they'd arrived at the college and had lugged all Hannah's worldly possessions up the twisting wooden staircase to her room and prepared to leave her to settle in on her own.

'Oh, Mum,' Hannah had said, when the hanky made its appearance again, 'I'll be fine, no worries. I'll ring you every week.'

'I'm not crying for you,' Sarah had mumbled. 'I'm crying for me.'

This had made Hannah laugh, which had made Sarah cry even more, knowing how much she would miss the sound of her daughter's happy, unaffected laughter.

But Hannah had been true to her word and had made her weekly phone calls. There'd been much talk of all the things she had thrown herself into. She'd joined the college rowing team, though she didn't know if she'd last the course as she wasn't as fit as some of the others; she'd gone along to the Oxford Union and added her voice to the debate on euthanasia; she'd been for a picnic in Christ Church Meadow; she'd had a visit from Jamie; and she'd busked in Cornmarket with another flute player who lived on the same staircase as her. 'It was brilliant, Mum,' she'd crowed. 'We made over twenty pounds in two hours. The tourists are such mugs.' There was even talk of the odd tutorial and lecture.

To all this reported activity, Trevor's only comment was, 'What about the Christian Union? Have you joined that?'

He hadn't liked her answer. 'No, but I've been along to a Buddhist meeting.'

That night, with his worst fears confirmed, Trevor had asked the Slipper Gang to pray for Hannah. 'Pray that she's not put on the path to temptation,' he'd told them.

Sarah's prayers were of a wholly more basic nature: 'Don't let her throw her opportunity away as I did.'

Being back in Brasenose for those few hours while they'd helped Hannah unpack had not been as awful as Sarah had dreaded. When she'd been there in the summer with Ali, she had balked at entering the college because it held so many poignant memories for her, mostly of deep regret. Being there with Hannah had been different: there had been no time to dwell on her self-reproach by wandering the immaculate quads, reliving long-ago days and reminding herself of blighted chances. No, there had been no time for such maudlin retrospection: she had been too preoccupied with letting go of her daughter.

It had seemed the bravest, most difficult thing she'd ever done.

Letting go was something Elliot was sorely tempted to do. Gervase was due to meet him in his office in ten minutes, and the way Elliot was feeling he would give anything to be able to take out his frustration on the man. He closed his eyes and, for a few unprofessional moments, saw himself giving the over-privileged bastard the pasting of his life. He was shoving him up against the wall and punching that supercilious expression right off his face. Then he was kicking him to the ground and—

His eyes snapped open, and he leaned back in his chair, let out his breath and unclenched his fists. No. That was going too far. It was all very well using Gervase as a mental punch-bag to chase away the maelstrom of his anger and frustration, but the scenes of blood and chipped bones were signs that things were getting out of hand. Perhaps it was time to put a stop to the supposedly therapeutic imagery.

He lowered his gaze to the file on his otherwise clear desk and read through the points he'd made last night at home. When he'd finished, he checked his watch and saw that it was five past six. As usual Gervase was late. He drummed his fingers impatiently, swivelled restlessly in his chair, then got to his feet. He went and stood at the panoramic window that looked out across the city, where offices all over Manchester glimmered in the fading light. Rivulets of water sluiced down the glass and above him the lacklustre sky was throwing a literal wet blanket over the remains of the day. Nine floors down, neighbouring office workers, some with umbrellas but most without, were hurrying to escape the heavy downpour. It was a murderously depressing view. Not what he needed at all. He turned away and went back to his desk.

After weeks of not hearing from Rachel Vincent he'd received a wary call from her. They'd arranged to meet in Altrincham last Monday evening at the Cresta Court Hotel and, after some gentle persuasion, she had told him the real reasons why she had left so suddenly. None of what she said came as a surprise, but Elliot had needed to hear from her what he had thus far suspected. He'd tried to encourage her to put in writing what she'd just shared with him, but at first she'd refused, claiming that if word got out her career would hit the skids faster than a runaway train. She was now working for a rival firm of accountants where the same prehistoric breed of male ruled supreme. 'Let's face it, Elliot,' she'd said, 'we all know that the Gervases of this world get away with it because they think sexual harassment is a big joke.'

In the end he had convinced her that, if that attitude was ever to be eradicated, women like her had to speak out. 'I'll make you an offer,' he'd said. 'Help me get rid of Gervase and there'll be a job for you.'

'My old job?' she'd asked doubtfully.

'No, with Gervase gone there'll be some shuffling to do. I think it's time there was a female partner, don't you?'

Elliot returned his attention to the file on his desk and looked at the letter Rachel had written for him, a copy of which was now on file in London with their senior personnel officer. It was two pages of carefully worded condemnatory evidence cataloguing Gervase's repeated harassment of some of the younger women in the office. According to Rachel's testimony, Gervase picked his victims with care, choosing those who were unmarried and, in particular, those who valued their career prospects highly enough that they wouldn't report him for fear of reprisals. He had approached Rachel several times, and on one occasion had turned up at her house late one evening with a bottle of wine suggesting that they cement their professional relationship in the time-honoured manner. When she'd refused and had sent him packing, he had begun to make things difficult in the office, culminating in the fiasco with Hayes and Clarke and the under-budgeted fee. It looked as if Gervase had deliberately agreed an unrealistically low fee with the client over the phone and had then let Rachel bill for the correct amount, which was a cool hundred thousand pounds over the apparent budget. He'd then informed her of what he'd done, saying that if she didn't resign he would claim that it was she who had miscalculated the incorrect fee. What's more, he would argue that it had been a deliberate act of sabotage after she'd made improper advances towards him – which, naturally, he had turned down – and of course, as everybody knows, hell has no fury like a woman scorned. As an act of petty revenge for not having had his way with her it stank, and given the clear account of events with which Rachel had provided him, Elliot was sure that Gervase would now have to own up to his appalling underhandedness.

Except there was always the worry that a slimy piece of work like Gervase could smooth-talk his way out of the deepest hole.

If all else failed, Elliot did have another trick up his sleeve for showing

Gervase the door. He didn't want to have to resort to such tactics but, if need be, he would. As partner-in-charge it was down to him to safeguard those who worked for the firm, and with the likes of Gervase roaming the building it seemed that no woman was safe.

Fifteen minutes late, Gervase finally breezed in. He didn't even acknowledge that he'd kept Elliot waiting.

'So, what can I do for you?' he asked, when he had made himself at home in the chair opposite Elliot and automatically tried to take a surreptitious look at the file a few feet away from him. 'Some problem you need help with, is it?'

Biding his time, Elliot regarded him for a few seconds. 'Problem is the right word,' he said, his mask of indifference set firmly in place, 'and it would appear that you're *it*.'

'Not with you, old chap. Is it National Riddle Day or something?'

'Sexual harassment mean anything to you?'

Gervase laughed and crossed one of his fat thighs over the other. 'Sexual harassment,' he said loftily. 'I'll tell you what that is. It's a lot of frigid women making a song and dance about something that comes quite naturally to chaps like us.'

'In what way?'

'Sorry, don't quite understand you.'

'Perhaps you'd explain what it is that comes quite naturally to you.' Elliot's tone was neutral and deceptively mild, betraying nothing of the trap he had waiting for Gervase.

Gervase studied his face warily. 'Would you mind awfully getting to the point?'

'Very well. The point is, I've received an extremely serious complaint about your behaviour in the office towards some of our female personnel. Anything to say?'

'Sounds like a lot of cock and bull.'

'I should warn you that a copy of the letter of complaint is with Personnel in London and they'll be sending somebody up here next week to investigate the allegations. Anything to say now?'

Gervase uncrossed his legs and tossed his head defiantly. 'You're one hell of a piece of work, Anderson. How you must be loving this. This hasn't got anything to do with sexual harassment, this is about *us*. This is nothing but a class issue.'

'I don't think that's what Rachel Vincent would call it.' Elliot shifted his gaze from Gervase's insolent face to the file at his fingertips.

Gervase's eyes narrowed malevolently and also came to rest on the file. 'And what's that bitch been saying?'

'Bitch,' repeated Elliot drily. 'That's an emotive word.'

'Then try this one. Bastard. Because that's what you are.'

'Thank you, I appreciate your directness.' Elliot's voice was as icy cool as the look in his eyes.

'I'll fight you over this,' Gervase lashed out, his arrogant swaggering now turning to bullying threats. 'You won't get rid of me that easily. It'll be her word against mine. You'll end up with egg on your face and an early-retirement package.'

'I doubt that very much. Divorce, as you well know, is an expensive occupation.'

Gervase stopped in his tracks. 'Divorce? What the hell are you driving at?'

'I wonder how Fiona will react when she realises that you'll be facing a charge of sexual harassment. It will hardly go with the image she's cultivated for herself down at the *Club*.' He drew out this last word contemptuously.

But Gervase laughed nastily. 'I think you'll find you're clutching at straws there. Fiona will be right behind me if she knows what's good for her.'

'But not, I suspect, if she hears about you and Dawn. Presumably a second divorce settlement would stretch even your *old* money.'

With a rush of fury, Gervase leaped to his feet. He rested his hands on the desk and leaned in towards Elliot, his breath betraying the extended lunch he'd enjoyed earlier, a lunch that had been topped off by several brandies and a cigar. 'You're nothing but a slippery bastard,' he snarled menacingly, 'a slippery bastard who can't hack it with anyone not from the same shitty working-class background that you crawled out of.'

Elliot didn't even flinch. He stared impassively into Gervase's odious face and said, 'At least I'm an honest slippery bastard.'

Gervase backed off. He went and stood by the window. 'So what's your problem exactly, Elliot? Jealous of somebody having more fun than you? Is that it? Are you so sexually tight-arsed since Ali dumped and divorced you that you can't stand the thought of anyone else getting lucky?'

At the reference to his private life, all Elliot could think was that this was the man responsible for keeping him on the phone the night Isaac had died. If Gervase hadn't made that call, Isaac might still be alive. The desire to smash his fist into the other man's slack jaw was so powerful that Elliot nearly allowed himself the pleasure of doing exactly that. He saw himself punch Gervase so hard that his flabby body flew back against the window and crashed through the glass to his certain death on the cold, wet pavement below.

This wildness of thought lasted no more than a second but it was long enough for Elliot to pull himself together and meet Gervase's words with composed authority. 'You can fight the allegations and make things extremely messy for all parties concerned, and I mean *all* parties, or you can own up to what you've done and resign.'

'That's a load of crap and you know it. Either way I lose.'

'Yes, I suppose you do. Now, if you don't mind, I have things to do.'

'Bugger you to hell and back, Anderson.' And giving Elliot the finger, Gervase stormed out of the office.

It was dark and raining even harder when Elliot, weary and dispirited, reached Timbersbrook. He parked his car and made a dash for the door. Sam was in the kitchen doing battle with a piece of pork tenderloin that he was knocking seven bells out of with a rolling-pin. 'I'm trying to show it exactly who's boss,' he said, with a grin, taking another well-aimed blow.

Without removing his raincoat, Elliot reached for the bottle of red wine that Sam had opened. He poured himself a glass and said, 'Not dissimilar from what I've been doing this afternoon.'

'Oh, aye? Been flexing those big honcho muscles of yours, have you?'

'Something like that.'

'Want to talk about it?'

'Not really.'

'Suit yourself. Supper won't be ready for at least another hour so if you want to be unsociable you've plenty of time for a swim.'

'Is that a subtle way of saying, "Get your miserable face out of here"?'

'Hey, back up, pal, I only meant that maybe you could do with a bit of unwinding, that's all.'

They stood staring at one another for a few hostile seconds until Elliot said, 'I'm sorry, Dad. You're right, a swim would probably do me good.'

Sam watched his son leave the kitchen and, once again, cursed the way things had turned out. Elliot and Ali had been so close to getting back together again when she had gone and pulled off the most unbelievably dumb stunt. When Elliot had come home that day after his trip to the States and explained what Ali had just told him, Sam hadn't known what to think of her. In the days that followed, he had found himself hating her for what she was putting Elliot through, but then gradually he calmed down and suggested to Elliot that maybe he'd been a bit hasty.

'Forget it,' Elliot had said. 'I never want to see her again. And please don't go behind my back and talk to her as if on my behalf. If nothing else, promise me that.'

Sam had so far stuck to his promise, but now he was wondering if it wouldn't be okay for him to see Ali, at least to let her know that not all the Andersons had abandoned her. Though he knew that his son was suffering, he didn't want Ali miserable either.

Over supper in the kitchen that evening he decided to test the water with Elliot.

Resignedly, Elliot said, 'You must do what you think is right.'

'You wouldn't consider talking to her yourself, then?'

'Don't push it, Dad.'

'Look, son, she made a huge error of judgement—'

'Is that what you call it?'

'Hey, don't get clever with me. But have you tried looking at it from another angle?'

'Any suggestions?'

'Well, how about this? She betrayed you physically but not mentally . . . not in her heart?'

'Sorry, but that almost makes it worse. What she did was so calculating, so premeditated.'

'We both know what she did was wrong,' Sam said sadly, 'and by now she knows that herself, so what harm a tiny act of forgiveness, eh?'

Elliot pushed away his unfinished meal. 'I wouldn't describe it as a tiny act of forgiveness.'

'So she made a mistake and you're too big and grand these days to forgive her, is that it?'

'Of course I'm not.'

'Seems that way to me.'

'Well, good for you.'

In bed that night, Elliot lay in the darkness thinking about what his father had said. He knew that it made sense, but he just couldn't bring himself to forgive Ali. Perhaps he was being stubborn, but he couldn't get it out of his mind that while professing to love him she had taken Trevor to her bed. Hadn't she realised how he would feel? Hadn't it occurred to her that he loved her so all-consumingly, so possessively, that he would be crazy with jealousy and that it would make him question what she really felt for him?

But, as angry as he was, he knew he was still deeply in love with Ali. She was an integral part of his being and always would be. She was everything he wasn't. She was his spontaneity, his sense of fun. In short, she made him feel complete. Like a perfectly balanced piano concerto, she was the colourful, triumphant cadenza to his more lyrically haunting melody.

And haunted was what he felt.

Since that fateful day in August at the mill, he had been grieving again for what might have been. The nightmares about Isaac had returned, and his every waking moment when he couldn't focus his thoughts on work was filled with a dreadful desire to take out his mood on the first person who got in his way.

He'd always seen himself as a fair man, but he wondered now if he hadn't let his personal life interfere with his professional one. Certainly Gervase was doing the firm no favours by harassing the women at the office, but had it been right for Elliot to use his knowledge about him and Dawn as a lever to oust him?

More importantly, had he let his grief over Isaac get the better of him? Had he allowed it to cloud his judgement?

He turned over in a futile attempt to sleep, and as he listened to the rain beating against the window, Gervase's last words echoed inside his head: *Bugger you to hell and back, Anderson.*

Oh, no worries, Gervase, I'm already there.

'Airports,' grumbled Ali, as she crossed one leg over the other and tapped the air impatiently with her foot. 'I can't stand them. Little more than air-conditioned palaces of the damned.'

Daniel smiled and offered her a small glass dish of cashew nuts. 'It could be worse,' he said. 'We could be travelling economy.'

She took a handful and gave the executive lounge of Brussels airport a withering glance. 'Well, praise and thanks to our lustrous and most generous clients for treating us to business class, then. A shame they couldn't have laid on a Lear jet for our own personal use.' She recrossed her legs and looked at her watch. 'How much longer are we going to be kept hanging around?'

'It won't be long now. Do you fancy another drink?'

She nodded and got quickly to her feet. 'I'll get them. It'll give me something to do.'

Daniel watched her go over to the hospitality bar, and couldn't help noticing how thin she was. Her appearance wasn't helped either by the severity of the black suit she was wearing: it drained her of all colour and drew attention to the unmistakable fact that she was washed out with tiredness. Dog-tired himself and knowing how little sleep Ali was surviving on, he had no idea how she was managing to stay upright, never mind work the hours she was currently putting in. When he was knackered, he invariably adopted what Richard described as his manner of a man past caring, but Ali was the opposite: she became edgy and uptight and even more restless and impatient than she normally was. And these past few months, since August, he had never known her so restless. She was always at the office before and after him – long after him mostly: some nights, as late as ten o'clock, he phoned the office to see if she was still there. But she'd grown wise to him tracking her movements and had stopped answering the phone. He'd tried other tactics to tear her away from her desk, inviting her for dinner with him and Richard or asking her to join them for an evening at the theatre. She was no fool, though, and had seen straight through him. 'I know what you're up to, Daniel, and as grateful as I am, there's no need. I'm fine. Really I am.'

But Daniel knew that she was far from fine. It was all very well claiming that the long hours she was working were doing wonders for their business – she was acquiring dozens of new clients, some of them quite prestigious – but it couldn't go on. 'It keeps me from thinking of Elliot,' she told him, when he'd literally taken her by the shoulders one morning at the office and told her to slow down.

Covering his mouth with a hand, Daniel gave in to a jaw-stretching yawn; it really had been a long, exhausting day. They'd been on the early flight out to Brussels, sat through countless meetings, then when they'd arrived back at the airport they'd been told that a small fire on the runway earlier that afternoon had delayed all incoming and outgoing flights by at least three hours. They'd toyed with the idea of checking into a hotel for the night, but had decided against it, both preferring the thought of half a night's sleep in their own beds to a disturbed one in a hotel room. Though it was debatable how much sleep Ali would get wherever she was. Sleep, he guessed, was something of a luxury to her, these days.

He saw her turn away from the bar and start walking towards him. She looked so fragile and young, and yet ... and yet she was far from fragile. Without doubt she was made of tougher stuff than he was. He couldn't begin to understand how he would have reacted if he had gone through half of what she had. For one thing he couldn't have deliberately denied himself Richard's love – not even for a friend like Ali. But, then, maybe that just proved the old gender theory that essentially men were selfish, that by ensuring they always put themselves first their survival was guaranteed. It was generally accepted that the female of the species was the one who always went the extra mile and made the greatest sacrifices – and in this instance, Ali was making one hell of a sacrifice.

She handed him his drink and sat down beside him. 'You look tired,' she remarked.

'That's rich coming from you.'

She stared at him over the rim of her glass. 'Meaning?'

He shrugged. 'Nothing you don't already know.'

She sat back in her chair. 'Don't start, Daniel. Not another lecture about me working too hard. It's not what I need to hear.'

He sipped his wine thoughtfully. 'You realise, don't you, that your time limit's nearly up?'

She looked away and rested her gaze on one of the flight information monitors.

'Ali, you've got a week and then I talk to Elliot. That was the agreement.'

'A few more weeks wouldn't hurt you,' she said softly, still not looking at him.

'Oh, yes, it would. It hurts me every day when I think of what you're doing to yourself.'

'Then don't think about it.'

He put down his glass and turned to face her. 'Look at me, Babe. Look me straight in the eye and tell me what you see.'

She scowled and pursed her lips. 'Stop being so melodramatic, Daniel. People are watching.'

She was right: a few yards away, a large, heavy-set man with a distinctive set of Belgian whiskers was staring at them over his copy of *Le Soir*. But Daniel didn't care, he took hold of Ali's chin and forced her to look at him. 'Tell me what you see.'

'I see *you*, Daniel. What else am I supposed to say?'

'So you don't see a friend who loves and cares for you? A friend who wants only the best for you.'

She turned her head away. 'And what you're blind to is that's exactly what I want for Sarah.'

Daniel ran a hand through his hair in frustration. 'Ali, you've given both Sarah and Elliot plenty of time to reconsider how they feel about you. If they were going to change their opinion of what you did, they would have done so by now.'

'But a few more weeks might make all the difference. Oh, come on, Daniel, give me more time. I know Sarah, she never does anything without putting a lot of thought into it. Coming to terms with what I did is not something she's going to rush in to. Once she's accepted why I did what I did, she'll get in touch. I know she will.'

'Ali, you're stringing me along. Face it, this is never going to work. We're not just talking about Sarah making the decision to leave Trevor, are we? She's actually got to divorce him while still under the impression that adultery took place, isn't that right? And even if she went through with it, you'd never be able to tell her the truth because it would make a mockery of everything she believes in.'

'But none of that would matter if she realised why I did it and could forgive me.'

'And if she never could?'

For the first time in their conversation, Ali hesitated. Tears sprang into her dark eyes and she gulped down the rest of her drink. 'I can't let myself think that,' she said, 'any more than I can allow myself to think that Elliot won't forgive me.'

And that was the cornerstone of her hope, thought Daniel. Ali had to keep faith with the belief that Elliot loved her so much that, no matter what, he would forgive her. If that happened, Daniel suspected that Ali would have the strength to wait however long it took for Sarah also to absolve her. But he doubted it would happen. As long as Elliot believed Ali had been unfaithful to him he would continue to think the worst of her and consign her to this everlasting misery. He put his arm round her shoulder and drew her to him. 'False hope is a soul-destroying business, Babe,' he said gently. 'I know you want to believe that Elliot will do the decent thing, but wouldn't it be better to tell him the truth and hope that you can convince him that it's in Sarah's interests to keep her in ignorance of what really happened that night?'

'No, it's too big a risk,' she said vehemently. Then, in a more conciliatory tone, 'Please, Daniel, instead of making it worse for me, why don't you help me? Elliot holds the key to this mess. Time's a great healer and the more of it that passes, the greater chance there is of him eventually forgiving me, and of Sarah getting the future she deserves.'

'Would you like me to speak to Elliot?'

Ali lifted her head from Daniel's shoulder. Fleetingly she considered saying yes, but then thought better of it. What if Daniel found himself unable to keep from Elliot the true course of events that night at the mill?

Sensing her hesitation and the reason behind it, Daniel said, 'If I'd wanted to go behind your back, I would have done so before now – and don't think there haven't been days when I wasn't tempted. Of course, if you don't trust me—'

'It's not a matter of not trusting you,' she cut in, 'it's . . . Oh, it's no good, you just have to accept that this is between Elliot and me. Only the two of us can resolve it.'

'You mean you have to get through this on your own, don't you?'

'Yes. Yes I do.'

He reached for his drink and took a long swallow. 'You know, Babe, sometimes I wish you didn't feel the need to be so bloody strong.'

'I can't help it, it's the way I am.'

'It's not a crime admitting that you need help. Millions of us do it every day of our lives.'

'But I have asked you for help.'

He looked up into her face. 'No, you haven't. You've asked me to stand back and leave you to it.'

'But it's what I want. Why can't you see that?'

He let out a weary sigh of defeat. 'All right, I'll do as you say. But I'm striking another deal with you. You have to ease off work. You're practically killing yourself with the hours you're putting in. I want to see some colour in that sad little face of yours and a decent bit of weight on you. And, what's more, we'll review matters in December. Is that clear?'

Much later that night, when at last Ali reached home, she pulled off her clothes and crawled into bed. She felt overwhelmingly exhausted and suddenly wished that she didn't feel the need, as Daniel had put it, always to be so bloody strong. She held Mr Squeezy against her chest and eventually fell asleep dreaming that it was Isaac in her arms.

48

October had given way to November, and the short wintry days of December had brought forth the annual feeding frenzy of retail madness. Sarah had taken a day off from sewing and had brought Grace to Chester to do her Christmas shopping, but she wasn't enjoying the outing as much as she had thought she would. Unusually for her she was exhausted and finding it difficult not to lose her temper when yet another pushchair rammed her from behind or a flailing elbow dug into her side.

A little after four o'clock, when the crowds were showing signs of thinning, Grace suggested that they stopped for a cup of tea and a mince-pie. 'My treat,' she said, as they found themselves a table in the nearest café in Bridge Street. The tinsel-decorated windows were steamed up and the waitresses were as short on politeness as they were on spare tables and festive pastries. With only a couple of cherry scones left in the display cabinet, Grace and Sarah's choice was soon made and despatched to them with a singular lack of care and attention.

'Christmas,' said Grace, as she mopped up the milk the waitress had slopped when the small, inelegant metal jug had been thumped on to the table. 'That special time of goodwill to all men.'

'Poor woman, I bet she wishes she was at home, as I do.'

Grace stopped what she was doing. She put the milk-soaked napkin into the overflowing ashtray and said, 'I'm sorry, Sarah, I didn't realise this was proving such a trial for you. Would you rather we finished and went back to the car?'

Sarah immediately regretted what she'd said. 'Oh, Grace, I'm sorry, I could have put that better.'

'Indeed not. If that's how you feel then that's exactly what you should say. I'd much rather have the truth from you than a polite white lie. Do you want to tell me what's wrong, or shall I mind my own business?'

Sarah stirred her tea with a buckled spoon. 'You're giving me the choice?'

Grace smiled. 'Don't I always?'

'No. No, you don't. With your sweet-tongued questions you always get right to the heart of the matter and make me confront things that are best left untouched.'

'You know, Sarah, I've never had you down as a coward, but now I'm beginning to think that you are.'

'Are you trying to bait me?'

'A fish only rises to the bait when it's hungry.'

'Or if it's curious.'

Grace cut her scone in half and slowly buttered both pieces. When she'd finished, she said, 'And, of course, you're neither of those things, are you, Sarah?'

Sarah drank some tea and wished that Grace would keep quiet. She was tired of her questions. She was especially tired of fielding them.

Hungry.

Curious.

They were both obvious metaphors for something else. She found herself wishing that the seat opposite her was filled by Ali. At least Ali wouldn't mess around with stupid metaphors. She'd be straight in there with a direct question: 'So what's bugging you today?' she'd say. 'A touch of the holier-than-thou Trevors?'

'I'm annoying you, aren't I, Sarah?'

In response to Grace's perceptive question, Sarah put down her cup. 'Yes, I'm afraid you are.'

'Well, then, there's an honest answer if ever I heard one. But am I the cause of your annoyance or merely a symptom?'

Before Sarah could reply, the people at the table next to them gathered together their bags of shopping and made a noisy exit. After they'd gone, she said, 'I feel that you're the cause, but very probably you're not. I think I'm annoyed with everybody.'

'But I would imagine there's one person who's annoying you more than most.'

'Are you referring to Trevor?'

'Oh, no, Sarah, not Trevor. I was thinking of you.'

'Me?'

'When we start accusing everybody else of irritating us, it's often because we're the person with whom we're most irritated. How's that sticking-plaster going, by the way? Still missing Ali?'

'Yes. And if you want to know the truth I was just wishing that you were her.'

'So what would you give to have her friendship reinstated?'

'That's an unfair question.'

'Only because you consider it so.'

'But you know why I can't see her. I'm protecting my marriage ... preserving it.'

Grace chewed thoughtfully on the last mouthful of her scone. She dusted the crumbs off her fingers and checked to see if there was any more tea in the pot. There wasn't. She replaced the lid and said, 'And is it working? Is your marriage in a better state than it was before you got rid of Ali's threat to it?'

'We're still together.'

'You mean you're still bound by guilt.'

'It's got us this far.'

For the first time in their friendship, Sarah heard Grace's normally gentle voice become heated with exasperation. 'Sarah,' she said, 'are you really prepared to make such an extreme sacrifice? Can you really go on living with somebody you don't love? And, quite apart from it not being fair to you, what about being fair to Trevor? Where, might I ask, is your integrity in all of this?'

'It's integrity that's keeping me with Trevor.'

'Nonsense. It's fear. You're wrapped in fearful thinking, terrified of making the decision you know you should have made a long time ago. You need to strip away the layers with which you've protected yourself and rediscover the real you, the genuine Sarah complete with all her self-esteem.'

Sarah picked up the buckled spoon from her saucer and tried to straighten it. Despite her efforts, it remained twisted. She dropped it back into the saucer. 'But I'm too afraid,' she said in a low voice. 'Can't you see that?'

Grace's expression softened. 'I know,' she said gently, 'and I also know that once you've made that important decision you'll be able to start forgiving yourself, because until you do you're never going to be truly at peace.'

'That's all very well, but when I've added yet another sin to the pile I've already accumulated, where will that leave me?'

'Oh, Sarah, there you go again being so hard on yourself. Why can't you accept that you've done your best? Stop hanging your guilty conscience on the peg of your faith, which you've turned into nothing more valid than a lucky talisman. And moreover, you—'

Sarah opened her mouth to speak, but Grace was having none of it. She quelled Sarah's protestations with a raised hand and said, 'Please, let me finish. I'm well aware that for somebody such as yourself forgiveness seems well out of your grasp, but some day you'll see that you were mistaken.'

'Perhaps some transgressions are irredeemable.'

Grace smiled suddenly. 'Trying to do God's job for him, are you, Sarah? Deciding what He can and cannot take on?'

Sarah didn't respond. Nor did she return Grace's smile.

'You know,' said Grace kindly, 'sometimes in our lives we have to admit defeat and hand over the burden of what we're not able to resolve. Maybe this is one of those occasions.'

Still Sarah didn't say anything.

When Grace had paid their bill, they left the warm, fuggy atmosphere of the café and stepped into the biting cold wind of early evening. It was dark as they made their way to the multi-storey car park, and as they plodded along with their heavy bags, Sarah felt even more weighed down than she had earlier. She knew that everything Grace had just said she had said with the right motive. She knew also that it made sense. But knowing the right thing to do and actually carrying it out was another matter. She wasn't brave enough to tell Trevor the truth. How could she tell him that their marriage had been a sham? How could she turn on him so brutally? Especially since the summer when he'd been trying so hard to please her. So intense had been his displays of loyalty and devotion that she had grown worried he might regain an interest in sex. To her relief, and shame, her fears on this score remained unfounded.

Keeping herself busy through the autumn and winter had seemed the best way to stop her thoughts wandering beyond the boundaries of her situation, that and writing long, chatty letters to Hannah, as if by concocting a happy fairy-tale version of the daily goings-on at Smithy Cottage it might magically become a reality. But nothing she did could disguise the one terrible, inescapable truth: she was desperately lonely. With no Hannah around and no Ali at the other end of a phone, there was no one to take the edge off her misery. Grace had tried to cheer her, she knew, but Grace wasn't Hannah, and she certainly wasn't Ali. But, then, nobody could ever replace Ali. Any feelings of rancorous envy that Sarah had thought she harboured towards Ali had vanished, along with her anger. She knew now that, more than anything, she wanted Ali's friendship back. But it was impossible. It was either Ali or her marriage. The two just weren't compatible.

All multi-storey car parks are the same and the one in which Sarah had left her car was no exception: it was dark and smelly, and now that it was night, it felt intimidating. They took the lift up to the third floor and when they stepped out, they were met by a loud shriek. It was the cry of a girl. They couldn't see anybody, but as they moved away from the lift and towards the car they heard a further scream, followed by the ominous sound of male laughter. It was coming from beyond the pay-and-display ticket machine. 'Stay here,' Sarah instructed Grace. She dumped her shopping and went to investigate. She found a group of scuffling lads, one of whom – the largest and indisputably the ugliest – had a gruesome selection of nuts and bolts skewered through the fleshier, more protruding of his features. He was holding a girl by the hair and had her on the ground with one of his huge booted feet resting on her stomach. Among the onlookers was another girl, standing by with a helpless look on her face. Without a thought for her own safety, Sarah waded in. 'What the hell do you think you're doing?' she shouted at the youth. 'What kind of pathetic bully are you? Let go of her. Didn't you hear me? I said let go.' Her voice echoed, shrill and fierce, in the cavernous dimly lit car park.

Amazingly he did as she said, but then, stepping over the girl, he came towards Sarah challengingly. He towered over her and pushed his face down into hers. His stale breath smelt as bad as he looked. 'Just a bit of fun.' He smirked. 'What's it to you?'

'Fun?' she repeated with disgust. 'You call that fun?' She turned her attention to the girl, who was now on her feet, standing next to the other girl. They made an identical pair with their shaggy permed hair, leather jackets and tiny skirts. Giggling nervously, they were exchanging glances with the lads, whom they obviously knew. They looked old enough to know better but young enough to have been at home enjoying an episode of *Grange Hill*. Sensing that the situation wasn't as menacing as she had thought at first, and that it was probably a case of horseplay that had got out of hand, Sarah let rip at the girl who'd been on the ground. 'And what were you thinking of, letting him treat you like that? Don't you have any self-respect? Don't you understand anything about being a woman? Now clear off and go home.'

Not waiting for a reply from the stunned group, she stalked away to where she'd left Grace.

'Goodness,' said Grace, when they were climbing into the car. 'What a tough little thing you are beneath that marshmallow exterior.'

Sarah drove towards the exit and didn't speak until they were out on the streets, heading for the Nantwich road. 'I hope I didn't embarrass you back there,' she said.

'Embarrass me? I'm immensely proud of you. Not everyone would have had the courage to take on such a grotesque-looking Goliath.'

'I couldn't help myself. I can't stand people who take advantage of others.'

'Or girls who get themselves into a situation they don't know how to get out of?'

'Them too. Just what did she think she was doing? Didn't either of those girls realise the danger they were putting themselves in?'

'They looked very young.'

'That's hardly an excuse to behave so irresponsibly.'

They drove the rest of the journey in silence. Sarah dropped Grace off, then continued the hundred yards or so to Smithy Cottage. The lights were on in the house and she carried the bags of shopping up to the spare bedroom, then dumped them on the bed. When she came downstairs Trevor was waiting for her. There wasn't a trace of sawdust in his hair or on his clothes so she assumed that he'd been hard at the Apocalyptic Age again. Angry, she thought of yet another day's potential earnings lost in the name of God.

'Sarah,' he said, 'I've invited the group round tonight. Any chance of you rustling up a cake or something?'

'Why?'

'Because everyone enjoys your cakes.'

She frowned. 'I didn't mean that. I meant why have you invited the group round? It's not the usual night to get together.'

'Ah,' he said awkwardly. Was it her imagination or did he look shifty? 'Um . . . it's a special evening,' he went on, 'something I feel called to do. It might set the ball rolling for other evenings like it. I truly think it will be a good thing for the group. Very liberating.'

Uninterested in this latest hare-brained scheme that Trevor felt 'called' to pursue, she sighed a weary sigh of resignation and went to the freezer for some mince pies she'd made at the weekend. Well, whatever he had planned, it really didn't matter. Nothing he ever did had any direct bearing on her.

An hour and a half later, she found she couldn't have been more wrong.

They'd messed about in the hall with their shoes and slippers, they'd had their quiet time, and now they were chomping their mince pies and sipping their coffee, waiting patiently for their very own oracle to speak to them.

Sarah was waiting too. There was something different about Trevor this evening, an air of mystery in which he was clearly revelling. He'd put himself centre-stage and was loving every minute of it. 'Why are we here,

Trevor?' Dave had asked earlier, to which Trevor had replied enigmatically, 'All shall shortly be revealed.'

Shirley had been just as curious as Dave, but had tried to conceal it with a reference to her back. 'It won't take long, will it, Trevor? Only my back isn't good tonight and won't cope with sitting in the same position for too long.'

'Right, then,' said Trevor, putting his empty plate under his chair. 'I know you're probably all wondering why I've arranged this meeting, and I thank you for turning out in the cold, but by the time you leave here I sincerely hope that you'll be warmed by, and armed with, the essence of what fired those early Christians – the spirit of true faith, which is to love and to forgive.'

Suddenly he got to his feet, for what Sarah could only think was extra effect – and it might have worked had not a piece of pastry been stuck in his beard – and said, 'I want to tell you a true story of a husband and a wife, a husband who committed an act of adultery and a godly wife who committed an act of faith and forgiveness.'

Sarah froze.

He wouldn't dare.

Surely not.

But Trevor did dare, and he held the room spellbound for the next twenty minutes as he told them of his personal encounter with the Devil. 'It was my appointed time of temptation,' he told them, 'and, being the poor wretch I am, I failed the test. I was offered sin on a platter and I feasted on it. But the point I want to make is that if a mature Christian such as myself can succumb to the charm of the Devil then what hope for others not so secure in their walk with Christ?' He gave them no opportunity to respond, ignored Sarah's pleas for him to stop, but blundered on enthusiastically with his testimony, aligning himself with Old Testament heroes such as Samson, Gideon, Barak and Moses, at the same time dressing the whole thing up in childish, Sunday-school language: Ali was Satan's messenger, he the innocent lamb, Sarah the water of forgiveness.

Sarah closed her eyes, realising that this was the future. Now that Trevor had revealed his sin of sins to a real audience there would be no stopping him. He would become a poor man's version of one of those cringe-making American TV evangelists spurting tears at the drop of a confession. She could even imagine him being a guest speaker at Christian men's breakfast meetings up and down the country baring his testimonial all.

He would be insufferable.

And he would make her life insufferable. He would hold her up as a model Christian wife – when she was anything but.

Her blood ran cold and, with a chilling calm, she knew that she had to stop him. She had to make him see that this madness could not go on. But, more importantly, she knew that she could not carry on living the lie.

She no longer felt sorry for Trevor. She no longer wanted to protect him from the truth. In fact, it was time he faced the truth. She hoped his faith was real enough to carry him through the days ahead. 'Trevor,' she said, just as he was drawing breath to continue his tale of good versus bad, 'I think you should sit down.'

'In a minute, Sarah, I haven't finished. I was just—'

'Trevor, sit down!' She spoke with the same anger that had earlier compelled her to take on the thug in the car park.

He did as she said and everyone looked at her expectantly, their amazed curiosity shining in their eyes. 'Trevor,' she began, 'I really can't allow you to cast me in the role of sainted wife who finds it in her heart to forgive her husband his momentary loss of control.'

'But that's just your natural Christian modesty preventing you from—'

'Be quiet, and don't open your mouth until I've finished. And, for goodness sake, get the crumbs out of your beard!'

He goggled at her, as did everybody else.

'There's something very important that you should know, Trevor,' she began again. 'In a sense I do forgive you for what happened with Ali because ... because you were set up. You were used. Without my knowledge, Ali planned the whole thing. She lured you into her bed so that, on the basis of you committing an act of adultery, it would give me the necessary grounds and courage, I might say, to leave you. A pity, really, that she went to all that trouble because, when it comes down to it, I'm leaving you of my own accord. I'm very sorry, Trevor, but I've never been the wife you deserved. I only hope that one day you can forgive me.'

The silence that followed couldn't have been greater. Sarah got to her feet and swept out of the room. All she was conscious of, as she headed for the hall and the unknown world beyond, was Trevor's open-mouthed expression of horrified disbelief and the rustle of paper as somebody – probably Elaine – flicked through their Bible for a helpful piece of scripture.

My God, I've done it, she thought, grabbing her coat and bag and shutting the door after her. I've finally done it.

The cold night air stung her cheeks as she pulled on her coat and considered what to do next. Grand exits were all very well, but they only worked if you had somewhere to go.

Grace was her answer.

She hurried along the lane in the light of the glowing street lamps, hoping that Grace would be in.

She was. Callum was there too.

Seeing the look of agitation on Sarah's face, Grace said, 'Callum, would you mind giving me a few minutes alone with Sarah? Perhaps you'd like to pour us a drink.'

When he'd disappeared, Sarah told Grace what she'd just done.

'And how do you feel?' asked Grace, when she had told her everything, including Trevor's ghastly testimony.

'Slightly euphoric.'

'Enjoy it while you can, it'll soon pass. If I know you, you'll be wallowing in guilt within the hour.'

'I'm not sure that I will. But, oh, my goodness, Grace, what do you suppose made Trevor do such a daft thing? And after weeks of insisting on absolute secrecy.'

'For some the need to confess outweighs the consequences. In Trevor's case, it's possible that the need to be absolved had to be on a grand scale.

Given his rather self-seeking personality, what better way to shake off his guilt than to make a public confession and receive a public act of forgiveness?'

'But supposing the group doesn't forgive him?'

Grace smiled. 'After the treatment you've just dished out?'

Sarah allowed herself a small smile. 'Was it very brutal of me, do you think?'

'A little. But don't go fretting over it. I presume you didn't tell him about Hannah.'

Sarah shook her head vehemently. 'No. And I never will. He should be allowed to keep that much of our marriage.'

'Only time will tell on that score. Now, is it all right if Callum brings us those drinks?'

'Oh, please, I feel I could do with one. By the way, I don't mind him knowing. I'm sure he would be discreet.'

Grace laughed. 'If there's one thing you can rely upon with my son the solicitor it's discretion.' She went out to the kitchen where Callum had gone, to return with him and a tray of glasses.

'Sherry,' said Callum, passing a glass to Sarah. 'My mother's answer to any emergency. I'm sorry about you and Trevor. Speaking as one who's been there, done it and got the battle scars, are you sure that what you're doing is the answer?'

'It's not a spur-of-the-moment decision,' Sarah said, realising that she'd taken the best part of two decades to reach it.

'Sorry,' he said, 'none of my business. I'll keep quiet and let you two do all the talking.'

'That would be a first,' said Grace, good-humouredly. She smiled at her son, then returned her attention to Sarah. 'I'd offer you a bed for the night, Sarah, but I really think you should put a little more distance between you and Trevor. Why don't you go and see Ali?'

'Do you think she'd have me?'

'Now, what do you really think? Go into the hall and ring her. Go on, do it now. Before the rush of adrenalin fades.'

A few minutes later Sarah came back into the sitting room.

'That was quick,' Grace said. 'Wasn't she in?'

'Oh, she was there all right, I just didn't tell her why I was coming to see her. Do you mind if I ring for a taxi?'

'I mind very much, given that Callum has just offered to drive you.'

Sarah turned to Callum. 'I couldn't possibly expect you to do that. It's so far and completely out of your way.'

'Sarah, there's no point in arguing with my mother. Or me, for that matter. Have your drink and then we'll go.'

Once again Sarah found herself standing on a cold doorstep. She kissed Grace's soft cheek and said, 'Thank you for all your help, and I'm sorry I was such terrible company earlier today.'

'I'll forgive you. Now remember, when the euphoria wears off, think of what an empowering day you've had. Not only did you stand up to a bully twice your size but you took the first all-important step towards creating a new life for yourself.'

'Come on, ladies,' said Callum, his breath freezing in the cold night air. 'It's too bloody nippy out here for protracted farewells.' He kissed his mother goodbye, then opened the passenger door of his Mercedes estate for Sarah. A hard frost had settled on the windscreen but, within seconds of switching on the engine, the thin layer of sparkling crystals began to melt.

For the first few minutes of the journey neither of them spoke, until Callum said, 'Has my mother ever mentioned my divorce to you?'

Surprised, Sarah said, 'No. Should she have?'

'No. But usually people who don't know the circumstances wonder why I ended up with custody of Jamie when it's more usual for the mother to keep the children.'

Sarah admitted that this had crossed her mind.

'I fought to the death for Jamie and I'd do it again, if the need arose.'

'Was she such a terrible wife and mother?'

'Yes,' he said simply. 'She had a major problem with monogamy and when Jamie was six years old she wanted to take him to live in Acapulco with her then current lover. I came home from work one day to find the house empty and a note saying what she was doing. I intercepted her at the airport and literally snatched Jamie out of her arms. The bloodiest of custody battles then ensued. I was scared to leave him for a moment in case she took him.'

'How awful. Where is she now?'

'No idea. The trail went cold years ago. Do you intend to divorce Trevor?'

Again his question took her by surprise, as did his abrupt tone. 'I don't know, I haven't thought that far. I just know I can't live with him any more.'

'Think very hard about it, Sarah. Divorce can be a hellish business.'

'So can marriage.'

He smiled. 'Okay, we've covered the divorce issue. Tell me who this bully was that you stood up to today. Or was that a thinly veiled reference on my mother's part to Trevor?'

'Trevor may be many things but he's not an out-and-out bully.' She told him about the incident in the car park.

'No wonder my mother wanted you to remind yourself of your hidden depths. What made you wade in like that?'

'It's a long story. We need to turn right here, by the way. Look, there's Ali's windmill, you can see its lights.'

If ever Sarah needed a symbol of light at the end of the tunnel, this was it.

49

Sarah insisted that Callum drop her off at the top of the lane to the mill, saying that she wanted to walk the remaining few hundred yards.

'Are you sure?' he asked. 'It's very dark, and it's probably icy. My mother would never forgive me if we heard on the news about a frozen body that was found in a ditch and it turned out to be you.'

'I'll be fine. And thank you for the lift, it was very kind of you.'

'No problem. Take care, won't you? And if you need a solicitor, you know where to find me.' He handed her a business card from his wallet. 'No doubt I'll see you sometime when Hannah and Jamie are back from college for Christmas. Good luck.'

Sarah watched him drive away. Then, with the freezing night air cutting through her overcoat, she began the short walk. She soon realised that Callum had been right. She could hardly see where she was going and in places the ground was treacherous with patches of ice. Once or twice she slipped and nearly went over, but undaunted she pressed on. Just as she'd reached the safety of the illuminated area of the mill and was able to walk more steadily, the door opened and a burst of light spilled out in front of her. In the centre of it was Ali.

Suddenly doubt gripped Sarah. Supposing Ali was distant? What if she had hurt her friend irrevocably by refusing to see her?

'Is that you, Sarah?'

'Yes,' she called, 'it's me.' She hastened her step and came face to face with Ali. They looked at one another, then everything was a mad blur of tears, hugs and incoherent apologies.

When they finally drew apart, Ali said, 'Come on in, you're about frozen to death.' She pulled Sarah inside, banged the door shut, took her coat and hung it up. 'Let's get you upstairs and into the warm.'

They sat on the rug in front of the fire, their faces flushed from the heat of the burning logs as well as from their tears.

'I couldn't believe it when I heard your voice on the phone,' said Ali. 'You don't know how much I've missed you.'

'Oh, yes, I do,' Sarah said. 'It's been the same for me. Not a day's gone by when I haven't wanted to talk to you and find out how you were. I'm sorry for hurting you in the way I did. I said some terrible things to you.'

Never had Ali felt so humbled. She had thought she'd never see Sarah again, that she had lost her friend for ever. Losing Sarah's friendship had been almost as bad as losing Isaac. Never had she felt so isolated. Although she was quite used to living alone, the solitariness she'd experienced of late had become a painful ordeal: each evening when she came home from the office she was stifled by it. The mill had felt much too large for her, and in bed at night the wind kept her awake as it murmured a mournful lament. It was only when she was at work with Daniel that the monotony of her sadness was broken. She didn't know what she would have done without him to lift her spirits. When she could no longer keep it from them, her parents had tried to help too, but because she'd lied about the true nature of her split from Elliot – she'd said that they had had a row – she'd found their love and support only added to her shame. Even Alastair had called her from Singapore. 'Hey, little sis, what the hell's going on? Mum and Dad have just spoken to me. Is there really no hope?' So touched was she by her brother's unexpected sympathy that she'd disintegrated into a flood of tears – unprecedented in their relationship, which was bonded with super-strength, I'm-tougher-than-you sibling rivalry. He'd even offered to speak to Elliot: 'Do you think he'd listen to me?' She'd mumbled something about it being hopeless and that he wasn't to flaunt his huge wealth on another overseas call.

And, irony of ironies, she hadn't been able to get out of her head that wretched piece of homework on Romans 7:15–25 that Trevor had set her, about the choice between right and wrong and how we always get it wrong. Well, she'd certainly done that.

But for all the harm Ali had caused, here was Sarah, the injured party, offering her the olive branch of peace. She chewed her thumbnail and said, 'You had every right to say what you did. It's me who has to apologise.'

Sarah smiled. 'I can't condone what you did, Ali, and I know you thought you were helping me, but I've come here tonight to tell you that I've left Trevor, not because of anything you did but because I finally found the courage to face the consequences of my own actions.'

Ali was stunned. 'You've really left him? Left him – as in *left* him?'

'Yes, a couple of hours ago.'

'But you seem so calm.'

'That's the weird thing, I am calm.'

'I always knew there was more to you than met the eye. How on earth did Trevor take it?'

'I'm not sure. I didn't give him much chance to respond.'

Ali frowned. 'What – you've written him a letter?'

Sarah told her about Trevor baring his soul to the group and her reaction to it. 'Do you think it was very unfair of me to finish our marriage in so humiliating a fashion for him?'

'I don't know whether unfair is the right word, but it would have certainly got the message home to him. I take my hat off to you, girl. When you come out fighting, you don't take any hostages, do you?'

'I didn't stop to think. I was acting on an impulse far stronger than anything I've ever experienced before. I just knew I had to put a stop to the madness.'

'Well, I'll tell you who'd be proud of you, Sarah the Impudent.'

They both laughed.

'But you realise you've turned Trevor into the biggest martyr this side of Joan of Arc, don't you?' said Ali. 'The Slipper Gang will be all over him, ready to have him canonised. You'll have done yourself no favours in their eyes either and you'll be the talk of Astley Hope for years to come.'

'I know and it's awful of me but I don't care.'

Ali gave her a hug. 'I want to say how proud I am of you and that I know you've done the right thing, but somehow it doesn't seem appropriate. From my own experience the end of a marriage is nothing to celebrate.'

'But we could celebrate the renewal of our friendship, couldn't we?'

'Good idea. No, don't move, stay here and throw another log on the fire while I do the honours.' She came back shortly with a bottle of red wine and two glasses. She filled them both and passed one to Sarah. 'To us,' she said, clinking her glass against Sarah's.

'And to the future, whatever it may be,' added Sarah.

'As to your immediate future,' Ali said, after she'd taken a reflective sip of her wine, 'you'll stay here with me, won't you?'

Sarah smiled. 'I was rather banking on that.'

Ali smiled too. 'So was I. I could do with the company.'

Sarah contemplated her friend. She was saddened at the change in Ali's appearance. She was pale and drawn, with dark smudgy shadows beneath her eyes. She was also much too thin. 'Is this the bit when I ask after Elliot?' she enquired gently.

Ali turned away and stared into the flickering flames of the fire, the soft light accentuating the shadows in her face. 'I haven't seen him since August,' she said. 'Losing him a second time feels immeasurably worse than before. It's reopened all the wounds that had begun to heal. For that brief spell in the summer the edge was taken off my grief for Isaac. It was as though we each had a part of Isaac within us, and when we were together we created a more complete memory of him. It made his death more bearable. But all that's gone now.'

'Oh, Ali, I'm so sorry.'

'Don't be, it was entirely of my own making. I made the same mistake with Elliot as I did with you. I took his forgiveness for granted. I thought that because he loved me he'd forgive me. So far I've been proved wrong.'

'Perhaps in time he will, when he—' But Sarah's words were cut short as Ali whipped round to face her. 'What is it, Ali?' she asked, alarmed.

'I've just realised something. But before I say anything, explain to me, hand on heart, and be prepared to swear on whatever is most precious to you, the bottom-line reason why you've left Trevor.'

Sarah looked confused. 'I don't understand.'

'Please, Sarah, it's important. Was it anything to do with my going to bed with him?'

Seeing the wild look of agitation in Ali's fiercely determined eyes, Sarah said, 'No, it wasn't. But I told you that a few minutes ago.'

'So what did it, then? What made you see reason at last?'

'I finally confronted the past, I suppose. Not only that, I realised that nothing I did was ever going to make my marriage right. I also knew I no longer felt sorry for Trevor, that I didn't feel beholden to him. Or beholden to a faith that I'd hidden behind – but that's another story, which I shan't bore you—'

'So adultery doesn't come into it?'

Sarah shook her head.

'You're positive? Absolutely positive? One hundred per cent sure?'

'Ali, what are you getting at?'

Ali took a gulp of her wine. 'There's something you have to know. I didn't do the unthinkable with Trevor. Trevor and I never had sex. It didn't happen.'

'But you said you did. And Trevor said that he and you—'

'I lied.'

'You lied?'

'Yes! Oh, heaven help me, but I lied. I'm not proud of what I did, you have to believe me, but I didn't seduce him as he thinks I did. It's worse than that. Much worse. I spiked his drink so that he'd crash out and wake up with only patchy recollections of the night before. That way I could make him believe anything I wanted. I undressed him and put him in my bed and the rest . . . the rest was pure fabrication on my part. Oh, Sarah, I'm so sorry. I should never have done it.'

Sarah took a few minutes to digest this dramatic turnaround in Ali's story. Her first and rather uncharitable thought was for Trevor and where it left him with his testimonial tale of the platter of temptation on which he thought he'd feasted. Her second thought was to be given more information.

'But, Ali, why didn't you tell me the truth sooner?'

'Because I wanted to keep the door open for you. If I'd withdrawn the lie it would have all been for nothing.'

'But why didn't you tell Elliot the truth? You could have told him what you'd really done.'

'No, I couldn't. He would have made me admit to you that Trevor was no guiltier of adultery than I was. You know what a straight, honest soul he is.'

Sarah was horrified at the sacrifice her friend had made for her. 'But, Ali, you lost Elliot in the process.'

'I very nearly lost you both.'

'Oh, Ali, you've got to speak to Elliot. You have to tell him you didn't go to bed with Trevor.'

But suddenly all Ali's earlier relief at knowing that the agony of her deception was over was replaced with doubt and melancholy. She returned her gaze to the flames. 'Perhaps it would do no good,' she said. 'He might think I was lying in the hope of winning him back.'

'Then I'll talk to him.'

'Maybe that wouldn't work either. He'd say I'd put you up to it.'

'But there has to be a way.'

'I'm not sure there is. If Elliot wanted to think well of me, he would have by now. I have to be realistic, I've turned myself into a classic wolf-crier. I'm a convicted liar whom no one will believe. It's probably only what I deserve.'

Seeing that Ali was close to tears again, Sarah put her arm round her. 'Hey there, you're not the only one who's a liar. What about my monumental piece of deceit with Trevor over Hannah? You can't steal my thunder on that.'

'Have you told him about it?'

'No.'

Ali sniffed and took another sip of wine. 'You know, I've given a lot of thought to Hannah's father, and I think I've figured out who he is.'

'You have?'

'Yes. It's my brother Alastair, isn't it?'

Sarah smiled and then she laughed. 'How did you reach that conclusion?'

'Quite easily, really. He was always trailing after you whenever you came down to Sanderling and I know you had a soft spot for him because you were always defending him. What's more, he came to see us in Oxford occasionally. But what I can't get my head round is why you didn't tell him you were pregnant. He would have married you, I know he would.'

'He wouldn't have had any choice, would he? You'd have been there with your shotgun.'

Ali smiled. 'So why didn't you tell him you were carrying his child?'

'For the simple fact that I wasn't. He isn't Hannah's father.'

'But he must be.'

'Ali, I think I know who I have and have not slept with.'

'But if it wasn't Alastair, who was it? I don't recall there being any other men on the scene at Oxford.'

Sarah took a hesitant sip on her wine. She lowered the glass and said, 'He was a tutor and I should have known better.'

'A tutor! Which one? Oh, my God, not Mr Creepy-I'm-so-Sleazy, the one in cowboy boots who chain-smoked, wore his jeans too tight and tried it on with all the first-years? Sarah, it wasn't?'

'Not even close.'

'Thank goodness for that. Who, then?'

'His name was John and he was on a sabbatical from Yale.'

Ali stared at her open-mouthed. 'Not John-John-Show-Us-Your—'

'The very one.'

'But he was a serial womaniser, Sarah. How on earth did you fall for him?'

'I didn't.'

'You just went with him for the sex?'

Sarah's face coloured. 'No!'

'What then?'

'He – he took advantage of me.'

Ali looked horrified. 'You're not saying he raped you, are you?'

Sarah thought of the two girls in the car park that afternoon and of what they'd got themselves into. 'I got myself into a situation with him. Then, when I changed my mind, he . . .'

'He wouldn't let you, is that it?'

'He was very persuasive and I was very naïve.'

'Sarah, the man was a complete bastard. Why didn't you tell me?'

'I was ashamed of myself for being so stupid and gullible, and I knew that you'd kick up a huge fuss and have the college authorities baying for his blood.'

'Too right I would have. It was lucky for him I never found out. Didn't he leave suddenly that year?'

'Yes. Shortly after I'd slept with him he had to go back to the States – his father was dying and he was needed at home. So, you see, there wasn't any point in telling him I was pregnant.'

'Oh, Sarah, what a dreadful mess. Will you ever tell Hannah?'

'I don't know. But if I do, that day's a long way off.'

'And what if she wanted to track down her real father? How would you feel about that?'

'A bridge to be crossed, if and when. But for now I think I have enough to contend with, don't you?'

At work the following morning, Ali received an unexpected phone call from Sam. She was just telling Daniel about last night when Margaret put the call through.

'How are you fixed for lunch?' he asked, without preamble.

'When were you thinking?' answered Ali. It was the first contact she'd had with Sam since the summer and, knowing what he must be thinking of her, she felt horribly embarrassed to be talking to him.

'Today,' he said.

She checked her diary. 'Okay,' she agreed. 'What time?'

'One o'clock at Franco's. And, Ali, no worries on my account, I'll be unarmed.'

'Thanks, Sam, I'll see you then.'

She put the phone down and saw that Daniel was staring at her over the top of his glasses.

'Do I detect Elliot's father at work again?' he asked.

'If only it were that easy.'

'Sounds to me as if it could be. Now that you've told Sarah the truth, you go right ahead and spill the real coffee-beans to Sam, then wait for the brew to filter back to Elliot. What do you reckon to him being on the phone the minute you get home tonight?'

'I'd rather put money on Elliot thinking that Sam and I have concocted this latest version of events as a last-ditch attempt to get us back together.'

Daniel regarded Ali as she switched her attention from him to the agreement she was preparing for a new client. She'd lost even more weight since October – weight that she could ill-afford to lose – and it didn't suit her. She looked as though she was wasting away. He hadn't seen her this bad since Isaac died. And it was coming up for that time of the year again. A week tomorrow was the anniversary of Isaac's death and he knew that over the coming days she would put herself through the same torture she'd gone through in previous years. He had made up his mind at home last night that at the end of this week he'd pull the plug on Ali's madness. But now it looked as if he wouldn't need to.

*

Ali reached Franco's five minutes late, but was disappointed to find that she was there before Sam. She was shown to the table he had booked for them and the waiter took her coat. 'Anything to drink while you're waiting for your companion?' he asked. Something in the way he used the word 'companion' made her wonder – hope – that maybe this was a clever ploy on Sam's part to bring her and Elliot together. She sat down and ordered a glass of mineral water. She would have preferred something stronger to steady her nerves, but thought that the combination of booze and her current agitation would not be a good mix.

Restlessly she scanned the menu on the holly-festooned chalkboard to the right of her, more out of the need to do something than to choose what to eat. She couldn't remember the last time she'd enjoyed a meal. When she'd tired of studying the menu, she glanced round at the other diners and listened to the record being piped through the restaurant. It was Whitney Houston singing 'I Will Always Love You'. Snatches of the lyrics struck home – 'bittersweet memories, that is all I'm taking with me, so goodbye, please don't cry, we both know I'm not what you need . . .'

Ali willed herself to stay calm. It's nothing but a sentimental song, she told herself. So what if it's a little close for comfort and reflects just how you should feel towards Elliot? Too right you're not what he needs. He needs the love of a good, sensible wife who won't give him any trouble. One who will love him and bring him only joy. He needs a head-case like you like he needs both his arms chopped off. But as stern as she was with herself, her emotions got the better of her and tears rolled down her cheeks. She fumbled in her bag for a tissue, but was out of luck. With nothing else for it, she grabbed the carefully folded linen napkin from the table and wiped her eyes with it. Bang goes my mascara, she thought, burying her face in the starchy fabric and blowing her nose noisily. She was mid-blow when she heard a familiar voice. 'So how's my favourite ex-daughter-in-law?'

She peered up from the napkin and saw Sam. She was so pleased to see his cheery face, yet disappointed that it wasn't Elliot, that she started to cry again.

'Oh, love,' he said, bending down to her, 'am I such a sight for sore eyes?'

'Yes, you are. Oh, Sam, I'm sorry, I don't seem able to stop blubbing, these days. The slightest thing sets me off.'

'Well, you go right ahead and while you're doing that I'll get us both a decent drink.' He attracted the attention of a waiter, who was doing a poor job at pretending not to notice what was going on and ordered two glasses of Scotch. 'No ice,' he said, 'this is strictly medicinal. There now,' he said, when the drinks were brought to their table, 'down the hatch in one and you'll feel a lot better.'

She tossed the drink back and wiped her eyes. 'How am I looking?' she asked.

'Like a very tired, unhappy panda.'

She groaned. 'I'm sorry.'

'And I'm sorry too. I wish now that I'd got in touch with you sooner, but the Boy Wonder wouldn't hear of it. Divided loyalty is a bloody awful thing.'

'How is Elliot?'

'A pain to live with. Perpetually snappy. Perpetually brooding. And perpetually miserable.'

She groaned again. 'And it's all my fault. I'm sorry.'

'Now quit apologising and help me decide what to eat.'

'Nothing for me. I'm in no fit state to keep anything down.'

'You'll have something to eat, my girl, or there'll be trouble. I'll order you an omelette and a small green salad. And for me, a nice big peppered steak should just about do it.'

When the waiter had taken their order and left them alone, Ali said, 'Why aren't you cross with me, Sam?'

He shook out his napkin and placed it on his lap. 'I was at first. I was bloody furious with you. You know what I'm like where Elliot's concerned and I could have said some pretty ungentlemanly things to you that day when he came home and told me what you'd done with Trevor. But then, as is generally the way with these matters, I cooled off and wanted to try to see it from where you were standing.'

'Was the view any clearer?'

'Not really.'

'Has Elliot calmed down at all?'

Sam sucked in his lips and shook his head. ''Fraid not, love. He's adamant that he doesn't want to see you again.'

'But, Sam, I didn't do it.'

'Come again?'

'I didn't sleep with Trevor. It was all a lie to make Sarah leave him.'

'Whoa there, you've lost me. Start at the beginning and tell me exactly what you did.'

Sick as she was of the story, Ali went through it again, just as she had last night with Sarah. Then she told Sam about Sarah leaving Trevor. 'She's forgiven me, Sam. Do you think Elliot could ever do the same?'

Sam sat back in his chair and let out his breath. 'Wow, Ali. They sure as hell broke the mould when they made you.'

'Are you being rude or paying me a compliment?'

'I'm saying you're a one-off.'

'Yeah,' she said miserably, 'and it's just as well, or imagine the mess the world would be in.'

Their meal arrived, and for a few minutes provided them with a distraction. Ali pushed her food round the plate until Sam said, 'Ali, eat your lunch. You're nowt but a waif and at your age it doesn't hang well on you.'

She burst out laughing. 'Give it to me straight, Sam, why don't you?'

He smiled and his dark eyes twinkled. 'That's better. Now, tell me what you're doing for Christmas.'

Ali tackled a tiny mouthful of omelette. 'I can't believe it's as good as a whole year since you were last asking me that.'

'And are you hedging as you did this time last year?'

'No,' she said, 'I'm not. I had thought of going to my parents, but now that Sarah's moved in with me a change of plan might be on the cards. We haven't got as far as discussing any of it and, of course, there's Hannah to consider, but I guess there's a chance that we'll have a quiet Christmas at the mill. How about you and Elliot? Going away again?'

'No. Elliot hasn't had time to think about a holiday. He's been too busy chasing his arse over some flash git at work.'

'Don't tell me, Gervase Merchant-Taylor?'

'Yeah, that's the man. He's been had for sexual harassment. It's raised a rare old stink, I can tell you. People up and down from London all the time. And from what I can make of all the phone calls the Boy Wonder's been making late at night, there's been more drama going on in that one office block than in all the soaps on telly put together.'

'Has he got rid of Gervase?'

'Oh, aye.'

'Bet that pleased him.'

'Not that you'd notice. You know what an inscrutable bugger he can be. Now, come on, love, I've nearly finished my steak and you've hardly made an impression on that omelette of yours.'

In the cold, sleety rain, Sam walked Ali back to her office, just as he had last year. This time, though, they were spared any poignant reminders of Isaac, and sheltering under their umbrellas, Sam kissed her goodbye. 'I'll do my best with Elliot, Ali,' he said. 'I'll tell him exactly what you've told me. And if my oh-so-cultured son has got a penn'orth of sense, he'll get in touch with you. Now take the greatest of care, won't you?'

Ali waited by the phone all that evening.

She pounced on it every time it rang at the weekend.

She did the same at work the following week.

But there was no call from Elliot.

Nothing.

His silence told her all she needed to know.

50

It was a week now since Sarah had moved in with Ali. Most of her thoughts were wrapped up in disentangling herself from the fallout of leaving Trevor, but each day she became increasingly concerned for her friend's welfare.

Lying in bed, Sarah listened to what had just woken her – Ali's soft footsteps on the wooden floor beneath her. She raised her head from the pillow, reached for her alarm clock and strained her eyes in the darkness to make out the time. A quarter past five. She sighed and lowered her head back on to the pillow. This was the fourth morning in a row that Ali had been unable to sleep beyond five o'clock. Then Sarah realised what day it was: the anniversary of Isaac's death. Poor Ali. She wondered whether she ought to offer to go with her when she made her visit to the church in Great Budworth. But instinct told her that Ali would reject such an offer. Sharing her grief had never been easy for her, and there was little hope that this had changed. All Sarah could do was be there for Ali when she came home that evening.

Just as Ali had been there for her this week, when Sarah had begun the task of coming to terms with the last eighteen years. Grace had been right when she'd said that she had to strip away the layers and rediscover the real Sarah. Nearly two decades of fearful thinking had enslaved her will – to use yet another of Grace's phrases. Ali's interpretation of her state of mind was less eloquent: 'Sarah,' she'd said over breakfast, the morning after she'd left Trevor, 'you're totally screwed up.'

'That's good coming from you,' Sarah had retaliated.

'Okay, so we're both screwed to hell and back. Any chance of this God of yours putting in an appearance and straightening us out?'

'Oh, so suddenly there is a God?'

'I didn't say that.'

'You're not wavering, are you, Ali?'

'God forbid.'

When Ali had left for work, Sarah had considered how best to let Hannah know what she had done. She had no idea how her daughter would react and her greatest fear was that she would condemn her and want to dissociate herself. Telling her over the telephone seemed inappropriate, so she had tried to write a letter. But the torn-up pieces of paper on the floor at her feet, as she had sat hunched over the kitchen table, bore witness to the difficulty she was having in expressing herself.

In the end the dilemma was taken out of her hands. Hannah phoned her, just as she was despairing of ever finding the right words.

'Mum, I've just had the weirdest conversation with Dad. He says you've had some sort of breakdown and that I'm not to worry because he'll sort everything. What the hell's he going on about?'

Steeling her courage, she had told Hannah the truth. 'Oh, Hannah, I wish I had had a breakdown. That would be so much easier for your father to cope with.'

'Bloody hell, Mum! You mean you've left him?'

'Hannah, please don't—' But Sarah couldn't carry on. She wanted to say, 'Please don't judge me,' but what right did she have to tell Hannah how to regard her?

'Please don't what, Mum?'

'Don't think too badly of me.'

There was a suspenseful pause.

'Hannah?'

'So what's brought this on? Okay, he can be a cent short of a dollar, but you've stuck with him this long. Why the sudden need to change things?'

'Because I have to. And ... because I don't love him.'

'Is there somebody else?'

'No. Absolutely not.'

'You don't sound very upset. It seems as if you've been planning this for some time.'

Her question had sounded too much as if it were an accusation and Sarah had countered with, 'You don't sound very upset either. You sound angry, but not upset.'

'I'm in shock.'

'Well, so am I.'

There was another pause.

'Look, Mum, I've got to go. I've got a lecture. I'll speak to you sometime.'

The word 'sometime' had resonated down the line with angry hurt and had stung Sarah into saying, 'Hannah, I love you, please try not to worry.' She had wanted to add, 'And please don't hate me for what I've done,' but hadn't wanted to risk putting that thought into her daughter's head.

'I'm bound to worry, Mum. I'd be a strange person if I didn't. Now, I really have to go, my money's running out.'

There were a million questions Sarah wanted to ask. A million things she wanted to say, just to keep the reassuring sound of Hannah's voice in her ear. But all she said was, 'One more thing, Hannah. How did you know where to find me?'

'Where else would you be?'

After she'd put down the phone and before she gave in to a burst of self-pitying tears, she wrote a short letter to Hannah in which she threw herself on her precious daughter's mercy. She sealed the envelope at once, stuck a stamp on it and, before she lost her nerve, walked in the icy rain to the nearest postbox. She was dripping wet and chilled to the bone when she returned to the mill. She lit the fire in the sitting room, made herself a cup of hot chocolate and, while warming her shivering body in front of the fire, she wrote a plan of action. It was time to start taking a firm line with herself. There was to be no more wallowing in self-pity. She had made a decision to leave her husband and she was going to get on with it as best she could. Ironically, it was a case of for better or for worse.

At the top of the page she wrote, 'Speak to Trevor'.

Is that it? she asked herself, when ten minutes later that was all she'd written on the lined page of foolscap. It wasn't much of a campaign of action.

She spoke to him that night. An hour after Ali returned from work, she drove Sarah over to Astley Hope. Sarah had insisted that Ali stayed in the car while she went inside to talk to Trevor. She hadn't phoned ahead to make sure he would be there, but instead had left it to chance.

Chance presented her with Trevor in a mood of hopeful reconciliation. He offered cups of tea and a promise that he'd never refer to the previous evening again, if that's what she wanted. Without once looking at her, he said, 'I know you've been under a lot of stress, what with Hannah going away to college, but there's nothing we can't work out together. Shirley's given me the address of a retreat for married couples that we could go on. She says ...'

Still the same old Trevor, she thought, as he rambled on, pretending that there was an easy alternative to the dreadful suggestion she had made. He was still prepared to live with his head jammed into the sand. 'Trevor,' she said firmly, watching him reach for the teapot from the draining-board, 'please listen to me. I meant every word of what I said last night. It may have been very wrong of me to tell you in front of the group and, believe me, I never intended it to happen that way. In fact I never intended it to happen at all, but it really is the way I feel. It's what I want. What I need to do.'

He stopped fiddling with the teapot, raised his eyes to her for a fraction of a second, then lowered his gaze back to the small brown teapot in his hand and stared at it as if he wasn't quite sure what it was or how it had got there. Then he threw it across the kitchen. It smashed against the back door, the pieces scattering all over the floor. Only the spout and handle remained intact.

At last, she thought, a genuine emotion. She waited for his verbal outburst to follow suit. Almost hoped that it would. But he didn't even raise his voice. Bizarrely he reached for another teapot from the cupboard to the right of the kettle, which was boiling fiercely, sending a cloud of steam into the cold kitchen.

'And just how did you intend to tell me that you wanted to end our marriage?'

'I never intended to. I thought ... I thought I could go on.'

'Go on?' he repeated. 'You make it sound as if it was a trial. An ordeal.'

She lowered her eyes from his bewildered face. How could she tell him the truth? That every day for her had been a trial. 'I'm sorry,' she said, knowing that it wasn't enough. An apology was never going to undo the harm she'd caused. 'I never meant to hurt you,' she added.

'But you have, Sarah. You and Ali.' He turned his back to her and made the tea that she knew she wouldn't drink. She wanted to make him stop what he was doing, but knew that he needed to occupy himself with something while they were having this unthinkable conversation. At last he swung round to look at her again and said, 'Sarah, I'm prepared to forgive you if you promise me that you'll seek help. This isn't the first time you've behaved irrationally and I'm sure that there's a perfectly reasonable explanation for what's triggered this madness. Shirley says it's probably an early menopause. Apparently lots of women go through similar episodes of confusion.'

Her heart sank. He was never going to face the truth. His make-believe world, which was way up there on some surreal plane, didn't have the foundations for such a weight of concrete reality. 'And what would you say was a reasonable explanation for Ali's behaviour?' she asked scathingly. 'Was that merely an episode of hormonal confusion too?'

His face hardened. 'That woman is totally beyond my comprehension. And if we're to make a go of our marriage, you would have to promise me that you wouldn't have anything more to do with her.'

'I'm afraid that's not possible, Trevor.'

'That sounds as though you're prepared to choose Ali over me.'

'Trevor,' she said in exasperation, 'listen to me, please. I'm leaving you because I don't love you. Not because I prefer Ali's friendship or because I'm having a funny hormonal turn. Is that clear enough for you?'

'And what about my rights? Don't I, as your husband, have a say in what happens to our marriage?'

'You deserve the right to be free of me, to live a life that's free of lies and guilt.'

'But you're my wife. Your duty is—'

'Trevor, if you so much as dare to quote a piece of scripture at me I shall leave without another word.'

But that was exactly what he did do. And, just as she'd warned him, she turned on her heel and went up to the spare bedroom. A few minutes later she came down the stairs carrying her sewing-machine and several rolls of fabric. She went out to Ali's car, dumped them in the boot and returned to the house, where she proceeded to stuff a selection of clothes and other personal possessions into carrier bags. Trevor didn't try to stop her. He stayed in the kitchen, at the table, his head in his hands, murmuring to himself. He was praying. Other women might have been moved by the sight of a man beseeching God to save his marriage, but all it did to Sarah was confirm her conviction that if Trevor had spent less time chatting to God and more time talking to her their marriage might not have needed saving.

With the last of the bags in the car, she went back into the house and gave Trevor a final parting shot of honesty. She told him that Ali hadn't seduced him that night at the mill. She wanted to believe that her motive for telling him the truth was an honourable one, that she didn't want him to go through the rest of his life thinking that he'd committed a terrible sin – but she was more inclined to think less of herself: she suspected that she wanted to deflate that well-disguised bit of his male ego that was indubitably proud that he'd slept with an attractive woman like Ali. That he couldn't recall having done so was immaterial – no doubt even his slow-working, virtuous brain could fill in the gaps for him.

His final words were, 'May God forgive you. You and Ali.'

It was not so much the bestowing of a benediction as a snarled, fist-clenched threat. It pained Sarah that they should part so acrimoniously, but as Ali had said during the drive back to the mill, 'Sarah, there's no reasoning with a fanatic when he starts wielding his beliefs as a weapon.'

Realising that there was little chance of her getting back to sleep, Sarah slipped out of bed, pulled on her dressing-gown, and went downstairs to join Ali in her nocturnal potterings. She found her in the sitting room, curled up on the sofa beneath the quilt Sarah had made for her last Christmas. She was fast asleep and could easily have been mistaken for a small child. The image was further enhanced by the poignant sight of Mr Squeezy's head poking out from the quilt. Quietly retracing her steps, Sarah went back upstairs to her bedroom.

Once again she lay in the darkness and, unable to sleep, her thoughts turned to Hannah.

Since that brief phone call and the letter she had sent her, Hannah had phoned almost every day. After each conversation Sarah had felt sufficiently encouraged to hope that her daughter's understanding and acceptance of the situation were increasing. It was generally acknowledged that children were extraordinarily selfish, and while Hannah's relationship with her father this past year had not been as happy as in previous years, it was clear that she didn't want the status quo changed; neither did she relish being saddled with the stigma of coming from a broken family.

'Your mind's obviously made up,' she said to Sarah during one conversation. 'There's nothing I can say to make you reconsider, is there?'

'Nothing at all,' she'd said.

'What will you do?'

'I don't know exactly.'

'God, Mum, don't you think you've been a bit hasty? You should at least have put a plan together.'

'Something will come up, I'm sure.'

It was strange to experience the sensation of their roles having been reversed. Suddenly Hannah was the questioning I-know-better adult and Sarah was the shoulder-shrugging teenager.

Hannah was also in regular contact with Trevor. 'How is he?' Sarah had asked only yesterday.

'He seems okay. The Worthies are rallying round him like bees to a honey-pot. He says he's going on a retreat for Christmas. It'll be some retreat – he's going with the entire Slipper Gang! Just imagine, if it's one of those places where you have to keep your gob shut the whole time they'll explode, the lot of them. By the way, Jamie's coming across from Bristol to give me a lift home. That okay with you?'

The fact that Hannah was able so soon, and so easily, to flit in and out of the unpleasant subject of her parents' broken marriage, gave Sarah further cause to hope that eventually all would be well.

*

Ali left for work just after eight, leaving Sarah wondering how much longer her friend could go on as she was. She hadn't touched the bowl of cereal Sarah had set out for her, or the piece of peanut-butter toast she'd hoped would tempt her. Ali had taken no more than a few sips of her tea before she'd reached for her briefcase and said, 'I'll be off now.'

Maybe once she's got this day over with she'll start to pick up, Sarah told herself, as she watched Ali's car headlamps pick out the frosty hedgerow as she disappeared down the dark lane. But she knew that it wasn't just Isaac's death that was causing Ali so much misery.

Most of her heartache was caused by Elliot.

Poor Ali, she had banked on him getting in touch with her after she'd had lunch with Sam, but there hadn't been a single word from him.

Sarah cleared away Ali's untouched breakfast, then went upstairs to sort out the room on the top floor of the mill. It was Ali's study, but over the Christmas holiday it was to be Hannah's bedroom. In a genuine and sincere attempt not to be partisan, Sarah had said that maybe Hannah ought to stay with her father for a few days before he went off on his retreat with the Slipper Gang. Her suggestion had been met with an indifferent 'Yeah, maybe.' She had not tried to justify her lack of enthusiasm for the idea and Sarah had not enquired why.

Thinking about it now as she made up the camp bed, Sarah concluded that Hannah was very much her own woman and carried a lot less self-doubt on her shoulders than Sarah had at that age. She wondered if this was a trait inherited from her biological father. Certainly he'd never had a problem with self-doubt. In all the years she'd carried the guilty secret of his presence in her life, she had rarely given him much thought. Through the necessity of trying to forget what she'd done, she had been, for the most part, successful in blocking him out. Occasionally, though, she had pondered on the scenario of accidentally bumping into him and imagining the conversation they would have. But the scene always ran along the same lines: he couldn't remember who she was, let alone recall ever having gone to bed with her. But it was also true that she could scarcely bring his face to mind. Vague recollections told her that he'd been blond with blue eyes and a strong jaw, but other than that she had little to work on when trying to think if Hannah bore any physical resemblance to him.

She had never been angry or bitter with John for getting her pregnant – how could she be when she had such a lovely daughter? – but that day last week in Chester when she'd come across the lad who was using his strength to dominate the girl at his feet, an explosion of suppressed anger had erupted within her. It had reminded her all too sharply of how she had got herself into a situation that had led to her being pregnant. She had thought herself totally in control of what was going on – after all, she knew what John's reputation was – but vanity had got the better of her. She'd allowed herself to go along with his notorious easy charm and naturally flirtatious manner. It won't go any further, she'd told herself, as he'd brushed her cheek with his lips. I'll stop him before anything happens, she thought, as she shivered at the touch of his fingers on her neck. But when he'd slipped his hand inside her dress she'd realised her mistake. She'd tried to wriggle out of his grasp but he'd pulled her to him and started to part her legs. Part of her – the part that was dizzy with desire – wanted him to carry on with what he was doing but the other part wanted to run. She didn't want this. Not this way. Not with a man she didn't love. She tried again to free herself but he smiled his bewitching smile and said, 'I won't hurt you, Sarah. It'll be okay. I promise you everything will be all right.'

Stupid girl that she was, she had believed him. The very next day she had heard him boasting in the college library to a fellow American how easy she'd been. 'Ten points for a virgin,' he'd laughed, 'and another five because she's prettier than the usual ones.'

She smoothed out the duvet on the camp bed, then went and stood at the window. It was light now and a bright sun shone down on the surrounding fields, which were white with frost. In the distance she could see the row of terraced cottages where Ali's cleaner, Lizzie, lived. A thin trail of smoke rose from one of the chimneys and Sarah thought how snug and cosy the little houses looked. The other morning Lizzie had mentioned that the tenant of the middle cottage was thinking of moving out in the next few months, and that the owner would be keen to find a new tenant. 'It's a bit grotty,' Lizzie had said, 'only two bedrooms and the kitchen is minute, barely room to swing a mouse, never mind a cat. But the rent's dirt cheap.' And, although she was more than happy to stay here with Ali, Sarah knew that there would come a time when she would have to stand on her own two feet . . . and that little cottage would be just perfect for her.

When she had told Hannah she didn't have a plan for her future, it wasn't strictly true. She had vague ideas of setting herself up in business. Why keep slogging away for a shop, which determined her work and wages, when she could be mistress of her own destiny? The only difference would be that she would have to seek out her customers – but the money she could earn would be so much more than she was currently being paid. It was worth a try. What did she have to lose?

Gazing out across the fields, and watching a crow flap its broad, languid wings as it swooped from one telegraph pole to another, she thought with satisfaction that she had come a long way in just a week.

'And who would have thought that possible?' she said aloud. Eight days ago she had been trying to hold together a life that seemed intent on falling apart. She had tried so hard to keep everything neat and tidy, safe and secure. She realised now how wearing it had been. 'Fighting the inevitable is a futile and profoundly exhausting occupation,' Grace had told her on the phone, when she'd called to see how she was getting on. 'We never understand what a heavy burden it is that we're carrying until we let go of it.'

It didn't seem right to describe her marriage as a burden, but in essence that was exactly what it had become. She felt sorry for Trevor and would probably always feel guilty that she had used him as she had, but as she stared into the empty blue sky, she had the strongest feeling that from the death of her old life a new and better one would emerge.

For Trevor too.

She hoped that God wouldn't mind if she took a break from religion. 'It's nothing personal,' she said, addressing the perfect canopy of blue, 'only I think I need to take stock of what it all really means.'

Just then the telephone rang. She moved away from the window and picked up the receiver from the extension on the desk. She was surprised to hear Daniel's voice.

'Hello, Sarah,' he said. 'I hope you believe in miracles, because this is the best. I've just had a call from Elliot.'

Later that afternoon, Ali left her car outside the post office in Great Budworth and made her way towards the sandstone church. She followed the path round to the furthest side of the churchyard and thought how inappropriate and insensitive it was that, on a day such as this, the sun was shining. But although it was indecently bright, there was no warmth to it and the air was cold and raw. She hurried on briskly, passing *Robert Ashworth* along with *Amy and Joseph Riley* and didn't slow her pace until she was at the foot of Isaac's small grave. She stooped to the frozen ground and laid out her offering of white roses. 'Oh, Isaac,' she murmured, 'thank goodness you're not here to see how much I've hurt your father. I've been so careless with him.'

She pulled off her gloves and tugged at the weeds to ward off her misery. But it didn't work and, without being able to stop it, she felt herself dragged down into the dark depths of her grief and anguish. All she could think of was the overwhelming need to hold her child. 'Just to hold you once more,' she whispered, 'just once would do it.' She closed her eyes and pictured herself cradling Isaac, breathing in his sweet baby smell, touching his soft, silky cheek, stroking his fine blond hair. The illusion felt so very real to her that the poignancy of it ripped through her. She lost every ounce of control and wept helplessly.

Blinded by the tears streaming down her face, she thought, for the craziest of moments, that Isaac was near her ... that he had just touched her. She held her breath, squeezed her eyes shut and allowed herself to think that he *was* there. But when she felt the pressure on her shoulder increase, she opened her eyes and saw that she wasn't alone. Elliot was crouching beside her.

'How long have you been there?' she mumbled, through her choking sobs, too weak to stand or move away from him.

'Long enough,' he answered, his own voice thick with emotion. Carefully he added his flowers to hers, and then, with extreme gentleness, lifted her to her feet. He led her to a nearby bench and sat her down beside him. Then, removing a handkerchief from his coat pocket, he raised her face to his and wiped away the tears from the ash grey arcs under her tired eyes. It was the most loving act and made her cry all the more.

'Stop, please,' she said, taking the handkerchief from him and pressing it to her face. 'You're making it worse.'

Distressed to see how changed she was since he last saw her, he said, 'I've made a lot of things worse, haven't I?'

With eyes that were so terribly sad, she met the intensity of his gaze. 'We both have,' she said. And then: 'Why didn't you ring me, Elliot? After I had lunch with Sam, I waited every day for you to call. Every day.'

'I'm sorry, but I was still cross with you. It was petty, I know, but I was angry because you had put your friendship for Sarah before your love for me.'

She hardly dared to ask the next question for fear of being rejected again, but she forced herself. 'And do you still feel that way?'

'No. That enormously influential lateral thinker, and your great advocate, Sam, put me straight last night. He said that I'd got it all wrong and that what you'd actually done was put Sarah's happiness before your own.'

'He's right, that's exactly what I did ... I just didn't realise how big a sacrifice it would be. Or how painful.'

He took her icy hand in his and raised it to his lips. 'You're a woman of extraordinary conviction, Ali, and I love you for it. But promise me one thing. Promise you'll never do anything as unwise or as reckless as that again.'

She nodded and blinked away the threat of fresh tears. 'I promise.'

'Good.'

'Does that mean you're giving me another chance to get it right between us?'

He shook his head. 'No. I'm giving us both a chance to get it right.'

'But you deserve better, Elliot.'

'Anyone else would bore me. I need the challenge of you.'

She almost smiled. 'I can't think why.'

He drew her closer to him, held her cold face in his hands and kissed her slowly and deeply. 'But I can,' he said at last, tilting his head back to look into her eyes, 'and that's all that matters.'

'But is it enough?'

'Oh, I think so.'

He kissed her again. Then, leaning tranquilly into each other, they stared in silence at the view beyond the churchyard, to the frost-whitened fields that were criss-crossed with stark, wintry hedges and trees. A skein of birds flew overhead, their formation as precise and perfect as the blue of the sky. With not a word passing between them, they each lowered their gaze to the grave of their son a few yards from where they were sitting.

Elliot said, 'We won't ever get over his death, Ali, not fully, but together we might learn to live with it.'

'I hope you're right,' she said faintly, then with a small smile, she added, 'You usually are.'

He squeezed her hand. 'Not always.'

She sighed and gave a little shiver. 'I hate it here,' she said, with heartfelt sadness. 'I wish I could derive some comfort from it but I can't. I doubt I ever will.'

'I'm hoping that after today you might feel differently.' He rose from the bench and held out a hand to her. 'I hope you approve of what I've done. I wanted to give you a happy memory of this place. It was the best I could do at such short notice.'

She looked at him quizzically.

'Come on,' he said, and pulled her to her feet. He led her back up the path towards the church. But as they neared the lych-gate, Ali stopped in her tracks. There, in front of the churchyard wall, was Sarah. Daniel was there too. So was Richard. And, with a grin that was stretched from ear to ear, so was Sam. He looked at Elliot and said, 'Well, Romeo, is it all sorted? Did you kiss and make up? Are we on for a celebratory drink?'

One of his rare-as-gold-dust smiles flickered across Elliot's face and, after exchanging an intimate glance of tenderness with Ali, he put his arm around her and said, 'Oh, aye, Dad, about as sorted as it's ever likely to be.'

Sam laughed heartily. 'Well, thank God for that!'

The Holiday

To Edward and Samuel
with all my love

And Special thanks to Maureen

'Show me a hero and I will write you a tragedy.'
F. Scott Fitzgerald

1

In the beginning God made man, and when he'd got it completely right, he made Theodore Vlamakis.

This thought, though perhaps lacking in originality, came to Laura Sinclair as she gazed out at the dazzling horizon where a cerulean sky met a sea of aquamarine, and where, closer to the shore, their nearest neighbour and good friend, Theo was swimming. She watched him emerge from the clear blue water and make his way up the pebbly beach. Even by Greek standards he was deeply tanned, and with his strong muscular physique, which he kept in check by swimming at least twice a day and for an hour at a time, he made a striking impression. When he'd finished drying himself off, smoothed back his short wet hair and slipped on a pair of sunglasses, Laura found herself speculating on just how far his tan went up those long legs.

All the way, probably. Theo was not a man who did anything by half.

She sighed nostalgically, recalling a time when her own legs had been lean and firm, when cellulite and thready veins were things her mother worried about.

Banishing such depressing forty-something thoughts, she continued watching Theo as he also took a moment to enjoy the view. He really was in all respects completely and utterly gorgeous. It didn't even matter that he was a vain forty-two-year-old serial romancer; it merely added to his charm.

Beneath the exterior of rich, dark smoothness he was also a man of considerable kindness. When she and Max had flown over at the weekend, he had arrived within minutes with a picnic basket of freshly baked bread, wafer-thin slices of salami, sun-ripened tomatoes just picked from his own garden and a bottle of chilled champagne. 'To celebrate the start of your summer here in Áyios Nikólaos,' he had said, his thumbs working deftly at the cork as he insisted they leave their unpacking till later.

She watched him turn from the water, sling a towel around his neck, and move along the beach towards the path that meandered up the hillside to his villa. As he did so, he tilted his head and glanced in her direction. She waved down to him and he returned the greeting. She invited him to join her for a drink by raising her arm and making a cup with her hand. He nodded and held up a thumb. She went inside and prepared a Campari and soda for herself, and oúzo with ice for him.

They had met Theo quite by chance, last spring when he'd been on the same flight as them bound for Corfu. Sitting in the window seat next to

663

Max, he had been delighted to learn that they were spending the next three weeks on his beloved island, hoping to buy a holiday home. He claimed to have the very property for them. 'It is newly built and completely perfect. You will fall in love with it, I know you will,' he had enthused. 'I designed it myself, so take it from me, you will not find anything better, other than my own house and you cannot have that, it is mine. It is a part of me.' They soon came to know that this was typical Theo-speak: he was never slow in declaring his feelings or his enthusiasm, or revealing his pride, which in another man would probably have come across as conceit.

He had been right though: both she and Max had fallen in love with Villa Petros the moment they saw it. Tucked into the verdant hillside of cypress trees, and with its easy access to the secluded beach below, it was just as Theo had promised. The deal was struck without any second thoughts, and with Theo's help they had spent most of last year decorating and furnishing the house to make it their own. Now they would be able to enjoy it properly. It would be their first real holiday in Áyios Nikólaos and Laura was looking forward to spending the entire summer there. It was just a shame that Max wouldn't be able to do the same. He would have to make at least one trip home to keep an eye on work, although having organised a little den of *Boy's Own* high-tech wizardry in the villa, there was no worry of him not knowing what was going on at the office.

The running of his own firm – a management consultancy he had set up in the mid-eighties – was a source of pride and satisfaction for Max. In its infancy, it had looked as if the risk he had taken in leaving his then well-paid and secure job would backfire on him, but the business took off and became a major success. So successful that if he wanted to he could sell the company tomorrow, retire, and they would still be able to live as comfortably as they did now. But Max was only forty-nine and Laura couldn't imagine him retiring. Not ever. He was an energetic doer, incapable of sitting still for more than two minutes – unless, of course, he happened to be watching the tennis on telly, and in particular the current coverage of Wimbledon. Tennis was his passion, and since they had arrived, he had been glued to the huge flat-screen television he had bought for his high-tech den. 'Go on, get your racket to the ball!' – was a frequently heard cry that broke the peace and quiet of Villa Petros.

By the time she was back out on the terrace with a tray of drinks, Theo had appeared. He was even better-looking close up, with his instantly engaging smile. In the time it had taken him to climb the hillside, his hair had dried in the baking heat to reveal the streaks of grey running through it, which did nothing to detract from his attractiveness. Not for the first time Laura thought how unfair it was that grey hair didn't do the same for women.

He threw his towel over the arm of a chair in a gesture of easy familiarity and came towards her. '*Kaliméra*, my darling Laura,' he said, giving her a languid kiss on each cheek and a cool touch on the shoulder. 'But look at you, you are turning pink. Why is it that you English women never take proper care of your bodies?'

'Perhaps it's because we live in hope of a devastatingly handsome man doing it for us.'

He laughed, then spied a bottle of sun cream on the table where their drinks lay and guided her to a lounger in the shade. 'In that case, I must not disappoint you. Now, lie down. I will do your back first.' He poured factor fifteen into the palm of his hand and worked it into her skin with slow, sensual movements, starting with her shoulders, his fingers drifting downwards with small circular movements.

'Thank you for dinner last night, by the way,' Laura said, trying to pretend that she wasn't finding the experience quite as pleasurable as she was. 'Max and I really enjoyed it. You're becoming quite a cook.'

'It is the bachelor life. One has to learn to do these things.'

'Well, when the time comes you'll make someone a wonderful husband.'

'Like your Max?'

'Yes, just like my Max. And if I weren't such a happily married woman,' she added, as his fingers slipped beneath the straps of her swimsuit, 'I might feel compromised by what you're doing.' She turned over.

'Ah, Laura, how it hurts me to know that you are immune to my charm.'

'Nonsense! It's good for you to have at least one woman in this world who is a friend and not a jealous lover.'

He poured another dollop of sun cream into his palm and gently rubbed it into her thigh. She hoped he wouldn't pay too much attention to this less than perfect area of her body. 'You think all the women in my life have a jealous spirit?' he asked, his hand lingering on her hip.

'Of course. They must have.'

'But why? I only try to make them happy?'

'Because, you silly vain man, they must hate knowing that they're just one of many.'

'Can I help it if women find me irresistible?'

'Oh, Theo, what a typically arrogant Greek man you are. It would serve you right if one day you fell in love with a woman who had enough sense to tell you to get lost.'

He grinned. 'But I have already, Laura. You.'

She pushed him away with a laugh and crossed the terrace for their drinks. She handed him his oúzo. 'Sorry, but the ice has almost melted to nothing.'

'Like my chance of seducing you,' he said, with a wink. Then changing his tone, as though the game was over, he said, 'When are you expecting Max back from the airport with the first of your houseguests?'

Laura glanced at her watch. 'In about an hour. That's if Izzy's plane has landed on time.'

'And this Easy, whom you mentioned last night during dinner, tell me more. What does she look like? Is she as beautiful as you? Does she have your pretty auburn hair and delicate complexion?'

'Her name's pronounced *Izzy* and she's far prettier than I am. She's younger, slimmer, and with hair that doesn't need to be chemically enhanced as mine does. And I'd appreciate it if you allowed her to settle in before you go offering her the benefit of your charming beachside manner. Just keep your distance.'

He raised one of his thick eyebrows. 'Why must you continually think the worst of me, Laura? I always respect women. I give them plenty of space. I never crowd them. That isn't my style.'

'Would that be before or after you've broken their hearts?'

Theo took a long sip of his drink and eyed her thoughtfully. 'You are protective towards this friend. Am I right? You think she could come to harm with me?'

'Yes, to both questions.'

'Why? What has happened to this Izzy that you feel the need to wrap her in cotton wool?'

'Oh, the usual. A stupid man who took pleasure in humiliating her.'

'Ah, the cruelty of some men,' he said, with a wry smile. 'She is divorced, then?'

'No. Fortunately for her she wasn't married to the idiot.'

'But there is a new boyfriend on the scene? Or is she still searching for her Mr Right?'

Laura shook her head. 'There's no new boyfriend, and if I know Izzy, she's probably decided that Mr Right is a figment of every young girl's imagination and that—'

'But Max is your Mr Right, isn't he?' Theo interrupted. 'He is far from being a figment of your imagination. He is very real.'

Laura thought of the wonderful man to whom she had been married for twenty-one years and smiled. They had met when she had just turned twenty and was recovering from the break-up of a relationship she should never have got herself into. Stupidly, she had been having an affair with her boss. Always a mistake, that, and especially if he's married. It had been the silliest thing she had ever done, but she'd believed his every word, that his marriage was over, that any day now he would be leaving his wife. In the end, and after he'd tired of her, he had called a halt to their relationship by giving her the sack. With her pride in tatters, she had gone home to her parents for a weepy cry on their shoulders and had met Max at a ball.

From the moment he had asked her to dance there had been an instant attraction between them, but knowing that she was on the rebound she had held off from his advances, not wanting to hurt him any more than she wanted to be hurt again. But his warmth and exuberance won her over, and within the year they were married. The following spring their daughter Francesca was born. Their marriage had been full of love, laughter and happiness, but above all else, it was founded on trust. 'Yes,' she said finally, in answer to Theo's question, 'Max is my Mr Right. But Izzy hasn't been so fortunate. She was landed with Mr Wrong and her outlook has been appropriately coloured.'

'Then I will make a pleasant surprise for her. I will be her Mr Sweep-Me-Off-My-Feet.'

Laura rolled her eyes. 'My goodness, what a self-deprecating man you are.'

'But wouldn't it make her feel better? Wouldn't it lift her jaded spirits?'

'What? Have some Lothario trying to get her into bed and then be waving her goodbye before the sheets are cold the following morning?'

'You are so very cynical, Laura. Did someone do that to you a long time ago? Before the wonderful Max?'

She frowned. 'Most women get that treatment at some stage in their lives.'

'Well, I promise you, I will be more subtle. Much more sensitive.'

'You mean you'd give her breakfast?'

He smiled. 'We shall have to see, won't we?'

Laura was concerned. 'You are joking, aren't you?'

'It is strange, but the more you protect her, the more I feel the need to rise to the challenge.'

'Now, look here, Theo, Izzy's a dear friend. She's coming for a restful holiday, she doesn't need—'

'But a little romance might help her relax even more.'

She watched Theo stretch out his long brown legs as he made himself more comfortable in the chair beside her and wondered if there wasn't an element of truth in what he was suggesting. After what Izzy had gone through this last year, maybe a light-hearted holiday romance would be the very thing to boost her self-confidence. Maybe it was time for Izzy to have a little fun, and if anyone was capable of giving her that, then surely it was Theo.

'By the way,' she said, deciding it was time to change the subject – it didn't do to let Theo bask in his own magnificence for too long – 'when does your guest arrive from England?'

'Tomorrow afternoon.'

'And how long is he staying?'

'Most of the summer, I think. He has the artistic temperament and needs peace and quiet to work on his latest book.'

'He's a writer?'

'Yes. He writes dark tales of death and destruction. His name is Mark St James. You have heard of him, perhaps?'

'I most certainly have. Max is a big fan. How exciting! Will we get to meet him?'

'If you are good to me I will give it some thought.' Then, leaning forward in his seat, he stroked her leg provocatively. 'We could strike a deal: your wounded Izzy for my infamous author. What do you say?'

'And there was me on the verge of asking you to stay for lunch. Suddenly I've changed my mind.'

'As your Max would say, *no problemo*. I have an appointment for lunch anyway. But I could come for dinner tonight. I will dress myself up ready to make the big impression on the lovely Izzy.'

2

Izzy had spent the last three hours sitting next to a hyperactive child, who had divided his time between pushing past her to go and play with the gadgets in the toilet and bouncing in his seat so that he could spill his foil-wrapped meal more effectively than any muck-spreader. 'He's so excited about the holiday,' his mother kept saying, and showing no sign of restraining him as his trainer-clad feet kicked at the seat in front. 'He's never flown before.' And hopefully never will again in my company, Izzy had thought.

But now, and having retrieved her luggage from the carousel, she was scanning the arrivals hall for a familiar face. She wasn't used to travelling alone, and though it wasn't a large airport, it still made her feel lost and unsure. But Max was easy to spot in the crowd of chatting holiday reps and taxi drivers, and not just because he was waving madly at her and wearing a brightly coloured shirt, but because he had such silvery-white hair. Laura often joked that he had started going grey while he was still in his twenties due to a misspent youth, but Max insisted that it was because he had fallen in love with Laura so unexpectedly that the shock had nearly killed him.

He greeted Izzy with one of his cheery bear hugs, which lifted her off her feet and made her think, as it had the first time she had met him, how like Steve Martin he was. It was a game she played: when she met someone for the first time, she matched them up with a celebrity lookalike. In Max's case it had come to her in a flash. He was Steve Martin in appearance, with his twinkling eyes and short white hair, and he was certainly Steve Martin in manner, with his quirky, self-effacing sense of humour. 'The good thing about Max,' Laura would say, 'is that if he ever loses his marbles no one will notice.' At heart he was essentially a big kid, and right now, as he took control of her trolley and steered it through the crowd, occasionally shouting 'Coming through,' Izzy knew that if Laura had been here, she would have been rolling her eyes at his antics.

Big kid or not, she couldn't deny how relieved she was to be in Max's safe hands, even if he was now standing on the back of the speeding trolley like a latter-day Ben Hur and she was having to run to keep up with him. And though it was against all the rules laid down by the book she had been trying to read on the plane – *One Hundred Ways To Be A Thoroughly Modern Woman* – was it really such a sin to want to hand over responsibility and let somebody else take the strain?

'How was your flight?' Max asked, when they were standing outside in the bright sunshine and were loading her luggage into the back of an open-topped Jeep.

'Fine,' she said, 'although I came close to shoving a horrible child through the emergency exit at thirty-five thousand feet. Otherwise I don't have a minute's delay or a case of drunken air rage to report.'

'How very disappointing. Okay, then, that's the bags in, climb aboard and we'll be off. There's a bottle of Coke in the glove compartment if you're in need of a cold drink. Help yourself.'

She fished out the bottle, which was wrapped in a special thermal casing, and drank from it gratefully. 'As usual, Max, you've thought of everything. You're a life-saver.'

'*No problemo.* Now in the words of my sweet old grandmother, Bette Davis, fasten your seat-belt, it's going to be a bumpy ride. These Jeeps are all very well, but the suspension's hard enough to rattle your eyes out of their sockets.'

Izzy had never been to Corfu before and she took in the journey with interest. After skirting the edge of Corfu Town, Max picked up the coastal road, and before long the landscape changed from urban scruff to rural charm.

'Breathtaking, isn't it?' he shouted, above the noise of the engine and the wind that was slapping their faces and sending Izzy's hair flying. Ahead was a glassy sea of translucent blue and a carpeted headland of lush green that went right down to the edge of a stretch of bleached white sand. It surpassed all Izzy's expectations. As though sensing her delight, Max remained silent and concentrated on the road, which twisted and turned through the spectacular scenery.

It seemed madness now that only a few days ago Izzy had nearly decided not to come. She had paid her mother a visit, to see if she would be all right without Izzy for the summer. It had been a weekend of pure, nerve-jangling hell: forty-eight hours of being cooped up with Prudence Jordan, a woman who had graduated with honours in How To Be A Repressive, Bitter Old Woman. Most of their time together had been spent in the small square sitting room at the back of the bungalow in which Izzy had grown up. The room was heavily sprigged with flowery décor – the sagging sofa and armchairs, the curtains, the lampshades, the wallpaper, the carpet, everything, had been given the floral treatment – and presiding over this horticultural nightmare was an army of china statues, lined up along the two low windows that looked out on to the garden, with their nasty unblinking, all-seeing eyes. They seemed to watch Izzy as she and her mother sanded down their teeth on stale Battenberg cake and drank tea that could have creosoted garden sheds.

A fidgety woman who could never be still, lest she was taken for an idle good-for-nothing, Prudence would switch from pressing cup after cup of the throat-stripping tea on Izzy to ignoring her and knitting furiously. She clashed the old metal needles together, the taut, cheap wool squeaking and setting Izzy's teeth and nerves further on edge. Prudence was a compulsive knitter and had been for nearly ten years. It had started when the local church had launched a campaign calling for volunteers to make six-inch squares to be sewn into blankets and sent to Rwanda. Her mother had thrown herself into the mission with determined zeal but hadn't known when to stop. A decade on, and even though the plight of that part of Africa was no longer as desperate as it had been, she was still at it. Somewhere there was probably an enormous stockpile of patchwork blankets waiting to be unpicked and recycled into useful balls of wool.

'And while you're off enjoying yourself with your fancy high-and-mighty friends, leaving me alone,' her mother had flung across the room, 'where will you be if I need your help?'

'Where I've always been, squashed under your thumb,' was the honest answer, but Izzy said mildly, 'We've been through this before. I've given you the number for the villa, and Auntie Trixie only lives four miles away. She'd be—'

'Your auntie Patricia's a fool.'

It was always a case of 'your' auntie Patricia, never 'my' sister Trixie.

'Auntie Trixie isn't a fool, Mum.'

'Well, you would say that. You're two of a kind, aren't you?'

It was a well-aimed blow. Seven years ago Auntie Trixie had brought shame to the family by divorcing her womanising, beer-bellied husband; more recently Izzy had brought the family name into further disrepute by living in sin with a man, then being careless enough to let him slip away before she had got a ring on her finger.

'If you had picked more wisely at the outset, you wouldn't be in the mess you are,' her mother had consoled her last autumn, as Izzy got through each day convincing herself that tomorrow would be better, that tomorrow she would put Alan behind her. But it hadn't been that easy. She had thrown too much of herself into their relationship. They had just celebrated three years of being together when he had sprung on her that he felt they should take responsibility for their feelings and explore where they were going wrong.

Wrong?

That was the first she had heard of it going anywhere other than straight ahead, turn right, turn left, then up the aisle to the altar.

Though perhaps those weekends he had spent in Blackpool visiting his ailing great-aunt in the old people's home, the sudden change in clothes and aftershave, the frequent mood swings and need for personal space should have set the alarm bells of suspicion ringing. In truth, they had been chiming faintly, but she had told herself to ride it out, to see it through. It was a concept she had been taught from an early age. But she had failed the test so many times. All she had learnt from it was that she was destined to fail because she always made the wrong choice.

'Isobel Jordan,' her mother would say, her hands on her aproned hips, 'I see you've still not finished that embroidery. Do you want to know why? It's because you picked the most difficult one, didn't you? You always think you know best, but you don't ... So you're giving up on the recorder lessons? Well, that doesn't surprise me. I said you'd be too lazy to practise ... You always did pick the biggest sweet in the shop then find it tasted of nothing.'

The most frequent piece of advice was: 'You know what your problem is, young lady? You don't have the conviction to see anything through. You're a butterfly brain, just like your auntie Patricia.'

Now, with well-practised constraint, Izzy said, 'I'm sure if there was a real problem you wouldn't let your differences with your sister get in the way of her helping you, should the need arise. Which I doubt very much it will. You look extremely well to me.' She marvelled at her courage and self-control. There had even been a hint of assertiveness to her voice.

In response her mother gave her a flinty look, and slipped seamlessly into another line of attack. 'Have you been seeing that counsellor again?' She uttered the word *counsellor* with weighty disapproval. Prudence had never forgiven Izzy for airing her dirty washing in public.

Counselling had been Alan's idea. According to him, it had been the means by which they would explore and face the negative feelings that were destroying their relationship.

It turned out that it was an easy way for him to tell her he was leaving her for somebody else, that her own behaviour had driven him to it; a typical bit of playacting on his part. She supposed that he had thought the counsellor would protect him when Izzy learned the truth. That the non-threatening environment of her office, with its marshmallow pink walls, its comfortable chairs, the carefully positioned box of tissues, the thoughtful cups of coffee and the counsellor's earnest, reassuring voice, would keep the peace.

He could not have misjudged it more.

Once the truth was out, Izzy had leapt up, grabbed her untouched cup of coffee and thrown its cold contents at him. Then she had passed the therapist the tissues, told her to mop up the mess and to stick her non-threatening environment up her Freudian slip. 'How's that for naming that emotion?' she had added, flinging open the door to make her getaway, 'and guess what, I think I've just released the feeling and now I'm going to move beyond it!'

'No, I'm not seeing her again,' Izzy replied evenly, proud that she was still on top of this conversation. Then, she reached forward to put her cup on the coffee table, and somehow dropped her cake plate to the floor, scattering pink and yellow crumbs over the carpet.

So much for being a grown woman of thirty-one! She was instantly a fumbling, nervous six-year-old, waiting for the inevitable reprimand and wishing she could hide at the bottom of the garden with her father. With a sad, faraway look in his eye he had spent his time feeding leaves and small branches into a charred metal bin with a funny little chimney. His hair and clothes had always smelt of smoke, and Izzy could never pass a bonfire without being reminded of her father and the wall of silence that had surrounded him.

'Still as clumsy as ever, then,' her mother tutted. 'I suppose you want me to fetch you a clean plate from the kitchen, do you?' She made the journey to the kitchen sound like a two-month trek across the freezing wastelands of Siberia.

That night, Izzy had slept in her old bedroom. The mattress of her childhood bed, lumpy and unyielding, smelling of mothballs, had ensured a nostalgically restless night. As had the memories invoked by that poky room, with its flaking paintwork, swirly patterned carpet, tiny knee-hole dressing table and teak-effect shelves, which held an assortment of old board games and incomplete jigsaws, which only saw the light of day at Christmas.

Lying in bed, trying to sleep, she had felt the familiar sensation of being trapped inside an airtight plastic box. She always felt like this when she came home. A few hours into any visit with all the secrets and memories stored in the ageing wallpaper and carpets, and the walls of the gloomy bungalow began to move in on her. As a child she had promised herself she would remember how many times she had hidden in this room, under this bed, wanting to escape the charged atmosphere but she hadn't been able to keep a tally: the occasions had been too numerous.

Any time spent with Prudence left her feeling drained, and this time she had been consumed with guilt that she had even considered a holiday.

Emotional blackmail was a relatively new trick of her mother's. It had surfaced last year, on the day they had buried her father, and a month before Alan had left her.

'I suppose one good thing will come out of his death,' her mother had said, as she had nodded to Izzy to pass round the corned-beef sandwiches to the mourners who had gathered awkwardly in the sitting room. 'It will bring Isobel and me closer together. She's all I have now.'

Her father had spent the last six weeks of his life in his dressing-gown, a blue and green tartan affair that had seemed to get the better of him, outgrowing his frail body, making him look small and redundant, diminished. He had had a stroke, had lost the power of speech and the use of his right arm and leg, and had spent most of his time staring out of the window, through the army of unblinking statues, at his beloved garden. Until Prudence had it covered with crazy paving. How unnecessarily cruel that had seemed to Izzy. She had visited as often as she could, reduced to tears each time she saw how fast her father was declining, flinching at her mother's no-nonsense rough handling of him, seeing the glimmer of light go out of his eyes, not that it had ever been very bright. He died on a Friday afternoon, his life trickling away quietly as Izzy set off on the long drive to see him, and his wife knitted another taut square while watching Richard Whiteley and Carol Vorderman on *Countdown*.

His death caused barely a dent in her mother's daily routine. She had her hands full anyway, what with the new postman to whip into shape and a young milkman who still hadn't learnt to close the gate quietly at six in the morning. If Prudence missed her husband at all, it was because she had no one on whom to take out her frustration.

Which was why Izzy was getting the full treatment.

Laura had shaken Izzy out of her guilt. 'She's a wicked old woman for trying to manipulate you like that,' she had said on the phone. Knowing Izzy as well as she did, she had called to make sure that the visit to Prudence had passed without incident. 'And what if she did snuff it while you were here with us enjoying yourself? So what? We'd get you back in time for the funeral. What more could she want?'

Izzy hadn't known Max and Laura for long, but it felt as though they knew her better than anybody else did. They had met when Izzy had moved up to Cheshire to start her new job and she had been renting a tiny cottage in the village where Max and Laura lived. She had been reversing into a small space in the high street, a manoeuvre she normally avoided at all costs – bonnet first or find a larger space, was her rule – but she had been in a hurry and there was nowhere else. Come on, she told herself, an articulated lorry could get in there. A thud, followed by a light tinkle of glass, told her, however, that she had failed. As she stepped out of the car to inspect the damage, her heart sank. Of all the cars she could have rubbed bumpers with, she had picked the shiniest of black Porsches. Damn! This would be expensive. She was just writing a note of apology for the car's owner when a voice said, 'Oh, dear, what a terrible shame. Will it be very difficult to replace the parts for your lovely old car?' The smiling man with his silvery-white hair didn't seem bothered by his smashed headlamp, or the dent in the moulded bumper. He placed his shopping on the passenger seat, bent down to inspect the ruined chrome-work on Izzy's Triumph Herald, then said, 'You look a bit shaken, are you okay?'

'I'm so sorry. This could only happen to me. I knew I shouldn't have tried to park here.'

They exchanged addresses and phone numbers, and the following evening she had called on him with the necessary insurance details and a bottle of wine to add weight to her apology. His wife had answered the door of their fabulously large house and insisted she stay for a drink with them – 'Max said a beautiful girl had bumped into him in the high street,' she had laughed, leading the way through to the kitchen where the smell of cooking reminded Izzy that she had passed on lunch that day. 'I thought he was exaggerating his good fortune as usual. But it seems I was wrong.'

Meeting Max and Laura had been Izzy's good fortune, though, for since that chance encounter she had made two very good friends.

She was a great believer in chance, though she had to admit it didn't always work in her favour.

3

Laura had set the table for lunch at the shaded end of the veranda, where the low, sloping eaves of the villa provided the most protection from the fierce midday sun. While Max poured the wine and Laura drizzled locally produced olive oil over a large pottery bowl of salad leaves and diced cucumber, Izzy took a moment to catch her breath. She and Laura hadn't stopped talking and laughing since Max had parked the Jeep an hour ago at the front of the villa and brought her inside.

Laura had given her an immediate guided tour, seeking approval, rather than fawning admiration. 'Stunning' was the word that kept tripping off Izzy's tongue, as she was shown each beautifully decorated and furnished room. The walls had either been washed with fresh white paint or a more subtle tone of buttermilk; dazzling watercolours of seascapes added splashes of vibrant colour. The floors were all of cool, polished marble or white tiles and in places were covered with antique rugs that were attractively worn and faded and helped to give the villa a lived-in look.

The sitting room, the largest and most spectacular of all the rooms, faced the sea, and its row of french windows opened directly on to the veranda, which ran the full length of the house. This was edged with a low, colonnaded wall that was painted white and lined with earthenware pots filled with shocking pink pelargoniums and pretty marguerites. It was here, in the shade, that they were having lunch and the mood round the table was as bright and informal as the setting.

'So what's it to be, Izzy?' asked Max, taking a hunk of bread from the basket in front of him and mopping up the pool of golden olive oil on his plate. 'An adventurous boat trip into Kassiópi with Captain Max or a swim and a gossip with Laura?'

'Hands off,' Laura intervened, before Izzy had a chance to reply. 'Izzy's mine for the rest of the afternoon.'

Max topped up Izzy's glass. 'Looks as though you're in for a tongue-wagging session.'

'I won't be fit for anything if I carry on drinking at this rate.'

'Oh, baloney! Alcohol intake doesn't count when you're on holiday, didn't you know that?'

'Is that true of calories?' asked Laura, giving Max's hand a playful slap as he reached for another piece of bread.

'Yes, my sweet,' he laughed. 'Nothing's ever the same when you're away from home. The value system changes completely.'

'Ah, so that's why so many people have a fling when they're on holiday,' joked Izzy.

'Well, not that I'm speaking from personal experience,' said Max, 'but you're probably right. It's like getting done for speeding in a foreign country – it doesn't mean anything because without any points on your licence it doesn't matter. Why? Thinking of giving it a whirl?'

'Heavens, no!'

'Perhaps you should,' said Laura.

Izzy looked at her, shocked. Was this really the woman who, only a few days ago, had agreed with her over coffee that she ought to give men a miss for a while? 'If I'm not mistaken, that's a slightly different tune from the one you've been whistling of late.'

'You're right, but maybe it's time to take stock and see what's out there.'

'But a holiday romance. It would be so shallow. So meaningless. So—'

'And potentially so much fun,' cut in Laura.

Since she had started reading that book on the plane Modern Woman seemed to have taken up residence inside Izzy's head. *Don't listen to her*, she warned. *In your current state you need an emotional entanglement like a fish needs a hook in its mouth.*

'It would be rather reckless, wouldn't it?' said Izzy, trying to be sensible but already tempted by a picture of herself wandering along the beach with a handsome man beneath a moonlit sky.

'But having fun doesn't have to be reckless,' persisted Laura. 'If you understood at the start what the outcome would be, that you would both know and accept that you'd be waving goodbye at the end of the holiday, where would be the harm?'

'Is it really possible to do that?' asked Izzy doubtfully, knowing that she was an all-or-nothing girl.

'There's only one way to find out,' smiled Laura. 'Give it a try.'

That afternoon when Max retreated to his den to watch Henri Le Conte in the over-thirty-fives doubles, Laura and Izzy changed into their swimsuits and took the path down to the beach. Tied to a post at the end of a wooden jetty that belonged to Villa Petros, two boats bobbed in the water; one was small and modest, the other a much more expensive affair.

'The little one is ours and the gin palace is owned by our neighbour,' explained Laura, catching Izzy's eye. 'He leaves it here because the water is too rough by his place and it would get smashed to pieces on the rocks. Fancy swimming out to the raft?'

They left their towels on the rocks and slipped into the cool, clear water. The raft wasn't far and they were soon climbing up the metal rungs and lying stretched out on their fronts on the sun-warmed decking. Though it was securely anchored, there was still a pleasing sense of motion and, with her eyes shut, Izzy felt as though she was drifting aimlessly. 'Is every day going to be as perfect as this?' she murmured, resting her head in the crook of her arm.

'I told you you'd like it. And, trust me, it just gets better and better.'

'You live a charmed life, you know that, don't you?'

Laura turned on to her side. 'I'd hate anyone to think that I don't know exactly how lucky I am.'

Concerned that she may have inadvertently upset her friend, Izzy opened her eyes. 'I'm sorry, I wasn't implying you took it for granted, I only meant—'

'It's okay. I know what you were getting at. But I'm all too aware that Max's little empire could come crashing down at any time, taking everything with it. Including us. If that happens, then so be it. We'd have to adapt and get on with it. Meanwhile, I'm quite happy to live by the creed that he's worked jolly hard for what he's got and I don't see any reason why he shouldn't make the most of it while he can.'

'A sound enough creed in anyone's book.'

They lay in silence, listening to the water lapping at the sides of the raft, and Izzy thought of her own rather more modest life at home. As a teacher in a small prep school her prospects were never going to reach the stratosphere of Max and Laura's gold-edged lifestyle. On the whole she had always enjoyed teaching, but she was conscious that recently what had appealed most to her about her job were the long holidays. That could mean only one thing: a change was due. She had been at the school for too long. She was growing stale. Also she disliked, no, hated, the new head, a woman who had been brought in to wield the axe. At the end of term, last Friday, there had been so many redundancies made that Izzy was sure it was only a matter of time before she herself was dismissed. Art teachers were hardly a high priority. If cuts were to be made, it was a generally held view that any old fool could teach the little dears to cut and paste.

She frowned guiltily. She shouldn't be here lazing in the sun on a raft, she should be at home scanning the *Times Educational Supplement* for a new job. But, hey, let the head make her redundant first.

It might even be for the best, given that her parting shot at the end of term had been that in the autumn the remaining members of staff were to dress in power suits. Power suits! What would she, an art teacher, do in a crisp two-piece? She didn't have anything in her wardrobe that remotely resembled one. Her clothes, at best, could be described as 'individual', or maybe 'eccentric', but 'cheap' was closer to the truth. The racks and rails of her local branch of Help the Aged were her favourite stamping ground for last season's fashion statements. Not that she was a complete fashion slouch – she knew a good label when she saw one and wasn't slow in handing over an extra pound for quality, especially if she needed something for a special occasion. But a power suit?

Other than school, little else was going on in Izzy's life, and had she been in danger of missing this, her mother had been only too quick to point it out to her. 'I had hoped to be a grandmother by now,' she had muttered on the phone, when Izzy was officially a single woman again. 'With your inability to maintain a steady relationship there's no chance of that ever happening, I suppose.'

'I'm sorry to have denied you that pleasure,' Izzy had said.

'There's no need to take that tone with me, young lady. A couple of grandchildren, is that really so much to ask for?'

In the circumstances, yes, it was.

Izzy had wanted children, but Alan had refused to entertain the idea. Just as he had refused to talk about marriage. 'We're okay as we are,' he would say. 'Why go changing things?'

Izzy sat up and looked towards the shore where a selection of villas nestled into the hillside. 'Tell me about your neighbours,' she said. 'You and Max have often mentioned Theo, the man who sold you the villa, especially what a sex-god he thinks he is, but what about the others? What are they like?'

Laura sat up too and pointed to the furthest villa along the bay to the left. 'That's owned by an elderly French couple who have been coming here for over twenty years. They live in Paris and tend to keep themselves to themselves. And to the right is a villa with yellow shutters. Do you see it? It's just peeping through the trees.'

Izzy squinted in the glare of the bright sun. 'Yes.'

'That's owned by an Englishwoman, but nobody ever sees her. She used to come here for holidays with her husband, and when he died five years ago she moved in permanently.'

'So why doesn't anyone see her?'

Laura shrugged. 'Don't know. Everyone just accepts that she's a recluse and lets her get on with it. Now, do you see the tatty little pink house?'

Again Izzy squinted her eyes. 'Yes.'

'That's owned by another Brit. But he's let it go to rack and ruin and struggles to rent it to tourists. Apparently it's a mess inside and out. Moving up the hillside, there's a tiny little villa that's owned by a German businessman. According to the local gossip, he's not coming this summer, so it will probably be rented too.'

'Aren't there any locals who live here?'

'A few, but not many. Behind the German villa is where Dimitri and Marietta live. They own one of the jewellery shops in Kassiópi and spend their summers here, running the shop.'

'And where do they spend their winters?'

'In Athens, like Theo.'

'So which is his place?'

Laura pointed to the right of Villa Petros, to the tip of the lush green headland. 'That's his. It's lovely, isn't it? Quite the best house in Áyios Nikólaos. It used to be an olive press but he's done a wonderful job of extending and renovating it. It's a bit of a hobby for him.'

Izzy gazed up at the attractive mellow stone villa. 'What does he do when he's not renovating old houses – and flirting with you?'

Laura smiled. 'You've been listening to Max too much.'

Izzy smiled too. 'He may have mentioned Theo's interest in you.'

'It's just a game he plays. It's nothing serious. No, what he's really into is property. And lots of it. He owns half of Athens, if you believe a fraction of the scurrilous stories Angelos shares with Max.'

'And who's Angelos?'

'He and his wife practically run Áyios Nikólaos. Without them we'd be sunk. They take care of our villa, as well as Theo's and several others.

Angelos does all the gardening and maintenance work, and Sophia does the cleaning. Look, that's their house, to the left of ours and further up the hill. You'll meet them soon. They're nice, very friendly.'

Izzy stretched her arms over her head and yawned. She had been up since five and was beginning to feel tired. 'And what about tomorrow, anything in mind for us to do?'

'We've got nothing planned. That's the beauty of coming here. It's total relaxation. What's more, I don't even have to cook tonight. Max is going to impress you with his barbecue skills. It'll just be the four of us.'

'Four?'

'Don't worry, it's only Theo joining us for the evening. Come on, I need to get out of the sun. Give me a head start and I'll race you back to the beach.'

4

With a beer in his hand, Max was more than happy to be left to his own devices to deal with the intricate operation of lighting the barbecue. He waved Laura away with a stand-aside-and-leave-this-to-me expression and told her to go and relax.

Only too pleased to escape the rising cloud of smoke, she picked up her Campari and soda and went over to the group of wicker chairs, positioned to give them the best view of the setting sun when they settled there after their meal.

She leaned back into one and wondered how the evening would go. She was mildly surprised that Theo wasn't here already. Her initial concern over him sweeping Izzy off her feet had done a surprising U-turn. She had a good feeling about the effect his company would have on Izzy. She didn't know of a single woman who wouldn't relish being flattered by an attractive man. The reverse was also true, of course. Men found the flirtatious attention of a beautiful woman an irresistible draw. The difference between the two was that men were inclined to take the passing attention of a woman seriously – Wow, I always knew I was a catch! – while women treated it as they would a fragrant waft of freesias: lovely, but not lasting.

Which was as close as one could get to describing Theo. He was lovely, all right, but any intimate relationship with him would almost certainly be short and sweet.

Throughout last summer when she and Max had occasionally stayed with Theo while the finishing touches were being put to Villa Petros, Laura had seen him in action with a number of women he brought with him from Athens. She had asked him once if he ever grew tired of the rapid turnaround in his love life.

'You are implying that I lead a shallow existence, Laura, is that it? Well, do not worry yourself on my account, I am quite happy as I am.'

She didn't doubt that he was happy, she just wondered if he could be happier.

Max had agreed with her, saying that he was a curious man. 'When he's having a drink on his own with me he's quite different,' he said, during one of their many conversations about Theo, 'but put a woman in front of him and it's as if a switch flicks – he goes into super-charged charmer mode.'

Hearing a change in the strength of the waves on the rocks below, Laura turned her gaze out to sea. One of the many Minoan ferries that passed this way between Brindisi and the port at Corfu Town was gliding across the horizon. Its smooth passage made her wonder just how smooth Theo would be this evening. What kind of a performance would he put on for Izzy's benefit?

And how would Izzy react?

Laura had deliberately not told her anything of the conversation she had had with Theo that morning. If she did, Izzy would automatically be on her guard, which would create an atmosphere of hostility between them. That would be a great shame.

No. It was much better that Izzy worked Theo out for herself, in her own time and in her own way, and decided just how seriously to take him. If she had any sense she would treat him in exactly the same way Laura did. Besides, Laura didn't want anything to spoil Izzy's holiday. After the tough year she had had, what with Alan, her father dying, and her dreadful mother to contend with, a relaxing summer was the least she deserved.

The sound of footsteps on the stony path below the terrace told her that Theo was about to make his entrance. 'Act one, scene one,' she muttered to herself, getting up from her chair and going to meet him.

On seeing him she burst out laughing: he was carrying a bottle in each hand and between his teeth there were two long-stemmed roses. She took the wine from him and led him to where Max was opening another beer.

'Oh, Theo,' gushed Max, 'red roses! How sweet! Really, you shouldn't have.'

'Ignore him,' said Laura. 'It's the fumes from the barbecue coals, they go straight to his head. One of those roses for me?'

'But of course, my darling Laura. Though only if I am permitted a kiss in exchange.' He leaned into her, was about to kiss her mouth when she neatly twisted her head and he had to make do with her cheek.

'She's getting too quick for you, Theo,' laughed Max. 'Now what can I get you to drink? Beer, wine, oúzo, gin and ... Ah, Izzy, there you are.'

Both Laura and Theo turned to see Izzy coming towards them. She was dressed in a black camisole top with a calf-length flowing skirt, also in black, and on her feet she wore a pair of espadrilles. Even though she had spent scarcely any time in the sun that day, she was already exhibiting a tan. With her shoulder-length dark brown hair pulled back into a loose plait, she looked all of twenty-five. Laura would have liked to study Theo's face closely to see what his initial reaction was, but the telephone rang inside the villa.

'Can you get that, love?' Max said. 'I've just put the kebabs on. If it's for me,' he shouted after her, 'and it seems urgent, tell them I'll call back later.'

'It looks as if we shall just have to introduce ourselves,' said Theo. 'Theo Vlamakis, friend to Max and Laura Sinclair, and hopefully soon to become your friend.' He offered Izzy the rose. 'To wish you a relaxing holiday here in Áyios Nikólaos. May today be the start of a happy love affair.'

Izzy took the rose from him, 'A love affair?' she repeated, thinking that he was George Clooney to a T. He had the same short dark hair, flecked with grey, and the same thick eyebrows above a pair of magnetic black eyes. Dressed in cream linen trousers with a pale peach short-sleeved shirt that showed a finely worked gold chain at his throat, there was no mistaking the aura of natural glamour and appeal about him.

'Yes, a love affair with Corfu and its beguiling people, of course,' he said. 'Now it is your turn. You have to introduce yourself.'

Self-conscious, but charmed by his words and manner, Izzy held out her hand and said, 'Izzy Jordan, friend to Max and Laura Sinclair, and I've a confession to make. I've heard a lot about you already.'

He gave a ceremonious little tilt of his head, took her hand and raised it to his lips. 'I am very pleased to meet you, Izzy Jordan. Though it seems you have the advantage. I know hardly anything about you. Is it very bad what Laura has confided in you about me? Does she make me sound like the empty-headed buffoon?'

Izzy laughed and withdrew her hand. Goodness, he was smooth. 'She speaks very highly of you, as a friend and a neighbour.'

'That's good. That means we step out in the right direction, you and me.'

'Theo, if you could lay off the Ionian charm for a couple of seconds, perhaps you'd be kind enough to get Izzy a drink.'

Dutifully leading her over to the table of drinks, Theo said, 'That Max, he has such a sharp tongue on him. Like so many English men, he is jealous of his Greek counterpart. We Greek men, we cannot understand how the English ever reproduce, especially the ones with the stiff-upper-lip public-school background. You know, Izzy, a night of passion for Max is sharing a beer with his highly esteemed Fergie.'

'What? The Duchess of York?' said Izzy, trying hard not to laugh.

'No,' grinned Theo, 'your great man of the people, Sir Alex Ferguson.'

'Theo, if you don't give it a rest, you'll feel the sharp end of one of these kebab sticks! Now, get the girl a drink.'

It wasn't until Max was serving the fruits of his labours and insisting that Theo and Izzy sit down that Laura reappeared. 'Who was that on the phone?' he asked.

'Francesca.'

Max stopped what he was doing. 'Nothing wrong, is there? She's not changed her mind about coming?'

Laura smiled. 'Poor old Daddy missing his beloved daughter, is he? Don't worry, she's still coming. She just wanted a chat.'

'Ah, mother-and-daughter stuff, was it?'

'Yes. Big bust-up with the boyfriend.'

Max tipped the last of the swordfish kebabs on to the large plate of seafood in the middle of the table and said, 'Good. He was an idiot. Didn't have an original thought in his head. He thought he was so cool and radical when all the time he was a jumped-up little jerk.'

'Aha, there speaks the father who thinks there is not a young man alive good enough for his daughter,' said Theo. 'Poor old Max, you would much rather be the one to choose a husband for her.'

Izzy knew quite a bit about the now ex-boyfriend. She had met him just once, but it had been enough to understand why Max was so glad to know that he had seen the last of him. He had been one of those slow-witted ecowarrior types with nose and eyebrow rings and dreadlocks crawling down his back. He had been a vegetarian as well, and Izzy recalled a beanburger that Laura had made specially for him, which he had prodded at rudely and said he couldn't eat because he could smell garlic in it. He was a far cry from what she knew was Max's idea of a perfect boyfriend for Francesca: he had to be motivated and smart, and if he could possibly manage it, straight out of the Tim Henman mould of clean-cut good looks and behaviour.

'Hah, baloney, to you, Theo!' Max retaliated. 'Just wait until you have children of your own before you start casting aspersions on my partiality.' Then, turning to Laura, 'She's okay, though, isn't she?'

'Relax, she's fine, currently denouncing all men as bastards. By the way, she asked if she could bring a friend with her when she comes over.'

'Anyone we know?'

'Sally Bartholomew.'

'What, *the* Sally? Man-eating Sally? A girl who can lasso a man to the ground with her own stockings. You said no, didn't you?'

Ignoring his question, Laura reached for the wine-cooler. 'Now then, who needs a refill? Darling, you're not going to wear those oven gloves all evening, are you?'

Max took them off and tossed them on to the table, then sat next to his wife. 'Go on, then, tell me the worst. How long is she staying?'

While Laura filled Max in on the details, Izzy offered Theo the plate of barbecued seafood.

'No, please,' he said, taking the dish from her, 'you are the guest here, I will serve you.'

'But you're a guest too.'

'No. I am just plain old Theo from next door.'

Izzy smiled. 'That sounds suspiciously like a man fishing for a compliment.'

He narrowed his dark eyes and looked puzzled. 'I am sorry. Fishing? What is the allusion here? I do not understand. Your English must be too refined for me.'

'Don't listen to a word, Izzy,' said Max, leaning across the table, helping himself to a jumbo-sized prawn and ripping it apart. 'Theo's English is as good as yours and mine, if not better. He was educated in England at one of those fancy public schools he was just condemning, and my guess is he learned very young to put people at a disadvantage with his linguistic ability. Usually pretty young girls. So be warned.'

Theo passed the plate he was holding to Laura. 'Is your husband going to be as bad-tempered for the rest of the evening just because a nymphet is coming to stay?'

'Lord, will you listen to him?' roared Max. But there was no anger to his voice. Giving Izzy a smile, he said, 'You see what you've let yourself in for this summer?'

'Ah, poor Izzy,' said Theo, turning to her and holding out a perfectly peeled prawn for her to take. 'I don't think you will stay sane here for long. Promise me, if you get tired of these crazy people you will come to me for a place of sanctuary. Villa Anna is so tranquil. I think it would suit you better. Eh? What do you say?'

Izzy took the proffered prawn. 'Thank you, but who's to say that I'm not as crazy as Max and Laura?'

By the time they had finished their meal and were sitting in the wicker chairs with a tray of liqueur bottles to choose from, the sun was setting, casting a coppery glow over the wide open sky, and across the darkening water, where the swelling outline of Albania could still be seen, lights were twinkling like stars. It was a beautiful sight and for a few minutes they all sat quietly enjoying it.

Laura was thinking how restrained Theo was being. Compared to how she had seen him in the past, with women far less attractive than Izzy, he was playing it very cool. She hadn't seen him once attempt to touch her, nor had he commented on her appearance. For an Englishman this would have been par for the course, but for a Greek with a sex-god reputation to live up to it was unheard-of. Was Theo smarter than she had given him credit for? Perhaps so. Instead of smothering Izzy in ready-made flattery he had chatted to her so far about life in England, the school where she taught, and how she had been unfortunate enough to meet her and Max. He had laughed at her description of bumping into Max's Porsche. 'It serves him right for having such an ostentatious car,' he had said.

'That's rich coming from you,' retorted Max. 'What about the pimp-mobile you have here on the island? BMWs are as rare as hen's teeth in these parts, never mind the Z3.'

'You see how easy it is to rile poor old Max?' Theo had said to Izzy. 'Always he is coming from the defensive point of view.'

The sun had now slipped below the horizon, and Max asked Theo about his friend, who was arriving the following day. 'You never mentioned before that you knew Mark St James.'

'I am sure there are lots of people you know that you have not told me about.'

'But this is different. Mark St James is an author. Quite a well-known one at that. One of my favourites.'

Theo drained his glass of Metaxá and shrugged. 'You are entitled to your hero-worship, but to me he is just a friend. No more, no less.'

'Is he the one whose books have been on the telly back home?' asked Izzy. 'The writer they describe as *Cracker* meets *Silence of the Lambs*?'

'Yes that's him,' said Max. 'Those adaptations of his books make a welcome change from all those bonnet dramas. Have you read any of his stuff?'

'No. I'm not sure they're quite my cup of tea.'

'You should give them a try,' urged Max. 'The psychology is brilliant. You really feel that he knows the mind of a criminal. It's rather disturbing, but you almost sympathise with the killer by the end of one of his books.'

'It is his forte,' said Theo, leaning forward to settle his empty glass on the low table. 'He studied criminal psychology at university. He knows his subject inside out.'

'How did you meet him?' asked Izzy.

'Ah, the perceptive Izzy. I see that the unlikely match of two such men intrigues you. But it is true, opposites really do attract. We met at college, and hit it off straight away. Mark thought I was a poncy fascist, and I thought he was an arrogant, foul-mouthed, narrow-minded bore.'

Izzy smiled. 'So what changed your opinion of each other?'

For a second Theo looked serious and stared into the darkening sky. 'He saved my life,' he said quietly. Then, 'But that's a story I will leave for Mark to tell you. Now, it is time for me to do some work. I have many phone calls to make. *Kaliníhta*, one and all.' He got to his feet, followed swiftly by the rest of them. He rested his hands on Laura's shoulders and kissed her cheeks. 'As ever, my darling, you were the perfect hostess.' He shook hands with Max, then turned to Izzy. 'Now that we are practically old friends, am I permitted to kiss you goodnight?'

He gave her a look and a smile that might easily have talked a girl into falling in love with him.

5

Theo considered himself a lucky man. Just as Churchill and Napoleon had functioned on little sleep, so did he. He had worked until two in the morning, had risen at six fully refreshed, and by half past seven had been for a swim, showered, dressed and walked up the dusty potholed lane to see Nicos and his wife, who ran the local supermarket. He had returned a short while later with his breakfast: a melon and a *kataifi*, a finely shredded pastry bulging with almonds and soaked in honey. He was eating this now while sitting on the flower-filled terrace overlooking the sea. The scent of the roses enhanced the delicious sweetness of the cake.

His sweet tooth, according to his grandmother, was his only weakness, but then she had always seen him through such blinkered eyes, could never accept that he might be fallible. All over Greece there were women just like her, responsible for giving Greek children, and especially boys, the reputation of being the most indulged children in the world. Certainly Anna Vlamakis had seen to it that her only grandchild was the most pampered and fêted.

'You are spoiling that boy beyond redemption,' his parents would complain. But Anna ignored their pleas for restraint and took delight in presenting him to her friends and neighbours as a handsome prodigy who could do no wrong. From an early age he had developed a talent for talking to adults without feeling in awe of them, or being self-conscious in their presence. It made him a precocious star turn whenever Anna showed him off. As she frequently did.

After each visit he made to his grandmother in Corfu, his exasperated parents would say that he had returned to Athens with a head bigger than his shoulders and neck could support. It was as well that she had not lived any closer in those early days of his childhood, or she would have been the ruin of him. Though, of course, there might be some, including his old friend Mark, who would say that she had done exactly that.

His father had worked for the diplomatic service, and when he was posted to the Greek embassy in London, both his parents must have breathed a sigh of relief. At last, distance would ensure that Anna Vlamakis' influence was kept to a minimum. But their relief was short-lived: his father's duties increased rapidly, which meant that his mother was also busy, helping him host dinners and parties for visiting dignitaries. The inevitable happened: they agreed that he should spend the long holidays from school with his grandmother in Corfu.

Theo had loved Anna's old town-house in Kérkyra with its faded Venetian façade, pretty courtyard, and ever-changing view of the harbour and old fort. He especially enjoyed going out with her. After her customary afternoon siesta, she would take him through the dark maze of narrow streets – some so narrow he could stretch out his arms and touch both walls – to her favourite *zaharoplastía*, a sweet-shop that sold mouth-watering cakes, and biscuits decorated with sesame seeds, coconut, apricots or chocolate. While Anna chatted with the owner, Theo would be left to make their choice, and when the cardboard boxes had been filled and tied with a ribbon they would go on to visit her friends for tea. Like Anna, these ladies had also outlived their husbands and were wealthy enough to have few worries in the world. Over pastries and liqueurs, they would share with him *risqué* stories of their many lovers, during and after their marriages, smiling at each other and watching his face to see if he was shocked by their scandalous revelations. But nothing they said ever shocked him: he was too fascinated by the world of love and sensual desire they spoke of with such wistful longing.

On other days Anna would take him to the Esplanade where they would watch a cricket match while sitting in the cool shade of one of the elegant Listón bars. Often they were joined by Thomas Zika, a local businessman and lifelong admirer of his grandmother. He spoke in hushed tones, and wore a suit and tie even on the hottest of days. He was an amazing linguist and encouraged Theo to be the same, talking to him in English one minute, Italian the next.

But the days Theo enjoyed most were those he spent in the elegant high-ceilinged drawing rooms of Anna's widowed friends. It was from those ladies that he had learned the importance of passion. His grandmother said that no one had ever lived until they had experienced what she called a Grand Passion. When he was of an age to understand things better, he had asked Anna why she had never accepted one of Thomas Zika's many proposals. 'Ah, Theo,' she had said, sipping her dry martini, which she had taught him to mix, 'it is true that Thomas loves me, and it is also true that I am very fond of him. But I do not love him. I would rather keep matters as they are. He is a close friend, perhaps the closest I have ever had, and I would not want to risk losing that by marrying him.'

'So you think it is always better to travel through life not taking any risks?'

'No. That is not what I am saying. My marriage to your grandfather was the risk I took and it was my moment of Grand Passion. I have no desire to replace or even add to the memory of what I have already experienced and keep treasured in my heart.'

'But you could have something different with Thomas.'

Smiling she had said, 'Perhaps if he were more persistent I might reconsider. But he seems to have resigned himself quite happily to what we have.'

'Maybe he is frightened to press you any harder, that one more proposal will turn you against him.'

'What a lot of thought you have given to this, Theo. But I'm afraid you will have to accept that Thomas and I have reached an impasse and are both happy to live with it.'

With such an upbringing, it was no surprise that Theo tended to surround himself with women. He felt most at ease when in their company. With the exception of a few close friends and one or two business associates, he seldom trusted men.

He attributed this wariness to his time at school in England. He had hated the boarding-school just outside London to which his parents had sent him, and it was many years before he truly forgave them for forcing him into the barbarism of the English public-school system. After the life he had lived so far, it had come as a profound culture shock. He was in no way effeminate, but the regime he was expected to follow at school, with its tough macho image, appalled him. Naturally he suffered a degree of bullying for being a foreigner, but he fought back by beating his tormentors on and off the playing-fields. He pursued the goals and accolades they coveted, and with such vigour and success that in the end they accepted him into their world. After all, it was better to have the enemy in your own pocket than in someone else's.

It was during his adolescence that he lost his virginity. He was seventeen and was spending nearly all of his free time with the wife of the new classics master. He was a dull man in his late thirties, with a pretty wife ten years his junior. Living in a small cottage within the school grounds, she was bored and lonely. To give her something to do, her husband had unwisely suggested that she help Theo perfect his English. Which she did, and a lot more besides.

She had been the only person he had missed when he left a year later. He had thought of returning to Athens, either to go to university there or to embark upon his national service, but with his parents still in London, he gave in to their wishes and stayed on in England. They wanted him to study in London, but he refused the university place he was offered there and went to Durham instead.

In Durham he experienced true bone-numbing coldness for the first time in his life. The freezing North Sea wind that came across the flat terrain cut through the layers of clothing with which he tried to protect himself as he cycled across town for a lecture. The rain was worse, icy cold, horizontal, and wetter than anything he had ever known; it slashed at his face, leaving him breathless and barely able to see the road in front of him. It was on such a raw, freezing cold day that he had met Mark.

He had heard of Mark St James already – his reputation, as they say, went well before him. He was a political activist intent on saving his generation, if not the world, from the evils of capitalism. His presence was advertised throughout college in the form of the posters he put up wherever he could, vilifying the leaders of the free world's major industrial nations, proclaiming them to be no better than the devil's disciples. When he wasn't organising a protest march or a silent sit-in, he was braving the elements selling copies of whatever radical paper he was currently supporting.

It was 1976 when punk rock was bursting on to the scene and, with his hair spiked and dyed an aggressive peroxide blond, his skinny legs covered in black PVC bondage trousers, decorated with zips and chains, the rest of him blanketed in an oversized, hand-knitted sweater that would not have looked out of place in a dog basket, the infamous Mark St James was a distinctive sight as he stood in the market-place in front of the church, ignored by the busy Saturday morning shoppers.

Theo had watched him through the steamed-up window of the café where he was having a late breakfast of coffee and doughnuts, and had admired his fellow student for his dedication to the cause. He was about to order a second mug of coffee when he noticed that it was raining again. Shivering at the thought of yet more icy rain, he suddenly felt compelled to go and offer this foolish young man a hot drink.

'Fuck off!' was the snarled response.

'Considering I am the first person to offer you anything other than a look of disparagement, don't you think you are being just a little hasty?'

An expression of hostile disdain flickered across the gaunt face, which appeared underfed and pinched with cold. The sneering blue-eyed gaze then trailed over Theo's clothes – cashmere coat and scarf, Italian leather gloves, black woollen trousers and shiny burgundy-coloured loafers.

'You're that flash Greek, aren't you?' His voice was low and husky, as though he was recovering from a bout of laryngitis.

Theo knew all too well that this was how he was labelled in some quarters, but hearing it uttered with such menacing contempt made him wince. 'I am only offering you a drink, not an opportunity to enslave you with my misguided political views.'

The look thawed and with a curl of lips that were chapped and bruised with cold, he said, 'Yeah, okay then. Who knows? I might be able to show a poncy fascist where he's going wrong.'

For the next fifteen minutes Theo was attacked for everything he had or hadn't done: global capitalism, world poverty, institutional power that was corrupt and killing those who weren't already starving to death, and ultimately for being too stupid to understand the manifesto that this angry young nihilist claimed would save the world from itself. And as if that wasn't enough, he was held personally responsible for the plight of the crumbling Acropolis in Athens. 'You realise, don't you,' Mark said, leaning forward in his chair and pointing a surprisingly clean and slender finger at Theo's face, 'it's the shit from all your cars that's the problem? The Acropolis is two thousand four hundred years old, it's survived God knows how many invasions, and you're wrecking it with your stinking pollution. So figure this one out, pretty boy, what the hell are you going to do to stop it?'

'Goodness, after such a display of sweet reason you mean I get a turn to speak? Well, I believe, and without my intervention, that help is at hand. UNESCO is sponsoring a rescue fund.'

'Yeah, but will it be enough?'

'Is anything we do enough?'

'Better something than nothing.'

'Which is why I offered you a cup of coffee. But now I must be on my way. I have an essay to write. It was good talking to you. Even if you are an arrogant, foul-mouthed, narrow-minded bore. Goodbye. Oh, and you should do something about that sore throat. Standing around in the cold will not do it any good. Trust me on that, if nothing else.'

They didn't see one another again until the following week when Theo was enjoying a late breakfast once more and watching Mark trying to sell his ideology to uninterested passers-by. This time, though, it was Mark who made the approach. He caught sight of Theo through the café window and marched straight over, comically restricted by his ridiculous trousers. He threw open the door, letting in a tornado of cold air, and sat uninvited in the chair opposite Theo. 'I object to being described as a narrow-minded bore,' he said angrily, causing several middle-aged women at a nearby table to raise their eyebrows and clutch at their handbags.

'But arrogant and foul-mouthed still stands, eh?'

'At least I'm not screwing every woman in Durham.'

'So who is?'

'You are, you bourgeois, time-wasting little—'

'Oh, please, spare me another come-the-revolution tirade. Now I hate to correct you, but your information is not all it could be. There are still a few women who I have yet to get into bed. Coffee? Or would you prefer hot chocolate? I see your throat is no better.'

'I'll have tea. Ordinary tea – none of that bloody fancy stuff. And if it's any of your sodding business I haven't got a sore throat. This is my normal speaking voice.'

'Then perhaps you would be kind enough to lower it so as not to disturb or intimidate the good ladies here.' He turned his head and gave them his most charming smile, the one he had used while visiting his grandmother's widowed friends.

When Theo had told Izzy last night that it was true about opposites attracting, he could not have described his friendship with Mark any better. There always had been, and always would be, a conflict of egos between them. They were two very strong characters, but because they were so different in nature, they amused and continually confounded each other. It was a real mystery to Theo, in these early days of their friendship, as to why an essentially shy, reserved person, who only wanted to be left alone, forced himself into a position of antagonism that made him such an obvious focus of attention.

Though they openly despised each other on those two initial encounters, they also secretly admired each other. Theo couldn't help but be impressed by Mark's convictions, and though it was a long time before he ever admitted it, Mark was envious of Theo's track record with girls.

'I can't believe they fall for that smooth-bugger routine,' he said one evening, many months later, when they were sitting cross-legged on the floor of his room and eating a curry he had just cooked in the kitchen he shared with twelve other students.

'An air of sophistication is what they like,' Theo had answered, casting a critical eye over Mark's untidy room. The walls were papered with posters of the Sex Pistols, Che Guevara and the Jam; the single bed was covered with unwashed clothes; a small bookcase was filled to capacity with psychology textbooks, and the desk was hidden beneath a tide of files and papers. 'Of course, the money helps,' he added, 'that and my astonishingly good looks.'

'And you think *I'm* an arrogant bastard!'

'Ah, but my arrogance is not based on immature angst and confused anger, as yours is. Mine comes from confidence.'

Now Theo poured himself some more orange juice from the iced jug on the table and stared at the lovely view. Just as yesterday, the sea was as smooth as glass and a hazy early-morning mist hung languidly over the horizon. It was unusually calm, this narrow strait of water between Corfu and Albania. Normally it was a wind-surfer's paradise, especially in the afternoon when the breeze really whipped up. Sometimes the water became dangerously rough and the tourists who innocently hired boats in the morning, expecting a pleasant day of cove-hopping, got rather more than they had bargained for. One saw them all the time, low-powered motor boats struggling against strong waves, the men pretending they had it all under control, and the women slipping on their life-jackets and worrying whether they would see home again.

He shifted his gaze to look along the hillside towards Villa Petros. There was no sign of movement on the terrace or the veranda, and he guessed that its occupants were still asleep. He pictured Max and Laura lying together, Max with one arm placed protectively around his wife's pale, freckled shoulders, and Laura, her auburn hair fanned slightly across the pillow. They were a couple made for each other, perfectly in tune with the other's needs, and still perfectly in love after so many years.

A twinge of envy crept up on him. Not ugly, covetous envy for another man's wife, but a gentle twisting yearning that one day somebody would love him with the constancy with which Laura must always have loved Max.

He pushed the thought away.

It was futile to think along those lines. He could never expect somebody to love him with the intensity he craved, not when it seemed unlikely that he would be capable of offering the same in return. His track record, of which Mark had once been envious, proved that he simply wasn't cut out for long-term monogamous commitment. And almost certainly it was too late for him to change the habit of a lifetime.

His thoughts turned to Izzy. It had been pure idle amusement on his part to tease Laura that he could help her friend to enjoy her holiday, and it had touched him to see her concern. He would never do anything to upset or annoy Laura. Though that first glimpse of Izzy last night had made him wonder: there was no denying that he had felt the irresistible pull an attractive woman always exerted on him. It was the freshness of her face that had appealed. There was no artifice to her. No elaborate hairstyle. No ostentatious jewellery. No makeup. He couldn't even recall if she was wearing any perfume. But she had moved with a beguiling grace that made her unconsciously lovely. She was without pretension, and from her sombre grey eyes, which were both gentle and enquiring, he had guessed that a lot was going on inside her head, and not all of it happy.

She was very different from the women he usually felt attracted to. In fact, she was the complete opposite.

Just as he and Mark had once been. And still were, in many respects: resisting polarities, but with a very real synergy between them, was what Mark said of them.

He leaned back in his seat, stretched his arms over his head, and smiled at the coincidence. 'Well, well, well,' he said aloud. 'We shall just have to wait and see what the Fates have in store for us.'

Mark didn't like coincidences. As far as he was concerned he had experienced too many of them just recently, and none had been good.

But the woman in the seat beside him was not of the same opinion. She was rather drunk and seemed to think that because he was bound for the same holiday destination as she and her husband, some high priestess of fate was at work.

He put her at somewhere in her mid-fifties, and decided she was undergoing a serious identity crisis, kidding herself that she was still in her twenties. She was wearing a pair of Christian Dior sunglasses, a tight cream lace dress, and with a head of scuzzy showbiz blonde hair, she was a real middle-aged designer dolly-babe. She was brittle thin, too, and he had the feeling that if he accidentally knocked her he'd set off an avalanche of body parts. Her lipstick had partially rubbed off and she was left with an outline of lip-liner: it gave her a clown-like drawn-on smile.

Between her and her husband – a man of zero conversational skills but a fine comb-over: you could almost count the strands clinging to his pate – they had bought enough booze from the drinks trolley to ensure that Messrs Gordon and Johnnie Walker would be rubbing their hands with delight.

'You know what, darlin', I was told I'd have an important encounter with a fair-haired man today,' she had said, once they were pushing through the thick bank of clouds that were raining on a miserably wet Manchester below, 'but she didn't mention about him having such a sexy voice. You got a cold?'

'Sorry?' he had said, knowing that he would be. He was sorrier still that he had decided to fly from Manchester instead of Newcastle. Why the hell had he agreed to be a guest speaker for that dinner Waterstone's had put on? If he had said no, as he normally did, he wouldn't have changed his flight arrangements at the last minute and be sitting here next to this wretched woman.

With an irritating jingle-jangle of silver bangles on her skinny wrist, she leaned into him. 'My tarot companion said I'd meet a man who fits your description exactly. Tall, fair-haired and wearing jeans. It's you.'

It could also have been any number of other men on board the plane, but he kept this piece of information to himself, discretion invariably being the better part of valour.

'I hate flying,' she went on, undeterred by his silence, 'so last night I gave my tarot reader a quick tinkle. Just to put my mind at rest. If it's my turn to go, I told her, I want some warning. Like enough to book a later flight! But you're going to bring me luck. You're going to change my life.'

She believed it too. Every last gibbering word of pound-a-minute make-believe. But then she would, wouldn't she? She was probably barking mad. Had to be.

His thoughts were interrupted again as she decided, since he was going to be playing such an important part in her life, that it was time they were properly introduced. Unscrewing the metal cap of one of the miniature bottles she had stashed in her vanity case, she told him her name was Liberty-Raquel Fitzgerald. After raising the bottle of crème-de-menthe to her lips and draining half in one well-practised swig, she added, 'This is my husband, Bob. He doesn't say much. Say hello, Bob.' Silent Bob obviously knew the score and did as he was told. He then got back to his book; a book Mark recognised only too well.

With nothing else for it, he knew that if he was going to get any peace he would have to lose himself in the in-flight movie: a soft-focus costume drama. He was just reaching for his headphones when she told him where she and Silent Bob would be staying.

His brain, which had thus far been lying dormant with boredom, did a double-take. 'Where did you say?'

'Áyios Nikólaos,' she repeated. Then, seeing what she mistook for well-I-never astonishment on his face, but which was actually horror, she said, 'No! Don't tell me, darlin', that's where you're staying! Whereabouts?'

He told her, not so much to provide her with the information but to clarify exactly where she would be in relation to him. Was it possible that there was more than one Áyios Nikólaos? No, he couldn't be that lucky.

The exchanging of geographical details confirmed what he foolishly thought were his worst fears, but then she said, 'We're there for most of the summer. Bob's looking to invest in property on the island. Isn't that right, Bob?' A nod indicated that she was correct. 'How about you? How long are you on holiday for?'

'It's a flexible arrangement,' he said evasively. 'When I've had enough I'll be going home.' At this rate, some time tomorrow.

She rattled her jewellery at him again and pressed a long red nail into the flesh of his forearm. 'But you know that you won't be leaving before you've fulfilled your obligation to me, don't you?'

His dumb expression made her go on.

She pressed the nails further into his skin. 'You know, to change my life. It's written in the stars. It's going to happen. I just know it is. I've got a really good feeling about you.'

He wished he could say the same of her.

6

The view from Izzy's bedroom window was enchanting, and with nobody else up on the first morning of her holiday, she was taking advantage of being able to absorb the magical beauty without interruption.

Despite the threat of mosquitoes, she had slept the night with only the shutters across her window, and the gauzy white muslin drapes had billowed gently as a cooling breeze had filled the room. She had fallen asleep to the rhythmic sound of the sea lapping at the shore below and had woken to the same. Now, as she sat on the small balcony that faced the sea, she could hear the muted clang of a church bell, and a second-shift cockerel crowing. Coming from the nearby eucalyptus trees was the motorised tone of chirruping cicadas.

It was such a heavenly morning she wished she had the talent to capture its essence. She glanced down at the sketchpad on her lap and looked at what she had achieved so far. Even to her self-critical eye, it didn't look too bad. She waggled her paintbrush in the jar of water on the table at her side, dabbed it into her tray of watercolours and resumed work again on the hazy lilac sky that was washed with a soft, pearly opalescence.

When Max and Laura had invited Izzy to spend the summer with them, her first thought had been to rush out and treat herself to a new set of paints and sketchpads. From then on she had been counting the days until the holiday, imagining the sheer bliss of being surrounded by so much beauty and having time to try to capture it on paper. It was perhaps an exaggeration, but it felt as though she was being given the chance to let her creativity have some fun. Normally constrained by the nature of her job, it was being given a moment of freedom in which to indulge itself.

At times, an art teacher's job was the most frustrating on earth. Or maybe it was just her. Perhaps the nurturing of creative young minds through rolling out Plasticine and making coil pots wasn't what she was cut out to do. Occasionally the children she taught were responsive to what she was trying to share with them, but too often they saw the lessons as an excuse to let off steam after the rigidity of too much formal teaching too early in their lives. Now and then a child responded to what she was trying to show them, but invariably she spent a large proportion of the lessons preventing paint fights, or washing glue off expensive school uniform. There were days when she fantasised that she could line up the worst of the troublemakers and fire a hose of red paint at them. This was after she had smothered them in glue and feathers. And also after she had locked them in the art cupboard overnight with nothing to eat but pasta tubes and sugar paper.

It didn't take an Ofsted inspector to tell her she was in the wrong job. She knew that she wasn't a particularly good teacher – not in the modern sense: her crowd-control technique was not all that it might be, and these days that seemed to be what mattered. But she had a genuine love of her subject and wished that she could instil just a fraction of it into her pupils. Oh, to have a budding Van Gogh in the class who, with just a few dabs of a brush, could portray the depths of a man's soul. Or a child who could draw with the rhythmic, spiritual intensity of William Blake. Surely it had to happen one day. The great artists of tomorrow had to go to school, didn't they? So why couldn't just one pass through her hands?

Because, as her mother had frequently told her, she was always in the wrong place at the wrong time doing the wrong thing. It would be just her luck that a future Picasso attended one of the neighbouring schools while she got lumbered with a fraud like Damien Hurst or that woman with the disgusting bed.

It had definitely been a case of being in the wrong place at the wrong time when she had met Alan.

She had moved up to Cheshire in the summer, and by the end of her first term in her new school she was suffering daily headaches and had found herself squinting late at night in bed as she tried to read. She became worried that something was seriously wrong with her. A tumour, for instance. A tumour that, if she played her cards right, would only be the size of a pea and would merely cause her to go blind. More likely it would be the size of a tangerine, pressing on a crucial bit of her brain, waiting to kill her when she was least expecting it. Ingrid Boardman, head of maths at school and the full-time wearer of bifocals – the person who had loaned her *One Hundred Ways To Be A Thoroughly Modern Woman* – had suggested that before she started writing out a will, Izzy might consider getting her eyes tested. She gave Izzy the address of her own optician and the next day she made an appointment. But when she turned up for her appointment and gave her name to the young receptionist she was informed that there was no record of a Miss Jordan booked in for that afternoon. 'Are you sure you've got the right day?' the cheeky youngster asked her. 'Today is Saturday.'

Annoyed that her ability to make an appointment was being queried, she said, 'Of course I'm certain. And I also know that tomorrow is Sunday.'

Giving Izzy a surly teenage pout, the girl got up from her swivel chair. 'I'll go and see what Mr Leigh says about this,' she said, and with such menace Izzy half expected Mr Leigh, whoever he was, to come and box her ears. While she waited, she tried on a selection of spectacle frames. It was extraordinary how many different styles there were to choose from. Just for a laugh she put on a pair of thick-rimmed Jarvis Cocker frames. She looked hideous: a cross between Nana Mouskouri and Michael Caine. She gave the mirror a dead-pan expression and mouthed in her best Cockney, 'Not a lot of people know I'm a transvestite.'

'I think you'll find they're a touch heavy for a face with features as delicate as yours,' said a voice from behind her.

She spun round. It was the dreaded Mr Leigh. Except he didn't look so very dreadful. His hair was dark and springy, and like the rest of him – eyes quickly surveying her, hands slipping a pen into his breast pocket, mouth breaking into a wide smile and body bouncing energetically across the carpet as he came towards her – it gave the impression of only just being under control. He was a lot younger than she had expected – only a little older than herself, in fact. She snatched off the ugly frames, embarrassed, and fumbled to get them back on to the rack. He came over, took them from her, and slipped them easily on to the appropriate hooks. He wasn't very tall, but what he lacked in height he made up for with his shoulders: they were massively broad. He had rugby prop forward written all over him, and if he hadn't been dressed in a white jacket she might have thought his profession was hanging around seedy nightclubs pitching drunken undesirables on to the streets. She decided, there and then, that she would go quietly.

'My receptionist says there seems to be some kind of mix-up,' he said, smoothly interrupting her flustered thoughts. 'According to the diary you don't have an appointment, but you're in luck, I've a free slot so I could fit you in now.'

'Oh, well, if you're sure it's no trouble,' she said.

After the receptionist had taken the necessary details from her, she was shown through to a room where the lights were romantically dimmed. 'What made you think you needed to have your eyes tested?' he asked, indicating for her to sit in a raised black chair.

She told him about the squinting and the headaches.

'What work do you do?'

'I'm a teacher.'

'Under a lot of stress, are you?'

'Not really.'

'Stress,' he said. 'It's a real killer. Marriage, divorce, bereavement, moving house, they're the big four that wreak havoc on the body. Especially the eyes. Have you experienced any of these things in the last few months?'

'I've moved house and changed my job,' she admitted. She wondered whether it was worth mentioning her mother too. Perhaps not.

'Moved house *and* changed your job,' he repeated, shaking his head and whistling through his teeth, not unlike a garage mechanic diagnosing a terminally sick car. 'Well, Miss Jordan, let's take a look, shall we?' He reached into a drawer, pulled out a strange-looking piece of equipment, then lunged into her face and pressed it against her right eye. 'Don't look into the light,' he said too late. He smelt of aftershave and Polo mints and she wondered if the latter was to cover up the smell of tobacco. I could never go out with anyone who smoked, she found herself thinking. But his hands don't smell of cigarettes, she pointed out, and he is quite good-looking. In fact, he's rather nice. The old Abba song, '*Look into his angel eyes and you'll be hypnotised,*' popped into her mind.

When he finished, he pronounced her to be in possession of near-perfect vision. 'You've got nothing to worry about other than slightly lazy eye muscles.' He explained some eye exercises to do twice a day that would help, then asked if she would have a drink with him that night.

'Oh, um isn't that rather unethical?' she asked, taken aback by his directness.

He grinned mischievously. 'Only if you tell anyone.'

It was when he had shown her to the door and she was crossing the road to call in at the chemist, before going back to her car, that she had noticed another optician's further along the row of shops. With an awful sinking feeling she knew that this was where she should have been for the last hour. Skulking guiltily past the shop window, she contented herself with the thought that had she gone there she wouldn't now be considering what to wear for her date that evening.

It's Fate, she told herself, with cheery smugness.

But it was a long time before she realised the extent of her foolishness. Before that happened, Alan had thoroughly charmed her, he had fully absorbed her into his life, had made her his own. And she had loved it. There had been walks in the country, picnics by the river, trips to the theatre and thrilling white knuckle rides at a theme park. There had been candle-lit dinners, roses, chocolates and the best champagne. There had even been a surprise weekend in the Cotswolds where he had told her he loved her and asked her to move in with him. As lavish and as clichéd as it all was, it was impossible to resist. Having only recently moved to the area and not knowing anybody beyond the school gates of her new job – this was before she had met Max and Laura – a relationship with somebody as self-assured and fun-seeking as Alan was just what she thought she needed. She was only too willing to fall in love with a man who treated her with such a flourish of generosity, even if at times it felt as though he was being a little possessive. But given the circumstances, what girl wouldn't have been blinded by the amount of false glitter being showered upon her?

With hindsight she could see that one of the attractions Alan held for her was that she had hoped to gain some of his confidence from him, as if his energy and strength of character would magically rub off on her. In the end, when everything went wrong, all it did was chip away at her self-esteem. But that was later, much later, when he must have realised that she wanted more from him than he was able to give.

Commitment.

That was when he must have decided it was time to move on. For him the fun was over. Commitment meant being serious. Commitment meant acting like a grown-up, and that was something Alan wasn't very good at. He liked playing the part of charming, boyish rogue. Seemingly he could only do that by having a relationship with a girlfriend who was merely passing through rather than a wife who was here to stay.

Mark saw Theo before his friend caught sight of him. Flash git, he thought, seeing how much he stood out from the crowd of stockily built taxi-drivers, the older men fingering their worry-beads, the younger ones smoking and chatting up the holiday reps. He pushed his trolley towards Theo. 'Hasn't anyone told you that men over forty shouldn't wear their trousers so tight?' he said.

Theo's face broke into a wide grin. He removed his sunglasses and embraced Mark in the ebullient, rousing hug Greek men find so acceptable, but which would have the majority of Englishmen running in the opposite direction.

Mark pushed him away. 'Get off, you exhibitionist. You only do that to annoy me.'

'Yes, but it gives me such pleasure to know that I'm embarrassing you.' Then, looking at the lone bag on Mark's trolley and the clothes he was wearing – faded jeans with an old T-shirt, which even Mark had to admit had seen better days – he said, 'Is that all the luggage you have brought with you?'

'I've come here to write, Theo. Bear that in mind, won't you? Now, can we hurry up and get the hell out of here? There's somebody I don't want to see again for as long as I—'

But he was interrupted by a loud voice he had hoped never to hear again. It was that awful dolly-babe woman yoo-hooing across the crowded arrivals hall with Silent Bob pushing a trolley of Louis Vuitton cases. She came over to him.

'Gawd, it's a real bun-fight round that conveyor belt, isn't it?' she said. 'And you were so quick getting away from the carousel I thought we wouldn't have the chance to arrange a little get-together.' Then, peering at Theo over the top of her sunglasses and giving him a more than passing look of interest, she said, 'Is he your taxi-driver?'

Mark opened his mouth to put her right, but Theo was ahead of him. With a respectful click of his heels, he stepped forward and said, 'I am Theodore Vlamakis. I am not just ordinary driver to *Meester* Saint James. I am his personal chauffeur. *Meester* Saint James very important man.'

She stared at Mark with renewed interest. She was clearly impressed.

But Mark was furious. 'Thank you, *Theodore*,' he said, with heavy emphasis. 'Perhaps we could get going now.'

'And your friends?'

'My what?' hissed Mark.

Theo grinned like a simpleton. 'Could we not give them a lift?'

'He speaks very good English, doesn't he?'

'Better than is good for him at times,' answered Mark coolly. 'But he's forgetting the size of my car. Sadly it isn't big enough for all of us. Not with so much luggage. Isn't that right, *Theodore*?' He gave Theo a warning look that dared him to contradict what he had just said.

Theo bowed neatly from the waist. 'As usual, *Meester* Saint James, you are right and I am wrong. Come, give me your luggage and I will keep my big stupid mouth shut while you say a nice bye-bye to your friends.'

'What the hell did you think you were doing back there?' demanded Mark when they were driving away from the airport.

'I'm sorry, but I could not help myself. Your face. Ah, it was the picture. Now tell me all about her.'

'I'd rather not. She's an experience I'd prefer to put behind me.' Nevertheless, he told Theo about the crazy conversation he had been subjected to throughout his flight.

'And her name, can it really be Dolly-Babe? That is a new one on me.'

'No, I'm afraid that's what I've christened her. Her real name is even more unlikely. It's Liberty-Raquel.'

Theo laughed. 'You mentioned that she and her husband are staying near us in Áyios Nikólaos? Did she tell you the name of their villa?'

'Yeah, Villa Mimosa. Mean anything to you?'

Theo laughed again. He pressed his foot on the accelerator and shot past a taxi, a dark blue Mercedes that was already moving at warp speed. Mark shuddered. He had forgotten, as he always did when they were apart for any length of time, how fast Theo drove. And how very Greek he really was.

7

At Laura's suggestion, she and Izzy were walking into Kassiópi for lunch. Max had stayed behind, claiming that Greg Rusedski needed his support for his big match that afternoon. 'You go without me,' he had said, 'you'll have much more fun on your own. You could bring me back a newspaper if there's anything decent left to read.'

The dusty little track they were following ran steeply through a large olive grove. At the foot of the trees, and wound around their trunks, were bundles of black netting which, as Laura had just explained, would be stretched out later in the year when it was time to harvest the olives. Though they were in the shade of the trees, the scorching heat of the midday sun forced them to walk at a comfortably unhurried pace. Also, the island was known for its tortoises, which roamed at will, and Laura was hoping they would catch sight of one in the clumps of parched grass. 'I nearly trod on one last year,' she said. 'It was so small it must have been a baby.'

Izzy pulled a face and took extra care where she put her feet.

The path soon levelled and they strolled along a wider, much clearer stretch of ground, where the air was fragrant with the smell of wild garlic and thyme. Laura pointed towards a tumbledown shed. 'Look,' she said, 'there's Zac.'

Zac was a large, scrawny dog of no discernible breed, with a ragged coat the colour of caramel. A short length of rope tied him to a wooden post and at their approach he jumped up, pushed his nose through the chain-link fence and wagged his tail, which was decorated with an assortment of dried leaves and twigs. To Izzy's surprise, Laura pulled a bone-shaped biscuit out of her bag and slipped it through the fence. Zac's tail went into overdrive and he devoured the biscuit in seconds. His nose came back through the fence and he wagged his tail hopefully. Then he barked loudly.

The noise summoned an elderly woman from a small stone building that, until now, Izzy hadn't noticed. She looked as ancient and gnarled as the surrounding olive trees and Izzy would have loved the opportunity to sketch her. The flesh beneath her jaw hung in two wobbling hanks at either side of her throat, her hair, iron-grey and wiry, was held down by a severe black headscarf, and the shabby dress she was wearing, which was partially covered by a floral overall, was also black; dark wrinkled tights and a pair of laced canvas shoes protruded beneath. In her large bony hands she held a broom. She gave Zac a sharp poke with it, instantly silencing him. She looked very fierce but when she turned to the cause of the commotion she gave Laura and Izzy a smile that was friendly and hospitable. Her parted lips displayed a gummy mouth, with a single badly stained tooth.

'How do you know the dog's name?' Izzy asked, after Laura had exchanged a few faltering words of Greek with the woman and they were on their way again.

'From Theo, of course. He knows everyone round here. You mustn't think he restricts his charm to pretty girls. The old women get the same treatment. He's very fair with his attentions.'

They walked on in silence, until Izzy ventured. 'He is rather nice, though, isn't he, in spite of all that charm?' She had been dying to bring up Theo in their conversation that morning, but hadn't dared for fear of making Laura think that she might be interested in him. In fact, she wasn't quite sure what to make of him. His attractiveness, much heralded by Laura, was everything she had been led to expect, but what lay beneath the glamorous image? Take away the stylish clothes, the trappings of his affluent lifestyle and the affectations he must have spent years cultivating, the boyish vanity and gregarious charm, and what would you be left with? What was he really like when he wasn't intent on making an impression on those around him?

In answer to her question, Laura said, 'Oh, he's nice, all right. Fatally so, I should think. Now, here's another friend I want to introduce you to. Max and I have christened him Neddy.'

Disappointed, Izzy acquainted herself with a tired old donkey. He was a sad, spindly-legged creature with a leathery, sagging body that clung to a frame of jutting bones. Like Zac, he, too, was going nowhere and was securely tied. 'The locals don't take very good care of their animals, do they?' Izzy said, as Laura delved into her bag again and this time brought out a carrot.

'It's a different culture,' Laura responded, patting Neddy's dusty coat. 'They can't afford to be sentimental over animals like we are at home. Here they're kept for one purpose and one purpose only. To work.'

'And when they're too old to work?'

'An all-too-short retirement awaits them. Which is what Neddy's enjoying. Aren't you, old boy?' She flicked away the flies that were buzzing round the sores near his rheumy eyes and gave him another carrot.

They carried on walking, and as the olive trees receded, houses appeared and the path joined a narrow lane of tarmac that twisted and turned its way down the hill into Kassiópi. Cats lay dozing in the sun on the side of the road, and in the shade of an open doorway, two elderly women sat gossiping on kitchen chairs, their stockinged and slippered feet resting on an upturned plastic crate. In the house next door, a baby lay sleeping contentedly in a pram while its mother watered the flowers in the terracotta pots on the spotless doorstep.

Izzy had expected Kassiópi to be busy and was surprised to find the streets deserted and quietly slumbering in the heat. 'Where is everybody?' she asked, when Laura suggested they make their way down to the harbour.

'Frying on the beach. That's why I like coming here at this time of the day. There are no jostling crowds of holidaymakers. Now, before I forget, just let me nip in here and get Max his paper.' Leaving Laura to hunt through the revolving racks of British, German and Italian newspapers, Izzy explored the rails of fake designer T-shirts and leather belts.

'He'll just have to make do with the *Express*,' Laura said, when she rejoined Izzy. She showed her what was headline news back home. 'Mother of Two Absconds with Schoolboy Lover.'

'Good Lord, whatever possessed the silly woman?' said Izzy.

Laura laughed. 'Not everyone is as cautious as you, Izzy.'

'Obviously. But she must be mad to do it – the press will crucify her. They'll turn her into a latter-day Lucrezia Borgia.'

'If she isn't one already. Come on, let's head for a drink and a bite to eat.'

The taverna Laura chose overlooked the picturesque horseshoe-shaped harbour where, in the sleepy afternoon peace, brightly coloured boats of varying shapes and sizes bobbed at anchor. A young waiter took their order and, within no time at all, they were relaxing in their chairs beneath a yellow and white striped awning with two plates of kalamári in front of them and a carafe of red wine to share.

'So, apart from thinking that Theo was rather nice,' said Laura, passing Izzy her napkin, 'what else did you conclude from last night?'

Izzy smiled to herself. So, what she had said about Theo back in the olive grove hadn't gone unnoticed by Laura. 'That it must be the easiest thing in the world to fall in love with him,' she said, 'or at least to think that you loved him. It would probably only ever be infatuation.'

'That's a very cynical view to take. Is it based on the belief that you think he's incapable of anything more?'

'I guess so.'

'Well, you've got to agree that makes him ideal material for a holiday romance.'

'Absolutely. But if you're thinking of him and me, forget it.'

'Why?'

'Because I'm not his type.'

'Says who?'

'Oh, come off it, Laura. You know perfectly well that the type of woman Theo would be attracted to would be a stunning beauty. She'd be tall, blonde, acquiescent, and mind-blowingly good in bed.'

'And who's been telling you that you're not mind-blowingly good in bed?'

Izzy lowered her eyes.

Laura frowned. 'Do I detect more of Alan's handiwork? Don't tell me, he took the trouble to tell you you were no good.'

Picturing the scene in that pink room and the therapist asking them to comment on their sex life, Izzy felt her insides melt. It had been so cruel of him. So humiliating. She knew she should be over all this nonsense by now, but it was still there niggling away at her, taunting her at the slightest provocation.

'It's like being with a child,' Alan had said, leaning forward in his chair, eager to share with someone the details of their most intimate moments. 'She does everything I ask, but it doesn't work.'

'Doesn't work?' the woman had repeated. 'In what way?'

There was a silence while Alan just stared at Izzy. She found this more unnerving than any of the hurtful accusations he had thrown at her. It had been too reminiscent of those chilly, silent pauses that had punctuated her relationship with her mother. From an early age Izzy had learned that conversation, no matter how trivial or how stilted, defused a tricky situation. It meant, though, that she had a worrying tendency to blurt out the first thing that came into her head. She did it then, with Alan staring at her.

'Can I help it that I'm not as experienced as he'd prefer?' she had murmured, mortified that he could do this to her, horrified at the extent of his betrayal.

She had played right into his hands and, giving her a pitying look, he had returned his attention to the therapist. 'She doesn't turn me on, that's the nuts and bolts of it. And you can see why, can't you? You can see why it would be such a lacklustre performance.'

'Perhaps you should be telling Izzy this, and not me,' the woman had said. Her gaze and neutral tone never faltered.

'Yes, Alan,' she had agreed, her own voice spiralling dangerously out of control. 'If it was always so bad, why did you keep up the pretence? Why did you bother? And more importantly,' her voice wobbled, 'if I didn't turn you on, how did you ever manage to get an . . . well, to go through with it?'

'You see what I mean?' he had said to the other woman, a triumphant smile snaking across his face. 'She can't even bring herself to say the word erection. Is it so bad to want a woman in bed with me and not an embarrassed child? Look, she's flinching.'

The hour-long session had finished on that appalling note and they had driven home in silence. They went to bed that night each intent on proving the other wrong. It was a disaster. A ghastly humiliating disaster. She ended up in tears and Alan, victorious, declared her useless. 'You need help, Izzy,' he had said, coming out of the bathroom without a stitch on.

She had turned away from the sight of his naked body and wondered if he was right. The truth was, she wasn't very experienced. A brief encounter here, a regrettable dalliance there, had done nothing to alter her opinion that sex seemed guaranteed to undermine a girl's confidence. In the complex world of everybody's birthright to complete satisfaction, how did she rate? Was she doing it right? How did her technique compare with that of Alan's previous lovers? He often spoke of his past relationships, referring to them as stepping-stones. 'And they've led me to you, Izzy,' he had said, the first time they had slept together.

Nervously she had followed his lead and allowed him to strip away her clothes and as he dropped them on the floor, her instinct, even in such a moment, was to tidy them into a neatly folded pile – jeans at the bottom, sweater on top, socks tucked into shoes. Or had it been a need to distract him? Or a distraction for herself?

He must have sensed her awkwardness for he said, 'Relax Izzy, you're quite safe with me.'

'Sexually repressed' was what he had called her three years on in that silly pink room. Funny that it had taken him so long to reach that conclusion. Funny, too, that it had never bothered him until he felt the desire to leave her for somebody else.

'Well?' prompted Laura, when Izzy still hadn't responded. 'Did he claim that you were neither use nor ornament in bed?'

'Actually, he was more explicit than that,' Izzy said, forcing herself to be honest. 'He said I was sexually repressed. Also that I was boring.'

Laura burst out laughing. But soon stopped. 'Oh, Izzy, don't look so hurt, I wasn't laughing at you. Please don't think that. It's Alan I'm laughing at. When men start throwing accusations about like that, you can bet your bottom dollar that it's their own inadequacies they're running from. Did you never stop to think that maybe he was a bit lacking in that department? That by blaming you he was hiding from his own problems? All that counselling stuff he put you through was just a ruse in which he hoped to bury the truth with his horrible lies and twisted accusations.'

'Do you really think so?'

Laura's face hardened. 'Yes I do. What's more, and I promised myself I'd never say this, but Max and I never liked him, and the sooner you get over him the better. You need to prove to yourself that he was wrong. And wrong with a capital W. If I were a doctor, you know what I'd prescribe you?'

'Don't tell me, an intensive course of holiday romance.'

Laura smiled. 'Got it in one. What you need is a relationship that has perfectly defined boundaries. When your holiday comes to an end, you walk away with your pride and dignity fully intact. And because love was never asked to join in, there's no danger of you getting hurt. For the first time in your life you could be in control of something. Who knows? You might prove to yourself that you're not such a disaster in bed as Alan has made you think you are.' She pointed to the front page of the *Express*, and added, 'That's probably what that woman is doing. I bet she's led a really boring existence, been dictated to all her marriage and has now finally done something about it. Her life will never be the same again. When the moment of passion has died she'll sell her story to the highest bidder and make herself some money. She'll be a celebrity. Hats off to her, I say.'

'But what about the boy?'

'He'll sell his story too, if he's got any sense. Let's not delude ourselves that he's a poor shy little lad who doesn't know what he's doing. Odds on, he's up for it just as much as she is.'

'And what effect will it have on him when he's older? How will he view women?'

'Time will tell. But for now, let's worry about your neurosis, shall we?'

'Which in particular? Alan? Or my mother?'

'Oh, Lord, I'd need another carafe of wine to find the enthusiasm or strength to dissect your mother. No, I've a better idea. Let's discuss you and Theo. What would you do if he did take a liking to you? How would you react?'

'With distrust, I suppose.'

'And what if he was able to allay your suspicions, what then?'

Izzy lowered her knife and fork. 'I'm not sure he, or any other man, would be able to do that.'

A determined note came into Laura's voice. 'Look, we both know that Alan was a creep of the highest order, but you've got to get it into your head that not all men are as cruel as him. You'll have to let one of them slip under the wire at some time in the not-too-distant future.'

'I know, I know, but you're speaking from the comfort zone of your own marriage to Max, which is bound to make you hold men in higher regard than I ever could.'

'I haven't always been married to Max. There was a time before him, a time when I was hurt just as badly as you.'

This was news to Izzy. Because Max and Laura were so happy and well suited, she had never thought of them with other partners. 'Really? You've never mentioned it before.'

'It's not something I like to remind myself of.'

'Why, because it still hurts?'

'No,' Laura said emphatically. 'Because I was so stupid, and on two counts. Stupid to believe a word he ever uttered, and stupid enough to let him cause me a single moment of pain. But if there's one thing I've learned from the experience, it's that Max proved to me that not all men are such pigs. It's only the occasional rotten apple that gives the rest of the barrel a bad name.'

'And you're determined that I should learn that lesson as well?'

'Is that so very bad of me?'

'It would explain why I feel that you're literally throwing Theo at me.'

Laura smiled. 'Go on, hand on heart, tell me you wouldn't be tempted if he made a play for you. *Well,* wouldn't you?'

'Laura, I can honestly say, with my hand on my heart, that I'm not going to answer any more of your daft questions. Another glass of wine?'

8

Theo was on the phone, and with the likelihood of the call going on for some time yet – judging from the expression on his face and the rapidity of his words – Mark decided to leave him to it. It always amused Mark that when Theo was speaking in his native tongue he could never work out whether an enthusiastic exchange was taking place or a heated argument: the tone was always the same, hugely expressive and bordering on volatile.

He went through to the kitchen; a large rectangular room with rough uneven walls of stone that, in places, were more than twenty inches deep. There were no fitted cupboards, just two enormous wooden dressers that held a variety of brightly coloured crockery and glassware. At the furthest end there was a small walk-in pantry where the shelves were neatly packed with everyday requirements, including at least a dozen different varieties of olive oil. In front of one of the dressers, and in the middle of the room, was a chunky oblong table with six wooden chairs around it; they varied in size and design, and Mark guessed they were handmade. Beneath a small window that looked out on to a vegetable plot and a glimpse of the sea, there was a white ceramic sink; it was modern but masquerading discreetly as old. Next to this, and taking up most of the available wall space, was a massive American fridge. Mark opened its shiny blue door and helped himself to a glass of water. He added ice to it and strolled through the rest of the house, out on to the terrace. He paused for a few minutes in the dazzling sunshine to slip on his sunglasses, the heat coming at him as a hammer-blow, before going down the stone steps to the area of garden that overlooked the swimming-pool.

Villa Anna was not at all what he had expected. Having stayed with Theo many times in Athens, he had made the assumption that his friend's recently acquired and renovated country retreat would be a replica of the many soulless apartments Theo had lived in over the years. But he should have known better than to presume anything of Theo. A friendship that had spanned more than two decades should have prepared him for the unexpected. Villa Anna wasn't even a toned-down version of the chic minimal furnishings and discordant sculptures with which Theo normally surrounded himself: instead it was a comfortable home with leanings towards tasteful modesty rather than expensive artifice. The cluttered shelves of books that lined the irregular, sloping stone walls, the simply framed sketches, the family photographs, the blend of faded rugs and muted fabrics, and the antique furniture – some of which Mark recognised as having once belonged to Anna Vlamakis – gave an air of permanency to the house. It's a home, had been Mark's first thought when Theo had unlocked the front door and brought him inside, less than half an hour ago.

So, was this where his friend was finally putting down some roots?

If it was, Mark could understand it. His own memories of previous trips to Corfu, together with the little he had seen so far of Áyios Nikólaos, was enough to make him see that Theo had found himself an ideal bolthole for when he tired of the madness of Athens.

Wanting to explore further, Mark followed a winding gravel path bordered on either side by bushes of scarlet oleander and large urns of broad-leafed ferns. It took him to a small clearing that was almost at the very tip of the headland. To his right was the bay of Áyios Nikólaos with its narrow stretch of beach, gently sloping hillside of cypress trees and clusters of villas, and to his left, a verdant coastline that led, he supposed, to the nearest village. Theo had given him a brief run-down on the local geographical landmarks during the drive from the airport, but until he saw it for himself it would mean nothing.

Back home he, too, lived near the sea: the North Sea. Admittedly the water wasn't as clear, or anywhere near as warm, but in its own way the view he lived with was just as spectacular as this. He had lived in Robin Hood's Bay for the last six years, in a three-storey Georgian house he had bought on the proceeds from his first book. It had originally been built for a sea captain in the mid-eighteenth century and had a great sense of history. Over the years it had been well documented by countless local historians. Living in a historic landmark was a pain at times, but he wasn't alone in that: practically everyone in the tightly packed village suffered from the same affliction. Perched on the cliff edge with its maze of little streets and the jumble of cottages with their distinctive pan-tiled roofs and an identity that was firmly anchored in fishing and smuggling, Robin Hood's Bay was a real tourist pull. People came from all over to *ooh* and *aah* at its quaintness, especially in the summer. In the winter months, when few people had the urge to cope with the cold rain and gusting winds that came in off the sea, the village became a different place altogether. It was that time of year that Mark liked best. A grim bleakness descended on the landscape and gave him the sense of brooding isolation that inspired his writing and which had become his trademark. When Theo had made his first visit in the depths of one of the coldest winters Mark had known, he had shaken his head and said, 'So, this is where you intend to hide for the rest of your life, is it?'

'Who said anything about hiding?'

'You have another word for it?'

There had been an element of truth in what Theo had said. After a long period in his life when everything he had touched had seemingly gone wrong, he had felt the need to disappear, to submerge himself in another world. But for all Theo's initial cynicism, he had soon come to realise why Mark had chosen to live where he had. 'It is a place of paradox,' he said, when he made his second visit in the height of summer and saw the carefree crowds of holidaymakers sunning themselves in the harbour with their ice-creams, heard the laughter of children playing in the rock pools, watched the fishing-boats coming in after a day at sea, and strolled through the expanse of purple-flowering heather that covered the moors only a few miles away, 'but I can see that this quaint little village suits you well. It reflects perfectly the dark and dour side to you, and the quirky mercurial bit you keep for those who know you best. But it is good, I see an improvement in you already. You are not so uptight.'

Theo had been right, as he so often was. Robin Hood's Bay suited him well: it felt comfortably secure and made few demands of him. That was how he wanted to live. Quietly. Unobtrusively. Doing what he enjoyed most, which was writing, and with nothing of his past to cast a shadow over his new life.

And that was what he had achieved, until February of this year when his latest novel, *Silent Footsteps*, was published. Within a week of the book hitting the shelves, he had received the first of the letters. To begin with he had ignored them, treating the typewritten notes as nothing more than the weird work of a crank. But then a familiar pattern emerged, and he began to feel spooked. The crank, whoever he was, was carrying out a copycat version of the killer's actions in *Silent Footsteps*. The story-line had revolved around a stalker who had written repeatedly to his victims telling them that he was their friend, that he was looking out for them. He always started the message in the same way: 'Remember, you're never alone. I am your friend.' It was classic stalker mentality: the stalker's need to feel involved in his victim's life, to become the focus of that person's every waking thought. But it wasn't just the wording of the letters that concerned Mark, it was the postmark on each envelope that caused him the most anxiety: the crank was replicating the sequence of postmarks that Mark had written into his book. The order in which the letters arrived was identical to the pattern in *Silent Footsteps*: Winchester first, followed by Salisbury, Lincoln, Norwich, Chester, Liverpool, Guildford, Durham, and finally Hereford. They were all cities that had cathedrals of notable interest, but while there hadn't been any particular reason why Mark had used this in his novel – it had simply been one of those lucky ideas plucked from the ether, which seemed to work well in the plot he was pursuing – the man, or woman for that matter, who was behind the letters Mark had so far received must have chosen the places with a very specific purpose in mind: to put the wind up him. It made him think, What if this person is serious? What if he's *deadly* serious?

Determined not to overreact, he had thrown the letters away, consigning the unspoken threat they contained to the rubbish bin where it belonged.

Fleetingly he had considered going to the police, but even in a quiet backwater such as Robin Hood's Bay there were more tangible crimes to deal with than the letters of a saddo who had nothing better to do with his time. No actual threat was being made, so it would be understandable if the police put it low on their list of priorities to follow up. Besides which, if he had taken the matter to them, within hours the local rag would have got hold of it, followed no doubt by a keen-eyed freelancer for one of the nationals. And how would that look? Sure, his publishers might like the thought of all the free publicity, but for Mark it would just be an excuse for his past to be dredged up once more. It would also play straight into the hands of the stalker. When he saw for himself, in black and white, the success he was having in rattling his victim, the stalker's insecure ego would get a terrific boost. Self-aggrandisement, big-time!

Though he wasn't being stalked as intensely as the characters in his novel – there had been no phone calls and no visible presence as such – Mark understood the very real sense of torment to which an innocent victim was subjected. The invasion of one's privacy means nothing until you experience at first hand what it feels like to read a letter written by somebody who has made it their business to watch and follow you.

Then, six weeks ago, the letters stopped, Hereford being the last point of contact. Anyone else might have breathed a sigh of relief and thought that the stalker had got bored with the game. But Mark was far from relieved. More than anyone, he knew the plot of *Silent Footsteps* and felt that the absence of the stalker's presence in his life was more threatening than when it had been there, and for the simple fact that in his novel, like a lull before a storm, a silence always came before the victim's death.

So the big joke was, if life was going to imitate art fully, Mark was going to meet his death before he was good and ready for it.

Soft footsteps on the gravel path behind him had him spinning round on his heel. 'Goddamnit, Theo! What the hell are you doing creeping up on me like that?'

That evening Theo cooked them supper. 'I'm told by my neighbours Max and Laura that my cooking is something to be admired,' he said. 'Your verdict, please.'

Mark chewed on a tender piece of lamb that was appetisingly pink and flavoured with oregano and lemon juice. 'Not bad,' he said, 'not bad at all.'

'Praise indeed from the maestro who introduced me to Pot Noodles and taught me to cook Spam curries on a Baby Belling. Ah, the spicy shite days, how I miss them. Can I get you anything else to drink?'

'No, this is fine.'

'More ice?'

'Theo, everything is fine. Stop fussing. You're worse than a Jewish mother.'

Theo poured some more wine for himself and thought that everything was far from fine. Mark was not the picture of health he had been when they had last met. He had lost weight and was distinctly on edge. But, then, who could blame him? Theo was glad now that he had been so insistent that his friend should spend the summer with him. Last month when Mark had told him about the crazy business with the letters he had been sent, he had said at once, 'Trust your instinct, Mark. If you think you are in any danger, come and stay with me.' He had been shocked to think that Mark had been on the receiving end of such a sinister campaign of fear, but more shocked that his old friend had not confided in him sooner. 'Even if you don't think you're in danger, I think you should still get away. It would do you good.' He had known that because Mark didn't try to refute this advice, he was genuinely concerned for his own welfare. Which, in years gone by, he hadn't always been too interested in.

Throughout his twenties and early thirties Mark had put himself through the very worst kind of hell. Addiction had nearly killed him. It had cost him his marriage, his home, countless jobs, most of his friends, very nearly his family but, worst of all, every last scrap of his self-esteem. He had sunk so low he had seemed an impossible case, deliberately isolating himself from anyone who had ever been close to him, including Theo. In desperation Mark's family had turned to him for help. 'You're the only one he has ever listened to,' Mark's mother had said. 'We've tried to help him, really we have, but he simply won't accept that a rehabilitation centre would do him any good. He says he's beyond help. He says . . . he says he wants to die. Oh, please, Theo, please help us.'

Theo had known for a long time that Mark was in trouble. Back in Durham he had often witnessed Mark drunk and seen how alcohol darkened his mood, how it revealed the savage anger in him, as well as the unimaginable self-hate. He had tried on several occasions to step in and make Mark see what he was doing to himself, but without success. Helpless, he had had to stand back and watch his friend's gradual decline as he turned ever more to alcohol and drugs. Though it had been painful to admit, he had known that if his friend was ever going to get better he was going to have to reach rock bottom.

After the conversation with Mark's mother, Theo flew over and tracked him down. He was living, if one could call it that, in a squalid, cockroach-infested bed-sit. The room was poorly lit, the single window obliterated by a piece of dirty cloth hanging from a broken rail. The walls were grubby and peeling, the carpetless floor littered with filthy clothes, the sink piled high with unwashed crockery. It was a stifling hellhole, the air fetid with the stench of sweat, alcohol and despair. And sitting hunched on a damp, uncovered mattress against a wall was Mark. Except it wasn't Mark. It wasn't the vigorous strong-minded, volatile man Theo had known from college, a man whose sharp humour and clarity of thought could cut through the most persuasive argument. To his horror, he was looking at the remnants of a dying man. He had known real anger in that moment as he had held out a hand to Mark and helped him to his feet. Anger that, somewhere beyond those walls, people were making money from Mark's misery.

The rancid smell of that awful room had lingered in Theo's nostrils as he had driven Mark the length of the country and admitted him to the clinic his parents had found for him.

'How did you manage it?' they asked Theo. 'How did you make him get in the car with you?'

'I didn't need to do anything,' he told them. 'It was as if he was waiting for me.'

That was the picture Theo had of Mark for many years to come. The ashamed acceptance in his painfully thin body, the unshaven face fixed on Theo with eyes hollow and dark, pleading, reproachful, as though saying, 'What took you so long? I could have died.'

The pain of that encounter eight years ago had never left Theo. He imagined that it must haunt Mark too. And though Mark had made a full recovery, he would probably be the first to say that, if the circumstances were right, it might happen all over again. 'I have to remind myself that once an alcoholic, always an alcoholic,' he had said when he came out of the clinic. Out of deference to his friend's ability to turn his life round, and knowing that it would only be by the most extraordinary effort of will that Mark would be able to stay clean, Theo had been fanatical about not having alcohol in his apartment when Mark came to stay. He even hid packets of paracetamol and aspirin where he thought no one would dream of looking. 'Go easy, pal,' Mark had told him one day when he had caught him turning the apartment upside down because he had a headache and couldn't find any aspirin. 'Temptation is there every day, with or without your hindrance. It's me who can't handle the booze and pills, not you. It's also bloody insulting. Stop treating me like a criminal. Have you tried the fridge? That's where Kim used to try to hide things from me. An empty egg box was a favourite of hers.'

It still felt insensitive to drink in front of Mark, but in spite of that, Theo made himself do it so that his friend would never think he doubted that he had the strength of character to say no to temptation.

Their meal was finished now, and turning their chairs round, they faced the sea and the darkening sky. Theo looked at Mark's pale face. 'You won't be spending the entire summer working, will you?' he asked.

Without turning his head, Mark said, 'Probably. Why?'

'No reason.'

'Oh, come on, Theo. You've always been lousy at subtlety. What are you really saying?'

'Okay. I think this business with the stalker has affected you more than you are letting on. I think that when I surprised you in the garden and nearly made you jump out of your skin, for a split second, you were more than just alarmed.'

9

'How about we invite Theo to join us?' asked Max. He had just proposed that they take the boat out for the morning to go cove-hopping, then stop for lunch at one of his favourite tavernas in Áyios Stéfanos.

'You're forgetting, he's got company,' said Laura, looking up from *Captain Corelli's Mandolin* and noting that, as usual, her husband was incapable of sitting still for longer than ten minutes without searching for something to occupy him. He had already swept the veranda and terrace and watered the plants, despite paying Sophia and Angelos to do it for them; he was now repositioning the umbrella above her sun-lounger so that she was safely in the shade. She tilted her wide-brimmed hat back on her head, looked at him over the top of her sunglasses and added, 'I don't think we should bother him, do you? Not today. We don't want to make a nuisance of ourselves.'

'Who said anything about bothering anyone?' Max said indignantly. 'I don't call it making a nuisance of ourselves by being friendly. Naturally I was including Theo's friend in the invitation.'

Laura exchanged a smile with Izzy, who was stretched out in the sun a few feet away, tanning nicely. 'Of course you were, darling.'

'Okay, okay,' he said, 'so I'm as transparent as polished glass. And what if I am curious to meet the man behind so many good books?'

Laura laughed. She closed *Captain Corelli*, slipped the paperback on to the floor, and held out her arms to Max. 'My husband, the star-struck little boy, wants to rub shoulders with his hero. How sweet.'

He leaned down to her and gave her a kiss. 'I thought perhaps you could go and see if they'd like to come,' he said, when he emerged from nuzzling her breasts.

She pushed him away with a playful shove and rearranged her swimsuit. 'Why me? Why not you?'

'It'll be more of a temptation coming from you. You know how Theo panders to your every whim.'

'But this isn't *my* whim,' she teased, 'it's *yours*. Try asking Izzy to help you out. I'm sure Theo would be just as persuaded by her. If not more.'

Izzy raised her head. 'Oh, no, you don't,' she said. 'Don't go including me in this.'

'I think it's a brilliant idea,' said Laura, warming to the suggestion and seeing it as a way to push Izzy in Theo's direction. 'How could he say no to you, especially if you go just as you are in that very-nearly bikini?'

Izzy flushed. She had known she would regret buying such a skimpy little thing. It had been one of those impulse buys that was supposed to boost her confidence, confirm her independence. You see, she was telling her mother, this is what I can wear when you're not around. Except it wasn't really working: her mother's disapproving influence was only a stone's throw away. Self-conscious, she sat up, pulled on her sun-top, and wondered if she would ever shake off the nagging voice that followed her wherever she went.

In the end Laura put Max out of his misery and agreed to go and see Theo. She tied a sarong around her waist and set off. When she reached Villa Anna she found him sitting on the terrace reading a newspaper while eating his breakfast.

'An unexpected pleasure,' he said, rising to his feet and bending his head to kiss her cheek beneath her hat. He hadn't shaved yet and his stubbly chin grazed her skin. It was not an unpleasant sensation. His shirt was unbuttoned and flapped loosely at his sides in the breeze. 'Please, sit down. I am having a late breakfast. Would you care to keep me company. A drink? Or maybe something to eat?'

'No, thanks. I'm here on an errand.'

'Oh?'

'I'm sorry, but it's Max. He's dying to meet your friend and has sent me here to invite you both to join us on a little boat trip down to Áyios Stéfanos.'

He gave her a shrewd look. 'And why did Max not come here himself?'

Laura smiled.

'Aha, the cunning Max. He is a man with so much guile. So you are the bait, are you? What a dangerous game he plays.'

'Dangerous?'

He bit into the cake on the plate in front of him. 'Yes,' he said, when he had finished chewing. 'Am I not the hungry shark who might be tempted to snap up the bait in one delicious mouthful?'

'Now, Theo, you really must stop fantasising like this.'

He licked his fingers provocatively. 'Sadly, it is all I am allowed.'

'Well, I wish you'd transfer your affections to a more worthwhile recipient.'

'So tell me, how is the lovely Izzy? Did I play the situation well the other night during dinner? Is she madly in love with me already?'

His quickness of thought – not to say his arrogance – surprised even Laura. 'You really are the most dreadful man. Of course she isn't in love with you. What on earth makes you think she'd fall for a shallow flirt like you?'

He made a pretence of considering her question before answering it. 'Mm . . . could it be because I am a devastatingly handsome devil? Charming too. Not to say witty.'

'And let's not forget how self-effacing you are.'

'I was coming to that.' He poured himself a glass of orange juice. 'Are you sure you won't join me?'

'No, thanks. So what did you think of Izzy?'

A slow smile spread over his face. 'She is the perfect *ingénue*. She is as innocent as a child and as sweet and as delicate as a rose.'

Laura groaned. 'Good heavens, what a lot of ghastly sentimental twaddle you do come up with.'

'Twaddle?'

'It means rubbish. Nonsense.'

'Aha. You want me to describe her in the manner of a typical Englishman, is that it? Okay. So be it. I think she would be an excellent shag.'

'*Theo!*'

He feigned a look of innocence. 'What now? Am I too blunt for you?'

'Is there no middle ground with you?'

He shook his head. 'I prefer extremes. But if you want I'll be honest with you . . . but only this once. I thought she was very nice. So nice, that I promise that I will do my best not to encourage her to fall in love with me.'

'How very thoughtful of you.'

'I think so too.'

'But what if *you* fall in love with *her*?'

He dabbed at the sticky crumbs on his plate, then licked his finger. 'Ah, now, that would be a fine state of affairs, would it not? It would be an interesting conundrum for me to resolve.'

'And novel, I would imagine.'

'Oh, highly original.' He pushed the plate away from him, got to his feet, and walked over to a rosebush. He snapped the stem of a delicate white bloom, breathed in its scent, then handed it to Laura.

She, too, drew in its fragrance. 'Have you never really been in love, Theo?' she said, after he had sat down again.

He faced her, his head slightly tilted. 'No, I don't believe I have.'

'Not ever?'

He paused. 'Perhaps once or twice I have come close.'

'But you never felt like pursuing it?'

He shrugged. 'I have a low boredom threshold.'

'Or maybe a fear of commitment.' Her words, like the scent of the rose, hung between them.

Removing his sunglasses, he looked at her closely. 'Why is it, Laura, that again and again I let you start these conversations with me?'

'Because . . .' she hesitated '. . . because deep down you love talking about yourself.'

He laughed. 'Ah, Laura, you know me so well. Now then, about Max and his desire to meet his hero. Let me go and find Mark and see what he has to say. I have to warn you, though, he is not very sociable just at the moment. My instinct tells me that you might have to make do with only my company for the day.'

*

713

Theo's instinct was right, that and the fact that he knew his friend implicitly.

'Oh, well,' said Max, when Theo and Laura broke the news to him, 'another time perhaps.'

'I'm sorry to disappoint you,' said Theo, 'but Mark sends his apologies. He is keen to spend the day working. The creative soul is a single-minded and determined taskmaster.'

But Mark's reason to stay behind had less to do with the driven artistic soul that Theo was now describing, and everything to do with fear: he was terrified of boats and water, and Theo had known all along that no invitation, however sweetly put, would have encouraged Mark to spend the day afloat.

Fear, though not actually voiced as such, had figured largely in their conversation last night about the letters Mark had received back in England. Theo had not been taken in by Mark's attempt to make light of it, or his denial that he was on edge. 'I'm tired, that's all,' he had said, 'in need of a holiday, so please, give me a break, will you, and cut the patronising pep talk? You're making me out to be some kind of convalescing invalid.' He had taken the same tone just a moment ago when Theo had asked if he minded him joining Max and Laura for the day: 'Of course I don't. I've got plenty of work to occupy me here. I'd rather have the peace and quiet.'

'Very well, I shall leave you to your writing. You will find plenty to eat in the—'

'Yes, I know where to look for food if I'm hungry. Just stop worrying about me.'

Helping Max to launch the boat, Theo untied the rope from the post on the jetty, and stepped lightly into the back of the small craft. He had offered the use of his own boat, but Max had laughed, telling him that it would do him good to rough it in theirs for a change. 'You English,' Theo had joked, 'you are so hung up on the concept that size does not matter!'

There was only one seat left for him and it was next to Izzy. 'Do you mind if I sit here with you?' he asked.

She smiled and shifted along the bench to make room for him. As he sat down he noticed the looks that passed between Max and Laura. Ah, so they were watching his every move, were they? They were playing a little game with him. He smiled to himself. Well, he could either go along with their expectations or he could play the game his own way.

Alone on the terrace in the shade of the vine-covered pergola that stretched from one end of Theo's house to the other, Mark was reading through the notes he had made late last night, long after Theo had gone to bed. He was underlining those he thought worthy of being added to the manuscript of his latest book, and crossing out with a single neat stroke anything he thought superfluous. The notebook was nearly full, yet there wasn't one page of messy scribble within its pristine pages. It always amazed people that he was so orderly. They tended to regard his unimaginative dress code

– faded jeans, T-shirt and CAT boots – as an indication of how he ran his life, that it would be as casual and thoughtlessly thrown together. In the chaotic mind-blown days of his addiction, this had certainly been the case, but not now. Now he was obsessively organised. His home was ruthlessly cleansed of all irrelevant clutter; his days were planned meticulously; his every hour was accounted for. 'A tidy mind is a happy mind' was a stupid maxim, but as trite as it was, it was a theory that held sufficient water for him to believe it. In the early days of his recovery he had been comforted by the petty rituals he had contrived for himself, using them to ground his mental state in the real world and not the hell he had inhabited previously. Now they were a matter of routine.

The desire to be so regulated and orderly was a side-effect of his brief spell in the clinic that had helped him to overcome his addiction, which had encompassed a variety of substances, but predominantly cocaine and alcohol. Hand in hand, they had been his partners in crime, partners that had taken him to the brink, convincing him, with each deadly, deceitful step they took him towards his downfall, that they were the only friends he needed, that they, and they alone, would give him the confidence and sense of worth he lacked.

By his mid-twenties he had been drinking with a determined vengeance that had nothing to do with social drinking. It was warfare. A war against himself. It wasn't the taste he craved, it was the obliterating effect he needed: the desire to drink was as strong as the need to eat, if not stronger. Seeking refuge in sleep – and a sleep in which he wasn't jerked awake by nightmares – he would fill himself with beer and whisky chasers until he collapsed on the bed and slept comatose for at least half the night.

Drugs came later, when desperation kicked in.

It was several months after he had married Kim, something he should never have done. He had done it primarily to annoy his parents, but also he believed that by marrying Kim he would be cutting himself off from his past, that he would be free of the destructive demons that had always plagued him. For a time it had worked and he and Kim were okay together. Not exactly happy and trouble-free with fairy-tale roses growing up the trellis of blissful matrimony – that would have been impossible in his state of severe alcohol dependency – but it had been a period of remission. Until, out of the blue, the old demons showed up. He had thought Kim was having an affair, but instead of confronting her, he put more energy into his drinking until eventually, knowing he couldn't go on as he was, he turned to cocaine: it would slow him down and take the pressure off, he thought. But it didn't. In no time at all, he was addicted, not so much to the drug but to the person he became when he was high. Without that buzz, he was nothing. A nobody. He got to the point where he couldn't get out of bed or go to the local shop for a loaf of bread unless his confidence had been fuelled by a line or two. What little sense of value he had soon went, as did his money. Without a moment's hesitation he would spend a week's wages in a single evening. Nothing mattered to him any more.

A year later he was uttering the immortal words, 'Hi, I'm Mark and I'm an addict.'

His first few days in the clinic had been a nightmare. He had truly believed he was going to die. His whole body had cried out for his faithful old buddies who never let him down, who boosted his self-esteem and gave him the strength he depended on to get through another day. The first day he had cursed and raged that he had ever set eyes on the traitor who had pretended he was a friend and brought him here. In his wild confusion he blamed Theo for everything wrong in his life. On his second day he tried to escape, never once thinking that his behaviour was that of a desperate madman. It had seemed so reasonable to him: he was being denied the two things that made his life worth living, so why wouldn't he make a run for it?

But escape wasn't on offer at the clinic. When the worst agony of the shakes and sweats of detox had passed he was given a timetable of what to do and firmly encouraged to stick to it. The hope was that it would keep his mind off the inner voice that told him all he needed was one small drink to ease him through the next hour. There was a never-ending regime of therapy to get through: group therapy of share and tell; individual therapy; even family therapy towards the end of his stay. He had never been so bloody busy. There was also time for private contemplation. This was always a low point for him. He never wanted to be alone with the person he hated so much – at least, not when he wasn't coked-up or drunk and there was nothing to hide behind. That was another thing about the clinic he hadn't been able to cope with initially: there was nowhere for him to hide, no quiet corners to lose himself in; the whole place was designed and run so that all was laid bare.

For some people the road to recovery starts within days of being admitted, but for Mark it was three weeks before he began to open up. The trigger had come from, of all things, the music that was played in the evenings. It was the only form of entertainment provided: no television, radio, papers, or magazines were available. The selection of music was not what he normally listened to – his taste had always been for satisfyingly aggressive rock – but here he was forced to listen to music his parents had tried to make him appreciate. And during this one evening at the clinic, when he had been eating his supper along with all the other inmates, his attention had been drawn away from the conversation he had been having with a guy who had been addicted to sex since the age of fifteen and he had listened with near mesmerised attentiveness to Mozart's Requiem. As though hearing it for the first time, he felt himself floating out of his body, soaring on the powerful, swelling notes, experiencing the heartbreaking magic of such an uplifting and glorious piece of choral work. He had started to shiver, as though an icy cold wind had ripped through the room, and then a searing heat had exploded deep within his chest. Then his head was in his hands and his hands were wet with tears. He was sobbing, his shoulders were shaking, his chest heaving. There was a voice, not his, surely not his, saying that he was sorry. Sorry that he was so screwed up. Sorry, too, that he had screwed up so many others. People gathered round him.

They held him. They cried with him. Then they took him away and he slept. Really slept.

The following morning, the man everyone called Bones – because his surname was McCoy – was assigned to talk to him. They sat in a room that had been stripped down to nothing more than two chairs and a desk, a floor of moss green carpet tiles, four walls of magnolia woodchip and a window. There was nothing to distract him – again, nothing to hide behind: no comfortable armchairs, no potted plants or soothing colour schemes designed to draw out deeply rooted fears. Slumped in his chair, his legs extended, crossed at the ankles, his hands hanging at either side of him, Mark had viewed the man before him. He was very small, not much more than five feet tall, with short, stumpy legs. He wore a cardigan with sleeves that were too long for his arms, and straight away Mark could see that his manner was annoyingly slow and thoughtful. But to an addict, who was used to his head buzzing at full tilt, everyone else always appeared to be moving at half speed. It was difficult to take him seriously, though – he looked like he would be more at home washing his car or trimming the hedge than working in a rehab clinic playing hardball with sex addicts and junkies.

First he asked Mark what had particularly moved him about the music he had heard the night before.

'It was the beauty of it,' he said simply, affecting an air of indifference and raising a foot to his knee to pick at a shoelace. 'It detached me from reality. Or what I see as reality.'

'Sounds like your average kind of trip. What exactly did it separate you from?' Silence.

Bones stared at him, waiting patiently for an answer. In the absence of one, he got up and opened the window. He sat down again. 'Do I need to repeat the question, or rephrase it, perhaps?' His tone was bland.

But, like a tiny pull on a thread, it somehow tugged an answer out of him. 'From the ... the death of a friend.'

It had taken real gut-wrenching courage to utter those words. Okay, he hadn't been able to look Bones in the eye but, if nothing else, his efforts should have been rewarded with at least a round of applause. But all he had got was: 'You mean the painful memory of that friend's death?'

'What else?'

Bones surveyed him thoughtfully. 'Mark, you've been here for three weeks now, and to my knowledge, this is the first time you've mentioned this. Why's that?'

'Why the hell do you think?'

'It's not what *I* think that's at stake.'

They had two-stepped like that for some time, and with each exchange, Mark gained a vicarious thrill in knowing he could outwit this inferior little man, who every now and then did nothing more constructive than dip his hand into his desk drawer and pull out a sweet.

His parents had tried this same trick on him when he was thirteen, taking him to see several child psychologists in the hope that he would walk away reborn. They had even tried hypnosis, but that had just been more of a challenge for him as he had forced his brain to keep alert, not to let it be fooled by the smooth tone of the doctor. But nothing had worked: he had always been too smart to let anyone know what he was really thinking.

But Mark was about to discover that Bones didn't always play by the book. Gentle and ponderous he could be, but as the weeks went by, Mark came to realise that he had seriously underestimated the man. When it was necessary Bones had no compunction in pulling the rug from under Mark, then watching him crack open his head on the hard floor of his arrogance.

'Now, Mark,' he said, on that first meeting after thirty minutes of prevaricating, 'I know that this whole scenario of ink blots and potty-training theories offends your intellect. After all, you're a former student of criminal psychology, what possible help could I offer a fine man like you? Who in their right mind would want to share their innermost feelings with an insignificant person such as me? But think on this while you're devoting yourself to blagging your way through this session. If you're so clever, what are you doing here?' He held up his hand. 'No, that was a rhetorical question. For now, I am doing all the talking. And I'll tell you what you're doing here, Mark. You're here because you're not in your right mind. In fact, you're in dire need of a clear-thinking outsider to give you a true perspective of yourself. And guess what, I'm just the man for the job. But don't worry that you'll become too dependent on me, I won't allow that to happen. The needy love–hate relationship you fear might develop between us if you open up to me will not take root. Believe me, I am too good at psychoanalysis for that to happen.'

'I'm bowled over by your modest claims.'

'And I by your scarcely controlled rage and dislike of me. But that's enough of the flattery. Let's get this straight, you're an alcoholic and a substance user, and it's down to me to help you get your head clean. The fact that you're here at all means that, deep down, you knew your number was up. And here's an interesting point I want you to consider, and consider well. An intellectual understanding of addiction isn't enough. You need to have an emotional response to it. So tell me about this friend who died and for whom you're still mourning. Or was it a girl? A girlfriend, perhaps?'

Another silence.

'Take your time. There's no hurry.'

But still Mark couldn't speak. And then, unbelievably, this extraordinary little man had the gall to stare straight at him and start whistling Joe Cocker's 'Let The Healing Begin'.

He didn't know how it happened, just as he couldn't explain the icy-cold feeling he had experienced the night before followed by the explosion of white heat in his body, but a tiny key slowly turned inside him and Mark heard himself say, 'His name was Niall and . . . and he drowned.'

Hearing the noise of a small engine, Mark raised his gaze from his notebook and looked down into the bay. Beneath a cloudless sky, where the turquoise water glinted in the glare of the sun, a motor-boat was cutting smoothly through the waves. Even at this distance he could hear its occupants laughing and joking. It made him wonder how Theo was getting on.

10

Izzy stood poised, every muscle taut, her toes clinging to the smooth rock, her arms in front of her, her eyes focused on the crystal clear water below. Modern Woman was threatening to push her in if she didn't get a move on, but her mother was alerting her to the dangers that lurked beneath the surface of the water. *Reckless! Wantonly reckless! This is just how people end up with their backs broken.*

It was her own fault, of course. She shouldn't have been so silly as to follow the crowd. Just because everyone else had thought it a good idea to drop anchor and spend time diving off the rocks, there had been no need for her to join in. She could have swum happily to the shore and left them to it. But oh, no, she'd had to pretend she wasn't frightened and could go along with them.

'It's quite safe, Izzy,' encouraged Max. 'There aren't any hidden rocks where you are.'

'He's right,' agreed Laura. 'It's so deep none of us have ever reached the bottom.'

'Perhaps if I jumped with you, it would help.' It was Theo, and somehow he had sneaked up behind her without her noticing. But, far from reassuring her, his presence only added to her trepidation. The sight of him with water trickling from his hair, down his neck and shoulders to his chest had her heart shifting to her mouth.

'I know I'm being silly,' Izzy said nervously, 'but I've – I've always been frightened of diving or jumping into the unknown.'

No! How could she have said that? It was a classic blurt-out-and-repent-at-leisure comment. An open invitation for him to take advantage of her.

Which he did.

'Then take my hand and I will show you what fun it can be.' And before she had a chance to protest he had grasped her hand, counted, '*Éna, dhío, tría*', and taken her with him. She screamed, but remembered just in time to close her mouth. And her eyes. She hit the water feet first, then sank into the cold and the dark, bubbles escaping from her mouth. A helpless, tumbling Alice came into her mind. As well as the thought that at least she had changed out of her skimpy little bikini and worn something that would hopefully stay on. At last she floated up to the surface. Theo was waiting for her. 'Now, was that so very scary?'

She pushed her hair out of her face and blinked salt water from her eyes. She managed a shaky laugh. 'I survived.'

He smiled. 'Another go?'

'Um ...'

'The answer you are looking for is yes, Izzy. Come, now I will teach you to dive properly. Jumping is for babies.'

Max and Laura had swum to the shore and Izzy could feel them watching her with Theo. 'The trick is to balance the weight and to lean forward,' he said, showing her the correct position to adopt. Shyly, she copied the line of his body, but he turned to her and gently lowered her arms. 'There, that's better. You don't want them too high. Now, this is how you use your hands to cut through the water. You see? Like this.'

After a few hesitant dives her nerves subsided and she began to get the hang of it. By her sixth attempt he proclaimed her a fast learner. 'Congratulations, you are as good as Laura.'

'Is that good?' she asked, swimming alongside him.

'It is very good.'

She turned on to her back and floated, letting the hot sun warm her face. She felt euphoric. She had overcome one of those niggling phobias she had had ever since she was a small child and the sense of achievement was fantastic. She closed her eyes and continued floating happily, smiling to herself, cherishing the feeling.

'You have a lovely body,' Theo remarked, after a few minutes' silence, 'and beautiful legs to go with it.'

Self-conscious, she flipped on to her front.

He laughed. 'Englishwomen are not used to compliments, are they? Anyone would think I had just insulted you.'

'You're probably right.'

'What? You think I insulted you?'

'No. I mean, we're not used to such open flattery.'

'Did your boyfriend not tell you what I have just said?'

'Um ... not exactly. Not in so many words.'

'Which words did he choose?'

'I can't really remember.'

'Ah, well, if they had been the right words they would have been memorable. Did he hurt you very badly?'

She blushed and swam away from him. She wasn't used to discussing her problems with a man. Not even with Max who, through Laura, knew most of the details of her pathetic relationship with Alan. And now, apparently, so did Theo. 'How much of my hapless love-life has Laura discussed with you?' she asked, as he swam parallel to her.

'Hardly anything. Just that there was a boyfriend who was very cruel to you.'

'He wasn't that bad.'

'So why do you let his cruelty linger on? Surely he is past history. He is gone. It is time for you to be happy.'

'I am happy.'

'Are you? You don't always look it.'

His directness made her defensive, and equally candid. 'Well, I'm *sorry* I look so miserable, but when you've given every little bit of yourself to a person and then they smash you apart, it's hard not to keep playing the same game of putting yourself back together. It becomes a habit.'

'Did you really love him so much?'

'Fool that I was, yes, I did. Or perhaps I only thought I did.'

'But that could be hindsight distorting the memory. Let us conclude that you did love him. Did you plan to marry?'

'I was keener than he was. As daft as it sounds, I saw us having children and growing old together. I suppose that must sound very dull to a man like you.'

He frowned. 'Why do you say that?'

'You don't give the impression of being the type to be interested in settling down.'

'Ah, you believe, just as Laura does, that I want to spend the rest of my life playing the field. That I am destined to spend an eternity chasing pretty young girls even when I am wrinkled and white-haired and hobbling round on a stick. Is that the future you predict for me?'

For a moment he looked quite cross, his thick brows drawn together, his eyes narrowed. At a loss to know what to say to placate him, and feeling that she ought to, she said, 'I'm sorry, I didn't . . .' but her words trailed away as in one fluid movement he swam up to her, placed a hand behind her neck and kissed her on the mouth.

The kiss, so sudden, so unexpected, was over almost before she had realised what he was doing, and when he pulled away, he smiled and said, 'Perhaps I just haven't been lucky enough to meet the right woman to settle down with.'

Izzy stared at him, stunned. Where had that come from?

Though it wasn't yet high season, the waterfront at Áyios Stéfanos was busy with boats searching for a mooring spot at the rows of wooden jetties. Max waited patiently for a large tourist-filled caïque to manoeuvre itself into position before he, too, found a suitable space alongside a stylish yacht with a Norwegian flag. He cut the engine and the boat drifted gently into place. Theo helped him secure it, and when all was done they strolled along the jetty to Galini's.

Max had had the foresight to book a table in advance, and it was just as well: the taverna, with its ringside view of the pretty sheltered harbour and all its comings and goings, was almost full. But, then, Áyios Stéfanos was always popular: it was one of the most visited beauty spots along this part of the coast, and despite the number of tourists who came to the small fishing village, it had lost little of its original charm. Theo had considered buying a property here for himself, but in the end he had decided that he preferred the quiet of Áyios Nikólaos with its less obvious congregation of tourists. It always amused him that even on holiday the British needed to be with likeminded folk. Just as they required tea made in a proper pot – none of this bag-in-a-cup nonsense – they needed a safety-net of their own culture around them. Right across the island one could see the invading colonies massing accordingly: the lively youngsters in the south of the island down at Kávos with its sun, sea, sex and cheap package deals; the Kensington-on-Sea crowd in Áyios Stéfanos, with its air of sophistication and quality, and further north, the middle ground of Kassiópi, where the mix of nationalities and type was greatest. But what annoyed Theo most about the British on holiday was their lack of integration. Some visitors came to the island year after year, but never made an effort to get to know the people who lived here or learn to speak Greek. Not even *kaliméra*, or *kalispéra*. Why be so insular? It was beyond him.

They were shown to their table and Max immediately ordered some drinks. The waiter listened politely as he tried to get his tongue round the words and phrases Theo had been teaching him, but only when he stumbled over the word for ice and looked to Theo for help did he come to his aid. '*Págho*,' he said, with a smile.

'Another five minutes and I'd have got it,' laughed Max, when the waiter left them alone.

'Another five minutes and it would have melted,' teased Laura. She opened her menu. 'I don't know about the rest of you but I'm starving. And as for you, Izzy, you must be exhausted after all that expert diving tuition.' She shot Theo a sly sidelong glance.

He gave her a knowing look in return, then immersed himself in his menu. So, she had seen him kiss Izzy, had she? He had wondered at the time if she had noticed. But, as predictable as his actions might have seemed to Laura, it had come as something of a surprise to him. An irrational impulse had seized him and he wished for the life of him that he could explain it.

The waiter returned with their drinks. After they had been handed round, Theo raised his oúzo and ice to his lips and glanced across the table to where Izzy was talking to Max. He knew from the many affairs he'd had, that she really wasn't his type. She was too quiet, too serious, too unsure of herself. Too sexually unaware. And yet ... and yet there was something about her, something that intrigued him. But what was it? He looked at her hard, studying her face for the answer. It was a face, he decided, that would stay young for many years; a face that would probably grow more beautiful as she aged, and aged gracefully. But there was more to it than that. There was something irresistibly cautious in her expression and he sensed that she was a long way from trusting him. Or trusting any man, for that matter. Was that the attraction, then? Was it, he wondered, with disturbing cynicism, that he saw her as the archetypal vulnerable young girl who needed her broken heart mending? Was it just the machismo challenge?

Aware that a worrying amount of introspection was creeping into his thoughts, he tossed back the remains of his oúzo and turned to Laura on his right to lighten his mood.

'So, Laura,' he said in a low voice, 'what did you think of my little display? Was it just as you would have wanted?'

'Are you referring to the diving lessons? Or what went on afterwards?' Her tone was playful.

'I think you know very well what I am referring to.'

'You played your part beautifully. But, a word of warning, you're not to hurt her. You go only as far as she's prepared to go.'

'Of course. I remember the promise I made this morning, no hearts to be broken. Mine included.'

'What's that about a broken heart?' asked Max, his conversation with Izzy having come to an end.

Theo was saved from lying by the sound of a commotion coming from the jetty nearest to the taverna. They all strained to see what was going on. Somebody, an English woman, was shouting, her furious words skimming across the water faster and more threatening than any tidal wave. 'You stupid, *stupid* man! Gawd help us, couldn't you see us coming?'

Theo smiled. It was Mark's friend, Dolly-Babe.

One of the waiters went to investigate and, no doubt, to ingratiate himself with a potential customer. Anywhere else in the world the woman would have been shooed away as an undesirable punter, but here in Greece business was business.

'What a hoot of a woman,' said Laura, 'and just look what she's wearing. That dress must have been sprayed on.'

She looked much the same as when Theo had met her at the airport and he watched her struggle to climb out of the boat, her legs pinned together at the knees by the impossible tightness of her dress. The young waiter extended his hand and she took it without a word of thanks. Her husband – baggy shorts, florid shirt, white socks, shoes and peaked cap – was left to manage as best he could. Eventually they approached the taverna and the waiter, spying a free table, guided them towards it.

'Oh, no, that won't do at all,' Dolly-Babe said. 'I need to be in the shade. The sun does terrible things to your skin. How about that one over there?' She pointed to a table a few yards away from where Theo and his friends were sitting and which was in full shade. 'Lovely,' she said, settling herself into the chair. 'A crème-de-menthe for me – and, Bob, what'll you have?'

'A large beer.'

The waiter looked apologetic. He was very young, and Theo guessed that his English probably wasn't up to full speed yet. 'Sorry, no crème-de-menthe,' he said.

'What? No crème-de-menthe?'

'You like oúzo? Oúzo very good.'

Dolly-Babe looked positively scandalised, as if she had just been offered a glass of meths. 'No, I don't like oúzo.'

'Retsína?'

She added another expression of disgust to her face. 'Gin. I'll have a gin and tonic, but go easy on the ice. Got that? Oh, and make it a double. A generous double.' She used her hands to indicate that it was a large glass she wanted.

The waiter nodded obligingly, as though he was too stupid to notice her patronising manner, but Theo knew that, despite the young man's faultless courtesy, he would be sorely tempted to spit in her drink before he served it to her.

She took out a lipstick and a small mirror from her handbag and touched up her makeup. She was just messing with her hair when she raised her eyes and caught sight of Theo. She stopped what she was doing. 'Bob!' she hissed across the table. '*Bob!* Look! Isn't that the driver, you know, the driver of that man who sat next to me on the plane? No, there, behind you. I know they all look the same, but I'm sure I'm right. Coo-ee!' A flutter of red nails waved in Theo's direction.

'Good gracious,' said Max, who also had been watching what was going on, 'she's waving at you, Theo. Do you know her? Someone from your past?'

Theo waved back politely, and out of the corner of his mouth, said, 'Max, please, do I look the type to have a past that would include her? Ah, she's coming over. I will explain later, but for now, will you do me the kindness of following my lead?'

'Hello there. What a coincidence meeting you here.'

Theo got to his feet. He bowed and held out his hand. 'All goes well with you on your holiday?'

She laughed loudly. 'Well, it was until some fool Italian geezer drove into our boat. Still, no real damage done. But take it from me, if there had been there'd be hell to pay for.' She raised her sunglasses and cast a curious eye over Theo's companions. 'More people you work for?' she asked.

'Yes. Today Theo Vlamakis *ees* captain of their ship. I bring them here for lunch.'

A stifled snigger from Laura went unnoticed by Dolly-Babe.

'Perhaps I introduce everyone to you? Yes? *Thees ees Meester* Sinclair and *hees* wife, and *thees ees Mees Issy* Jordan.'

'Hi,' she said to everyone. 'I'm Liberty-Raquel Fitzgerald, and over there is my Bob. Where are you all staying?'

'Áyios Nikólaos,' said Max, 'and you?'

'Snap. We're there too. Arrived yesterday. In fact, we were on the same plane that Mr Vlama-vlam-whatsisname here was meeting.'

'Whereabouts in Áyios Nikólaos are you staying?' asked Laura. She seemed to have got the sniggering under control now and sounded all politeness.

'Villa Mimosa. Apparently it's very near Mr St James's place.' She turned back to Theo. 'Mr St James not with you today?'

Theo made another self-deprecating little bow. 'Sadly, no.'

She looked disappointed.

'You have me pass on a message, maybe?'

She hesitated, and Theo could see that she was debating with herself whether or not a foreigner could really be trusted. 'No, that's all right,' she said at length. 'I'll call on him in person. That's probably the best thing to do. But perhaps you could help me. Exactly which villa is it he's staying in? Is it that big posh one right on the end?'

There seemed no point in lying to her, she would find out easily enough anyway, so Theo reluctantly told her that it was indeed the big posh house that Mr St James was staying in.

'I thought it might be,' she said. 'Well, then, I'd best be getting back to my Bob or he'll think I've abandoned him.' She suddenly looked at Izzy. 'You want to be careful sitting in the sun like that, you'll end up with wrinkles. See this complexion,' she used a red nail as a pointer, 'as good as the day I was born with it. And how have I kept it that way? Sunscreen and lots of shade. That's how. Oh, it looks like Sunny-Jim Spiros has pulled his finger out and found us some drinks at last. See you.'

As soon as she was out of earshot, everyone fell on Theo for an explanation.

'Who on earth is she? And why does she think you work for your friend Mark?' asked Laura.

Theo explained about Mark being trapped on the plane with her and her husband and the nicknames he had given them, and his own response at the airport. 'It was a joke on my part. She gave me such a look I could not help myself.'

'What kind of look?' asked Izzy.

'Like this.' He ran his eye over her body, leaving nobody in any doubt what he meant. It was a look that could have peeled a banana. Izzy blushed and lowered her eyes.

'That's a bit rich coming from you, Theo,' said Max. 'Isn't that what you do to every pretty girl who passes your way?'

'But that is different. Greek men are expected to behave like that. Besides, it is second nature to us.'

'Is it, indeed?'

'Ah, but, Laura, it was also her manner. She made the assumption that so many of you Brits make, that because I was Greek I was good for little more than driving a taxi. Believe me, there is nothing that annoys a Greek more than to have his country rubbished, or his humble and generous nature mistaken for stupidity.'

'And you think that's what she was doing?'

'Yes,' said Theo fiercely. 'I was Zorba the Greek to her. A rustic peasant. A parody to be laughed at.'

'But Zorba was a noble and wise man,' Izzy said softly, 'a little excessive, maybe, but not a bad stereotype.'

Hearing Izzy's gentle words and the contrast they made with his own, Theo suddenly realised how petulant he sounded. He raised his hands, his palms facing his friends. '*Lipáme,*' he apologised, with a light laugh, 'please forgive me. In my desire to defend my nation I got a little carried away. I was, as you say, very much on my low horse.'

Nobody was brave enough to correct his English, and the conversation moved on to what they were going to eat. Having already made her choice, Izzy peered discreetly at Theo over the top of her menu. What a surprising man he is, she thought, and not just because he dishes out kisses so freely. Beneath all that light-hearted flirty banter, there was quite a different person. There was a man with strong views, who was quite prepared to reveal foolish ignorance and prejudice in others.

He might not like to believe it, she reflected, disappearing again behind her menu, but he wasn't so dissimilar from the fictional character of Alexis

Zorba. Neither man was afraid to confront his desires, and to do so quite openly. Especially their love of women.

She suspected that there was a lot more to Theo Vlamakis than at first met the eye.

11

By the time they had finished their lunch and paid their bill it was late afternoon. It was still very hot with a perfectly clear sky, but the wind had risen, and the sea was much rougher than when they had set off.

'I hope you're a good sailor,' Max said to Izzy, as they left behind them the calm water of the picturesque harbour and embraced the first of the choppy waves. The boat reared up out of the water then dropped with a suddenness that jolted Izzy almost out of her seat. She placed her hands firmly either side of her and gripped the bench. It was just as well she did: the next wave was bigger than the first and made even Laura give a scream of alarm.

'You'd better hold on tight,' Max shouted over his shoulder, his words only just audible as the wind gusted and whipped them out of his mouth. Spray was coming into the boat, and stung as it struck Izzy's cheek. It was like *The Cruel Sea* but without the duffel coats and cocoa! She wondered if there were any life-jackets on board. She wasn't a bad swimmer and thought she could probably make it to the shore, but what if . . . what if the boat capsized and they were all stuck under it? Or supposing she banged her head and knocked herself unconscious? What then? She gripped the bench harder still, willing her panicky thoughts away.

'There's no need to worry,' said Theo, sitting once again at her side, 'Max knows what he is doing. It is only dangerous if one tries to go too fast.' Then, with a wink, he said, 'His boat may be smaller than mine, but his engine is powerful enough to get us home safely.' He put a protective arm round her shoulders and invited her to lean into him. It was not an invitation she had any intention of turning down. Right then she would have happily accepted reassurance from a peckish Hannibal Lecter.

They weren't the only ones struggling against the elements. In front of them was a boat Izzy recognised, whose departure from the waterfront at Áyios Stéfanos they had watched with amusement. Its departing grace had matched that of its earlier arrival. But this had been after its occupants had joined them for a post-lunch coffee and glass of Metaxá and they had been treated to a brief run-down on the lives of Bob and Dolly-Babe Fitzgerald. Dolly-Babe had done most of the talking but occasionally her husband squeezed a word in. He was here on business, doing a recce of several new resorts that were being built in the south of the island. 'No good looking round here,' he had said. 'Too expensive. Though if I could get a foot in the door, I wouldn't say no. Strikes me this place is in dire need of a massive overhaul.'

'I think you will find *thees* area *ees* protected from any further development,' Theo had said, still maintaining the charade of ignorant taxi-driver and piling on the exaggerated accent.

'What? You mean there's a restriction on any new building work? You sure about that?'

Izzy had wondered how Theo would react to having his word doubted. But with perfect composure, he said, 'It *ees* an area of *houtstanding* beauty. The government *weeshes* it to remain so.'

After this Bob went back to being Silent Bob and Dolly-Babe took up the conversation, telling them how she had met Bob – her diamond in the rough, as she called him. She had been a croupier on a cruise ship and it had been love at first sight with this self-made man who had cracked his first million at the age of twenty-eight from owning a caravan park. Nothing to do with money, then? Izzy had wanted to ask. 'He was my destiny,' Dolly-Babe had said, giving Bob a dig in the ribs with one of her sharp little elbows, 'it was in the cards. And I don't mean the Black Jack cards!' Her raucous laughter had had heads turning their way.

They had gained on the Fitzgerald boat now and Izzy could see Bob at the helm. His wife, pale-faced and shrieking, was telling him in no uncertain terms to slow down. She was also holding on desperately to the remains of her windswept hair-do. When she realised they weren't alone on the high seas, a look of relief passed over her face. Max slowed his speed and came in alongside. 'Ahoy, there,' he said jovially, 'everything all right?'

Bob's response was restricted to an I-can't-see-what-all-the-fuss-is-about expression, but Dolly-Babe's wide-eyed look of near-hysteria told a different story.

'If the engine isn't up to it, it's best to take it slowly,' Max advised. 'It gets even rougher round the next headland.'

'You see?' shouted Dolly-Babe at her husband, who was wearing the look of a man who didn't appreciate the helpful tip he was being given by somebody in a bigger boat than his. His weary face reminded Izzy of her father's expression in the car whenever her mother had instructed him on how best to overtake. 'I told you not to go so fast,' continued Dolly-Babe. 'I knew I was right and you were wrong.' She turned back to Max, as if to say something else, but the combination of a strong swell of water beneath their boats and an increase of pressure from Bob's hand on the throttle had her toppling backwards. She landed with an undignified bump on her skinny bottom and lost one of her high-heeled slip-on shoes. 'Bleeding hell, Bob!' she yelled, just managing to steady herself. 'What the sweet Fanny Adams do you think you're doing? I could have gone overboard.'

Something in Silent Bob's eyes suggested this thought had occurred to him. And not just once.

'Well, so long as you're okay,' Max said. He let out the throttle, turned the boat sharply away, sending up an arc of white spray, and went on ahead. Izzy noticed, though, that he was thoughtful enough not to leave too great a gap between the two boats.

'He is all heart, is he not?' said Theo, in her ear and above the noise of the engine.

'Who, Max?'

'Yes. He is so kind-hearted he would not dream of leaving them to the mercy of the sharks. You are beginning to look very pale. Are you going to be sick?'

They were beyond the headland that Max had warned Silent Bob about and the increase in the pitch and roll of the boat was causing Izzy's stomach to reconsider lunch. 'I hope not,' she said, closing her eyes and mentally crossing her fingers.

From the terrace of Villa Anna, and with the benefit of a pair of binoculars he had found in Theo's study, Mark saw two boats approaching. As they drew nearer he was able to make out Theo and his friends in the leading boat – Theo had his arm around a dark-haired girl, no surprises there – and in the other ... was that dreadful couple from the plane.

He kept the powerful glasses fixed on the two boats, swinging them from one to the other. He checked out Theo's friends: a man with silver hair was doing all the hard work, probably Max Sinclair, and an attractive woman, his wife presumably, was sitting beside him smoothing back her auburn hair as the wind kept blowing it into her face. And behind them was the girl with Theo. She looked a lot younger than everyone else, in her mid-twenties, perhaps, and of them all seemed to be enjoying herself least. Perhaps she wasn't appreciating the attentions of the pram-chaser sitting next to her, thought Mark wryly.

He watched the two boats battle their way into the shallow, more sheltered water of the bay, until at last they slowed their engines and dropped anchor. The silver-haired man was out first, followed swiftly by Theo who went to assist Silent Bob. They must all be mad, thought Mark, as he watched them chatting on the jetty. From the safety of the terrace, where he had spent most of the day working, he had seen the rapid change in the sea conditions as a strong wind had sprung up, and had wondered how much it would affect Theo and his friends' homeward journey.

He went and sat in one of the chairs by the pool, which was in full sun. He stripped off his shirt and decided that he had finished work for the day. He was pleased with the amount he had got done. He had fully expected, given the dramatic upheaval in his routine, not to get anything of any worth written. Normally when he was working, he had to stick to a strict code of conduct; so ritualistic it was absurd. The first draft of a manuscript was always hand-written in blue ink – real ink from a fountain pen, never a biro. He used W.H. Smith A4 Jotter Pads, with a ruled left-hand margin, though he never wrote close up to it, he always had to leave a further half-inch space clear. There was no reason why he did this, he just had to do it. He put his written pages into black lever-arch files, never any other colour, and any notes he added to the pages once they'd reached the file had to be written in pencil, never pen. It went without saying that he had his collection of lucky pens and pencils. And sure, the next step was lunacy, when he'd be claiming he couldn't work unless he was wearing his lucky boxers. He also had to have music playing in the background, especially when he was doing the final draft on his PC. For his last book he had listened constantly to Bruce Springsteen. He didn't always hear the music, but he heard its absence keenly. It was a cheap brain-washing trick that never failed to fool his subconscious into getting down to work.

Here, though, sitting in Theo's garden with only the cicadas for musical accompaniment, he had been a ritual down, and had had to crank up his brain as best he could. It would be a nice irony if, when he returned home, he was only able to write with the sound of a hundred-piece cicada orchestra playing for him. Fortunately he had already made a good start on the first draft of his latest novel – *Flashback Again* – so at least he had a shove of momentum behind him before he had started this morning.

Flashback Again was his sixth novel, and was proving to be his most ambitious. There were times when he woke in the middle of the night convinced that the plot was unfeasible, convinced, too, that his run of luck was on the verge of ending. As irritating as these disturbed nights were, they were nothing compared to those he had once lived with. During his days as an alcoholic, he had been tormented with nightmares of the most ferocious realism. Nightmares that began with the same hypnotic feel to them but climaxed with a brutal and horrifying dénouement that had him staggering to the nearest sink or loo. He rarely had anything in his stomach, other than alcohol, and he would vomit so violently that he coughed up blood. Unable to get back to sleep he often got dressed and prowled the streets, looking for something to obliterate the fear.

Writing had been Theo's idea. He had put it to Mark when he had insisted that his friend stay with him in Athens after he was discharged from the clinic. They had been sitting in a taverna in Pláka, the old quarter that lay at the foot of the Acropolis, where quiet winding streets and balconies of fragrant jasmine made it an oasis of calm in a crazy city. Athens was robust, disorderly, a place of haphazard growth, where classical old and insolent new rubbed shoulders to create a stupendous disharmony.

'We need to think seriously about what you are going to do next,' Theo had said.

The statement, as true as it was, panicked Mark. In his fragile, vulnerable state, the here and now was all he could cope with. Anything more freaked him out. But he had known that Theo was right: he had to have a plan. He was all too aware of the danger in not having any structure to his days. Previously drugs and alcohol had filled the void in his life; now he had to find something new. If he didn't, he might falter and screw up again.

'I think you should invest your past in your future,' Theo had continued.

'Any suggestions?'

'Yes. Write a book.'

'Just like that?'

'Why not? Despite the number of brain cells you must have destroyed, you are still highly intelligent and more than capable of writing a novel. You have plenty going on inside that head of yours to write at least half a dozen books.'

'It takes more than intelligence. It takes creativity, discipline, and a hell of a lot of determination.'

'You have all of those things, Mark. Think back to our college days when you wrote for those student magazines. Your stuff was far superior to anything else they carried. Think also of the discipline and determination you needed to keep up with the onerous task of feeding your addiction over the years. But that is all behind you. Now it is time for you to divert that energy and allow yourself to reach your full capacity.'

Of course, Theo had only been voicing what had been in Mark's mind ever since he could remember. What big-headed student hadn't imagined that he would produce a life-affirming work of fiction that would set the world alight with its magnificent prose and original line of thought? But it was only now as an adult, now that his head was clear for the first time, that he allowed himself to pursue what had previously been little more than pie in the sky.

Theo had been right on the button when he had said that Mark's past was the key to his future. With his wealth of first-hand experience of fear, writing a psychological thriller had seemed the most natural step for him to take. Fear, after all, begets fear. And who better to play to the dark side of the imagination than somebody who had been there since he was a child?

He wrote his first book in less than nine months while he remained in Athens with Theo. Once or twice, in the early days of his recovery, when Theo needed to travel overseas Mark went with him. 'Believe me, it is not that I don't trust you,' Theo had said, during a flight to Sydney where he was currently negotiating a deal to snap up some prime water-front properties in the harbour, 'It is more a case of keeping an eye on my investment.'

'Theo, you're an obscenely rich, upper-class Greek suburbanite. What the hell kind of investment do you see in me?'

'Ah, but one never knows how things will turn out. Maybe one day you will be the wealthy author and I the penniless Greek peasant. I would then call in my debt.'

'You're forgetting, we're quits. I saved your rotten life and now you've saved mine. The debt's already settled, and seeing as my life is infinitely more valuable than yours, I reckon you owe me.'

The 'debt' had been a long-standing joke between the pair, though its origins were not the least bit funny. In Durham, about a month after they had first met, Mark had been walking aimlessly about the town late one night, as he often did if he couldn't sleep. He had walked along the towpath, down by the river, then headed for the cathedral. There was nobody about, probably because it was so damned cold: a bitter, bone-blasting wind was slicing straight through him, stinging his eyes, making them water. It had rained earlier, and the streets were wet and shining in the soft light cast from the lamps. He stood for a moment to admire the chunky no-nonsense Norman architecture of the cathedral, and to shelter from the worst of the wind. He was just cursing the lack of buttons on his second-hand greatcoat and blowing on his hands to warm them when he heard a scuffling sound, followed by a cry. He retraced his steps to where he thought the noise was coming from and peered into the shadowy gloom of a litter-strewn alleyway. There he saw two lads kicking the hell out of some poor bloke on the ground. The sickening thud of boot on bone galvanised him, as did the sight of the victim's expensive shoes and clothes.

'Hey, you two,' he yelled, 'anybody can work over a ponce like that. How about a real fight?' He shrugged off his coat, threw it on top of a pile of overflowing bin-bags and cardboard boxes, and walked towards them. He must have looked a menacing sight – viciously dyed hair, Doc Martens and a snarl that would have threatened the hardiest mugger. 'Come on, then,' he challenged, 'one at a time, or both together, it makes no odds to me.' He raised his fists and they came at him. He had never approved of the expensive school his parents had sent him to, but now he was grateful for it, especially for the choice of sports on offer, which had included boxing. The first thug received a broken nose for his trouble and ran off. The second, however, was more determined and pulled a wide, jagged-edged knife on Mark. He dodged out of the way to begin with, as the blade flashed and swooped within inches of his face, but then he tripped, lost his balance and fell against the wall. It was a mistake his assailant leaped on, and in one swift movement the cold steel was thrust deep into his side, and was left there as the mugger hightailed it into the darkness. Reeling with pain, and disbelief that this was happening to him – it was a bloody high price to pay for a night of insomnia in anyone's book! – he held his breath, drew out the knife and watched his blood flow through the grubby whiteness of his T-shirt and down his jeans. Clutching his side, he went over to the motionless figure lying on the ground in a filthy puddle. 'You'd better not be dead after all the trouble I've just gone to,' he muttered. But for all his bravado, he flinched at the bloodied mess that had been Theo's face. Pretty boy no more. He bent down to feel for a pulse and nearly lost consciousness at the pain that ripped through him. He pressed his fingers to Theo's neck, located a faint ticking, then, like the thieves before him, rifled through his pockets, knowing that if anyone would have what he needed it would be this flash git. He found what he was looking for and, pushing the clean, neatly folded handkerchief against his side, he got to his feet. He retrieved his coat from the pile of rubbish, covered Theo with it, then made his way to where he knew there was a phone box. He called for an ambulance and staggered back to the alleyway, shivering with cold and shock.

The ambulance soon arrived and Theo, still showing no real sign of life, was put on a stretcher. It was only when Mark dropped the blood-soaked handkerchief from his side, that the extent of his own injury was realised.

He was hailed as a hero by Theo and his family, as well as by the college authorities. Even his own parents, unused to lavishing praise on their youngest son, applauded his bravery.

But he still felt like the same old loser he had always been.

12

Theo had said his goodbyes and was now climbing the steep path up to Villa Anna, but even when he had put a sizeable distance between him and the jetty, he could still make out Dolly-Babe's jarring voice. She was talking about him as though he couldn't hear or, more probably, as though he was an imbecile who couldn't understand her.

'You'd think he'd make more of an effort, wouldn't you?' she was saying. 'He's a bit too casual for my liking. If I was employing him I'd expect him to wear trousers for work, not shorts. And, if you'll take a tip from me, it doesn't do to be too familiar with the hired help. The next thing you'll know, he'll be taking you for a ride. I suppose he will pass on my message to Mr St James. You never can be sure with his type. Charming, but totally unreliable.'

Theo laughed to himself and was still smiling when he came upon Mark lazing comfortably in a chair beside the pool. His eyes were closed and he looked unusually relaxed and at ease, stripped off to the waist and with his arms raised behind his head. Theo could see the line of the scar that remained from the wound Mark had received on the night he had saved a relative stranger's life. It had laid down the foundations of their friendship and bonded it for ever. They were told by the medical staff at the hospital that they were probably both lucky to be alive. Theo's skull had been fractured, his nose broken and Mark had very nearly had his spleen ruptured. It was while they were lying in adjacent beds the following morning that Theo had thanked Mark for coming to his aid. Through his bruised, swollen lips he had said, 'It is not everyone who would have been brave enough to do what you did. I am very grateful.'

'I didn't feel as if I had any choice,' had been the terse response.

'You could have pretended not to hear and walked away.'

'I'm not that kind of guy. My only regret is that it wasn't a more worthwhile life I'd saved. What the hell were you doing out so late anyway? Some sensible woman denied you access to her bed, did she?'

'I had been to a party.'

'And hadn't got lucky? Hah! Serves you right.'

The exchange was brought to an end with the arrival of Theo's parents. Sweeping into the ward, and seeing the state of him, his mother had burst into a paroxysm of tears. 'It looks worse than it really is,' he said, in an attempt to placate her, his voice raised above her noisy sobbing. Everyone in the ward was watching them, their curiosity aroused by the uninhibited cacophony of a language they couldn't understand. In an effort to calm the situation, Theo indicated Mark and told his parents that if it hadn't been for him he wouldn't be there. 'You must thank him,' he said. 'He was very brave.' Sadly, his words only fuelled his mother's hysteria, but his father glanced across to the other bed and took in the dyed hair. He went over and introduced himself, holding out a cautious hand and regarding the young man, who made such a curious contrast to his son. 'I am very pleased to meet you. You were injured also in the attack?'

'One of them had a knife. It was my own fault, I should have moved quicker.'

Theo's father looked shocked. 'We owe you so much. If there is ever anything we can do to help you, you must allow us to do so. Have you and Theo been friends for long?'

Theo had heard the trace of politely disguised disbelief in his father's voice – surely his son didn't mix with this type of person?

'No,' had been Mark's blunt reply. 'I just happened to be passing.'

If he had expected his remark to end the conversation, it didn't. Instantly his status in Theo's parents' eyes went up: he, a passing stranger, had saved the life of their only son.

'And your parents, are they here too?'

The same blunt reply. 'No.'

Taking a moment off from her weeping, Theo's mother said, 'But they are coming later to see you?'

'They don't know anything about this. And they don't need to know. I'll be out of here at the first opportunity.'

'But what will you do?' Theo had asked. 'Who will take care of you?'

Mark gave him a withering stare as if to say, 'You might be a soft mummy's boy, but some of us can cope on our own. I'll manage, just as I always have.'

When a nurse joined them and insisted that her patients needed to rest, Theo motioned to his father to come back to his side. He spoke in Greek so that Mark wouldn't understand what he was saying and, hoping that Mark wouldn't be too furious with him, he asked his father to see if he could get in touch with Mark's parents.

Later that evening, Mr and Mrs St James arrived, white with worry. But it soon became clear that their concern for their son was as great as his disregard for them. Growing up in a culture that valued families, especially mothers who were loved and revered, Theo was horrified to see how rude and cruel Mark was to his.

'Come to see if I've died yet?' he said, as they stood looking down at him. 'Well, sorry to disappoint you, but I'm going to be around for a while yet.'

Theo could see from their faces that they were not unused to such brutal comments. He wondered what had gone on in their family to make Mark vent such hatred towards them.

'You're looking very serious,' Mark said, lowering his arms and squinting into the sun as he looked up at Theo. 'Though from what I saw of you in the boat, it looked as if your charm was having no great effect. Perhaps that's why you look so miserable.'

Theo spotted the binoculars beneath Mark's seat, and smiled. 'As you well know, what you see on the surface is not always the true picture.'

'Oh, come off it, Theo, you're losing it. And, besides, she's way too young for you. There's nothing dignified about an ageing pram-chaser.'

Theo raised an eyebrow. 'And, there speaks the man with a string of successful relationships behind him.'

'Yeah, well, relationships aren't my thing. But at least I gave marriage a go, as brief as it was, which is more than can be said of you. Do you want a drink? I was just going in for one.' Up on his feet, he added, 'Oh, and by the way, somebody phoned while you were out. I left his message on your desk in your study. He said you were to ring him soon as you could.'

Minutes later, when they had poured themselves a drink and Theo had dealt with the phone call, they went back outside into the sunshine by the pool. Theo said, 'She is not so very young, you know.'

'Who?'

'The girl in the boat.'

'And does this girl in the boat, who is *not so very young*, have a name?'

'Izzy. Izzy Jordan. She is staying with my neighbours, the Sinclairs.'

'And?'

Theo leaned back in his chair. 'I cannot put my finger on it, but there is something about her that is quite appealing.'

With a wry laugh, Mark said, 'You mean she's a woman?'

'There is that.'

'And with a click of your fingers you assume you can have her, don't you? God, you make me sick. You don't change, do you?'

'Aha, the green-eyed monster makes his appearance once more.'

'Oh, shut up! Of course I'm not jealous. Just deeply cynical.'

'You never have been able to stomach my success with—'

'Please, Theo, not that old number. If I wanted to spend all my time chasing a cracking pair of legs, then I would do exactly that. What's more, I'd make a better job of it than you!'

Theo grinned. 'So you noticed her legs, did you?'

'I was speaking generally,' snapped Mark.

'Well, my old friend,' he taunted, 'all I will say is that if she is too young for me, she is too young for you also.'

'Look, I told you, I wasn't talking specifically. It was a stupid chauvinistic turn of phrase. And, anyway, didn't you just say she was older than she looks?'

Theo conceded the point to Mark, sipped his drink and listened to the waves crashing on the rocks below. It always amused him when they argued like this. It was a familiar routine they went through, an enjoyable game they had played since they were students: Mark, full of cynical, vitriolic disapproval, and he full of his own self-importance, as they battled it out each trying to prove the other wrong. In the old days there had been no surer way to fire Mark up. 'Oh, I nearly forgot to tell you,' he said brightly, 'I have good news, and I have bad. Which do you want first?'

'Go on, then, give me the bad. You know how I like to punish myself.'

'Your ladyfriend, Dolly-Babe, she is determined to meet you again. She is talking of inviting you to have a cosy drink with her and Silent Bob. She wants Max and Laura and Izzy to go as well, and is planning to call round and make her invitation in person.'

Mark's face darkened. 'Well, she can forget it. I shan't be going. I trust you did the decent thing and made a suitable excuse for me.'

Theo shifted in his seat.

'Theo? You did, didn't you?'

'I could not easily turn down an invitation on your behalf. You have to remember, she still thinks I am no more than the hired help for the wealthy visitors to the island.' He explained how he had pretended to be employed by Max and Laura for the day, and also how Dolly-Babe must have decided at the last minute that he was trustworthy enough to pass on a message. 'She thinks this is your villa and that I am your live-in chauffeur.'

'You idiot. What are you going to do when she finds out the truth?'

He shrugged. 'What do I care what she says or thinks any more than she cares for what I think or do?'

'So if that was the bad news, cheer me up with the good.'

'Ah, the good news is that you will see less of me than you thought. That phone call was a summons for me to return to Athens the day after tomorrow. Yes, I thought that would cheer you. You will have the place to yourself. It will be a pleasant and peaceful holiday for you.'

'You're forgetting, I'm not here on holiday, I'm here to work.'

'Well, what have you got to say for yourself?'

Max had taken himself off for a late-afternoon siesta, leaving Laura and Izzy alone on the veranda, which meant that Laura was now giving Izzy a thorough grilling on the events of the day. 'I saw him kiss you,' she said, 'so don't try and make out that nothing happened.'

'It wasn't much of a kiss, it was only—'

'Not much of a kiss! This is Theo we're discussing. How many times in your life have you been kissed by a man as heart-stoppingly gorgeous as him?'

Izzy blushed. 'I was going to say it was so quick that it was over before I had a chance to think about it.'

Laura gave her a cunning smile. 'But you've had plenty of time since. Time in the boat as well when he had his arm around you.'

'Sorry to disappoint you, but I felt too sick in the boat to think of anything other than getting my feet back on *terra firma*. Is it always as bad as that? Because if so, count me out on any other expeditions that involve water.'

'It was particularly rough this afternoon. We're probably in for a run of similar days. But back to you and Theo.'

'Oh, Laura, don't be absurd. I'm sure he did it out of force of habit. Or, more likely, he did it to see how I would react.'

'From where I was sitting, I thought you were very cool about it.'

'What did you expect me to do? Slap his face? It was only a kiss.' As nonchalant as she forced herself to sound, Izzy knew that was the last thing she felt when she thought of Theo. She had known him no longer than a blink of an eye, but it was long enough to know that he made her feel nervous.

It was nervousness born of the fear that he might be capable of making her do something she would regret.

13

Early the next morning, without disturbing Max and Laura, Izzy crept out of the villa and went for a walk along the beach. The air was fresh and clean, and the sea sparkled as though someone had been up all night polishing it. There was nobody else about as the bleached white stones crunched noisily beneath her feet and she felt guilty to be disturbing the serenity of the day. *There you go again, Isobel Jordan, ruining it for everyone else! Can't you ever be quiet?*

She paused to admire the stunning view where, across the soft blue of the water, a layer of mist entwined itself around the Albanian hills. Slipping her bag of sketching things off her shoulder, she sat down, rummaged for her pencil and paper, and cast her eyes for something to sketch. She settled on the half-way point in the bay, to her right, focusing on one particular spot, where a small formation of circular rocks jutted out like chunky discs from a toy construction kit.

Minutes later, and unhappy with her drawing, she put it aside and lay back on the stones, which were already warm from the sun. She closed her eyes and thought how lucky she was to be here. It was so kind of Max and Laura to invite her to spend the summer with them. But, then, that was Max and Laura all over, generous and big-hearted, eager for those around them to enjoy life as much as they did. She had been touched by this spirit of generosity right from the outset of getting to know them. 'It was lucky I was parked in your way,' Max had joked. 'You've got to be very careful who you tangle bumpers with these days. There are some strange people about.'

'Yes, darling,' Laura had said, 'you for one! Would you like to stay for supper, Izzy? It's only a lamb hotpot, nothing special.' The invitation had taken her by surprise. She had caused goodness knows how many hundreds of pounds' worth of damage to a man's car and here was his wife offering her a meal. She accepted the invitation and stayed until nearly midnight, not realising how the time was flying by as they laughed and chatted. As he helped Izzy into her coat when she insisted that she really had to go, Max had said to Laura, 'Why don't you invite Izzy to go along to that pseudo-intellectual-artsy-fartsy group you've recently joined?'

Laura had laughed. 'It might not be Izzy's idea of a fun evening. To be honest, I'm not sure that it's mine. I've only been to three sessions, but it seems to be an excuse for a lot of legitimised snobbery in the name of appreciating art.'

But that was how Izzy's friendship with Laura had really taken off. They had become allies as they sat at the back of the class in the draughty village hall, trying not to laugh at the pretentious lecturer as he pranced about the creaking wooden floor with his bow-tie, *pince-nez* and hand-embroidered waistcoats. 'Brian Sewell meets Lionel Blair,' Izzy had whispered to Laura, two minutes into the first class. Luckily the lecturer was so caught up in the sound of his own pedantic voice that he didn't hear them sniggering. However, from then on one or two other members of the group went out of their way to give them looks of open hostility. 'Oh dear, I'll be getting you a terribly bad name,' Izzy had said in the car on the way home, later that evening.

'No worse than it already is,' Laura had said. 'Don't forget the crazy man I'm married to.'

With her head resting on the stones, Izzy was alerted to the sound of footsteps. She sat up and saw Theo approaching. He was dressed for a swim, which meant that, other than a towel slung loosely around his shoulders, he was wearing only a pair of swimming shorts. Seeing her, he raised his hand and made his way along the sunlit beach.

'Hello, Izzy,' he said, drawing level and sitting beside her, 'you're up very early.'

'So are you.'

'Ah, with me, it is habit. And you? What is your excuse?'

'It seems a shame to waste a single moment here. It's so lovely. I'm beginning to wonder if I'll be able to leave when it's time to go back to England.'

'But that is such a long way off. There is no need for you to think of that now. Allow yourself to enjoy what you have today, don't spoil it with tomorrow's anxieties. You have been drawing, eh?' He reached a hand over her legs to the discarded sketchpad. He studied it for a few seconds then raised his eyes to the rocky outcrop she had drawn. 'This is very good. Do you draw people as well?'

'I do, but not very well. I can't do noses. It doesn't matter who they are, they all end up with the same nose.'

'Anyone's in particular?'

She laughed. 'A Medici hawk-nose, so don't ever ask me to do your portrait.'

He laughed too and held her gaze. 'Would you have dinner with me tonight?'

When she didn't say anything, he passed her the sketchpad. 'My question has surprised you?'

'Um . . . What about your guest?'

'You want him to join us?'

She could see that he was teasing her. 'I meant, won't it be rude leaving him on his own?'

'He is a good friend. He will not mind. Or maybe you are prevaricating. Perhaps you do not want to have dinner with me. Is it possible that you don't trust me?'

Yes, he was definitely teasing her. But as his dark eyes bored into hers, she found herself wondering whom she trusted less. Him with his smooth, worldly charm, or herself with her pitiful inexperience.

As if sensing her thoughts, he said, 'I will behave very well with you, Izzy. I will be the perfect gentleman. You will be quite safe.'

Now, where had she heard that before?

Then suddenly it wasn't Theo sitting next to her, but Alan. Alan making the same claim – *You're quite safe with me.*

Instantly any notion of saying yes to Theo was blown away. A tornado of anger ripped through her, Theo was after only one thing, and once he'd got it, he would be on his way, laughing quietly to himself with not a thought for her feelings.

What a monumental fool she had so very nearly made of herself.

And how much easier could she have made it for him?

Well, this was one notch on the bedpost that he wouldn't be carving.

To the sound of Modern Woman cheering in approval, Izzy slid her things into her bag and stood up. 'You're right,' she said, looking down at him, 'I don't trust you. But don't take it personally. Enjoy your swim.' To her ears, there was no bitterness in her words, just a reassuring ring of finality. And triumph. This was an important victory for her self-esteem.

Puzzled, Theo watched Izzy stride away. Was it something he had said?

Over breakfast at Villa Anna, he put the same question to Mark. 'Clearly I said something to offend her, but I cannot think what it was.'

Mark laughed. 'I told you yesterday. It's time to face up to it – you're losing it, mate.'

Banging his cup of coffee down on the table, and spilling some, Theo said, 'Mark, please, I am being serious.'

'Hey, easy there, Casanova. So why does it bother you so much that she turned you down? Is it really such a strange phenomenon for you?'

'I know what you're thinking, that it's merely vanity, but it is more than that, I promise you. I am concerned that I may have upset her.'

'And that bothers you?'

'You seem surprised.'

'Well, put it this way. We could sit here until this evening putting together a list of all the women you must have upset at some time or other in a life given over to the thrill of the chase. Admittedly your game-plan never included deliberately hurting them, but think how used they must have felt when you moved on to the next conquest.'

'Oh, but you're wrong. They used me as much as I used them.'

'Maybe some of them did, but I bet the majority thought they would mean something more to you than a casual affair. As deluded as they were, I guarantee that they all thought they would be the one to change you.'

'To tie me down?'

Mark shook his head. 'No. To make you fall in love with them.'

'But you know as well as I do, nobody can make another person fall in love with them.'

'But isn't that what you've always tried to do? Isn't that why you continually pursue one woman after another? You want them to love you.

Just as I pursued drugs and alcohol with such conviction, so you have used women. I don't think it's labouring the point when I say you're probably addicted to the attention women give you.'

Even if Theo had got an answer for Mark's outrageous statement, which he hadn't, he was let off the hook by the appearance of Angelos, who had come to clean the pool and tend the garden.

Another time.

14

Until now Max had been listening to Laura and Izzy's conversation with only half an ear, but something in their tone diverted his attention from his breakfast-time reading of the latest exploits of the old-enough-to-know-better woman and her schoolboy lover. The story, though no longer front-page news, was maintaining a good head of steam. Apparently they were still on the run, their whereabouts a mystery, but they were popping up everywhere: there had been sightings of them in Taunton, Hull, Dublin and the Algarve.

'But why, Izzy? Why did you say no to him?'

Lowering his paper and glancing at his wife's face, Max thought he detected more than just mild disbelief in her expression. 'Well, if anyone's interested in my opinion,' he said, 'as fond as I am of Theo, I think it serves the cocky devil right. It's about time somebody gave him a metaphorical knee in the groin. Well done, Izzy. Good for you.'

'You're only saying that because you're jealous,' said Laura, giving him a look he couldn't quite fathom.

'Jealous, my little honey-pie?' he responded, trying to share a conspiratorial wink with Izzy, but failing miserably. Her eyes were on Laura. 'Of what precisely?'

'Like most men, you're envious of one of your number who has a flair for—' She stopped short, as if thinking better of what she had been going to say.

'What flair would that be?' asked Izzy, her face like thunder. 'Would it by any chance have something to do with him thinking he has the ability to lead the stupidest of fools straight to his bed? And is that what you want for me? A one-night stand that leaves me feeling used and abused? Well, is it?'

'Of course not,' Laura said defensively, 'but you're deliberately and wildly distorting the situation.'

Max didn't consider himself the most observant or sensitive of men, but even he sensed the air of tension around the breakfast table. He had never seen Izzy look cross before. He had seen her miserable and upset, but never angry. Especially not towards Laura. Back at home when Laura and Francesca were having one of their occasional spats, he would leave them to it, retreating to the sanctuary of the office, but here escape wasn't going to be so easy. He folded his paper carefully, put it on the ground beside his chair and said, 'I know I'm a dull old fellow when it comes to finer feelings and sub-plots, but has something been going on of which I've been kept in ignorance? Or are you both having a bad bout of PMT?'

When Laura didn't respond, even after he had thrown in the patronising query about PMT – he had thought it might unite the women and consequently defuse the moment – his suspicions were aroused. There was more going on here than he had imagined. 'Laura, you haven't gone behind Izzy's back and tried to fix her up with Theo, have you? Not Theo. Not him of all men.'

Both Max and Izzy waited for Laura to deny the accusation.

But Laura didn't.

Which was proof enough to confirm her guilt.

'It's not as bad as you're making out,' she said. Her words were directed at Max but her eyes were on Izzy. 'Oh, come on, Izzy, we discussed it. We agreed it might be good for you. Just a bit of fun.'

'No, Laura, you took the line that it would be good for me. And had I known that you and Theo were already in cahoots planning my seduction I would never have listened to a word you had to say about him.'

'I thought it would give you a lift – you know, give you back some of your self-esteem.'

'Oh, well, that makes perfect sense. I see it all now. There I'd be, thinking how wonderful it was that Theo was paying me so much attention and I'd have you to thank for my self-esteem being so high it was in need of oxygen.' Her voice was tight with cynicism.

To his dismay, Max knew it was down to him to bring about a truce. He did it almost every day at work, bringing headstrong and opposing views to meet half-way to find a compromise, but caught between the woman he loved, who had obviously meddled too far, and a close friend who was giving out more distress signals than a sinking ship, he knew which of the two options he'd rather deal with. Emotions were best left to experts. 'I'm sure you meant well, Laura,' he said tactfully, 'but I really do think you should apologise to Izzy.'

All three sat in silence for some moments. Until, at last, Laura offered Izzy a hesitant, conciliatory smile. 'I'm sorry,' she said, 'truly I am. You know I wouldn't do anything to hurt you. Am I forgiven?'

Max turned to Izzy, willing her to accept the olive branch. And to add a note of reviving humour to the mood round the table, he said, 'Come on, Izzy, I know Laura was way off the mark with what she did, but let's face it, only a fool would take a man like Theo seriously.' As soon as the words were out, he realised it was the worst thing he could have said. He received a kick under the table from Laura and a look from Izzy of mingled fury and pain. Appalled at his clumsiness, he wished now that he'd not got involved.

Izzy could see his discomfort and knew that all she had to do to make everything right was swallow her pride and laugh the matter off. But she couldn't. She was too choked with anger – which was made all the worse by knowing that she had been in danger of taking Theo seriously. Of *wanting* to take him seriously.

Not trusting herself to speak, she stood up and left Laura and Max to finish breakfast on their own.

'Should I go after her and apologise?' she heard Max say, as she headed for the beach.

'No,' said Laura. 'Between us, I think we've both said and done enough. Let's give her space to cool off.'

By the time Izzy had stomped part-way down the steep hillside in the baking sun and had lingered awhile to take in the fragrant scent of pine on the air, her fury had begun to subside. She suspected that in such beautiful surroundings it would be difficult for anyone to maintain a bad mood for long. It was probably what made the Corfiots as warm and gregarious as they were. Life was too good to harbour a grudge for more than a couple of minutes. She pressed on down the path and along the beach, towards the rocky outcrop she had tried earlier to draw. She knew that, as a guest in somebody else's house, she was behaving atrociously. She also knew that she was far more angry with herself than she was with Max and Laura.

Only a fool would take a man like Theo seriously.

'Well, there's no bigger fool than Izzy Jordan,' she muttered. She threw herself on the hot white stones and sighed. Then did a double-take.

She wasn't alone. A man was sitting on one of the rocks a few yards from her. She had seen him here before, had noticed him from her balcony when she had been painting the bay. He was sideways on to her, and though she couldn't make out all of his face, she could see that his attention was held by a fishing-boat rising and falling on the swell of the incoming tide. He was very still, and had an absorbed, faraway look. He didn't look relaxed, though: his lean, rangy frame was taut, his back and shoulders slightly rounded, as if he were ready for flight, should the need arise. Suddenly she longed to have her sketchpad to hand. He had an interesting face, what she could see of it, with a side profile that was pale, angular, and caught in a frown of concentration. She could only see his left eye, but she liked the way it was narrowed against the sun, and the starburst of lines that creased his skin. He was clean-shaven, with fair hair long enough to be messed up by the warm sea breeze. Every now and then he pushed it out of his face with long fingers. The sleeves of his T-shirt, one slightly ripped under the armpit, flapped loosely in the wind and accentuated the thinness of his arms. Unlike Theo, he didn't look like a man who gave much thought to his appearance. She wondered who he was and which villa he was staying at. Was it possible that he was Theo's writer friend, Mark St James? He was about the right age.

Drawing her knees up to her chest and clasping her arms around them, she closed her eyes and concentrated her thoughts so that by the time she returned to the villa she would be able to commit him to paper.

Watching the men on the boat finish hauling in their bundles of yellow nets, metal weights banging on the side of the boat, shaking heads indicating their disappointment at catching only a couple of slippery grey squid, Mark was reminded of similar scenes he had witnessed back in Robin Hood's Bay when, at the end of the day, the fishermen brought home empty lobster pots.

As the boat puttered away, he turned his head towards the shore. He recognised Izzy instantly, and while her eyes were shut he took the opportunity to see what it was about her that had Theo so intrigued. Based on what he knew about Theo's taste in women, his conclusion was vague. It had to be her naturalness, he surmised, after he had taken in the slender figure dressed in khaki shorts and vest top; the long evenly tanned legs drawn up so that she was resting her chin on them, and the loose, dark-brown shoulder-length hair that was being tossed in the wind. She was what he called a low-maintenance girl and he found himself thinking that there was a comfortable haphazardness about her that he strongly approved of. And, with growing certainty, he decided that this was what appealed to Theo. He was captured by her lack of sophistication. She would make a change from the glamorous, hard-faced beauties he usually went in for.

He continued to watch her, struck by the odd pose she had adopted, and for such a length of time. With her eyes squeezed shut, it was as if she was concentrating hard on something. Maybe she was meditating.

He had been encouraged to have a go at meditation when he was in rehab, which he hadn't found easy, given that he had spent a lifetime running away from what went on in his disorderly brain – sitting in silence and trying to be at peace with a person who had scared the hell out of him ever since he could remember was not something to which he'd taken. Bones had suggested that perhaps he should forget whose head he was trying to get inside, and after whistling Carole King's 'You've Got A Friend', while unwrapping a Murraymint, the sly old devil had said, 'Think of somebody you admire. A friend, perhaps. A friend who has had a great influence on you.'

In other words, think of the man who cared enough to bring you here.

Irritating as the suggestion was, it had worked. By focusing on Theo and the reasons why they were friends, he had found himself dwelling less on the negative facets of his own life and more on the positive. It was a lesson in counting one's blessings.

Back in Durham, lying alongside Theo in the hospital after his parents had made their unexpected, futile visit, he had turned on Theo with a savagery that even now he was ashamed to recall. 'I suppose that was your bloody doing, was it? Had a word with somebody, did you? Flashed some cash to pull some strings?'

'But why would you not wish for your parents to know that you needed their help?' Theo had asked.

'Listen, pal, I don't need my parents' help. Got that? In fact, it's the last bloody thing I need. And I certainly don't need your interference. So butt out of my life or I'll finish off what those fools couldn't manage last night.'

Luckily for him, Theo had paid no attention to anything he said and when they were discharged from hospital Theo enlisted Mr and Mrs Vlamakis' help to take care of him. While Mark had no qualms in telling his own parents to shove off, he was not so rude as to treat Theo's parents in the same offhand manner. He realised quickly that he had no choice but to give in to their offers of help. They took one look at the room he was living in and whisked him away to stay in some five-star luxury accommodation: a recently restored town-house, which they had bought for Theo at the start of term. Only when Mr Vlamakis was convinced that his son and heir was going to survive his ordeal did he return to London, leaving his wife to fuss over her charges. And fuss she did.

'You might just as well give in gracefully,' Theo told him one evening, when his mother was in the kitchen preparing yet another meal of gigantic proportions to build up their strength. 'My mother will not rest until she has you fully recovered.'

It was during those weeks that Mark had grown grudgingly to like Theo. If nothing else, he had to admire him for his tenacity. It didn't matter how rude Mark was, Theo simply flung aside his insults with a single-minded determination that was unshakeable.

'Why are you doing this for me?' Mark asked him one night, when Theo's mother was on the phone to her husband giving him the latest update on Theo's progress – to their great relief, the cuts and bruises to his handsome face were relatively superficial and there would be no long-term scarring: the skull fracture was healing and prompt surgery had also ensured that his nose would eventually be as good as new.

'Because in spite of everything you do and say I find myself liking you.'

'Well, you shouldn't.'

'Why not?'

'I'll bring you bad luck.'

Theo had laughed. 'So far history has proved you wrong. Have you forgotten already that you saved my life? It was the greatest of luck for me that you were passing that night.'

From that day on, Theo swore that if ever Mark needed his help, it would be there for the asking. It was one of his typically over-the-top gestures but, all the same, it was a promise he more than lived up to. And although in theory he and Theo had cancelled the debt between them, Mark still felt that Theo was in credit. Anyone would have done what Mark had done, that cold wintry night in Durham, but not everybody would have had sufficient faith or patience to stand by Mark during the worst of his addiction days, then support him on the long, painful road to recovery.

Once again he turned his gaze back to the girl on the stones, and the thought occurred to him that if Theo was serious about this Izzy – and Mark had every reason to believe that he was, judging from his mood at breakfast – then maybe he could help. A few choice words from him and perhaps she would view Theo more favourably. He smiled to himself, thinking of the irony that he, of all people, should consider himself qualified to further Theo's love-life.

He was still mulling over this thought when he realised that the girl was on her feet and walking along the beach towards the path that would take her up the hillside. Well, if he had hoped to put a good word in on his friend's behalf, he had just lost his opportunity.

15

The following week slipped by in a languid haze of quiet inertia and as the month of July progressed, bringing the height of the holiday season ever nearer, there was an increase in visitors to the island. In Kassiópi, the shops and bars, the tavernas and apartments were steadily filling, adding an extra width to the smiles on the faces of their owners. Inland, the temperature continued to soar, but the wind that blew in across the water brought a refreshing coolness to Áyios Nikólaos. And this morning, as Izzy lay in bed watching the muslin drapes billowing gently at the open french windows, she thought she had seldom felt so happy or relaxed.

Even the ridiculous scene that had taken place last week with Max and Laura caused her only an occasional pang of guilt. When she had returned to the villa after calming down on the beach, she had found Laura on her own and apologised straight away. 'I'm sorry,' she had said. 'I behaved worse than a stroppy teenager. Forgive me, please?'

'I'm sorry too,' Laura had said. 'I shouldn't have been acting so deviously. Max has all but put me over his knee and smacked my bottom.'

'And don't think I wouldn't try it,' he had called from his den, where he was reading a roll of faxes that had come in that morning. Then he had poked his head out through the open window and said, 'I'm sorry too, Izzy, for shooting my big mouth off without first engaging my heat-fried brain.'

'Oh, stop being so nice the pair of you,' she had said, 'you're making me feel a hundred times worse, I'm shrivelling up with embarrassment.'

'Don't do that, there's little enough of you as it is. Now stop pestering me, I've got work to do, an honest crust to earn. Talking of which, we're out of bread. Any chance of you two making yourselves useful by going shopping?'

'Yes, O Master,' Laura had laughed, 'and when we get back shall we throw ourselves at your feet and worship you?'

'Now you're talking. By the way, ask Nicos if he's got any of that decent olive oil he keeps under the counter. Tell him he's not to palm us off with that overpriced stuff he sells to the tourists.'

'Anything else, O Bossy One?'

'Yes, you can take some travellers' cheques and change them. We're running low on cash.'

'He's missing work, bless him,' Laura had muttered to Izzy, with a smile, when Max had disappeared from view, 'feeling the need to assert himself.'

On the way up the hill to the supermarket, Izzy had tried to explain to

Laura why she had been so cross. 'It wasn't you I was angry with, it was me,' she had said, as they plodded breathlessly in the dry heat. 'I realised that I was stupidly following the same old route I've been down before. Needy old Izzy, so desperate for a bit of affection she was gullible enough to be flattered by a good-looking man and not care about the consequences. Honestly I could kick myself for my naïvety.'

'You don't think you're being too hard on yourself?' Laura said. 'After all, he was only inviting you to have dinner with him.'

'Oh, come on, men like Theo expect something in return, it's an unspoken agreement. They think they're on a promise.'

'Not necessarily. And anyway, it's down to you whether or not you go along with such an unspoken agreement.'

'But don't you see? That's the whole problem. I'd be taken in by him, wouldn't I? A few nice words, a kiss or two, and heaven only knows what I'd be getting myself into.'

'Well, let's forget about Theo and all his kind. We've got to decide what we're going to do with our time before the hordes arrive. I recommend a week of doing nothing because, believe me, when Francesca and Sally arrive along with Max's parents, it'll be a non-stop whirl of activity.'

The weather was so hot over the following days that they had given in to lethargy and lazed around the villa and the beach. Their only exercise, other than swimming, was their evening walk into Kassiópi where they had supper in the harbour. Sometimes they were too lazy to do even that and one of them would draw the short straw and drive. They didn't see anything of Theo. According to a message relayed by Sophia and Angelos, he had flown back to Athens on business leaving his house-guest to work in peace. 'You don't suppose we ought to see if he'd appreciate an evening's worth of company?' Max had asked hopefully. He was still anxious to meet the elusive Mark St James. 'It seems rude not to check on him, just to see if he's okay.'

But Laura had been firm. 'Sophia and Angelos are there every other day,' she said. 'If there was a problem they'd be on to it.'

'You don't think he would—'

Laura had sat on his lap, silenced him with a kiss, and told him to wait until Theo returned. 'If you're good I might invite them both for dinner when your parents and the girls are here. I'll even flirt outrageously with Theo to ensure he brings his friend with him. How does that sound?'

Max had kissed her back. 'Not too outrageously, I hope.'

Yawning now, and stretching her arms above her head, Izzy decided it was time to get up. Everyone was arriving today and she had promised to help Laura with some of the last-minute arrangements.

She found her friend in the kitchen, pouring olive oil over a large piece of meat. 'Lamb with rosemary and garlic,' she said, when she saw Izzy. 'I know it's a disgusting sight at this time of the day, but I thought I'd get it prepared now before it gets so hot that I won't feel like doing it. Just pass me that salt mill, will you?'

They worked together steadily for the next couple of hours. While Laura concentrated on the evening meal, Izzy got on with making a selection of scones and cakes.

'I know it's madness,' said Laura, as Izzy weighed out flour and sugar, 'but wherever they are in the world, Max's parents have to stop what they're doing and have afternoon tea. It's quite an obsession with them. Though I'm probably the nuttier one for pandering to them. After today I shan't go on spoiling them – they'll be on local cakes and pastries.'

Izzy had met Corky and Olivia Sinclair several times before and knew that they were a wonderful couple who enjoyed life to the full. Max joked that whenever they came to stay an air-raid warning had to be sounded so that anyone with a weak disposition could head for the hills.

'As you know, for a pair of septuagenarians they're extremely boisterous,' Laura said now, as she stood at the sink washing her hands. 'They'll be far more trouble than Francesca and Sally, and that's saying something.'

In the preceding days, there had been much talk of Nympho Sally, as Max called Francesca's friend, and Izzy had been told why he was so terrified of her. At a Christmas party last year, she hadn't realised that he was Francesca's father and had come on to him like a pouting, hip-wiggling Marilyn Monroe, dangling a piece of mistletoe in front of his nose and making a pass at him. Even when she had found out who he was, she hadn't seemed bothered. 'She wasn't the slightest bit embarrassed,' Max said.

'Unlike my poor innocent husband,' laughed Laura.

'And the worst of it was she wasn't drunk.'

'Weren't you a tiny bit flattered?'

'No, Izzy, I wasn't. Terrified, more like. So I'd appreciate it if you both promise not to leave me alone with her.'

'Oh, go on with you,' Laura teased, 'you're flattering yourself. She's got all those handsome waiters in Kassiópi to amuse her. You won't get a look in.'

'Thank God for that.'

'And let's not forget Theo,' Izzy had added. 'Sounds like she's bound to make a play for him. Perfect sugar-daddy material.'

Max had laughed heartily. 'A match made in heaven. Oh, thank you, Izzy, you've quite cheered me.'

But Laura had pulled a face at them. 'I think the pair of you are being quite unfair to Theo. He's nowhere near as bad as you're making him sound. I bet you any money you like that there's more to him than meets the eye.'

And now, as Izzy took the tray of scones out of the oven and slipped them on to a wire rack, she recalled that she, too, had thought the same when they were having lunch in Áyios Stéfanos. Well, maybe there were hidden depths to Theo, but one thing she was sure of: if there were any depths to explore it wouldn't be her who would risk getting the emotional bends from trying to fathom him out.

Max was the spitting image of his father, and seeing them together always amused Laura; it gave her a clear view of what her husband would be like in years to come. There were the obvious similarities between them: they were the same height, the same width – which naturally they disputed, each claiming the other had the larger paunch – and had the same hair colouring, with Max's nearly as white as his father's. But beyond that there was the same thoughtfulness for others, as well as a shared artless and self-deprecating humour, and neither was afraid to shoot straight from the hip. Corky was doing so now.

They were sitting outside in the shade on the terrace having tea, Francesca and Sally having gone down to the beach to make a start on their tans. 'You look as if you've gained some more weight,' Corky was saying to Max. 'Those shorts look a tad tight to me.' He was gloating with delight, having just boasted for the last ten minutes that he had lost half a stone. He gave his not-obviously depleted waistline a pat. 'You've been living too much of the high life,' he continued. 'It'll be your downfall, mark my words.'

'In your dreams, Dad,' said Max, while discreetly sucking in his stomach. 'Snake-hips Max is what Laura calls me, these days. Isn't that right, cupcake?'

She smiled back at him. 'Among other things, darling. More to eat, anyone?' She offered the last of the chocolate sponge cake Izzy had made that morning, there being nothing else left on the table: Corky and Olivia had all but licked the plates clean – goodness knows where they put it all. Or where they got their energy. They had only been here for a few hours but they had already devoured a hearty lunch, gone for a walk, unpacked their cases and stored them neatly under their beds. Laura felt drained of what little energy she had started out with. It was worse than having a houseful of teenagers. 'How about you, Olivia? Another slice of cake?'

She shook her head. 'I'd love another cup of tea, though. Any more in the pot?' Olivia could drink tea for England. There was nobody to touch her. She had even brought with her a supply of Twinings English Breakfast.

Izzy rose from the table. 'It won't be worth drinking now, I'll make you some fresh.'

'Oh, thanks, Izzy. Now what about you, Corky? Have you got room for another slice?'

Max's father looked longingly at the cake.

'Best to keep it all tidy,' he said. 'You can't keep food lying about in this heat.'

By the time Izzy had returned with a fresh pot of tea, every last crumb had gone and Corky and Olivia wanted to know the itinerary for the days ahead.

'I thought we could go over to the other side of the island tomorrow and show you Paleokastrítsa,' Laura said, thinking of the long climb up the hill to the monastery, hoping it might tire them out and make them want to have a day off to recover. The suggestion had Corky reaching for his guidebook. 'Here we are,' he said, flicking to the appropriate page. '"Paleokastrítsa,"' he read aloud, '"sixteen miles from Corfu Town and the island's most celebrated beauty spot."' He turned the book round and held it aloft so that everyone could see where they would be going. He pointed out the monastery perched high on the hill.

'Looks to me like a first-rate HT2 expedition,' Olivia said knowledgeably.

'Yes,' agreed Corky. 'Probably NS, as well.'

In response to Izzy's questioning look, Max explained. 'Hats, Trainers and two litres of water. It's how they grade their days out. They do this every holiday they go on.'

'And what's NS? No Smoking?'

'No,' laughed Corky. 'No Shorts. I bet the monastery will only let us chaps in if we're wearing regulation long trousers.'

'In that case, don't forget NC,' added Olivia.

'No Cameras?' suggested Izzy.

'Nice try,' said Corky, 'but it's No Cleavage.'

A sudden peal of laughter had them peering down into the bay towards the raft where Francesca and Sally were both sunbathing topless. Olivia smiled. 'The girls will have to cover up if they're going to come with us. Any more tea in that pot?'

Having offered again to make some more tea, Izzy stood at the kitchen window looking out at Max's parents on the veranda. They were older than her mother, yet seemed a generation younger. Not a word of complaint had passed their lips since they had arrived; not one fault had they found with their flight, their fellow passengers, the heat, or the peculiar Corfiot plumbing that necessitated separate arrangements for toilet paper. 'How quaint,' had been Olivia's remark when this had been explained to her. In comparison, Prudence Jordan would have been snorting her disapproval all the way back to the airport for the next flight home. What a difference there was between her mother and them. Taking life at face value, they threw themselves into it with enthusiasm, determined to enjoy themselves. Her poor mother was incapable of doing the same: she had never allowed herself the pleasure of being happy. And was that, perhaps, what Izzy would end up doing? Was she, like her mother, destined to be a lonely old woman because she was too frightened to let go and have a little fun? Was that why she had turned down Theo's dinner invitation? Scared that she might have been caught out enjoying herself?

No. That was nonsense. She had said no because she had seen straight through his wily charm. For once she had been sensible.

But wasn't sensible another word for boring?

She took the freshly made tea outside and saw that, down in the bay, Francesca and Sally were on their feet preparing to dive off the raft. Their happy shrieks as they jostled each other made her smile and think of the day she had learned to dive with Theo.

Further along the bay somebody else was watching Francesca and Sally. He had seen them earlier on the plane, then later at the carousel when they had been waiting for their luggage.

'How old do you reckon?' Nick Patterson said, over his shoulder to his brother.

Reluctantly, Harry looked up from the book he had started reading during the flight, Lawrence Durrell's *Prospero's Cell.* 'What're you on about now?'

Nick pointed down the hillside, towards the beach. 'I asked how old you thought they were.'

Harry pushed his glasses up on to his nose, and after a few seconds, said, 'Same as us, probably. Maybe a bit older. It's hard to tell at this distance. You know I'm no expert.'

'Older isn't good. Older is seriously bad news. The chicks don't go for younger. Well, not at this age they don't.'

Calling them chicks wouldn't help either, thought Harry. 'Then give it up as a bad job before you waste any more time on them.'

'No way. If we're going to be stuck here playing Happy bloody Families while Mum and Dad go through a traveller's pack version of their mid-life crisis routine, then I might just as well have something to do.'

Harry returned his attention to his book. He didn't want to think about his parents. And certainly not his father. As a young child he had longed to have a father who was normal, in the sense of having a regular job sitting behind a desk bossing others about and coming home late to eat his supper while watching the television and occasionally complaining that his sons played their music too loud. Instead, he had been lumbered with a pseudo-Bohemian who had been going through an extended state of middle-aged neurosis since, well ... probably since the age of five. Not a day went by when his father wasn't consumed with some personal or professional disaster. Nobody else was allowed to have problems of their own as he veered from one drama to the next: of losing his hair, what there was of it; of suspecting he had some unmentionable disease of the prostate; of living in fear that he was being talked about, countered by an even greater fear that he wasn't being talked about.

He worked in the film industry, and when he told people this, he made it sound as though he and Steven Spielberg were best mates and constantly on the phone to each other. He had done it to Nick and Harry's friends, years ago, trying to impress them with his stories of whom he had recently rubbed shoulders with – a euphemism for standing in the queue in the canteen and watching Michael Parkinson help himself to a plate of steak and kidney pudding. But that was in the days of his career with the BBC, before he had suffered the ignominy of being made redundant. Now he worked for an independent film company that put together small-budget documentaries. His last project had recently gone out on Channel Four and was yet another example of his late-night shock-and-titillate explorations of the human mind and body. As Nick often said, 'Oh, man, it's okay to be obsessed with sex when you're in your prime, but it's sick to see your ageing hippie father parading his hang-ups on telly.'

Their mother rarely watched his programmes but, then, she was seldom at home – there was always some committee or cause she felt compelled to support. When the first episode of *Sexual Rites of Passage* had been due to go out last month, his father had approached her and asked her if she would watch it because he would appreciate her opinion. She had glared at him and said, 'You really want my honest view on why, yet again, you're pedalling pornography, Adrian? Well, in my opinion, you need help. The sooner the better. Was there anything else?'

Between them, Harry's parents took up far too much space in his life. He was still cross with them, and himself, that he had agreed to come on this holiday. With the end of his third year at college drawing to a close, he and his friends had decided to go backpacking in Turkey – it was to have been their last fling before finals next year. His father had put paid to that by whingeing on at him that this would probably be their last family holiday and Harry had stupidly given in.

'Fancy a swim?' asked Nick.

Knowing that he wouldn't get any peace unless he did, he said, 'Oh, go on, then.'

Francesca and Sally might have given the impression that they hadn't noticed Nick and Harry at the airport but, like any girls their age, their testosterone antennae had been picking up signals loud and clear. They weren't entirely impressed with what was coming their way on the beach, but were prepared to reserve judgement for now.

'How old do you reckon?' asked Sally, swimming over to Francesca.

'Too young for you.'

'I could make an exception.'

'Oh, yes? Which one of them has caught your eye?'

'The tall dark-haired one with glasses. He looks as if butter wouldn't melt.'

Francesca laughed. 'Yeah, and you'd like to be the one to prove otherwise. So you're leaving me the small funky one, are you?'

'Well, the Jamiroquai look is more your bag, isn't it? And the hair of the dog might make you feel better.'

'He looks nothing like Carl. Carl never wore his hair in pigtails.'

'Oh, who cares? It's a generic look. Shall we stick around to find out what they're like?'

'Nah, there's plenty of time for that. For now let's play hard to get. On the count of three we make for the shore and sashay our way back up to the villa.'

16

Theo returned to Áyios Nikólaos late that evening. Mercifully, there had been no delay to the short flight from Athens, and the drive along the winding coast road from the airport had been a clear run. He felt tired but elated as he approached the rutted track that led to his villa. He had got exactly what he had wanted from his week in Athens, and had outwitted two of his arch business rivals. There was nothing to beat the thrill of a chase that culminated in a successfully clinched deal. He knew that the day when he no longer experienced the same level of excitement would be the day he retired gracefully. But that was a long way off. For now, his hunger was as keen as ever. As was his golden touch. A Midas touch that Mark used to say would be his undoing. But Mark didn't know the half of his success. Few people did. He kept the extent of his wealth between himself and the handful of lawyers and accountants he had known for many years and whom he trusted implicitly. Mark didn't know – any more than the financial pundits in Athens who liked to keep abreast of his affairs – about the portfolio of stocks and shares he had steadily accrued, or the many companies he controlled.

But for all Mark liked to criticise him – 'You're a flash show-off with more money than sense' – Theo was a modest man. While it was true that he had always appreciated the good things money could provide, he now favoured a simpler approach to life, which was why he had made his first real home here in Áyios Nikólaos. Much as he enjoyed Athens, with all its thrusting energy, it gave him no real sense of belonging. It was clear to him that Athens was where he worked, and Corfu was where he lived, where he could be himself.

After he had showered and changed, he found Mark in the kitchen cooking supper.

'Don't go getting the wrong idea about this,' Mark said, as he slipped a cheese and herb omelette on to a plate and passed it to Theo, 'I'm only playing at doting housewife just this once. Wine?'

They ate outside. The evening was very still, with only the faintest of breezes to rustle the leaves on the nearby eucalyptus trees and stir up the scent of basil from one of the pots on the terrace. Though it was dark, it was still warm and the balmy night sky flickered with bats as they swooped and circled overhead. Attracted by the candles on the table, a broad-winged moth was risking its short life by fluttering around the flames, and below them in the bay an incoming tide quietly washed the arc of stones. This is undeniably my home, thought Theo, with contentment, as he stared out at the inky water and the moon streaking its shimmering silvery light across the surface.

'You have had a good week?' he asked Mark, breaking the comfortable silence between them. 'The writing went well?'

'Not bad. How about you? Made yourself another bag of gold?'

'Several,' he said noncommittally, keeping to himself that he would sell on the decrepit office block he had just acquired for a handsome profit after he had had it restored and refurbished into luxurious apartments. 'And were you left alone,' he asked Mark, 'or did the determined Dolly-Babe pay a call as she threatened?'

'Thankfully I've seen no one, other than Angelos and Sophia, and Nicos up at the shop. It's been very quiet. Just how I like it. Though I did have a call from my publisher or, more accurately, the fool of a new publicist who's been appointed to take care of me.'

Theo tried to keep the smile from his face. He knew of old what a lousy self-promoter Mark was, and how he despised anyone else's attempts to do it for him. 'And what did that poor lamb to the slaughter want of you?'

'Oh, the usual, a bit more of my soul.'

'Any bit in particular?'

'Yes, the part I'd rather keep to myself.'

'Ah, I see it all. They want you to agree to be interviewed, is that it?' Theo still had the video tape of one of Mark's rare TV appearances in which he had presented the inexperienced interviewer with, possibly, her worst moment. She had innocently asked him if he ever thought he would get married again, only to have flung back at her, 'That's none of your goddamn business!'

Mark nodded. 'Yeah, it's a familiar tale – sell the personal story to sell the book. Sod the product, let's hit 'em with brand definition. And while they're doing that they'll turn me into some kind of bloody media tart.'

'What did you tell them?'

'What do you think?'

'I should imagine that the line was sizzling with your hot-tempered response.'

Running his fingers through his hair, then leaning forward to flick them at the moth, Mark took a moment to think about what Theo had just said. His response had, indeed, been hot-tempered, and had resulted in a stunned silence from the girl. She hadn't known what to say in the face of his adamant refusal to be swept along with her plans for hyping his book.

'You've had such an interesting and colourful life,' she had twittered. 'It would be a fabulous hook on which to hang the publicity campaign.'

An interesting and colourful life.

Hell on wheels!

Was the whole nightmare experience that he had lived through, and been lucky to survive, to be labelled as nothing more than an *interesting and colourful* episode?

Well, they could all go to hell. Goddamnit, the books had sold well in the past without him having to prostitute himself, which meant there was no good reason why he should have to start doing so now.

It was at times like this that he regretted ever writing under the name Mark St James. With hindsight he should have used a pseudonym and kept his anonymity, but in the early days of his recovery he had needed to reaffirm who he really was. It had been a mistake. He had realised that as soon as his private life suddenly became public property. With the overnight success of his first book, which went straight into the bestseller lists – in the UK, the States and Germany – and was then televised, press interviews had been expected of him. Once it was known that he had been an alcoholic and substance abuser, journalists only wanted to know how many bottles of vodka he had got through a day, or how much his cocaine habit had cost him. That it had very nearly cost him his life was of no real significance to them. He was a story in himself. He was a ready-made package of saleable interest.

When he had finished his third novel he stopped playing ball. He gave them the finger and retreated behind a wall of silence. No more interviews. No more days-of-hell-and-road-to-recovery stories. He had had enough. Disappointed, his publishers had had to find a new way to promote him. Working off the slipstream of his previous bestsellers, they came up with the Enigmatic Reclusive Mark St James, an angle, cloying as it was, that had worked just fine.

Until now, when some slip of a girl had proposed to resurrect the old approach. 'I've been going through the press cuttings from way back,' she'd said, 'and it strikes me that you never once told anyone why you'd been an alcoholic. And I'm wondering if this isn't a line we could follow now. What do you think?'

Struggling to control his anger, he had said, 'I think you're wasting your time as well as mine. The answer's no. Goodbye.'

For all that, she had hit on a point that many before her had missed. Or perhaps they had deliberately overlooked it. The reason behind another person's misery is usually so uninteresting that it's invariably pushed aside. People only want to know about the seedy details of an addict's decline into the underworld, to know just how low someone could fall, smug in the knowledge that it could never be them. Addiction is always somebody else's problem, somebody else's destructive weakness. There are those who slip into it without realising and others, like him, who throw themselves in head first, wanting to drown in the bittersweet nirvana it offers.

Seeing that Theo was watching him and waiting for him to speak, he said, 'I probably wasn't as polite as I should have been, but I needed to make her understand that I have no intention of doing any more interviews. Besides, you know as well as I do, you live and die by the stuff you're reported to have said.'

Pouring more wine into his glass, Theo said, 'Please, Mark, this is me you are talking to. You do not have to justify yourself with simple old Theo. I know better than anyone that you see yourself as an artist and not a performing dog. Perish the thought that anyone would ever confuse the two with you.'

'Bastard! Now you're just trying to make me sound pretentious.'

Theo smiled. 'And with so little effort.'

'Can I help it that I don't have anything of great worth to say? If I thought I had some deep emotional philosophy to pass on to mankind, then I'd be the first to pontificate.'

'But that's just the point. You do have something worthwhile to say. Your books are full of dire warnings of man's failings.'

'Now who's sounding pretentious?'

The next day, and with Albania lost behind early-morning cloud, Theo went for a swim in the sea. Floating on his back he glanced up the hillside and saw Laura staring down at him. He waved and gestured for her to join him. Within minutes she was on the beach and easing herself into the cool, refreshing water.

'We got your message from Angelos,' she said, swimming out to him. 'How was Athens?'

'Hotter than the devil's breath, though slightly more fragrant. But only just. I hear from Mark, who has been my ears and eyes in my absence, that you have guests. Does that mean you and Max are too busy to join me for dinner tonight?'

She groaned. 'By this afternoon I'll be fit for bed and little else.'

He raised an eyebrow. 'Really, Laura, you must stop putting such outrageous thoughts into my head.'

She splashed water at him. 'I meant that I'll be too tired for anything other than sleep. We've got Max's parents here, along with Francesca and her friend Sally.'

'Aha, yes, I recall now. Sally is the girl Max was so keen to see again. Is she behaving herself?'

'More or less. Two lads arrived on the same plane as they did yesterday – they're staying in the house over there.' She pointed in the direction of the faded pink villa further along the bay. 'I think she and Francesca are waiting to see what they have to offer. If anything.'

There was a pause, but not an insignificant one.

'And how is Izzy?'

'She's very well.'

They swam out towards the raft and climbed up on to it. Keeping his voice as neutral as he could, as he stared up at the soft blue sky, Theo said, 'Tell me, Laura, has Izzy spoken to you about me?'

Squeezing the water out of her hair, Laura said, 'Why? Should she have?'

He kept his face turned upwards. 'I think that just before I went away I might have inadvertently upset her. Did she mention it to you? Only I would hate to be responsible for annoying the sweet girl.'

There was another pause while Laura thought what to say. She had already run into trouble with Izzy over discussing her with Theo and she was reluctant to upset her friend again, but seeing the amount of effort that Theo was putting into his apparently casual interest in Izzy's welfare, she decided it wouldn't do any harm for him to be told the truth. Perhaps he was being serious for once.

'So what you are saying,' he said, when she had finished, 'is that I reminded her of this dreadful Alan?'

'That's about the height of it. You must have come on too strong with her. But why the concern, Theo? This can't be the first time you've upset a member of the opposite sex. Or is it just that you can't cope with being turned down?'

Laura's words were uncomfortably similar to those that Mark had uttered a short while ago and Theo didn't like the sound of them. Why was it that everyone made such unjust assumptions about him? Would it shock them to know that he, too, had feelings? That he could genuinely feel something for a woman? Mark had accused him of using women to fill a void, which Theo had wanted to refute vigorously at the time, but last week when he was lying in bed with one of his more regular companions – a woman he knew to be actively seeking a ring for her finger – he had pondered on Mark's theory and had not liked the conclusion he had reached.

Without answering Laura's question, he touched her shoulder lightly and said, 'Come, despite the early hour of the day, you are already turning pink in the sun. It's time to swim back to the beach and return you safely to Max.'

When they reached the shore, Laura said, 'We're all off to Paleokastrítsa for the day, but why don't you join us for a drink tonight? Bring your friend, Mark, if he'll come. You know how anxious Max is to meet him.'

'Thank you, that would be nice. *Ti óra?*'

Laura smiled, took a moment to think, and counted on her fingers. '*Enyá i óra.*'

'Bravo! Nine o'clock it is, then. Have fun today in Paleokastrítsa. Take care in the sun, though – it is going to be very hot, I fear.'

17

Theo was right. The day was proving to be one of the hottest of the summer so far, and Paleokastrítsa had been awarded a rating of HT4 – Hats, Trainers and four litres of water. 'A cracking-the-flagstones scorcher of a day,' Corky had called it, as the sun blazed down on them. However, while Laura was finding that the heat was getting to her, Max's parents were showing no sign of tiring. They had led the way in hiring a boat to explore the small coves and grottoes; they had swum in water the colour of pure turquoise; they had skipped like mountain goats up the steep path to the monastery; they had rattled off several rolls of film and bought a dozen or so postcards. And now, as Laura lay dozing on the crowded beach in the shade of an umbrella, they were off with Max inspecting the local shops. She turned to Izzy and said, 'You see what I mean about Corky and Olivia? They're exhausting, aren't they?'

'I think they're wonderful.'

'Oh, they're wonderful, all right, and I love them to pieces. It's just that I wish I had half their energy. They make me feel so inadequate when they're around. All I feel good for is a long, long sleep. I should have done what the girls opted to do – stayed at home and relaxed.'

Izzy laughed. 'I'm not sure that relaxing was entirely what Francesca and Sally had on their minds.' Sitting on her balcony first thing that morning, she had heard them in the room next to hers discussing their plans for the day. It seemed to involve an awful lot of hard work, namely being as visible as they could manage, yet maintaining an air of distant allure. Izzy hadn't yet seen the two young men whose presence in the bay warranted such meticulous scheming, but Olivia had mentioned them yesterday afternoon when the girls had come up to the house after their swim and declared them both to be of above-average appearance. 'Aren't they the two good-looking boys who were on the plane with us?' she had asked her granddaughter, as the girls stood staring down on to the beach. 'It might be nice for you to get to know one another.' Francesca's casual, 'Mm . . . were they on the plane with us? I don't recall,' had amused Izzy and she had been tempted to tiptoe across the veranda and take a peek at them.

A yawn from Laura prompted her to say, 'What you need is an early night.'

'Chance would be a fine thing,' said Laura. 'Just as well Theo and Mark are joining us this evening. At least Max's parents won't be able to get the cards out and keep us up into the wee small hours.'

'They're not into bridge, are they?' asked Izzy, with a sinking heart. It was one of those games that terrified her. Alan and his parents had played it. They would sit around the little felt-topped card table and stare at one another in deadly combative silence, which in turn made her uptight and nervous and caused her mind to wander from her cards. It had to be the most boring pastime ever invented.

'Bridge? Good Lord, no,' said Laura. 'Canasta's their game. I'll warn you now, though, they like nothing more than a convert, and once they've roped you in you'll never be the same again. They'll fill you up with wine and thrash you senseless. You won't see your bed before three in the morning. Some of the worst hangovers Max and I have ever had have been inflicted on us by his own parents at one of their curry-and-Canasta evenings.'

Izzy thought it sounded a lot more fun than bridge. She closed her eyes and sank into a happy state of pre-sleep contentment. She listened to what was going on around her on the crowded beach: the crying of a small fractious child; the bickering of a couple with a strong Brummy accent, each blaming the other for having forgotten to pack the camera; the insistent voice of a German, who was reading aloud from his newspaper; and the flirtatious laughter of a group of young Italian girls, who were as stunningly pretty as they were vain.

Having spent so much time in the quiet seclusion of Áyios Nikólaos, the brash commercialism of Paleokastrítsa had come as something of a culture shock. Despite the warnings in the guidebooks that the area was one of the island's top tourist attractions, nothing had prepared Izzy for the sight that had met them after they had driven through the twisting, rural landscape and arrived to find hundreds of people spilling out of rows of coaches and all dashing for the sun-loungers and fringed umbrellas on the beach. For all that, though, the resort was breathtakingly beautiful, with its unbelievably clear water and dramatic cliffs, and Izzy was glad she had tagged along for the day. Thinking that Max and Laura might prefer to spend a day alone with his parents, she had mentioned to them last night that she would stay behind, but they would have none of it. 'For heaven's sake, stop being so considerate,' Laura had said.

'Quite right,' Max had agreed. 'You're not an optional extra, Izzy, you're here on holiday with us, so you can jolly well pull your weight when it comes to joining in with the fun. There'll be no slacking from anybody.'

It was a funny phrase to use – *optional extra* – but it came close to how, as a child, Izzy had sometimes seen herself. Though a more precise analogy was that she had viewed herself as one of those free gifts in the cereal packet: something that nobody needed.

She couldn't be the first person who had grown up knowing that her birth had not been a much longed-for event. There had certainly been no planning for hers, no sense of joyful anticipation. But how could there have been, when her mother had been through the process once before, pinning all her happiness and expectations on a tiny boy who had died within days of his arrival in the world?

Without him knowing it, that child's whole life had been mapped out for him in his mother's mind. He would have been perfect in every way; the gifted son every parent would have wanted. Clever. Handsome. Kind. Loving. Musical. Artistic. Nothing would have been beyond his capabilities. He would have excelled at school, college, and in his career. And it would have been no ordinary career. He would have been dynamic. A key player. A man to be admired.

Izzy knew all this because her mother had raised her on a daily diet of everything her dead brother would have been. No one else would listen. No one cared enough. Izzy had taken it upon herself to be her mother's audience and had listened attentively, as if her life depended on it.

It was an unworthy thought, but she believed that John Richard Jordan had been fortunate not to survive. He had got off lightly. How could he have hoped ever to live up to his mother's expectations?

No expectations had been laid down for Izzy when, five years later, she had been born. From an early age she heard her mother arguing with her father, blaming him for whatever trouble Izzy had caused that day, blaming him for her very existence.

One of her earliest memories was of feeling sorry for her father. How awful it must be for him, she had thought, watching his sad face as he sat reading a book. From then on she had tried hard to please her mother, always to keep on her good side. Because if she could do that, she told herself, her father wouldn't be blamed and he might smile at her. With steadfast determination she learned where it was safe to tread, and where the landmines of her mother's black moods were hidden. She learned the importance of being invisible and when to hide from her mother when she was in the throes of one of her terrifying rages, which came from nowhere but always had to run its course.

It was such a strain and it made her an uneasy child, never comfortable with herself – or with anyone else, for that matter. She was quick to make mistakes and quicker still to be flustered over the slightest things. She was accident-prone too, which only added to her mother's frustration. She tried to be careful – to pick up her feet, to watch where she was going, to hold the glass properly, not to bang the door shut – but it rarely worked and a stinging hand would catch her on the back of her head, making her eyes feel loose and her ears ring. Often she would go to school with vivid bruises on her arms and legs and had to pretend to anyone who asked that she had tripped and fallen over in the garden.

She had assumed, in the way that children do with their trusting, unquestioning acceptance, that whatever went on at home was normal, that all children had to dodge blows. Didn't all mothers scream at their daughters that they hated them, that they wished they were dead? It never occurred to her that it could be different. Not until it was too late, when shame kept her mouth shut, preventing any words of disloyalty slipping out.

She had never forgotten the day she broke one of her mother's statues. Or its consequences. She was helping to clear away the breakfast things when she accidentally knocked a tight-lipped lady in a rose-pink crinoline dress off the draining-board where, along with her silent partners, she was waiting to be dusted. Only five years old, Izzy knew she was in trouble. She had stared down at her feet, at the pieces of china on the grey-tiled floor, then slowly, holding her breath, she had found the courage to raise her eyes to her mother's face. For the longest of moments their eyes had met and held. Then hands reached out to her, and the room began to move, the walls bending like those weird mirrors at the funfair.

She was being shaken.

Up and down, backwards and forwards, her head snapping painfully on her neck.

Then she was spinning, round and round.

Everything was moving.

The kitchen clock whizzed by.

Followed by the cooker.

Then the big cupboard where they kept their coats and shoes, the carpet-sweeper with the little swirly brushes that stuck out at the front and back.

She saw the table she had been helping to clear: the plates; the bowls; the packet of cornflakes; the metal teapot, and the little milk jug. But it was all moving so fast, their shapes and colours blurred in a whirlpool of surreal confusion, just like in *The Wizard of Oz.*

Faster and faster the room went.

She felt hot.

Clammy.

Dizzy.

And frightened that she was going to be sick.

Her legs felt loose as they dangled beneath her. One of her slippers flew off. Her teeth were clattering inside her head. Her ribs were hurting, something was crushing them. She wanted to scream but she could hardly breathe. She closed her eyes, wanting it to stop. Then suddenly there was a crash and a thud that hurt more than anything else had. But at last it had stopped. The room was still.

When she opened her eyes nothing made sense. Everything was a mess. Her mother was on her knees, surrounded by upturned chairs, bits of broken china and glass. She was crying. Her father was there. And he was shouting. She had never heard him shout before. It scared her more than all the blood that was coming from her head. Frightened, she began to cry. 'I'm sorry,' she sobbed, when she felt her father's arms around her, 'I didn't mean to do it.'

18

It was a poor excuse he had given, and not for one moment did Mark think Theo had been taken in by his claim that he needed to work that evening. Besides, his friend understood well enough that a neighbourly drinks get-together was never going to be high on his list of hot options. So, having passed up the opportunity to spend an evening dodging a zealous hostess with an overflowing drinks tray, he was going for a quiet walk around Kassiópi to explore the harbour.

He set off shortly after Theo had left for next door. The day he had arrived, Theo had shown Mark a footpath situated just yards from the end of his oleander-lined drive. It went through the nearby olive grove and, according to his friend, was a handy short-cut into Kassiópi. He followed the stony, uneven path for a while then remembered with annoyance that Theo had said it was advisable to take a torch when using this route late at night. It was light now, but give it a couple of hours and it would probably be pitch black. Well, he could either risk it or come back the long way via the road, though even then he would have the last hundred yards of ankle-turning potholed track to negotiate in the darkness. Despite his misgivings he pressed on, the parched grass swishing at the bottoms of his jeans, the low branches of the olive trees nearly catching his head, and the cool evening air rich with the scent of wild garlic and thyme.

The rock-studded path rose steeply, deceptively so, until finally it flattened out and he came to a clearing. He paused to catch his breath, and cursed himself for his lack of fitness. Then he heard something move behind him. He stiffened. He turned slowly. Nothing. He let out his breath, swallowed the lump of fear that had lodged in his throat, then pushed a hand through his hair. Just as he had convinced himself he had imagined it, he caught a faint rustle of something – *someone* – moving in the dried tangle of undergrowth. A rush of adrenaline surged through his blood-stream and he clenched his fists.

Then he saw it.

Relief made him laugh out loud. 'Jeez, a bloody tortoise!' He went over to take a closer look. 'Well, I was pretty sure this wasn't bandit country,' he said, bending down to inspect the scaly expressionless face. Beady eyes peered back at him, then the long neck, face and curved stumpy legs withdrew into the safety of the shell. 'Don't blame you, mate,' said Mark, straightening up. 'I know the feeling.'

He had only been walking a short while when a dog leaped up against a fence and barked at him. Once again the suddenness made him start. Not only am I the most unfit man who ever lived, he thought angrily, I'm probably the most neurotic. His annoyance stayed with him as he walked on. How long was it going to take him to lose this irrational fear and realise that he was quite safe? There was no way that the nutter who had been sending him those letters back in England could be stalking him here. Nobody, other than his agent, publishers and family knew he was here.

Rule number one, he told himself firmly, going over familiar ground, don't let it get to you. It's what goes on inside your head that causes all the damage. It's what all stalkers set out to do. They want their victim to become as obsessed with them as they are with you.

But it didn't matter how many times he repeated this calming mantra to himself, or reminded himself that he had written an entire novel based on the theory of what goes on in a stalker's mind, he couldn't shake off the anger that this unknown man – and, yes, he was sure it was a man – had the power to invade his life in the way he had. That even here, thousands of miles from home, his pernicious presence could still get to Mark.

Back in England Mark had got used to looking over his shoulder: it had become part of his routine. It had turned a walk up the hill to the post office into a bizarre parody of Cold War espionage. Locking his door, he would glance right, then left, walk a little distance, then stop to retie a shoelace, or maybe pause in front of the gift shop to take a furtive look around him. But it was always the same; the only person acting strangely was himself. Paranoid was not a word he wanted to start using about his behaviour – it reminded him of his cokehead days – but it was there waiting in the wings of his mind.

By the time he reached Kassiópi, he had calmed down and was looking forward to sitting in a bar with a cup of coffee and watching the world go by. It was busier than he had expected, and as he walked along the main street, lost in the crowd of suntanned tourists looking for somewhere to eat, he took pleasure from knowing that he was just another anonymous face in the crowd. He chose what appeared to be the busiest bar and a table close to the road, which gave him the best vantage-point to see everything that was going on.

Across the road was a small square, occupied mostly by the village elders. Sitting on green wrought-iron seats, chatting and smoking, their lives seemed untouched by the noisy, incongruous mix of people around them. No doubt they had seen it all before: the young British men with their cropped hair, earrings and tattoos; the Scandinavian contingent marked out by their startlingly blond hair, long legs and enormous feet in Ellesse flip-flops; and the girls, of whatever nationality, wearing more makeup than clothing. It was probably a safe bet to say that nothing surprised these local folk any more.

A waiter took Mark's order and brought it to him with smooth efficiency. To his shame, and even after such a long-standing friendship with Theo, 'Éna kafé parakaló,' was just about the extent of Mark's Greek. At college he had secretly envied Theo's effortless ability to switch between English, German, Italian and Greek. Not that he had ever said as much. In those days he could never have openly admitted that Theo, or anyone else, was better at something than him. But age and experience had mellowed him and now he had no trouble in giving Theo the credit he deserved. But, then, he had always known that Theo was a far better man than he was or ever could be. He had hinted as much to Bones, during one of their spilling-the-guts-of-his-deepest-and-innermost-feelings sessions. 'And is that something you wish you could be?' had been Bones's measured response.

'What are you getting at now?'

'I was asking if it was important to you to feel that you were Theo's equal. Or, indeed, anybody's equal. Because you don't, do you, Mark? Beneath the outward show of swaggering arrogance and conceit that has taken everybody else in, you know that it's all a lie. You're convinced that you're nobody's equal. Am I right?'

'Equality is something we have to strive for.'

'Is it? How strange. I thought we were put on this earth with nothing but our circumstances dividing us from others. So what is it about Theo that makes you think he's more special than you are? I recall only a few weeks ago, when he brought you here, you were claiming he was nothing short of . . .' he lowered his eyes to the notes he had made in his file '. . . ah, yes. "An effing devil in cashmere" is what you called him. My, how quickly your opinion has changed.'

Bones's pathetic attempt at irony had provoked a smile from Mark. But not an answer. Which was a mistake. Up until then, and in the manner of a predatory cat chasing a frightened mouse, Bones had been playing with him. Now, in the silence that had fallen between them, he went in for the kill.

'So, tell me more about the boating accident,' he said. 'Yesterday you told me about your friend dying, but now I want you to go further. When you knew your friend was drowning and you couldn't reach him, what did you feel?'

'I was a twelve-year-old boy. What the hell do you think I felt?'

'I don't know, Mark, I wasn't there.'

'Then use your imagination.'

'Mark, listen to me, you will only discover your true worth when you are brave enough to let someone help you confront the repressed memories of that tragic day.'

'They're not repressed. They're there all the time. Every day. Every night.'

'I'm sure they are, but you're not facing them. You're just cramming the lid down on them, keeping them at bay. And how much more strength will it take, do you think, to keep that lid down?'

But Bones was asking too much of him. In response, his body betrayed him: his skin crawled, and then his scalp pricked painfully. And, though the room was cool – Bones always insisted on having the window open – he felt sickeningly hot. His nerves were raw. He clenched his fists, knowing that if he didn't, the trembling would kick in. Then came the final betrayal. The reassuring voice that told him a drink would help him through it. A comforting glass of whisky. Or vodka. Or anything. The whispering grew louder. And louder still until it was a roaring, insistent demand inside his head. *Get me a drink!*

He tried to think of what Bones had told him to do when this happened: to think of his own strength overcoming the power of the fear that made him want to drink. 'Always remember,' Bones had said, 'it's not the drink you have to resist, but the giving in to the fear of the past.'

Bones must have known what was going on in his mind, for he said, 'Come and stand at the window with me, Mark. There's something I want to show you.'

Surprised by his own obedience, he struggled to his feet. He knew it was a diverting technique, but he was beyond caring. He leaned against the window-ledge for support, briefly closed his eyes, and breathed in the fresh morning air, taking great gulps of it as though trying to cheat his body with a fix of oxygen rather than alcohol. Beside him Bones rattled on about the amazing view, about the prettiness of the steeple on the nearby church and how it had been saved in the early eighties from toppling over. 'Nobody believed it could be saved,' he said, going back to his desk. 'Everyone said it would have to be pulled down, but there it is, as beautiful, as perfect as the day it was built. Just goes to show, doesn't it?'

Thumping his fists on the window-ledge, Mark shouted, 'Enough! I get the analogy.'

'Good. So let's recap. Niall was your best friend and you were on holiday together.'

He sighed, knowing there was no escape. If he was ever going to be truly exorcised and free of the constant shadow-boxing with the memory of Niall's death, he would have to put himself through this. Very slowly, still fighting the need in his body for a drink, he took up the story. He and Niall had been on a school camping holiday. They should have been joining in with a table-tennis tournament with another school party also staying at the outward-bound centre, but neither had fancied it. At Mark's suggestion they sneaked down to the small marina with something more exciting in mind. It was usually Mark's idea that they do something they weren't supposed to do, which had repeatedly brought his parents into conflict with Niall's. Mr and Mrs Percival didn't approve of Mark: they claimed he was a bad influence on their only son, leading him astray and encouraging him to do things he wouldn't otherwise have dreamed of doing. But the disapproval went deeper than that: not to put too fine a point on it, the St James family was loaded, and Niall's was not. It didn't help either that Mr Percival worked for Mark's father. At that age, the two boys could see no problem with this, but Niall's parents saw the disparity in their lifestyles as divisive and a blatant reminder of everything they couldn't offer their son.

But this supposed disparity between Mark and Niall was the last thing on their minds that day as they knelt on the wooden pontoon untying one of the dinghies. They were both foolish enough to think that, after three lessons, they could handle a boat, especially one as small as this.

Slipping away unseen, they congratulated themselves on their smartness. The wind was strong and it wasn't long before they had skittered out to sea, far away from the sailing centre. What they didn't know was that they were heading straight towards a squall, a brief localised storm. The first they knew about it was a mass of low-lying clouds, black and threatening, rolling towards them. Then the rain started, heavy drops that splattered against their faces. They began to wonder if they had been so smart after all. But as quickly as the clouds had appeared, they passed over and the sky brightened. Their earlier mood of cocksure confidence returned. Had they known better, they would have realised that worse was to come. The rain fell again harder this time, the wind gathered and the temperature dropped. Huge waves buffeted the boat and they tried to remember what the sailing instructor had taught them. But it was no use: fear had blotted out everything they had been told. The rain was coming down so hard that Mark couldn't even see the shore. Everything was an endless roll of turbulent, impenetrable grey. The sea was grey and the sky was leaden. The sail was straining in the fierce wind and there didn't seem to be anything they could do to control the dinghy. Pulling on the rudder or sail did nothing. They were helpless, at the mercy of the sea and weather.

It was then that Mark began to get a sense of the danger they were in. With no lifejackets on board, what would happen if they capsized? And just as he had thought this, the sky lit up with a flash of lightning. It made them both jump and, hanging on to each other, panic set in. With growing horror, they watched mountainous waves grow and swell. Tossed from one to the next, they were powerless. But when the final violent gust of wind hit they never saw it coming. The boat went over and, knowing that Niall wasn't as strong a swimmer as he was, Mark had screamed, 'Hold on to me,' as the billowing sea swallowed them up.

But the strength of the water pushed them clean away from the boat, and when eventually Mark surfaced there was no sign of Niall.

He dived back under the water, kicking his legs, pulling at the ice-cold water with his arms. But still he couldn't see his friend. Out of breath, he rose to the surface again, filled his lungs with air and dived once more. Again and again, he dived, surfaced and dived, desperate to reach Niall in time. The salt water was stinging his eyes, his chest was aching as though it would burst and his fingers were numb with cold.

Suddenly he saw Niall. He was trapped under the hull of the boat. He swam over and pulled frantically at his arms to free him. But even as he was doing this, he knew it was too late. Hooking a hand under his chin, he dragged him to the surface and tried to hold him against the overturned boat. Choking for breath, he screamed at Niall to wake up. He tried to give him mouth-to-mouth, but it was no good, he couldn't hold him still for long enough. With tears running down his cheeks he knew that Niall was dead. And knew, too, that it was his fault. He prayed then that the waves would take him and that he, too, would die.

But he didn't die. His sense of self-preservation wouldn't allow it to happen, and with the worst of the storm now over he managed to extend the centreboard on the boat and right it. Just as he was clambering in, a lifeboat alerted by the local coastguard came speeding into view. He was wrapped in a blanket and told he had had a lucky escape.

'Well done, Mark,' Bones had said, when he had finished. 'That was good. Very good. Now, in tomorrow's session we'll explore why you've persisted in acting out this old conflict. And if there's time, we'll look at why you're still behaving like an angry teenager masquerading as an intellectual-ising adult opposing anyone in authority, or those you think lucky enough to have their lives neatly sewn up. We might even touch base with your parents. The hinterland of bad parenting is always a rich vein to tap into. My spies tell me that *chilli con carne* is on the menu for lunch. Do you think I ought to risk it? Or should I steer clear?'

That was the extraordinary thing about being in a rehab clinic: one minute you could be dissecting the carnage of your most intimate experiences, and the next you could be mulling over something as mundane as what to have for lunch.

Wanting to order another cup of coffee, Mark looked about him to catch the eye of a passing waiter. The bar was busier than when he had arrived. Darkness had brought with it dazzling Vegas-style neon lights advertising Woodpecker Cider, Heineken, Becks and Amstel beer. And to complement the bright lights, the music had been turned up – Will Smith was getting jiggy with it and doing another of his rap-meets-Stevie-Wonder numbers on a large-screen TV hung from the ceiling in a corner of the bar – and a vibrant party atmosphere was in the air.

He decided to move on. His coffee already paid for, he left a tip on the table, stepped into the road and strolled down towards the harbour. Not that it was much of a stroll: the streets were packed and he had to run the gauntlet of numerous knick-knack stalls. There was something for everyone, or so they claimed. You could have your portrait done, buy yourself some cheap silver jewellery, have your name written on a grain of rice – for some strange reason – have your hair braided or a temporary tattoo applied. He was certainly spoiled for choice! And if none of that appealed, he could always go for the Albanian woman selling cheap, unromantic polyester roses and those silly light-up wristbands.

Beneath a sky of midnight blue, the still water in the harbour was ablaze with the reflection of coloured lights from all the bars, shops and restaurants around the quay. It was just as busy down here as at the top of the town, but seeing that one of the benches at the harbour's edge was free, Mark headed over to it. He had just settled himself, pulled out his notebook and pen from his shirt pocket, when he heard a voice from behind him.

'Hello there. Mind if we join you?'

It was Dolly-Babe with Silent Bob in tow.

Oh, joy! Now, why the hell hadn't he done the sensible thing and gone along with Theo's plans for the evening? It served him right for lying, he supposed.

Theo had gone for the honest option when he had arrived at Villa Petros. He hadn't thought it fair to keep fobbing his friends off with lame excuses about Mark's work so he told them the truth.

'I'm sorry,' he said, when Laura had offered him a chair on the veranda and Max had poured him a glass of wine, 'but not only is Mark a very private man, he used to be an alcoholic. The invitation to spend the evening with a reprobate boozer like you, Max, is not good for him.'

'Oh, Theo,' said Laura, 'why didn't you say something sooner?'

'Because I am a man of discretion. Mark's affairs are his own.'

'Now you come to mention it,' said Max, 'I recall something about him in the papers. Can't think why I hadn't thought of it before. If my memory serves me right, he went through a hell of a time of it, didn't he?'

Theo nodded. 'He did.' And then, more cheerfully, 'Now where are you hiding your parents Max? And what about Francesca and the nymphomaniac Sally, are they not here?'

'The girls have gone into Kassiópi. And Mum and Dad are doing sterling stuff in the kitchen with Izzy; they're stacking the dishwasher and tidying up.'

'Aha, you have been cracking the whip over them, have you?'

'Let's just say that they have an abundance of energy, and Laura thought it a good idea to put it to use. And it looks as if they've done their chores for the day – here they come. Let me introduce you.'

Rising to his feet, Theo shook hands first with Olivia then Corky. 'What a beautiful mother you have Max,' Theo said.

Max smiled. 'Now you can understand why I had to marry someone equally beautiful.'

Laura went to him and gave him a kiss. 'You old smoothie, you.'

Seeing Izzy standing on the edge of the group and sensing her awkwardness, Theo moved towards her. 'One big happy family, eh? You have parents like these?'

'Um . . . no. My father died last year. What about you?'

'I'm fortunate to have both my parents still alive. I'm sorry about your father. Were you very close?' As soon as the question was out, Theo regretted it. He saw her eyes fill and her lips tauten until they were white. She looked intensely unhappy. He mentally kicked himself. What was it with him, that he always managed to say the wrong thing? He had come here this evening determined to make amends for upsetting her on the beach that day, and now look what he had done. 'Come,' he said brightly, 'while Max is busy schmoozing his wife, let me get you a drink. You must be thirsty after all that work in the kitchen.'

'No, really,' she said, resisting his hand as it touched her elbow to steer her across the terrace, 'I don't need one.' Her voice was as stiff as the look she gave him.

He let go of her, realising that his spontaneous gesture had been to her a gross act of intrusion. 'I'm sorry,' he said, perplexed, and racking his brains for some way to put her at ease. In the end all he could think of was to repeat his apology, and quickly, before she moved away from him. 'Izzy, please, I am sorry. Will you give me a chance?'

'What for?'

Even he was surprised by what he had just said. Used to thinking fast on his feet, he now found himself completely deficient. Automatically he reached out to her arm again, thinking his touch would instil in her a sense of reassurance. Just in time, he stopped himself. More physical contact and she might slap his face. 'I'm not really sure myself,' he said at last. 'All I know is that I would like the opportunity to apologise to you properly. The last time we spoke I upset you, and tonight I have done it again. Please, won't you—' But he was interrupted as Max joined them.

'Now, stop pestering poor Izzy, Theo. You're needed over here. My parents are keen to learn some Greek and we've appointed you their teacher.'

He allowed himself to be dragged back to the rest of the group, and as he set about entertaining them by imitating their inaccurate pronunciation, he watched Izzy's face grow steadily more sombre. He had a strong urge to leap from his chair and go to her. More than anything he wanted to see her face light up with a smile.

19

Izzy was never going to be able to get back to sleep. She had tossed and turned for most of the night and when eventually she had dozed off, it had been only for a couple of hours.

She kicked off the sheet, which had twisted itself into a wrinkled second skin around her, and went and stood outside on the balcony. The sky was pearly-pink, fresh and beautiful, glowing in the dawn light. Still and subdued, the smooth surface of the sea glistened serenely, scarcely a trace of a wave breaking against the shore.

Images of smashed china, of her mother crying, of her father cradling her in his arms had kept her awake. She had thought she was over her father, but after yesterday she realised that all she had been doing since his death was to keep on adding yet more layers of pretence to cover the cracks in their relationship. She understood now that the tears she had shed for him since the day he had died were nothing compared to the unshed tears of confused sadness and regret that she must have been storing up since she was a child.

She had been cross with herself yesterday for reliving that morning in the kitchen when her mother had lost control. Cross, because it had provoked too many other memories, too many other disturbing incidents. She had never blamed her mother for what she had done. Her mother had been ill with depression, her self-control precariously balanced as she struggled through each day as fraught and uptight as those little squares she knitted later in life.

After that terrible day her mother was admitted to a psychiatric hospital and arrangements were made for Izzy to go into a children's home. To this day, Izzy never knew why she had been put in the home – it was not a subject that was ever discussed in front of her. Why hadn't her father taken care of her? Or her aunt?

Her memories of the place were mostly a kaleidoscope of hazy but evocative sensations, of smells and sounds – but there were other more vivid flashes of recollection.

It had been just before Christmas that she had been taken there. She knew it was Christmas, because on a table at one end of the echoey dormitory she had slept in there had been a small silver tree draped in red tinsel and wonky decorations speckled with glitter that the other children had made. The floor had been shiny clean and smelt of polish and disinfectant, but the clanking bed with its austere metal frame and peeling white paint had seemed dirty. The sheets had been like paper, hard and starched; the woollen blanket, rough and scratchy, and the pillow had smelt of vomit. Above the bed there was a flickering light and a window criss-crossed with metal bars.

Mealtimes were noisy and chaotic. The food wasn't what she was used to. One day she had been forced to eat a bowl of rice pudding sprinkled with brown sugar. That night she was sick, and pushed into a freezing cold bath. When she had been lifted out, shivering and frightened, somebody had dressed her, changed the plaster on her head, and taken her back to bed where the sheets had been changed. Impatient hands had tucked her in, jolted the mattress with quick-tempered movements. She was given a stern warning that she wasn't to be sick again. With the smell of unfamiliar soap in her nostrils, and pinned down by the taut bedclothes, she had cried herself quietly to sleep, terrified of causing any more trouble and thinking – *knowing* – that this was her punishment for having broken one of her mother's precious statues.

Her greatest fear was that if she wasn't good she might stay for ever in this prison. And it was a prison, she knew that, for why else were there bars at the windows? She missed her own small bedroom, where she could hide under the ancient wooden bed that had once belonged to her father, and which was so high she had to climb up on to it. It was there, hidden in the dark and by the light of a torch, that she would draw her pictures, slipping them beneath the rug if she heard the sound of her mother's sharp, impatient footsteps approaching.

Her father visited her at the home.

As she was so young, and had no grasp of time, she never knew when he would arrive. She would sit waiting anxiously for him in one of the playrooms, watching the other children dig around in the large toy boxes. She would close her eyes and imagine that when she opened them he would be there, that he had come to take her home.

The people in charge tried to make her join in, but she wouldn't. The other children frightened her: they were all bigger, noisier too. They seemed quite happy to be there. The only toy she played with was a box of Fuzzy-felt. While she waited for her father to come, she would sit at a table near a window – just to make sure she didn't miss him, or that he didn't miss her – and watch the snow fall while putting together brightly coloured scenes of make-believe happiness: a house with a red door, a tree with green apples, a yellow sun, a mummy with curly brown hair, a daddy with long legs and a black triangle for a hat, and a little girl with a pet dog at her feet. Except there wasn't a dog in the faded and stained box, it had got lost, so she had made do with a pig. It was from another box of shapes and she knew it looked silly, its fat pink body dwarfing the rest of the picture, but she had wanted it to be as complete in her mind as she could make it.

She hated it when her father had to leave. It seemed that he had only just arrived when he was getting his coat back on, patting her shoulder and saying goodbye. She would watch him from the window as he walked away, his collar pulled up, his head hunched into his shoulders. Sometimes he waved, sometimes he didn't. When he didn't wave, she would carefully, and very slowly, dismantle the Fuzzy-felt picture, and return the pieces to its box.

She had no idea how long she was there, but she was sure it was weeks rather than days because the artificial Christmas tree disappeared. When she went home nobody spoke about what had happened. Her mother seemed different. Quieter. Slower. More watchful. Which made her even more scary.

As time went by, Izzy began to wonder if the home had been a frightening dream. But one look in the mirror told her that she hadn't imagined it. Reflected back at her were the familiar silvery grey eyes – poor man's blue, as her mother called them – and a vivid scar on her right temple that hadn't been there before. Something else new about her was that she couldn't bear to have her face immersed in water – it brought back that petrifying night when she had been sick and plunged into the bath of icy-cold water.

The following Christmas, when Auntie Trixie had been staying with them Izzy had heard her say, 'Well, thank goodness Isobel was so young when she went into that dreadful home, she doesn't remember it.' The crashing silence that had filled the room had convinced Izzy that she had not dreamed her time away from her parents. It also reaffirmed what she had pieced together from snatches of grown-up conversation: that it was a subject best not mentioned. And though her mother's mood swings were less marked, Izzy lived in dread of doing anything that might upset her, and which would result in a return to that prison. She moved around the bungalow as though on eggshells, trying to make herself less obtrusive.

Exhausted with the strain, she soon became a bundle of nerves, jumping if her mother spoke her name too sharply, flinching if a hand moved too fast. She searched constantly for ways to help, to make everything right.

Yet nothing she did helped. She was destined to cause trouble, to be in the wrong place at the wrong time.

But it was all such a long time ago. It shouldn't still affect her. But it did, of course. She wouldn't be human if when the threads of her childhood tweaked she didn't feel it. She realised now, with guilty confusion, that she felt angry with her father – that he had never protected her from her mother, and angrier still that he had left her in that home.

This newly identified emotion wrapped itself around her heart and squeezed painfully.

For once, Mark was up before Theo. He made himself a pot of coffee and took it out on to the terrace, with his A4 notepad and fountain pen. His intention was to work, but as he sat at the wooden table where he had found Theo last night when he got back from Kassiópi, he suspected this would not be the case. For one thing, it was too quiet – he was up so early that not even the cicadas had got going yet – and the second reason was that he was annoyed with Theo for making a fool of himself.

'I've upset her again,' he had said forlornly last night, as Mark had sat down with him, noting the empty bottle of Metaxá and the unusually miserable expression on his friend's face. 'What is wrong with me, eh? And please, do not suggest that I'm losing it. Do that, and I will happily smash this bottle over your big ugly head.'

Having arrived back from Kassiópi, expecting to share his tale of having bumped into Dolly-Babe and Silent Bob, Mark had been unprepared for this impromptu late-night heart-to-heart. It wasn't often that Theo got drunk.

'Izzy?' he had asked.

'Well, of course it's Izzy,' snapped Theo. 'Who else would it be?'

'So what did you say this time?'

'I put my foot straight into it.' He groaned, holding his head. 'No deeper could I have gone.'

'Oh, come on, it can't be that bad.' Mark's tone was slightly impatient. Since he had kicked the bottle into touch he had a limited supply of patience for anyone else's alcohol-induced ramblings. Was this really the man who ran a mini empire and had an intellect sharp enough to slice bread?

Theo raised his head and looked at him petulantly. 'You think I am play-acting, eh? You think I am behaving in the manner of a spoilt child who can't get his way, is that it?'

Mark looked at him thoughtfully, seeing two very different men. There was Theo the sharp, practical businessman, and Theo the sentimental and hopelessly romantic philosopher. It was probably a fair summing up of your typical Greek man. 'You've always been a spoilt child, Theo,' he said, 'so I'm not going to refute that. But what I think you're experiencing, and for the first time, is what the rest of us mere mortals have to endure more regularly. The phenomenon of rejection. Welcome to the club. I wish I could say that membership was exclusive, but I'm afraid it isn't. So tell me where it went wrong.'

'*Ti hálya!* I blundered in where angels—'

'Keep to English, Theo, and just get to the point.'

He did.

'But that's a mistake anyone could have made,' said Mark, once again feeling that his friend was turning the episode into an over-the-top Greek tragedy. It still puzzled him why and how this girl had got under Theo's skin in the way that she had. 'How were you to know that she hasn't got over her father's death? My advice is not to take it personally. The next time you see her, just apologise as discreetly and courteously as you can.'

'That is easier said than done. The look she gave me, it could have yammered a nail into a wall.'

Mark had laughed. 'I think you mean *hammered*. I also think you've drunk too much. I guarantee that in the morning you'll see I'm right.'

He gave up on the idea of working. He wasn't in the mood. He finished his cup of coffee and decided to go for a walk, as he frequently did at this time of the day when he could be sure of having the beach to himself.

But today he found he didn't have that luxury. Perched on the rock where he often sat was the cause of Theo's problems. He stopped short, was about to retrace his steps and slip away unseen when she turned and looked straight at him. He could see she had been crying. That she still was.

Few men know what to do when confronted with tears, and Mark was no exception. He would also be the first to agree that listening isn't instinctive to men. Without another thought, he pretended he hadn't seen her and started walking in the direction he had just come. He didn't need this. There was no reason for him to get involved in somebody else's emotional problems. But gradually he slowed down and thought of Theo. What if Theo had turned his back on him all those years ago? What if he hadn't searched for him until he had found him in that hell-hole of a squat? And what if Bones hadn't been patient enough, or thick-skinned enough, to ignore the abuse Mark had flung at him?

But this was different. He was a stranger to this girl. How could he possibly help her?

But a stranger could sometimes be of more use than one's friends or family. A stranger could offer an objective view, a detached analysis of the problem.

And if that wasn't straight from Bones's gob, he didn't know what was.

He came to a standstill. Okay, he told himself. I'll do it this once. I'll interfere, just this once. For the first time in my life I'll be Mark the Comforter. He was relieved when he approached her to find that she had stopped crying. He noticed, though, that it was now her turn to pretend she hadn't seen him, and even when he was standing no more than a few feet from her, she still kept her head resolutely turned away. He felt oddly cheated. Here he was, prepared to do his bit, and she was trying to ignore him. So much for Mark the Bloody Comforter. But he had come this far, he was damned if he was going to let her get off without offering her some glib piece of reassuring advice. The least she could do was play along and stop him from feeling such a prize idiot.

He cleared his throat to speak, but couldn't think of one sensible thing to say. He might earn his living by the pen and be known for writing realistic dialogue, but in this situation it was clear he was no spontaneous soother. And as she continued to ignore him, he despaired of ever finding the right words.

And the longer the silence continued between them, the worse it became. He was well and truly caught between a rock and a hard place – creep away once more and look a fool, or brazen it out and look as big a fool. Then, luckily for him, the matter was taken out of his hands.

'I'm sorry, I'm taking your place, aren't I?' Her voice was soft, lower than he had expected.

'Sorry? Place?'

She swung her legs round and hopped down until she was level with him. 'I've seen you sitting here most days. It's where you like to come first thing in the morning when nobody's about, isn't it? I'll leave you to it.'

Her words had been rushed, and her grey gaze slid over him, elusive as quicksilver. He detected within her a nervous energy that wasn't dissimilar from what he was feeling. 'No, don't do that. Well, not unless you have to,' he said.

Their roles reversed again and now it was she who hesitated. 'I . . . I ought to be getting back.'

'To the Sinclairs'?'

She gave him a puzzled look. 'You know them?'

'I know *of* them,' he said. It was as good a way as any to break the ice. 'I also know that your name is Izzy. I'm staying next door with Theo.'

'Oh, so you *are* who I thought you were.'

'And who might that be? Anyone I know?'

Her lips curved into a shy smile. 'The phantom Mark St James. Max was beginning to think that Theo was only pretending to know you.'

'Well, now you'll be able to put him right.' He inclined his head towards the rocks. 'Won't you stay a little longer? I'd hate to feel I'd chivvied you away.'

'But then you won't have your opportunity to sit here and enjoy the view.'

'We could compromise, enjoy the view together. Then I wouldn't feel guilty thinking that I'd cut short your enjoyment.' He could see that his suggestion had surprised her. For that matter, he had surprised himself.

'Okay,' she agreed. 'So long as you're sure.'

Thinking that he would tell Theo not to mess with this girl, that she was far too sweet to be spoiled by him, he helped her back up on to the rock where she had been sitting. 'At least this way we both get to ease our consciences,' he said, when they were settled. Staring out over the stretch of water, they watched a ferry slide along the imperceptible line of the horizon. As its progress continued, a swell of water travelled across the narrow strait, until it finally broke into a series of noisy, crashing waves on the shore, churning up the sand, shifting the stones and pebbles. When the ship had passed, the water reverted to its former steady calm; a gently rippling swathe of silk. And for two people who had never met before, they sat in a curiously companionable silence, taking in the pale, golden sunlight and a translucent sky that hadn't yet fully woken to its mantle of dazzling blue.

Only minutes before, Izzy had been cursing the appearance of somebody else on the beach, but now she was glad of the distraction he had brought with him, grateful that his presence alone had magically stemmed her tears: tears she had allowed to get the better of her.

Her earlier attempt at drifting off to sleep again had been futile, just as she had known it would be, so she had dressed and come down here. It had seemed the perfect place to lose her maudlin thoughts but, sadly, it had only added to them. The beauty and serenity of the secluded cove were supposed to have cleared her mind and coaxed her into a peaceful state of all's-right-with-the-world, and to a degree it had worked, yet at the same time the perfection had caught her off guard. In the end, she had given in to her feelings: a good cry was what she needed, she told herself, as the tears gathered momentum and made her feel much worse. And if it hadn't been for the man sitting next to her, she would probably still be bawling her eyes out. She felt she ought to thank him for rescuing her from herself, but she suspected it would embarrass him. She had witnessed all too plainly the expression on his face just before he had turned and walked away. But what else could he have done? She had been taken aback, though, when he had reappeared by her side. She wondered now what had changed his mind.

Had it simply been his determination to have his fix of early-morning solitary space?

She winced at her unfortunate choice of words. Last night, and after Theo had left, Max had filled her in on part of the conversation she had missed while she had been in the kitchen with Corky and Olivia, and the reason why Theo's friend had turned down their invitation to join them for a drink. She didn't know anything about alcoholism or drugs, and couldn't imagine what it must be like to live each day so thoroughly out of control. Or what might drive a person into such a hopeless situation. She thought of the day she had seen him here sitting on these very rocks, and how she had thought he had an interesting face, not knowing that, at some stage in his life, he must have been unutterably wretched.

Taking a sideways glance at him, she decided that her original description still held good. Not quite what you'd call handsome, but definitely interesting. Close up, the angular lines of his face were a little more pronounced, his nose a touch longer and straighter, and his mouth firmer. But what she hadn't been able to appreciate before was the colour of his eyes. They were a brilliant blue, which surprised her: for some reason she had expected brown. She was also surprised by the depth of sensitivity she saw within them. Recalling the charcoal sketch she had done of him from memory, and which was in her sketchpad in the bag at her feet, she realised she might have drawn him quite differently had she caught a glimpse of those eyes: they would have softened the harsh, dramatic features she had given him.

They had been silent for some minutes now and, worried that he might feel she was being rude and ignoring him again, she asked the first question that came into her head. 'I bet you get asked this all the time, but is it very lonely being a writer?'

'Not really. You have to take into account that when I'm working I'm surrounded by some of the weirdest, most absorbing people in the world. Take it from me, psychopaths are anything but dull.'

His voice was low and husky, nearly as compelling as his eyes. 'What a strange life you must lead.'

'Yeah, I know, I should get out more. But I enjoy what I do. It gives me the ideal excuse not to join in with the rest of the world. I can be an official observer without ever having to participate. So what do you do for a living?'

'I'm a teacher.'

'Ooh, now that's what I call a scary job. What do you teach?'

'Apart from idiots?'

He turned and beamed his extraordinary blue gaze on her. 'Do I detect a schoolmarm with attitude?'

'A frustrated art teacher, actually.'

'Is there any other kind?'

'Mm ... I think you're right. It would be a reassuring thought if art teachers the world over were as frustrated as I was. I'd feel normal then.'

'Normal is boring. Have no truck with it. So when you grow up, what will you do?'

'What do you mean when I grow up?'

He smiled and caused her again to reconsider the anatomy of his face. The lifting of the corners of his mouth softened all those angles and lines.

'Easy there, girl, I was paying you a compliment. Isn't it every woman's wish to be thought younger than she really is?'

'Not if it puts her at a disadvantage.'

He pushed a hand through his fine collar-length blond hair, which was fairer at the tips than at the roots; she suspected he didn't visit the hairdresser too often. 'Bad experience with ageism?' he said.

'Regularly. Only last month I answered the door to a man collecting for some charity or other and he asked if my mother was at home.'

'What did you do? Bludgeon him to death for his cheek?'

'No, I put an extra fifty pence in his tin. He was collecting for the blind.'

He laughed. 'So, given that you're all grown-up, what would you rather be doing instead of teaching? Painting for a living, perhaps?'

She shook her head. 'A nice dream, but not a viable one, I'm afraid. The truth is, I'm not good enough.'

'Says who?'

'Um . . . says me.'

'And you'd know, would you? You're objective enough with your own creative endeavours, are you?' His low, gravelly voice sounded sharp, almost querulous. 'I'm sorry,' he said, and in a more gentle tone, 'I got carried away then. It just seemed as though you were being unnecessarily hard on yourself and, believe me, I know how that feels.'

Glancing up at his face and catching another glimpse of his eyes, she sensed that he meant what he was saying. It made her think how very different he was from his friend, Theo. And thinking now of Theo, she realised that she had been excessively hard on him last night. He hadn't deserved the treatment she had given him. It wasn't his fault that the words he had uttered about her father had cut her to the quick – *Were you very close?* How was he to know that closeness was the very thing she had never experienced with her father, that as a child it had been what she had craved above all else. Most daughters go through a period of idolising their fathers, but given the inflammatory atmosphere in which Izzy had grown up, she had needed hers as an ally. But he had never been there for her. He had turned a blind eye to what was going on. Until now, she had never wanted to think badly of him, but that was what her earlier outburst of tears had been about. The raw injustice of it all had finally pressed down on her, shocking her with its revelatory intensity. It was the sudden realisation that, after all these years, she had been harbouring a desperate need to tell him what she really thought of him. She wondered if the violent anger she had felt for Alan in that counsellor's room when she had thrown her cold coffee at him had had nothing to do with his stupid infidelity, but had been her latent desire to hurt her father, to let him know what it felt like to be so completely betrayed.

And, in a very small way, she had done the same thing to Theo last night. She decided to be bold and ask Mark if he would pass on her apologies to Theo. 'Would you do me a favour?' she asked.

'Depends what it is. If it involves gun running, I'm not your man.'

She smiled. 'No, this is quite legal. It's just that I've been very rude to Theo and, well, I think he deserves an apology. Do you think you could tell him that I'm sorry for being so short with him?'

He took a moment to consider her words, then said, 'You know, apologies are always best delivered in person. Why don't you come back to the villa now and tell him yourself?'

She hesitated. 'It's still quite early. Will he be awake?'

'Let's go and find out, shall we?'

20

All the way up to Villa Anna Izzy tried to work out how best to apologise to Theo. Too much of an apology and he would probably take it as a come-on, and he was in no need of encouragement. But too little and it would appear insincere. She wondered, too, why she had let herself be persuaded into this out-of-character act of spontaneity, and by someone she had only just met.

But all thoughts of what she would say were pushed aside when Mark opened a small wooden gate, and led her through a garden that was a sumptuous paradise of colour and scent. They found Theo floating on his back in the pool. His eyes were closed, and his body was a picture of relaxed pleasure. It was also naked.

'Theo,' Mark said, 'you might want to put something on, I've brought someone to see you.'

It was clear, from the expression on Theo's face as he opened his eyes and saw Izzy staring down at him, that he was shocked. Without a word, he swam to the shallow end where Mark was waiting for him with a towelling robe that had been hanging on the back of a chair. Izzy was surprised by his manner. She would have expected him to brazen it out, which would have been more in keeping with his behaviour to date. Was he genuinely embarrassed? Or was he just being a gentleman and saving her blushes? Either way, she found it rather endearing.

'I met Izzy down on the beach,' said Mark. 'We got chatting and I invited her to join us for breakfast. That all right with you?'

This was news to Izzy. She thought she was here to apologise and then go home. She didn't hear Theo's muttered answer but Mark simply laughed and said, 'I'll go and throw some breakfast together, leave you two to chat.'

'Perhaps this wasn't such a good idea,' Izzy said, when they were alone and she watched Theo tighten the belt on his robe. 'I shouldn't have accepted Mark's invitation.'

Theo's unshaven face, which until now had been clouded with what she had taken to be annoyance, suddenly cleared with one of his familiar smiles, his usual equanimity shining through. 'I'm glad that you did. I'm just sorry that you have found me in such a state of disrepair. I'm ashamed to admit it, but I have a hangover. A little too much Metaxá last night.' He raised a hand and touched his head lightly. 'Which was why you found me in the pool as you did. In my weakened state, the sea did not appeal. Please, sit down. Or perhaps you would like a look round. My garden is very beautiful at this time of day. The scent from the roses is quite magnificent.'

'Thank you, I'd like that.'

He slipped on a pair of smooth leather sandals and led the way. They followed a gravel path, lined at either side with stone urns containing luxuriant ferns and the occasional lemon and kumquat tree, until they came to a lower level that was a pretty oasis of green and cream. 'This is one of my favourite areas,' he said. Behind them was a towering Scots pine and the ground they stood on was soft and cushiony, where needles had dropped from the tree. The still morning air was heavy with the scent of pine, but a headier, more exotic and luscious fragrance came from the creamy blooms of a curved bed of exquisite roses. 'It may seem a little grand, but I call this my rose garden,' he said, fingering a petal that looked as perfect as it smelt. 'Some of these are very old – they came from my grandmother's garden. I would hate to lose a single one of them. It would be a great loss. Angelos is under strict orders to take good care of them. Especially when I'm not here.'

'How touchingly sentimental that sounds,' Izzy said.

For a couple of seconds he didn't say anything. Then: 'You think me incapable of sentiment, Izzy? You think I am not able to feel real emotion?' His tone was accusing, and the vehemence behind his words baffled her.

When she didn't answer, he turned away from her and said, 'Well, no matter. You would not be the first to jump to such a conclusion.'

He seemed so strangely introverted that she decided it was time to get her apology over and done with before she caused any more antagonism between them. 'Before I offend you further,' she said, 'I've got something I'd like to say.'

He returned his gaze to her, and stared at her keenly, his head slightly tilted. His attentiveness made it all the more difficult for her to get the words out.

'Um . . . I was very rude to you last night,' she pressed on, 'and . . . and I just wanted you to know that it wasn't anything to do with you. It was me. I was in a terrible mood and I took it out on you. I'm sorry. I just wanted you to know that.'

He came towards her, visibly lightened by what she had said. The gap between them suddenly seemed dangerously small and the atmosphere dangerously intoxicating with the potent fragrance of the flowers as the sunlight filtered through the trees.

'We have only known one another for a short time,' he said, 'but it seems to me that on several occasions I have annoyed and offended you. So I, too, would like to say that I am sorry. I think also that you have an opinion of me that, if I am honest, is one I have stupidly encouraged. But I would very much like to be given the opportunity to change that perception, if it isn't too late. What do you say? Do you think we could be friends?'

She smiled.

He took another step towards her. 'Is that a yes?'

'Um . . . a cautious yes.'

He reached for her hand, lifted it to his lips and kissed it, while all the time keeping his dark eyes on hers. 'There,' he said, lowering her hand and flashing a smile, 'that was not so bad, was it?'

Despite the presence of Modern Woman tapping her foot and warning that if she wasn't careful she'd be right back where she'd started, Izzy agreed that it wasn't.

21

Laura poured bottled water into the kettle and plugged it in. She put the empty plastic container in the bin and made a mental note to check how much they had left. What with her mother's insatiable desire for tea, they were getting through an inordinate amount of water. Last year she had made the mistake of using water straight from the tap, and while it was perfectly safe to do so, the brackish aftertaste was far from appetising or refreshing.

The tea made, she took it outside and was about to settle down with her book, which she still hadn't finished, when she heard footsteps behind her.

It was Francesca, looking as slothful and bleary-eyed as she herself felt. She dipped her head and kissed Laura's cheek. 'Morning, Mum.'

'It's a little early for you, isn't it? Couldn't you sleep?'

'Sally's snoring like an volcano.'

'Oh dear. Not a lot we can do about that. Do you want a cup of tea? I've just made a pot.'

'Nah, I'll make some coffee in a moment, when I've got myself together.' She yawned and stretched out on the sun-lounger beside Laura, her slim, lithe body already dressed for action in a fluorescent pink bikini. Since it was her first real opportunity to talk to her daughter on her own since she had arrived, Laura broached the subject of the recently departed boyfriend. She wanted to be sure that Francesca's apparent easy-come-easy-go attitude wasn't just a brave front. Regrets were seldom of any use and, as Max would be the first to say, the boy simply wasn't worth the trouble.

'Glad you came?' she asked. 'The change doing you good?'

Francesca turned her head. There were smudgy signs of eye makeup that hadn't been cleaned off from last night, and with her henna-dyed hair still loosely plaited and sticking out at either side of her ears, she reminded Laura of Pippy Longstocking from the books she used to read to her when she was little. 'Are we venturing into heart-to-heart territory?' Francesca asked.

'Only if you want to go there.'

'Cool it, Mum, you should know me better than that. For once I agree with Dad. Carl was a pillock and I'm not going to lose any sleep over him. Anyway, it looks as if Sally and I have got something better to interest us right here.'

'Some local colour?'

'No, home-grown is safer. Less risk of being misunderstood. We got chatting to them last night in Kassiópi.'

When she embarked upon these conversations Laura knew she was treading a difficult path: she wanted her daughter to confide in her, but at the same time she didn't want to acknowledge just how much of an adult Francesca was. She said, 'Would I be right in thinking it's the two lads from the pink villa?'

'You're remarkably well informed. Or has Dad been spying on me?'

Laura laughed. 'Are their parents with them?' She was wondering if she dared invite them for a drink so that she and Max could carry out a thorough inspection of the boys. After all, they had Sally's welfare to consider: while she was staying with them she was their responsibility whether she liked it or not.

'Yes,' confirmed Francesca, with an exaggerated roll of her eyes. 'So no worries about a shagathon taking place.'

'A shagathon,' repeated a voice from behind them. 'What a delightful expression. In our day we called it an orgy.'

It was Olivia. She patted the top of her granddaughter's head affectionately and pulled up a chair. 'Is that fresh tea?'

'Yes, it is. Francesca, would you fetch your grandmother a cup, please?'

In the brief space of time that they were alone, Laura said, 'You could at least pretend to be shocked.'

'But why?'

'I bet you wouldn't have let Max get away with anything half so outrageous. A shagathon indeed!'

Olivia smiled. 'But that's what's so good about the age we live in. Grandparents are allowed to behave as disgracefully as their grandchildren. It's the middle years when we're expected to conform. Take it from me, Corky and I have much more fun, these days.'

Laura groaned. 'I knew it would happen sooner or later – *Grans Behaving Badly*!'

Francesca returned with a cup for Corky, and the foresight to bring a few extras. 'For everyone else when they surface,' she said, plonking them on the table. 'I'm off for a swim. See you later.'

The first thing Harry saw when he pushed back the shutters, was a blurred outline of blue, white and green. He slipped on his glasses, and the blue became sky and sea, the white, sand, and the green, the verdant hillside. He stepped outside and leaned against the wrought-iron rail that separated his cramped bedroom terrace from the more spacious terrace below, where they congregated as a family for indigestible meals of combat and tension. He pushed his hands through his sleep-tousled hair and took in the splendour of the morning. It was then that he saw somebody swimming.

Squinting, he saw that it was Francesca, the more attractive of the two girls they had got talking to last night. And, naturally, because she was the most attractive, Nick had stepped in straight away and staked out the boundaries. They had been sitting in one of the bars in Kassiópi; he had been watching *Saving Private Ryan* on a large screen above the bar while his brother had been eyeing up the potential. The two girls had seen them the minute they had walked in but, in the way all girls did, they had pretended not to see them. 'Hold tight,' Nick had said, out of the corner of his mouth. 'Chick alert. I'll give them a few minutes to settle in, then I'll make a move on them. You can have the tall one. Mine's the one with the sticky-out plaits. Cute or what?'

'What if you're not her type?' Harry had said.

Nick had given him a look of mocking disbelief. 'Drink up, and I'll get us another round in.'

He had watched Nick saunter over to the bar and wondered why girls were always drawn to his brother. Even when he had been at junior school he could pull a crowd of them around him. But whatever cheesy line he had given these two, it had had the desired effect: they had followed him back to the table and introduced themselves. The tall one was called Sally, and the one his brother had labelled as cute was Francesca. It turned out that they were the same age as his brother, a few months short of twenty. Being older by two years he had felt alienated from them as a group, and had found his attention wandering from the conversation, letting it settle on Tom Hanks and his platoon. As a consequence they had probably written him off as boring. Well, so be it. What did it matter?

But as he watched Francesca diving from the raft opposite her parents' villa, he realised that it did matter. Just for once, he wanted people to think that he was as interesting as his brother.

With a rueful shake of his head, he went back into his room. What would be the point? Faced with the choice between him – Mr Dullsville – and his brother – Mr Hip-Hop-Goin'-With-The-Groove – who seemed to possess all the magnetic pull of a crushed-velvet Austin Powers, he wouldn't get a look in.

Smirking quietly to himself, Mark was impressed at the show Theo was putting on for Izzy's benefit. It was a top performance of carefully measured moves that he obviously thought would put her at ease. It had been Mark's intention to leave Theo and Izzy to eat their breakfast alone, but Theo had sought him out in the kitchen and said, 'Please, you must stay with me. I sense that she will be more relaxed with you acting as a chaperon.'

Watching the almost reverential manner in which he was treating her, Mark wondered if he had misjudged Theo. Wasn't it bound to happen, that sooner or later he would find a woman who would mean more to him than a potential bedroom tumble? And who was he to doubt his friend's ability to love? His past was hardly a glowing account of starry-eyed romance. Perhaps he had allowed his history of disastrous relationships to colour his opinion of what Theo might be capable of feeling for Izzy.

Or was he jealous?

The treachery of this thought appalled him. Was it possible that he was jealous that his friend might find happiness – while he might not?

It was such a disagreeable thought that he quickly manoeuvred it to the back of his mind, to the storehouse of conundrums he had yet to unravel. A writer's mind was packed with useful and not so useful fragments of information. He had a mental picture of his brain as an old-fashioned ironmonger's shop, its walls covered in shelves overflowing with bits and bobs. Trouble was, when he wanted to find anything in a hurry, he needed an ancient, efficient employee who could lay his hands instantly on exactly what Mark was looking for. Which was why he had to write things down: if he didn't he might never retrieve the irreplaceable flashes of inspiration that slipped in and out of his mind.

He had been on the verge of doing exactly this last night when he had been in the harbour. He had thought of something, which, at the time, had seemed earth-shatteringly important. But with the appearance of Dolly-Babe and Silent Bob, it had wriggled away. He hated losing ideas. It was like being robbed of something precious, and the perpetrators of this heinous crime had joined him on the bench.

'Did you get my message?' Dolly-Babe had asked.

He had decided to play dumb. 'Message?'

She tutted, giving him the benefit of alcohol-tainted breath. She leaned in close to him, so close he could see his bored face reflected back in her sunglasses – didn't she ever take them off? It was dark, for pity's sake. 'You know, you wanna watch that chauffeur of yours,' she said. 'I asked him to tell you that I wanted to invite you over to our villa for a drink.'

'It must have slipped his memory.'

Another tut.

'I was going to invite your neighbours as well, the Sinclairs. But I never got round to it. Bob's been rushed off his size nines. He's been dashing all over the island. Isn't that right, Bob?'

But Bob wasn't listening. He was talking quietly to somebody on his mobile phone.

'He's very busy,' she said, lowering her voice. 'Lots of irons in the fire. He's found some land for sale that he says is just the job.' And then, 'This is no coincidence, you know. Us seeing you this evening.'

'Really?'

She smiled. 'I gave Ria, my tarot reader, a call this morning, just to see what was in store for me. For Bob too.' She lowered her voice again. 'He's got some important decisions to make over the coming weeks and I want to be sure he knows what he's doing. Anyway, I asked her about the tall, fair-haired man who was going to bring me luck, and . . .' She paused, obviously building up the tension to an enthralling dénouement.

'And?' he filled in for her, providing the necessary drumroll.

'And she said we'd meet again. *Soon.*'

'How extraordinary.'

'There's no denying the psychic forces that surround us, is there?' she said. 'You feel it too, don't you?'

'Did she see anything else on your horizon?' he asked, curious to hear what further madness she could be convinced of.

'Well, the Eight of Cups showed up.'

His clueless expression invited her to expand. 'It's a card that promises new and bigger social horizons,' she said helpfully. 'New faces. New places. New experiences. New everything, in fact.'

It sounded a fair description of just about anybody's annual holiday. It was time for him to make his escape. 'It's been great seeing you again,' he lied, 'but I ought to be getting back.'

'We're off now as well. Where are you parked? Just here in the harbour?'

'No, I'm on foot.' Too late he realised his mistake. A lift home was eagerly pressed upon him, as was a firm invitation for him to drop in at Villa Mimosa. 'Don't be a stranger, call in for a chat any time,' she said, as they pulled up outside Theo's villa. 'It must be very dull being here all on your lonesome.'

Thanking them for the lift and watching their hire car disappear down the drive, he began to change his opinion of Dolly-Babe. Behind the glossy make-up, the too young designer frocks, the sunglasses and the ridiculous belief that some Mystic Meg at the other end of a telephone line had the answers to what lay ahead for her, there was a sad and lonely woman. A woman who, while her husband was playing the big wheeler-dealer, probably drank more than was good for her. It made him wonder what she was running away from.

They had long since finished breakfast – fresh figs, toast with local honey and a pot of coffee – and had moved into the shaded area of the terrace, which was covered by a pergola of twisted vine. Theo was explaining to Izzy how the fruit above their heads, green and tiny now, would grow into fat red grapes that would be harvested in the autumn and made into wine. She was looking at Theo with what Mark could only describe as a private half-smile, as though she had just thought of something that amused her. He was intrigued to know what it was.

'Don't you believe a word of it, Izzy,' he said, as he heard Theo trying to convince her that he would be taking off his socks and shoes to help Angelos tread the grapes. 'Can you imagine him risking his expensive hand-made clothes with such dirty work?'

'Ha! And do you see so much as a callus on my friend's hands?' asked Theo. 'He is no more a sweaty son of the soil than I am. Ever since I have known him, he has tried to make himself out to be a friend of the people, a working-class hero, but it is nothing more than an act with him. Don't let him fool you, Izzy.'

'I think if I have any sense at all I won't let either of you fool me,' Izzy said, with a laugh. 'Are you always like this?'

'Like what?' asked Theo.

'So rude and horrible to each other.'

'This is us being nice to each other,' said Mark. 'You should be around when we're going at it hammer and tong.'

'And who usually gets the upper hand?'

'You think that I, Theo Vlamakis, would let a fraud like Mark get the better of me? Tsk, tsk, Izzy, you disappointment me. I never lose at verbal fisticuffs.'

'The hell you don't! I let you win occasionally just so you don't lose heart.'

'But I allow you to think that you have let me win so that your poor little ego can give itself a pat on its back.'

'Oh, you poor sick bastard, how did you ever climb to the top of the food chain?'

Theo turned to Izzy with a triumphant smile. 'There! You see how easily I have won the argument? When Mark resorts to profanity, it is because he knows he is losing the debate. He is a hopeless case, but one I take pity on. More coffee?'

'No, thank you. I really ought to be going.' She glanced at her watch. 'Goodness! Just look at the time. Laura will be wondering where I am.' She picked up her bag, slipped it over her shoulder and got to her feet. 'I had no idea I'd been here so long. I hope I haven't kept you from anything important.'

'Not at all,' urged Theo. 'But calm yourself, there's no need to hurry. It is but a short walk to next door.'

They saw her to the wooden gate that led to the path which would take her back to Villa Petros. 'And thank you again for breakfast,' she said, as she turned to leave them, 'I really enjoyed it. You've both cheered me up.'

'You will come again, perhaps? When you are in need of more cheering up?'

She didn't answer Theo's question, but gave him a flicker of a smile. Then she waved goodbye and hurried away.

Watching her go, Theo sighed. 'You know, Mark, I was very cross with you earlier for bringing Izzy here when I was in no state to be seen, but it seems that once again I am in your debt. How did you persuade her to come?'

Mark shrugged. 'She mentioned that she felt bad about last night and asked if I would pass on an apology to you. I simply said that apologies were best made in person.'

'As easy as that?'

Mark slapped him on the back. 'Yeah, old mate, as easy as that.'

22

A week later when Theo asked Izzy to have dinner with him, the response at Villa Petros was mixed.

Laura just smiled knowingly behind *Captain Corelli*, which she still hadn't finished, and Max slipped into old-fashioned parental mode, warning Izzy not to take any nonsense from Theo. 'Don't give him so much as a hint of encouragement,' he muttered darkly, leaning against the balustrade on the terrace and watching Theo make his way back down the path towards his own villa.

Francesca nudged Sally. 'Good to see somebody else getting the treatment that's usually reserved for me.'

'I don't see why Izzy shouldn't encourage him,' said Olivia. 'He's a perfect dear, utterly adorable.'

'Oh, good Lord,' said Corky, glancing in Max's direction, 'I knew that late-night Greek lesson would be a mistake. That fellow's unleashed something dangerous in your mother.'

'Well, if Izzy changes her mind, I'll be more than happy to fill in for her,' said Sally. 'Two minutes' notice would be all I'd need to get this body buffed up ready for him.'

'More like an entire afternoon,' sniggered Francesca.

Sally dealt her a nifty swipe with the magazine she was reading. 'Two minutes and I'd be irresistible to him. I'd have him panting at my feet.'

'Yeah, but he'd still be two decades older than you,' laughed Francesca. She raised herself from her sun-lounger. 'Come on, let's go for a swim and see if those Patterson boys are out and about.'

Izzy watched the two girls gather together their towels, flip-flops, sunglasses and bottles of Ambre Solaire, then picked up Sally's well-thumbed copy of *Cosmopolitan*, opened it at random and hid behind it, not wanting to catch anybody's eye, especially not Laura's. Too much had already been said on the subject of her having dinner with Theo and she really didn't want the fuss to continue. She felt a little as though she had been tricked into accepting his invitation. He had made it in front of everyone and she had known that she would have looked rude and churlish if she had said no. Although, curiously enough, she hadn't wanted to say no.

Since last week when she had made her peace with Theo he had behaved with impeccable restraint towards her. Not that they had seen much of him. Like Max, he had been busy with work – much to Laura's disappointment Max had even flown home for three days of important meetings. But when she had seen Theo, it had been down on the beach, before anyone else was up and while she had been sketching the bay. He would come and sit next to her after his early-morning swim. Yesterday Mark had joined them too, though he hadn't swum.

'Don't you like swimming?' she had asked him.

'I could ask the same of you,' he had said.

'It's too early for me. Too cold. I need the sea to have warmed up before I venture in.'

'Then that's the excuse I shall use as well. May I see?'

She passed him her sketchpad and watched his face for his reaction.

'I thought you said you weren't any good at this game?'

She looked critically at the charcoal drawing, a view of the headland showing Theo's villa peeping through the cypress trees. 'It's one of my better attempts.'

'So what are the bad ones like?' He began flicking through the pages, but Izzy remembered that the pad contained the drawing she had done of him some weeks earlier and snatched it out of his hands.

'That bad, eh? Well, I suppose we all underestimate our talents.'

'Even you?'

He raised an eyebrow. 'Implying that I don't seem the type to be insecure?'

'You seem very confident to me.'

'It's all a front. I'm as riven as the next artistic soul.'

She laughed.

'Why do I get the feeling you're not taking me seriously?'

'Perhaps I should read one of your books. Maybe then I'd be able to judge you better. Reading between the lines, I might get to see the real you.'

He feigned a look of hurt pride and put a clenched fist to his heart. 'You mean you haven't read one of my novels? I'm deeply wounded.' Then, dropping the act, he said, 'So if you don't like my kind of fiction, what do you read?'

'All sorts,' she said evasively. She let a handful of sand slip through her fingers, strongly suspecting that he would frown upon her choice of reading matter which usually contained romance and a happy ending.

'And specifically?' he pressed. 'What was the last book you read?'

'Don't let him bully you, Izzy.' Theo had emerged from the water. 'He is too used to mixing with literary snobs to appreciate that some people read for pleasure and escape rather than to be lectured.'

'That's simply not true, Theo, as well you know. I've never been able to abide that affected attitude. Pejorative conceit is what I've always fought against. Perhaps you should let Izzy speak for herself.'

They both looked at her, each waiting for her to take their side.

'Um . . . I think I'd rather leave you both to it,' she said, feeling that she couldn't answer one without offending the other. She put her things into her bag and stood up.

'You see what you've done, Mark?' Theo exclaimed. 'With your intimidating arrogance you have scared her away.'

'Hey, she was fine until you poked your nose in.'

'Stop it, you two.' She had laughed. 'I have enough of bickering children during term-time. When I'm on holiday I expect a break from it.'

They had been quick to apologise, and Theo said, 'Come and have breakfast with us and we'll prove to you that we can behave quite civilly.'

'And if we misbehave you can scold us again,' smiled Mark. 'You do it so beautifully.'

'Another time perhaps,' she had said. 'It's my turn this morning to go up to Nicos and fetch the rolls and croissants for everybody.'

That had been yesterday, and this morning Theo had appeared with a present for her. It was a book. 'It's from both of us and is by way of an apology for behaving like two naughty schoolboys yesterday. You mentioned to Mark that you were interested in reading one of his books and he wondered if you would enjoy this one. It is his first, and possibly his least bloodthirsty, but by no means the least unnerving. Please, borrow it for as long as you wish.'

She had read the blurb on the jacket and, under everyone's gaze, had opened the book and read the printed dedication: 'To Theo, because he was stupid enough to care.' Underneath was written, in a large loose hand, 'Don't worry, I'm not going soft on you – Mark.'

Intrigued, she had asked, 'What did you care so much about?'

He had closed the book in her hands, flashed her one of his brilliant smiles, and said, 'Have dinner with me tonight and I'll tell you.'

Confident now that everybody was going to leave her alone, she put down Sally's magazine and reached for the book Theo had brought for her. Its title – *Culling The Good* – didn't give the impression that she was in for a light-hearted romp. She looked at the photograph of Mark on the inside back flap: it showed him leaning against a wall in a darkened archway, his arms folded across his chest. He was wearing a leather jacket and an air of open hostility. The photographer must have spent an age getting the light and shadows just right, ensuring that they fell across his cheekbones to accentuate their sharpness as well as hollow out his eyes and emphasise the slight twist to his mouth. His hair was shorter than it was now, savagely so, and gave him a chilling insolence that was as disagreeable as it was threatening. He looked quite terrifying, the kind of man anyone with any sense would cross the road to avoid late at night. "The new prince of darkness," was one of the quotes on the back of the book, and certainly the man in the picture gave the appearance of more than living up to that description. Yet it was difficult to equate the man she had met, who made her smile with his unexpected humour, with the bleak person portrayed here. She turned to the author's biographical notes, to see if she could learn more about him, but there was only the year in which he had been born and the wide-ranging number of jobs he had had a go at: she could quite easily see him as a cub reporter, but not as a milkman. Nor could she visualise him working in a funeral parlour. Perhaps it was *de rigueur* to have an off-the-wall CV if you were going to be a successful author.

Exactly on time, Theo brought his car to a halt outside Villa Petros. He had been ready for over half an hour, but Mark had insisted that he play it cool. 'Early just won't do at all,' he had said.

'And you would know, would you?' Theo had thrown at him, while fiddling with his keys and checking his shirt collar in the mirror.

'Okay, I might not have your experience, but I know for sure that women don't like to be surprised when they're getting ready. Hurry her through those last few moments and the evening could be a disaster. She'll spend the first thirty minutes worrying that her makeup isn't right, or cursing you for making her forget those essential pieces of jewellery.'

'Izzy doesn't wear makeup.'

'She might tonight. She might feel she has to impress you.'

Now, as Theo pressed the doorbell, he hoped that Mark was wrong, that Izzy didn't feel the need to impress him. The last thing he wanted was for her to have spoiled her natural charm by covering herself in what she didn't need. She was perfect just as she was. He thought of the night when he had first met her and hoped that he was in for a repeat performance.

Max opened the door to him and led him through to the sitting room. Straight away Theo sensed that the relationship between them had shifted from its customary friendliness.

'So, where are you taking Izzy?' asked Max. He spoke stiffly, with all the authority of a Victorian father. He might just as well have been standing with his back to the fireplace, his hands clasped behind him, ready to take a horsewhip to Theo. It was tempting to taunt him and he was on the verge of doing so when he heard voices. Francesca and Sally came in from the terrace through one of the open french windows.

'Hi, Theo,' said Francesca. She threw herself on to one of the sofas and kicked off her fluorescent orange flip-flops. 'All ready for your hot date with Izzy?'

He smiled. 'I was under the impression I was merely having dinner with her. It has now turned into a hot date, has it? What fun. I look forward to the evening with greater anticipation.' Out of the corner of his eye he saw Sally draping her slinky body along the length of the sofa to his right. She was doing her best to attract his attention, running a hand through her long hair and sighing exaggeratedly. Amused, he turned to Max and suggested they go outside.

'How is it going with your young house guest?' he asked, when they were beyond eavesdropping distance. He hoped the question might help to restore the equilibrium of their friendship.

'She's behaving herself quite well, really. She's been as good as gold, apart from that little display in there just now.'

'Well, to put your mind at rest, she is wasting her time with me.'

Max looked at him closely. 'It's not you and Sally I'm worried about.'

'Oh?'

'Come off it, Theo. Don't play the innocent with me. This thing you seem to have going with Izzy, you won't . . . well, you won't do anything to upset her, will you? I'm very fond of her and I'd hate to see her . . .' He cleared his throat and tried again. 'I'd hate to see her used in any way.'

Levelling his gaze on Max's concerned face, Theo said, 'Two questions,

Max. What "thing" is it you assume that I have going with Izzy, and why would I want to upset her?'

'You know jolly well what I mean. You have a certain attitude when it comes to women.'

Theo shook his head. 'No, Max. You have decided for me that I have a certain attitude towards women. You have leaped to a conclusion regarding my private life and refuse to see me in any other light. But I will give you this promise: I have no more intention of hurting Izzy than you did when you first got to know Laura.'

'But that was different. It was love that I felt for Laura, it wasn't any of this fly-by-night—'

'And there you go again, leaping to conclusions. Now, then, if I am not mistaken, I hear the object of your desire approaching.'

Both men rose to their feet, and at once Theo saw that his wish had been granted. Flanked by Laura and Olivia, the object of his own desire looked as charming as she had the first night they had met.

23

Shirley Maclaine singing, 'If My Friends Could See Me Now' from the film *Sweet Charity* kept going through Izzy's mind as Theo, smiling and relaxed, decked out sexily in a loose-fitting linen suit, sunglasses and a litre or two of intoxicating aftershave, drove at an alarming speed through the sluggish early evening traffic. As he zigzagged his BMW through the slower-moving cars that threatened to slow his progress he struck Izzy as a man who had been born to drive flashy sports cars.

With the invigorating cool air rushing at her face as they drove along narrow winding roads that took them high into the hills, she was glad that she had elected to wear her hair in a plait – she had known that two minutes in an open-topped car with her hair loose would have been asking for trouble.

Throughout the day Francesca and Sally had been full of useful fashion tips and advice for her evening out with Theo. Francesca had been keen to lend her some outlandish clothes from her wardrobe as well as give her a head of stumpy little bumps threaded with bits of rag, while Sally had advocated the I've-just-tumbled-out-of-bed-but-for-you-I'm-willing-to-get-back-in look. 'Forget Francesca's funky look. Wanton allure is what you want to go for,' she had urged. 'Take it from me, it works every time.'

So would hanging out her tongue and pasting a Bonk Me Now label to it, Izzy had thought. She turned down Sally's offer to let her plunder the bewildering depths of her makeup bag, shooed the girls away and got ready alone, determined not to associate herself with purses made from sows' ears.

Just as Izzy was wondering if there were any more heart-stopping hairpin bends to negotiate, they arrived at the restaurant. It was tucked into the hillside and a craggy-faced man called Spiros greeted them. He looked much older than Theo, but amazingly they were the same age. 'We were in the army together for our national service,' Theo explained. 'That was where Spiros learned to cook so badly.'

'Yes – and, as a military chauffeur, it was where Theo learned to drive so fast,' laughed Spiros. He led them through the air-conditioned interior of the restaurant and outside to a covered area that gave them a perfect view of the slope of the hill they had just climbed, and which stretched away into the lush green valley. The light was already fading and pretty lanterns glowed on the white-clothed tables. Only a few tables were empty, but Spiros guided them to one that was reserved.

No sooner had they taken their seats and Spiros had left them than a short, overweight woman, hot and flushed, appeared. Theo immediately got to his feet and embraced her. After much kissing and a voluble exchange of words, he turned to Izzy and introduced her: 'Izzy, this is Marika, Spiros' wife. She doesn't speak any English, but if you are very nice to her she will cook you the best meal of your life.'

Izzy held out her hand and smiled. '*Kalispéra*,' she said, adding hesitantly '*ti kanete?*'

The other woman's face lit up with approval, but her quick-fired response was way beyond the simple words and phrases Izzy had picked up so far, and she looked to Theo for help. Smiling, he said, 'Marika says she is very well and compliments you on your accent.' Another lively and incomprehensible blast of banter from Marika followed, involving a lot of head-shaking and even a wagging finger. When they were alone, Izzy asked him what else Marika had said – 'She sounded very cross with you.'

He laughed. 'She was saying how beautiful you were, and that you were probably far too good for me.'

Izzy blushed, reached for her menu and studied it hard.

Theo smiled to himself. It hadn't been exactly what Marika had said, but he had seen it as a perfect opportunity to pay Izzy a compliment without frightening her off. Marika had in fact told him that this was yet another attractive woman he had brought to their restaurant and when was he going to make a return visit with the same one?

It amused him that Izzy still took fright every time he said anything nice about her. No matter how sincere he tried to make his words sound, they never penetrated the barrier of embarrassed awkwardness she hid behind. He had mentioned it to Mark. 'It doesn't matter how serious I try to be, she clearly thinks I am falsely flattering her. The guard, it goes straight up.'

'She's intelligent and English, Theo. *Ergo*, she has a natural suspicion of foreign men such as you, who make it their business to trade flattery for sex.'

'I don't recall my being a foreigner presenting itself as a problem when we were students.'

'The girls then were young and foolishly taken in by your supposed Continental good looks and money. You were one of the swankiest students in college, infamous for your extravagant parties. Of course they fell for you. You were a good catch – you were the Aristotle Onassis of Old Durham Town.'

'So how am I to gain her trust?'

'Perhaps you never will. Maybe you should just give in to the fact that she doesn't fancy you.'

Thinking of what Mark had said, and glancing at Izzy's pensive face, Theo felt even more determined to convince her – and everybody else – that he was serious about her. He wasn't used to being denied what he wanted but, to his surprise, the experience was not without its appeal. It would make the moment when it came – and he was certain it would – that much more pleasurable. Denial, he was coming to know, was good for sharpening one's sexual appetite.

Once Spiros had taken their order, brought them their wine and then their starter, they both relaxed into the evening. It was Izzy who asked the first question. 'I've kept my part of the bargain and agreed to have dinner with you. Now you must keep yours.'

'And what would that be?'

'You said you'd tell me the significance of Mark's dedication to you in *Culling The Good.*'

'Ah, I see. Well, before I solve the mystery for you, tell me, have you started reading it, and if so, what do you think of it?'

'I haven't been able to put it down,' she said, truthfully. All that day she had been gripped by its dark, menacing pace. 'I can see that I'm going to have to view Mark in a whole new light.'

He laughed. 'You think, then, that he is more interesting after reading a few chapters of his book?'

She caught his mocking tone. 'Not quite, but it does leave me wondering what else he's got going on inside that head of his.'

'You would not be the first.'

This time Theo's words were weighted with a seriousness that made Izzy's curiosity get the better of her. 'The first night I met you, you said that Mark had saved your life. What happened to you?'

He helped himself to another piece of bread from the basket between them, wiped it across his plate of fried aubergine salad, and said, 'It was when we were students. Late one night, on my way home after a party, I was attacked by a couple of young gentlemen who were eager to part me from my wallet. It was lucky for me that Mark is such a hooligan and is able to fight so well.' Finishing what was in his mouth, he added, 'According to the doctors, I was fortunate that Mark was passing at the time. If it had not been for him—' He stopped abruptly.

'Go on,' she said softly. She sensed that for once Theo was in earnest.

But if he had been, it was short-lived. His face lit up with a sexy grin and he said, 'If it had not been for Mark I would not be here tonight enjoying myself with you.'

Annoyed, she fiddled with her wine-glass, twisting its stem between her fingers. 'I wish you wouldn't do that.'

'I should very much like for your every wish to be my command, but what is it exactly that I must stop doing?'

'You always ... oh, I don't know, but everything turns into a joke with you.'

'Why should that be a problem?'

'It means I never know where I stand with you.'

'You would rather I was more sombre?'

'Yes, if it meant I didn't think you were laughing at me.'

In an instant the smile was gone from his face. He reached across the table, took her wine-glass from her, then held her hand. 'Is that what you think I have been doing? Is that why you refuse to let your guard down with me?'

She tried to slip away her hand, but he grasped it firmly.

'Izzy, please, I want you to know that I would never laugh at you. I'm not playing some silly game. It is important to me that you understand that.'

Izzy wished the conversation hadn't taken this particular turn, and suddenly felt tense, wary of where Theo might think he could lead her. But then she chided herself for overreacting. She forced herself to relax, to listen to the plinkety-plink of the bouzoúki music coming from inside the restaurant. 'Did you ever see the film *Shirley Valentine*?' She asked at last, hoping that she had hit upon a way to make Theo understand why she was so cautious of him.

Without releasing her hand, he nodded. 'Yes, of course I have. And I think, much as it will amuse you, most Corfiot men aspire to be your esteemed Mr Tom Conti. But what is the point you are making?'

'Um ... Well, do you remember the part when she discovers that Tom Conti, with whom she has—'

'Yes,' he interrupted, 'the boat looked in danger of capsizing.'

'I wasn't thinking of that bit specifically. I was going to say, do you remember when she realises he's been using the same chat-up line for countless other female tourists?'

Letting go of Izzy's hand, Theo said, 'Ah, so you see me in the same role. You think that I try out the same old routine on any pretty girl who comes my way, is that it?'

She wanted to say, 'Swear that that isn't *exactly* what you do,' but said, 'Maybe you're a tiny bit more subtle.'

He frowned. 'Do you not find me just a little attractive, Izzy?'

'You have your moments,' almost tripped off her tongue, but she doused the confession with a sip of her wine.

Still frowning, he said, 'So how do I convince you that I have the potential to be totally different?'

'You could spend the rest of the evening by not trying to come on to me.'

'What? Not one compliment?'

She shook her head.

'Not one? "Your eyes are like the stars in the heavens—"'

'Definitely not!'

'How about a—'

'Nothing, Theo. You're to be completely straight with me. No silliness.'

'Am I allowed to touch you?'

She hesitated. It had been quite pleasant a few minutes ago when his strong square hand had held hers. 'No,' she said resolutely. There were to be no half measures.

'And what then? If I behave myself all evening, what will be my prize? A kiss maybe?'

With perfect timing, saving her from giving him an answer, Spiros came across the restaurant to take away their empty plates. He returned shortly with their main course, an extravagant seafood platter for them to share. Its crowning glory was a lobster, which Theo got to work on immediately, skilfully dissecting it and passing Izzy pieces of tender white meat. 'Now that I am too scared to open my mouth for fear of breaking our agreement,' he said, 'tell me about yourself. Where in England did you grow up and what kind of a child were you?'

'Well, I think it's fairly safe to say that I was a mistake. My mother didn't want me, and if she'd thought she could get away with it she would probably have lost me in the hospital where I was born. A large laundry basket would have done the trick.'

'Is that, as I have learned from Mark, a classic example of one of your famously ironic English jokes?'

'Actually, no. It's the truth.' To her surprise, she found herself telling him about the brother she had never known, whose tragically short life had eclipsed hers and had caused her mother's breakdown. She skirted briefly over her time in the children's home and the extent of what her mother had inflicted on her. She spoke with detached composure, as if it were someone else's story she was telling. Until now, she hadn't shared with anyone, not even Laura, the details of her childhood. It felt strange lifting the lid after so many years of silence. Part of her had always been afraid to admit what had gone on, as though she would be judged and found wanting in some way. That, maybe, it had been her fault.

'*Ti apésyo!*' Theo said, when she finished speaking.

'Sorry?'

'I said, that's terrible.'

'You're right. It was terrible that my mother's depression wasn't diagnosed sooner.'

'I meant it was awful for you.'

She gave a casual shrug, as if this had never occurred to her before. 'It's not a perfect world that we live in,' she said dismissively. 'All we can do is square our shoulders and put these things behind us.' It was sound advice, and she had tried hard to follow it all her life, but had never truly achieved it.

'So, having squared your shoulders in your typically English Dunkirk spirit, what kind of relationship do you have with your mother now?'

A picture of a vindictive Bette Davis serving up a dish of dead rats in *Whatever Happened to Baby Jane?* came into Izzy's mind. 'Um . . . a difficult one.'

Pouring more wine into their glasses, Theo looked at Izzy thoughtfully. Knowing he was heading into dangerous territory, he said, 'And your father, how did you get on with him?' He saw her hesitate, and waited for her to realign her composure.

'To be honest with you, I never really knew where I stood with him. I spent most of my childhood hoping desperately that he would notice me.'

Theo found it impossible to imagine that any father would not have wanted to hug a younger version of the woman he saw before him and tell her how special she was. 'He was distant with you?'

'I think he had to be. He was caught between my mother and me. We were both terrified of upsetting or annoying her.'

'You paint a picture that is very black. Were there no good times?'

'Of course there were. I loved school and I was always—'

'But nothing happy in your home life?'

'I suppose to a Greek man this must sound rather strange.'

He nodded. 'Families are very important to us. Generations live together and all in a degree of domestic harmony.'

'No arguments at all?'

'Ah, well, disagreements come naturally to us, but we blow up over them and then we carry on as though nothing has happened. We are used to living in close quarters with those we love and who drive us to distraction. Take Angelos and Sophia, for instance. Under the one roof they have Angelos' mother living with them, a classic matriarchal figure who makes most of the important decisions for the family. They have two young daughters still at school, and they have Giorgios who is in his early twenties and who is quite happy to remain at home. It probably has not occurred to him that he could leave his parents and find a place of his own. He will stay there until he marries. He might even move his bride in with him. And yet it works. Despite the heated disagreements and differences of opinions, they get along famously.'

'Goodness! It sounds the perfect recipe for disaster. Could you live like that?'

'I would prefer not to. But if my parents had nowhere to live, I would gladly have them live with me.'

The thought of her mother moving into Izzy's neat little flat bringing with her the army of china statues made Izzy shudder.

'You are cold? Would you like my jacket to keep you warm?'

'No,' she laughed, 'I was picturing the nightmare scene of my mother moving in with me.'

'Would it be so very bad?'

'It would be awful. Just one weekend with her is enough to sap the most resilient spirit. Within a month I'd lose what little sanity and self-confidence I've scraped together since I left home.'

'She would criticise you?'

'Constantly. It would be one snide comment after another. I'm a terrible disappointment to her.'

'But I, too, am a disappointment to my mother.'

'You?'

'Why, yes. All the time I have to listen to my mother asking me when I am going to settle down with a nice girl. She desperately wants a grandchild. She feels aggrieved not to have gained the same status as her friends, that of doting grandmother.'

'What do you tell her?'

He looked as though he was holding back a smile. 'I tell her that I'm waiting for the right woman.' Then, 'Have you never tried standing up to your mother?'

Izzy snorted. 'You're joking!'

'Why not? Why not be honest with her? Tell her that she has done her best so far to ruin your life but you are not prepared to let her spoil the rest.'

'You make it sound the most natural thing in the world.'

'That's because it is.'

'You haven't met Prudence Jordan.'

'I admit that is a pleasure I have been denied, but one that I would be curious to experience.'

Contemplating the dangerously attractive face before her, Izzy thought that it was something she would pay good money to see as well. Just what effect would Theo Vlamakis, with his dark-eyed charm and good looks, have on her mother? She pictured his broad-shouldered body restrained in her mother's flower-sprigged sitting room and heard Prudence say, 'Isobel tells me that you're *Greek*.' She would make it sound as if he was of an inferior race. Her mother considered foreigners a clumsy mistake on God's part, a bit of tinkering in his celestial workshop – *Just trying out an idea I had, Mrs Jordan, soon have it put right.* Knitting blankets for the overseas poor was all very well, but perish the thought she should have to entertain them for tea.

Across the valley, the setting sun had almost completed its descent, and as the light drained from the sky, their dessert arrived. Theo explained that it was a speciality of Marika's called *locamades* – a melt-in-the-mouth concoction of deep-fried batter covered in honey and dusted with cinnamon.

'You still haven't told me about the dedication in *Culling The Good*,' Izzy said, eyeing the dish with anticipation. 'Does it refer to something specific you did for Mark?'

'Aha, Izzy, you have all the makings of a fine detective. Nothing eludes you. But here, try one of these, they are delicious.' He held out his fork. She tried to take it from him, but he smiled and said, 'No innuendo intended, but open wide.' She did as he said. The warm sweetness melted in her mouth. Watching her lick her lips, he said, 'You should feel honoured. It is not for everyone that Marika makes this dish.'

When Marika herself had appeared at their table with the unasked-for dessert, he had known it was her way of giving her seal of approval to his dinner guest. She had only ever done it twice before. Would this be third time lucky? Realising he still hadn't answered Izzy's question, he speared another honeyed ball of sweetness on his fork, held it across the table for her, and said, 'Mark and I have a friendship that is unlike most others. Each of us has saved the other from an untimely death. And, no, I'm not exaggerating. Mark really did save my life that night back in Durham when I was a careless student with more money than sense. I made myself an easy target. I should have known better.'

'And Mark? How did you save his life?'

Theo hesitated. He knew better than anyone that his friend hated his past to be discussed. 'It is a very personal matter, and one that perhaps only Mark should share with you. But I will say this, what Mark did for me took an immense amount of courage and what I did for him needed no such thing, only patience. Not that he would agree with me. But that is so typical of the man – he likes to disagree with everything I say and do.'

'With anything in particular?'

'Ah, well, the list is long and varied, but perhaps my worst crime in his opinion is to be a fat capitalist pig.'

'And are you?'

'I like to think not. But who knows? Maybe I am. I enjoy what I do. I hope I don't sound arrogant if I say that I am proud of my success. I also have no shame in appreciating what money can do for a person. Used wisely it can be a powerful tool against a lot of unnecessary suffering in the world. But enough of me. What would your friends consider your worst crime to be?'

'Probably my inability to decide what I really want to do with the rest of my life.'

'A crime indeed, when you consider that you are only given the one. So what is wrong with your current existence that you feel you should be changing it?'

'I don't think I'm cut out for teaching.'

'You don't like children? You surprise me. I would have thought you would have been very good with them. I see you as being one of the most patient and understanding people I have come across.' And, with a smile, he added quickly, 'That is said as a comment on your ability as I see it, a fact, not a reflection of my feelings for you. It was not a compliment.'

'As a matter of fact I really like children,' she said, letting his remark pass with a smile of her own. 'The problem lies in the school I work in and what's going on there. We've got a headmistress who's on a mission to cleanse the staffroom of faces she doesn't like.'

'Does she like yours?'

'I couldn't tell you. So far I've done my best to keep out of her way, but I wouldn't be at all surprised to get home at the end of the summer and find a redundancy notice on my doormat.'

'Can she do that?'

'She can do more or less whatever she wants. She's been brought in by the school governors to solve the problem of dwindling numbers and escalating costs by a process of reshaping. Which is a nasty word for getting rid of dedicated, hardworking teachers.'

He was surprised at the depth of bitterness in her voice. 'So, change is in the air?'

She sighed. 'I guess so. But what exactly? That's what I should be deciding while I'm here on holiday.'

'That day we all went to Áyios Stéfanos,' he said thoughtfully, 'you said you saw yourself growing old with Alan and having children. Is that what you really want to do with your life, marry the man of your dreams and have a family?'

She sat back in her chair, horrified at what he had just said. But it was horribly near the truth. Yet how could she admit, in this intimidating age of women having it all, that if the circumstances were right she would be quite happy to give up work and devote herself to full-time motherhood? And was it fair that she should be made to feel guilty for wanting that, as though she was harbouring some awful subversive secret? When had it become socially unacceptable to be a full-time mother? And just where had the concept of choice gone, now that women always had to be on top?

She stared at Theo in the soft light cast from the glowing lantern on the table, searching his face for signs of cynicism. But, try as she might, she could detect no mockery in him. The reverse seemed to be true: he was gazing at her with such a look of sincerity that it forced her to speak the truth. 'Perhaps that's partly what has upset me so much this past year. Mistakenly, I thought I was in a relationship that had a natural progression towards marriage and children, something I'd always thought I would be lucky enough to have, then suddenly—'

'Then suddenly all your dreams were snatched away from you?'

She nodded. 'You know, when I was young I believed that if I wished hard enough my dreams would come true.'

'And now you don't believe that?'

She laughed, but it didn't sound a happy laugh. 'Dreams are for children. So is wishing.'

'I disagree. I think that to live without a dream is what causes so much misery in this world. Dreams, hopes, aspirations, those are the things that make each day worth waking up for. Mark had all that taken away from him for a time and it was the worst hell anybody could live through. If you have a dream, Izzy, you should hang on to it, no matter how far-fetched you imagine it to be. Don't let anyone talk you out of it. Now, shall I order coffee, or would you prefer one later when I invite you in for a night-cap?'

'Assuming that I'll accept?'

'Assuming that you will reward me for having behaved myself . . .' he glanced at his watch '. . . for nearly three whole hours.'

'Is that a record for you?'

He grinned. 'I think it is.'

24

It was eleven o'clock, and in one of the busy harbourside bars in Kassiópi, Francesca and Sally were just starting their evening. They had arranged to meet Nick and Harry, who were having dinner with their parents beforehand. Nick had described the evening as a command performance: 'It's Pa's fiftieth, so we've all got to be there in attendance lying through our back teeth convincing him fifty is the new forty. Some bloody hope!'

Having arrived early, the girls ordered two vodkas with Coke and sat back to take in the view of passers-by.

'How's that for an entry into the Biggest Bum in the Universe competition?' said Sally, indicating with her eyes a woman in tight white jeans, a low-cut top and shocking pink stilettos. 'What do you think she's going for, the Trailer Trash ensemble, or the Rover's Return look?'

'You're so cruel, Sally.'

'Not a malicious thought in my head, just speaking as I find. But take a look over there, I bet you could fry an egg on that back.'

Francesca winced at the sight of a pair of excruciatingly red shoulders branded by white strap marks where the top half of a bikini had been. 'Poor woman, she looks as though she should be in intensive care.'

'She looks completely gross, you mean.' Then noticing a man at a nearby table, Sally leaned in closer. 'Clock the guy behind you.'

Francesca twisted round to see who Sally was referring to. He was fair-haired, casually dressed, almost scruffily so, but not bad-looking in a lean, hawkish, lived-in way. He was sitting low down in his seat, his head resting on the back of the chair, one of his legs crossed over the other, a hand picking absently at the laces of his CAT boot as he gazed across the water. She watched him take out a small notebook and pen from his shirt pocket and scribble something down. She thought he looked vaguely familiar. 'Maybe he's got one of those faces,' she said, turning back to Sally and lowering her voice, 'but I feel as if I've seen him before.'

'Yeah, I know what you mean. He's kinda fit, wouldn't you say?'

'Not bad, if you go for the type who looks old enough to be married with a brood of runny-nosed children.'

'So where are they? I see no wife. I see no snivelling kids. And I'll tell you what else I don't see, a wedding ring.'

'He could be divorced.'

'Or widowed.'

'Perhaps he's a serial wife murderer. He bumps them off for the life insurance.'

'Yeah, a wife murderer who goes off on holiday with the spoils once the body's been cremated and the evidence has gone up in smoke.'

'And he's here hoping to pick up his next victim, trawling the streets of Kassiópi for a beautiful woman with a desire to die young. Shall I introduce you?'

Their laughter caused several heads to turn, including, and much to Sally's delight, the fair-haired man's. 'It's official,' she said, when he had turned away. She scooped out the slice of lemon from her drink and sucked it. 'He's divine and I wish he was mine.'

'Sorry to be the bearer of bad news, but I've just recognised who he is. He's Theo's friend, the one who's staying with him. Anyway, I thought you liked Harry. Isn't that why we're here tonight?'

'Oh, come off it, Francesca. You know very well I'm out of the running there. He doesn't even know I exist. It's quite clear he's got the hots for you and you've got his number. And don't give me any of that wide-eyed stuff. No, there's nothing else for it, I'll just have to do the honourable thing and get Nick off your back for you.'

'Sounds like you've got it all worked out. Ever thought to check with me and see what I think about it?'

Sally grinned. 'Go on, tell me I've got it wrong.'

Unable to deny what Sally was suggesting, Francesca smiled too. 'But Harry's so shy. He'll never get it together to ask me out.'

'Well, we'll just have to give him a shove in the right direction, won't we?'

'And what'll you do with Nick?'

'Oh, I'll let him do what he's best at, I'll give him the opportunity to shoot his mouth off the whole time.'

'Two of a kind, then,' laughed Francesca. 'A match made in heaven.'

Sally flicked her discarded lemon across the table; it landed in Francesca's lap. 'In the absence of anything better I'm not too proud to sweep up the crumbs. It's a shame about Theo fancying Izzy, isn't it?' She sighed. 'Looks, age and money. I could have been a happy woman.'

'You're dreadful, you really are. What is it with you and older men?'

'I was a deprived child, no father figure in my life.'

'Depraved, maybe, but your father's great.'

'Okay, I'll admit it. It's the sex. Older men are miles better at it. They've all the experience that idiots like Nick haven't. There's none of that awful fumbling around, looking for where things go. They're also keen to impress, to prove they're still up for it. It's a great combination.'

Francesca smirked. 'And you thought my dad would be good in bed with you. You're one sick girl.'

Coming as near as she would ever be to embarrassment, Sally flushed faintly and recrossed her legs. 'How was I to know he was your father? We hadn't been introduced or anything.' And changing the subject, she said, 'You know what really gets me about Izzy is that she doesn't seem interested in Theo. Or do you suppose she's just playing it super-cool?'

'Haven't a clue. But whatever she's doing, it seems to be working. Mum says he's been really persistent. The harder she's made it for him, the more he's pursued her. Oh, and about time too. Here's Nick and Harry.'

'Top banana to you, girls!' Nick greeted them. He plonked himself in the chair next to Francesca. 'So, how's it going? Sorry we're late, but the aged ones have trouble feeding themselves these days. It takes for ever. I tell you, when they start dribbling, I'll be long gone.'

Harry took the seat beside Sally. 'Excuse my intolerant brother, won't you? I'm hoping that one day he'll meet with a terrible accident and we'll all be put out of our misery.'

'Hey, who released your comedy valve, mate? You should be grateful that we're in the company of women and years of good breeding forbids me from taking a swing at you. Now, who's drinking what?'

They ordered a round of drinks, followed shortly by another. The bar was really busy now, and the warm night air was filled with raised voices and the pounding of a heavy pop-Latin beat. Having developed a headache after her second vodka and Coke, Francesca found that she wasn't in the mood for Nick's constant stream of jokes and putdown lines aimed at his brother. She liked him well enough, but he was one of those guys who liked himself better than anybody else did, and had long since lost touch with where the on-off switch was for his mouth. Harry was his brother's antithesis: was clean-cut and dead straight while Nick went for the funky surf gear and pony-tail look, and could have done with a lesson in opening up. She could see that he felt awkward in this situation. He was probably one of those anti-social students who spent most of the term with his door shut, his nose in a book. He certainly didn't seem the type to be off his head at some club every night. That was more his brother's scene. It used to be hers too. Well, not the off-her-head bit, it was the music she and Sally had been into. It was how she had met Carl. But now with the demise of her relationship with Carl she had the feeling she had outgrown it. Across the table, Sally, the perpetual thrill-seeker, was telling Nick all about one of the clubs in Manchester that had been a regular night out for them.

'You must have heard of the Tiger Lounge,' Sally was saying. 'It's dead famous. I can't believe you've been to Manchester and not heard of it.'

'So what's so special about it? What kind of music do they do?'

'The best in all things kitsch. Sixties, seventies, eighties. They even do classic movie themes. The last time we were there it was nothing but Andy Williams and Shirley Bassey.'

Francesca remembered that night all too well. She and Sally had spent most of the day getting ready for it, dressing in mini-skirts, and false nails and eyelashes. Another friend had done their hair for them, whipping it into outrageous beehives that they sprayed green. It was that night when she realised she had reached the end of the road with Carl. She had caught him chatting to a redhead in a fluffy pink bra top, and overheard him asking for her phone number and when he could see her again. She hadn't stuck around to hear the answer.

'Kitsch is great once in a while,' Nick shouted, above the music that seemed even louder now, 'but you can't beat a good rock festival. Ever been to Glastonbury, Sal?'

'No. Don't fancy all the mud.'

'You should give it a go. But I'll tell you what I'm doing next year. I'm planning a trip to Goa; that's where the hardcore ravers go. A mate of mine's been. He said the tropical beach parties are out of this world. Only trouble is, the drug laws are so harsh that if you get caught with so much as a Tic-Tac in your pocket, you'll end up in prison for the rest of your life. Another drink, anyone? How about you, Frankie? You're not saying much – losing the power of speech, are you?'

'No, just the will to live. And please, don't call me Frankie.'

'Oo-er, and what medication have you missed today?'

'You okay?' asked Sally.

'I've got a headache.'

'That's a woman for you.'

'Give it a rest, Nick, and leave her alone. Would you like a glass of water?' She looked gratefully across the table to Harry. 'Thanks,' she said, 'but I think I'll take some time out, go for a walk round the harbour. The music's too loud here.'

Making room for her to slip by, Harry rose uncertainly to his feet. Even more uncertainly, he said, 'Do you want some company?'

Avoiding Sally's eyes, she said, 'If you like.'

With the sound of Nick calling after them, 'Harry, behave yourself, don't go doing anything with Frankie that I'll regret,' they moved off.

'Do you want me to throttle him now or later?' Harry asked. 'It would be a pleasure either way.'

'When I'm feeling better I'll do it myself.'

They walked slowly round the harbour, dodging the swarms of scooters and the gangs of promenading Greek grandmothers with their pushchairs of sleeping children. 'There's a small bar further up the hill owned by a strange old woman in slippers,' Harry said. 'Would you like to sit there? It would at least be quiet.'

'What's strange about the old lady?'

'Well . . . I hardly like to mention it, but she suffers from an excess of facial hair.'

'A full set?'

'No. Only a moustache. It's possible, though, that she's working on growing a beard.'

In spite of the thumping pain in her head, Francesca smiled. 'Well, lead on and let me see for myself.'

The bar was blissfully quiet, just as Harry had said it would be, and almost at once she began to feel better. It was in a slightly elevated position with no more than half a dozen tables overlooking the harbour. They were the only customers and Francesca felt a pang of pity for the owner, who must barely scrape a living from the place. She was as old and strange as Harry had described, and after she had shuffled along in her sheepskin slippers with their drinks – a cup of coffee for Francesca and bottle of Amstel for Harry, who was also the lucky recipient of a beaming smile – she shuffled back to her wooden chair in the doorway of the bar and resumed her lace-making.

'How often do you come here?' asked Francesca. 'I'm getting the impression she knows you.'

'I sometimes hang out here when Nick's in one of his party moods.'

'Which is quite often, I should think. Does he ever stop?'

'Nope. The dweeb's been hyperactive since the day he was born.'

'But you prefer a more leisurely pace?'

'Is that a polite way of asking if I'm always this boring?'

'Whoa, the boy has a raw spot.'

'Doesn't everyone?'

'Some more tender and exposed than others. And I'd like it known that I didn't accuse you of being boring, you did it all yourself. Which is a shame, really, because you're not.'

'Patronising me now?'

She ripped open a sachet of white sugar and tipped it into her coffee. 'What is it with you? Don't you recognise a compliment when you hear one? Or have you been in your brother's shadow too long?'

He pushed his glasses back up on to his nose. 'Something like that, yes.'

'Then maybe it's time you did something about it.'

'Any suggestions?'

'Well, yes, seeing as you've asked. When we've finished our drinks you can walk me home. That's if you don't think you've drawn the short straw.'

As he poured the beer into his glass, Harry couldn't believe his luck. He had been wondering for days how to steal a march over his brother and get this girl on her own, and now it had happened. 'No, no, of course I don't think that,' he said, suddenly realising that she might take his silence for indifference. 'But I thought you and Sally would be staying on with Nick for—'

'The last thing I'm in the mood for is a long session in a nightclub with your brother strutting his top-banana stuff. I vote we leave them to it.'

'You're sure, then?'

'A rule you need to learn, Harry,' she said, dipping her finger into the froth of his beer then licking it off, 'we girls don't like to be accused of not knowing our minds. Do you think you can grasp that?'

He stared at her as though she had just committed an erotic act. 'I'll try,' he murmured.

Erotic acts were on Mark's mind as he walked home with the aid of a torch that, this time, he had remembered to bring with him. Though the moon was full, its silvery rays did not penetrate the dense foliage of the trees in the olive grove, and the stony path he was carefully negotiating was as black as his mood.

While sitting in the harbour in Kassiópi, he had been trying to get his head round the next chapter of his book, without success. It was the point in the story-line that invariably gave him the most difficulty. It concerned the protagonist's sex life, or rather the protagonist's prospective foray into some erotic action betwixt the sheets. If it weren't for his publisher's insistence that nearly all crime novels had to have a will-they-won't-they element of suspense, he wouldn't bother. 'But I'm writing psychological gore-fests not bloody bodice-rippers!' had been his response when his editor had first raised the question of whether or not he couldn't include some sexual chemistry between his characters. 'Just a touch,' his editor had reasoned bravely. 'It would engage the reader's interest further. It would also broaden the appeal of your novels.' It was back to that old number of him being a marketable commodity.

Stupidly he had let his principles fly out of the window and done what he had been asked to do. Which meant that because it had happened once it would go on happening. But it didn't get any easier. Theo said he was no good at it because (a) he was British – what did the British know about passion? – and (b) he lacked experience. Such a cheap sense of humour, that boy! Even relying on his imagination, which was as vivid as the next man's, if not more so, he still found that the sex scenes he wrote lacked emotion and spontaneity.

He had spent most of today trying to write this chapter but hadn't got anywhere with it. Not long after Theo had left to take Izzy out for dinner, he had decided to give himself a change of scene by going into Kassiópi for the evening, but that had proved as big a waste of time as the rest of the day had.

Maybe not entirely. People-watching could always be put to good use and he had been quietly amused by the group of youngsters sitting at a nearby table. The dynamics of any group of people never failed to interest him. It was always fascinating to see who was the leader and who were the followers, and in this instance, the smallest guy was the one with the biggest mouth and ego. Mark had recognised the two girls as part of the Sinclair contingent – he had seen them swimming out to the raft below their villa – and the lads were presumably the ones Izzy had said were staying with their parents in the pink villa next door to Dolly-Babe and Silent Bob's. It was funny how easily their little community had been put together. Here they all were, two thousand miles from home, but already they had restructured themselves into a microcosm of what they had come here to escape.

Climbing the first of the steady uphill slopes of the path, Mark wished that he, too, could escape. If he could find a way round that chapter, he would. But he knew there was no avoiding it: it had to be done, and soon, or it might make him freeze up. Writer's block was only ever a stone's throw away for any novelist, and he knew that the smallest problem could grow into a wall of self-doubt and neurosis. Then, with a wry smile, he thought, he should let Theo write it. After all, he was the one with all the experience.

That was the trouble with writing. It took up the vast majority of his time and made for a lousy social life. Most days he would get up early, work through till lunch, then make himself a sandwich. He would eat it standing at the sink planning his afternoon session, which inevitably struck through most of the evening, or he would go out for a walk along the coastal path to clear his head. If he was feeling generous to himself he might wander up the hill and have lunch at the village bookshop, where they had an extraordinary selection of second-hand books as well as a great café. On warm sunny days he ate outside on the terrace, fending off the gulls while eavesdropping on the tourists and gaining all sorts of fascinating insights into their lives.

Other than his writing and the writing group he led, he had no commitments to tie him to anyone or anything. Initially, that was exactly how he had wanted it. He hadn't wanted another person's life touching his. But once he had gained sufficient belief in himself that he was straight enough to consider a relationship little had come his way. It had seemed easier in the long run to cut his losses and absorb himself in his work. When he was on a roll there was nothing better, it gave him the ultimate high: the satisfying high that drugs and alcohol had never provided. What more mysterious and mind-altering process could there be than to sit down of a morning and, at the touch of his fingertips, lose himself in a world that at times was more real than the one in which he lived?

He turned to his right and stood at the end of Theo's drive. It was lit up every few yards by a series of mushroom-shaped lights. Outside the villa, he saw Theo's car. Surprised that his friend was back so soon, he hunted through his pockets for his key, then hesitated. Supposing Theo was back early because he and Izzy were on the verge of doing what the protagonist in his current book was supposed to be enjoying?

Theo wouldn't thank him for bursting in and ruining it. Do that and he'd never hear the last of it.

So, what should he do?

Go in and ruin everything for his friend, or wander down to the beach and wait for the lights to go out?

He favoured the last option. Edging his way quietly round the side of the house, he took the path down to the beach.

25

Theo knew that his garden made the perfect romantic setting, so he led Izzy to the edge of the terrace and put their glasses of Metaxá on the low wall, then watched her stare up at the stars that pricked the velvet night sky. He knew that the next few moments would be crucial. Turn on the charm now, and she would run. He had come so far this evening in gaining her trust and he didn't want to do anything to jeopardise that.

While driving back from the restaurant he had been trying to come to terms with exactly what he felt for Izzy. His conclusion had surprised him. Or had it?

Beside him on the terrace, Izzy said, 'I've had a wonderful evening, Theo. Thank you, it's been lovely.'

Any number of snappy one-liners came into his mind, but with iron-will restraint, he said, 'I'm delighted you enjoyed yourself. Do you think you would want to do it again sometime?'

She smiled cautiously. 'I might.'

'And has my behaviour met with your exacting standards?'

'Um . . . I think so.'

He moved in closer. 'Does that mean I get my prize?'

'Well, perhaps just a small one.'

'Not too small, I hope.'

Backing away from him, Izzy reached for her glass, took a sip of the smooth brandy and wondered why she was still keeping Theo at what she thought was a safe distance. Wasn't she being absurd? Why not go for it? What was to stop her seizing the day and enjoying a sparkle of brightness in an otherwise lacklustre life? It was only a kiss he wanted.

So why did the idea make her feel so nervous?

She took another sip of her drink and forced herself to face the truth. She was nervous that he might be disappointed in her. Doubtless he would be a skilled kisser and would know a good kiss from a bad one.

But as convinced as she was that Theo was about to try to kiss her, he didn't. Instead, he stepped away from her and began to pace the terrace.

'What is it?' she asked.

He came and stood in front of her again. 'I'm sorry,' he said, 'it's just that you make me feel nervous.'

'Nervous? I make *you* nervous?'

'Yes, Izzy. I know this sounds crazy when we have known each other for so little time, and yet . . . and yet . . .' His words fizzled out and he resumed his pacing.

'And yet, what?' she asked. What was going on here? Was she missing something?

He came to a sudden stop, just in front of her. 'I think there is a very real danger that I am falling in love with you.'

She stared at him dumbfounded. 'You're kidding, right?'

He looked hurt. 'From the moment I first saw you, you have had an extraordinary effect on me. Not so much as a kiss has passed between us, but I know I feel so very strongly for you.'

'But you know nothing about me.'

'I have learned more than you think. When you talk, Izzy, I listen. And tonight you have spoken a lot about yourself.'

There was no refuting this. Perhaps it was all the wine she had drunk, but she had shared with Theo more about herself than she had with anybody else. To fill in the silence she said, 'We have kissed, actually.'

'We have?'

'Yes, that day when you taught me to dive.'

He shook his head. 'That was no kiss.'

'Your lips touched mine, if I remember rightly. Sorry to be pedantic, but by my definition that makes it a kiss.'

With one of his brilliant smiles, he said, 'By my definition that was merely a touching of lips, it was not a touching of souls. Now this is what I call a kiss.'

In what seemed like one deft movement, he stepped in close, drew her to him and kissed her. But that's not fair, she thought, I wasn't ready! She willed herself to relax, to enjoy the sensation of Theo's firm mouth familiarising itself with hers. But it was no good. She felt stiff and awkward in his arms, conscious of everything she was doing wrong, or might do wrong.

It was at this moment, down on the beach where he was still killing time, that Mark looked up the hillside. In the light cast from the villa, he had no problem in identifying Theo and Izzy on the terrace above him and what they were doing. Troubled, he pushed his hands into his trouser pockets. For some reason that wasn't clear to him, he was disappointed that Izzy hadn't held out longer on Theo. Why was everything so bloody easy for the man?

He kicked at a rock, feeling that strange sixth-sense thing he got when his writing wasn't going well. It was what he called a plot snag. It was a warning sensation that pestered him, kept him awake at night, kept him from thinking straight, giving him no peace until he hit on what the problem was and where the answer lay. Sometimes it was days before the solution came to him.

He bent down, picked up a large, heavy stone and hurled it into the calm sea. It made a satisfyingly loud splash. So loud that it caused a distraction for the happy lovers above him.

'Is that you, Mark?' came Theo's voice. 'What are you doing down there?'

'Enjoying a late-night stroll. Why? What the hell are you doing up there?' His words had slipped out before he could stop them.

'Izzy is here and I'm supposed to be making her some coffee. Why not join us?'

By the time he had reached the terrace there was no sign of either Izzy or Theo. He went inside. Through an open door at the far end of the sitting room he saw that Theo was on the phone in his study. With both elbows resting on the desk, he appeared to be engaged in one of his typically heated Greek conversations and looked far from happy at having his attention diverted.

Mark found Izzy in the kitchen making the coffee. 'I'll get the mugs,' he said, reaching for them from a shelf on one of the dressers. He set them down on the chunky wooden table behind them. 'Good meal?' he asked, searching the tall fridge for a carton of milk.

'Yes, it was excellent. But I ate far too much.'

'Where did he take you?'

'I've no idea. It was way off in the hills. The people who run the taverna are friends of his.'

'Spiros and Marika?'

'That's right. Have you been there too?'

'Once or twice. As a matter of interest what did you have for your dessert?'

She gave him a puzzled look. 'Um . . . something delicious with a name I can't quite remember. *Loc-, loca—*'

'*Locamades?*'

'Yes, that's it,' she said. 'Why do you ask?'

'No special reason. It looks like Theo's going to be a while on the phone, let's take our coffee outside.'

They sat at a small table where Mark lit several candles designed to keep mosquitoes at bay. 'I'll leave you to add your own milk and sugar,' he said. Leaning back in his chair, he hooked one leg over the other and fiddled with a fraying shoelace. He stared morosely into the darkness. It had been the worst kind of day for him: depressingly uncreative. In his uncommunicative state, he knew he wasn't good company, that he should have stayed down on the beach until Izzy had gone home. But, then, common sense had never been his strong suit.

As though reading his mind, Izzy said, 'So how was your evening?'

He shifted his gaze, settled it on her face. 'Disappointing. I went into Kassiópi hoping that a change of scene might improve my mood.'

'And it didn't?'

'No.' The finality in his voice sounded harsh and discordant. Realising how rude he was being, he added, 'Sorry, I've had a bad day, got nothing of any worth done.'

'Do you get many days like this?'

'It varies.' He told her about his struggle with his protagonist's miserable love-life. 'It's an on-going thing I have with each book I write. You'd think it would get easier, but it doesn't.'

'I've made a start on *Culling The Good.*'

'And your verdict?'

'I'd be a fool if I sat here and told you I wasn't enjoying it.'

'You'd be surprised how brutally candid people can be. I'm continually criticised for being too grim and bleak, too realistic. Not that it bothers me. In-your-face realism is what I'm aiming to achieve. I want to offend. It means I've hit home, touched a nerve. I'm not interested in the cosy crime world of purple rinses, thatched cottages and mass redemption. I like to think that my books have a touch more gravitas and shock value in them than your average episode of *Scooby-Doo*.'

'Based on the little I've read so far of your book, I think that goes without saying. But perhaps you could answer this for me – it's something Max and I were discussing this afternoon. If all comedians are supposed to have a dark side, does it naturally follow that writers of your genre have a comedic side to them?'

In spite of his ill-humour, Mark smiled. 'Gee, you think?'

She smiled too. 'Perhaps I'll ask you again when you've had a better day. Do you suppose Theo is going to be much longer? I ought to be going, really.'

'I'll go and have a word with him, shall I?'

'Please. I don't have a key and I know that Max will be waiting up for me.'

'He will? Why? Doesn't he trust you?'

'It's not me he doesn't trust, it's Theo. Oh, perhaps I shouldn't have said that. You won't tell Theo, will you?'

'The lips are sealed. Hang on here a minute and I'll see what he's got to say.'

He returned shortly. 'Looks like Theo's going to be stuck for some time. He's asked me to do the honourable thing and walk you home or he'll get it in the neck from Max. That okay with you?'

'Mm . . . With the insight I now have of what goes on in your mind I'm not sure I want to go anywhere in the dark with you.'

He pulled out a small torch from his back pocket, switched it on, held it against his face, and let out a hollow, ghoulish laugh. 'You have nothing to fear, my dear. Take my hand and step into the madness of the world I inhabit.'

She laughed and allowed herself to be pulled across the garden towards the gate that led to the hillside path. 'Has anyone ever told you that you're quite mad?'

'That's really not the kind of thing you should say to a madman, especially if he's the one in charge of the torch.' He flicked it off and for a moment they were plunged into darkness.

When their eyes had adjusted, Izzy said, 'Look, over there.' She pointed through a gap in the cypress trees, down to the sea, where moonlight danced on the softly rippling surface and a man in a small fishing-boat with a lantern was casting his nets. 'Isn't that the most magical sight? See the way the light from his lantern is falling across the still water. It's almost phosphorescent. And those shadows, the way they glisten on the water.' She turned and faced him, her expression as eager and delighted as a child on Christmas morning. 'You're not looking,' she frowned.

'I was. I just got sidetracked by somebody getting over-excited with a perfect Kodak moment.'

She gave him a playful swipe on the arm. 'Like most men, you have no soul.'

'Oh, I sold that to the devil a long time ago.'

'Don't tell me, he returned it as faulty.'

'Why you little—' But he got no further as, laughing, she hared off into the darkness. He chased after her but she was lighter on her feet than he was and was soon nowhere to be seen. Then, suddenly, he heard a cry. Switching on the torch, he quickened his pace. When he found her, she was on the ground rubbing her ankle. He crouched beside her. 'You okay?'

'I think I've twisted it.'

'Can you wriggle your toes?'

She did as he said. 'Does that mean I haven't broken anything?' she asked, when all five toes seemed to be in working order.

'Sorry, haven't a clue.'

'Fat lot of use you are in an emergency.'

'Hey, easy there, time for a reality check. If I'm about to carry you up the rest of this hill you'd better be nice to me. What do you fancy, fireman's lift or Heathcliff carrying Cathy in his arms across the moors?'

'Oh, definitely the Heathcliff mode of transport.'

'Now, how did I know you'd go for that option?'

They made slow going, and despite the pain in her ankle, Izzy started to laugh.

'No,' he said, stumbling over some loose stones and staggering, 'no laughing, it's not allowed. If you laugh, I swear I'll drop you and watch you bounce all the way down to the beach.'

'No, you won't, you're enjoying yourself too much playing at being a super-hero.'

'I am? Hell, why didn't you tell me before?'

'If I'm not allowed to laugh, can I sing?'

'Go ahead,' he puffed, his arms feeling like lead, 'whatever does it for you, Izzy Jordan.'

'Jack and Jill went up the hill to fetch a pail of water ...'

He groaned. 'Beneath that pretty benign exterior, you enjoy living dangerously, don't you? How much further is it? Tell me there'll be oxygen when we reach the top.'

'We're on the final ascent now.'

He paused to catch his breath. 'Any chance of you radioing for assistance? I'm dying on my feet here.'

'Are you saying I'm overweight?'

'For a weakling like me, excessively so.'

They eventually made it to the top, and hearing their voices, Max and Corky, who were still up, came to investigate. Izzy introduced Mark and explained what had happened.

'I'm sorry I'm being such a nuisance,' she said after she had been helped to a sun-lounger and Max had despatched Corky to fetch an ice-pack from the freezer in the kitchen.

'Didn't I warn you no good would come of an evening out with Theo?' Max smiled.

'What bothers me most,' said Mark, kneeling on the ground to inspect Izzy's ankle, 'is that he trusted me to get Izzy home safely. I'll never hear the last of this.'

'It wasn't anybody's fault but my own. I shouldn't have been running away from you. Thanks for carrying me, it was very kind of you.'

He stood up. 'Stop right there. I'm no good with schmaltzy words of thanks. They bring me out in a nasty rash of embarrassment.'

'Can't suggest anything to help with a rash,' said Corky, appearing from behind, 'but this should help with the ankle.' He handed an ice-pack to Izzy along with a tea-towel. 'Thought that would do to strap it on with.' He also fished an elegant silver hip flask out of his trouser pocket. 'A snifter or two should help as well. What do you say?'

'I shouldn't really, I've already had plenty to drink.'

'Purely medicinal, my dear. Good for the shock.'

'What's good for what shock?'

Everybody turned to see Francesca coming across the terrace. She wasn't alone. Beside her was a tall, good-looking young man whom Izzy recognised as one of the Patterson boys.

'What on earth have you been up to, Izzy?' she asked, when she drew level and saw the ice-pack. 'A night out with Theo and you're an invalid.'

'I fell and did something painful to my ankle, and rather embarrassingly everyone's making too much fuss over me.'

'So where's Mum? Not like her to miss out on a good fussing session.'

'She's in bed,' said Max, 'as is your grandmother. So if you could keep your voice down to a dull roar we won't disturb them. Ahem, who's your friend?'

With an airy wave of her hand, Francesca introduced Harry. 'Everyone, this is Harry. And, Harry, this is my father. You can't miss him – he's the one sizing you up as a potential son-in-law. You're just the respectable sort of young man he'd choose for me. Do you fancy something to eat? I do. How about the rest of you?'

26

The next morning, Theo drove Izzy to the doctor's surgery in Kassiópi. After a thorough inspection, Dr Katerina Tsipa strapped up Izzy's impressively swollen ankle and declared it badly twisted. She prescribed some tablets to ease the swelling and complete rest. Her English was sufficient to get this across without too much difficulty, but Izzy was grateful that Theo was there to help her fill in the necessary forms and translate anything she didn't understand. Arrangements were made for a pair of crutches to be brought to the villa, which, when they arrived, gave Francesca and Sally hours of fun as they took it in turns to race up and down the veranda on them while shrieking at the top of their voices, 'Yo, ho, ho and a bottle of oúzo,' and 'Out of my way, Jim lad, or I'll be scraping the barnacles off your bum!'

For the following week, while Max and Laura took Corky and Olivia sightseeing, Izzy spent her days reading – she had finished *Culling The Good* and had moved on to *When Darkness Falls*, another of Mark's books. It was just as spine-tingling as *Culling The Good* but with an even higher body-count. The level of violence portrayed was far greater than she was used to reading, and the same was true of the language. She had never seen the F word so liberally employed and once or twice she found herself blushing at the extremes to which Mark had gone in expressing himself. The more she read, the harder it was for her to equate the author of these novels with the man she knew; the man who had carried her up the hill and displayed such a dry, ready wit. But there was no humour in what Mark wrote, only a grim portrayal of human nature at its worst. It struck her that he walked a fine line of creating stories that were essentially moralistic but without preaching.

When she needed a breather from all this carnage and drama, she caught up with news from home. If it could be classed as news.

It was definitely the silly season and the papers that Max brought back with him from his daily walk into Kassiópi were full of sensationalist trivia. In the absence of any newsworthy story, they were relying on the old standbys of royal cock-ups: the Duke of Edinburgh had, once again, insulted a minority group, and a lesser-known royal, one of those so far down the pecking order you could never remember their name, had apparently been caught speeding. But the one story that seemed set to run and run, and which had truly caught the public's imagination, was the tale of the mother of two and her schoolboy lover, who were still missing. 'At the rate they're going,' Laura had said, 'the boy will be old enough to marry her by the time anyone finds them.'

There were reports of the infamous pair – Christine and Mikey, the world and his wife were on first-name terms with them now – having been seen all over Europe. Most sightings had taken place in the Costas, though Ibiza was also mentioned, and a hotel in Reykjavik was claiming to have had the runaway lovers there for an overnight stay. 'They looked very much in love,' the manager was quoted as saying 'They were no trouble at all. Very quiet. Very clean. I do not know what the problem is. You British, you always have such a closed mind when it comes to sex.'

One of the papers had even set up a hotline. 'If you've seen this couple, phone this number,' the caption read, above a picture that made Christine look like a cross between Lily Savage and Myra Hindley. There was one of Mikey dressed in his school uniform, which had probably been taken when he was about eleven.

As soap operas went, it was up there with the best of them, riveting stuff.

When she wasn't reading, Izzy was playing cards with Max's parents. Just as Laura had predicted, they had seized upon the opportunity to teach her Canasta. The wine had flowed too, despite her protests that perhaps she shouldn't mix her tablets with alcohol.

'The odd drop won't make any difference,' Corky had said, filling her glass, 'It'll help you relax.'

'It'll also help her on her way to an almighty hangover,' Laura had said.

Her greatest frustration at being immobile was that she missed her early-morning sessions on the beach. Negotiating the steep hillside path was out of the question, her ankle just couldn't take any weight on it yet, and annoyingly she had to make do with tantalising glimpses of the bay from the small balcony off her bedroom or the terrace. To ease her frustration she spent the first couple of hours of each day painting and sketching. With so much free time on her hands, she could see that her technique was improving. So much so that Olivia had raved about some of her watercolours and bought a set from her to take home. Even Sally had picked one for herself.

During the day when everybody was out and the villa was quiet, she took the opportunity to write all the postcards she had been meaning to send ever since she had arrived. While she had been lax over keeping in touch with Ingrid and the other staff at school, her mother was up to date. Duty had forced Izzy to write a letter each week she had been away. And that was a proper letter, a full two-page inconsequential missive. A postcard just wouldn't do. In her mother's opinion they were far too informal. 'A lot of badly written sentences put together with little thought for grammar or punctuation,' she would say, if one slipped through her draught-proof letter-box. She also didn't want the postman reading her private mail.

And now, sitting in the shade on the veranda, everyone having gone off for the day in the boat, Izzy was trying to write once again to her mother. It was a tortuous, thankless endeavour.

'Dear Mother, how are you?' was all she had written so far.

It was a daft question. Prudence Jordan would, as ever, claim to be not long for this world. It was tempting to sidetrack her attention-seeking hypochondria by taking the radical approach: 'Hi Mum,' it would be great to write, 'I'm having a wonderful time here without you. The weather is as hot as the misguided handsome Greek man who professes to be falling in love with me.' But, of course, she never would. Any more than she would ever find the courage to stand up to Prudence as Theo had said she should.

That was as likely as her taking Theo seriously.

I think there is a very real danger that I am falling in love with you.

An extraordinary declaration that had been left hanging between them ever since that night. Due to Mark's appearance on the beach and the phone call Theo had had to take, there had been no time to pursue what Theo had meant by it. Nor had there been time to linger over that kiss. For which she was grateful. A humiliating post-mortem – 'Call that a kiss? *Ha!*' – was not what she needed.

The only time Izzy and Theo had been alone since then was when he had driven her to the doctor. His concern for her as he had helped her in and out of the car had made her laugh. Especially when he had insisted on carrying her into the surgery. 'No, Theo,' she had cried, 'put me down, and give me your arm.' But he wouldn't listen.

'It is all my fault that you have hurt yourself, so it is I who will carry you.'

'You make it sound like a punishment. You'll be falling on your sword next.'

When they left the surgery and were driving home, he had stopped the car in the shade of a tree just before they reached Max and Laura's driveway. 'Izzy,' he said, his face as earnest as she had ever seen it, 'I want you to know that what I said last night, it was not said flippantly. I meant every word.'

She had been worried, as she sat beside him, that he might try to kiss her again, and a tiny knot of panic formed in her stomach. A day-time kiss would really sort out the women from the girls. With no romantic moonlight to fill in the gaps and make up for any inadequacy on her part, she was well and truly on her own.

But the sudden blast of a horn from an approaching Jeep with an inflatable whale rearing up from the back seat resolved the problem for her. Parked in the narrowest stretch of the road, with no room for a car to overtake, Theo had had no alternative but to drive on.

Once Izzy was back at the villa, there was no chance for the two of them to be alone together. She could see from Theo's frown of frustration as everyone gathered around her to hear what the doctor had said that he knew he had lost his opportunity to have her to himself. She was torn between relief and feeling sorry for him. Though if she were completely honest, relief had the edge. She had just got used to having Theo as a friend when he had nudged their friendship to a level that made her feel uneasy with him again.

Before now, she hadn't stopped to think how important it was for her to feel she was in control. It was another reason why she was so wary of Theo. With his charming and persuasive manner he could take away any sense of control she thought she had, leaving her feeling irrationally frightened and defenceless. And it wasn't difficult to work out why this would be: as a child she had witnessed all too often the terrifying consequences of her mother's loss of control. She had seen, heard and felt things that had left an indelible impression on her young mind.

To lose control was bad.

To be in control was good.

It was as simple as that, and until now she hadn't realised how closely she had stuck to this subconscious rule. But looking back on her life, she could see that everything she had ever done had been carefully and calmly thought out and entirely of her own making. There had been no room for spontaneous outbursts.

And yet . . . and yet there had been the awful incident with Alan when she had lost her temper with him. More recently, there had been that embarrassing display of pique with Max and Laura over Theo.

So what did these slips of inner rage say about her? That, deep down, and if sufficiently provoked, she was as close to the edge as her mother had once been? Or did they mean, and please, God, let this be the answer, that she was capable of a lot more than she gave herself credit for? And, if so, where did that leave her with regard to Theo? Was it possible that, and with a bit more effort on her part, she could learn to let go when she was with him and enjoy a whole new sense of freedom?

When she thought of Theo in more rational moments, especially when he was being so nice to her, the way she was treating him didn't seem fair to him.

Since she had hurt her ankle – and between his many business commitments, which had taken him into Corfu Town and once to Athens – Theo had been a frequent visitor to the villa, often bearing gifts of the sweet and sticky variety for them all.

Yesterday he had joined them for lunch and brought her *When Darkness Falls.*

'How's Mark?' Max had asked, when they were all seated around the table. Much to Max's disappointment, he hadn't accompanied Theo on any of his visits.

'Working hard. He scarcely speaks to me these days. He is writing all hours. He says he is on a roll. Is that the right phrase?'

'Sounds like it could be.'

Then, lowering his voice to a low whisper and resting a hand on Izzy's leg under the table, he had said, 'So, Izzy, am I on a roll with you?'

She had blushed so much that, at the other end of the table, Laura had raised her eyebrows and smiled. Sally had noticed too and winked. But Max, bless him, unaware of the situation, had asked Theo what was taking him into Corfu Town later that afternoon. 'It's such a scorching day, it'll be murder.'

'I know, but I have an appointment I must keep.'

'Doctor or dentist?' asked Francesca.

'Neither. With a lawyer.'

'Oh, another acquisition?' asked Max.

'Yes. A piece of land. The contract has to be signed today, or the owner will sell to somebody else. Somebody less desirable.'

'In my experience, the rival businessman is always the one who is less desirable,' said Corky. 'Is it much land?'

Theo shrugged. 'A fair amount.' Izzy got the impression that he was being modestly evasive.

'On the island?'

He smiled at Olivia. 'What is this we are playing? A game of Twenty Questions?'

'Come on, Theo,' laughed Max, 'you've got us curious now. What are you up to? A spot of property developing here on Corfu?'

'If you must know, I am up to precisely the opposite. I am buying some land to prevent an area of great beauty from being spoiled.'

'How altruistic of you,' sighed Sally. 'I just love a man who does something for the good of everybody else, don't you, Izzy?'

'An admirable quality indeed,' Izzy said, without meeting Sally's eye – or anybody else's for that matter. 'Are we allowed to know where the land is, Theo?'

To everybody's surprise, he said, 'It's right here in Áyios Nikólaos, the olive grove that leads down into Kassiópi. I discovered last week that the family who own it have been offered a substantial amount of money to sell up. The buyer wants to erect several blocks of apartments.'

'But that's awful,' said Izzy, horrified. 'It would destroy the magic of this whole area.'

'Which is why I am buying the land and putting a stop to any such plans.'

Later, when Theo had left them to drive down the coast for his meeting, taking Sally and Francesca with him so that they could go shopping, Laura had got Izzy on her own and asked her what Theo had said to make her blush so dramatically. 'I've never seen anyone look so red. Or so guilty,' she added.

Since the night she had gone out for dinner with Theo, Izzy had kept Laura informed of most of what went on between them, and as far as Laura was concerned, she was on to a winner. 'Go for it, Izzy. He's crazy about you. We can all see it. Even Max is coming round and admits that he was perhaps a little quick to judge Theo.'

'But I'm scared of him,' Izzy had confessed. 'I know it's silly, but I can't relax when I'm on my own with him.'

'That's because you haven't learned to trust him. Or, more accurately, because you haven't learned to trust yourself to trust again. You think that because you made one error of judgement, you'll keep on doing it. Just relax with him and you'll find that everything will slip into place. I guarantee it.'

But that, Izzy said to herself, resuming her letter to her mother, is not as easy as Laura thinks it is. There were far too many reasons why it would be simpler for her to keep well away from Theo.

And, besides, what would be the point?

Why get involved with a man who, in all probability, when her holiday ended, she would never see again?

27

That evening, Laura sank into her chair on the terrace beside Izzy, who, as she so often was these days, was engrossed in her book. Exhausted – too tired even to admire the setting sun, she closed her eyes, grateful that Corky and Olivia had gone into Kassiópi with Francesca and Sally.

As kind, as thoughtful and as fun as they were, her in-laws were running her ragged. With most of the sights now ticked off on their extensive list of places to visit, Laura was almost out of ideas and energy to keep them amused.

Why couldn't they be lazier? A little more like her own parents.

Why this constant need to be so active?

And why on earth did she feel so dog-tired? Surely she should be used to the heat by now. Last night during supper Francesca had caught her with her eyelids drooping and had teased her that she was hitting the menopause. 'When all those hot flushes kick in we won't need to bother with a log fire in the winter,' she had laughed. 'We'll sit in front of you and warm our toes.'

Oh, the cruelty of youth.

Olivia had suggested a course of HRT, saying she wished she had been young enough to take advantage of it when she had gone through the change. 'My hot flushes were so awful, they were more like tropical rainstorms,' she had said. 'I had several fainting phases as well. Very unpleasant.' Maybe, with all that behind her, it was no wonder that Olivia was so full of beans.

She and Max had done their best to occupy his parents, taking them far and wide. They had been to Kanóni to see the much-photographed Mouse Island with its chapel tucked into the cypress trees. Another day they had been to the top of Corfu's highest mountain, Mount Pantokrator, all 2,972 feet of it. They had been lucky with the weather: the sky had been crystal clear, and they had been able to make out Paxos, and even a glimpse of mainland Greece. They had also been to Corfu Town and had covered what to Laura had felt like every square inch of it. They had taken in the new and old fortresses, the paper money museum, the leather and jewellery shops, of which there were hundreds, and all had had to be inspected before Max's mother decided what to treat herself to. Then they had sat in the cool, gloomy interior of the beautiful old church of St Spiridon, with its towering campanile and red onion dome, which they all decided bore an uncanny resemblance to a fireman's helmet. In true Anglican fascination, they had watched locals hurrying in during their lunch-break to light candles and plant ritualistic kisses on the tomb of their much-loved patron saint, their lips murmuring prayers of hope and exultation. They had finished the day by relaxing over a drink in the quiet, arcaded street of the Listón where Max and Corky had got involved in the drama of a local cricket team showing a guest side from England how the game should be played.

On another day they had taken the boat out and explored the coastline south of Kassiópi, spending an afternoon at Kalámi Bay where Corky was keen to see where Gerald Durrell had lived as a boy. Then they had moved on to Kouloúra where several minutes of *For Your Eyes Only* had been filmed. 'Not one of the best Bond movies, I'll grant you,' Corky had said, when they stopped off for lunch at a waterside taverna. His comment had inevitably led to a discussion as to which had been the best 007 extravaganza. Olivia claimed that Sean Connery was the only true Bond, though she was prepared to give Pierce Brosnan the benefit of the doubt. But Francesca claimed that the early movies had been nothing but a blatant display of misogyny. 'You should all be ashamed of yourselves,' she said, with disdain. 'Ian Fleming hated women – you can see it in the way they were portrayed in those early films, targets of sexual and physical abuse every time.' That shut them all up. There was nothing like a verbal knuckle-rapping from the younger generation to put the older one in its place.

The following day they had visited the Achillíon. Originally built as a hideaway palace of over-the-top kitsch for the Empress Elizabeth of Austria, a lonely, unhappy woman with a penchant for statues, it was now one of the island's most popular sights. Its more recent claim to fame – other than having been a casino for some years – was that, like Kouloúra, it, too, had been used as a setpiece in *For Your Eyes Only*. After several hours of admiring statues and taking photographs, Laura had assumed – had hoped – they were set for home, but Olivia had suddenly been consumed by an irresistible urge to venture into the nearby distillery where they had been roped into tasting and, unbelievably, buying several bottles of kumquat liqueur. It was terrible stuff, so sweet it had turned Laura's mouth inside out. She couldn't think what Olivia was going to do with it all, apart from contribute it to the Christmas tombola she and Corky organised every year for their local church.

Having rested for a short while, Laura now opened her eyes and said to Izzy, 'Whatever shall I do with Max's parents for the rest of their stay? The thought of yet another crowded beauty-spot fills me with dread. I wish it had been my ankle that had got twisted. It would have let me off the hook nicely.'

'You could tell them there's nothing else worth seeing,' Izzy said, lowering her book.

'But they've got their guidebooks to prove me wrong.'

'Then your only course of action is to tell them the truth. Honesty is always the best policy.'

'I quite agree with you, Izzy.'

They turned to see Max coming towards them with a bottle of wine and three glasses. 'Which is as good a cue as any to say that I'm not just your wine waiter for the evening, but the bearer of bad news.'

Laura took the glass he offered her. 'Oh, and what's that?'

'I've just been on the phone to Phil from the office. I have to go home sooner than I thought.'

'Trouble?'

He sat down in the chair next to Laura and smiled. 'Nothing a whiz kid like me can't handle. Do you mind very much?'

'Yes,' she pouted. 'Lots. When are you planning on going?'

'I thought I could leave with Mum and Dad on Friday, if I can get on the flight. A later one, if not.'

Unable to keep the disappointment out of her voice, Laura said, 'How long do you think you'll be away this time?'

'Difficult to say until I get a feel for what needs doing. It's a new client we'd be mad to lose out on. But at least you'll still have Izzy for company, not forgetting the girls. How about we have a lavish, all button-popping meal in Kassiópi the night before I go?'

'I suppose that might soften the blow.'

The next morning, while lying in bed next to Max, Laura had a change of heart. 'Let's not eat out on Thursday night,' she said, 'let's have a party instead. It'll be more fun.'

'But won't that make more work for you? You keep saying how tired you are.'

'Such concern for your poor ageing wife does you credit. But I'm being more cunning than you think. I'm relying on your parents to take over. You know how they love organising a party. This will keep them busy for the rest of their holiday.'

'You clever old thing, you.'

During breakfast, and just as Laura had predicted, Corky and Olivia seized on the idea.

'Why don't we make it a theme party?' suggested Olivia.

'Fancy dress, you mean?' asked Sally.

'Oh dear, does that sound very dull to you? In our day fancy-dress parties were all the rage.'

'No way, it sounds cool. How about we do the whole Greek myth scene?'

Across the table, Laura saw Max roll his eyes and knew what he was thinking – Sally licensed to thrill in nothing but a transparent sheen of gossamer.

A guest list was immediately drawn up. Francesca took charge of this. At the top she wrote Theo's name. Laura saw her give Izzy a sly look, which Izzy tried to ignore, but the colour of her cheeks gave her away. Laura smiled to herself and said, 'Do you think we could persuade Mark to come along as well?'

'We can but try,' said Francesca, adding his name, then Harry and Nick.

'You'd better include their parents,' Laura said. 'It's about time we met them.'

'Subtle, Mum,' said Francesca, twirling the pencil between her fingers, then tapping it against her teeth. 'I was wondering when you'd get round to checking them out.'

Since the night Izzy had hurt her ankle and Francesca had brought Harry home, the Patterson boys had put in more than the occasional appearance. Usually late at night. Much to Francesca's amusement, Max had taken a liking to Harry, referring to him as PM – Promising Material. 'He's clean, good-looking and polite. What more could I want for my daughter?' he teased her. 'And just think, he might even be the type to hold down a steady and well-paid job when the time comes.'

'You're so woefully predictable, Dad!' had been Francesca's response.

The guest list was extended to include Dimitri and Marietta, who ran the jewellery shop in Kassiópi; and Sophia and Angelos, plus Giorgios and his two younger sisters.

'You know who we can't miss off the list, don't you?' said Max.

Everybody looked at him.

'The Fitzgeralds.'

'You're right,' said Laura. 'It would be very rude to exclude them. Go on, Francesca, add their names. And we'll have to remember to tell Theo that his little game of pretending to be Mark's chauffeur will have to come to an end before then. I don't want Dolly-Babe being made to look a fool in front of everybody.'

'Oh, you're all heart, Mum.'

'Now then,' said Olivia, after she had fetched one of the many books she had brought with her – *Who's Who in Greek Mythology*. 'Who shall we dress up as?' She flicked through the pages until one caught her eye. 'Aha, anyone fancy being Medea?'

'What's she famous for?' asked Sally.

'Wasn't she the one who was into rejuvenation?' said Izzy, flexing her ankle experimentally – she had removed the strapping last night in bed to see if she could manage a day without its support. 'She chopped up an old ram, popped it into the cauldron of bubbling potion and out leaped a young lamb.'

'She was also a ruthless so-and-so,' added Corky. 'Keen to teach Jason a lesson for his infidelity, she murdered their children.'

'Hey, I like her style,' laughed Sally, 'a woman not to tangle with. Read on, Mrs S, and let's see who else you've got for us.'

Quietly relieved that everyone was now absorbed in preparing for the party, Laura slipped away to the far end of the terrace where she lay down on a sun-lounger. Happy in the knowledge that she no longer had to entertain the troops, she closed her eyes and, without meaning to, was soon dozing. She dreamed that, on his return to England, Max impressed his new client by dressing up as Hercules and wrestling his competitors to the floor.

28

While everyone else was trying to decide which mythological character they wanted to be at the party, Francesca and Sally knocked up some invitations on Max's computer and offered to deliver them.

Their first port of call was Nick and Harry. 'It makes sense to start off at the furthest point and work our way back,' said Francesca, as they took the path down to the beach.

'It wouldn't have anything to do with being keen to see Harry, would it?'

Francesca pretended she hadn't heard what Sally had said, but it wasn't a million miles from the truth. Rarely did she and Sally keep anything of a personal nature from each other, but in this instance Francesca was keen to preserve a degree of privacy. Not that there was much to tell. Well, not by Sally's standards, anyway. But discussing Harry with anyone might taint what Francesca felt for him. Though she wasn't entirely sure what it was. He was so unlike any previous boyfriend she had had. Maybe that was the appeal.

But what she did or did not feel for Harry was beside the point. Three nights ago, without meaning to, she had annoyed and upset him. They had been on their own, Nick and Sally having gone to a bar for another all-night session, and they were walking home through the olive grove. It was nearly two o'clock in the morning and they were following the small beams of light cast from their torches. The path had seemed steeper and bumpier in the dark and, in her high platform shoes, the going was even harder. It wasn't long before she missed her step, and because Harry was the kind of bloke he was, gentle and caring, his hand was immediately there to stop her going over. 'You don't need to let go,' she had said, feeling his hand loosen on her arm once she had regained her balance. It sounded as if she was teasing him, and she probably was, just a little, but she quite fancied the thought of him holding her hand. Without a word, he slipped his hand into hers and they continued on their way.

It had been a long time since she had felt like this – cherished, as though she mattered. It made her wonder what she had ever seen in a jerk like Carl – whose idea of a romantic moment was to lick his lips and say, 'How about it?' She cringed at the memory of him saying this the first time they had met, at a party. How could she have fallen for such a crass line? What on earth had been the attraction? Perhaps her parents had been right that the whole episode had been her need to rebel, to shock her father into believing that she was all grown-up. She realised now that, far from shocking him, she had only disappointed him.

She had been so deep in thought that she missed her footing again, and if it hadn't been for Harry she would have fallen flat on her face. He held on to her tightly, his fingers digging into her arm. 'You okay?' he asked.

'Thanks to you I am,' she said, her face raised to his. Aware of how close their bodies were, she waited to see what he would do.

The wait was worth while.

Every delicious, anticipatory second of it.

He removed his glasses, and very slowly brought his mouth down to hers. His timing was supreme: not too fast, not too slow, just perfect. And when he got down to it – when he got into his stride and held her to him – she realised she had never been kissed so beautifully.

'You've done this before, haven't you?' she said, when at last he let her go.

'Not like this I haven't.'

His honesty, and the sweet, tender way in which he was looking at her, squinting to focus on her face, made her smile. She reached up and pulled his head down to her again. But after the briefest of kisses, he gently pushed her from him.

'What's wrong?' she asked.

Suddenly he looked awkward. His glasses were in place again, as was his shy reserve. 'Nothing's wrong,' he mumbled, more to himself than to her. He wasn't even meeting her gaze now.

'Liar,' she retorted. 'Tell me what's wrong.' She sensed rejection only a short slippery step away and didn't like the idea. Not so soon after Carl.

'I'm sorry,' he said, still not looking at her, 'it's just . . . if we carry on I'm not sure I'd know how to stop myself from . . .'

This was the last thing she had expected him to say, and relief made her laugh. 'From what?' she asked, curious to see how he would answer.

'I think you know. I also think you're having a joke at my expense.' In the shadowy darkness, his face was tight with condemnation.

'Hey, there, Mr Sensitive, before you start accusing me of teasing you, how about you considering that the boot might be on the other foot? No girl likes being kissed – a kiss that would score highly in the history of your one hundred best snogs, and then have a repeat sample denied her.'

He nudged his glasses. 'Are you always this stroppy when a guy tries to act decently?'

'No!' she snapped. 'It's a first. I've never met a bloke who hasn't tried to grope me at the first opportunity.'

He frowned. 'So where does that leave me? Mr Bloody Boring again, I suppose. Someone you and Sally can have a good laugh at.'

She hesitated. 'Actually, it makes you a refreshing change. So quit blathering, and if it isn't too much of a turn-on for you, give me your hand so I can get home in one piece.'

'I'll do my best to contain myself,' he responded, his expression stern, which was at odds with his normally good-natured face.

They walked on in stony, nerve-jarring silence. At the gate to Villa Petros, he let go of her hand and was all set to leave without another word when she touched his arm lightly and said, 'I'm sorry that you thought I was laughing at you. I wasn't, really. It was relief. It was—'

But he wasn't interested in what she had to say. 'Goodnight, Francesca.' He turned and left her.

She let herself in and went to bed. But she couldn't sleep. All she could think of was turning the clock back to that moment in the olive grove when Harry had kissed her, and before she had blown it with him. Not for the first time in her life, her hot-headedness had got the better of her.

That had been three nights ago and she hadn't seen him since. And now, as she and Sally approached the pink villa that Harry and his family were renting, she wondered how he would react to seeing her again.

'It's a bit of a wreck, isn't it?' said Sally, as they pushed through the tangle of overgrown bushes and weeds that had invaded the path. Everything about the villa looked tired and worn out. The faded walls had long since lost their original vibrancy and the green paintwork on the shutters was peeling badly. Even the bougainvillaea clinging to one of the walls looked as if it had had enough.

Without catching a glimpse of Mr and Mrs Patterson, Francesca and Sally could hear them. It was obvious from the raised voices coming from inside the villa that an argument was in full swing. Nick had often referred to the warring tension between 'the aged ones' but Francesca hadn't taken him seriously. Now she knew he hadn't been exaggerating. 'Perhaps we ought not to bother them,' she said, thinking of Harry and how he would hate her to see his parents like this. 'Let's leave them till later.'

'What? And miss out on embarrassing them? No way.'

When they reached the terrace they saw Nick and Harry. They were dressed for the beach, in swimming shorts with a towel slung over a shoulder, snorkels and masks in hand. Despite the commotion still going on inside the villa, Nick was instantly all smiles. 'Welcome to the madhouse. As you can no doubt hear the lovebirds, Ma and Pa Patterson, are a bit preoccupied with each other at the moment so I shan't introduce you. We have to make allowances, love blinds them. We're off for a swim, want to join us?'

Sneaking a look at Harry, Francesca said, 'Later, maybe.' She handed over the invitation to Nick. 'Mum and Dad are giving a party and you're all invited.'

With Sally's help, she explained about the party and its theme. 'If you're stuck for ideas, we've got a brilliant book on Greek mythology we could lend you.'

'And, please, don't say you want to be Hercules, Nick,' said Sally. 'We've got them queuing up for him.'

But Nick dismissed Hercules out of hand. 'The man was a fool going along with all those tedious labours. I think I'll go as Cronus.'

'Who was he?' asked Francesca. Nick had never struck her as being the sharpest knife in the cutlery box and she was amazed that he knew anything about Greek mythology.

Throwing a look over his shoulder, towards the villa where the noise had at last died down, Nick said, 'At his mother's request, Cronus hacked off his dad's genitals with a sickle and tossed them into the sea. It was poor old Gaia's answer to the vasectomy.'

'They were a sick old bunch, weren't they?' laughed Sally.

'What will you be going as, Francesca?' Harry asked, and Francesca, who until now had been sure that he was doing his best to avoid eye-contact with her, met his gaze.

'I haven't decided yet,' she said, 'though I did wonder about Cassandra.'

He pushed up his glasses. 'Cassandra,' he repeated, keeping his eyes on her. 'The daughter of Hecuba and Priam whose fate it was never to be believed.'

She smiled. 'That's her. Good choice or not?'

His mouth twitched amiably. 'I'd have to reserve judgement.'

'You do that, then.'

'Sure you don't want to join us for a swim now?' he asked.

'I'd love to but we've got the rest of these invitations to deliver. See you later perhaps?'

'That would be nice.'

Once they had left the boys and were out of earshot, Sally said, 'A seriously weird family, wouldn't you say, all that arguing?'

'Explains why Nick's such a head-case, doesn't it?'

'So where does Harry fit in, then?'

Francesca laughed. 'He has to be adopted. Nobody as normal as he is could have been conceived by such genetically impaired parents.'

They headed for their next port of call, Villa Mimosa. This was a large, buttermilk-coloured, two-storeyed house about a hundred yards higher up the hillside and just beyond a smaller villa that seemed uninhabited. In the baking midday sun, the steep climb left them both breathless. With the sound of cicadas chirruping noisily all around them, they paused to catch their breath and to take in the view below them. Down on the beach, Nick and Harry were swimming in the sparkling sea, their snorkels poking up through the choppy waves. Thinking of the brief exchange, just now, with Harry, Francesca was hopeful that another of his off-the-chart kisses might be on offer. She smiled at the prospect.

'Come on,' she said, turning round and climbing further up the path. 'We'll burn if we stand here much longer. Let's go and see if Dolly-Babe's in.'

They found her reclining on a sun-lounger in the shade of a large canvas parasol. She was wearing a white swimsuit that couldn't have been designed with swimming in mind – it was a dazzling sight of pearls and rhinestones. But Francesca was more struck by the two very upright boobs thrusting through the glitter – silicone-enhanced for sure. When Dolly-Babe saw the girls, she put down her glass and hurriedly tied a sarong around her tiny waist. 'Can I help you?' she asked, lowering her sunglasses and peering at them in a less-than-welcoming fashion.

Francesca explained who they were and handed over the invitation.

'Ooh,' said Dolly-Babe, her demeanour undergoing a dramatic change. 'A party! That's nice. Care to join me for a drink, girls?' She slipped on a pair of gold-trimmed Prada mules that had Sally's tongue hanging out with envy and tip-tapped inside the house, returning minutes later with an open bottle of chilled wine and two extra glasses. 'Now, then,' she said, when they had settled into their chairs and raised their glasses, 'what kind of a bash is it that your parents are throwing?'

Sally took up the reins of the conversation – it was now one party girl to another. But Dolly-Babe looked unsure when she learned that it was to be a fancy-dress do. 'I don't see my Bob going for that somehow,' she said doubtfully. 'It's as much as he can do to put on a shirt and tie to go out for dinner. He never likes any fuss.'

'It's nothing too over the top,' Francesca said. 'You don't have to make your costume too elaborate, just enough to hint at your character. For instance, if your husband wanted to come as Atlas, all he'd have to do was draw a map of the world on a balloon and stick it to his shoulder.'

The idea of her husband wearing nothing more complicated than a balloon attached to his shoulder seemed to allay Dolly-Babe's fears. 'But what about me? I know diddley-squat about Greek myths. What do you think I should go as?'

With the tumble of dyed blonde hair perched on top of her head, Francesca wanted to say that Medusa would be an easy option, but she felt that Dolly-Babe might not think that funny. Sally told her about Medea. Murdered children and all.

'Gawd help us! Isn't there someone more, well, you know, nice and attractive? A bit more glamorous – like me?'

'We could lend you a book if you want,' Sally offered. Then, seeing a pile of magazines on the table between them, she said, 'Are you into the psychic world, Mrs Fitzgerald?'

'Call me Liberty-Raquel, darlin', and, yes, I am. Are you?'

'Kind of.'

This was news to Francesca. She helped herself to one of the magazines and flicked through it. 'Psychic Perception – All Your Financial Problems Solved', was the title of one of its main articles.

'So have you had any really weird experiences?' asked Sally. 'You know, like you knew what somebody was about to do or say? I get that a lot.'

Yes, thought Francesca, like you know exactly what I'm thinking of you right now and what I'll say to you later. But if she had thought her friend was teasing Dolly-Babe, she soon discovered she was wrong. Sally was in earnest. This was a whole new side to her friend that Francesca had not known existed. Amused, she continued flicking through the pages of the magazine. There was a big feature on 'Spiritual Astrology for a Better Sex Life', followed by a piece on 'The Truth Behind Spontaneous Human Combustion'. There was even a piece about casting love spells to push your potential partner in the right direction. Love, sex and money seemed to be the chief concerns of the magazine. So, no different from any other coffee-table glossy, you could say. Except that there seemed to be a lot of emphasis on money. An extraordinary number of clairvoyants, psychics, mediums and tarot readers were all willing to chat to you on the phone via your credit card.

'I went to a fortune-teller once,' she heard Sally say. 'It was a gang of us from school. We just did it for a laugh. But this woman who read my hand, she knew all about me. She knew things I'd never told anyone.'

'Ria's the same,' Dolly-Babe said, draining her glass and refilling it. She offered them the bottle, but they both refused. 'Ria's my personal psychic medium, and you know what? She told me I'd be going to a party while I was here.'

'She did?'

'Yes. She read the cards for me and the Eight of Cups was there.'

'What does that mean?'

'It signifies an expansion of social horizons. And I'll tell you something else. Ria says that your neighbour Mr St James is a part of my stay here. Ria says that he's going to play an integral part in my life. I just wish I knew what it was. It's so nerve-racking waiting to see what it's all about.'

Francesca felt as if she had escaped from the Land People Forgot when she and Sally finally got away. She said as much as they retraced their steps down to the beach, then on towards Villa Anna to see Theo.

'I don't know why you have such a closed mind to the psychic world,' Sally said huffily. 'It seems perfectly reasonable to me.'

'Well, coming from the girl who was unhinged enough to make a pass at my father, I'll take that with a handful of salt. I can't believe you're buying into all that rubbish.'

'It's the new rock and roll, didn't you know?'

'More like the new cash 'n' carry. I was checking out the classifieds in that magazine while you were chatting to Dolly-Babe, and it was page after page of "Most Credit Cards" accepted. It's a colossal con. It's for people too dumb to figure out that it's all a case of *que sera, sera*.' Then, seeing that she wasn't getting anywhere, she said, 'Did you see the expression on her face when I told her who her precious Mr St James was?'

'Sure did. Talk about the penny dropping.'

Both she and Sally had assumed that although Dolly-Babe did not know who Theo was, she knew who Mark was, so when they had made some reference to him being here to work on his latest book, she had shrieked, 'Well, Gawd bless us! You know, I kept thinking he was familiar, but for the life of me I couldn't put my finger on it.' It turned out that her husband had been taking one of Mark's novels to bed with him each night and a black and white photograph of the author had stared at her across their bed. Francesca thought this spoke volumes about a woman who had just been claiming to be intuitive and perceptive.

After their long, sweaty uphill climb, there was no one in at Villa Anna so they left the party invitation on a table on the terrace, weighting it down with a stone, and decided to go for a swim. They had had enough of playing Postman Pat. The remaining invitations could wait.

29

Mark was giving himself a rare break from his strict writing routine and was spending the day in Corfu Town with Theo.

They had come into town for the memorial service to Theo's grandmother, Anna Vlamakis. She had been dead for eighteen years, but tradition was that on each anniversary of her death a special service of remembrance was held. Mark thought it a much more positive and substantial way to think of one's departed relations than leaving an occasional bunch of flowers on a grave in a windswept cemetery.

Here, courtesy of the Greek Orthodox Church, the friends and relatives who had gathered to remember Anna Vlamakis had now moved on from the spiritual words of comfort to what had been her favourite restaurant in the Listón, to celebrate her memory in gregarious Greek fashion.

Back in the late 1970s and early 1980s Mark had met the old lady several times on trips to Corfu, and had liked her immensely, despite the appalling way in which she indulged her only grandson. He had never been to Greece before he had met Theo, and when their unlikely friendship had developed, Theo had invited him to spend part of the 1978 summer vacation in Athens and Corfu.

Mark had been torn between the plans he had already made and the idea of actually allowing himself some fun. He had planned to stay on in Durham and work his way through the summer, serving behind the bar of a pub, and in his free time advance his grandiose theories that would one day save the world from itself. Going home to his parents, like his fellow students, and working for the family firm had not been a consideration. However, after a short tussle with his conscience, he threw some clothes into a rucksack and justified the trip by telling himself that travel broadened the mind. There was even a chance that he might get some writing done. In those days anger and the injustices of the world fuelled his work. His prose was then an outpouring of vitriolic loathing for the oppressors of the state. In other words, it was all hot air. But at the time, and in his youth, and in his hunger to make a difference to the world, it had been important to him. He was moderately successful at getting into print and had several articles published, mostly in a variety of home-spun rags that had a penchant for protest politics and the round-them-up-and-shoot-them genre of journalism. These were the people he hung out with, political activists whose main aim was to create a classless society.

So, not surprisingly, he kept his holiday plans to himself that particular summer when he flew off to Athens with a man who represented everything he opposed: wealth, privilege, and a set of handmade leather luggage that was as ostentatious as it was offensive to somebody who, in those days, was a zealous vegetarian and didn't even wear leather shoes.

Theo's parents, Christiana and Thanos Vlamakis, now living in Athens, had greeted him in their luxurious apartment overlooking the busy harbour with the same warmth and sincerity they had extended towards him in Durham. They were as effusive as they were hospitable and frequently embarrassed him by introducing him to their friends and neighbours as the man who had saved Theo's life, embellishing the tale with more drama each time they told it. 'Make them stop,' he had pleaded with Theo. 'I can't stand it. Any more of it and I swear I'll turn back the clock and kill you myself!'

But Theo had laughed and told him to make the most of his hero status. 'Is it my fault that they have put you on a pedestal?'

'Cut the crap, Theo, and tell your parents to do the same.'

'Don't be so self-absorbed. Be generous enough to let them enjoy themselves at your expense.'

And the old maxim that a good story never goes away was perfectly true, for even now over lunch, Christiana was telling the myth once more to some elderly relatives who had flown in from Thessaloníki. Though she was talking in Greek, Mark could understand what she was saying by her body language and the way she kept smiling at him. He shot Theo a look that meant 'Distract her', but Theo merely smiled and carried on talking to a larger-than-life man on his right, who had the most extraordinarily shaggy eyebrows. He was the priest who had just conducted the service and, in his flowing black robes, complemented by a fuzzy white beard with nicotine stains around his mouth and a hearty, full-throated laugh, his presence gave the proceedings an air of robust jollity. There was no po-faced piety about him as he held out his wine-glass to be replenished and took a lip-smacking slurp.

Sitting on Mark's left was a quiet ghost of a man. He looked about a hundred and ten, and so frail that a gust of wind might blow him away. He was in a wheelchair pushed close to the table and was dressed in a suit that must once have fitted him properly. The same was true of his shirt; above a buttoned collar, a tightly knotted tie drooped mockingly at his neck, exposing loose, translucent flesh. Resting on his lap, like a curled-up cat, was an ancient Panama, poignantly shabby and knocked about. Its owner was Thomas Zika and Mark had met him on his first visit to Corfu when he and Theo had been staying with Anna. It was widely known within the family that Thomas Zika had been very much in love with Theo's grandmother and Mark had always thought it a great waste that in the autumn of their lives the pair had never married.

The skin on the old man's head was parched and taut across his skull and only a few wispy strands of white hair remained. His features, made delicate by the passing of time, were set in a face so pale and waxen it looked as if the sun might shine straight through it. His eyes were dim and watery, and uncomfortably red-rimmed, with just a few lashes. Poking out through gaping cuffs, trembling vein-streaked hands were trying to grip a knife and fork; no matter how hard he tried, the medallions of turbot kept slipping away from him.

Mark returned his attention to his plate. He had only taken a few mouthfuls when he felt a light touch on his elbow. 'I wonder, young man, if you would be so kind as to help me.' The voice, hushed and tremulous, was barely audible; Mark had to strain to catch it. 'I should hate to die of starvation,' Thomas Zika continued. 'At my age it would seem so very undignified.'

Mark smiled at him and discreetly took his cutlery.

'You have changed a great deal since I saw you last,' said Thomas Zika, when Mark had completed his task.

'With respect, Mr Zika, it's a long time since we last met. It must be more than twenty years.'

'Can it really be as long as that?'

'I'm afraid it is.'

'But you are happier now?'

The gaze from the watery, bloodshot eyes was as perceptive as the question. 'I like to think so,' Mark replied.

'The years have been good to you?'

'Some good, some not so good.'

The old man nodded slowly, thoughtfully. 'We always learn most from the bad times, the years of being in the wilderness. Would you agree?'

Mark smiled to himself. It was as if he was back in the rehab clinic with Bones.

'You find what I have said amusing?'

'I'm sorry, it's just that you reminded me of someone.'

'Ah, a wise old counsellor? Or perhaps a stupid old man, who should have learned by now to mind his own business?'

'You were right the first time.'

'Excellent. That is eminently better than the latter.'

After a long pause, Thomas Zika said, 'Would it be asking very much of you to help me further? It seems that my hands are determined to disobey my every command today. If you would harpoon the pieces, I think I could manage to steer them on a homeward course.'

It was a relief for Mark to help him, and unexpectedly he pictured himself doing the same for his father one day.

Time was when he couldn't have been in the same room as his father without wanting to strike him down. That was when he had used him as a focus for all the anger he had within him. His mother and two older brothers had come in for their share too, but irrationally it was his father he had most wanted to hurt. And, as a teenager, it had been so easy to rile him: the cutting sarcasm, the cruel home truth, the biting irony, and the withering contempt. Relentlessly he would goad his father, seeing him as nothing more than a moving target that was no match for his superior intellect. But the harder he pushed, the more his father withdrew. He kept up the pressure, just waiting for the day when his father would lose control. But it never came.

It was power he had wanted. Power over his father and his family. He craved it as much as he later craved drugs and alcohol. He was obstinate and ruthlessly antagonistic. An unlovable son who taunted his parents into sending him away to school – 'Go on, then, if you dare, prove how little you care.' And when at last they had reached the end of their tether and sent him away, he claimed a victory over them, awarding himself the moral high ground, asserting that he had been right all along. He was the most disruptive and obnoxiously offensive son any family could have been cursed with.

He was no easier at school. Sullen but volatile, he made few friends, the other children preferring to keep their distance from him. They were frightened of him: frightened of his anger; of what it could do to him, what it could do to them. And because his mood swings were so unpredictable, some of the older, braver boys called him Skitzy. He was twice suspended for smoking on school premises, and very nearly expelled just before O levels for turning the air blue with his language when a teacher caught him drinking in a nearby pub one lunchtime. His parents were summoned, and after they had begged the head to reconsider and an apology had been extracted from Mark, he was given a last chance. He watched them drive away afterwards, his mother holding a handkerchief to her face, his father tight-lipped and ashen.

It pained him now to think how close he had come to destroying his parents. But unleashing his anger had been his only source of comfort, his only means of survival: to reject his parents before they rejected him.

Making his peace with his family had been one of the many humbling experiences he had had to go through to complete the process of cleaning himself up. Bones had said that it was essential for his recovery that he underwent some family-therapy sessions. At first he had resisted the suggestion. Violently. 'No!' he had cried, leaping from his seat and nearly knocking it over. 'No, I'm not ready for that.' His desperate voice had bounced off the bare walls of the austere room. From nowhere, his body was covered in a sheen of sweat. The white noise of his panic filled his head and his guts dissolved. Then the need for a drink flooded his system. A drink to drown the fear. Going over to the open window, he fought hard to resist his addiction by focusing on his breathing. He looked across the fields to the restored church spire, but his eyes took in none of it. His face was tight with recollection as he visualised the last time he had seen his parents.

He had let himself into their house late one night, using the key he had had for years, but until then had never used. This was no social call: he was there to steal from them. He had been out of work for nearly a year – employers are hard to come by when you're a full-time alcoholic and living in a squat permanently off your head. He had sold everything he owned, and scrounged from those who had anything worth scrounging.

His parents had discovered him in the dining room, clearing out a Georgian cabinet of silver knick-knacks. He was carelessly tipping them into a large bin-liner when the light was switched on. It was a toss-up as to who looked more shocked, him or them. His mother, standing a few inches behind his father, had gasped and clutched at the neck of her nightdress as if a blast of cold air had just swept in. His father, once he had gathered his wits together and realised what was going on, had said, 'At least have the decency to leave your mother the photographs.'

Looking down at what was in his hand, Mark had seen that he was about to add to his bag of booty a silver-framed picture of himself as a small boy. A smiling, untroubled face stared back at him; a happy child with a happy future ahead of him. Suddenly the awful reality of what he was doing hit him. With all the force of mainlining straight into his bloodstream, it made him hesitate. Made him wonder if there wasn't another way.

But it only lasted for a matter of seconds.

'I need money,' he said, and tossed the photograph into the bin-liner. He heard the glass break as it banged against another piece of silver. The threat he was making was so clear that he might just as well have been holding a gun to his parents' heads.

His father tightened the belt on his dressing-gown. 'How much ... this time?'

'How much can you spare ... this time?'

'Put the bag down and come with me.'

His father's flat voice had its usual effect on him, made him feel as though he was no more significant than one of his employees. Without looking at his mother, Mark followed his father the length of the house to his study, remembering a time when he had played here with his brothers, racing them up and down the long corridor and hallway, skidding to a halt on their knees as they flew across the polished wooden floor, rucking up rugs, bumping into panelled walls, their happy laughter filling the house while their mother gently rebuked them for their recklessness.

He stood in front of the walnut desk, and watched his father write a cheque. 'I'm giving you this on the understanding that, from now on, you leave us alone. You've done your damnedest to destroy yourself, I won't allow you to do the same to your mother. You're not to come here again.'

He snatched the cheque from his father's hand. 'I can live with that. I'm not too proud to know that I'm being paid off to safeguard your finer feelings.' He folded the crisp piece of paper in half and slipped it into his pocket, his mind already heading for the door to get out of the house, out of their lives. 'But satisfy my morbid curiosity, don't you care about me at all?'

The cool steely gaze – whose blueness matched Mark's own eyes – stared back at him, never wavering. 'No. I've had enough. I've done all that I possibly could for you. My conscience is clear.'

It was the longest conversation he had had with his father in years.

He was as good as his word and kept his side of the bargain by staying away. Until one day, coming round from a drinking binge that had lasted nearly a week – a week of which he had no recollection – he wrote his mother a letter. It was only a few melodramatic, disorientated lines saying that he was sorry for all the trouble he had caused and that he wished that he was dead.

Had it been a cry for help?

Almost certainly.

One instinctively knows when one has had enough. When it's time to come quietly.

Within two weeks Theo was helping him into a car and driving him through the night to a rehab clinic.

Bringing him out of his reverie, Bones had said, 'Mark, please sit down. You really have nothing to fear from such a meeting with your family, and everything to gain.'

Sinking into his chair, desperate now, he had begged, 'Please, I'm not ready. It's too soon. Give me more time.' Refusing to see his parents was the last line in his defence. Remove that and he would be vulnerable and exposed again.

But Bones was having none of his excuses. 'You have to learn to coexist, Mark. The new man you are becoming has to live alongside the man you once were. There must be no shame involved. There will never be a more perfect time to see your parents. Now, shall we say Monday afternoon for the first meeting?'

They had been through a similar process when Bones had suggested that it might be helpful and appropriate for Mark to see Theo. All the other 'guests' at the clinic had a regular time for meeting friends and family from the outside world but he hadn't wanted to see anyone: he had felt too raw and ashamed. But Bones was a persistent sod and arranged for Theo to come and see him.

'Is it very bad, this place I have brought you to?' Theo had asked, as they wandered the grounds in the bright spring sunshine shortly after they had been put through their paces by Bones.

'Let's just say it's growing on me.'

They sat on a wooden bench overlooking a small lake and watched a squadron of ducks swim by. 'I have known you all this time, Mark, and yet before this day you never told me about your friend drowning. I feel that I have let you down because you didn't feel able to confide in me. Have I been such a poor friend to you?'

'Hey, it's me on the guilt trip, okay? Don't go trying to steal my thunder.'

'But I do feel guilty. I'm disappointed with myself that I never saw through your subterfuge. Your act of wanting single-handedly to save the world should have alerted me to what you were really doing.'

'And what was that?'

'Trying to make an atonement for a young boy's death that you blamed yourself for. Oh, how very clever you were, I didn't ever suspect. Nor did I really understand just how successful you were at alienating yourself from everybody.'

'I wasn't entirely successful. I let you get close, didn't I?'

'And for that I feel truly honoured. But tell me what this strange little man whom you call Bones has taught you.'

'Oh, the usual half-baked theory that I have to learn to love myself.'

Looking stern, Theo said, 'Please, Mark, do not be so flippant. Respecting oneself is crucial. Why can you not do that?'

'Who knows? By the time Bones has finished with me I might be able to.'

It was when it was time for Theo to leave that Mark felt his emotions slide out of control. Theo had hugged him goodbye, a fierce, heart-filled hug that had taken the breath out of his chest and made him cling to his friend like a frightened child standing with his mother at the school gate for the first time. He had never forgotten the compassion on Theo's face as he released his hold. Or his words: 'I will come back for you, Mark,' he had soothed, his eyes misting over, 'I won't let you down.'

Before the first meeting with his parents, he had had all weekend to stew in a ferment of anxiety and fear. How could he face them after everything he had done?

Would they come?

Perhaps his mother might, but his father? Would he feel that this was just one more aspect of his son's dismally weak character with which he didn't want to be associated?

Monday afternoon arrived, and in what was initially an excruciating ordeal, the last remaining spectres of his nightmare were finally laid to rest.

Bones started the proceedings by passing round a family-sized box of Maltesers and saying, in a carefully lowered voice that was clearly designed to draw them into a cosy circle of intimacy, 'Well, everyone, we live in a society that is only too keen to make us feel guilty. We can't throw away a shampoo bottle without thinking we should recycle it.'

Mark could see that Bones's unassuming manner was putting his mother at ease, but there wasn't a trace of a thaw in his father as he sat bolt upright in his chair, his face rigid with tension and disapproval. He was dressed for battle – suit, tie, shoes gleaming, eyes averted, defences bristling.

'What I thought we'd look at first,' Bones carried on, 'is how everyone likes to have a scapegoat. Nowadays we use the term quite lightly, but its true significance is based on the desire to get rid of the thing, or person, whom we consider to be the cause of all our problems. Even in our enlightened age, there's nothing better than to be able to blame something, or someone, for whatever is going wrong at a particular time. An unhappy husband will leave his wife for another woman because he believes the wife to be the one holding him back or not understanding him, for making him miserable. The truth is, he is holding himself back with his own misunderstanding of the many problems he refuses to acknowledge as his. Scapegoating goes on all the time. We blame the Russians or Michael Fish for bad weather. We blame politicians for the rising—'

'Are you saying that . . . that all this is our fault?' The question was barked with ferocious defensiveness.

'No, Mr St James, I am not blaming you. Far from it. I'm suggesting that you are blaming yourself for not being able to help Mark work through the unresolved anger of a tragic accident. But if I may be allowed to explain further. When Mark really began to get out of control, you soon found yourselves turning him into a scapegoat for your own feelings of inadequacy and failure. In some small measure it lessened the guilt for you, out of sight, out of mind. No, please, don't look so shocked. It was a position he deliberately forced you into. You had little choice in the matter. He already saw himself as the scapegoat for Niall's death and wanted to take things further by proving to those closest to him that he should be thoroughly punished for what he had done. So he bullied you into sending him away to school. I'm afraid he manipulated you perfectly by turning himself into the family's black sheep. Paradoxically he imagined it would make him feel confident and empowered to know that he was in charge of you all. By then there was no stopping him. He began to see himself as the superhuman carrier of collective guilt.' A smile passed over Bones's face. 'And I think you would both agree with me that he is certainly arrogant enough to believe that he was up to the job.'

And so it went on, Bones talking, his parents listening, as he gently guided them through the dark maze in which they had been trapped. He spoke of the need for them all to challenge the past, to look it right in the eye and see it for what it was – something that no longer existed. The atmosphere gradually became less charged. His mother said, 'What hurt me most was that he wouldn't let me touch him.' She looked at Mark, reached out to his hand. 'I so badly wanted to wrap you in love, to hold you, to make you realise that you were loved. But you pushed me away so many times that I gave up trying.'

Unable to speak, he squeezed her hand. He looked at his father, to see how he was coping, knowing that it wouldn't be easy for him. His father's body had gone slack, his head was bowed low, his chin almost touching his chest. With a shock, Mark realised his father was crying. In response he felt his throat constrict and the backs of his eyes prickle. He caught Bones gesturing to him to pass his father the box of tissues on the desk. But he couldn't. His body wouldn't move. It was paralysed by too much family history. Resentment. Bitterness. And a mutual fear of each other.

'Mark, I think your father might like a tissue. Would you pass him one, please?'

As cunning as ever, Bones had forced him to confront yet another ghost. He reached for a triple-strength Kleenex and, like a white flag of surrender, passed it to his father.

The head still bowed, there was an embarrassed murmur of thanks, followed by a loud trumpeting blow. But then the real tears flowed, and seeing his father's rock-hard exterior crumbling away, Mark lost it as well. For the first time since he had been a small boy he wept openly in front of his parents, the tears streaming down his cheeks. In response, a heavy weight magically rose from his shoulders. The relief was enormous. And, without disturbing them, Bones quietly left them to it.

He soon returned with a tray of civilising tea and a plate of custard creams, as well as a list of thought-provoking questions for each of them to consider for when they met the following day. 'What we'll need to address,' he said, dunking a biscuit into his tea and crossing one of his stumpy little legs over the other, 'is the concern that every parent feels in these situations. Where did we go wrong? My job is to convince you that you didn't.'

'But . . . but we should have done more,' Mark's father said, sounding as if he was having to squeeze the words through a throat that was tightly bunched. 'We should never have given up on him. I . . . I blame myself. If I had—'

Bones jumped on him from a great height.

'Fault is not being apportioned,' he said firmly, 'not today, tomorrow or any other day. Mark and I haven't invited you here to point the finger of blame at you, or accuse you of negligence. You're here because you have a shared history that, as painful as it is, needs explaining. Nobody, and I can't stress this enough, *nobody* is to blame. It is extremely important to remember that each of you was presented with an impossible no-win situation. You all did what came naturally to you. As parents you tried your best to help and understand him, but couldn't. He was beyond your reach. There's no shame in admitting that. No shame in admitting that you couldn't stop your son from hitting the self-destruct button. It was an impossible situation that you all dealt with in the only way you knew how.' He paused to offer them a second cup of tea. 'You know, the life we want,' he went on, tinkling his teaspoon against his cup, 'is rarely the life we have. All we can ever do is bridge the gap to the Promised Land.'

After that they were at least able to communicate with each other on a new, improved level. The resentment, bitterness and mutual fear he and his father had felt for each other gave way to tolerance and understanding, a glimmer of hope that life could be better.

And all these years on, they were still working at that bridge Bones had spoken of. Mark was a part of his parents' lives once again, and he suspected that they were just a little bit proud of him. His father, who normally didn't have time to read, never failed to get hold of his latest book the moment it was out – he always refused a free copy, saying that he wanted the pleasure of walking into their local bookshop and asking for his son's latest novel.

As for his brothers, Peter and Hugh – the clever bastards, he had always called them – he now had two sisters-in-law as well as three nieces and a nephew. He was a constant source of amusement to the children. They knew that their uncle Mark wasn't like other uncles. Last Christmas, his youngest niece had climbed on to his lap and asked him if all families had a skeleton like theirs hidden away in a cupboard. He had laughed and instantly made up a spine-tingling story about the one kept in the attic of his parents' house where they were all staying. He described how it came out of its box on the stroke of midnight and wandered around the house. The next morning, Peter had had a go at him for scaring Susie half to death and keeping her awake all night.

But there was one thing for which he was especially grateful to his brothers, and that was their enthusiasm for running the family business now that their father had retired: a business that had been in the family for three generations.

And what exactly was the family business?

It was, of all things, a brewery.

As Theo would say, 'How is that for a nice touch of your typically English irony?'

30

They were the last to leave the restaurant. Thanos and Christiana Vlamakis, along with the elderly relatives from Thessaloníki, took a taxi to the airport to catch their flights home, the priest went off in a haze of Metaxá to the Esplanade to watch a cricket match and Theo and Mark helped Thomas Zika back to his apartment on Kapodistriou Street. They had only a short distance to cover, but by the time Mark had pushed the old man's wheelchair through the busy tourist-filled streets, he was hot and perspiring.

Home for Mr Zika was on the fourth floor of a tall, thin building that backed on to a maze of shadowy little streets and tiny shops. From the front it looked out across to the old fortress and the turquoise sea beyond. Originally built for the old aristocracy of the town, the Venetian-style house, with its elegant proportions, wrought-iron balconies and shuttered windows must have been a beautiful and impressive home in its glory days; now it was just another example of faded grandeur. Its yellow paintwork was dirty and peeling, its stonework crumbling like blocks of salt. Split into goodness knows how many apartments, it still had only one lift and they had to wait patiently for it to descend to their level. It was of the ancient metal-cage variety and clanked and juddered slowly and disconcertingly, up to the fourth floor. Taking Mr Zika's key Theo let them in. The first thing that struck Mark as they entered the apartment was the cool temperature. After the searing heat in the street, it came as a welcome relief. He had read once that all old people's houses feel cold; it was the seeping away of the owner's lifeblood that made them like that. It was not the cheeriest theory.

Theo led the way, manoeuvring the wheelchair down a dim passage that was only just wide enough for it. They came to a high-ceilinged drawing room that smelt strongly of age and polish – years and years of polish that must have been assiduously applied to the delicate pieces of furniture that took up most of the available space in the large rectangular room. Burnished to a high gloss, tables, writing-desks, glass-fronted cabinets all vied for their own bit of space. Oriental rugs, some overlapping in places, covered the floor, marble-based lamps illuminated gloomy corners, and soft light bounced off glowing bronze statues and porcelain vases. A tapestry drooped on one of the walls, its colours muted, its silk surround ripped and sagging. It partially disguised a worrying crack in the plaster that had carved itself a forty-five-degree groove right up to the ornate cornice of the ceiling where a dusty chandelier hung. Faded drapes framed the tall, narrow windows and sunlight fought to penetrate the barrier of discoloured netting that looked as though it might turn to dust at a touch. The steady ticking of an ormolu clock on the mantelpiece added to the clutter of a room that made Mark feel uncomfortably on edge. But, then, turning to his right, he saw something that made him feel instantly at home.

Covering an entire wall, from floor to ceiling, were rows of leatherbound books. There were as many English titles as there were Greek ones and his hands twitched to reach out and touch them. 'You're a man after my own heart, Mr Zika,' he said, indicating the tightly packed shelves.

'Please, call me Thomas,' the old man said, as Theo helped him into a wing-backed armchair, where beside him was a small table with a chessboard on it; it looked as if a game was in progress. 'I think you have earned that right, after all the assistance you have given me. And go ahead, acquaint yourself with a few of my oldest friends.' He sank back into the seat and sighed deeply, a long, painful wheeze. He looked tired, as though he were only hanging on to life by a gossamer thread of strained will. 'If you would care to wait, Eleni, my housekeeper, will be here shortly and we could ask her to make us some coffee. But perhaps you are eager to be on your way.'

Stooping to tuck a blanket around the old man's legs, Theo murmured something that Mark didn't catch, but the gist of which became apparent when Theo went to make the coffee himself. While he was out of the room, Mark helped himself to a book from one of the shelves. The dusty smell of the mould-spotted leather reminded him of a thousand old bookshops in which he had browsed. He sat next to Thomas, showed him what he had picked out and fingered the pages with the greatest of care. After a while he sensed that tiredness was making Thomas vague and distracted. The lucid man with whom he had chatted in the restaurant was gone. Now he was murmuring indistinctly to himself, his eyelids drooping, his hands lying inert on his lap. It wasn't long before faint snoring added to the rhythmic ticking of the clock on the mantelpiece. Quietly replacing the book on the shelf, Mark went in search of Theo. 'I don't think Thomas will be wanting any coffee,' he said. 'He's asleep.'

The kitchen was small and dingy, with a free-standing cupboard against one wall and a fridge that vibrated noisily against the leg of a cumbersome old gas cooker. A pale blue Formica-topped table with chrome legs held an assortment of papers, unopened envelopes and a tin of pens and pencils. Above this was a thin shelf, on which a set of old pans was stacked. The poky room made a sharp contrast with the cluttered but opulent drawing room.

'I will make him some anyway,' Theo said, turning off the tap and looking for a cloth to dry the cups he had just washed. 'He never sleeps for long.'

'How old is he?'

'At the last count he was ninety-five. He does well for his age, eh?'

'Extraordinarily well. I can't imagine either of us still being around at that age. I'm not sure I'd want to go on for that long. What would be the point?'

'Ah, my friend, I would relish the thought that one day you would be as wise and as content as dear old Thomas, a man who needs only to play himself at chess and read his beloved books to be happy.'

'To hell with that, you'd just enjoy seeing me helpless.'

Theo narrowed his eyes and passed him a delicate bone-china cup of coffee, the gold line of its rim almost rubbed away. 'It was very kind what you did for Thomas over lunch,' he said. 'It isn't everyone who would have done that, and with such courteous compassion.'

'I suspect it was harder for Thomas to ask for my help than for me to give it.'

'But that is always the case. You of all people know that to be true.'

When they returned to Áyios Nikólaos, they found the party invitation that had been left for them on the terrace.

'And what excuse do you expect me to give my friends this time?' asked Theo, coming out from the house where he had changed to go for a swim. 'That you have a headache?'

Mark followed him to the pool. 'Why do you say that?'

'Because I know you so well. You would rather stay here and bury yourself in the violent make-believe land of your imagination than show your face at a fancy-dress party and risk enjoying yourself in the real world.'

Watching Theo dive into the water and swim a length before coming up for air, Mark thought of Thomas Zika and how they had left him to the company of his books and the ticking of his clock, which cruelly echoed the long-drawn-out loneliness of what remained of his life. He said, 'Well, just to prove how wrong you are, Theodore Know-It-All Vlamakis, I will go.'

Theo turned over on to his back and laughed. 'Now this I have to see. Mark St James dressed up as a Greek god. Ha, ha, ha!'

His laughter continued long after Mark had left him to gloat over such an improbable notion.

31

As it turned out Theo was denied a laugh at Mark's expense. On the morning of the party he received a phone call that had him changing his plans for the following week. Leaving his study, he went to look for Mark. He found him working on the terrace in the shade, his head bent over an A4 pad of paper, his hand moving steadily across the page. Reluctant to interrupt, Theo stood for a moment, marvelling at the creative process in which his friend was so absorbed. It was something he could never do. His brain was too restless to apply itself to just one task. He didn't have the single-minded determination, or the patience, to sit still long enough to be a writer. He bored easily and needed a variety of challenges if his attention was to be held.

Which was why he had spent most of life diversifying in the way that he had. When asked what he did for a living he usually said he did nothing more than dabble in property. But there were plenty of other things he got up to. He could never go anywhere without noticing a potential investment. It didn't matter how big or small it was, or how improbable; if he thought he could do something with it, he would immediately make enquiries and put forward an appropriate offer. Whether it was a run-down petrol station, a struggling taverna, or a large chain of shops that had lost its direction, he would bring in his own hand-picked management team and turn the business round. Once it was up and running, he would be looking for the next project to occupy him. And if he acted quickly, his next project was within his grasp.

Back in Athens a whisper of a rumour had started. It was in connection with the chain of hotels owned by the Karabourniotis family and, according to the word that had reached his office, the family was looking for an investor to help ease their growing financial difficulties. But Theo wasn't interested in putting money into anything that he didn't own outright, not when he knew he would have to stand back and watch his investment thrown away on yet more bad decisions and rising debts. If his fingers were going to delve into this particular pie, it would only be through a straight buy-out.

Not for a split second had it entered his head to leave it to his legal boys and accountants to meet with the Karabourniotis family, not when he believed in the personal approach. Besides, he knew them well, and knew just how proud old man Yiannis Karabourniotis was. Seeking help from outside his family was the last thing he would have wanted; it would have been his last desperate resort. Theo suspected that his greedy sons had driven him to this point, that they had been frittering away the profits on themselves rather than reinvesting in the hotels by modernising and expanding. This was another reason why Theo wanted to deal directly with Yiannis. Yiannis would never publicly criticise his sons, so the whole business would need careful handling and Theo trusted only himself to do that.

'How much longer are you going to stand there distracting me?' asked Mark, jolting him out of his thoughts.

'You will be relieved to know that I need to be in Athens again. I leave after lunch.'

Mark put down his pen and leaned back in his chair. 'How long will you be away this time?'

'I'm touched. You are missing me already?'

'Like a dog deprived of his fleas.'

'An unpleasant analogy, but in answer to your question, I don't know. A week seems probable.' He explained why he was going.

'So why the interest?' asked Mark. 'What's so special about these hotels that you feel you have to make another of your boardroom raids on them?'

'When I have so much already? Is that what you're getting at?'

'Yes. Exactly that.'

'Aha, the same old Mark. What a delight it is to know that despite your own success you still despise mine. It is quite simple. I want the hotels because they are there. They are available. If not me putting money on the table, it will be somebody else making a ruthless hostile bid. And, forgive my arrogance, but I believe I will offer Yiannis Karabourniotis the best deal.'

'What will you do with them?'

'Make them highly successful, of course.'

'But what makes you think you can succeed where he has failed?'

'I will not have two greedy sons milking my company. And if you have finished prosecuting me, I must go and pack. Then I shall wander next door and see Izzy.'

He had little to pack: running two households meant that he had everything he needed in both places. Each of his wardrobes was a mirror image of the other: suits, shirts, ties and shoes, as well as a selection of more casual clothes were duplicated. It was an extravagance – a bloody crime, as Mark frequently told him – but one he could easily justify. Packing consisted of a simple reorganisation of his briefcase for the week ahead. He then phoned his housekeeper in Athens to warn her that he would be arriving later that afternoon. Katina had worked for him for many years and knew his habits well. She lived close by so his unpredictable comings and goings were of little inconvenience to her. She assured him that she would have everything ready for his arrival. When he had put down the phone he changed into a suit and went next door.

It had been a curious week since he had told Izzy what he felt for her. Even more curious was that, during his busy week of travelling between Athens and Corfu, his feelings for her had not changed. She was never far from his thoughts. While she had been held captive at Villa Petros resting her ankle, the chance to see her alone had been non-existent. To his annoyance and frustration, there always seemed to be somebody about. He had thought of calling her from Athens on several occasions, but had known that there would have been people all around her making it impossible for them to have the kind of conversation he desired. The Fates, it seemed, were conspiring against them.

Or were they?

Surely if he really wanted to get her alone he would have made it happen. Wasn't that what he excelled at? Didn't he always make things happen according to his wishes? So why, then, had he not scooped up the lovely Izzy in his arms, carried her away and made love to her as he wanted to?

Was he frightened of doing that? Because in taking that step he might destroy what he had so carefully built up? She was so wary of him that he knew he still had a long way to go in gaining her confidence and her trust. If he moved in too fast he might jeopardise everything.

But there was another possibility to explain why he was treating her with such patience. It was a theory with which Mark had confronted him over supper one evening. 'You fancy yourself in the role of a disillusioned, soul-searching, worldly man wanting to be redeemed by the love of a sweet young girl. You see her as Jane Eyre to your Rochester, Rebecca to your Maxim de Winter, Fanny Price to—'

'Yes, Mark, I have grasped the subtlety of your words, you are not the only one to have trawled the pages of these fine books. But I'm afraid I think you are spending too much time in the world of fiction. You are so used to making things up, you don't know what is real and not real.'

'Oh, come on, own up to it. You're intrigued by the idea of harnessing a love as refreshing as the one you think Izzy can offer you. But what then? What will you do when you have succeeded in capturing her heart?'

'At the rate I'm going, I doubt that will ever happen.'

'Of course it will. You never fail at anything you're determined to have.'

'In business that might be true, but this is different. Izzy is not a commodity to be negotiated for.'

'I'm relieved to hear it.'

And this was what had started to worry Theo. With his sledgehammer comments, had Mark come close to what was really going on between him and Izzy? Had the division between his professional and his personal life become blurred? Did he view her as one of those must-have businesses? Was there a chance that his feelings for her were based purely on the desire always to have his own way? Was it the thrill of the chase that excited him? And if so, as Mark had said, 'What then?' Having won her heart, was there a danger that he would grow bored with it and search for another?

And wasn't that what he had always done?

But he didn't want to believe this. He wanted to believe that, at long last, the impossible had happened: Theodore Vlamakis had finally met the woman for whom he would forsake all others.

He was so deep in thought, his head bowed in concentration, that he let out a startled cry of surprise when he came face to face with the very woman he had been thinking about. 'Izzy,' he said when he had recovered himself, 'I was just on my way to see you.' Looking down at her ankle, he added, 'Should you be putting so much strain on it?'

She smiled. 'I'm testing it, but the others don't know, so please don't tell them. They'll be very cross with me.'

'And I, too, shall be very cross with you if you come to any more harm. Where are you going?'

'Down to the beach. I'm tired of just staring at it.' She indicated the bag on her shoulder. 'I wanted to find some driftwood to sketch. I feel like an escaped prisoner on the run.'

'May I join you?'

She looked at his clothes doubtfully. 'Won't you spoil your suit?'

'I promise I will be very careful with it.'

'You make a lot of promises, don't you?'

'But, I promise you, I keep them all.' He flashed her one of his best star-bright smiles. 'Now, I won't take any arguments, you must give me your hand.'

Why, thought Izzy as she slipped her hand through his, does he make everything sound so provocative? And why does he still scare me so much?

Laura had said it was because he made her reconsider everything she thought she knew about herself. 'He makes you wonder what it would be like to live a little dangerously. Instead of watching everyone else having a good time from behind the glow-white net curtains of your so-called respectable upbringing, Theo challenges you to dance naked in the street while kicking over the milk bottles and rattling the neighbours' dustbin lids.'

Maybe Laura was right.

When they were down on the beach, sitting on the stones, Theo, having removed his jacket and checked that his trousers wouldn't come to any harm, said, 'Do you realise this is my first opportunity to be with you on your own since you hurt your ankle? I might be forgiven for thinking that you have been hiding from me.'

Ignoring the implication of his words, she dug around in her bag for her sketchpad. Keeping her head down, she said, 'Up on the path you mentioned that you were coming to see me. Why?'

He selected a perfectly white stone the size of an egg from between his polished shoes and wrapped his fingers around it. 'I have to return to Athens again and I wanted to see you before I went. I am leaving in half an hour.'

'Will you be away for long?'

'A week. Perhaps longer. It depends how quickly I can get what I want.'

He threw the stone into the water and turned his head to fix his dark eyes on hers. There was a determination in his gaze that made her realise that no matter how hard she tried to have a normal conversation with him, he always had his own agenda. *It depends how quickly I can get what I want.* He never missed a trick, did he? 'You'll miss Max and Laura's party tonight,' she said, hunting through her bag again, this time for a pencil.

'I will miss more than that. I will miss you.'

'No, you won't,' she said brightly, 'you'll be far too busy.'

A hand came to rest on hers through the canvas of the bag. She glanced up to see a look of annoyance on his face. 'Please,' he said, 'do not take that oh-so-English mother-knows-best tone with me. If I say I will miss you, Izzy, I mean exactly that.'

He's just like a little boy, she thought. The moment he thinks he isn't being taken seriously, or there's a danger he can't get his own way, he takes offence. While she was pondering on this, he said, 'I have something for you.'

From the inside pocket of his jacket, he pulled out a mobile phone. She looked at it, puzzled.

'It is so that I can speak to you in private while I am away. Switch it on late at night when you are no longer chaperoned and I will call you while you are in bed.' And as though to show her that his cross-little-boy act had gone, he grinned and said, 'Every night I will tell you a bedtime story.'

She laughed nervously. 'With a happy ending, I hope.'

'Well, Izzy, I would say that depends on you, doesn't it?' He leaned in and very gently kissed her. It was a small, brief kiss. Nothing to get too worked up over. But a tiny knot of panic tightened in her stomach. 'The ball,' he murmured, while stroking a finger the length of her jaw, 'as you English say, is in your court.'

32

Once Theo had left for the airport, Mark concentrated on the chapter he had started that morning. He was keen to finish it, and in view of the prolonged roll he was on, it seemed a shrewd move on his part to capitalise on his current good fortune.

It had been like this ever since he had overcome the problem of creating a credible will-they-won't-they love-interest scenario between his protagonist and the killer's next victim. He was feeling so confident about the way the book had developed a life of its own that he was beginning to think it was his best yet. And it was all down to one person. It was a shame, though, that he would never be able to give her the credit for inspiring him. That was out of the question. His actions might easily be misconstrued and he didn't want to cause any ructions. Least of all between himself and Theo.

As unexpected as it was, the source of his inspiration was none other than Izzy. Without her knowing it she had freed his imagination and enabled him to create a far more realistic sub-plot than he had hitherto put together.

Bones would have a field day with what he had done. 'You're nothing but a grave robber,' he could hear the man saying, 'stripping people of their lives for your own gratification.' And, yes, he supposed he was a bit of a Dr Frankenstein when it came down to it. He never thought twice about hoovering up snippets of other people's lives; it was simply part and parcel of being a writer. But in this instance, he had gone one step further. He had helped himself to a whole person; he had dropped Izzy into his novel. He didn't kid himself that she would be flattered by what he had done, not if she knew she had become his protagonist's lover, and certainly not if she knew she was next in line to get the chop at the hands of a psychotic killer. It was hardly the most honourable thing to do, or the best way to ingratiate himself with a fellow human being.

The idea had come to him the evening he had failed in his duty to get Izzy safely home – a point Theo had been at pains to labour when he had returned to Villa Anna. 'Did I ask you to chase her up the path and make her nearly break her neck? No! I asked you to make sure that she reached home in one piece.' He had been unable to sleep that night and as he lay tossing and turning, listening to the waves gently lapping against the rocks down in the bay, the solution had suddenly come to him. Switching on the bedside lamp, he had reached for his notebook and pen and feverishly scribbled the tumble of thoughts rushing to get out of his head. By the following morning he had the next three chapters planned and was eager to make a start.

Previously he had tended to echo the seriousness of the book's theme in his protagonist's sexual relationships, which meant that the bedroom scenes, in his view, lacked spontaneity. Graphic and raw, there was no tenderness, no love, not even a sense of euphoria when his protagonist finally got his leg over. It was sex to order. Sex in the name of duty. Just doing my job, ma'am.

But now he saw a way to change all that. Why not create a contrast of emotions within the book? Like the chiaroscuro effect of light and dark in a painting, could he not employ the same technique in his writing? And wouldn't the juxtaposition of some light-hearted sexual interaction make the evil undercurrents of the story appear even more threatening? It would surely add another dimension. The reader would be lulled into a false sense of security, making the outcome all the more shocking. Instinctively he had known it was the right course to follow and had got to work with renewed vigour.

As absurd as it was, it had been nothing more than the act of staggering up the hillside with Izzy in his arms and their shared laughter that had triggered off this new change of direction. But as simple and seemingly insignificant as this moment might have appeared to anybody else, for him it had allowed the chapters that had earlier floored him to flow effortlessly from his pen. When Theo had commented on the noticeable increase in his output and asked where the inspiration had come from, Mark had kept quiet, feeling slightly ashamed that he was using Izzy in such a dubious manner. He was acutely aware that it was wholesale exploitation and he didn't want Theo to know the depths to which he had sunk. Especially as during the last week or so Theo had shown all the signs of becoming possessively protective of Izzy. He didn't like to think of the outrage Theo would feel if he knew that the woman with whom he fancied himself in love was being vicariously exploited by his oldest friend.

But, this reservation aside, he was delighted with the way his work was going and wondered what his editor would make of it.

He also wondered what Bones would make of it. 'What's this, Mark? *You* writing about love and passion? Whatever next?'

No psychoanalyst worth his Freud and Gestalt can resist the temptation to dissect a client's sex life, and Bones had been no exception.

'Women,' he had said, opening a drawer and rustling a bag of jelly-babies at the start of one of their sessions, 'friend or foe?'

'That's a ludicrous statement,' Mark had countered. 'It can never be as simplistic as that.'

'Okay, let me come in from another angle. How many people have you ever really connected with, apart from Theo?'

'Why do you assume I have with Theo?'

'Are you afraid to admit that you have? Afraid to show that you're capable of caring for another person?'

He didn't answer Bones. Just stared him out. Then, to annoy him, Bones started whistling another of his tunes – 'Try A Little Tenderness'.

'Shut the hell up, will you?'

The whistling stopped and Bones popped a jelly-baby into his mouth. He chewed slowly, the sweet smell of artificial strawberry juice coming at Mark across the desk. 'And your answer?'

'As, no doubt, you've already concluded, apart from Theo I've never been really close to anyone.'

'Good.'

'It's good that I've never connected with anyone?'

'No, good that I extracted that confession from you without the use of thumbscrews.' He reached for another sweet. 'Now, then, back to you and women. How do you view them?'

'Have you ever thought that perhaps you have a serious sugar habit?'

'Deflecting the question and sending it off course by lobbing a personal criticism is neither original nor constructive, Mark. Does the idea of somebody ransacking your sexual history disturb you?'

'No.'

'Then try giving me an answer.'

'I don't think I can.'

'Perhaps you should allow me to do some of your thinking for you.'

'I thought therapists weren't supposed to do that. I thought—'

'Another attempt to deflect me? Really, Mark, why do you insist on doing this?'

'Because it's marginally more interesting than anything else going on here.'

'You're bored?'

'Out of my mind.'

'Talking of which, let's get back to it. Would you say that you were a success in bed? A sexual dynamo?'

'I've had my moments.'

'Mm ... As intrigued as I am by your so-called moments, let's think about the earth-moving pleasures you've given the women in your life. Were you good at that? A thrilling success?'

'Depends how one measures success.'

'And still you insist on shilly-shallying around with me. Which, you should have learned by now, only forces me to be more direct. Were you able to make your lovers climax?'

Watching Bones bite the head off a green jelly-baby, he said, 'Is any man really sure he's hitting the right buttons?'

The rest of the jelly-baby went the way of its head. 'I assure you, when the right buttons are pressed, you know all about it.'

This was the first time Mark had viewed Bones as a man who had a life outside the clinic. Was it possible that this little man with his insatiable sweet tooth was a super-stud in bed?

'Something amusing you?'

'Yes. You sounded as if you were boasting there for a minute.'

'Interesting that you should view it that way. But putting the question of my sexual prowess to one side, shall we take a moment to hold yours up to the light and see how transparent it is?'

It didn't take Bones long to establish the obvious, that Mark's experience with women was pretty shallow. That he had interpreted emotional dependency as weakness. That he had been unable to commit himself. And that nothing lasted because nothing meant anything to him.

As Kim would have been the first to confirm.

Poor Kim. She really hadn't known what she was getting into when she had married him. It had been a disaster from the outset. Marrying solely to provide the necessary wings to fly in the face of his parents' disapproval was never going to be a solid foundation for a lasting relationship. Kim must have known what he had done, but perhaps, and if only to appease his conscience, he had always hoped that she had had her own game plan when she had agreed to go through with the marriage. After all, on paper he looked like he was worth the effort. As the youngest son and potential heir to a thriving family business, he must have seemed a good investment to a girl who had spent most of her childhood being shuffled from one foster family to another, and her young adult years camped out at Greenham Common, before going north to support the miners in her continued search for a sense of belonging.

It was during the miners' strike, and in a leaking, bone-shaking Bedford van on his way to help Arthur Scargill beat Ian MacGregor and *la* Thatcher, that Mark had met Kim. He had come upon her as she was trying to hitch a lift. Her hair was braided into rainbow-coloured dreadlocks and she was dressed in dungarees several sizes too large for her with a donkey jacket turned up at the collar to keep out the rain. She was grateful to climb in alongside him to escape the downpour when he stopped to offer a lift, but street-wise enough to let him know she was no fool. 'Don't think you can try anything on with me,' she had warned him. 'I've got a knife and I'm not afraid to use it.'

'And good morning to you, fair maiden,' he had said.

'Oh, fancy yourself as a clever dick, do you?' she had responded. 'Well, like I say, make a move on me and I'll cut it off for you.'

Their whirlwind romance, as he had sarcastically described it for Bones's benefit, consisted of several months of communal living until the miners' strike came to an end. Then he wrote to his parents to inform them that he was getting married. 'The least you could do for me is be there at the register office,' he had written.

'That was really telling them, wasn't it, Mark?' Bones had said, when he recounted the scene of his marriage vows being witnessed by his stony-faced parents and brothers. Kim had dressed for the occasion by getting her nose pierced and wearing one of those multi-coloured, hand-knitted Peruvian hats with ear-flaps, while he had excelled himself with a pair of dirty combat trousers and a T-shirt with a picture of Lenin on the front. 'You badly wanted to rub their noses in the mire of your unhappiness, didn't you?' Bones remarked. 'What better way than to say, "Look, this is what you've driven me to do."?'

His parents gave him some money to put down on a small flat. Guilt-money, every penny of it, he had convinced himself, as he and Kim set up home and played at Mr and Mrs Domestic Harmony. But within a short while he had lost his job, his wife and the flat. Gone, too, was every scrap of his political ideology. There seemed no point in it. What difference did it make anyway? The void he was left with he filled with booze. When things got out of hand he tried a stint of going on the wagon, but it didn't help. He got the shakes and depression kicked in. And to beat the depression he upped the amount of cocaine he was taking to give him the lift he needed. But all that happened was that the drug used up what little energy he had so when the comedown hit him he felt worse than ever. His depression deepened, he became jittery and paranoid, and as panicky as hell. And though he was exhausted, he couldn't sleep, not with his brain racing at full tilt. He knew he needed help, but he was powerless to seek it. It was easiest just to keep on drinking.

'And where was Theo when all this was going on?' Bones had asked him. 'Wasn't he summoned to your wedding like your family?'

'No.'

'Why not?'

'I didn't want him there.'

'Didn't want him to see how fast you were sliding out of control?'

'Something like that.'

'And what was his reaction when you finally got round to bringing him up to date?'

'He asked me if I was happy.'

'And were you?'

'I told him I was.'

'That wasn't what I asked.'

'Well, of course I wasn't happy. I was having a blast of a time shoving corpses into cheap plywood coffins by day and avoiding my wife by night. A real recipe for joy.'

'I'll come back to your wife in a minute, but for now, tell me why you took a job surrounding yourself with the dead. Was that a satisfying career move, or a brilliant piece of macabre irony on your part? Or was it a mental reminder like one of those we stick on the fridge with a cute magnet – "Must remember to pay the television licence." Except in this case it was "Must remember what a dead body looks like, lest I forget the horror of Niall's death"?'

'I needed a job—'

'With a first-class honours degree in criminal psychology you could have got something more appropriate than working in a small-town under-taker's.'

'It seemed appropriate at the time.'

'Yes, I think you probably did see it as appropriate, particularly the element of macabre irony. A society dying on its feet, and you there to help bury it. Was that the big joke?'

'If you say so.'

'And who did you share this joke with? Kim?'

'No.'

'Theo?'

'No. No one.'

'So, it was a side-splitting laugh a minute with yourself? Except it wasn't funny, was it? It was, and please excuse the pun, a deadly serious affair. There was to be no escape from the spectre of your childhood. Rubbing shoulders with all those rotting corpses was your reward for failing Niall, wasn't it? Couldn't you have come up with something more subtle?'

'It was the best I could do in the circumstances.'

'Well, now, the sharpness in your voice tells me that you've had enough. But to finish with, let me leave you with this thought. You've never held down a job for more than seven months and your track record for staying in a lasting relationship is laughable. Is this a coincidence? Laziness? Or a fear of failure?'

It went without saying that every word uttered by Bones scored a bull's-eye. Since Kim had left him, when she couldn't put up with his drinking any longer, he had lost all interest in forming any kind of relationship, let alone a lasting one. He also felt disgusted with himself that he had treated Kim so badly, and the scant remains of any decency he still had held him back from doing the same to anyone else. As for work, he didn't want to do anything that might stretch him or give him a sense of achievement. By not accepting the challenge in the first place he could be sure not to fail. But it went a little deeper, as Bones took the trouble to point out to him.

'This is standard-issue stuff from the school of survival, Mark. Ever since Niall's death you allowed yourself nothing of any real worth, only the dregs of the barrel that nobody else was interested in having. It meant that if they were taken away, as Niall was, you wouldn't get hurt.'

It was a harsh summing-up of his brief marriage, but sadly it was true. If he hadn't been so self-absorbed he would have realised that Kim was chock full of her own emotional problems from her childhood, and that she needed his help, not his drunken black moods.

Looking back on those days – days and nights when she had stayed away from the flat because she had been terrified of what he might do next – it all felt like a terrible dream sequence. None of it seemed real. The shame of it was, he had never had the opportunity to say how sorry he was. Not long after their divorce he had read of her death in the local paper. She had got her life together far better than he had at that time, and was working in a supermarket, stacking shelves. She had finished her shift late one night, stepped out into the road to catch her bus home and was knocked down by a stolen car being driven by a fourteen-year-old boy. Death had been instantaneous. One minute she had probably been looking forward to her supper of beans on toast – one of her favourite meals, especially if the beans had those funny little sausages with them – and the next she was lying face down in the gutter, surrounded by a group of strangers checking her for any vital signs. Her untimely death should have given him food for thought, forced him to take stock. But no. What grief he had felt for her he obliterated by going on a three-day bender. As always, his response to anything that might touch him was to get drunk.

He let out his breath and leaned back in his chair. Yes. It was done. He had finished the chapter. Objective achieved.

He replaced the cap on his fountain pen – a gift from Theo when he had started work on his first novel – and stretched his arms up over his head. He could feel a day's worth of tension in his shoulders and neck, the muscles taut after sitting still for so many hours.

To help him unwind, he decided to go for a walk to the shop to buy another film for his camera. As he strolled along the hot, dusty road, he tried to decide what to do about the Sinclair party that evening.

Theo's parting shot when he had left for the airport had been, 'Fifty of your strong English pounds says that you are such a miserable killjoy you won't go to Max and Laura's tonight.'

It was tempting to let Theo have the last word and be done with it. A quiet evening alone would not be such a bad thing. He was used to his own company. But from nowhere a picture of Thomas Zika playing chess with himself to get through the long, lonely hours came into his mind.

It was as though he was being shown a glimpse of what the future held for him.

It was a future he didn't much care for.

33

While she was fetching a drink for Virginia Patterson and taking time out from her annoyingly overbearing manner, the roar of conversation and laughter told Laura that the party was a success. Not only had everybody made the effort to dress up, but they all seemed to be enjoying themselves. They made a curious gathering, and she didn't mind admitting that initially she had had misgivings about one or two of their guests getting on with each other. But it seemed that there was nothing like a change of identity, albeit a superficial one, to help lower the social mask one normally hid behind. And, looking at everyone on the terrace, who had come similarly wrapped in a white cotton sheet, she pictured the stripped beds they must have left behind in their villas.

Dressed as Hercules, Max was one of the few who wasn't wearing a sheet. He had plumped for shorts and a Lion King beach towel he had bought in Kassiópi. He had made a tail out of plaited string and sewn it to the bottom edge of the towel, which hung off him like a cloak; anyone who came near him, received a swish of his tail and a flash of his biceps.

Corky was dressed as Zeus, and to complete his sartorial sheeted elegance he had hung a lightbulb round his neck, stuck a three-foot-long cotton wool beard to his chin and fixed a lightning bolt made of cardboard to his chest. Olivia was stylishly decked out as Hera, Zeus's wife, and she had made herself a sceptre out of a garden cane borrowed from Angelos, which she had wrapped in cooking foil and used to keep Corky in line by poking him with it whenever the mood took her.

The girls had predictably gone for the not-wearing-very-much look. Francesca, dressed as Hebe, the goddess of youth, was barefoot, having laced her feet and lower legs with rose pink ribbons. The sheet she wore, or what there was of it – and Laura was sure that some of her precious bed linen had been sacrificed in the name of adornment – stopped a few inches below her bottom and was held in place by more of the rose pink ribbon to give her a perfect Playtex Cross-Your-Heart-bra outline. She was wearing her hair loose and her lips were heavily painted with red lipstick. Max had swished her with his tail and called her a pouting Botticelli tart.

Like Izzy, Sally had kept her costume a secret right up until the moment she made her entrance into the kitchen earlier that evening, before their guests had arrived. The look on Max's face when he saw her summed up their collective fear.

'Is that a muslin drape from your bedroom window that you're nearly wearing?' Laura had asked, wishing she had the body to do the same but fearing for every man's blood pressure.

'It is,' said Sally, performing a little twirl for them. 'Can you guess who I am?' She held up a makeshift bow and arrow, which action parted the folds in the diaphanous layers of muslin and exposed her breasts. When nobody answered – they were all too stunned – she said, 'I'm Artemis, the huntress.'

Francesca had laughed loudly. 'But she was a virgin.'

Sally grinned. 'Yeah, well, a little artistic licence goes a long way.'

'I'll say. Does it extend to wearing any knickers?'

'I'm wearing a flesh-coloured thong. Look, can't you see?'

It was an offer that had Max and his father averting their eyes and suggesting it was time for a drink.

Izzy appeared, then, dressed in what the girls called her Lara Croft khaki shorts and vest top. She was carrying a spear made from a garden cane and an impressive shield, made of cardboard and beautifully painted in shades of silver to match the spear. Though her ankle had more or less healed, this evening it was bandaged again and a toy arrow stuck out from her heel where a few drops of red paint had been dabbed on. 'Achilles,' she said, 'in case you were wondering.'

'My goodness, haven't we all been inventive?' said Olivia, 'How do you think our guests will fare? Will they pass muster?'

The guests, as Laura looked at them all now, had been equally creative, and the only repeat character was that of Hebe. While Francesca was more than qualified to play the part of the goddess of youth, Dolly-Babe was pushing the boundaries of belief a smidgen too far.

The Fitzgeralds had been the first to arrive and, just as Francesca and Sally had predicted, Bob's only concession to the theme of the party was a balloon at the end of a short length of string pinned to the shoulder of his shirt. It made him look as though he had two heads. It also made him conspicuously awkward, as it bobbed beside his right ear as though agreeing with his every word as he talked to Corky about problems with his business ventures on the island. He sounded more than a little put out that he wasn't finding things as straightforward as he had expected. He was full of conspiracy theories: of cartels that were freezing out honest men like him, and of red tape that magically appeared from nowhere if the locals didn't like the look of you. 'I had a neat little number all lined up with some old peasant who didn't have a clue what he was sitting on, and just as I was about to get a contract organised, he refused to sell. Said he'd had a better offer. Better offer, my arse!'

Laura hadn't caught the rest of the conversation because Dolly-Babe had turned to her and said, 'Gawd, I wish he'd shut up. If I've heard him go on about losing that piece of land once, I've heard it a million times.' Laura suspected from the smell of Dolly-Babe and the way she swayed as she leaned into her that she had already had a head start on the drinking before she arrived. 'So what do you think of my costume?'

'Oh, very nice,' Laura had said, casting her eyes over a sparkly Spandex figure-hugging dress that Tina Turner would have been proud of, and a head of hair that was piled higher than normal and threaded through with sequin-covered ribbons.

'You know, I spent ages trying to decide who to come as, but then I thought, Come on, gal, who else could you be but Hebe, the goddess of youth?'

'Snap,' Francesca had said, joining them from across the terrace. 'I'm her as well.'

Barefoot confidence meets barefaced cheek, Laura had thought, with a private smile.

'Well, Gawd bless us,' Dolly-Babe had cried. 'You know, it was a close-run thing, it was her, or that Afro ... Afro ...' She had clicked her fingers as if to summon up the name. It had worked. Well, almost. 'You know, that one into love, Afrodykey.'

The Pattersons had arrived next.

Courtesy of the girls, everyone at Villa Petros had been given an advance-warning thumbnail sketch of Mr and Mrs Patterson and Laura wasn't at all sure that it had been a good idea to invite them, but having seen so much of their sons she had crossed her fingers and hoped for the best.

Within seconds of hearing and seeing Virginia Patterson, Laura had been plucked from the present and dumped in the past of her schooldays and, in particular, on to the frozen hockey-field where a formidable games mistress had bullied the spirit out of her. Dressed in a crumpled white sheet, her plump feet pushed into flat Ecco sandals, Nick and Harry's mother had come as Athena, the goddess of wisdom and strength, and now, as she took the glass of Pimm's that Laura had just fetched for her, it sounded worryingly as if she was going to play her character a little too exact. 'Of course, if I'd had more warning I would have made a better job of my costume,' she said airily.

Yes, thought Laura, you might have taken the trouble to iron the sheet. And just as the horrible woman was getting into her stride, her words dried up and her eyes narrowed. Following her gaze, Laura saw that she had caught sight of Sally, who, it had to be said, looked as if she would be more at home in a soft-porn movie than at a holiday drinks party. Behind her large-framed glasses, Virginia's beady gaze immediately turned to her husband who was making no attempt to hide the fact that he was feasting his eyes on the gossamer vision as she drifted into the arms of his younger son. The good feeling Laura had enjoyed only moments earlier evaporated, to be replaced with concern, as if the mix of people here tonight was going to prove explosive.

But that was nonsense, she told herself. What could possibly go wrong? She looked around the terrace as though seeking confirmation that all would be well, that everyone was still enjoying themselves. Seeing nothing to alarm her, she thought what a shame it was that Theo had had to rush back to Athens that afternoon. 'I suppose that means Mark won't come,' Sally had said, when Izzy told them the bad news, and she crossed his name off the guest list along with Theo's. Giorgios' name already had a line through it: he was working in Kassiópi tonight.

'You sound disappointed,' Francesca had laughed.

'It's all right for you, you've got Harry. Now I'm definitely lumbered with Nick.'

Excusing herself from the circle of guests, Laura went inside the villa to fetch a tray of *mezéthes* that Sophia had prepared. When she came back out she saw Virginia Patterson being approached by Dolly-Babe. Feeling the need to intervene, or at least supervise the conversation between these two unlikely bedfellows, she quickly joined them and offered the tray of food.

'I shouldn't really,' said Dolly-Babe, her long-nailed hand playing eeny-meeny-miny-mo. 'Mm ... they all look so delish. What are these?'

'I'm not really sure, I didn't make them, but they might be spinach pies.'

'*Spanakópita.*'

Dolly-Babe's hand hesitated and she looked up at Virginia. 'Spanky-what?'

'*Spanakópita,*' repeated Virginia, with an irritating tone of lofty supremacy. 'That's the correct Greek name for them.'

Oh, Lord, thought Laura. Was there going to be no let-up from this woman's need to feel superior to them all? But ever the polite hostess, she said, 'Nick and Harry were telling me that you live in London. Whereabouts?'

'Dulwich. You're from the north, aren't you?' She made it sound as if Laura came from the wrong side of the tracks.

Oh, go on, thought Laura, don't hold back, ask about our pigeons and whippets. 'Our families are both from Worcestershire,' she said lightly, 'but Max and I have lived in Cheshire for many years now.'

'Now there's a coincidence. My Bob and me, we lived in Cheshire for a while. In Alderley Edge.'

'I've heard of that,' said Virginia. 'Wasn't there a lot of talk recently on the radio about it being a den of pagans?'

'That was well out of order, all that stuff and nonsense. Bob and me took great offence to being called pagans. Why, I'm the most spiritual person you'd ever meet.'

'Really? How interesting.' Virginia's voice was spectacularly condescending as she scanned the terrace for a kindred Dulwich soul, but found only her husband leaning in too close to Izzy and taking a peek down her front. Clearly annoyed, Virginia thrust her Pimm's to her lips and spiked her nose on the cocktail stick loaded with slices of fruit. Laura had to look away to hide a smirk. She saw Olivia coming towards them.

'Laura,' she said eagerly, 'you'll never believe what Nick's just been telling us. Apparently Christine and Mikey are here. He says he saw them on the beach this afternoon.'

'Friends from England?' asked Dolly-Babe.

Olivia laughed. 'Goodness me, no! Christine and Mikey are the runaway lovers. You know, the ones in the newspapers. Haven't you been following their story? We have. Avidly. Isn't that right, Laura?'

Laura cringed with hypocritical embarrassment. It was all very well showing a keen interest in private towards some racy tabloid titillation, but to admit it in public, and in front of a woman like Virginia Patterson who probably never sullied her mind with anything less worthy than a broadsheet, was too much.

'What? You mean that disgusting woman and the teenage boy? They're here?' Dolly-Babe's voice was shrill with disapproval. 'Gawd, it makes me sick every time I read about them. She's old enough to be his mother.'

'Talking about the runaway lovers?' asked Francesca with Sally, Nick and Harry in tow.

'Nick, I think you have some explaining to do,' said his mother. 'What's all this about you claiming to have seen—'

'Relax, Mum, I saw them all right.'

'So why didn't you mention it?'

He shrugged. 'Didn't think you'd be interested.'

'But are you sure it was them?' Laura asked Nick.

'I'm pretty sure. The age gap is a giveaway.'

'So if they really are here, where do you suppose they're staying?' asked Olivia.

Angelos and Sophia gave them the answer. The couple were staying in the villa owned by the German businessman from Frankfurt.

'But that's next door to us!' cried Dolly-Babe and Virginia Patterson together.

From across the terrace, Izzy was only half listening to Adrian Patterson. She was much more interested in what Laura and the others were discussing. She had already tried to give him the slip by saying she needed to go in search of a drink, only for him to follow her.

She had had more than enough of him with his sleazy smile and innuendo-loaded talk of what he did for a living. She had always wondered what kind of person made those dreadful TV programmes. Well, now she knew. The awful thing was, he probably thought she was impressed by what he did. She felt him pressing against her side as he stepped in closer still. 'You'll have to excuse me,' she said, her patience snapping, 'I promised Laura I'd help in the kitchen.' She walked away as fast as her ankle would let her.

Only when she was sure she was going to be left alone – when she saw Adrian Patterson talking to Silent Bob – did she slip outside again. She went and leaned against the wall at the edge of the terrace, away from where everyone else was gathered. Though it was dark now, with insects buzzing around the flaming torches that Max and Corky had lit, the night air felt warm and a soft breeze blew in from the sea. She closed her eyes and took a deep breath of contentment.

'I'm sorry to see that your ankle has taken a turn for the worse,' said a low voice from behind her. It was so distinctive, it could belong to no one else. 'Hello, Mark, we didn't expect to see you tonight. What a lovely surprise.'

Still looking at her *faux*-bloodstained bandage and toy arrow, he said, 'Yeah, well, I've surprised myself. Achilles, I presume?'

'How very astute.' Then over his shoulder, Izzy suddenly caught sight of Adrian Patterson heading towards her. 'There's somebody I'm trying to avoid,' she said, slipping behind Mark so that she was out of sight. 'I don't suppose you'd do me a favour by sticking around for a few minutes, would you?'

'Always happy to oblige. Who are you hiding from?'

'I'll point him out later.' When the coast was clear, she said, 'Do you want a drink? There's loads to choose from; wine, Pimm's, beer –' she stopped. 'Oh, I'm sorry, I forgot, you don't, do you?' She felt herself colour.

'Hey, cut yourself some slack. It's my problem, not yours.'

'But it must be so awful for you in these situations.'

'Judging from the look on your face, it's worse for those who think they've put their foot in it.'

'So what can I get you? Coke? Fruit juice? Water? You're smiling. What's wrong? Have I said something stupid again?'

'Private joke. Some fizzy water would be fine. And when you come back, you can give me a run-down on everybody here and warn me of anyone I need to give a wide berth. Or should I come with you to keep you safe from whoever it is who's been bothering you?'

Seeing that Corky was now chatting to Adrian Patterson, she said, 'No, stay here, it looks as if I'll be okay for a while.'

Mark watched her go, then turned to look across the water towards the twinkling lights of Albania and congratulated himself on having made it. While it was nowhere near as bad, he was reminded of his first AA meeting. It had taken all his courage to walk through that door that night and take his seat among the group, and he had had to employ the same sort of determination to get himself here tonight.

And it wasn't just about proving Theo wrong – though a bet was a bet, and this was one that he had clearly won – it had been more about convincing himself that he could change his life if he so wished. Once he had made the decision to be sociable, he had realised that he was looking forward to seeing Izzy again. He hadn't seen her since he had been so absorbed in his writing, and although he had spent great chunks of time with her in his imagination, he had missed the real Izzy, especially their chats down on the beach. As he waited for her to come back with his drink, he found himself thinking that she was the first woman he had ever bothered to get to know.

Women . . . friend or foe? Bones had once asked.

Well, the answer in this case was unequivocal: he viewed Izzy as a friend.

Hearing footsteps behind him, he turned round expectantly, assuming it would be Izzy. But it wasn't. It was Dolly-Babe, dressed up as the Queen of Spandex, and she was heading straight for him. Oh, Lord, it was true, there really was no peace for the wicked. Not for him anyway.

34

There was nowhere for him to hide, so he braced himself for another assault on his patience, which, as Theo would be only too quick to mention, was an attribute he didn't have in abundance. She sidled in very close, a skinny freckled arm reaching out to him. For a brief moment he felt the full weight of her – such as it was – as she steadied herself against him and slopped wine down the front of his shirt.

'Aha, Mr St James. I have a confession to make.' Her face, unlike her pale arms, was flushed and glowing, and her extraordinary hair looked as though it was on the verge of a landslide.

'Really?' Oh, great!

'Yes. I had no idea who you were until a few days ago.' She wagged a finger at him.

Looking at her unfocused eyes, he wondered if she was seeing two of him.

'But, you know, you could have said something.'

He edged discreetly away from her. 'I stand corrected,' he said, 'fully rebuked.'

She laughed loudly, and moved towards him again. 'But I always suspected that there was something, well, a bit different about you.'

'In what way?'

'You're like me, you see what's going on.' She gave a comically theatrical swivel of her eyes. 'You feel it, don't you? That's why you're a writer. You channel your powers into your books.'

It was tempting to enquire in which direction she thought her powers were channelled, but he refrained from doing so. It was child's play to make fun of somebody like Dolly-Babe.

'Any more news from your psychic friend back home?' he asked pleasantly. 'Looks as though she got it right about the party, didn't she?'

Her face lit up, which made him feel all the more sorry for her: how easily pleased she was. 'Ria's a gem,' she said. 'I don't know what I'd do without her. But you know what? My horoscope said something interesting today – except it was for yesterday, seeing that we get the papers a day late. I'm a Gemini. What star sign are you?'

'Aquarius.'

'I knew it! I just knew you had to be Aquarius.'

'Any reason why?'

She beamed a wide, garishly pink smile at him. 'It's obvious, darlin'. Aquarians are original, independent and creative. As a writer, that must be you to a T. Now, listen to this and tell me what you think. My horoscope said I've got to get out of the rut I've made for myself. "Why wait for fate to take its course?" was what it said.' She drained her glass of wine in a long, thirsty swig. 'What do you think it means?'

That you need to cut back on your drinking, was the answer screaming inside his head, but Mark knew better than anyone that a comment like that would only have Dolly-Babe reaching for another drink of denial. And talking of drinks, where was Izzy with his water? He looked over Dolly-Babe's shoulder and saw, to his relief, Izzy coming towards them.

'Sorry I was so long,' she said, giving him his glass and smiling at Dolly-Babe, 'but I was intercepted. Everyone's talking about our new neighbours.'

'Oh, who are they?' asked Mark.

Dolly-Babe's eyes flashed with a fury that seemed quite out of place. 'Don't ask, it's too awful for words. The thought of that poor boy and that shameless woman makes my blood boil. And don't go giving me that argument that it's every young boy's fantasy to be seduced by an older woman. It's not natural. She's taking advantage of him. He's nothing but a child.' She shuddered.

Sharing a look of surprise with Mark at the vehemence behind Dolly-Babe's words, Izzy said, 'Have you been following the story in the papers about the mother of two running off with her teenage lover?'

'On and off.'

'Well, they're here in Áyios Nikólaos.'

'And staying in the villa next door to us!' cut in Dolly-Babe. 'I've a good mind to ring the papers myself and tell them where that dreadful woman is. She needs shooting, she does.' She raised her glass to her lips, saw that it was empty, and added, in a voice that sounded alarmingly bitter, 'I need a refill.'

They watched her move with exaggerated care through the chairs, tables and guests on the terrace. 'You know, I can't help feeling sorry for her,' said Izzy.

'I was thinking much the same myself a few moments ago.'

'You were?'

'Don't sound so thunderstruck. Didn't you have me down as the understanding, sensitive type?'

She looked at him hard. 'Not quite. I imagined you would be more interested in casting her as a victim in one of your novels – the ageing woman strangled by her blonde hair attachments, her long nails ripped off, her high heels—'

'Then you've got me all wrong. I choose my victims with much more care and thought.'

'So why do you suppose she's taking the moral high ground on the runaway lovers? I would have expected her to take the stance of more power to middle-aged women like herself.'

'I doubt that she sees herself as middle-aged. Show me a man or woman who claims they don't give a damn about growing old and I'll show you a liar.'

'I hadn't thought of that.'

'That's because you're fortunate enough still to have youth and beauty on your side.'

She smiled. 'You know that she's come as Hebe, don't you?' Then, casting an eye over his jeans and denim shirt with the sleeves rolled up to his elbows, she said, 'You're going to have to help me out with your costume. It's so subtle I must be missing it.'

He stood back from her, so she could see him better. 'I'm in disguise. Go on, guess which god I am.'

'Any clues?'

'Go for irony.'

'Mr Grecian 2000?'

'Do you mind? The hair's pure Bobby Shaftoe, not a wisp of grey. Try again.'

'Mm . . . Hercules?'

'And why would that be ironic? Don't you see me as a heroic hunk of masculinity?'

'Well, if you don't want me to insult you further, you'd better tell me who you're supposed to be.'

'I'm disappointed in you. I thought I could rely on you of all people. I'm Dionysus, god of wine. Who else could I possibly come as?'

In the far reaches of his mind, he heard Bones saying, 'It's always the same with you, Mark, isn't it? Go ahead, just throw another log of irony on the fire of your wretchedness.' And seeing that she didn't know what to say, and that the joke had fallen flat on its face, he said, 'It's a funny old thing, but we're a nation that simply doesn't cut the mustard when it comes to laughing at the afflicted.'

'It does leave us rather stranded.'

'But laughing at oneself is sometimes the best medicine of all.'

'When you were an alcoholic, could you laugh at yourself?'

Disconcerted by her directness, he took a thoughtful sip of his mineral water. 'No. In those days I wasn't capable of finding anything remotely funny.'

A sudden burst of loud bouzoúki music coming from behind them made them turn towards the villa, where on the veranda a space had been cleared and Angelos and Sophia were teaching Max and Laura some fancy Greek dancing; Laura had the hang of it, but Max was all over the place.

'Just as well you decided to join us here tonight,' said Izzy, 'or the noise would have disturbed you horribly. What made you come?'

Again he was surprised by her candour. 'Because I was invited.'

'You've turned down other invitations from Max and Laura. Why did you accept this one, and without Theo to hold your hand?'

'Goodness, you certainly know how to make a guy feel welcome, don't you?'

She smiled. 'Sorry, it's my curious nature getting the better of me. None of us expected you to come on your own.'

'Well, tell you what, help me become invisible and I'll think about satisfying that appalling curiosity of yours.'

'Invisible?'

'Her glass suitably refilled, Dolly-Babe is heading in our direction and, as sympathetic as I am towards her problems, I'm not in the mood to waste an entire evening on her. Fancy a walk on the beach?'

They slipped away unnoticed, but when Mark realised that Izzy's ankle still wasn't strong enough to negotiate the steep path at any real speed, he said, 'Theo would kill me with his bare hands if you hurt yourself again in my company, so there's nothing else for it, I'll have to carry you.'

'There's no need, I can manage. Really, I can.'

Ignoring her, he swung her off her feet and resumed their descent. 'Hold on tight, and no laughing. I said no laughing, Izzy! Don't you ever do as you're told?'

'Oh, all the time, just not when I'm with you.'

'Dear God, you're enough to drive a man to drink!'

'That's not funny, Mark.'

'Then behave yourself and stop wriggling, or you'll have my downfall on your conscience.'

'Has anyone ever told you you're a cruel and heartless man?'

'No, they wouldn't dare.'

They carried on down the hill in silence, the lively music from the villa growing more distant with every step.

'Mark?'

'Yes.'

'I know it's none of my business, but what made you become an alcoholic?'

He tightened his grip on her. 'You make it sound like a career choice. And you're right, it is none of your business.'

Another silence passed between them.

'I'm sorry. Was that a question too far?'

'Yes. What's got into you? You're not normally this nosy.'

'It's reading your novels. They've set me thinking. Made me wonder about the real you.'

'Well, don't bother. I'll give you fair warning, no good will come of it. Now, what d'yer know? We've made it in one piece.' He lowered her to the stones, faced the water's edge, and stretched out his arms dramatically. 'For your special delectation, Miss Jordan, I give you a romantically deserted moonlit beach. And a broken man into the bargain.' He rubbed his back meaningfully.

'But just think, you've got the return journey to look forward to.'

He groaned. 'Nothing else for it, I'll have to send for reinforcements.'

'Now, what was that you were saying about Hercules?'

'Hey, nice try, little lady, but if you want that kind of man, you're banging on the wrong door. I don't do heroics. Definitely not my call.'

'That's not what Theo says.'

'Oh, yes? And what has the mentally challenged Mr Theodore Vlamakis been saying about me?'

'He said you saved his life.'

'Did he now?'

'And did you?'

He frowned and rolled up one of his sleeves, which had come unfurled with all the exertion. 'Theo loves to exaggerate these things. It's the Greek way. Come on, let's walk. That's if your ankle's okay?'

'It's fine. And in case you're worried, I can manage the path perfectly well on my own. I just have to take it slowly.'

He smiled. 'Now you tell me.'

When they had got as far as the rocky outcrop, she said, 'Theo told me you were very brave to do what you did.'

'My, but you're a persistent little soul, aren't you?'

'No, just plain old-fashioned nosy.'

'So if I spin you a yarn of what a wonderfully brave chap I am, will you promise to shut up?'

'Hand on heart.'

'Okay, then, sit yourself down and when you're comfortable, I'll begin.' He settled beside her on the rock where they had first met. The tide was high, and the barely moving water was lapping softly at the stones beneath them. 'Now, what do you want to know first? Why I wasted a huge chunk of my life on drink, or why it was so easy for me to take on two thugs who were kicking the hell out of somebody I scarcely knew?'

'Um ... you decide. You're the story-teller.'

'Okay. Here we go. Once upon a time, there was a small boy called Mark. There was nothing remotely unusual about him, he was pretty much your bog standard normal kid. Not particularly bright. Not particularly stupid. His parents were kind and loving, and he had two brothers who never gave him a moment's trouble, apart from being a lot smarter than he was, but, hey, you can't have everything. One day everything changed. At the age of twelve, Mark's best friend died and because he blamed himself, he turned into a monster who took out his anger and confused self-loathing on anyone within spitting distance. Especially his bewildered parents. Time passed and, much against the odds, he worked hard enough at school to get himself to college where he met a flash Greek upstart who represented everything this angry young man despised. You could say it was hate at first sight. Then, one very cold wintry night, he came across the aforementioned flash Greek upstart lying on the ground having his face rearranged by two lads who were interested in a redistribution of the contents of his wallet. With nearly a decade of anger stored up in this one skinny frame – a physique that never did improve with age, I might say – violence held no fear for our boy. Not even from a knife-wielding thug who stabbed him for his trouble.' He paused. 'You will say if I'm boring you, won't you?'

She shook her head, transfixed. 'No, please, carry on.'

'Well, the two young men paradoxically became good friends. They left college: one went on to become the disgustingly successful businessman you now know and love, and the other went from bad to worse. Still haunted by the death of his young friend, he opened his mouth and poured into it a magic brew called Instant Gratification, not seeing the label underneath that said "Danger and Self-delusion This Way". It was potent stuff. So long as he was full of the magic brew his world didn't seem so bad. But the more he drank, the more he wanted. Then one day, he was offered some better magic. Cocaine. Oh, how he loved this stuff. And how it loved him. They couldn't get enough of each other. They became inseparable. But before long, he realised he was in seriously deep shit. But, behold! Help was to hand. Theo, his fairy godmother, came to his rescue, carried him off to a clinic where a weird man called Bones with a sugar dependency waved a magic wand, and taught him to see the error of his ways. And surprisingly enough, from that point on, everybody lived happily ever after. Well, more or less.'

In the silence that followed, Izzy kept her eyes ahead of her on the curved disc of moon that was hanging in the clear night sky. She didn't trust herself to turn and look at Mark. She had found his story, despite his self-deprecating tone, so poignant that she was worried she might embarrass him by crying. She knew, though, that what she was feeling for him – for all the pain he must have suffered as a child – was mixed up with the confusion of emotions she had from her own childhood. Though their experiences were different, she could relate to him. She felt also that he might be one of the few people who would truly understand the sense of could-have-done-better that had always been with her. That dreadful sense of disappointment that had followed her all her life.

'Have I embarrassed you?' he asked, breaking into her thoughts. 'I'm sorry if I've made you feel uncomfortable.'

Hearing the touching concern in his soft husky voice did her no good. Her throat clenched and the tears started, and there seemed no way of stopping them. 'I'm sorry,' she mumbled, her head still turned from him, 'it's my own fault. I shouldn't have kept on at you. It serves me right.' And still the tears came. Oh, why wouldn't they stop? And why did she never have a tissue when she needed one? She sensed him moving beside her, then felt the firm but gentle pressure of his hand on hers.

'Do I detect a fellow-sufferer of self-recrimination?'

She sniffed as discreetly as she could and looked at him. 'I don't suppose you've got a tissue, have you?'

He dug around in his trouser pockets. '*Voilà!* You're in luck. An unused handkerchief.'

She took it from him and pressed it to her eyes.

'You can use it for your nose as well,' he said. 'I don't mind. There'll be no extra charge.'

She managed a small smile. 'Then you'd best cover your ears, this won't be very ladylike.'

'Don't mind me, just blast away.'

She did and felt much better for it. 'Sorry about that. I kept thinking of you as that young boy. It must have been so awful for you, blaming yourself like that. How did your friend die?'

'A boating accident. We didn't know what we were doing. He drowned and I survived, but wished I hadn't. As simple and as complicated as that.'

'Is that why you never go swimming, or out in Theo's boat with him?'

He nodded. 'Being in or on water freaks the hell out of me.'

She frowned. 'But didn't you say you live by the sea?'

'I didn't say I was sane, now, did I? It's a personal challenge I set myself a long time ago. Was I up to it? Could I cope with such a tangible reminder?'

'And can you?'

He seemed to hold this thought for a moment as he looked down at the dark water beneath them. He said, 'I'm sitting here, aren't I? So what's your story? What nerve did I inadvertently tweak? Theo hinted that you didn't have the Rebecca of Sunnybrook Farm childhood.'

'Something like that.'

'Care to be more specific? After forcing my sordid past out of me, I think it's the least you can do in return. Let's call it share-and-tell time.'

She gave him a tiny shrug. 'There's not much to tell.'

His hand moved back to hers. 'You sure about that?'

At his gentle persuasion, she told him about her mother, how terrified she had been of her, and of the death of the baby that had been such a destructive force within her family. She spoke about her father too. How she had quietly idolised him, and that it was only now that she realised just how angry she was that he hadn't done more to help, not just her but her mother as well. She said, 'I feel guilty that I feel so much anger towards him now that he's dead. It doesn't seem right.'

'Forget any thought of what you think is right or wrong. Just acknowledge what you feel or it will continue to hold you back from enjoying the life you're entitled to.'

'Is that how you see me? Somebody who's holding back?'

He gave her a reassuring smile. 'Honest answer?'

'Yes.'

'I see two Izzies. One who doubts her strengths and talents because they've never been encouraged and, as a consequence, settles for the status quo because it's safer that way. And then there's this other Izzy, the one who's perceptive, witty and just longing to break free and live dangerously. A woman who could do anything she wanted if she would only be generous enough to give herself the chance.'

'If she were to let go of the past, you mean?'

'Sounds easy enough, I know. But you're talking to a man who knows better than most how much courage it takes to walk away from the only life you've ever allowed yourself . . . or felt that you deserved.'

When she didn't respond, Mark said, 'So you know what this means, don't you?'

'What?'

'It makes us a right couple of damaged goods sitting on the shelf of life's patched-together casualties. But one thing's for sure, we're quite normal. Despite what you might think, everybody has something niggling away inside them. As the old REM song goes, "Everybody Hurts".'

'Even Theo?'

'Well, maybe he's the exception. Though he does have one rather pressing problem at the moment.'

'Really? Is that why he's gone back to Athens again?'

He looked at her closely, trying to figure out whether she was being deliberately obtuse. He decided she wasn't. 'Izzy, you're his problem.'

'Me?'

'He's genuinely very fond of you and doesn't know how to convince you that he's serious.'

She said nothing but slid her gaze down and absorbed herself in examining the stitching on the hem of her shorts.

'Look, tell me to butt out if you want, but what do you feel for him?'

She raised her head. 'He's lovely, truly he is. He's funny, kind, and – and very attractive, but he . . .' Her voice trailed off.

'But what?'

'He frightens me.'

'Theo? He's as harmless as a wet sponge. He'd never hurt you, Izzy, I swear it. I'd stake my last Rolo on it.'

She shook her head. 'I didn't mean it in that way. It's difficult to explain, but I can't fully relax when I'm with him. I keep thinking that I could never make the grade with him. Take the time when he kissed me that night he took me out for dinner. It was hopeless. I was so tense, all I could think of while he was kissing me was a mental checklist: arms engaged, lips puckered, nose to the side. Stop laughing, it's true. That's exactly what I was doing.'

'I'm not laughing.'

'Then what's that tee-hee sound coming from your mouth?'

'It's disbelief.'

She gave him a shove and he shoved her back.

'You know, if you could get over this kissing problem, you'd see Theo in an altogether different light.'

'Don't tell me, all I need is an intensive course of kissing therapy. But believe me, I've had it with therapists, whatever their speciality.'

'How so?'

'When my boyfriend was trying to find a way to leave me, he insisted that we saw a therapist. She was very nice, but—'

'But you didn't trust her, right?'

'Correct. I didn't trust her at all. In fact I was convinced she was in cahoots with Alan. I was quite rude to her.'

'You couldn't have been as rude to her as I was to Bones. I threatened to kill him. There, I've shocked you. You'll think twice now about sitting on these rocks again with me late at night and all alone.'

She smiled. 'But shocking people is what you do best. Your books tell me that much.'

'I don't only live to shock people.'

'What else do you do, then?'

'Well, I'm a fair cook, so I tell myself. Chicken tikka masala on a Friday night being a locally acclaimed wonder of mine.'

'Mm . . . Anything else you're good at?'

'You want more? There's no satisfying some folk. Hey, but wait, I'm also great at kidnapping people from parties. Yeah, I can see you're impressed by that.'

'Well, close to it.'

'Do you want to go back and join the throng?'

'Not really. Not when there's a hairy-faced Pa Patterson trying to get a look down my front.'

'Ah, so he was the one you were keen to avoid, was he? I'm glad to have been of use. But if I'd known it was going to turn into an all-night session I would have thought to bring some food down with us.'

'Yes, for an expert kidnapper, that was a careless oversight on your part.'

'Are you always this picky?'

'Funnily enough, only with you.'

'Oh, shucks, now you're just trying to make me feel special.'

She laughed. 'Have you ever thought of writing comedy?'

'Is that a sneaky put-down?'

'No, I was being serious. You're very funny.'

'I've been accused of many things, but having a sense of humour is not one of them.'

'Well, I think you're funny. You make me laugh.'

'I also made you cry.'

'So you did. It would have to be bittersweet comedy in that case.'

'Okay, I'll ring my editor tomorrow and give her the good news. "Sorry," I'll tell her, "but I've taken expert advice and I'm scrapping the winning formula and going for cheap laughs. I'm going to be the new King of Comedy!"'

'You'd have to change the publicity shot of you on the back of the books and learn to lighten yourself up. No more scowling Prince of Darkness.'

'I'm beginning to go off the idea already.'

'I knew it. No staying power.'

'That's a bloke for you. First sign of a struggle and we're off.'

They laughed companionably, then sat in silence while a ferry passed on the horizon, its diamond white lights shining in the darkness, the throbbing sound of its powerful engine reverberating across the water. When it had disappeared, Mark said, 'What will you do about Theo?'

'I don't think I can do anything about him. I get the feeling he's a law unto himself. The cooler I play it with him, the harder he pursues me. I've given him no encouragement, really I haven't.'

'I know that sometimes it seems you'd have to shoehorn him out of that massive ego of his, but you mustn't be fooled by the exterior packaging. If you really got to know him you'd see that he's as normal and down-to-earth as you and me.'

'He wouldn't thank you for saying that.'

No, he wouldn't, thought Mark. She was quite right. If Theo had a fault it was his vanity. He had never seen himself as normal and down-to-earth. Back in Durham he had always liked being the one who stood out from the crowd. And in the intervening years nothing had changed: he still enjoyed his good looks, his expensive clothes, the choice of luxurious homes, the flashy cars and, of course, the attention they drew. 'So you don't see it ever working between the two of you? Not even as a holiday romance?'

She pulled the toy arrow from the bandage around her ankle, placed it between them, and swung her feet so that the backs of her boots tapped lightly against the rocks they were sitting on. 'No, I don't. I'm not his sort, not at all. You know that, deep down, don't you?'

'Whoa, there, don't go bringing me into this. This is between you and Theo.'

'But it's true. You must have seen him over the years with millions of girls, none of whom were like me.'

'Hundreds, not millions. He's not that good a catch.'

She gave him another playful shove and caught him with an elbow in the ribs.

He caught his breath, groaned and clasped his side. 'Watch it, Izzy, that's where I was stabbed.'

Her hands went to her face. 'Oh, Mark, I'm so sorry. Are you okay?'

He opened his eyes slowly and grinned. 'Had you going, there.'

'Don't ever do that to me again. You frightened me half to death.' She raised her hand again to give him a playful slap, but he caught her wrist and held it tightly.

'Oh, no, you don't,' he laughed, 'once is quite enough.' She laughed too, and in the soft moonlight, her face wreathed in smiles, it was the strangest thing, but he suddenly found himself entirely conscious of the moment. Without once raising his glance from Izzy's face, he knew that the sky above them was a glorious canopy of velvety darkness, that the stars were bright and shining, that the moon was a perfectly sculptured half-disc of light. He was aware, too, that the breeze that had blown all day had dropped, and that the sea was calm, soundless and glassy. His senses told him it really was the most beautiful night.

Yet more beautiful than any of this was the girl beside him. As motionless as he was, she was staring back at him with steady, unblinking eyes: eyes that earlier had been so sad but which were now bright with some new emotion he wasn't sure he recognised or understood. What he did understand, though, was his sudden desire to kiss her. Common sense told him not to do it. But when had he ever allowed common sense over the threshold of his intentions?

Loosening his grip on her slender arm, but still holding it, he lowered his gaze to her lips and with the slightest of movements, inclined his head. His intent couldn't have been clearer. If she moves away, I shan't kiss her, he told himself, as though this would exonerate him of any wrongdoing. But if she stays where she is, I will.

35

It was an amazing kiss.

A clean sweep of a kiss that was silky and smooth.

Slow.

Gentle.

Intensely erotic.

With his hand on the nape of her neck he drew her closer, wanting more of the sweet warmth of her mouth, a mouth that was so deliciously inviting he couldn't think why she had ever doubted her ability to kiss Theo.

The thought of Theo invoked common sense. He should bring matters to an immediate close. He should clear his throat and mumble some kind of gentlemanly apology: 'Sorry, but I really don't know what came over me.'

But to hell with that! He knew exactly what he was doing and wanted to go on doing it for as long as he could.

As inevitably as night follows day, the moment came to an end, brought to a halt by the intrusive sound of a small fishing-boat crossing the water in front of them. He stroked her hair away from her face, tucked it behind her ear. 'I suppose one of us should say, "How did that happen?"'

'It was you,' she said, with a shy half-smile. 'You started it.'

'Not true. It was all down to you. You turned those lovely eyes on me. What was I supposed to do?'

'But it was you who lowered your head.'

'You didn't have to respond. In my mind I gave you the choice to back out. Look, I'll show you, this is all I did.'

He tilted his head and kissed her again. When she started to laugh, he stopped. She said, 'You tricked that one out of me.'

'So I did. But, in my defence, you make it so easy for me.'

'I'm not easy.'

She sounded cross, and realising his blunder, he reached out to her hand. 'I didn't mean it that way.'

The night air hung listlessly around them. The tide must have turned, for now the sea was sucking at the pebbly shore beneath their feet. 'But it's what it looks like,' she murmured. 'First Theo, now you.'

'What it looks like isn't what it is. I know that and so do you.'

She raised her eyes. 'I wouldn't want you to think that I'm the kind of girl who—'

'You made your feelings for Theo very clear when we were talking. I wouldn't have kissed you if I'd thought you were serious about him.'

Though he spoke with conviction, Mark wasn't so sure that he was speaking the truth. Remembering the night he had seen Theo kissing Izzy, he understood now that it hadn't been disappointment he had felt as he'd stood on the beach looking up at them, it had been jealousy. The realisation confirmed what he had suspected about himself that day he had first met Izzy and took her back to Villa Anna to see Theo – he really had been jealous that his friend might find happiness and he might not. And not just any old happiness, but the chance to be loved by someone as special as Izzy. It was a disturbing conclusion that needed some thought. But now wasn't the time. Now he wanted to make Izzy feel comfortable with him again. He said, 'We could pretend it never happened, that we didn't kiss. Or make out that it was an act of impetuous madness.'

'We could ... if that's what you wanted.'

'Doesn't it also depend on what you want?'

She looked up at him, her eyes wide and faintly troubled again. 'Why did you kiss me?'

'Because I wanted to. And because it felt entirely the right thing to do. Can I ask the same of you?'

'No.'

'Hey, I sense a degree of disparity going on here.' Her expression relaxed and he felt hopeful again. Hopeful. What an odd word to use. Hopeful of what? What did he expect to come out of all this? 'So who gets to have the final word on the subject? You or me?'

'Be my guest, take the floor.'

'Okay. Here goes. I'd like it going on record that you need have no worries about your kissing technique. Your fears are totally ill-founded. Not that I'm claiming to be an expert, you understand, but I reckon with a bit more encouragement you could really make a go of it.'

'Kissing for a living?'

'Mm ... not quite what I had in mind.'

'And who would give me the necessary encouragement?'

He cleared his throat, slicked back his hair, and straightened an imaginary tie at his neck. 'I could make a start first thing in the morning.'

She laughed, picked up the arrow that was between them, turned it over in her hands and stroked the feathers. Impulsively, he took it from her and held it to his heart. 'Argh, you've got me right here, Izzy.'

She snatched it away from him. 'You're barmy. Completely barmy.'

'Actually, and just between you and me, this is the sanest I've ever felt.' He put his arm around her.

She relaxed into him, rested her head against his. 'Do you suppose after I've practised another kiss on you we ought to get back to the party?'

'Why, Sugar Lips, I do declare you're making me blush with your forward ways. But it's not a bad idea. Though if I don't think you're up to standard, you could be stuck here for a while.'

She gave him a nudge with her elbow. 'I thought you said I was good.'

'Easy there, Tiger, always room for improvement.'

Having insisted that Max and his parents had done more than their fair share of organising the party, Laura had packed them off to bed, and she and Izzy were in the kitchen, tidying up the last of the glasses.

Izzy knew that for the last hour Laura had been dying to get her on her own and subject her to an intensive question-and-answer session. When she and Mark had returned to the party, they had bumped into Laura as they had emerged from the path, so it was a foregone conclusion that she would want to know what Izzy had been up to with him.

'I thought it was strange when I couldn't find you anywhere,' Laura said now, as she opened the dishwasher and stood back to let the cloud of steam escape. 'It was Dolly-Babe who told me that she'd seen the pair of you sneaking away down the hillside like a couple of lovers in search of a smoochy hideaway. She was very put out. She was hoping to have Mark all to herself.'

'That's what he was afraid of.'

'Ah, so he used you as protection, did he? Very cunning of him. So, Izzy, how many holiday flings do you need?'

'It's not like that!' she cried indignantly. 'Despite what you all thought, I was never having a fling with Theo.'

'Calm down, I was only teasing. I think it's great that you're testing the water from more than one puddle, so to speak. And he is rather gorgeous with that dead sexy voice of his, I can quite see the attraction. But putting your string of conquests to one side, you'll never guess what went on here while you were enjoying your secret assignation down on the beach.'

Izzy couldn't believe her luck that so convenient a diversion was to hand and quickly grasped it. 'Don't tell me, Ma and Pa Patterson had a fight?'

'No, worse than that. Angelos was doing his best to teach Dolly-Babe to dance the light fantastic, and with more than a glass or two of oúzo inside of him, he let it slip who Theo really was. Not only that, it turns out the land that Bob was after was the olive grove here in Áyios Nikólaos that Theo bought. It all got very unpleasant with the pair of them thinking they'd been made fools of. They stomped off in a fearful fit of pique.'

'Goodness! Do you think Theo knew all along that it was Bob who had designs on the olive grove?'

'Of course he knew. Theo might like to give the impression of being a charming happy-go-lucky man for whom everything falls into his lap by haphazard chance, but to be as successful as he is it takes a ruthlessly sharp mind that's as astute as it is devious. With that land being right on his doorstep he would have known exactly who was behind the offer and what plans Bob had for it, so he had made certain that there was no likelihood that Bob could set them in motion.' She yawned hugely. 'Oh dear, that's it as far as I'm concerned, I'm going to bed. I'm all in. I'm definitely getting old, I can't take these late nights any more. I just hope the girls don't make too much noise when they get in – I could do with an uninterrupted night's sleep. You coming?'

But Izzy didn't follow Laura to bed. Her head was too full of that evening's events. She made herself a mug of tea and went and sat on the terrace. All the villa lights had been switched off and sitting in the darkness she felt the night wrap its cool aura of calm around her.

But the aura of calm didn't last for long.

A horribly familiar voice inside her head said, *And just what did you think you were doing down there on the beach, and for all the world to see?*

You know what, she answered her mother back, I was having the time of my life! There! What do you say to that? Mm ... gone quiet on me, have you? Well, good. Because if ever there was a man worth disgracing myself for, this is the one.

She closed her eyes, defiantly shutting out her mother's unwanted presence, and relived every heart-stopping moment of that first kiss with Mark.

How it had happened was still a mystery to her. One minute they had been laughing and joking and the next, she had found herself wishing he would kiss her. And just as this thought had formed itself, he had lowered his eyes and tilted his head, and she had realised he was thinking the same. And the best thing was, there hadn't been a single attack of doubt or nerves throughout. It had felt so right between them. All she had been conscious of was the dreamy pleasure his soft warm lips were giving her. It had seemed so natural, so unforced and unhurried. And so sublimely wonderful.

Unlike the kiss she had had with Theo. How scared she had been that he would find her wanting. That he would think she was less of a woman than he was used to.

But Mark hadn't made her feel like that.

When eventually they had decided they ought to rejoin the party, Mark had offered to carry her up the path again, but she had put her foot down and said she could manage just fine. 'Am I allowed to hold the hand of Little Miss Independent, then?' he had asked.

'I think that would be okay.'

But, of course, he had done more than that. Half-way up the hillside, he had stopped and said, 'Do you remember? This is where you fell and hurt yourself. We'd better not take any chances, I'll take hold of both your hands.'

'But that would mean I couldn't walk.'

'True. But it would enable me to kiss you again, safe in the knowledge that those lethal hands and elbows of yours couldn't take another shot at me.' He had treated her to a repeat performance of that trick of slowly lowering his head. 'And would that be all right?' he had asked, holding back from her and making the moment all the more seductive and irresistible. 'I'd hate to be accused of presuming anything of you.'

The combination of his husky voice, little more than a whisper, the smell of his aftershave mingling with the heady scent of the cypress trees around them, and the heat of his body reaching out to her, all came together and hit her in the form of an all-consuming bolt of desire. It was a shockwave of pure lust that travelled at high speed the length and breadth of her. Tilting her head back, she closed her eyes and waited for him to kiss her.

But when a few seconds had passed and he hadn't, she opened her eyes. 'What's the hold-up?' she asked.

Holding her face in his long, smooth fingers, he said, 'I was just taking a good look at you. Committing you to memory.'

'Why?'

'Because I can't imagine a better way to remember this evening. Can I see you tomorrow?'

'Where?'

'On the rocks where we were just sitting ... where I first met you.'

'Okay, I'll be there. Early, before everyone else is up.'

Thinking of the scene now, and looking at her watch, Izzy saw that it was only a matter of hours before she would be with Mark again. She hugged this happy thought to her, holding it tight, wanting to squeeze every delicious impetuous hope out of it. She didn't care a jot if she was crying for the moon, it was the best feeling in the world, and while it lasted, she was determined to enjoy it.

Further round the bay, at Villa Anna, Mark was also sitting in the dark. Staring at the sea, he was watching the outgoing tide breaking the surface of the water. Nearer to him, and down on the shore, he could hear the waves building in strength as they clawed at the sand and stones, dislodging what they could within their deceptively embracing touch.

The shifting tide echoed his own agitated state. And restless with a surfeit of energy he went and leaned against the low wall on the edge of the terrace. He suddenly wished that he had had the nerve to entice Izzy back here to spend the night with him.

He sighed heavily, ran his hands through his hair and told himself to think of something else. Something marginally less erotic than the thought of undressing Izzy and making love to her.

Think of Theo and what the hell you're going to say to him when you speak to him next! Oh, by the way, Theo, I've got this thing going with Izzy. No hard feelings, eh?

36

Francesca was regretting the amount she had had to drink. She was feeling sick and each time she closed her eyes the noisy packed-out bar they were squeezed into would spin round inside her head. She should never have knocked back all those tequila slammers. She had only done it to teach Harry a lesson. To show him that this was how you had a good time.

Earlier on, and already a bit tipsy, she had been boasting to Nick what a great kisser his brother was. She had then tried to kiss Harry in front of everyone, but he wouldn't let her. 'Don't, Francesca,' he had said, his face reddening, 'not here. Not like this.' But she had kept on until in the end he had unhooked her hands from around his neck and pushed her away. 'I'd rather kiss you when you were sober and knew what you were doing.' His voice had been as hard as steel. So had his eyes.

Humiliated right down to her varnished toenails, she had turned on him. 'Oh, lighten up,' she had shouted above the pounding beat of a disco anthem. But he had stood there looking down at her with that disapproving expression on his face.

'Yeah,' Nick had joined in, 'stop being such a pain, shape up or push off.'

He had done neither. He had simply remained where he was, watching her coolly, his brows drawn together, making her feel like a naughty child. In defiance, she had ordered another round of drinks. 'You're embarrassing me,' she had said, bumping against him as she slipped off her bar stool and spilled tequila down his trousers. 'This is adult time, why don't you just go?'

And he had. Without another word, he had gone.

Now she was wishing he hadn't. She hated herself for having treated him so badly. Feeling sick and miserable, she also wished she hadn't listened to Nick's suggestion that they leave her parents' party, get changed and head into Kassiópi. She had been enjoying herself up until then. She and Harry had been having a great laugh together – they had even joined in with all that Greek dancing with her parents. But it was Sally who had said, 'Oh, come on, don't be boring. Let's go.' She knew the real reason why Nick had wanted to come: he had wanted to meet up with that bloke from Glasgow, the one with the accent as thick as cold custard who had been supplying him with his wacky-baccy. According to Giorgios, it came across from Albania. Occasionally it would wash up on the shore; that was when a delivery went wrong, when the Corfiot coastguards would appear on the scene unexpectedly, and the terrified Albanians would shove the lot overboard. Some of the waiters they had got to know joked that they spent the winter months when all the tourists had gone home sampling what came ashore.

She was no prude, but Nick was a mug for smoking the stuff. God knows what was in it. A bloody fool, that's what he was. And it was all his fault that she was stuck here drunk, and that Harry had left her. She wanted to go home, wanted to be sick in the privacy of her own bathroom, then lie on the bed and crash out. But she wasn't so drunk that she was going to risk walking through the olive grove in the dark on her own. Dad would go mad if he discovered she had done that. Technically she might be a full-blown adult, but to him she was still his little girl. In her wretchedly self-pitying state she felt tears welling in her eyes. Blinking them away, she knew she had no choice but to wait for Nick and Sally to decide that they had had enough and were ready to leave. Though knowing how they liked to party, she was probably in for a long wait.

As it turned out, once Nick had found his Glaswegian friend and had got what he had come for, he didn't feel the need to hang about. 'Right then, girls,' he said, tucking an arm through theirs, 'shall we go?'

They made slow progress. Sally was in a worse state than Francesca, and leaving the bright lights of Kassiópi behind them, and propping themselves up on each other, they entered the darkness of the olive grove. None of them had a torch, and once again Francesca wished that Harry was with them.

'If Captain Sensible was here, we'd have no problem seeing where we were going,' said Nick, as if picking up on her thoughts. 'Wouldn't you know that he'd take the bloody torch with him?'

'Don't talk about him like that.'

'Oo-er, listen to her,' jeered Nick. 'She's really got the hots for him.'

'Shut up, Nick, and keep walking before I land one on you. Save your energy for your brain, what there is of it.'

'I think I'm going to be sick,' groaned Sally. She staggered away from them and vomited into the bushes. It had the effect of making Francesca follow suit. No more booze for the rest of the holiday, she promised herself, as she emptied the contents of her stomach. No more tequilas. And definitely no more nights out with Nick.

When they had finished, they found Nick slumped on the ground, his back resting against the trunk of an olive tree, his head tilted upwards. 'Something to clear the mind,' he said, waving a clumsily put-together reefer, its end glowing red in the darkness.

'You're an idiot, Nick, smoking that junk.'

'After what you've just deposited in the bushes, Frankie girl, I'll take that as a case of pots and kettles. You need to learn to chill out. You're getting to be as bad as my brother. Perhaps you're seeing too much of each other. Wish I knew what it is you see in a dork like him when you could have me.'

'I've told you before, don't call me Frankie! And if you really want to know, your brother's worth ten of you.'

'Oh, come on the pair of you, stop arguing,' said Sally. 'Let's get going. Give me a puff of that, Nick. It'll help me feel better.'

By the time they had reached the bay, Nick was laughing and joking. He insisted that they go down to the beach. 'It's a beautiful night, girls,' he said, staring up at the moon and slipping his arms around them once more. In his mellowed state he was all love and peace. So was Sally. 'Oh, yes, my cool sisters of swing,' he sang out expansively, 'it's a real beautiful night for catching the vibe. You know what we should do, we should go for a swim.'

It was a crazy idea and Francesca was having none of it. To her horror, Sally agreed with Nick, and giggling loudly, she flung her arms around him and kissed him. 'I never knew until now just how brilliant you were, Nick.'

'But you're both off your heads,' Francesca protested. 'You're mad even to think of it.'

They paid her no heed, slipped out of their clothes, held hands, and ran into the water.

Annoyed and resigned, Francesca watched them go. She was so tired and fed up, she was tempted to leave them to it, to climb the hill and go to bed. But something told her not to leave her friend. If Sally came to any harm, she would never forgive herself. Once again, she had no choice but to wait for Nick and Sally to get bored and come to their senses.

She sat down on the stones and instantly what little energy she had drained out of her. Her head felt like a ball of lead wobbling on her neck and the need to sleep was so overwhelming that she lay back and closed her eyes.

As long as I can hear them, she told herself drowsily, everything will be okay.

37

Mark was watching the scene below him with rising apprehension.

He had been on the verge of going to bed when he heard voices drifting up from the beach. Putting down the book he had been reading, he had gone to the edge of the terrace to see what was going on. Straining his eyes in the darkness, he had recognised Max and Laura's daughter, Francesca, and her friend, Sally. The younger of the Patterson boys – the shambling, feckless one with long hair – was with them. And by the look of them they were drunk, staggering about, laughing and joking, raising their voices more than was necessary. His blood had run cold when he had seen Sally and the boy strip off and throw themselves into the water.

An excess of alcohol and a late-night swim was not a wise combination, and as he stood now, rooted to the spot, he saw them swimming further and further away from the safety of the shore. Seeing Francesca lie back on the stones as though she was settling in for the night only added to his fears.

You're overreacting, he told himself, they'll be fine. Stop worrying. They're old enough to look after themselves. Just read your book and mind your own business.

He turned away from the sea and retraced his steps to his chair. He had taken no more than two paces when he heard a cry. A girl's cry. He spun on his heels and peered into the darkness.

Laughter drifted up to him on the gathering breeze. It was the boy. Floating on his back, his arms stretched out either side of him, he seemed to be finding something hysterically funny in the sky above him.

The fear that had wedged itself in Mark's throat subsided and once again he told himself not to be such a fool. But then he realised something was wrong with the picture he was looking at. Something was missing.

The girl whose cry he had heard, where was she?

He strained his eyes to pick out the whiteness of her body in the water. Where the hell was she?

From the terrace of Villa Petros, Izzy had also observed what was going on. She, too, concluded that something was wrong and headed for the beach as fast as she could.

She found that Mark had got there a few seconds ahead of her. The look of alarm on his face, confirmed her fears. 'Sally,' she said breathlessly, 'where is she?'

'I don't know, I can't see her. The tide's going out, she must have drifted with it. You wake Francesca and I'll shout to the boy. What's his name?'

'Nick. It's Nick.'

Standing at the water's edge, and though he couldn't see the boy, Mark began shouting to him. 'Nick,' he bellowed, 'Nick, can you hear me?'

There was no answer.

He tried calling to Sally. But there was no answer from her either.

Nor could Izzy get any response from Francesca. No matter how hard she shook her, Francesca slept on. All she got from the girl was an incoherent mumbling before she turned on to her side and sank further into a deep state of blackout. Giving up on her, Izzy went and joined Mark.

'It's no good,' he said. 'They're not answering me.'

Then in the silence they both heard a cry.

Followed by another, and another.

Keeping the panic from his voice, and ignoring the nausea in the pit of his stomach, Mark kicked off his shoes. 'Go and get help. I'll swim out to them.'

'But, Mark, you can't, you—'

'Go! Go on!'

She watched him plunge into the water, before turning to race back up the hillside. But just as she reached the path, disaster struck. Her ankle gave way and she keeled over in pain.

In order to overcome the phobic instinct that had been with him for the last thirty years, Mark knew that he had to use the raw terror of those memories – of Niall's open-eyed death mask of a face – to strengthen his body. If he couldn't do that, if he let the memories overwhelm him, he would never survive.

In the distance, he saw what he thought was a head bobbing in the darkness. Pushing his arms through the water, kicking his legs as hard as he could, he heard the terrified shouts for help. But it was only one voice he could hear, and it was such a deep-throated cry of fear he couldn't decide whether it was Sally or the boy.

He swam on.

Harder.

Faster.

But the gap didn't seem to be closing. Now that he was so far from the shore, the waves were building, buffeting him relentlessly, and the effort just to stay afloat was harder to sustain. His stomach was cramping and the muscles in his legs were bunching. It was a struggle just to keep his breathing going. To keep the rhythm. To use the memories. Not to give in to them.

A sudden wave caught him off-guard and salty water hit the back of his throat. Panicked and choking, he swallowed it. And then his nerve went. It was all too terrifyingly familiar: the powerful swell of the sea, the sense of uselessness, the deep, deep, coldness.

His body was no longer responding to anything he told it to do: it had turned to stone. A wave covered him, then another, and as he slipped beneath the surface he knew it was over. He had cheated death as a child, but this time it would not be denied. It was futile to fight it. Why not let the Grim Reaper have his way? It would be over in seconds.

He opened his mouth and water flooded in. The searing and strangely echoing coldness of it filled his head and lungs, but suddenly his chest heaved with a desperate need for air, and he realised that although his leaden brain might have been fooled into admitting defeat, some other part of him wasn't prepared to give in.

A new strength rushed through him, and he propelled himself to the surface. Coughing and spluttering, he gasped for air, fought for his life as the waves continued to buffet him. Treading water, he got his breathing under control again and looked around for any sign of Nick or Sally, not holding out much hope of finding them, not now.

At first he thought he had imagined it, but then he heard it again. A faint cry for help. Straining his stinging eyes in the darkness, he saw a flash of movement scarcely twenty yards from him.

It was Sally trying to stay afloat.

Adrenaline pumped through him and he swam over to her. She saw him and the relief showed in her panic-stricken face. She sank into his arms, frightened and exhausted, but he wasn't prepared for her weight and they both went under. Down and down they went. Deeper and deeper. Her cold body slithered out of his grasp and he lost her. Kicking his feet, he swam to the surface, got his breath back, then dived down for her. It was so dark he couldn't see anything. The salt water was burning his eyes. Suddenly he felt a hand. He grabbed at it and, with a tremendous surge of energy, hauled her upwards. But she wasn't moving and her freezing cold body was a dead weight in his arms. A grotesquely distorted image of Niall's face flew into his mind.

Anger and despair ripped through him. *No!* It couldn't happen twice.

He held on tightly to Sally's motionless body, and with one arm around her chest, and treading water, he prayed that he had the strength to get them both back to the shore.

He turned to start the long, hard swim, but was momentarily dazzled by a flare of light. In his shocked, exhausted state, he didn't register what it was. But as the light grew nearer and brighter, and he heard the low throaty roar of an engine, he realised it was a boat coming to help.

'Whoever you are,' he murmured wretchedly, his mind plummeting back to that moment when the lifeboat had come for him and Niall, 'you're too late.'

38

Izzy caught sight of Mark and Sally in the water and, her heart racing with relief, she pushed against the throttle, nearly knocking herself off her feet as the boat lurched forward in her haste to reach them. Ignoring the pain in her ankle as she tried to stand firm, she gunned the boat straight ahead. She came in close, cut her speed, and leaned over the side of the boat to Mark.

'I think she's dead,' was all he said as between them they heaved Sally's lifeless body into the boat.

Izzy's heart sank. Dead? No! Oh, please, no. Not this outrageous young girl who had made them all laugh. Not this fun-loving soul who was so bright and vivacious with everything before her. Leaving Mark to haul himself in, she felt for a pulse, determined to find one. He had to be wrong. Pressing her fingers against Sally's throat, she held her breath, blocked out everything else around her, willed the faintest flicker of life to reveal itself. Desperation made her think she had imagined it, and hardly trusting herself, she moved her fingers, then tried again. But yes. There it was. A pulse. No more than a flutter, but a sign of hope. Summoning all her first-aid knowledge, she started working at Sally's chest to expel the water that had tried to claim her, then tilting her head back and pinching her nose, she breathed into her cold mouth. The taste of salt, vomit and alcohol on Sally's lips made her want to retch, but she carried on relentlessly, filling her own lungs with air before steadily breathing it into Sally. She would not let her die. 'Come on, Sally,' she murmured, her hands pumping at the girl's chest, her brain fighting to chase away the fear that she might fail. 'Come on, Sally, you can do this. Come on.' A sudden gurgling sound, followed by a twitch of movement beneath her hands, instantly renewed Izzy's dwindling hopes. She turned Sally on to her side and said to Mark, 'Have a look in that seat cupboard. Laura sometimes keeps spare towels in there.'

After a brief fumble, Mark passed Izzy two large beach towels and helped her wrap Sally, who was now shaking violently. 'What about the boy?' he asked. His voice was a rasping whisper, his breathing heavy, and crouching beside her, water pooling on the deck from his dripping jeans and shirt, she could hear his teeth chattering. Shivering with cold, his hair plastered to his head, his eyes dark and wild against the paleness of his face, she knew he was in shock. 'He's okay,' she said, touching his arm to reassure him. 'He made it to the raft, that's where I left him.' And thinking it might help Mark to recover by having something to do, she added, 'Do you want to get us back?' He stared at her blankly, as though not understanding. Then he nodded and moved to the front of the boat. After studying the controls, he turned it round and headed for the raft. Above the sound of the engine and Sally's stifled sobs, Izzy could hear him cursing to himself. She had never heard such language: it was a furious litany of obscenities that made her wince as she cradled Sally in her arms.

Nick was waiting for them at the raft. He climbed in and took the towel Izzy offered him.

'Is she okay?' he asked, bending down to take a look at Sally. She was still crying and didn't seem aware of his presence.

'She'll be fine,' Izzy said, then, distracted by flashing beams of light on the shore by the jetty, she saw that Francesca was on her feet and that Max and Laura were with her. Corky was there too. The sound of the boat starting up must have disturbed them.

Pandemonium broke out when they got to the jetty. Everyone started talking at once. Max was beside himself with relief, thanking Mark and Izzy for what they had done, and Laura, who had been consoling Francesca, reached out to Sally and held her tightly. But there was anger too. Francesca's relief that Sally was all right made her turn on Nick. 'This is all your fault,' she yelled at him. 'It was your idea to go swimming. I told you not to, that you were both too drunk and too high. But you wouldn't listen.' She was screaming at him, tears running down her cheeks. 'If you hadn't been so keen to get off your head on dope none of this would have happened!'

Max's face turned white. 'Drugs?' he hissed. 'What drugs?' He flashed his torch on Nick's face.

'Nothing heavy,' said Nick, blinking in the light and clutching the towel around him. He was nothing like the cocky lad they were used to seeing. With his long hair clinging to his head and neck, and his thin legs poking out from beneath the towel, he looked pitifully young and vulnerable. 'It was only a joint, you know, just recreational.'

From behind Izzy, where he had been pulling on his boots, Mark stepped forward and squared himself up in front of Nick. He took hold of him, lifted him clean off his feet and shook him. Really shook him. 'You crazy little bastard,' he raged. Then throwing him to the ground, he shouted again: 'Spare us! Only a joint! Don't you get it? Don't you understand that because of you and your joint several people very nearly died here tonight? Can you live with that? Or maybe you're so arrogant you think you can.'

Without another word, he stalked away into the darkness, leaving them not knowing what to say or do next.

It was Corky who took command. He helped Nick to his feet, and said, 'Righty-ho, drama over. Let's get everyone up to the villa and into some dry clothes. Laura, you take Sally, Max, you look after Francesca, Izzy, you and I will bring up the rear with young Nick.'

'Um ... sorry to be a nuisance, Corky,' Izzy said, as everyone started to move, 'but I'm afraid I've turned my ankle again.' In view of what had happened she felt ridiculous bringing attention to herself but she knew she wouldn't be able to make the steep path without help. When she had decided that the best way to help Mark was to use Max and Laura's boat, every step she had taken to the jetty had made her cry out with pain. Now her calf was swelling and throbbing unbearably.

It had been a terrible risk she had taken, but it had been all she could think to do. Max had shown her how to handle the boat on one of their many trips out in it, but she wasn't sure how to start the engine. Then she remembered where Max kept a spare key and had been relieved to find that it was no more difficult than a car. The outboard motor had sprung into action first go. She had hauled in the anchor, untied the mooring rope, switched on the bow light and headed out into the bay to find Mark and the others.

Now, as Corky helped her and Nick up the path, a shiver went through her as she thought how differently it might all have ended if she hadn't been able to start the engine.

In the warm of the villa, and while Max phoned the emergency number for the local doctor's surgery, Laura made them tea. In the ensuing commotion Olivia was roused from her sleep and immediately fussed over Sally, wrapping her in Corky's dressing-gown, and when that proved insufficient to stop her shivering as she lay on the sofa, Francesca holding her hand, she instructed Corky to fetch a blanket.

Feeling sorry for Nick, who was being held responsible for the near tragedy, Izzy limped across the sitting room and sat next to him. He was fully dressed now, in the clothes that he had earlier stripped off, but he was still cold and a little shaky. She put a comforting arm around his shoulders.

'I think it would be best if I got going,' he murmured, his head bent down to the floor.

'No,' she said firmly. 'Have some tea first, then somebody will take you home.'

He shook his head dejectedly. 'It would have been better if I'd drowned out there. It would save my parents the job of killing me when they discover what I've done.'

'Don't ever say that,' she rebuked him. 'Treat this as a warning not to be so stupid again. You and Sally survived by the skin of your teeth. Be glad for that.'

He looked up at her. 'That bloke who saved Sally, why did he go berserk with me?'

'Let's just say he had his reasons. And if you've got any sense, you'll give what he said some thought.'

The next morning, sitting on the veranda in the shade of the pergola, everyone was subdued with shock and lack of sleep. The plans that had earlier been set in motion for the day had been dramatically altered. Max, Corky and Olivia wouldn't be the only ones flying back to England: understandably, Sally wanted to go home too, to be with her parents.

Max had phoned them after the doctor had confirmed that, though badly shaken, Sally was physically in good shape for somebody who had nearly drowned. Nobody had envied Max the job of explaining to Mr and Mrs Bartholomew what had happened, and his relief when he had handed the phone to Sally had been considerable. In the harsh brightness from the overhead spotlights in the kitchen where he sat at the table, his head bowed, he looked as if he had aged ten years in that one night.

With the decision made that Sally was to fly home, Laura had said that she would go too.

'But why?' Max had said, 'there's no need.'

'Yes, there is, I know what you'll do – you feel so bad about this, you'll take Sally home to her parents and accept the blame for what's happened.'

'We could make sure he doesn't do that,' Corky said, 'we'll go with him.'

'Thanks, but I'd rather be there myself.'

'In that case, I'm coming with you,' said Francesca.

Because it was clear that the holiday was now over for them all, Izzy said that perhaps she ought to return home as well.

But Max wouldn't hear of it. 'No, Izzy, with your ankle the way it is, you're not going anywhere. Besides, there's no reason for you to leave. Make the most of some quiet time on your own. Angelos and Sophia will take care of you. You won't have to do a thing.'

'Yes,' agreed Laura, 'please stay. It's not fair that your holiday should be cut short. Francesca and I will probably be back in a couple of days, with Max following on as soon as he's done what he needs to.'

'Are you sure?'

'Yes. Very sure,' said Max, getting up from his chair and coming over to where she was sitting, her ankle heavily strapped and resting on a low table. He kissed the top of her head. 'After what you did last night, this is the least we can do for you. If you and Mark hadn't seen what was going on, the telephone call I had to make to Sally's parents would have been very different.'

Just before lunch Max and Laura went to see Mark. They wanted to thank him for what he had done. They came back from Villa Anna a short while later, disappointed.

'He wasn't in,' Max said. 'I feel really bad that we haven't been able to thank him. It was quite a risk he took swimming that far out to save Sally and I want him to know how grateful we are.'

Izzy kept to herself just how big a risk it must have been for Mark. *Being in or on water freaks the hell out of me.* She wondered at his extraordinary courage in doing what he had. She also remembered that they had agreed to meet down on the beach that morning, but that had been before the events of last night had overtaken them all.

An hour before everyone had to leave for the airport, they had visitors.

It was Harry with his parents. There was no sign of Nick. The relaxed atmosphere on the terrace immediately evaporated, and under the pretext of some last-minute packing, Corky and Olivia made themselves scarce. When Izzy struggled to her feet to make her exit and join them inside the villa, Virginia Patterson said, 'Don't go on our account, not when it's you we need to thank.'

From her flat, unemotional tone, Francesca thought she had never heard gratitude so poorly expressed. Neither was there any evidence of it in the ghastly woman's face.

'It wasn't just me,' Izzy replied, settling down again. 'It's Mark you should really be talking to.'

'We've tried,' said Harry, 'but there's no answer. He must be out.' His gaze moved from Izzy and came to rest on Francesca where she was sitting between her parents, both of whom were suddenly bristling as if they needed to vent their feelings.

'Thank you, Harry,' said his mother, 'but I think your father and I are capable of handling this on our own.'

'Yes,' chipped in her husband, 'that's if you would allow us to get a word in.'

It was such an unnecessary put-down that Francesca coloured with indignation for Harry. How dare his parents treat him so offhandedly? But then she recalled how shamefully she had treated him last night, and knew she had to put things right between them before she left for home. In a voice loaded with contempt for his mother and father, she said, 'Seeing as you're not needed by your parents, Harry, perhaps you'd like to come and have a word with me. There's something I'd like to say to you.'

She led him to the far end of the terrace where she knew they wouldn't be heard or observed. Knowing she was short of time, she took the direct approach. 'Look, I just want to say that I know I behaved appallingly last night, and I'm really sorry. The minute you left I regretted what I'd said. God knows what I was fired up on, but I'm more sorry than I can say. Perhaps if I hadn't got so drunk . . .' she paused and stared down into the bay, 'none of this mess would have happened . . . I might have been able to stop Nick and Sally.'

'I think it was me who fired you up,' he said softly. 'Maybe if I hadn't humiliated you, you wouldn't have felt the need to get drunk.'

'When *you* humiliated *me*?'

'Yes. When I wouldn't kiss you.'

She looked shamefaced. 'I should never have tried to force you to do that. I knew you wouldn't want to, not in front of everyone, but I still went ahead and did it. I wanted to prove to you, and your brother, that you could knock the spots off him any day.'

He smiled shyly. 'Really?'

'Yes, really. You're miles more interesting than him. And it's about time you realised that. You should also stand up to your parents. They were bloody awful to you just now.'

'Anything else?'

'Yes, I'd like to kiss you goodbye, if it wouldn't be too horrible for you.'

'You're leaving?'

'Change of plan. I'm going back home today with Sally and my grandparents. Mum and Dad are going as well. It seems the right thing to do.'

'What time's your flight?'

'Soon.' She checked her watch. 'We've got to leave in three-quarters of an hour.'

He moved in closer. 'So it had better be a proper goodbye kiss, then?'
She nodded. 'One to remember.'

Manoeuvring her up against a pillar, and taking off his glasses, he stroked
the side of her face then kissed her for the longest and sweetest moment.
When he stopped and drew away from her, he said, 'Do you think you'd
like to keep in touch, back in England?'

She smiled. 'Now, what do you think?'

He replaced his glasses. 'I think the rest of my holiday is going to be
extremely dull without you.'

The villa seemed very quiet when everyone had gone. Izzy had been alone in
it before, when she had first hurt her ankle, but this time it was different. It
was as if an unhappy spirit was lurking somewhere in the large house,
following her about.

Sitting on the terrace, looking down on to the beach, she tried to occupy
herself by reading *When Darkness Falls*. She had only four chapters left,
which meant the tension was building to its climax, but despite the quality
of the writing she couldn't keep her mind fixed on the plot. It kept
wandering off, worried about the story's creator. Where was he? What was
he doing? She had hoped he might come and see her, but of course he
wasn't to know that she was immobile again. There hadn't been time last
night for her to explain why she had disregarded his instruction to fetch the
others.

Her mind wasn't put at ease when later that evening Sophia came to cook
her a light supper. She was full of apologetic mutterings that she and her
husband had not known of the drama that had taken place and been on
hand to help. She was also furious that drugs had been involved.

'It is the Italians and Albanians,' she said, banging Laura's expensive Le
Creuset frying-pan down on the cooker and cracking eggs into a bowl.
'They are bringing it here to our perfect island and ruining everything. If I
ever got hold of them, they would know about it!'

Her angry outburst complete, she then went on to tell Izzy that Angelos
had been to Villa Anna that afternoon to see to the pool and had reported
back to his wife that there was no sign of anybody in or around the house.
'It is very strange,' Angelos had told her, 'the shutters are all across the
windows, as if nobody is there. And Theo's guest rarely goes out during the
day. Always he is working. Writing. Writing. Writing. He has his favourite
spot in the shade where he sits every day. But not today. Perhaps he has
finished his book?'

Izzy knew this couldn't be so. Mark had told her last night that he was
only a third of the way through it.

She went to bed early that night but was soon woken by the sound of
ringing. She fumbled for the bedside lamp, rubbed her eyes and tried to
work out what had disturbed her. It was a while before she remembered the
mobile phone Theo had given her. She leaped out of bed and, too late,
remembered her ankle. Agonising pain shot through her and she limped
over to the dressing-table. She looked at the compact little device wondering
how to switch it on, then pressed a likely button and heard Theo's voice.

'Izzy,' he said, 'is that you?'

'Yes.'

'You sound sleepy. Were you in bed? It's very early. Are you unwell?'

'No, I'm not unwell, just tired. The last twenty-four hours have been rather hectic.' She told him about Nick and Sally.

'Dear God in heaven, that's terrible. And Mark actually went into the water to rescue Sally?'

'Theo,' she said, 'I might be being silly, but I'm worried about Mark. He told me last night of his fear of water, about the friend of his who drowned when he was a boy. And after he'd saved Sally, it was obvious he was in a state of shock, and since then nobody has seen him. Angelos called at the villa today and said there was no sign of him.'

'You're right to be worried, Izzy. I'll ring him now and call you back later.'

Within minutes the mobile was ringing again. 'I can't get an answer from him, Izzy. Now, please, it is a lot to ask of you, I know, but will you do me a favour? There is a key under a flowerpot by the door at the back of the house. I want you to go inside and make sure that my friend is all right. If he is angry that you have invaded his privacy, tell him it is his own fault. Tell him he should have answered the phone. But whatever the outcome, call me. My number is on my desk in my study.'

39

Izzy hadn't told Theo the one important factor that was going to make her mission nigh on impossible – her re-injured ankle. The doctor who had checked out Sally had also taken a look at her and told her what she knew already: she was back to square one, and rest, plenty of it, was the only cure. Fortunately she still had the crutches and with these, she was now making slow progress down the path and along the hillside to Theo's house; concentrating hard on not missing her footing in the dark. Also, she was trying to suppress the fear that something terrible had happened to Mark. Without him having said as much, she knew that Theo's concern for him was the same as hers; that the shock of what he had made himself do last night might have had him knocking back a restorative drink. A restorative drink that might have done him untold harm.

Her daunting journey complete, she leaned against the gate to Theo's villa physically and mentally exhausted. Her whole body ached from the effort, and she stood for a moment to catch her breath, to rub away the tension in her shoulders and to rest her good leg. Ahead of her, and beneath a star-pricked sky, the low-roofed house was in darkness. The bushes around her stirred in the mild breeze, and far off in the distance she could hear a dog barking.

She pressed on to the door Theo had told her to use, flashed the torch over the steps and saw the pot he had mentioned. He hadn't thought to tell her how large it was, though, or that it contained a hydrangea that came up almost to her waist. Resting the crutches against the wall, she bent down and tried to rock the pot to one side. Angelos must have watered it that day for it was damp and even heavier than she expected. She gave it another shove and tilted it sufficiently to grab the key before letting it down with a heavy thud. Wiping the moist soil off her hands, she raised the key to the lock, then hesitated. Shouldn't she give Mark the opportunity to open the door rather than blunder in and perhaps embarrass him? He might have chosen to do nothing more worrying than shut himself away for the day to work.

The most rational explanation was that he wasn't in, that he was enjoying a late supper in Kassiópi. Or, like her, he had simply gone to bed early.

As plausible as these suggestions were, they didn't satisfy her.

She gave a gentle tap at first, then a more vigorous knock. 'Mark, are you in there? It's me, Izzy.' Not getting any response, she inserted the key and turned the handle. She stood in the dark, eerie silence, getting her bearings in a house she had only ever been inside twice before. Closing the door behind her, she thought she heard a noise, and suddenly she was scared, her heart in her mouth, her brain conjuring up chilling murder scenes from the books she had read of late. 'Irrational,' she muttered under her breath. 'Get a grip.' She crossed the stone floor of the sitting room and went towards the kitchen, where she thought the noise had come from.

She found him hunched over the kitchen table, his head clasped in his hands. He was so still, she thought for a moment that he was asleep. Then a worse thought hurtled into her head ... that he was dead. 'Mark?'

He raised his head slowly and revealed a face of gaunt agony. His skin was grey and lined, his eyes dull and bloodshot, distant, unseeing. His hair was awry from where he must have been raking his hands through it, and it gave him a wild, almost manic appearance. He was dressed in the clothes he had worn last night; crinkled and patchy with salt, they smelled of stale sweat and vomit. But, thank God, there was no smell of alcohol on him. 'Mark,' she said, 'please, what can I do to help?'

He pressed the heels of his hands to his eyelids as if to clear his thoughts and summon the energy to speak to her. 'If you could bear it, would you hold me, please?' he murmured. His voice was thick, a faint husk of a whisper, and the pain in it made her react at once. Very gently, she took him in her arms, cradled his head against her and absorbed the tremor that was running through him. They stayed like that for an age, disconnected from time or their surroundings; it might have been for ten minutes, it might have been for ever.

The shrill ringing of the telephone made them both start.

'I know who it will be,' said Izzy, reluctantly releasing him. She moved across the kitchen on her crutches to the phone that hung on the wall beside the tall American-style fridge.

'I couldn't take the suspense,' said Theo. 'Is he all right? Please, God, say he's well and ready to abuse me with a tirade of foul language for my interference.'

'Yes and no,' she said truthfully. 'Hold on a moment.' She covered the receiver with her hand. 'It's Theo, Mark. Will you speak to him, please? Just put his mind at rest that you're okay. He knows about you rescuing Sally.'

He came stiffly to the phone and took it from her. 'It's okay, Theo,' he said tiredly, 'I haven't done anything silly. I'm just a bit out of it, that's all. Was it you who sent me the guardian angel? Well, how else would she have known about the key? And, no, of course I'm not mad with you. I'm more grateful than I can say. Look, I'll speak to you tomorrow. Now isn't the time. Yeah, cheers, mate.'

He put the phone back on the wall and turned to Izzy.

'You're not cross I came, are you?' she asked nervously.

'How could I be?'

'Why didn't you open the door when I called to you?'

He dragged his hands over his face, distorting his features. 'I don't know. It was as if I was paralysed. I haven't been able to think straight all day ... not since last night.' As if noticing the crutches for the first time, he said, 'What have you done to your ankle?'

Sensing that he wasn't ready yet to discuss what he had gone through, she told him. 'But that's not important. I'm more concerned about you. Have you eaten anything today?'

'No.' He looked down at himself and shook his head wearily. 'I'm sorry, I must look and smell pretty disgusting.'

'Nothing that a shower won't put right. Do you think you can manage that?'

While he was in the shower, Izzy put his clothes into the washing-machine and set it whirring. She made him some tea and took it through to his bedroom, doing her best not to spill it on Theo's expensive rugs as she made the precarious journey on one crutch from one end of the villa to the other, taking in a couple of steps and a narrow archway that she had to tackle sideways on.

His bedroom came as a surprise. It was meticulously tidy: there were no clothes lying around, no coins, pens or combs cluttering the surfaces, no book left face down with its spine cracked, no socks lurking in the corner of the room, not even a pair of shoes left haphazardly on the floor. The white cotton sheets on the bed were unwrinkled and the pillows perfectly placed – clearly Mark hadn't slept there the previous night. As she pulled the top sheet back in readiness for him, he appeared behind her in a clean pair of boxer shorts and a black REM T-shirt. He still looked tired and haggard, but there was a reassuring glimmer of light in his eyes now.

'I know this will sound like the worst chat-up line in the history of come-ons,' he said, smoothing back his hair and casting his gaze over the bed, 'but would you stay with me tonight?'

She tried to keep the shock from her face, but must have failed miserably, for he said, 'Slow down, Izzy, I don't mean it in the way you're thinking. I ... I just don't want to be alone. I'd like to know that you were there.'

'Okay,' she said, 'if you think it would help.'

He gave her one of his T-shirts and she changed in the bathroom. He had already turned out the lamp when she joined him, but in the moonlight that peeped in through the shutters at the open window, she could see that his eyes were closed. She could also see the harsh contours of his ravaged face, which betrayed his suffering. He must have spent that day reliving an experience he would never be able to obliterate fully from his memory. It struck her then, as odd a thought as it was, that she had never come up with one of her silly celeb-lookalikes for him. It's because he's unique, she thought. He's a man like no other. And, thinking that he might already have dozed off, she slipped noiselessly under the sheet beside him. But he wasn't asleep and with his back to her, he said, 'Thank you for doing this, Izzy.' She moved a little closer and placed an arm tenderly around him. She felt his shoulder quiver and realised just how tense he still was. Gradually she sensed his thin, angular body relax, until finally he fell asleep.

She lay wide awake in the semi-darkness, listening to his uneven breathing, wondering at the extraordinary situation she had got herself into. Could this really be Izzy Jordan, that well-known shall-I-shan't-I ditherer; the proponent *par excellence* of 'Oh, I couldn't possibly do that'; the neurotic woman who listened to voices in her head for guidance? Come to think of it, Modern Woman and Prudence Jordan had been slacking recently.

Didn't her mother have anything to say about her scandalously immoral daughter, who was currently lying in bed with a former addict.

'Well, I don't care what you think,' she imagined herself saying to her mother. 'Mark might have had more than his fair share of problems, but he's the first man I feel truly comfortable with.'

She thought about this, and realised it was true. What's more, she trusted him, or more precisely, she had trusted herself to trust again. He was so honest, so direct. And so easy to be with. There was no chicanery to him. She never felt as though he was setting a trap for her.

With these thoughts running through her head, she soon fell asleep and dreamed that she was back in the children's home. She was standing anxiously at the window waiting for her father to appear through the snow. Except it wasn't her father who arrived to see her, it was Mark, and she wasn't a child, she was an adult. He was helping her to put away the box of Fuzzy-felt shapes, telling her that the tears always dry. No matter how many tears, they all dry in the end.

Beams of early-morning sunlight were penetrating the shutters, enabling Mark to watch Izzy as she slept next to him. With her hair swept back from her face, she looked so peaceful, and so very beautiful. But there was something different about her that he couldn't quite put his finger on. Then he understood what it was. He had never seen her with her hair pulled back from her forehead before. He noticed an ugly two-inch scar just into the hairline of her right temple and wondered how somebody so intrinsically cautious could have received such an injury. A car accident perhaps? He winced at the thought and dispelled it immediately. He didn't want to imagine her coming to any harm.

Last night on the phone with Theo, he had referred to Izzy as his guardian angel, and even now, this morning, when he was thinking straight at last, he could think of no better description. Goodness knows how much longer he would have remained sitting in that petrifyingly inert state if she hadn't turned up. The awful horror of being so vividly reminded of Niall's death had disarmed him of the power of reasoned thought. All his brain would allow him to focus on was that he had so very nearly failed again. And he would have failed if it hadn't been for Izzy: if she hadn't had the sense to use Max's boat that girl would have died. Him too, probably.

But that wasn't entirely why he had lost it yesterday. Coming up from the beach, after his explosive outburst at that idiot Patterson boy, he had come face to face with temptation for the first time in years. The craving for a drink had hit him so suddenly, had been so strong, it had completely freaked him out. Cold fear had made him nauseous and he had only just made it in time to the villa before he was violently ill. He was shaking, and sweat poured off him. Shocked at the strength of the craving, he hadn't trusted himself to move from the chair in the kitchen, terrified that just a single step might take him to where he knew Theo kept his hoard of oúzo and Metaxá. And, as he desperately fought to keep his nerve, his mind had swirled in the vortex of Niall's drowning and his funeral. Mark's parents hadn't wanted him to attend it, they had said he was too young, that he had already gone through enough, but he had insisted on going. Afterwards he had wished he hadn't. Niall's mother had been distraught with grief-stricken anguish. She sobbed throughout the service in the little church, loudly and without restraint, and later collapsed against her husband at the graveside. Mrs Percival's inconsolable sorrow had left an indelible impression on his tormented mind. Even so young he had felt the need to comfort these heartbroken people, to take their grief from them. But what could he offer them when he was a living reminder of all they had lost? They never said anything, but he could see it in their eyes, the bitter reproach – Why couldn't it have been you who drowned? And in that moment, as he had stared at them across the gaping hole in the ground, the body of his friend just feet away, Mark would have given anything to trade his life for their son's.

And, of course, for the best part of twenty years that was exactly what he tried to do. If it hadn't been for Theo, he might have succeeded.

What a lot he had to thank Theo for.

Then, gazing down at Izzy's sleeping face, he thought that he had a lot to thank her for too. He couldn't remember much about being on the boat with her, but he could recall the determined way in which she had worked to bring Sally back from the dead. To his shame, he had been convinced her efforts were in vain.

Turning his thoughts to last night, a flicker of a smile crossed his face as he thought of Izzy's endearingly prim expression when he had asked her to stay with him. Only twenty-four hours earlier he had been fantasising about getting her into bed, but last night all he had wanted was to feel her arms around him so that he would sleep, and surer still that she would keep him safe ... safe from the weakness that would always be with him. To his amazement, she had trusted him enough to do as he asked.

Few people had ever really trusted him, and who would blame them? Not so long ago he had lied, cheated and stolen from his own family and friends, but here he was, lying next to this innately good person who trusted him implicitly.

And if Izzy trusted him so completely, what did he feel for her?

Difficult to say.

Or was it?

Didn't being with her make perfect sense? Hadn't he always, right from the start, felt comfortable with her? And hadn't he looked forward to their chats on the beach? And what of his writing? Wasn't it time now to be honest about his use of her in his book? Pretending that she was nothing but a lucky hit of inspiration was a classic example of deluded thinking that would fool no one. That was the real reason why he hadn't told Theo the truth behind his new-found roll of creativity. Theo would see straight through him.

So what did it all mean? That while he had been setting her up as the love interest for his protagonist in his novel he had been nurturing a whacking great desire to sleep with her?

Or did it go deeper than that?

Did he see something in her that was lasting and emotionally satisfying? The potential for a long-term relationship, perhaps?

It was a little after nine o'clock when Izzy woke. Her first thought was of Mark, and seeing that the other side of the bed was empty, she didn't bother to dress but went in search of him.

He was outside in the garden, sitting on the low white wall in the bright sunshine. Dressed and shaved, he was looking better than he had last night, much more his normal self. He smiled when he saw her and came to meet her in the shade of the terrace as she leaned on her crutches, wishing she could be rid of them and fling her arms around him.

'How are you feeling?' she asked.

He kissed her cheek. 'A little wobbly, but a lot better . . . thanks to you.'

'I didn't do very much. I only—'

He silenced her with a kiss, this time on the lips. 'You were there when I needed you. So do me the kindness of accepting my thanks with good grace. Breakfast?'

'Just a mug of tea would do.'

'Tea it is, then. And don't even think of following me. Sit down and allow yourself to be waited on.'

It was a beautiful day. The sky was vast and uncompromisingly clear, and beneath it the sea stretched away into a hazy infinity of shimmering blue. A delicate warm breeze fanned the leaves on the nearby olive tree, and down in the bay, the sound of waves breaking gently against the rocks accompanied the early-morning shift of cicadas, who were already in fine voice. It was a glorious morning and contrasted sharply with the disturbing events of the last couple of days.

During the night Izzy had heard Mark moaning in his sleep, as if caught in the grip of some deeply rooted terror. Once or twice she had reached out to him, tried to soothe him, but it had had no effect.

'I've made you some toast,' he said, reappearing sooner that she had expected, 'just in case you were being polite.'

She looked at the tray he was carrying. 'Toast as well as chicken tikka masala. You were holding back on me.'

'Doesn't do to give too much away too soon.' He sat opposite, picked up a mug of tea to pass to her, but paused with it mid-air. 'You know, I really am grateful for last night. If it hadn't been for you I might . . . Well, who knows what I might have been driven to do?'

She took the mug from him. 'It's Theo who deserves the thanks. He phoned me and when I told him how concerned I was because nobody had seen you he made me come and make sure you were okay.' She took a small sip of her tea and added, 'He's a very good friend to you.'

'I know. Which makes what I feel for you all the more complicated.'

Not looking at him, or asking what exactly it was that he felt for her, she said, 'I would never want to come between the two of you.'

'It wouldn't come to that.' And changing the subject, he said, 'So tell me, how's Sally?'

She told him that Sally had been given a clean bill of health by the doctor Max had called out, about the Pattersons coming to see them, and how everyone had left yesterday afternoon.

'Leaving you home alone?'

'I did suggest that maybe I should cut short my holiday, but Max and Laura wouldn't hear of it. They said they'd be back soon and that everything would return to how it was. Laura will probably come ahead of Max, so I shan't be on my own for too long.'

'I'm glad they persuaded you to stay on ... and that you're alone.'

She raised her eyes and met his. They were the same colour as the sky above them, just as clear, just as breathtakingly beautiful. 'I'm glad too,' she murmured.

His lips twitched with a smile. 'Eat your toast and stop flirting with me, Izzy.'

She feigned indignation. 'I wasn't flirting with you. The very thought.'

'Yes you were, and unless you want to find yourself being carried off to bed, I'd advise you to go easy on any more direct eye-contact.'

'Are you threatening me?'

'No, merely propositioning you.'

'Oh, I don't think that's ever happened to me before. So, what you're saying is, if I behave myself we'll just carry on having a quiet breakfast together. Whereas if—'

Slowly rising from his chair, he came round to her side of the table. 'Whereas if you keep looking at me the way you are, I'll have no choice but to do something about it. It's entirely up to you.'

She pushed herself to her feet, smiled flirtatiously and hooked her hands around his neck. 'Well, in that case, ready when you are.'

Laughing, he picked her up, carried her inside and lowered her on to the bed where they had slept the night. He kissed her lovingly, but when she began to remove what little clothing she was wearing, he waved her hands aside. 'How about you let me handle that, Izzy? I think I can remember what to do.'

40

'So tell me again about this dunderhead Alan who didn't know a G-spot from his Air on a G-string?'

It was a week later and they were by the pool, following a failed attempt at taking an afternoon nap – a siesta seemed such a waste to Mark when there were other things he would much rather be doing with Izzy. Now, as he rubbed sun cream on to her back, he felt pretty damn smug with himself. More than once in the last few days he had thought of Bones's words about knowing when the right buttons had been pressed and, credit where credit was due, the man had known his stuff. Lying in the drowsy afterglow of their first time in bed together, Izzy had left him in no doubt that the buttons had been well and truly pressed. Not just once, but several times. 'Do it again, Mark,' she had sighed, her arms wrapped around him.

'I'm not as young as you, Izzy.' He had laughed. 'I need to rest up for a while.'

'No, you don't,' she had murmured, her lips brushing his ear, while one of her hands drifted across his chest, caressing his hot skin with light, sensual movements. She soon proved him wrong – that he was in no need of rest – and later, when they had refuelled on supplies brought in on a tray from the kitchen and they were sitting cross-legged on the bed, she had told him about her last boyfriend, who had convinced her that she was a non-starter when it came to sex.

'Well, if you'd like me to write him a letter disputing that theory of his,' he had told her, as he trailed a finger over the smooth curve of her shoulder, 'I'd be more than pleased to do so.'

Taking his hand and kissing each of his fingertips, she said, 'You know what? I couldn't give a damn what he thought about me.'

'Tut tut, Miss Jordan, you're using language your mother wouldn't approve of.'

'I think I'm doing a lot more that my mother wouldn't approve of.'

'Time to extend the list, then. I'd hate to short-change her. What shall we play now?' And manoeuvring her on to her back, he had begun kissing her, working his mouth down the length of her body.

'No, Mark, not again.'

'You're only saying that.'

'Oh, go on, then.'

'A little more enthusiasm, if you wouldn't mind . . .'

'Why do you want to know so much about that rat?' she asked now, and in answer to his question.

'No reason.'

'You're lying, Mark.'

'Oh, gee, you're too smart for me, Izzy. But it's a guy thing, you wouldn't appreciate it.'

She turned over and sat up. 'Try me.'

He screwed the lid back on the sun-tan lotion. 'Okay,' he conceded, 'it makes me feel incredibly good about myself to know that where he couldn't cut the mustard I can. Makes me sound a bit of a rat as well, doesn't it?' he added.

She smiled. 'Like you said, it's a guy thing.'

'Not cross with me, then?'

'No, not cross with you.'

'Good, because I couldn't think of anything worse. I'd have to spend the rest of the day on my hands and knees grovelling to you. I'd have to raid every florist's on the island and surround you with flowers of apology. I'd have to dream up so many extravagant gestures of love that you'd—'

'Throwing your money at me now, are you?'

'I might not look the part, but Theo's not the only one with bags of gold under his mattress.'

'Is that so?'

He caught the edge of mockery to her voice. 'Hey, I'm a household name, didn't you know?'

'What, like Andrex?'

He laughed. 'Phew, for a moment there I was running the risk of being in awe of myself.'

Angelos paid them a visit later that afternoon while Mark was working. He brought with him a carrier-bag of home-grown tomatoes and cucumbers, and after checking the pool, he went round the garden watering Theo's beloved plants. He hadn't said anything, but Mark knew that Angelos and his wife must have guessed what was going on between him and Izzy: they couldn't have failed to notice that she was never at Villa Petros and that only one bed at Villa Anna was being slept in. He hoped to God that Theo had no cause to get in touch with either Angelos or Sophia while he was in Athens: he didn't want his friend to hear the news from anyone but him. Initially he had thought that it would have to be done face to face when Theo returned, but it was proving so difficult for either of them to talk to Theo on the phone without feeling guilty that this morning they had agreed they couldn't keep lying to him, that they would have to break it to him the next time he called.

They had gone to ridiculous lengths to keep the truth from Theo, each of them chatting separately with him on the phone – Izzy spoke to him on the mobile he had given her, and Mark on one of the phones inside the house. There had been no question of Mark staying with Izzy at Max and Laura's place: after last week, when Mark hadn't answered the phone, Theo was now keeping a regular tab on him, calling most evenings when he had finished work and had returned to his apartment. 'You really don't have to do this, Theo,' Mark had told him, only last night.

'I know that, but I want to. It serves you right for frightening me so badly. I've just been talking to Izzy. She sounded odd to me. Is she lonely without Max and Laura, do you think?' And to make Mark feel even more of a conniving bastard, Theo had asked him to keep an eye on her. 'For some unaccountable reason she likes you, so maybe you could go and see her and cheer her up.'

'Yeah, I'll see what I can do.'

'So how is the work going? You are still writing at speed?'

'Like a rocket on high-octane fuel.'

'Excellent. I have a feeling this book will be your best, Mark. The muse is performing well for you, eh? Long may it continue.'

It was a sentiment he privately echoed. Izzy was the perfect muse. Though she was with him so much of the day and night, she was no distraction. When he wanted to work she was more than happy to sit reading quietly or go for a swim in Theo's pool. Often she would get out her drawing and painting things and sit for hours dabbling, as she modestly called it. Yesterday he had turned the page of his notepad and caught her sketching him. When he insisted that she showed him what she had done, he had been amazed by how well she had captured his likeness. 'You've made me look very serious,' he said. 'Couldn't you have given me a smile?'

'But you weren't smiling at the time, you were deep in concentration. That was what I was trying to show. And anyway, the Prince of Darkness can't wear a cheeky-chappy grin when he's exploring the dark night of the soul.'

It was then that he decided to come clean about using her for his novel.

'Do I die?' she asked, in that candid way she did sometimes.

'I haven't decided.'

'What? You don't know the outcome of the book?'

'Not in this instance.'

'Oh, well, if it's all the same to you, I'd prefer to live.'

'I'll see what I can do.'

Her only frustration was that he wouldn't let her go wandering off on her own. Her ankle was a lot stronger now – she no longer needed the crutches, and was able to go for short walks – but he wouldn't hear of her going far. 'Quit the wheedling and the pouty look, Izzy. What if you fell and couldn't make it back?'

'I'd rely on you coming to find me.'

'Forget it. I've done all the carrying up and down that bloody hillside I'm ever going to do. One more session like that and I'll give myself a hernia. And what use would I be to you, then? Satisfying your insatiable sexual appetite will be the last thing I'll be good for.'

Her mouth dropped open and the colour rushed to her face.

He loved the way he could still shock and embarrass her. 'Too late now to be feigning a chaste innocence, Izzy. Remember, it's in my arms that you show your true colours.'

Apart from Angelos and Sophia, and Izzy's chats with Max and Laura on the phone, they hadn't seen or spoken to anyone else. They had caught the odd glimpse of the Patterson boys on the beach, but had seen nothing of the runaway lovers – if it really was them staying here, and Mark had his doubts – or the Fitzgeralds, not that he expected Dolly-Babe to come calling. Not now. Izzy had told him about the olive grove Theo had bought from under Bob's nose and he had asked Theo on the phone why he hadn't thought to mention it to him.

'What was there to tell? I bought a piece of land. It is not the first or the last investment I will make without running it by you for your approval.'

'So there was nothing vindictive in what you did?'

'Vindictive? You think protecting my immediate environment from being developed into a cheap and nasty resort is an act of malicious intent on my part?'

'You're deliberately missing the point. Did you enjoy getting one over Dolly-Babe and Silent Bob because they treated you like an ignorant oik?'

'But, Mark, it is you who are deliberately missing the point. I stole nothing from them, they did not own the land, it was not theirs.'

'True, and now it's yours.'

'Yes, now it's mine. And as you so often say, once again I have had my own way.'

Angelos wound up the hose and put it back into the store cupboard where he kept the rest of his garden tools and the chemicals for the pool, then waved and was gone.

Izzy raised her arms above her head and stretched languidly. 'I suppose I ought to write to my mother.' She sighed.

Mark finished constructing the sentence he had in his head, got it down on paper and said, 'And tell her what?'

'That the weather is still hot and sunny and that I'm still having a wonderful time.'

'Nothing about meeting a devilishly attractive man who's fast developing a compulsive disorder to have sex with you every other hour.'

'Mm ... Perhaps I'll keep that for the next missive.'

He smiled at her dead-pan expression, noting that she was learning to parry his attempts to make her blush. 'How often do you write to your mother?'

'As often as my conscience gets the better of me.'

'So how many times since you've been here on holiday? To the nearest unit of ten will do.'

'You horrible man.'

'It's taken years of counselling to hone me down to this level of astuteness. But I reckon I could whittle you into shape by 2050.'

She pulled a face. 'I'll be an old woman by then. What a dreadful thought.'

'Spare a thought for me. In eight years' time I'll be eligible to go on a Saga holiday.'

She laughed, leaned over and kissed him. 'Now, that I'd like to see.'

He pulled her on to his lap. 'Then you'd best stick around, kidda.'

*

He worked steadily for the rest of that afternoon, his mind flying along with the plot. If there was any one thing he wanted to get across in his novels, it was that a society that underestimates the destructive nature within each and every one of its members was a society beyond help. By exploring man's most basic flaws – those of wanting to be in a position of power and the need for recognition – he wanted to prove that murderers aren't a different species, that they are *us*. That they do not, contrary to popular opinion, walk around giving off an unmistakable air of evil, enabling everybody else to give them a wide berth. More often than not, the most successful murderers are clever, charming and seductive, with a chameleon-like ability to switch from apparent good to abhorrent evil.

Creating a monster on the page was no problem to him; it came more easily than crafting the victims. He always found it perfectly straightforward to justify why somebody had committed a heinous crime. Essentially he saw his novels not so much as whodunits but as whydunits, which peeled away the layers of deceit, corruption and greed to get to the truth. He particularly liked the idea of shaking the reader out of any complacency he might harbour about his own safe little world. Yes, my friend, this really could be you! But for the grace of God, it might have been you who turned into the monster who murders, rapes and molests.

It had always intrigued him that, when studying the mind of a criminal, there was no denying the recognisable facets of one's own personality staring back at one. He had been talking to Izzy about this in bed the other night when she had asked him about the theme of his latest book – normally he hated to discuss what he was currently working on. 'It's about a man who survived a classroom massacre when he was a boy,' he had told her. 'By wrestling the killer to the floor, he saved the rest of his classmates from being butchered.'

'So he's the hero, the goodie?'

Smiling at her black-and-white simplification of good versus bad, he had said, 'Well, he was the hero then, but now he's the baddie.'

'But why?'

'He never truly recovered from the trauma. I mean, would any of us survive mentally unscathed from such an ordeal? Clinically speaking he's psychotic, out of touch with reality.'

'But what makes him want to kill?'

'Oh, the usual, voices in the head. Visions.'

She had chewed her lower lip. 'I have voices in my head.'

'I'll wager they're not on the scale I'm talking about.'

'So what's this book going to be called?'

'*Flashback Again*. And before you ask why, it's because the killer starts suffering from flashbacks to the time he survived the massacre. He believes it's a call for him to track down the other survivors and kill them.'

She had flinched, then rolled on top of him, and said, 'Just think, I'm in bed with the strange man who creates all this despicable horror.'

He had pulled the sheet over her head and growled in her ear, 'Be very afraid, Izzy. Be very afraid.'

*

The evening sky was a glorious infusion of indigo that had seeped into swathes of bright sapphire. Stars pricked at the darker patches and the moon, still quite low, spilled its light across the shimmering sea. Thinking how glad he was that he had accepted Theo's offer to spend the summer with him, Mark tried to recall when, if ever, he had been so relaxed and happy.

He had arrived here in June, as nervy and jumpy as hell, half frightened to death of his own shadow, but now look at him. It was ages since he had given his *Silent Footsteps* copy-cat stalker any thought, and now that he had successfully distanced himself from what had been going on at home, he felt he had been an idiot to let it get the better of him.

The only cloud hanging over him now was making his confession to Theo. During supper, he and Izzy had decided that tonight was definitely the night. Out of the corner of his eye, he caught Izzy glancing apprehensively at the mobile on the table between them. 'Let's not wait for him to ring us,' he said decisively, 'let's call him and get it over and done with.'

She checked her watch. 'Do you think he'd be home this early?'

'We could give it a try.' He reached for the phone and tapped in Theo's number. It rang and rang, and just as he was on the verge of giving up, he heard Theo's slightly breathless voice. This was it, then.

'Theo, it's Mark. Is it a good time to talk?'

'It's fine, but wait a moment while I pour myself a drink. I've just this minute got in. You would not believe how hot Athens is.' Hearing the clink of ice against glass, Mark could almost smell the oúzo Theo was pouring as he moved about his apartment carrying his cordless phone with him. 'There, that's better. Now I am sitting down and I am all yours. There is nothing wrong, I hope?'

'Why do you say that?'

'It's just that it is so rare for you to ring me. How is Izzy? Have you seen her today? Did you do as I asked? Have you cheered her up?'

'Um ... yes, in a manner of speaking. And ... and she's very well. Oh, hell, Theo, there's no easy way to tell you this, I just hope you can forgive me.'

'Why, what have you done?' Theo's tone was instantly wary.

'I'm sorry, Theo, but I've—' He stalled hopelessly. He cleared his throat, tried again. 'The thing is, Izzy and I ... well, we've kind of been seeing each other.'

The silence said it all.

Mark's gaze locked with Izzy's and she squeezed his hand. 'Say something, Theo. I'm getting the feeling you could beat the hell out of me.'

Still nothing.

'Would it help if I got down on my knees and said I was sorry?'

'Oh, please, save the theatrical drama for your novels.'

'Look, you have to believe me, I didn't mean to do it. It wasn't deliberate, I couldn't help myself.'

'Or stop yourself, it would seem.'

Mark had never heard Theo's voice so cold. 'You're right,' he muttered, 'I couldn't.'

Another silence.

Until, 'How long have you been *kind of seeing* Izzy, as you so delicately put it?'

'Since the night of the party.' It was almost the hardest part of the confession, letting Theo know that the deceit had been going on for as long as it had.

'And ... and do you think it is serious between the pair of you?'

Mark kept his gaze on Izzy's anxious face. 'Yes. Much to my amazement, I think it is.'

'Then it is settled. There is nothing more to be said.'

'Of course there is, and don't you dare try taking that line with me, Theo.'

'Which line would you prefer me to take?' The coldness had thawed, and in its place was dry cynicism.

'I don't know. But one that ensures our friendship isn't damaged.'

There was another lengthy pause, during which Mark heard the clink of ice again. In his mind's eye, he saw Theo swirling the glass round in his hand, tilting back his head and draining the drink in one. But then he heard the unexpected sound of laughter. 'Theo?'

'It is all right, my friend, I am just beginning to see the funny side of it.'

'You are?'

'Yes. You have never before coveted anything I had or aspired to anything I have accomplished, and yet here you are, stealing the prize that, quite possibly, I wanted most.'

'It wasn't like that.'

'I know, but let a defeated man have his pride. Is Izzy there with you?'

'Yes, she is.'

'If she will speak to me, put her on.'

Mark passed the phone to Izzy. 'It's okay,' he whispered, 'the worst is over.'

'Theo,' she said, 'I'm sorry, truly I am. We never intended—'

'Ah, Izzy, come on now. All is fair in love and war and, besides, you were always honest with me, you did not deliberately mislead me. It is I who have misled myself. But to show you how magnanimous I can be, Mark is my best friend and, more than anyone, I know that he deserves somebody as special as you. Now take good care of one another. And, please, do try to have a civilising effect on him for me.'

'I'll do my best.'

They went to bed that night and lay in each other's arms with a clear conscience at last. But when they woke the following morning, a clear conscience was the last thing on their minds.

41

They were roused by the sound of insistent knocking.

'If that's Angelos with another bag of cucumbers, I'll swing for him,' fumed Mark. He pulled on a pair of shorts and stomped off to answer the door. Izzy hurried after him. If Angelos was about to get it in the neck from Mark she ought to be on hand to defuse the situation.

But it wasn't Angelos. It was two men they had never seen before. One was young and red-haired, in tight jeans and a black tank top, and the other was in shorts with hairy white legs; his face was hidden behind a camera – a camera that was making a fast, mechanical whirring sound.

'Mark St James?' enquired Carrot Top, a notebook and pen emerging from his back pocket. 'Didn't wake you, did we?' The camera whirred again.

'What the—' Then, changing tack, Mark hurriedly started to close the door. But he wasn't fast enough. A foot was already in place.

'Just a few words, that's all.' Another whirr from the camera.

'What about?'

'It's about your neighbours across the bay, Christine and Mikey. You did know they were staying here, didn't you?'

'What if I did?'

'Oh, come on,' urged Carrot Top, 'it's the story of the summer. Give us a break. You know what a tough business this is. A word or two is all I need.' Izzy guessed he had slipped into what he imagined was his congenial let's-be-mates-about-this routine. 'Bet your publisher wouldn't say no to a bit of free publicity for you, eh?'

'What my publisher wants doesn't necessarily correlate with what I want. But if it's my neighbours' story you're after, go and see them. I'm sure they'd be as delighted to see you as I am.'

'We can't get near them. They've barricaded themselves in.'

'You do surprise me.'

'So, then, how about it? Why not help us out?'

'Well, boys, I'd love to, but it's like this, I know damn all. Now, if it occurs to me that I could be of any assistance, I'll let you know. Now have a nice day, y'all.'

Izzy had to stop herself laughing at the tone Mark was using. If he put any more syrupy sarcasm into his words they'd be able to make flapjacks with them!

'This your girlfriend, then?' asked Carrot Top, his tactics changing abruptly.

'That's none of your business.'

'Like to say a few words?' Carrot Top leaned in towards Izzy. She backed away. Suddenly it didn't seem so funny. 'Oh, go on, don't be shy. It's . . .' he flicked through his notebook '. . . Izzy Jordan, isn't it? Surely you've got a view that you'd like to share with us. And if not that, what about you and Mr St James saving the lives of that young girl and her boyfriend? Not just drunk apparently, they'd been smoking something a bit dodgy, hadn't they? Nasty combination. Lucky for them you were around. I'm sure you don't need me to tell you it's a great story. So, how about it?'

'I think the expression she's hunting for is "no comment",' said Mark firmly. 'So if you'd be so good as to remove your foot from my threshold, I'd be eternally grateful. And if you don't, I'll have to slam the door on it very hard, very painfully. Now, are we through with the small-talk?'

Reluctantly Carrot Top and his sidekick went on their way, leaving Izzy and Mark to speculate on how they had discovered the runaway lovers' hiding place.

'Do you suppose Dolly-Babe actually carried out her threat?' Izzy asked, when they were sure that the coast was clear and they had taken their breakfast outside. 'I would never have had her down as the type to interfere like that. It seems so vindictive and mean-spirited. What's it got to do with her?'

'No doubt she was as keen as the next person to have her fifteen minutes of fame. And, don't forget, one of the tabloids was offering a reward for anyone who could lead them to the star-crossed lovers.'

'Yes, but surely the Fitzgeralds aren't short of money.'

Mark shrugged. 'Who knows? Things aren't always what they seem.' Then, raising Theo's binoculars to his eyes and sweeping them across the bay, he let out a whistle. 'Take a look.' He passed her the glasses.

'I don't believe it,' she said, after she had focused on what he had seen. Squeezed into the garden at the front of the villa the runaway lovers were renting, there was a cluster of men and women. The cans of lager and cameras were a dead giveaway. Tabloid bounty-hunters without a doubt. And, just as Carrot Top had said, it looked as if Christine and Mikey had barricaded themselves in. The villa's bottle-green shutters were resolutely in place providing an impenetrable barrier for the zoom lenses that were trained on the windows for the first sign of movement from within.

Moving her field of vision further up the hillside, Izzy focused on the villa where Dolly-Babe and Silent Bob were staying. 'Oh, my goodness,' she exclaimed.

'What?'

'It's Dolly-Babe. She's posing for the cameras in a rhinestone-encrusted swimsuit. Lord, you'd think it was *Hello!* taking pictures of her. Here, see for yourself.'

Mark took the binoculars. 'And, if I'm not mistaken, she's being interviewed.' Shifting the glasses a couple of inches to the left, he said, 'Hey, guess what, the same's going on down at the Pattersons' place.'

'What? Ma Patterson in a rhinestone swimsuit?'

'Now, wouldn't that be a sight? No, there's no sign of her. It's your personal cleavage inspector, Pa Patterson, being interviewed.'

As she picked at the bread roll on the table in front of her, Izzy's face was solemn. 'It's not funny, really, is it? And how did that journalist know my name?'

Mark put the binoculars down. 'Odds on that Dolly-Babe has shared more than is necessary. After all, it would be simplicity itself to inveigle any amount of gossip out of her.'

'But why bring us into it? What have we got to do with it?'

'Damn all. But that would never stop a seasoned hack from gathering as much colour and gossip as he could to bulk up a story. You've got to keep in mind that there's no real news back home so they'll get what they can elsewhere. A cheap flight to the sun for a day or two and a nice little scoop for their editor. What do you say to us getting out of here for the day?'

'I'd say let's do it. Let's go somewhere quiet and free of nosy-parkers. How do you fancy Old Períthia?' Old Períthia was the deserted village high in the hills behind Áyios Nikólaos. Max and Laura had taken Corky and Olivia to see it during their visit, but Izzy had missed out on that excursion because she had been resting her ankle.

'Sounds good to me,' said Mark, 'but how will we get there? Is there a bus?'

'We could take Max and Laura's Jeep. She keeps telling me on the phone that we can use it any time we want.'

'There's just one small snag. Will you be able to drive?' He cast his eyes doubtfully to her ankle.

'I don't see why not. But don't you want to drive? I thought men hated being a passenger when there was an opportunity to get their hands on a steering-wheel.'

'Part of my sordid past, I'm afraid. I was disqualified after smashing into a tree while chemically enhanced. I was lucky to walk away. Cowardice has made me reluctant to reapply for my licence.' He looked uncomfortable, his eyes fixed on some far-off point on the horizon.

'Goodness, you've really lived, haven't you?'

He gave a short laugh. 'Why is it that I can never shock you with my past deeds, Izzy? You're supposed to shake your head and tut with disapproval at my wicked recklessness.'

'Mm ... would it help if I did?'

But before Mark had a chance to reply, a movement in the oleander bushes to their right distracted him. His glance froze. A figure was slipping away down the hillside; a flash of red hair told them it was Carrot Top.

'Definitely time to get the hell out of here,' Mark said grimly.

The wind snatched at the map in Mark's hands as Izzy drove along the road towards Kassiópi. She had only driven the Jeep a couple of times so she took it slowly, especially when they had passed Kassiópi and Mark instructed her to take the next left towards the village of Loútses. The road narrowed and instantly became steeper. The higher they climbed the fewer cars they saw and, following the twists and turns through the terraced hillside, they eventually came to an open stretch of road that looked back towards Kassiópi and the stark, yellowish-brown mountains of Albania across the glimmering sea. It was a magnificent view and Izzy stopped the car so that they could take a look. They stood in the breathless heat and, without the noise of the engine, it was blissfully quiet, save for a faraway church bell that was clanging softly, its mellow timbre blending harmoniously with the sweet soprano trill of birdsong. She reached for her camera from the back seat and took several pictures. When she turned round, Mark snapped his own camera at her. 'Not fair,' she grumbled. 'I wasn't ready.'

'Tough.' He smiled and tapped her head, dislodging her baseball cap.

They drove on, climbing ever higher. The increase in altitude made her ears pop and, not long afterwards, they saw a row of cars parked neatly to one side of the road. But she didn't stop. She was determined to park as near as she could to the deserted village. There was no point in pushing it with her ankle, the less walking she had to do the better. Luck was with her. There was a space at the top of the line of cars, into which she managed to squeeze the Jeep.

They followed the well-trodden path and soon came to the first of the ruins. The small single-storey house had lost its door, but had retained its old wooden shutters. Devoid of paint, and now the colour of ash, they hung crookedly from twisted hinges. Through gaps in the stonework, bushy plants grew in wild abundance. Roof tiles lay scattered on the ground, broken and chipped, some ground to dust. They stepped into the gloomy interior. It was unexpectedly dank and chilly. A musty smell of age and decay mingled with the more forceful stench of cat pee. Izzy tried to imagine what it must have been like when a large, boisterous family had lived here, but she couldn't. This soulless, crumbling little house with its dungeon atmosphere was too far removed from the pretty whitewashed homes she had glimpsed during her holiday, with their starched white lace curtains at sparkling clean windows and beaded curtains at the swept and polished doorways.

She slipped her hand through Mark's. 'It's sad, isn't it,' she murmured, 'to see something so uncared-for?'

He didn't reply but led her back out into the bright sunshine where a young German couple were studying their guidebooks. Exchanging smiles, they went on further towards the centre of the village where there was supposed to be a taverna that served lunches. But instead of heading straight for it, they took path through yet more ruins, walking at a slow, leisurely pace, perfectly in step with each other. When they came to a low wall, where a large, ancient olive tree lowered its silvery-leafed branches and provided a welcome canopy of shade in the baking heat of the midday sun, they climbed over the wall and lay on the parched grass. Nobody else had ventured this far and they were alone. Breathing in the smell of wild garlic and listening to the persistent thrum of the cicadas, which in the secluded, deserted place seemed even louder than usual, Izzy closed her eyes and wondered how the crazy media circus was getting on back in Áyios Nikólaos.

Was it really possible that Dolly-Babe had blown the whistle, just as she had threatened at the party? And if it had been her who was responsible, why had it taken a week for the press to arrive? And just how much extra gossip was Dolly-Babe being persuaded to part with? She decided she would ring Max and Laura that evening. If there was any danger of those journalists printing the story about Nick and Sally, it would be better if they knew about it in advance. As for old Ma Patterson, she would probably die on the spot at the thought of her cultured Dulwich friends reading about her younger son's holiday escapade.

While Izzy hoped that Nick had learned something from the near tragedy, she also hoped he wouldn't beat himself up over it too much. The anger that had made Mark lash out at the boy that night had shocked her at the time, but given what he had just forced himself to do, she could fully understand it.

During their first day together, Mark had apologised for his loss of control. Not quite meeting her eye, he had said, 'I'm sorry you had to see me like that, but I lost it. If I'd had the strength, God alone knows what I would have done to that boy.' He had gone on to say how impressed he had been with her life-saving skills. 'You were straight into it. When did you learn how to do that?'

'At school. We have to do regular first-aid refresher courses.'

'Just as well you were such a diligent student. Any chance of you practising some more mouth-to-mouth on me?'

They were in bed and leaning on top of her, he had kissed her long and lingeringly, working his tongue deep into her mouth. Lifting his head, he had said, 'And just why the hell did you let that fool of a boyfriend convince you that you were hopeless in bed, Izzy? Take it from me, you're dynamite.' Holding her close, he had swept away the hair from her face and planted a soft kiss on her forehead. Seeing the scar on her temple, he had said 'How did you get that?'

He had made no comment when she had finishing telling him, but kissed her with such gentle tenderness that her body had ached with desire for him.

'What are you thinking of?'

She opened her eyes, turned her head and saw that Mark was looking at her. 'You've a smile on your face that could melt cheese,' he said.

'I was just contemplating the effect your finely tuned bedroom technique has on me.'

'So, I'm good, am I?'

She sighed, 'Oh, more than good. A supreme artist.' But, wanting to tease him, she added, 'Well, not bad for an old guy.'

He groaned. 'It's a terrible thought, but when you were curled up on the sofa watching *Blue Peter*, I was at university.'

'And what were you doing when *I* was at university?'

He thought about this, as though doing the sums on the eleven-year gap between them. He said, 'Hitting the bottle with a vengeance.' He raised himself up on an elbow. 'And what about your own talent in the bedroom? The King of Comedy can only do his best when he's working with the classiest material.'

Without answering, she plucked at a long piece of grass and used it to trace the outline of his jaw and mouth. His lips twitched and he took the grass from her hand and did the same to her. It tickled and she started to laugh. 'No,' he said, when she pushed him away, 'what's sauce for the goose is good for the gander.' But she ignored him, rolled on to his chest, and snatched the piece of grass out of his grasp. 'You're playing with fire, Miss Jordan,' he warned, and suddenly she was on her back and he was lying on top of her and one of his hands was undoing the button on her shorts.

'Mark, *no!*'

'This one's on me, Izzy, treat yourself. Go with it.' His fingers began to move, slowly, expertly.

'But someone might see,' she whimpered, trying desperately to hang on to reason, but already her body was betraying her and responding swiftly to his touch.

'Who cares? Live a little. Have some fun.'

And she did.

Again and again.

Wave after wave of exquisite pleasure.

She lay in stunned silence afterwards, languid and limp, staring up at the silver leaves dancing in the breeze above them, shocked that he could arouse her so effortlessly. 'That must be an all-time record,' he said, brushing his lips over hers. 'You were over the finishing line before I'd fired the starting gun.'

'It's you. You have this terrible effect on me.'

'I'm glad to hear it, but face facts, my darling, you're a hussy.'

'Oh, Lord, am I?'

'Yes, shamelessly so. But don't ever change, that's just how I like you.'

She closed her eyes. Hussy. It was official; she was a hussy. That's what this gorgeous man with his husky voice and extraordinary life had turned her into. She was a woman who now lay on the sun-baked earth in the scorching heat, experiencing the fastest orgasm known to mankind. She smiled to herself, feeling like the cat who had got more than the cream. How's that for living dangerously? she thought. How's that for dancing naked in the street and kicking over the milk bottles and rattling the dustbin lids? Opening her eyes, she said, 'With Alan I used to fake it, just to hurry things along.'

He lay on his back and laughed loudly. 'Oh, please, keep those confessions coming. I just love to hear them.'

'And what about your previous lovers? Did you have the same effect on them?' She could tell from his silence that she had surprised him.

'Bones asked me much the same question in the clinic,' he said eventually.

'And your answer?'

He shifted his position so that he was sitting with his shoulders resting against the wall. 'As humiliating as it was I had to admit that I made a lousy lover. Probably on a par with your Alan.'

She sat up next to him, her legs stretched out alongside his. Touching the inner side of his thin wrist, she lightly trailed a finger the length of a vein. 'So it was more than just a guy thing, the interest in Alan?'

'Shucks, Izzy, you've caught me out again.'

'So what was the problem?'

'I hadn't met you.'

'No, seriously.'

'I *was* being serious.' He stroked her hand. 'Low self-esteem also played its part, of course. That and the drugs.'

'I thought they kind of buoyed you up, you know, made you want to do it all the more.'

'For some people they do. Maybe in the early stages. But mix it with a barrel-sized cocktail of whisky and vodka and you're lucky if you can walk straight, never mind impress the girls. Cocaine made me feel invincible, as if I was running like the wind, but all I was doing was running on the spot. I was going nowhere.'

'Did no one try to stop you?'

'In the beginning, yes. But you have to remember, I didn't have many friends. Relationships don't last when you're abusing yourself, not when you're self-absorbed and insensitive to anybody else's problems. And, anyway, the few people I knew put my behaviour down to the fact that I'd always been a difficult bastard. Though once I suspected people were looking out for me, I became cunning. I drank on my own, kept things hidden.'

'Even from Theo?'

'Especially from Theo. I couldn't bear to see the disappointment in his face whenever he saw me drunk. He didn't bother with censure, he just tolerated me as though I was a badly behaved child who was letting him down. I'm relieved in a way that he never saw me at my worst, when I thought I could drink myself sober.'

'And what were you like at your worst?'

He let go of her hand and plucked at the parched grass between them. 'Oh, mood swings that covered everything from violent rage to weeping self-pity. A restless and paranoid concern only for myself. A need to put others down before they did it to me. And, most importantly, a hard-nosed determination never to admit I was out of control. I was like the Grand Old Duke of York: when I was up, I was very up and when I was down, I was down on my knees, head in the gutter. I did some pretty awful things and I can't dignify any of them. There are no excuses I can offer.'

Sliding her palm under his hand, she slipped her fingers between his and squeezed them gently. And thinking of the night she had found him all alone in the darkness at Villa Anna, she said, 'Mark, what would happen if you did have a drink?'

'It would probably kill me.' He spoke the words quite calmly, as if he had told her nothing more significant than what time it was. 'I have to accept that I have an addictive personality, and that the programme of recovery I embarked upon all those years ago is with me for life. I'm still in touch with Bones by phone and letter, and once a year I pay him a visit so that he can ask me a lot of absurd questions. He calls it my MOT – Mark's Ongoing Therapy.' He gave her a wry smile. 'Of course, I only go to humour him.'

She smiled too. 'Of course.'

A tiny sparrow flew down from the olive tree above them and landed a few yards from their feet. Keeping very still, they watched it hop towards them as it pecked hopefully, but in vain, at the dusty ground. It soon gave up and flew off in search of more promising pastures.

'So tell me, Izzy. Have I put you off?'

'Put me off what?'

'Getting involved with me.'

'I think I'm already involved with you,' she said softly, and even more faintly, 'heart, body and soul involved.'

'Heart, body and soul,' he echoed, staring straight ahead of him. 'Would that be the same as love?'

Caught between wanting to tear out her heart with her bare hands to give him, and protecting herself from being hurt again, she said, 'I'm not sure. You tell me.'

He turned his head, held her face in his hands, and kissed her lightly. 'We'll have to see, won't we?'

That evening back in Áyios Nikólaos, where the bay was now empty of journalists and photographers, Izzy phoned Laura. She was mortified to learn that Max and Laura had already had several newspapers contact them about Sally nearly drowning.

'All we can do is wait and see what they come up with,' Laura said. 'If there's anything to report, we'll fax you a copy first thing in the morning.'

They spent the night at Villa Petros and early the next morning, when they opened the door of Max's den, Izzy and Mark were horrified at what they found: a long roll of printed fax paper stretched right across Max's desk and cascaded down on to the white-tiled floor.

42

It was all there in hideous black and white.

The exposure of Christine and Mikey's whereabouts in Corfu had been thoroughly detailed, including their subsequent return to England, where, and in the words and pictures of the *Sun*, the *Mirror* and the *News of the World*, Mikey had been reunited with his open-armed parents. Most photographs showed a smiling, cocky lad who looked about twenty and who had clearly had the time of his life. In contrast, the *Mail* showed a picture of Christine, her head bent, her shoulders sagging, her eyes hidden behind sunglasses. For her, the fun was over. Not only was she going to have to face her husband and children but, at the insistence of Mikey's parents, the police had every intention of pressing charges. Izzy felt sorry for her: whatever dream she had been chasing, it had now become a fully fledged nightmare.

With the tawdry details of the runaway lovers exhaustively dealt with – and Mikey had not been shy in giving the tabloid boys what they wanted, though one suspected that any moment his canny parents might get Max Clifford involved – the journalists had gone on to fill up the pages with an exposé of what they called, the Jag-and-gin crowd who holidayed in this idyllic part of Corfu and who were apparently abusing local kindness and hospitality with their careless middle-class arrogance.

Not even the fuzzy reproduction quality of the fax machine could take the edge off the disreputable savagery of the journalists' self-righteous knives. Headline after headline, paragraph after paragraph gave a wildly distorted version of who they all were and what they had been up to. Max and Laura were shown to be wealthy, uncaring parents who had slept on while their drunken daughter's drug-taking friend had nearly drowned. Mr and Mrs Patterson were portrayed as parents who had a lax attitude towards the taking of recreational drugs by their out-of-control junkie sons, with Mr Patterson caricatured as a sixties throw-back hippie who made sleazy low-budget documentaries. And the Fitzgeralds – the ex-croupier and the self-made man – were held up as paragons of moral decency for blowing the cover of an evil woman leading an impressionable young boy astray.

Mark had been similarly misrepresented. 'Bestselling Novelist and One-time Addict Mark St James in Drugs Drowning Drama' was one headline.

Izzy could feel Mark's growing annoyance as together they scanned the long roll of paper. There were several photographs of him; one she recognised from the covers of his books, and another of the pair of them standing wide-eyed and startled in the doorway of Theo's villa – she in just a T-shirt, which mercifully covered everything, and him bare-chested and in his shorts. There was a caption describing her as 'Mr St James's Holiday Companion'. It made her sound as though he had found her through an escort agency. But the paragraph that incensed her most was the one that had been put together as a result of Carrot Top eavesdropping on a private conversation. Mark was portrayed as having a cavalier attitude towards his previous problems, that smashing a car into a tree when off his head was an everyday occurrence for him. Furious, Izzy wondered at Carrot Top's nerve. 'It's so wrong,' was all she could say. 'How dare they do this to you?'

'It's how it works.' He threw the paper on to Max's desk and walked away. She didn't go after him, sensing that perhaps he wanted to be alone. Carefully folding the long piece of paper, she placed it neatly on the desk and phoned Max and Laura.

Within seconds Laura had answered. She sounded upset and told Izzy Max was so angry that he had already been in touch with the company lawyer to see if anything could be done. 'I've never seen him so cross,' she said. Izzy could hear that she was close to tears. 'And we've had Sally's parents on the phone. They're livid and blaming us for what happened. They've called us irresponsible.'

'But that's ridiculous. Sally's an adult. It was down to her what she drank or smoked. You mustn't blame yourself, Laura. Promise me that. Do you want me to come back?'

'No, there's no need. Stay there. We'll be joining you as soon as we can next week. We'd come sooner only I've got a doctor's appointment arranged.'

'Nothing wrong, is there?'

'I doubt it, but Max is insisting I get checked out. You know what a worrier he can be. I keep telling him it's my age, but he won't listen. I think he's anxious that it could be something serious. And wouldn't that be the last thing we need on top of all this? How's Mark?'

'Angry.'

'He needn't be. I thought he came out of it a lot better than the rest of us.'

'Yes, but I get the feeling he doesn't like his past being dredged up in such lurid detail.'

'Well, if you get the opportunity go and see that ghastly Dolly-Babe and tell her she ought to be ashamed of herself for what she's done. And to think I almost felt sorry for her at the party. Now all I feel like doing is wringing her scrawny old neck! My only consolation is that she looks such a tart in the photographs of her sprawled on a sun-lounger with all that cellulite on show!'

'You haven't sent any of those pictures. Why not?'

'Oh, didn't I? Well, I certainly meant to. I'll do it when we've finished talking.'

A short while later, the fax machine sprang into life again and Izzy ripped off the length of paper. Laura was right. Dolly-Babe hadn't fared at all well – not so much *Hello!* as *Oh, My Gawd!*

*

The following morning, because his father couldn't resist reading about himself, Harry was dispatched to the supermarket to buy a copy of every English paper that had arrived in Kassiópi bearing yesterday's news. When he got back to the villa the rest of his family were waiting for him. They each grabbed a paper from him and soon found what they were looking for. Even his mother was eagerly flicking through the pages, despite her earlier protestations that she wouldn't be reduced to such vulgarity.

'I don't believe it,' his father cried. 'They've got my age wrong! How could they think I was sixty?'

'Because you look sixty,' said Virginia. Her tone was cruel and bitter. 'That dreadful Fitzgerald woman has implied that since we're neighbours here, it makes us friends.' Shuddering at the thought, she returned her attention to the paper.

'But sixty!'

'I don't think your age is the issue here, Dad,' snapped Harry. He folded the paper he had been reading and put it aside. 'They've made complete jerks of us.'

'I don't know what you're so worried about, they've barely mentioned you. Probably because you're so boring.'

Harry turned to his brother, tempted, just this once, to put the advantage of his height and weight to good use. Predictably Nick's subdued sackcloth-and-ashes routine had been all too brief; now he was well on the road to reverting back to his old irritating self. It had been too much to expect that the novelty of the reformed character he had sworn to become would last more than a week. 'Blame by association is enough to be going on with, Nick,' he said. He stood up. 'And if you've got any sense, you'll all realise that what's printed here about our family isn't far off the mark.'

He left them arguing among themselves and headed down to the beach where he sat on the pebbles and stared out at the sea. They were returning home in three days' time and he couldn't wait to leave. Spending the summer with his parents had been a crazy idea. He should never have agreed to it. He should have stuck to his guns and gone backpacking round Turkey.

But if he had done that he would never have met Francesca.

He threw a stone into the water and watched the ripples extend further and further in the calm sea. Nothing happens in isolation, he thought. Everything is connected.

He got to his feet and decided to walk into Kassiópi and ring Francesca from one of the public phones in the harbour. He had held off until now, not wanting to push it with her, but after reading all that stuff in the papers he wanted to see how she and her family were taking it.

Mark said goodbye to his agent and rang off. He had phoned Julian to make sure that his wish to keep his private life out of the press would be respected.

He stood at the kitchen window that overlooked the terrace and wondered whether Izzy would mind if they went back to Theo's villa. They had spent the night here at Max and Laura's so that they could be on hand for the first of the faxes, but now he wanted to get on with some work. He was about to interrupt her shower to ask her this when the phone rang. Though he knew it couldn't be for him, he picked it up anyway. Without preamble, a shrill voice demanded to speak to Isobel Jordan. 'I'm afraid she's busy at the moment,' he said.

'Nothing new in that. She's always too busy to speak to her mother.'

Ah, so here was the infamous Prudence Jordan. He leaned back against the wall and settled in for a chat. 'She's in the shower, Mrs Jordan. Can I get her to return your call?'

'A shower at this time of day? But it's nearly lunchtime.'

'Maybe for you but for us it's well past lunchtime. But, then, we don't have any restrictions on the use of bathrooms here.' He couldn't resist tossing in that final comment just to see how she would react. He heard a sharp intake of breath, and sensed her uncurling herself, like a coiled snake.

'To whom am I speaking?'

He smiled to himself. Now the fun would start. 'My name's Mark, and I'm a friend of your daughter.'

He caught another sharp inhalation of breath. 'You're the one in the newspaper, aren't you? You're the drunk she's hitched herself up with.'

He'd had worse, but as opening accusations went, it wasn't bad. 'She may well have hitched up with me, Mrs Jordan, but as for being a drunk—'

'Oh, don't think you can be clever with me, young man. Just because you're a writer, don't imagine for one moment you can twist my words round to make me look silly.'

'I wouldn't dream of it, not when you're so capable of doing that all on your own.'

He missed her reply as, out of the corner of his eye, he saw Izzy come into the kitchen. Fresh from the shower, she was still wet and wearing only a towel, her hair pulled back sleekly from her face. It made her look even younger. He beckoned her over.

'Who is it?' she mouthed.

'Your mother,' he whispered. 'We're getting along like a house on fire.'

Her eyes opened wide and she clutched at the towel. 'Give it to me, let me speak to her.'

After a brief tussle, he passed her the receiver, and in a voice that he knew was loud enough for Izzy's mother to hear, said, 'Say goodbye to the old witch from me, won't you?'

Izzy visibly paled as she took the receiver. 'No, Mum, he was joking. Of course he didn't mean it.'

'Says who?'

'Please, Mark,' she begged.

He put his head next to hers so that he could hear what was being said.

'What's wrong, Mum? Why have you phoned?'

'I might have known you would try and take the innocent approach, but I suppose you're proud of yourself, aren't you, parading your reputation in the papers for all the world to see? Did you stop to think what people would think? Or how it would make me look? It was your aunt who showed me. She rushed straight here soon as she could to have a gloat at my expense. A drunk and a drug addict, the paper says. How could you, Isobel? He'll be totally unreliable. He'll probably get you hooked as well. He'll lie to you and steal from you, they do that. They can't stop themselves.'

'*Mother!* This is ridiculous. Mark's put all that behind—'

'Well, he would tell you that, wouldn't he? But you know what they say, once a drunk, always a drunk. And he'll have brought all his problems on himself, see if I'm not wrong. Weak-willed, that's what he'll be. But be it on your own head. Don't come crying to me when he's used and abused you. Though God knows what he sees in a simpleton like you. Or perhaps that's the appeal.'

This was too much for Mark, and he wrenched the phone out of Izzy's hand. 'I'm well aware, Mrs Jordan, that you've had problems of your own over the years, but the only one who's using and abusing your daughter is *you*! Now, if you don't mind, I'm going to cut you off so that I can try and undo some of the harm you've caused.'

'Well, really—'

But that was as far as Mark allowed her to go. He slammed the phone down and took Izzy in his arms. Tears were filling her eyes and he stroked them away. He kissed her forehead. 'She's going to make a formidable mother-in-law for some poor sod,' he said, lifting her chin and willing a smile back on to her face.

'Only a very stupid man would want to marry me,' she murmured faintly.

'Or how about a very stupid man who was wildly in love with you?'

43

A week later, and with the furore caused by the invasion of bounty-hunters for the British press now behind them, Angelos brought Izzy and Mark the news that somebody new had come to stay in what had been the Pattersons' villa – they had gone home to Dulwich. He also told them that the Fitzgeralds were vacating Villa Mimosa in the next couple of days. With his ear pressed so firmly to the grape-vine, Angelos was able to tell them that Silent Bob had at last got himself a foothold in the property market on the island. He had joined forces with a Norwegian businessman, and between them they were providing the financial backing for a holiday village to be built in the south of Corfu, which would unashamedly appeal to the young crowd. With the contract signed, he was now keen to pack up, return home and see to his other business interests.

Nothing had been seen of the pair, not on the beach, not up at the supermarket, not even in Kassiópi in one of the tavernas. But, then, as Mark had said, the embarrassment of seeing herself in the papers as others saw her was probably keeping Dolly-Babe firmly indoors, away from prying eyes.

The news that the Fitzgeralds would soon be leaving had Izzy suddenly wanting to see Dolly-Babe for one last time: there were questions she wanted answering. She wanted to know how the journalists had unearthed so much about Nick and Sally's near-drowning accident. Details had been printed that Dolly-Babe just couldn't have known. She hadn't been there, so how had she known that Nick and Sally had been drunk, or that they had been smoking an illegal substance? It was possible that Nick might have told the journalists what had happened, but Izzy couldn't imagine Mrs Patterson letting her son speak so unguardedly.

Determined to have her answer, and fired up on curiosity that just wouldn't go away, she decided to go and have it out with Dolly-Babe before it was too late and she lost her chance. Sitting on the terrace with Mark she told him what she had in mind.

Hardly raising his head from his notepad, he said, 'Fine by me, just so long as you don't expect me to come with you.'

'That's okay, I'll go on my own. I'd rather not witness her fawning all over you.'

Now he did look at her. 'Pumpkin pie, you're not jealous of the thing I've got going with that woman, are you?'

She waved his comment aside. 'You're welcome to her, Mark. Just say the word and I'll be on my way.'

He sucked on the end of his pen. 'It's a hard choice, you or Dolly-Babe. You'll have to let me sleep on it. What do you intend saying to her?'

'I haven't decided yet. But one thing I will get out of her is a promise that she'll apologise to Max and Laura tomorrow afternoon when they arrive. It's the least she could do in the circumstances for acting so maliciously. She may have felt slighted over that silliness with Theo, but she went too far in her desire to get her own back.'

'My, my, what a fierce little tiger you've turned into.'

Walking up the hillside in the hot sunshine towards her prey, Izzy did indeed feel as though she had turned into a different person. Not only was she a hussy – a shameless one at that – she was now a predatory cat preparing to pounce on somebody who had hurt her friends.

Well, maybe that wasn't entirely true. It was perhaps only a thin veneer of courage that she had acquired. Not thick enough yet to deal with her mother, she suspected.

After that terrible phone conversation, Izzy had dreaded the telephone ringing again and her mother hurling more words of bitterness at her. Mark's solution was to return to Theo's villa where there would be no danger of Prudence Jordan tracking her down. 'But I'm running away from her, aren't I? I should be able to stand my ground. I should face up to—'

'Ssh,' he had said, holding her tight, 'It'll come. When you're ready, it'll come.'

She hadn't even been brave enough to check the answerphone when she went back each day to make sure that the villa hadn't been broken into overnight. Again, Mark had helped. He had come with her to shield her from the task of listening to any potentially poisonous outbursts from her mother. To her relief, there were no furious messages left for her, only a much friendlier one from Laura giving Izzy their flight details. Tagged on to the end of it was: 'I suppose you're not there because you're with that gorgeous tortured soul again. I hope you're not indulging in unprotected sex, Izzy. See you soon.'

Mark had looked at her with cool amusement. 'Perhaps you ought to ring her and put her mind at rest, tell her that we're being eminently sensible and grown up.'

In bed that night as Mark lay staring up at the ceiling, his hands laced behind his head, he had said, 'What would you do if you did find you were pregnant? After all, condoms do have a failure rate.'

She had frozen into a rigid block of uncertainty. How had he sneaked that up on her so stealthily? And why? When a man asked a question like that it usually meant one thing: that he was getting cold feet. He had never actually said *I love you*, but was he now worrying that he had implied it by his actions? Was he now searching for an escape route? Her mother's triumphant face swam before her: *That's what you get for being so quick to leap into his bed! It's only ever about sex.*

'Um . . . I don't know.'

'But you must.'

Oh, heavens, what could she say? There was no right answer. Tell him she would want to keep the baby and he would think she would use it as a bargaining tool to trap him – *See, now you'll have to marry me.* But say she would get rid of it and he would think she was callous and cold-hearted: a wicked woman quite prepared to throw away his child. It was hopeless, she couldn't win.

In the silence that was stretching uncomfortably between them, he said, 'Let me put it to you this way, would it be so very bad if you were pregnant?'

'But I'm not, am I?' she sidestepped.

He turned to face her. 'What's wrong? It's a simple enough question. Nail it for me, Izzy.'

She swallowed. 'But it isn't that simple. There's more going on behind your words than you're admitting to.'

'Really. Such as?'

'You're ... you're setting a trap for me.'

He rolled on to his side and kissed her. 'Stop trying to make me feel cheap, Izzy.' Pushing back the sheet, he placed a warm hand over her stomach. It was the most loving and tender of acts. 'Do you think I'd make a good father?' There was a look in his eyes and a depth of emotion in his voice she had never seen or heard before.

'No,' she said lightly, the sensual warmth of his palm spreading through her, 'you'd frighten your children to death with your horrific bedtime stories.'

'And if I promised to stick to the Brothers Grimm for their bedtime tales?'

'Mm ... maybe then you'd be okay.'

He lowered his head and pressed his lips to where his hand had been. 'So what's your answer?'

'It depends what you're really asking me.'

'I think you know what I'm getting at. I'm asking how you'd feel, one day, having my children within the context of a death-do-us-part situation.'

Half laughing, but half terrified, she looked at him nervously. Was he serious? 'But, Mark, you scarcely know me. You – you ...' But the words fizzled out. What could she say? As crazy as it was, especially in view of the short space of time they had known each other, she knew that, given the opportunity, and as reckless as it was, she would happily run off into the sunset with Mark, and on any day he cared to name. But was it really possible that he felt the same for her?

'I know what you're thinking,' he said, 'that we haven't known each other for long, but you must feel what I do, that it feels so right when we're together. These last two weeks have been the best of my life. This is more than just a holiday romance between us, Izzy.'

'But supposing it only feels right between us because we're here? Maybe back in England, when it's cold and raining and we're trudging round Tesco's bickering over biological versus non-biological washing powder, the magic won't be there.'

'Then we'll wait and see. I'm not saying that we should rush into anything, I just want us to plan to be together.'

He sounded so sure.

So very intense.

Slipping her arms around his neck, she kissed him. 'By the way,' she said, 'it would have to be non-biological. I have sensitive skin.'

A slow, sexy smile passed across his face. 'Now there's a coincidence. So have I.'

Dolly-Babe was all contrition. 'I can't apologise enough,' she kept saying, as she led Izzy towards the shade of a large candy-striped awning and invited her to sit down. 'I wanted to come and see you all to say I was sorry, but Bob wouldn't let me, and I didn't dare go behind his back. He's so very angry about losing that olive grove, and losing it to a man who tricked us. Though I don't suppose you would have wanted to see me anyway.' Her words were hurried and a little too joined together, her gaze anywhere but on Izzy, and her hands busy with the animal-print sarong that matched her swimsuit, straightening it this way, then that way.

'Is Bob here?' asked Izzy, looking towards the villa, and hoping he wasn't.

'No. He's gone down to Kávos where he's investing in some kind of holiday village. He won't be back till late. It's work, work, work for him. Never stops. But that's my Bob. Never happy unless he's a-wheeling and a-dealing. It's how he's got to be so successful. Millionaire by the age of twenty-eight – did I ever tell you that? Caravan park. Who'd have thought there was any *gelt* in caravans? Can't stand them myself. Horrible things. Give me claustrophobia. Fancy a drink?'

'No, thanks.'

There was a well-sampled bottle of red wine on the table between them and an empty under Dolly-Babe's chair. With shaking hands, she topped up her glass then clattered the bottle down on the table. 'Sure you won't join me?'

Izzy shook her head and wondered if this was what Dolly-Babe's life was like back in England: Silent Bob away all the time, leaving his wife bored and alone, day after day. It made her think of one of Mark's casual throwaway lines about the loneliness of the long-distance drinker. It caused her to see Dolly-Babe quite differently. She saw a determined pride in the older woman's face, a sad need to preserve the façade of her fading youth. She probably thought it was all she had left.

'I suppose you've come here to find out why I got in touch with the papers?'

Izzy nodded. 'Yes, I am. I don't understand why you interfered.'

Dolly-Babe slipped on her sunglasses, and got busy with her sarong again. She was pleating it now. 'How old do you reckon I am?' she asked finally.

Goodness! How on earth was she to answer that? 'Ooh . . . um . . . I don't know.'

'It's okay. I know I'm a figure of fun to young girls like you. But you wait until your only true gift starts to let you down.' Bitterness poured out from her.

'Youth isn't our only asset.'

'It is when you haven't got anything else to offer, such as a brain. Unlike you, I haven't had a fancy education. My learning's been done at the school of hard knocks.' She drank from her glass in a long thirsty gulp. 'I'm fifty-one, and sixteen years ago I proved beyond all doubt that I was a brainless fool.' She fell silent, contemplating the glass in her hand.

Izzy said, 'We've all done things we regret, and it certainly doesn't mean we're any more stupid than the next person.'

Dolly-Babe looked at her sharply. 'How about getting pregnant and giving up the baby? How does that rate on the stupidity stakes? Because that's what I did.'

Izzy was at a loss what to say. She had come here wanting retribution on behalf of Mark and her friends and now she was feeling sorry for Dolly-Babe. 'I don't think that was a mark of stupidity,' she said, finding her voice at last, 'more an act of great courage. It couldn't have been easy for you. What happened?'

Taking another swallow of wine, Dolly-Babe said, 'It was before I'd met Bob. I'd just started work on a cruise ship as a croupier. It was a great life. I was earning good money, travelling the world, and meeting any number of men. Then I got pregnant. There was no way I could keep the baby, and with no one to turn to for help, I had to give it up. I know you're thinking I was being selfish, and probably I was, but at the time having kids wasn't what I wanted. I was having too much fun. So I had the baby, gave it away and went back to my old job. Not long after that I met Bob. But as the years have gone on, I've . . . well, you know . . . I've wondered about him. Yeah, I didn't mention that, did I, that he was a boy? Nice-looking little lad, thatch of black hair like you wouldn't believe, and a cute little nose.' She turned her head, stared down into the bay, her thoughts obviously on that tiny baby she had known for so short a time. 'Gawd, just listen to me!' she said suddenly, with false brightness. 'It's confession time at the OK Corral.' She sniffed loudly and reached for another drink.

'Did you never think of finding him?'

She shook her head violently. 'Bob doesn't know anything about it. He's got very strong views on matters like that. Likes things to be proper, no nasty secrets. The irony is, he's always wanted children, especially a son, but we haven't been able to have any. How's that for a cruel trick on nature's behalf? Punishment or what?'

'You could have adopted?'

'No, like I said, Bob's got strong views, his own, or not at all. And, besides, we were too old by then. We were in our early forties by the time we sussed that he was firing blanks. The adoption agencies would have laughed in our faces.'

'So, the thing with Christine and Mikey was all about your son?' ventured Izzy.

'I know it sounds dumb, but yes, yes, it was. I kept thinking that it could have been my son being seduced by that dreadful woman. Not that I'm saying Mikey's the child I gave away. Gawd, no, I'm not that daft. No, it was just the connection I'd made in my head. It was the age, you know, him being the same as my lad. It seems crazy now, hearing myself say all this. To be honest, it's a bit of a relief.'

'Don't you have anyone at home you can talk to?'

'No. Once I got married that was it. The life I'd led before was wrapped up and put away the moment Bob put this ring on my finger.'

Izzy eyed the impressive cluster of diamonds on Dolly-Babe's hand and wondered sadly if it had been worth it.

Hearing the phone ring, Mark hurried inside to answer it.

'Good and bad news for you,' Theo greeted him, his former good humour completely reinstated, as it had been for some days – to his shame, Mark wasn't so sure that he would have been able to forgive Theo so easily had the tables been turned.

He said, 'Go on, then, give it to me.'

'The good news is that the lengthy discussions I've had with old man Karabourniotis have not been for nothing. I have, at last, acquired the hotels I wanted.'

'Oh, I get it, and the bad news is that you're coming back?'

'Aha, always the step ahead of me, Mark. Yes, that is the bad news, so please, tidy up the love-nest the pair of you have created for yourselves. As from tomorrow you will have to keep the noise down at bedtime. Hearing Izzy's cries as you have her spiralling into a state of ecstasy will be too much of a torment for me.'

'I'll see what I can do.'

They talked some more. Theo wanted to know if there had been any more excitement in Áyios Nikólaos during his extended absence. 'No, it's all gone quiet. The Pattersons left with their tails firmly wedged between their legs. Harry, the only decent one among them, came to say goodbye and to thank Izzy and me for even thinking of saving his brother from drowning.'

'And Dolly-Babe and Silent Bob? What of them?'

'According to Angelos, they'll be leaving pretty soon. In fact, that's where Izzy is right now. She went marching off to extract an apology from Dolly-Babe for Max and Laura who, by the way, are also returning tomorrow afternoon.'

'Ah, that's good. I look forward to seeing Laura. I will be able to resume my flirting with her, now that I am no longer forcing myself to behave in front of Izzy. It will be just like old times. And to celebrate such happiness I will cook us all a meal.'

Finishing their call, Mark went back outside. He blinked in the bright sunlight, and awarded himself a short break from work. He decided to go for a walk along the beach. He didn't bother locking up as he would only be gone a few minutes and, besides, Corfu was the safest place he had ever known. Wasn't that what Theo had said when he had been urging him to come and spend the summer in Áyios Nikólaos?

Less than half an hour later, he was retracing his steps and enjoying a lightness of heart that was becoming familiar to him. Life had taken on a whole new dimension. There was a serene calmness to his days, which gave him a wonderful clarity of thought and hope for the future. Hell, he'd even started talking long-term plans with Izzy. Who'd have thought it?

For so much of his life he had worn bullet-proof armour to protect himself from any attack on his emotions, and now here he was fully exposed and loving every minute of it. What he had with Izzy, he had never known before. The funny thing was it didn't surprise him. There had been no earth-shattering moment of realisation that he loved her, not even a seismic jolt of his heart. It had slowly but surely crept up on him ever since their first meeting back in June.

He would never have believed that in less than two months he could have formed a relationship that had moved on to such a profoundly satisfying level of companionship. He knew, though, that he would do everything in his power to keep it that way. He had experienced very little real peace of mind in his life, and now that Izzy had given it to him, and in such abundance, he'd be damned if he let it slip out of his grasp. Being so perfectly connected with Izzy made him realise how narrow and one-tracked his life had been before. She truly touched the best in him, revealed a side of his personality he hadn't known existed.

And what would Bones make of it all? Would he warn him that there was a danger he might become too dependent on Izzy? Or would he just sit there looking all benign and whistling one of his blasted tunes? What would it be? 'Love Changes Everything' perhaps?

He pushed open the gate to Theo's garden and wandered over to the terrace, wanting to get out of the blistering August heat. He stood with relief in the cool shade of the pergola. He was just thinking of getting himself a drink when he stopped in his tracks. There on the table, where he had been working earlier, was an envelope with his name on it.

The writing was unmistakable – small, cramped and slanting to the left. It was just like all the other letters he had received back in England.

44

Mark sat down to read the letter.

It didn't take long.

All it said was: ARE YOU READY?

He crumpled the piece of white A4 in his hand, crushing it so hard he half expected to see it disintegrate into a pile of dust. He dropped it to the ground.

He bent forward, clasped his head. It was madness. How could this be happening? How had the stalker found him?

The answer came to him in a sickening bolt of comprehension.

How had Izzy's mother known about the pair of them?

She had read it in the newspapers back home, that's how. Even his parents had got in touch after reading about him at their Buckinghamshire breakfast table.

So, thanks to Dolly-Babe and those bloodsucking journalists, his whereabouts had been handed on a plate to whoever was stalking him.

ARE YOU READY?

They were the very same words he had written in *Silent Footsteps*. It was the last communication the stalker made before he killed his victim.

He closed his eyes, rubbed at his temples. This couldn't be for real. Whoever had done this, surely they didn't really want to kill him. Wasn't it just a sick joke that had slipped beyond the usual boundaries of loony-tune behaviour?

He let out his breath, realising that he had been holding it in. A coldness was gripping his insides. His heart was racing, thumping painfully in his chest. His every instinct shouted that this was no joke. Somebody was playing with him in deadly earnest. This was serious. Somebody had a grudge against him and was determined to make him pay for some imagined crime he had committed.

But who?

Who had he ever crossed – and to the extent that they had been prepared to track him down half-way across Europe so they could extract their revenge?

No, it was no joke. For somebody to have come this far, they meant business.

He thought of everyone he knew – or thought he knew – back in Robin Hood's Bay. He pictured the small writers' group he taught in the village hall, seeing their faces one by one. Okay, some pretty off-the-wall folk attended the weekly get-togethers, but not one of them seemed so kooky as to want him dead. Not even Lionel Bridges, whom he had had to take aside one night when the class was over and ask him to ease off the pornography he insisted on writing and reading aloud to the group. Lionel wrote under the ridiculous pseudonym of Shona Mercy, and caused no end of offence and embarrassment to some of the more genteel lady members, including Deirdre, a grey-haired spinster who cleaned for Mark once a week.

Deirdre had full and frequent access to his home and correspondence, which gave her plenty of opportunity and the means to stalk him, but he simply couldn't accept that she had a malicious bone in her body. Since her retirement as a school secretary, she took care of her elderly mother, who was in her nineties and whose health was failing, and now spent her free time writing what he called chintzy poetry.

No, not even the most far-fetched Agatha Christie plot would have her down as a potential killer: she was much too delicate and refined for such rough work. When she had applied for the job as his cleaner he had been so surprised he had asked her why she wanted to do it – he couldn't imagine her baby pink little hands scrubbing out his bath. 'It's not the money, pet,' she had told him, 'I just need to be out from under Mother's feet occasionally.'

Then there was Dale, the young garage mechanic who wrote bloodcurdling Gothic horror à la Bram Stoker and Anne Rice. In fact, he lived and breathed Gothic horror, spending his weekends and holidays working at the Dracula Experience in Whitby – the one-time home of his hero Bram Stoker. With the aid of a pair of fangs and a black cape lined with red silk, his job was to scare the punters, which he said he loved doing. But had the ghoulish world of vampires worn thin for Dale? Had he looked around and seen a more satisfying way to thrill himself?

He went through the other members of the group, but could find no reason for any of them to want to terrorise him, let alone kill him.

He cast his mind further, beyond Robin Hood's Bay to London. Had he offended some writer at one of the countless literary dinners he was invited to? Someone from the Crime Writers' Association perhaps? Someone who felt aggrieved that he had got the award that they had thought was theirs. But that was madness. Okay, the priesthood of crime writers was known for attracting a weird and cranky old bunch who took themselves too seriously, but not your actual real-life murderer, surely?

No, the probable culprit was one of his readers. Somebody he didn't know. An obsessed fan who was psychotically at the mercy of a controlling inner voice. He let his thoughts wander down this more convincing path, recalling any number of strange incidents he had encountered at his book signings, which invariably brought out the anorak crowd. Once, in Leeds, a woman had turned up purely to tear him off a strip for using such foul language in his novels, calling him an affront to the English language. Another time, down in Plymouth, there had been a man dressed in black biker gear with a stark skull of a face. He wouldn't speak but silently, almost menacingly, he had pulled the latest Terry Pratchett book out of a carrier-bag and thrust it at him to sign. Mark had tried to explain that he wasn't

Mr Pratchett, cracking a joke that he wished he was, but the man had deepened the scowl on his gaunt face and pushed the book further towards him. He had signed it just to be rid of the screwball.

But no amount of recollection was helping Mark. It was an exercise he had been through before, anyway. He had got nowhere then, and he was getting nowhere now. With a bitter sense of irony, he thought that maybe it was the publicity department at his publisher's who were behind the letters; after all they had every reason to hate him. Perhaps they had decided to get their own back on him for being such an awkward bugger.

So lost in his thoughts was he that he didn't hear the slow footsteps approaching. Nor did he sense the hands raised behind his head. Not until they were covering his eyes.

'Guess who?'

He leaped in the air so violently he nearly knocked Izzy off her feet. 'Holy shit, Izzy!' he cried, his voice ringing out with raw nervous energy. 'What the hell do you think you're doing?' He fell back into the chair, his whole body flooded with the electricity of so much adrenaline pumping through it. 'You scared me half to death.'

She sat beside him, her face pale with shock.

'I'm sorry,' she murmured, 'it was meant to be a joke. I didn't mean to frighten you.'

He heard the anxious concern in her voice and saw her distress. He forced a smile. 'Hey, it's okay. It's me. My fault. I shouldn't be such a nervous wreck.' And, straining to add some normality to the situation, he said, 'How'd you get on with Dolly-Babe? Did you take her to task?' He took a surreptitious kick at the ball of paper by his foot, knocking it under the table out of Izzy's line of sight.

That evening, and while soaking up the quiet cool of the night and watching the stars come out, Izzy was positive she wasn't imagining it: Mark was acting strangely.

He had spent most of the evening ignoring her, glancing frequently at the growing shadows in the garden as the sky darkened and the trees grew taller and more solid. Restless and uptight, he was withdrawn and uncommunicative. She had asked him several times if he was okay.

'Sure I am,' he had said. 'Why wouldn't I be?' He had spoken easily enough, but his jaw tightened and there was a darkness in his eyes, which were alert beneath the fine sun-bleached fringe.

To gain his interest, she had tried telling him about Dolly-Babe and the baby she had given away all those years ago. But his attention had soon wavered. For something to talk about now, she returned to the subject once more. 'You were right all along,' she said. 'Poor Dolly-Babe certainly has had her problems to deal with, hasn't she?'

'Yeah, I guess it would explain her obsession with the psychic world,' he said absentmindedly, fingers picking at a shoelace, his gaze skimming the top of Izzy's head. 'There's nothing like diverting one's thoughts from the past by trying to predict the future.'

'I asked her how she knew so much about Nick and Sally, and she said she'd got it from Sophia. Apparently Laura had told Sophia everything, so at least my curiosity is settled on that account. And the reason it was a week before the journalists turned up was that at first they didn't believe her. They thought she was just another crackpot, but then they got a tip-off from somebody at the airport.' Izzy could see that she had lost him again, that his mind wasn't even half on their conversation – so where on earth was it? 'And later I thought I'd tie you to the bed and tickle you with a feather duster,' she added.

'Yeah, that makes sense.' His gaze had switched to the far end of the garden and his fingers were drumming an irritating tattoo on the table.

'Or would you prefer a wet kipper?'

'Whatever you think. I'll leave it to you.'

After a long pause, his fingers stopped moving. He turned sharply. 'A wet what?'

'Ah, I've got your attention now, have I? Come on, Mark, tell me what's wrong. Ever since I got back from Dolly-Babe's you've been acting oddly.' She saw him hesitate and knew then with certainty that something had happened when she had been away from him. 'Did someone phone you with bad news? It's not Theo, is it?'

He shook his head. 'It's nothing. Nothing that you need worry about.' His tone was casual but not convincing.

'But if something's bothering you—'

'Please, Izzy, just leave it. I don't want you involved. In fact you're the last—' But he stopped himself short. 'Forget it, it was ... it was my publisher, that's all. They always rattle me like this.'

As Izzy slept, Mark lay wide awake beside her. The room was unbearably hot. It was the hottest and muggiest night he had known, but nothing would persuade him to open a window. While Izzy had been in the bathroom getting ready for bed, he had checked all the doors and windows, making doubly sure that they were locked. Coming out of the bathroom Izzy had commented on the stuffiness of the bedroom and had suggested she open a window to let some air in, but he had told her not to, that he was fed up with being bitten in the night by all the mosquitoes that made straight for him. Accepting this without argument, she had climbed into bed and fallen asleep almost immediately, her head resting against his shoulder.

As sleep continued to elude him, he thought of what he had said to Izzy outside on the terrace, or what he had very nearly said – *I don't want you involved. In fact you're the last ...* What he had been going on to say was that Izzy was the last person he wanted anywhere near him right now.

If a crazy psycho had come here to Áyios Nikólaos to satisfy an inner voice that was telling him to kill Mark St James, then what was to stop him having a go at Izzy as well?

He didn't know what to do for the best.

Should he get Izzy the hell out of here and on a plane back to England – frightening her silly in the process – or should he keep quiet and go on watching their backs until the threat had passed?

But the threat might not pass.

If the stalker was going to stick to the script of *Silent Footsteps*, an attempt would be made on his life.

He had never felt surer about anything.

45

The day started as idyllically as any other morning Izzy had woken to during her holiday – the sky was a faultless blue, the sun dazzling, the air fragrant with the scent of pine, and the sea glimmering peacefully in the bay below – but a cloud of tension hung over her, and it just wouldn't go away.

It emanated from Mark, and nothing he said or did helped to lift the bad feeling that had descended upon her since yesterday evening. Every time she looked at him she could see that he was unreachable, that his distracted thoughts were elsewhere. His troubled face and distant eyes only confirmed her belief that something was terribly wrong. Though he had sat at the table in his usual working spot in the shade, she knew he hadn't written a single word all morning. She had frequently caught him staring at her, his expression dark and puzzling. It was as if he was worried about her. But why? Or had she got it wrong? Had she annoyed him? Had she said or done something?

She had tried wheedling the truth out of him, but had got nowhere. He was a firmly closed book to her. He didn't seem to want her near him, preferring to sit in remote silence, yet neither did he want her where he couldn't see her. When she had said she was going down to the beach for a swim, he had asked her what was wrong with Theo's pool.

'Nothing,' she had said. 'I just fancied a dip in the sea. It'll be cooler.'

'Then I'll come with you. I could do with a change of scene.' He was on his feet before he had even got the words out.

Now, and while she swam in the refreshing water, he was sitting on the shore, tense and watchful, his hand shielding his eyes from the glare of the sun as he scrutinised her every movement. And scrutinised everybody else's movements on the beach. Especially anyone who came near her.

'Paranoid' was the word that kept going through her head.

It was as if a switch had been flicked inside him and he had become a different man. A man who jumped at the slightest movement or sudden noise; a man who suspected trouble at every turn.

What on earth had got into him?

She was so concerned, she wished that Theo was here already. He was arriving later that afternoon, but for Izzy his arrival couldn't come fast enough. She felt sure that if anyone could get Mark to relax and open up, it would be Theo.

Not in any particular hurry to get home, Theo ignored the turning for

Áyios Nikólaos and drove on to Kassiópi so that he could buy what he wanted to cook for dinner that evening. Parking his car between two open-topped Jeeps, he strolled round the harbour to his favourite bar for a drink before he went shopping. He greeted its owner, Michalis, with a warm handshake and asked how business was.

Michalis gave the obligatory could-be-better shrug and said, '*Étsi kyétsi.*'

Theo smiled, knowing that business was always good for Michalis. As well as this popular harbour bar, he also owned several apartments in Kassiópi, another bar up in Róda, and a villa in Majorca, where he and his wife spent their winters once the olives had been harvested from their highly productive olive groves. '*Étsi kyétsi*' meant that Michalis was confident he would be banking enough money this season to extend his interest further on the island, ready for next spring. 'And your mother?' Theo enquired. 'The last I heard of her from Sophia and Angelos was that she had been unwell.'

'Ah, plenty of life in her yet,' Michalis said, with a hearty laugh, 'Eighty-five and still able to lift a shovel. She was helping my son, Andonis, to repair a drain only the other day.'

'You work her too hard,' remonstrated Theo.

Michalis threw his hands in the air. 'It is her, not me, she is not happy unless she is busy. You know how it is.'

Theo knew exactly how it was. Greek women: the older they got, the more determined and fiercely independent they became. His grandmother had been the same. Despite advice and warnings from her doctor to slow down, she had continued to live her life just as she had always lived it: to the fullest. Taking it easy had been anathema to her.

Waiting for Michalis to bring him his drink, Theo watched a brightly painted caïque disgorge a group of noisy, sunburnt tourists, most of whom started heading towards Michalis' bar. Still dressed in his expensive handmade suit, and despite having removed his tie and unbuttoned his collar, Theo knew that the contrast between his appearance and that of this crowd of scruffy holidaymakers could not have been greater. One man, wearing only shiny football shorts and trainers and a pair of boxer shorts on his shaved head – was this the ultimate in sun protection? – was staring at him as though he were mad. One of us has a problem with his mental faculties, thought Theo, as he removed his jacket and hung it carefully on the back of his chair, but it is not me.

Michalis brought him his oúzo and ice, and after a further exchange of words, he left Theo alone so that he could tend to the needs of the rest of his customers – the Full English Breakfast Plonkers, as he called them, the ones who thought plates of chips and mushy peas were sold the world over. 'What? No mushy peas, mate? Are you having me on?' But in spite of their ridiculous foibles, the British punters were well liked here: their plump wallets were open all hours when they were on holiday. Unlike those of the Scandinavians, who, according to Michalis, were so tight they preferred to stay in self-catering accommodation and cook for themselves.

Sipping his drink, and his thoughts turning closer to home, Theo wondered if he would be successful in hiding his feelings of envy and disappointment when he saw Mark and Izzy together. Though he had gone to great lengths to convince Mark that he held no grudge towards him, he hadn't been able to pretend to himself that he was happy with the way things had worked out. The trick was to make light of the matter, he knew, which so far he had managed to do. But that had been on the telephone when there had been no danger of his expression betraying him. He had deliberately lied to Mark about the necessity of prolonging his stay in Athens – he had acquired the chain of hotels early on – but he had not had the courage to return home immediately. So he had stayed and immersed himself in work; routine stuff he could easily have organised by phone, fax or e-mail from the comfort of his villa here on Corfu. From somewhere he had found the strength to tease Mark that it was so good and generous of him to let the eager lovers have their time together. Not a word had he said about his own cowardly need to keep away because he didn't trust himself to behave in a reasonable manner.

He had always viewed Mark as the brother he had never had. Well, now he felt like calling in a brother's privilege, that of knocking Mark's teeth out for stealing his girl!

He drained his glass, left what he owed Michalis on the table, and crossed the harbour to the shops. It was time to get on. Time to stop feeling sorry for himself and maybe even admit that, on this occasion, he had lost to a better man.

Izzy was in the shower after her swim and, knowing she would be there for some time yet, Mark went outside. Taking a deep breath, he steeled himself and pulled an envelope from his pocket.

It had been waiting for him when they came up from the beach, casually left on the doorstep for anyone to see. Luckily Izzy hadn't spotted it – she had been hanging her towel over the line between the two olive trees at the side of the house, and he had stuffed it into his pocket before she reappeared.

Glancing over his shoulder to check that she hadn't cut short her shower, he ripped open the envelope.

I'VE CHANGED MY MIND. IT WON'T BE YOU.

That was it.

It might not appear much, but in essence it paved the way for a whole new nightmare. The stalker was writing his own script now.

I'VE CHANGED MY MIND. IT WON'T BE YOU.

It could mean only one thing. The deranged person had changed his mind over his choice of victim.

With shaking hands he slid the note back inside the envelope. What the hell was he going to do? The intent of the threat could not be clearer. Whoever it was must have been spying on him and Izzy and decided to hurt him in the worst possible way. He was going for Izzy, he just knew it.

How could he protect her?

He paced the terrace, his thoughts tumultuous and chaotic. He forced his brain to think straight, to conjure up a credible solution.

Home.

That was it.

Get Izzy home to England.

Hide her.

Keep her safe.

But as fast as these thoughts flitted through his head, he knew it wouldn't work.

Hiding, running, how long could that go on? How long could he live with the uncertainty? He suddenly thought of the day he had confessed to Izzy about using her in his latest novel, when he had also admitted that he didn't know what would ultimately happen to her character. He remembered her smiling and saying, 'Oh, well, if it's all the same to you, I'd prefer to live.' He recalled too, his response: 'I'll see what I can do.'

The memory of those glibly spoken words made him feel physically sick. Sick, because when confronted with the real thing he didn't know how the hell he was going to protect her.

As if realising he was still pacing the terrace, and that it served no purpose, he came to an abrupt stop, spun on his heel and bolted inside the villa, fear and despair driving him to make sure Izzy was all right. He banged on the bathroom door and called to her, 'You okay in there?'

The door opened almost instantly. 'Yes, why, have you come to soap my shoulders for me?' She smiled at him as she wrapped herself in a towel. 'Because if so, you're too late. Or maybe there was a certain scene from *Psycho* you wanted to run through with me?'

He couldn't think of anything to say, so he forced himself to smile and pulled her hot damp body to him. He squeezed his eyes shut, blocking out the gruesome image to which she had just alluded and the indisputable and painful truth in all this mess: if anything happened to Izzy, he would never know peace of mind again.

Theo had been in the villa only a short while – he had scarcely exchanged his suit for a pair of shorts to go swimming – before he knew that something was wrong.

At first he had put it down to the three of them feeling uncomfortable with each other and, given the circumstances, it was perhaps to be expected. But he had soon realised that he was picking up on a much greater problem. Had the happy couple had a falling-out already?

'You are acting the part of a genuinely possessive lover, eh?' he said to Mark, when they were alone by the pool, and alone only because Izzy had insisted that she returned to Max and Laura's villa to be there to greet them when they arrived from the airport. Theo had been surprised at the strength of Mark's vehement objection to her going, but had said nothing, watching instead the agitated manner in which he had tried to dissuade her. He had even suggested that he go with her.

'No,' she had laughed, 'that's not fair to Theo. You stay here and chat while I make sure everything's ready for Max and Laura.'

'But Sophia and Angelos have seen to that. They were there this morning. What else needs doing, for pity's sake?'

But his words hadn't detained her and she had gone with an assurance that they would all be together that evening for supper.

Getting no response from Mark about him being a possessive lover, Theo said, 'You will scare her off if you continue to treat her like a caged bird.' He floated on his back, stared up at the cloudless blue sky and waited for Mark to say something. A tiny, wholly unworthy part of him was pleased that all was not well between him and Izzy.

'When you've finished your swim, I want to show you something,' Mark said.

Theo rolled over on to his front and swam to the shallow end of the pool where Mark was looking down at him. 'You sound serious. What is it?'

'Finish your swim, then I'll tell you.'

He raised himself out of the water, shook the water from his hair, and wrapped a towel around his waist. 'It is finished. I am at your disposal.'

Mark led him across the garden, up the steps of the terrace and inside the villa. To Theo's surprise, Mark took him into his study where he opened one of his desk drawers. 'I hope you don't mind me hiding these here, but I didn't want Izzy to see them. You'll understand why. The first came yesterday, the other today.'

Theo took a crumpled piece of paper from Mark's outstretched hand, a neatly folded one too. 'Tell me this is a coincidence, Mark,' he said, after he had read the two letters. 'Or, better still, convince me that all authors get strange mail like this when they're on holiday.'

'I wish I could. I wish, too, that I didn't feel so genuinely scared by whoever is behind them. He must have seen me in the newspapers back in England and come out here straight away. I might just as well have mailed him your address. God, Theo, if this lunatic's intention is to frighten me, he's doing a bloody good job of it.'

All the petty, rancorous thoughts of a few moments earlier were gone as Theo stared at the letters. Now he felt nothing but protective concern. 'His actions prove beyond doubt that he is serious, Mark, and I'm afraid I don't believe that he only wants to frighten you. My instinct says that his intentions go further than that.' Theo understood now, all too clearly, that what he had thought were the actions of a possessive lover had been a rational man's attempts to keep the woman he cared for safe, and without alarming her. 'Mark, if this person really wanted to hurt you, how do you think he would go about it?'

There was no hesitation to Mark's reply. 'You know the answer to that as well as I do. He would try to harm somebody who mattered to me.'

'Then we have to act. We must go to the police.'

'Other than providing us with a round-the-clock guard to catch our stalker red-handed as he plays Mr Postman again, I don't think they can do anything.'

'If that is what it takes, then that is what I shall insist upon. You must bear in mind, Mark, that the Greek police are not the same as your soft English bobbies. Here on Corfu they take a firm line with anyone they consider to be having a detrimental effect on another person's well-being.

They enjoy a very real sense of power, and because they carry a gun they have a bark that is as fierce as any bite, believe me.'

'Okay, if you think there's a chance of them helping, then so be it.'

'Good. Tomorrow morning we will go together into Kassiópi and show this stalker that he has made a gross error of judgement by coming here to play his sadistic games. This man has to be found, he has to be confronted once and for all, or this madness could carry on for ever. If he is allowed to, he will keep you dangling by threatening to kill those closest to you until he has driven you insane.'

'Thanks for making it such a stark reality for me.'

'I am only saying aloud what you must have already thought. Now, why don't we go and see how Izzy is getting on? She should not be out of our sight. We need to ensure that somebody is always with her. I would suggest also that you do your best to settle her mind. I could tell from her manner and the way she was looking at you that she is worried about you. Try to make light of the fact that you have been acting strangely. And while the police are hunting your stalker, I think it would be a wise precaution if I take you both to stay with me in Athens.'

'But won't that alert Izzy and make her think something is wrong?'

'I will word my invitation so beautifully she will not be at all suspicious of our motives. Come, Mark, trust me, have I not always taken good care of you?'

46

Darkness had closed in around them and in the soft glow of candlelight Izzy could feel the anxiety of the last twenty-four hours gradually loosen its hold on her. Max and Laura were in wonderfully high spirits, laughing and joking throughout dinner, bouncing their good humour off Theo, and making it impossible for the rest of them not to respond with equal ebullience. Even Mark seemed more relaxed. She glanced at him over a flickering candle; his eyes no longer held the tense, distracted look they had worn earlier. She wondered if Theo's arrival had helped him resolve whatever problem had been bothering him, because since Theo's return he had been a lot less edgy. He caught her watching him and, giving her a small smile, he extended a hand across the table. She reached out and touched just the ends of his fingers with the tips of hers. It was a deliberately discreet and intimate gesture, which Izzy had thought would go unnoticed by the others. But she was wrong.

'No, no, *no!*' cried Theo from her left. His voice was so loud, so sudden, it made her start, and without any warning, he slapped his own hand down on top of theirs. 'I will not allow it,' he said sternly. 'I refuse to sit here playing the hairy green gooseberry. Is it not bad enough that I have to put up with watching Max and Laura acting like a couple of young teenagers? Must I endure your mishy behaviour as well?'

'It's *mushy* behaviour,' laughed Max, putting an arm around Laura's shoulders. 'And, anyway, a man can't help loving his wife, especially one as beautiful as mine.' He kissed her cheek, then with his lips against her ear he whispered something. Laura gave him a small nod, and Izzy noticed a particular smile on her lips that she now realised had been there ever since her friends had arrived at the villa that afternoon. Except now it was bigger.

'We only found out yesterday,' said Max, his face breaking into a grin that widened by the second, 'and it just goes to show that you're never too old. Laura and I are doing a Tony and Cherie Blair, we're going to be parents all over again. And just so that you know how to react, we're both as pleased as punch. Well, now that the shock's wearing off, we are,' he added.

Izzy went straight to Laura and hugged her. 'That's such amazing news. Congratulations. I suppose that explains why you were so tired all the time. Did you have any idea?'

'None whatsoever. At my age pregnancy isn't the first thing that springs to mind when you're feeling under the weather, especially as I've been taking the pill all these years, if a little slapdashly at times. I thought perhaps the heat was getting the better of me. Or, worse, that I was entering the twilight zone of hot flushes and dizzy moments. But Max insisted I saw a doctor when we were in England and, hey presto, one pregnant geriatric mother diagnosed.'

Shaking Max's hand and smiling broadly, Theo said, 'You old dog, Max, it seems I have thoroughly underestimated you!' Then he leaned across the table and kissed Laura. 'Congratulations, my darling, I'm so pleased for you. It is indeed heart-warming news.'

Laura smiled. 'You don't think we're too old?'

'Heavens, no!' said Izzy. 'Though Max might have to start his training sooner rather than later if he isn't going to bring shame on the family name at all those school sports days you've got to look forward to now.'

Max groaned. 'Oh, thanks, Izzy. But I'm hoping by then they'll have invented the three-legged zimmer-frame race.'

'And what does Francesca have to say to this good news?' asked Theo.

'Her exact words were: "Well, Dad, I always wanted a baby brother or sister to boss around, so I guess this is better late than never."'

'And Corky and Olivia, what do they think of you two rascals?'

'They're delighted. As are my parents. My mother is thinking that perhaps she could go in for some kind of fertility treatment and get in on the act.'

'Well, I think it is quite brilliant what you have done,' said Theo, 'and I look forward to next year when you spend your summer here with little Sinclair junior.' He suddenly clapped his hands. 'This is definitely something to celebrate. Champagne it is! We must drink to your good health and for a baby boy as even-tempered as his beautiful mother.'

'You wouldn't by any chance be ignoring the possibility that it might be a girl?' suggested Mark.

Theo shook his head decisively. 'No. My intuition says that it will be a sturdy little boy to keep his father on his toes.' He rose from his chair.

'Would you like some help, Theo?' asked Izzy, also rising to her feet and hoping he would say yes. It seemed an ideal chance to get him on his own and talk about Mark: until now there had been no such opportunity.

'Thank you, Izzy, that's very kind of you.'

But they were alone only for a few moments, and before Izzy had so much as decided on her opening gambit, Mark appeared in the kitchen with a stack of dirty plates.

'I thought I'd bring these in,' he said, opening the dishwasher and bending down to it.

'You see, Izzy?' said Theo, as he pulled out a bottle of Veuve Clicquot from the bottom of the fridge. 'You see how he doesn't trust me for a single minute to be alone with you. He comes in here under the pretext of being helpful, but really he wants to be very sure I will not push you down on to the kitchen table and kiss you long and hard. I pose an interesting threat to him, eh?'

'The day I feel threatened by you, Theo, is the day the sun stops shining.

Now, shall we just get on with serving the champagne? Laura says she only wants a small glass and I'd like some more water.'

'Oh, Izzy, can you hear the harsh quality to his words? Are you sure you would not like to reconsider what you have got yourself into? It isn't too late to change your mind. A lady is allowed to do so.'

'But this one has no intention of doing so,' said Izzy, glad to hear the familiar put-downs between Mark and Theo. After the stilted conversations she had had with Mark since yesterday, it came as a refreshing change to listen to their customary rivalry. 'And if I could get a word in between you two,' she added, 'you're going to have to give me a clue where you keep your glasses, Theo.'

He pointed to a cupboard, gave her a tray, then said to Mark, 'She is insolent as well as stubborn, that girl, you will need to watch her.'

'Something I have every intention of doing,' replied Mark, as Theo went ahead with the bottle, which he was going to open outside. And, wanting to assure Izzy that all was well – just as Theo had instructed him to do earlier that afternoon – Mark took the tray of glasses she had just arranged and set it on the dresser behind them. 'I'm sorry I've been so preoccupied lately,' he said, holding her hands, 'I should have warned you that I get like that sometimes. I hope I haven't upset you.'

She looked at him as though carefully considering his words. He thought for a nasty moment that she didn't believe him, that she had guessed the truth. 'But you're okay now?' she asked.

Relieved that she didn't seem to have rumbled him, he rested his hands on her shoulders, drew her closer. 'Right now at this very minute I'm more than okay. What man in his right senses wouldn't feel completely okay if he were standing here in my shoes?' He kissed her deeply. Then he slipped his hands around her waist, determined to convince her that he was his old self, and said, 'Now what exactly was it Theo had in mind for you on the table?'

She laughed and laced her fingers behind his neck. 'Never mind Theo, what do *you* have in mind?'

'Why, Sugar Lips, you're doing it again. You're leading me astray.'

'Only following your lead, Mark. Nothing more.'

He kissed her once more. But only briefly. 'Come on, we'd better get back out there or we'll never get any peace from Theo.'

'So there you are,' said Max, when they reappeared on the terrace, 'We were just debating whether we'd have to resort to glugging the bubbly straight from the bottle.'

'And don't tell me that would be a first for you,' laughed Izzy.

Taking the tray of glasses from Izzy, Theo poured them their drinks, and while everyone entered into the spirit of out-toasting one another, Mark once again let the conversation go over his head. He was finding it an impossible strain to pretend that everything was fine. Staring into the dark night sky, he noticed that a strong warm breeze had sprung up and was sending eerie patches of thick cloud scudding across the moon. In front of him, just a few inches away, the candles on the table were flickering as the wind almost blew them out. He wished with all his heart that the wind was strong enough to blow away the weight of worry and fear that was dragging him down. Despite Theo's confident assurances that all would be well – that they could disappear to Athens leaving the local police to track down the stalker – he simply didn't believe that matters could be so easily resolved. His lack of faith in Theo's unshakeable convictions reminded him of the waking-in-the-middle-of-the-night sensation he occasionally experienced when his subconscious was working overtime on a plot that wouldn't come together as he wanted it to. It was as if there was an important detail he and Theo were both overlooking; a fatal flaw in their logical reasoning.

He tuned back into the conversation just in time to hear Theo hotly defending his nation. 'Believe me, Greece's domestic economic health is better than you English like to think it is,' he was saying, 'its international standing in the wider community is—'

'Hey, there's no need to get so defensive, Theo,' Mark cut in irritably, 'Everyone sitting round this table knows the contribution you make towards keeping the domestic economy afloat here, and we're all very proud of you. So give it a rest, will you? I thought this was a party and that we were meant to be enjoying ourselves.'

'Hear, hear,' agreed Max.

Theo rolled his eyes. 'Please, the pair of you, take your patronising sarcasm and stick it up your anally retentive English jacksies!'

'But that's where we keep your precious Elgin Marbles.'

'Max Sinclair, now you are just playing dirty with me. How did I ever get involved with such a disreputable bunch of people? What have I ever done to you to deserve this cruel treatment? Truly, sitting here with you, I cannot think of anything worse. Hand on heart, you are my worst nightmare.'

They all laughed, but then, and in the midst of the light-hearted moment, a disembodied voice said, 'None of you has any idea of what a worst nightmare is. But after tonight, well, maybe you just might.'

Their laughter died instantly. Coming towards them in the shadowy darkness was the figure of a man, and though Mark could make out little more than a silhouetted outline, he saw all too clearly that the man was holding a gun, and that he was pointing it straight at him.

47

Mark's first thought was: this is it.

His second thought was to take charge and make sure no one fancied himself a hero.

'Nobody move,' he whispered, scarcely opening his mouth to speak when the initial gasps of alarm had passed and silence had fallen on them. 'It's me he's come to see, so just sit tight.'

He sounded so much calmer than he felt. Gooseflesh was running amok all over him and the rush of adrenaline coursing through his body was greater than any chemically induced hit he had ever experienced: his heart was pounding as if it would burst clean out of his ribcage. Squinting, he tried to get a better look at the man.

Whoever he had imagined to be behind the letters, it was not this thin, ageing, insignificant little man hiding in the shadows. It was tempting to think that they could easily outfight him. But though they undoubtedly had size and numbers on their side, this lunatic sure as hell had the upper hand: he had a gun.

Rising slowly from his seat, so slowly it was hurting the muscles in the backs of his legs, he tried to move a little nearer. His movements were too obvious, though, and the man started waving the gun, acting every inch the madman who wouldn't think twice about using it. But then he probably was a madman, wasn't he, and thinking twice was an occupational hazard he would avoid at all costs?

'*Sit down!*' They all jumped at the voice that screeched crazily out of control. Laura clutched at Max who had his arm around her, and Izzy, her eyes frantic with terror, reached out to Theo. 'I said sit down!'

'Do as he says, Mark,' urged Theo, his expression pleading with him not to do anything that would endanger their lives.

But ignoring both his friend's words and those of his stalker, Mark calmly held up his hands in a see-no-tricks-up-my-sleeves gesture. 'It's okay,' he said. 'It's me you want, and it's me you've got. Let's talk.' He moved a few inches further forward, his main concern now to shield Izzy. Her place at the table meant that she was nearest to this nutter. The man might be pointing the gun at Mark, but that last letter had said, I'VE CHANGED MY MIND. IT WON'T BE YOU.

'Who says I want to talk?' The question was defiant, the tone level.

'If you've come here to kill me, I think the least you can do is explain why.' From his side, Mark heard Izzy let out a small cry of disbelief. He willed her not to say anything. Please, God, don't let her move. Make her invisible. 'So how about it?' he continued, stealing another small step on his pursuer. 'After all, it's a condemned man's right to have one last request.' How reasonable he was making it sound. He could have been negotiating with a salesman in a car showroom, asking for alloy wheels to be thrown in for free.

'I know what you're doing,' the man said, 'I'm not a fool. You think a bit of negotiating will solve this. It won't. Though if it's talk you want, then, yes, I'll go along with you. But you stay right where you are. No nearer, do you hear?'

Knowing that it might be his last chance, Mark gave an exaggerated shrug of agreement and stepped neatly in front of Izzy; the first part of his mission accomplished. Now all he had to do was play for sufficient time for a miracle to happen. 'So who are you?' he asked.

The man's response was to tilt back his head and laugh. It was a horrible, twisted laugh. The sign of a man who had slipped into that dark place of the soul where right and wrong had crossed over. 'I'm disappointed in you,' he sneered. 'I know it's been a long time, but I would have thought your powers of deduction would have made the connection by now.' And, as if it had been planned right down to the exact second, he moved forward, the clouds that had been covering the moon slid by and a shaft of silvery light shone down on the terrace. The man's face was suddenly, and shockingly, visible.

Recognition hit Mark with a sickening bolt of horror. Take away the wilderness of grey hair, the pallid skin that was wrinkled and loose, the stoop of the wire-thin shoulders and it was Mr Percival ... Niall's father. 'But ... but why?' he murmured, finally finding his voice. 'Why are you doing this?'

There was another burst of hideous laughter, and a look of pure malice in the eyes that stared back at Mark. 'Because I hate you. I've hated you for thirty years. You as good as murdered our only child. It was your fault he died.'

'But I was a child myself.' The defensiveness in his words made Mark feel as if he had never moved on from being that frightened boy of twelve who had clung to an upturned hull of a boat while the waves had crashed over him.

'You were a devil child. You were always making Niall do things he didn't want to do. You were a wicked, malignant influence on him. It should have been you who died, not Niall.'

'Don't you think that there were times when all I wanted to do was to turn back the clock? Didn't you ever consider that I'd spent most of my life wishing it had been me who had drowned?'

'Easy words now when you're trying to save your own skin. But I know you're incapable of feeling any real emotion. Real emotion was living with that nightmare every day, coming home from work and knowing my son wouldn't be there. Waking up in the morning and knowing—' His voice broke, but he quickly carried on again. 'It was too much for his mother. She never recovered, never had a happy thought in her head. Because of what you did, grief drove her mad. She spent most of her time shut away in a psychiatric hospital, not knowing what day of the week it was, not knowing who I was. As surely as you killed Niall, you destroyed her. Thanks to you, she took her own life eight months, one week and two days ago. So, tell me, how does it feel to be accountable for two deaths?'

Numb with the realisation that this man had suffered so much, was so desperate to square the account, and that the evening could only have one tragic outcome, Mark couldn't speak. He couldn't even shake his head to deny what he was being accused of. And, despite the intense warmth of the night, he felt chilled to the bone. Sweat was pouring off him, running down his back, trickling between his shoulder-blades. He tried to think straight. Tried to concentrate on what Niall's father had just told him, to make sense of it.

Eight months ago when his wife had killed herself, that was January . . . in February *Silent Footsteps* had been published . . . A week later he had received the first of the letters. He forced himself to speak, to wrench the words out of his parched throat. 'So you want revenge for both those deaths? Is that what you've come here for?'

'Doesn't that seem reasonable?'

'No. I'm sorry, it doesn't.' For a surreal moment they were back in the car showroom and he was haggling over those bloody alloy wheels again.

'And I am sorry too, but this has gone on for long enough. It is time for this madness to stop.' It was Theo, up on his feet and standing next to Mark.

Swinging his arm, Niall's father pointed the gun at Theo. '*I* will decide when this comes to an end. Not unless you want to die first.' His eyes had turned glassy and his face glistened with a sheen of sweat. His expression was that of a frenzied killer.

'Please, Theo,' Mark murmured, 'no heroics. Sit down and let him say what he needs to say.' Keeping his gaze steadfastly on the gun, he sensed, rather than watched, Theo reluctantly sit down. He took a deep, steadying breath, and knowing all too well that negotiating their way through this was their only hope, the dialogue, such as it was, had to be kept going. He said, 'If you'd hated me for so long, why didn't you kill me before? Why wait?'

'Oh, don't get me wrong, I thought about killing you all those years ago. Night after night when I couldn't sleep, I saw myself taking you out in a boat and leaving you to drown. Some nights I would imagine myself holding you under the water, watching you flail your legs and arms just as Niall must have done. It didn't help with the insomnia, but it was better than counting sheep.'

'Oh, God help us, you're one sick bastard.'

It was Max who had spoken, and Niall's father's eyes hovered maniacally over him. Terrified that he might just go ahead and squeeze the trigger for the sheer hell of it, Mark distracted him by saying, 'So what stopped you?'

The unhinged gaze swivelled back to him. 'I wanted you to suffer. And I knew that, in a small way, you already were.'

'You knew about my addiction?'

'Oh, yes. I knew all about that. I knew everything you were doing. I made it my business to shadow you.'

'You were stalking me even then?'

'Every step. I saw what you were doing to your family, how you were making your parents suffer. How you were throwing everything they had given you right back in their faces. You were destroying them as much as you were destroying yourself. If it hadn't been such sweet justice, I might have felt sorry for them. But I didn't. I didn't want to waste a single emotion on people who had looked down their noses at us. They never thought our Niall was good enough to be a friend for their precious son. I was only an employee and what right did my son have to fraternise with the likes of you? Whereas the truth was, Niall was too good for you.'

The mind-deforming bitterness that this man had harboured for all these years was so strong that Mark could feel it coming out of him like a poisonous cloud of evil. It must have consumed him for so long that it was as much a part of him as his legs and arms were. 'So what was the plan? I assume you had one?'

'You assume correctly. I decided that I wanted to wait until you had recovered and had something worth taking, a life you enjoyed and would want to preserve. I watched you become a success, making something of yourself at last.' He paused and swallowed hard. 'Do you have any idea how painful that was? To see you succeeding and knowing that my son had been denied that right. That all he had was twelve pitifully short years before he was left to rot in the ground.'

'But surely my miserable life wasn't ever worth taking?'

'To an extent, I'd agree with you. Which is why I've got something better in mind for you. I knew you'd hand it to me on a plate in the end. And reading about your so-called bravery in the newspapers, how you and your girlfriend had saved that girl's life, well, I saw then that the moment had come. I'm right, aren't I?'

It was just as Mark had suspected. 'Yes,' he said simply, and seeing the hand tighten its grip on the gun, he knew that time was running out. He had to think of a new direction in which to take Niall's father; he had to channel his thoughts somewhere different. He thought of Bones – calm, detached Bones – and how he would deal with this situation. Steeling himself, he said, 'How did you feel when you read about me saving that girl?'

There was a flicker of some new emotion in the crazed face before him. But there was no answer to the question.

He pressed on. 'Did it make you think about the unfairness of our world? The indiscriminate giving and taking of life? Did it make you want to scream to whoever would listen that it wasn't fair?'

'*No!* It made me hate you even more.'

'Why? Because I'd proved myself where once I had failed? Don't you think that I tried my damnedest to save your son? That I would have wanted to save my friend? But you never wanted to believe that, did you? At the mercy of your own guilt for not being there when Niall needed you most, you turned me into your personal scapegoat, didn't you? Somebody had to take the blame for you failing your son ... and then your wife, so why not me?'

Tears suddenly sprang into the old man's eyes. 'That's a lie! It was you. *You!* You didn't try hard enough. You didn't care enough. If you had, you would have saved Niall. But your kind doesn't care. They don't care about anyone but themselves.' His voice was cracking up and the strength of his grip on the gun had lessened; the slim barrel was drooping so low, it was pointing at Mark's feet. For a split second Mark thought of taking his chance and hurling himself forward to seize the gun. But he knew the gap between them was too great. He would never make it in time. There was nothing else for it but to keep the dialogue going and inch his way forward. He took the smallest of imperceptible steps, but got no further. The gun was back into position and aimed squarely at his chest.

'I warned you. No nearer. You think I won't do it, don't you? You think I'm just a crazy old fool who hasn't got the guts.'

Tears were streaming down the old man's cheeks, his hands, mottled and stringy with veins, were shaking. Mark could see that he was dangerously close to the edge, which meant that anything might happen. 'I don't think anything of the kind,' he said soothingly. 'It's taken a lot of courage to get this far. A lot of smart planning too.' He was acting out a classic talk-them-down trick – convince them you thought they were a genius and they loved nothing more than to prove it to you; he had used it several times in his books.

Wiping his face on the back of a hand, Niall's father pulled himself together, seemed to hold himself firm. 'Smarter than you'd ever know.'

'Clever of you to use the sequence of events in *Silent Footsteps*. A nice touch, that.'

'I thought you'd appreciate it. Just as you'll appreciate that I have absolutely nothing to lose by what I'm about to do. I've lost my son and my wife, I have nothing left. So here's one more nice touch for you. You have two seconds to choose who I kill. Your closest and oldest friend. Or your girlfriend. Sorry, you weren't fast enough, time's up. I'll choose for you.' And with an agility that took Mark completely off-guard, he moved so that he now had a clear view of Izzy and was aiming the gun straight at her, his fingers already squeezing the trigger.

'No!'

It was a scream so loud and violent, Mark felt his jaw snap, and in an explosion of energy he threw himself in front of Izzy.

He heard the shot and the cries, but most of all felt the massive jolt of agonising pain rip through him. From then on he was conscious only of a blurred sense of pandemonium breaking out, and as his legs crumpled beneath him, he dropped to the ground and another jolt of pain hit him.

He heard and felt nothing more.

48

Theo's recollection of what had happened was already taking on a vagueness that was the result of acute shock. It was fortunate that he had given his statement to the policemen from Kassiópi several hours ago, because if he was asked now for the details he might not be so lucid. Certain elements of the night were already jumbled in his head.

At the time he had been fully in control, organising everything, the ambulance, the police, and, with Max's help, trying to stem the flow of blood, of which there had been so much. A pool of it had formed on the terrace, and in the panic one of them had stepped into it and made macabre red footsteps on the stone paving.

Now, as he stood alone at the window, his haunted reflection staring back at him while trying once again to recall the sequence of events, he found that he could not picture that dreadful moment when the gun had gone off. He could not bring himself to focus on what he had seen, knowing only that in those last insane seconds he had been powerless to help his friend.

Before that, he could remember the wind blowing the candles, hot wax splashing on to the table, the sound of the sea breaking on the rocks below and thinking: This can't go on. We have to stop it. All the talking in the world is not going to stop this man from killing each and every one of us.

And just as he had thought this, the crazy little man had started saying that Mark had to choose whom he was going to kill. It was at this point that his memory was now distorting the picture. He could see and feel himself wanting to move. Wanting to push Izzy out of the way, but he hadn't been able to. Fear had immobilised him. Just as now the after-shock was immobilising his brain. All it would allow him to remember were the moments before the first shot was fired and everything that happened immediately after the second.

He was on the ground beside Izzy. She was shaking and screaming as she knelt over Mark's blood-soaked body – his head was covered with it, as was his chest and back. It had taken both Max and Laura to pull her off so that he could see if there was any chance of saving him. 'He's dead,' she kept crying. 'He's dead. He's dead.' Laura had held her tight, doing her best to soothe and comfort her, but was unable to find the words to deny what they could see for themselves.

But Mark had defied them. He wasn't dead. And that was when Theo had taken control. If Mark was going to survive, they needed to act immediately: they had to get him to hospital.

By the time the ambulance arrived, Mark still hadn't regained consciousness and his pulse was faint, barely there at all. The amount of blood he had lost seemed so great that Theo was convinced the long journey to Corfu Town would be futile. He would never make it that far.

He should have had more faith in his friend's tenacity to live, though. Mark did make it to the clinic that Theo insisted he be taken to and it was here, right now, that he was being operated on. All Theo knew at this point was that Mark had been shot in the chest and that he had cracked his head badly when he had fallen to the ground. He had no idea how critical his injuries were, or what his chances of recovery were.

Max and Laura had stayed behind at the villa, but Izzy had insisted on coming with Theo. Now they could do nothing but wait for someone to come and tell them the news. Although they never actually voiced their fears to each other, Theo knew that Izzy was preparing herself for the worst. Just as he was.

He turned at the sound of a door opening and saw that she was back from the bathroom. White-faced and hollow-eyed, her clothes still stained with Mark's blood, she said, 'Any news?'

He shook his head.

She came and stood next to him at the window. 'Why didn't he tell me he was being stalked?'

'He didn't want to frighten you. Especially when he realised you might be in danger.' He felt her shiver beside him and put his arm around her.

'I knew there was something wrong, but he wouldn't talk to me.'

'You mustn't be cross with him. It shows the depth of his feelings for you. He was trying to protect you.'

'That man ... Niall's father. He was very ill, wasn't he?'

'Yes. He was truly sick at heart. There would have been nothing anyone could have done for him. It's a hard truth, but I believe it's best that he killed himself.'

'Did you explain everything to the police?'

'Everything. But I expect there will be more questions to answer tomorrow. Or, rather, later today.' He glanced at his watch, and as he did so, the door behind them opened. They both turned to see who it was, knowing that this was what they had been waiting for. Holding Izzy's hand, Theo spoke in Greek to the doctor, wanting to protect her for as long as he could, to be the one to break it to her. He could at least do that much for Mark.

But there was no need to protect Izzy. The news was good. Mark was going to be all right. Though his right lung had been punctured by the bullet, which had gone clean through his chest and out of his back, the doctor was matter-of-fact about the operation he had just performed.

'It's a routine procedure,' he assured them. 'We've re-inflated the lung and sewn it up, nothing to worry about, really.' He went on to say that Mark had one of the toughest skulls he had come across and it had saved him from any damage to his brain when he had collapsed and hit his head. 'Given the severity of the cut to his head, another skull might have crushed like an egg, but not this one.' There had been a slight cause for concern at the length of time Mark had been unconscious, as a result of the fall, but all the tests showed so far that he was going to be just fine.

It was generally agreed between Izzy and Theo that Mark made a lousy patient. They told him so, three days later during one of his griping sessions about the constant prodding and poking that went on whenever he tried to sleep. 'It's like they think I'm a laboratory experiment for them to play with in moments of boredom,' he complained.

'An expensive laboratory experiment that I am paying for,' Theo corrected him over his shoulder, as he left the room to give Izzy and Mark some time alone.

It was a comment that provoked a snarl of such ferocity from Mark that Izzy burst out laughing. 'You have no idea how good it is to hear you whingeing like this,' she said.

'I'm not whingeing,' he snapped.

'You are. You're behaving atrociously.'

'Then get me out of here.'

She looked at his gaunt face, the blackened arcs beneath his sunken eyes, the dressing that was stuck to the side of his head – and where a large patch of his hair had been shaved off – and at the layers of bandages strapped around his chest. 'According to the doctor you're not going anywhere for at least another three days,' she said firmly.

'Don't try bossing me about,' he scowled, while trying to suppress a yawn, 'you're not at school now, Miss Jordan.'

He fell asleep shortly afterwards. He slept a lot, but lightly, and only for brief periods of time. Leaning back in the chair by the side of his bed, Izzy closed her eyes. She wasn't sleeping properly either; her nights were filled with chaotic, exhausting nightmares. Recurrently she would hear Mark's cry that fateful night. *'No!'* It clung to her, a whorl of a scream that went on for ever, wailing its siren of terror and desperation. She frequently dreamed of Mark being shot, of holding him in her arms, watching helplessly as his life ebbed away, taking with it her every hope of happiness. Usually the dreams were a replay of what had really happened – including Niall's father holding the gun to his own head and ending his life, just as he had on the terrace. But last night she had dreamed that Niall's father was alive, that they were all back in England, that having killed Mark he was now stalking her. 'There's no one to protect you now, Izzy,' he was saying, as he crept up behind her, 'no one to die in your place.'

Max, Laura and Theo had commented this morning on how tired and drained she looked. She had tried to make light of it, insisting that she was fine. 'A few sleepless nights never hurt anyone,' she had said, keeping to herself the depth of her shock at what had happened. She couldn't come to terms with the fact that she had come so close to dying, that if it hadn't been for Mark's selfless act of courage she would probably be dead.

Though she was desperate for rest, Izzy found the corridor outside Mark's room too noisy for her to sleep. There was a constant squeak of shoes on the polished floor, a steady hum of voices, a persistent ringing of telephones. Giving up on the idea of snatching a nap while he slept, she went to look at the cards and flowers grouped together on the table at the end of his bed. His parents and brothers had been the first to get in touch after Theo had called them to explain what had happened. They had then phoned Mark to make sure he really was okay, as had his agent and publisher who had read of the incident in the papers back home. Max and Laura had visited several times, bringing with them newspapers and chocolates, neither of which he had so much as glanced at. The largest bunch of flowers, and easily the most ostentatious, was from Dolly-Babe and Silent Bob. Their card wished him a speedy recovery and contained a postscript of their home address – they had left for England yesterday morning – 'Just in case you're ever passing our way,' Dolly-Babe had scribbled.

'About as likely as me being left alone in this hell-hole,' had been Mark's muttered response, when he had read it.

As the days progressed, Izzy grew concerned. Far from making a steady recovery as they had been told he would, Mark seemed to be slipping into a decline. The doctor said he thought Mark was depressed.

'It's as if he's given up,' the doctor told her and Theo, 'as though he doesn't care one way or the other if he gets better.'

'Would it help if he was discharged and nursed where he felt more relaxed?' asked Theo.

The doctor shook his head. 'No. He's not to be moved. Not yet. Not until I'm happy with his mental state.'

A little over a week after he had been admitted, Mark told Izzy that he thought it would be better if she stopped coming to see him.

She was devastated, and felt as though the air had been knocked out of her. 'But why? What have I done?' She had to steady herself against the back of a chair.

He looked straight at her and, with not an ounce of emotion in his voice or expression, he said, 'Let's face it, Izzy, it was never going to work between us. It was nothing more than a holiday fling with a few extra excitements on the side. It's over. Please don't make a drama of it. I'm tired, I'd like to sleep now. To be left alone.'

Mark watched her go for the last time, turned his head into the pillow and buried it as far as it would go.

Early next morning he had a visitor.

A furious visitor.

Theo.

He marched in and, for a good five minutes, ranted and raved at Mark. Then he paced the room and ranted some more, resorting to his native tongue when he ran out of English. The attack was as thorough as it was vociferous.

'Have you quite finished?' Mark asked him, when at last the room fell quiet.

But clearly Theo hadn't. 'Do you have any idea what you have done to that poor girl?' he demanded. 'She is distraught with what you have told her. Inconsolable.'

'She'll get over it.' He made his voice sound far away, distant, uncaring. Just as he had yesterday with Izzy, when he had hoped that the carefully added note of irritation in his final words would hasten her departure and bring about an end to the pain of seeing the heart-shattering destruction he was wreaking. Outwardly he might have given a convincing performance of indifference, but inwardly he had been a broken man. He had never felt so sure about a decision, yet so hurt by it.

Theo wheeled round on him, glared angrily. 'I doubt that. She feels more for you than anyone else ever will.'

'Maybe now she does, but when she gets back to England she'll put this summer behind her. Put it down to experience and think of it as an interesting holiday romance.'

'And will you? Will you return to your sad, lonely little world and imagine that she didn't storm the castle to reach your heart and touch you in some beautiful, lasting way?'

'Don't start getting sentimental on me, Theo. Keep the purple prose for some other mug who'll listen.'

'I would rather be sentimental than afraid to grab the chance of enjoying the life I was meant to live.'

'I'm afraid I don't possess your giddy, optimistic approach. For some of us, the real world can only ever be a disappointment.'

As though he had used up all his anger, Theo came and sat in the chair next to the bed. He leaned forward, his hands clasped between his legs. 'Just explain to me why. What has changed your feelings for her?'

Mark had known that it would come to this, that he would have to give Theo a reasonable explanation. An act of cold indifference was never going to satisfy him. 'I have to end it, Theo,' he said quietly. 'I'm not doing this out of self-interest. I'm doing this for Izzy. Surely you can see that. Everything I touch I either spoil or destroy. Izzy was very nearly killed because of me. I simply won't let myself put her at risk again.'

Theo stared at him in astonishment. 'But, Mark, that is nonsense. It is irrational beyond belief. You do not spoil everything you come in contact with. Far from it.'

'Really? What about Niall, and his parents? All three of them dead at the last count. And what about the pain I caused my family? And even you, days after meeting me you wind up mugged.'

'And what of all the good things that have occurred because of you, eh? Any other man would be satisfied with saving just the one life, but no, you have to score a hat-trick of saving three: mine, Sally's and Izzy's. A super-human feat, a record to be proud of, perhaps.'

'Well, you know what Scott Fitzgerald said: "Show me a hero and I will write you a tragedy." Now please, Theo, don't make this any harder for me.

Tell Izzy whatever you think will make her feel better, but don't waste your breath trying to make me change my mind. It won't work.'

49

The holiday was over.

Despite what Max and Laura thought.

They were keen for Izzy to stay on for another week, to leave when they did. But she had told them several times already that it would be better if she went home as originally arranged. 'You deserve to have some time alone before you have to go back as well,' she said now, as they tried once again to dissuade her from going.

'Just a few more days,' Laura implored, passing her a plate. 'It would do you good.'

Izzy settled the plate on the table in front of her. 'But my flight's booked,' she said wearily. She was tired of having to defend her decision.

'And can be changed just like that,' said Max, snapping his thumb and middle finger together. 'Really, Izzy, we don't want you to leave, not yet. Not like this. It's too soon after everything that's happened.'

'Max is right,' Theo joined in. 'It's much too soon.'

'It's nearly a fortnight. And, anyway, school starts next week. I have to go home. There are things I have to organise.'

Nobody said anything more, and in the silence Izzy watched Theo open the box of pastries he had brought with him, his fingers working at the knot in the ribbon, his brow furrowed. Wretchedness was making her irritable and impatient, and she suddenly wanted to snatch the box out of his hands and slash at the ribbon with a pair of scissors.

Since the night of the shooting, and when he hadn't been at the hospital visiting Mark, Theo had spent even more of his time at Villa Petros. It was as if he had formed a pact with Max and Laura, as though the three of them couldn't get through a single day without a conversation about the shooting, as if one more conversation would exorcise the painful memories. She couldn't bring herself to tell them that she didn't want to keep going over the same well-trodden ground. She didn't want to be reminded of how lucky she was to be alive, not when she felt so numb and miserable. For that reason alone, she needed to get away. She was banking on going home to get back to normality. To put the summer behind her.

To put Mark behind her.

But she knew that would never happen. She would never forget him. They might not have known one another for very long, but the distance she and Mark had covered together was greater and more meaningful than anything else she had known. She had trusted him completely . . . had given herself, heart, body and soul, to him.

Theo had explained to her what lay behind Mark's apparent dismissal, and while it didn't change matters, it at least gave her the reason why he had suddenly, and inexplicably, rejected her. As Theo had been at pains to point out, Mark's reasoning might be irrational and misguided, but it meant that she could accept that there wasn't anything more she could have done. Unlike her break-up with Alan, Mark hadn't left her feeling humiliated and used, or guilty.

And wasn't this exactly what Laura had wanted for her? A holiday fling to prove to herself that she was up for a bit of fun with no strings attached? No broken hearts. No recriminations. Only a wonderful sense of empowerment.

But it wasn't that simple.

Her heart was hanging in there by the sheerest of threads. Which was why everybody was treating her so carefully. They had turned her into a fragile ornament that they weren't quite sure where to place for the best. She loved them for their kindness, but wished they would stop. A little rough handling would be so much better. A rap on the knuckles and a stern word or two telling her to pull herself together would be easier to cope with. Her mother's uncaring approach would be perfect. *So, he had his fun and dumped you, did he? I warned you. You've only yourself to blame. How very foolish you've been. Here, make yourself useful and dry the dishes.* Modern Woman would help too. She would stand with her hands on her hips: *Hey, lighten up, sister, and count yourself lucky you got out while you still could. He was always going to be trouble.*

As they sat on the terrace enjoying the late-afternoon sun, Izzy sensed the conversation bouncing over and around the only subject she was interested in.

Mark.

How was he?

Had his depression lifted?

Had he asked after her?

Did he, like her, lie awake at night reliving those days they had spent together?

He had been discharged from the hospital at the weekend and Theo had come to see Izzy the morning after, just as he had promised he would. 'He is better for being with me,' he had told her, 'but only because he is more comfortable cursing my interference and ineptitude than that of a pretty young nurse.'

'He will be all right, though, won't he?'

'Don't worry, Izzy, I will see to it that he makes a full recovery. As to the confused workings of his mind, which is governing his heart, well, that I cannot speak for. I wish it were different. Truly I do. I had such high hopes for you both.'

'So did I,' she murmured . . .

Now unable to wait another moment to ask the question she most wanted answered, she interrupted Theo, who was telling Max and Laura some story about Angelos over-watering his flowers. 'How's Mark?' she said. Instantly three wary faces stared back at her. If I were a grief-stricken widow, this is how they would treat me, she thought. 'How is he?' she repeated.

Theo put down the pastry he was eating. He licked the crumbs from his fingers. 'He is getting stronger. Putting on a little weight also.'

'Is he writing?'

'In the morning, yes, for a couple of hours. But by the afternoon he is too tired, which, as you can imagine, frustrates him. Not to put too fine a point on it, he is a raging pain by about three o'clock. I have to go back to Athens the day after tomorrow, so I am taking him with me. I hope the change of scenery may do him good. If not, I will put him on the first available plane for England and let him fend for himself.'

'No, you won't.' Laura smiled. 'You're too kind-hearted to do that.'

He sighed. 'Maybe that's true, but I swear he is testing my patience to its outer limits.' Then changing the subject, he said, 'How quiet it is going to be for you and Max with us all gone. It might even feel like a proper holiday for you.' He picked up the remains of his cake and smiled one of his charming but infinitely roguish smiles. 'But promise me you will rest your legs during this pregnancy, Laura. I don't want to see you next summer with varicose veins.'

Both Max and Laura laughed at his irrepressible warmth and good humour.

This is how I must try and remember my holiday, Izzy thought, as she made herself join in with the laughter; a happy and carefree time.

Early next morning, as arranged, Theo came to take Izzy to the airport. 'I have business in town to attend to,' he had told Max yesterday, 'so I might as well save you the journey.'

The goodbyes were as tearful as Izzy had dreaded. Although she knew she would be seeing her friends in a week's time, it felt so final. This really was the end of a magical dream. Even if she came back again – and everybody said she must – it could never be the same.

The airport was horribly crowded with hundreds of holidaymakers queuing to check in their luggage. Theo waited with her and she was conscious of people staring at him as though they thought they should recognise him. Dressed in one of his immaculate lightweight suits with a pale blue shirt and tie, and dark glasses, there was a flamboyant film-star quality about him. She thought back to the first time she had met him and how like George Clooney she had thought he was. 'Do you get this trouble wherever you go?' she asked, after a woman had stopped her trolley to have a better look at him.

He lowered his sunglasses and smiled. 'It's you they are staring at, not me.'

'Mm ... they're probably wondering what I'm doing with such a gorgeous man.'

He laughed. And laughed loudly. 'My God, Izzy. At last, you have paid me a compliment. I have waited all summer to hear you say something pleasant about me. No, no, don't start crying. Not here, or people will get entirely the wrong idea.'

'Am I allowed to shed a tear now?' she asked, when she had checked in her luggage and had joined the queue to go through passport control.

'A very small one. I don't want my suit to be ruined by a flood of tears. It might shrink and that would never do.' He hugged her tightly. 'Okay, that's enough emotion,' he said, releasing her from his arms. 'Too much and I will let the side down with you. Take good care of yourself, Izzy, and keep in touch. I want to know how you get on with your dreadful headmistress, what cunning revenge you have in store for her. Max and Laura are bullying me to visit them in England, so we will meet again quite soon, I'm sure. And, of course, next year you will come to Corfu again. No, don't look so doubtful, Izzy, you will come again, I know you will. This place suits you. The island has its regular visitors who just can't keep away. Mark my words, you will be one of them.'

She smiled extra hard at his words.

'There, you see how brave you have become? What inner strength you have found here on holiday?' He kissed her cheeks and then, 'And lastly, this.' He pressed his lips firmly to hers. 'Be lucky, Izzy. Be happy.'

With her head leaning against the small window of the aeroplane, she watched the landscape beneath her. When the island had disappeared completely she felt a sharp tug on the thread that was holding her heart together. No more tears, she told herself sternly. Just accept that once again Chance has played its little game with you. Now you have happiness, now you don't.

She slept through most of the flight, dreaming of the coming autumn term at school and discovering on her first day back that she had a child protégé in the new intake: a small blond-haired boy who could knock Picasso into a Cubist cocked hat.

Home had never looked more dreary or unwelcoming. It had all the cheer of the Arctic tundra.

She had chosen this ground-floor flat after her split with Alan because she had thought it had such a warm, cosy feel to it, but now as she pushed open the front door and lugged her bag into the hall, then gathered up the mountain of mail from the mat, she thought it cursed with gloom. Nothing could have matched more appropriately the sense of desolation she had come home with. She was reminded of the abandoned house she and Mark had looked at in Old Períthia.

It's the rain, she told herself, as she stood in the middle of the sitting room staring out through the window on to the communal lawn she shared with the rest of the residents of the converted house.

That and the grey sky.

And the sub-zero temperature of a typically English summer's day.

It's not the flat, she chided her flagging spirits. The flat is fine. It's your home. Your only home, so you'd better get used to being in it again.

There, that was telling her.

To soften the lacklustre light from outside, she switched on two small lamps and set to with her unpacking.

Thanks to Laura insisting that anything that needed washing she throw into the machine yesterday morning, everything was clean and neatly folded, so it took her no time at all to put it away.

Dealing with the backlog of mail was rather different, however. It took her over an hour to sort it into piles: action needed sometime in the future, and action required first thing in the morning. There was one letter, though, that she had deliberately left till last. She had recognised the stark white envelope the moment she had seen it and had put it aside to be dealt with when she was feeling stronger. It was from school and could mean only one thing: she was being given a mealy-mouthed redundancy package.

A perfect and fitting end to her holiday.

She didn't know whether she was disappointed or relieved when she opened the letter in bed that night and read that she hadn't been given the elbow after all.

Amazingly, she had been promoted.

In real terms it wouldn't amount to much. She would be working longer hours with greater responsibility and for not much more money.

Still, it would look good on her CV when she got round to looking for a new job.

Switching off the bedside lamp, she thought, Oh, well, business as usual, then. Nothing turns out the way I think it will.

When would she ever learn?

50

'I have to go,' Mark said, 'you know I do. It's time.'

'But are you sure you're ready?'

'Come on, Theo, you were there when the doctor gave me the all-clear.'

Theo shook his head doubtfully. 'To travel on your own, though ... Supposing you feel unwell? What if—'

'We could play the What-if game for ever and a day,' cut in Mark. 'No, like I say, I'm ready to go home.' He picked up a small white pebble and hurled it into the sea. Too late he realised his mistake and winced at the pain. To his disgust he had been advised to wear a sling to restrict his arm movements and protect the damaged muscles in his chest and shoulder, but he had dispensed with it at the first opportunity, claiming he no longer needed it, that he didn't want the fuss or bother of it. Nothing would make him admit otherwise that a punctured lung, even if it had made a full recovery, hurt like hell if he coughed or breathed too deeply. And if he moved too sharply, as he just had, his body declared pay-back time.

Sitting beside him, Theo must have noticed him wince. He flashed Mark a look of impatience. 'You see? I'm right, you are still in pain, you are not ready to go home yet. And with that dreadful haircut you look like a half-starved refugee. They'll stop you at the airport, accuse you of being an illegal immigrant.'

With a rueful smile, Mark ran his left hand – the one that didn't pull on his weakened muscles – through the stubble on his head. Three days ago, while still in Athens with Theo, he had acquired the mother of all haircuts. Fed up with looking in the mirror each morning and seeing the bare patch on his scalp where it had been stitched back together, he had decided to go for the buzz-cut look to even things out. He had walked into the nearest barber's and had the lot as good as shaved off. When Theo had got back from work late that night, he had taken one look at him and dropped his jaw to the floor. 'That, my friend, is going to take some getting used to!'

Just as Theo had said it would, the change of scene had been good for Mark. The sense of having been-there-done-that was not lost on him. It was, after all, in Athens, that he had stayed while getting his head together after he had left the rehab clinic and tried to decide what to do next with his life.

While Theo was at his office, an elegant, stately, refurbished town-house in a quiet square a short walk from his apartment, Mark had spent the mornings writing. But it hadn't gone well. Slow and tortuous, it was like pulling teeth. Another change of environment and associated disruption to his routine hadn't helped. In the afternoon he tried to rest, as he had been advised. When he couldn't sleep, despite being so tired, he would tune out by flicking through the channels on Theo's state-of-the-art television, but the sheer awfulness of Greek daytime viewing was in a class of its own and had had him riveted. Greek soaps, he had decided, were produced, directed and acted by comic geniuses, only they didn't know it. There were more gasps of surprise, rivers of tears and shock-horror scenes in one half-hour slot than in a month's worth of British and Aussie soaps combined. But it hadn't induced sleep, and resorting to the old standby of Sky and CNN to help him nod off, he kept wondering why Theo bothered with such an expensive piece of kit when the home-grown programmes available to him were so bad. The answer was in the stash of videos and DVDs he found in an elegant cabinet in the corner of the marble-floored sitting room. Since his last visit to Theo in Athens, it was apparent his friend had developed a taste for his own little bit of Merry Olde England in the form of *Only Fools and Horses*, *Monty Python* and *Blackadder*. There was even a shelf dedicated to some of the BBC's best costume drama over the last twenty years. It was an extraordinary hoard that made Mark smile and had him wondering if this was how his friend kept his English up to scratch.

In the evenings, when he had a resurgence of energy, he and Theo would go out for a meal. They went for walks too, strolling round Theo's favourite areas of the city, invariably finishing up in the Pláka district and watching the world go by. They had had dinner with Theo's parents several times and, as ever, Christiana Vlamakis had lavished an excess of concern on him.

'Oh!' she had cried, patting his arm when Theo told her the details of the shooting. 'You are not a safe man to be around.'

He must have flinched when she had said this, as Theo had hurriedly gabbled something to her that was incomprehensible to his ears but which had the effect of making Christiana cluck around him for the rest of the evening.

'It was a figure of speech my mother used,' Theo said, during the drive back to his apartment that night. 'I don't want you brooding on those words of hers.'

'She's right, though, isn't she?'

'You know my view on that subject, so please do not bait me. I think you are mad to give any credence to such a tomfoolish theory.'

'Credence to such *tomfoolery* is the expression, you want.'

'Pah!'

It was the nearest they got to discussing Izzy. And, for that, Mark was grateful. There was nothing more to be said. She had gone back to England to get on with her life without him. That was the end of the story he had written for them.

Yet, as he sat here on the beach in Áyios Nikólaos with Theo towelling himself off after his swim, and recalling the many times he had enjoyed Izzy's company in this same spot, he didn't try to kid himself that he was better off without her. He knew very well that having Izzy in his life was infinitely better than not having her in it. But that was a luxury of thought he would not allow himself to dwell on. She was better off without him. Safer, too.

He knew Theo would disagree with him, which was why there was no point in discussing it with his friend, but he was convinced that he wasn't destined to live a normal life. The happy-ever-after scenario that others enjoyed would always elude him.

Two days later, his return to England went as smoothly as he could have hoped for, apart from Theo making a fuss at the airport and insisting that he be helped on to the plane and met at the other end. 'You are not to lift that heavy luggage. You must lose that appalling pride of yours and ask for help.'

'Sure you wouldn't prefer me to be pushed about in a wheelchair?'

Theo had slapped his forehead with his hands. 'Now, why had I not thought of that?'

'No, Theo, *don't!*'

'Okay, I'll let it go for fear of you turning nasty. Now prepare yourself, I am about to thoroughly embarrass and annoy you.'

Which he did, embracing Mark and smacking two great big kisses on either side of his face.

While listening to the lunchtime news on the radio and waiting for the kettle to boil, Mark realised that it was one of those rare moments since his return, three days ago, when the phone wasn't ringing and he had the house to himself.

Once word had gone round the village that he was home, everybody wanted to come and see him. The shooting had found its way into a number of the British papers, including the local rag, the *Whitby Gazette*. Coming so soon after the near-drowning accident it must have been a story too good to pass up. As a consequence, there was a fascination on the part of those he knew, even vaguely, to hear the grisly details straight from the horse's mouth.

Deirdre had been the first to call round, bringing with her a Victoria sponge cake, some gingerbread and scones, a pot of home-made lemon curd and a cheese and onion quiche. 'Well, pet,' she had said, settling the stack of Tupperware boxes on the worktop, removing her shoes and stepping into her slippers, 'you've been having a time and a half of it, haven't you?'

Lionel Bridges had been next to pay him a visit, followed swiftly by Dale, who brought with him his latest girlfriend: a raven-haired oddity, who also worked part-time at the Dracula Experience in Whitby. They told him they were moving in together, renting a tiny terraced house called Karma Cottage. He had had to stop himself smiling at the thought of them ever having children: they'd be straight out of the Addams Family! The rest of the writers' group soon made an appearance, and it was as well that Deirdre had been so thoughtful and kind as everyone who called on him with offers of help – did he need a lift to the hospital, the doctor's, or the supermarket? – was hungry. And while they happily tucked into the cakes and scones they took it in turns to ask him the questions that were burning holes in their tongues. Lionel – always a man for detail – had been straight off the starting block, wanting to know what sort of gun had been used. Mark had had to admit that he didn't know. 'Sorry, Lionel,' he had said, 'not my instrument of death. Wouldn't know a Bren gun from a tommy-gun.' It was true. He had never used them in his novels; he preferred his killers to be more ingenious. For some peculiar reason he had the idea that there was something horribly prosaic about a life being ended by a mere bullet.

But now that the initial interest in him had been satiated, he was being allowed time on his own. With the exception of the nightly phone calls from Theo and the early-morning ones from his family, he had been left, at last, to catch some much-needed breath.

He made himself a mug of tea and took it up to the first floor, to his study, which stretched from the front of the house to the back. He had chosen this room to work in because it had such great views: out across the cliff edge and the boundless sea, or to the rolling hills of the north Yorkshire moors. Sitting in his sea captain's chair – another of his self-deprecating sick jokes – he put his feet on his desk and sipped his tea thoughtfully. He had been looking forward to this moment, hoping that the familiar would ground him. He let his eyes roam the neatly organised shelves at either side of the chimney-breast where a potted history of his life could be put together from the books, records and CDs he had collected over the years.

Above the fireplace was a Victorian watercolour. It was a beautiful, restful landscape, all fading light and muted shades of colour, painted by a highly thought-of artist who had lived in the village at the turn of the century. Oddly enough, it had been the first present he had bought himself with his first advance from his publisher. Whenever Theo saw it, he said it represented the lesser-spotted St James's underbelly of sentimentality. It also provoked him to make fun of Mark's inability to spend the money he earned. 'You are useless with money,' he would say. 'You don't have a clue what it can do for you.'

'That's because I don't have the imagination for it,' he would protest.

'Rubbish! It's guilt. You spent so many years lecturing the world on the perils of capitalism you can't bring yourself to enjoy it.'

Swivelling his seat, Mark switched his gaze to the blank screen of his computer. It reminded him that he hadn't got round to checking his e-mails. He decided that as they had made it this far without his attention, they could wait a while longer.

His tea finished, it was time to get started on some work. What with all the visitors and interruptions he had had, he hadn't had a chance to get anything written, and when he didn't write he got twitchy. And twitchy was bad. Twitchy encouraged doubts to rise to the surface of his brain, nagging little maggots of anxiety that crawled around hinting that he was way off-course with the plot, the narrative, the dialogue.

He set out his things.

Notepad.

Pens.

Pencils.

Next he inserted a CD into the hi-fi, switched it on, reread the last few pages of what he had written and held the fountain pen poised over the blank page.

And that was as far as he got.

Two hours later, and discounting the words, 'Chapter Forty-Eight', not another word had appeared on the page.

Everything was in order, just as it should be: the ambience was right, the tools were right, so what the hell was the problem?

He had no answer.

He changed the CD. Replaced U2's *The Joshua Tree* with Bob Dylan's 'Blowin' in the Wind' and sat down again, pen poised.

Nothing.

He resharpened his pencils, fitted a new ink cartridge into his pen, ripped out the top page of the A4 pad of paper – well, it might be jinxed – reheaded it, gave Bob Dylan his marching orders and slipped in his lucky CD, REM's *Up* – fingers crossed, it had always worked well for him in the past.

But still nothing.

The page was blank.

And remained so for the rest of that day and the following week.

It was a disaster.

How could this have happened? How could that old enemy of every author, the dreaded writer's block, have worked such a perfect number on him? No matter what he did, there was a complete absence of creative thought going on inside his head. Nothing would come to him. He was all out of words and ideas. It was a catastrophe.

Uncannily he recalled his thoughts while sitting in Theo's garden at the start of his visit, when he had laughed at himself for being so wrapped up in the futility of ritual and joked that he would get so used to writing with a musical backdrop of cicadas that he wouldn't be able to work without it.

No more than coincidence, he told himself firmly. Don't give it another thought.

But without the collusion of his book to work on, he knew that he was being forced into a corner. His brain was denying him the one thing he had used as a defence mechanism to ward off the terror of that night when Niall's father had tried to shoot Izzy. By focusing his thoughts on the plot of his book, continually readjusting pages of dialogue in his mind, mentally checking that every I was dotted and every T crossed, that no stone of narrative was unturned, it had, until now, successfully kept him busy. Kept him from dwelling on Izzy . . . what she meant to him. Without that vital weapon of defence, he was now at the mercy of his imagination. He had started having long-drawn-out dream sequences in which he was repeatedly trying to save Izzy from being shot. He usually managed to wake himself before the real terror set in, but in the early hours of this morning he had woken in a sweat-drenched tangle of sheets, screaming Izzy's name – he hadn't reached her in time and she was dying.

Now, as he stood in the kitchen making himself some breakfast, he shuddered at the rawness of the memory. He slapped two pieces of buttered toast together and went outside to the small garden that overlooked the cliff edge and the sea. He listened to the screech of seagulls wheeling overhead and watched a group descend on the rooftops of his neighbours' houses. On the other side of the low wooden fence, he heard his immediate neighbour open his back door. Bill Watkins was a sprightly octogenarian who, notoriously, was as deaf as a post, but after a brief exchange of smiles while the old man threw a bag of rubbish into his dustbin, Mark turned away embarrassed, convinced that Bill must have heard him screaming like a banshee through the wall.

So what's next on the agenda of madness? he asked himself.

Another week of being unable to write?

More nightmares?

Or are you going to do something about it?

I could ring Theo and talk it over with him, he answered the contentious voice of his conscience.

Yeah, and you could be as evasive with him as you always are.

In the end, though, he did ring Theo. But his own problems were pushed aside when Theo said, 'What a coincidence, I was going to call you. But I'm afraid it's not—'

'You're not coming over, are you?' interrupted Mark, slipping effortlessly into their usual line of derogatory banter and finding some relief in it.

'No, you're quite safe. But it saddens me to tell you that poor old Thomas Zika died in his sleep last night.'

'I'm sorry, Theo. He didn't have any family left, did he? Who will arrange the funeral?'

'Oh, I will see to that. It is to be a very small affair. My parents are flying over. They were very fond of him. As I was.'

Me too, thought Mark, when later he put down the phone and remembered how protective he had felt towards Thomas on the day of Anna's memorial service. He felt sad. Sad because Thomas had lived so very long and never truly had what he wanted in life. He had contented himself to love Theo's grandmother from afar, but wouldn't he have preferred to be married to her? Why had he been so prepared to compromise his own wishes and desires? Why hadn't he pursued Anna more determinedly?

These thoughts stayed with him for the rest of that day – another day of not being able to write – and he knew it was no coincidence that whenever he pictured Thomas Zika in that restaurant, unable to feed himself, he transferred himself into Thomas's place. Would he end up the same, never knowing what it might have been like with Izzy, never taking that risk to find out just how fulfilling a life they might have shared?

He ran a tired hand over his jaw, pressed the heels of his palms against his closed eyes, imagining all too clearly the solitary games of chess that awaited him.

And what if his current mental state continued and he could never write again?

It was a terrifying thought.

Previously his writing had been his point of reference. It had compensated in some way for not having a relationship, but now he had neither.

So what or who are you afraid of? asked the voice that had questioned him in the garden earlier that morning.

He suddenly smiled to himself, thinking of Izzy and how she had admitted to hearing voices in her head.

Going upstairs to his study, he realised that he had actually thought of her without it hurting. It was progress. It made him wonder if he could face looking at the photographs he had just had developed. He hadn't looked at them yet, unsure whether he wanted to be reminded so vividly of what he had jettisoned. His fingers hesitated over the package on his desk, but he rejected the temptation. Not yet. It was too soon.

He sat down and toyed with the idea of sneaking up on his notepad and seeing if he could get some words written.

But fear of failing again made him switch on his computer to check his e-mails instead. There were the usual messages from his publisher keeping him informed of stuff they thought he gave a monkey's for; a message from his father who had recently joined the ranks of the Silver Surfers and now spent an obsessive number of hours browsing the Internet; a note from Lionel asking if he could drop round with some chapters from the steamy pen of Shona Mercy for him to read – top-shelf eroticism was not what Mark needed right now – and lastly, and this one had him leaning forward in his seat, a message from Bones, who was just back from a brief working secondment in California. His message said that on his return to work at the clinic, he had been shown the newspapers regarding Mark's latest exploits – a colleague had kept them for him thinking he might be interested.

Five minutes later as he was dialling Bones's home number, Mark was aware of yet another voice banging on inside his head.

It was Dolly-Babe, jangling her bangles and telling him Bones's e-mail was a SIGN.

Yeah, he thought, a sign that I'm desperate.

'It's not a bad time to call, is it?' he asked, when Bones picked up.

'Hello, Mark. Now, would that be bad in the sense of—'

'Don't you ever cut yourself some slack?'

'Just a little joke. You know, I was thinking of having an answerphone message that said: "Sorry, none of my multiple personalities are here to listen to you, but I'll deal with you just as soon as I've found myself."'

'I wouldn't bother.'

'So, what can I do for you? I was wondering when I'd hear from you.'

'Why do you assume I want something?'

'Well, for one thing it's nearly midnight and for another you've recently flirted with death again. Not once, but twice. How am I doing?'

'You're slipping, you missed out on the girl.'

'On the contrary, I was saving her. And that wasn't meant to be a pun on your fine heroic deeds. Now tell me everything. It's late, so no games of mental hide and seek. Do that and I'll put the phone down on you.'

He did as Bones instructed.

When he fell quiet, Bones said, 'Good. So where shall we dive in first?'

'Anywhere you like. Why I can't write. Why I've started having nightmares about the shooting and why I told the woman I love to get the hell out of it and leave me alone because she'd be better off without me, that I'd only bring her bad luck.'

There was a long pause, during which Mark half expected to hear the familiar, almost reassuring rustle of a sweet wrapper. 'Well?' he said irritably. 'I thought there were to be no games.'

'Mm ... There's a word I'm looking for. A word that covers your last point. Now what is it? It begins with a C. Help me, Mark, you're the one who's good with words.'

'Hell! I didn't think I'd have to play Twenty Questions!'

'Come on. You can do it.'

'Okay, how about Conditioning?'

'No.'

'Convergent thinking?'

'No. And that's two words. I said one.'

'Causal attribution?'

'Are you listening to me?'

'God, not one of Freud's old cookies, Castration anxiety?'

'Now you're just showing off. No, the word I was thinking of begins with a C, followed by an R, an A and finally a P.'

'Crap?'

'Yes. Your head must be full of it, Mark, if you're arrogant enough to think that the world revolves around your petty little actions. How many times do I have to tell you, it is not your job to save mankind from itself?'

'But—'

'No buts, this is where I get tough with you. You've phoned me at this ridiculously late hour, not to seek my advice but to have me confirm and sanction what was already in your mind, hoping I'd give you the necessary permission and blessing to go ahead. Don't interrupt, I haven't finished! It's bloody obvious why you're having nightmares and even more obvious why you can't write, even to a swollen-headed fool like you. But, as usual, you're deliberately hiding from the truth. I bet you've even told yourself you don't deserve this lucky break. I'm right, aren't I?'

'Maybe.'

'And after everything I've taught you, you still come up with a hare-brained thought such as that! Will you never learn? By the way, you say that you love this woman, have you by any chance been brave enough to tell her you love her?'

'Er ... not in so many words.'

'I thought not. The same old Mark. Scared of being vulnerable. Scared of a committed relationship. But I notice you didn't use the word in the past tense, which means that subconsciously you haven't consigned the relationship to the wastepaper basket, so I would suggest that you do something about it. Go and tell her that you love her. I guarantee your nightmares will stop and your writing will flow. If I'm wrong I shan't charge you for this consultation. How's that?'

'Oh, go suck a Murraymint!'

'That's my boy!'

'But what if she doesn't love me? She's never actually said she does.'

'That's a risk you'll just have to take. My guess is she's worth the gamble. Or would you rather you never found out? Now listen to me, and listen well.'

'You're not going to start whistling one of your bloody awful tunes, are you?'

'I was tempted a few minutes ago, Genesis's 'Throwing It All Away' struck me as fitting. But, no, I was going to ask if you consider yourself to be a success in bed with this woman?'

Mark laughed, then winced. His chest still wasn't up to it. 'If you really want to know, I'd say we were a corona of excellence.'

Bones laughed too. 'I said you were good with words, Mark. I like that. You see her as the heavenly body and you as the halo of light. A sparkling image on which to end our conversation. Keep me posted, won't you? Think happy thoughts, Mark. Goodnight.'

51

By the second week of the autumn term, Izzy knew she didn't have a child
protégé lurking among the new intake, despite what the parents might like
to believe of their offspring. 'He's so artistic, so amazingly good with his
hands,' was a boast she had frequently heard since she had trained to be a
teacher. And Mrs Claremont, an insipid mother of the oh-don't-do-that-
darling variety, who had already bestowed on the school a generous offering
of three ready-made, badly-behaved boys had felt the need to make the
same proud boast of her latest, hopefully last, contribution. 'He likes
nothing more than to really get stuck in,' she had gushed on the first day of
term, when she had presented a moon-faced child of five to Izzy. Claremont
number four looked more like a bruising seven-year-old, and at eight
thirty-five in the morning, with his tie already askew, and his shirt bubbling
over the top of his grey shorts, he had certainly looked the type to want to
get stuck into anything and everything. The muckier the better, probably.
The more annoying the better.

Two weeks on and Claremont number four had lived up to Izzy's
predictions. He was an utter menace in the art room, lacking the ability to
concentrate for more than three minutes at a time and wrecking anything
he touched. He was also a bully, picking on nearly everybody in the class,
terrorising them with his bigger build and strength. He took special pleasure
in making fun of a timid little girl called Gemma, who spent most of their
art lessons sniffing back the threat of tears and twisting a prettily
embroidered handkerchief around her fingers. She was such an unhappy
child that Izzy had sat down with her at the end of Friday afternoon's
lesson, just before last break, and asked her if she was all right. A tiny nod
was all she received for an answer.

'Have you made any friends?' she asked, suspecting not: the child was
new to the school and hadn't come up from the kindergarten like most of
the others had.

A sideways shake of her head confirmed Izzy's suspicions.

'That's a shame. Friends are important. Do you know what would make
you lots of friends?'

Another sideways shake of her head.

Izzy leaned in close to her and whispered into her ear. Then, with a
reassuring smile, she said, 'Do you think you could do that?'

'I think so.'

'Good. So why don't you practise getting that voice a little louder over the weekend and then give it a go in our next art lesson on Monday afternoon?'

It was now Monday afternoon, first period after lunch and Izzy had the staffroom all to herself. Not having a lesson to teach, she was supposed to be genning up on the latest edict from the headmistress about the new report system she was implementing. Computerised report cards were replacing the out-of-date A4 sheets of paper upon which teachers with handwriting as poor as any GP's could disguise the unpalatable truth behind scribbled lines of false praise.

But computerised report cards, or whatever else the headmistress wanted to introduce, held no interest for Izzy. Looking out of the window, down on to the playing-fields where on one side a group of boys in muddy shorts were being taught to run headlong into an enormous battering ram, and on the other, girls were chasing each other with hockey sticks and showing scant regard for anybody's safety, she knew that soon none of this would matter to her. Some time in the new year she would be gone.

No one knew of her plans to leave, not even Max and Laura with whom she had spent Saturday evening. They had come to her for supper; it was her small, rather inadequate way of thanking them for such a wonderful holiday. Laura was looking fabulously well on her pregnancy and was clearly going through the blooming stage. Snuggled up on the sofa with Max, she was a picture of health and happiness, and bursting with energy and enthusiasm. As was Max. Much to Izzy's surprise he had told her that evening that he was thinking of selling his hugely successful management consultancy.

'Are you serious?' Izzy had asked him.

'Very. I've even got somebody sniffing round wanting to make an offer. It's a good one too. I'd be a fool not to take it.'

'But what will you do?'

'That's what I want to know, Izzy.' Laura had laughed. 'I have visions of him wearing a zip-up cardie and following me round the supermarket like Victor Meldrew, saying, "How much? I don't believe it!"'

'I'm not sure what I'll do,' Max had said, shrugging off Laura's joke. 'Something new, something different. Small-scale consultancy work on my own terms would be tempting. I missed so much of Francesca's early years, I'll be darned if I'm going to make that mistake again. So we'll just have to see.'

It was Izzy's view exactly about her own future, except while Max wouldn't have to worry where his next penny was coming from as he waited for something new and different to land in his lap, she would have worry in spades over the coming months.

Discovering that she was pregnant had seen to that.

Misfortune couldn't ever just rain on Izzy Jordan with a soft pitter-patter, oh, no! She had to be swept away on a tidal wave of rotten luck.

Not that the baby was bad luck. The baby was wonderful, but it was a frightening prospect. She would be entitled to maternity leave, of course, but what then? How would she be able to afford decent childcare on her salary and run her flat? She would probably have to sell it, buy something smaller, live in a cheaper area.

And how would she ever live down the shame her mother would make her feel?

A child born out of wedlock in the Jordan family!

A single-parent family!

A government statistic!

Scandalous!

Still, there was always the hope that her mother would be so appalled she would never speak to her again.

There was also the shame she would bring on school to consider. Once it became impossible to hide the bump under her power suit – yes, as absurd as it was she had succumbed to the horror of wearing a skirt and jacket – the head would never stand for anything as sordid as an unmarried mother-to-be on the staff. What sort of a message would that give the youngsters, to say nothing of the awkwardness of explaining her situation to the board of governors?

And what about Mark?

When she had used the pregnancy-testing kit yesterday evening and had seen that she had hit the jackpot, her first thought was of the expression in Mark's eyes that night in bed when he had asked her if she thought he would make a good father. She would have to tell him, of course. It was only fair. And even if she did keep it from him – and the thought had occurred to her – when Max and Laura found out she was pregnant they would be sure to tell Theo, and in turn, Theo would be bound to let Mark know. But what mustn't happen was for Mark to think she was using the baby as a bargaining tool. She would never do that.

But for all the chaos ahead, she was really quite calm. Surprisingly so. She had no idea what she was going to do, how she was going to juggle the consequences of her summer away, but some inner force of optimism was gently leading her by the hand. It was as if the tiny baby inside her knew best. 'Hey,' it was saying, 'trust me on this, I've got it all worked out.'

The children were coming in from the playing-fields now. She looked at her watch. Ten minutes and the bell would summon her for her next class.

It wasn't until she saw Gemma looking anxiously over her shoulder to where Claremont number four was preparing to take aim with a bit of spit-soggy tissue that she remembered her chat with the shy little girl on Friday afternoon. 'Gemma,' she said, standing in front of her desk, 'I'd like you to be my personal helper this lesson. You can start by passing round the sheets of paper we need.' She watched the child move nervously round the two large squares of desks, sliding a piece of orange A3 to everyone as they laughed, chatted, scraped chair legs on the tiled floor, slipped on their art overalls and rummaged noisily through their pencil cases. In contrast to their happy, relaxed faces, Gemma's was a study of fixed concentration. Poor child, thought Izzy, recognising the expression she had worn most of her school days when she had been terrified of making a mistake. Just as she had been all her childhood, frightened to death of dropping the responsibility she had been given but wanting so much to prove that she could do it.

When Gemma was two boys away from David Claremont, Izzy saw him raise his fingers to flick his revolting handmade missile at her. Gemma saw it too. She looked him straight in the eye and said, 'David Claremont, you're nothing but a silly baby and if you can't behave, you should go back to being in the kindergarten class where you belong with all the other silly babies.'

She was word-perfect, had remembered every word Izzy had whispered into her ear. Not only that, her diction had been as clear as a bell, as authoritative as any teacher's, and from the expression on her face, she was suddenly walking on air. She didn't seem at all bothered that she was now the focus of everybody's attention, that everyone had stopped what they were doing and were staring at her, wondering, no doubt, where this new, assertive Gemma had come from. Izzy noticed a few smiles of admiration around the classroom, as well as the frown on Claremont number four's face. There was even a hint of a trembling lower lip.

If it was the only lesson Izzy ever taught a child, she knew it would be the best one. She was going out on a high, if nothing else.

But, meanwhile, she had a lesson of doing creative things with pasta tubes and lentils to make the most of. Not even the thought of clearing up the floor afterwards lowered her spirits as she saw the dramatic change she had wrought in Gemma. Gone was the threat of tears, gone was the twisted handkerchief, and in place was a smile of heady achievement as she continued to help Izzy, handing out what was needed.

Forty minutes later when it was a toss-up between describing the nearly finished pieces of work as art or have done with it and call it a pasta and lentil bake bound with glue, the shadowy figure of the headmistress appeared at the half-glass-panelled door. Izzy hoped that it was nothing more than one of her regular patrols to make sure that everybody was where they were supposed to be and that they weren't enjoying themselves too much. But the handle turned and in she came.

Oh, Lord, what did this mean? Had she got wind of her pregnancy? But how? Nobody knew, she had told no one. Her panicky thoughts were abruptly distracted by a cry of 'Oh, Miss, look at what David's done! He's got glue everywhere!'

Perfect! Just what she needed. This would really impress the head.

She turned to see what the dreadful child had done now and groaned at the sight of him. He was covered in white PVA glue. The stupid boy must have lifted the pot over his head and poured it over himself. It was a wickedly tempting thought to roll his chubby body round the floor and cover him in pasta and lentils, then staple him by his ears to the display wall. From behind her she could hear the head muttering about it being an inappropriate moment, that perhaps they would call back a little later when Miss Jordan wasn't quite so busy.

Izzy groaned to herself again. Oh, this was really bad. A prospective parent was being shown round the school and had just witnessed the art teacher's singular lack of talent for keeping a class of five-year-olds under control. But then she heard a man say, presumably the prospective father, 'How refreshing to see such a hands-on technique being employed. Do you mind if we don't rush away?'

Oh, thanks, buddy, she thought, stooping to untie the knot of Claremont number four's art overall. Brilliant. She had caught herself one of those sly parents, who wanted to see how she was going to handle things. But then she stopped what she was doing. That had been no prospective parent. Not with that voice.

Slowly, hardly daring to believe what she had heard, she straightened up and turned round.

It *was* him.

It really was Mark.

He looked different somehow. Smarter than she had ever seen him, as if he had tried to dress the part of a prospective parent. The baseball cap was a mistake, though.

'I think it would be better, Mr St James, if we came back later,' the head insisted, looking pointedly at Izzy. 'We're extremely proud of the new science laboratories we had built last autumn. Mr Weston is our head of—'

His gaze on Izzy, Mark said, 'I'm not interested in science. Science is for geeks. Art and literature, that's what does it for me.'

His words, together with his forthright tone, brought an instant hush to all the children, as well as a cold glint to the headmistress's eyes. Izzy recognised it as the look of a headmistress who had decided that this parent would be trouble, that no matter how strapped for cash the school was, she could do without his money. 'Perhaps the library would be of more interest to you,' she said briskly. 'This way.' She held open the door, and gave him space to pass.

'In a minute,' he said, making no attempt to move and keeping his gaze on Izzy. 'I want to see more of this classroom. Why don't you deal with the sticky problem child while Miss Jordan gives me the low-down on what goes on in here?'

Izzy was almost quaking at his sheer nerve. She hid her face by trying to untie the wretched knot on Claremont number four's overall, but she knew that the head had to do as Mark had suggested or appear grossly discourteous and unprofessional. She felt a pang of sympathy for the moon-faced child as he was hauled from his seat and all but dragged outside to his awaiting punishment.

The classroom was still unnaturally quiet as Mark approached her, his boots crunching twirls of pasta with each step he took.

'Well, Miss Jordan, how about it?'

She forced herself to look at him. 'How about what?' How could he do this? How could he just wander in here without warning her? And why?

He came within a few inches of her. His voice was so low she had to strain to catch it. 'Is that the power suit you told me about? It makes you look different. Very high maintenance.'

'I'm afraid I haven't really got an awful lot to show you, what with it being the start of a new term,' she said, for the benefit of all ten pairs of ears that were listening; she had never known a class to be so attentive. Then, in a frantic whisper, 'What on earth are you doing here, Mark? Why have you come?'

'To apologise. I've undergone a reality check. I've been a complete fool.'

She led him to the back of the classroom, towards the big cupboard in the alcove where she hoped they could speak without being overheard. 'The theme we'll be covering this term,' she said, as he followed closely behind, 'is autumn. We'll be using as many media as we can to capture the spirit of the season.' She slowed her step, lowered her voice. 'And when you've apologised, what then?'

What then? was the million-dollar question that had plagued Mark every mile he had covered by taxi and train since first thing that morning. During the long journey he kept thinking of his conversation with Bones, and how easily Bones had shaken the truth out of him. Until that moment, he hadn't said out loud that he loved Izzy. When he had been with her, he had skirted every which way around the simple phrase – I love you – never quite committing himself to it, never letting her know the extent of his feelings. The truth was, he had been scared of what his love for Izzy meant to him. When he had come close to losing her that night in Corfu, it had frightened him to know just how painfully vulnerable his love for her made him. But all those days and weeks without her had taken their toll, and he had known that he couldn't go on pretending to himself that he was protecting her by ending their relationship. The only person he had been protecting was himself. And, as usual, Bones had been the one to cut straight to the heart of the matter, forcing him to see things clearly.

Getting off the train at Manchester and finding himself a taxi for the remainder of his journey, he had worried that Izzy would refuse to speak to him – after what he had done to her, she had every right to turn him away. Which was why he had engineered their meeting as he had. Coward that he was, he had hoped that by seeing her like this, so publicly, she would be at a disadvantage and less likely to be angry with him. It had been simplicity itself convincing that money-grabbing snob of a headmistress over the phone that he was interested in sending his non-existent children to her school – he had made out he had four all under the age of eight – and an appointment had been instantly made. And, as public venues went, this fitted the bill perfectly: all these goggling children couldn't keep their eyes off them.

'It's the *what then* that I've come here to resolve,' he said, his voice still low, 'I could get poetic and talk about how much I miss you. I could say how the sky was dark without you, how the sun never shone, and that the stars had dropped out of the heavens, but there'd be a danger you'd laugh at me. I could also confess that I can't write without you in my life. But that might make it appear as though I have a cheap ulterior motive in coming here, so I'd better not mention that. Which leaves me just the one option to prove I'm being sincere.'

They were standing in the shelter of a large alcove now, facing an open cupboard, their backs to the class of children who had started up a rumble of activity; chairs were being scraped across the floor and voices were raised. It was probably going to be the only moment of privacy they got before some nosy child came to see what was going on, so seizing his chance, Mark lifted Izzy's chin with his hand, bent his head and kissed her. It was the lightest of kisses, their lips barely touching. 'Do you remember that day at Old Períthia,' he murmured, still kissing her, 'when I asked you if being involved with somebody, heart, body and soul, was the same as being in love?'

She nodded.

'Well, I'm here to say that it is the same. I love you with all my heart, with all my unattractive body and with all my ragged, unworthy soul.' He pulled away, looked into her face. 'Tell me that being an irreplaceable part of my life is enough for you, Izzy. Tell me that you love me.'

'Oh, Mark, it's more than enough. And, yes, of course I love you, how could you ask? But please, we have to stop this. You'll get me the sack.'

'Wouldn't I be doing you a favour, getting you away from that awful headmistress?'

'Not if she refuses to give me a good reference.'

'I'll write you all the references you'll ever need. Come on, Izzy, make a break for it, let's get out of here. I don't mind getting you the sack for a furtive kiss, but I draw the line at young minds being perverted by the sight of their teacher being made love to in the art cupboard, which is what we'll end up doing if we stay here a minute longer.'

'But I can't possibly leave them.'

'Yes, you can. It's easy. You just give me your hand.'

His madness took her as far as the doorway, where, having crunched across the floor, they found their escape thwarted by a partially scrubbed Claremont number four and a furious-looking headmistress. Izzy's nerve ran out on her, went and hid in the furthest corner of the room. Now sanity and reason would step in and make her realise it couldn't be that simple.

'Mr St James,' said the head, looking none too pleased, 'if you feel you've quite exhausted the delights of the art room, perhaps we could—'

'Sorry,' he said, pushing rudely past her, 'I'd love to stop and chat, but Miss Jordan has a pressing engagement I'm rather keen for her to fulfil. And as for the delights of the art room, believe me, I'm bowled over by them.'

Oh, my goodness, Izzy thought, as they raced to the front of the school to where her Triumph Herald was parked, it really is going to be as simple as he says.

Hardly aware of the short drive back to her flat, or of the speed at which they had tumbled into bed and made love, Izzy sank into the softness of the pillows behind her and looked across the room to the framed sketch she had drawn of Mark when she had first set eyes on him. How intensely serious he had seemed that day on the rocks as he looked out across the water, not at all the witty, unpredictable and loving man she had come to know.

'By the way,' she said, 'I just want you to know that you are totally and utterly mad, Mr St James.'

He lay with his head half on her chest and half on her stomach. 'I suspected that might be the case,' he responded, without looking up.

'Why didn't you phone or at least write to me?'

'I thought about it but decided a personal appearance was more appropriate. I'll never forget the expression on your face when you saw it was me.'

She stroked his spiky hair, what there was of it, understanding now why he had worn the baseball cap. One look at his brutally cut hair and the terrible scar, complete with stitch marks, on the side of his head and he would have been refused entry to the school; the headmistress would probably have called the police saying an escaped convict was on the loose. 'You realise, thanks to you, that I'm going to be the talk of the staffroom,' she said. 'For days and weeks to come I'll be the only topic of conversation.'

'I'd hoped to turn you into a legend at the very least. I want you to become known as the reckless art teacher who abandoned her pupils to run off home to have sex with a complete stranger in the middle of the afternoon.'

Reckless, she repeated to herself. Well, she had certainly become that. She closed her eyes and wondered how he would react if she told him she was pregnant, that right now, he was just a few inches from the heartbeat of his child. Feeling his weight lift from her, she opened her eyes. He had raised himself up on an elbow and was staring at her.

'You've got a strange look on your face,' he said, 'one that says you know the punchline that nobody else knows.'

She smiled hesitantly. 'Maybe I do. Maybe I don't.'

Kissing her forehead, he said, 'Well, I'll leave you to your secrets, then. I need a shower.'

'Help yourself. But you'll have to make do with girlie shower gel. It's all I have.'

He grinned. 'Who knows? It might bring out my feminine side.'

She had almost fallen asleep when she sensed she wasn't alone. Turning over, she saw that Mark was standing at the foot of the bed. He smelt of Timotei shower gel and was wearing her lilac bathrobe, the sleeves of which were hopelessly too short for his long thin arms. But it was what he had in his hands that really caught her attention. It was the box containing the pregnancy testing kit she had thrown into the bin in the bathroom last night. Oops.

'Is this the punchline?' he asked, holding out the package for her to see.

She searched his face for a clue to his thoughts. But his expression was unreadable. Scared, she suddenly wondered if she had got it wrong about him wanting to be a father. Or maybe he did fancy it, but not just yet. She sat up straight, held the duvet against her. 'We weren't as careful as we thought we were. Does it ... does it change anything?'

A silence passed, his eyes not on her, but on the pregnancy-testing kit. At last he looked at her. 'Too damned right it does!'

52

The combined christening party for Maximilian Cornelius Lewis Sinclair and Beth St James – Mark had been adamant there would be no fancy names for a child of his – was a suitably joyous occasion.

It was a warm summer's day in the middle of June, the party of close friends and family had spilled out into Max and Laura's pretty garden, and as Theo held Beth in his arms and posed with Mark while Izzy took their photograph, he felt it was the proudest moment of his life.

'You are the luckiest man alive,' he said to Mark, when Izzy had left them to photograph somebody else, 'I hope you appreciate everything you have.'

'Including my mother-in-law?'

'Ah, well, you win some, you lose some. But at least she is here and on speaking terms with you.'

'Oh, she's on speaking terms all right, she never stops speaking to us. She phones every other day to check that Beth is sleeping in the right position, that Izzy isn't feeding her too often, or too little, and that we're using the correct nappies, not the ones she's just read are carcinogenic.'

Theo chuckled. 'It's a fair price to pay for your good fortune. And your own parents? How do they feel towards their latest grandchild?'

Both men looked across the lawn, to where Izzy was patiently trying to line up the St James family – including a host of children who wouldn't keep still – to have their picture taken. The scene reminded Theo of Mark and Izzy's wedding day earlier that year in Robin Hood's Bay. They had married on a bitter winter's morning and the photographer had had less than five minutes to take his pictures outside the small Methodist chapel before they died of hypothermia. The reception had been a modest affair back at the house, and because no cars were allowed into the quaint little village, they had to walk down the main street in a flurry of snow before cutting through a criss-cross of sheltered narrow passageways. But at least they had had the pleasure of thawing out in front of a roaring log fire while drinking mugs of life-saving hot chocolate. Serving hot chocolate instead of alcohol as a welcome for their guests had been Izzy's inspired idea. 'So much more practical than champagne on a day like this,' she had said, as they warmed their frozen hands gratefully on the mugs of reviving sweetness. It had been particularly good to see Mark's parents in such happy circumstances, their obvious love for and pride in their youngest son, who had taken such a long and tortuous route to happiness.

In answer to Theo's question, Mark said, 'They're delighted with Beth. You'd think she was their first grandchild.'

Refraining from saying that perhaps Beth was special because she was the one grandchild they had thought they would never have, Theo said, 'And judging from their faces, it looks as if they're just as delighted with Izzy.'

Mark smiled. 'Yeah, she's worked her magic on them as well. Shall I have Beth now so that you can get yourself a drink?'

Theo held on to the tiny sleeping child possessively. 'No need, I am quite happy as I am. It's a shame your old mentor, Bones, isn't here. I would have liked the opportunity to meet him again after all these years. He missed your wedding also.'

'It's his way of keeping his professional distance, I guess.'

'If it had been me I would have jumped at the chance to rejoice over one of my biggest success stories. And talking of stories, what's the latest news of *Flashback Again*?'

'The general opinion is that it's my finest hour. "Popular while remaining literate," is what the literati are saying. As if they know anything. There's even talk of a film.'

'Aha! Didn't I tell you? Didn't I say that I had a good feeling about this one? You should listen to your old friend more often. He knows what he is talking about.' The loudness of his voice stirred the sleeping baby in his arms. Two little feet kicked from under the silk christening gown, then a pair of eyes opened wide: they were grey and solemn, just like Izzy's. 'She is quite adorable,' sighed Theo, 'and so very like her mother.'

'Really? I hadn't noticed.' Bending down to take a closer look, Mark stroked his daughter's delicate cheek, 'Can't see it myself.'

'Oh, surely you cannot be so blind that you—' Theo stopped short, realising that Mark was teasing him. 'Oh, he of so little heart and soul.'

'That's not what Izzy says about me. In fact when we're in bed she—'

'Please,' cried Theo, clasping Beth closer to him to cover her ears, 'spare the child your saucy bedroom tales! Now, behave yourself and tell me when you are coming to stay. You will be coming, won't you? You'll both need a holiday after the year you've had. Max and Laura are flying over in a couple of weeks. Why don't you join them?'

Mark shook his head. 'Not a chance. Last summer was a little too action-packed for us. We've decided to go somewhere else. We thought walking in the Himalayas would suit us better.'

'What? Are you mad? How could you be thinking of taking my precious little goddaughter to the Himalayas?'

'He's not, Theo,' said Izzy from behind him. 'He's winding you up. Shall I have Beth for you? Give your arms a rest. I know she's only a few weeks old but she gets heavier by the minute.'

Again Theo held on tight. 'No, I am fine. And I shall not part with her until you have told me when you are coming to stay.'

'We were going to talk to you about that. Go on, Mark, you ask him, it was your idea.'

Theo detected an air of discomfort in his friend.

'It's no big deal,' Mark said, 'but we wondered if you would help find us a house to buy. With all the tourists that descend on the village in the summer, it gets so busy, we thought—'

'No, Mark,' corrected Izzy, with a smile, '*you* thought.'

He scowled and pushed at his hair, which had mercifully recovered from the savage attack on it last year. 'Yeah, okay,' he said. '*I* thought that if we had our own place in Áyios Nikólaos I'd be able to get more work done during the summer months. There'd be fewer distractions.'

A small smile appeared on Theo's face. Then it widened into a ridiculously huge grin. He lifted Beth so that her little yawning face was inches away from his. 'You hear that, Beth?' he said, planting a kiss on the end of her nose. 'That was your father speaking. Now I know he is everything he was meant to be. A happily married middle-aged man with a beautiful wife and daughter and fast becoming a fat, capitalist pig. Ah, ah, ah, Johnny Two Homes St James! He'll be renewing his driving licence next just so that he can own a flashy car like your uncle Theo.'

'If you weren't holding my child, I'd ram this fist right where I've always wanted to shove it!'

'Oh, admit it, Mark! Admit, just this once, that you have undergone a wonderfully radical shift of perspective on what is important in your life.'

Laughing to herself, Izzy took Beth from Theo and left them to it. She wandered across the lawn to where Max had fixed a rope swing to the branch of an old apple tree for when his son was old enough to play on it. 'He's planning ahead with everything,' Laura had told Izzy on the phone, during one of their long catch-up sessions. 'I'm just glad he saw sense and didn't sell the business and become a part-time house-husband or he would have been fussing around with Lord knows what else.'

After testing the swing to see if it would take her weight, Izzy lowered herself on to the wooden seat. She shifted Beth in her arms so that she was comfortable and gazed at her lovingly. 'You were right,' she murmured softly. 'You told me you had everything worked out. You just didn't tell me how well you'd got it sorted.'

Since Mark had made his extraordinary appearance in her classroom that day last autumn, her life had changed beyond recognition. She had never been so happy, or felt so self-assured. She knew now that the two were inextricably linked, for how else would she have found the nerve to do what she did last September?

Before the headmistress had had a chance to demand an explanation for her appalling behaviour and consequently sack her, Izzy had marched into her office the following morning to carry out a pre-emptive strike. Disappointed not to find the head skulking in her lair, she had caught sight of an offensively insipid calendar of Anne Hathaway-style cottages on the wall. Taking a pen from the head's mahogany desk tidy, she flipped September over and sketched in a man urinating down the smoking chimney-pot of October's half-timbered thatched cottage. 'How's that for putting your fire out, you horrible old dragon?' she muttered. Hearing footsteps on the wooden floor outside, she hurriedly turned back the page, replaced the pen in the desk tidy, and greeted the headmistress with a polite smile. 'I've brought you this,' she said, dropping an envelope on to the desk.

'It's my resignation. I'm leaving, as of now, this very minute. Not very professional, I know, but under the circumstances I'm sure you won't want me to stay.'

Later that morning, and after phoning Laura to tell her what was going on, she locked the door to her flat and set out with Mark on the long drive to her new home. 'No doubts?' Mark had asked, when they stopped for petrol and a bite to eat at a Little Chef on the A1. 'After all, Miss Jordan, this is a little rash for you, very out of character.'

Kissing him, she had said, 'My only doubt is whether my poor old car will make the journey. Now buckle up and tell me how much further we have to go.'

'It's all the way or nothing, Izzy.'

'Would there be any other way with you?'

And that, she knew, would always be the case. Her life with Mark would never be boring; it would never contain anything as dull as a half-measure. It would always be an exhilarating roller-coaster ride of extremes. When he had fully taken in the fact that she was pregnant, he had swung through every emotion. From euphoria that he was going to be a father, to maudlin concern that she might not have told him. 'How did you think you were going to manage on your own?' he had asked, his eyes moist, his voice thick.

'How any other single mother would manage.'

'But you would have told me, wouldn't you?'

'Yes,' she had said firmly. 'I was always going to tell you. I just didn't know when or how. I didn't want you to think I was forcing your hand.'

'You know your trouble, Izzy, you're too bloody considerate.'

'Sweet of you to say.'

They had stayed up all night, discussing what they would do next.

'I want you to come and live with me,' he had said. He was adamant. 'Tell that headmistress to go shove her job where the sun don't shine, and become a kept woman.' Her doubtful expression provoked him to add, 'What scares you most? Standing up to that despotic she-devil, or accepting the position of being my live-in lover?'

'Oh, definitely the latter.'

'So what exactly is it that you're not sure about?'

'I'd need to know if it was a permanent position. I couldn't—'

'Bloody hell, Izzy! I don't believe you. Of course it's permanent.'

'You never said.'

'Well, I'm saying it now. And if needs be I'll get you a ring first thing tomorrow morning to convince you.'

'Is that a proposal?'

He frowned. 'Yeah, okay. I could have put it better, but will it do for now?'

'Why? Will you have something better up your sleeve at a later date?'

Pushing her back on to the bed, he had said, 'You'll have to wait and see.'

A month later he proposed 'properly' when he took her on a midnight walk on the beach in Robin Hood's Bay. Despite the cold, it was a beautiful night, with a full moon pinned to the cloudless sky like a sheriff's badge, its silvery light tiptoeing across the waves behind them. 'Now, would you say this was romantic enough for you?' he had asked, getting down on one knee in the damp sand and rummaging through his coat pockets. 'Damn it, where the hell did I put it? I had it a moment ago.' He was suddenly a mass of volatile nerves. He cursed some more, then eventually found the ring in his jeans pocket. 'Oh, for heaven's sake, Izzy, stop laughing! This is supposed to be one of those perfect moments you'll never forget.'

She grabbed hold of his collar, pulled him to his feet and kissed his cold lips. 'Believe me, I'll never forget it. It'll stay with me for the rest of my life. I'll always love you, Mark, but promise you'll never go mainstream on me. I'm not sure I could handle you being normal. And, by the way, the answer's yes.'

'Yes?'

'Among all that cursing and fumbling I'm assuming there was a proposal of marriage.'

The sound of laughter made Izzy look up. Nearer the house Corky was telling Laura's parents something that had them laughing loudly. To the left of them, Max and Harry were deep in conversation – Harry had recently graduated and much to Francesca's horror there was talk of him joining her father's firm. Laura's horror was that there might be a danger of Ma and Pa Patterson becoming a part of their family. 'Imagine having to be nice to them on a permanent basis,' she had told Izzy. A scary prospect indeed.

Sitting in the shade of the house, and showing Francesca how she should be holding her baby brother, was Izzy's mother. How poignant the sight of Beth and little Max must be for her, Izzy thought sadly. Having given birth to her own child and experienced the bond of motherhood, she couldn't think how she would cope if Beth was suddenly snatched from her. If five weeks was all she was allowed to have with her child, what desperate depths of depression might she sink to? She held Beth tightly and watched her mother across the garden.

When she had summoned the courage to take Mark home to meet her mother, Prudence had been perfectly vile to him. In that hateful little bungalow with its ghastly memories, her mother had asked Mark why he thought she would be remotely interested in meeting him. 'After the way you spoke to me on the telephone, you should consider yourself lucky that I've let you over the threshold.'

'I thought you would want to meet the man who was going to marry your daughter,' he said lightly.

'Marry? Who said anything about you marrying?'

'I just did. It's why we've come to see you. We're planning on getting married in January. We thought you'd want to know.'

Pouring herself another cup of tea, her cold eyes appraising him, she said, 'A tawdry affair in a dreadful register office, no doubt. You needn't waste an invitation on me, I shan't be there.'

Turning to Izzy, he said, 'Well, I should think that comes as quite a relief to you, Izzy, doesn't it? At least now we'll be able to enjoy the day.'

How could he have said that? How could he have been so brazen? But if she had thought Mark had been blunt in what he had said so far, she was well off-beam. His worst was yet to come.

'Are you going to just sit there and let this monstrously rude man speak to me in that way?' her mother demanded.

'Look, Mum, it doesn't have to be like this between us. Why don't you—'

'Like what precisely? What are you getting at? And why is this tea so weak? How many bags did you put in the pot? I knew I should have done it myself. I never could trust you to do anything right, not even something as simple as making the tea. You know how I prefer it to be—'

'Quite honestly, Mrs Jordan,' interrupted Mark, and in a voice that was sublimely cordial, 'I don't give a flying fuck how you prefer your tea. We've come here today to tell you we're getting married and that you're going to be a grandmother sometime at the beginning of May. Now, that may be of interest to you or it may not. But while Izzy and I go for a walk to rid ourselves of your choking bitterness, why don't you mull over those details and see what you really think of them. But get this, when we return I expect you to be civil. Is that clear? One foot wrong, and I promise you will never *ever* see your grandchild. Nod if you understand what I have just said.'

If every staring statue in that room had shattered in the awesome silence that followed as her mother gave an imperceptible nod, Izzy wouldn't have been surprised. They left her sitting in her chair, speechless, her tea-cup wobbling in its saucer. When they returned an hour later, resigned to driving straight back up to Yorkshire instead of staying the night, as planned, they found Prudence in the kitchen, at the sink, peeling a mound of potatoes and listening to *Sing Something Simple* on the radio.

'Which would you prefer,' she asked, as they joined her, 'roast or mashed potatoes with your chicken? I thought we'd eat at six, I'm not one for eating late. Izzy, you'd better sit down and rest. Too much running around won't do the baby any good. Are you taking any iron supplements?'

It was extraordinary. Like the ECT treatment she had all those years ago, it was as if the shock of Mark's words had erased all the earlier unpleasantness from her mother's mind. She cooked them supper, and while they ate, she enquired politely after Mark's writing, offered to knit a selection of matinée jackets for the baby, and when it was bedtime, she even allowed them to sleep together.

So had that been the answer, then? Would years of misery have been avoided if only Izzy had had the guts to fire off a round or two of Anglo-Saxon at her mother as Mark had?

She would never know, and maybe it didn't matter. What they had now between them, as new and fragile as it was, was more important than what might have been. The pink jackets and mittens her mother had made for Beth – and there were plenty of them – might be hopelessly too large for her, but it was a heart-warming and reassuring sign that they were moving in the right direction. The fraught tension that had gone into those horribly distorted squares for the cold and hungry in some faraway African village had been replaced with garments that were beautifully made, if a little old-fashioned. 'So long as she doesn't start knitting me a Val Doonican sweater, I don't care how many things she knits or how grim they are,' Mark had said, when yet another parcel arrived in the post revealing a further addition to their unborn baby's wardrobe.

In that same delivery, there had been a letter from Dolly-Babe. Unbeknown to Izzy, when Mark had returned home last summer, he had penned a note to Dolly-Babe thanking her for the flowers she had sent him while he had been in hospital in Corfu. He had also mentioned that drinking wasn't going to help her forget the past – he had tried it himself. Izzy had no idea how he had had the nerve to write such a letter, or how he had actually worded it, but the response, when it finally came months later, was to thank him for his advice:

I was that angry with you when I first read your letter that I threw it in the bin. Bloody awful cheek, I thought. That girlfriend of yours must have been shooting her big mouth off to you, telling you stuff that was confidential. But all that day when Bob was out, I couldn't stop thinking about what you'd written, and what Ria had said about you changing my life. Anyway, to cut a long story short, I've been attending one of those groups you suggested, you know the kind of thing – 'My name is Liberty-Raquel and I'm an alcoholic.' Not that I am, of course, but you've got to meet them half-way, haven't you? Well, you don't need me to tell you that, I'm sure. There are people in the group much worse than me. Drink, you wouldn't believe it! Or what they knock back. Last week a woman admitted to drinking nail-varnish remover, said she couldn't get enough of it! But for all that, they're not a bad crowd and it does get me out of the house, so I'd just like to say thanks – thanks for giving me a kick up the backside.

'So you did help change her life in the end, didn't you?' Izzy had said to Mark, when she had finished reading the letter.

With typical bad grace, he had growled, 'Say so much as one word of my having fulfilled a psychic's prediction and I'll invite her to stay with us!'

Beth wriggled restlessly in her arms and Izzy nudged at the grass beneath her feet and set the swing moving to and fro. The rocking motion instantly settled the baby and Izzy smiled at the thought of Mark carrying out his threat. He might be one of the most unpredictable and daring people she knew, but she doubted that even he would go that far to prove he was as good as his word.

'And what, pray, Mrs St James, are you thinking of to make you smile like the proverbial Cheshire cat?'

'Really, Mr St James, creeping up behind me like that and cross-examining me with your impertinent questions! Isn't a wife allowed to have a few secrets from her husband?'

Coming round to stand in front of her, Mark placed his hands at shoulder height on the ropes of the swing and looked down at her. 'I knew marriage would be a mistake. I liked you better when you were a scarlet woman lying in the sun, baring and confessing your all.'

'Ssh, you'll make your daughter blush.'

'Just like her mother, then.' He reached out to take Beth so that Izzy could get to her feet. 'So what were you smiling about?'

'You, of course. You know how funny I think you are.'

'Mm ... I keep forgetting what a highly twisted sense of humour you have.'

She laughed. 'If I have, it's only developed since I met you.'

Slipping a hand around her waist, he drew her close. 'Are you up for a full-frontal kiss right under your mother's nose?'

'Oh, I think I could manage that.'

'My, how you've changed your tune. Now brace yourself, Izzy, this is going to be a big one.'

From across the garden, Theo watched his friend kiss the woman he had once hoped would feel for him what she so clearly felt for Mark. He felt no envy, just a deep, satisfying sense of contentment.

'Well, Theo, it isn't quite what you had in mind almost a year ago when you thought you might sweep Izzy off her feet, is it?'

He turned to see Laura at his side. He took the glass of wine she had brought for him. 'How very unkind of you to remind me of my arrogance that day on the terrace with you. But I'm not too proud to admit that it's been a good lesson for me.' Then, looking back at Mark and Izzy, he said, 'They've done an excellent job of sweeping each other off their feet, haven't they? They truly bring out the best in one another.'

She squeezed his arm. 'Cheer up, Theo, you'll find your Miss Right one day. Just when you're least expecting it, there she'll be, all gorgeous and utterly in love with you.'

'And in the meantime, do I have your permission to flirt with you?'

'What? With my awful legs?'

'Oh, my darling Laura, please don't tell me you've let yourself go. Did I not warn you about those varicose veins? Did I not tell you to rest your legs during your pregnancy? What you need is a good holiday to recuperate, and I know just the place, where the sun shines all day and the pace of life comes to a grinding stop.'

She burst out laughing. 'The pace of life comes to a grinding stop? You must be joking!'

He grinned. 'Well, excluding the everyday drama of a middle-aged mother and her schoolboy lover turning up in the bay, a near-fatal drowning, a tragic shooting, people falling in love and the careless conception of a couple of charming babies, I think you'll agree that the pace was pretty slow and made for the perfect holiday.'

She raised her glass against his. 'And let's not forget our perfect friend and neighbour, Mr Theodore Vlamakis who made it all possible. Thank you Theo. You're an exceptional man.'

'Now that's something I won't dispute. Cheers!'